THE OXFORD BOOK OF THE
AMERICAN SOUTH

THE OXFORD BOOK OF THE
AMERICAN SOUTH

TESTIMONY, MEMORY, AND FICTION

Edited by

Edward L. Ayers
Bradley C. Mittendorf

New York   Oxford
OXFORD UNIVERSITY PRESS
1997

Dedicated to Martha H. Mittendorf and Billie L. Ayers

Oxford University Press

Oxford   New York
Athens   Auckland   Bangkok   Bogotá   Bombay
Buenos Aires   Calcutta   Cape Town   Dar es Salaam
Delhi   Florence   Hong Kong   Istanbul   Karachi
Kuala Lumpur   Madras   Madrid   Melbourne
Mexico City   Nairobi   Paris   Singapore
Taipei   Tokyo   Toronto

and associated companies in
Berlin   Ibadan

Published by Oxford University Press, Inc.,
198 Madison Avenue, New York, New York 10016

Library of Congress Cataloging-in-Publication Data
The Oxford book of the American South : Testimony, memory, and fiction /
edited by Edward L. Ayers and Bradley C. Mittendorf
p.   cm.   Includes index.
ISBN 0-19-508522-1
1. American literature—Southern States.   2. Southern States—
Literary collections.   I. Ayers, Edward L., 1953– .
II. Mittendorf, Bradley C., 1967– .   III. Title: Book of the American South.
PS551.097   1997
810.8'03275—dc21   96-45135

1 3 5 7 9 8 6 4 2

Printed in the United States of America on acid-free paper

Contents

Contents

Consequences

Hard Times

Contents

⪥

The Turning

Preface

Sixteen volumes of the Library of Southern Literature appeared before an unexpectant world between 1908 and 1913. The Library's editors hoped the impressive matched set — 6,560 pages "compiled under the direct supervision of southern men of letters"—would refute the suspicion that the South had little literature worth publishing, much less anthologizing. Though the Library met with gratitude and enthusiasm in the South, critics outside the region ridiculed the massive collection as old-fashioned in both style and politics.

Things are different now. Writers such as William Faulkner, Eudora Welty, Zora Neale Hurston, Robert Penn Warren, James Agee, Richard Wright, and Ralph Ellison seemed miraculously to emerge from the Southern shadows in the decades after the Library of Southern Literature. New authors speaking in distinctly Southern accents about distinctly Southern situations have emerged ever since. Fiction and nonfiction from the American South enjoy a respect and recognition no one could have imagined at the beginning of the twentieth century.

With such riches to choose from, how were we to select what might go into *The Oxford Book of the American South*? Our determination to include a broad range of Southerners has not been difficult, for women writers, black writers, and white writers of every background have left eloquent legacies. Faced with more brilliant writing than we could possibly contain between the pages of a single volume, we have tried to create a unified book rather than a mere series of readings, a portrait of a society unfolding in time. To that end, we have favored writing by Southerners about the South, and we have embraced not only fiction but also memoirs, diaries, and essays. Because certain passions have surfaced time and again in more than two hundred years of Southern writing, we have chosen readings that express those passions: the complexities of race, the fierceness and solace of religious faith, the absurdity and hilarity of everyday life, the temptations and consequences of violence, the entanglements of family, the distances that separate the rich from the poor, the ambivalence toward the outside world, and the tenaciousness of memory.

We obviously had to make some hard decisions. We have regretfully neglected authors who, by other criteria, might seem more gifted artists than some included here. There is not as much from the Colonial Era as we would have liked nor as many fiction writers from the prolific decades of the late twentieth century. We reluctantly excluded several genres entirely, such as folklore, poetry, and professional history, because we could find no effective way to integrate them with the rest of the book. We have sometimes used sections of novels and have sometimes cut material from within nonfiction works. We hope that readers will turn to the original books to get the full story and we take solace from knowing that anthologies gathered for other purposes will include many of those authors left out here.

Like so much Southern writing, this book is about memory, about imagining and reimagining the past. Each of the book's four parts corresponds with a major period in the South's history. The volume opens with the slave era of the late eighteenth and early nineteenth centuries and then recounts the tumult between the Civil War and World War I. The remarkable cultural renaissance and crippling economic depression of the 1920s and 1930s constitute the third part of this book. The final section documents the complicated and still unfolding story of the contemporary South. Within each section, writers appear in a sort of chorus. First to speak are those who witnessed the events firsthand, and they are followed in turn by people of subsequent generations. Sometimes the similarities and continuities across the years are remarkable; at other times, it is the silence and contempt that stand out.

We provide a brief introduction to each historical period, along with a sketch of each writer's background, but we do not outline lessons and point out morals. Readers will discover for themselves the rich surprises that lie within and among the selections that follow, the threads that tie passages together across decades and centuries. While the book's selections can be sampled in any order, those within each part connect and resonate with special force. Each story, portrait, or argument can stand alone, but it gains depth and meaning from being part of a whole.

No honest survey of Southern writing over the last two centuries could steer clear of controversy. While some writers in this book celebrate the South and evoke its virtues, others speak with bitterness, disappointment, or anger. Some express their love of the South through a language of exasperation, longing, and regret; some do not love the South at all. Regardless of their tone, all the authors here speak of the South with a sense of wonder. For anyone who comes to know the place, it could hardly be otherwise.

THE OXFORD BOOK OF THE
AMERICAN SOUTH

The Old South

During the seventeenth century the beleaguered military outpost of Jamestown slowly spread into ragged tobacco farms. Indentured servants from Britain did much of the work, though slaves from Africa became increasingly common in towns and on plantations. Disease, warfare, and demoralization reduced the presence of native peoples, while the Europeans lived longer and saw more of their children survive. Trade, farming, and land speculation made many white men prosperous.

The Southern colonies became ever more wedded to slavery while the institution became more marginal in the areas to the north. Hundreds of thousands of Africans, kidnapped or taken in war, eventually found themselves in the ports of Virginia, Georgia, South Carolina, and Louisiana. They labored as slaves in tobacco fields, rice swamps, and cane rows. They worked in imposing mansions and in raw cabins, in village shops and on remote farmsteads. Africans gradually became African Americans, forming families and blending their diverse languages and religions into something new and sustaining.

The owners of the slaves became the richest men and women in the British mainland colonies and the leaders of the revolution against the mother country. They wrote the founding documents and led the new nation through its first tentative decades. Though not proud of slavery, the leaders of the South saw no pressing need to abolish the institution immediately; it appeared to be on its way toward a very gradual end, as it was in the North. They agreed that their involvement in the world slave trade would end at the beginning of the new century.

Cotton and Eli Whitney's cotton gin changed everything in the nineteenth century, including white Southerners' vague vision of slavery's demise. The crop grew luxuriantly, its potential stretching as far to the southwest as anyone could imagine. The Cherokee, Choctaw, and Chickasaw peoples, standing in the way, were driven or enticed off the land. The world longed for cotton and the need for labor seemed limitless on the frontiers of Alabama, Mississippi, Louisiana, and Texas. Virginia and the Carolinas supplied that labor, selling thousands of slaves every year to the booming states farther south. Restless white farmers moved their wives, babies, and slaves to the freshest cotton land. Churches and courthouses went up in one new county after another, bringing tenuous order to the rough society piling in around them. The two-thirds of white people who owned no slaves watched both slaveholders and slaves warily. Generally, though, common whites did much as they pleased.

Lines quickly hardened between the regions after 1820, creating The North and The South. Many white Northerners felt affronted by the growing numbers and power of the slaveholders; some, coming to consider slavery not merely archaic but sinful, advertised their beliefs to the world. White Southerners abandoned any public ambivalence about slavery, explaining to themselves and to others that black people were fit only for servitude, that the rich and powerful South was part of God's plan for the spread of Christianity and progress. White Southerners, proud, defensive, and defiant became ever more conscious of themselves as a people set apart from their fellow citizens.

White people and black people made elaborate, lopsided, and unspoken bargains with one another. Slaveowners would keep slaves' families together and protect them from violence at the hands of other whites; African Americans would work and appear contented. Many on both sides violated the bargain. Slaveowners often sold, abused, and violated slaves; slaves fought back, in ways both obvious and hidden. The whites who held no slaves sometimes seemed eager to join in the bargain; at other times, they became fearful and resentful of black and white alike. The white women of the South, told that they benefited from slavery, nevertheless worried about temptations the institution presented to their sons and husbands. The slave South, apparently so simple, was in fact complicated top to bottom, constantly changing, continually shifting beneath people's feet.

The selections that follow describe this society from fourteen different perspectives, mixing devotion, outrage, humor, sadness, and confusion. They range from an eighteenth-century naturalist's evocation of a southern Eden, to a slave woman's description of the hell created by a sexually abusive master, to a 1986 novel imagining the bonds between a young runaway slave mother and a white woman abandoned by her husband. Slavery appears here from the perspective of a young African seized from his home, from Thomas Jefferson's Enlightenment-era speculations on racial differences, and from a heartfelt defense of bondage on the grounds of divine will. The selections include the journal of a devout traveling minister, the religious visions of the leader of the largest slave revolt in the nation's history, and a white novelist's interpretation of that revolt. Several selections tell of fights: one for frontier bragging rights, one for the dignity of a slave, and one feud over nothing in particular. Two Southerners, writing eighty years after the fall of the slave South, wrestle with the mysteries of that time and place, sifting through the memories and stories, trying to learn how such things came to be.

from *Travels*

William Bartram (1739–1823)

When the botanist William Bartram traveled alone through Georgia, eastern Florida, Alabama, and the Carolinas in 1773, the Native Americans he encountered nicknamed him "Pucpuggy," or "The Flower Hunter." His account of the land and the people he saw on those journeys, published in 1791, offers a haunting, romanticized glimpse of the upcountry South before the arrival of the white and black people who would soon transform the landscape.

After riding near two miles through Indian plantations of Corn, which was well cultivated, kept clean of weeds, and was well advanced, being near eighteen inches in height, and the Beans planted at the Corn-hills were above ground; we left the field on our right, turning towards the mountains, and ascending through a delightful green vale or lawn, which conducted us in amongst the pyramidal hills, and crossing a brisk flowing creek, meandering through the meads, which continued near two miles, dividing and branching in amongst the hills. We then mounted their steep ascents, rising gradually by ridges or steps one above another, frequently crossing narrow fertile dales as we ascended: the air felt cool and animating, being charged with the fragrant breath of the mountain beauties, the blooming mountain cluster Rose, blushing Rhododendron and fair Lilly of the valley. Having now attained the summit of this very elevated ridge, we enjoyed a fine prospect indeed; the enchanting Vale of Cowee, perhaps as celebrated for fertility, fruitfulness and beautiful prospects as the Fields of Pharsalia or the Vale of Tempe; the town, the elevated peeks of the Jore mountains, a very distant prospect of the Jore village in a beautiful lawn, lifted up many thousand feet higher than our present situation, besides a view of many other villages and settlements on the sides of the mountains, at various distances and elevations; the silver rivulets gliding by them, and snow white cataracts glimmering on the sides of the lofty hills; the bold promontories of the Jore mountain stepping into the Tanase river, whilst his foaming waters rushed between them.

After viewing this very entertaining scene, we began to descend the mountain on the other side, which exhibited the same order of gradations of ridges and vales as on our ascent; and at length rested on a very expansive, fertile plain, amidst the towering hills, over which we rode a long time, through magnificent high forests, extensive green fields, meadows and lawns. Here had formerly been a very flourishing settlement; but the Indians deserted it in search of fresh planting land, which they soon found in a rich vale but a few miles distance over a ridge of hills. Soon after entering on these charming, sequestered, prolific fields, we came to a fine little river, which crossing, and riding over fruitful strawberry beds and green lawns, on the sides of a circular ridge of hills in front of us, and going round the bases of this promontory, came to a fine meadow on an arm of the vale, through which meandered a brook, its humid vapours bedewing the fragrant strawberries which hung in heavy red clusters over the grassy verge. We crossed the rivulet; then rising a sloping, green, turfy ascent, alighted on the borders of a grand forest of stately trees, which we penetrated on foot a little distance to a horse-stamp, where was a large squadron of those useful creatures, belonging to my friend and companion, the trader, on the sight of whom they assembled together from all quarters; some at a distance saluted him with shrill neighings of gratitude, or came prancing up to lick the salt out of his hand, whilst the younger and more timorous came galloping onward, but coyly wheeled off, and fetching a circuit stood aloof; but as soon as their lord and master strewed the crystaline salty bait on the hard beaten ground, they all, old and young, docile and timorous, soon formed themselves in ranks and fell to licking up the delicious morsel.

It was a fine sight; more beautiful creatures I never saw; there were of them of all colours, sizes and dispositions. Every year, as they become of age, he sends off a troop of them down to Charleston, where they are sold to the highest bidder.

Having paid our attention to this useful part of the creation, who, if they are under our dominion, have consequently a right to our protection and favour, we returned to our trusty servants that were regaling themselves in the exuberant sweet pastures and strawberry fields in sight, and mounted again. Proceeding on our return to town, continued through part of this high forest skirting on the meadows: began to ascend the hills of a ridge which we were under the necessity of crossing; and having gained its summit, enjoyed a most enchanting view; a vast expanse of green meadows and strawberry fields; a meandering river gliding through, saluting in its various turnings the swelling, green, turfy knolls, embellished with parterres of flowers and fruitful strawberry beds; flocks of turkies strolling about them; herds of deer prancing in the meads or bounding over the hills; companies of young, innocent Cherokee virgins, some busy gathering the rich fragrant fruit, others having already filled their baskets, lay reclined under the shade of floriferous and fragrant native bowers of

Magnolia, Azalea, Philadelphus, perfumed Calycanthus, sweet Yellow Jessamine and cerulean Glycine frutescens, disclosing their beauties to the fluttering breeze, and bathing their limbs in the cool fleeting streams; whilst other parties more gay and libertine, were yet collecting strawberries, or wantonly chasing their companions, tantalising them, staining their lips and cheeks with the rich fruit.

The sylvan scene of primitive innocence was enchanting, and perhaps too enticing for hearty young men long to continue idle spectators.

In fine, nature prevailing over reason, we wished at least to have a more active part in their delicious sports. Thus precipitately resolving, we cautiously made our approaches, yet undiscovered, almost to the joyous scene of action. Now, although we meant no other than an innocent frolic with this gay assembly of hamadryades, we shall leave it to the person of feeling and sensibility to form an idea to what lengths our passions might have hurried us, thus warmed and excited, had it not been for the vigilance and care of some envious matrons who lay in ambush, and espying us, gave the alarm, time enough for the nymphs to rally and assemble together. We however pursued and gained ground on a group of them, who had incautiously strolled to a greater distance from their guardians, and finding their retreat now like to be cut off, took shelter under cover of a little grove; but on perceiving themselves to be discovered by us, kept their station, peeping through the bushes; when observing our approaches, they confidently discovered themselves, and decently advanced to meet us, half unveiling their blooming faces, incarnated with the modest maiden blush, and with native innocence and cheerfulness, presented their little baskets, merrily telling us their fruit was ripe and sound.

We accepted a basket, sat down and regaled ourselves on the delicious fruit, encircled by the whole assembly of the innocent jocose sylvan nymphs: by this time the several parties, under the conduct of the elder matrons, had disposed themselves in companies on the green, turfy banks.

My young companion, the trader, by concessions and suitable apologies for the bold intrusion, having compromised the matter with them, engaged them to bring their collections to his house at a stipulated price: we parted friendly.

And now taking leave of these Elysian fields, we again mounted the hills, which we crossed, and traversing obliquely their flowery beds, arrived in town in the cool of the evening.

from *The Interesting Narrative of the Life of Olaudah Equiano, or Gustavus Vassa, the African*

Olaudah Equiano (1745–1797)

Olaudah Equiano, born in what is now Nigeria, was kidnapped into slavery at age eleven and sent to the Americas in 1756. He lived briefly in Virginia before being bought by an officer in the British navy and working for several years on British warships. After being sold to a Quaker merchant in the Caribbean, Equiano saved money and purchased his freedom in 1766. In 1789, he published his *Narrative*, one of the first written by a former slave. The story of his capture and sale to Virginia resembles that of many others among the half million Africans brought to what would become the United States.

My father, besides many slaves, had a numerous family, of which seven lived to grow up, including myself and a sister, who was the only daughter. As I was the youngest of the sons, I became, of course, the greatest favorite with my mother, and was always with her; and she used to take particular pains to form my mind. I was trained up from my earliest years in the art of war: my daily exercise was shooting and throwing javelins; and my mother adorned me with emblems, after the manner of our greatest warriors. In this way I grew up till I was turned the age of eleven, when an end was put to my happiness in the following manner: — generally when the grown people in the neighborhood were gone far in the fields to labor, the children assembled together in some of the neighboring premises to play; and commonly some of us used to get up a tree to look out for any assailant, or kidnapper, that might come upon us—for they sometimes took those opportunities of our parents' absence, to attack and carry off as many as they could seize. One day as I was watching at the top of a tree in our yard, I saw one of those people come into the yard of our next neighbor but one to kidnap, there being many stout young people in it. Immediately on this I gave the alarm of the rogue, and he was surrounded by the stoutest of them, who entangled him with cords, so that he could not escape till some of the grown people came and secured him. But, alas! ere long it was my fate to be thus attacked, and to be carried off, when none of the grown people were nigh. One day, when all our people were gone out to their works as usual, and only I and my dear sister were left to mind the house, two men and a woman got over our walls, and in a moment seized us both, and, without giving us time to cry out, or make resistance, they stopped our mouths, and ran off with us into the nearest wood. . . .

. . . I continued to travel, sometimes by land, sometimes by water, through different countries and various nations, till, at the end of six or seven months after I had been kidnapped, I arrived at the sea coast. . . .

The first object which saluted my eyes when I arrived on the coast, was the sea, and a slave ship, which was then riding at anchor, and waiting for its cargo. These filled me with astonishment, which was soon converted into terror, when I was carried on board. I was immediately handled, and tossed up to see if I were sound, by some of the crew; and I was now persuaded that I had gotten into a world of bad spirits, and that they were going to kill me. Their complexions, too, differing so much from ours, their long hair, and the language they spoke, (which was very different from any I had ever heard) united to confirm me in this belief. Indeed, such were the horrors of my views and fears at the moment, that, if ten thousand worlds had been my own, I would have freely parted with them all to have exchanged my condition with that of the meanest slave in my own country. When I looked round the ship too, and saw a large furnace of copper boiling, and a multitude of black people of every description chained together, every one of their countenances expressing dejection and sorrow, I no longer doubted of my fate; and, quite overpowered with horror and anguish, I fell motionless on the deck and fainted. When I recovered a little, I found some black people about me, who I believed were some of those who had brought me on board, and had been receiving their pay; they talked to me in order to cheer me, but all in vain. I asked them if we were not to be eaten by those white men with horrible looks, red faces, and long hair. They told me I was not: and one of the crew brought me a small portion of spirituous liquor in a wine glass, but, being afraid of him, I would not take it out of his hand. One of the blacks, therefore, took it from him and gave it to me, and I took a little down my palate, which, instead of reviving me, as they thought it would, threw me into the greatest consternation at the strange feeling it produced, having never tasted any such liquor before. Soon after this, the blacks who brought me on board went off, and left me abandoned to despair.

I now saw myself deprived of all chance of returning to my native country, or even the least glimpse of hope of gaining the shore, which I now considered as friendly; and I even wished for my former slavery in preference to my present situation, which was filled with horrors of every kind, still heightened by my ignorance of what I was to undergo. I was not long suffered to indulge my grief; I was soon put down under the decks, and there I received such a salutation in my nostrils as I had never experienced in my life: so that, with the loathsomeness of the stench, and crying together, I became so sick and low that I was not able to eat, nor had I the least desire to taste any thing. I now wished for the last friend, death, to relieve me; but soon, to my grief, two of the white men offered me eatables; and, on my refusing to eat, one of them held me fast by the hands, and laid me across, I think the windlass, and tied my feet, while the other flogged me severely. I had never experienced any thing of this kind before, and although not being used to the water, I naturally feared that element the first time I saw it, yet, nevertheless, could I have got over the nettings, I would have jumped over the side, but I could not; and besides, the crew used to watch us very closely who were not chained down to the decks, lest we should leap into the water; and I have seen some of these poor African prisoners most severely cut, for attempting to do so, and hourly whipped for not eating. This indeed was often the case with myself. In a little time after, amongst the poor chained men, I found some of my own nation, which in a small degree gave ease to my mind. I inquired of these what was to be done with us? they gave me to understand, we were to be carried to these white people's country to work for them. I then was a little revived, and thought, if it were no worse than working, my situation was not so desperate; but still I feared I should be put to death, the white people looked and acted, as I thought, in so savage a manner; for I had never seen among any people such instances of brutal cruelty; and this not only shown towards us blacks, but also to some of the whites themselves. One white man in particular I saw, when we were permitted to be on deck, flogged so unmercifully with a large rope near the foremost, that he died in consequence of it; and they tossed him over the side as they would have done a brute. This made me fear these people the more; and I expected nothing less than to be treated in the same manner. I could not help expressing my fears and apprehensions to some of my countrymen; I asked them if these people had no country, but lived in this hollow place? (the ship) they told me they did not, but came from a distant one....

... The stench of the hold while we were on the coast was so intolerably loathsome, that it was dangerous to remain there for any time, and some of us had been permitted to stay on the deck for the fresh air; but now that the whole ship's cargo were confined together, it became absolutely pestilential. The closeness of the place, and the heat of the climate, added to the number in the ship, which was so crowded that each had scarcely room to turn himself, almost suffocated us. This produced copious perspirations, so that the air soon became unfit for respiration, from a variety of loathsome smells, and brought on a sickness among the slaves, of which many died—thus falling victims to the improvident avarice, as I may call it, of their purchasers. This wretched situation was again aggravated by the galling of the chains, now became insupportable; and the filth of the necessary tubs, into which the children often fell, and were almost suffocated. The shrieks of the women, and the groans of the dying, rendered the whole a scene of horror almost inconceivable. . . .

. . . At last, we came in sight of the island of Barbadoes, at which the whites on board gave a great shout, and made many signs of joy to us. We did not know what to think of this; but as the vessel drew nearer, we plainly saw the harbor, and other ships of different kinds and sizes, and we soon anchored amongst them, off Bridgetown. Many merchants and planters now came on board, though it was in the evening. They put us in separate parcels, and examined us attentively. They also made us jump, and pointed to the land, signifying we were to go there. We thought by this, we should be eaten by these ugly men, as they appeared to us; and, when soon after we were all put down under the deck again, there was much dread and trembling among us, and nothing but bitter cries to be heard all the night from these apprehensions, insomuch, that at last the white people got some old slaves from the land to pacify us. They told us we were not to be eaten, but to work, and were soon to go on land, where we should see many of our country people. This report eased us much. And sure enough, soon after we were landed, there came to us Africans of all languages. . . .

We were not many days in the merchant's custody, before we were sold after their usual manner, which is this:—On a signal given, (as the beat of a drum,) the buyers rush at once into the yard where the slaves are confined, and make choice of that parcel they like best. The noise and clamor with which this is attended, and the eagerness visible in the countenances of the buyers, serve not a little to increase the apprehension of terrified Africans, who may well be supposed to consider them as the ministers of that destruction to which they think themselves devoted. In this manner, without scruple, are relations and friends separated, most of them never to see each other again. I remember, in the vessel in which I was brought over, in the men's apartment, there were several brothers, who, in the sale, were sold in different lots; and it was very moving on this occasion, to see and hear their cries at parting. O, ye nominal Christians! might not an African ask you—Learned you this from your God, who says unto you, Do unto all men as you would men should do unto you? Is it not enough that we are torn from our country and friends, to toil for your luxury and lust of gain? Must every tender feeling be likewise sacrificed to your avarice? Are the dearest friends and relations, now rendered more dear by their separation from their kindred, still to be parted from each other, and thus prevented from cheering the gloom of slavery, with the small comfort of being together, and mingling their sufferings and sorrows? Why are parents to lose their children, brothers their sisters, or husbands their wives? Surely, this is a new refinement in cruelty, which, while it has no advantage to atone for it, thus aggravates distress, and adds fresh horrors even to the wretchedness of slavery.

I now totally lost the small remains of comfort I had enjoyed in conversing with my countrymen; the women too, who used to wash and take care of me were all gone different ways, and I never saw one of them afterwards.

I stayed in this island for a few days; I believe it could not be above a fortnight; when I, and some few more slaves, that were not saleable amongst the rest, from very much fretting, were shipped off in a sloop for North-America. On the passage we were better treated than when we were coming from Africa, and we had plenty of rice and fat pork. We were landed up a river a good way from the sea, about Virginia county, where we saw few or none of our native Africans, and not one soul who could talk to me. I was a few weeks weeding grass, and gathering stones in a plantation; and at last all my companions were distributed different ways, and only myself was left. I was now exceedingly miserable, and thought myself worse off than any of the rest of my companions; for they could talk to each other, but I had no person to speak to that I could understand. In this state, I was constantly grieving and pining, and wishing for death rather than any thing else.

from *Notes on the State of Virginia*

Thomas Jefferson (1743–1826)

Thomas Jefferson wrote *Notes on the State of Virginia* in 1781, five years after his draft of the Declaration of Independence and while he served as governor of the new state. It was privately printed in Paris in 1785 and first made available by a U.S. publisher in 1788. This, his only book, was composed in response to questions posed to him by French officials with whom Jefferson shared many ideals of reason and progress. Jefferson praised Virginia for its wholesome environment and devotion to agriculture, but he also wrestled with the troubling aspects of the place where he had been born and where he would die. Obviously ambivalent about slavery, Jefferson took refuge in "scientific" notions of race, persuading himself and others that black people were fundamentally, biologically, different from whites, unfit for the freedom he had done so much to define for other Americans. His influence would be immense.

The political economists of Europe have established it as a principle, that every State should endeavor to manufacture for itself; and this principle, like many others, we transfer to America, without calculating the difference of circumstance which should often produce a difference of result. In Europe the lands are either cultivated, or locked up against the cultivator. Manufacture must therefore be resorted to of necessity not of choice, to support the surplus of their people. But we have an immensity of land courting the industry of the husbandman. Is it best then that all our citizens should be employed in its improvement, or that one half should be called off from that to exercise manufactures and handicraft arts for the other? Those who labor in the earth are the chosen people of God, if ever He had a chosen people, whose breasts He has made His peculiar deposit for substantial and genuine virtue. It is the focus in which he keeps alive that sacred fire, which otherwise might escape from the face of the earth. Corruption of morals in the mass of cultivators is a phenomenon of which no age nor nation has furnished an example. It is the mark set on those, who, not looking up to heaven, to their own soil and industry, as does the husbandman, for their subsistence, depend for it on casualties and caprice of customers. Dependence begets subservience and venality, suffocates the germ of virtue, and prepares fit tools for the designs of ambition. This, the natural progress and consequence of the arts, has sometimes perhaps been retarded by accidental circumstances; but, generally speaking, the proportion which the aggregate of the other classes of citizens bears in any State to that of its husbandmen, is the proportion of its unsound to its healthy parts, and is a good enough barometer whereby to measure its degree of corruption. While we have land to labor then, let us never wish to see our citizens occupied at a workbench, or twirling a distaff. Carpenters, masons, smiths, are wanting in husbandry; but, for the general operations of manufacture, let our workshops remain in Europe. It is better to carry provisions and materials to workmen there, than bring them to the provisions and materials, and with them their manners and principles. The loss by the transportation of commodities across the Atlantic will be made up in happiness and permanence of government. The mobs of great cities add just so much to the support of pure government, as sores do to the strength of the human body. It is the manners and spirit of a people which preserve a republic in vigor. A degeneracy in these is a canker which soon eats to the heart of its laws and constitution.

. . .

... There must doubtless be an unhappy influence on the manners of our people produced by the existence of slavery among us. The whole commerce between master and slave is a perpetual exercise of the most boisterous passions, the most unremitting despotism on the one part, and degrading submissions on the other. Our children see this, and learn to imitate it; for man is an imitative animal. This quality is the germ of all education in him. From his cradle to his grave he is learning to do what he sees others do. If a parent could find no motive either in his philanthropy or his self-love, for restraining the intemperance of passion towards his slave, it should always be a sufficient one that his child is present. But generally it is not sufficient. The parent storms, the child looks on, catches the lineaments of wraths, puts on the same airs in the circle of smaller slaves, gives a loose to the worst of passions, and thus nursed, educated, and daily exercised in tyranny, cannot but be stamped by it with odious peculiarities. The man must be a prodigy who can retain his manners and morals undepraved by such circumstances. And with what execration should the statesman be loaded, who, permitting one half the citizens thus to trample on the rights of the other, transforms those into despots, and these into enemies, destroys the morals of the one part, and the *amor patriæ* of the other. For if a slave can have a country in this world, it must be any other in preference to that in which he is born to live and labor for another; in which he must lock up the faculties of his nature, contribute as far as depends on his individual endeavors to the evanishment of the human race, or entail his own miserable condition on the endless generations proceeding from him. With the morals of the people, their industry also is destroyed. For in a warm climate, no man will labor for himself who can make another labor for him. This is so true, that of the proprietors of slaves a very small proportion indeed are ever seen to labor. And can the liberties of a nation be thought secure when we have removed their only firm basis, a conviction in the minds of the people that these liberties are of the gift of God? That they are not to be violated but with his wrath? Indeed I tremble for my country when I reflect that God is just; that his justice cannot sleep forever; that considering numbers, nature and natural means only, a revolution of the wheel of fortune, an exchange of situation is among possible events; that it may become probable by supernatural interference! The Almighty has no attribute which can take side with us in such a contest. But it is impossible to be temperate and to pursue this subject through the various considerations of policy, of morals, of history natural and civil. We must be contented to hope they will force their way into every one's mind. I think a change already perceptible, since the origin of the present revolution. The spirit of the master is abating, that of the slave rising from the dust, his condition mollifying, the way I hope preparing, under the auspices of heaven, for a total emancipation, and that this is disposed, in the order of events, to be with the consent of the masters, rather than by their extirpation.

. . .

. . . It will probably be asked, Why not retain and incorporate the blacks into the State, and thus save the expense of supplying by importation of white settlers, the vacancies they will leave? Deep-rooted prejudices entertained by the whites; ten thousand recollections, by the blacks, of the injuries they have sustained; new provocations; the real distinctions which nature has made; and many other circumstances, will divide us into parties, and produce convulsions, which will probably never end but in the extermination of the one or the other race. To these objections, which are political, may be added others, which are physical and moral. The first difference which strikes us is that of color. Whether the black of the negro resides in the reticular membrane between the skin and scarf-skin, or in the scarf-skin itself; whether it proceeds from the color of the blood, the color of the bile, or from that of some other secretion, the difference is fixed in nature, and is as real as if its seat and cause were better known to us. And is this difference of no importance? Is it not the foundation of a greater or less share of beauty in the two races? Are not the fine mixtures of red and white, the expressions of every passion by greater or less suffusions of color in the one, preferable to that eternal monotony, which reigns in the countenances, that immovable veil of black which covers the emotions of the other race? Add to these, flowing hair, a more elegant symmetry of form, their own judgment in favor of the whites, declared by their preference of them, as uniformly as is the preference of the Oranootan for the black woman over those of his own species. The circumstance of superior beauty, is thought worthy attention in the propagation of our horses, dogs, and other domestic animals; why not in that of man? Besides those of color, figure, and hair, there are other physical distinctions proving a difference of race. They have less hair on the face and body. They secrete less by the kidneys, and more by the glands of the skin, which gives them a very strong and disagreeable odor. This greater degree of transpiration, renders them more tolerant of heat, and less so of cold than the whites. Perhaps, too, a difference of structure in the pulminary apparatus, which a late ingenious experimentalist has discovered to be the principal regulator of animal heat, may have disabled them from extricating, in the act of inspiration, so much of that fluid from the outer air, or obliged them in expiration, to part with more of it. They seem to require less sleep. A black after hard labor through the day, will be induced by the slightest amusements to sit up till midnight, or later, though knowing he must be out with the first dawn of the morning. They are at least as brave, and more adventuresome. But this may perhaps proceed from a want of forethought, which prevents their seeing a danger till it be present. When present, they do not go through it with more coolness or steadiness than the whites. They are more ardent after their female; but love seems with them to be more an eager desire, than a tender delicate mixture of sentiment and sensation. Their griefs are transient. Those numberless afflictions, which render it doubtful whether heaven has given life to us in mercy or in wrath, are less felt, and sooner forgotten with them. In general, their existence appears to participate more of sensation than reflection. To this must be ascribed their disposition to sleep when abstracted from their diversions, and unemployed in labor. An animal whose body is at rest, and who does not reflect, must be disposed to sleep of course. Comparing them by their faculties of memory, reason, and imagination, it appears to me that in memory they are equal to the whites; in reason much inferior, as I think one could scarcely be found capable of tracing and comprehending the investigations of Euclid; and that in imagination they are dull, tasteless, and anomalous. It would be unfair to follow them to Africa for this investigation. We will consider them here, on the same stage with the whites, and where the facts are not apochryphal on which a judgment is to be formed. It will be right to make great allowances for the difference of condition, of education, of conversation, of the sphere in which they move. Many millions of them have been brought to, and born in America. Most of them, indeed, have been confined to tillage, to their own homes, and their own society; yet many have been so situated, that they might have availed themselves of the conversation of their masters;

many have been brought up to the handicraft arts, and from that circumstance have always been associated with the whites. Some have been liberally educated, and all have lived in countries where the arts and sciences are cultivated to a considerable degree, and all have had before their eyes samples of the best works from abroad. The Indians, with no advantages of this kind, will often carve figures on their pipes not destitute of design and merit. They will crayon out an animal, a plant, or a country, so as to prove the existence of a germ in their minds which only wants cultivation. They astonish you with strokes of the most sublime oratory; such as prove their reason and sentiment strong, their imagination glowing and elevated. But never yet could I find that a black had uttered a thought above the level of plain narration; never saw even an elementary trait of painting or sculpture. In music they are more generally gifted than the whites with accurate ears for tune and time, and they have been found capable of imagining a small catch. Whether they will be equal to the composition of a more extensive run of melody, or of complicated harmony, is yet to be proved. Misery is often the parent of the most affecting touches in poetry. Among the blacks is misery enough, God knows, but no poetry.

from the Reverend Francis Asbury's *Journal*

Francis Asbury (1745–1816)

Francis Asbury, born in England and ordained a Wesleyan ("Methodist") minister in 1767, volunteered to be a missionary to the American colonies. Asbury was the only Methodist missionary to remain in the colonies throughout the American Revolution and became superintendent of the Methodist Church in 1784. Devoting himself to spreading the influence of the church, Asbury rode horseback throughout the South preaching and helping to organize new churches. His exhausting travels and labors, described in the journal he kept from 1771 to 1816, helped transform his prayers into reality: the Methodist Church joined the Baptists and Presbyterians as one of the three great denominations of the South. His journal was published in its entirety in 1821.

Tuesday 2 January 1787. We rode near fifty miles on our way to Westmoreland; next day, by hard riding, we came to Pope's, in Westmoreland; but I have not been more weary many times in my life.

Saturday & Sunday. Attended the quarterly meeting in the Northern Neck: there were many simple and loving testimonies delivered in the love-feast.

Thursday 11. Rode through the snow to Fairfield. Here a Capt. R. had turned the people out of the barn in which worship was held, and threatened to take brother Paup to jail if he did not show his authority for preaching; after all this vapouring of the valiant Captain, when the affair was brought before the court, Captain R——found it convenient to ask pardon of our brother, although he sat upon the bench in his own cause: —so the matter ended. The Lord is at work in the Neck: more than one hundred have been added to the society since conference, who are a simple, loving, tender people.

We had a good time on Friday the 12th; I spoke on Acts xxvi. 18. I think God has spoken by me to S——s, a wild man—but the Lord can tame him: O Lord, speak for thyself!

Sunday 14. We had a crowd at the Presbyterian meeting-house in Lancaster, to whom I delivered a very rough discourse: it was a close and searching time, and we had many communicants, both white and coloured.

Tuesday 16. Preached at the church on the love of Christ. I find it hard to the flesh to ride fifteen or twenty miles every day and perform the duties of my station; especially when indisposed and suffering therefrom the bodily pain incident thereto. Lord, give me patience! I feel uncommon affection for the people here.

Wednesday 17. I had a crowd of careless sinners at Mrs. Ball's, who is a famous heroine for Christ. A lady came by craft and took her from her own house, and with tears, threats, and entreaties urged her to desist from receiving the preachers, and Methodist preaching; but all in vain. She had felt the sting of death some years before, and was a most disconsolate soul; having now found the way, she would not depart therefrom.

Thursday 18. Rode ten miles to the ferry; but being unable to cross, I returned to Mrs. B.'s: next morning I came away before day, and reached Shackford's.

Saturday 20. Preached at Douglas's — very low in body and spirit.

Sunday 21. & Monday 22. Cold times in religion in this circuit, (Gloucester) compared with the great times we have had in Lancaster.

Tuesday 23. Came off early, and preached in Yorktown to some well-behaved women. Dined with Mr. Mitchell, and went on to dear brother Weldon's whose heart and hands were open.

Wednesday 24. According to appointment, I attended at Williamsburg. I had about five from the country, and about fifteen hearers from the town, besides a few blacks and children. I spoke with freedom on "They made light of it." I returned through the rain, but hope to receive no harm.

> He guards our souls, he keeps our breath,
>   Where thickest dangers come:
> Go, and return; secure from death,
>   Till God commands thee home.

Friday 26. We waited four hours in the rain before we could cross the ferry at Old Jamestown; it was two hours after night when we came to brother Morings.

Tuesday 30. We held a quarterly meeting at Craney Island; the weather prevented many from attending. I was blessed in the company of the preachers.

Wednesday 31. I enlarged on "What shall the end be of them who obey not the Gospel of God?" I observed to them that the Gospel had once been taken away from them; and that they ought to lay it seriously to heart, lest it should be the case again. We had some quickening in the sacrament and at the love-feast. Thence I went through Portsmouth, and preached on "Ye are now returned to the Shepherd and Bishop of your souls."

Saturday, February 3. Visited my old friend Fullford: he is feeble in body, and not much at ease in his worldly possessions, yet happy in God.

Brother Poythress frightened me with the idea of the Great Swamp, the east end of the Dismal; but I could not consent to ride sixty miles round; so we ventured through, and neither we nor our horses received any injury.—Praise the Lord!—Our passing unharmed through such dangers and unhealthy weather, feelingly assures me that I am kept by the immediate interposition of His providence I preached in the new chapel.—I hope not in vain. I am now surrounded with waters, and hideous swamps, near the head of Pasquotank-River.

NORTH CAROLINA.—Thursday 9. Came on, wet and unwell to Proby's. Went on to Nixonton, where I had many to hear, and was blessed in my own soul, and, I think, spoke to the cases of some of my audience.

Friday 10. I had a long ride of nearly fifty miles to Gates county. We stopped at one Newby's, one of the society of Friends, who entertained us kindly. We reached sister Gibson's, cold and weary. The poor flesh complains, but my soul enjoys peace and sweetness.

Sunday 11. We had a large congregation, and an open time at Knotty-Pine chapel.—Here we have a little revival.

Tuesday 13. I had about sixty people at Wicocon: I spoke as I felt on Jer. xiii. 11. I mourned over the people and left them.

I came to Hardy's, where I spoke with some light on Matt. xxii. 5. I unhappily ran a splinter into my leg which has alarmed me.

I found we had to go twelve miles by water, and send the horses another way. O what a world of swamps, and rivers, and islands, we live in here! I met brother B——and A——; two devoted young men; the former, a native of Maryland; the latter of Virginia. At the desire of several of the brethren I preached at Washington, where many collected in the courthouse, whom I addressed on my favourite text, 1 Tim. i. 15. Three miles on the water, and riding three more on roads under the water, (such is the inundated state of the country,) made our jaunt unpleasant.

Thursday 22. We set off for Newbern. Stopped at Kemps Ferry, kept by Curtis, where we were kindly entertained, *gratis*. I feel heaviness through labour and temptation, yet I am given up to God.

Friday 23. I arrived at Newbern. I felt the power of death as I journeyed along. We rode round the town, and could get no certain information about preaching, brother Cole being absent. We were at last taken in at Mr. Lathrop's. The place and people were in such a state, that I judged, by my own feelings, it would be as well to leave them just as I found them—and so I did.

Tuesday 27. It was rather a dry time at the love-feast and sacrament. There was some life and melting while I enforced "Look unto me, and be ye saved, all ye ends of the earth." We then rode to H——'s on Island Creek. I went alone into the woods, and had sweet converse with God. At

night we were poorly provided against the weather; the house was unfinished; and, to make matters worse, a horse kicked the door open, and I
took a cold, and had the toothache, with a high fever.

Thursday, March 1. I had more hearers, and they were more attentive
than I expected: I trust it was a profitable time. Rode to brother Johnson's
— without the labour of slaves he manages to have abundance for man
and beast.

Tuesday 6. My horse is stiff, and almost foundered, and there is an
appearance of a swelling on his head. I have always had hard struggles to
get to Charleston—Lord, give me patience, and bear me up!

Wednesday 7. Crossed the main fork of Black-River, and came through
a wild country to Colonel R——'s: the Colonel's wife is a tender, devoted
woman.

Thursday and Friday 8, 9. Directed our course to the south: crossed
Cape Fear, and reached Drowning-Creek. Rested a day at W——'s, a kind
people, but without religion.

SOUTH CAROLINA. — Sunday 11. Preached at Robinson's new courthouse. Rode in the evening to M——'s. Crossed Little Pee-Dee; stopped
at S——'s; ate a morsel, and came on to Buck Swamp.

Thursday 15. Preached at the new church at S——'s: here I heard that
Doctor Coke was in Charleston. Proceeded thence to the widow Port's,
where I had much ado to prevail on brother H. to stay.

We rode nearly fifty miles to get to Georgetown. Here the scene was
greatly changed: almost the whole town came together to hear the word
of the Lord.

We arrived in Charleston, and met Doctor Coke. Here we have already
a spacious house prepared for us; and the congregations are crowded and
solemn.

Sunday 25. I enlarged on, "I had rather be a door-keeper in the house
of God, than to dwell in the tents of wickedness;" at night again on Isai.
xlv. 22. We held our conference in this city.

Tuesday 27. We exchanged sentiments on matters freely.

Wednesday 28. The Doctor treated on the qualifications and duties of
a deacon.

Thursday 29. Our conference ended.

Friday 30. I left the city, and rode thirty miles, although my horse had
been injured by over-feeding. Next day I rode forty miles through the rain,
and begged a lodging with Doctor W.

Sunday, April 1. We came to Santee Ferry, and there was such an over-
flowing of water in our route that we had to swim upon our horses several
times: my horse performed so well that I was not wet much higher than
my knees: that day we rode thirty miles, and the next day fifty miles, and

came to Moore's. Here we met with brother R. Swift, who had been near death, but then was recovering: we advised him to go with us for his life. The people here begin to feel, and yield to the power of truth.

Wednesday 4. At Camden I preached on "They made light of it:" thence we rode on to quarterly meeting, where I met with a multitude of people who were desperately wicked — but God hath wrought among them: we had little rest by day or night.

Friday 6. Rode forty miles to preaching at Jackson's; and then to brother Pace's.

Saturday 7, and Sunday 8. Attended Anson quarterly meeting, in North Carolina: the Doctor preached on the love of Christ, and I on "the grace of God that bringeth salvation;" sacrament followed.

From Saturday to Saturday, I have rode about three hundred miles, and have preached only about half the time: O may the Lord seal and water his own word, that all this toil of man and beast be not in vain.

from *The Confessions of Nat Turner*

Nat Turner (1800–1831)

Nat Turner, born into slavery in Southampton County, Virginia, in 1800, felt himself marked early in his life for a special purpose. He preached Christian sermons throughout the county and beyond, telling listeners of his visions. Turner interpreted signs such as eclipses to mean that he must lead an insurrection against the whites who held blacks in slavery. On August 22, 1831, Turner and a small cadre of other slaves began a rebellion, killing five people at one home and then moving through Southampton County. Turner's band, joined by more than sixty other slaves, killed over fifty whites during the next forty hours. Military and police forces stifled the rebellion before it could reach the county seat of Jerusalem, but Turner escaped. He evaded capture until late October, when he was accidentally discovered. Turner was hanged on November 11, 1831, but not before being interviewed by Thomas Gray, his court-appointed attorney. The interview, as reported by Gray, quickly became an influential document, read widely in the South. It has remained both fascinating and controversial ever since, the boundary between fact and fiction, between Turner and Gray, unclear and intriguing.

Agreeable to his own appointment, on the evening he was committed to prison, with permission of the jailer, I visited NAT on Tuesday the 1st November, when, without being questioned at all, he commenced his narrative in the following words:—

SIR,—You have asked me to give a history of the motives which induced me to undertake the late insurrection, as you call it—To do so I must go back to the days of my infancy, and even before I was born. I was thirty-one years of age the 2d of October last, and born the property of Benj. Turner, of this county. In my childhood a circumstance occurred which made an indelible impression on my mind, and laid the ground work of that enthusiasm, which has terminated so fatally to many, both white and black, and for which I am about to atone at the gallows. It is here necessary to relate this circumstance—trifling as it may seem, it was the commencement of that belief which has grown with time, and even now, sir, in this dungeon, helpless and forsaken as I am, I cannot divest myself of. Being at play with other children, when three or four years old, I was telling them something, which my mother overhearing, said it had happened before I was born—I stuck to my story, however, and related somethings which went, in her opinion, to confirm it — others being called on were greatly astonished, knowing that these things had happened, and caused them to say in my hearing, I surely would be a prophet, as the Lord had shewn me things that had happened before my birth. And my father and mother strengthened me in this my first impression, saying in my presence, I was intended for some great purpose, which they had always thought from certain marks on my head and breast—[a parcel of excrescences which I believe are not at all uncommon, particularly among negroes, as I have seen several with the same. In this case he has either cut them off or they have nearly disappeared] — My grandmother, who was very religious, and to whom I was much attached—my master, who belonged to the church, and other religious persons who visited the house, and whom I often saw at prayers, noticing the singularity of my manners, I suppose, and my uncommon intelligence for a child, remarked I had too much sense to be raised, and if I was, I would never be of any service to any one as a slave—To a mind like mine, restless, inquisitive and observant of every thing that was passing, it is easy to suppose that religion was the subject to which it would be directed, and although this subject principally occupied my thoughts—there was nothing that I saw or heard of to which my attention was not directed—The manner in which I learned to read and write, not only had great influence on my own mind, as I acquired it with the most perfect ease, so much so, that I have no recollection whatever of learning the alphabet—but to the astonishment of the family, one day, when a book was shewn me to keep me from crying, I began spelling the names of different objects—this was a source of wonder to all in the neighborhood, particularly the blacks—and this learning was constantly improved at all opportunities—when I got large enough to go to work, while employed, I was reflecting on many things that would present themselves to my imagination, and whenever an opportunity occurred of looking at a book, when the school children were getting their lessons, I would find many things that the fertility of my own imagination had depicted to me before; all my time, not devoted to my master's service, was spent either in prayer, or in making experiments in casting different things in moulds made of earth, in attempting to make paper, gunpowder, and many other experiments, that although I could not perfect, yet convinced me of its practicability if I had the means. I was not addicted to stealing in my youth, nor have ever been—Yet such was the confidence of the negroes in the neighborhood, even at this early period of my life, in my superior judgment, that they would often carry me with them when they were going on any roguery, to plan for them. Growing up among them, with this confidence in my superior judgment, and when this, in their opinions, was perfected by Divine inspiration, from the circumstances already alluded to in my infancy, and which belief was ever afterwards zealously inculcated by the austerity of my life and manners, which became the subject of remark by white and black. — Having soon discovered to be great, I must appear so, and therefore studiously avoided mixing in society, and wrapped myself in mystery, devoting my time to fasting and prayer—By this time, having arrived to man's estate, and hearing the scriptures commented on at meetings, I was struck with that particular passage which says: "Seek ye the kingdom of Heaven and all things shall be added unto you." I reflected much on this passage, and prayed daily for light on this subject — As I was praying one day at my plough, the spirit spoke to me, saying "Seek ye the kingdom of Heaven and all things shall be added unto you.["] *Question* — what do you mean by the Spirit. *Ans.* The Spirit that spoke to the prophets in former days—and I was greatly astonished, and for two years prayed continually, whenever my duty would permit — and then again I had the same revelation, which fully confirmed me in the impression that I was ordained for some great purpose in the hands of the Almighty. Several years rolled round, in which many events occurred to strengthen me in this my belief. At this time I reverted in my mind to the remarks made of me in my childhood, and the things that had been shewn me — and as it had been said of me in my childhood by those by whom I had been taught to pray, both white and black, and in whom I had the greatest confidence, that I had too much sense to be raised, and if I was, I would never be of any use to any one as a slave. Now finding I had arrived to man's estate, and was a slave, and these revelations being made known to me, I began to direct my attention to this great object, to fulfil the purpose for which, by this time, I felt assured I was intended. Knowing the influence I had obtained over the minds of my fellow servants, (not by the means of conjuring and such like tricks—for to them I always spoke of such things with contempt) but by the communion of the Spirit whose revelations I often communicated to them, and they believed and said my wisdom came from God. I now began to prepare them for my purpose, by telling them something was about to happen that would terminate in fulfilling the great promise that had been made to me — About this time I was placed under an overseer, from whom I ran away — and after remaining in the woods thirty days, I returned, to the astonishment of the negroes on the plantation, who thought I had made my escape to some other part of the country, as my father had done before. But the reason of my return was, that the Spirit appeared to me and said I had my wishes directed to the things of this world, and not to the kingdom of Heaven, and that I should return to the service of my earthly master—"For he who knoweth his Master's will, and doeth it not, shall be beaten with many stripes, and thus have I chastened you." And the negroes found fault, and murmurred against me, saying that if they had my sense they would not serve any master in the world. And about this time I had a vision—and I saw white spirits and black spirits engaged in battle, and the sun was darkened—the thunder rolled in the Heavens, and blood flowed in streams—and I heard a voice saying, "Such is your luck, such you are called to see, and let it come rough or smooth, you must surely bare it." I now withdrew myself as much as my situation would permit, from the intercourse of my fellow servants, for the avowed purpose of serving the Spirit more fully—and it appeared to me, and reminded me of the things it had already shown me, and that it would then reveal to me the knowledge of the elements, the revolution of the planets, the operation of tides, and changes of the seasons. After this rev-elation in the year 1825, and the knowledge of the elements being made known to me, I sought more than ever to obtain true holiness before the great day of judgment should appear, and then I began to receive the true knowledge of faith. And from the first steps of righteousness until the last, was I made perfect; and the Holy Ghost was with me, and said, "Behold me as I stand in the Heavens"—and I looked and saw the forms of men in different attitudes—and there were lights in the sky to which the chil-dren of darkness gave other names than what they really were—for they were the lights of the Saviour's hands, stretched forth from east to west, even as they were extended on the cross on Calvary for the redemption of sinners. And I wondered greatly at these miracles, and prayed to be informed of a certainty of the meaning thereof—and shortly afterwards, while laboring in the field, I discovered drops of blood on the corn as though it were dew from heaven—and I communicated it to many, both white and black, in the neighborhood—and I then found on the leaves in the woods hieroglyphic characters, and numbers, with the forms of men in different attitudes, portrayed in blood, and representing the figures I had seen before in the heavens. And now the Holy Ghost had revealed itself to me, and made plain the miracles it had shown me—For as the blood of Christ had been shed on this earth, and had ascended to heaven for the salvation of sinners, and was now returning to earth again in the form of dew—and as the leaves on the trees bore the impression of the figures I had seen in the heavens, it was plain to me that the Saviour was about to lay down the yoke he had borne for the sins of men, and the great day of judgment was at hand. About this time I told these things to a white man, (Etheldred T. Brantley) on whom it had a wonderful effect—and he ceased from his wickedness, and was attacked immediately with a cutaneous eruption, and blood ozed from the pores of his skin, and after praying and fasting nine days, he was healed, and the Spirit appeared to me again, and said, as the Saviour had been baptised so should we be also —and when the white people would not let us be baptised by the church, we went down into the water together, in the sight of many who reviled us, and were baptised by the Spirit—After this I rejoiced greatly, and gave thanks to God. And on the 12th of May, 1828, I heard a loud noise in the heavens, and the Spirit instantly appeared to me and said the Serpent was loosened, and Christ had laid down the yoke he had borne for the sins of men, and that I should take it on and fight against the Serpent, for the time was fast approaching when the first should be last and the last should be first. *Ques.* Do you not find yourself mistaken now? *Ans.* Was not Christ crucified. And by signs in the heavens that it would make known to me when I should commence the great work—and until the first sign appeared, I should conceal it from the knowledge of men—And on the appearance of the sign, (the eclipse of the sun last February) I should arise and prepare myself, and slay my enemies with their own weapons.

from *Georgia Scenes*

Augustus Baldwin Longstreet (1790–1870)

Augustus Baldwin Longstreet, though born and raised in Georgia, received his legal education in the North. Returning to his native state to practice law, Longstreet traveled through the frontier districts of the southwest part of the state in the late 1810s and early 1820s, making political and social contacts and observing the raw society around him. After Longstreet became a newspaper editor, he tried to portray the customs, speech, and values of people he had encountered on his travels. These sketches, mixing affection with amusement, were collected and published in *Georgia Scenes* in 1835; they met with warm reviews and widespread sales. Longstreet subsequently became a Methodist minister and president of several Southern colleges and universities.

In the younger days of the Republic, there lived in the county of——, two men, who were admitted on all hands to be the very best men in the county — which, in the Georgia vocabulary, means they could flog any other two men in the county. Each, through many a hard fought battle, had acquired the mastery of his own battalion; but they lived on opposite sides of the Court House, and in different battalions; consequently they were but seldom thrown together. When they met, however, they were always very friendly; indeed, at their first interview, they seemed to conceive a wonderful attachment to each other, which rather increased than diminished, as they became better acquainted; so that, but for the circumstance which I am about to mention, the question which had been a thousand times asked "Which is the best man, Billy Stallions, (Stallings,) or Bob Durham?" would probably never have been answered.

Billy ruled the upper battalion, and Bob the lower. The former measured six feet and an inch, in his stockings, and without a single pound of cumbrous flesh about him weighed a hundred and eighty. The latter, was an inch shorter than his rival, and ten pounds lighter; but he was much the most active of the two. In running and jumping, he had but few equals in the county; and in wrestling, not one. In other respects they were nearly equal. Both were admirable specimens of human nature in its finest form. Billy's victories had generally been achieved by the tremendous power of his blows; one of which had often proved decisive of his battles; Bob's, by his adroitness in bringing his adversary to the ground. This advantage he had never failed to gain, at the onset, and when gained, he never failed to improve it to the defeat of his adversary. These points of difference, have involved the reader in a doubt, as to the probable issue of a contest between them. It was not so, however, with the two battalions. Neither had the least difficulty in determining the point by the most nat-ural and irresistible deductions *a priori*: and though, by the same course of reasoning, they arrived at directly opposite conclusions, neither felt its confidence in the least shaken by this circumstance. The upper battalion swore "that Billy only wanted one lick at him to knock his heart, liver and lights out of him; and if he got two at him, he'd knock him into a cocked hat." The lower battalion retorted, "that he wouldn't have time to double his fist, before Bob would put his head where his feet ought to be; and that, by the time he hit the ground, the meat would fly off his face so quick, that people would think it was shook off by the fall." These disputes often led to the *argumentum ad hominem*; but with such equality of success on both sides, as to leave the main question just where they found it. They usually ended, however, in the common way, with a bet; and many a quart of old Jamaica, (whiskey had not then supplanted rum,) were staked upon the issue. Still, greatly to the annoyance of the curious Billy and Bob contin-ued to be good friends.

Now there happened to reside in the county, just alluded to, a little fel-low, by the name of Ransy Sniffle: a sprout of Richmond, who, in his ear-lier days, had fed copiously upon red clay and blackberries. This diet had given to Ransy a complexion that a corpse would have disdained to own, and an abdominal rotundity that was quite unprepossessing. Long spells of the fever and ague, too, in Ransy's youth, had conspired with clay and blackberries, to throw him quite out of the order of nature. His shoulders were fleshless and elevated; his head large and flat; his neck slim and translucent; and his arms, hands, fingers and feet, were lengthened out of all proportion to the rest of his frame. His joints were large, and his limbs small; and as for flesh, he could not with propriety be said to have any. Those parts which nature usually supplies with the most of this article— the calves of the legs for example—presented in him the appearance of so many well drawn blisters. His height was just five feet nothing; and his average weight in blackberry season, ninety-five. I have been thus partic-ular in describing him, for the purpose of showing what a great matter a little fire sometimes kindleth. There was nothing on this earth which delighted Ransy so much as a fight. He never seemed fairly alive, except when he was witnessing, fomenting, or talking about a fight. Then, indeed, his deep sunken grey eye, assumed something of a living fire; and his tongue acquired a volubility that bordered upon eloquence. Ransy had been kept for more than a year in the most torturing suspense, as to the

comparative manhood of Billy Stallings and Bob Durham. He had
resorted to all his usual expedients to bring them in collision, and had
entirely failed. He had faithfully reported to Bob all that had been said
by the people in the upper battalion "agin him," and "he was sure Billy
Stallings started it. He heard Bill say himself to Jim Brown, that he could
whip him, *or any other man in his battalion;*" and this he told to Bob —
adding, "Dod burn his soul, if he was a little bigger, if he'd let any man
put upon his battalion in such a way." Bob replied, "If he (Stallings)
thought so, he'd better come and try it." This Ransy carried to Billy, and
delivered it with a spirit becoming his own dignity, and the character of
his battalion, and with a coloring well calculated to give it effect. These,
and many other schemes which Ransy laid, for the gratification of his
curiosity, entirely failed of their object. Billy and Bob continued friends,
and Ransy began to lapse into the most tantalizing and hopeless despair,
when a circumstance occurred, which led to a settlement of the long disputed question.

It is said that a hundred game cocks will live in perfect harmony
together, if you will not put a hen with them: and so it would have been
with Billy and Bob, had there been no women in the world. But there
were women in the world, and from them, each of our heroes had taken
to himself a wife. The good ladies were no strangers to the prowess of their
husbands, and strange as it may seem, they presumed a little upon it.

The two battalions had met at the Court House, upon a regimental
parade. The two champions were there, and their wives had accompanied
them. Neither knew the other's lady, nor were the ladies known to each
other. The exercises of the day were just over, when Mrs. Stallings and
Mrs. Durham stept simultaneously into the store of Zepheniah Atwater,
from "down east."

"Have you any Turkey-red?" said Mrs. S.

"Have you any curtain calico?" said Mrs. D. at the same moment.

"Yes, ladies," said Mr. Atwater, "I have both."

"Then help me first," said Mrs. D., "for I'm in a hurry."

"I'm in as great a hurry as she is," said Mrs. S., "and I'll thank you to
help me first."

"And pray, who are you, madam!" continued the other.

"Your betters, madam," was the reply.

At this moment Billy Stallings stept in. "Come," said he, "Nancy, let's
be going; it's getting late."

"I'd o' been gone half an hour ago," she replied, "if it hadn't been for
that impudent huzzy."

"Who do you call an impudent huzzy? you nasty, good-for-nothing,
snaggle-toothed gaub of fat, you," returned Mrs. D.

"Look here woman," said Billy, "have you got a husband here? If you have, I'll *lick* him till he learns to teach you better manners, you *sassy* heifer you." At this moment something was seen to rush out of the store, as if ten thousand hornets were stinging it; crying "Take care—let me go—don't hold me—where's Bob Durham?" It was Ransy Sniffle, who had been listening in breathless delight, to all that had passed.

"Yonder's Bob, setting on the Court-house steps," cried one. "What's the matter?"

"Don't talk to me!" said Ransy. "Bob Durham, you'd better go long yonder, and take care of your wife. They're playing h———l with her there, in Zeph. Atwater's store. Dod deternally durn my soul, if any man was to talk to my wife as Bill Stallions is talking to yours, if I didn't drive blue blazes through him in less than no time."

Bob sprang to the store in a minute, followed by a hundred friends; for the bully of a county never wants friends.

"Bill Stallions," said Bob, as he entered, "what have you been saying to my wife?"

"Is that your wife?" inquired Billy, obviously much surprised, and a little disconcerted.

"Yes, she is, and no man shall abuse her, I don't care who he is."

"Well," rejoined Billy, "it an't worth while to go over it — I've said enough for a fight: and if you'll step out, we'll settle it!"

"Billy," said Bob, "are you for a fair fight?"

"I am," said Billy. "I've heard much of your manhood, and I believe I'm a better man than you are. If you will go into a ring with me, we can soon settle the dispute."

"Choose your friends," said Bob; "make your ring, and I'll be in it with mine, as soon as you will."

They both stept out, and began to strip very deliberately; each battalion gathering round its champion—except Ransy, who kept himself busy, in a most honest endeavor to hear and see all that transpired in both groups, at the same time. He ran from one to the other, in quick succession—peeped here, and listened there—talked to this one—then to that one—and then to himself—squatted under one's legs, and another's arms; and in the short interval between stripping and stepping into the ring, managed to get himself trod on by half of both battalions. But Ransy was not the only one interested upon this occasion:—the most intense interest prevailed every where. Many were the conjectures, doubts, oaths and imprecations uttered, while the parties were preparing for the combat. All the knowing ones were consulted as to the issue; and they all agreed to a man, in one of two opinions: either that Bob would flog Billy, or Billy would flog Bob. We must be permitted, however, to dwell for a moment upon the opinion of 'Squire Thomas Loggins; a man, who it was said, had never failed to predict the issue of a fight, in all his life. Indeed, so unerring had he always proved, in this regard, that it would have been counted the most obstinate infidelity, to doubt for a moment, after he had delivered himself. 'Squire Loggins was a man who said but little; but that little was always delivered with the most imposing solemnity of look and cadence. He always wore the aspect of profound thought, and you could not look at him without coming to the conclusion, that he was elaborating truth from its most intricate combinations.

"Uncle Tommy," said Sam Reynolds, "you can tell us all about it, if you will—how will the fight go?"

The question immediately drew an anxious group around the 'Squire. He raised his teeth slowly from the head of his walking cane, on which they had been resting—pressed his lips closely and thoughfully together —threw down his eye brows—dropped his chin—raised his eyes to an angle of twenty three degrees—paused about half a minute, and replied: "Sammy, watch Robert Durham close in the beginning of the fight—take care of William Stallions in the middle of it—and see who has the wind at the end." As he uttered the last member of the sentence, he looked slyly at Bob's friends, and winked very significantly; whereupon they rushed, with one accord, to tell Bob what Uncle Tommy had said. As they retired, the 'Squire turned to Billy's friends, and said, with a smile: "Them boys think I mean that Bob will whip."

Here the other party kindled into joy, and hastened to inform Billy how Bob's friends had deceived themselves as to Uncle Tommy's opinion. In the meantime, the principals and seconds, were busily employed in preparing themselves for the combat. The plan of attack and defence, the manner of improving the various turns of the conflict, "the best mode of saving wind," &c. &c. were all discussed and settled. At length, Billy announced himself ready, and his crowd were seen moving to the centre of the Court House Square; he and his five seconds in the rear. At the same time, Bob's party moved to the same point, and in the same order. The ring was now formed, and for a moment the silence of death reigned through both battalions. It was soon interrupted, however, by the cry of "clear the way!" from Billy's seconds; when the ring opened in the centre of the upper battalion, (for the order of march had arranged the centre of the two battalions on opposite sides of the circle,) and Billy stept into the ring from the east, followed by his friends. He was stript to the trowsers, and exhibited an arm, breast and shoulders, of the most tremendous portent. His step was firm, daring and martial; and as he bore his fine form a little in advance of his friends, an involuntary burst of triumph broke from his side of the ring; and at the same moment, an uncontrollable thrill of awe, ran along the whole curve of the lower battalion.

"Look at him!" was heard from his friends—"just look at him."

"Ben, how much you ask to stand before that man two seconds?"

"Pshaw, don't talk about it! Just thinkin' about it's broke three o' my ribs a'ready!"

"What's Bob Durham going to do, when Billy lets that arm loose upon him?"

"God bless your soul, he'll think thunder and lightning a mint julip to it."

"Oh, look here men, go take Bill Stallions out o' that ring, and bring in Phil Johnson's stud horse, so that Durham may have some chance! I don't want to see the man killed right away."

These and many other like expressions, interspersed thickly with oaths of the most modern coinage, were coming from all points of the upper battalion, while Bob was adjusting the girth of his pantaloons, which walking had discovered, not to be exactly right. It was just fixed to his mind, his foes becoming a little noisy, and his friends a little uneasy at his delay, when Billy called out, with a smile of some meaning, "Where's the bully of the lower battalion? I'm getting tired of waiting."

"Here he is," said Bob, lighting, as it seemed from the clouds in the ring, for he had actually bounded clear of the head of Ransy Sniffle, into the circle. His descent was quite as imposing as Billy's entry, and excited the same feelings, but in opposite bosoms.

Voices of exultation now rose on his side.

"Where did he come from?"

"Why," said one of the seconds, (all having just entered,) "we were girting him up, about a hundred yards out yonder, when he heard Billy ask for the bully; and he fetched a leap over the Court House, and went out of sight; but I told them to come on, they'd find him here."

Here the lower battalion burst into a peal of laughter, mingled with a look of admiration, which seemed to denote their entire belief of what they had heard.

"Boys widen the ring, so as to give him room to jump."

"Oh, my little flying wild cat, hold him if you can! and when you get him fast, hold lightning next."

"Ned what you think he's made of?"

"Steel-springs and chicken-hawk, God bless you!"

"Gentlemen," said one of Bob's seconds, "I understand it is to be a fair fight; catch as catch can, rough and tumble:—no man touch 'till one or the other hollos."

"That's the rule," was the reply from the other side.

"Are you ready?"

"We are ready."

"Then blaze away my game cocks."

At the word, Bob dashed at his antagonist at full speed; and Bill squared himself to receive him with one of his most fatal blows. Making his calculation from Bob's velocity, of the time when he would come within striking distance, he let drive with tremendous force. But Bob's onset was obviously planned to avoid this blow; for contrary to all expectations, he stopt short just out of arms reach; and before Billy could recover his balance — Bob had him "all under-hold." The next second, sure enough, "found Billy's head where his feet ought to be." How it was done, no one could tell; but as if by supernatural power, both Billy's feet were thrown full half his own height in the air, and he came down with a force that seemed to shake the earth. As he struck the ground, commingled shouts, screams and yells burst from the lower battalion, loud enough to be heard for miles. "Hurra my little hornet!" — "Save him!" — "Feed him! — Give him the Durham physic till his stomach turns!" Billy was no sooner down than Bob was on him, and lending him awful blows about the face and breast. Billy made two efforts to rise by main strength, but failed. "Lord bless you man, don't try to get up! — *Lay* still and take it! — you *bleege* to have it."

Billy now turned his face suddenly to the ground, and rose upon his hands and knees. Bob jerked up both his hands and threw him on his face. He again recovered his late position, of which Bob endeavored to deprive him as before; but missing one arm, he failed, and Billy rose. But he had scarcely resumed his feet before they flew up as before, and he came again to the ground. "No fight gentlemen!" cried Bob's friends, "the man can't stand up! — Bouncing feet are bad things to fight in." His fall, however, was this time comparatively light; for having thrown his right arm round Bob's neck, he carried his head down with him. This grasp, which was obstinately maintained, prevented Bob from getting on him, and they lay head to head, seeming, for a time, to do nothing. Presently they rose, as if by mutual consent; and as they rose, a shout broke from both battalions. "Oh, my lark!" cried the east, "has he foxed you? Do you begin to feel him! He's only beginning to fight—He ain't got warm yet."

"Look yonder!" cried the west—"didn't I tell you so! He hit the ground so hard, it jarred his nose off. Now ain't he a pretty man as he stands! He shall have my sister Sall just for his pretty looks. I want to get in the breed of them sort o' men, to drive ugly out of my kin folks."

I looked and saw that Bob had entirely lost his left ear, and a large piece from his left cheek. His right eye was a little discolored, and the blood flowed profusely from his wounds.

Bill presented a hideous spectacle. About a third of his nose, at the lower extremity, was bit off, and his face so swelled and bruised, that it was difficult to discover in it any thing of the human visage—much more the fine features which he carried into the ring.

They were up only long enough for me to make the foregoing discoveries, when down they went again, precisely as before. They no sooner touched the ground than Bill relinquished his hold upon Bob's neck. In this, he seemed to all, to have forfeited the only advantage which put him upon an equality with his adversary. But the movement was soon explained. Bill wanted this arm for other purposes than defence; and he had made arrangements whereby he knew that he could make it answer these purposes; for when they rose again, he had the middle finger of Bob's left hand in his mouth. He was now secure from Bob's annoying trips; and he began to lend his adversary most tremendous blows, every one of which was hailed by a shout from his friends. "Bullets! — *Hoss* kicking! — Thunder!"—"That'll do for the face—now feel his short ribs, Billy!"

I now considered the contest settled. I deemed it impossible for any human being to withstand for five seconds, the loss of blood which issued from Bob's ear, cheek, nose and finger, accompanied with such blows as he was receiving. Still he maintained the conflict, and gave blow for blow with considerable effect. But the blows of each became slower and weaker, after the first three or four; and it became obvious, that Bill wanted the room, which Bob's finger occupied, for breathing. He would therefore, probably, in a short time, have let it go, had not Bob anticipated his politeness, by jerking away his hand, and making him a present of the finger. He now seized Bill again, and brought him to his knees — but he recovered. He again brought him to his knees; and he again recovered. A third effort, however, brought him down, and Bob on top of him. These efforts seemed to exhaust the little remaining strength of both; and they lay, Bill undermost, and Bob across his breast, motionless, and panting for breath. After a short pause, Bob gathered his hand full of dirt and sand, and was in the act of grinding it in his adversary's eyes, when Bill cried "ENOUGH!"—Language cannot describe the scene which followed—the shouts, oaths, frantic jestures, taunts, replies and little fights; and therefore I shall not attempt it. The champions were borne off by their seconds, and washed: when many a bleeding wound, and ugly bruise, was discovered on each, which no eye had seen before.

Many had gathered round Bob, and were in various ways congratulating and applauding him, when a voice from the centre of the circle cried out: "Boys, hush and listen to me!" It proceeded from 'Squire Loggins, who had made his way to Bob's side, and had gathered his face up into one of its most flattering and intelligible expressions. All were obedient to the

'Squire's command. "Gentlemen," continued he, with a most knowing smile, "is — Sammy — Reynold — in — this — company — of — gentlemen." "Yes," said Sam, "here I am." "Sammy," said the 'Squire, winking to the company, and drawing the head of his cane to his mouth with an arch smile, as he closed, "I—wish—you—to tell—cousin—Bobby—and—these—gentlemen here present—what—your—uncle—Tommy—said —before—the—fight—began." "Oh! get away, Uncle Tom," says Sam, smiling, (the 'Squire winked,) "you don't know nothing about *fighting*." (The 'Squire winked again.) "All you know about it, is how it'll begin; how it'll go on; how it'll end; that's all. Cousin Bob, when you going to fight again, just go to the old man, and let him tell you all about it. If he can't, don't ask nobody else nothing about it, I tell you." The 'Squire's foresight was complimented in many ways by the by-standers; and he retired, advising "the boys to be at peace, as fighting was a bad business."

Durham and Stallings kept their beds for several weeks, and did not meet again for two months. When they met, Billy stepped up to Bob and offered his hand, saying: "Bobby you've *licked* me a fair fight; but you wouldn't have done it, if I hadn't been in the wrong. I oughtn't to have treated your wife as I did; and I felt so through the whole fight; and it sort o' cowed me."

"Well Billy," said Bob, "let's be friends. Once in the fight, when you had my finger in your mouth, and was pealing me in the face and breast, I was going to hollo; but I thought of Betsy, and knew the house would be too hot for me, if I got whipt, when fighting for her, after always whipping when I fought for myself."

"Now, that's what I always love to see," said a by-stander: "It's true, I brought about the fight; but I wouldn't have done it, if it hadn't o' been on account of *Miss*, (Mrs.) Durham. But dod eternally durn my soul, if I ever could stand by and see any woman put upon — much less *Miss* Durham. If Bobby hadn't been there, I'd o' took it up myself, be durned if I wouldn't, even if I'd o' got whipt for it—But we're all friends now." The reader need hardly be told, this was Ransy Sniffle.

Thanks to the Christian religion, to schools, colleges, and benevolent associations, such scenes of barbarism and cruelty, as that which I have been just describing, are now of rare occurrence: though they may still be occasionally met with in some of the new counties. Wherever they prevail, they are a disgrace to that community. The peace officers who countenance them, deserve a place in the Penitentiary.

from *Narrative of the Life of Frederick Douglass*

Frederick Douglass (1818–1895)

Frederick Douglass was born a slave on a plantation in Maryland, the son of a white man. His owner's wife taught the young Douglass the rudiments of reading before her husband forced her to quit, but Douglass continued secretly to educate himself. The more he learned the more he resented everything about slavery, and he continually devised ways to resist and escape. At age twenty, he managed to flee and join antislavery forces in the North; at twenty-three, he was asked to testify publicly about his life in slavery. Douglass quickly became one of the most famous spokesmen for abolition, speaking with such ability that many who heard him doubted that he had ever been a slave. In 1845, he published his *Narrative* to document his life as a slave and to persuade Northerners to join the crusade against the institution. Douglass became a leading force in the movement and in the fight for black freedom during the Civil War and for decades afterward.

I left Master Thomas's house, and went to live with Mr. Covey, on the 1st of January, 1833. I was now, for the first time in my life, a field hand. In my new employment, I found myself even more awkward than a country boy appeared to be in a large city. I had been at my new home but one week before Mr. Covey gave me a very severe whipping, cutting my back, causing the blood to run, and raising ridges on my flesh as large as my little finger. The details of this affair are as follows: Mr. Covey sent me, very early in the morning of one of our coldest days in the month of January, to the woods, to get a load of wood. He gave me a team of unbroken oxen. He told me which was the in-hand ox, and which the off-hand one. He then tied the end of a large rope around the horns of the in-hand ox, and gave me the other end of it, and told me, if the oxen started to run, that I must hold on upon the rope. I had never driven oxen before, and of course I was very awkward. I, however, succeeded in getting to the edge of the woods with little difficulty; but I had got a very few rods into the woods, when the oxen took fright, and started full tilt, carrying the cart against trees, and over stumps, in the most frightful manner. I expected every moment that my brains would be dashed out against the trees. After running thus for a considerable distance, they finally upset the cart, dashing it with great force against a tree, and threw themselves into a dense thicket. How I escaped death, I do not know. There I was, entirely alone, in a thick wood, in a place new to me. My cart was upset and shattered, my oxen were entangled among the young trees, and there was none to help me. After a long spell of effort, I succeeded in getting my cart righted, my oxen disentangled, and again yoked to the cart. I now proceeded with my team to the place where I had, the day before, been chopping wood, and loaded my cart pretty heavily, thinking in this way to tame my oxen. I then proceeded on my way home. I had now consumed one half of the day. I got out of the woods safely, and now felt out of danger. I stopped my oxen to open the woods gate; and just as I did so, before I could get hold of my ox-rope, the oxen again started, rushed through the gate, catching it between the wheel and the body of the cart, tearing it to pieces and coming within a few inches of crushing me against the gate-post. Thus twice, in one short day, I escaped death by the merest chance. On my return, I told Mr. Covey what had happened, and how it happened. He ordered me to return to the woods again immediately. I did so, and he followed on after me. Just as I got into the woods, he came up and told me to stop my cart, and that he would teach me how to trifle away my time, and break gates. He then went to a large gum-tree, and with his axe cut three large switches, and, after trimming them up neatly with his pocket-knife, he ordered me to take off my clothes. I made him no answer, but stood with my clothes on. He repeated his order. I still made him no answer, nor did I move to strip myself. Upon this he rushed at me with the fierceness of a tiger, tore off my clothes, and lashed me till he had worn out his switches, cutting me so savagely as to leave the marks visible for a long time after. This whipping was the first of a number just like it, and for similar offences.

I lived with Mr. Covey one year. During the first six months, of that year, scarce a week passed without his whipping me. I was seldom free from a sore back. My awkwardness was almost always his excuse for whipping me. We were worked fully up to the point of endurance. Long before day we were up, our horses fed, and by the first approach of day we were off to the field with our hoes and ploughing teams. Mr. Covey gave us enough to eat, but scarce time to eat it. We were often less than five minutes taking our meals. We were often in the field from the first approach of day till its last lingering ray had left us; and at saving-fodder time, midnight often caught us in the field binding blades.

Covey would be out with us. The way he used to stand it, was this. He would spend the most of his afternoons in bed. He would then come out fresh in the evening, ready to urge us on with his words, example, and frequently with the whip. Mr. Covey was one of the few slaveholders who could and did work with his hands. He was a hard-working man. He knew by himself just what a man or a boy could do. There was no deceiving him.

His work went on in his absence almost as well as in his presence; and he had the faculty of making us feel that he was ever present with us. This he did by surprising us. He seldom approached the spot where we were at work openly, if he could do it secretly. He always aimed at taking us by surprise. Such was his cunning, that we used to call him, among ourselves, "the snake." When we were at work in the cornfield, he would sometimes crawl on his hands and knees to avoid detection, and all at once he would rise nearly in our midst, and scream out, "Ha, ha! Come, come! Dash on, dash on!" This being his mode of attack, it was never safe to stop a single minute. His comings were like a thief in the night. He appeared to us as being ever at hand. He was under every tree, behind every stump, in every bush, and at every window, on the plantation. He would sometimes mount his horse, as if bound to St. Michael's, a distance of seven miles, and in half an hour afterwards you would see him coiled up in the corner of the wood-fence, watching every motion of the slaves. He would, for this purpose, leave his horse tied up in the woods. Again, he would sometimes walk up to us, and give us orders as though he was upon the point of starting on a long journey, turn his back upon us, and make as though he was going to the house to get ready; and, before he would get half way thither, he would turn short and crawl into a fence-corner, or behind some tree, and there watch us till the going down of the sun.

Mr. Covey's *forte* consisted in his power to deceive. His life was devoted to planning and perpetrating the grossest deceptions. Every thing he possessed in the shape of learning or religion, he made conform to his disposition to deceive. He seemed to think himself equal to deceiving the Almighty. He would make a short prayer in the morning, and a long prayer at night; and, strange as it may seem, few men would at times appear more devotional than he. The exercises of his family devotions were always commenced with singing; and, as he was a very poor singer himself, the duty of raising the hymn generally came upon me. He would read his hymn, and nod at me to commence. I would at times do so; at others, I would not. My non-compliance would almost always produce much confusion. To show himself independent of me, he would start and stagger through with his hymn in the most discordant manner. In this state of mind, he prayed with more than ordinary spirit. Poor man! such was his disposition, and success at deceiving, I do verily believe that he sometimes deceived himself into the solemn belief, that he was a sincere worshipper of the most high God; and this, too, at a time when he may be said to have been guilty of compelling his woman slave to commit the sin of adultery. The facts in the case are these: Mr. Covey was a poor man; he was just commencing in life; he was only able to buy one slave; and, shocking as is the fact, he bought her, as he said, for *a breeder*. This woman was named Caroline. Mr. Covey bought her from Mr. Thomas Lowe, about six miles from St. Michael's. She was a large, able-bodied woman, about twenty years old. She had already given birth to one child, which proved her to be just what he wanted. After buying her, he hired a married man of Mr. Samuel Harrison, to live with him one year; and him he used to fasten up with her every night! The result was, that, at the end of the year, the miserable woman gave birth to twins. At this result Mr. Covey seemed to be highly pleased, both with the man and the wretched woman. Such was his joy, and that of his wife, that nothing they could do for Caroline during her confinement was too good, or too hard, to be done. The children were regarded as being quite an addition to his wealth.

If at any one time of my life more than another, I was made to drink the bitterest dregs of slavery, that time was during the first six months of my stay with Mr. Covey. We were worked in all weathers. It was never too hot or too cold; it could never rain, blow, hail, or snow, too hard for us to work in the field. Work, work, work, was scarcely more the order of the day than of the night. The longest days were too short for him, and the shortest nights too long for him. I was somewhat unmanageable when I first went there, but a few months of this discipline tamed me. Mr. Covey succeeded in breaking me. I was broken in body, soul, and spirit. My natural elasticity was crushed, my intellect languished, the disposition to read departed, the cheerful spark that lingered about my eye died; the dark night of slavery closed in upon me; and behold a man transformed into a brute!

Sunday was my only leisure time. I spent this in a sort of beast-like stupor, between sleep and wake, under some large tree. At times I would rise up, a flash of energetic freedom would dart through my soul, accompanied with a faint beam of hope, that flickered for a moment, and then vanished. I sank down again, mourning over my wretched condition. I was sometimes prompted to take my life, and that of Covey, but was prevented by a combination of hope and fear. My sufferings on this plantation seem now like a dream rather than a stern reality.

Our house stood within a few rods of the Chesapeake Bay, whose broad bosom was ever white with sails from every quarter of the habitable globe. Those beautiful vessels, robed in purest white, so delightful to the eye of freemen, were to me so many shrouded ghosts, to terrify and torment me with thoughts of my wretched condition. I have often, in the deep stillness of a summer's Sabbath, stood all alone upon the lofty banks of that noble bay, and traced, with saddened heart and tearful eye, the countless number of sails moving off to the mighty ocean. The sight of these always affected me powerfully. My thoughts would compel utterance; and there, with no audience but the Almighty, I would pour out my soul's complaint, in my rude way, with an apostrophe to the moving multitude of ships:—

"You are loosed from your moorings, and are free; I am fast in my chains, and am a slave! You move merrily before the gentle gale, and I sadly before the bloody whip! You are freedom's swift-winged angels, that fly round the world; I am confined in bands of iron! O that I were free! O, that I were on one of your gallant decks, and under your protecting wing! Alas! betwixt me and you, the turbid waters roll. Go on, go on. O that I could also go! Could I but swim! If I could fly! O, why was I born a man, of whom to make a brute! The glad ship is gone; she hides in the dim distance. I am left in the hottest hell of unending slavery. O God, save me! God, deliver me! Let me be free! Is there any God? Why am I a slave? I will run away. I will not stand it. Get caught, or get clear, I'll try it. I had as well die with ague as the fever. I have only one life to lose. I had as well be killed running as die standing. Only think of it; one hundred miles straight north, and I am free! Try it? Yes! God helping me, I will. It cannot be that I shall live and die a slave. I will take to the water. This very bay shall yet bear me into freedom. The steamboats steered in a north-east course from North Point. I will do the same; and when I get to the head of the bay, I will turn my canoe adrift, and walk straight through Delaware into Pennsylvania. When I get there, I shall not be required to have a pass; I can travel without being disturbed. Let but the first opportunity offer, and, come what will, I am off. Meanwhile, I will try to bear up under the yoke. I am not the only slave in the world. Why should I fret? I can bear as much as any of them. Besides, I am but a boy, and all boys are bound to some one. It may be that my misery in slavery will only increase my happiness when I get free. There is a better day coming."

Thus I used to think, and thus I used to speak to myself; goaded almost to madness at one moment, and at the next reconciling myself to my wretched lot.

I have already intimated that my condition was much worse, during the first six months of my stay at Mr. Covey's, than in the last six. The circumstances leading to the change in Mr. Covey's course toward me form an epoch in my humble history. You have seen how a man was made a slave; you shall see how a slave was made a man. On one of the hottest days of the month of August, 1833, Bill Smith, William Hughes, a slave named Eli, and myself, were engaged in fanning wheat. Hughes was clearing the fanned wheat from before the fan, Eli was turning, Smith was feeding, and I was carrying wheat to the fan. The work was simple, requiring strength rather than intellect; yet, to one entirely unused to such work, it came very hard. About three o'clock of that day, I broke down; my strength failed me; I was seized with a violent aching of the head, attended with extreme dizziness; I trembled in every limb. Finding what was coming, I nerved myself up, feeling it would never do to stop work. I stood as long as I could stagger to the hopper with grain. When I could stand no longer, I fell, and felt as if held down by an immense weight. The fan of course stopped; every one had his own work to do; and no one could do the work of the other, and have his own go on at the same time.

Mr. Covey was at the house, about one hundred yards from the treading-yard where we were fanning. On hearing the fan stop, he left immediately, and came to the spot where we were. He hastily inquired what the matter was. Bill answered that I was sick, and there was no one to bring wheat to the fan. I had by this time crawled away under the side of the post and rail-fence by which the yard was enclosed, hoping to find relief by getting out of the sun. He then asked where I was. He was told by one of the hands. He came to the spot, and, after looking at me awhile, asked me what was the matter. I told him as well as I could, for I scarce had strength to speak. He then gave me a savage kick in the side, and told me to get up. I tried to do so, but fell back in the attempt. He gave me another kick, and again told me to rise. I again tried, and succeeded in gaining my feet; but, stooping to get the tub with which I was feeding the fan, I again staggered and fell. While down in this situation, Mr. Covey took up the hickory slat with which Hughes had been striking off the half-bushel measure, and with it gave me a heavy blow upon the head, making a large wound, and the blood ran freely; and with this again told me to get up. I made no effort to comply, having now made up my mind to let him do his worst. In a short time after receiving this blow, my head grew better. Mr. Covey had now left me to my fate. At this moment I resolved, for the first time, to go to my master, enter a complaint, and ask his protection. In order to this, I must that afternoon walk seven miles; and this, under the circumstances, was truly a severe undertaking. I was exceedingly feeble; made so as much by the kicks and blows which I received, as by the severe fit of sickness to which I had been subjected. I, however, watched my chance, while Covey was looking in an opposite direction, and started for St. Michael's. I succeeded in getting a considerable distance on my way to the woods, when Covey discovered me, and called after me to come back, threatening what he would do if I did not come. I disregarded both his calls and his threats, and made my way to the woods as fast as my feeble state would allow; and thinking I might be overhauled by him if I kept the road, I walked through the woods, keeping far enough from the road to avoid detection, and near enough to prevent losing my way. I had not gone far before my little strength again failed me. I could go no farther. I fell down, and lay for a considerable time. The blood was yet oozing from the wound on my head. For a time I thought I should bleed to death; and think now that I should have done so, but that the blood so matted my hair as to stop the wound. After lying there about three quarters of an hour, I nerved myself up again, and started on my way, through bogs and briers, barefooted and bareheaded, tearing my feet sometimes at nearly every step; and after a journey of about seven miles, occupying some five hours to perform it, I arrived at master's store. I then presented an appearance enough to affect any but a heart of iron. From the crown of my head to my feet, I was covered with blood. My hair was all clotted with dust and blood; my shirt was stiff with blood. My legs and feet were torn in sundry places with briers and thorns, and were also covered with blood. I suppose I looked like a man who had escaped a den of wild beasts, and barely escaped them. In this state I appeared before my master, humbly entreating him to interpose his authority for my protection. I told him all the circumstances as well as I could, and it seemed, as I spoke, at times to affect him. He would then walk the floor, and seek to justify Covey by saying he expected I deserved it. He asked me what I wanted. I told him, to let me get a new home; that as sure as I lived with Mr. Covey again, I should live with but to die with him; that Covey would surely kill me; he was in a fair way for it. Master Thomas ridiculed the idea that there was any danger of Mr. Covey's killing me, and said that he knew Mr. Covey; that he was a good man, and that he could not think of taking me from him; that, should he do so, he would lose the whole year's wages; that I belonged to Mr. Covey for one year, and that I must go back to him, come what might; and that I must not trouble him with any more stories, or that he would himself *get hold of me*. After threatening me thus, he gave me a very large dose of salts, telling me that I might remain in St. Michael's that night, (it being quite late,) but that I must be off back to Mr. Covey's early in the morning; and that if I did not, he would *get hold of me*, which meant that he would whip me. I remained all night, and, according to his orders, I started off to Covey's in the morning, (Saturday morning,) wearied in body and broken in spirit. I got no supper that night, or breakfast that morning. I reached Covey's about nine o'clock; and just as I was getting over the fence that divided Mrs. Kemp's fields from ours, out ran Covey with his cowskin, to give me another whipping. Before he could reach me, I succeeded in getting to the cornfield; and as the corn was very high, it afforded me the means of hiding. He seemed very angry, and searched for me a long time. My behavior was altogether unaccountable. He finally gave up the chase, thinking, I suppose, that I must come home for something to eat; he would give himself no further trouble in looking for me. I spent that day mostly in the woods, having the alternative before me, — to go home and be whipped to death, or stay in the woods and be starved to death. That night, I fell in with Sandy Jenkins, a slave with whom I was somewhat acquainted. Sandy had a free wife, who lived about four miles from Mr. Covey's; and it being Saturday, he was on his way to see her. I told him my circumstances, and he very kindly invited me to go home with him. I went home with him, and talked this whole matter over, and got his advice as to what course it was best for me to pursue. I found Sandy an old adviser. He told me, with great solemnity, I must go back to Covey; but that before I went, I must go with him into another part of the woods, where there was a certain *root*, which, if I would take some of it with me, carrying it *always on my right side*, would render it impossible for Mr. Covey, or any other white man, to whip me. He said he had carried it for years; and since he had done so, he had never received a blow, and never expected to while he carried it. I at first rejected the idea, that the simple carrying of a root in my pocket would have any such effect as he had said, and was not disposed to take it; but Sandy impressed the necessity with much earnestness, telling me it could do no harm, if it did no good. To please him, I at length took the root, and, according to his direction, carried it upon my right side. This was Sunday morning. I immediately started for home; and upon entering the yard gate, out came Mr. Covey on his way to meeting. He spoke to me very kindly, bade me drive the pigs from a lot near by, and passed on towards the church. Now, this singular conduct of Mr. Covey really made me begin to think that there was something in the *root* which Sandy had given me; and had it been on any other day than Sunday, I could have attributed the conduct to no other cause than the influence of that root; and as it was, I was half inclined to think the *root* to be something more than I at first had taken it to be. All went well till Monday morning. On this morning, the virtue of the *root* was fully tested. Long before daylight, I was called to go and rub, curry, and feed, the horses. I obeyed, and was glad to obey. But whilst thus engaged, whilst in the act of throwing down some blades from the loft, Mr. Covey entered the stable with a long rope; and just as I was half out of the loft, he caught hold of my legs, and was about tying me. As soon as I found what he was up to, I gave a sudden spring, and as I did so, he holding to my legs, I was brought sprawling on the stable floor. Mr. Covey seemed now to think he had me, and could do what he pleased; but at this moment—from whence came the spirit I don't know—I resolved to fight; and, suiting my action to the resolution, I seized Covey hard by the throat; and as I did so, I rose. He held on to me, and I to him. My resistance was so entirely unexpected, that Covey seemed taken all aback. He trembled like a leaf. This gave me assurance, and I held him uneasy, causing the blood to run where I touched him with the ends of my fingers. Mr. Covey soon called out to Hughes for help. Hughes came, and, while Covey held me, attempted to tie my right hand. While he was in the act of doing so,

I watched my chance, and gave him a heavy kick close under the ribs. This kick fairly sickened Hughes, so that he left me in the hands of Mr. Covey. This kick had the effect of not only weakening Hughes, but Covey also. When he saw Hughes bending over with pain, his courage quailed. He asked me if I meant to persist in my resistance. I told him I did, come what might; that he had used me like a brute for six months, and that I was determined to be used so no longer. With that, he strove to drag me to a stick that was lying just out of the stable door. He meant to knock me down. But just as he was leaning over to get the stick, I seized him with both hands by his collar, and brought him by a sudden snatch to the ground. By this time, Bill came, Covey called upon him for assistance. Bill wanted to know what he could do. Covey said, "Take hold of him, take hold of him!" Bill said his master hired him out to work, and not to help to whip me; so he left Covey and myself to fight our own battle out. We were at it for nearly two hours. Covey at length let me go, puffing and blowing at a great rate, saying that if I had not resisted, he would not have whipped me half so much. The truth was, that he had not whipped me at all. I considered him as getting entirely the worst end of the bargain; for he had drawn no blood from me, but I had from him. The whole six months afterwards, that I spent with Mr. Covey, he never laid the weight of his finger upon me in anger. He would occasionally say, he didn't want to get hold of me again. "No," thought I, "you need not; for you will come off worse than you did before."

This battle with Mr. Covey was the turning-point in my career as a slave. It rekindled the few expiring embers of freedom, and revived within me a sense of my own manhood. It recalled the departed self-confidence, and inspired me again with a determination to be free. The gratification afforded by the triumph was a full compensation for whatever else might follow, even death itself. He only can understand the deep satisfaction which I experienced, who has himself repelled by force the bloody arm of slavery. I felt as I never felt before. It was a glorious resurrection, from the tomb of slavery, to the heaven of freedom. My long-crushed spirit rose, cowardice departed, bold defiance took its place; and I now resolved that, however long I might remain a slave in form, the day had passed forever when I could be a slave in fact. I did not hesitate to let it be known of me, that the white man who expected to succeed in whipping, must also succeed in killing me.

from *Social Relations in Our Southern States*
Daniel R. Hundley (1832–1899)

Daniel R. Hundley, born in Alabama in 1831, knew both the North and the South. After going to college in Kentucky, he received a law degree from Harvard and moved to Chicago in 1856 to practice law. Appalled by the deterioration of relations between the regions, Hundley wrote *Social Relations in Our Southern States* (1860) to help defuse conflict by explaining the South to the North. His rambling book offered a series of clear-eyed portrayals of white Southerners and, in the section reprinted here, an explanation of why slavery should not be abolished, an explanation that echoed those of many moderate white Southerners. When the Civil War broke out the year after his book appeared, Hundley returned to Alabama, joined the Confederacy, became colonel of his regiment, and was twice captured and imprisoned by Union troops. After the war, he remained in Alabama, farming and practicing law.

A great many philanthropic men, possessing too exalted an opinion of human kind, are ever seeking to find fault with God (either directly or indirectly) for the misery and sin which are in the world. They will not consent to acknowledge that man is, when unregenerate, essentially a bestial sort of animal, grovelling in ignorance and vice, and influenced at all times by such sentiments only as are inspired either through fear or self-interest. Filled with their own idea of what a man ought to be, they delude themselves into the belief that he would be the beau ideal of their imagination, had God never allowed the devil to leave Hell; for they do not consider that there is in every man a private devil of his own, which can turn his bosom into a hell or heaven as the man himself of his own free will shall choose to act.

All such short-sighted and one-ideaed philosophers are in the main miserable—full of impracticable theories, and ever disposed to be skeptical as regards any kind of religious belief. Though boastful of their charity and humanity, however, their hearts are filled instead with all bitterness, being perfect strangers to that heavenly Love, which "suffereth long and is kind;" for they seem to delight in looking at the darker aspects only of every subject, and refuse to perceive that their Creator is always

"From seeming evil still educing good."

46

Hence, they are the genuine representative of Procrustes in this present nineteenth century: whoever does not agree with them in sentiment, they damn incontinently, pronouncing anathema maranatha upon the heads of all such. Hence also, they may be fitly styled the latter-day Popes, from whose decrees there is no appeal. Yea, verily, as was predicted of Anti-Christ, they do not scruple to set themselves up as superior to the authority of the Holy Scriptures, and boldly and impiously teach for doctrines the whims and caprices of men. Thus they denounce what Abraham, the chosen friend of God, and what the Jews, his chosen people, all practised, as the "sum of all villanies." And they likewise pronounce Jesus Christ an impostor, because (as they blasphemously assert) he was influenced to let slavery alone from political considerations, although he did not allow these to prevent him from overturning the old Jewish laws allowing of concubinage and fornication. And in precisely a similar spirit do they denounce St. Paul, because he, acting as the inspired Apostle of Christ, sent Onesimus, a runaway slave, back to his master, and enjoined upon all other slaves to count their masters worthy of all honor, especially those masters who were fellow-believers of the glorious Gospel which Paul preached.

Now, on the minds of such men we do not expect to produce the slightest impression, by any thing we may have to say touching the condition of the negro slaves in our Southern States. Their understandings are as impervious to logical sequences, as the hide of the two-horned rhinoceros is to rifle-balls. They may be called, indeed, not inaptly the pachydermatous race of bipeds. Like the tree mobwana of Central Africa, no matter how much you may clip, and pollard, bark, or even cut them down, they still flourish and seem to draw their nourishment from thin air alone. But, from an intimate acquaintance with many Northerners who have been seduced by the ceaseless clamor of such senseless babblers, to entertain strong anti-slavery convictions; we feel assured that we shall not labor in vain while endeavoring to present a fair and truthful statement of the result to themselves, as well as to the rest of mankind, of the forced labor of the Negroes in our Southern States.

We are well persuaded that many good men, pious men — men of earnest natures and delicate sensibilities, not in the North alone but even in the South — do honestly look upon slavery as both a great moral evil and an equally great social curse. And when we consider their early prejudices and peculiar cast of mind, we can not greatly blame them because they sincerely are of opinion, that, had the peculiar institution never been introduced into this country, we should all have been much better off as a people and as individuals. For, well we know, they do not consider, while entertaining the honest convictions they do, that they thus assail the wisdom and goodness of the Great Ruler of Nations; that they are carping at the overruling-providence of the Omniscient Being, in whose sight the wisest of men barely rise to the rank of fools. Alas! so short-sighted are we all. "I could write down twenty cases," says Cecil, "wherein I wished that God had done otherwise than he did; but which I now see, had I had my own will, would have led to extensive mischief."

And the experience of Cecil is the experience of all mankind. We are all miserably short-sighted, and hardly a day passes but we are disposed to find fault with *what is*; but the morrow invariably proves to us, that we could not possibly have benefited matters had we had the power. So, at the present time, many of us are hourly expecting and hoping that God will signally rebuke the sin of slavery, and by a special interposition of Divine Providence bring what we conceive to be the greatest of evils to an instant and final end. In our folly, we do not consider that Jehovah never would have permitted the first human-freighted ship to leave the shores of Africa for the New World, had he not designed a beneficial result should flow from the introduction of the sable children of the tropics into the fruitful fields of our own temperate latitude. Yes, Madam, with our conception of the nature of Deity, we can not believe that the All-wise Ruler would purposely allow a great evil to grow and increase to such magnitude, as to become indeed the very centre and pivot of the world's commerce; merely to signalize his disapprobation of it by the overthrow of the world's property, when he might have crushed it in the beginning without harm to a single individual. We honestly believe, therefore, God had a design in permitting the old Slave-trade—a design to bless and benefit the human race.

What! God have a hand in the horrors of the Middle Passage? Consider, Madam, the horrors of war, of pestilences, and famines. God surely has a hand in all these. Consider the horrors of our Revolutionary struggle, and, above all, the sad fate of the poor Indian, whom your own Puritan ancestors helped to drive off, at the point of the bayonet, from the hunting-grounds of his fathers, to the unknown wildernesses of the West. Will you deny that God had a hand in all this? And yet the Red-men have faded from before the presence of the Pale-faces, as the morning mists melt away before the rising sun. We have slain in battle many more of them, than ever perished of blacks in the Middle Passage, and at the same time we have utterly corrupted the living with our damnable fire-water, thus rendering them useless to themselves and to the world; neither have we converted any numbers of them to Christianity, as is the case with millions of the Africans held in bondage on the American Continent. Still, in the face of these facts, your anti-slavery minister will tell you in all soberness, that God had a hand in removing the savages in order to make room for the saints. And he will tell you the simple truth. We have no fault to find with him for entertaining such a belief. But we do find fault with him for turning upon the men of the South in the same breath, and saying to them in regard to their negroes, what the lawyer said to his client when told *whose* bull it was did the goring: "Ah! that alters the case." Yes, thou Reverend Pharisee, we do blame you for your inconsistency, while acknowledging the hand of God in the merciless slaughter of whole tribes of artless children of the forest, in order to make room for the children of civilization; in refusing to perceive the benign Providence that snatched the idolatrous children of the desert from their cannibalism and their bloody human sacrifices, to place them under the control and tutorage of enlightened men and women of a superior race.

from *Incidents in the Life of a Slave Girl*

Harriet Jacobs (1813–1897)

Harriet Jacobs, born into slavery in Edenton, North Carolina, was orphaned while still a young child. She was taught to read by her owner's wife and, by her own account, experienced a relatively pleasant childhood. Her happiness ended, however, when her owner began to abuse her sexually. Desperate, Jacobs hid for several years in a small crawlspace above a storeroom in her grandmother's home. Finally escaping to the North, Jacobs became active in the antislavery movement and, at the urging of several female abolitionists, wrote *Incidents in the Life of a Slave Girl*, published in Boston in 1861. Jacobs's painful, frank, and psychologically complex account, neglected for many years, has recently become recognized as one of the most illuminating narratives of a former slave.

During the first years of my service in Dr. Flint's family, I was accustomed to share some indulgences with the children of my mistress. Though this seemed to me no more than right, I was grateful for it, and tried to merit the kindness by the faithful discharge of my duties. But I now entered on my fifteenth year—a sad epoch in the life of a slave girl. My master began to whisper foul words in my ear. Young as I was, I could not remain ignorant of their import. I tried to treat them with indifference or contempt. The master's age, my extreme youth, and the fear that his conduct would be reported to my grandmother, made him bear this treatment for many months. He was a crafty man, and resorted to many means to accomplish his purposes. Sometimes he had stormy, terrific ways, that made his victims tremble; sometimes he assumed a gentleness that he thought must surely subdue. Of the two, I preferred his stormy moods, although they left me trembling. He tried his utmost to corrupt the pure principles my grandmother had instilled. He peopled my young mind with unclean images, such as only a vile monster could think of. I turned from him with disgust and hatred. But he was my master. I was compelled to live under the same roof with him — where I saw a man forty years my senior daily violating the most sacred commandments of nature. He told me I was his property; that I must be subject to his will in all things. My soul revolted against the mean tyranny. But where could I turn for protection? No matter whether the slave girl be as black as ebony or as fair as her mistress. In either case, there is no shadow of law to protect her from insult, from violence, or even from death; all these are inflicted by fiends who bear the shape of men. The mistress, who ought to protect the help-less victim, has no other feelings towards her but those of jealousy and rage. The degradation, the wrongs, the vices, that grow out of slavery, are more than I can describe. They are greater than you would willingly believe. Surely, if you credited one half the truths that are told you con-cerning the helpless millions suffering in this cruel bondage, you at the north would not help to tighten the yoke. You surely would refuse to do for the master, on your own soil, the mean and cruel work which trained bloodhounds and the lowest class of whites do for him at the south. . . .

I longed for some one to confide in. I would have given the world to have laid my head on my grandmother's faithful bosom, and told her all my troubles. But Dr. Flint swore he would kill me, if I was not as silent as the grave. Then, although my grandmother was all in all to me, I feared her as well as loved her. I had been accustomed to look up to her with a respect bordering upon awe. I was very young, and felt shamefaced about telling her such impure things, especially as I knew her to be very strict on such subjects. Moreover, she was a woman of a high spirit. She was usu-ally very quiet in her demeanor; but if her indignation was once roused, it was not very easily quelled. I had been told that she once chased a white gentleman with a loaded pistol, because he insulted one of her daughters. I dreaded the consequences of a violent outbreak; and both pride and fear kept me silent. But though I did not confide in my grandmother, and even evaded her vigilant watchfulness and inquiry, her presence in the neigh-borhood was some protection to me. Though she had been a slave, Dr. Flint was afraid of her. He dreaded her scorching rebukes. Moreover, she was known and patronized by many people; and he did not wish to have his villainy made public. It was lucky for me that I did not live on a dis-tant plantation, but in a town not so large that the inhabitants were igno-rant of each other's affairs. Bad as are the laws and customs in a slave-holding community, the doctor, as a professional man, deemed it prudent to keep up some outward show of decency.

THE JEALOUS MISTRESS

Mrs. Flint possessed the key to her husband's character before I was born. She might have used this knowledge to counsel and to screen the young and the innocent among her slaves; but for them she had no sympathy. They were the objects of her constant suspicion and malevolence. She watched her husband with unceasing vigilance; but he was well practised in means to evade it. What he could not find opportunity to say in words he manifested in signs. He invented more than were ever thought of in a deaf and dumb asylum. I let them pass, as if I did not understand what he meant; and many were the curses and threats bestowed on me for my stupidity. One day he caught me teaching myself to write. He frowned, as if he was not well pleased; but I suppose he came to the conclusion that such an accomplishment might help to advance his favorite scheme. Before long, notes were often slipped into my hand. I would return them, saying, "I can't read them, sir." "Can't you?" he replied; "Then I must read them to you." He always finished the reading by asking, "Do you understand?" Sometimes he would complain of the heat of the tea room, and order his supper to be placed on a small table in the piazza. He would seat himself there with a well-satisfied smile, and tell me to stand by and brush away the flies. He would eat very slowly, pausing between the mouthfuls. These intervals were employed in describing the happiness I was so foolishly throwing away, and in threatening me with the penalty that finally awaited my stubborn disobedience. He boasted much of the forbearance he had exercised towards me, and reminded me that there was a limit to his patience. When I succeeded in avoiding opportunities for him to talk to me at home, I was ordered to come to his office, to do some errand. When there, I was obliged to stand and listen to such language as he saw fit to address to me. Sometimes I so openly expressed my contempt for him that he would become violently enraged, and I wondered why he did not strike me. Circumstanced as he was, he probably thought it was better policy to be forbearing. But the state of things grew worse and worse daily. In desperation I told him that I must and would apply to my grandmother for protection. He threatened me with death, and worse than death, if I made any complaint to her. Strange to say, I did not despair. I was naturally of a buoyant disposition, and always I had a hope of somehow getting out of his clutches. Like many a poor, simple slave before me, I trusted that some threads of joy would yet be woven into my dark destiny.

I had entered my sixteenth year, and every day it became more apparent that my presence was intolerable to Mrs. Flint. Angry words frequently passed between her and her husband. He had never punished me himself, and he would not allow any body else to punish me. In that respect, she was never satisfied; but, in her angry moods, no terms were too vile for her to bestow upon me. Yet I, whom she detested so bitterly, had far more pity for her than he had, whose duty it was to make her life happy. I never wronged her, or wished to wrong her; and one word of kindness from her would have brought me to her feet.

After repeated quarrels between the doctor and his wife, he announced his intention to take his youngest daughter, then four years old, to sleep in his apartment. It was necessary that a servant should sleep in the same room, to be on hand if the child stirred. I was selected for that office, and

informed for what purpose that arrangement had been made. By managing to keep within sight of people, as much as possible, during the day
time, I had hitherto succeeded in eluding my master, though a razor was
often held to my throat to force me to change this line of policy. At night
I slept by the side of my great aunt, where I felt safe. He was too prudent
to come into her room. She was an old woman, and had been in the family many years. Moreover, as a married man, and a professional man, he
deemed it necessary to save appearances in some degree. But he resolved
to remove the obstacle in the way of his scheme; and he thought he had
planned it so that he should evade suspicion. He was well aware how
much I prized my refuge by the side of my old aunt, and he determined to
dispossess me of it. The first night the doctor had the little child in his
room alone. The next morning, I was ordered to take my station as nurse
the following night. A kind Providence interposed in my favor. During
the day Mrs. Flint heard of this new arrangement, and a storm followed. I
rejoiced to hear it rage.

After a while my mistress sent for me to come to her room. Her first
question was, "Did you know you were to sleep in the doctor's room?"

"Yes, ma'am."

"Who told you?"

"My master."

"Will you answer truly all the questions I ask?"

"Yes, ma'am."

"Tell me, then, as you hope to be forgiven, are you innocent of what I
have accused you?"

"I am."

She handed me a Bible, and said, "Lay your hand on your heart, kiss
this holy book, and swear before God that you tell me the truth."

I took the oath she required, and I did it with a clear conscience.

"You have taken God's holy word to testify your innocence," said she.
"If you have deceived me, beware! Now take this stool, sit down, look me
directly in the face, and tell me all that has passed between your master
and you."

I did as she ordered. As I went on with my account her color changed
frequently, she wept, and sometimes groaned. She spoke in tones so sad,
that I was touched by her grief. The tears came to my eyes; but I was
soon convinced that her emotions arose from anger and wounded pride.
She felt that her marriage vows were desecrated, her dignity insulted; but
she had no compassion for the poor victim of her husband's perfidy. She
pitied herself as a martyr; but she was incapable of feeling for the condition of shame and misery in which her unfortunate, helpless slave was
placed.

Yet perhaps she had some touch of feeling for me; for when the conference was ended, she spoke kindly, and promised to protect me. I should have been much comforted by this assurance if I could have had confidence in it; but my experiences in slavery had filled me with distrust. She was not a very refined woman, and had not much control over her passions. I was an object of her jealousy, and, consequently, of her hatred; and I knew I could not expect kindness or confidence from her under the circumstances in which I was placed. I could not blame her. Slaveholders' wives feel as other women would under similar circumstances. The fire of her temper kindled from small sparks, and now the flame became so intense that the doctor was obliged to give up his intended arrangement.

I knew I had ignited the torch, and I expected to suffer for it afterwards; but I felt too thankful to my mistress for the timely aid she rendered me to care much about that. She now took me to sleep in a room adjoining her own. There I was an object of her especial care, though not of her especial comfort, for she spent many a sleepless night to watch over me. Sometimes I woke up, and found her bending over me. At other times she whispered in my ear, as though it was her husband who was speaking to me, and listened to hear what I would answer. If she startled me, on such occasions, she would glide stealthily away; and the next morning she would tell me I had been talking in my sleep, and ask who I was talking to. At last, I began to be fearful for my life. It had been often threatened; and you can imagine, better than I can describe, what an unpleasant sensation it must produce to wake up in the dead of night and find a jealous woman bending over you. Terrible as this experience was, I had fears that it would give place to one more terrible.

My mistress grew weary of her vigils; they did not prove satisfactory. She changed her tactics. She now tried the trick of accusing my master of crime, in my presence, and gave my name as the author of the accusation. To my utter astonishment, he replied, "I don't believe it: but if she did acknowledge it, you tortured her into exposing me." Tortured into exposing him! Truly, Satan had no difficulty in distinguishing the color of his soul! I understood his object in making this false representation. It was to show me that I gained nothing by seeking the protection of my mistress; that the power was still all in his own hands. I pitied Mrs. Flint. She was a second wife, many years the junior of her husband; and the hoary-headed miscreant was enough to try the patience of a wiser and better woman. She was completely foiled, and knew not how to proceed. She would gladly have had me flogged for my supposed false oath; but, as I have already stated, the doctor never allowed any one to whip me. The old sinner was politic. The application of the lash might have led to remarks that would have exposed him in the eyes of his children and grandchildren. How often did I rejoice that I lived in a town where all the inhabitants knew each other! If I had been on a remote plantation, or lost among the multitude of a crowded city, I should not be a living woman at this day.

The secrets of slavery are concealed like those of the Inquisition. My master was, to my knowledge, the father of eleven slaves. But did the mothers dare to tell who was the father of their children? Did the other slaves dare to allude to it, except in whispers among themselves? No, indeed! They knew too well the terrible consequences.

My grandmother could not avoid seeing things which excited her suspicions. She was uneasy about me, and tried various ways to buy me; but the neverchanging answer was always repeated: "Linda does not belong to *me*. She is my daughter's property, and I have no legal right to sell her." The conscientious man! He was too scrupulous to *sell* me; but he had no scruples whatever about committing a much greater wrong against the helpless young girl placed under his guardianship, as his daughter's property. Sometimes my persecutor would ask me whether I would like to be sold. I told him I would rather be sold to any body than to lead such a life as I did. On such occasions he would assume the air of a very injured individual, and reproach me for my ingratitude. "Did I not take you into the house, and make you the companion of my own children?" he would say. "Have I ever treated you like a negro? I have never allowed you to be punished, not even to please your mistress. And this is the recompense I get, you ungrateful girl!" I answered that he had reasons of his own for screening me from punishment, and that the course he pursued made my mistress hate me and persecute me. If I wept, he would say, "Poor child! Don't cry! don't cry! I will make peace for you with your mistress. Only let me arrange matters in my own way. Poor, foolish girl! you don't know what is for your own good. I would cherish you. I would make a lady of you. Now go, and think of all I have promised you."

I did think of it.

THE LOVER

There was in the neighborhood a young colored carpenter; a free-born man. We had been well acquainted in childhood, and frequently met together afterwards. We became mutually attached, and he proposed to marry me. I loved him with all the ardor of a young girl's first love. But when I reflected that I was a slave, and that the laws gave no sanction to the marriage of such, my heart sank within me. My lover wanted to buy me; but I knew that Dr. Flint was too wilful and arbitrary a man to consent to that arrangement. From him, I was sure of experiencing all sorts of opposition, and I had nothing to hope from my mistress. She would have been delighted to have got rid of me, but not in that way. It would have relieved her mind of a burden if she could have seen me sold to some distant state, but if I was married near home I should be just as much in her husband's power as I had previously been,—for the husband of a slave has no power to protect her. Moreover, my mistress, like many others, seemed to think that slaves had no right to any family ties of their own; that they were created merely to wait upon the family of the mistress. I once heard her abuse a young slave girl, who told her that a colored man wanted to make her his wife. "I will have you peeled and pickled, my lady," said she, "if I ever hear you mention that subject again. Do you suppose that I will have you tending *my* children with the children of that nigger?" The girl to whom she said this had a mulatto child, of course not acknowledged by its father. The poor black man who loved her would have been proud to acknowledge his helpless offspring.

Many and anxious were the thoughts I revolved in my mind. I was at a loss what to do. Above all things, I was desirous to spare my lover the insults that had cut so deeply into my own soul. I talked with my grandmother about it, and partly told her my fears. I did not dare to tell her the worst. She had long suspected all was not right, and if I confirmed her suspicions I knew a storm would rise that would prove the overthrow of all my hopes.

This love-dream had been my support through many trials; and I could not bear to run the risk of having it suddenly dissipated. There was a lady in the neighborhood, a particular friend of Dr. Flint's, who often visited the house. I had a great respect for her, and she had always manifested a friendly interest in me. Grandmother thought she would have great influence with the doctor. I went to this lady, and told her my story. I told her I was aware that my lover's being a free-born man would prove a great objection; but he wanted to buy me; and if Dr. Flint would consent to that arrangement, I felt sure he would be willing to pay any reasonable price. She knew that Mrs. Flint disliked me, therefore, I ventured to suggest that perhaps my mistress would approve of my being sold, as that would rid her of me. The lady listened with kindly sympathy, and promised to do her utmost to promote my wishes. She had an interview with the doctor, and I believe she pleaded my cause earnestly; but it was all to no purpose.

How I dreaded my master now! Every minute I expected to be summoned to his presence; but the day passed, and I heard nothing from him. The next morning, a message was brought to me: "Master wants you in his study." I found the door ajar, and I stood a moment gazing at the hateful man who claimed a right to rule me, body and soul. I entered, and tried to appear calm. I did not want him to know how my heart was bleeding. He looked fixedly at me, with an expression which seemed to say, "I have half a mind to kill you on the spot." At last he broke the silence, and that was a relief to both of us.

"So you want to be married, do you?" said he, "and to a free nigger."

"Yes, sir."

"Well, I'll soon convince you whether I am your master, or the nigger fellow you honor so highly. If you *must* have a husband, you may take up with one of my slaves."

What a situation I should be in, as the wife of one of *his* slaves, even if my heart had been interested!

I replied, "Don't you suppose, sir, that a slave can have some preference about marrying? Do you suppose that all men are alike to her?"

"Do you love this nigger?" said he, abruptly.

"Yes, sir."

"How dare you tell me so!" he exclaimed, in great wrath. After a slight pause, he added, "I supposed you thought more of yourself; that you felt above the insults of such puppies."

I replied, "If he is a puppy I am a puppy, for we are both of the negro race. It is right and honorable for us to love each other. The man you call a puppy never insulted me, sir; and he would not love me if he did not believe me to be a virtuous woman."

He sprang upon me like a tiger, and gave me a stunning blow. It was the first time he had ever struck me; and fear did not enable me to control my anger. When I had recovered a little from the effects, I exclaimed, "You have struck me for answering you honestly. How I despise you!"

There was silence for some minutes. Perhaps he was deciding what should be my punishment; or, perhaps, he wanted to give me time to reflect on what I had said, and to whom I had said it. Finally, he asked, "Do you know what you have said?"

"Yes, sir; but your treatment drove me to it."

"Do you know that I have a right to do as I like with you,—that I can kill you, if I please?"

"You have tried to kill me, and I wish you had; but you have no right to do as you like with me."

"Silence!" he exclaimed, in a thundering voice. "By heavens girl, you forget yourself too far! Are you mad? If you are, I will soon bring you to your senses. Do you think any other master would bear what I have borne from you this morning? Many masters would have killed you on the spot. How would you like to be sent to jail for your insolence?"

"I know I have been disrespectful, sir," I replied; "but you drove me to it; I couldn't help it. As for the jail, there would be more peace for me there than there is here."

"You deserve to go there," said he, "and to be under such treatment, that you would forget the meaning of the word *peace*. It would do you good. It would take some of your high notions out of you. But I am not ready to send you there yet, notwithstanding your ingratitude for all my kindness and forbearance. You have been the plague of my life. I have wanted to make you happy, and I have been repaid with the basest ingratitude; but though you have proved yourself incapable of appreciating my kindness, I will be lenient towards you, Linda. I will give you one more chance to redeem your character. If you behave yourself and do as I require, I will forgive you and treat you as I always have done; but if you disobey me, I will punish you as I would the meanest slave on my plantation. Never let me hear that fellow's name mentioned again. If I ever know of your speaking to him, I will cowhide you both; and if I catch him lurking about my premises, I will shoot him as soon as I would a dog. Do you hear what I say? I'll teach you a lesson about marriage and free niggers! Now go, and let this be the last time I have occasion to speak to you on this subject."

Reader, did you ever hate? I hope not. I never did but once; and I trust I never shall again. Somebody has called it "the atmosphere of hell;" and I believe it is so.

For a fortnight the doctor did not speak to me. He thought to mortify me; to make me feel that I had disgraced myself by receiving the honorable addresses of a respectable colored man, in preference to the base proposals of a white man. But though his lips disdained to address me, his eyes were very loquacious. No animal ever watched its prey more narrowly than he watched me. He knew that I could write, though he had failed to make me read his letters; and he was now troubled lest I should exchange letters with another man. After a while he became weary of silence; and I was sorry for it. One morning, as he passed through the hall, to leave the house, he contrived to thrust a note into my hand. I thought I had better read it, and spare myself the vexation of having him read it to me. It expressed regret for the blow he had given me, and reminded me that I myself was wholly to blame for it. He hoped I had become convinced of the injury I was doing myself by incurring his displeasure. He wrote that he had made up his mind to go to Louisiana; that he should take several slaves with him, and intended I should be one of the number. My mistress would remain where she was; therefore I should have nothing to fear from that quarter. If I merited kindness from him, he assured me that it would be lavishly bestowed. He begged me to think over the matter, and answer the following day.

The next morning I was called to carry a pair of scissors to his room. I laid them on the table, with the letter beside them. He thought it was my answer, and did not call me back. I went as usual to attend my young mistress to and from school. He met me in the street, and ordered me to stop at his office on my way back. When I entered, he showed me his letter, and asked me why I had not answered it. I replied, "I am your daughter's property, and it is in your power to send me, or take me, wherever you please." He said he was very glad to find me so willing to go, and that we should start early in the autumn. He had a large practice in the town, and I rather thought he had made up the story merely to frighten me. However that might be, I was determined that I would never go to Louisiana with him.

Summer passed away, and early in the autumn Dr. Flint's eldest son was sent to Louisiana to examine the country, with a view to emigrating. That news did not disturb me. I knew very well that I should not be sent with *him*. That I had not been taken to the plantation before this time, was owing to the fact that his son was there. He was jealous of his son; and jealousy of the overseer had kept him from punishing me by sending me into the fields to work. Is it strange that I was not proud of these protectors? As for the overseer, he was a man for whom I had less respect than I had for a bloodhound.

Young Mr. Flint did not bring back a favorable report of Louisiana, and I heard no more of that scheme. Soon after this, my lover met me at the corner of the street, and I stopped to speak to him. Looking up, I saw my master watching us from his window. I hurried home, trembling with fear. I was sent for, immediately, to go to his room. He met me with a blow. "When is mistress to be married?" said he, in a sneering tone. A shower of oaths and imprecations followed. How thankful I was that my lover was a free man! that my tyrant had no power to flog him for speaking to me in the street!

Again and again I revolved in my mind how all this would end. There was no hope that the doctor would consent to sell me on any terms. He had an iron will, and was determined to keep me, and to conquer me. My lover was an intelligent and religious man. Even if he could have obtained permission to marry me while I was a slave, the marriage would give him no power to protect me from my master. It would have made him miserable to witness the insults I should have been subjected to. And then, if we had children, I knew they must "follow the condition of the mother." What a terrible blight that would be on the heart of a free, intelligent father! For *his* sake, I felt that I ought not to link his fate with my own unhappy destiny. He was going to Savannah to see about a little property left him by an uncle; and hard as it was to bring my feelings to it, I earnestly entreated him not to come back. I advised him to go to the Free States, where his tongue would not be tied, and where his intelligence would be of more avail to him. He left me, still hoping the day would come when I could be bought. With me the lamp of hope had gone out. The dream of my girlhood was over. I felt lonely and desolate.

Still I was not stripped of all. I still had my good grandmother, and my affectionate brother. When he put his arms round my neck, and looked into my eyes, as if to read there the troubles I dared not tell, I felt that I still had something to love. But even that pleasant emotion was chilled by the reflection that he might be torn from me at any moment, by some sudden freak of my master. If he had known how we love each other, I think he would have exulted in separating us. We often planned together how we could get to the north. But, as William remarked, such things are easier said than done. My movements were very closely watched, and we had no means of getting any money to defray our expenses. As for grandmother, she was strongly opposed to her children's undertaking any such project. She had not forgotten poor Benjamin's sufferings, and she was afraid that if another child tried to escape, he would have a similar or a worse fate. To me, nothing seemed more dreadful than my present life. I said to myself. "William *must* be free. He shall go to the north, and I will follow him." Many a slave sister has formed the same plans.

A PERILOUS PASSAGE IN A SLAVE GIRL'S LIFE

After my lover went away, Dr. Flint contrived a new plan. He seemed to have an idea that my fear of my mistress was his greatest obstacle. In the blandest tones, he told me that he was going to build a small house for me, in a secluded place, four miles away from the town. I shuddered; but I was constrained to listen, while he talked of his intention to give me a home of my own, and to make a lady of me. Hitherto, I had escaped my dreaded fate, by being in the midst of people. My grandmother had already had high words with my master about me. She had told him pretty plainly what she thought of his character, and there was considerable gossip in the neighborhood about our affairs, to which the open-mouthed jealousy of Mrs. Flint contributed not a little. When my master said he was going to build a house for me, and that he could do it with little trouble and expense, I was in hopes something would happen to frustrate his scheme; but I soon heard that the house was actually begun. I vowed before my Maker that I would never enter it. I had rather toil on the plantation from dawn till dark; I had rather live and die in jail, than drag on, from day to day, through such a living death. I was determined that the master, whom I so hated and loathed, who had blighted the prospects of my youth, and made my life a desert, should not, after my long struggle with him, succeed at last in trampling his victim under his feet. I would do any thing, every thing, for the sake of defeating him. What *could* I do? I thought and thought, till I became desperate, and made a plunge into the abyss.

And now, reader, I come to a period in my unhappy life, which I would gladly forget if I could. The remembrance fills me with sorrow and shame. It pains me to tell you of it; but I have promised to tell you the truth, and I will do it honestly, let it cost me what it may. I will not try to screen myself behind the plea of compulsion from a master; for it was not so. Neither can I plead ignorance or thoughtlessness. For years, my master had done his utmost to pollute my mind with foul images, and to destroy the pure principles inculcated by my grandmother, and the good mistress of my childhood. The influences of slavery had had the same effect on me that they had on other young girls; they had made me prematurely knowing, concerning the evil ways of the world. I knew what I did, and I did it with deliberate calculation.

But, O, ye happy women, whose purity has been sheltered from childhood, who have been free to choose the objects of your affection, whose homes are protected by law, do not judge the poor desolate slave girl too severely! If slavery had been abolished, I, also, could have married the man of my choice; I could have had a home shielded by the laws; and I should have been spared the painful task of confessing what I am now about to relate; but all my prospects had been blighted by slavery. I wanted to keep myself pure; and under the most adverse circumstances, I tried hard to preserve my self-respect; but I was struggling alone in the powerful grasp of the demon Slavery; and the monster proved too strong for me. I felt as if I was forsaken by God and man; as if all my efforts must be frustrated; and I became reckless in my despair.

I have told you that Dr. Flint's persecutions and his wife's jealousy had given rise to some gossip in the neighborhood. Among others, it chanced that a white unmarried gentleman had obtained some knowledge of the circumstances in which I was placed. He knew my grandmother, and often spoke to me in the street. He became interested for me, and asked questions about my master, which I answered in part. He expressed a great deal of sympathy, and a wish to aid me. He constantly sought opportunities to see me, and wrote to me frequently. I was a poor slave girl, only fifteen years old.

So much attention from a superior person was, of course, flattering; for human nature is the same in all. I also felt grateful for his sympathy, and encouraged by his kind words. It seemed to me a great thing to have such a friend. By degrees, a more tender feeling crept into my heart. He was an educated and eloquent gentleman; too eloquent, alas, for the poor slave girl who trusted in him. Of course I saw whither all this was tending. I knew the impassable gulf between us; but to be an object of interest to a man who is not married, and who is not her master, is agreeable to the pride and feelings of a slave, if her miserable situation has left her any pride or sentiment. It seems less degrading to give one's self, than to submit to compulsion. There is something akin to freedom in having a lover who has no control over you, except that which he gains by kindness and attachment. A master may treat you as rudely as he pleases, and you dare not speak; moreover, the wrong does not seem so great with an unmarried man, as with one who has a wife to be made unhappy. There may be sophistry in all this; but the condition of a slave confuses all principles of morality, and, in fact, renders the practice of them impossible.

When I found that my master had actually begun to build the lonely cottage, other feelings mixed with those I have described. Revenge, and calculations of interest, were added to flattered vanity and sincere gratitude for kindness. I knew nothing would enrage Dr. Flint so much as to know that I favored another; and it was something to triumph over my tyrant even in that small way. I thought he would revenge himself by selling me, and I was sure my friend, Mr. Sands, would buy me. He was a man of more generosity and feeling than my master, and I thought my freedom could be easily obtained from him. The crisis of my fate now came so near that I was desperate. I shuddered to think of being the mother of children that should be owned by my old tyrant. I knew that as soon as a new fancy took him, his victims were sold far off to get rid of them; especially if they had children. I had seen several women sold, with his babies at the breast. He never allowed his offspring by slaves to remain long in sight of himself and his wife. Of a man who was not my master I could ask to have my children well supported; and in this case, I felt confident I should obtain the boon. I also felt quite sure that they would be made free. With all these thoughts revolving in my mind, and seeing no other way of escaping the doom I so much dreaded, I made a headlong plunge. Pity me, and pardon me, O virtuous reader! You never knew what it is to be a slave; to be entirely unprotected by law or custom; to have the laws reduce you to the condition of a chattel, entirely subject to the will of another. You never exhausted your ingenuity in avoiding the snares, and eluding the power of a hated tyrant; you never shuddered at the sound of his footsteps, and trembled within hearing of his voice. I know I did wrong. No one can feel it more sensibly than I do. The painful and humiliating memory will haunt me to my dying day. Still, in looking back, clamly, on the events of my life, I feel that the slave woman ought not to be judged by the same standard as others.

The months passed on. I had many unhappy hours. I secretly mourned over the sorrow I was bringing on my grandmother, who had so tried to shield me from harm. I knew that I was the greatest comfort of her old age, and that it was a source of pride to her that I had not degraded myself, like most of the slaves. I wanted to confess to her that I was no longer worthy of her love; but I could not utter the dreaded words.

As for Dr. Flint, I had a feeling of satisfaction and triumph in the thought of telling *him*. From time to time he told me of his intended arrangements, and I was silent. At last, he came and told me the cottage was completed, and ordered me to go to it. I told him I would never enter it. He said, "I have heard enough of such talk as that. You shall go, if you are carried by force; and you shall remain there."

I replied, "I will never go there. In a few months I shall be a mother."

He stood and looked at me in dumb amazement, and left the house without a word. I thought I should be happy in my triumph over him. But now that the truth was out, and my relatives would hear of it, I felt wretched. Humble as were their circumstances, they had pride in my good character. Now, how could I look them in the face? My self-respect was gone! I had resolved that I would be virtuous, though I was a slave. I had said, "Let the storm beat! I will brave it till I die." And now, how humiliated I felt!

I went to my grandmother. My lips moved to make confession, but the words stuck in my throat. I sat down in the shade of a tree at her door and began to sew. I think she saw something unusual was the matter with me. The mother of slaves is very watchful. She knows there is no security for her children. After they have entered their teens she lives in daily expectation of trouble. This leads to many questions. If the girl is of a sensitive nature, timidity keeps her from answering truthfully, and this well-meant course has a tendency to drive her from maternal counsels. Presently, in came my mistress, like a mad woman, and accused me concerning her husband. My grandmother, whose suspicions had been previously awakened, believed what she said. She exclaimed, "O Linda! has it come to this? I had rather see you dead than to see you as you now are. You are a disgrace to your dead mother." She tore from my fingers my mother's wedding ring and her silver thimble. "Go away!" she exclaimed, "and never come to my house, again." Her reproaches fell so hot and heavy, that they left me no chance to answer. Bitter tears, such as the eyes never shed but once, were my only answer. I rose from my seat, but fell back again, sobbing. She did not speak to me; but the tears were running down her furrowed cheeks, and they scorched me like fire. She had always been so kind to me! So kind! How I longed to throw myself at her feet, and tell her all the truth! But she had ordered me to go, and never to come there again. After a few minutes, I mustered strength, and started to obey her. With what feelings did I now close that little gate, which I used to open with such an eager hand in my childhood! It closed upon me with a sound I never heard before.

Where could I go? I was afraid to return to my master's. I walked on recklessly, not caring where I went, or what would become of me. When I had gone four or five miles, fatigue compelled me to stop. I sat down on the stump of an old tree. The stars were shining through the boughs above me. How they mocked me, with their bright, calm light! The hours passed by, and as I sat there alone a chilliness and deadly sickness came over me. I sank on the ground. My mind was full of horrid thoughts. I prayed to die; but the prayer was not answered. At last, with great effort I roused myself, and walked some distance further, to the house of a woman who had been a friend of my mother. When I told her why I was there, she spoke soothingly to me; but I could not be comforted. I thought I could bear my shame if I could only be reconciled to my grandmother. I longed to open my heart to her. I thought if she could know the real state of the case, and all I had been bearing for years, she would perhaps judge me less harshly. My friend advised me to send for her. I did so; but days of agonizing suspense passed before she came. Had she utterly forsaken me? No. She came at last. I knelt before her, and told her the things that had poisoned my life; how long I had been persecuted; that I saw no way of escape; and in an hour of extremity I had become desperate. She listened in silence. I told her I would bear any thing and do any thing, if in time I had hopes of obtaining her forgiveness. I begged of her to pity me, for my dead mother's sake. And she did pity me. She did not say, "I forgive you;" but she looked at me lovingly, with her eyes full of tears. She laid her old hand gently on my head, and murmured, "Poor child! Poor child!"

from *The Adventures of Huckleberry Finn*

Mark Twain (1835–1910)

Mark Twain was born Samuel Clemens in Missouri in 1835. Both a journeyman printer and a steamboat pilot on the Mississippi River in his youth, Clemens served an abbreviated stint in the Confederate Army in 1861 and moved to the West during the war. There, he adopted his pen name and became one of the most popular lecturers and writers in the nation. In *Huckleberry Finn* (1884), Twain explored the antebellum South from the vantage point of a young white boy and a runaway slave accompanying him on a raft floating down the Mississippi. The book offers a biting portrait of white Southerners and a complicated, conflicted view of black Americans. *Huckleberry Finn* was controversial when it appeared and has remained so ever since.

Col. Grangerford was a gentleman, you see. He was a gentleman all over; and so was his family. He was well born, as the saying is, and that's worth as much in a man as it is in a horse, so the Widow Douglas said, and nobody ever denied that she was of the first aristocracy in our town; and pap he always said it, too, though he warn't no more quality than a mudcat himself. Col. Grangerford was very tall and very slim, and had a darkish-paly complexion, not a sign of red in it anywheres; he was clean-shaved every morning all over his thin face, and he had the thinnest kind of lips, and the thinnest kind of nostrils, and a high nose, and heavy eyebrows, and the blackest kind of eyes, sunk so deep back that they seemed like they was looking out of caverns at you, as you may say. His forehead was high, and his hair was gray and straight and hung to his shoulders. His hands was long and thin, and every day of his life he put on a clean shirt and full suit from head to foot made out of linen so white it hurt your eyes to look at it; and on Sundays he wore a blue tail-coat with brass buttons on it. He carried a mahogany cane with a silver head to it. There warn't no frivolishness about him, not a bit, and he warn't ever loud. He was as kind as he could be—you could feel that, you know, and so you had confidence. Sometimes he smiled, and it was good to see; but when he straightened himself up like a liberty-pole, and the lightning begun to flicker out from under his eyebrows, you wanted to climb a tree first, and find out what the matter was afterwards. He didn't ever have to tell anybody to mind their manners—everybody was always good-mannered where he was. Everybody loved to have him around, too; he was sunshine most always — I mean he made it seem like good weather. When he turned into a cloud-bank it was awful dark for half a minute, and that was enough; there wouldn't nothing go wrong again for a week.

When him and the old lady come down in the morning all the family got out of their chairs and give them good day, and didn't set down again till they had set down. Then Tom and Bob went to the sideboard where the decanter was and mixed a glass of bitters and handed it to him, and he held it in his hand and waited till Tom's and Bob's was mixed, and then they bowed and said, "Our duty to you, sir, and madam"; and *they* bowed the least bit in the world and said thank you, and so they drank, all three, and Bob and Tom poured a spoonful of water on the sugar and the mite of whisky or apple-brandy in the bottom of their tumblers, and give it to me and Buck, and we drank to the old people too.

Bob was the oldest and Tom next—tall, beautiful men with very broad shoulders and brown faces, and long black hair and black eyes. They dressed in white linen from head to foot, like the old gentleman, and wore broad Panama hats.

Then there was Miss Charlotte; she was twenty-five, and tall and proud and grand, but as good as she could be when she warn't stirred up; but when she was she had a look that would make you wilt in your tracks, like her father. She was beautiful.

So was her sister, Miss Sophia, but it was a different kind. She was gentle and sweet like a dove, and she was only twenty.

Each person had their own nigger to wait on them—Buck too. My nigger had a monstrous easy time, because I warn't used to having anybody do anything for me, but Buck's was on the jump most of the time.

This was all there was of the family now, but there used to be more — three sons; they got killed; and Emmeline that died.

The old gentleman owned a lot of farms and over a hundred niggers. Sometimes a stack of people would come there, horseback, from ten or fifteen miles around, and stay five or six days, and have such junketings round about and on the river, and dances and picnics in the woods daytimes, and balls at the house nights. These people was mostly kinfolks of the family. The men brought their guns with them. It was a handsome lot of quality, I tell you.

There was another clan of aristocracy around there—five or six families — mostly of the name of Shepherdson. They was as high-toned and well born and rich and grand as the tribe of Grangerfords. The Shepherdsons and Grangerfords used the same steamboat-landing, which was about two mile above our house; so sometimes when I went up there with a lot of our folks I used to see a lot of the Shepherdsons there on their fine horses.

One day Buck and me was away out in the woods hunting, and heard a horse coming. We was crossing the road. Buck says:

"Quick! Jump for the woods!"

We done it, and then peeped down the woods through the leaves. Pretty soon a splendid young man came galloping down the road, setting his horse easy and looking like a soldier. He had his gun across his pommel. I had seen him before. It was young Harney Shepherdson. I heard Buck's gun go off at my ear, and Harney's hat tumbled off from his head. He grabbed his gun and rode straight to the place where we was hid. But we didn't wait. We started through the woods on a run. The woods warn't thick, so I looked over my shoulder to dodge the bullet, and twice I seen Harney cover Buck with his gun; and then he rode away the way he come — to get his hat, I reckon, but I couldn't see. We never stopped running till we got home. The old gentleman's eyes blazed a minute — 'twas pleasure, mainly, I judged — then his face sort of smoothed down, and he says, kind of gentle:

"I don't like that shooting from behind a bush. Why, didn't you step into the road, my boy?"

"The Shepherdsons don't, father. They always take advantage."

Miss Charlotte she held her head up like a queen while Buck was telling his tale, and her nostrils spread and her eyes snapped. The two young men looked dark, but never said nothing. Miss Sophia she turned pale, but the color come back when she found the man warn't hurt.

Soon as I could get Buck down by the corn-cribs under the trees by ourselves, I says:

"Did you want to kill him, Buck?"

"Well, I bet I did."

"What did he do to you?"

"Him? He never done nothing to me."

"Well, then, what did you want to kill him for?"

"Why, nothing — only it's on account of the feud."

"What's a feud?"

"Why, where was you raised? Don't you know what a feud is?"

"Never heard of it before — tell me about it."

"Well," says Buck, "a feud is this way: A man has a quarrel with another man, and kills him; then that other man's brother kills *him*; then the other brothers, on both sides, goes for one another; then the *cousins* chip in — and by and by everybody's killed off, and there ain't no more feud. But it's kind of slow, and takes a long time."

"Has this one been going on long, Buck?"

"Well, I should *reckon!* It started thirty years ago, or some'ers along there. There was troubled 'bout something, and then a lawsuit to settle it; and the suit went agin one of the men, and so he up and shot the man that won the suit—which he would naturally do, of course. Anybody would."

"What was the trouble about, Buck?—land?"

"I reckon maybe—I don't know."

"Well, who done the shooting? Was it a Grangerford or a Shepherdson?"

"Laws, how do *I* know? It was so long ago."

"Don't anybody know?"

"Oh, yes, pa knows, I reckon, and some of the other old people: but they don't know now what the row was about in the first place."

"Has there been many killed, Buck?"

"Yes; right smart chance of funerals. But they don't always kill. Pa's got a few buckshot in him; but he don't mind it 'cuz he don't weigh much, anyway. Bob's been carved up some with a bowie, and Tom's been hurt once or twice."

"Has anybody been killed this year, Buck?"

"Yes; we got one and they got one. 'Bout three months ago my cousin Bud, fourteen year old, was riding through the woods on t'other side of the river, and didn't have no weapon with him, which was blame' foolishness, and in a lonesome place he hears a horse a-coming behind him, and sees old Baldy Shepherdson a-linkin' after him with his gun in his hand and his white hair a-flying in the wind; and 'stead of jumping off and taking to the bush, Bud 'lowed he could outrun him; so they had it, nip and tuck, for five mile or more, the old man a-gaining all the time; so at last Bud seen it warn't any use, so he stopped and faced around so as to have the bullet-holes in front, you know, and the old man he rode up and shot him down. But he didn't git much chance to enjoy his luck, for inside of a week our folks laid *him* out."

"I reckon that old man was a coward, Buck."

"I reckon he *warn't* a coward. Not by a blame' sight. There ain't a coward amongst them Shepherdsons—not a one. And there ain't no cowards amongst the Grangerfords either. Why, that old man kep' up his end in a fight one day for half an hour against three Grangerfords, and come out winner. They was all a-horseback; he lit off of his horse and got behind a little woodpile, and kep' his horse before him to stop the bullets; but the Grangerfords stayed on their horses and capered around the old man, and peppered away at him, and he peppered away at them. Him and his horse went home pretty leaky and crippled, but the Grangerfords had to be *fetched* home—and one of 'em was dead, and another died the next day. No, sir; if a body's out hunting for cowards he don't want to fool

any time amongst them Shepherdsons, becuz they don't breed any of that
kind."

Next Sunday we all went to church, about three mile, everybody a-
horseback. The men took their guns along, so did Buck, and kept them
between their knees or stood them handy against the wall. The
Shepherdsons done the same. It was pretty ornery preaching—all about
brotherly love, and such-like tiresomeness; but everybody said it was a
good sermon, and they all talked it over going home, and had such a powerful lot to say about faith and good works and free grace and prefore-
ordestination, and I don't know what all, that it did seem to me to be one
of the roughest Sundays I had run across yet.

About an hour after dinner everybody was dozing around, some in their
chairs and some in their rooms, and it got to be pretty dull. Buck and a
dog was stretched out on the grass in the sun sound asleep. I went up to
our room, and judged I would take a nap myself. I found that sweet Miss
Sophia standing in her door, which was next to ours, and she took me in
her room and shut the door very soft, and asked me if I liked her, and I
said I did; and she asked me if I would do something for her and not tell
anybody, and I said I would. Then she said she'd forgot her Testament, and
left it in the seat at church between two other books, and would I slip out
quiet and go there and fetch it to her, and not say nothing to nobody. I
said I would. So I slid out and slipped off up the road, and there warn't
anybody at the church, except maybe a hog or two, for there warn't any
lock on the door, and hogs likes a puncheon floor in summer-time because
it's cool. If you notice, most folks don't go to church only when they've
got to; but a hog is different.

Says I to myself, something's up; it ain't natural for a girl to be in such
a sweat about a Testament. So I give it a shake, and out drops a little piece
of paper with *"Half past two"* wrote on it with a pencil. I ransacked it, but
couldn't find anything else. I couldn't make anything out of that, so I put
the paper in the book again, and when I got home and upstairs there was
Miss Sophia in her door waiting for me. She pulled me in and shut the
door; then she looked in the Testament till she found the paper, and as
soon as she read it she looked glad; and before a body could think she
grabbed me and give me a squeeze, and said I was the best boy in the
world, and not to tell anybody. She was mighty red in the face for a
minute, and her eyes lighted up, and it made her powerful pretty. I was a
good deal astonished, but when I got my breath I asked her what the paper
was about, and she asked me if I had read it, and I said no, and she asked
me if I could read writing, and I told her "no, only coarsehand," and then
she said the paper warn't anything but a bookmark to keep her place, and
I might go and play now.

I went off down to the river, studying over this thing, and pretty soon I noticed that my nigger was following along behind. When we was out of sight of the house he looked back and around a second, and then comes a-running, and says:

"Mars Jawge, if you'll come down into de swamp I'll show you a whole stack o' water-moccasins."

Thinks I, that's mighty curious; he said that yesterday. He oughter know a body don't love water-moccasins enough to go around hunting for them. What is he up to, anyway? So I says:

"All right; trot ahead."

I followed a half a mile; then he struck out over the swamp, and waded ankle-deep as much as another half-mile. We come to a little flat piece of land which was dry and very thick with trees and bushes and vines, and he says:

"You shove right in dah jist a few steps, Mars Jawge; dah's whah dey is. I's seed 'm befo'; I don't k'yer to see 'em no mo'."

Then he slopped right along and went away, and pretty soon the trees hid him. I poked into the place a ways and come to a little open patch as big as a bedroom all hung around with vines, and found a man laying there asleep—and, by jings, it was my old Jim!

I waked him up, and I reckoned it was going to be a grand surprise to him to see me again, but it warn't. He nearly cried he was so glad, but he warn't surprised. Said he swum along behind me that night, and heard me yell every time, but dasn't answer, because he didn't want nobody to pick him up and take *him* into slavery again. Says he:

"I got hurt a little, en couldn't swim fas', so I wuz a considerable ways behine you towards de las'; when you landed I reck'ned I could ketch up wid you on de lan' 'dout havin' to shout at you, but when I see dat house I begin to go slow. I 'uz off too fur to hear what dey say to you—I wuz 'fraid o' de dogs; but when it 'uz quiet ag'in I knowed you's in de house, so I struck out for de woods to wait for day. Early in de mawnin' some er de niggers come along, gwyne to de fields, en dey tuk me en showed me dis place, whah de dogs can't track me on account o' de water, en dey brings me truck to eat every night, en tells me how you's a-gittin' along."

"Why didn't you tell my Jack to fetch me here sooner, Jim?"

"Well, 'twarn't no use to 'sturb you, Huck, tell we could do sumfn—but we's all right now. I ben a-buyin' pots en pans en vittles, as I got a chanst, en a-patchin' up de raf' nights when—"

"*What* raft, Jim?"

"Our ole raf'."

"You mean to say our old raft warn't smashed all to finders?"

"No, she warn't. She was tore up a good deal—one 'en of her was; but dey warn't no great harm done' only our traps was mos' all los'. Ef we hadn' dive' so deep en swum so fur under water, en de night hadn't been so dark, en we warn't so sk'yered, en ben sich punkin-heads, as de sayin' is, we'd a seed de raf'. But it's jis' as well we didn't, 'kase now she's all fixed up ag'in mos' as good as new, en we's a got a new lot o' stuff, n de place o' what 'uz los'."

"Why, how did you get hold of the raft again, Jim—did you catch her?"

"How I gwyne to ketch her en I out in de woods? No; some er de nig-gers foun' her ketched on a snag along heah in de ben', en dey hid her in a crick 'mongst de willows, en dey wuz so much jawin' 'bout which un 'um she b'longs to de mos' dat I come to heah 'bout it pretty soon, so I ups en settles de trouble by tellin' 'um she don't b'long to none uv'um, but to you en me; en I ast 'm if dey gwyne to grab a young white genlman's propaty, en git a hid'n for it? Den I gin 'm ten cents apiece, en dey 'uz mighty well satisfied, en wisht some mo' raf's 'ud come along en make 'em rich ag'in. Dey's mighty good to me, dese niggers is, en whatever I wants 'm to do fur me I doan' have to ast 'em twice, honey. Dat Jack's a good nigger, en pooty smart."

"Yes, he is. He ain't ever told me you was here; told me to come, and he'd show me a lot of water-moccasins. If anything happens *he* ain't mixed up in it. He can say he never seen us together, and it'll be the truth."

I don't want to talk much about the next day. I reckon I'll cut it pretty short. I waked up about dawn, and was a-going to turn over and go to sleep again when I noticed how still it was—didn't seem to be anybody stirring. That warn't usual. Next I noticed that Buck was up and gone. Well, I gets up, awondering, and goes down-stairs—nobody around; everything as still as a mouse. Just the same outside. Thinks I, what does it mean? Down by the woodpile I comes across my Jack, and says:

"What's it all about?"

Says he:

"Don't you know, Mars Jawge?"

"No," says I, "I don't."

"Well, den, Miss Sophia's run off! 'deed she has. She run off in de night some time—nobody don't know jis' when; run off to get married to dat young Harney Shepherdson, you know—leastways, so dey 'spec. De fam-bly foun' it out 'bout half an hour ago—maybe a little mo'—en' I *tell* you dey warn't no time los'. Sich another hurryin' up guns en hosses *you* never see! De women folks has gone for to stir up de relations, en ole Mars Saul en de boys tuck dey guns en rode up de river road for to try to ketch dat young man en kill him 'fo he kin git acrost de river wid Miss Sophia. I reck'n dey's gwyne to be mighty rough times."

"Buck went off 'though waking me up."

"Well, I reck'n he *did!* Dey warn't gwyne to mix you up in it. Mars Buck he loaded up his gun en 'lowed he's gwyne to fetch home a Shepherdson or bust. Well, dey'll be plenty un 'm dah, I reck'n, en you bet you he'll fetch one ef he gits a chanst."

I took up the river road as hard as I could put. By and by I begin to hear a guns a good ways off. When I came in sight of the log store and the wood-pile where the steamboats lands I worked along under the trees and brush till I got to a good place, and then I clumb up into the forks of a cottonwood that was out of reach, and watched. There was a wood-rank four foot high a little ways in front of the tree, and first I was going to hide behind that; but maybe it was luckier I didn't.

There was four or five men cavorting around on their horses in the open place before the log store, cussing and yelling; and trying to get a couple of young chaps that was behind the woodrank alongside of the steam-boat landing; but they could'nt come it. Every time one of them showed himself on the river side of the woodpile he got shot at. The two boys was squatting back to back behind the pile, so they could watch both ways.

By and by the men stopped cavorting around and yelling. They started riding towards the store; then up gets one of the boys, draws a steady bead over the wood-rank, and drops one of them out of his saddle. All the men jumped off of their horses and grabbed the hurt one and started to carry him to the store; and that minute the two boys started on the run. They got halfway to the tree I was in before the men noticed. Then the men see them, and jumped on their horses and took out after them. They gained on the boys, but it didn't do no good, the boys had too good a start; they got to the woodpile that was in front of my tree, and slipped in behind it, and so they had the bulge on the men again. One of the boys was Buck, and the other was a slim young chap about nineteen years old.

The men ripped around awhile, and then rode away. As soon as they was out of sight I sung out to Buck and told him. He didn't know what to make of my voice coming out of the tree at first. He was awful surprised. He told me to watch out sharp and let him know when the men come in sight again; said they was up to some devilment or other — wouldn't be gone long. I wished I was out of that tree, but I dasn't come down. Buck begun to cry and rip, and 'lowed that him and his cousin Joe (that was the other young chap) would make up for this day yet. He said his father and his two brothers was killed, and two or three of the enemy. Said the Shepherdsons laid for them in ambush. Buck said his father and brothers ought to waited for their relations — the Shepherdsons was too strong for them. I asked him what was become of young Harney and Miss Sophia. He said they'd got across the river and was safe. I was glad of that; but the way Buck did take on because he didn't manage to kill Harney that day he shot at him—I hain't ever heard anything like it.

All of a sudden, bang! bang! bang! goes three or four guns—the men had slipped around through the woods and come in from behind without their horses! The boys jumped for the river—both of them hurt—and as they swum down the current the men run along the bank shooting at them and singing out, "Kill them, kill them!" It made me so sick I most fell out of the tree. I ain't a-going to tell *all* that happened—it would make me sick again if I was to do that. I wished I hadn't ever come ashore that night to see such things. I ain't ever going to get shut of them—lots of times I dream about them.

I stayed in the tree till it begun to get dark, afraid to come down. Sometimes I heard guns away off in the woods; and twice I seen little gangs of men gallop past the log store with guns; so I reckoned the trouble was still a-going on. I was mighty downhearted; so I made up my mind I wouldn't ever go anear the house again, because I reckoned I was to blame, somehow. I judged that that piece of paper meant that Miss Sophia was to meet Harney somewheres at half past two and run off; and I judged I ought to told her father about that paper and the curious way she acted, and then maybe he would 'a' locked her up, and this awful mess wouldn't ever happened.

When I got down out of the tree I crept along down the riverbank a piece, and found the two bodies laying in the edge of the water, and tugged at them till I got them ashore; then I covered up their faces, and got away as quick as I could. I cried a little when I was covering up Buck's face, for he was mighty good to me.

It was just dark now. I never went near the house, but struck through the woods and made for the swamp. Jim warn't on his island, so I tramped off in a hurry for the crick, and crowded through the willows, red-hot to jump aboard and get out of that awful country. The raft was gone! My souls, but I was scared! I couldn't get my breath for most a minute. Then I raised a yell. A voice not twenty-five foot from me says:

"Good lan'! is dat you, honey? Doan' make no noise."

It was Jim's voice—nothing ever sounded so good before. I run along the bank a piece and got aboard, and Jim he grabbed me and hugged me, he was so glad to see me. He says:

"Laws bless you, chile, I 'uz right down sho' you's dead ag'in. Jack's been heah; he says he reck'n you's ben shot, kase you didn' come home no mo'; so I's jes' dis minute a-startin' de raf' down towards de mouf er de crick, so's to be all ready for to shove out en leave soon as Jack comes ag'in en tells me for certain you *is* dead. Lawsy, I's mighty glad to git you back ag'in, honey."

I says:

"All right—that's mighty good; they won't find me, and they'll think I've been killed, and floated down the river—there's something up there that 'll help them think so—so don't you lose no time, Jim, but just shove off for the big water as fast as ever you can."

I never felt easy till the raft was two mile below there and out in the middle of the Mississippi. Then we hung up our signal lantern, and judged that we was free and safe once more. I hadn't had a bite to eat since yesterday, so Jim he got out some corn-dodgers and buttermilk, and pork and cabbage and greens—there ain't nothing in the world so good when it's cooked right—and whilst I eat my supper we talked and had a good time. I was powerful glad to get away from the feuds, and so was Jim to get away from the swamp. We said there warn't no home like a raft, after all. Other places do seem so cramped up and smothery, but a raft don't. You feel mighty free and easy and comfortable on a raft.

from *The Mind of the South*

W. J. Cash (1900–1941)

W. J. Cash grew up in Gaffney, South Carolina, a cotton-mill town where his father managed a company store. Cash, like many young white Southerners in the 1920s, found the iconoclasm of pundits such as H. L. Mencken an attractive antidote to the boosterism and romanticism of the latest "New South." Never at ease with himself or his society, Cash witnessed much as a journalist in Charlotte that confirmed his belief that the South's own people and the nation did not see the region clearly. He worked on *The Mind of the South* through much of the 1920s and 1930s, developing a sweeping interpretation of the region's history. Soon after the book was published in early 1941, generally to warm reviews, Cash committed suicide in Mexico City, where, accompanied by his new wife and funded with a prestigious fellowship, he had gone to work on a novel.

What the Old South of the legend in its classical form was like is more or less familiar to everyone. It was a sort of stage piece out of the eighteenth century, wherein gesturing gentlemen move soft-spokenly against a background of rose gardens and dueling grounds, through always gallant deeds, and lovely ladies, in farthingales, never for a moment lost that exquisite remoteness which has been the dream of all men and the possession of none. Its social pattern was manorial, its civilization that of the Cavalier, its ruling class an aristocracy coextensive with the planter group—men often entitled to quarter the royal arms of St. George and St. Andrew on their shields, and in every case descended from the old gentlefolk who for many centuries had made up the ruling classes of Europe.

They dwelt in large and stately mansions, preferably white and with columns and Grecian entablature. Their estates were feudal baronies, their slaves quite too numerous ever to be counted, and their social life a thing of Old World splendor and delicacy. What had really happened here, indeed, was that the gentlemanly idea, driven from England by Cromwell, had taken refuge in the South and fashioned for itself a world to its heart's desire: a world singularly polished and mellow and poised, wholly dominated by ideals of honor and chivalry and *noblesse*— all those sentiments and values and habits of action which used to be, especially in Walter Scott, invariably assigned to the gentleman born and the Cavalier.

Beneath these was a vague race lumped together indiscriminately as the poor whites — very often, in fact, as the "white-trash." These people belonged in the main to a physically inferior type, having sprung for the most part from the convict servants, redemptioners, and debtors of old Virginia and Georgia, with a sprinkling of the most unsuccessful sort of European peasants and farm laborers and the dregs of the European town slums. And so, of course, the gulf between them and the master classes was impassable, and their ideas and feelings did not enter into the make-up of the prevailing Southern civilization.

But in the legend of the New South the Old South is supposed to have been destroyed by the Civil War and the thirty years that followed it, to have been swept both socially and mentally into the limbo of things that were and are not, to give place to a society which has been rapidly and increasingly industrialized and modernized both in body and in mind — which now, indeed, save for a few quaint survivals and gentle sentimentalities and a few shocking and inexplicable brutalities such as lynching, is almost as industrialized and modernized in its outlook as the North. Such an idea is obviously inconsistent with the general assumption of the South's great difference, but paradox is the essence of popular thinking, and millions — even in the South itself — placidly believe in both notions.

These legends, however, bear little relation to reality. There was an Old South, to be sure, but it was another thing than this. And there is a New South. Industrialization and commercialization have greatly modified the land, including its ideology, as we shall see in due course. Nevertheless, the extent of the change and of the break between the Old South that was and the South of our time has been vastly exaggerated. The South, one might say, is a tree with many age rings, with its limbs and trunk bent and twisted by all the winds of the years, but with its tap root in the Old South. Or, better still, it is like one of those churches one sees in England. The facade and towers, the windows and clerestory, all the exterior and superstructure are late Gothic of one sort or another, but look into its nave, its aisles, and its choir and you find the old mighty Norman arches of the twelfth century. And if you look into its crypt, you may even find stones cut by Saxon, brick made by Roman hands.

The mind of the section, that is, is continuous with the past. And its primary form is determined not nearly so much by industry as by the purely agricultural conditions of that past. So far from being modernized, in many ways it has actually always marched away, as to this day it continues to do, from the present toward the past.

It follows, therefore, that to get at its nature we shall have first of all to examine into the question of exactly what the Old South was really like.

. . .

How account for the ruling class, then? Manifestly, for the great part, by the strong, the pushing, the ambitious, among the old coon-hunting population of the backcountry. The frontier was their predestined inheritance. They possessed precisely the qualities necessary to the taming of the land and the building of the cotton kingdom. The process of their rise to power was simplicity itself. Take a concrete case.

A stout young Irishman brought his bride into the Carolina upcountry about 1800. He cleared a bit of land, built a log cabin of two rooms, and sat down to the pioneer life. One winter, with several of his neighbors, he loaded a boat with whisky and the coarse woolen cloth woven by the women, and drifted down to Charleston to trade. There, remembering the fondness of his woman for a bit of beauty, he bought a handful of cotton seed, which she planted about the cabin with the wild rose and the honeysuckle—as a flower. Afterward she learned, under the tutelage of a new neighbor, to pick the seed from the fiber with her fingers and to spin it into yarn. Another winter the man drifted down the river, this time to find the half-way station of Columbia in a strange ferment. There was a new wonder in the world—the cotton gin—and the forest which had lined the banks of the stream for a thousand centuries was beginning to go down. Fires flared red and portentous in the night—to set off an answering fire in the breast of the Irishman.

Land in his neighborhood was to be had for fifty cents an acre. With twenty dollars, the savings of his lifetime, he bought forty acres and set himself to clear it. Rising long before day, he toiled deep into the night, with his wife holding a pine torch for him to see by. Aided by his neighbors, he piled the trunks of the trees into great heaps and burned them, grubbed up the stumps, hacked away the tangle of underbrush and vine, stamped out the poison ivy and the snakes. A wandering trader sold him a horse, bony and half-starved, for a knife, a dollar, and a gallon of whisky. Every day now—Sundays not excepted—when the heavens allowed, and every night that the moon came, he drove the plow into the earth, with uptorn roots bruising his shanks at every step. Behind him came his wife with a hoe. In a few years the land was beginning to yield cotton—richly, for the soil was fecund with the accumulated mold of centuries. Another trip down the river, and he brought home a mangy black slave—an old and lazy fellow reckoned of no account in the rice-lands, but with plenty of life in him still if you knew to get it out. Next year the Irishman bought fifty acres more, and the year after another black. Five years more and he had two hundred acres and ten Negroes. Cotton prices swung up and down sharply, but always, whatever the return, it was almost pure velvet. For the fertility of the soil seemed inexhaustible.

When he was forty-five, he quit work, abandoned the log house, which had grown to six rooms, and built himself a wide-spreading frame cottage. When he was fifty, he became a magistrate, acquired a carriage, and built a cotton gin and a third house—a "big house" this time. It was not, to be truthful, a very grand house really. Built of lumber sawn on the place, it was a little crude and had not cost above a thousand dollars, even when the marble mantel was counted in. Essentially, it was just a box, with four rooms, bisected by a hallway, set on four more rooms bisected by another hallway, and a detached kitchen at the back. Wind-swept in winter, it was difficult to keep clean of vermin in summer. But it was huge, it had great columns in front, and it was eventually painted white, and so, in this land of wide fields and pinewoods it seemed very imposing.

Meantime the country around had been growing up. Other "big houses" had been built. There was a county seat now, a cluster of frame houses, stores, and "doggeries" about a red brick courthouse. A Presbyterian parson had drifted in and started an academy, as Presbyterian parsons had a habit of doing everywhere in the South—and Pompeys and Caesars and Ciceros and Platos were multiplying both among the pickaninnies in the slave quarters and among the white children of the "big houses." The Irishman had a piano in his house, on which his daughters, taught by a vagabond German, played as well as young ladies could be expected to. One of the Irishman's sons went to the College of South Carolina, came back to grow into the chief lawyer in the county, got to be a judge, and would have been Governor if he had not died at the head of his regiment at Chancellorsville.

As a crown on his career, the old man went to the Legislature, where he was accepted by the Charleston gentlemen tolerantly and with genuine liking. He grew extremely mellow in age and liked to pass his time in company, arguing about predestination and infant damnation, proving conclusively that cotton was king and that the damyankee didn't dare do anything about it, and developing a notable taste in the local liquors. Tall and well-made, he grew whiskers after the Galway fashion—the well-kept whiteness of which contrasted very agreeably with the brick red of his complexion—donned the long-tailed coat, stove-pipe hat, and string tie of the statesmen of his period, waxed innocently pompous, and, in short, became a really striking figure of a man.

Once, going down to Columbia for the inauguration of a new Governor, he took his youngest daughter along. There she met a Charleston gentleman who was pestering her father for a loan. Her manner, formed by the Presbyterian parson, was plain but not bad, and she was very pretty. Moreover, the Charleston gentleman was decidedly in hard times. So he married her.

When the old man finally died in 1854, he left two thousand acres, a hundred and fourteen slaves, and four cotton gins. The little newspaper which had recently set up in the county seat spoke of him as "a gentleman of the old school" and "a noble specimen of the chivalry at its best"; the Charleston papers each gave him a column; and a lordly Legaré introduced resolutions of respect into the Legislature. His wife outlived him by ten years—by her portrait a beautifully fragile old woman, and, as I have heard it said, with lovely hands, knotted and twisted just enough to give them character, and a finely transparent skin through which the blue veins showed most aristocratically.

. . .

Such is the epic, in little, of the rise of the ruling class in the great South. And yet—maybe I go too fast. Maybe, in fact, it is only a part of the epic. Certainly it happened like that over and over again. In many parts, as in Mississippi, it even happened, because of the almost unparalleled productivity of the soil, in accelerated tempo, and so went even further. But I suspect that something else happened, too. Behind the figure of my Irishman bulk the outlines of others, all of them fashioned from darker colors—others adumbrated in the passage I have already quoted from the old Alabama observer, Judge Baldwin, concerning the downfall of the Virginians.

Let us consider his testimony a little further. He is describing the conditions the Virginians could not meet:

"The country was just settling up. Marvelous reports had gone forth of the fertility of the virgin lands; and the productions of the soil were commanding a price remunerating to slave labor as it had never been remunerated before. Emigrants came flocking from all quarters of the Union, especially from the slave-holding States. The new country seemed to be a reservoir, and every road leading to it a vagrant stream of enterprise and adventure. Money, or what passed for money, was the only cheap thing to be had. Every crossroad and every avocation presented an opening— through which a fortune was seen by the adventurer in near perspective. Credit was a thing of course. To refuse it—if the thing was ever done— was an insult for which a bowie-knife was not too summary a means of redress. The State banks were issuing their bills by the sheet, like a patent steam printing press its issues; and no other showing was asked of the applicant for the loan than an authentication of his great distress for money. . . .

"Under this stimulating process, prices rose like smoke. Lots in obscure villages were sold at city prices; lands, bought at the minimum cost of government, were sold at from thirty to forty dollars per acre, and considered dirt cheap at that. In short, the country had got to be a full ante-type of California, in all except the gold. . . . Money got without work, by those unaccustomed to it, turned the heads of its possessors, and they spent it with a recklessness with which they had gained it. . . .

"In the fullness of time, the new era had set in—the era of the second great experiment of independence; the era, namely, of credit without capital, and enterprise without honesty. . . . The condition of society may be imagined;—vulgarity—ignorance—fussy and arrogant pretension—unmitigated rowdyism—bullying insolence, if they did not rule the hour, seemed to wield unchecked dominion. . . ."

The dim figures behind my Irishman become plainer. From the frenzied scene described here—a scene strikingly reminiscent of the Florida of a decade ago, and, indeed, of the whole United States throughout the 1920's—there emerge certain very definite personalities: the boomer, the shark, and, in teeming profusion, that typical slicker of the old backwoods, the horse-trader.

Inevitable figures, of course. In theory, the frontier is the land of equal opportunity for all. In theory, its rewards are wholly to industry, to thrift, to luck—to my Irishman. In practice, they are just as often to cunning, to hoggery and callousness, to brutal unscrupulousness and downright scoundrelism. In practice, on any frontier which holds out large prospects, and where, accordingly, men congregate in numbers, where events move swiftly and competition is intense, there invariably arises the schemer—the creator and manipulator of fictitious values, the adept in spurring on the already overheated imaginations of his fellows—and, in his train, a whole horde of lesser swindlers and cheats. And when the bankruptcies which they breed are done with, when the frontier is past and its final rewards totaled up, these, or many of them, anyhow, are likely to have five thousand acres where my Irishman had two thousand.

Strictly, of course, what our observer reports here applies only to the Mississippi Valley, but, in degrees, I think it holds good for all the cotton country and all the great South. Everywhere, in some measure, the advance of the plantation was accompanied by a fevering of imagination and a surge upward in values, and everywhere the knave and the horse-trader turned these things to account. Did they, in fact, come finally to make up the greater part of the planter class? To say that outright would be to go too far, no doubt; but if we were to modify it to say men distinguished by something of the same hard and coarse stamp as the horse-trader at least, we should not perhaps be greatly wide of the truth. "Vulgarity—ignorance—fussy and arrogant pretension—unmitigated rowdyism—bullying insolence . . .": these are significant words from one who was himself a Southerner and a patriot.

There is other evidence to the same general effect. On the eve of the Civil War, Frederick Law Olmsted, first of all that host of Yankee journalists who were presently to overrun the country below the Potomac, was snarling over the *nouveaux* he found about Vicksburg, and adding:

"The farce of the vulgar rich has its foundation in Mississippi, as in New York and Manchester, in the rapidity with which certain values have advanced, especially that of cotton, and simultaneously, that of cotton land and Negroes. Of course, there are men of refinement and cultivation among the rich planters of Mississippi, and many highly estimable and intelligent persons outside of the wealthy class, but the number of such is smaller in proportion to that of the immoral, vulgar, and ignorant newly-rich than in any other part of the United States."

A few years earlier he had already set down an opinion but little if at all more favorable to the seaboard states of the South.

Olmsted, however, has been called prejudiced. Maybe he was. But nobody will accuse D. R. Hundley, author of *Social Relations in Our Southern States*, published at Philadelphia in 1860, of being so. A Charleston lawyer of good family, he wrote his book primarily as a defense of "the chivalry" against the attacks of Yankee critics. Yet, in the long run, his conclusions do not differ materially from those of Olmsted. For, though he is full of enthusiasm for the Southern gentlemen, he says flatly that such gentlemen were less numerous among the planters than what he calls Cotton Snobs—as he depicts them, parvenus and unprincipled boors.

In the light of all this, is it possible still to maintain that the ruling class of the great South was, in the full sense and as a whole, an aristocracy? Or that it was anything, for the great part, but the natural flower of the backcountry grown prosperous? To ask it is to answer it. There were many gentlemen in the South, as even Olmsted grants. There remained always, of course, the Virginians; for, though gradually overshadowed and swallowed up into the new master class of cotton, the little aristocracies clung tenaciously to their tradition. Moreover, what I have said about their general failure in the cotton country must not be taken to apply too absolutely. If they nowhere succeeded in large numbers, if they nowhere accounted for the majority of successes in any considerable district, some of them (some of the completely realized aristocrats and a great many more of those gentlemen farmers who had grown up beside them) did nevertheless succeed. There were few parts of the South, indeed, in which it was not possible to find two or three—occasionally a small colony—of them.

And besides these, there were everywhere, and from the beginning, other men, moving along on the level of my Irishman or scaling up to a higher type yet, to individuals and families with a heritage of education and polite breeding—men of a plain tradition, to whom personal decency and upright integrity were a matter of course. But none of these last could properly be reckoned aristocrats. Their birth was comparatively humble, and their breeding middle-class.

The ruling class as a body and in its primary aspect was merely a close clique of property—and one of which the personnel, because of the rapid clip at which estates changed hands during the era of speculation, can hardly have even approximated fixation before 1840. Its emergence to power can be exactly gauged by the emergence of Andrew Jackson—born in a log cabin in the Carolina wilderness — who first achieved political importance as its more or less explicit protagonist. It reached its bloom in Calhoun, the son of a plain and slaveless farmer of the midlands of South Carolina, and in William L. Yancey, a Carolina upcountryman who achieved fame and fortune on the Alabama frontier.

. . .

The matter of the derivation of the poor white, indeed, goes further than I have yet said. Not only is it true that he sprang from the same general sources as the majority of the planters, but even that, in many cases, he sprang from identical sources—that he was related to them by the ties of family. In any given region the great planter who lived on the fertile lands along the river, the farmer on the rolling lands behind him, and the cracker on the barrens back of both were as often as not kindred. And in sections half a thousand miles apart the same connection could be traced between people of the most diverse condition.

The degree of consanguinity among the population of the old Southern backcountry was very great. As I have suggested, economic and (for all the considerable variation in original background) social distinctions hardly existed prior to the invention of the cotton gin; certainly few existed to the point of operating as an effective barrier to intermarriage. And the thin distribution of the people often made it necessary for the youth, come of marrying age, to ride abroad a considerable way for a wife. Hence by 1800 any given individual was likely to be cousin, in one degree or another, to practically everybody within a radius of thirty miles about him. And his circle of kin, of course, overlapped more or less with the next, and that in turn with the next beyond, and so on in an endless web, through the whole South.

What happened when the cotton gin tossed the plantation ferment into this situation is obvious. Given a dozen cousins—brothers, if you wish —one or two would carve out plantations at home (in the Carolinas or Georgia, say); another or two, migrating westward, might be lucky enough to do the same thing there; four or five, perhaps attempting the same goal, would make just enough headway to succeed as yeoman farmers; and the rest would either fail in the competition or, being timid and unambitious,

would try the impossible feat of standing still in this world of pushing men
—with the result that, by processes I need not describe, they would gradually be edged back to poorer and poorer lands. In the end, they—or the
weakest and least competent of their sons—would have drifted back the
whole way: would definitely have joined the ranks of the crackers. And
once there, they would be more or less promptly and more or less fully
forgotten by their more prosperous kinsmen.

That this is really what took place is a proposition which does not
depend on mere supposition or dogmatic statement. Whoever will take
the trouble to investigate a little in any county in the South—outside the
areas occupied by the colonial aristocracies, at any rate—will be immediately struck by the fact that the names of people long prominent locally,
people emphatically reckoned as constituting the aristocracy, are shared
by all sorts and conditions of men. Stay awhile in any town of the land,
and presently some gentleman native to the place will point you out a
shuffling, twisted specimen, all compact of tangled hair, warts, tobacco
stains, and the odor of the dung-heap, and with a grandiloquent wave of
the hand and a mocking voice announce: "My cousin, Wash Venable!"
What he means, of course, is what he means when he uses the same gesture and the same tone in telling you that the colored brother who attends
to his spittoons is also his cousin—that you will take him seriously at your
peril. What he means is that the coincidence of names is merely a little
irony of God, and that the thing he says is clearly not so.

But, though he may know it only vaguely if at all, it more often than
not is so just the same. It is not necessary to rest on the reflection that,
while it is plausible enough that some such coincidences should arise
from mere chance, it seems somehow improbable that a hundred such
coincidences in the same county, ten thousand such coincidences in the
South generally, can be so explained. If one gets out into the countryside
where the "cousin" lives, one is pretty sure to come upon definite and concrete evidence. Maybe there will be an old woman—there nearly always
is an old woman — with a memory like a Homeric bard's, capable of
moving easily through a mass of names and relationships so intricate that
the quantum theory is mere child's play in comparison. And scattered
here and there all about the South are one-gallus genealogists, somewhat
smelly old fellows with baggy pants and a capacity for butchering the
king's English, but shrewd withal and, like the old woman, capable of
remarkable feats of memory. From such sources one may hear the whole
history of the Venables, beginning with Big John, who used to catch squirrels with his hands and whoop with laughter when they bit him, down to
seventh cousin Henry's third wife and the names that had been selected
for the babies that were born dead. One may discover, indeed, that the

actual relationship between the mocking gentleman in the town and "Cousin Wash" is somewhat remote. But—it was not so remote in the Old South.

Perhaps there are limits beyond which this should not be pushed, but they are not narrow. I am advised by those who know Virginia better than I do that even there, if only one goes back far enough, it is often quite possible to establish such connections. And I have myself traced the origin of many of the names ensconced in the beautiful old red brick houses which dot the lovely landscape of bluegrass Kentucky to a group of families in the piedmont country of North Carolina — families which, to my personal knowledge, perfectly illustrate, in their native habitat, the account I have set down here.

. . .

But all this was as nothing compared to the influence which the conditions created by the plantation were to exert. For here, indeed, reality would retreat to the farthest verge; here, as a corollary to things I have already told you, the very drive of the belly would recede and recede until it operated on our Southerner as gently as it has ever operated on mortal man outside some idyllic Pacific island paradise.

In this world he was to have freedom from labor beyond the wildest dream of the European peasant and the New England farmer wrestling with a meager soil in a bitter, unfriendly climate. If he were a planter, then he — whose ancestors, in likelihood, had for many generations won their daily bread under the primitive curse—found himself free from every necessity of toil, free from all but the grateful tasks of supervision and mastery, free to play the lord at dignified ease. If he were a plain farmer, with few slaves or none, then there was the fact that the growing of cotton (or of corn, for that matter) in this country required no more than three or four months of labor in the year. And finally, if he were a poor white strictly, that was to have to work least of all.

As he escaped toil, so also he escaped that other bane of the European peasant and the Yankee farmer: the haunting specter of want. He would never go actually hungry; for the possession of some sort of land and hence some sort of subsistence, you will recall, was almost universal. And even if, through some mischance, his own larder was empty, a kindly neighborhood communism, brought over from the backcountry, saw to it that he was fed, and without harrowing his dignity on the rack of formalized charity. Shelter could be no problem in a land in which pinewoods remained always a nuisance, to be disposed of by wholesale burning. If winter came, it never came so sternly that it could not be banished from the draftiest of huts by a few causal faggots. As for clothing, the little that was wanted need never be ragged, unless, and by exception, his women were lazy; it was too easy for them to grow a bit of cotton for spinning, or even to help themselves to the nearest field of a planter.

In the absolute, certainly, there was much of privation and downright misery in the lot of the poor white, and often in that of the yeoman farmer as well. But these people did not contemplate absolutes. They continued always to reckon their estate in terms established on the frontier. As they themselves would have phrased it from the depths of a great complacency, they found it "tol'able, thankee, tol'able."

But in this complacency itself of course, we return directly upon the handiwork of the plantation; the loss of social and economic focus on the part of the masses, the divorce of pride from the idea of effort and achievement—the whole complex of extraordinary results proceeding from the curious combination of forces at play in this world.

And that this complex constituted a tragic descent into unreality on the part of these masses I need hardly tell you. Nothing is plainer than that, out of every sensible consideration of his own interest, the common white of the South ought early to have developed some decided awareness of his true position. For these walls which bound him in were very real: they not only barred him off from any advance *en masse*; they also, slowly, obscurely, but certainly and constantly, involved his degradation.

But if this was so, it is also to be noted that the loss of social and economic focus carried his escape from the drive of the belly forward to its ultimate term. His leisure was, as it were, *reamed out*. If he did not come, as has sometimes been charged against him, actually to hold labor as such in contempt (the heritage of the frontier and his laborious European fathers was too potent in him for that; all he ever really despised was "nigger work"—work that smacked of servility or work in gangs under the orders of a boss), he did nevertheless wax vastly indifferent to it, as something in which there was no point. And his energies were freed almost entirely for other ends.

The plantation, however, involved even more than these things. As we know, it had fetched in the Negro. But the Negro is notoriously one of the world's greatest romantics and one of the world's greatest hedonists. I am well aware that, when it is a question of adapting himself to necessity, he is sometimes capable of a remarkable realism. But in the main he is a creature of grandiloquent imagination, of facile emotion, and, above everything else under heaven, of enjoyment.

And in this society in which the infant son of the planter was commonly suckled by a black mammy, in which gray old black men were his most loved story-tellers, in which black stalwarts were among the chiefest heroes and mentors of his boyhood, and in which his usual, often practically his only, companions until he was past the age of puberty were the black boys (and girls) of the plantation—in this society in which by far the greater number of white boys of whatever degree were more or less shaped by such companionship, and in which nearly the whole body of whites, young and old, had constantly before their eyes the example, had constantly in their ears the accent, of the Negro, the relationship between the two groups was, by the second generation at least, nothing less than organic. Negro entered into white man as profoundly as white man entered into Negro — subtly influencing every gesture, every word, every emotion and idea, every attitude.

from *The Making of a Southerner*
Katharine Du Pre Lumpkin (1897–1988)

Katharine Du Pre Lumpkin, a Georgian, traveled through much of that state and South Carolina during her childhood. Though her father, a Confederate veteran, viewed the South uncritically, Lumpkin's exposure to poor whites and blacks led her to question Southern orthodoxies. After going to graduate school in New York, Lumpkin worked for the Young Women's Christian Association and published books about Southern social conditions. In 1946, while serving as research director for the Institute of Labor Studies, she wrote *The Making of a Southerner*, her autobiography. The section included here is a sympathetic portrayal of men such as her father, raised for mastery in the Old South and confronted with the turmoil of the Civil War and emancipation. Lumpkin, a critic of the South, strove to understand the perspectives of those who perpetuated segregation.

By the time young Will was ten he would know a great deal about the work on the plantation. He would be familiar with what was to be done as each season came around. In a general way he could have told when it was cotton chopping time, and when cotton picking. He would have a notion of how many acres were put into different crops. He would know the kind of care stock must be given, also farm implements, also something of the expense of upkeep for the slaves, perhaps the names of the merchants with whom his father usually traded for the goods for slave clothing, and the place he habitually bought their shoes. He would certainly know, because he had watched it so many times, how the work was laid out, how the gangs were alloted their tasks, and which of the slaves were good workers and which had especially to be watched. More plainly than anything else, he would know that in his circumstances of life on a slave plantation the white master did not do any farm work himself. His slaves did the actual manual labor. His part was to tell the slaves what to do. This was the very essence of arrangements. His part as white master would one day be to supervise and direct and issue orders to his slaves.

A boy of ten could even realize that his responsibilities as master would not be light ones. He could sense very early how much time and worry his father put into making the plantation pay. He did not understand, it is true, until much later—indeed, until catastrophe was almost upon his family—how poorly the old place was paying in the years leading up to the Civil War; or how its land was being worn out by uneconomical use of it; or how financially serious it was to have many of the family slaves passing their "prime." Yet in spite of the times he lived in, which were not such as to breed a feeling of quite serenity in men whose major capital was in slaves, young Will would quite naturally assume throughout his boyhood that all would remain as it had been, that one day he would have to carry the duties which his father early in life was beginning to teach him.

Believing this, he would all the more surely believe all he learned from teaching and example as to the nature of his slaves and what their attitude should be towards him. He would know as a fact beyond argument or question that his black slaves deserved and needed their slavery. Undoubtedly he heard the point argued and proof offered for it. This was not because any doubts lurked in his elders' minds. It was a time when abolitionist talk was rife. Southern slaveowners had become very sensitive. They did not believe the criticisms of their "peculiar institution" to be justified, and of course they answered back. But when it came to the quite conversations of their firesides, the tenor of their jokes, the worries of management, the problems of what they regarded as their chattels' innate vagaries which made them different from white men, in all these their minds moved back again into the familiar grooves.

There was also the other side to the matter. It was in the very nature of slavery that the chattel should render the master unquestioning obedience. This lesson was instilled into Father almost from babyhood. To be sure as a boy he could not indiscriminately order his father's slaves around. He quickly learned his limits. He could give orders to Pete, his body servant. Pete belonged to him. Even in Pete's case, if he disapproved of what his young master wished, there were courts of appeal in Aunt Winnie and his mistress. Father, as a little boy, might get angry with his mammy, Aunt Winnie, and try to order her around because he felt she was black and he was the young master. Winnie, however, would not have been greatly troubled by this, except that the child she loved was being extremely naughty. His parents, she knew, would uphold Aunt Winnie, at least while their son was very small. He would never dare speak other than respectfully to Uncle Jerry. Actually, while small, he stood in awe of the slave foreman's imposing presence and his obvious authority among the slaves. But he would most certainly know some day even Jerry would have to obey when the young master spoke. He was even "scared" of Runaway Dennis, he said. Aunt Winnie used to frighten him into being good by saying, "Runaway Dennis will get you." So Father told us, "As a little boy I was always afraid of runaway Negroes." But as a boy would, he probably had ideas as to how he would handle a runaway Negro when he was master. He could "order" the "little darkies" to do this or that. No doubt he did upon many occasions. But if he were too arrogant and "bossy"—and what child would not be under similar circumstances?—they had ways of refusing to play with him; if necessary they could invent something Aunt Winnie had "ordered" them to do to get away from a quarrelsome "young master." With all these "ifs" and "buts," however, young Will grew up knowing in his conscious mind that these black people on his father's place belonged to his father, and would one day belong to him. He was their "young master" and someday would have the authority to elicit from them the same obedience his father commanded. He would know in his very bone and blood as a court decision once put it, "The power of the master must be absolute, to render the submission of the slave perfect. It would not do to allow the rights of the master to be brought into discussion. . . . The slave, to remain a slave, must be sensible that there is no appeal from his master."

My father had only a few years to live as "young master" among his slaves. There were five at best after his tenth birthday, and the better part of these were spent during a raging war which patently threatened his heritage. Nevertheless, until the very end, he went on expecting to be even as his father had been. He continued to think of himself as one day riding over his own acres, knowing every field, stream, hill, and pasture, as he knew the palm of his hand. He would look on every building and fence and know it had either come down to him, built by his forebears, or had been planned by himself and constructed under his direction. He would expect to know when an animal was ailing, the poultry had a disease, the gin required a new part for its running, or rust had formed on the threshing machine. Above all, he would know his slaves, each by name, and each for his good points and his foibles, most of them being inherited, or the children of those who had been handed down. He would expect constantly to guide and discipline and keep them contented by skillful handling. First and last, he would know that every plan, every decision, every quandary nagging his mind, save those of marketing his cotton and purchasing supplies from the outside, resolved itself into a human problem, if it could be so called: the problem of managing his black dependents. He would know he was master in all things on his plantation, everything, nothing excepted, including the life of his slaves. With it he would know that his station was secure as a Southern gentleman.

It would seem it left a special stamp on men who lived this life. But more particularly in a special way it stamped their sons, who were reared to expect it and then saw it snatched away.

from *The Confessions of Nat Turner*

William Styron (1925–)

William Styron, born in Newport News, Virginia, served in the Marine Corps during World War II and returned to the States to attend college, work as an editor in New York, and write novels. In 1967, Styron's *The Confessions of Nat Turner,* a fictional account of the Southampton slave uprising of 1831, became front-page news. While the book received the Pulitzer Prize, the attempts of a white writer to imagine the thoughts of the most famous slave insurrectionist brought Styron immediate and bitter criticism. Black critics, in particular, charged that Styron imposed baseless sexual and psychological motivations upon Turner. Readers may compare the original confessions with Styron's fictional interpretation.

M y brothers!" I cried. "Stop yo' laughin' and listen to me! Leave off from that laughin', brothers, and listen to a minister of the Holy Word!" A hush fell over the Negroes and they stirred restlessly, turned toward me, puzzlement and wonder in their eyes. "Come closer!" I commanded them. "This here is no time for laughin'! This is a time for weepin', for *lamentation!* For rage! You is *men,* brothers, *men* not beasts of the field! You ain't no four-legged dogs! You is *men,* I say! Where oh where, my brothers, is yo' pride?"

Slowly, one by one, the Negroes drew near, among them Will and Sam, who climbed up from the road and stood gazing at me as they mopped their faces with gray slimy wads of waste cotton. Still others shuffled closer —young men mostly, along with a few older slaves; they scratched themselves out of nervousness, some eyes darted furtively across the road. But all were silent now, and with a delicious chill I could feel the way in which they had responded to the fury in my words, like blades of sawgrass bending to a sudden wind. And I began to realize, far back in the remotest corner of my mind, that I had commenced the first sermon I had ever preached. They became still. Brooding, motionless, the Negroes gazed at me with watchful and reflective concern, some of them hardly drawing a breath. My language was theirs, I spoke it as if it were a second tongue. My rage had captured them utterly, and I felt a thrill of power course out from myself to wrap them round, binding us for this moment as one.

"My brothers," I said in a gentler tone, "many of you has been to church with yo' mastahs and mist'esses at the Whitehead church or up Shiloh

90

way or down at Nebo or Mount Moriah. Most of you hasn't got no religion. That's awright. White man's religion don't teach nothin' to black folk except to obey ole mastah and live humble—walk light and talk small. That's awright. But them of you that recollects they Bible teachin' knows about Israel in Egypt an' the peoples that was kept in bondage. Them peoples was Jewish peoples an' they had names just like us black folk—like you right there, Nathan, an' you, Joe—Joe is a Jewish name—an' you there, Daniel. Them Jews was just like the black folk. They had to sweat they fool asses off fo' ole Pharaoh. That white man had them Jews haulin' wood an' pullin' rock and thrashin' corn an' makin' bricks until they was near 'bout dead an' didn't git ary penny for none of it neither, like ev'y livin' mothah's son of us, them Jews was in *bondage.* They didn't have enough to eat neither, just some miser'ble cornmeal with weevils in it an' sour milk an' a little fatback that done got so high it would turn a buzzard's stomach. Drought an' hunger run throughout the land, just like now. Oh, my brothers, that was a sad time in Egypt fo' them Jews! It was a time fo' weepin' an' lamentation, a time of toil an' hunger, a time of *pain!* Pharoah he whupped them Jews until they had red whelps on 'em from head to toe an' ev'y night they went to bed cryin', 'Lord, Lord, when is you goin' to make that white man set us free?'"

There was a stirring among the Negroes and I heard a voice in the midst of them say, "Yes, yes," faint and plaintive, and still another voice: "Mm-huh, dat's *right!*" I stretched out an arm slowly, as if to embrace them, and some of the crowd moved nearer still.

"Look aroun' you, brothers," I said, "what does you see? What does you see in the air? What does you see blowin' in the air?" The Negroes turned their faces toward the town, raised their eyes skyward: there in amber translucent haze the smoke from the distant fires swam through the streets, touching the gallery, even as I spoke, with its acrid and apple-sweet taste of scorched timber, its faint smell of corruption.

"That there is the smoke of *pestilence,* brothers," I went on, "the smoke of pestilence an' death. The same smoke that hanged over the Jews in bondage down there in Egypt land. The same smoke of pestilence an' death that hanged over them Jews in Egypt hangs over all black folk, all men whose skin is black, yo' skin and mine. An' we got a tougher row to hoe even than them Jews. Joseph he was at least a man, not no four-legged dog. My brothers, laughter is good, laughter is bread and salt and buttermilk and a balm for pain. But they is a time for ev'ything. They is a time for weepin' too. A time for rage! And in bondage black folk like you an' me must weep in they rage. *Leave off* from such dumb laughter like just now!" I cried, my voice rising. "When a white man he lift a hand against one of us'ns we must not laugh but rage and weep! 'By the rivers of Babylon, there we sat down, yea, we wept when we remembered Zion!' That's right!" ("Mum-huh, dat's right!" came the voice again, joined by another.) "'We hanged our harps upon the willows, for they that carried us away captive required of us a song. How shall we sing the Lord's song in a strange land?' *That's right!*" I said, the words bitter on my tongue. "White man make you sing an' dance, make you shuffle, do the buck-an'-wing, play 'Ole Zip Coon' on the banjo and the fiddle. 'They that carried us away captive required of us a song.' Yes! Leave off from that singin', leave off from that banjo, leave off from that buck-an'-wing! They is a time for ev'ything. This is no time fo' singin', fo' laughter. Look aroun' you, my brothers, look into each other's eyes! You jest seen a white man pit brother 'gainst brother! Ain't none of you no four-legged beasts what can be whupped an' hurt like some flea-bit cur dog. You is men! You is *men*, my dear brothers, look at yo'selves, look to yo' *pride!*"

As I spoke, I saw two older black men at the rear of the crowd mutter to each other and shake their heads. Glances of puzzlement and worry crossed their faces and they sidled off, disappeared. The others still listened, intent, brooding, nearly motionless. I heard a soft sigh and a gentle "Amen." I raised my arms to either side of me and extended my hands, palms outward, as if in benediction. I felt the sweat pouring from my face.

"In the visions of the night, brothers," I continued, "God spoke to Jacob an' He said, 'I am God, the God of thy father: fear not to go down into Egypt, for I will there make of thee a great nation.' An' Jacob went down into Egypt an' the peoples of Israel multiplied an' Moses was born. Moses he was born in the bulrushers an' he delivered the Jews out of Egypt an' into the Promised Land. Well, there they had a powerful lot of troubles too. But in the Promised Land them Jewish peoples they could stand up an' live like *men*. They become a great nation. No more fatback, no more pint of salt, no more peck of corn fo' them Jews; no more overseers, no more auction blocks; no more horn blow at sunrise fo' them mothahs' sons. They had chicken with pot likker an' spoonbread an' sweet cider to drink in the shade. They done got paid an honest dollar. Them Jews become *men*. But oh, my brothers, black folk ain't never goin' to be led from bondage without they has *pride*! Black folk ain't goin' to be free, they ain't goin' to have no spoonbread an' sweet cider less'n they studies to love they own *selves*. Only then will the first be last, and the last first. Black folk ain't never goin' to be no great nation until they studies to love they own black skin an' the beauty of that skin an' the beauty of them black hands that toils so hard and black feet that trods so weary on God's earth. And when white men in they hate an' wrath an' meanness fetches blood from that beautiful black skin then, oh *then*, my brothers, it is time not fo' laughing but fo' weeping an' rage an' lamentation! *Pride!*" I cried after a pause, and let my arms descend. "Pride, pride, *everlasting* pride, pride will make you free!"

I ceased speaking and gazed at the rapt black faces. Then I finished slowly and in a soft voice: "Arise, shine; for thy light is come, an' the glory of the Lord is risen upon thee. Amen."

The Negroes were silent. Far off in Jerusalem, through the hot afternoon, a church bell let fall a single chime, striking the half-hour. Then the Negroes one by one straggled away across the gallery, some with troubled looks, some stupid and uncomprehending, some fearful. Others drew toward me, radiant; and Henry, who was deaf, who had read my lips, came up close to me and silently clasped my arm. I heard Nelson say, "You done spoke de truth," and he too drew near, and I felt their warmth and their brotherhood and hope and knew then what Jesus must have known when upon the shores of Galilee he said: *"Follow me, and I will make you fishers of men."*

. . .

"Last but not least," Gray said, *"item.* And a durned important item it is, too, Reverend, also attested to by witnesses both black and white and by widespread evidence so unimpeachable as to make this here matter almost a foregone conclusion. And that is that you not only had a fantastic amount of niggers who did *not* join up with you but there was a whole countless number of other niggers who was your active *enemies.* What I mean in simple terms, Reverend, is that once the alarm went out, there was niggers *everywhere*—who were as determined to protect and save their masters as you were to murder them. They was simply livin' *too well!* All the time that you were carryin' around in that fanatical head of your'n the notion that the niggers were going to latch on to your great mission, as you put it, an' go off to some stinkin' swamp, the actual reality was that nine out of ten of your fellow burrheads just wasn't buyin' any such durn fool ideas. Reverend, I have no doubt that it was your own race that contributed more to your fiasco than anything else. It just ain't a race made for revolution, that's all. That's another reason that nigger slavery's goin' to last for a thousand years."

He rose from his seat across from me. "Well, I got to go, Reverend. I'll see you tomorrow. Meanwhile, I'll put down in my deposition to the court which precedes your confession that the defendant shows no remorse for his acts, and since he *feels* no guilt his plea will be that of 'not guilty.' Now, one last time, are you *sure* you feel no remorse at all? I mean, would you do it again if you had the chance? There's still time to change your mind. It ain't goin' to save your neck but it'll surer'n hell look better for you in court. Speak up, Reverend."

When I made no reply to him he left without further word. I heard the cell door slam shut and the bolt thud home in the slot with its slippery chunking sound. It was almost night again. I listened to the scrape and rustle of fallen leaves as the cold air swept them across the ground. I reached down to rub my numb and swollen ankles and I shivered in the wind, thinking: Remorse? Is it true that I really have no remorse or contrition or guilt for anything I've done? Is it maybe because I have no remorse that I can't pray and that I know myself to be so removed from the sight of God? As I sat there, recollecting August, I felt remorse impossible to know or touch or find. All I could feel was an entombed, frustrate rage — rage at the white people we had killed and those we had failed to kill, rage at the quick and the dead, rage above all at those Negroes who refused us or fled us or who had become the enemy — those spiritless and spineless wretches who had turned against us. Rage even at our own minuscule force, which was so much smaller than the expected multitude! For although it ravaged my heart to accept it, I knew that Gray was not wrong: the black men had caused my defeat just as surely as the white. And so it had been on that last day, that Wednesday afternoon, when after having finally laid waste to twoscore dwellings and our force of fifty had rallied in the woods to storm Major Ridley's place, I had caught sight for the first time of Negroes in great numbers with rifles and muskets at the barricaded veranda, firing back at us with as much passion and fury and even skill as their white owners and overseers who had gathered there to block our passage into Jerusalem. (The alarm had gone out at least by the morning of the day before, our schedule was disastrously upset, and we had met resistance everywhere for many hours. The Ridley place, which straddled the road into town, was now an ominous fortress yet it had to be taken — and quickly: it was our last chance — if we were to break through and dash the last mile on horseback, seizing Jerusalem before it became an armed camp.) Far up on the veranda of the old stately brick house now barricaded by wagons and crates and hogsheads I could see twenty-five or thirty Negroes owned by the white gentry near town — coachmen, cooks, some field hands maybe but I could tell from what they wore mostly gardeners and house nigger flunkies, even a clutch of bandannaed yellow kitchen girls passing ammunition. I heard the voice of Major Ridley above the steady fusillade of gunfire — "That's the spirit, boys!" he cried to the defenders, black and white alike. "That's the spirit! Fire away, lads! Lay on the lead! We'll turn the rascals back!" — and the volleys swelled tempestuously down upon us with a noise like the continual crackle of lightning, ripping twigs and leaves from the green summer trees.

Then I recall Hark saying to me as we crouched behind the great stump of a felled oak, shouting above our own rifle fire: *Look at dem black fuckahs shootin' at us!* And I thought, lying to myself: Yes, they're black but they've been forced, dragooned by white men who have threatened them with their very lives. Negroes would not fire back like that of their own free will, at least not in those numbers. And all this I kept thinking desperately even as I signaled and we charged the house (but far within I knew better: had not pitifully less than a hundred joined us? When I had expected hundreds? Had not I with my own eyes seen fifty more Negroes flee at our approach all along the way, scattering to the woods?)—our men now moving on foot and crouched in a ragged skirmish line behind hedged and sun-dappled boxwood and maple trees. Each of us was mercilessly exposed, the force not outnumbered but outpositioned and outgunned in a lopsided uphill assault, and intimidated nightmarishly less by white men now than by the sight of a horde of housebound and privileged town and up-county Negroes sending coolly aimed gunfire into our black ranks. At last we had to fall back and disperse into the woods. I saw my men streaming off in panic everywhere. Unmounted horses burst for the meadows. My mission had become totally shattered, blown apart like gunpowder on the wind. Then the ghastly final mortal mischief. Two of my men had made it to within twenty yards of the veranda and then were both killed as I watched: one of these was Will, raging to the end with a sublime fury beyond mere valor, beyond even madness; the other was my old great Henry, who, lacking ears to judge the whereabouts of danger, caught a musket ball in the throat. He fell like a dead tree.

Hark too had fallen wounded far behind me as we made our withdrawal down the slope. I got up from where I had stumbled to go back for him but he was too near the veranda; as he struggled from the lawn with a hand clutched to his bloodied shoulder I saw three barechested Negroes who were dressed in the pantaloons of coachmen charge from the house under covering fire and kick him back to earth with booted feet. Hark flopped about in desperation but they kicked him again, kicked him with exuberance not caused by any white man's urging or threat or exhortation but with rackety glee, kicked him until I saw droplets of blood spray from his huge and jagged wound. Then they dragged him past one of the barricade wagons and underneath the veranda and two of the Negroes kept aiming booted kicks at his shoulder even as they disappeared from sight. I fled, escaped then. And I remember feeling sick with rage and with the knowledge of defeat, and later that night after my troops dissolved forever (the twenty of us who remained in a final fire-fight with a dozen mounted Isle of Wight County militia along the rim of humid twilit woods, some of my men too weary, some too demoralized or drunk—yes, *Gray was right* —to refrain from slipping away once and for all into the trees, thereupon to steal back home, harboring wild hopes that in the confusion their adventure with me might not have been noticed) and I too lit off alone, hoping against hope that I could find Nelson or Austin or Jack and regroup and swim across the river for a three- or four-man attack by stealth on the armory—but knowing even as night came down over the woods and the voices of white men hallooed in the dark and the drumming of far-off cavalry hooves echoed from the roads that such a hope trembled on lunacy — an accusation kept howling somewhere in the black defeated hollow of my brain: *It was the niggers that beat you! You might have took Ridley's. You might have made Jerusalem if it wasn't for those bootlickin' black scum of white men's ass-suckin' niggers!*

The following morning after I had slept for the first time in days, alone just as sunrise shimmered up cool and hazy over the pinelands, I sneaked out of the woods in search of food and soon happened upon the Vaughans' place where Nelson's troops had slain four people. Kitchen fires were still smoldering from the day before, the spacious white house lay deserted and still. As I crept past the chicken shed and into the barnyard I heard a grunting and a snuffling noise, and saw two razorback wild hogs devouring the body of a man. It must have been the overseer. The corpse was parted from its head and I knew that the last face the man had ever seen had been that of Will. I watched the hogs rooting at the man's intestines for a moment and I was without feeling; the iniquitous mud-smeared beasts may as well have been feeding upon slops or offal. Yet after I had taken some food from the plundered, littered kitchen and had prepared a sack of bacon and meal to help me through the first part of my flight to the woods, I was afflicted by fear and uneasiness. It had been my custom for many years, as I have said before, to spend part of this hour of the day in prayer and meditation, but when I went back to the border of the woods and knelt there to ask God's guidance in the coming time of solitude—to request that He show me the ways and necessities for my salvation now that my cause in His name was irrevocably lost—I found to my terrible distress that for the first time in my life I was unable even to think. Try as I might, I could not cause a prayer to pass my lips. The God I knew was slipping away from me. And I lingered there in the early morning and felt as alone and as forsaken as I had ever felt since I had learned God's name.

And so while I sat shivering in the November wind I listened to the sounds of late afternoon welling up from the town, and the rage withered within me and died away. Again the emptiness and desolation returned: the same ache of loneliness that had not really left me once since that morning at the edge of the woods and during the long weeks I had hidden out in my little swampland cave — the same inability to pray. And I thought: Maybe in this anguish of mine God is trying to tell me something. Maybe in His seeming absence He is asking me to consider something I had not thought of or known before. How can a man be allowed to feel such emptiness and defeat? For surely God in His wisdom and majesty would not ordain a mission like mine and then when I was vanquished allow my soul to be abandoned, to be cast away into some bottomless pit as if it were a miserable vapor or smoke. Surely by this silence and absence He is giving me a greater sign than any I have ever known . . .

I rose wearily from the cedar plank and hobbled the length of the chain to the window. I gazed out into the fading light. Faint from the end of the rutted dirt road, by the water's edge, I heard the sound of a mandolin or a guitar and the voice of a young girl singing. Sweet and gentle, from some white, delicate throat I would never see, the song floated up along the river shore on a breath of wind. Bright pinpoints of snow flickered through the dusk and the music mingled in my spirit with a lost fragrance like that of lavender.

"She is far from the land where her young hero sleeps . . ."

Tenderly the voice rose and fell, then faded away, and another girl's voice called out softly—"Oh, Jeanie!"—and the sweet lavender smell persisted in my memory, making me stir with longing and desire. I thrust my head into my hands and leaned against the cold bars, thinking: No, Mr. Gray, I have no remorse for anything. I would do it all again. Yet even a man without remorse, in the face of death, may have to save one hostage for his soul's ransom, so I say yes, I would destroy them all again, all—But for one . . .

. . .

"Dar! She gone!" Will roared, gesturing with his broadax to the other Negroes, who had begun to straggle across the yard. "Does you want her, preacher man, or she fo' me?"

Ah, how I want her, I thought, and unsheathed my sword. She had run into the hayfield, and when I too rounded the corner of the house I thought she had slipped away, for there was no one in sight. But she had merely fallen down in the waist-high grass and as I stood there she rose again—a small and slender figure in the distance—and resumed her flight toward a crooked far-off fence. I ran headlong into the field. The air was alive with grasshoppers: they skimmed and flickered across my path, brushed my skin with brittle momentary sting. I felt the sweat streaming into my eyes. The sword in my right hand hung like the weight of all the earth. Yet I gained on Margaret quickly, for she had tired fast, and I reached her just as she was trying to clamber over the rotted pole fence. She made no sound, uttered no word, did not turn to plead or contend or resist or even wonder. Nor did I speak—our last encounter may have been the quietest that ever was. Beneath her foot one of the poles gave way in crunching powdery collapse and she tripped forward, bare arms still out-thrust as if to welcome someone beloved and long-unseen. As she stumbled thus, then recovered, I heard for the first time her hurtful, ragged breathing, and it was with this sound in my ears that I plunged the sword into her side, just below and behind her breast. She screamed then at last. Litheness, grace, the body's nimble felicity—all fled her like ghosts. She crumpled to earth, limp, a rag, and as she fell I stabbed her again in the same place, or near it, where pulsing blood already encrimsoned the taffeta's blue. There was no scream this time although the echo of the first sang in my ears like a far angelic cry; when I turned aside from her fallen body I was troubled by a steady soughing noise like the rise and fall of a summer tempest in a grove of pines and realized that it was the clamor of my own breathing as it welled up in sobs from my chest.

I lurched away from her through the field, calling out to myself like one bereft of mind. Yet hardly had I taken a dozen steps when I heard her voice, weak, frail, almost without breath, not so much voice as memory—faint as if from some distant and half-forgotten lawn of childhood: Oh Nat I hurt so. Please kill me Nat I hurt so.

I stopped and looked back. "*Die*, God damn your white soul," I wept. "Die!"

Oh Nat please kill me I hurt so.

"Die! Die! Die! Die!"

The sword fell from my hand. I returned to her side and looked down. Her head was cradled against the inside of her arm, as if she had composed herself for sleep, and all the chestnut streaming luxuriance of her hair had fallen in a tangle amid the hayfield's parched and fading green. Grasshoppers stitched and stirred in restless fidget among the weeds, darting about her face.

"I hurt so," I heard her whisper.

"Shut your eyes," I said. I reached down to search with my fingers for a firm length of fence rail and I could sense once more her close girl-smell and the fragrance of lavender, bitter in my nostrils, and sweet. "Shut your eyes," I told her quickly. Then when I raised the rail above her head she gazed at me, as if past the imponderable vista of her anguish, with a grave and drowsy tenderness such as I had never known, spoke some words too soft to hear and, saying no more, closed her eyes upon all madness, illusion, error, dream, and strife. So I brought the timber down and she was swiftly gone, and I hurled the hateful, shattered club far up into the weeds.

For how long I aimlessly circled her body—prowled around the corners of the field in haphazard quest for nothing, like some roaming dog—how long this went on I do not recollect. The sun rose higher, boiling; my own flesh was incandescent, and when at the farm I heard the men call for me their voices were untold distances away. By the edge of the woods I found myself seated on a log, head in my hands, unaccountably thinking of ancient moments of childhood—warm rain, leaves, a whippoorwill, rushing mill wheels, jew's-harp strumming—centuries before. Then I arose again and resumed my meaningless and ordained circuit of her body, not near it yet ever within sight as if that crumpled blue were the center of an orbit around whose path I must make a ceaseless pilgrimage. And once in my strange journey I thought I heard again her whispery voice, thought I saw her rise from the blazing field with arms outstretched as if to a legion of invisible onlookers, her brown hair and innocent school gown teased by the wind as she cried: "Oh, I would fain swoon into an eternity of love!" But then she vanished before my eyes—melted instantly like an image carved of air and light—and I turned away at last and went back to join my men.

. . .

All day after that we swept north through the countryside. Despite certain unforeseen halts and delays, our advance was everywhere successful. The Porter place, Nathaniel Francis's, Barrow's, Edwards's, Harris's, Doyle's—each was overrun, and each was the scene of ruthless extermination. We missed laying hold of Nathaniel Francis himself (much later I learned from Hark that he had been away at the time in Sussex County), and so it was one of the lesser ironies of our mission—and a source of bitter disappointment to both Sam and Will—that almost the only white man in the county who owned a truly illustrious reputation for cruelty to Negroes escaped the blade of our retribution. His ending would have had a quality all its own. Such are the fortunes of war. By early afternoon I had regained my stability and composure; my strength came back, I felt immeasurably better and took heart and vigor from our rapid gains. Under the influence of Nelson—but also because of my actions at the Whitehead place—Will had become somewhat more subdued, and I felt that finally he was under a semblance of control. By late afternoon there was no one who was white left alive along the twenty miles we had traveled.

Even so, our work of death was not absolutely exhaustive, not complete, and I am far from sure that this was not the ruination of my mission, since it took but a single soul to raise the alarm. And I must admit to a failing on my own part which may have caused more than anything else the fact of the resistance we began to encounter the following day and which slowed us to a fatal pace. For as I told Gray, late that afternoon just before twilight at the Harris farm we had seen a young white girl of fourteen or so flee to the woods, screaming her terror as she rushed into the haven of a grove of juniper trees. And Gray himself had established that it was this girl who had managed to reach the Williams place near dark, allowing that fortunate man to hide his family and his slaves and to ride off north, spreading the alarm. In turn it had been that alarm which may or may not (I cannot be certain) have given the enemy their ultimate advantage and tipped the balance against us. What I failed to confide to Gray is that it had not been "us" who had seen her but I alone, rocking weary in the saddle as dusk descended and my men killed and ransacked and looted the Harris house. I heard her faint frantic cry, saw a flicker of color as she vanished into the darkening thicket of trees.

I might have reached her in a twinkling—the work of half a minute—but I suddenly felt dispirited and overcome by fatigue, and was pursued by an obscure, unshakable grief. I shivered in the knowledge of the futility of all ambition. My mouth was sour with the yellow recollection of death and blood-smeared fields and walls. I watched the girl slip away, vanished without a hand laid upon her. Who knows but whether we were not doomed to lose. I know nothing any longer. Nothing. Did I really wish to vouchsafe a life for the one that I had taken?

from *Dessa Rose*

Sherley Anne Williams (1944–)

Sherley Anne Williams, a Californian, has explored the African American experience through poetry, short stories, literary criticism, and the novel *Dessa Rose* (1986). Her novel imagines slavery from two alternating points of view: that of a young slave woman who has had a baby while running away, and that of a young white woman abandoned by her husband on their north Alabama plantation. The two women find their lives entangled, the social demands of race and gender in conflict with their inarticulate desires for understanding and connection.

The white light the raftered ceiling. Dessa had seen this all before. She watched the white woman sitting in the light from the long window. Her hair was the color of fire; it fell about her shoulders in lank whisps. Her face was very white and seemed to radiate a milky glow; her mouth was like a bloody gash across it. Dessa closed her eyes. Only the Quarters had been a dream. Mammy, Martha. Kaine's face danced before her eyes. She was the one who was missing; she had been sold away. This was a bed and these were sheets. She clutched them in her hands.

The white woman sat in a rocker across from the bed. Next to her was a large cradle; next to it another piece of furniture Dessa couldn't identify. A large cupboard stood in a corner on the other side of the rocker; near the corner was a door. Dessa stared at it but could not move.

They had come for her at night. Nathan, Cully, and Harker, whom she hadn't known. Jemina, praising the Lawd in scared whispers, had opened the cellar door and unlocked her chains. Free, and scrambling up the steep steps, Dess had focused all of her attention on the stranger's whispered instructions, refusing to think beyond the next step. She was free and she walked on, mindful of his hand on her arm, uncaring of anything else save his cautions and the putting of one foot in front of the other. Silently, she had thanked the Lawd, Legba, all the gods she knew, for Harker and Cully and Nathan, for Jemina herself. She would not be a slave anymore in this world.

They had walked for a long time, Harker going before her, holding back low branches and vines, his voice whispering the presence of obstacles on the path so she could avoid them. It had taken a while for her feet to remember the gliding shuffle that, slow as it appeared, ate up ground. The coffle had taught her that, just as it had Cully and everyone else who had ever spent more than a day on one. She had learned quickly after the first few hours of hobbing along with the manacle rubbing her ankle raw. She had known without being told that if she fell, one of the drivers would be along with the whip. Her feet were remembering: The muscles of her calves and thighs protested some and it took all of her concentration to keep their protests from drowning out the remembrance of her feet. She didn't speak. She didn't think either. She was free; maybe not as free as she would ever be but she knew, without needing to think about it, that she'd never be less free than she was now, striding, sometimes stumbling toward a place she'd never seen and didn't know word one about.

She remembered laughing weakly, leaning against the thin mulatto boy, an arm around her, an awkward pat on her shoulder. ". . . the midwife back at the farm say less your time real near . . ." (Farm? Had he— A *white* woman—) Her own foot in the stirrup, Cully pushing from behind, she mounted the horse before Harker. And leaning back against his chest, tears sliding silently down her cheek. She had not known how bad she felt, how scared, how— She had lost track of place, of time, dozing only to be jostled awake by the dull throbbing in her back, some pounding in her head, starting up out of some unremembered dreams to feel the sinewy arms around her, the beard-stubbled cheek against her face, "Got you" on a smoky breath. At some point they rested, probably more than once; she remembered the sky through a canopy of trees, the smell of roasting meat, "Rest," her face against some coarse material, the warmth of someone's flesh and the dull throbbing in her back. She was bumped up and down and something, in her womb, she guessed, somewhere deep inside her, the baby pinched its lining in its fist. It had rained, hard and soaking, and Harker laughed, "There go the trail and the scent," as he pulled out an oil-cloth and draped her in it. But the wetness of the rain was mixed with that other, sudden, drenching liquid that made the horse rear, nearly killing them both, embarrassing her half to death. What would Harker think, her having no more bladder control than this? And little else: the anxious broad-nosed face, a fiercely muttered "Shush!" and "Bear down, bear down! You got to help." The core of her body uprooted, Lawd, the pain, the blood . . .

The white woman's mouth was like an open wound across the milky paleness of her face. She sat, one shoulder bare, a child held against her breast. "Got enough?" She tickled the baby under the chin and raised it to her shoulder, patting its back and murmuring. The baby was big, a year old, maybe, or more, with plump white arms and legs, wisps of light-colored hair on its smooth white head. The child burped loudly and grinned; the white woman laughed. "Well, I guess you did get your fill."

Dessa closed her eyes; her lashes clotted wetly against her cheeks. Her stomach was flat, the muscles flaccid; her breasts, swollen and tender, felt on fire. Lawd, where my baby at; where is my child? She could feel the sodden rag between her thighs, sticky with blood. "Where my child?" She didn't know she had spoken aloud until she heard the gasp,

"Right here."

And opened her eyes.

The white woman, the shoulder still bare, the curly black head and brown face of a new baby nestled at her breast, faced her now. "See?"

"Naaaaaawwwww!" The scream rushed out of her on an explosion of breath. She saw the glass-colored eyes buck before her own squeezed tight. The covers weighed her arms and legs; some voice screamed, "Annabelle. Annabelle, get Ada! She starting up again!" Hands, herself crying weakly, a cool cloth on her forehead and something at her breasts.

"See? See? He know his mama. See, he just want to eat."

Dessa looked down. The brown baby was in her arms, his dark eyes staring up at her unwinkingly. She touched a tiny fist; it opened to grasp her finger. She looked up. She had never seen the tall brown-skinned woman before.

"Let me fix them pillows so you can nurse more better." The woman bent over Dessa, her hands moving deftly. Dessa lay quietly but warily. "There, now; you turn just a little on your side and you both be more comfortable. Well, go on; put the nipple in his mouth."

Dessa looked down quickly, then up at the woman's smiling face. She did as she was told, gingerly touching her breast and awkwardly guiding it toward the baby's mouth. The nipple touched his cheek and he turned his head toward it, his mouth opening to grasp and clamping tightly around it, all in one sudden movement. A sharp pain shot through her breast at the first tug and she gasped.

"You got to get used to that," the woman said conversationally. "Pain going get worse before it get better—that is, if you ain't dried up. It's a mercy if you not, way you been carrying on." She laughed. "Attacking white folks and scaping all crost the country in the dead of night." Laughing again and shaking her head. "I told her don't be coming in here less one of us was with her. But you think Miz Ruint going listen at me?"

At least she could understand these words even if they still made no sense to her. Who was this woman? Where was "Harker?"

"She sent the boy at him. He be here directly. You go on see at that baby. He getting some, huh?" she asked, peeking over at the nursing baby. "It be all right, now."

Every pull of the baby's lips sent a thrill of pain through Dessa's breast. She looked up at the woman and smiled before she closed her eyes.

. . .

Rufel watched the colored girl, not as she had at first from the rocker by the window, rocking gently as she nursed the babies or shelled peas. The colored girl was young. Don't look no more than twelve or thirteen, Rufel had thought. Couldn't be more than fourteen, she would say to herself, don't care what Ada said. She disliked disagreeing with Ada. The older darky had an abrupt way of speaking that Rufel found daunting. Rufel herself was not, of course, a child to be corrected by some middle-aged darky—Who knew no more about birthdays, she would continue sullenly to herself, than "planting time" and "picking time." Why, even Mammy hadn't known how old she was or even her own birthdate. That was why they—*she*, Rufel, "Miz 'Fel," had chosen Valentine's Day as Mammy's birthday. Mammy had refused to accept a date— "This way I don't have to *age*, see," she had joked, "I just gets a little older." Eyes full and shiny, a smile fluttering about her bee-stung lips— Rushing from the wound of that memory, Rufel would silently declare, All darkies know about is old age.

Rufel would sew or rock for a minute, until another point occurred to her. Thirteen, even fourteen was young to have a baby, even for a darky. Well. Rocking again, maybe sewing, fifteen. But no older and Ada talked about her as if she were a grown woman. Even if the girl were eighteen, as Ada said, she was too young to live as a runaway, hand to mouth, Rufel thought scornfully, like the rest of these darkies. And Ada was no better than the rest of them. Why, any white person that came along could lay claim to them, sell them, auction them off to the highest bidder. They should thank their lucky stars she was a kindhearted person. Bertie— But she resolutely closed her mind against the thought of her husband. She had done what she could do. He would see that when he came. Rufel would resume her task, all the while watching the colored girl. If she didn't want to go back to her people—

The wench was the color of chocolate and Rufel would stare at her face as she tossed or, more frequently now, slept quietly, at the thin body that barely made an impression in the big feather bed. The girl would be all right. Rocking again or returning to the rocker if she had stood as she sometimes did to fetch some article, to stretch, or just to look more closely at the colored girl.

Ada and Harker said she—they called her Dessa—had been sold south by a cruel master. She certainly acted mean enough to have been ruined by a cruel master—kicking and hitting at whoever got in the way the few times Rufel had seen her roused from stupor. But the girl's back was scarless and to hear Ada tell it, every runaway in the world was escaping from a "cruel master." Ada herself claimed to have escaped from a lecherous master who had lusted with her and then planned the seduction of Ada's daughter, Annabelle. Rufel didn't believe a word of that. She could see nothing attractive in the rawboned, brown-skinned woman or her lanky, half-witted daughter—and would have said as much but Mammy had cut her off before she could speak, thanking Ada for her help and God that Ada had escaped from her old master.

Vexed, Rufel had bit her lip, remembering then what the utter non-sense of the darky's statement had made her forget. They needed Ada. That was the plain fact of it.

Often, misery washed over her. She would struggle against the familiar tide, feeding her indignation at Ada's story. At least Uncle Joel and Dante, the darkies Bertie had brought back from that last trip, had stayed, she would remind herself then. And, forgetting her angry, and silent, exasperation at Bertie's conviction that he had somehow gotten the best of a deal that netted him an old darky and a crippled one, took some satisfaction in their loyalty to the place. Mammy said they had been some help at harvest, but the real work was done by the darkies Ada knew. Still, Rufel hadn't been able to resist pointing out Ada's lie to Mammy.

"No white man would do that," she'd insisted; unless he tied a sack over her head first, she had continued maliciously to herself. Mammy, folding linen—*black hands in the white folds, Mammy's hand against her face, and even then, maybe, that scaly, silvery sheen creeping over the rich, coffee-colored skin*—had paused. "Why, Mammy, that's—" Rufel wasn't sure what it was and stuttered. "That's—"

"Miz Rufel!" Mammy had said sharply. "You keep a lady tongue in your mouth. Men," Mammy had continued with a quailing glance as Rufel opened her mouth, voice overriding Rufel's attempt to speak, "men can do things a *lady* can't even guess at."

Rufel knew that was true but could not bring herself to concede this openly. "Well—" She had tossed her head, flicking back locks of hair that tumbled in perpetual disarray from the artless knot atop her head. "Everyone know men like em half white and whiter," she had finished saucily.

"Miz Rufel," Mammy had snapped. "Lawd know it must be some way for high yeller to git like that!" Shaking out a diaper with a low pop and folding it with careful precision across her lap. "Ada have a good heart and at least she know how to work that danged old stove."

Mammy's retort about the stove had silenced Rufel. She shared Mammy's antipathy for the beastly and expensive contraption Bertie had so proudly installed in the kitchen lean-to during the first months of their marriage. Its management had baffled every cook they ever owned; meals were most often late or the food burned, when the darky could manage to get the fire going at all. None of them had ever understood how to regulate cooking temperatures by sticking a hand into the oven and counting until it had to be withdrawn, the method prescribed by the manufacturer. And it took Mammy's constant supervision to see that the stove was kept clean and blackening applied to prevent the rust of its many surfaces and joints. To his credit, Bertie had seldom complained about the tardy and overdone meals (often he was not there to share them), and usually laughed when Rufel apologized for the quality of the meals set before him. How, he would ask, could she be expected to teach darkies to regulate the temperature of the stove when most of them couldn't count beyond one or two? Still, Rufel felt she had failed in a crucial duty and she was both relieved and piqued that Ada seemed to have an instinct where the operation of the stove was concerned.

Despite Ada's considerable skill in the kitchen, Rufel still itched sometimes to throw the lie back in Ada's face (White man, indeed! Both of them probably run off by the mistress for making up to the master), but she was glad she hadn't provoked Mammy that day. Mammy had probably not believed Ada's story herself, Rufel thought now, but had not wanted to antagonize Ada. Mammy, perhaps even then foreseeing her own death, trying to secure the help Rufel would need until Bertie came back, knew Rufel would need that scheming Ada. No, Rufel had concluded, hurrying now lest she be trapped in grief and fear, the "cruel master" was just to play on her sympathy.

But—maybe—there were no people for this wench to return to. Timmy had said the other darkies called her the "debil woman." His blue eyes had rolled back into his head and he had bared his baby teeth in a grotesque grin as he said it. Repulsed by his mimicry, she had scolded him for the mockery. "But that's the way they do it, mamma; and laugh and slap their thighs." He had imitated that also and she had relaxed, a little surprised at how seriously she had taken the joke. And it was a joke, she told herself, a foolish nickname, "debil woman" (He talk plain when he with me, she thought defensively). What could there be to fear in this one little sickly, colored gal? Oh, she was wild enough to have some kind of devil in her, Rufel would think, smiling, remembering the way the girl's eyes had bucked the first time she awakened in the bedroom, just the way Mammy's used to when something frightened her. Mammy, Mammy's hands in her hair—Sudden longing pierced Rufel. Mammy's voice: "Aw, Miz 'Fel"; that was special, extra loving, extra.

Rufel squeezed her eyes tight. She—the colored girl—had probably been scared out of her wits at finding herself in a bed. Even in her fevered state, she would know that no darky could own a room like this. It was a spacious and light-filled chamber, handsomely proportioned and stylishly finished from the highly polished golden-oak flooring to the long, French-style windows that faced the morning sun. Even the open-beam ceiling, so long an ugly reminder of that good-for-nothing darky's unfinished work, seemed, since Mammy had hit upon the idea of painting the rough wood white, almost elegant. The highboy and matching cupboard, the cedar clothespress and thin-legged dressing table with its three-quarter mirror had come with her from Charleston; the crib and the half-sized chest had been made by the estate carpenter at Dry Fork as the Prestons' christening gift for Timmy. She had only to look at these to see Dry Fork again—not as she had come to know it during her lying-in with Timmy and the weeks she had spent there regaining her strength, as a bustling, virtually self-sufficient, miniature village, but as she had seen it on her first visit, the year she and Bertie went to Montgomery to buy a cook: the stately mansion built in the English style with an open court in front, the circular carriage drives and broad walks, the gardens opening before it: large flowers beds and mounds, empty at that season but since pictured in her mind in a riot of blooming colors, rose, snowball, hyacinth, jonquil, violet. A mockingbird sang perpetually from bowers of honeysuckle and purple wisteria, perfumed and heavy with spring blossoms.

There was no comparison, of course, between the Glen and such magnificence; you couldn't build an establishment like Dry Fork in five or even ten years. Not without slaves, not without "capital." Unconsciously, Rufel quoted Bertie, and shrugged, impatient with herself. What could a darky have to compare the Glen with? Certainly it offered a better home than any runaway could hope to have. Even that scheming Ada didn't want to go back out in the wild.

And, if the darky wasn't from around here— No angry owners or slave catchers had descended on the house as Rufel had half expected would happen. She had been in the yard drawing water from the well, because that idiot girl of Ada's had forgotten to do it, the morning Harker rode in with the girl. She had been startled by the sight of darkies on horses and frightened when she recognized Harker. What would these darkies steal next? And: She would have to say something; people might not come way out here looking for a chicken or a pig, but somebody would want to know about these horses. The darkies had been as startled as Rufel, but, after the briefest hesitation, had continued walking their horses toward the kitchen lean-to. "Harker." She had stepped into their path—and seen the girl strapped in the litter Harker pulled behind his horse. There was something in the ashen skin, like used charcoal, the aimless turning of the head that had kept Rufel silent. The baby had started to cry, a thin wail muffled by layers of covering. The girl's eyes had fluttered open and seemed to look imploringly at Rufel before rolling senselessly back into her head.

"Go get Ada," Rufel had ordered without hesitation. "Take her on into the house; bring the bucket," she said as she bent to look for the baby.

She shouldn't have done it; Rufel had been over that countless times, also. If anybody ever found out. If they had been followed. But nothing of that had entered her head as she picked her way carefully up the steep back steps, the baby hugged close to her body. The girl's desolate face, the baby's thin crying—as though it had given up all hope—had grated at her; she was a little crazy, she supposed. But she could do something about this, about the baby who continued to cry while she waited in the dim area back of the stairs for the darkies to bring the girl in. Something about the girl, her face— And: She—Rufel—could do something. That was as close as she came to explaining anything to herself. The baby was hungry and she fed him. Or she would imagine herself saying to Mammy, "Well, I couldn't have them bringing a bleeding colored gal in where Timmy and Clara were having breakfast," wheedling a little, making light. As long as the girl wasn't from around here— Though it would serve the neighbors right, she thought, resentful now, if the darky did belong to someone around here. Many times as Bertie had gone looking for a darky and been met with grins and lies. Truly, it would not surprise her to learn that some jealous neighbor had been tampering with their slaves, just as Bertie had always said, urging them to run away.

Harker and Ada swore the darky wasn't from around here. In fact, Harker said the girl was from Charleston. Not that Rufel believed that for a minute; Ada had probably put him up to that, hoping to touch Rufel's heart. But, if the girl were from Charleston. Here Rufel would stop short, hearing once again Mammy's anxious voice, urging her to write the family, for surely they would send for Rufel to visit, seeing again the glittering ballrooms of her first Charleston season. Usually—for if it wasn't this longing or memory, it would be some other—she would put aside whatever task she worked on, gather up the babies if she had been nursing, and find something in the sitting room that needed doing.

No one asked and she rarely thought to question herself after the first day or so. She knew there was more to the girl's story than the darkies were telling, and now and then she did wonder briefly what could have forced the girl out into the woods with her time so near. Even in the comfort and splendor of Dry Fork, having Timmy had been an ordeal, and Rufel refused to dwell on the agony of Clara's birth. Well, darkies did have their own way of doing things and whatever the real story was, it couldn't, she thought, amount to much. Rufel sometimes suspected that the girl was the sweetheart of one of the new darkies, and was made uneasy by the idea. They couldn't start using the Glen like a regular hideaway, she would think fearfully, and push the speculation aside. The colored girl would wake and tell her story— Whether or not she believed it, Rufel, recalling the long hours she had spent with Mammy, talking idly or in companionable silence, thought it would be something to pass the time.

Rufel leaned now against the bedroom door and watched the colored girl, who lay curled on her side in the big feather bed, facing the door. The colored girl had not stirred at the sound of the closing door and after a moment Rufel continued across the room to the curtained doorway in the adjacent wall. This girl couldn't go on acting crazy forever, she thought impatiently, talking all out of her head, laying up like she was still half dead. Rufel pushed aside the curtain with a swish and entered the narrow antechamber where her seven-year-old son, Timmy, slept. It had been her dressing room in the original plan of the house. The boy had slept in the room since early spring and its plain neatness was a sign of his growing independence. He acted more like nine or ten than the eight he would be in November, spending long hours with Uncle Joel and Dante as they tended the stock and garden, with Ada in the cook-shed, or with Annabelle, when she could catch him and there was nothing better to do.

She should keep him closer, Rufel thought as she put away his clothing in neat piles on the open shelves above his makeshift bed, keep him away from the darkies. Send him to the field school at the crossroads— But Bertie would return and be mortified to find his son sharing a desk with common red-necks. And where would she get the two dollars a month to keep him there? I can't just keep him cooped up in here with me all day, she thought wearily. And the darkies talked before him as they would not with her; it was through him that Rufel kept some kind of track of the comings and goings in the Quarters. She was not entirely convinced that some of those darkies were not Bertie's nigras taking his continued absence as an opportunity to slip back and live free. Neither she nor Timmy would ever recognize them. Mammy had been the one who knew them all.

Finished, Rufel turned and stood in the doorway, peeking between the curtains; she could just see the top of the girl's head in the pillows. Rufel shrugged between the curtains and started toward the bedroom door but stopped as she neared the bed. The girl had turned over; her profile was a sooty blur against the whiteness of the pillow. Her eyes were closed, the lashes lost in the darkness of her face. When open, they looked like Mammy's, a soft brownblack set under sleepy, long-lashed lids. And big. Once, when Rufel had had to restrain her, the girl had seemed to look at her, to recognize her. Even as Rufel watched, the girl's expression had changed to fear and loathing. It was over in a moment. The girl had renewed her efforts to get out of the bed and Rufel had called to Ada for help. Sometimes, when the girl's eyes fluttered open, their gaze sweeping past her without recognition, Rufel thought she had imagined that momentary expression. And it was silly to suppose the girl had really recognized her, even if she were from Charleston. And never, never had Rufel done anything to anyone to deserve such a look. But to see eyes so like Mammy's, staring such hatred at her. It had given Rufel quite a turn. She wanted the girl to wake up, wanted to see that look banished from her face.

The girl lay unmoving and Rufel continued to the door. It was time for this darky to wake up. Rufel turned as a thought hit her, and, back to the corridor door, eyed the colored girl. Perhaps she had changed her position slightly, but she lay still now under Rufel's gaze. "You not doing a thing but playing possum," Rufel said loudly. The girl did not respond and, turning with a flounce, Rufel stepped into the wide central hall, closing the door behind her.

The Civil War and Its Consequences

The Civil War was the most important event in the history of the South. Free or slave, black or white, male or female, rich or poor, the war changed the landscape of people's lives. From the moment it began, the war unleashed changes few could have imagined. To the surprise of virtually everyone, it brought slavery to an abrupt end. It brought death to one fourth of the white men of military age in the South. It brought a lifetime of suffering to those Southerners who survived as wounded veterans or as widows and orphans. It brought the devastation of the agricultural economy. It brought an ignominious end to the national political power of the white South.

At the same time, the Civil War brought freedom to a people denied it for two hundred and fifty years. It brought them the right to marry and keep their children under the family's own roof. It brought them the opportunity to worship as they wished, where they wished, with whom they wished. It brought the chance for people to keep something of what they produced with their own hands and brains. It brought the first glimpse of political rights, of being able to say what one thought about matters of common concern. It brought the possibility of learning to read, write, and figure, of seeing what lay beyond the next plantation or the dusty crossroads.

The years following the war were marked by their own kind of struggle. In some ways, that struggle was more desperate for being private, hidden. Old boundaries had been destroyed and only the crudest ones could be rebuilt. Whites labored to define whiteness, to wall and protect it with segregation. Blacks labored to define freedom, to decide what they had to have and what they could live without for the time being. Politics became ugly and civic life atrophied.

The economic realm seemed to hold the most promise. Whites professed themselves glad to be free of slavery and its obligations. Landowners began to abandon the plantations to tenants, moving to towns where stores, mills, and railroads offered novel ways to make money. Young black men moved regularly, looking for better jobs on the railroads or in the lumber camps. Boosters claimed that the South had become new, reborn in a stronger and prouder form. And some people did become rich in the new order. But more Southerners became poorer instead, as they divided farms among their children, as they went into mills where they barely earned a living, or as they moved from one tenant shack to another.

Southern writers struggled to make sense of this turmoil. Diaries and memoirs of the Civil War recorded the sense of disbelief and confusion that accompanied secession and then defeat, the transformation of defiance into doubt and resignation. The fiction written about the Confederacy in later years imagined the war as experience, metaphor, and farce, trying to find a larger meaning in so much suffering. The fiction written about the former slaves imagined the exultation and disbelief, the uncertainty and hard decisions that followed hard on the heels of freedom.

Black Southerners knew all about freedom from having watched it from a distance. They seized the opportunity to define what they wanted and needed, but the promise soon evaporated. The African American writing of the post-Reconstruction era here tells of the way people survived slavery, of making their way in the New South, of burying a child in the red soil of the South. The writing by whites in the postwar era, much of it by women, speaks of losses, dangers, and uncertainties that, though out of sight, were no less powerful as a result. The final selection here comes from the most popular book ever written about the South. Composed seventy years after the war, it stresses the bonds between blacks and whites, the triumph over hard times, and the faith in tomorrow, translating the Civil War and its consequences into terms Americans choose to believe.

War

from *The Civil War Diary of Sarah Morgan*

Sarah Morgan (1842–1909)

Sarah Fowler Morgan came of age in Baton Rouge, the daughter of a respected judge. Though she and her father supported the Union during the secession crisis, both invested their loyalty in the Confederacy once the Civil War began. Early in 1862, twenty-year-old Morgan began keeping a diary, recording her passionate but conflicted ideas about Yankees and Southerners, men and women, loyalty and patriotism. The diary is marked by defiance, conciliation, and, ultimately, grief. Morgan eventually moved to South Carolina, wrote for a leading newspaper there, and married its editor. Upon his murder fifteen years later, Morgan moved to Paris to live with her son. She died there but is buried in Charleston, South Carolina. Her diary was published in 1913 and a newly edited version appeared in 1991.

May 9th (1862)

Our lawful (?) owners have at last arrived. About sunset day before yesterday, the Iroquois anchored here, and a graceful young Federal stepped ashore, carrying a Yankee flag over his shoulder, and asked the way to the Mayor's office. I like the style! If we girls of B.R. had been at the landing instead of the men, that Yankee should never have insulted us by flying his flag in our faces! We would have opposed his landing except under a flag of truce; but the men let him alone, and he even found a poor Dutchman willing to show him the road! He did not accomplish much; said a formal demand would be made next day, and asked if it was safe for the men to come ashore and buy a few necessaries, when he was assured the air of B.R. was very unhealthy for Federal soldiers at night. He promised very magnanimously not [to] shell us out, if we did not molest him; but I notice none of them dare set their feet on terra-firma, except the officer who has now called three times on the Mayor, and who is said to tremble visibly as he walks the streets.

Last evening came the demand: the town must [be] surrendered immediately; the federal flag Must be raised, they would grant us the same terms they granted to New Orleans. Jolly terms those were! The answer was worthy of a Southerner. It was "the town was defenseless, if we had cannon, there were not men enough to resist; but if forty vessels lay at the landing,—it was intimated that we were in their power, and more ships coming up—we would not surrender; if they wanted, they might come Take us; if they wished the Federal flag hoisted over the Arsenal, they might put it up for themselves, the town had no control over Government property." Glorious! What a pity they did not shell the town! But they are taking us at our word, and this morning they are landing at the Garrison, and presently the Bloody banner will be floating over our heads. "Better days are coming, we'll all go right."

"All devices, signs, and flags of the confederacy shall be suppressed." So says Picayune Butler. Good. I devote all my red, white, and blue silk to the manufacture of Confederate flags. As soon as one is confiscated, I make another, until my ribbon is exhausted, when I will sport a duster emblazoned in high colors, "Hurra! for the Bonny blue flag!" Henceforth, I wear one pinned to my bossom—not a duster, but a little flag—the man who says take it off, will have to pull it off for himself: the man who dares attempt it—well! a pistol in my pocket will fill up the gap. I am capable, too.

This is a dreadful war to make even the hearts of women so bitter! I hardly know myself these last few weeks. I, who have such a horror of bloodshed, consider even killing in self defense murder, who cannot wish them the slightest evil, whose only prayer is to have them sent back in peace to their own country. *I* talk of killing them! for what else do I wear a pistol and carving knife? I am afraid I *will* try them on the first one who says an insolent word to me. Yes, and repent for ever after in sack cloth and ashes! O if I was only a man! Then I could don the breeches, and slay them with a will! If some few Southern women were in the ranks, they could set the men an example they would not blush to follow. Pshaw! there are *no* women here! We are *all* men!

. . .

... So yesterday the town was in a foment because it was reported the Federal officers had called on the Miss Morgans, and all the gentlemen [were] anxious to hear how they had been received. One had the grace to say "If they did, they received the best lesson there that they could get in town; those young ladies would meet them with the true Southern spirit." The rest did not know; they would like to find out. I suppose the story originated from the fact that we were unwilling to blackguard—yes, that is the word—the Federal officers here, and would not agree with many of our friends in saying they were liars, thieves, murderers, scoundrels, the scum of the earth, etc. Such epithets are unworthy of ladies, I say, and do harm, rather than advance our cause. Let them be what they will, it shall not make me less the lady; I say it is unworthy of anything except low newspaper war, such abuse, and will not join in.

I have a brother-in-law in the Federal army that I love and respect as much as anyone in the world, and shall not readily agree that his being a Northerner would give him an irresistible desire to pick my pockets, and take from him all power of telling the truth. No! There are few men I admire more than Major Drum, and I honor him for his indepedence in doing what he believes Right. Let us have liberty of speech, and action in our land, I say, but not gross abuse and calumny. Shall I acknowledge that the people we so recently called our brothers are unworthy of consideration, and are liars, cowards, dogs? Not I! If they conquer us, I acknowledge them as a superior race; I will not say we were conquered by cowards, for where would that place us? It will take a brave people to gain us, and that the Northerners undoubtedly are. I would scorn to have an inferior foe; I fight only my equals. These women may acknowledge that *cowards* have won battles in which their brothers were engaged, but I, I will ever say *mine* fought against brave men, and won the day. Which is most honorable? To the glory of our nation be it said, that it is only the women who talk that way. The men are all fighting, and these poor weak females sit over their knitting and pour out a weak, spiteful, pitiful stream of deluted [sic] rage against Cowards (?) their husbands and brothers think it worth while to fight against!

I hate to hear women on political subjects; they invariably make fools of themselves, and it sickens me to see half a dozen talking at once of what *they* would do, and what ought to be done; it gives me the greatest disgust, so I generally contrive to absent myself from such gatherings, as I seldom participate. But in this cause, it is necessary for me to express my opinion, sometimes, so I give it here, that I may not believe in after years I am quite a weathercock. I was never a secessionist, for I quietly adopted father's views on political subjects, with out meddling with them; but even father went over with his state, and when so many outrages were committed by the fanatical leaders of the North, though he regretted the Union, said "Fight to the death for our liberty." I say so too, I would want to fight until we win the cause so many have died for. I dont believe in Secession, but I do in Liberty. I want the South to conquer, dictate its own terms, and go back to the Union for I believe that apart, inevitable ruin awaits both.

It is a rope of sand, this Confederacy founded on the doctrine of Secession, and will not last many years—not five. The North Cannot subdue us. We are too determined to be free. They have no right to confiscate our property to pay debts they themselves have incurred. Death as a nation, rather than Union on such terms! We will have our Rights secured on so firm a basis, that it can never be shaken. If by power of overwhelming numbers they conquer us, it will be a barren victory over a desolate land. We, the natives of this loved soil will be beggars in [a] foreign land; we will not submit to despotism under the garb of Liberty. The north will find herself burdened with an unparalelled [sic] debt, with nothing to show for it, except deserted towns, and burning homes, a standing army which will govern with no small caprice, and an improverished land. England will then be ready to step in, and Crash! the American Commonwealth will disappear in the British Monarchy.

Therefore I say, let us conquer, make our *own* terms, and be a band of brothers in deed, and in truth; and so I pray daily "God bless our Southern Nation, and grant us peace in the name of Jesus Christ!" If that be treason, make the most of it!

May 17th

One of these days, when we are at peace, and all quietly settled in some corner of this wide world without anything particularly exciting to alarm us every few moments, and with the knowledge of what is the Future to us now, and will be the Past to us then, seeing it has all come right in the end, and has been for the best, we will wonder how we could ever have been foolish enough to await each day and hour with such anxiety, and if it were really possible that half the time as we lay down to sleep, we did not know but that we might be homeless and beggars in the morning. It will look unreal then; we will say it was imagination; but it is bitterly true now.

The Yankees left us some four days ago, to attack Vicksburg, leaving their flag flying in the Garrison, without a man to protect it, with the understanding that the town would be held responsible for it. It was meant for a trap, and the bait took, for night before last it was pulled down, and torn to pieces. Now, unless Will will have the kindness to sink a dozen of their ships up there—I hear he has command of the lower batteries—they will be back in a few days, and will execute their threat of shelling the town. If they do, what will become of us? All we expect, in the way of earthly property, is as yet mere paper; which will be so much trash if the South is ruined, as it consists of debts due father by many planters for professional services rendered, who, of course, will be ruined too, so all money is gone.

That is nothing; we will not be ashamed to earn our bread, so let it go. But this house, is really something to us, a shelter from the weather at least, if all associations and pecuniary values were put aside, and our servants too, we are loath to part with. Here the Yankees are on the side of the river, longing for an opportunity of "giving us a lesson," and a band of guerillas now organizing just back of us who will soon number over two thousand, are generally eager to have a "brush" with the enemy. With fire front and rear what chance is there for poor Baton Rouge? We will be burnt up in a few hours, with these people fighting over our heads, as it were.

The men say all women and children must be removed. Where to? Charlie suggests Greenwell for us. If we go, even if the town is spared the ordeal of fire, our house will be broken open by the soldiers and pillaged, for Butler has decreed that no unoccupied house will be respected. If we stay and witness the fight, if *they* are victorious, we are subject to hourly insult, for I understand that the officers who were here said "if the people did not treat them decently, they would know what it was, when Billy Wilson's crew got here. *They* would give them a lesson!" That select crowd is now in the city. Heaven help us when they will reach here! It is these small cities which suffer the greatest outrages. What are we to do?

A new proclamation from Butler has just come. It seems that the ladies have an ugly way of gathering their skirts when the Federals pass, to prevent contact, and some even turn up their noses—unladylike to say the least, but which may be owing to the odor they have, which is said to be unbearable even at this early season of year. Butler says, whereas the so called *ladies* of New Orleans insult his men and officers, he gives one and all, permission to insult *any* or all who so treat them, then and there, with the assurance that the women will not receive the slightest protection from the government, and the men will all be justified. I did not have time to read it, but repeat it as it was told me by mother who is in perfect despair at the brutality of the thing.

These are our brothers? None for me! Let us hope for the honor of this nation that Butler is not counted among the *gentlemen* of the land. And so, if any man takes a fancy to kiss me, or put his arm around me, he will be upheld in the outrage if he only says I pulled my dress from under his feet? That will justify them! And if we decline receiving their visits, it is another excuse to insult us, on the plea of prior insult to them!

O my brothers, George, Gibbes and Jimmy, never did we more need protection! where are you? If Charlie must go, we are defenseless. Come to my bosom O my discarded carving knife, laid aside under the impression (fate it seems) that these were *gentlemen* sent to conquer us. Come, I say, and though sheathless now, I will find you a sheath in the body of the first man who attempts to Butlerize—or brutalize—(the terms are synonymous) me! I didn't kiss *my* sweetheart even! shall I let some northern beggar take the first? With the blessing of Heaven, no! It is a hard case to kiss someone's [*sic*] else, if you cant kiss your own sweetheart. If I was only a man! I dont know a woman here who does not groan over her misfortune in being clothed in petticoats: why cant we fight as well as the men?

Still not a word from the boys: we hear Norfolk has been evacuated but no particulars, and George was there, Gibbes is where ever Johnston is, supposed to be on the Rappahannock, but we have not heard from either for more than six weeks, and all communication is now cut off. And Jimmy—I groan in spirit every time I think of him. Suppose he is lying sick, or perhaps dying, on the road? I wont think of it. I shut my eyes tightly and say please God take care of him. O if He will only send back the boys in safety how thankful we shall be! I know our fate though; the men of our family who are worth something, will die off in their prime: while we worthless women, of no value or importance to ourselves or the rest of the world, will live on, useless trash in creation. Pleasant, is it not?

O for Peace! If it were not for the idea that it must dawn on us before many months were over, I would lie down and die at once. Hope alone sustains me. Yet I do not say give up: let us all die first. But Peace—! what a blessing it would be! No one who has not passed through such times can appreciate it. Think of meeting your brothers and friends again—such as are spared! Think of the blessing of lying down in quiet at night, and waking in safety in the morning, with no thought of bomb shells breaking the silence of the night, or of thieving lawless soldiers searching for plunder. Think of settling quietly into the life Heaven has appointed for you, whether in comfort or poverty, content because He sends it, and because either will be rest, and quiet at last!

O Peace! how it will be appreciated by those who have suffered in this struggle! I fore warn all not to consider me a responsible creature when it is once declared. I shall be insane with delight I know. I have a bad habit of hugging people when I am very happy, so every one who does not wish to be embraced had better keep away. I remember we were all standing at Mrs Brunot's gate, in a crowd of some three hundred people watching the militia drill, last October, when father joined us and told us of the battle of the Passes. Jimmy was there, and I knew every officer engaged: we had won, and I was so wild with delight that I came near killing Dena by hugging, and laughed with tears streaming down my face, and father said he must never tell me news in the streets again.

. . .

This war has brought out wicked, malignant feelings that I did not believe could dwell in woman's heart. I see some with the holiest eyes, so holy one would think the very spirit of Charity lived in them and all Christian meekness, go off in a mad tirade of abuse and say with the holy eyes wonderously changed "I hope God will send down plague, Yellow fever, famine, on these vile Yankees, and that not one will escape death." O what unutterable horror that remark causes me as often as I hear it! I think of the many mothers, wives and sisters who wait as anxiously, pray as fervently in their far away lonesome homes for their dear ones, as we do here; I fancy them waiting day after day for the footsteps that will never come, growing more sad, lonely, and heartbroken as the days wear on, I think of how awful it would be to me if one would say "your brothers are dead," how it would crush all life and happiness out of me; and I say "God forgive these poor women! They know not what they say!" O woman! into what loathsome violence you have debased your holy mission! God will punish us for our hardheartedness.

Not a square off, in the new theater, lie more than a hundred sick soldiers. What woman has stretched out her hand to save them, to give them a cup of cold water? Where is the charity which should ignore nations and creeds, and administer help to the Indian or Heathen indifferently? Gone! all gone in Union versus Secession! *That* is what the American War has brought us. If I was independent, if I could work my own will without causing others to suffer for my deeds. I would not be poring over this stupid page, I would not be idly reading or sewing. I would put aside woman's trash, take up Woman's duty, and I would stand by some forsaken man and bid him God speed as he closes his dying eyes. *That* is Woman's mission! and not Preaching and Politics. I say I would, yet here I sit! O for liberty! the liberty that *dares* do what conscience dictates, and scorns all smaller rules!

If I could help these dying men! Yet it is as impossible as though I was a chained bear. I cant put out my hand. I am threatened with Coventry because I sent a custard to a sick man who is in the army, and with the anathema of society because I said if I could possibly do anything for Mr Biddle — at at a distance — (he is sick) I would like to very much. [Sentence lined through] [Word erased] thinks we have acted shockingly in helping Col. McMillan, and that we will suffer for it when the Federals leave. I would like to see the *man* who *dared* harm my father's daughter! But as he seems to think our conduct reflects on him, there is no alternative. Die, poor men, without a woman's hand to close your eyes! We women are too *patriotic* to help you! I look eagerly on, cry in my soul "I wish —"; you die, God judges me. Behold the woman who dares not risk private ties for God's glory and her professed religion! Coward, helpless woman that I am! If I was free! —

5th [February 1865]

Not dead! not dead! O my God! Gibbes is *not* dead! Where [sic]

O dear God! another? Only a few days ago came a letter so cheerful and hopeful — we have waited and prayed so patiently — at my feet lies one from Col. Steedman saying he is dead. Dead! suddenly and without a moment's warning summoned to God! No! it cannot be! I am mad! O God have mercy on us! my poor mother! And Lydia! Lydia! God comfort you! My brain seems fire. Am I mad? Not yet! God would not take him yet! He will come again! Hush! God is good! Not dead! not dead! O Gibbes come back to us!

11th [February]

O God O God have mercy on us! George is dead! Both in a week! George our sole hope—our sole dependence.

March

Dead! dead! Both dead! O my brothers! what have we lived for except you? We who would so gladly have laid down our lives for yours, are left desolate to mourn over all we loved and hoped for, weak and helpless; while you, so strong, noble, and brave, have gone before us without a murmur. God knows best. But it is hard—O so hard! to give them up without a murmur!

We cannot remember the day when our brothers were not all in all to us. What the boys would think; what the boys would say; what we would do when the boys came home, that has been our sole thought through life. A life time's hope wrecked in a moment—God help us! In our eyes, there is no one in the world quite so noble, quite so brave, quite so true as our brothers. And yet they are taken—and others useless to themselves and a curse to their families live on in safety, without fear of death. This is blasphemy. God knows best; I will not complain. But when I think of drunken, foolish, coarse Will Carter with horses and dogs his sole ambition, and drinking and gambling his idea of happiness, my heart swells within me. He lives, a torment to himself and a curse to others—he will live to a green old age as idle, as ignorant, as dissipated as he is now.

And Gibbes, Harry, and George, God's blessings he bestowed on us awhile—are dead. My brothers! my dear brothers! I would rather mourn over you in your graves, remembering what you were, than have you change places with that man. Death is nothing in comparison to dishonor.

If we had had any warning or preparation, this would not have been so unspeakably awful. But to shut ones eyes to all dangers and risks, and drown every rising fear with "God will send them back; I will not doubt his mercy," and then suddenly to learn that your faith has been presumption—and God wills that you shall undergo bitter affliction—it is a fearful awakening! What glory have we ever rendered to God that we should expect him to be so merciful to us? Are not all things His, and is He not infinitely more tender and compassionate than we deserve?

We have deceived ourselves willfully about both. After the first dismay

121

on hearing of Gibbes' capture, we readily listened to the assertions of our friends that Johnson's Island was the healthiest place in the world, that he would be better off, comfortably clothed and under shelter, than exposed to shot and shell, half fed, and lying on the bare ground during Ewell's winter campaign. We were thankful for his safety, knowing Brother would leave nothing undone that could add to his comfort. And besides that, there was the sure hope of his having him paroled. On that hope we lived all winter—now confident that in a little while he would be with us, then again doubting for awhile, only to have the hope grow surer afterwards. And so we waited and prayed, never doubting he would come at last. He himself believed it, though striving not to be too hopeful lest he should disappoint us, as well as himself. Yet he wrote cheerfully and bravely to the last. Towards the middle of January, Brother was sure of succeeding, as all the prisoners had been placed under Butler's control. Ah me! How could we be so blind? We were sure he would be with us in a few weeks! I wrote to him that I had prepared his room.

On the 30th of January came his last letter, addressed to me, though meant for Sis. It was dated the 12th—the day George died. All his letters pleaded that I would write more frequently—he loved to hear from me; so I had been writing to him every ten days. On the third of February I sent my last. Friday the fifth, as I was running through Miriam's room, I saw Brother pass the door, and heard him ask Miriam for mother. The voice, the bowed head, the look of utter despair on his face, struck through me like a knife. "Gibbes! Gibbes!" was my sole thought; but Miriam and I stood motionless looking at each other without a word. "Gibbes is dead" said mother as he stood before her. He did not speak; and then we went in.

We did not ask how, or when. That he was dead was enough for us. But after a while he told us uncle James had written that he had died at two o'clock on Thursday the twenty first. Still we did not know how he had died. Several letters that had been brought remained unopened on the floor. One, Brother opened, hoping to learn something more. It was from Col. Steedman to Miriam and me, written a few hours after his death, and contained the sad story our dear brother's last hours. He had been in Col. Steedman's ward of the hospital for more than a week, with headache and sore throat; but it was thought nothing; he seemed to improve, and expected to be discharged in a few days. On the twenty first he complained that his throat pained him again. After prescribing for him, and talking cheerfully with him for some time, Col. Steedman left him surrounded by his friends, to attend to his other patients. He had hardly reached his room when someone ran to him saying Capt. Morgan was dying. He hurried to his bedside, and found him dead. Capt. Steedman, sick in the next bed, and those around him said he had been talking pleasantly with them, when he sat up to reach his cup of water on the table. As soon as he drank it he seemed to suffocate; and after tossing his arms wildly in the air, and making several fearful efforts to breathe, he died.

O Gibbes! Gibbes! When you took me in your arms and cried so bitterly over that sad parting, it was indeed your last farewell! My brothers! my brothers! Dear Lord how can we live without our boys?

Sewed to the paper that contained the last words we should hear of our dear brother, was a lock of hair grown long during his imprisonment. I think it was a noble, tender heart that remembered that one little deed of kindness, and a gentle, pitying hand that cut it from his head as he lay cold and stark in death. Good heart that loved our brave brother, kind hand that soothed his pain, you will not be forgotten by us!

And keenly as we felt his loss, and deeply as we mourned over him who had fought with the bravest of the brave through more than thirty battles, to die a prisoner in a strange land — there was one for whom we felt a keener grief — the dear little wife who loved him so perfectly, whose life must henceforth be a blank before her. God help my poor little sister! "Hush, mother, hush," I said when I heard her cries. "We have Brother, and George and Jimmy left, and Lydia has lost all!" Heaven pity us! George had gone before—only He in mercy kept the knowledge of it from us for awhile longer.

On Thursday the eleventh, as we sat talking to mother, striving to make her forget the weary days we had cried through with that fearful sound of dead! dead! ringing ever in our ears, some one asked for Miriam. She went down, and presently I heard her thanking some body for a letter. "You could not have brought me anything more acceptable! It is from my sister, though she can hardly have heard from us yet!" I ran back, and sitting at mother's feet, told her Miriam was coming with a letter from Lydia. Mother cried at the mention of her name. O my little sister! you know how dear you are to us!

"Mother! Mother!" a horrible voice cried, and before I could think who it was, Miriam rushed in holding an open letter in her hand, and perfectly wild. "George is dead!" she shrieked and fell heavily to the ground. O my God! I could have prayed thee to take mother too, when I looked at her! I thought—I almost hoped she was dead, and that pang spared! But I was wild myself. I could have screamed!—laughed! "It is false! do you hear me mother? God would not take both! George is not dead!" I cried trying in vain to rouse her from her horrible state or bring one ray of reason to her eye. I spoke to a body alive only to pain; not a sound of my voice seemed to reach her; only fearful moans showed she was yet alive. Miriam lay raving on the ground. Poor Miriam! her heart's idol torn away. God help my darling! I did not understand that George *could* die until I looked at her. In vain I strove to raise her from the ground, or check her wild shrieks for death. "George! only George!" she would cry; until at last with the horror of seeing both die before me, I mastered strength enough to go for the servant and bid her run quickly for Brother.

How long I stood there alone, I never knew. I remember Ada coming in hurriedly and asking what it was. I told her George was dead. It was a relief to see her cry. I could not; but I felt the pain afresh, as though it were her brother she was crying over, not mine. And the sight of her tears brought mine too. We could only cry over mother and Miriam; we could not rouse them; we did not know what to do. Some one called me in the entry. I went, not understanding what I was doing. A lady came to me, told me her name, and said something about George; but I could not follow what she said. It was as though she were talking in a dream. I believe she repeated her words several times, for at last she shook me and said "Listen! Rouse yourself! the letter is about George!" Yes, I said; he is dead. She said I must read the letter; but I could not see, so she read it aloud.

It was from Dr Mitchell, his friend who was with him when he died, telling of his sickness and death. He died on Tuesday the twelfth of January, after an illness of six days, conscious to the last and awaiting the end as only a Christian, and one who has led so beautiful a life, could, with the grace of God, look for it. He sent messages to his brothers and sisters, and bade them tell his mother his last thoughts were of her, and that he died trusting in the mercy of his Saviour. George! our pride! our beautiful, angel brother! *Could* he die? Surely God has sent all these afflictions within these three years to teach us that our hopes must be placed Above, and that it is blasphemy to have earthly idols!

The letter said that the physicians had mistaken his malady which was inflamation of the bowels, and he had died from being treated for something else. It seemed horrible cruelty to read me that part; I knew that if mother or Miriam ever heard of it, it would kill them. So I begged Mrs. Mitchel [sic] never to let them hear of it. She seemed to think nothing of the pain it would inflict; how could she help telling if they asked? she said. I told her I must insist on her not mentioning it; it would only add suffering to what was already insupportable; if they asked for the letter, offer to read it aloud, but say positively that she would not allow any one to touch it except herself, and then she might pass it over in silence.

I roused Miriam then, and sent her to hear it read. She insisted on reading it herself; and half dead with grief held out her hands, begging piteously to be suffered to read it alone. I watched then until I was sure Mrs. Mitchel would keep her promise. Horrible as I knew it to be from strange lips, I knew by what I experienced that I had saved her from a shock that might cost her her life; and then I went back to mother. No need to conceal what I felt there! She neither spoke nor saw. If I had shrieked that he died of ill treatment, she would not have understood. But I sat there silently with that horrible secret, wondering if God would help me bear it, or if despair would deprive me of self-control and force me presently to cry it aloud, though it should kill them both.

At last Brother came. I had to meet him downstairs and tell him. God spare me the sight of a strong man's grief! Then Sister came in, knowing as little as he. Poor Sister! I could have blessed her for every tear she shed. It was a comfort to see some one who had life or feeling left. I felt as though the whole world was dead. Nothing was real, nothing existed except horrible speechless pain. Life was a fearful dream through which but one thought ran—"dead—dead."

Miriam had been taken to her room more dead than alive—mother lay speechless in hers. The shock of this second blow had obliterated, with them, all recollection of the first. It was a mercy I envied them; for I remembered both until loss of consciousness would have seemed a blessing. I shall never forget mother's shriek of horror when towards evening she recalled it. O those dreadful days of misery and wretchedness! It seems almost sacrilege to refer to them now. They are buried in our hearts with our boys—thought of with prayers and tears.

How will the world seem to us now? What will life be without the boys? When this terrible strife is over, and so many thousand return to their homes, what will peace bring us of all we hoped? Jimmy! dear Lord, spare us that one! but I have always felt Jimmy must die young—and we have been so cast down that hope seems almost presumption in us. So we send our hearts over the waves after our last one, while our souls hardly dare pray "God spare him!"

from "Co. Aytch"

Sam Watkins (1839–1901)

Sam Watkins of Columbia, Tennessee, was twenty-one and attending a local college in the spring of 1861 when he enlisted in Company H of the First Tennessee Regiment. Watkins found himself in a dauntingly long list of major battles, with Shiloh, Murfreesboro, Chickamauga, and Atlanta among them. Out of one hundred and twenty men who enlisted in his company, he was one of only seven who survived. Watkins composed "Co. Aytch" twenty years after his enlistment, writing for a local audience, and it was published in 1882. Watkins adopts an ironic and modest tone far different from the self-serving and inflated language common among such memoirs.

THE BLOODY CHASM

In these memoirs, after the lapse of twenty years, we propose to fight our "battles o'er again."

To do this is but a pastime and pleasure, as there is nothing that so much delights the old soldier as to revisit the scenes and battle-fields with which he was once so familiar, and to recall the incidents, though trifling they may have been at the time.

The histories of the Lost Cause are all written out by "big bugs," generals and renowned historians, and like the fellow who called a turtle a "cooter," being told that no such word as cooter was in Webster's dictionary, remarked that he had as much right to make a dictionary as Mr. Webster or any other man; so have I to write a history.

But in these pages I do not pretend to write the history of the war. I only give a few sketches and incidents that came under the observation of a "high private" in the rear ranks of the rebel army. Of course, the histories are all correct. They tell of great achievements of great men, who wear the laurels of victory; have grand presents given them; high positions in civil life; presidents of corporations; governors of states; official positions, etc., and when they die, long obituaries are published, telling their many virtues, their distinguished victories, etc., and when they are buried, the whole country goes in mourning and is called upon to buy an elegant monument to erect over the remains of so distinguished and brave a general, etc. But in the following pages I propose to tell of the fellows who did the shooting and killing, the fortifying and ditching, the sweeping of the streets, the drilling, the standing guard, picket and videt, and who drew (or were to draw) eleven dollars per month and rations, and also drew the ramrod and tore the cartridge. Pardon me should I use the personal pronoun "I" too frequently, as I do not wish to be called egotistical, for I only write of what I saw as an humble private in the rear rank in an infantry regiment, commonly called "webfoot." Neither do I propose to make this a connected journal, for I write entirely from memory, and you must remember, kind reader, that these things happened twenty years ago, and twenty years is a long time in the life of any individual.

I was twenty-one years old then, and at that time I was not married. Now I have a house full of young "rebels," clustering around my knees and bumping against my elbow, while I write these reminiscences of the war of secession, rebellion, state rights, slavery, or our rights in the territories, or by whatever other name it may be called. These are all with the past now, and the North and South have long ago "shaken hands across the bloody chasm." The flag of the Southern causes has been furled never to be again unfurled; gone like a dream of yesterday, and lives only in the memory of those who lived through those bloody days and times.

EIGHTEEN HUNDRED AND SIXTY-ONE

Reader mine, did you live in that stormy period? In the year of our Lord eighteen hundred and sixty-one, do you remember those stirring times? Do you recollect in that year, for the first time in your life, of hearing Dixie and the Bonnie Blue Flag?

. . .

Well, here we were, again "reorganizing," and after our lax discipline on the road to and from Virginia, and after a big battle, which always disorganizes an army, what wonder is it that some men had to be shot, merely for discipline's sake? And what wonder that General Bragg's name became a terror to deserters and evil doers? Men were shot by scores, and no wonder the army had to be reorganized. Soldiers had enlisted for twelve months only, and had faithfully complied with their volunteer obligations; the terms for which they had enlisted had expired, and they naturally looked upon it that they had a right to go home. They had done their duty faithfully and well. They wanted to see their families; in fact, wanted to go home anyhow. War had become a reality; they were tired of it. A law had been passed by the Confederate States Congress called the conscript act. A soldier had no right to volunteer and to choose the branch of service he preferred. He was conscripted.

From this time on till the end of the war, a soldier was simply a machine, a conscript. It was mighty rough on rebels. We cursed the war, we cursed Bragg, we cursed the Southern Confederacy. All our pride and valor had gone, and we were sick of war and the Southern Confederacy.

A law was made by the Confederate States Congress about this time allowing every person who owned twenty negroes to go home. It gave us the blues; we wanted twenty negroes. Negro property suddenly became very valuable, and there was raised the howl of "rich man's war, poor man's fight." The glory of the war, the glory of the South, the glory and the pride of our volunteers had no charms for the conscript.

We were directed to re-elect our officers, and the country was surprised to see the sample of a conscript's choice. The conscript had no choice. He was callous, and indifferent whether he had a captain or not. Those who were at first officers had resigned and gone home, because they were officers. The poor private, a contemptible conscript, was left to howl and gnash his teeth. The war might as well have ended then and there. The boys were "hacked," nay, whipped. They were shorn of the locks of their glory. They had but one ambition now, and that was to get out of the army in some way or other. They wanted to join the cavalry or artillery or home guards or pioneer corps or to be "yaller dogs," or anything.

[The average staff officer and courier were always called "yaller dogs," and were regarded as non-combatants and a nuisance, and the average private never let one pass without whistling and calling dogs. In fact, the general had to issue an army order threatening punishment for the ridicule hurled at staff officers and couriers. They were looked upon as simply "hangers on," or in other words, as yellow sheep-killing dogs, that if you would say "booh" at, would yelp and get under their master's heels. Mike Snyder was General George Maney's "yaller dog," and I believe here is where Joe Jefferson, in Rip Van Winkle, got the name of Rip's dog Snyder. At all times of day or night you could hear, "wheer, hyat, hyat, haer, haer, hugh, Snyder, whoopee, hyat, whoopee, Snyder, here, here," when a staff officer or courier happened to pass. The reason of this was that the private knew and felt that there was just that much more loading, shooting and fighting for him; and there are the fewest number of instances on record where a staff officer or courier ever fired a gun in their country's cause; and even at this late day, when I hear an old soldier telling of being on some general's staff, I always think of the letter "E." In fact, later in the war I was detailed as special courier and staff officer for General Hood, which office I held three days. But while I held the office in passing a guard I always told them I was on Hood's staff, and ever afterwards I made those three days' staff business last me the balance of the war. I could pass any guard in the army by using the magic words, "staff officer." It beat all the countersigns ever invented. It was the "open sesame" of war and discipline.]

Their last hope had set. They hated war. To their minds the South was a great tyrant, and the Confederacy a fraud. They were deserting by thousands. They had no love or respect for General Bragg. When men were to be shot or whipped, the whole army was marched to the horrid scene to see a poor trembling wretch tied to a post and a platoon of twelve men drawn up in line to put him to death, and the hushed command of "Ready, aim, fire!" would make the soldier, or conscript, I should say, loathe the very name of Southern Confederacy. And when some miserable wretch was to be whipped and branded for being absent ten days without leave, we had to see him kneel down and have his head shaved smooth and slick as a peeled onion, and then stripped to the naked skin. Then a strapping fellow with a big rawhide would make the blood flow and spurt at every lick, the wretch begging and howling like a hound, and then he was branded with a red hot iron with the letter D on both hips, when he was marched through the army to the music of the "Rogue's March." It was enough. None of the General Bragg's soldiers ever loved him. They had no faith in his ability as a general. He was looked upon as a merciless tyrant. The soldiers were very scantily fed. Bragg never was a good feeder or commissary-general. Rations with us were always scare. No extra rations were ever allowed to the negroes who were with us as servants. No coffee or whisky or tobacco were ever allowed to be issued to the troops. If they obtained these luxuries, they were not from the government. These luxuries were withheld in order to crush the very heart and spirit of his troops. We were crushed. Bragg was the great autocrat. In the mind of the soldier, his word was law. He loved to crush the spirit of his men. The more of a hang-dog look they had about them the better was General Bragg pleased. Not a single soldier in the whole army ever loved or respected him. But he is dead now.

Peace to his ashes!

We became starved skeletons; naked and ragged rebels. The chronic diarrhoea became the scourge of the army. Corinth became one vast hospital. Almost the whole army attended the sick call every morning. All the water courses went dry, and we used water out of filthy pools.

Halleck was advancing; we had to fortify Corinth. A vast army, Grant, Buell, Halleck, Sherman, all were advancing on Corinth. Our troops were in no condition to fight. In fact, they had seen enough of this miserable yet tragic farce. They were ready to ring down the curtain, put out the footlights and go home. They loved the Union anyhow, and were always opposed to this war. But breathe softly the name of Bragg. It had more terror than the advancing hosts of Halleck's army. The shot and shell would come tearing through our ranks. Every now and then a soldier was killed or wounded, and we thought what "magnificent" folly. Death was welcome. Halleck's whole army of blue coats had no terror now. When we were drawn up in line of battle, a detail of one-tenth of the army was placed in our rear to shoot us down if we ran. No pack of hounds under the master's lash, or body of penitentiary convicts were ever under greater surveillance. We were tenfold worse than slaves; our morale was a thing of the past; the glory of war and the pride of manhood had been sacrificed upon Bragg's tyrannical holocaust. But enough of this.

THE BULL OF THE WOODS

On our way to Lafayette from Lee & Gordon's mill, I remember a ludicrous scene, almost bordering on sacrilege. Rosecrans' army was very near us, and we expected before three days elapsed to be engaged in battle. In fact, we knew there must be a fight or a foot race, one or the other. We could smell, as it were, "the battle afar off."

One Sabbath morning it was announced that an eloquent and able LL. D., from Nashville, was going to preach, and as the occasion was an exceedingly solemn one, we were anxious to hear this divine preach from God's Holy Word; and as he was one of the "big ones," the whole army was formed in close column and stacked their arms. The cannon were parked, all pointing back toward Chattanooga. The scene looked weird and picturesque. It was in a dark wilderness of woods and vines and overhanging limbs. In fact, it seemed but the home of the owl and the bat, and other varmints that turn night into day. Everything looked solemn. The trees looked solemn, the scene looked solemn, the men looked solemn, even the horses looked solemn. You may be sure, reader, that we felt solemn.

The reverend LL. D. had prepared a regular war sermon before he left home, and of course had to preach it, appropriate or not appropriate; it was in him and had to come out. He opened the service with a song. I did remember the piece that was sung, but right now I cannot recall it to memory; but as near as I can now recollect here is his prayer, *verbatim et literatim:*

"Oh, Thou immaculate, invisible, eternal and holy Being, the exudations of whose effulgence illuminates this terrestrial sphere, we approach Thy presence, being covered all over with wounds and bruises and putrifying sores, from the crowns of our heads to the soles of our feet. And Thou, O Lord, art our dernier resort. The whole world is one great machine, managed by Thy puissance. The beautific splendors of Thy face irradiate the celestial region and felicitate the saints. There are the most exuberant profusions of Thy grace, and the sempiternal effux of Thy glory. God is an abyss of light, a circle whose center is everywhere and His circumference nowhere. Hell is the dark world made up of spiritual sulphur and other ignited ingredients, disunited and unharmonized, and without that pure balsamic oil that flows from the heart of God."

When the old fellow got this far, I lost the further run of his prayer, but regret very much that I did so, because it was so grand and fine that I would have liked very much to have kept such an appropriate prayer for posterity. In fact, it lays it on heavy over any prayer I ever heard, and I think the new translators ought to get it and have it put in their book as a sample prayer. But they will have to get the balance of it from the eminent LL. D. In fact, he was so "high larnt" that I don't think anyone understood him but the generals. The colonels might every now and then have understood a word, and maybe a few of the captains and lieutenants, because Lieutenant Lansdown told me he understood every word the preacher said, and further informed me that it was none of your one-horse, old-fashioned country prayers that privates knew anything about, but was bang-up, first-rate, orthodox.

Well, after singing and praying, he took his text. I quote entirely from memory. "Blessed be the Lord God, who teaches my hands to war and my fingers to fight." Now, reader, that was the very subject we boys did not want to hear preached on—on that occasion at least. We felt like some other subject would have suited us better. I forget how he commenced his sermon, but I remember that after he got warmed up a little, he began to pitch in on the Yankee nation, and gave them particular fits as to their geneology. He said that we of the South had descended from the royal and aristocratic blood of the Huguenots of France, and of the cavaliers of England, etc.; but that the Yankees were the descendants of the crop-eared Puritans and witch burners, who came over in the Mayflower, and settled at Plymouth Rock. He was warm on this subject, and waked up the echoes of the forest. He said that he and his brethren would fight the Yankees in this world, and if God permit, chase their frightened ghosts in the next, through fire and brimstone.

About this time we heard the awfullest racket, produced by some wild animal tearing through the woods toward us, and the cry, "Look out! look out! hooie! hooie! hooie! look out!" and there came running right through our midst a wild bull, mad with terror and fright, running right over and knocking down the divine, and scattering Bibles and hymn books in every direction. The services were brought to a close without the doxology.

This same brave chaplain rode along with our brigade, on an old string-haltered horse, as we advanced to the attack at Chickamauga, exhorting the boys to be brave, to aim low, and to kill the Yankees as if they were wild beasts. He was eloquent and patriotic. He stated that if he only had a gun he too would go along as a private soldier. You could hear his voice echo and re-echo over the hills. He had worked up his patriotism to a pitch of genuine bravery and daring that I had never seen exhibited, when fliff, fluff, fluff, *fluff*, FLUFF, *FLUFF*—a whir, a BOOM! and a shell screams through the air. The reverend LL. D. stops to listen, like an old sow when she hears the wind, and says, "Remember, boys, that he who is killed will sup tonight in Paradise." Some soldier hallooed at the top of his voice, "Well, parson, you come along and take supper with us." Boom! whir! a bomb burst, and the parson at that moment put spurs to his horse and was seen to limber to the rear, and almost every soldier yelled out, "The parson isn't hungry, and never eats supper." I remember this incident, and so does every member of the First Tennessee Regiment.

PRESENTMENT, OR THE WING OF THE ANGEL OF DEATH

Presentment is always a mystery. The soldier may at one moment be in good spirits, laughing and talking. The wing of the death angel touches him. He knows that his time has come. It is but a question of time with him then. He knows that his days are numbered. I cannot explain it. God has numbered the hairs of our heads, and not a sparrow falls without His knowledge. How much more valuable are we than many sparrows?

We had stopped at Lee & Gordon's mill, and gone into camp for the night. Three days' rations were being issued. When Bob Stout was given his rations he refused to take them. His face wore a serious, woe-begone expression. He was asked if the was sick, and said "No," but added, "Boys, my days are numbered, my time has come. In three days from today, I will be lying right yonder on that hillside a corpse. Ah, you may laugh; my time has come. I've got a twenty dollar gold piece in my pocket that I've carried through the war, and a silver watch that my father sent me through the lines. Please take them off when I am dead, and give them to Captain Irvine, to give to my father when he gets back home. Here are my clothing and blanket that any one who wishes them may have. My rations I do not wish at all. My gun and cartridge-box I expect to die with."

The next morning the assembly sounded about two o'clock. We commenced our march in the darkness, and marched twenty-five miles to a little town by the name of Lafayette, to the relief of General Pillow, whose command had been attacked at that place. After accomplishing this, we marched back by another road to Chickamauga. We camped on the banks of Chickamauga on Friday night, and Saturday morning we commenced to cross over. About twelve o'clock we had crossed. No sooner had we crossed than an order came to double quick. General Forrest's cavalry had opened the battle. Even then the spent balls were falling amongst us with that peculiar thud so familiar to your old soldier.

Double quick! There seemed to be no rest for us. Forrest is needing reinforcements. Double quick, close up in the rear! siz, siz, double quick, boom, hurry up, bang, bang, a rattle de bang, bang, siz, boom, boom, boom, hurry up, double quick, boom, bang, halt, front, right dress, boom, boom, and three soldiers are killed and twenty wounded. Billy Webster's arm was torn out by the roots and he killed, and a fragment of shell buried itself in Jim McEwin's side, also killing Mr. Fain King, a conscript from Mount Pleasant. Forward, guide center, march, charge bayonets, fire at will, commence firing. (This is where the LL. D. ran.) We debouched through the woods, firing as we marched, the Yankee line about two hundred yards off. Bang, bang siz, siz. It was a sort of running fire. We kept up a constant fire as we advanced. In ten minutes we were face to face with the foe. It was but a question as to who could load and shoot the fastest. The army was not up. Bragg was not ready for a general battle. The big battle was fought the next day, Sunday. We held our position for two hours and ten minutes in the midst of a deadly and galling fire, being enfiladed and almost surrounded, when General Forrest galloped up and said, "Colonel Field, look out, you are almost surrounded; you had better fall back." The order was given to retreat. I ran through a solid line of blue coats. As I fell back, they were upon the right of us, they were upon the left of us, they were in front of us, they were in the rear of us. It was a perfect hornets' nest. The balls whistled around our ears like the escape valves of ten thousand engines. The woods seemed to be blazing; everywhere, at every jump, would rise a lurking foe. But to get up and dust was all we could do. I was running along by the side of Bob Stout. General Preston Smith stopped me and asked if our brigade was falling back. I told him it was. He asked me the second time if it was Maney's brigade that was falling back. I told him it was. I heard him call out, "Attention, forward!" One solid sheet of leaden hail was falling around me. I heard General Preston Smith's brigade open. It seemed to be platoons of artillery. The earth jarred and trembled like an earthquake. Deadly missiles were flying in every direction. It was the very incarnation of death itself. I could almost hear the shriek of the death angel passing over the scene. General Smith was killed in ten minutes after I saw him. Bob Stout and myself stopped. Said I, "Bob, you weren't killed, as you expected." He did not reply, for at that very moment a solid shot from the Federal guns struck him between the waist and the hip, tearing off one leg and scattering his bowels all over the ground. I heard him shriek out, "O, O, God!" His spirit had flown before his body struck the ground. Farewell, friend; we will meet over yonder.

When the cannon ball struck Billy Webster, tearing his arm out of the socket, he did not die immediately, but as we were advancing to the attack, we left him and the others lying where they fell upon the battle-field; but when we fell back to the place where we had left our knapsacks,

Billy's arm had been dressed by Dr. Buist, and he seemed to be quite easy. He asked Jim Fogey to please write a letter to his parents at home. He wished to dictate the letter. He asked me to please look in his knapsack and get him a clean shirt, and said that he thought he would feel better if he could get rid of the blood that was upon him. I went to hunt for his knapsack and found it, but when I got back to where he was, poor, good Billy Webster was dead. He had given his life to his country. His spirit is with the good and brave. No better or braver man than Billy Webster ever drew the breath of life. His bones lie yonder today, upon the battlefield of Chickamauga. I loved him; he was my friend. Many and many a dark night have Billy and I stood together upon the silent picket post. Ah, reader, my heart grows sick and I feel sad while I try to write my recollections of that unholy and uncalled for war. But He that ruleth the heavens doeth all things well.

AFTER THE BATTLE

We remained upon the battlefield of Chickamauga all night. Everything had fallen into our hands. We had captured a great many prisoners and small arms, and many pieces of artillery and wagons and provisions. The Confederate and Federal dead, wounded, and dying were everywhere scattered over the battlefield. Men were lying where they fell, shot in every conceivable part of the body. Some with their entrails torn out and still hanging to them and piled up on the ground beside them, and they still alive. Some with their under jaw torn off, and hanging by a fragment of skin to their cheeks, with their tongues lolling from their mouth, and they trying to talk. Some with both eyes shot out, with one eye hanging down on their cheek. In fact, you might walk over the battlefield and find men shot from the crown of the head to the tip end of the toe. And then to see all those dead, wounded and dying horses, their heads and tails drooping, and they seeming to be so intelligent as if they comprehended everything. I felt like shedding a tear for those innocent dumb brutes.

Reader, a battlefield, after the battle, is a sad and sorrowful sight to look at. The glory of war is but the glory of battle, the shouts, and cheers, and victory.

A soldier's life is not a pleasant one. It is always, at best, one of privations and hardships. The emotions of patriotism and pleasure hardly counterbalance the toil and suffering that he has to undergo in order to enjoy his patriotism and pleasure. Dying on the field of battle and glory is about the easiest duty a soldier has to undergo. It is the living, marching, fighting, shooting soldier that has the hardships of war to carry. When a brave soldier is killed he is at rest. The living soldier knows not at what moment he, too, may be called on to lay down his life on the altar of his country.

The dead are heroes, the living are but men compelled to do the drudgery and suffer the privations incident to the thing called "glorious war."

A NIGHT AMONG THE DEAD

We rested on our arms where the battle ceased. All around us everywhere were the dead and wounded, lying scattered over the ground, and in many places piled in heaps. Many a sad and heart-rending scene did I witness upon this battlefield of Chickamauga. Our men died the death of heroes. I sometimes think that surely our brave men have not died in vain. It is true, our cause is lost, but a people who loved those brave and noble heroes should ever cherish their memory as men who died for them. I shed a tear over their memory. They gave their all to their country. Abler pens than mine must write their epitaphs, and tell of their glories and heroism. I am but a poor writer, at best, and only try to tell of the events that I saw.

One scene I now remember, that I can imperfectly relate. While a detail of us were passing over the field of death and blood, with a dim lantern, looking for our wounded soldiers to carry to the hospital, we came across a group of ladies, looking among the killed and wounded for their relatives, when I heard one of the ladies say, "There they come with their lanterns." I approached the ladies and asked them for whom they were looking. They told me the name, but I have forgotten it. We passed on, and coming to a pile of our slain, we had turned over several of our dead, when one of the ladies screamed out, "O, there he is, Poor fellow! Dead, dead, dead!" She ran to the pile of slain and raised the dead man's head and placed it on her lap and began kissing him and saying, "O, O, they have killed my darling, my darling, my darling! O, mother, mother, what must I do! My poor, poor darling! O, they have killed him, they have killed him!" I could witness the scene no longer.

"DEAD ANGLE"

The First and Twenty-seventh Tennessee Regiments will ever remember the battle of "Dead Angle," which was fought June 27th, on the Kennesaw line, near Marietta, Georgia. It was one of the hottest and longest days of the year, and one of the most desperate and determinedly resisted battles fought during the whole war. Our regiment was stationed on an angle, a little spur of the mountain, or rather promontory of a range of hills, extending far out beyond the main line of battle, and was subject to the enfilading fire of forty pieces of artillery of the Federal batteries. It seemed fun for the guns of the whole Yankee army to play upon this point. We would work hard every night to strengthen our breastworks, and the very next day they would be torn down smooth with the ground by solid shots and shells from the guns of the enemy. Even the little trees and bushes which had been left for shade, were cut down as so much stubble. For more than a week this constant firing had been kept up against this salient point. In the meantime, the skirmishing in the valley below resembled the sounds made by ten thousand wood-choppers.

Well, on the fatal morning of June 27th, the sun rose clear and cloudless, the heavens seemed made of brass, and the earth of iron, and as the sun began to mount toward the zenith, everything became quiet, and no sound was heard save a peckerwood on a neighboring tree, tapping on its old trunk, trying to find a worm for his dinner. We all knew it was but the dead calm that precedes the storm. On the distant hills we could plainly see officers dashing about hither and thither, and the Stars and Stripes moving to and fro, and we knew the Federals were making preparations for the mighty contest. We could hear but the rumbling sound of heavy guns, and the distant tread of a marching army, as a faint roar of the coming storm, which was soon to break the ominous silence with the sound of conflict, such as was scarcely ever before heard on this earth. It seemed that the arch-angel of Death stood and looked on with outstretched wings, while all the earth was silent, when all at once a hundred guns from the Federal line opened upon us, and for more than an hour they poured their solid and chain shot, grape and shrapnel right upon this salient point, defended by our regiment alone, when, all of a sudden, our pickets jumped into our works and reported the Yankees advancing, and almost at the same time a solid line of blue coats came up the hill. I discharged my gun, and happening to look up, there was the beautiful flag of the Stars and Stripes flaunting right in my face, and I heard John Branch, of the Rock City Guards, commanded by Captain W. D. Kelley, who were next Company H, say, "Look at that Yankee flag; shoot that fellow; snatch that flag out of his hand!" My pen is unable to describe the scene of carnage and death that ensued in the next two hours. Column after column of Federal soldiers were crowded upon that line, and by referring to the history of the war you will find they were massed in column forty columns deep; in fact, the whole force of the Yankee army was hurled against this point, but no sooner would a regiment mount our works than they were shot down or surrendered, and soon we had every "gopher hole" full of Yankee prisoners. Yet still the Yankees came. It seemed impossible to check the onslaught, but every man was true to his trust, and seemed to think that at that moment the whole responsibility of the Confederate government was rested upon his shoulders. Talk about other battles, victories, shouts, cheers, and triumphs, but in comparison with this day's fight, all others dwarf into insignificance. The sun beaming down on our uncovered heads, the thermometer being one hundred and ten degrees in the shade, and a solid line of blazing fire right from the muzzles of the

Yankee guns being poured right into our very faces, singeing our hair and clothes, the hot blood of our dead and wounded spurting on us, the blinding smoke and stifling atmosphere filling our eyes and mouths, and the awful concussion causing the blood to gush out of our noses and ears, and above all, the roar of battle, made it a perfect pandemonium. Afterward I heard a soldier express himself by saying that he thought "Hell had broke loose in Georgia, sure enough."

I have heard men say that if they ever killed a Yankee during the war they were not aware of it. I am satisfied that on this memorable day, every man in our regiment killed from one score to four score, yea, five score men. I mean from twenty to one hundred each. All that was necessary was to load and shoot. In fact, I will ever think that the reason they did not capture our works was the impossibility of their living men passing over the bodies of their dead. The ground was piled up with one solid mass of dead and wounded Yankees. I learned afterwards from the burying squad that in some places they were piled up like cord wood, twelve deep.

After they were time and time again beaten back, they at last were enabled to fortify a line under the crest of the hill, only thirty yards from us, and they immediately commenced to excavate the earth with the purpose of blowing up our line.

We remained here three days after the battle. In the meantime the woods had taken fire, and during the nights and days of all that time continued to burn, and at all times, every hour of day and night, you could hear the shrieks and screams of the poor fellows who were left on the field, and a stench, so sickening as to nauseate the whole of both armies, arose from the decaying bodies of the dead left lying on the field.

On the third morning the Yankees raised a white flag, asked an armistice to bury their dead, not for any respect either army had for the dead, but to get rid of the sickening stench. I get sick now when I happen to think about it. Long and deep trenches were dug, and hooks made from bayonets crooked for the purpose, and all the dead were dragged and thrown pell mell into these trenches. Nothing was allowed to be taken off the dead, and finely dressed officers, with gold watch chains dangling over their vests, were thrown into the ditches. During the whole day both armies were hard at work, burying the Federal dead.

Every member of the First and Twenty-seventh Tennessee Regiments deserves a wreath of imperishable fame, and a warm place in the hearts of their countrymen, for their gallant and heroic valor at the battle of Dead Angle. No man distinguished himself above another. All did their duty, and the glory of one is but the glory and just tribute of the others.

After we had abandoned the line, and on coming to a little stream of water, I undressed for the purpose of bathing, and after undressing found my arm all battered and bruised and bloodshot from my wrist to my shoulder, and as sore as a blister. I had shot one hundred and twenty times that day. My gun became so hot that frequently the powder would flash before I could ram home the ball, and I had frequently to exchange my gun for that of a dead comrade.

Colonel H. R. Field was loading and shooting the same as any private in the ranks when he fell off the skid from which he was shooting right over my shoulder, shot through the head. I laid him down in the trench, and he said, "Well, they have got me at last, but I have killed fifteen of them; time about is fair play, I reckon." But Colonel Field was not killed —only wounded, and one side paralyzed. Captain Joe P. Lee, Captain Mack Campbell, Lieutenant T. H. Maney, and other officers of the regiment, threw rocks and beat them in their faces with sticks. The Yankees did the same. The rocks came in upon us like a perfect hail storm, and the Yankees seemed very obstinate, and in no hurry to get away from our front, and we had to keep up the firing and shooting them down in self-defense. They seemed to walk up and take death as coolly as if they were automatic or wooden men, and our boys did not shoot for the fun of the thing. It was, verily, a life and death grapple, and the least flicker on our part, would have been sure death to all. We could not be reinforced on account of our position, and we had to stand up to the rack, fodder or no fodder. When the Yankees fell back, and the firing ceased, I never saw so many broken down and exhausted men in my life. I was as sick as a horse, and as wet with blood and sweat as I could be, and many of our men were vomiting with excessive fatigue, over-exhaustion, and sunstroke; our tongues were parched and cracked for water, and our faces blackened with powder and smoke, and our dead and wounded were piled indiscriminately in the trenches. There was not a single man in the company who was not wounded, or had holes shot through his hat and clothing. Captain Beasley was killed, and nearly all his company killed and wounded. The Rock City Guards were almost piled in heaps and so was our company. Captain Joe P. Lee was badly wounded. Poor Walter Hood and Jim Brandon were lying there among us, while their spirits were in heaven; also, William A. Hughes, my old mess-mate and friend, who had clerked with me for S. F. & J. M. Mayes, and who had slept with me for lo! these many years, and a boy who loved me more than any other person on earth has ever done. I had just discharged the contents of my gun into the bosoms of two men, one right behind the other, killing them both, and was re-loading, when a Yankee rushed upon me, having me at a disadvantage, and said, "You have killed my two brothers, and now I've got you." Everything I had ever done rushed through my mind. I heard the roar, and felt the flash of fire, and saw my more than friend, William A.

Hughes, grab the muzzle of the gun, receiving the whole contents in his hand and arm, and mortally wounding him. Reader, he died for me. In saving my life, he lost his own. When the infirmary corps carried him off, all mutilated and bleeding he told them to give me "Florence Fleming" (that was the name of his gun, which he had put on it in silver letters), and to give me his blanket and clothing. He gave his life for me, and everything that he had. It was the last time that I ever saw him, but I know that away up yonder, beyond the clouds, blackness, tempest and night, and away above the blue vault of heaven, where the stars keep their ceaseless vigils, away up yonder in the golden city of the New Jerusalem, where God and Jesus Christ, our Savior, ever reign, we will sometime meet at the marriage supper of the Son of God, who gave His life for the redemption of the whole world.

from *Red Hills and Cotton: An Upcountry Memory*

Ben Robertson (1903–1943)

Ben Robertson, of Clemson, South Carolina, became a prominent journalist in the 1920s and 1930s, covering national affairs for major newspapers. Going to England at the outbreak of World War II, Robertson alternated between writing about the war raging around him and the South Carolina of his youth. *Red Hills and Cotton*, published in 1942, affectionately evoked that society and tried to describe its mysteries to a later age. The year after its publication and shortly after accepting an offer to become the chief of the New York *Herald-Tribune*'s London bureau, Robertson died in a plane crash in Portugal.

Many people in trouble came to my grandfather for advice and help—the politicians, the preachers, the kinfolks, the colored folks, the tenants. He talked to them all on the piazza. Once I remember my Uncle Jule came to tell my grandfather and all the rest of us that we ought to go right away to the Panhandle of Texas. My Uncle Jule had caught Panhandle fever, and he wanted the last one of us to sell out in Carolina, pack up, and head straight for Texas. This was a kind of fever we have always been susceptible to—we have always been tempted by panhandles and gold mines and far-off bottom lands and distant valleys, by western places that have just been waiting for us to come into them and make a million dollars. Often too it has been easier for us to go somewhere than it has been to stay at home. My Uncle Jule this time was excited; he was sure that the Texas Panhandle was the coming country, things were bound to boom in that country. So he talked and we sat on the piazza and listened. He said: "I'm going." Turning then to my Uncle Jim, he asked: "How do you feel, Jim?" My Uncle Jim was a rambling man; he too had been having problems at home—cotton was under seven cents, bills for fertilizer were owing. "I'm interested," said my Uncle Jim. With that assurance, my Uncle Jule then turned toward my Uncle Wade. But before he could say anything further, my grandfather interrupted. "Boys," said he, "now just you hold on—I don't want too many of you going out there at one time. If too many of you go, I might not have money enough to get you all back."

Out on the wide quiet piazza, my grandfather always sat in a low straight chair—the chair he turned upside down whenever he took his nap. My grandmother was a lady who liked a rocking-chair; she would sit in a broad hickory rocker and rock. The rest of us would sit on the slabs of granite that composed the front steps. Shortly after dusk, our Great-Uncle Bob would arrive from his house down the creek, and he would drop down on the edge of the porch with one foot on the hard sandy ground. The immense Southern night would descend on us all and then the talk would start—my grandmother would rock, and we would listen, and our grandfather and our Great-Uncle Bob would tell us about the Civil War. We would sit in the tremendous starlight, and sometimes a warm, worn breeze would stir, and we would sit still and listen to the story the two men loved to tell. Thirty years have passed since then, but I can still close my eyes and hear them—hear their Southern voices, hear the katydids in the oak trees, the droning chorus of the crickets; hear a hound dog howling, a lean mourning sound; hear still farther away the lonesome remote rumbling of a train.

"After holding ourselves in readiness for battle through the night, on Sunday a.m., just at sunrise, General Scott opened fire on us from the opposite side of the stream. By eight o'clock we discovered his army had crossed the steam—the Civil War had started." My grandfather would hesitate there for a full effect. He had a feeling for story-telling, for the effects. "Two companies were left to guard the bridge and the rest of us had no more sense than to go for them at a double-quick pace. We soon found ourselves facing the enemy in an open field where the battle was on in earnest. Your Cousin Taylor was killed in the very first volley." Again our grandfather would pause. "Elisha Ferguson fell mortally wounded. It was soon discovered that the enemy was endeavoring to surround us. At this juncture General Bee made along our lines apparently as cool as if nothing serious was on hand. General Bee gave orders to fall back on the Henry house, a distance of eight hundred yards, where we would continue the fight. General Bee was killed before we reached the Henry house." We all knew about General Bee—they had brought him back to South Carolina for burial, he was in the burying ground at the foot of our valley. Our grandfather would continue: "Well, by two o'clock in the afternoon if we had known anything about war, we might readily have concluded we were in on the eve of a massacre, but we didn't know anything then about war. An hour later we were wiser—a man learns a lot about war even in the first battle."

On and on. The Seven Days' Battle, the Wilderness. General Jackson in the valley of the Shenandoah. General Lee. The sound of the Yankees' pickaxes, digging under Petersburg. And Richmond, always Richmond. To save Richmond. It became a holy place to us, a place to be loved forever like Plymouth Rock and Valley Forge and the Mississippi River. On and on. The katydids and the crickets. The hound dog. Another train, echoing through the sleeping hills. My grandfather would finish. My Uncle Bob would start over. "We were at Fredericksburg, and our men held their fire until the Yankees were almost on us ... the slaughter was desperate. I passed over the field of battle a few hours later and the dead were so numerous that many of them were being placed in a common grave."

The campaign would turn to the Tennessee. "Chickamauga, and that was the bloodiest battle of the war. In Virginia we often fought foreign-born men whom Northerners had hired to take their places, but there at Chickamauga it was us against men from Ohio, Indiana, and Illinois—it was us against our brothers."

Whenever our grandfather and our Great-Uncle Bob had finished talking, we would sit on for a while, alone on the piazza in the great motionless night, and our hearts would nearly break within us. We had lost, we had lost.

Very often they would talk to us about Jackson and Lee. My grandfather and my Great-Uncle Bob had been privates in the armies of those generals, but they had known them—sometimes they had talked to them, often had been near by. The relationship between everyone in the Confederate Army seemed always to have been intimate, to have been brotherly and close. Often Confederate privates had brothers who were colonels—our Cousin Bob had been a colonel, and my grandfather had saved him at Lookout Mountain. He had placed the cousin colonel, wounded, on the back of old Grayboy, one of our horses, and, being himself too tired to walk, our grandfather had held on to Grayboy's tail and the horse had brought them both to safety. Within our own family, there were privates, sergeants, captains and a colonel in the Confederate Army. It was a democratic army, a personal army, and my grandfather and my Great-Uncle Bob all their lives loved Lee and Jackson like their father. They seemed to have felt when those generals were camped with them that they and the rest of the Confederate Army were their personal protectors. It is the way we have always felt in the South toward our leaders. Once one of my aunts went to the battlefield at Kings Mountain when President Hoover was there to dedicate a memorial to our people who had been killed in 1780 in that battle. My aunt came back home astonished at the number of secret-service men and guards that had been thrown around the President. "Who did they think they were protecting him from?" asked my aunt. "There was nobody there except us—just the Governor and the president of the university and a lot of home-folks from the cotton mills and the farms." It was shocking to my aunt to see a President of the United States

142

surrounded by a guard in South Carolina. She and all the rest of us have always regarded ourselves as the protectors of the President—as protectors even of President Herbert Hoover.

. . .

My kinfolks did not live in magnolia groves with tall white columns to hold up the front porches. We did not care for magnolias—they were swampy; and as for the white columns, we considered them pretentious. We did not call our farms plantations in the Upcountry, and we did not call ourselves old Southern planters—we were old Southern farmers. We were plain people, intending to be plain. We believed in plain clothes, plain cooking, plain houses, plain churches to attend preaching in on Sunday. We were Southerners, native-born and of the heart of the South, but we preferred the ways of Salem, Massachusetts, to those of Charleston, South Carolina. Charleston was a symbol to us—it represented luxury and easy soft living and all the evils of Egypt. Charleston believed in a code that shocked us. It was Cavalier from the start; we were Puritan.

The leading Charlestonians were descended from gentlemen in England, and they actually talked about who was a gentleman born and who was not. We said God help us if we ever became that kind of gentleman; gentleman with us had to win his title by the quality of his acts. Charlestonians had come to the colony of South Carolina with money and china dishes and English silver. We had come down along the mountains from Pennsylvania with nothing—we had walked. The North was our mother country—John Knox and Plymouth, the church without a bishop, the country without a king, and when we named a town in South Carolina by the name of Chester, we were naming it for Chester in Pennsylvania, not for the Chester in Britian. We gave our places Northern names and Biblical names—Chesterfield, York, Ebenezer, Mount Zion, Bethany Grove, Pisgah; and we called places for whimsies that struck our fancy—Nine Times, Lickety Split Creek, Honea Path, Due West. Once in the early days our kinfolks named a creek for a good, faithful hound dog —it is still called that on the map. It must have been a magnificent feeling to march down a continent, giving names to town sites and to mountains and streams. That must have marked the start of our real feeling for freedom. We understand in our country why Walt Whitman liked to sing the names of American rivers, why for apparently no reason at all he listed them one after another. We know what swept Thomas Wolfe when he wrote of the golden Catawba, of the Swannanoa, of the Little Tennessee —it was lightning from his heart.

Charlestonians too had the same sort of love for place names that we had—they gave good original names to Hell Hole Swamp, to Christ Church Parish—but they named other swamps and parishes for Lord

Colleton and Lord Ashley and for the Earl of Craven. Charlestonians settled a lowland; we came into a hill region—it was inevitable that we should have fought. From the beginning, the difference in our views was fundamental, and the time was bound to come when there would not be room enough in Carolina for two such conceptions of a state. There would not be space enough even in the South, nor even in the whole of the West. One of us had to whip the other to a farewell and a frazzle. In Carolina from 1750 to 1860 we lost to Charleston; since that time Charleston has lost to us. The Charleston idea, which also became the Mobile-Natchez idea, the idea of all the low countries and deltas, was beaten by the troops of the Federal Union, and Charleston in losing took all of us in all of the upcountries along with it. Our Upcountry idea is an idea within a beaten idea, and has been a conquered idea too for eighty years, but we have not let it slip from us. We know what we want. We are Southern Jeffersonian Puritans who have never given in to Alexander Hamilton's state. Sometimes I think there is more of Salem in our Southern hills today than is left even in Salem. We still believe in reform —in reform and more reform, slow and steady and never letting up, and when necessary we believe in revolution. We are not fearful of revolution. It has its place.

John C. Calhoun lived at the foot of our valley, where Twelve Mile and Keowee come together to form the Seneca, but Calhoun was not popular with our kinfolks. His land came almost up to our land, but that did not matter. His people were the same sort of people ours were, and our feud with him, like every other kind of feud we ever had with anyone, was personal. Our kinfolks and his had traveled together in the same caravans for nearly a hundred years before Calhoun became Calhoun; we remembered when his grandmother was scalped at Longcane in 1760; we remembered his father, Patrick Calhoun, who was as afraid as we were of voting for the new Federal Constitution. John C. Calhoun was an Upcountry Carolinian, but he also was a politician, and everybody knows what often happens to a politician. He sold us out. The cause of the Lowcountry became his cause—we were not important enough in 1815 for Mr. John C. Calhoun.

Personally and politically we opposed Calhoun; we personally disliked his wife. She made fun of Mrs. Rachel Jackson for smoking a corncob pipe, and Mrs. Jackson was a Donelson—she was one of our cousins, and we did not stand for any public ridicule of our kinfolks. My Great-Aunt Narcissa said: "We certainly did not stand for a Charlestonian making fun of our kin." Mrs. Calhoun was a Charlestonian.

Calhoun very early in his cold and ambitious and great political career married his Charleston wife; she had a plantation and some money. He

144

kept his legal residence in the Upcountry in our district—our Courthouse continued to be his Courthouse, but that became merely a technicality, for after his marriage we never again saw him very often. He built columns on his house at the foot of our valley, planted magnolias in his yard, and our Great-Aunt Narcissa told us: "He even had himself sprinkled in the church of Charleston," the Protestant Episcopal church.

We preferred the Baptist, Methodist, and Presbyterian churches in the Upcountry to the church that copied the royal church of England. We were opposed to Episcopal ritual, to vested choirs, to stained-glass windows, and we in the Baptist and Presbyterian churches completely loathed the idea of an American church creating bishops. "Bishops," my Great-Aunt Narcissa said, "are kings—they even dress in purple." Mary, the colored woman, told us once that the reason the Charleston folks belonged to the Episcopal church was that they ran about all the week having such a good time that when Sunday came they were so worn out they wanted to rest, they wanted a church that would not disturb them, that would leave them to their quiet. The Upcountry folks, said Mary, worked through the week, and when Sunday came, they wanted to enjoy themselves, so they liked the Baptist church, which gave to everyone the liberty to rise up and shout.

Charleston as we looked down upon it was a worldly place, a sea city trading with remote London and Canton in heathen China. It had silks and a theater and artists came there to paint the portraits of the Rutledges and Ravenels. In the hills we were continental, pure back-woods, and we had determined to turn our backs on all foreign countries. We were going to get rich quick somehow in our Upcountry. We were going to accept Christ as our personal Saviour, and forget Europe with all of its squabbles and wars and worn-out religious faiths. In America we were going to build the greatest, freest, best nation the world had ever known.

Our spoons in the Upcountry were pewter, our clothes were spun on the loom, our beautiful curly maple and solid walnut furniture was made by hand, by some of the kinfolks. We lived only two hundred and fifty miles from Charleston, but we seldom went there unless there was a constitution to sign or a charter was up for discussion. We knew more about Texas and California than we knew about Charleston. We were a land people in the hills, were inland in our mind and in our experience, and our knowledge of Charleston's ocean was limited to the sound we listened to in the pink conch shell that held open the front hall door. The sea to us was a mystery. It was far off and we never forgot what our Grandmother Bowen said to us about it—that she would wait until she reached heaven to see the sea; that the first places she would look down upon from on high would be the Holy Land and the ocean.

Charleston was worldly and sumptuous, with the wicked walking on every side, but it too was American and Western, standing for a country without a king. It was Southern also and its relationship with us in the hills was always a family affair. It was hard on us for a hundred and ten years, and we have been hard on it for the past eighty. An Upcountry politician, running for the United States Senate, told the people of Charleston once that he did not care for their vote—the grass could grow in the Charleston streets for all that it mattered to him. And there was an Upcountry woman who had engraved on her tomb: "Born 1810—Died 1890. Lived Fifty Years." The other thirty years, it was explained, had been passed in Charleston. We have hated the lovely old city, but at the same time we have admired it—it has always had strength of mind and sometimes it has had genius. During the harried generation before the Civil War, it developed into a city state, into a sort of American Athens; it all but ruled the whole nation and bidding for glory, it swept us and all the rest of the South straight into secession. One of our tragedies in the hills was that we did not hate Charleston enough; we were not opposed to it with complete violence nor with absoluteness of conviction. Our relationship with Charleston was like that of our Great-great-Uncle Billy and our Great-great-Uncle Alf—we did not speak to Charleston but we would knock down any stranger who spoke of it with a jeer. After all, Charleston is Carolinian—even if its streets are flat. It does not please us even now to hear Yankees ridiculed in Europe.

The Charleston idea and the hill idea of the Southern Scotch Irish have had this in common throughout the South since the beginning: both have been against the Northern factory system, both have been fearful of the sort of state the Northern capitalists intended to set up in the United States. Almost all Southerners still are afraid of letting themselves fall into the Northern power of money. Even now we put more faith in a cotton bale than we put in money. We are primary people, we believe in tangible things—in abstract thought, but in tangible things. In faith, in love, in cotton bales, in acres of lands, in mules. We do not understand shares and stocks, the use of money to make money. We want to own our own jobs, to work for a man whom we know personally, to live in our own house or in the house of a person with whom we are acquainted. We do not believe in a system that forces us to deal with an owner's agent. Again and again we come back to the central focus of all our economic fear—to the impersonal life, to the mechanical that kills you.

Our tragedy in the Southern hills was that before we had been beaten by the North in the Civil War we already, within the South, had been beaten by Charleston. Even before Fort Sumter was fired on we had lost in the hills. We had lost and all the time we had been as fearful almost of the sort of national life Charleston stood for as we had been afraid of the money-harnessing schemes of the Yankees. In the South both the hill people and the Charlestonians wanted a rural nation, but Charleston believed in a country of great estates, we in one of small ones. In the Upcountry, however, we lacked the absolute courage of our conviction; too often we also had coveted great estates. Ours seldom were as great as the plantations of the lowland gentry, but very often they were great enough—we would own a thousand acres of land. The Charleston system was based on slavery, ours on our own hands, yet we also bought slaves—we gave the sons land when they married, and the daughters slaves as their dowry. Sometimes we bred slaves as a crop, raising and selling them like cotton on the market.

My Great-Aunt Narcissa was a fierce Upcountry democrat, yet she had a personal servant. That personal servant, that slave, that thousand acres of land was the clay link in our fine steel chain; so when the pressure came we gave way. The folks in Salem said slavery was a nightmare, a crime, a horror, the sum of all wickedness; they said we were dirty, unkempt, poverty-stricken, ignorant, vicious. Our Baptist church in our valley was called Salem Baptist Church, but when 1860 was reached, we sent our delegate to the Carolina convention to vote with Charleston. Upcountry and Lowcountry—we seceded.

We had never intended to fight that war on a question of Negro slavery; we had wished to fight it on the proposition of a rural against an urban civilization, on human rights against money rights. We wanted time to abolish our slavery and we did not want another slavery thrust upon us. We were Puritans in the hills, spiritual people, and it was a profound blow to find ourselves maneuvered into a position of being obliged to defend Negro slavery with guns. Secession, too, smote us to the depths of our conscience. We loved the United States, the Union was like the Ark of the Covenant, it was holy. Our leaving the Union still troubles us in the true Biblical manner—into the third and fourth generations. It grieves us because we have always believed in the final triumph of good, and we have never been able to defend secession to ourselves after our losing the war. Right somehow makes its own might. It is evil that loses, and when God let us lose, it bowed our spirit to the dust. The surrender at Appomattox broke us economically, but it did us a far deeper injury than that: defeat put us spiritually on the defensive. We have been punished for eighty years for defending black slavery, but we still have our original conception, and we know in our hearts it is right. For us in the South, it is not complicated this time by slaves.

Our Grandmother Bowen would talk to us through the long summer heat at the house on Wolf Creek about our cause that had lost and had not lost. To justify secession seemed always on her mind, an essential that she must explain. It disturbed her incessantly, and she would repeat to us time and again the legal reasons that had made it lawful under the Constitution for us to dissolve the Union. The Union had been a pact, a mutual agreement, and in any court of law a compact under circumstances could be abolished. This was a sad predicament in which to find my grandmother, for she in her inner being did not believe in legal arguments, in appealing to courts. She believed in absolute right and wrong, in moralities, not in legalities. Furthermore, the arguments she gave to us about secession were not hers at all, but had been concluded for her by the cold expedient mind of John C. Calhoun, the man she had never admired. My grandmother trusted the heart, not the mind. She believed in the flame within, in touching the secret life, in inspiring human beings to act because of love and generosity and pity.

She held, like my grandfather, that the United States under the rule of the North had mistaken its great purpose in the world. And like my grandfather, she too cautioned us throughout her life: don't give in, your time will come, work and hold on, wait. My grandmother loathed the crudeness of the system that had developed the new cities beyond the Potomac River. This system existed on ruthlessness, on wealth and power, rather than on duty, and it had to win at any cost. Any cost. She had rules, a set of standards, and if success did not come within these, then she believed in accepting failure. There was a time to lose, she said. The passage she quoted most from the Bible was from the third chapter of Ecclesiastes: "To every thing there is a season, and a time to every purpose: a time to be born and a time to die; a time to plant, and a time to pluck up that which is planted; a time to kill, and a time to heal; a time of war, and a time of peace."

The new Northern system shocked my grandmother by its lack of social responsibility, by its lack of obligation—it took profits, it attempted to shift on to others its rightful losses. My grandmother could not understand how a corporation could hire men when times were good and then drop them from the payroll when times were hard; she held to the old rural relationship of landlord and tenant. A landlord provided a tenant with a house and fatback and meal, the ultimate necessities, no matter what happened to the price of cotton. Factories, like farms, said my grandmother, should be small; ownership should be dispersed. It made her sad to see more and more families from our valley move off to live in the strangeness of big cities. Her entire instinct warned her against leaving the fields, against working for organizations controlled by the new leaders who had organized vast accumulations of dollars.

A human being, my grandmother said, was responsible to others than himself — to the general community. And my grandmother's Southern individualism never included the individual right to make money at the community's cost. She was an old-fashioned Southern woman, conservative in a Southern way and radical; she had that very old radicalism that has always been latent in the South.

Yankees, according to my grandmother, lived off the sweat of human beings, and to impress upon us how intense was her disapproval of such persons, she sometimes would assemble us and say in a pleading, commanding voice: "Don't you dare marry a Yankee — marry someone in Carolina if you can, and if you can't find anyone suitable in Carolina, then look for someone in Georgia, but don't you marry a Yankee. They are just pigtracks." The grimness of my grandmother's life was Yankees.

from *Know Nothing*

Mary Lee Settle (1918–)

Mary Lee Settle grew up in a prominent family in Charleston, West Virginia, and worked as an actress and a model before serving in World War II. She has been a prolific writer, especially of historical fiction. Her most important work is the Beulah Quintet, a series focused on an imagined county in West Virginia. The selection here is from the middle novel of the five, *Know Nothing* (1960). It evokes the season of secession, juxtaposing the death of a marble-white Virginia lady with the uncertainties of a Confederate unit forming across the mountains in what became West Virginia.

Dr. Noah Kregg drove his gig carefully across the ice of the Gloriana. Down in the river valley the wind was not high and the snow drifted against his face softly, almost too thick for him to see the narrow carriage road which led from Kregg's Crossing through the still whiteness up the hill to the high flat plateau of Albion. He could not even hear his horse's hoofs on the icy road, and could barely make out a difference in the whiteness where twin vapors heaved out of the animal's nose from the climb and the cold.

He tried to keep his impatience and worry from making him use his whip, for fear the horse would slip on the ice; something besides the cloying river valley winter cold made his usually placid face stern and gray, made him take the valuable last minutes to think, think again, impotent and angry, what in the hell a man could do. He forced himself to consider logically, as a man of science, to remember what the old doctor in Lynchburg had taught him when, as a poor member of the Kregg clan, he had gone to learn to be a doctor in his office, because God had meant a poor Kregg to work for his training, not expect some frivolous shower of blessing from his cousins to take him to Edinburgh.

"Concentrate on the organs," the old man had said. "I never saw a woman die there wasn't something pheesically wrong. Pheesically. You leave the other to the ladies' novels."

But he knew it wasn't, in that blind snow, and in that blind despair he had to face at Albion, a thing of the organs.

For three years he had watched while Melinda Kregg wasted away before his eyes, when they would let him tend her instead of carting her away to some highfalutin foreign doctor who took their money and didn't know the Kreggs—how the pattern of their living and dying went. He forced himself to remember, as if that would help, the pale, graceful young woman whom Crawford had brought back to Albion. The first thing he had noticed about her was that she seldom laughed, and when she did, its gaiety seemed to break through from some secret place hidden inside her. He had seen the first seven years of the marriage, happy enough as marriages went, not warm, but considerate, polite, not tender.

But then, in his own secret heart, Dr. Noah didn't believe much in marriage. He couldn't honestly say he'd seen a great deal come from Kregg marriages anyhow. It was something they had, a family heaviness, like big noses or profligacy that he had seen run through the blood of other families he knew. He could have been describing Albion itself and set down that memory to the permeating influence of the mansion from which he had tended Crawford's parents to their graves at Kregg's Crossing Church.

When the horse pulled the gig up onto the huge plateau, the wind roared and stung. It swept the snow in frail racing veils across the wide lawn, a sea of white, the strong wind clearing glimpses of the black James River far in the distance below Albion's cliffs. The horse faltered with its weight, and absent-mindedly he touched her flank with the whip to urge her on. Through the cruel veils of snow he could see Albion, huge and solid, its thick white columns so anchored they seemed to ignore the driving storm. He brushed his hand across his tear-stung eyes to clear them.

People said that Melinda hadn't ever recovered from the birth of her third child. That August day, three summers before, he had stood beside her great bed after the labor and seen her turn her face away and stare out through the great columns at the sky. Her skin was still glossy with pain, but she had that dim quiet look of hers that dared even pain to make her react. When he tried to show her the healthy red baby girl in his two strong hands, she went on staring.

Dr. Noah could hardly admit it to himself, because of the way he had been brought up, because science fought with the stern Kregg God planted in his mind, but he had to observe, and he had seen too often that an excess of religion wasn't good for a woman's health. He had seen Melinda Kregg grasp at Crawford's God with a will of iron and lose and lose her strength to its blinding force.

Albion loomed huge above the tiny gig. He heard a door slam. One of the Negroes ran out, his head down against the battling wind, to tether his horse.

Miasma. He glanced again at the thin black snake of the James far below him. Was it true that miasma brought fever, that the land atmosphere could enter the waiting body as the wind was trying to enter him as he waited for the Negro to take his horse? Could the world a woman lived in kill her? He didn't know. He took his black bag from the seat beside him, sick at having to face them, not knowing, stripped by thought of any knowledge of the human mysterious body he might have ever thought he had. He told himself not to be a fool—simple winter fever, call it winter fever. A woman didn't have to die of winter fever.

Inside Albion's black and white marble hall it was warm, protected against the dark, snow-drifting February day. Crawford walked out of the drawing room to meet him, his footsteps echoing through the great space of the hall, and waited without saying a word while he blew the cold from his nose to keep from looking too much at Crawford's face, as frozen as the ice outside.

He could sense the young man struggling to make contact, say anything, and his habitual, "What's the news from downriver?" made Dr. Noah look up at last from the barrier of his handkerchief, bland and smiling, radiating comfort.

"It's going to be all right, Crawford. The convention's still holding out again secesh. After all, it's six weeks since Christmas when South Carolina went. We'll hold out from both sides, damn them."

Crawford didn't say a word. Dr. Noah faltered on. "If Virginny holds out we can stop the damned thing." He took Crawford's arm and couldn't avoid it any more. "I came as quick as I could."

"Toey says she's some better." Crawford still avoided looking at him. Without speaking again they matched steps up the wide winding staircase. Dr. Noah kept his eyes on the marble head, below them in the stairwell, of one of those statues Crawford and Melinda had brought back from Europe, as if any amount of naked statues and dim-looking paintings could keep Albion from being Albion, solid, cold Albion, where in all their married life they had hardly made a dent in its rich and bleak splendor. Beyond the open double doors of the drawing room he could see the fine old polished harpsichord with the Lacey name on it, which Melinda preferred to the fine piano Crawford had bought her. When she played it in the evening, her own face was as cool and fragile and thin as the fine notes she flicked from it and sent precisely into the after-supper dead calm. Sometimes she read poetry aloud, preoccupied, and in the last years the Old Testament or Saint Paul, while he sat, family cousin asked to supper once a month, and listened to her, punishing herself with words long beyond her strength, while Crawford kept trying to persuade her to stop and let herself be carried to bed.

Toey must have heard them coming. The quiet, dim Negro woman slipped out of the door of the master chamber and closed it softly behind her.

"I didn't want to talk in front of her," she whispered to Dr. Noah, even in the hall. "She's some better, but she jest wore out. She had the bloody dyree all night. It's quit now." She went on with a rush, warning, "Don' act like you notice nothin like that. She frets about it, don' think it's nice. I done tole her looks pretty. She's always askin if she looks pretty!" The word was not whispered, but said in an exasperated questioning whine. Toey began to cry.

"Come on, Toey, now quit that. I need you." Dr. Noah patted her arm.

The master chamber at Albion was as impersonal as the rest of the house. Not a piece of furniture had been moved or changed since Crawford's mother's time. The great bed was propped high with pillows for Melinda's heart, and in them she looked dry and weightless; there was some new excitement which made her smile when she saw the two men, but she said nothing.

Beside the bed a little girl played with colored blocks, her pinafore tucked up above her knees, and her soft chestnut curls tangled, neglected by death. She was so absorbed in her game she didn't look up.

"I want to bleed the patient," Dr. Noah told Crawford, ashamed of himself for the act of authority he put on like a coat when he went into a sickroom, but with everything else so tentative, the act itself helped. At least, he'd always hoped so. "You'd better take little Lacey out of here."

"She won't let her go at all, Marse Noah. She jest frets somethin awful," Toey whispered again.

They looked at each other and didn't need to mention it, that part of Melinda's sickness which made her cling to the baby she had rejected.

"Crawford, take her over across the room then."

Awkwardly, Crawford picked up the startled baby. She began to cry, disturbed at her game.

"Keep her still. Let her play with your watch."

Melinda had seen Crawford. "Darling." Her puffed lips, broken out from the fever, cracked into a private smile.

"I'll be right here," Crawford said without looking at her, and began to jog Lacey until she stopped crying and watched him, surprised.

"My dear." Dr. Noah took Melinda's hand to feel her pulse, too fast and weak for him to have to time. By habit, he took out his watch and frowned. "Now my dear, I'm going to bleed you. You'll get relief from the fever. It won't hurt."

"Toey," Melinda whispered, "do I look pretty? Does my hair look pretty?"

"Yes ma'am." Toey sighed. Her brown hand pushed the already dead hair back, hardly touching it as if she knew it hurt Melinda.

Dr. Noah, getting his lancet and uncovering Melinda's arm, watched the woman in the bed. It was curious how the dying — he corrected his mind — the very sick lost personality, became so alike, suppliant, childish, sometimes pleading, but always that physical receding he could never understand, as much as he'd seen it, as if they waited to be called back, hopelessly.

He nodded for Toey to hold the bleeding bowl, and plunged the lancet into the exposed vein of Melinda's arm. Her blood flowed dark into it, lapping the sides of the white bowl as Toey's hands shook.

When he had judged a pint and had seen Melinda's face go paler, the fever flush fading satisfactorily, Dr. Noah applied the tourniquet and nodded as if he were pleased.

Toey took the bowl and poured Miss Melinda's blood into the clean chamber pot. She'd seen so much of it go there it made her cry again, but she kept on kneeling down so that nobody would see her and fuss.

"Darling," she heard Miss Melinda say, "please come here." She sounded better. Toey could see Marse Crawford's fine leather boots, kind of hesitating across the room, the heels not touching the floor.

When Dr. Noah saw the look of pure joy Melinda gave her husband he began to believe in miracles.

"Oh darling." That rapid thin voice like her pulse raced. Crawford seemed hardly to hear her.

"You were never out of my mind. I know you thought about me and it wasn't bad to do that. That's a safe place to be, in a mind. No surprises."

"Miss Melinda, try to sleep." Dr. Noah released the tourniquet for the first time.

Her voice flowed on, weaker. ". . . like holding a baby inside you and never letting it be born. But we had a baby. We had Lacey. Winsome handsome Lacey . . ." She looked at Crawford and closed her eyes.

" You don't say anything. That's because you're a gentleman. That's important." She giggled. "It's a big lie. A big fool lie."

Crawford interrupted her. The man looked awed, afraid of the tenderness.

"Melinda, you *must* prepare to meet your Maker."

Melinda was whispering. When her voice went down Toey got up and ran to the side of the bed, cold with fear.

"Aw, take her hand, please, Marse Crawford." Her begging jarred the room. Crawford didn't move. Toey took the dry hand and pressed it. Melinda's eyelids moved.

"Do you think that He will be a gentleman, too, darling? No wonder the sky is so lonesome-looking."

The room was still. The woman in the bed seemed to sleep. Dr. Noah pushed Toey's hand aside and grabbed her pulse. It had stopped. It began again.

From the pillows she began again with it. Toey was the only one who bent down to catch what she said.

"Darling, take me out of this hotel soon. I want to go home. Please darling . . ."

She couldn't open her eyes. The diarrhea had begun again, soaking the bed, filling the room with a sweet foul bloody smell.

"Tell Crawford I'm sorry."

The doctor was too intent on her pulse to notice what she said, but Crawford heard it, and glanced at him, startled.

Melinda began to giggle, so faintly that even Toey had to strain to hear her. "I just thought of something. Listen . . ." She giggled again. The fine weak sound died. Toey watched her face flatten as if something had pushed her deeper into the bed, then come forward again, relaxed, white and smooth as wax. Her eyes were open. Toey's unthinking woman's hands came forward, caressing them shut again.

"Oh my God, Marse Crawford, she died laughin," she moaned and went on moaning as she breathed.

Across the room Lacey began to howl, neglected and panicked.

Dr. Noah led Crawford out of the chamber as he always did the husband, as he would have a sleepwalker. "It is the will of God," he told him to break the man's shambling stupor.

"Is it?" Crawford answered bitterly and leaned against the wall to stare at the old fool who could not know that for the last day Melinda had thought that he was Johnny Catlett.

When the snow melted in the western Virginia mountains late in the spring of 1861, the Gauley River rose higher than usual, even for the season. In places it flooded the late May cornfields, but as the Fincastle Greys rode farther up the river, the smaller fields were dry and the spring-pale green fingers of corn thrust up in neat rows in the dark earth.

By its size, Johnny read how far they had traveled east and north into the mountains. At Beulah the early corn had already grown ten inches in the warm rich receptive river valley. As they crossed the ford of Gauley and followed through the hill farms of Nicholas County, it was only six inches, the frail color of the delicate new leaves which made the mountains so young for a few weeks every year. He could not look at a well-planted field without pride; no farmer could. He studied and by habit wished for mild wind, tender sun, and gentle rain to raise the year's young.

A man should not go to war in the spring when every growing thing was so young and needing care. The time to go was the fall of the year when the crops were harvested and men went to fight as they would go to hunt.

Stretched out behind him on the sunny road were the thirty-six men who had joined him. After four days they rode more silently, testing the strength of their horses, the excitement, the hunter's joy gone. Once in a while one of the men broke into song to lure the others. He could hear someone behind him singing softly.

"With a wing wing waddle and a Jack Frost straddle,
To my John Bar battle to my long ways home."

The isolated song, no one joining it, sounded lonely on the narrow road, winding into the indifferent ever-rising mountains. A sweet breeze played in the treetops and made them sigh. Johnny rode with his head down as if he were dozing, to keep young Preston Carver, who rode beside him, from talking.

He heard one of the men call, "Cap'n Johnny!"

Another one said, "Haish! He's dozin.'"

"My, ain't he a one? He'll make usn a sodjer. He don't give a damn whether he lives or dies."

He could sense adoring eighteen-year-old Preston in his cherry-red uniform the girls designed, and his shoulder curls, turn around and grin with the men.

The new boy asked, low to keep him from hearing, "Who air he?"

"Oh, hell," the man who had been singing told him. "He's a real gintleman from downriver, owns a heap of niggers. Anyhow, hit don't matter, you're in the calvary now, boy."

The boy's joining was the first pure act of war he had seen, and even with the shock of it, Johnny had to smile to himself. They had camped the night before at a farm where a gnarled unsmiling woman let them sleep in the hay-barn so long as they promised not to smoke. They had thought she was alone.

It was hard to find a farm that would take them. Some of the people didn't want the soldiers stealing their food. Not a few had stood at the gates and stared with such hatred in their eyes that Johnny could read their feelings without asking, and rode on.

An old man had called out, "God help ye, mis'able sinners!"

One of the men behind him yelled, "Amen, Brother Ben!"

He had approached the old woman by riding up and asking for drinking water.

"I reckon what you're arter is a place to sleep," she told him calmly, looking straight at him as if she weren't the kind you had to waste time with. "Well, I'm fer ye. I seen ye comin. We don't hanker arter no free niggers burnin up ever'thing. Ye kin have the barn." Then she added, "Don't go tellin thim damned Yankee Bullers up the road. They ain't got no sense nohow."

As Johnny had stood, that night outside the barn, watching and wondering who had planted the straight clean ranks of young corn in fields all around the unpainted board house, he heard a thumping that seemed to come from the direction of the springhouse. She told them she had locked it because she didn't want any of them getting into her milk. He decided it was that stubborn plow horse of Kelly's, as big a fool as he was.

They were mounted early, but not too early to see her set the new milk down by the springhouse door. She still didn't open it.

As they rode away, he looked back. She was taking the lock off. A tall boy ran out and off to the stable, with her after him. The men reined up to watch and laugh. The boy rode out of the stable on a sheepskin saddle, straight past his mother, swerving as she tried to catch the horse. He cleared the snake-fence.

She called after him, "You come right back hyar, Jedediah!"

He was already galloping across the cornfield, riding over the tender corn he had planted so carefully. Johnny watched the horse's hoofs flail it down.

"You bring that thar horse back, Jedediah," the old woman screamed, impotent.

The boy, sixteen, Johnny judged, joined on the end of the troop, seeming to pay no attention at the men's laughter. They rode on out of the sound of the woman's voice.

"My brother's done gone to Grafton. She's about to work me to death. I been locked in the springhouse for three days. Ain't had nothing to eat but milk and it give me the dyree," was all the boy said to Kelly, who had dropped back to ride beside him.

"'Fore Gawd," he said once they were out of sight of the farm, "hit feels right good to jine the calvary."

Johnny gave the order to halt, the sun at noon. They spread out into a field beside the road to unsaddle their horses and let them graze. He could see Preston Carver coming toward him, eager.

"Preston, you watch these men and see that they're saddled up in half an hour. We want to be in Marlinton before night. I'm going on up to the top and look around."

The boy, his red uniform now covered with dust and dark with sweat at the legs from his horse, saluted smartly and turned back to the men.

"'Tention!" he yelled.

They had all lain down on the ground and were getting out their tobacco.

"Shut up, Pressy," somebody called. "Quit actin like you got on your big brother's britches."

Preston looked beseechingly around for Johnny, but he had already ridden away up toward the top of the rise. He watched him go, handsome, easy in the saddle, his straight body, his fine horse, his brave ostrich-feather plume casting a running shadow in the road.

Beyond the rise Johnny dismounted and tethered his horse. In front of him the deep valley and the forbidding, evocative range of Alleghenies were blue in the distance. He sank down to rest against a tree, hardly seeing it all any more, away for a moment from the men, thinking of the boy and the trampled corn.

Did a man go to war as to a lover, to a war he didn't believe in and knew they couldn't win, to suicide of an already dying country, broken and old, and young again every year, only to escape his life, or did he go because he no longer cared? Johnny felt unburdened, as if the hope of years, the pain and the yearning, had slipped like an unstrapped load from his back and left him light and empty with grief. Events in the winter piled on events: the election of Lincoln, the mindless anger and fear, the trapped feeling of a surrounded state, the efforts to keep balance, as he knew Virginia could, the final narrow vote that had severed her from the Union, with a waiting South and a waiting North poised on each side of her. Finally there were no more voices of silence, and she had flushed with fear and panic like a grouse, toward the South. He, Captain Johnny, felt swept up as a swimmer by the sudden flood of fear, but still with his head above water, trying as so many had to speak for calm.

At night he faced the new brave brag of the women around him, watching him at the table with awe, to see if he had made up his mind, as he, silent and troubled, still unable to believe the point of balance had been lost, waited to know what he ought to do. Their feminine warlike passion, born of boredom and fed on old fear and new pride, pushed at him.

The letter that Melinda was dead had come in March. After that he drowned in opinion and let himself be carried, doing what unconsciously they wanted him to do, a hollow careless civilized man, showing nothing to their prying eyes after the news.

Although his mother cried and pointed out that no man with over twenty Negroes was expected to go, that Dan wasn't going because he had a family, he could see the steel pride of sacrifice in her eyes behind her sorrow.

On the seventh of April, Sara drove up from Canona with the children to go back to the orchard farm for the spring planting. She told them, standing bravely in the dining room, refusing even to join them for supper, that Lewis had given up his preaching and decided he could serve God better in the Union Army. Her mother had bowed her head to the table as if she had been struck down, and Leah had only stared at her until she backed out of the room, and Cousin Amelia watched her hands in her lap, embarrassed.

Johnny jumped up and followed her to the door and took her into his arms to let her cry.

"I cain't understand all this hatred," she kept saying. "I just cain't understand it, though I pray for guidance."

She moved away from him then and, turning in the path, said, "Women are more righteous but they have less mercy than men. The Lord bless and keep you. The Lord make His face to shine upon you and give you peace, Johnny." He had stood, his heart touched for the first time since Melinda's death, until he could no longer hear the clop of her horses in the dark. After he could no longer hear her he went into his office and sat blankly watching one page of a book, too deadened to think any more, wishing to God he could cry.

The sweating mare was drawing flies. Johnny took off his hat to wave them away. When did you let go, when did you let yourself drown in the world, cease to care? He remembered old Telemachus and the nigger-belly catfish. All his life he had been trying to swim away from that great mouth, that hungry jaw, never knowing that he would some day have the energy or even the desire for flight taken from him, and stop struggling, as they said a swimmer did when he was drowning, cease to care with his body.

from *The Legacy of the Civil War*

Robert Penn Warren (1905–1989)

Robert Penn Warren, poet, critic, historian, and novelist, was born and raised in Guthrie, Kentucky, a small town near the Kentucky-Tennessee border. Educated at Vanderbilt University, University of California, Yale, and New College, Oxford, as a Rhodes scholar, Warren made his public debut as a writer with *John Brown: The Making of a Martyr* in 1929. He soon followed with his contribution to the Agrarian symposium *I'll Take My Stand* in 1930. In 1946, he won the Pulitzer Prize for *All the King's Men,* in which he challenges the reader to confront vexing moral dilemmas: pragmatism versus idealism, the illusion of innocence, the conflict between father and son, and the past's bearing on the present. In the selection here, taken from *The Legacy of the Civil War: Meditations on the Centennial* (1961), he explores the ways in which twentieth-century Southerners use the Confederate defeat as an excuse for the region's shortcomings.

L et us leave in suspension such debates about the economic costs of the War and look at another kind of cost, a kind more subtle, pervasive, and continuing, a kind that conditions in a thousand ways the temper of American life today. This cost is psychological, and it is, of course, different for the winner and the loser. To give things labels, we may say that the War gave the South the Great Alibi and gave the North the Treasury of Virtue.

By the Great Alibi the South explains, condones, and transmutes everything. By a simple reference to the "War," any Southern female could, not too long ago, put on the glass slipper and be whisked away to the ball. Any goose could dream herself (or himself) a swan—surrounded, of course, by a good many geese for contrast and devoted hand-service. Even now, any common lyncher becomes a defender of the Southern tradition, and any rabble-rouser the gallant leader of a thin gray line of heroes, his hat on saber-point to provide reference by which to hold formation in the charge. By the Great Alibi pellagra, hookworm, and illiteracy are all explained, or explained away, and mortgages are converted into badges of distinction. Laziness becomes the aesthetic sense, blood-lust rising from a matrix of boredom and resentful misery becomes a high sense of honor, and ignorance becomes divine revelation. By the Great Alibi the Southerner makes his Big Medicine. He turns defeat into victory, defects into virtues. Even more pathetically, he turns his great virtues into absurdities—sometimes vicious absurdities.

It may, indeed, be arguable that in economic matters the Southerner (like the Westerner) is entitled to some grievance, and an alibi—there was, for instance, such a thing as the unfavorable freight-rate differential. But the Southerner isn't nearly as prompt to haul out the Great Alibi for economic as for social and especially racial matters. And the most painful and costly consequences of the Great Alibi are found, of course, in connection with race. The race problem, according to the Great Alibi, is the doom defined by history — by New England slavers, New England and Middlewestern Abolitionists, cotton, climate, the Civil War, Reconstruction, Wall Street, the Jews. Everything flows into the picture.

Since the situation is given by history, the Southerner therefore is guiltless; is, in fact, an innocent victim of a cosmic conspiracy. At the same time, the Southerner's attitude toward the situation is frozen. He may say, in double vision of self-awareness, that he wishes he could feel and act differently, but cannot. I have heard a Southerner say: "I pray to feel different, but so far I can't help it." Even if the Southerner prays to feel different, he may still feel that to change his attitude would be treachery—to that City of the Soul which the historical Confederacy became, to blood spilled in hopeless valor, to the dead fathers, and even to the self. He is trapped in history.

As he hears his own lips parroting the sad clichés of 1850 does the Southerner sometimes wonder if the words are his own? Does he ever, for a moment, feel the desperation of being caught in some great Time-machine, like a treadmill, and doomed to an eternal effort without progress? Or feel, like Sisyphus, the doom of pushing a great stone up a hill only to have the weight, like guilt, roll back over him, over and over again? When he lifts his arm to silence protest, does he ever feel, even fleetingly, that he is lifting it against some voice deep in himself?

Does he ever realize that the events of Tuscaloosa, Little Rock, and New Orleans are nothing more than an obscene parody of the meaning of his history? It is a debasement of his history, with all that was noble, courageous, and justifying bleached out, drained away. Does the man who, in the relative safety of mob anonymity, stands howling vituperation at a little Negro girl being conducted into a school building, feel himself at one with those gaunt, barefoot, whiskery scarecrows who fought it out, breast to breast, to the death, at the Bloody Angle at Spotsylvania, in May, 1864? Can the man howling in the mob imagine General R. E. Lee, CSA, shaking hands with Orval Faubus, Governor of Arkansas?

Does the man in the mob ever wonder why his own manly and admirable resentment at coercion should be enlisted, over and over again, in situations which should, and do, embarrass the generosity and dignity of manhood, including his own? Does he ever consider the possibility that whatever degree of dignity and success a Negro achieves actually enriches, in the end, the life of the white man and enlarges his worth as a human being?

There are, one must admit, an impressive number of objective difficulties in the race question in the South—difficulties over and beyond that attributable to Original Sin and Confederate orneriness; but the grim fact is that the Great Alibi rusts away the will to confront those difficulties, at either a practical or an ethical level. All is explained—and transmuted.

The whole process of the Great Alibi resembles the neurotic automatism. The old trauma was so great that reality even now cannot be faced. The automatic repetition short-circuits clear perception and honest thinking. North as well as South (for the North has its own mechanism for evading reality), we all seem to be doomed to reënact, in painful automatism, the errors of our common past.

from *Jubilee*

Margaret Walker (1915–)

Margaret Walker, the daughter of college professors, grew up in Alabama, Mississippi, and New Orleans, Louisiana, where she heard many stories of the South from her grandmother. During the 1930s, Walker went north for college at Northwestern and worked in the Federal Writers' Project. After receiving her M.A. and publishing a book of poetry, she taught from 1949 to 1979 at Jackson State University in Mississippi. While teaching, she completed her Ph.D. work for the University of Iowa and received her doctorate for *Jubilee* (1966), a novel Walker had been working on since she was nineteen. The novel, inspired by the stories of her great-grandmother Walker had heard as a girl, imagines the Civil War and emancipation from the point of view of slaves on the cusp of freedom.

> *Hurrah, hurrah, we bring the Jubilee*
> *Hurrah, hurrah, the flag to make you free!*

A NOISE LIKE THUNDER ... A CLOUD OF DUST

January 1, 1865, the Emancipation Proclamation was repeated in Georgia. But the telegraph poles and wires had all been damaged or cut by Sherman's men in their march to Savannah and the sea, so there was no news, and the people in the backwoods knew nothing. The first three or four months passed without any news from the eastern war front and with little news from Tennessee where the last western battles were being fought around Nashville.

Vyry persuaded Caline and May Liza as well as Miss Lillian that they should try to plant some kind of crop.

"What for?" asked May Liza. "Big Missy never could get the last harvest."

"We got to eat," said Vyry, "and we got the younguns to feed. Leastwise Miss Lillian got hern, and I got mine."

Vyry took the initiative, and to the amazement of the whole household she set the plow in the field and made more than a dozen long furrows in one day. When the other women saw her determination they grudgingly helped her plant corn, collards, pease, okra, mustard and turnip salad, tomato plants, potatoes, and onions. Miss Lillian seemed to pay less attention to what was going on around her as the days passed, but she smiled and gave her approval to their plans.

The first green shoots were in the fields by the middle of May and Vyry looked at their "crop" with pride and pleasure. Life on the plantation was no longer pure drudgery, with every hour one of hard driving labor. Things were not so hard, but an almost deserted farm with no men was not easy either. Vyry's children were growing. Minna was a quiet one, docile, obedient, and easily controlled, but Vyry was having difficulty trying to train Jim to work.

Early one morning, about the third week in May, Vyry was in the kitchen cooking when all the children came running to alarm the house. They could hear a noise like thunder and the sky was black. Caline and May Liza closed the upstairs windows against a possible thunder storm. But as the rumbling noise grew louder and the black sky obscured the sunlight, they heard voices singing with drums and bugles sounding and in a few minutes they saw that the black cloud was dust from the horses hooves of a great army of men riding and singing:

Hurrah, hurrah, we bring the jubilee
Hurrah, hurrah, the flag to make you free
. . . .
While we go marching through Georgia!

They rode up to the steps, and in less than fifteen minutes soldiers and horses were over-running the place. They came like a crowd of locusts and the noise was so great that suddenly there was bedlam. Miss Lillian had only just finished dressing and, as Caline said, "I don't believe she ever got her shoes buttoned, and her hair was still hanging down her back in one long yellow plait like she went to bed."

The commanding officer, a major-general, came to the front door and knocked. When May Liza saw for the first time the Union blue uniform, she was so flustered and excited she kept curtseying and bobbing up and down saying, "Come in sir, come right in sir, and make yourself at home."

He smiled and said, "Is your mistress home?"

"Yassah, yassah, she'll be down terreckly. Won't you have a seat in the parlor sir? That's where gentlemens generally goes."

"I'll wait here till she comes, thank you."

Miss Lillian came down the long stairs slowly, her skirts trailing, her blue eyes looking more calm than stricken, and only her husky voice sounding a little startled.

"Good morning, sir."

"Good morning, madam, are you the mistress of this place?" Miss Lillian looked around as though expecting Big Missy to answer and then again at the soldier, his hat in his hand.

"Yes. I reckon I am. I'm the only one left."

"The only one left?" He was puzzled.

"Of my family. My mother and my father, my husband and my brother are all out there." And she pointed vaguely toward the cemetery.

He still looked puzzled and seeing his bewilderment she hastened to say with more alertness than usual but with no asperity, "They're dead."

He saw her agitation because she was ringing her hands. Now he fully understood.

"I'm sorry ma'am. How many slaves do you have on the place?"

"Slaves?"

"Yes, servants?"

"Oh, about five, I guess. Vyry and Caline and May Liza and Vyry's children. I think the rest must have all run away."

"Well ma'am, I am ordered to have all your slaves appear in the yard, and in the presence of you and the witnessing soldiers, hear me read the proclamation freeing them from slavery."

"Oh." Her voice trembled only ever so slightly. "Mister Lincoln's proclamation? I told Mama he had set the slaves free." And then she turned toward the cord to ring the parlor bell, but seeing May Liza and Caline standing gaping in the inner door, she called instead.

"Liza, call Vyry and tell her to get her children and you and Caline come out on the porch. This gentleman has something he wants to tell you."

Vyry would never forget the scene of that morning of the front veranda as long as she lived. Miss Lillian stood in the door with her two children, Bob and Susan, and her arms were around their shoulders. Standing beside Vyry were Caline and May Liza, their faces working though they were trying to look solemn while the man read the paper. Vyry scarcely heard a word he said. It was all she could do to keep Jim still because he wanted to dance a jig before the reading was over. Minna stood quietly beside her mother, holding a corner of Vyry's apron in her hand and, like Miss Lillian's children, she stared curiously at the soldiers. Vyry caught snatches of the long document as the man's voice droned on, "Shall be . . . forever free" and she was caught up in a reverie hearing that magic word. Could it be possible that the golden door of freedom had at last swung open? She mused further, watching the long lines of soldiers standing on Marse John's plantation, and still coming in long lines from the big road, and she was thinking, *There must be no end of them.*" Her ears caught the words:

And I hereby enjoin upon the people so declared to be free to abstain from all violence, unless in necessary self-defense; and I recommend to them that, in all cases when allowed, they labor faithfully for reasonable wages.

He was folding the paper before Vyry realized that the tears were running down her face. Then she turned to go back inside to her kitchen and her cooking.

Jim could restrain himself no longer. The ten-year-old little boy grabbed his six-year-old sister and, lifting her in his arms, began to dance his jig and sing,

> You is free, you is free!
> Minna you is free!
> You free as a jaybird setting on a swinging limb.
> Jubilee, you is free!
> Jubilee, you is free!

And Minna, who was puzzled but excited, smiled and tried to catch some of the contagion of her brother's wild spirits. She laughed and clapped her hands and said, "Free? Free? Free?"

When Vyry got back to her kitchen she found it overrun with soldiers. They had eaten her pan of biscuits and the ham she had cooked for breakfast and the big coffee pot was empty. They were, moreover, all over the barnyard catching the chickens and wringing their necks and hollering, "Fried chicken for breakfast! Come and get it! Fried chicken!" And they took a big black wash pot and made a fire under it in the backyard and inside the kitchen they were breaking open the cabinets taking food out and emptying the flour bin and getting out the lard. Vyry stepped back in amazement. "Scuse me ma'am," then seeing she wasn't the young missus they began to beg her to cook some more food, saying they were hungry.

"If yall will just get outa my way, I'll fix some more food."

Perhaps, if she had known what she was saying, and getting herself into that day, she might have gone out of the kitchen and let them have it. But instinctively she ran them out of the kitchen and began to make pans of biscuits and fry chicken. She fried chicken all day long. She stood so long, cooking as fast as they could scald the chickens and pick the feathers off and dress them, that at last she was too numb to feel anything and she lost track of the time and how late the day was getting.

In the meantime the soldiers were ransacking everything. They broke open the smokehouse and emptied it of all hams and shoulders and middlings, the sides of beef, and the dried mutton. They gathered basketsful of eggs, cleaned out the springhouse of milk and butter and cream and cheese; loaded the corn into wagons, gathered up all the ducks and geese and turkeys and tied them with strings and ropes. Vyry heard a great yell go up when they found Marse John's liquor. They drank up or carted away all the whiskey, brandy, rum, and wine that was left on the place. They turned loose all the horses and ran some away while they hitched others to all the wagons on the place, the carriage, barouche, and buggy. They found two new calves and took these and all others with the cows. They left an old pesky bull in the pasture. They gave the hogs and pigs a merry chase with sticks and they ran through muddy pig sties catching the slippery, slimy, squealing animals, mud, slops and all, in their arms and boxing them into pens. They set the gin house, that was full of cotton, on fire and burned it to the ground. They took molasses and started strewing it all over the place, in and out of the Big House, up and down stairs and through the parlors making trickling streams all over Big Missy's fine scarlet carpets. They yanked down the heavy silk and velvet portieres and broke up half the furniture.

Behind the soldiers came still another motley lot, more than a mile of freed slaves following the army. They had bundles of rags and some had pots and pans and squawking chickens and other fowl. They were in wagons and on foot, riding mules and driving little oxcarts. There were gray-haired men and women, young mothers with their babies at the breast and streaming lines of children walking. These people were also hungry, and some were sick and diseased with running sores. One poor old gray-haired woman was driving a cart pulled by a team of goats and she had in the cart every possible thing she could carry, such as sacks of seed and meal, squawking chickens, geese, ducks, and a shoat, iron cooking pots and skillets, a wash pot, quilts and croker sacks, and a big tin coffee pot. One of the soldiers observing her said, "Hey, Auntie, where'd you get all this stuff? You look like the children of Israel coming out of Egypt!" The soldiers laughed but the old black woman answered indignantly, "I buyed it."

"You buyed it? Buyed it with what? Worthless Confederate specie?" And they laughed again.

"Nossah. I buyed it with myself. I work for Marster nigh on to fifty years; ever since I been big enough to hold the hoe. I ain't never even much had enough to eat, had to scrounge around for scraps half the time. When we come away to freedom everything turn wrong-side-outwards. I just took what was mine, cause I buyed it with myself."

Somewhere among the motley crowd was Jim, the houseboy. When Caline and May Liza appeared in the kitchen with him, Vyry was flabbergasted.

"Vyry, look who's here?" said May Liza, much more gaily than usual, although she had been bubbling over with joy all day.

"And he come to take me away!"

This was the most surprising news of all to Vyry. All these years she had never thought of Jim and May Liza as sweethearts, but they had worked all their lives in the Big House and Jim was a man in his forties. Come to think of it, May Liza had to be near the same age. Caline was much older. Vyry had never known exactly how old Caline was, but when she was a child and Aunt Sally was cooking in the Big House, Caline was a much younger woman than Aunt Sally. Caline was a middle-aged woman now, more than twice the age of Vyry. Vyry was twenty-eight years old, now that freedom had come to her, but she had not let her mind wander past the business of the morning. It was the middle of the afternoon when Jim appeared. May Liza had her few things tied in a bundle and so did Caline.

"Yall ain't gwine now, is you?"

"Yes we is. We's gwine right now," said May Liza, "Jim says our best bet is to follow the army and they'll be all getting away from here by sundown."

"Why don't you come, too, Vyry?" said Jim. "Me and May Liza is getting married today and Caline gwine live with us soon as we can find a place to stay."

"Where yall gwine, and whichaway is the army headed?"

"We's gwine down in Alabamy. The army is headed that-away now. And Vyry, you might as well, cause I seen the last of Randall Ware."

Vyry's heart lurched painfully at the mention of Randall Ware's name. Her voice was unsteady as she answered Jim.

"What you mean, you seen the last of him, and whereabouts was he at?"

"Last I seen he was sick in Atlanta. Too sick to follow Uncle Billy when he came through Georgia marching to the sea. I seen him on a litter. He was wasted until he was too poor to stand on his feets and he had the fever so bad I doubt he coulda lasted another week. They was sending all the sick and wounded back to Chattanooga and I reckon thereabouts is where they brung him. He bound to be in his grave now. You better come with us."

Vyry felt so weak she had to sit down, and then she trembled so for a moment she couldn't speak. When she did find her voice she was surprised to hear herself saying, "Naw. I don't believe he's dead. I feel like he mighta been sick and couldn't get here by now, but he told me to wait here for him until the war was over . . ."

"Well the war's over now. Mister Lincoln's dead and buried. . . ."

"Aw, naw he ain't!"

"Yeah, and Lee had done surrendered to Grant before ever Mister Lincoln got shot."

"Who shot him? The Confederate soldiers?"

"Naw, but it was a southern white man what shot him. He say some kind of gibberish in a foreign tongue bout Mister Lincoln was a tyrant."

"What is that?"

"I think it means a overbearing ruler like a king."

"Lawd, ain't that a pity! I reckon he done it cause Mister Lincum was trying to help the poor colored peoples."

"Yeah, it just like Brother Zeke said that time, Mister Lincoln sure enough the colored peoples' Moses. He make old Pharaoh get up and git!"

"Where you seen Brother Zeke?"

"He died in the Union camp where me and your free man Randall Ware was before Randall Ware taken sick. I was right there when Brother Zeke died and I helped to bury him."

"Lawd, I sure hates to hear that. He sure was a good man."

"That's just what we says. Now, is you gwine with us?"

"Naw, Jim, I ain't leaving here now. I gotta feeling he ain't dead and I'm duty bound to wait. But I sure hates to see yall go, and I thanks you just the same."

"Wellum we gwine," said Caline. "I been here all my life and I ain't never seen nothing but this here piece of Georgia woods and I'm sick to my stomach of this here place. I wants to travel and see some more of the world before I die. I had me a husband once, Big Boy, but they sold him away and I think they sold him down in Alabamy. Course that was years ago and I don't know where he's at now, living or dead. I ain't got no where to go, but I'm gwine. I'm free, and I ain't staying here no more."

"I ain't heard tell nothing from Randall Ware but once until today. My youngun, Minna, were a young nursing baby when he went away and she nigh on to seven summers old. I got his younguns and I prays to Gawd to see they daddy one more time in this life. I feels like something down deep inside of me would tell me was he dead. I ain't got nowhere to go, neither, but I'm duty bound to wait."

The sun was still high in the sky when Jim and May Liza and Caline left Marse John's plantation and Vyry told them goodbye. She was still working in the kitchen. Miss Lillian and Bob and Susan came in the kitchen where she was cooking, saying they were hungry, and she fed them fried chicken and bread and went to the back door to call Jim and Minna.

"Maw, ain't we gwine with the soldiers?" asked Jim as he stuffed his mouth full of chicken.

"Whoever give you that notion?" asked Vyry.

"Aw Maw, everybody what's anybody is gwine with the soldiers. We's free ain't we? We ain't got to stay here and work no more is we?"

"Yes, son, we's free and we ain't got to stay, but being free don't mean we ain't gotta work, and anyhow I promise your daddy I'd wait here for him."

Jim was crestfallen, but slightly mollified with the promise of his own father. He was excited, however, over the prospect of going with the soldiers and secretly he had been getting a bundle of rags together, too, to follow the army.

Vyry really hadn't promised Randall Ware to wait, but she had promised so long in her mind to stay where he could find her that now it did not make sense for her to go. In the first place, where would they go? She knew that sometime in the future, unless Randall Ware was really dead, he would make it back to his blacksmith shop and grist mill in nearby Dawson. He could make money and make a living for them and give her and their children a home. Maybe her children would even learn to read and write, as he could, and cipher on their hands. She wasn't ready to leave the plantation, not yet.

Jim went outside to tell a newly found friend, a man who was among the contraband freedmen, "My Maw says naw, we ain't gwine with the army. She waiting here for us daddy."

"Oh, I see. How long your daddy been gone?"

"I dunno. I can't hardly remember him. I musta been real little."

"And your sister were a baby?"

"Yassah, I reckon so."

Jim was sharing his fried chicken with his new friend, and the man ate awhile and said nothing. But he was still with the children around the back door of the kitchen when Vyry finally quit cooking and made ready to go to her old cabin for the night.

"Dragged Fighting from His Tomb"

Barry Hannah (1942–)

Barry Hannah, a Mississippian with a masters degree from the University of Arkansas, has taught at Clemson University and at the Universities of Alabama and Mississippi. His boldly imagined, often outrageous, novels and short stories have received much attention. In "Dragged Fighting from His Tomb," published in his 1978 collection *Airships*, Hannah subverts the traditional Civil War narrative, replacing the expected tone of reverence and distance with a distinctly modern tone, ribald and sarcastic, talking in the voice of the man who shot Jeb Stuart.

It was a rout.

We hit them, but they were ready this time.

His great idea was to erupt in the middle of the loungers. Stuart was a profound laugher. His banjo-nigger was with him almost all the time, a man who could make a ballad instantly after an ambush. We had very funny songs about the wide-eyed loungers and pickets, the people of negligent spine leisuring around the depots and warehouses, straightening their cuffs and holding their guns as if they were fishing poles. Jeb loved to break out of cover in the clearing in front of these guards. He offered them first shot if they were ready, but they never were. It was us and the dirty gray, sabers out, and a bunch of fleeing boys in blue.

Except the last time, at Two Roads Junction in Pennsylvania.

These boys had repeaters and they were waiting for us. Maybe they had better scouts than the others. We'd surprised a couple of their pickets and shot them down. But I suppose there were others who got back. This was my fault. My talent was supposed to be circling behind the pickets and slaying every one of them. So I blame myself for the rout, though there are always uncertainties in an ambush. This time it was us that were routed.

We rode in. They were ready with the repeating rifles, and we were blown apart. I myself took a bullet through the throat. It didn't take me off my mount, but I rode about a hundred yards out under a big shade tree and readied myself to die. I offered my prayers.

"Christ, I am dead. Comfort me in the valley of the shadow. Take me through it with honor. Don't let me make the banshee noises I've heard so many times in the field. You and I know I am worth more than that."

I heard the repeating rifles behind me and the shrieks, but my head was

171

a calm green church. I was prepared to accept the big shadow. But I didn't seem to be dying. I felt my neck. I thrust my forefinger in the hole. It was to the right of my windpipe and there was blood on the rear of my neck. The thing had passed clean through the muscle of my right neck. In truth, it didn't even hurt.

I had been thinking: Death does not especially hurt. Then I was merely asleep on the neck of my horse, a red-haired genius for me and a steady one. I'd named him Mount Auburn. We took him from a big farm outside Gettysburg. He wanted me as I wanted him. He was mine. He was the Confederacy.

As I slept on him, he was curious but stable as a rock. The great beast felt my need to lie against his neck and suffered me. He lay the neck out there for my comfort and stood his front heels.

A very old cavalryman in blue woke me up. He was touching me with a flagstaff. He didn't even have a weapon out.

"Eh, boy, you're a pretty dead one, ain't you? Got your hoss's head all bloody. Did you think Jeb was gonna surprise us forever?"

We were alone.

He was amazed when I stood up in the saddle. I could see beyond him through the hanging limbs. A few men in blue were picking things up. It was very quiet. Without a thought, I already had my pistol on his thin chest. I could not see him for a moment for the snout of my pistol.

He went to quivering, of course, the old fool. I saw he had a bardlike face.

What I began was half sport and half earnest.

"Say wise things to me or die, patriot," I said.

"But but but but but but," he said.

"Shhh!" I said. "Let nobody else hear. Only me. Tell the most exquisite truths you know."

He paled and squirmed.

"What's wrong?" I asked.

A stream of water came out the cuff of his pants.

I don't laugh. I've seen pretty much all of it. Nothing a body does disgusts me. After you've seen them burst in the field in two days of sun, you are not surprised by much that the mortal torso can do.

"I've soiled myself, you gray motherfucker," said the old guy.

"Get on with it. No profanity necessary," I said.

"I believe in Jehovah, the Lord; in Jesus Christ, his son; and in the Holy Ghost. I believe in the Trinity of God's bride, the church. To be honest. To be square with your neighbor. To be American and free," he said.

"I asked for the truths, not beliefs," I said.

"But I don't understand what you mean," said the shivering home guard. "Give me an example."

"You're thrice as old as I. You should give *me* the examples. For instance: Where is the angry machine of all of us? Why is God such a blurred magician? Why are you begging for your life if you believe those things? Prove to me that you're better than the rabbits we ate last night."

"I'm better because I know I'm better," he said.

I said, "I've read Darwin and floundered in him. You give me aid, old man. Find your way out of this forest. Earn your life back for your trouble."

"Don't shoot me. They'll hear the shot down there and come blow you over. All the boys got Winchester repeaters," he said.

By this time he'd dropped the regiment flag into a steaming pile of turd from his horse. I noticed that his mount was scared too. The layman does not know how the currents of the rider affect that dumb beast he bestrides. *I've seen a thoroughbred horse refuse to move at all under a man well known as an idiot with a plume. It happened in the early days in the streets of Richmond with Wailing Ott, a colonel too quick if I've ever seen one. His horse just wouldn't move when Ott's boys paraded out to Manassas. He screamed and there were guffaws. He even cut the beast with his saber. The horse sat right down on the ground like a deaf beggar of a darky. Later, in fact during the battle of Manassas, Colonel Ott, loaded with pistols, sabers and even a Prussian dagger, used a rotten outhouse and fell through the aperture (or split it by his outlandish weight in iron) and drowned head down in night soil. I saw his horse roaming. It took to me. I loved it and its name (I christened it afresh) was Black Answer, because a mare had just died under me and here this other beast ran into my arms. It ran for me. I had to rein Black Answer to keep him behind General Stuart himself. (Though Jeb was just another colonel then.) I am saying that a good animal knows his man. I was riding Black Answer on a bluff over the York when a puff went out of a little boat we were harassing with Pelham's cannon from the shore. I said to Black Answer, "Look at McClellan's little sailors playing war down there, boy." The horse gave a sporty little snort in appreciation. He knew what I was saying.*

It wasn't a full fifteen minutes before a cannon ball took him right out from under me. I was standing on the ground and really not even stunned, my boots solid in the dust. But over to my right Black Answer was rolling up in the vines, broken in two. That moment is what raised my anger about the war. I recalled it as I held the pistol on the old makeshift soldier. I pulled back the hammer. I recalled the eyes of the horse were still bright when I went to comfort it. I picked up the great head of Black Answer and it came away from the body very easily. What a deliberate and pure expression Black Answer retained, even in death.

What a bog and labyrinth the human essence is, in comparison. We are all overbrained and overemotioned. No wonder my professor at the University of Virginia pointed out to us the horses of that great fantast Jonathan Swift and his Gulliver book. Compared with horses, we are all a dizzy and smelly farce. An old man cannot tell you the truth. An old man, even inspired by death, simply foams and is addled like a crab.

"Tell me," I said, "do you hate me because I hold niggers in bondage? Because I do not hold niggers in bondage. I can't afford it. You know what I'm fighting for? I asked you a question."

"What're you fighting for?"

"For the North to keep off."

"But you're here in Pennsylvania, boy. You attacked *us*. This time we were ready. I'm sorry it made you mad. I'm grievous sorry about your neck, son."

"You never told me any truths. Not one. Look at that head. Look at all those gray hairs spilling out of your cap. Say something wise. I'm about to kill you," I said.

"I have daughters and sons who look up to me," he said.

"Say I am one of your sons. Why do I look up to you?" I said.

"Because I've tried to know the world and have tried to pass it on to the others." He jumped off the horse right into the droppings. He looked as if he were venturing to run. "We're not simple animals. There's a god in every one of us, if we find him," he said.

"Don't try to run. I'd kill you before I even thought," I said.

His horse ran away. It didn't like him.

On the ground, below my big horse Mount Auburn, the old man was a little earthling in an overbig uniform. He kept chattering.

"I want a single important truth from you," I said.

"My mouth can't do it," he said. "But there's something here!" He struck his chest at the heart place. Then he started running back to the depot, slapping hanging limbs out of his way. I turned Mount Auburn and rode after. We hit the clearing and Mount Auburn was in an easy prance. The old man was about ten yards ahead, too breathless to warn the troops.

In an idle way I watched their progress too. Captain Swain had been killed during our ambush. I saw the blueboys had put his body up on a pole with a rope around his neck, a target in dirty gray. His body was turning around as they tried out the repeaters on him. But ahead of me the old man bounced like a snowtail in front of Mount Auburn. We were in a harrowed field. The next time I looked up, a stand of repeaters was under my left hand three strides ahead. I was into their camp. Mount Auburn stopped for me as I picked up a handful of the rifles by the muzzles.

The old man finally let out something.

"It's a secesh!" he shouted.

Only a couple looked back. I noticed a crock of whiskey on a stool where the brave ones were reloading to shoot at Captain Swain again. I jumped off Mount Auburn and went in the back door of the staff house. I kicked the old man through the half-open door and pulled Mount Auburn into the room with me, got his big sweaty withers inside. When I looked around I saw their captain standing up and trying to get out his horse pistol. He was about my age, maybe twenty-five, and he had spectacles. My piece was already cocked and I shot him square in the chest. He backed up and died in another little off-room behind his desk. A woman ran out of the room. She threw open the front door and bullets smacked into the space all around her. She shut the door. A couple of bullets broke wood.

"Lay down," I said.

She had a little Derringer double-shot pistol hanging in her hand. The old man was lying flat on the floor behind the desk with me.

The woman was a painted type, lips like blood. "Get down," I told her. She was ugly, just lips, tan hair, and a huge bottom under a petticoat. I wondered what she was going to try with the little pistol. She lay down flat on the floor. I asked her to throw me the pistol. She wouldn't. Then she wormed it across to us behind the big desk. She looked me over, her face grimy from the floor. She had no underwear and her petticoat was hiked up around her middle. The old man and I were looking at her organ.

"Wha? War again?" she said. "I thought we already won."

The woman and the old man laid themselves out like a carpet. I knew the blueboys thought they had me down and were about ready to come in. I was in that position at Chancellorsville. There should be about six fools, I thought. I made it to the open window. Then I moved into the window. With the repeater, I killed four, and the other two limped off. Some histrionic plumehead was raising his saber up and down on the top of a pyramid of crossties. I shot him just for fun. Then I brought up another repeater and sprayed the yard.

This brought on a silence. Nothing was moving. Nobody was shooting. I knew what they were about to do. I had five minutes to live, until they brought the cannon up. It would be canister or the straight big ball. Then the firing started again. The bullets were nicking the wall in back of me. I saw Mount Auburn behind the desk. He was just standing there, my friend, my legs. Christ, how could I have forgotten him? "Roll down, Auburn!" I shouted. He lay down quick. He lay down behind the thick oak desk alongside the slut and the old man.

Then what do you think? With nothing to do but have patience until they got the cannon up, somebody's hero came in the back door with a flambeau and a pistol, his eyes closed, shooting everywhere. Mount

Auburn whinnied. The moron had shot Auburn. This man I overmurdered. I hit him four times in the face, and his torch flew out the back door with one of the bullets.

I was looking at the hole in Auburn when the roof of the house disappeared. It was a canister blast. The sound was deafening. Auburn was hurting but he was keeping it in. His breaths were deeper, the huge bold eyes waiting on me. I had done a lead-out once before on a corporal who was shot in the buttocks. He screamed the whole time, but he lives now, with a trifling scar on his arse, now the war is over. You put your stiletto very hard to one side of the hole until you feel metal—the bullet—and then you twist. The bullet comes out of the hole by this coiling motion and may even jump up in your hand.

So it was with the lead in Auburn's flank. It hopped right out. The thing to do then is get a sanitary piece of paper and stuff it into the wound. I took a leaf from the middle of the pile of stationery on the captain's table, spun it, and rammed it down.

Auburn never made a complaint. It was I who was mad. I mean, angry beyond myself.

When I went out the front door with the two repeaters, firing and levering, through a dream of revenge—fire from my right hand and fire from my left—the cannoneers did not expect it. I knocked down five of them. Then I knelt and started shooting to kill. I let the maimed go by. But I saw the little team of blue screeching and trying to shoot me, and I killed four of them. Then they all ran off.

There was nothing to shoot at.

I turned around and walked back toward the shack I'd been in. The roof was blown off. The roof was in the backyard lying on the toilet. A Yank with a broken leg had squirmed out from under it.

"Don't kill me," he said.

"Lay still and leave me alone," I said. "I won't kill you."

Mount Auburn had got out of the house and was standing with no expression in the bare dirt. I saw the paper sticking out of his wound. He made an alarmed sound. I turned. The Yank with a broken leg had found that slut's double-barreled Derringer. I suppose she threw it up in the air about the time the roof was blown over.

He shot at me with both barrels. One shot hit my boot and the other hit me right in the chin, but did nothing. It had been misloaded or maybe it wasn't ever a good pistol to begin with. The bullet hit me and just fell off.

"Leave me alone," I said. "Come here, Auburn," I called to the big horse. "Hurt him."

I went back in the house while Mount Auburn ran back and forth over the Yank. I cast aside some of the rafters and paper in search of the old man and the slut. They were unscathed. They were under the big desk in a carnal act. I was out of ammunition or I would have slaughtered them too. I went out to the yard and called Mount Auburn off the Yank, who was hollering and running on one leg.

By the time the old man and the slut got through, I had reloaded. They came out the back slot that used to be the door.

"Tell me something. Tell me something wise!" I screamed.

He was a much braver man than I'd seen when I'd seen him in the shade of the tree.

"Tell me *something*. Tell me *something wise!*" I screamed.

"There is no wisdom, Johnny Reb," the old man said. "There's only tomorrow if you're lucky. Don't kill us. Let us have tomorrow."

I spared them. They wandered out through the corpses into the plowed rows. I couldn't see them very far because of the dirty moon. I was petting Mount Auburn when Jeb and fifteen others of the cavalry rode up. Jeb has the great beard to hide his weak chin and his basic ugliness. He's shy. I'm standing here and we've got this whole depot to plunder and burn. So he starts being chums with me. Damned if I don't think he was jealous.

"You stayed and won it, Howard, all on your own?" he says.

"Yes, sir. I did."

"There's lots of dead Christians on the ground," he said. "You've got blood all over your shirt. You're a stout fellow, aren't you?"

"You remember what you said to me when you came back and I was holding Black Answer's head in my hands when he'd been shot out from under me?"

"I recall the time but not what I said," said Jeb Stuart.

"You said, 'Use your weeping on people, not on animals,'" I said.

"I think I'd hold by that," said Stuart.

"You shit! What are we doing killing people in Pennsylvania?" I screamed.

"Showing them that we can, Captain Howard!"

They arrested me and I was taken back (by the nightways) to a detention room in North Carolina. But that was easy to break out of.

I rode my horse, another steed that knew me, named Vermont Nose.

I made it across the Mason-Dixon.

Then I went down with Grant when he had them at Cold Harbor and in the Wilderness. My uniform was blue.

I did not care if it was violet.

I knew how Stuart moved. We were equal Virginia boys. All I needed was twenty cavalry.

I saw him on the road, still dashing around and stroking his beard.

"Stuarrrrrrrrt!" I yelled.

He trotted over on his big gray horse.

"Don't I know this voice?" he said.

"It's Howard," I said.

"But I sent you away. What uniform are you wearing?"

"Of your enemy," I said.

They had furnished me with a shotgun. But I preferred the old Colt. I shot him right in the brow, so that not another thought would pass about me or about himself or about the South, before death. I knew I was killing a man with wife and children.

I never looked at what the body did on its big horse.

Then Booth shot Lincoln, issuing in the graft of the Grant administration.

I am dying from emphysema in a Miami hotel, from a twenty-five-year routine of cigars and whiskey. I can't raise my arm without gasping.

I know I am not going to make it through 1901. I am the old guy in a blue uniform. I want a woman to lie down for me. I am still functional. I believe we must eradicate all the old soldiers and all their assemblies. My lusts surpass my frame. I don't dare show my pale ribs on the beach. I hire a woman who breast-feeds me and lets me moil over her body. I've got twenty thousand left in the till from the Feds.

The only friends of the human sort I have are the ghosts that I killed. They speak when I am really drunk.

"Welcome," they say. Then I enter a large gray hall, and Stuart comes up.

"Awwww!" he groans. "Treason."

"That's right," I say.

In 1900 they had a convention of Confederate veterans at the hotel, this lonely tall thing on the barbarous waves. I was well into my third stewed mango, wearing my grays merely to be decorous. I heard a group of old coots of about my age hissing at a nearby table. It became clear that I was the object of distaste.

I stood up.

"What is it?" I asked them.

I was answered by a bearded high-mannered coot struck half dead by Parkinson's disease. He was nodding like a reed in wind. He rose in his colonel's cape. Beside him his cane clattered to the floor.

"I say I saw you in the road, dog. I'm a Virginian, and I saw it by these good eyes. You killed Jeb Stuart. *You!* Your presence is a mockery to us of the Old Cause."

"Leave me alone, you old toy," I said.

I raised my freckled fists. His companions brought him down.

When the convention left, I dressed in my grays again and walked to the beach. Presently Charlie came out of the little corral over the dune, walking Mount Auburn's grandchild. If President Grant lied to me, I don't want to know. I have proof positive that it came from a Pennsylvania farm in the region where we foraged and ambushed.

It was an exquisitely shouldered red horse, the good look in its eye.

Charlie let me have the rein and I led the animal down to the hard sand next to the water. It took me some time to mount. My overcoat fell over his withers.

"You need any help, Captain Howard?" Charlie asked.

" I don't need a goddamned thing except privacy," I said.

There was nothing on the beach, only the waves, the hard sand, and the spray. The beauty I sat on ran to the verge of his heartburst. I had never given the horse a name. I suppose I was waiting for him to say what he wanted, to talk.

But Christ is his name, this muscle and heart striding under me.

"Shiloh"

Bobbie Ann Mason (1940–)

Bobbie Ann Mason is from Kentucky, the daughter of a dairy farmer. After graduating from the University of Kentucky and working in publishing in New York, Mason earned a Ph.D. in English from the University of Connecticut in 1972. She writes fiction as well as literary criticism, publishing her first book of fiction, *Shiloh and Other Stories*, in 1982. In the title story, Mason writes not of the battle but of the meaning the place holds — and does not hold — for the displaced residents of the latter-day South. Mason, who now lives in rural Pennsylvania, has published several important novels since her debut.

Leroy Moffitt's wife, Norma Jean, is working on her pectorals. She lifts three-pound dumbbells to warm up, then progresses to a twenty-pound barbell. Standing with her legs apart, she reminds Leroy of Wonder Woman.

"I'd give anything if I could just get these muscles to where they're real hard," says Norma Jean. "Feel this arm. It's not as hard as the other one."

"That's 'cause you're right-handed," says Leroy, dodging as she swings the barbell in an arc.

"Do you think so?"

"Sure."

Leroy is a truckdriver. He injured his leg in a highway accident four months ago, and his physical therapy, which involves weights and a pulley, prompted Norma Jean to try building herself up. Now she is attending a body-building class. Leroy has been collecting temporary disability since his tractor-trailer jacknifed in Missouri, badly twisting his left leg in its socket. He has a steel pin in his hip. He will probably not be able to drive his rig again. It sits in the backyard, like a gigantic bird that has flown home to roost. Leroy has been home in Kentucky for three months, and his leg is almost healed, but the accident frightened him and he does not want to drive any more long hauls. He is not sure what to do next. In the meantime, he makes things from craft kits. He started by building a miniature log cabin from notched Popsicle sticks. He varnished it and placed it on the TV set, where it remains. It reminds him of a rustic Nativity scene. Then he tried string art (sailing ships on black velvet), a macramé owl kit, a snap-together B-17 Flying Fortress, and a lamp made out of a model truck, with a light fixture screwed in the top of the cab. At first the kits were diversions, something to kill time, but now he is thinking about building a full-scale log house from a kit. It would be considerably cheaper than building a regular house, and besides, Leroy has grown to appreciate how things are put together. He has begun to realize that in all the years he was on the road he never took time to examine anything. He was always flying past scenery.

"They won't let you build a log cabin in any of the new subdivisions," Norma Jean tells him.

"They will if I tell them it's for you," he says, teasing her. Ever since they were married, he has promised Norma Jean he would build her a new home one day. They have always rented, and the house they live in is small and nondescript. It does not even feel like a home. Leroy realizes now.

Norma Jean works at the Rexall drugstore, and she has acquired an amazing amount of information about cosmetics. When she explains to Leroy the three stages of complexion care, involving creams, toners, and moisturizers, he thinks happily of other petroleum products—axle grease, diesel fuel. This is a connection between him and Norma Jean. Since he has been home, he has felt unusually tender about his wife and guilty over his long absences. But he can't tell what she feels about him. Norma Jean has never complained about his traveling; she has never made hurt remarks, like calling his truck a "widow-maker." He is reasonably certain she has been faithful to him, but he wishes she would celebrate his permanent homecoming more happily. Norma Jean is often startled to find Leroy at home, and he thinks she seems a little disappointed about it. Perhaps he reminds her too much of the early days of their marriage, before he went on the road. They had a child who died as an infant, years ago. They never speak about their memories of Randy, which have almost faded, but now that Leroy is home all the time, they sometimes feel awkward around each other, and Leroy wonders if one of them should mention the child. He has the feeling that they are waking up out of a dream together—that they must create a new marriage, start afresh. They are lucky they are still married. Leroy has read that for most people losing a child destroys the marriage—or else he heard this on *Donahue*. He can't always remember where he learns things anymore.

At Christmas, Leroy bought an electric organ for Norma Jean. She used to play the piano when she was in high school. "It don't leave you," she told him once. "It's like riding a bicycle."

The new instrument had so many keys and buttons that she was bewildered by it at first. She touched the keys tentatively, pushed some buttons, then pecked out "Chopsticks." It came out in an amplified fox-trot rhythm, with marimba sounds.

"It's an orchestra!" she cried.

The organ had a pecan-look finish and eighteen present chords, with optional flute, violin, trumpet, clarinet, and banjo accompaniments. Norma Jean mastered the organ almost immediately. At first she played Christmas songs. Then she bought *The Sixties Songbook* and learned every tune in it, adding variations to each with the rows of brightly colored buttons.

"I didn't like these old songs back then," she said. "But I have this crazy feeling I missed something."

"You didn't miss a thing," said Leroy.

Leroy likes to lie on the couch and smoke a joint and listen to Norma Jean play "Can't Take My Eyes Off You" and "I'll Be Back." He is back again. After fifteen years on the road, he is finally settling down with the woman he loves. She is still pretty. Her skin is flawless. Her frosted curls resemble pencil trimmings.

Now that Leroy has come home to stay, he notices how much the town has changed. Subdivisions are spreading across western Kentucky like an oil slick. The sign at the edge of town says "Pop: 11,500"— only seven hundred more than it said twenty years before. Leroy can't figure out who is living in all the new houses. The farmers who used to gather around the courthouse square on Saturday afternoons to play checkers and spit tobacco juice have gone. It has been years since Leroy has thought about the farmers, and they have disappeared without his noticing.

Leroy meets a kid named Stevie Hamilton in the parking lot at the new shopping center. While they pretend to be strangers meeting over a stalled car, Stevie tosses an ounce of marijuana under the front seat of Leroy's car. Stevie is wearing orange jogging shoes and a T-shirt that says CHATTA-HOOCHEE SUPER-RAT. His father is a prominent doctor who lives in one of the expensive subdivisions in a new white-columned brick house that looks like a funeral parlor. In the phone book under his name there is a separate number, with the listing "Teenagers."

"Where do you get this stuff?" asks Leroy. "From your pappy?"

"That's for me to know and you to find out," Stevie says. He is slit-eyed and skinny.

"What else you got?"

"What you interested in?"

"Nothing special. Just wondered."

Leroy used to take speed on the road. Now he has to go slowly. He needs to be mellow. He leans back against the car and says, "I'm aiming to build me a log house, soon as I get time. My wife, though, I don't think she likes the idea."

"Well, let me know when you want me again," Stevie says. He has a cigarette in his cupped palm, as though sheltering it from the wind. He takes a long drag, then stomps it on the asphalt and slouches away.

Stevie's father was two years ahead of Leroy in high school. Leroy is thirty-four. He married Norma Jean when they were both eighteen, and their child Randy was born a few months later, but he died at the age of four months and three days. He would be about Stevie's age now. Norma Jean and Leroy were at the drive-in, watching a double feature (*Dr. Strangelove* and *Lover Come Back*), and the baby was sleeping in the back seat. When the first movie ended, the baby was dead. It was the sudden infant death syndrome. Leroy remembers handing Randy to a nurse at the emergency room, as though he were offering her a large doll as a present. A dead baby feels like a sack of flour. "It just happens sometimes," said the doctor, in what Leroy always recalls as a nonchalant tone. Leroy can hardly remember the child anymore, but he still sees vividly a scene from *Dr. Strangelove* in which the President of the United States was talking in a folksy voice on the hot line to the Soviet premier about the bomber accidentally headed toward Russia. He was in the War Room, and the world map was lit up. Leroy remembers Norma Jean standing catatonically beside him in the hospital and himself thinking: Who is this strange girl? He had forgotten who she was. Now scientists are saying that crib death is caused by a virus. Nobody knows anything, Leroy thinks. The answers are always changing.

When Leroy gets home from the shopping center, Norma Jean's mother, Mabel Beasley, is there. Until this year, Leroy has not realized how much time she spends with Norma Jean. When she visits, she inspects the closets and then the plants, informing Norma Jean when a plant is droopy or yellow. Mabel calls the plants "flowers," although there are never any blooms. She always notices if Norma Jean's laundry is piling up. Mabel is a short, overweight woman whose tight, brown-dyed curls look more like a wig than the actual wig she sometimes wears. Today she has brought Norma Jean an off-white dust ruffle she made for the bed; Mabel works in a custom-upholstery shop.

"This is the tenth one I made this year," Mabel says. "I got started and couldn't stop."

"It's real pretty," says Norma Jean.

"Now we can hide things under the bed," says Leroy, who gets along with his mother-in-law primarily by joking with her. Mabel has never really forgiven him for disgracing her by getting Norma Jean pregnant. When the baby died, she said that fate was mocking her.

"What's that thing?" Mabel says to Leroy in a loud voice, pointing to a tangle of yarn on a piece of canvas.

Leroy holds it up for Mabel to see. "It's my needlepoint," he explains. "This is a *Star Trek* pillow cover."

"That's what a woman would do," says Mabel. "Great day in the morning!"

"All the big football players on TV do it," he says.

"Why, Leroy, you're always trying to fool me. I don't believe you for one minute. You don't know what to do with yourself—that's the whole trouble. Sewing!"

"I'm aiming to build us a log house," says Leroy. "Soon as my plans come."

"Like *heck* you are," says Norma Jean. She takes Leroy's needlepoint and shoves it into a drawer. "You have to find a job first. Nobody can afford to build now anyway."

Mabel straightens her girdle and says, "I still think before you get tied down y'all ought to take a little run to Shiloh."

"One of these days, Mama," Norma Jean says impatiently.

Mabel is talking about Shiloh, Tennessee. For the past few years, she has been urging Leroy and Norma Jean to visit the Civil War battleground there. Mabel went there on her honeymoon—the only real trip she ever took. Her husband died of a perforated ulcer when Norma Jean was ten, but Mabel, who was accepted into the United Daughters of the Confederacy in 1975, is still preoccupied with going back to Shiloh.

"I've been to kingdom come and back in that truck out yonder," Leroy says to Mabel, "but we never yet set foot in that battleground. Ain't that something? How did I miss it?"

"It's not even that far," Mabel says.

After Mabel leaves, Norma Jean reads to Leroy from a list she has made. "Things you could do," she announces. "You could get a job as a guard at Union Carbide, where they'd let you set on a stool. You could get on at the lumberyard. You could do a little carpenter work, if you want to build so bad. You could—"

"I can't do something where I'd have to stand up all day."

"You ought to try standing up all day behind a cosmetics counter. It's amazing that I have strong feet, coming from two parents that never had strong feet at all." At the moment Norma Jean is holding on to the kitchen counter, raising her knees one at a time as she talks. She is wearing two-pound ankle weights.

"Don't worry," says Leroy. "I'll do something."

"You could truck calves to slaughter for somebody. You wouldn't have to drive any big old truck for that."

"I'm going to build you this house," says Leroy. "I want to make you a real home."

"I don't want to live in any log cabin."

"It's not a cabin. It's a house."

"I don't care. It looks like a cabin."

"You and me together could lift those logs. It's just like lifting weights."

Norma Jean doesn't answer. Under her breath, she is counting. Now she is marching through the kitchen. She is doing goose steps.

Before his accident, when Leroy came home he used to stay in the house with Norma Jean, watching TV in bed and playing cards. She would cook fried chicken, picnic ham, chocolate pie — all his favorites. Now he is home alone much of the time. In the mornings, Norma Jean disappears, leaving a cooling place in the bed. She eats a cereal called Body Buddies, and she leaves the bowl on the table, with the soggy tan balls floating in a milk puddle. He sees things about Norma Jean that he never realized before. When she chops onions, she stares off into a corner, as if she can't bear to look. She puts on her house slippers almost precisely at nine o'clock every evening and nudges her jogging shoes under the couch. She saves bread heels for the birds. Leroy watches the birds at the feeder. He notices the peculiar way goldfinches fly past the window. They close their wings, then fall, then spread their wings to catch and lift themselves. He wonders if they close their eyes when they fall. Norma Jean closes her eyes when they are in bed. She wants the lights turned out. Even then, he is sure she closes her eyes.

He goes for long drives around town. He tends to drive a car rather carelessly. Power steering and an automatic shift make a car feel so small and inconsequential that his body is hardly involved in the driving process. His injured leg stretches out comfortably. Once or twice he has almost hit something, but even the prospect of an accident seems minor in a car. He cruises the new subdivisions, feeling like a criminal rehearsing for a robbery. Norma Jean is probably right about a log house being inappropriate here in the new subdivisions. All the houses look grand and complicated. They depress him.

One day when Leroy comes home from a drive he finds Norma Jean in tears. She is in the kitchen making a potato and mushroom-soup casserole, with grated-cheese topping. She is crying because her mother caught her smoking.

"I didn't hear her coming. I was standing here puffing away pretty as you please," Norma Jean says, wiping her eyes.

"I knew it would happen sooner or later," says Leroy, putting his arm around her.

"She don't know the meaning of the word 'knock,'" says Norma Jean. "It's a wonder she hadn't caught me years ago."

"Think of it this way," Leroy says. "What if she caught me with a joint?"

"You better not let her!" Norma Jean shrieks. "I'm warning you, Leroy Moffitt!"

"I'm just kidding. Here, play me a tune. That'll help you relax."

Norma Jean puts the casserole in the oven and sets the timer. Then she plays a ragtime tune, with horns and banjo, as Leroy lights up a joint and lies on the couch, laughing to himself about Mabel's catching him at it. He thinks of Stevie Hamilton—a doctor's son pushing grass. Everything is funny. The whole town seems crazy and small. He is reminded of Virgil Mathis, a boastful policeman Leroy used to shoot pool with. Virgil recently led a drug bust in a back room at a bowling alley, where he seized ten thousand dollars' worth of marijuana. The newspaper had a picture of him holding up the bags of grass and grinning widely. Right now, Leroy can imagine Virgil breaking down the door and arresting him with a lungful of smoke. Virgil would probably have been alerted to the scene because of all the racket Norma Jean is making. Now she sounds like a hard-rock band. Norma Jean is terrific. When she switches to a Latin-rhythm version of "Sunshine Superman," Leroy hums along. Norma Jean's foot goes up and down, up and down.

"Well, what do you think?" Leroy says, when Norma Jean pauses to search through her music.

"What do I think about what?"

His mind has gone blank. Then he says, "I'll sell my rig and build us a house." That wasn't what he wanted to say. He wanted to know what she thought—what she *really* thought—about them.

"Don't start in on that again," says Norma Jean. She begins playing "Who'll Be the Next in Line?"

Leroy used to tell hitchhikers his whole life story—about his travels, his hometown, the baby. He would end with a question: "Well, what do you think?" It was just a rhetorical question. In time, he had the feeling that he'd been telling the same story over and over to the same hitchhikers. He quit talking to hitchhikers when he realized how his voice sounded — whining and self-pitying, like some teenage-tragedy song. Now Leroy has the sudden impulse to tell Norma Jean about himself, as if he had just met her. They have known each other so long they have forgotten a lot about each other. They could become reacquainted. But when the oven timer goes off and she runs to the kitchen, he forgets why he wants to do this.

The next day, Mabel drops by. It is Saturday and Norma Jean is cleaning. Leroy is studying the plans of his log house, which have finally come in the mail. He has them spread out on the table—big sheets of stiff blue paper, with diagrams and numbers printed in white. While Norma Jean runs the vacuum, Mabel drinks coffee. She sets her coffee cup on a blue-print.

"I'm just waiting for time to pass," she says to Leroy, drumming her fingers on the table.

As soon as Norma Jean switches off the vacuum, Mabel says in a loud voice, "Did you hear about the datsun dog that killed the baby?"

Norma Jean says, "The word is 'dachshund.'"

"They put the dog on trial. It chewed the baby's legs off. The mother was in the next room all the time." She raises her voice. "They thought it was neglect."

Norma Jean is holding her ears. Leroy manages to open the refrigerator and get some Diet Pepsi to offer Mabel. Mabel still has some coffee and she waves away the Pepsi.

"Datsuns are like that," Mabel says. "They're jealous dogs. They'll tear a place to pieces if you don't keep an eye on them."

"You better watch out what you're saying, Mabel," says Leroy.

"Well, facts is facts."

Leroy looks out the window at his rig. It is like a huge piece of furniture gathering dust in the backyard. Pretty soon it will be an antique. He hears the vacuum cleaner. Norma Jean seems to be cleaning the living room rug again.

Later, she says to Leroy, "She just said that about the baby because she caught me smoking. She's trying to pay me back."

"What are you talking about?" Leroy says, nervously shuffling blue-prints.

"You know good and well," Norma Jean says. She is sitting in a kitchen chair with her feet up and her arms wrapped around her knees. She looks small and helpless. She says, "The very idea, her bringing up a subject like that! Saying it was neglect."

"She didn't mean that," Leroy says.

"She might not have *thought* she meant it. She always says things like that. You don't know how she goes on."

"But she didn't really mean it. She was just talking."

Leroy opens a king-sized bottle of beer and pours it into two glasses, dividing it carefully. He hands a glass to Norma Jean and she takes it from him mechanically. For a long time, they sit by the kitchen window watching the birds at the feeder.

Something is happening. Norma Jean is going to night school. She has graduated from her six-week body-building course and now she is taking an adult-education course in composition at Paducah Community College. She spends her evenings outlining paragraphs.

"First you have a topic sentence," she explains to Leroy. "Then you divide it up. Your secondary topic has to be connected to your primary topic."

To Leroy, this sounds intimidating. "I never was any good in English," he says.

"It makes a lot of sense."

"What are you doing this for, anyhow?"

She shrugs. "It's something to do." She stands up and lifts her dumbbells a few times.

"Driving a rig, nobody cared about my English."

"I'm not criticizing your English."

Norma Jean used to say, "If I lose ten minutes' sleep, I just drag all day." Now she stays up late, writing compositions. She got a B on her first paper—a how-to theme on soup-based casseroles. Recently, Norma Jean has been cooking unusual foods—tacos, lasagna, Bombay chicken. She doesn't play the organ anymore, though her second paper was called "Why Music Is Important to Me." She sits at the kitchen table, concentrating on her outlines, while Leroy plays with his log house plans, practicing with a set of Lincoln Logs. The thought of getting a truckload of notched, numbered logs scares him, and he wants to be prepared. As he and Norma Jean work together at the kitchen table, Leroy has the hopeful thought that they are sharing something, but he knows he is a fool to think this. Norma Jean is miles away. He knows he is going to lose her. Like Mabel, he is just waiting for time to pass.

One day, Mabel is there before Norma Jean gets home from work, and Leroy finds himself confiding in her. Mabel, he realizes, must know Norma Jean better than he does.

"I don't know what's got into that girl," Mabel says. "She used to go to bed with the chickens. Now you say she's up all hours. Plus her a-smoking. I like to died."

"I want to make her this beautiful home," Leroy says, indicating the Lincoln Logs. "I don't think she even wants it. Maybe she was happier with me gone."

"She don't know what to make of you, coming home like this."

"Is that it?"

Mabel takes the roof off his Lincoln Log cabin. "You couldn't get *me* in a log cabin," she says. "I was raised in one. It's no picnic, let me tell you."

"They're different now," says Leroy.

"I tell you what," Mabel says, smiling oddly at Leroy.

"What?"

"Take her on down to Shiloh. Y'all need to get out together, stir a little. Her brain's all balled up over them books."

Leroy can see traces of Norma Jean's features in her mother's face. Mabel's worn face has the texture of crinkled cotton, but suddenly she looks pretty. It occurs to Leroy that Mabel has been hinting all along that she wants them to take her with them to Shiloh.

"Let's all go to Shiloh," he says. "You and me and her. Come Sunday."

Mabel throws up her hands in protest. "Oh, no, not me. Young folks want to be by theirselves."

When Norma Jean comes in with groceries, Leroy says excitedly, "Your mama here's been dying to go to Shiloh for thirty-five years. It's about time we went, don't you think?"

"I'm not going to butt in on anybody's second honeymoon," Mabel says.

"Who's going on a honeymoon, for Christ's sake?" Norma Jean says loudly.

"I never raised no daughter of mine to talk that-a-way," Mabel says.

"You ain't seen nothing yet," says Norma Jean. She starts putting away boxes and cans, slamming cabinet doors.

"There's a log cabin at Shiloh," Mabel says. "It was there during the battle. There's bullet holes in it."

"When are you going to *shut up* about Shiloh, Mama?" asks Norma Jean.

"I always thought Shiloh was the prettiest place, so full of history," Mabel goes on. "I just hoped y'all could see it once before I die, so you could tell me about it." Later, she whispers to Leroy, "You do what I said. A little change is what she needs."

"Your name means 'the king,'" Norma Jean says to Leroy that evening. He is trying to get her to go to Shiloh, and she is reading a book about another century.

"Well, I reckon I ought to be right proud."

"I guess so."

"Am I still king around here?"

Norma Jean flexes her biceps and feels them for hardness. "I'm not fooling around with anybody, if that's what you mean," she says.

"Would you tell me if you were?"

"I don't know."

"What does *your* name mean?"

"It was Marilyn Monroe's real name."

"No kidding!"

"Norma comes from the Normans. They were invaders," she says. She closes her book and looks hard at Leroy. "I'll go to Shiloh with you if you'll stop staring at me."

. . .

On Sunday, Norma Jean packs a picnic and they go to Shiloh. To Leroy's relief, Mabel says she does not want to come with them. Norma Jean drives, and Leroy, sitting beside her, feels like some boring hitchhiker she has picked up. He tries some conversation, but she answers him in monosyllables. At Shiloh, she drives aimlessly through the park, past bluffs and trails and steep ravines. Shiloh is an immense place, and Leroy cannot see it as a battleground. It is not what he expected. He thought it would look like a golf course. Monuments are everywhere, showing through the thick clusters of trees. Norma Jean passes the log cabin Mabel mentioned. It is surrounded by tourists looking for bullet holes.

"That's not the kind of log house I've got in mind," says Leroy apologetically.

"I know *that*."

"This is a pretty place. Your mama was right."

"It's O.K.," says Norma Jean. "Well, we've seen it. I hope she's satisfied."

They burst out laughing together.

At the park museum, a movie on Shiloh is shown every half hour, but they decide that they don't want to see it. They buy a souvenir Confederate flag for Mabel, and then they find a picnic spot near the cemetery. Norma Jean has brought a picnic cooler, with pimiento sandwiches, soft drinks, and Yodels. Leroy eats a sandwich and then smokes a joint, hiding it behind the picnic cooler. Norma Jean has quit smoking altogether. She is picking cake crumbs from the cellophane wrapper, like a fussy bird.

Leroy says, "So the boys in gray ended up in Corinth. The Union soldiers zapped 'em finally, April 7, 1862."

They both know that he doesn't know any history. He is just talking about some of the historical plaques they have read. He feels awkward, like a boy on a date with an older girl. They are still just making conversation.

"Corinth is where Mama eloped to," says Norma Jean.

They sit in silence and stare at the cemetery for the Union dead and, beyond, at a tall cluster of trees. Campers are parked nearby, bumper to bumper, and small children in bright clothing are cavorting and squealing. Norma Jean wads up the cake wrapper and squeezes it tightly in her hand. Without looking at Leroy, she says, "I want to leave you."

Leroy takes a bottle of Coke out of the cooler and flips off the cap. He holds the bottle poised near his mouth but cannot remember to take a drink. Finally he says, "No, you don't."

"Yes, I do."

"I won't let you."

"You can't stop me."

"Don't do me that way."

Leroy knows Norma Jean will have her own way. "Didn't I promise to be home from now on?" he says.

"In some ways, a woman prefers a man who wanders," says Norma Jean. "That sounds crazy, I know."

"You're not crazy."

Leroy remembers to drink from his Coke. Then he says, "Yes, you *are* crazy. You and me could start all over again. Right back at the beginning."

"We *have* started all over again," says Norma Jean. "And this is how it turned out."

"What did I do wrong?"

"Nothing."

"Is this one of those women's lib things?" Leroy asks.

"Don't be funny."

The cemetery, a green slope dotted with white markers, looks like a subdivision site. Leroy is trying to comprehend that his marriage is breaking up, but for some reason he is wondering about white slabs in a graveyard.

"Everything was fine till Mama caught me smoking," says Norma Jean, standing up. "That set something off."

"What are you talking about?"

"She won't leave me alone—*you* won't leave me alone." Norma Jean seems to be crying, but she is looking away from him. "I feel eighteen again. I can't face that all over again." She starts walking away. "No, it *wasn't* fine. I don't know what I'm saying. Forget it."

Leroy takes a lungful of smoke and closes his eyes as Norma Jean's words sink in. He tries to focus on the fact that thirty-five hundred soldiers died on the grounds around him. He can only think of that war as a board game with plastic soldiers. Leroy almost smiles, as he compares the Confederates' daring attack on the Union camps and Virgil Mathis's raid on the bowling alley. General Grant, drunk and furious, shoved the Southerners back to Corinth, where Mabel and Jet Beasley were married years later, when Mabel was still thin and good-looking. The next day, Mabel and Jet visited the battleground, and then Norma Jean was born, and then she married Leroy and they had a baby, which they lost, and now Leroy and Norma Jean are here at the same battleground. Leroy knows he is leaving out a lot. He is leaving out the insides of history. History was always just names and dates to him. It occurs to him that building a house out of logs is similarly empty—too simple. And the real inner workings of a marriage, like most of history, have escaped him. Now he sees that building a log house is the dumbest idea he could have had. It was clumsy of him to think Norma Jean would want a log house. It was a crazy idea. He'll have to think of something else, quickly. He will wad the blueprints into tight balls and fling them into the lake. Then he'll get moving again. He opens his eyes. Norma Jean has moved away and is walking through the cemetery, following a serpentine brick path.

Leroy gets up to follow his wife, but his good leg is asleep and his bad leg still hurts him. Norma Jean is far away, walking rapidly toward the bluff by the river, and he tries to hobble toward her. Some children run past him, screaming noisily. Norma Jean has reached the bluff, and she is looking out over the Tennessee River. Now she turns toward Leroy and waves her arms. Is she beckoning to him? She seems to be doing an exercise for her chest muscles. The sky is unusually pale—the color of the dust ruffle Mabel made for their bed.

Consequences

"Letter to the Union Convention, 1865"

Black Citizens of Tennessee

Few private letters and diaries of African Americans survive from the Civil War era, but the voluminous record of pleas, arguments, and demands they sent to the federal government stand as powerful testimony. That record is now being compiled and edited by a skilled team of historians, revealing sides to the war and emancipation never before seen. In this selection, a petition to a convention of white unionists in Tennessee in the waning days of the war, black men argue eloquently for their rights as citizens and as people. There is no record of a response.

[*Nashville, Tenn., January 9, 1865*]

To the Union Convention of Tennessee Assembled in the Capitol at Nashville, January 9th, 1865:

We the undersigned petitioners, American citizens of African descent, natives and residents of Tennessee, and devoted friends of the great National cause, do most respectfully ask a patient hearing of your honorable body in regard to matters deeply affecting the future condition of our unfortunate and long suffering race.

First of all, however, we would say that words are too weak to tell how profoundly grateful we are to the Federal Government for the good work of freedom which it is gradually carrying forward; and for the Emancipation Proclamation which has set free all the slaves in some of the rebellious States, as well as many of the slaves in Tennessee.

After two hundred years of bondage and suffering a returning sense of justice has awakened the great body of the American people to make amends for the unprovoked wrongs committed against us for over two hundred years.

Your petitioners would ask you to complete the work begun by the nation at large, and abolish the last vestige of slavery by the express words of your organic law.

Many masters in Tennessee whose slaves have left them, will certainly make every effort to bring them back to bondage after the reorganization of the State government, unless slavery be expressly abolished by the Constitution.

We hold that freedom is the natural right of all men, which they them-selves have no more right to give or barter away, than they have to sell their honor, their wives, or their children.

We claim to be men belonging to the great human family, descended from one great God, who is the common Father of all, and who bestowed on all races and tribes the priceless right of freedom. Of this right, for no offence of ours, we have long been cruelly deprived, and the common voice of the wise and good of all countries, has remonstrated against our enslavement, as one of the greatest crimes in all history.

We claim freedom, as our natural right, and ask that in harmony and co-operation with the nation at large, you should cut up by the roots the system of slavery, which is not only a wrong to us, but the source of all the evil which at present afflicts the State. For slavery, corrupt itself, corrupted nearly all, also, around it, so that it has influenced nearly all the slave States to rebel against the Federal Government, in order to set up a gov-ernment of pirates under which slavery might be perpetrated.

In the contest between the nation and slavery, our unfortunate people have sided, by instinct, with the former. We have little fortune to devote to the national cause, for a hard fate has hitherto forced us to live in poverty, but we do devote to its success, our hopes, our toils, our whole heart, our sacred honor, and our lives. We will work, pray, live, and, if need be, die for the Union, as cheerfully as ever a white patriot died for his country. The color of our skin does not lesson in the least degree, our love either for God or for the land of our birth.

We are proud to point your honorable body to the fact, that so far as our knowledge extends, not a negro traitor has made his appearance since the beginning of this wicked rebellion.

Whether freeman or slaves the colored race in this country have always looked upon the United States as the Promised Land of Universal free-dom, and no earthly temptation has been strong enough to induce us to rebel against it. We love the Union by an instinct which is stronger than any argument or appeal which can be used against it. It is the attachment of a child to its parent.

Devoted as we are to the principles of justice, of love to all men, and of equal rights on which our Government is based, and which make it the hope of the world. We know the burdens of citizenship, and are ready to bear them. We know the duties of the good citizen, and are ready to per-form them cheerfully, and would ask to be put in a position in which we can discharge them more effectually. We do not ask for the privilege of cit-izenship, wishing to shun the obligations imposed by it.

Near 200,000 of our brethren are to-day performing military duty in the ranks of the Union army. Thousands of them have already died in battle, or perished by a cruel martyrdom for the sake of the Union, and we are ready and willing to sacrifice more. But what higher order of citizen is there than the soldier? or who has a greater trust confided to his hands? If we are called on to do military duty against the rebel armies in the field, why should we be denied the privilege of voting against rebel citizens at the ballot-box? The latter is as necessary to save the Government as the former.

The colored man will vote by instinct with the Union party, just as uniformly as he fights with the Union army.

This is not a new question in Tennessee. From 1796 to 1835, a period of thirty-nine years, free colored men voted at all her elections without question. Her leading politicians and statemen asked for and obtained the suffrages of colored voters, and were not ashamed of it. Such men as *Andrew Jackson*, President of the United States, Hon. *Felix Grundy*, John Bell, Hon. *Hugh L. White, Cave Johnson,* and *Ephraim H. Foster,* members of the United States Senate and of the Cabinet, Gen. *William Carroll, Samuel Houston,* Aaron V. Brown, and, in fact, all the politicians and candidates of all parties in Tennessee solicited colored free men for their votes at every election.

Nor was Tennessee alone in this respect, for the same privilege was granted to colored free men in North Carolina, to-day the most loyal of all the rebellious States, without ever producing any evil consequences.

If colored men have been faithful and true to the Government of the United States in spite of the Fugitive Slave Law, and the cruel policy often pursued toward them, will they not be more devoted to it now than ever, since it has granted them that liberty which they desired above all things? Surely, if colored men voted without harm to the State, while their brethren were in bondage, they will be much more devoted and watchful over her interests when elevated to the rank of freemen and voters. If they are good law-abiding citizens, praying for its prosperity, rejoicing in its progress, paying its taxes, fighting its battles, making its farms, mines, work-shops and commerce more productive, why deny them the right to have a voice in the election of its rulers?

This is a democracy—a government of the people. It should aim to make every man, without regard to the color of his skin, the amount of his wealth, or the character of his religious faith, feel personally interested in its welfare. Every man who lives under the Government should feel that it is his property, his treasure, the bulwark and defense of himself and his family, his pearl of great price, which he must preserve, protect, and defend faithfully at all times, on all occasions, in every possible manner.

This is not a Democratic Government if a numerous, law-abiding, industrious, and useful class of citizens, born and bred on the soil, are to be treated as aliens and enemies, as an inferior degraded class, who must have no voice in the Government which they support, protect and defend, with all their heart, soul, mind, and body, both in peace and war.

This Government is based on the teachings of the Bible, which prescribes the same rules of action for all members of the human family, whether their complexion be white, yellow, red or black. God no where in his revealed word, makes an invidious and degrading distinction against his children, because of their color. And happy is that nation which makes the Bible its rule of action, and obeys principle, not prejudice.

Let no man oppose this doctrine because it is opposed to his old prejudices. The nation is fighting for its life, and cannot afford to be controlled by prejudice. Had prejudice prevailed instead of principle, not a single colored solider would have been in the Union army to-day. But principle and justice triumphed, and now near 200,000 colored patriots stand under the folds of the national flag, and brave their breasts to the bullets of the rebels. As we are in the battlefield, so we swear before heaven, by all that is dear to men, to be at the ballot-box faithful and true to the Union.

The possibility that the negro suffrage proposition may shock popular prejudice at first sight, is not a conclusive argument against its wisdom and policy. No proposition ever met with more furious or general opposition than the one to enlist colored soldiers in the United States army. The opponents of the measure exclaimed on all hands that the negro was a coward; that he would not fight; that one white man, with a whip in his hand could put to flight a regiment of them; that the experiment would end in the utter rout and ruin of the Federal army. Yet the colored man has fought so well, on almost every occasion, that the rebel government is prevented, only by its fears and distrust of being able to force him to fight for slavery as well as he fights against it, from putting half a million of negroes into its ranks.

The Government has asked the colored man to fight for its preservation and gladly has he done it. It can afford to trust him with a vote as safely as it trusted him with a bayonet.

How boundless would be the love of the colored citizen, how intense and passionate his zeal and devotion to the government, how enthusiastic and how lasting would be his gratitude, if his white brethren were to take him by the hand and say, "You have been ever loyal to our government; henceforward be voters." Again, the granting of this privilege would stimulate the colored man to greater exertion to make himself an intelligent, respected, useful citizen. His pride of character would be appealed to this way most successfully; he would send his children to school, that they might become educated and intelligent members of society. It used to be thought that ignorant negroes were the most valuable, but this belief probably originated from the fact that it is almost impossible to retain an educated, intelligent man in bondage. Certainly, if the free colored man be educated, and his morals enlightened and improved, he will be a far better member of society, and less liable to transgress its laws. It is the brutal, degraded, ignorant man who is usually the criminal.

One other matter we would urge on your honorable body. At present we can have only partial protection from the courts. The testimony of twenty of the most intelligent, honorable, colored loyalists cannot convict a white traitor of a treasonable action. A white rebel might sell powder and lead to a rebel soldier in the presence of twenty colored soldiers, and yet their evidence would be worthless so far as the courts are concerned, and the rebel would escape. A colored man may have served for years faithfully in the army, and yet his testimony in court would be rejected, while that of a white man who had served in the rebel army would be received.

If this order of things continue, our people are destined to a malignant persecution at the hands of rebels and their former rebellious masters, whose hatred they may have incurred, without precedent even in the South. Every rebel soldier or citizen whose arrest in the perpetration of crime they may have effected, every white traitor whom they may have brought to justice, will torment and persecute them and set justice at defiance, because the courts will not receive negro testimony, which will generally be the only possible testimony in such cases. A rebel may murder his former slave and defy justice, because he committed the deed in the presence of half a dozen respectable colored citizens. He may have the dwelling of his former slave burned over his head, and turn his wife and children out of doors, and defy the law, for no colored man can appear against him. Is this the fruit of freedom, and the reward of our services in the field? Was it for this that colored soldiers fell by hundreds before Nashville, fighting under the flag of the Union? Is it for this that we have guided Union officers and soldiers, when escaping from the cruel and deadly prisons of the South through forests and swamps, at the risk of our own lives, for we knew that to us detection would be death? Is it for this that we have concealed multitudes of Union refugees in caves and canebrakes, when flying from the conscription officers and tracked by bloodhounds, and divided with them our last morsal of food? Will you declare in your revised constitution that a pardoned traitor may appear in court and his testimony be heard, but that no colored loyalist shall be believed even upon oath? If this should be so, then will our last state be worse than our first, and we can look for no relief on this side of the grave. Has not the colored man fought, bled and died for the Union, under a thousand great disadvantages and discouragements? Has his fidelity ever had a shadow of suspicion cast upon it, in any matter of responsibility confided to his hands?

There have been white traitors in multitudes in Tennessee, but where we ask, is the black traitor? Can you forget how the colored man has fought at Fort Morgan, at Milliken's Bend, at Fort Pillow, before Petersburg, and your own city of Nashville?

When has the colored citizen, in this rebellion been tried and found wanting?

In conclusion, we would point to the fact that the States where the largest measure of justice and civil rights has been granted to the colored man, both as to suffrage and his oath in court, are among the most rich, intelligent, enlightened and prosperous. Massachusetts, illustrious for her statesmen and her commercial and manufacturing enterprises and thrift, whose noble liberality has relieved so many loyal refugees and other sufferers of Tennessee, allows her colored citizens to vote, and is ever jealous of their rights. She has never had reason to repent the day when she gave them the right of voting.

Had the southern states followed her example the present rebellion never would have desolated their borders.

Several other Northern States permit negro suffrage, nor have bad effects ever resulted from it. It may be safely affirmed that Tennessee was quite as safe and prosperous during the 39 years while she allowed negro suffrage, as she has been since she abolished it.

In this great and fearful struggle of the nation with a wicked rebellion, we are anxious to perform the full measure of our duty both as citizens and soldiers to the Union cause we consecrate ourselves, and our families, with all that we have on earth. Our souls burn with love for the great government of freedom and equal rights. Our white brethren have no cause for distrust as regards our fidelity, for neither death nor life, nor angels, nor principalities, nor powers, nor things present, nor things to come, nor height, nor depth, nor any other creature, shall be able to separate us from the love of the Union.

Praying that the great God, who is the common Father of us all, by whose help the land must be delivered from present evil, and before whom we must all stand at last to be judged by the rule of eternal justice, and not by passion and prejudice, may enlighten your minds and enable you to act with wisdom, justice, and magnanimity, we remain your faithful friends in all the perils and dangers which threaten our beloved country.

[59 *signatures*]
And many other colored citizens of Nashville

"Dave's Neckliss"

Charles W. Chesnutt (1858–1932)

Charles W. Chesnutt crossed a number of lines in his lifetime. Though born in Cleveland, Ohio, the grandson of a white man and the son of free blacks, Chesnutt grew up in Fayetteville, North Carolina, where his family returned after the Civil War. He attended a school funded by the Freedman's Bureau and then worked as a teacher and school principal in Charlotte and in Fayetteville. Despite his success, Chesnutt resented the racial oppression of the South and moved his family to Cleveland in 1884, where he worked first as a court reporter and then as founder of a successful legal stenography company. Chesnutt also had a passion for writing and began publishing short stories in 1885. "Dave's Neckliss" (1889), like others of these early stories, was among the first written in black dialect by a black writer, using the language to convey not only authenticity but moral complexity. Chesnutt's work dealt primarily with the South, and especially with themes of interracial sex and the phenomenon of people legally defined as "black" whose relatively light skin color enabled them to pass as white. Chesnutt met with much praise for his early stories, but his powerful and controversial novels found only a diminishing readership. He stopped writing fiction in the early twentieth century, devoting his energies to business and organizations dedicated to improving the lives of African Americans.

Have some dinner, Uncle Julius?" said my wife. It was a Sunday afternoon in early autumn. Our two women-servants had gone to a camp-meeting some miles away, and would not return until evening. My wife had served the dinner, and we were just rising from the table, when Julius came up the lane, and, taking off his hat, seated himself on the piazza.

The old man glanced through the open door at the dinner table, and his eyes rested lovingly upon a large sugar-cured ham, from which several slices had been cut, exposing a rich pink expanse that would have appealed strongly to the appetite of any hungry Christian.

"Thanky, Miss Annie," he said, after a momentary hesitation, "I dunno ez I keers ef I does tas'e a piece er dat ham—ef yer'll cut me off a slice un it."

"No," said Annie, "I won't. Just sit down to the table and help yourself; eat all you want, and don't be bashful."

Julius drew a chair up to the table, while my wife and I went out on the piazza. Julius was in my employment; he took his meals with his own family, but when he happened to be about our house at meal times, my wife never let him go away hungry.

I threw myself into a hammock, from which I could see Julius through an open window. He ate with evident relish, devoting his attention chiefly to the ham, slice after slice of which disappeared in the spacious cavity of his mouth. At first the old man ate rapidly, but after the edge of his appetite had been taken off he proceeded in a more leisurely manner. When he had cut the sixth slice of ham (I kept count of them from a lazy curiousity to see how much he *could* eat) I saw him lay it on his plate; as he adjusted the knife and fork to cut it into smaller pieces, he paused, as if struck by a sudden thought, and a tear rolled down his rugged cheek and fell upon the slice of ham before him. But the emotion, whatever the thought that caused it, was transitory, and in a moment he continued his dinner. When he was through eating, he came out on the porch, and resumed his seat with the satisfied expression of countenance that usually follows a good dinner.

"Julius," I said, "you seemed to be affected by something, a moment ago. Was the mustard so strong that it moved you to tears?"

"No, suh, it wa'n't de mustard; I wuz studyin' 'bout Dave."

"Who was Dave, and what about him?" I asked.

The conditions were all favorable to story-telling. There was an autumnal languor in the air, and a dreamy haze softened the dark green of the distant pines and the deep blue of the Southern sky. The generous meal he had made had put the old man in a very good humor. He was not always so, for his curiously undeveloped nature was subject to moods which were almost childish in their variableness. It was only now and then that we were able to study, through the medium of his recollection, the simple but intensely human inner life of slavery. His way of looking at the past seemed very strange to us; his view of certain sides of life was essentially different from ours. He never indulged in any regrets for the Arcadian joyousness and irresponsibility which was a somewhat popular conception of slavery; his had not been the lot of the petted house-servant, but that of the toiling field-hand. While he mentioned with a warm appreciation the acts of kindness which those in authority had shown to him and his people, he would speak of a cruel deed, not with the indignation of one accustomed to quick feeling and spontaneous expression, but with a furtive disapproval which suggested to us a doubt in his own mind as to whether he had a right to think or to feel, and presented to us the curious psychological spectacle of a mind enslaved long after the shackles had been struck off from the limbs of its possessor. Whether the sacred name of liberty ever set his soul aglow with a generous fire; whether he had more than the most elementary ideas of love, friendship, patriotism, religion — things which are half, and the better half, of life to us; whether he even realized except in a vague, uncertain way, his own degradation, I do not know, I fear not; and if not, then centuries of repression had borne their legitimate fruit. But in the simple human feeling, and still more in the undertone of sadness, which pervaded his stories, I thought I could see a spark which, fanned by favoring breezes and fed by the memories of the past, might become in his children's children a glowing flame of sensibility, alive to every thrill of human happiness or human woe.

"Dave use' ter b'long ter my ole marster," said Julius; "he wuz raise' on dis yer plantation, en I kin 'member all erbout 'im, fer I wuz ole 'nuff ter chop cotton w'en it all happen'. Dave wuz a tall man, en monst'us strong: he could do mo' wuk in a day dan any yuther two niggers on de plantation. He wuz one er dese yer solemn kine er men, en nebber run on wid much foolishness, like de yuther darkies. He use' ter go out in de woods en pray; en w'en he hear de han's on de plantation cussin' en gwine on wid dere dancin' en foolishness, he use' ter tell 'em 'bout religion en jedgemen'-day, w'en dey would haf ter gin account fer eve'y idle word en all dey yuther sinful kyarin'son.

"Dave had l'arn how ter read de Bible. Dey wuz a free nigger boy in de settlement w'at wuz munst'us smart, en could write en cipher, en wuz alluz readin' books er papers. En Dave had hi'ed dis free boy fer to l'arn 'im how ter read. Hit wuz 'g'in de law, but co'se none er de niggers didn' say nuffin ter de w'ite folks 'bout it. Howsomedever, one day Mars Walker—he wuz de oberseah—foun' out Dave could read. Mars Walker wa'n't nuffin but a po' bockrah, en folks said he couldn' read ner write hisse'f, en co'se he didn' lack ter see a nigger w'at knowed mo' d'n he did; so he went en tole Mars Dugal'. Mars Dugal' sont fer Dave, en ax' 'im 'bout it.

"Dave didn't hardly knowed w'at ter do; but he couldn' tell no lie, so he 'fessed he could read de Bible a little by spellin' out de words. Mars Dugal' look' mighty solemn.

"'Dis yer is a se'ious matter,' sezee;' it's 'g'in de law ter l'arn niggers how ter read, er 'low 'em ter hab books. But w'at yer l'arn out'n dat Bible, Dave?"

"Dave wa'n't no fool, ef he wuz a nigger, en sezee:

"'Marster, I l'arns dat it's a sin fer ter steal, er ter lie, er fer ter want w'at doan b'long ter yer; en I l'arns fer ter love de Lawd en ter 'bey my marster.'

"Mars Dugal' sorter smile' en laf' ter hisse'f, like he 'uz might'ly tickle' 'bout sump'n, en sezee:

"'Doan 'pear ter me lack readin' de Bible done yer much harm, Dave.

Dat's w'at I wants all my niggers fer ter know. Yer keep right on readin', en tell de yuther han's w'at yer be'n tellin' me. How would yer lack fer ter preach ter de niggers on Sunday?'"

"Dave say he'd be glad fer ter do w'at he could. So Mars Dugal' tole de oberseah fer ter let Dave preach ter de niggers, en tell 'em w'at wuz in de Bible, en it would he'p ter keep 'em fum stealin' er runnin' erway.

"So Dave 'mence' ter preach, en done de han's on de plantation a heap er good, en most un 'em lef' off dey wicked ways, en 'mence' ter love ter hear 'bout God, en religion, en de Bible; en dey done dey wuk better, en didn' gib de oberseah but mighty little trouble fer to manage 'em.

"Dave wuz one er dese yer men w'at didn' keer much fer de gals—leastways he didn' 'tel Dilsey come ter de plantation. Dilsey wuz a monst'us peart, good-lookin', gingybread-colored gal—one er dese yer high-steppin' gals w'at hol's dey head up, en won' stan' no foolishness fum no man. She had b'long ter a gemman over on Rockfish w'at died, en whose 'state ha' ter be sol' fer ter pay his debts. En Mars Dugal' had be'n ter de oction, en w'en he seed dis gal a-cryin' en gwine on 'bout bein' sol' erway fum her ole mammy, Aun' Mahaly, Mars Dugal' bid 'em bofe in, en fotch 'em ober ter our plantation.

"De young nigger men on de plantation wuz des wil' atter Dilsey, but it didn' do no good, en none un 'em couldn' git Dilsey fer dey junesey,(1) tel Dave 'mence' fer ter go roun' Aun' Mahaly's cabin. Dey wuz a fine-lookin' couple, Dave en Dilsey wuz, bofe tall, en well-shape', en soopl'. En dey sot a heap by one ernudder. Mars Dugal' seed 'em tergedder one Sunday, en de nex' time he seed Dave atter dat, sezee:

"'Dave, w'en yer en Dilsey gits ready fer ter git married, I ain' got no rejections. Dey's a poun' er so er chawin'-terbacker up at de house, en I reckon yo' mist'iss kin fine a frock en a ribbin er two fer Dilsey. You er bofe good niggers, en yer neenter be feared er bein' sol' 'way fum one ernudder long ez I owns dis plantation; en I 'spec' ter own it fer a long time yit.'

"But dere wuz one man on de plantation w'at didn' lack ter see Dave en Dilsey tergedder ez much ez marster did. W'en Mars Dugal' went ter de sale whar he got Dilsey en Mahaly, he bought ernudder han', by de name er Wiley. Wiley wuz one er dese yer shiny-eyed, double-headed little niggers, sha'p ez a steel trap, en sly ez de fox w'at keep out'n it. Dis yer Wiley had be'n pesterin' Disley 'fo' she come ter our plantation, en had nigh 'bout worried de life out'n her. She didn' keer nuffin fer 'im, but he pestered her so she ha' ter th'eaten ter tell her marster fer ter make Wiley let her 'lone. W'en he come ober to our place it wuz des ez bad, 'tel bimeby Wiley seed dat Dilsey had got ter thinkin' a heap 'bout Dave, en den he sorter hilt off aw'ile, en purten' lack he gin Dilsey up. But he wuz one er dese yer 'ceitful niggers, en w'ile he wuz laffin' en jokin' wid de yuther han's 'bout Dave en Dilsey, he wuz settin' a trap fer ter ketch Dave en git Dilsey back fer hisse'f.

"Dave en Dilsey made up dere min's fer ter git married long 'bout Christmas time, w'en dey'd hab mo' time fer a weddin'. But 'long 'bout two weeks befo' dat time ole Mars 'mence' ter lose a heap er bacon. Eve'y night er so somebody 'ud steal a side er bacon, er a ham, er a shoulder, er sump'n fum one er de smoke-'ouses. De smoke-'ouses wuz lock', but somebody had a key, en manage' ter git in some way er 'nudder. Dey's mo' ways 'n one ter skin a cat, en dey's mo' d'n one way ter git in a smoke-'ouse — leastways dat's w'at I hearn say. Folks w'at had bacon fer ter sell didn' hab no trouble 'bout gittin' rid un it. Hit wuz 'g'in de law fer ter buy things fum slabes; but Lawd! dat law didn' 'mount ter a hill er peas. Eve'y week er so one er dese yer big covered waggins would come 'long de road, peddlin' terbacker en w'iskey. Dey wuz a sight er room in one er dem big waggins, en it wuz mon-st'us easy fer ter swop off bacon fer sump'n ter chaw er ter wa'm yer up in de winter-time. I s'pose de peddlers didn' knowed dey wuz breakin' de law, caze de niggers alluz went at night, en stayed on de dark side er de waggin; en it wuz mighty yard fer ter tell *wa't* kine er folks dey wuz.

"Atter two er th'ee hund'ed pounds er meat had be'n stol', Mars Walker call all de niggers up one eben', en tol' 'em dat de fus' nigger de cot stealin' bacon on dat plantation would git sump'n fer ter 'member it by long ez he lib'. En he say he'd gin fi' dollars ter de nigger w'at 'skiver' de rogue. Mars Walker say he s'picion one er two er de niggers, but he couldn' tell fer sho, en co'se dey all 'nied it w'en he 'cuse em un it.

"Dey wa'n't no bacon stole' fer a week er so, 'tel one dark night w'en somebody tuk a ham fum one er de smoke-'ouses. Mars Walker des cusst awful w'en he foun' out de ham wuz gone, en say he gwine ter sarch all de niggers' cabins; w'en dis yer Wiley I wuz tellin' yer 'bout up'n say he s'pi-cion' who tuk de ham, fer he seed Dave comin' 'cross de plantation fum to'ds de smoke-'ouse de night befo'. W'en Mars Walker hearn dis fum Wiley, he went en sarch' Dave's cabin, en foun' de ham hid under de flo'.

"Eve'ybody wuz 'stonish'; but dere wuz de ham. Co'se Dave 'nied it ter de las', but dere wuz de ham. Mars Walker say it wuz des ez he 'spected: he didn' b'lieve in dese yer readin' en prayin' niggers; it wuz all 'pocrisy, en sarve' Mars Dugal' right fer 'lowin' Dave ter be readin' books w'en it wuz 'g'in' de law.

"W'en Mars Dugal' hearn 'bout de ham, he say he wuz might'ly 'ceived en disapp'inted in Dave. He say he wouldn' nebber hab no mo' confer-dence in no nigger, en Mars Walker could do des ez he wuz a mineter wid Dave er any er de res' er de niggers. So Mars Walker tuk'n tied Dave up en gin 'im forty; en den he got some er dis yer wire clof w'at dey uses fer to make sifters out'n en tuk'n wrap' it roun' de ham en fasten it tergedder at de little een'. Den he tuk Dave down ter de blacksmif shop, en had Unker Silas, de plantation blacksmif, fasten a chain ter de ham, en den fasten de yuther een' er de chain roun' Dave's neck. En den he says ter Dave, sezee:

"'Now, suh, yer'll wear dat neckliss fer de nex' six mont's; en I 'spec's yer ner none er de yuther niggers on dis plantation won' steal no mo' bacon dyoin' er dat time.'

"Well, it des 'peared ez if fum dat time Dave didn' hab nuffin but trouble. De niggers all turnt ag'in 'im, caze he be'n de 'casion er Mars Dugal' turnin' 'em all ober ter Mars Walker. Mars Dugal' wa'n't a bad marster hisse'f, but Mars Walker wuz hard ez a rock. Dave kep' on sayin' he didn' take de ham, but none un 'em didn' b'lieve him.

"Dilsey wa'n't on de plantation w'en Dave wuz 'cused er stealin' de bacon. Ole Mist'iss had sont her ter town fer a week er so fer ter wait on one er her darters w'at had a young baby, en she didn' fine out nuffin' 'bout Dave's trouble 'tel she got back ter de plantation. Dave had patien'ly endyoed de finger er scawn, en all de hard words w'at de niggers pile' on 'im, caze he wuz sho' Dilsey would stan' by 'im, en wouldn' b'lieve he wuz a rogue, ner none er de yuther tales de darkies wuz tellin' 'bout 'im.

"W'en Dilsey come back fum town, en got down fum behine de buggy whar she b'en ridin' wid ole Mars, de fus' nigger 'ooman she met says ter her,

"'Is yer seed Dave, Dilsey?'

"'No, I ain' seed Dave,' says Dilsey.

"'Yer des oughter look at dat nigger; reckon yer wouldn' want 'im fer yo' junesey no mo'. Mars Walker cotch 'im stealin' bacon, en gone en fasten' a ham roun' his neck, so he can't git it off'n hisse'f. He sut'nly do look quare.' En den de 'ooman bus' out laffin' fit ter kill herse'f. W'en she got thoo laffin' she up'n tole Dilsey all 'bout de ham, en all de yuther lies w'at de niggers be'n tellin' on Dave.

"W'en Dilsey started down ter de quarters, who should she meet but Dave, comin' in fum de cotton-fiel'. She turnt her head ter one side, en purten' lack she didn' seed Dave.

"'Dilsey!' sezee.

"Dilsey walk' right on, en didn' notice 'im.

"'Oh, Dilsey!'

"Dilsey didn' paid no 'tention ter 'im, en den Dave knowed some er de niggers be'n tellin' her 'bout de ham. He felt monst'us bad, but he 'lowed ef he could des git Dilsey fer ter listen ter 'im fer a minute er so, he could make her b'lieve he didn' stole de bacon. It wuz a week er two befo' he could git a chance ter speak ter her ag'in; but fine'ly he cotch her down by de spring one day, en sezee:

"'Dilsey, w'at fer yer won' speak ter me, en purten' lack yer doan see me? Dilsey, yer knows me too well fer ter b'lieve I'd steal, er do dis yuther wick'ness de niggers is all layin' ter me—yer knows I wouldn' do dat, Dilsey. Yer ain' gwine back on yo' Dave, is yer?'

"But w'at Dave say didn' hab no 'fec' on Dilsey. Dem lies folks b'en tellin' her had p'isen her min' 'g'n Dave.

"'I doan wanter talk ter no nigger,' says she, 'w'at be'n whip' fer stealin', en w'at gwine roun' wid such a lookin' thing ez dat hung roun' his neck. I's a 'spectable gal, *I* is. W'at yer call dat, Dave? Is dat a cha'm fer ter keep off witches, er is it a noo kine er neckliss yer got?'

"Po' Dave didn' knowed w'at ter do. De las' one he had 'pended on fer ter stan' by 'im had gone back on 'im, en dey didn' 'pear ter be nuffin mo' wuf libbin' fer. He couldn' hol' no mo' pra'r-meetin's, fer Mars Walker wouldn' low' 'im ter preach, en de darkies wouldn' a' listen' ter 'im ef he had preach'. He didn' eben hab his Bible fer ter comfort hisse'f wid, fer Mars Walker had tuk it erway fum 'im en burnt it up, en say ef he ketch any mo' niggers wid Bibles on de plantation, he'd do 'em wuss'n he done Dave.

"En ter make it still harder fer Dave, Dilsey tuk up wid Wiley. Dave could see him gwine up ter Aun' Mahaly's cabin, en settin' out on de bench in de moonlight wid Dilsey, en singin' sinful songs en playin' de banjer. Dave use' ter scrouch down behine de bushes, en wonder w'at de Lawd sen' 'im all dem tribberlations fer.

"But all er Dave's yuther troubles w'a'n't nuffin side er dat ham. He had wrap' de chain roun' wid a rag, so it didn't hurt his neck; but w'eneber he went ter wuk, dat ham would be in his way; he had ter do his task, how-somedever, des de same ez ef he didn' hab de ham. W'eneber he went ter lay down, dat ham would be in de way. Ef he turn ober in his sleep, dat ham would be tuggin' at his neck. It wuz de las' thing he seed at night, en de fus' thing he seed in de mawnin'. Wheneber he met a stranger, de ham would be de fus' thing de stranger would see. Most un 'em would 'mence' ter laf, en whareber Dave went he could see folks p'intin' at him, en year 'em sayin':

"'W'at kine er collar dat nigger got roun' his neck?' er, ef dey knowed 'im, 'Is yer stole any mo' hams lately?' er 'W'at yer take fer yo' neckliss, Dave?'

"Fus' Dave didn' mine it so much, caze he knowed he hadn' done nuf-fin. But bimeby he got so he couldn' stan it no longer, en he'd hide hisse'f in de bushes w'eneber he seed anybody comin', en alluz kep' hisse'f shet up in his cabin atter he come in fum wuk.

"It wuz monst'us hard on Dave, en bimeby, w'at wid dat ham eberlastin' en eternally draggin' roun' his neck, he 'mence' fer ter do en say quare

things, en make de niggers wonder ef he wa'n't gittin' out'n his mine. He
got ter gwine roun' talkin' ter hisse'f, en singin' corn-shuckin' songs, en
laffin' fit ter kill 'bout nuffin. En one day he tole one er de niggers he had
'skivered a noo way fer ter raise hams—gwine ter pick 'em off'm trees, en
save de expense er smoke-'ouses by kyoin' 'em in de sun. En one day he
up'n tole Mars Walker he got sump'n pertickler fer ter say ter 'im; en tole
'im he wuz gwine ter show 'im a place in de swamp whar dey wuz a whole
trac' er lan' covered wid ham-trees.

"W'en Mars Walker hearn Dave talkin' dis kine er fool-talk, en w'en
he seed how Dave wuz 'mencin' ter git behine in his wuk, en w'en he ax'
de niggers en dey tole 'im how Dave be'n gwine on, he 'lowed he reckon'
he 'd punish' Dave ernuff, en it mou't do mo' harm dan good fer ter keep
de ham on his neck any longer. So he sont Dave down ter de blacksmif-
shop en had de ham tuk off. Dey wa'n't much er de ham lef' by dat time,
fer de sun had melt all de fat, en de lean had all swivel' up, so dey wa'n't
but th'ee er fo' poun's lef'.

"W'en de ham had be'n tuk off'n Dave, folks kinder stopped talkin'
'bout 'im so much. But de ham had be'n on his neck so long dat Dave had
sorter got use' ter it. He look des lack he'd los' sump'n fer a day er so atter
de ham wuz tuk off, en didn' 'pear ter know w'at ter do wid hisse'f; en
fine'ly he up'n tuk'n tied a lighterd-knot ter a string, en hid it under de flo'
er his cabin, en w'en nobody wuzn' lookin' he'd take it out en hang it
roun' his neck, en go off in de woods en holler en sing; en he allus tied it
roun' his neck w'en he went ter sleep. Fac', it 'peared Dave done gone
clean out'n his mine. En atter a w'ile he got one er de quarest notions you
eber hearn tell un. It wuz 'bout dat time dat I come back ter de plantation
fer ter wuk—I had be'n out ter Mars Dugal's yuther place on Beaver Crick
fer a mont' er so. I had hearn 'bout Dave en de bacon, en 'bout w'at wuz
gwine on on de plantation; but I didn' b'lieve w'at dey all say 'bout Dave,
fer I knowed Dave wa'n't dat kine er man. One day atter I come back,
me'n Dave wuz choppin' cotton tergedder, w'en Dave lean' on his hoe, en
motion' fer me ter come ober close ter 'im; en den he retch' ober en w'is-
pered ter me.

"'Julius,' sezee, 'did yer knowed yer wuz wukkin' 'long yer wid a ham?'

"I couldn' 'magine w'at he meant. 'G'way frum yer, Dave,' says I. 'Yer
ain' wearin' no ham no mo'; try en fergit 'bout dat; 't ain'gwine ter do yer
no good fer ter 'member it.'

"'Look a-year, Julius,' sezee, 'kin yer keep a secret?'

"'Co'se I kin, Dave,' says I. 'I doan go roun' tellin' people w'at yuther
folks says ter me.'

"'Kin I trus' yer, Julius? Will yer cross yo' heart?'

"'I cross my heart. 'Wush I may die ef I tells a soul,' says I.

"Dave look at me des lack he wuz lookin' thoo me en 'way on de yuther side er me, en sezee:

"'Did yer knowed I wuz turnin' ter a ham, Julius?'

"I tried ter 'suade Dave dat dat wuz all foolishness, en dat he oughtn' ter be talkin' dat-a-way—hit wa'n't right. En I tole 'im ef he'd des be patien', de time would sho'ly come w'en eve'thing would be straighten' out, en folks would fine out who de rale rogue wuz w'at stole de bacon. Dave 'peared ter listen ter w'at I say, en promise' ter do better, en stop gwine on dat-a-way; en it seem lack he pick' up a bit w'en he seed dey wuz one pusson didn' b'lieve dem tales 'bout 'im.

"Hit wa'n't long atter dat befo' Mars Archie McIntyre, ober on de Wim'b'le'ton road, 'mence' ter complain 'bout somebody stealin' chickens fum his hen-'ouse. De chickens kep' on gwine, en at las' Mars Archie tole de han's on his plantation dat he gwine ter shoot de fus' man he ketch in his hen-'ouse. In less'n a week atter he gin dis warnin', he cotch a nigger in de hen-'ouse, en fill' 'im full er squir'l-shot. W'en he got a light, he 'skivered it wuz a strange nigger; en w'en he call' one er his own sarven's, de nigger tole 'im it wuz our Wiley. W'en Mars Archie foun' dat out, he sont ober ter our plantation fer ter tell Mars Dugal' he had shot one er his niggers, en dat he could sen' ober dere en git w'at wuz lef' un 'im.

"Mars Dugal' wuz mad at fus'; but w'en he got ober dere an hearn how it all happen', he didn' hab much ter say. Wiley wuz shot so bad he wuz sho' he wuz gwine ter die, so he up'n says ter ole marster:

"'Mars Dugal',' sezee, 'I knows I's be'n a monst'ous bad nigger, but befo' I go I wanter git sump'n off'n my mine. Dave didn' steal dat bacon w'at wuz tuk out'n de smoke-'ouse. *I* stole it all, en I hid de ham under Dave's cabin fer ter th'ow de blame on him—en may de good Lawd fergib me fer it.'

"Mars Dugal' had Wiley tuk back ter de plantation, en sont fer a doctor fer ter pick de shot out'n 'im. En de ve'y nex' mawnin' Mars Dugal' sont fer Dave ter come up ter de big house; he felt kinder sorry fer de way Dave had be'n treated. Co'se it wa'n't' no fault er Mars Dugal's but he wuz gwine ter do w'at he could fer ter make up fer it. So he sont word down ter de quarters fer Dave en all de yuther han's ter 'semble up in de yard befo' de big house at sun-up nex' mawnin'.

"Yearly in de mawnin' de niggers all swarm' up in de yard. Mars Dugal' wuz feelin' so kine dat he had brung up a bairl er cider, en tole de niggers all fer ter he'p deyselves.

"All de han's on de plantation come but Dave; en bimeby, w'en it seem lack he wa'n't comin', Mars Dugal' sont a nigger down ter de quarters ter look fer 'im. De sun wuz gittin' up, en dey wuz a heap er wuk ter de done, en Mars Dugal' sorter got ti'ed waitin'; so he up'n says:

"'Well, boys en gals, I sont fer yer all up yer fer ter tell yer dat all dat 'bout Dave's stealin' er de bacon wuz a mistake, ez I s'pose yer all done hearn befo' now, en I's mighty sorry it happen'. I wants ter treat all my niggers right, en I wants yer all ter know dat I sets a heap by all er my han's w'at is hones' en smart. En I want yer all ter treat Dave des lack yer did befo' dis thing happen', en mine w'at he preach ter yer; for Dave is a good nigger, en has had a hard row ter hoe. En de fus' one I ketch sayin' anythin' 'g'in Dave, I'll tell Mister Walker ter gin 'im forty. Now take ernudder drink er cider all roun', en den git at dat cotton, fer I wanter git dat Persimmon Hill trac' all pick' ober ter-day.'

"W'en de niggers wuz gwine 'way, Mars Dugal' tole me fer ter go en hunt up Dave, en bring 'im up ter de house. I went down ter Dave's cabin, but couldn' fine 'im dere. Den I look' roun' de plantation en in de aidge er de woods, en 'long de road; but I couldn' fine no sign er Dave. I wuz 'bout ter gin up de sarch, w'en I happen' fer ter run 'cross a foot-track w'at look' lack Dave's. I has wukked 'long wid Dave so much dat I knowed his tracks: he had a monst'us long foot, wid a holler instep, w'ich wuz sump'n skase 'mongs' black folks. So I followed dat track 'cross de fiel' fum de quarters 'tel I got ter de smoke-'ouse. De fus' thing I notice' wuz smoke comin' out'n de cracks: it wuz cu'ous, caze dey hadn't be'n no hogs kill' on de plantation fer six mont' er so, en all de bacon in de smoke-'ouse wuz done kyoed. I couldn' 'magine fer ter sabe my life w'at Dave wuz doin' in dat smoke-'ouse. I went up ter de do' en hollered:

"'Dave!'

"Dey didn' nobody answer. I didn' wanter open de do', fer w'ite folks is monst'us pertickler 'bout dey smoke-'ouses; en ef de oberseah had a-come up en cotch me in dere, he mou't not wanter b'lieve I wuz des lookin' fer Dave. So I sorter knock at de do' en call' out ag'in:

"'O Dave, hit's me—Julius! Doan be skeered. Mars Dugal' wants yer ter come up ter de big house—he done 'skivered who stole de ham.'

"But Dave didn' answer. En w'en I look' roun' ag'in en didn' seed none er his tracks gwine way fum de smoke-'ouse, I knowed he wuz in dere yit, en I wuz 'termine' fer ter fetch 'im out; so I push de do' open en look in.

"Dey wuz a pile er bark burnin' in de middle er de flo', en right ober de fier, hangin' fum one er de rafters, wuz Dave; dey wuz a rope roun' his neck, en I didn' haf ter look at his face mo' d'n once fer ter see he wuz dead.

"Den I knowed how it all happen'. Dave had kep' on gittin' wusser en wusser in his mine, 'tel he des got ter b'lievin' he wuz all done turnt ter a ham' en den he had gone en built a fier, en tied a rope roun' his neck, des lack de hams wuz tied, en had hung hisse'f up in de smoke'ouse fer ter kyo.

"Dave wuz buried down by de swamp, in de plantation buryin'-groun'. Wiley didn' died fum de woun' he got in Mars McIntyre's hen-'ouse; he got well atter a w'ile, but Dilsey wouldn' hab nuffin mo' ter do wid 'im, en 't wa'n't long 'fo' Mars Dugal' sol' 'im ter a spekilater on his way souf—he say he didn' want no sich a nigger on de plantation, ner in de county, ef he could he'p it. En w'en de een' er de year come, Mars Dugal' turnt Mars Walker off, en run de plantation hisse'f atter dat.

"Eber sence den," said Julius in conclusion, "w'eneber I eats ham, it min's me er Dave. I lacks ham, but I nebber kin eat mo' d'n two er th'ee poun's befo' I gits ter studyin' 'bout Dave, en den I has ter stop en leab de res' fer ernudder time."

There was a short silence after the old man had finished his story, and then my wife began to talk to him about the weather, on which subject he was an authority. I went into the house. When I came out, half an hour later, I saw Julius disappearing down the lane, with a basket on his arm.

At breakfast, next morning, it occurred to me that I should like a slice of ham. I said as much to my wife.

"Oh, no, John," she responded, "you shouldn't eat anything so heavy for breakfast."

I insisted.

"The fact is," she said, pensively, "I couldn't have eaten any more of that ham, and I gave it to Julius."

"The Little Convent Girl"

Grace King (1852–1932)

Grace King, the daughter of a prominent New Orleans lawyer, fled to the family's plantation when the Union took the city in 1862. After the war, having lost much of their wealth, the family lived for several years in a working-class neighborhood. King began writing to tell the story of New Orleans from the perspective of someone sympathetic to and deeply familiar with the particular customs of the city. Throughout the latter nineteenth century, King produced a series of stories and novels devoted to that purpose. Though her fiction sometimes succumbed to romanticization, "The Little Convent Girl" (1893) is a subtle and complex narrative, one that deals in the harsh world of racial definition in the postwar South.

She was coming down on the boat from Cincinnati, the little convent girl. Two sisters had brought her aboard. They gave her in charge of the captain, got her a state-room, saw that the new little trunk was put into it, hung the new little satchel up on the wall, showed her how to bolt the door at night, shook hands with her for good-by (good-bys have really no significance for sisters), and left her there. After a while the bells all rang, and the boat, in the awkward elephantine fashion of boats, got into midstream. The chambermaid found her sitting on the chair in the state-room where the sisters had left her, and showed her how to sit on a chair in the saloon. And there she sat until the captain came and hunted her up for supper. She could not do anything of herself; she had to be initiated into everything by some one else.

She was known on the boat only as "the little convent girl." Her name, of course, was registered in the clerk's office, but on a steamboat no one thinks of consulting the clerk's ledger. It is always the little widow, the fat madam, the tall colonel, the parson, etc. The captain, who pronounced by the letter, always called her the little *convent* girl. She was the beau-ideal of the little convent girl. She never raised her eyes except when spoken to. Of course she never spoke first, even to the chambermaid, and when she did speak it was in the wee, shy, furtive voice one might imagine a just-budding violet to have; and she walked with such soft, easy, carefully calculated steps that one naturally felt the penalties that must have secured them—penalties dictated by a black code of deportment.

She was dressed in deep mourning. Her black straw hat was trimmed with stiff new crape, and her stiff new bombazine dress had crape collar and cuffs. She wore her hair in two long plaits fastened around her head tight and fast. Her hair had a strong inclination to curl, but that had been taken out of it as austerely as the noise out of her footfalls.

Her hair was as black as her dress; her eyes, when one saw them, seemed blacker than either, on account of the bluishness of the white surrounding the pupil. Her eyelashes were almost as thick as the black veil which the sisters had fastened around her hat with an extra pin the very last thing before leaving. She had a round little face, and a tiny pointed chin; her mouth was slightly protuberant from the teeth, over which she tried to keep her lips well shut, the effort giving them a pathetic little forced expression. Her complexion was sallow, a pale sallow, the complexion of a brunette bleached in darkened rooms. The only color about her was a blue taffeta ribbon from which a large silver medal of the Virgin hung over the place where a breastpin should have been. She was so little, so little, although she was eighteen, as the sisters told the captain; otherwise they would not have permitted her to travel all the way to New Orleans alone.

Unless the captain or the clerk remembered to fetch her out in front, she would sit all day in the cabin, in the same place, crocheting lace, her spool of thread and box of patterns in her lap, on the handkerchief spread to save her new dress. Never leaning back—oh, no! always straight and stiff, as if the conventual back board were there within call. She would eat only convent fare at first, notwithstanding the importunities of the waiters, and the jocularities of the captain, and particularly of the clerk. Every one knows the fund of humor possessed by a steamboat clerk, and what a field for display the table at meal-times affords. On Friday she fasted rigidly, and she never began to eat, or finished, without a little Latin movement of the lips and a sign of the cross. And always at six o'clock of the evening she remembered the angelus, although there was no church bell to remind her of it.

She was in mourning for her father, the sisters told the captain, and she was going to New Orleans to her mother. She had not seen her mother since she was an infant, on account of some disagreement between the parents, in consequence of which the father had brought her to Cincinnati, and placed her in the convent. There she had been for twelve years, only going to her father for vacations and holidays. So long as the father lived he would never let the child have any communication with her mother. Now that he was dead all that was changed, and the first thing that the girl herself wanted to do was to go to her mother.

The mother superior had arranged it all with the mother of the girl, who was to come personally to the boat in New Orleans, and receive her child from the captain, presenting a letter from the mother superior, a fac-simile of which the sisters gave the captain.

It is a long voyage from Cincinnati to New Orleans, the rivers doing their best to make it interminable, embroidering themselves *ad libitum* all over the country. Every five miles, and sometimes oftener, the boat would stop to put off or take on freight, if not both. The little convent girl, sit-ting in the cabin, had her terrible frights at first from the hideous noises attendant on these landings—the whistles, the ringings of the bells, the running to and fro, the shouting. Every time she thought it was shipwreck, death, judgment, purgatory; and her sins! her sins! She would drop her crochet, and clutch her prayer-beads from her pocket, and relax the con-straint over her lips, which would go to rattling off prayers with the veloc-ity of a relaxed windlass. That was at first, before the captain took to fetching her out in front to see the boat make a landing. Then she got to liking it so much that she would stay all day just where the captain put her, going inside only for her meals. She forgot herself at times so much that she would draw her chair a little closer to the railing, and put up her veil, actually, to see better. No one ever usurped her place, quite in front, or intruded upon her either with word or look; for every one learned to know her shyness, and began to feel a personal interest in her, and all wanted the little convent girl to see everything that she possibly could.

And it was worth seeing—the balancing and *chasséeing* and waltzing of the cumbersome old boat to make a landing. It seemed to be always attended with the difficulty and the improbability of a new enterprise; and the relief when it did sidle up anywhere within rope's-throw of the spot aimed at! And the roustabout throwing the rope from the perilous end of the dangling gang-plank! And the dangling roustabouts hanging like drops of water from it—dropping sometimes twenty feet to the land, and not infrequently into the river itself. And then what a rolling of barrels, and shouldering of sacks, and singing of Jim Crow songs, and pacing of Jim Crow steps; and black skins glistening through torn shirts, and white teeth gleaming through red lips, and laughing, and talking and—bewildering! entrancing! Surely the little convent girl in her convent walls never dreamed of so much unpunished noise and movement in the world!

The first time she heard the mate—it must have been like the first time woman ever heard man—curse and swear, she turned pale, and ran quick-ly, quickly into the saloon, and—came out again? No, indeed! not with all the soul she had to save, and all the other sins on her conscience. She shook her head resolutely, and was not seen in her chair on deck again until the captain not only reassured her, but guaranteed his reassurance. And after that, whenever the boat was about to make a landing, the mate would first glance up to the guards, and if the little convent girl was sitting there he would change his invective to sarcasm, and politely request the colored gentlemen not to hurry themselves—on no account whatever; to take their time about shoving out the plank; to send the rope ashore by post-office—write him when it got there; begging them not to strain their backs; calling them mister, colonel, major, general, prince, and your royal highness, which was vastly amusing. At night, however, or when the little convent girl was not there, language flowed in its natural curve, the mate swearing like a pagan to make up for lost time.

The captain forgot himself one day: it was when the boat ran aground in the most unexpected manner and place, and he went to work to express his opinion, as only steamboat captains can, of the pilot, mate, engineer, crew, boat, river, country, and the world in general, ringing the bell, first to back, then to head, shouting himself hoarser than his own whistle—when he chanced to see the little black figure hurrying through the chaos on the deck; and the captain stuck as fast aground in midstream as the boat had done.

In the evening the little convent girl would be taken on the upper deck, and going up the steep stairs there was such confusion, to keep the black skirts well over the stiff white petticoats; and, coming down, such blushing when suspicion would cross the unprepared face that a rim of white stocking might be visible; and the thin feet, laced so tightly in the glossy new leather boots, would cling to each successive step as if they could never, never make another venture; and then one boot would (there is but that word) hesitate out, and feel and feel around, and have such a pause of helpless agony as if indeed the next step must have been willfully removed, or was nowhere to be found on the wide, wide earth.

It was a miracle that the pilot ever got her up into the pilot-house; but pilots have a lonely time, and do not hesitate even at miracles when there is a chance for company. He would place a box for her to climb to the tall bench behind the wheel, and he would arrange the cushions, and open a window here to let in air, and shut one there to cut off a draft, as if there could be no tenderer consideration in life for him than her comfort. And he would talk of the river to her, explain the chart, pointing out eddies, whirlpools, shoals, depths, new beds, old beds, cut-offs, caving banks, and making banks, as exquisitely and respectfully as if she had been the River Commission.

It was his opinion that there was as great a river as the Mississippi flowing directly under it—an underself of a river, as much a counterpart of the other as the second story of a house is of the first; in fact, he said they were navigating through the upper story. Whirlpools were holes in the floor of the upper river, so to speak; eddies were rifts and cracks. And deep under the earth, hurrying toward the subterranean stream, were other streams, small and great, but all deep, hurrying to and from that great mother-stream underneath, just as the small and great overground streams hurry to and from their mother Mississippi. It was almost more than the little convent girl could take in: at least such was the expression of her eyes; for they opened as all eyes have to open at pilot stories. And he knew as much of astronomy as he did of hydrology, could call the stars by name, and define the shapes of the constellations; and she, who had studied astronomy at the convent, was charmed to find that what she had learned was all true. It was in the pilot-house, one night, that she forgot herself for the first time in her life, and stayed up until after nine o'clock. Although she appeared almost intoxicated at the wild pleasure, she was immediately overwhelmed at the wickedness of it, and observed much more rigidity of conduct thereafter. The engineer, the boiler-men, the firemen, the stokers, they all knew when the little convent girl was up in the pilot-house: the speaking-tube became so mild and gentle.

With all the delays of river and boat, however, there is an end to the journey from Cincinnati to New Orleans. The latter city, which at one time to the impatient seemed at the terminus of the never, began, all of a sudden, one day to make its nearingness felt; and from that period every other interest paled before the interest in the immanence of arrival into port, and the whole boat was seized with a panic of preparation, the little convent girl with the others. Although so immaculate was she in person and effects that she might have been struck with a landing, as some good people might be struck with death, at any moment without fear of results, her trunk was packed and repacked, her satchel arranged and rearranged, and, the last day, her hair was brushed and plaited and smoothed over and over again until the very last glimmer of a curl disappeared. Her dress was whisked, as if for microscopic inspection; her face was washed; and her finger-nails were scrubbed with the hard convent nailbrush, until the disciplined little tips ached with a pristine soreness. And still there were hours to wait, and still the boat added up delays. But she arrived at last, after all, with not more than the usual and expected difference between the actual and the advertised time of arrival.

There was extra blowing and extra ringing, shouting, commanding, rushing up the gangway and rushing down the gangway. The clerks, sitting behind tables on the first deck, were plied, in the twinkling of an eye, with estimates, receipts, charges, countercharges, claims, reclaims, demands, questions, accusations, threats, all at topmost voices. None but steamboat clerks could have stood it. And there were throngs composed of individuals every one of whom wanted to see the captain first and at once: and those who could not get to him shouted over the heads of the others; and as usual he lost his temper and politeness, and began to do what he termed "hustle."

"Captain! Captain!" a voice called him to where a hand plucked his sleeve, and a letter was thrust toward him. "The cross, and the name of the convent." He recognized the envelop of the mother superior. He read the duplicate of the letter given by the sisters. He looked at the woman—the mother—casually, then again and again.

The little convent girl saw him coming, leading some one toward her. She rose. The captain took her hand first, before the other greeting, "Good-by, my dear," he said. He tried to add something else, but seemed undetermined what. "Be a good little girl—" It was evidently all he could think of. Nodding to the woman behind him, he turned on his heel, and left.

One of the deck-hands was sent to fetch her trunk. He walked out behind them, through the cabin, and the crowd on deck, down the stairs, and out over the gangway. The little convent girl and her mother went with hands tightly clasped. She did not turn her eyes to the right or left, or once (what all passengers do) look backward at the boat which, however slowly, had carried her surely over dangers that she wot not of. All looked at her as she passed. All wanted to say good-by to the little convent girl, to see the mother who had been deprived of her so long. Some expressed surprise in a whistle; some in other ways. All exclaimed audibly, or to themselves, "Colored!"

It takes about a month to make the round trip from New Orleans to Cincinnati and back, counting five days' stoppage in New Orleans. It was a month to a day when the steamboat came puffing and blowing up to the wharf again, like a stout dowager after too long a walk; and the same scene of confusion was enacted, as it had been enacted twelve times a year, at almost the same wharf for twenty years; and the same calm, a death calmness by contrast, followed as usual the next morning.

The decks were quiet and clean; one cargo had just been delivered, part of another stood ready on the levee to be shipped. The captain was there waiting for his business to begin, the clerk was in his office getting his books ready, the voice of the mate could be heard below, mustering the old crew out and a new crew in; for if steamboat crews have a single principle,—and there are those who deny them any,—it is never to ship twice in succession on the same boat. It was too early yet for any but roustabouts, marketers, and church-goers; so early that even the river was still partly mist-covered; only in places could the swift, dark current be seen rolling swiftly along.

"Captain!" A hand plucked at his elbow, as if not confident that the mere calling would secure attention. The captain turned. The mother of the little convent girl stood there, and she held the little convent girl by the hand. "I have brought her to see you," the woman said. "You were so kind—and she is so quiet, so still, all the time, I thought it would do her a pleasure."

She spoke with an accent, and with embarrassment; otherwise one would have said that she was bold and assured enough.

"She don't go nowhere, she don't do nothing but make her crochet and her prayers, so I thought I would bring her for a little visit of 'How d' ye do' to you."

There was, perhaps, some inflection in the woman's voice that might have made known, or at least awakened, the suspicion of some latent hope or intention, had the captain's ear been fine enough to detect it. There might have been something in the little convent girl's face, had his eye been more sensitive—a trifle paler, maybe, the lips a little tighter drawn, the blue ribbon a shade faded. He may have noticed that, but—And the visit of "How d' ye do" came to an end.

They walked down the stairway, the woman in front, the little convent girl — her hand released to shake hands with the captain—following, across the bared deck, out to the gangway, over to the middle of it. No one was looking, no one saw more than a flutter of white petticoats, a show of white stockings, as the little convent girl went under the water.

The roustabout dived, as the roustabouts always do, after the drowning, even at the risk of their good-for-nothing lives. The mate himself jumped overboard; but she had gone down in a whirlpool. Perhaps, as the pilot had told her whirlpools always did, it may have carried her through to the underground river, to that vast, hidden, dark Mississippi that flows beneath the one we see; for her body was never found.

"Désirée's Baby"

Kate Chopin (1851–1904)

Kate Chopin was born Katherine O'Flaherty in St. Louis in 1851 to a prominent Catholic family. Chopin identified with the Confederacy, in whose service a beloved half-brother died. In 1870, at age nineteen, she married Oscar Chopin and moved to New Orleans; they later relocated to their plantations in northern Louisiana. When both her husband and mother died in the early 1880s, Chopin began writing, in part to support herself. Though viewed in the past as one of the many innocuous local-color writers of the late nineteenth century, Chopin pushed the boundaries of that school. Twenty-three of Chopin's short stories and sketches were collected in *Bayou Folk* (1894). Among the collected pieces was "Désirée's Baby," an exploration of the tension between love and race. Chopin touched off her greatest controversy with the publication of her final novel, *The Awakening*, in 1899, which tells the tale of a young woman who commits adultery and suicide. The harsh reception of that book, now considered a classic, shattered Chopin's confidence as a writer. She died of a brain hemorrhage in 1904.

As the day was pleasant, Madame Valmondé drove over to L'Abri to see Désirée and the baby.

It made her laugh to think of Désirée with a baby. Why, it seemed but yesterday that Désirée was little more than a baby herself; when Monsieur in riding through the gateway of Valmondé had found her lying asleep in the shadow of the big stone pillar.

The little one awoke in his arms and began to cry for "Dada." That was as much as she could do or say. Some people thought she might have strayed there of her own accord, for she was of the toddling age. The prevailing belief was that she had been purposely left by a party of Texans, whose canvas-covered wagon, late in the day, had crossed the ferry that Coton Maïs kept, just below the plantation. In time Madame Valmondé abandoned every speculation but the one that Désirée had been sent to her by a beneficent Providence to be the child of her affection, seeing that she was without child of the flesh. For the girl grew to be beautiful and gentle, affectionate and sincere,—the idol of Valmondé.

It was no wonder, when she stood one day against the stone pillar in whose shadow she had lain asleep, eighteen years before, that Armand Aubigny riding by and seeing her there, had fallen in love with her. That was the way all the Aubignys fell in love, as if struck by a pistol shot. The wonder was that he had not loved her before; for he had known her since his father brought him home from Paris, a boy of eight, after his mother died there. The passion that awoke in him that day, when he saw her at the gate, swept along like an avalanche, or like a prairie fire, or like anything that drives headlong over all obstacles.

Monsieur Valmondé grew practical and wanted things well considered: that is, the girl's obscure origin. Armand looked into her eyes and did not care. He was reminded that she was nameless. What did it matter about a name when he could give her one of the oldest and proudest in Louisiana? He ordered the *corbeille* from Paris, and contained himself with what patience he could until it arrived; then they were married.

Madame Valmondé had not seen Désirée and the baby for four weeks. When she reached L'Abri she shuddered at the first sight of it, as she always did. It was a sad looking place, which for many years had not known the gentle presence of a mistress, old Monsieur Aubigny having married and buried his wife in France, and she having loved her own land too well ever to leave it. The roof came down steep and black like a cowl, reaching out beyond the wide galleries that encircled the yellow stuccoed house. Big, solemn oaks grew close to it, and their thick-leaved, far-reaching branches shadowed it like a pall. Young Aubigny's rule was a strict one, too, and under it his negroes had forgotten how to be gay, as they had during the old master's easy-going and indulgent lifetime.

The young mother was recovering slowly, and lay full length, in her soft white muslins and laces, upon a couch. The baby was beside her, upon her arm, where he had fallen asleep, at her breast. The yellow nurse woman sat beside a window fanning herself.

Madame Valmondé bent her portly figure over Désirée and kissed her, holding her an instant tenderly in her arms. Then she turned to the child.

"This is not the baby!" she exclaimed, in startled tones. French was the language spoken at Valmondé in those days.

"I knew you would be astonished," laughed Désirée, "at the way he has grown. The little *cochon de lait!* Look at his legs, mamma, and his hands and fingernails, — real finger-nails. Zandrine had to cut them this morning. Is n't it true, Zandrine?"

The woman bowed her turbaned head majestically, "Mais si, Madame."

"And the way he cries," went on Désirée, "is deafening. Armand heard him the other day as far away as La Blanche's cabin."

Madame Valmondé had never removed her eyes from the child. She lifted it and walked with it over to the window that was lightest. She scanned the baby narrowly, then looked as searchingly at Zandrine, whose face was turned to gaze across the fields.

"Yes, the child has grown, has changed," said Madame Valmondé, slowly, as she replaced it beside its mother. "What does Armand say?"

Désirée's face became suffused with a glow that was happiness itself.

"Oh, Armand is the proudest father in the parish, I believe, chiefly because it is a boy, to bear his name; though he says not,—that he would have loved a girl as well. But I know it is n't true. I know he says that to please me. And mamma," she added, drawing Madame Valmondé's head down to her, and speaking in a whisper, "he has n't punished one of them —not one of them—since baby is born. Even Négrillon, who pretended to have burnt his leg that he might rest from work—he only laughed, and said Négrillon was a great scamp. Oh, mamma, I'm so happy; it frightens me."

What Désirée said was true. Marriage, and later the birth of his son had softened Armand Aubigny's imperious and exacting nature greatly. This was what made the gentle Désirée so happy, for she loved him desperately. When he frowned she trembled, but loved him. When he smiled, she asked no greater blessing of God. But Armand's dark, handsome face had not often been disfigured by frowns since the day he fell in love with her.

When the baby was about three months old, Désirée awoke one day to the conviction that there was something in the air menacing her peace. It was at first too subtle to grasp. It had only been a disquieting suggestion; an air of mystery among the blacks; unexpected visits from far-off neighbors who could hardly account for their coming. Then a strange, an awful change in her husband's manner, which she dared not ask him to explain. When he spoke to her, it was with averted eyes, from which the old love-light seemed to have gone out. He absented himself from home; and when there, avoided her presence and that of her child, without excuse. And the very spirit of Satan seemed suddenly to take hold of him in his dealings with the slaves. Désirée was miserable enough to die.

She sat in her room, one hot afternoon, in her *peignoir*, listlessly drawing through her fingers the strands of her long, silky brown hair that hung about her shoulders. The baby, half naked, lay asleep upon her own great mahogany bed, that was like a sumptuous throne, with its satin-lined half-canopy. One of La Blanche's little quadroon boys—half naked too—stood fanning the child slowly with a fan of peacock feathers. Désirée's eyes had been fixed absently and sadly upon the baby, while she was striving to penetrate the threatening mist that she felt closing about her. She looked from her child to the boy who stood beside him, and back again; over and over. "Ah!" It was a cry that she could not help; which she was not conscious of having uttered. The blood turned like ice in her veins, and a clammy moisture gathered upon her face.

She tried to speak to the little quadroon boy; but no sound would come, at first. When he heard his name uttered, he looked up, and his mistress was pointing to the door. He laid aside the great, soft fan, and obediently stole away, over the polished floor, on his bare tiptoes.

She stayed motionless, with gaze riveted upon her child, and her face the picture of fright.

Presently her husband entered the room, and without noticing her, went to a table and began to search among some papers which covered it.

"Armand," she called to him, in a voice which must have stabbed him, if he was human. But he did not notice. "Armand," she said again. Then she rose and tottered towards him. "Armand," she panted once more, clutching his arm, "look at our child. What does it mean? tell me."

He coldly but gently loosened her fingers from about his arm and thrust the hand away from him. "Tell me what it means!" she cried despairingly.

"It means," he answered lightly, "that the child is not white; it means that you are not white."

A quick conception of all that this accusation meant for her nerved her with unwonted courage to deny it. "It is a lie; it is not true, I am white! Look at my hair, it is brown; and my eyes are gray, Armand, you know they are gray. And my skin is fair," seizing his wrist. "Look at my hand; whiter than yours, Armand," she laughed hysterically.

"As white as La Blanche's," he returned cruelly; and went away leaving her alone with their child.

When she could hold a pen in her hand, she sent a despairing letter to Madame Valmondé.

"My mother, they tell me I am not white. Armand has told me I am not white. For God's sake tell them it is not true. You must know it is not true. I shall die. I must die. I cannot be so unhappy, and live."

The answer that came was as brief:

"My own Désirée: Come home to Valmondé; back to your mother who loves you. Come with your child."

When the letter reached Désirée she went with it to her husband's study, and laid it open upon the desk before which he sat. She was like a stone image: silent, white, motionless after she placed it there.

In silence he ran his cold eyes over the written words. He said nothing. "Shall I go, Armand?" she asked in tones sharp with agonized suspense.

"Yes, go."

"Do you want me to go?"

"Yes, I want you to go."

He thought Almighty God had dealt cruelly and unjustly with him; and felt, somehow, that he was paying Him back in kind when he stabbed thus into his wife's soul. Moreover he no longer loved her, because of the unconscious injury she had brought upon his home and his name.

She turned away like one stunned by a blow, and walked slowly towards the door, hoping he would call her back.

"Good-by, Armand," she moaned.

He did not answer her. That was his last blow at fate.

Désirée went in search of her child. Zandrine was pacing the sombre gallery with it. She took the little one from the nurse's arms with no word of explanation, and descending the steps, walked away, under the live-oak branches.

It was an October afternoon; the sun was just sinking. Out in the still fields the negroes were picking cotton.

Désirée had not changed the thin white garment nor the slippers which she wore. Her hair was uncovered and the sun's rays brought a golden gleam from its brown meshes. She did not take the broad, beaten road which led to the far-off plantation of Valmondé. She walked across a deserted field, where the stubble bruised her tender feet, so delicately shod, and tore her thin gown to shreds.

She disappeared among the reeds and willows that grew thick along the banks of the deep, sluggish bayou; and she did not come back again.

Some weeks later there was a curious seen enacted at L'Abri. In the centre of the smoothly swept back yard was a great bonfire. Armand Aubigny sat in the wide hallway that commanded a view of the spectacle; and it was he who dealt out to a half dozen negroes the material which kept this fire ablaze.

A graceful cradle of willow, with all its dainty furbishings, was laid upon the pyre, which had already been fed with the richness of a priceless *layette*. Then there were silk gowns, and velvet and satin ones added to these; laces, too, and embroideries; bonnets and gloves; for the *corbeille* had been of rare quality.

The last thing to go was a tiny bundle of letters; innocent little scribblings that Désirée had sent to him during the days of their espousal. There was the remnant of one back in the drawer from which he took them. But it was not Désirée's; it was part of an old letter from his mother to his father. He read it. She was thanking God for the blessing of her husband's love: —

"But, above all," she wrote, "night and day, I thank the good God for having so arranged our lives that our dear Armand will never know that his mother, who adores him, belongs to the race that is cursed with the brand of slavery."

from *Up from Slavery*

Booker T. Washington (1856–1915)

Booker T. Washington, born into slavery in Franklin County, Virginia, in 1856, moved with his family just after the Civil War to West Virginia, where he worked at a salt furnace. In the selection here, Washington tells the story of his journey from West Virginia to Hampton Institute and then to Tuskegee Institute. Washington became known as the most prominent African American in the late nineteenth century, though many black people resented his message of political accommodation and distrusted his reliance on wealthy white Northerners. Washington's autobiography, *Up from Slavery*, published in 1901, followed the American tradition of the self-made man's account of his success. It became a best-seller, popular among whites as well as blacks.

THE STRUGGLE FOR AN EDUCATION

One day, while at work in the coal-mine, I happened to overhear two miners talking about a great school for coloured people somewhere in Virginia. This was the first time that I had ever heard anything about any kind of school or college that was more pretentious than the little coloured school in our town.

In the darkness of the mine I noiselessly crept as close as I could to the two men who were talking. I heard one tell the other that not only was the school established for the members of my race, but that opportunities were provided by which poor but worthy students could work out all or a part of the cost of board, and at the same time be taught some trade or industry.

As they went on describing the school, it seemed to me that it must be the greatest place on earth, and not even Heaven presented more attractions for me at that time than did the Hampton Normal and Agricultural Institute in Virginia, about which these men were talking. I resolved at once to go to that school, although I had no idea where it was, or how many miles away, or how I was going to reach it; I remembered only that I was on fire constantly with one ambition, and that was to go to Hampton. This thought was with me day and night.

After hearing of the Hampton Institute, I continued to work for a few months longer in the coal-mine. While at work there, I heard of a vacant position in the household of General Lewis Ruffner, the owner of the salt-furnace and coal-mine. Mrs. Viola Ruffner, the wife of General Ruffner, was a "Yankee" woman from Vermont. Mrs. Ruffner had a reputation all through the vicinity for being very strict with her servants, and especially with the boys who tried to serve her. Few of them had remained with her more than two or three weeks. They all left with the same excuse: she was too strict. I decided, however, that I would rather try Mrs. Ruffner's house than remain in the coal-mine, and so my mother applied to her for the vacant position. I was hired at a salary of $5 per month.

I had heard so much about Mrs. Ruffner's severity that I was almost afraid to see her, and trembled when I went into her presence. I had not lived with her many weeks, however, before I began to understand her. I soon began to learn that, first of all, she wanted everything kept clean about her, that she wanted things done promptly and systematically, and that at the bottom of everything she wanted absolute honesty and frankness. Nothing must be sloven or slipshod; every door, every fence, must be kept in repair.

I cannot now recall how long I lived with Mrs. Ruffner before going to Hampton, but I think it must have been a year and a half. At any rate, I here repeat what I have said more than once before, that the lessons that I learned in the home of Mrs. Ruffner were as valuable to me as any education I have ever gotten anywhere since. Even to this day I never see bits of paper scattered around a house or in the street that I do not want to pick them up at once. I never see a filthy yard that I do not want to clean it, a paling off of a fence that I do not want to put it on, an unpainted or unwhitewashed house that I do not want to paint or whitewash it, or a button off one's clothes, or a grease-spot on them or on a floor, that I do not want to call attention to it.

From fearing Mrs. Ruffner I soon learned to look upon her as one of my best friends. When she found that she could trust me she did so implicitly. During the one or two winters that I was with her she gave me an opportunity to go to school for an hour in the day during a portion of the winter months, but most of my studying was done at night, sometimes alone, sometimes under some one whom I could hire to teach me. Mrs. Ruffner always encouraged and sympathized with me in all my efforts to get an education. It was while living with her that I began to get together my first library. I secured a dry-goods box, knocked out one side of it, put some shelves in it, and began putting into it every kind of book that I could get my hands upon, and called it my "library."

Notwithstanding my success at Mrs. Ruffner's I did not give up the idea of going to the Hampton Institute. In the fall of 1872 I determined to make an effort to get there, although, as I have stated, I had no definite idea of the direction in which Hampton was, or of what it would cost to go there. I do not think that any one thoroughly sympathized with me in my ambition to go to Hampton unless it was my mother, and she was troubled with a grave fear that I was starting out on a "wild-goose chase." At any rate, I got only a half-hearted consent from her that I might start. The small amount of money that I had earned had been consumed by my stepfather and the remainder of the family, with the exception of a very few dollars, and so I had very little with which to buy clothes and pay my travelling expenses. My brother John helped me all that he could, but of course that was not a great deal, for his work was in the coal-mine, where he did not earn much, and most of what he did earn went in the direction of paying the household expenses.

Perhaps the thing that touched and pleased me most in connection with my starting for Hampton was the interest that many of the older coloured people took in the matter. They had spent the best days of their lives in slavery, and hardly expected to live to see the time when they would see a member of their race leave home to attend a boarding-school. Some of these older people would give me a nickel, others a quarter, or a handkerchief.

Finally the great day came, and I started for Hampton. I had only a small, cheap satchel that contained what few articles of clothing I could get. My mother at the time was rather weak and broken in health. I hardly expected to see her again, and thus our parting was all the more sad. She, however, was very brave through it all. At that time there were no through trains connecting that part of West Virginia with eastern Virginia. Trains ran only a portion of the way, and the remainder of the distance was travelled by stage-coaches.

The distance from Malden to Hampton is about five hundred miles. I had not been away from home many hours before it began to grow painfully evident that I did not have enough money to pay my fare to Hampton. One experience I shall long remember. I had been travelling over the mountains most of the afternoon in an old-fashioned stage-coach, when, late in the evening, the coach stopped for the night at a common, unpainted house called a hotel. All the other passengers except myself were whites. In my ignorance I supposed that the little hotel existed for the purpose of accommodating the passengers who travelled on the stage-coach. The difference that the colour of one's skin would make I had not thought anything about. After all the other passengers had been shown rooms and were getting ready for supper, I shyly presented myself before the man at the desk. It is true I had practically no money in my pocket with which to pay for bed or food, but I had hoped in some way to beg my way into the good graces of the landlord, for at that season in the mountains of Virginia the weather was cold, and I wanted to get indoors for the night. Without asking as to whether I had any money, the man at the desk firmly refused to even consider the matter of providing me with food or lodging. This was my first experience in finding out what the colour of my skin meant. In some way I managed to keep warm by walking about, and so got through the night. My whole soul was so bent upon reaching Hampton that I did not have time to cherish any bitterness toward the hotel-keeper.

By walking, begging rides both in wagons and in the cars, in some way, after a number of days, I reached the city of Richmond, Virginia, about eighty-two miles from Hampton. When I reached there, tired, hungry, and dirty, it was late in the night. I had never been in a large city, and this rather added to my misery. When I reached Richmond, I was completely out of money. I had not a single acquaintance in the place, and, being unused to city ways, I did not know where to go. I applied at several places for lodging, but they all wanted money, and that was what I did not have. Knowing nothing else better to do, I walked the streets. In doing this I passed by many food-stands where fried chicken and half-moon apple pies were piled high and made to present a most tempting appearance. At that time it seemed to me that I would have promised all that I expected to possess in the future to have gotten hold of one of those chicken legs or one of those pies. But I could not get either of these, nor anything else to eat.

I must have walked the streets till after midnight. At last I became so exhausted that I could walk no longer. I was tired, I was hungry, I was everything but discouraged. Just about the time when I reached extreme physical exhaustion, I came upon a portion of a street where the board sidewalk was considerably elevated. I waited for a few minutes, till I was sure that no passers-by could see me, and then crept under the sidewalk and lay for the night upon the ground, with my satchel of clothing for a pillow. Nearly all night I could hear the tramp of feet over my head. The next morning I found myself somewhat refreshed, but I was extremely hungry, because it had been a long time since I had had sufficient food. As soon as it became light enough for me to see my surroundings I noticed that I was near a large ship, and that this ship seemed to be unloading a cargo of pig iron. I went at once to the vessel and asked the captain to permit me to help unload the vessel in order to get money for food. The captain, a white man, who seemed to be kind-hearted, consented. I worked long enough to earn money for my breakfast, and it seems to me, as I remember it now, to have been about the best breakfast that I have ever eaten.

My work pleased the captain so well that he told me if I desired I could continue working for a small amount per day. This I was very glad to do.

I continued working on this vessel for a number of days. After buying food with the small wages I received there was not much left to add to the amount I must get to pay my way to Hampton. In order to economize in every way possible, so as to be sure to reach Hampton in a reasonable time, I continued to sleep under the same sidewalk that gave me shelter the first night I was in Richmond. Many years after that the coloured citizens of Richmond very kindly tendered me a reception at which there must have been two thousand people present. This reception was held not far from the spot where I slept the first night I spent in that city, and I must confess that my mind was more upon the sidewalk that first gave me shelter than upon the reception, agreeable and cordial as it was.

When I had saved what I considered enough money with which to reach Hampton, I thanked the captain of the vessel for his kindness, and started again. Without any unusual occurrence I reached Hampton, with a surplus of exactly fifty cents with which to begin my education. To me it had been a long, eventful journey; but the first sight of the large, three-story, brick school building seemed to have rewarded me for all that I had undergone in order to reach the place. If the people who gave the money to provide that building could appreciate the influence the sight of it had upon me, as well as upon thousands of other youths, they would feel all the more encouraged to make such gifts. It seemed to me to be the largest and most beautiful building I had ever seen. The sight of it seemed to give me new life. I felt that a new kind of existence had now begun—that life would now have a new meaning. I felt that I had reached the promised land, and I resolved to let no obstacle prevent me from putting forth the highest effort to fit myself to accomplish the most good in the world.

As soon as possible after reaching the grounds of the Hampton Institute, I presented myself before the head teacher for assignment to a class. Having been so long without proper food, a bath, and change of clothing, I did not, of course, make a very favourable impression upon her, and I could see at once that there were doubts in her mind about the wisdom of admitting me as a student. I felt that I could hardly blame her if she got the idea that I was a worthless loafer or tramp. For some time she did not refuse to admit me, neither did she decide in my favour, and I continued to linger about her, and to impress her in all the ways I could with my worthiness. In the meantime I saw her admitting other students, and that added greatly to my discomfort, for I felt, deep down in my heart, that I could do as well as they, if I could only get a chance to show what was in me.

After some hours had passed, the head teacher said to me: "The adjoining recitation-room needs sweeping. Take the broom and sweep it."

It occurred to me at once that here was my chance. Never did I receive an order with more delight. I knew that I could sweep, for Mrs. Ruffner had thoroughly taught me how to do that when I lived with her.

I swept the recitation-room three times. Then I got a dusting-cloth and I dusted it four times. All the woodwork around the walls, every bench, table, and desk, I went over four times with my dusting-cloth. Besides, every piece of furniture had been moved and every closet and corner in the room had been thoroughly cleaned. I had the feeling that in a large measure my future depended upon the impression I made upon the teacher in the cleaning of that room. When I was through, I reported to the head teacher. She was a "Yankee" woman who knew just where to look for dirt. She went into the room and inspected the floor and closets; then she took her handkerchief and rubbed it on the woodwork about the walls, and over the table and benches. When she was unable to find one bit of dirt on the floor, or a particle of dust on any of the furniture, she quietly remarked, "I guess you will do to enter this institution."

I was one of the happiest souls on earth. The sweeping of that room was my college examination, and never did any youth pass an examination for entrance into Harvard or Yale that gave him more genuine satisfaction. I have passed several examinations since then, but I have always felt that this was the best one I ever passed.

. . .

When I first went to Hampton I do not recall that I had ever slept in a bed that had two sheets on it. In those days there were not many buildings there, and room was very precious. There were seven other boys in the same room with me; most of them, however, students who had been there for some time. The sheets were quite a puzzle to me. The first night I slept under both of them, and the second night I slept on top of both of them; but by watching the other boys I learned my lesson in this, and have been trying to follow it ever since and to teach it to others.

I was among the youngest of the students who were in Hampton at that time. Most of the students were men and women—some as old as forty years of age. As I now recall the scene of my first year, I do not believe that one often has the opportunity of coming into contact with three or four hundred men and women who were so tremendously in earnest as these men and women were. Every hour was occupied in study or work. Nearly all had had enough actual contact with the world to teach them the need of education. Many of the older ones were, of course, too old to master the text-books very thoroughly, and it was often sad to watch their struggles; but they made up in earnestness much of what they lacked in books. Many of them were as poor as I was, and, besides having to wrestle with their books, they had to struggle with a poverty which prevented their having the necessities of life. Many of them had aged parents who were dependent upon them, and some of them were men who had wives whose support in some way they had to provide for.

The great and prevailing idea that seemed to take possession of every one was to prepare himself to lift up the people at his home. No one seemed to think of himself. And the officers and teachers, what a rare set of human beings they were! They worked for the students night and day, in season and out of season. They seemed happy only when they were helping the students in some manner. Whenever it is written—and I hope it will be—the part that the Yankee teachers played in the education of the Negroes immediately after the war will make one of the most thrilling parts of the history of this country. The time is not far distant when the whole South will appreciate this service in a way that it has not yet been able to do.

EARLY DAYS AT TUSKEGEE

... In May, 1881, near the close of my first year in teaching the night-school, in a way that I had not dared expect, the opportunity opened for me to begin my life-work. One night in the chapel, after the usual chapel exercises were over, General Armstrong referred to the fact that he had received a letter from some gentlemen in Alabama asking him to recommend some one to take charge of what was to be a normal school for the coloured people in the little town of Tuskegee in that state. These gentlemen seemed to take it for granted that no coloured man suitable for the position could be secured, and they were expecting the General to recommend a white man for the place. The next day General Armstrong sent for me to come to his office, and, much to my surprise, asked me if I thought I could fill the position in Alabama. I told him that I would be willing to try. Accordingly, he wrote to the people who had applied to him for the information, that he did not know of any white man to suggest, but if they would be willing to take a coloured man, he had one whom he could recommend. In this letter he gave them my name.

Several days passed before anything more was heard about the matter. Some time afterward, one Sunday evening during the chapel exercises, a messenger came in and handed the General a telegram. At the end of the exercises he read the telegram to the school. In substance, these were its words: "Booker T. Washington will suit us. Send him at once."

There was a great deal of joy expressed among the students and teachers, and I received very hearty congratulations. I began to get ready at once to go to Tuskegee. I went by way of my old home in West Virginia, where I remained for several days, after which I proceeded to Tuskegee. I found Tuskegee to be a town of about two thousand inhabitants, nearly one-half of whom were coloured. It was in what was known as the Black Belt of the South. In the county in which Tuskegee is situated the coloured people outnumbered the whites by about three to one. In some of the adjoining and near-by counties the proportion was not far from six coloured persons to one white.

. . .

My first task was to find a place in which to open the school. After looking the town over with some care, the most suitable place that could be secured seemed to be a rather dilapidated shanty near the coloured Methodist church, together with the church itself as a sort of assembly-room. Both the church and the shanty were in about as bad condition as was possible. I recall that during the first months of school that I taught in this building it was in such poor repair that, whenever it rained, one of the older students would very kindly leave his lessons and hold an umbrella over me while I heard the recitations of the others. I remember, also, that on more than one occasion my landlady held an umbrella over me while I ate breakfast.

. . .

... The first month I spent in finding accomodations for the school, and in travelling through Alabama, examining into the actual life of the people, especially in the country districts, and in getting the school advertised among the class of people that I wanted to have attend it. The most of my travelling was done over the country roads, with a mule and a cart or a mule and a buggy wagon for conveyance. I ate and slept with the people, in their little cabins. I saw their farms, their schools, their churches. Since, in the case of the most of these visits, there had been no notice given in advance that a stranger was expected, I had the advantage of seeing the real, everyday life of the people.

In the plantation districts I found that, as a rule, the whole family slept in one room, and that in addition to the immediate family there sometimes were relatives, or others not related to the family, who slept in the same room. On more than one occasion I went outside the house to get ready for bed, or to wait until the family had gone to bed. They usually contrived some kind of a place for me to sleep, either on the floor or in a special part of another's bed. Rarely was there any place provided in the cabin where one could bathe even the face and hands, but usually some provision was made for this outside the house, in the yard.

The common diet of the people was fat pork and corn bread. At times I have eaten in cabins where they had only corn bread and "black-eye peas" cooked in plain water. The people seemed to have no other idea than to live on this fat meat and corn bread,—the meat, and the meal of which the bread was made, having been bought at a high price at a store in town, notwithstanding the fact that the land all about the cabin homes could easily have been made to produce nearly every kind of garden vegetable that is raised anywhere in the country. Their one object seemed to be to plant nothing but cotton; and in many cases cotton was planted up to the very door of the cabin.

. . .

The breakfast over, and with practically no attention given to the house, the whole family would, as a general thing, proceed to the cotton-field. Every child that was large enough to carry a hoe was put to work, and the baby—for usually there was at least one baby—would be laid down at the end of the cotton row, so that its mother could give it a certain amount of attention when she had finished chopping her row. The noon meal and the supper were taken in much the same way as the breakfast.

TEACHING SCHOOL IN A STABLE AND A HEN-HOUSE

I confess that what I saw during my month of travel and investigation left me with a very heavy heart. The work to be done in order to lift these people up seemed almost beyond accomplishing. I was only one person, and it seemed to me that the little effort which I could put forth could go such a short distance toward bringing about results. I wondered if I could accomplish anything, and if it were worth while for me to try.

. . .

About three months after the opening of the school, and at the time when we were in the greatest anxiety about our work, there came into the market for sale an old and abandoned plantation which was situated about a mile from the town of Tuskegee. The mansion house—or "big house," as it would have been called—which had been occupied by the owners during slavery, had been burned. After making a careful examination of this place, it seemed to be just the location that we wanted in order to make our work effective and permanent.

But how were we to get it? . . .

. . .

. . . A canvass was made among the people of both races for direct gifts of money, and most of those applied to gave small sums. It was often pathetic to note the gifts of the older coloured people, most of whom had spent their best days in slavery. Sometimes they would give five cents, sometimes twenty-five cents. Sometimes the contribution was a quilt, or a quantity of sugarcane. I recall one old coloured woman, who was about seventy years of age, who came to see me when we were raising money to pay for the farm. She hobbled into the room where I was, leaning on a cane. She was clad in rags; but they were clean. She said: "Mr. Washin'ton, God knows I spent de bes' days of my life in slavery. God knows I's ignorant an' poor; but," she added, "I knows what you an' Miss Davidson is tryin' to do. I knows you is tryin' to make better men an' better women for de coloured race. I ain't got no money, but I wants you to take dese six eggs, what I's been savin' up, an' I wants you to put dese six eggs into de eddication of dese boys an' gals."

Since the work at Tuskegee started, it has been my privilege to receive many gifts for the benefit of the institution, but never any, I think, that touched me so deeply as this one.

from *The Souls of Black Folk*

W. E. B. Du Bois (1868–1963)

W. E. B. Du Bois was born in Massachusetts in 1868. An excellent student, he received a B.A. from Fisk in 1888 and in 1895 became the first African American to receive a Ph.D. from Harvard. Taking a teaching position at Atlanta University in 1897, Du Bois explored and confronted the South in person and in the studies he directed of Southern society. Although he stayed at Atlanta until 1910, Du Bois and his wife never became comfortable there. The selection here from his greatest work, *The Souls of Black Folk* (1903), tells of the death of his young son in Atlanta; in that piece, Du Bois expresses the rage, sadness, and frustration that he submerged in his less personal writing. Du Bois went on to become the leading black intellectual of the twentieth-century United States, writing brilliant history, fiction, and sociology as well as leading political movements that laid the foundations for the civil rights movement. In 1963, he expatriated to Ghana, where he died that same year.

U nto you a child is born," sang the bit of yellow paper that fluttered into my room one brown October morning. Then the fear of fatherhood mingled wildly with the joy of creation; I wondered how it looked and how it felt, — what were its eyes, and how its hair curled and crumpled itself. And I thought in awe of her, — she who had slept with Death to tear a man-child from underneath her heart, while I was unconsciously wandering. I fled to my wife and child, repeating the while to myself half wonderingly, "Wife and child? Wife and child?"—fled fast and faster than boat and steam-car, and yet must ever impatiently await them; away from the hard-voiced city, away from the flickering sea into my own Berkshire Hills that sit all sadly guarding the gates of Massachusetts.

Up the stairs I ran to the wan mother and whimpering babe, to the sanctuary on whose altar a life at my bidding had offered itself to win a life, and won. What is this tiny formless thing, this newborn wail from an unknown world, — all head and voice? I handle it curiously, and watch perplexed its winking, breathing, and sneezing. I did not love it then; it seemed a ludicrous thing to love; but her I loved, my girl-mother, she whom now I saw unfolding like the glory of the morning—the transfigured woman.

Through her I came to love the wee thing, as it grew and waxed strong; as its little soul unfolded itself in twitter and cry and half-formed word, and as its eyes caught the gleam and flash of life. How beautiful he was, with his olive-tinted flesh and dark gold ringlets, his eyes of mingled blue and brown, his perfect little limbs, and the soft voluptuous roll which the blood of Africa had moulded into his features! I held him in my arms, after we had sped far away to our Southern home,—held him, and glanced at the hot red soil of Georgia and the breathless city of a hundred hills, and felt a vague unrest. Why was his hair tinted with gold? An evil omen was golden hair in my life. Why had not the brown of his eyes crushed out and killed the blue?—for brown were his father's eyes, and his father's father's. And thus in the Land of the Color-line I saw, as it fell across my baby, the shadow of the Veil.

Within the Veil was he born, said I; and there within shall he live,—a Negro and a Negro's son. Holding in that little head—ah, bitterly!—the unbowed pride of a hunted race, clinging with that tiny dimpled hand—ah, wearily!—to a hope not hopeless but unhopeful, and seeing with those bright wondering eyes that peer into my soul a land whose freedom is to us a mockery and whose liberty a lie. I saw the shadow of the Veil as it passed over my baby, I saw the cold city towering above the blood-red land. I held my face beside his little cheek, showed him the star-children and the twinkling lights as they began to flash, and stilled with an even-song the unvoiced terror of my life.

So sturdy and masterful he grew, so filled with bubbling life, so tremulous with the unspoken wisdom of a life but eighteen months distant from the All-life,—we were not far from worshipping this revelation of the divine, my wife and I. Her own life builded and moulded itself upon the child; he tinged her every dream and idealized her every effort. No hands but hers must touch and garnish those little limbs; no dress or frill must touch them that had not wearied her fingers; no voice but hers could coax him off to Dreamland, and she and he together spoke some soft and unknown tongue and in it held communion. I too mused above his little white bed; saw the strength of my own arm stretched onward through the ages through the newer strength of his; saw the dream of my black fathers stagger a step onward in the wild phantasm of the world; heard in his baby voice the voice of the Prophet that was to rise within the Veil.

And so we dreamed and loved and planned by fall and winter, and the full flush of the long Southern spring, till the hot winds rolled from the fetid Gulf, till the roses shivered and the still stern sun quivered its awful light over the hills of Atlanta. And then one night the little feet pattered wearily to the wee white bed, and the tiny hands trembled; and a warm flushed face tossed on the pillow, and we knew baby was sick. Ten days he lay there,—a swift week and three endless days, wasting, wasting away. Cheerily the mother nursed him the first days, and laughed into the little eyes that smiled again. Tenderly then she hovered round him, till the smile fled away and Fear crouched beside the little bed.

Then the day ended not, and night was a dreamless terror, and joy and sleep slipped away. I hear now that Voice at midnight calling me from dull and dreamless trance,—crying, "The Shadow of Death! The Shadow of Death!" Out into the starlight I crept, to rouse the gray physician,—the Shadow of Death, the Shadow of Death. The hours trembled on; the night listened; the ghastly dawn glided like a tired thing across the lamplight. Then we two alone looked upon the child as he turned toward us with great eyes, and stretched his string-like hands,—the Shadow of Death! And we spoke no word, and turned away.

He died at eventide, when the sun lay like a brooding sorrow above the western hills, veiling its face; when the winds spoke not, and the trees, the great green trees he loved, stood motionless. I saw his breath beat quicker and quicker, pause, and then his little soul leapt like a star that travels in the night and left a world of darkness in its train. The day changed not; the same tall trees peeped in at the windows, the same green grass glinted in the setting sun. Only in the chamber of death writhed the world's most piteous thing—a childless mother.

I shirk not. I long for work. I pant for a life full of striving. I am no coward, to shrink before the rugged rush of the storm, nor even quail before the awful shadow of the Veil. But hearken, O Death! Is not this my life hard enough,—is not that dull land that stretches its sneering web about me cold enough,—is not all the world beyond these four little walls pitiless enough, but that thou must needs enter here,—thou, O Death? About my head the thundering storm beat like a heartless voice, and the crazy forest pulsed with the curses of the weak; but what cared I, within my home beside my wife and baby boy? Wast thou so jealous of one little coign of happiness that thou must needs enter there,—thou, O Death?

A perfect life was his, all joy and love, with tears to make it brighter,— sweet as a summer's day beside the Housatonic. The world loved him; the women kissed his curls, the men looked gravely into his wonderful eyes, and the children hovered and fluttered about him. I can see him now, changing like the sky from sparkling laughter to darkening frowns, and then to wondering thoughtfulness as he watched the world. He knew no color-line, poor dear,—and the Veil, though it shadowed him, had not yet darkened half his sun. He loved the white matron, he loved his black nurse; and in his little world walked souls alone, uncolored and unclothed. I—yea, all men—are larger and purer by the infinite breadth of that one little life. She who in simple clearness of vision sees beyond the stars said when he had flown, "He will be happy there; he ever loved beautiful things." And I, far more ignorant, and blind by the web of mine own weaving, sit alone winding words and muttering, "If still he be, and he be There, and there be a There, let him be happy, O Fate!"

Blithe was the morning of his burial, with bird and song and sweet-smelling flowers. The trees whispered to the grass, but the children sat with hushed faces. And yet it seemed a ghostly unreal day,—the wraith of Life. We seemed to rumble down an unknown street behind a little white bundle of posies, with the shadow of a song in our ears. The busy city dinned about us; they did not say much, those pale-faced hurrying men and women; they did not say much,—they only glanced and said, "Niggers!"

We could not lay him in the ground there in Georgia, for the earth there is strangely red; so we bore him away to the northward, with his flowers and his little folded hands. In vain, in vain!—for where, O God! beneath thy broad blue sky shall my dark baby rest in peace,—where Reverence dwells, and Goodness, and a Freedom that is free?

All that day and all that night there sat an awful gladness in my heart, —nay, blame me not if I see the world thus darkly through the Veil,—and my soul whispers ever to me, saying, "Not dead, not dead, but escaped; not bond, but free." No bitter meanness now shall sicken his baby heart till it die a living death, no taunt shall madden his happy boyhood. Fool that I was to think or wish that this little soul should grow choked and deformed within the Veil! I might have known that yonder deep unwordly look that ever and anon floated past his eyes was peering far beyond this narrow Now. In the poise of his little curl-crowned head did there not sit all that wild pride of being which his father had hardly crushed in his own heart? For what, forsooth, shall a Negro want with pride amid the studied humil-iations of fifty million fellows? Well sped, my boy, before the world had dubbed your ambition insolence, had held your ideals unattainable, and taught you to cringe and bow. Better far this nameless void that stops my life than a sea of sorrow for you.

Idle words; he might have borne his burden more bravely than we,— aye, and found it lighter too, some day; for surely, surely this is not the end. Surely there shall yet dawn some mighty morning to lift the Veil and set the prisoned free. Not for me,—I shall die in my bonds,—but for fresh young souls who have not known the night and waken to the morning; a morning when men ask of the workman, not "Is he white?" but "Can he work?" When men ask artists, not "Are they black?" but "Do they know?" Some morning this may be, long, long years to come. But now there wails, on that dark shore within the Veil, the same deep voice, *Thou shalt forego!* And all have I foregone at that command, and with small complaint,—

all save that fair young form that lies so coldly wed with death in the nest I had builded.

If one must have gone, why not I? Why may I not rest me from this restlessness and sleep from this wide waking? Was not the world's alembic, Time, in his young hands, and is not my time waning? Are there so many workers in the vineyard that the fair promise of this little body could lightly be tossed away? The wretched of my race that line the alleys of the nation sit fatherless and unmothered; but Love sat beside his cradle, and in his ear Wisdom waited to speak. Perhaps now he knows the All-love, and needs not to be wise. Sleep, then, child,—sleep till I sleep and waken to a baby voice and the ceaseless patter of little feet—above the Veil.

from *The Deliverance*

Ellen Glasgow (1873[?]–1945)

Ellen Glasgow was very much a product of Richmond, Virginia. The daughter of the manager of the Tredegar Iron Works and a woman from an elite Tidewater family, Glasgow was frequently ill as a child and rarely attended school. Fascinated by science, Glasgow read Darwin and other iconoclastic thinkers. She prided herself on her independence of thought, tendencies encouraged by the unhappy circumstances of her teenage years, when her mother died after a breakdown and when her sister's fiancé committed suicide. Glasgow began to write early, eventually launching an ambitious fictional "social history" of Virginia. *The Deliverance* (1904), the third in the series, tells of the aftermath of the Civil War, when the Southern social order underwent wrenching change. Glasgow continued to write prolifically throughout the first decades of the new century, winning the Pulitzer Prize in 1942.

At Twelve o'clock the next day, Carraway, walking in the June brightness along the road to the Blake cottage, came suddenly, at the bend of the old ice-pond, upon Maria Fletcher returning from a morning ride. The glow of summer was in her eyes, and though her face was still pale, she seemed to him a different creature from the grave, repressed girl of the night before. He noticed at once that she sat her horse superbly, and in her long black habit all the sinuous lines of her figure moved in rhythm with the rapid pace.

As she neared him, and apparently before she had noticed his approach, he saw her draw rein quickly, and, screened by the overhanging boughs of a blossoming chestnut, send her glance like a hooded falcon across the neighbouring field. Following the aim of her look, he saw Christopher Blake walking idly among the heavy furrows, watching, with the interest of a born agriculturist, the busy transplanting of Fletcher's crop. He still wore his jean clothes, which, hanging loosely upon his impressive figure, blended harmoniously with the dull-purple tones of the upturned soil. Beyond him there was a background of distant wood, still young in leaf, and his bared head, with the strong, sunburned line of his profile, stood out as distinctly as a portrait done in early Roman gold.

That Maria had seen in him some higher possibility than that of a field labourer was soon evident to Carraway, for her horse was still standing on the slight incline, and as he reached her side she turned with a frank question on her lips.

"Is that one of the labourers—the young giant by the fence?"

"Well, I dare say he labours, if that's what you mean. He's young Blake, you know."

"Young Blake?" She bent her brows, and it was clear that the name suggested only a trivial recollection to her mind. "There used to be some Blake children in the old overseer's house—is this one of them."

"Possibly; they live in the overseer's house."

She leaned over, fastening her heavy gauntlet. "They wouldn't play with me, I remember; I couldn't understand why. Once I carried my dolls over to their yard, and the boy set a pack of hounds on me. I screamed so that an old Negro ran out and drove them off, and all the time the boy stood by, laughing and calling me names. Is that he, do you think?"

"I dare say. It sounds like him."

"Is he so cruel?" she asked a little wistfully.

"I don't know about that—but he doesn't like your people. Your grandfather had some trouble with him a long time ago."

"And he wanted to punish me?—how cowardly."

"It does sound rather savage, but it isn't an ordinary case, you know. He's the kind of person to curse 'root and branch,' from all I hear, in the good old Biblical fashion."

"Oh, well, he's certainly very large, isn't he?"

"He's superb," said Carraway, with conviction.

"At a distance—so is that great pine over there," she lifted her whip and pointed across the field; then as Carraway made no answer, she smiled slightly and rode rapidly toward the Hall.

For a few minutes the lawyer stood where she had left him, watching in puzzled thought her swaying figure on the handsome horse. The girl fretted him, and yet he felt that he liked her almost in spite of himself—liked something fine and fearless he found in her dark eyes; liked, too, even while he sneered, her peculiar grace of manner. There was the making of a woman in her after all, he told himself, as he turned into the sunken road, where he saw Christopher already moving homeward. He had meant to catch up with him and join company on the way, but the young man covered ground so quickly with his great strides that at last Carraway, losing sight of him entirely, resigned himself to going leisurely about his errand.

When, a little later, he opened the unhinged whitewashed gate before the cottage, the place, as he found it, seemed to be tenanted solely by a family of young turkeys scratching beneath the damask rose-bushes in the yard. From a rear chimney a dark streak of smoke was rising, but the front of the house gave no outward sign of life, and as there came no answer to his insistent knocks he at last ventured to open the door and pass into the narrow hall. From the first room on the right a voice spoke at his entrance, and following the sound he found himself face to face with Mrs. Blake in her massive Elizabethan chair.

"There is a stranger in the room," she said rigidly, turning her sightless eyes; "speak at once."

"I beg pardon most humbly for my intrusion," replied Carraway, conscious of stammering like an offending schoolboy, "but as no one answered my knock, I committed the indiscretion of opening a closed door."

Awed as much by the stricken pallor of her appearance as by the inappropriate grandeur of her black brocade and her thread lace cap, he advanced slowly and stood awaiting his dismissal.

"What door?" she demanded sharply, much to his surprise.

"Yours, madam."

"Not answer your knock?" she pursued, with indignation. "So that was the noise I heard, and no wonder that you entered. Why, what is the matter with the place? Where are the servants?"

He humbly replied that he had seen none, to be taken up with her accustomed quickness of touch.

"Seen none! Why, there are three hundred of them, sir. Well, well, this is really too much. I shall put a butler over Boaz this very day."

For an instant Carraway felt strangely tempted to turn and run as fast as he could along the sunken road—remembering, as he struggled with the impluse, that he had once been caught at the age of ten and whipped for stealing apples. Recovering with an effort his sense of dignity, he offered the suggestion that Boaz, instead of being seriously in fault, might merely have been engaged in useful occupations "somewhere at the back."

"What on earth can he have to do at the back, sir?" inquired the irrepressible old lady; "but since you were so kind as to overlook our inhospitable reception, will you not be equally good and tell me your name?"

"I fear it won't enlighten you much," replied the lawyer modestly, "but my name happens to be Guy Carraway."

"Guy—Guy Carraway," repeated Mrs. Blake, as if weighing each separate letter in some remote social scales. "I've known many a Guy in my day—and that part, as least, of your name is quite familiar. There was Guy Nelson, and Guy Blair, and Guy Marshall, the greatest beau of his time—but I don't think I ever had the pleasure of meeting a Carraway before."

"That is more than probable, ma'am, but I have the advantage of you, since, as a child, I was once taken out upon the street corner merely to see you go by on your way to a fancy ball, where you appeared as Diana."

Mrs. Blake yielded gracefully to the skilful thrust.

"Ah, I was Lucy Corbin then," she sighed. "You find few traces of her in me now, sir."

"Unfortunately, your mirror cannot speak for me."

She shook her head.

"You're a flatterer—a sad flatterer, I see," she returned, a little wistfully; "but it does no harm, as I tell my son, to flatter the old. It is well to strew the passage to the grave with flowers."

"How well I remember that day," said Carraway, speaking softly. "There was a crowd about the door, waiting to see you come out, and a carpenter lifted me upon his shoulder. Your hair was as black as night, and there was a circle round your head———"

"A silver fillet," she corrected, with a smile in which there was a gentle archness.

"A fillet, yes; and you carried a bow and a quiver full of arrows. I declare, it seems but yesterday."

"It was more than fifty years ago," murmured the old lady. "Well, well, I've had my day, sir, and it was a merry one. I am almost seventy years old —I'm half dead, and stone blind into the bargain, but I can say to you that this is a cheerful world in spite of the darkness in which I linger on. I'd take it over again and gladly any day—the pleasure and the pain, the light and the darkness. Why, I sometimes think that my present blindness was given me in order that I might view the past more clearly. There's not a ball of my youth, nor a face I knew, nor even a dress I wore, that I don't see more distinctly every day. The present is a very little part of life, sir; it's the past in which we store our treasures."

"You're right, you're right," replied Carraway, drawing his chair nearer the embroidered ottoman and leaning over to stroke the yellow cat; "and I'm glad to hear so cheerful a philosophy from your lips."

"It is based on a cheerful experience — I've been as you see me now only twenty years."

Only twenty years! He looked mutely round the soiled whitewashed walls, where hung a noble gathering of Blake portraits in massive old gilt frames. Among them he saw the remembered face of Lucy Corbin herself, painted under a rose-garland held by smiling Loves.

"Life has its trials, of course," pursued Mrs. Blake, as if speaking to herself. "I can't look out upon the June flowers, you know, and though the pink crape-myrtle at my window is in full bloom I cannot see it."

Following her gesture, Carraway glanced out into the little yard; no myrtle was there, but he remembered vaguely that he had seen one in blossom at the Hall.

"You keep flowers about you, though," he said, alluding to the scattered vases of June roses.

"Not my crape-myrtle. I planted it myself when I first came home with Mr. Blake, and I have never allowed so much as a spray of it to be plucked."

Forgetting his presence, she lapsed for a time into one of the pathetic day-dreams of old age. Then recalling herself suddenly, her tone took on a sprightliness like that of youth.

"It's not often that we have the pleasure of entertaining a stranger in our out-of-the-way house, sir—so may I ask where you are staying—or perhaps you will do us the honour to sleep beneath our roof. It has had the privilege of sheltering General Washington."

"You are very kind," replied Carraway, with a gratitude that was from his heart, "but to tell the truth, I feel that I am sailing under false colours. The real object of my visit is to ask a business interview with your son. I bring what seems to me a very fair offer for the place."

Grasping the carved arms of her chair, Mrs. Blake turned the wonder in her blind eyes upon him.

"An offer for the place! Why, you must be dreaming, sir! A Blake owned it more than a hundred years before the Revolution."

At the instant, understanding broke upon Carraway like a thunder-cloud, and as he rose from his seat it seemed to him that he had missed by a single step the yawning gulf before him. Blind terror gripped him for the moment, and when his brain steadied he looked up to meet, from the threshold of the adjoining room, the enraged flash of Christopher's eyes. So tempestuous was the glance that Carraway, impulsively falling back, squared himself to receive a physical blow; but the young man, without so much as the expected oath, came in quietly and took his stand behind the Elizabethan chair.

"Why, what a joke, mother," he said, laughing; "he means the old Weatherby farm, of course. The one I wanted to sell last year, you know."

"I thought you'd sold it to the Weatherbys, Christopher."

"Not a bit of it—they backed out at the last; but don't begin to bother your head about such things; they aren't worth it. And now, sir," he turned upon Carraway, "since your business is with me, perhaps you will have the goodness to step outside."

With the feeling that he was asked out for a beating, Carraway turned for a farewell with Mrs. Blake, but the imperious old lady was not to be so lightly defrauded of a listener.

"Business may come later, my son," she said, detaining them by a gesture of her heavily ringed hand. "After dinner you may take Mr. Carraway with you into the library and discuss your affairs over a bottle of burgundy, as was your grandfather's custom before you; meanwhile, he and I will resume our very pleasant talk which you interrupted. He remembers seeing me in the old days when we were all in the United States, my dear."

Christopher's brow grew black, and he threw a sharp and malignant glance of sullen suspicion at Carraway, who summoned to meet it his most frank and open look.

"I saw your mother in the height of her fame," he said, smiling, "so I may count myself one of her oldest admirers, I believe. You may assure yourself," he added softly, "that I have her welfare very decidedly at heart."

At this Christopher smiled back at him, and there was something of the June brightness in his look.

"Well, take care, sir," he answered, and went out, closing the door carefully behind him, while Carraway applied himself to a determined entertaining of Mrs. Blake.

To accomplish this he found that he had only to leave her free, guiding her thoughts with his lightest touch into newer channels. The talk had grown merrier now, and he soon discovered that she possessed a sharpened wit as well as a ready tongue. From subject to subject she passed with amazing swiftness, bearing down upon her favourite themes with the delightful audacity of the talker who is born, not made. She spoke of her own youth, of historic flirtations in the early twenties, of great beaux she had known, and of famous recipes that had been handed down for generations. Everywhere he felt her wonderful keenness of perception—that intuitive understanding of men and manners which had kept her for so long the reigning belle among her younger rivals.

As she went on he found that her world was as different from his own as if she dwelt upon some undiscovered planet—a world peopled with shades and governed by an ideal group of abstract laws. She lived upon lies, he saw, and thrived upon the sweetness she extracted from them. For her the Confederacy had never fallen, the quiet of her dreamland had been disturbed by no invading army, and the three hundred slaves, who had in reality scattered like chaff before the wind, she still saw in her cheerful visions tilling her familiar fields. It was as if she had fallen asleep with the great blow that had wrecked her body, and had dreamed on steadily throughout the years. Of real changes she was as ignorant as a new-born child. Events had shaken the world to its centre, and she, by her obscure hearth, had not felt so much as a sympathetic tremor. In her memory there was no Appomattox, news of the death of Lincoln had never reached her ears, and president had peacefully succeeded president in the secure Confederacy in which she lived. Wonderful as it all was, to Carraway the most wonderful thing was the intricate tissue of lies woven around her chair. Lies—lies—there had been nothing but lies spoken within her hearing for twenty years.

"Wash"

William Faulkner (1897–1962)

On the surface, William Faulkner's life possessed little drama. Born and raised in Mississippi, Faulkner dropped out of high school, lived with a friend at Yale, briefly joined the Royal Air Force, worked as postmaster at the University of Mississippi, traveled to Europe, and published a novel to little response. In 1929, however, Faulkner began to experiment with new forms of storytelling, first with *The Sound and the Fury,* and then in a remarkable series of novels over the next eight years. In his short story "Wash" (1934), Faulkner explores the postwar relationship between a former slave owner and Confederate officer, Thomas Sutpen, and his poor white helper, Wash Jones. Wash, who had persuaded himself that Sutpen thought of him as a friend, if not an equal, must decide what to do when he discovers otherwise.

Sutpen stood above the pallet bed on which the mother and child lay. Between the shrunken planking of the wall the early sunlight fell in long pencil strokes, breaking upon his straddled legs and upon the riding whip in his hand, and lay across the still shape of the mother, who lay looking up at him from still, inscrutable, sullen eyes, the child at her side wrapped in a piece of dingy though clean cloth. Behind them an old Negro woman squatted beside the rough hearth where a meager fire smoldered.

"Well, Milly," Sutpen said, "too bad you're not a mare. Then I could give you a decent stall in the stable."

Still the girl on the pallet did not move. She merely continued to look up at him without expression, with a young, sullen, inscrutable face still pale from recent travail. Sutpen moved, bringing into the splintered pencils of sunlight the face of a man of sixty. He said quietly to the squatting Negress, "Griselda foaled this morning."

"Horse or mare?" the Negress said.

"A horse. A damned fine colt.... What's this?" He indicated the pallet with the hand which held the whip.

"That un's a mare, I reckon."

"Hah," Sutpen said. "A damned fine colt. Going to be the spit and image of old Rob Roy when I rode him North in '61. Do you remember?"

"Yes, Marster."

"Hah." He glanced back towards the pallet. None could have said if the girl still watched him or not. Again his whip hand indicated the pallet. "Do whatever they need with whatever we've got to do it with." He went out, passing out the crazy doorway and stepping down into the rank weeds (there yet leaned rusting against the corner of the porch the scythe which Wash had borrowed from him three months ago to cut them with) where his horse waited, where Wash stood holding the reins.

When Colonel Sutpen rode away to fight the Yankees, Wash did not go. "I'm looking after the Kernal's place and niggers," he would tell all who asked him and some who had not asked — a gaunt, malaria-ridden man with pale, questioning eyes, who looked about thirty-five, though it was known that he had not only a daughter but an eight-year-old grand-daughter as well. This was a lie, as most of them—the few remaining men between eighteen and fifty—to whom he told it, knew, though there were some who believed that he himself really believed it, though even these believed that he had better sense than to put it to the test with Mrs. Sutpen or the Sutpen slaves. Knew better or was just too lazy and shiftless to try it, they said, knowing that his sole connection with the Sutpen plantation lay in the fact that for years now Colonel Sutpen had allowed him to squat in a crazy shack on a slough in the river bottom on the Sutpen place, which Sutpen had built for a fishing lodge in his bachelor days and which had since fallen into dilapidation from disuse, so that now it looked like an aged or sick wild beast crawled terrifically there to drink in the act of dying.

The Sutpen slaves themselves heard of his statement. They laughed. It was not the first time they had laughed at him, calling him white trash behind his back. They began to ask him themselves, in groups, meeting him in the faint road which led up from the slough and the old fish camp, "Why ain't you at de war, white man?"

Pausing, he would look about the ring of black faces and white eyes and teeth behind which derision lurked. "Because I got a daughter and family to keep," he said. "Get out of my road, niggers."

"Niggers?" they repeated; "niggers?" laughing now. "Who him, calling us niggers?"

"Yes," he said. "I ain't got no niggers to look after my folks if I was gone."

"Nor nothing else but dat shack down yon dat Cunnel wouldn't *let* none of us live in."

Now he cursed them; sometimes he rushed at them, snatching up a stick from the ground while they scattered before him, yet seeming to sur-round him still with that black laughing, derisive, evasive, inescapable, leaving him panting and impotent and raging. Once it happened in the very back yard of the big house itself. This was after bitter news had come down from the Tennessee mountains and from Vicksburg, and Sherman had passed through the plantation, and most of the Negroes had followed him. Almost everything else had gone with the Federal troops, and Mrs. Sutpen had sent word to Wash that he could have the scuppernongs ripening in the arbor in the back yard. This time it was a house servant, one of the few Negroes who remained; this time the Negress had to retreat up the kitchen steps, where she turned. "Stop right dar, white man. Stop right whar you is. You ain't never crossed dese steps whilst Cunnel here, and you ain't ghy' do hit now."

This was true. But there was this of a kind of pride: he had never tried to enter the big house, even though he believed that if he had, Sutpen would have received him, permitted him. "But I ain't going to give no black nigger the chance to tell me I can't go nowhere," he said to himself. "I ain't even going to give Kernel the chance to have to cuss a nigger on my account." This, though he and Sutpen had spent more than one afternoon together on those rare Sundays when there would be no company in the house. Perhaps his mind knew that it was because Sutpen had nothing else to do, being a man who could not bear his own company. Yet the fact remained that the two of them would spend whole afternoons in the scuppernong arbor, Sutpen in the hammock and Wash squatting against a post, a pail of cistern water between them, taking drink for drink from the same demijohn. Meanwhile on weekdays he would see the fine figure of the man — they were the same age almost to the day, though neither of them (perhaps because Wash had a grandchild while Sutpen's son was a youth in school) ever thought of himself as being so — on the fine figure of the black stallion, galloping about the plantation. For that moment his heart would be quiet and proud. It would seem to him that that world in which Negroes, whom the Bible told him had been created and cursed by God to be brute and vassal to all men of white skin, were better found and housed and even clothed than he and his; that world in which he sensed always about him mocking echoes of black laughter was but a dream and an illusion, and that the actual world was this one across which his own lonely apotheosis seemed to gallop on the black thoroughbred, thinking how the Book said also that all men were created in the image of God and hence all men made the same image in God's eyes at least; so that he could say, as though speaking of himself, "A fine proud man. If God Himself was to come down and ride the natural earth, that's what He would aim to look like."

Sutpen returned in 1865, on the black stallion. He seemed to have aged ten years. His son had been killed in action the same winter in which his wife had died. He returned with his citation for gallantry from the hand of General Lee to a ruined plantation, where for a year now his daughter had subsisted partially on the meager bounty of the man to whom fifteen years ago he had granted permission to live in that tumble-down fishing camp whose very existence he had at the time forgotten. Wash was there to meet him, unchanged: still gaunt, still ageless, with his pale, questioning gaze, his air diffident, a little servile, a little familiar, "Well, Kernel," Wash said, "they kilt us but they ain't whupped us yit, air they?"

That was the tenor of their conversation for the next five years. It was inferior whisky which they drank now together from a stoneware jug, and it was not in the scuppernong arbor. It was in the rear of the little store which Sutpen managed to set up on the highroad: a frame shelved room where, with Wash for clerk and porter, he dispensed kerosene and staple foodstuffs and stale gaudy candy and cheap beads and ribbons to Negroes or poor whites of Wash's own kind, who came afoot or on gaunt mules to haggle tediously for dimes and quarters with a man who at one time could gallop (the black stallion was still alive; the stable in which his jealous get lived was in better repair than the house where the master himself lived) for ten miles across his own fertile land and who had led troops gallantly in battle; until Sutpen in fury would empty the store, close and lock the doors from the inside. Then he and Wash would repair to the rear and the jug. But the talk would not be quiet now, as when Sutpen lay in the ham-mock, delivering an arrogant monologue while Wash squatted guffawing against his post. They both say now, though Sutpen had the single chair while Wash used whatever box or keg was handy, and even this for just a little while, because soon Sutpen would reach that stage of impotent and furious undefeat in which he would rise, swaying and plunging, and declare again that he would take his pistol and the black stallion and ride single-handed into Washington and kill Lincoln, dead now, and Sherman, now a private citizen. "Kill them!" he would shout. "Shoot them down like the dogs they are—"

"Sho, Kernel; sho, Kernel," Wash would say, catching Sutpen as he fell. Then he would commandeer the first passing wagon or, lacking that, he would walk the mile to the nearest neighbor and borrow one and return and carry Sutpen home. He entered the house now. He had been doing so for a long time, taking Sutpen home in whatever borrowed wagon might be, talking him into locomotion with cajoling murmurs as though he were a horse, a stallion himself. The daughter would meet them and hold open the door without a word. He would carry his burden through the once white formal entrance, surmounted by a fanlight imported piece by piece from Europe and with a board now nailed over a missing pane, across a velvet carpet from which all nap was now gone, and up a formal stairs, now but a fading ghost of bare boards between two strips of fading paint, and into the bedroom. It would be dusk by now, and he would let his burden sprawl onto the bed and undress it and then he would sit quietly in a chair beside. After a time the daughter would come to the door. "We're all right now," he would tell her. "Don't you worry none, Miss Judith."

Then it would become dark, and after a while he would lie down on the floor beside the bed, though not to sleep, because after a time—sometimes before midnight—the man on the bed would stir and groan and then speak. "Wash?"

"Hyer I am, Kernel. You go back to sleep. We ain't whupped yit, air we? Me and you kin do hit."

Even then he had already seen the ribbon about his granddaughter's waist. She was now fifteen, already mature, after the early way of her kind. He knew where the ribbon came from; he had been seeing it and its kind daily for three years, even if she had lied about where she got it, which she did not, at once bold, sullen, and fearful. "Sho now," he said, "Ef Kernel wants to give hit to you, I hope you minded to thank him."

His heart was quiet, even when he saw the dress, watching her secret, defiant, frightened face when she told him that Miss Judith, the daughter, had helped her to make it. But he was quite grave when he approached Sutpen after they closed the store that afternoon, following the other to the rear.

"Get the jug," Sutpen directed.

"Wait," Wash said. "Not yit for a minute."

Neither did Sutpen deny the dress. "What about it?" he said.

But Wash met his arrogant stare; he spoke quietly. "I've knowed you for going on twenty years. I ain't never yit denied to do what you told me to do. And I'm a man nigh sixty. And she ain't nothing but a fifteen-year-old gal."

"Meaning that I'd harm a girl? I, a man as old as you are?"

"If you was ara other man, I'd say you was as old as me. And old or no old, I wouldn't let her keep that dress nor nothing else that come from your hand. But you are different."

"How different?" But Wash merely looked at him with his pale, questioning, sober eyes. "So that's why you are afraid of me?"

Now Wash's gaze no longer questioned. It was tranquil, serene. "I ain't afraid. Because you air brave. It ain't that you were a brave man at one minute or day of your life and got a paper to show hit from General Lee. But you air brave, the same as you air alive and breathing. That's where hit's different. Hit don't need no ticket from nobody to tell me that. And

I know that whatever you handle or tech, whether hit's a regiment of men or a ignorant gal or just a hound dog, that you will make hit right."

Now it was Sutpen who looked away, turning suddenly, brusquely. "Get the jug," he said sharply.

"Sho, Kernel," Wash said.

So on that Sunday dawn two years later, having watched the Negro midwife, which he had walked three miles to fetch, enter the crazy door beyond which his granddaughter lay wailing, his heart was still quiet though concerned. He knew what they had been saying—the Negroes in cabins about the land, the white men who loafed all day long about the store, watching quietly the three of them; Sutpen, himself, his granddaughter with her air of brazen and shrinking defiance as her condition became daily more and more obvious, like three actors that came and went upon a stage. "I know what they say to one another," he thought. "I can almost hyear them: *Wash Jones has fixed old Sutpen at last. Hit taken him twenty years, but he has done hit at last.*"

It would be dawn after a while, though not yet. From the house, where the lamp shone dim beyond the warped doorframe, his granddaughter's voice came steadily as though run by a clock, while thinking went slowly and terrifically, fumbling, involved somehow with a sound of galloping hooves, until there broke suddenly free in mid-gallop the fine proud figure of the man on the fine proud stallion, galloping; and then that at which thinking fumbled, broke free too and quite clear, not in justification nor even explanation, but as the apotheosis, lonely, explicable, beyond all fouling by human touch: "He is bigger than all them Yankees that kilt his son and his wife and taken his niggers and ruined his land, bigger than this hyer durn country that he fit for and that has denied him into keeping a little country store; bigger than the denial which hit helt to his lips like the bitter cup in the Book. And how could I have lived this nigh to him for twenty years without being teched and changed by him? Maybe I ain't as big as him and maybe I ain't done none of the galloping. But at least I done been drug along. Me and him kin do hit, if so be he will show me what he aims for me to do."

Then it was dawn. Suddenly he could see the house, and the old Negress in the door looking at him. Then he realized that his granddaughter's voice had ceased. "It's a girl," the Negress said. "You can go tell him if you want to." She reentered the house.

"A girl," he repeated; "a girl"; in astonishment, hearing the galloping hooves, seeing the proud galloping figure emerge again. He seemed to watch it pass, galloping through avatars which marked the accumulation of years, time, to the climax where it galloped beneath a brandished saber and a shot-torn flag rushing down a sky in color like thunderous sulphur, thinking for the first time in his life that perhaps Sutpen was an old man like himself. "Gittin a gal," he thought in that astonishment; then he thought with the pleased surprise of a child: "Yes, sir. Be dawg if I ain't lived to be a great-grandpaw after all."

He entered the house. He moved clumsily, on tiptoe as if he no longer lived there, as if the infant which had just drawn breath and cried in light had dispossessed him, but it of his own blood too though it might. But even above the pallet he could see little save the blur of his granddaughter's exhausted face. Then the Negress squatting at the hearth spoke, "You better gawn tell him if you going to. Hit's daylight now."

But that was not necessary. He had no more than turned the corner of the porch where the scythe leaned which he had borrowed three months ago to clear away the weeds through which he walked, when Sutpen himself rode up on the old stallion. He did not wonder how Sutpen had got the word. He took it for granted that this was what had brought the other out at this hour on Sunday morning, and he stood while the other dismounted, and he took the reins from Sutpen's hand, an expression on his gaunt face almost imbecile with a kind of weary triumph, saying, "Hit's a gal, Kernel. I be dawg if you ain't as old as I am—" until Sutpen passed him and entered the house. He stood there with the reins in his hand and heard Sutpen cross the floor to the pallet. He heard what Sutpen said, and something seemed to stop dead in him before going on.

The sun was now up, the swift sun of Mississippi latitudes, and it seemed to him that he stood beneath a strange sky, in a strange scene, familiar only as things are familiar in dreams, like the dreams of falling to one who has never climbed. "I kain't have heard what I thought I heard," he thought quietly. "I know I kain't." Yet the voice, the familiar voice which had said the words was still speaking, talking now to the old Negress about a colt foaled that morning. "That's why he was up so early," he thought. "That was hit. Hit ain't me and mine. Hit ain't even hisn that got him outten bed."

Sutpen emerged. He descended into the weeds, moving with the heavy deliberation which would have been haste when he was younger. He had not yet looked full at Wash. He said, "Dicey will stay and tend to her. You better—" Then he seemed to see Wash facing him and paused. "What?" he said.

"You said—" To his own ears Wash's voice sounded flat and ducklike, like a deaf man's. "You said if she was a mare, you could give her a good stall in the stable."

"Well?" Sutpen said. His eyes widened and narrowed, almost like a man's fists flexing and shutting, as Wash began to advance towards him, stooping a little. Very astonishment kept Sutpen still for the moment, watching that man whom in twenty years he had no more known to make any motion save at command than he had the horse which he rode. Again his eyes narrowed and widened; without moving he seemed to rear suddenly upright. "Stand back," he said suddenly and sharply. "Don't you touch me."

"I'm going to tech you, Kernel," Wash said in that flat, quiet, almost soft voice, advancing.

Sutpen raised the hand which held the riding whip; the old Negress peered around the crazy door with her black gargoyle face of a worn gnome. "Stand back, Wash," Sutpen said. Then he struck. The old Negress leaped down into the weeds with the agility of a goat and fled. Sutpen slashed Wash again across the face with the whip, striking him to his knees. When Wash rose and advanced once more he held in his hands the scythe which he had borrowed from Sutpen three months ago and which Sutpen would never need again.

When he reentered the house his granddaughter stirred on the pallet bed and called his name fretfully. "What was that?" she said.

"What was what, honey?"

"That ere racket out there."

"'Twarn't nothing," he said gently. He knelt and touched her hot forehead clumsily. "Do you want ara thing?"

"I want a sup of water," she said querulously. "I been laying here wanting a sup of water a long time, but don't nobody care enough to pay me no mind."

"Sho now," he said soothingly. He rose stiffly and fetched the dipper of water and raised her head to drink and laid her back and watched her turn to the child with an absolutely stonelike face. But a moment later he saw that she was crying quietly. "Now, now," he said. "I wouldn't do that. Old Dicey says hit's a right fine gal. Hit's all right now. Hit's all over now. Hit ain't no need to cry now."

But she continued to cry quietly, almost sullenly, and he rose again and stood uncomfortably above the pallet for a time, thinking as he had thought when his own wife lay so and then his daughter in turn: "Women. Hit's a mystry to me. They seem to want em, and yit when they git em they cry about hit. Hit's a mystry to me. To ara man." Then he moved away and drew a chair up to the window and sat down.

Through all that long, bright, sunny forenoon he sat at the window, waiting. Now and then he rose and tiptoed to the pallet. But his granddaughter slept now, her face sullen and calm and weary, the child in the crook of her arm. Then he returned to the chair and sat again, waiting, wondering why it took them so long, until he remembered that it was Sunday. He was sitting there at mid-afternoon when a half-grown white boy came around the corner of the house upon the body and gave a choked cry and looked up and glared for a mesmerized instant at Wash in the window before he turned and fled. Then Wash rose and tiptoed again to the pallet.

The granddaughter was awake now, wakened perhaps by the boy's cry without hearing it. "Milly," he said, "air you hungry?" She didn't answer, turning her face away. He built up the fire on the hearth and cooked the food which he had brought home the day before: fatback it was, and cold corn pone; he poured water into the stale coffee pot and heated it. But she would not eat when he carried the plate to her, so he ate himself, quietly, alone, and left the dishes as they were and returned to the window.

Now he seemed to sense, feel, the men who would be gathering with horses and guns and dogs—the curious, and the vengeful: men of Sutpen's own kind, who had made the company about Sutpen's table in the time when Wash himself had yet to approach nearer to the house than the scuppernong arbor—men who had also shown the lesser ones how to fight in battle, who maybe also had signed papers from the generals saying that they were among the first of the brave; who had also galloped in the old days arrogant and proud on the fine horses across the fine plantations—symbols also of admiration and hope; instruments too of despair and grief.

That was whom they would expect him to run from. It seemed to him that he had no more to run from than he had to run to. If he ran, he would merely be fleeing one set of bragging and evil shadows for another just like them, since they were all of a kind throughout all the earth which he knew, and he was old, too old to flee far even if he were to flee. He could never escape them, no matter how much or how far he ran: a man going on sixty could not run that far. Not far enough to escape beyond the boundaries of earth where such men lived, set the order and the rule of living. It seemed to him that he now saw for the first time, after five years, how it was that Yankees or any other living armies had managed to whip them: the gallant, the proud, the brave; the acknowledged and chosen best among them all to carry courage and honor and pride. Maybe if he had gone to the war with them he would have discovered them sooner. But if he had discovered them sooner, what would he have done with his life since? How could he have borne to remember for five years what his life had been before?

Now it was getting toward sunset. The child had been crying; when he went to the pallet he saw his granddaughter nursing it, her face still bemused, sullen, inscrutable. "Air you hungry yit?" he said.

"I don't want nothing."

"You ought to eat."

This time she did not answer at all, looking down at the child. He returned to his chair and found that the sun had set. "Hit kain't be much longer," he thought. He could feel them quite near now, the curious and the vengeful. He could even seem to hear what they were saying about him, the undercurrent of believing beyond the immediate fury: *Old Wash Jones he come a tumble at last. He thought he had Sutpen, but Sutpen fooled him. He thought he had Kernel where he would have to marry the gal or pay up. And Kernel refused.* "But I never expected that, Kernel!" he cried aloud, catching himself at the sound of his own voice, glancing quickly back to find his granddaughter watching him.

"Who you talking to now?" she said.

"Hit ain't nothing. I was just thinking and talked out before I knowed hit."

Her face was becoming indistinct again, again a sullen blur in the twilight. "I reckon so. I reckon you'll have to holler louder than that before he'll hear you, up yonder at that house. And I reckon you'll need to do more than holler before you get him down here too."

"Sho now," he said. "Don't you worry none." But already thinking was going smoothly on: "You know I never. You know how I ain't never expected or asked nothing from ara living man but what I expected from you. And I never asked that. I didn't think hit would need. I said, *I don't need to. What need has a fellow like Wash Jones to question or doubt the man that General Lee himself says in a handwrote ticket that he was brave? Brave,*" he thought. "Better if nara one of them had never rid back home in '65"; thinking *Better if his kind and mine too had never drawn the breath of life on this earth. Better that all who remain of us be blasted from the face of earth than that another Wash Jones should see his whole life shredded from him and shrivel away like a dried shuck thrown onto the fire.*

He ceased, became still. He heard the horses, suddenly and plainly; presently he saw the lantern and the movement of men, the glint of gun barrels, in its moving light. Yet he did not stir. It was quite dark now, and he listened to the voices and the sounds of underbrush as they surrounded the house. The lantern itself came on; its light fell upon the quiet body in the weeds and stopped, the horses tall and shadowy. A man descended and stooped in the lantern light, above the body. He held a pistol; he rose and faced the house. "Jones," he said.

"I'm here," Wash said quietly from the window. "That you, Major?"

"Come out."

"Sho," he said quietly. "I just want to see to my granddaughter."

"We'll see to her. Come on out."

"Sho, Major. Just a minute."

"Show a light. Light your lamp."

"Sho. In just a minute." They could hear his voice retreat into the house, though they could not see him as he went swiftly to the crack in the chimney where he kept the butcher knife: the one thing in his slovenly life and house in which he took pride, since it was razor sharp. He approached the pallet, his granddaughter's voice:

"Who is it? Light the lamp, grandpaw."

"Hit won't need no light, honey. Hit won't take but a minute," he said, kneeling, fumbling toward her voice, whispering now. "Where air you?"

"Right here," she said fretfully. "Where would I be? What is ..." His hand touched her face. "What is ... Grandpaw! Grand...."

"Jones!" the sheriff said. "Come out of there!"

"In just a minute, Major," he said. Now he rose and moved swiftly. He knew where in the dark the can of kerosene was, just as he knew that it was full, since it was not two days ago that he had filled it at the store and held it there until he got a ride home with it, since the five gallons were heavy. There were still coals on the hearth; besides, the crazy building itself was like tinder: the coals, the hearth, the walls exploding in a single blue glare. Against it the waiting men saw him in a wild instant springing toward them with the lifted scythe before the horses reared and whirled. They checked the horses and turned them back toward the glare, yet still in wild relief against it the gaunt figure ran toward them with the lifted scythe.

"Jones!" the sheriff shouted; "stop! Stop, or I'll shoot. Jones! *Jones!*" Yet still the gaunt, furious figure came on against the glare and roar of the flames. With the scythe lifted, it bore down upon them, upon the wild glaring eyes of the horses and the swinging glints of gun barrels, without any cry, any sound.

from *Gone with the Wind*

Margaret Mitchell (1900–1949)

Margaret Mitchell, like the five generations of her family before her, was born in Atlanta. She briefly attended Smith College, returning to Atlanta in 1919 after her mother died of influenza. Married early to a man who became abusive, Mitchell divorced, worked as a reporter for an Atlanta newspaper, and remarried. In 1926, Mitchell resigned from the paper and began writing a story of the Civil War and Reconstruction set in Georgia. Though she completed the book in four years, she refused to submit it for publication until 1935. Immediately accepted by Macmillan, *Gone with the Wind* sold 1 million copies in its first six months, won the Pulitzer Prize against such competition as William Faulkner's *Absalom, Absalom!*, and was made into a movie that garnered ten Academy Awards. The novel, richer and more complex than the film, is the story of a rather unprincipled young Southern woman who, confronted with defeat and poverty that crush other people, survives and even flourishes. Mitchell, who published nothing else, was struck by a car and killed in 1949.

She looked from the alcove into the huge drawing room and watched the dancers, remembering how beautiful this room had been when first she came to Atlanta during the war. Then the hardwood floors had shone like glass, and overhead the chandelier with its hundreds of tiny prisms had caught and reflected every ray of the dozens of candles it bore, flinging them, like gleams from diamonds, flame and sapphire about the room. The old portraits on the walls had been dignified and gracious and had looked down upon guests with an air of mellowed hospitality. The rosewood sofas had been soft and inviting and one of them, the largest, had stood in the place of honor in this same alcove where she now sat. It had been Scarlett's favorite seat at parties. From this point stretched the pleasant vista of drawing room and dining room beyond, the oval mahogany table which seated twenty and the twenty slim-legged chairs demurely against the walls, the massive sideboard and buffet weighted with heavy silver, with seven-branched candlesticks, goblets, cruets, decanters and shining little glasses, Scarlett had sat on that sofa so often in the first years of the war, always with some handsome officer beside her, and listened to violin and bull fiddle, accordion and banjo, and heard the exciting swishing noises which dancing feet made on the waxed and polished floor.

Now the chandelier hung dark. It was twisted askew and most of the prisms were broken, as if the Yankee occupants had made their beauty a target for their boots. Now an oil lamp and a few candles lighted the room and the roaring fire in the wide hearth gave most of the illumination. Its flickering light showed how irreparably scarred and splintered the dull old floor was. Squares on the faded paper on the wall gave evidence that once the portraits had hung there, and wide cracks in the plaster recalled the day during the siege when a shell had exploded on the house and torn off parts of the roof and second floor. The heavy old mahogany table, spread with cake and decanters, still presided in the empty-looking dining room but it was scratched and the broken legs showed signs of clumsy repair. The sideboard, the silver and the spindly chairs were gone. The dull-gold damask draperies which had covered the arching French windows at the back of the room were missing, and only the remnants of the lace curtains remained, clean but obviously mended.

In place of the curved sofa she had liked so much was a hard bench that was none too comfortable. She sat upon it with as good grace as possible, wishing her skirts were in such condition that she could dance. It would be so good to dance again. But, of course, she could do more with Frank in this sequestered alcove than in a breathless reel and she could listen fascinated to his talk and encourage him to greater flights of foolishness.

But the music certainly was inviting. Her slipper patted longingly in time with old Levi's large splayed foot as he twanged a strident banjo and called the figures of the reel. Feet swished and scraped and patted as the twin lines danced toward each other, retreated, whirled and made arches of their arms.

> "'Ole Dan Tucker he got drunk — '
>   (Swing yo' padners!)
> 'Fell in de fiah an' he kick up a chunk!'
>   (Skip light, light ladies!)"

After the dull and exhausting months at Tara it was good to hear music again and the sound of dancing feet, good to see familiar friendly faces laughing in the feeble light, calling old jokes and catchwords, bantering, rallying, coquetting. It was like coming to life again after being dead. It almost seemed that the bright days of five years ago had come back again. If she could close her eyes and not see the worn made-over dresses and the patched boots and mended slippers, if her mind did not call up the faces of boys missing from the reel, she might almost think that nothing had changed. But as she looked, watching the old men grouped about the decanter in the dining room, the matrons lining the walls, talking behind fanless hands, and the swaying, skipping young dancers, it came to her suddenly, coldly, frighteningly that it was all as greatly changed as if these familiar figures were ghosts.

They looked the same but they were different. What was it? Was it only that they were five years older? No, it was something more than the passing of time. Something had gone out of them, out of their world. Five years ago, a feeling of security had wrapped them all around so gently they were not even aware of it. In its shelter they had flowered. Now it was gone and with it had gone the old thrill, the old sense of something delightful and exciting just around the corner, the old glamor of their way of living.

She knew she had changed too, but not as they had changed, and it puzzled her. She sat and watched them and she felt herself an alien among them, as alien and lonely as if she had come from another world, speaking a language they did not understand and she not understanding theirs. Then she knew that this feeling was the same one she felt with Ashley. With him and with people of his kind—and they made up most of her world—she felt outside of something she could not understand.

Their faces were little changed and their manners not at all but it seemed to her that these two things were all that remained of her old friends. An ageless dignity, a timeless gallantry still clung about them and would cling until they died but they would carry undying bitterness to their graves, a bitterness too deep for words. They were a soft-spoken fierce, tired people who were defeated and would not know defeat, broken yet standing determinedly erect. They were crushed and helpless, citizens of conquered provinces. They were looking on the state they loved, seeing it trampled by the enemy, rascals making a mock of the law, their former slaves a menace, their men disfranchised, their women insulted. And they were remembering graves.

Everything in their old world had changed but the old forms. The old usages went on, must go on, for the forms were all that were left to them. They were holding tightly to the things they knew best and loved best in the old days, the leisured manners, the courtesy, the pleasant casualness in human contacts and, most of all, the protecting attitude of the men toward their women. True to the tradition in which they had been reared, the men were courteous and tender and they almost succeeded in creating an atmosphere of sheltering their women from all that was harsh and unfit for feminine eyes. That, thought Scarlett, was the height of absurdity, for there was little, now, which even the most cloistered women had not seen and known in the last five years. They had nursed the wounded, closed dying eyes, suffered war and fire and devastation, known terror and flight and starvation.

But, no matter what sights they had seen, what menial tasks they had done and would have to do, they remained ladies and gentlemen, royalty in exile—bitter, aloof, incurious, kind to one another, diamond hard, as bright and brittle as the crystals of the broken chandelier over their heads. The old days had gone but these people would go their ways as if the old days still existed, charming, leisurely, determined not to rush and scramble for pennies as the Yankees did, determined to part with none of the old ways.

Scarlett knew that she, too, was greatly changed. Otherwise she could not have done the things she had done since she was last in Atlanta; otherwise she would not now be contemplating doing what she desperately hoped to do. But there was a difference in their hardness and hers and just what the difference was, she could not, for the moment, tell. Perhaps it was that there was nothing she would not do, and there were so many things these people would rather die than do. Perhaps it was that they were without hope but still smiling at life, bowing gracefully and passing it by. And this Scarlett could not do.

She could not ignore life. She had to live it and it was too brutal, too hostile, for her even to try to gloss over its harshness with a smile. Of the sweetness and courage and unyielding pride of her friends, Scarlett saw nothing. She saw only a silly stiff-neckedness which observed facts but smiled and refused to look them in the face.

As she stared at the dancers, flushed from the reel, she wondered if things drove them as she was driven, dead lovers, maimed husbands, children who were hungry, acres slipping away, beloved roofs that sheltered strangers. But, of course, they were driven! She knew their circumstances only a little less thoroughly than she knew her own. Their losses had been her losses, their privations her privations, their problems her same problems. Yet they had reacted differently to them. The faces she was seeing in the room were not faces; they were masks, excellent masks which would never drop.

But if they were suffering as acutely from brutal circumstances as she was—and they were—how could they maintain this air of gaiety and lightness of heart? Why, indeed, should they even try to do it? They were beyond her comprehension and vaguely irritating. She couldn't be like them. She couldn't survey the wreck of the world with an air of casual unconcern. She was as hunted as a fox, running with a bursting heart, trying to reach a burrow before the hounds caught up.

Suddenly she hated them all because they were different from her, because they carried their losses with an air that she could never attain, would never wish to attain. She hated them, these smiling, light-footed strangers, these proud fools who took pride in something they had lost, seeming to be proud that they had lost it. The women bore themselves like ladies and she knew they were ladies, though menial tasks were their daily lot and they didn't know where their next dress was coming from. Ladies all! But she could not feel herself a lady, for all her velvet dress and scented hair, for all the pride of birth that stood behind her and the pride of wealth that had once been hers. Harsh contact with the red earth of Tara had stripped gentility from her and she knew she would never feel like a lady again until her table was weighted with silver and crystal and smoking with rich food, until her own horses and carriages stood in her stables, until black hands and not white took the cotton from Tara.

Hard Times

Between 1915 and 1940, the grandchildren of Confederates and freedmen found themselves in a South replete with new opportunities to pursue and difficulties to endure. Military service during World War I provided many young Southerners, both black and white, with an expanded vision of the world. Whether out of desire or necessity, many ex-servicemen joined the others who abandoned the countryside. The fortunate ones found stable jobs in one of the growing industries; the majority endured hard times in a different setting.

Many black Southerners, denied the opportunities and wages available to white workers, used Southern cities as way stations on their trek north — a journey that came to be called the "Great Migration." Restricted politically by lynching, Jim Crow laws, and a resurgent Ku Klux Klan, blacks who remained in the South turned to their own institutions, most notably the church, to combat an unpredictable world.

In the eyes of many Americans, the South became synonymous with backwardness and bigotry. Controversy over biblical interpretation captured the attention of the South and of the rest of the nation in 1925 when the state of Tennessee prosecuted John Scopes for teaching evolution. While some Southerners gloried in their distance from what they saw as the corruption of the modern urban world, others despaired at the image and reality of the South. Young people became bored with the conventions and fixations of their elders, grew tired of hearing of the days before The War. They dreamed instead of the same fast cars, jazz music, and movie stars as did their counterparts in the rest of the country.

In the 1930s the Great Depression shook the already fragile economic and social landscape of the South. Farm tenants of both races became destitute and homeless; President Roosevelt labeled the region the nation's number one economic problem. Poverty cut across class lines, threatening the tenuous middle class as well as those at the bottom of the social order. Unable to cope with the problems locally as their relief rolls grew with each passing year, states looked to the federal government for help. New Deal projects such as the Tennessee Valley Authority provided many Southerners with jobs and training and set a precedent for federal intervention in state affairs.

Even as Southerners suffered in the 1930s, the nation discovered vibrant music and literature in the region. Blues performers regaled their listeners with stories of disappointment and heartache, all the while reassuring their audience that resilience and creativity were the keys to survival. Southern writers, black and white, gained national fame. Critics began to speak of a Southern Renaissance, of a completely unexpected outpouring of brilliant fiction and nonfiction.

The writing in this section tends to be direct and hard-hitting. Exposés as well as defenses of the South flourished in the 1920s and 1930s as writers struggled with one disturbing scene after another. Violence, anger, and disappointment pushed to the surface, along with romantic dreams of earlier days. Despite the widespread deprivation and suffering of the South during the Great Depression, more than a few writers later wrote of those years with tenderness, recalling them as hard times that pulled people together in ways no one would have predicted.

from *I'll Take My Stand*

Twelve Southerners

In 1930, a group of like-minded Vanderbilt University colleagues and students led by English professors John Crowe Ransom and Donald Davidson published *I'll Take My Stand: The South and the Agrarian Tradition*. Referred to as the Agrarians, they were disturbed by what they perceived to be Southerners' willingness to trade their agrarian way of life for the promise of a new industrial South. At the center of the intellectual debates of the 1930s concerning the South's cultural identity, they defended a Southern culture that they believed to be the nation's last bastion of civilized society. Members of the group included future novelist and poet Robert Penn Warren, historian Frank Owsley, and psychologist Lyle Lanier.

The authors contributing to this book are Southerners, well acquainted with one another and of similar tastes, though not necessarily living in the same physical community, and perhaps only at this moment aware of themselves as a single group of men. By conversation and exchange of letters over a number of years it had developed that they entertained many convictions in common, and it was decided to make a volume in which each one should furnish his views upon a chosen topic. This was the general background. But background and consultation as to the various topics were enough; there was to be no further collaboration. And so no single author is responsible for any view outside his own article. It was through the good fortune of some deeper agreement that the book was expected to achieve its unity. All the articles bear in the same sense upon the book's title-subject: all tend to support a Southern way of life against what may be called the American or prevailing way; and all as much as agree that the best terms in which to represent the distinction are contained in the phrase, Agrarian *versus* Industrial.

But after the book was under way it seemed a pity if the contributors, limited as they were within their special subjects, should stop short of showing how close their agreements really were. On the contrary, it seemed that they ought to go on and make themselves known as a group already consolidated by a set of principles which could be stated with a good deal of particularity. This might prove useful for the sake of future reference, if they should undertake any further joint publication. It was then decided to prepare a general introduction for the book which would state briefly the common convictions of the group. This is the statement. To it every one of the contributors in this book has subscribed.

Nobody now proposes for the South, or for any other community in this country, an independent political destiny. That idea is thought to have been finished in 1865. But how far shall the South surrender its moral, social, and economic autonomy to the victorious principle of Union? That question remains open. The South is a minority section that has hitherto been jealous of its minority right to live its own kind of life. The South scarcely hopes to determine the other sections, but it does propose to determine itself, within the utmost limits of legal action. Of late, however, there is the melancholy fact that the South itself has wavered a little and shown signs of wanting to join up behind the common or American industrial ideal. It is against that tendency that this book is written. The younger Southerners, who are being converted frequently to the industrial gospel, must come back to the support of the Southern tradition. They must be persuaded to look very critically at the advantages of becoming a "new South" which will be only an undistinguished replica of the usual industrial community.

But there are many other minority communities opposed to industrialism, and wanting a much simpler economy to live by. The communities and private persons sharing the agrarian tastes are to be found widely within the Union. Proper living is a matter of the intelligence and the will, does not depend on the local climate or geography, and is capable of a definition which is general and not Southern at all. Southerners have a filial duty to discharge to their own section. But their cause is precarious and they must seek alliances with sympathetic communities everywhere. The members of the present group would be happy to be counted as members of a national agrarian movement.

Industrialism is the economic organization of the collective American society. It means the decision of society to invest its economic resources in the applied sciences. But the word science has acquired a certain sanctitude. It is out of order to quarrel with science in the abstract, or even with the applied sciences when their applications are made subject to criticism and intelligence. The capitalization of the applied sciences has now become extravagant and uncritical; it has enslaved our human energies to a degree now clearly felt to be burdensome. The apologists of industrialism do not like to meet this charge directly; so they often take refuge in saying that they are devoted simply to science! They are really devoted to the applied sciences and to practical production. Therefore it is necessary to employ a certain skepticism even at the expense of the Cult of Science, and to say, It is an Americanism, which looks innocent and disinterested, but really is not either.

The contribution that science can make to a labor is to render it easier by the help of a tool or a process, and to assure the laborer of his perfect economic security while he is engaged upon it. Then it can be performed with leisure and enjoyment. But the modern laborer has not exactly received this benefit under the industrial regime. His labor is hard, its tempo is fierce, and his employment is insecure. The first principle of a good labor is that it must be effective, but the second principle is that it must be enjoyed. Labor is one of the largest items in the human career; it is a modest demand to ask that it may partake of happiness.

The regular act of applied science is to introduce into labor a labor-saving device or a machine. Whether this is a benefit depends on how far it is advisable to save the labor. The philosophy of applied science is generally quite sure that the saving of labor is a pure gain, and that the more of it the better. This is to assume that labor is an evil, that only the end of labor or the material product is good. On this assumption labor becomes mercenary and servile, and it is no wonder if many forms of modern labor are accepted without resentment though they are evidently brutalizing. The act of labor as one of the happy functions of human life has been in effect abandoned, and is practiced solely for its rewards.

Even the apologists of industrialism have been obliged to admit that some economic evils follow in the wake of the machines. These are such as overproduction, unemployment, and a growing inequality in the distribution of wealth. But the remedies proposed by the apologists are always homeopathic. They expect the evils to disappear when we have bigger and better machines, and more of them. Their remedial programs, therefore, look forward to more industrialism. Sometimes they see the system righting itself spontaneously and without direction: they are Optimists. Sometimes they rely on the benevolence of capital, or the militancy of labor, to bring about a fairer division of the spoils: they are Coöperationists or Socialists. And sometimes they expect to find super-engineers, in the shape of Boards of Control, who will adapt production to consumption and regulate prices and guarantee business against fluctuations: they are Sovietists. With respect to these last it must be insisted that the true Sovietists or Communists—if the term may be used here in the European sense—are the Industrialists themselves. They would have the government set up an economic super-organization, which in turn would become the government. We therefore look upon the Communist menace as a menace indeed, but not as a Red one; because it is simply according to the blind drift of our industrial development to expect in America at last much the same economic system as that imposed by violence upon Russia in 1917.

Turning to consumption, as the grand end which justifies the evil of modern labor, we find that we have been deceived. We have more time in which to consume, and many more products to be consumed. But the tempo of our labors communicates itself to our satisfactions, and these also become brutal and hurried. The constitution of the natural man probably does not permit him to shorten his labor-time and enlarge his consuming-time indefinitely. He has to pay the penalty in satiety and aimlessness. The modern man has lost his sense of vocation.

Religion can hardly expect to flourish in an industrial society. Religion is our submission to the general intention of a nature that is fairly inscrutable; it is the sense of our rôle as creatures within it. But nature industrialized, transformed into cities and artificial habitations, manufactured into commodities, is no longer nature but a highly simplified picture of nature. We receive the illusion of having power over nature, and lose the sense of nature as something mysterious and contingent. The God of nature under these conditions is merely an amiable expression, a superfluity, and the philosophical understanding ordinarily carried in the religious experience is not there for us to have.

Nor do the arts have a proper life under industrialism, with the general decay of sensibility which attends it. Art depends, in general, like religion, on a right attitude to nature; and in particular on a free and disinterested observation of nature that occurs only in leisure. Neither the creation nor the understanding of works of art is possible in an industrial age except by some local and unlikely suspension of the industrial drive.

The amenities of life also suffer under the curse of a strictly-business or industrial civilization. They consist in such practices as manners, conversation, hospitality, sympathy, family life, romantic love—in the social exchanges which reveal and develop sensibility in human affairs. If religion and the arts are founded on right relations of man-to-nature, these are founded on right relations of man-to-man.

Apologists of industrialism are even inclined to admit that its actual processes may have upon its victims the spiritual effects just described. But they think that all can be made right by extraordinary educational efforts, by all sorts of cultural institutions and endowments. They would cure the poverty of the contemporary spirit by hiring experts to instruct it in spite of itself in the historic culture. But salvation is hardly to be encountered on that road. The trouble with the life-pattern is to be located at its economic base, and we cannot rebuild it by pouring in soft materials from the top. The young men and women in colleges, for example, if they are already placed in a false way of life, cannot make more than an inconsequential acquaintance with the arts and humanities transmitted to them.

Or else the understanding of these arts and humanities will but make them the more wretched in their own destitution.

The "Humanists" are too abstract. Humanism, properly speaking, is not an abstract system, but a culture, the whole way in which we live, act, think, and feel. It is a kind of imaginatively balanced life lived out in a definite social tradition. And, in the concrete, we believe that this, the genuine humanism, was rooted in the agrarian life of the older South and of other parts of the country that shared in such a tradition. It was not an abstract moral "check" derived from the classics—it was not soft material poured in from the top. It was deeply founded in the way of life itself—in its tables, chairs, portraits, festivals, laws, marriage customs. We cannot recover our native humanism by adopting some standard of taste that is critical enough to question the contemporary arts but not critical enough to question the social and economic life which is their ground.

The tempo of the industrial life is fast, but that is not the worst of it; it is accelerating. The ideal is not merely some set form of industrialism, with so many stable industries, but industrial progress, or an incessant extension of industrialization. It never proposes a specific goal; it initiates the infinite series. We have not merely capitalized certain industries; we have capitalized the laboratories and inventors, and undertaken to employ all the labor-saving devices that come out of them. But a fresh labor-saving device introduced into an industry does not emancipate the laborers in that industry so much as it evicts them. Applied at the expense of agriculture, for example, the new processes have reduced the part of the population supporting itself upon the soil to a smaller and smaller fraction. Of course no single labor-saving process is fatal; it brings on a period of unemployed labor and unemployed capital, but soon a new industry is devised which will put them both to work again, and a new commodity is thrown upon the market. The laborers were sufficiently embarrassed in the meantime, but, according to the theory, they will eventually be taken care of, It is now the public which is embarrassed; it feels obligated to purchase a commodity for which it had expressed no desire, but it is invited to make its budget equal to the strain. All might yet be well, and stability and comfort might again obtain, but for this: partly because of industrial ambitions and partly because the repressed creative impulse must break out somewhere, there will be a stream of further labor-saving devices in all industries, and the cycle will have to be repeated over and over. The result is an increasing disadjustment and instability.

It is an inevitable consequence of industrial progress that production greatly outruns the rate of natural consumption. To overcome the disparity, the producers, disguised as the pure idealists of progress, must coerce and wheedle the public into being loyal and steady consumers, in order to keep the machines running. So the rise of modern advertising—along with its twin, personal salesmanship—is the most significant development of our industrialism. Advertising means to persuade the consumers to want exactly what the applied sciences are able to furnish them. It consults the happiness of the consumer no more than it consulted the happiness of the laborer. It is the great effort of a false economy of life to approve itself. But its task grows more difficult every day.

It is strange, of course, that a majority of men anywhere could ever as with one mind become enamored of industrialism: a system that has so little regard for individual wants. There is evidently a kind of thinking that rejoices in setting up a social objective which has no relation to the individual. Men are prepared to sacrifice their private dignity and happiness to an abstract social ideal, and without asking whether the social ideal produces the welfare of any individual man whatsoever. But this is absurd. The responsibility of men is for their own welfare and that of their neighbors; not for the hypothetical welfare of some fabulous creature called society.

Opposed to the industrial society is the agrarian, which does not stand in particular need of definition. An agrarian society is hardly one that has no use at all for industries, for professional vocations, for scholars and artists, and for the life of cities. Technically, perhaps, an agrarian society is one in which agriculture is the leading vocation, whether for wealth, for pleasure, or for prestige—a form of labor that is pursued with intelligence and leisure, and that becomes the model to which the other forms approach as well as they may. But an agrarian regime will be secured readily enough where the superfluous industries are not allowed to rise against it. The theory of agrarianism is that the culture of the soil is the best and most sensitive of vocations, and that therefore it should have the economic preference and enlist the maximum number of workers.

These principles do not intend to be very specific in proposing any practical measures. How may the little agrarian community resist the Chamber of Commerce of its county seat, which is always trying to import some foreign industry that cannot be assimilated to the life-pattern of the community? Just what must the Southern leaders do to defend the traditional Southern life? How may the Southern and the Western agrarians unite for effective action? Should the agrarian forces try to capture the Democratic party, which historically is so closely affiliated with the defense of individualism, the small community, the state, the South? Or must the agrarians—even the Southern ones—abandon the Democratic party to its fate and try a new one? What legislation could most profitably be championed by the powerful agrarians in the Senate of the United

States? What anti-industrial measures might promise to stop the advances of industrialism, or even undo some of them, with the least harm to those concerned? What policy should be pursued by the educators who have a tradition at heart? These and many other questions are of the greatest importance, but they cannot be answered here.

For, in conclusion, this much is clear: If a community, or a section, or a race, or an age, is groaning under industrialism, and well aware that it is an evil dispensation, it must find the way to throw it off. To think that this cannot be done is pusillanimous. And if the whole community, section, race, or age thinks it cannot be done, then it has simply lost its political genius and doomed itself to impotence.

from "Boom Town"

Thomas Wolfe (1900–1938)

Thomas Wolfe, born to a stone cutter and boardinghouse owner in Asheville, North Carolina, in 1900, was the first in his family to obtain a college degree. Determined to become a professional writer, he first concentrated on playwrighting but later found his home in novels and short stories. Although he maintained a cosmopolitan lifestyle—residing in New York and traveling in Europe—his native Asheville dominated his imagination. In his story "Boom Town" (1934), Wolfe's protagonist, John, returns to his hometown and discovers a growing city in the place of the country village where he grew up. Wolfe died following brain surgery in 1938 at the age of thirty-seven.

At one corner of the burial lot a tall locust tree was growing: its pleasant shade was divided between the family lot and the adjacent one where members of the mother's family, the Pentlands, had been buried. The gravestones in the family lot (which was set on a gentle slope) were arranged in two parallel rows. In the first row were buried John's brothers, Arthur McFarlane Hawke and Edward Madison Hawke, who were twins: also his mother's first child, Margaret Ann.

Facing these was the family monument. It was a square massive chunk of gray metallic granite, brilliantly burnished, one of the finest and most imposing monuments in the cemetery. It bore the family name in raised letters upon its shining surface, and on each end were inscriptions for his father and his mother. His father was buried at the end of the monument which faced the town. His inscription read: "William Oliver Hawke — born near Gettysburg, Pennsylvania, April 16, 1851 — Died, Altamont, Old Catawba, June 21, 1922." The mother's inscription was at the other end of the monument, facing her own people, and read: "Delia Elizabeth Hawke—née Pentland—Born at the Forks of Ivy, Old Catawba, February 16, 1860—Died—"

All of the monuments, save his father's and mother's, had, in addition to the name and birth and death inscription, a little elegiac poem, carved in a fine italicized script, and reading somewhat as follows:

Still is the voice we knew so well
Vanished the face we love

Flown his spirit pure to dwell
With Angels up above.
Ours is the sorrow, ours the pain
And ours the joy alone
To clasp him in our arms again
In Heaven by God's throne.

In the drowsy waning light of the late afternoon, John could see people moving across the great hill of the dead, among the graves and monuments of other burial lots. The place had the brooding hush a cemetery has on a summer day, and in the fading light even the figures of the people had a dream-like and almost phantasmal quality as they moved about.

The mother stood surveying the scene reflectively, her hands held at the waist in their loose strong clasp. She looked at the gravestones in the family lot, reading the little elegiac verses, and although she had read these banal phrases a thousand times, she did so again with immense satisfaction, framing the words with her lips and then nodding her head slowly and deliberately in a movement of emphatic affirmation, as if to say: "Ah-hah! That's it exactly!"

For a moment longer, she stood looking at the stones. Then she went over to Ed's grave, picked up a wreath of laurel leaves which someone had left there a few weeks before, and which had already grown withered and faded looking, and set it at the head of the grave against the base of the stone. Then she moved about among the graves, bending with a blunt, strong movement and weeding out tufts of the coarse grass which had grown weedily about the bases of some of the monuments.

When she had finished, she stood looking down at Margaret's stone, which was weathered, stained, and rusty looking. She read the inscription of the old faded letters, and then turning to her younger son, spoke quietly:

"This morning at eight o'clock, thirty-nine years ago, I lost the first child that I ever had. Your sister Margaret died today—July the fourteenth —four days less than nine months old. She was the most perfect baby I ever saw—the brightest and most sensible child for her age." And again she nodded her head slowly and deliberately, in a movement of powerful affirmation.

"Time went on, I had other children, kept my hands full, and to a certain degree," she said reflectively, "kept my mind off sorrow. No time for sorrow!" cried the mother, with the strong convulsive tremor of the head. "Too much to do for sorrow! ... Then, when years had passed, the hardest blow of all fell. Arthur was taken. It seemed I had given up all. Could have borne as well if all the others had been taken! I can't understand why!" And for a moment her brown worn eyes were wet. "But it had grown a part of me—felt somehow that he was to lead the others, and when I realized that he was gone, it seemed that everything was lost.

"I never got to know Ed," she said quietly. "I always wanted to talk to him, but could not. I felt a part of him was gone—maybe he felt so, too. It was hard to give Ed up, but I had suffered the first great loss in giving up his twin, the other part."

She paused, looking down at the two tombstones for a moment, and then said gravely and proudly: "I believe that they have joined each other, and if they are happy, I'll be reconciled. I believe I'll meet them in a Higher Sphere, along with all the members of our family—all happy and all leading a new life."

She was silent for another moment, and then, with a movement of strong decision, she turned away and looked out toward the town where already the evening lights were going on, were burning hard and bright and steady in the dusk.

"Come now, my sonny boys!" she cried briskly and cheerfully. "It's getting dark, and there are people waiting for us."

"Son," she said, laying her broad hand on John's shoulder in a warm, strong, and easy gesture, and speaking in the old half-bantering manner that she had used so often when he was a child, "I've been a long time livin' on this earth, and as the fellow says, the world do move. You've got your life ahead of you, and lots to learn and many things to do, but let me tell you something, boy!" And for a moment she looked at him in a sudden, straight, and deadly fashion, with a faint smile around the edges of her mouth. "Go out and see the world, and get your fill of wanderin', and then," she cried, "come back and tell me if you've found a better place than home! I've seen great changes in my time, and I'll see many more before I die, and there are great things yet in store for us—great progress, great inventions, it will all come true. Perhaps I'll not live to see it, but you *will*! We've got a fine town here, and we've got fine people here to make it go, and we're not done yet. I've seen it all grow up out of a country village—and some day we will have a great city here."

. . .

A great city? These words, he knew, had come straight from his mother's heart, from all the invincible faith of her brave spirit which had endured the anguish, grief, and suffering of a hundred lives and which would never change. That unshaken spirit would, he knew, face toward the future to the last hour of her life with this same unyielding confidence, and would be triumphant over all the ruinous error and mischance of life. And for her, he knew, this "great city" that she spoke of now was the city of her heart, her faith, her spirit—the city of the everlasting future, and her quenchless hope, the fortunate, good, and happy life that some day she was sure would be found here on the earth for all men living.

But that other city, this glittering and explosive shape of man's destructive fury which now stood sharply in their vision in the evening light— what did the future hold for that place and its people? In this strange and savage hunger for what she had spoken of as a better life, a greater city, in this delirium of intoxication which drove them on, there was really a fatal and desperate quality, as if what they hungered for was ruin and death. It seemed to him that they were ruined: it seemed that even when they laughed and shouted and smote one another on the back, the knowledge of their ruin was in them—and they did not care, they were drunk and mad and amorous of death.

But under all their flash and play of life, the paucity of their designs— the starved meagerness of their lives—was already apparent to them. The better life resolved itself into a few sterile and baffled gestures—they built an ugly and expensive house and bought a car and joined a country club; they built a larger, uglier, and more expensive house, bought a more expensive car, and joined a larger and more expensive country club—they pursued this routine through all the repetitions of an idiot monotony, building new houses, new streets, new country clubs with a frenzied haste, a wild extravagance, but nowhere was there food to feed their hunger, drink to assuage their thirst. They were stricken and lost, starved squirrels chasing furiously the treadmill of a revolving cage, and they saw it, and they knew it.

A wave of ruinous and destructive energy had welled up in them— they had squandered fabulous sums in meaningless streets and bridges, they had torn down the ancient public buildings, court house, and city hall, and erected new ones, fifteen stories tall and large enough to fill the needs of a city of a million people; they had leveled hills and bored through mountains, building magnificent tunnels paved with double roadways and glittering with shining tiles—tunnels which leaped out on the other side into Arcadian wilderness. It was mad, infuriate, ruinous; they had flung away the earnings of a lifetime and mortgaged those of a generation to come; they had ruined themselves, their children, and their city, and nothing could be done to stop them.

Already the town had passed from their possession, they no longer owned it, it was mortgaged under a debt of fifty million dollars, owned by bonding companies in the North. The very streets they walked on had been sold beneath their feet—and still they bought, bought, bought, signing their names to papers calling for the payment of a king's ransom for forty feet of earth, reselling the next day to other mad men who signed away their lives with the same careless magnificence. On paper, their profits were fabulous, but their "boom" was already over, and they could not see it. They were staggering below obligations to pay that none of them could meet—and still they bought.

And then, when it seemed that they had exhausted all the possibilities of ruin and extravagance in town, they had rushed out into the wilderness, into the calm eternity of the hills, into the lyrical immensities of wild earth where there was land enough for all men living, where any man could take as much earth as he needed, and they had madly staked off little plots and wedges of the wilderness, as one might try to stake a picket fence out in the middle of the ocean. They had given fancy names to all their plots and stakings—"Wild Boulders"—"Shady Acres"—"Eagle's Crest." They set prices to an acre of the wilderness that might have bought a mountain, and made charts and drawings, showing populous and glittering communities of shops, houses, streets, roads, and clubs in regions where there was no road, no street, no house, and which could not be reached in any way save by a group of resolute and desperate pioneers armed with axes, or by airplane.

These places were to be transformed into idyllic colonies for artists and critics and writers—all the artists and critics and writers in the nation—and there were colonies as well for preachers, doctors, actors, dancers, golfplayers, and retired locomotive engineers. There were colonies for everyone, and what is more, they sold them!

It was the month of July 1929—that fatal year which brought ruin to millions of people all over the country. They were now drunk with an imagined victory, pressing and shouting in the dusty tumult of the battle, most beaten where they thought their triumph the greatest, so that the desolate and barren panorama of their ruin would not be clearly known to them for several years to come.

. . .

And now, as John stood there looking at this new strange town, this incredible explosion of a town which had gone mad and frenzied over night, he suddenly remembered the barren night-time streets of the town he had known so well in his childhood. The gaunt pattern of their dreary and unpeopled desolation had burned its acid print upon his memory. Bare, wintry, and deserted—by ten o'clock at night those streets had been an aching monotony and weariness of hard light and empty pavements, a frozen torpor broken only occasionally by the footfalls of some prowler of the night, by desperate famished lonely men who hoped past hope and past belief for some haven of comfort, warmth, and love there in the wilderness, for the sudden opening of a magic door into some secret, rich, and more exultant life. They never found it. They were dying in the darkness, and they knew it—without a goal, a wall, a certain purpose, or a door.

For that was the way the thing had come. That was the way the thing had happened. Yes, it was there—on many a night long past and wearily accomplished in ten thousand little towns and in ten million barren streets where all the passion, hope, and hunger of the famished men beat like a great pulse through the fields of night—it was there and nowhere else that all this madness had been brewed.

And yet, what really had changed in life? Below their feet, the earth was still and everlasting as it had always been. And around them in the cemetery the air brooded with a lazy drowsy warmth. There was the cry of the sweetsinging birds again, the sudden thrumming of bullet noises in undergrowth and leaf, and the sharp cricketing stitch of afternoon, the broken lazy sounds from far away, a voice in the wind, a boy's shout, a cry, the sound of a bell, as well as all the drowsy fragrance of a thousand warm intoxicating odors—the resinous smell of pine, and the smells of grass and warm sweet clover. It was all as it had always been, but the town where he had spent his childhood and which lay stretched out before him in the evening light had changed past recognition: the town, with its quiet streets and the old frame houses, which were almost obscured beneath the massed leafy spread of trees, was now scarred with hard raw patches of concrete on which the sun fell wearily, or with raw clumps and growths of new construction — skyscrapers, garages, hotels, glittering residential atrocities of stucco and raw brick—or it was scored and scarred harshly by new streets and roads.

The place looked like a battle field; it was cratered and shelltorn with savage explosions of brick and concrete all over town. And in the inter-spaces the embowered remnants of the old and pleasant town remained, timid, retreating, overwhelmed, to remind one, in all this harsh new din, of foot-falls in a quiet street as men went home at noon, of laughter and quiet voices and the leafy rustle of the night. For this was lost!

This image of his loss, and theirs, had passed through his mind with the speed of light, the instancy of thought, and now he heard his mother's voice again:

"And you'll come back!" he heard her saying. "There's no better or more beautiful place on earth than in these mountains, boy—and some day you'll come back again," she cried with all the invincible faith and hopefulness of her strong heart.

An old and tragic light was shining like the light of dreams on the rocky little river which he had seen somewhere, somehow, from the windows of a train long, long ago, in his childhood, somewhere before memory began, and which wound its deathless magic in his heart forever. And that old and tragic light of fading day shone faintly on their faces, and suddenly they were fixed there like a prophecy with the hills and river all around them—and there was something lost, intolerable, foretold, and come to pass, and like old time and destiny—some magic that he could not say.

Down by the river's edge in darkness he heard the bell, the whistle, and the pounding wheel. It brought to him, as it had done ten thousand times in childhood, its great promise of morning, new lands, and a shining city.

And now, receding, far and faint, he heard again the whistle of the great train pounding on the rails across the river. It swept away from them, leaving the lost and lonely thunder of its echoes in the hills, the flame-flare of its terrific furnace for a moment, and then just heavy wheels and rumbling loaded cars — and, finally, nothing but the silence it had left behind it.

Now, even farther off and almost lost, he heard for the last time its wailing and receding cry, bringing to him again all its wild and secret prophecy, its pain of going, and its triumphant promise of new lands. He saw them fixed forever in his vision, and the lonely light was shining on their faces, and he felt an intolerable pain, an unutterable joy and triumph, as he knew that he would leave them. And something in his heart was saying like a demon's whisper of unbodied joy that spoke of flight and darkness, new earth he could touch and make his own again: Soon! Soon! Soon!

Then they all got into the car again and drove rapidly away from the green hill of the dead, the woman toward the certitude of lights, the people, and the town; the young man toward the train, the city, and the voyages—all of the gold-bright waters of the morning, the seas, the harbors, and the magic of the ships.

"Kneel to the Rising Sun"

Erskine Caldwell (1903–1987)

Erskine Caldwell spent his boyhood in various towns and hamlets across the Southeast. His father's position with the Associate Reformed Presbyterian Church required the family to move frequently, exposing young Caldwell to a broad range of Southerners. Never a dedicated student, he spent time at several colleges before deciding, in 1925, to pursue a career in journalism. After one year at the *Atlanta Journal,* Caldwell abandoned newspaper work to concentrate on his own writing. Describing a lynching in the rural South in "Kneel to the Rising Sun" (1935), he reminds us of the difficult choice many Southerners faced between what was right and what they thought necessary for survival. Perhaps the best-known Southern writer, his sixty books have been translated into forty languages and have sold more than 80 million copies.

A shiver went through Lonnie. He drew his hand away from his sharp chin, remembering what Clem had said. It made him feel now as if he were committing a crime by standing in Arch Gunnard's presence and allowing his face to be seen.

He and Clem had been walking up the road together that afternoon on their way to the filling station when he told Clem how much he needed rations. Clem stopped a moment to kick a rock out of the road, and said that if you worked for Arch Gunnard long enough, your face would be sharp enough to split the boards for your own coffin.

As Lonnie turned away to sit down on an empty box beside the gasoline pump, he could not help wishing that he could be as unafraid of Arch Gunnard as Clem was. Even if Clem was a Negro, he never hesitated to ask for rations when he needed something to eat; and when he and his family did not get enough, Clem came right out and told Arch so. Arch stood for that, but he swore that he was going to run Clem out of the country the first chance he got.

Lonnie knew without turning around that Clem was standing at the corner of the filling station with two or three other Negroes and looking at him, but for some reason he was unable to meet Clem's eyes.

Arch Gunnard was sitting in the sun, honing his jackknife blade on his boot top. He glanced once or twice at Lonnie's hound, Nancy, who was lying in the middle of the road waiting for Lonnie to go home.

277

"That your dog, Lonnie?"

Jumping with fear, Lonnie's hand went to his chin to hide the lean face that would accuse Arch of short-rationing.

Arch snapped his fingers and the hound stood up, wagging her tail. She waited to be called.

"Mr. Arch, I —"

Arch called the dog. She began crawling towards them on her belly, wagging her tail a little faster each time Arch's fingers snapped. When she was several feet away, she turned over on her back and lay on the ground with her four paws in the air.

Dudley Smith and Jim Weaver, who were lounging around the filling station, laughed. They had been leaning against the side of the building, but they straightened up to see what Arch was up to.

Arch spat some more tobacco juice on his boot top and whetted the jackknife blade some more.

"What kind of a hound dog is that, anyway, Lonnie?" Arch said. "Looks like to me it might be a ketch hound."

Lonnie could feel Clem Henry's eyes boring into the back of his head. He wondered what Clem would do if it had been his dog Arch Gunnard was snapping his fingers at and calling like that.

"His tail's way too long for a coon hound or a bird dog, ain't it, Arch?" somebody behind Lonnie said, laughing out loud.

Everybody laughed then, including Arch. They looked at Lonnie, waiting to hear what he was going to say to Arch.

"Is he a ketch hound, Lonnie?" Arch said, snapping his finger again.

"Mr. Arch, I —"

"Don't be ashamed of him, Lonnie, if he don't show signs of turning out to be a bird dog or a foxhound. Everybody needs a hound around the house that can go out and catch pigs and rabbits when you are in a hurry for them. A ketch hound is mighty respectable animal. I've known the time when I was mighty proud to own one."

Everybody laughed.

Arch Gunnard was getting ready to grab Nancy by the tail. Lonnie sat up, twisting his neck until he caught a glimpse of Clem Henry at the other corner of the filling station. Clem was staring at him with unmistakable meaning, with the same look in his eyes he had had that afternoon when he said that nobody who worked for Arch Gunnard ought to stand for short-rationing. Lonnie lowered his eyes. He could not figure out how a Negro could be braver than he was. There were a lot of times like that when he would have given anything he had to be able to jump into Clem's shoes and change places with him.

"The trouble with this hound of yours, Lonnie, is that he's too heavy on his feet. Don't you reckon it would be a pretty slick little trick to lighten the load some, being as how he's a ketch hound to begin with?"

Lonnie remembered then what Clem Henry had said he would do if Arch Gunnard ever tried to cut off his dog's tail. Lonnie knew, and Clem knew, and everybody else knew, that that would give Arch the chance he was waiting for. All Arch asked, he had said, was for Clem Henry to over-step his place just one little half inch, or to talk back to him with just one little short word, and he would do the rest. Everybody knew what Arch meant by that, especially if Clem did not turn and run. And Clem had not been known to run from anybody, after fifteen years in the country.

Arch reached down and grabbed Nancy's tail while Lonnie was won-dering about Clem. Nancy acted as if she thought Arch were playing some kind of a game with her. She turned her head around until she could reach Arch's hand to lick it. He cracked her on the bridge of the nose with the end of the jackknife.

"He's a mighty playful dog, Lonnie," Arch said, catching up a shorter grip on the tail, "but his wagpole is way too long for a dog his size, espe-cially when he wants to be a ketch hound."

Lonnie swallowed hard.

"Mr. Arch, she's a mighty fine rabbit tracker. I —"

"Shucks, Lonnie," Arch said, whetting the knife blade on the dog's tail, "I ain't ever seen a hound in all my life that needed a tail that long to hunt rabbits with. It's way too long for just a common, ordinary, everyday ketch hound."

Lonnie looked up hopefully at Dudley Smith and the others. None of them offered any help. It was useless for him to try to stop Arch, because Arch Gunnard would let nothing stand in his way when once he had set his head on what he wished to do. Lonnie knew that if he should let him-self show any anger or resentment, Arch would drive him off the farm before sundown that night. Clem Henry was the only person there who would help him, but Clem . . .

The white men and the Negroes at both corners of the filling station waited to see what Lonnie was going to do about it. All of them hoped he would put up a fight for his hound. If anyone ever had the nerve to stop Arch Gunnard from cutting off a dog's tail, it might put an end to it.

It was plain, though, that Lonnie, who was one of Arch's sharecroppers, was afraid to speak up. Clem Henry might; Clem was the only one who might try to stop Arch, even if it meant trouble. And all of them knew that Arch would insist on running Clem out of the country, or filling him full of lead.

"I reckon it's all right with you, ain't it, Lonnie?" Arch said. "I don't seem to hear no objections."

Clem Henry stepped forward several paces, and stopped.

Arch laughed, watching Lonnie's face, and jerked Nancy to her feet. The hound cried out in pain and surprise, but Arch made her be quiet by kicking her in the belly.

Lonnie winced. He could hardly bear to see anybody kick his dog like that.

"Mr. Arch, I . . ."

A contraction in his throat almost choked him for several moments, and he had to open his mouth wide and fight for breath. The other white men around him were silent. Nobody liked to see a dog kicked in the belly like that.

Lonnie could see the other end of the filling station from the corner of his eye. He saw a couple of Negroes go up behind Clem and grasp his overalls. Clem spat on the ground, between outspread feet, but he did not try to break away from them.

"Being as how I don't hear no objections, I reckon it's all right to go ahead and cut it off," Arch said, spitting.

Lonnie's head went forward and all he could see of Nancy was her hind feet. He had come to ask for a slab of sowbelly and some molasses, or something. Now he did not know if he could ever bring himself to ask for rations, no matter how much hungrier they became at home.

"I always make it a habit of asking a man first," Arch said. "I wouldn't want to go ahead and cut off a tail if a man had any objections. That wouldn't be right. No, sir, it just wouldn't be fair and square."

Arch caught a shorter grip on the hound's tail and placed the knife blade on it two or three inches from the rump. It looked to those who were watching as if his mouth were watering, because tobacco juice began to trickle down the corners of his lips. He brought up the back of his hand and wiped his mouth.

A noisy automobile came plowing down the road through the deep red dust. Everyone looked up as it passed in order to see who was in it.

Lonnie glanced at it, but he could not keep his eyes raised. His head fell downward once more until he could feel his sharp chin cutting into his chest. He wondered then if Arch had noticed how lean his face was.

"I keep two or three ketch hounds around my place," Arch said, honing the blade on the tail of the dog as if it were a razor strop until his actions brought smiles to the faces of the men grouped around him, "but I never could see the sense of a ketch hound having a long tail. It only gets in their way when I send them out to catch a pig or a rabbit for my supper."

Pulling with his left hand and pushing with his right, Arch Gunnard docked the hound's tail as quickly and as easily as if he were cutting a willow switch in the pasture to drive the cows home with. The dog sprang forward with the release of her tail until she was far beyond Arch's reach, and began howling so loud she could be heard half a mile away. Nancy stopped once and looked back at Arch, and then she sprang to the middle of the road and began leaping and twisting in circles. All that time she was yelping and biting at the bleeding stub of her tail.

Arch leaned backward and twirled the severed tail in one hand while he wiped the jackknife blade on his boot sole. He watched Lonnie's dog chasing herself around in circles in the red dust.

Nobody had anything to say then. Lonnie tried not to watch his dog's agony, and he forced himself to keep from looking at Clem Henry. Then, with his eyes shut, he wondered why he had remained on Arch Gunnard's plantation all those past years, sharecropping for a mere living on short rations, and becoming leaner and leaner all the time. He knew then how true it was what Clem has said about Arch's share-croppers' faces becoming sharp enough to hew their own coffins. His hands went to his chin before he knew what he was doing. His hands dropped when he had felt the bones of jaw and the exposed tendons of his cheeks.

As hungry as he was, he knew that even if Arch did give him some rations then, there would not be nearly enough for them to eat for the following week. Hatty, his wife, was already broken down from hunger and work in the fields, and his father, Mark Newsome, stone-deaf for the past twenty years, was always asking him why there was never enough food in the house for them to have a solid meal. Lonnie's head fell forward a little more, and he could feel his eyes becoming damp.

The pressure of his sharp chin against his chest made him so uncomfortable that he had to raise his head at last in order to ease the pain of it.

The first thing he saw when he looked up was Arch Gunnard twirling Nancy's tail in his left hand. Arch Gunnard had a trunk full of dogs' tails at home. He had been cutting off tails ever since anyone could remember, and during all those years he had accumulated a collection of which he was so proud that he kept the trunk locked and the key tied around his neck on a string. On Sunday afternoons when the preacher came to visit, or when a crowd was there to loll on the front porch and swap stories, Arch showed them off, naming each tail from memory just as well as if he had had a tag on it.

Clem Henry had left the filling station and was walking alone down the road towards the plantation. Clem Henry's house was in a cluster of Negro cabins below Arch's big house, and he had to pass Lonnie's house to get there. Lonnie was on the verge of getting up and leaving when he saw Arch looking at him. He did not know whether Arch was looking at his lean face, or whether he was watching to see if he were going to get up and go down the road with Clem.

The thought of leaving reminded him of his reason for being there. He had to have some rations before suppertime that night, no matter how short they were.

"Mr. Arch, I . . ."

Arch stared at him for a moment, appearing as if he had turned to listen to some strange sound unheard of before that moment.

Lonnie bit his lips, wondering if Arch was going to say anything about how lean and hungry he looked. But Arch was thinking about something else. He slapped his hand on his leg and laughed out loud.

"I sometimes wish niggers had tails," Arch said, coiling Nancy's tail into a ball and putting it into his pocket. "I'd a heap rather cut off nigger tails than dog tails. There'd be more to cut, for one thing."

Dudley Smith and somebody else behind them laughed for a brief moment. The laughter died out almost as suddenly as it had risen.

The Negroes who had heard Arch shuffled their feet in the dust and moved backwards. It was only a few minutes until not one was left at the filling station. They went up the road behind the red wooden building until they were out of sight.

Arch got up and stretched. The sun was getting low, and it was no longer comfortable in the October air. "Well, I reckon I'll be getting on home to get me some supper," he said.

He walked slowly to the middle of the road and stopped to look at Nancy retreating along the ditch.

"Nobody going my way?" he asked. "What's wrong with you, Lonnie? Going home to supper, ain't you?"

"Mr. Arch, I . . ."

Lonnie found himself jumping to his feet. His first thought was to ask for the sowbelly and molasses, and maybe some corn meal; but when he opened his mouth, the words refused to come out. He took several steps forward and shook his head. He did not know what Arch might say or do if he said "No."

"Hatty'll be looking for you," Arch said, turning his back and walking off.

He reached into his hip pocket and took out Nancy's tail. He began twirling it as he walked down the road towards the big house in the distance.

Dudley Smith went inside the filling station, and the others walked away.

After Arch had gone several hundred yards, Lonnie sat down heavily on the box beside the gas pump from which he had got up when Arch spoke to him. He sat down heavily, his shoulders dropping, his arms falling between his outspread legs.

Lonnie did not know how long his eyes had been closed, but when he opened them, he saw Nancy lying between his feet, licking the docked tail. While he watched her, he felt the sharp point of his chin cutting into his chest again. Presently the door behind him was slammed shut, and a minute later he could hear Dudley Smith walking away from the filling station on his way home.

Lonnie had been sleeping fitfully for several hours when he suddenly found himself wide awake. Hatty shook him again. He raised himself on his elbow and tried to see into the darkness of the room. Without knowing what time it was, he was able to determine that it was still nearly two hours until sunrise.

"Lonnie," Hatty said again, trembling in the cold night air, "Lonnie, your pa ain't in the house."

Lonnie sat upright in bed.

"How do you know he ain't?" he said.

"I've been lying here wide awake ever since I got in bed, and I heard him when he went out. He's been gone all that time."

"Maybe he just stepped out for a while," Lonnie said, turning and trying to see through the bedroom window.

"I know what I'm saying, Lonnie," Hatty insisted. "Your pa's been gone a heap too long."

Both of them sat without a sound for several minutes while they listened for Mark Newsome.

Lonnie got up and lit a lamp. He shivered while he was putting on his shirt, overalls, and shoes. He tied his shoelaces in hard knots because he couldn't see in the faint light. Outside the window it was almost pitch-dark, and Lonnie could feel the damp October air blowing against his face.

"I'll go help look," Hatty said, throwing the covers off and starting to get up.

Lonnie went to the bed and drew the covers back over her and pushed her back into place.

"You try to get some sleep, Hatty," he said; "you can't stay awake the whole night. I'll go bring Pa back."

He left Hatty, blowing out the lamp, and stumbled through the dark hall, feeling his way to the front porch by touching the wall with his hands. When he got to the porch, he could still barely see any distance ahead, but his eyes were becoming more accustomed to the darkness. He waited a minute, listening.

Feeling his way down the steps into the yard, he walked around the corner of the house and stopped to listen again before calling his father.

"Oh, Pa!" he said loudly. "Oh, Pa!"

He stopped under the bedroom window when he realized what he had been doing.

"Now that's a fool thing for me to be out here doing," he said, scolding himself. "Pa couldn't hear it thunder."

He heard a rustling of the bed.

"He's been gone long enough to get clear to the crossroads, or more," Hatty said, calling through the window.

"Now you lay down and try to get a little sleep, Hatty," Lonnie told her. "I'll bring him back in no time."

He could hear Nancy scratching fleas under the house, but he knew she was in no condition to help look for Mark. It would be several days before she recovered from the shock of losing her tail.

"He's been gone a long time," Hatty said, unable to keep still.

"That don't make no difference," Lonnie said. "I'll find him sooner or later. Now you go on to sleep like I told you, Hatty."

Lonnie walked towards the barn, listening for some sound. Over at the big house he could hear the hogs grunting and squealing, and he wished they would be quiet so he could hear other sounds. Arch Gunnard's dogs were howling occasionally, but they were not making any more noise than they usually did at night, and he was accustomed to their howling.

Lonnie went to the barn, looking inside and out. After walking around the barn, he went into the field as far as the cotton shed. He knew it was useless, but he could not keep from calling his father time after time.

"Oh, Pa!" he said, trying to penetrate the darkness.

He went farther into the field.

"Now, what in the world could have become of Pa?" he said, stopping and wondering where to look next.

After he had gone back to the front yard, he began to feel uneasy for the first time. Mark had not acted any more strangely during the past week than he ordinarily did, but Lonnie knew he was upset over the way Arch Gunnard was giving out short rations. Mark had even said that, at the rate they were being fed, all of them would starve to death inside another three months.

Lonnie left the yard and went down the road towards the Negro cabins. When he got to Clem's house, he turned in and walked up the path to the door. He knocked several times and waited. There was no answer, and he rapped louder.

"Who's that?" he heard Clem say from bed.

"It's me," Lonnie said. "I've got to see you a minute, Clem. I'm out in the front yard."

He sat down and waited for Clem to dress and come outside. While he waited, he strained his ears to catch any sound that might be in the air. Over the fields towards the big house he could hear the fattening hogs grunt and squeal.

Clem came out and shut the door. He stood on the doorsill a moment speaking to his wife in bed, telling her he would be back and not to worry.

"Who's that?" Clem said, coming down into the yard.

Lonnie got up and met Clem halfway.

"What's the trouble?" Clem asked then, buttoning up his overall jumper.

"Pa's not in his bed," Lonnie said, "and Hatty says he's been gone from the house most all night. I went out in the field, and all around the barn, but I couldn't find a trace of him anywhere."

Clem then finished buttoning his jumper and began rolling a cigarette. He walked slowly down the path to the road. It was still dark, and it would be at least an hour before dawn made it any lighter.

"Maybe he was too hungry to stay in bed any longer," Clem said. "When I saw him yesterday, he said he was so shrunk up and weak he didn't know if he could last much longer. He looked like his skin and bones couldn't shrivel much more."

"I asked Arch last night after suppertime for some rations—just a little piece of sowbelly and some molasses. He said he'd get around to letting me have some the first thing this morning."

"Why don't you tell him to give you full rations or none?" Clem said. "If you knew you wasn't going to get none at all, you could move away and find a better man to sharecrop for, couldn't you?"

"I've been loyal to Arch Gunnard for a long time now," Lonnie said. "I'd hate to haul off and leave him like that."

Clem looked at Lonnie, but he did not say anything more just then. They turned up the road towards the driveway that led up to the big house. The fattening hogs were still grunting and squealing in the pen, and one of Arch's hounds came down a cotton row beside the driveway to smell their shoes.

"Them fattening hogs always get enough to eat," Clem said. "There's not a one of them that don't weigh seven hundred pounds right now, and they're getting bigger every day. Besides taking all that's thrown to them, they make a lot of meals off the chickens that get in there to peck around."

Lonnie listened to the grunting of the hogs as they walked up the driveway towards the big house.

"Reckon we'd better get Arch up to help look for Pa?" Lonnie said. "I'd hate to wake him up, but I'm scared Pa might stray off into the swamp and get lost for good. He couldn't hear it thunder, even. I never could find him back there in all that tangle if he got into it."

Clem said something under his breath and went on towards the barn and hog pen. He reached the pen before Lonnie got there.

"You'd better come here quick," Clem said, turning around to see where Lonnie was.

Lonnie ran to the hog pen. He stopped and climbed halfway up the wooden-and-wire sides of the fence. At first he could see nothing, but gradually he was able to see the moving mass of black fattening hogs on the other side of the pen. They were biting and snarling at each other like a pack of hungry hounds turned loose on a dead rabbit.

Lonnie scrambled to the top of the fence, but Clem caught him and pulled him back.

"Don't go in that hog pen that way," he said. "Them hogs will tear you to pieces, they're that wild. They're fighting over something."

Both of them ran around the corner of the pen and got to the side where the hogs were. Down under their feet on the ground Lonnie caught a glimpse of a dark mass splotched with white. He was able to see it for a moment only, because one of the hogs trampled over it.

Clem opened and closed his mouth several times before he was able to say anything at all. He clutched at Lonnie's arm, shaking him.

"That looks like it might be your pa," he said. "I swear before goodness, Lonnie, it does look like it."

Lonnie still could not believe it. He climbed to the top of the fence and began kicking his feet at the hogs, trying to drive them away. They paid no attention to him.

While Lonnie was perched there, Clem had gone to the wagon shed, and he ran back with two singletrees he had somehow managed to find there in the dark. He handed one to Lonnie, poking it at him until Lonnie's attention was drawn from the hogs long enough to take it.

Clem leaped over the fence and began swinging the singletree at the hogs. Lonnie slid down beside him, yelling at them. One hog turned on Lonnie and snapped at him, and Clem struck it over the back of the neck with enough force to drive it off momentarily.

By then Lonnie was able to realize what had happened. He ran to the mass of hogs, kicking them with his heavy stiff shoes and striking them on their heads with the iron-tipped singletree. Once he felt a stinging sensation, and looked down to see one of the hogs biting the calf of his leg. He had just enough time to hit the hog and drive it away before his leg was torn. He knew most of his overall leg had been ripped away, because he could feel the night air on his bare wet calf.

Clem had gone ahead and had driven the hogs back. There was no other way to do anything. They were in a snarling circle around them, and both of them had to keep the singletrees swinging back and forth all the time to keep the hogs off. Finally Lonnie reached down and got a grip on Mark's leg. With Clem helping, Lonnie carried his father to the fence and lifted him over to the other side.

They were too much out of breath for a while to say anything, or to do anything else. The snarling, fattening hogs were at the fence, biting the wood and wire, and making more noise than ever.

While Lonnie was searching in his pockets for a match, Clem struck one. He held the flame close to Mark Newsome's head.

They both stared unbelievingly, and then Clem blew out the match. There was nothing said as they stared at each other in the darkness.

Clem walked several steps away, and turned and came back beside Lonnie.

"It's him, though," Clem said, sitting down on the ground. "It's him, all right."

"I reckon so," Lonnie said. He could think of nothing else to say then.

They sat on the ground, one on each side of Mark, looking at the body. There had been no sign of life in the body beside them since they had first touched it. The face, throat, and stomach had been completely devoured.

"You'd better go wake up Arch Gunnard," Clem said after a while.

"What for?" Lonnie said. "He can't help none now. It's too late for help."

"Makes no difference," Clem insisted. "You'd better go wake him up and let him see what there is to see. If you wait till morning, he might take it into his head to say the hogs didn't do it. Right now is the time to get him up so he can see what his hogs did."

Clem turned around and looked at the big house. The dark outline against the dark sky made him hesitate.

"A man who short-rations tenants ought to have to sit and look at that till it's buried."

Lonnie looked at Clem fearfully. He knew Clem was right, but he was scared to hear a Negro say anything like that about a white man.

"You oughtn't talk like that about Arch," Lonnie said. "He's in bed asleep. He didn't have a thing to do with it. He didn't have no more to do with it than I did."

Clem laughed a little, and threw the singletree on the ground between his feet. After letting it lie there a little while, he picked it up and began beating the ground with it.

Lonnie got to his feet slowly. He had never seen Clem act like that before, and he did not know what to think about it. He left without saying anything and walked stiffly to the house in the darkness to wake up Arch Gunnard.

Arch was hard to wake up. And even after he was awake, he was in no hurry to get up. Lonnie was standing outside the bedroom window, and Arch was lying in bed six or eight feet away. Lonnie could hear him toss and grumble.

"Who told you to come and wake me up in the middle of the night?" Arch said.

"Well, Clem Henry's out here, and he said maybe you'd like to know about it."

Arch tossed around on the bed, flailing the pillow with his fists.

"You tell Clem Henry I said that one of these days he's going to find himself turned inside out, like a coat sleeve."

Lonnie waited doggedly. He knew Clem was right in insisting that Arch ought to wake up and come out there to see what had happened. Lonnie was afraid to go back to the barnyard and tell Clem that Arch was not coming. He did not know, but he had a feeling that Clem might go into the bedroom and drag Arch out of bed. He did not like to think of anything like that taking place.

"Are you still out there, Lonnie?" Arch shouted.

"I'm right here, Mr. Arch. I —"

"If I wasn't so sleepy, I'd come out there and take a stick and—I don't know what I wouldn't do!"

Lonnie met Arch at the back step. On the way out to the hog pen Arch did not speak to him. Arch walked heavily ahead, not even waiting to see if Lonnie was coming. The lantern that Arch was carrying cast long flat beams of yellow light over the ground; and when they got to where Clem was waiting beside Mark's body, the Negro's face shone in the night like a highly polished plowshare.

"What was Mark doing in my hog pen at night, anyway?" Arch said, shouting at them both.

Neither Clem nor Lonnie replied. Arch glared at them for not answering. But no matter how many times he looked at them, his eyes returned each time to stare at the torn body of Mark Newsome on the ground at his feet.

"There's nothing to be done now," Arch said finally. "We'll just have to wait till daylight and send for the undertaker." He walked a few steps away. "Looks like you could have waited till morning in the first place. There wasn't no sense in getting me up."

He turned his back and looked sideways at Clem. Clem stood up and looked him straight in the eyes.

"What do you want, Clem Henry?" he said. "Who told you to be coming around my house in the middle of the night? I don't want niggers coming here except when I send for them."

"I couldn't stand to see anybody eaten up by the hogs, and not do anything about it," Clem said.

"You mind your own business," Arch told him. "And when you talk to me, take off your hat, or you'll be sorry for it. It wouldn't take much to make me do you up the way you belong."

Lonnie backed away. There was a feeling of uneasiness around them. That was how trouble between Clem and Arch always began. He had seen it start that way dozens of times before. As long as Clem turned and went away, nothing happened, but sometimes he stayed right where he was and talked up to Arch just as if he had been a white man, too.

Lonnie hoped it would not happen this time. Arch was already mad enough about being waked up in the middle of the night, and Lonnie knew there was no limit to what Arch would do when he got good and mad at a Negro. Nobody had ever seen him kill a Negro, but he had said he had, and he told people that he was not scared to do it again.

"I reckon you know how he came to get eaten up by the hogs like that," Clem said, looking straight at Arch.

Arch whirled around.

"Are you talking to me . . .?"

"I asked you that," Clem stated.

"God damn you, yellow-blooded . . ." Arch yelled.

He swung the lantern at Clem's head. Clem dodged, but the bottom of it hit his shoulder, and it was smashed to pieces. The oil splattered on the ground, igniting in the air from the flaming wick. Clem was lucky not to have it splash on his face and overalls.

"Now, look here . . ." Clem said.

"You yellow-blooded nigger," Arch said, rushing at him. "I'll teach you to talk back to me. You've got too big for your place for the last time. I've been taking too much from you, but I ain't doing it no more."

"Mr. Arch, I . . ." Lonnie said, stepping forward partly between them. No one heard him.

Arch stood back and watched the kerosene flicker out on the ground.

"You know good and well why he got eaten up by the fattening hogs," Clem said, standing his ground. "He was so hungry he had to get up out of bed in the middle of the night and come up here in the dark trying to find something to eat. Maybe he was trying to find the smokehouse. It makes no difference, either way. He's been on short rations like everybody else working on your place, and he was so old he didn't know where else to look for food except in your smokehouse. You know good and well that's how he got lost up here in the dark and fell in the hog pen."

The kerosene had died out completely. In the last faint flare, Arch had reached down and grabbed up the singletree that had been lying on the ground where Lonnie had dropped it.

Arch raised the singletree over his head and struck with all his might at Clem. Clem dodged, but Arch drew back again quickly and landed a blow on his arm just above the elbow before Clem could dodge it. Clem's arm dropped to his side, dangling lifelessly.

"You God-damn yellow-blooded nigger!" Arch shouted. "Now's your time, you black bastard! I've been waiting for the chance to teach you your lesson. And this's going to be one you won't never forget."

Clem felt the ground with his feet until he had located the other singletree. He stooped down and got it. Raising it, he did not try to hit Arch, but held it in front of him so he could ward off Arch's blows at his head. He continued to stand his ground, not giving Arch an inch.

"Drop that singletree," Arch said.

"I won't stand here and let you beat me like that," Clem protested.

"By God, that's all I want to hear," Arch said, his mouth curling. "Nigger, your time has come, by God!"

He swung once more at Clem, but Clem turned and ran towards the barn. Arch went after him a few steps and stopped. He threw aside the singletree and turned and ran back to the house.

Lonnie went to the fence and tried to think what was best for him to do. He knew he could not take sides with a Negro, in the open, even if Clem had helped him, and especially after Clem had talked to Arch in the way he wished he could himself. He was a white man, and to save his life he could not stand to think of turning against Arch, no matter what happened.

Presently a light burst through one of the windows of the house, and he heard Arch shouting at his wife to wake her up.

When he saw Arch's wife go to the telephone, Lonnie realized what was going to happen. She was calling up the neighbors and Arch's friends. They would not mind getting up in the night when they found out what was going to take place.

Out behind the barn he could hear Clem calling him. Leaving the yard, Lonnie felt his way out there in the dark.

"What's the trouble, Clem?" he said.

"I reckon my time has come," Clem said. "Arch Gunnard talks that way when he's good and mad. He talked just like he did that time he carried Jim Moffin off to the swamp—and Jim never came back."

"Arch wouldn't do anything like that to you, Clem," Lonnie said excitedly, but he knew better.

Clem said nothing.

"Maybe you'd better strike out for the swamps till he changes his mind and cools off some," Lonnie said. "You might be right, Clem."

Lonnie could feel Clem's eyes burning into him.

"Wouldn't be no sense in that, if you'd help me," Clem said. "Wouldn't you stand by me?"

Lonnie trembled as the meaning of Clem's suggestion became clear to him. His back was to the side of the barn, and he leaned against it while sheets of black and white passed before his eyes.

"Wouldn't you stand by me?" Clem asked again.

"I don't know what Arch would say to that," Lonnie told him haltingly.

Clem walked away several paces. He stood with his back to Lonnie while he looked across the field towards the quarter where his home was.

"I could go in that little patch of woods out there and stay till they get tired of looking for me," Clem said, turning around to see Lonnie.

"You'd better go somewhere," Lonnie said uneasily. "I know Arch Gunnard. He's hard to handle when he makes up his mind to do something he wants to do. I couldn't stop him an inch. Maybe you'd better get clear out of the country, Clem."

"I couldn't do that, and leave my family down there across the field," Clem said.

"He's going to get you if you don't."

"If you'd only sort of help me out a little, he wouldn't. I would only have to go and hide out in that little patch of woods over there a while. Looks like you could do that for me, being as how I helped you find your pa when he was in the hog pen."

Lonnie nodded, listening for sounds from the big house. He continued to nod at Clem while Clem was waiting to be assured.

"If you're going to stand up for me," Clem said, "I can just go over there in the woods and wait till they get it off their minds. You won't be telling them where I'm at, and you could say I struck out for the swamp. They wouldn't ever find me without bloodhounds."

"That's right," Lonnie said, listening for sounds of Arch's coming out of the house. He did not wish to be found back there, behind the barn where Arch could accuse him of talking to Clem.

The moment Lonnie replied, Clem turned and ran off into the night. Lonnie went after him a few steps, as if he had suddenly changed his mind about helping him, but Clem was lost in the darkness by then.

Lonnie waited for a few minutes, listening to Clem crashing through the underbrush in the patch of woods a quarter of a mile away. When he could hear Clem no longer, he went around the barn to meet Arch.

Arch came out of the house carrying his double-barreled shotgun and the lantern he had picked up in the house. His pockets were bulging with shells.

"Where is that damn nigger, Lonnie?" Arch asked him. "Where'd he go to?"

Lonnie opened his mouth, but no words came out.

"You know which way he went, don't you?"

Lonnie again tried to say something, but there were no sounds. He jumped when he found himself nodding his head to Arch.

"Mr. Arch, I —"

"That's all right, then," Arch said. "That's all I need to know now, Dudley Smith and Tom Hawkins and Frank and Dave Howard and the rest will be here in a minute, and you can stay right here so you can show us where he's hiding out."

Frantically Lonnie tried to say something. Then he reached for Arch's sleeve to stop him, but Arch had gone.

Arch ran around the house to the front yard. Soon a car came racing down the road, its headlights lighting up the whole place, hog pen and all. Lonnie knew it was probably Dudley Smith, because his was the first house in that direction, only half a mile away. While he was turning into the driveway, several other automobiles came into sight, both up the road and down it.

Lonnie trembled. He was afraid Arch was going to tell him to point out where Clem had gone to hide. Then he knew Arch would tell him. He had promised Clem he would not do that. But try as he might, he could not make himself believe that Arch Gunnard would do anything more than whip Clem.

Clem had not done anything that called for lynching. He had not raped a white woman, he had not shot at a white man; he had only talked back to Arch, with his hat on. But Arch was mad enough to do anything; he was mad enough at Clem not to stop at anything short of lynching.

The whole crowd of men was swarming around him before he realized it. And there was Arch clutching his arm and shouting into his face.

"Mr. Arch, I —"

Lonnie recognized every man in the feeble dawn. They were excited, and they looked like men on the last lap of an all-night fox-hunting party. Their shotguns and pistols were held at their waist, ready for the kill.

"What's the matter with you, Lonnie?" Arch said, shouting into his ear.

"Wake up and say where Clem Henry went to hide out. We're ready to go get him."

Lonnie remembered looking up and seeing Frank Howard dropping yellow twelve-gauge shells into the breech of his gun. Frank bent forward so he could hear Lonnie tell Arch where Clem was hiding.

"You ain't going to kill Clem this time, are you, Mr. Arch?" Lonnie asked.

"Kill him?" Dudley Smith repeated. "What do you reckon I've been waiting all this time for if it wasn't for a chance to get Clem. That nigger has had it coming to him ever since he came to this county. He's a bad nigger, and it's coming to him."

"It wasn't exactly Clem's fault," Lonnie said. "If Pa hadn't come up here and fell in the hog pen, Clem wouldn't have had a thing to do with it. He was helping me, that's all."

"Shut up, Lonnie," somebody shouted at him. "You're so excited you don't know what you're saying. You're taking up for a nigger when you talk like that."

People were crowding around him so tightly he felt as if he were being squeezed to death. He had to get some air, get his breath, get out of the crowd.

"That's right," Lonnie said.

He heard himself speak, but he did not know what he was saying.

"But Clem helped me find Pa when he got lost looking around for something to eat."

"Shut up, Lonnie," somebody said again. "You damn fool, shut up!"

Arch grabbed his shoulder and shook him until his teeth rattled. Then Lonnie realized what he had been saying.

"Now, look here, Lonnie," Arch shouted. "You must be out of your head, because you know good and well you wouldn't talk like a nigger-lover in your right mind."

"That's right," Lonnie said, trembling all over. "I sure wouldn't want to talk like that."

He could still feel the grip on his shoulder where Arch's strong fingers had hurt him.

"Did Clem go to the swamp, Lonnie?" Dudley Smith said. "Is that right, Lonnie?"

Lonnie tried to shake his head; he tried to nod his head. Then Arch's fingers squeezed his thin neck. Lonnie looked at the men wild-eyed.

"Where's Clem hiding, Lonnie?" Arch demanded, squeezing.

Lonnie went three or four steps towards the barn. When he stopped, the men behind him pushed forward again. He found himself being rushed behind the barn and beyond it.

"All right, Lonnie," Arch said. "Now which way?"

Lonnie pointed towards the patch of woods where the creek was. The swamp was in the other direction.

"He said he was going to hide out in that little patch of woods along the creek over there, Mr. Arch," Lonnie said. "I reckon he's over there now."

Lonnie felt himself being swept forward, and he stumbled over the rough ground trying to keep from being knocked down and trampled upon. Nobody was talking, and everyone seemed to be walking on tiptoes. The gray light of early dawn was increasing enough both to hide them and to show the way ahead.

Just before they reached the fringe of the woods, the men separated, and Lonnie found himself a part of the circle that was closing in on Clem.

Lonnie was alone, and there was nobody to stop him, but he was unable to move forward or backward. It began to be clear to him what he had done.

Clem was probably up a tree somewhere in the woods ahead, but by that time he had been surrounded on all sides. If he should attempt to break and run, he would be shot down like a rabbit.

Lonnie sat down on a log and tried to think what to do. The sun would be up in a few more minutes, and as soon as it came up, the men would close in on the creek and Clem. He would have no chance at all among all those shotguns and pistols.

Once or twice he saw the flare of a match through the underbrush where some of the men were lying in wait. A whiff of cigarette smoke struck his nostrils, and he found himself wondering if Clem could smell it wherever he was in the woods.

There was still no sound anywhere around him, and he knew that Arch Gunnard and the rest of the men were waiting for the sun, which would in a few minutes come up behind him in the east.

It was light enough by that time to see plainly the rough ground and the tangled underbrush and the curling bark on the pine trees.

The men had already begun to creep forward, guns raised as if stalking a deer. The woods were not large, and the circle of men would be able to cover it in a few minutes at the rate they were going forward. There was still a chance that Clem had slipped through the circle before dawn broke, but Lonnie felt that he was still there. He began to feel then that Clem was there because he himself had placed him there for the men to find more easily.

Lonnie found himself moving forward, drawn into the narrowing circle. Presently he could see the men all around him in dim outline. Their eyes were searching the heavy green pine tops as they went forward from tree to tree.

"Oh, Pa!" he said in a hoarse whisper. "Oh, Pa!"

He went forward a few steps, looking into the bushes and up into the treetops. When he saw the other men again, he realized that it was not Mark Newsome being sought. He did not know what had made him forget like that.

The creeping forward began to work into the movement of Lonnie's body. He found himself springing forward on his toes, and his body was leaning in that direction. It was like creeping up on a rabbit when you did not have a gun to hunt with.

He forgot again what he was doing there. The springing motion in his legs seemed to be growing stronger with each step. He bent forward so far he could almost touch the ground with his fingertips. He could not stop now. He was keeping up with the circle of men.

The fifteen men were drawing closer and closer together. The dawn had broken enough to show the time on the face of a watch. The sun was beginning to color the sky above.

Lonnie was far in advance of anyone else by then. He could not hold himself back. The strength in his legs was more than he could hold in check.

He had for so long been unable to buy shells for his gun that he had forgotten how much he liked to hunt.

The sound of the men's steady creeping had become a rhythm in his ears.

"Here's the bastard!" somebody shouted, and there was a concerted crashing through the dry underbrush. Lonnie dashed forward, reaching the tree almost as quickly as anyone else.

He could see everybody with guns raised, and far into the sky above the sharply outlined face of Clem Henry gleamed in the rising sun. His body was hugging the slender top of the pine.

Lonnie did not know who was the first to fire, but the rest of the men did not hesitate. There was a deafening roar as the shotguns and revolvers flared and smoked around the trunk of the tree.

He closed his eyes; he was afraid to look again at the face above. The firing continued without break. Clem hugged the tree with all his might, and then, with the faraway sound of splintering wood, the top of the tree and Clem came crashing through the lower limbs to the ground. The body, sprawling and torn, landed on the ground with a thud that stopped Lonnie's heart for a moment.

He turned, clutching for the support of a tree, as the firing began once more. The crumpled body was tossed time after time, like a sackful of kittens being killed with an automatic shotgun, as charges of lead were fired into it from all sides. A cloud of dust rose from the ground and drifted overhead with the choking odor of burned powder.

Lonnie did not remember how long the shooting lasted. He found himself running from tree to tree, clutching at the rough pine bark, stumbling wildly towards the cleared ground. The sky had turned from gray to red when he emerged in the open, and as he ran, falling over the hard clods in the plowed field, he tried to keep his eyes on the house ahead.

Once he fell and found it almost impossible to rise again to his feet. He struggled to his knees, facing the round red sun. The warmth gave him the strength to rise to his feet, and he muttered unintelligibly to himself. He tried to say things he had never thought to say before.

When he got home, Hatty was waiting for him in the yard. She had heard the shots in the woods, and she had seen him stumbling over the hard clods in the field, and she had seen him kneeling there looking straight into the face of the sun. Hatty was trembling as she ran to Lonnie to find out what the matter was.

Once in his own yard, Lonnie turned and looked for a second over his shoulder. He saw the men climbing over the fence at Arch Gunnard's. Arch's wife was standing on the back porch, and she was speaking to them.

"Where's your pa, Lonnie?" Hatty said. "And what in the world was all that shooting in the woods for?" Lonnie stumbled forward until he had reached the front porch. He fell upon the steps.

"Lonnie, Lonnie!" Hatty was saying. "Wake up and tell me what in the world is the matter. I've never seen the like of all that's going on."

"Nothing," Lonnie said. "Nothing."

"Well, if there's nothing the matter, can't you go up to the big house and ask for a little piece of streak-of-lean? We ain't got a thing to cook for breakfast. Your pa's going to be hungrier than ever after being up walking around all night."

"What?" Lonnie said, his voice rising to a shout as he jumped to his feet.

"Why, I only said go up to the big house and get a little piece of streak-of-lean, Lonnie. That's all I said."

He grabbed his wife about the shoulders.

"Meat?" he yelled, shaking her roughly.

"Yes," she said, pulling away from him in surprise. "Couldn't you go ask Arch Gunnard for a little bit of streak-of-lean?"

Lonnie slumped down again on the steps, his hands falling between his outspread legs and his chin falling on his chest.

"No," he said almost inaudibly. "No. I ain't hungry."

from *Their Eyes Were Watching God*

Zora Neale Hurston (1891[?]–1960)

Zora Neale Hurston was born in Eatonville, Florida — an all-black town — and overcame enormous odds to gain an education at Howard University and Barnard College. A student of anthropology and folklore, Hurston wove her observations of African American life into the fiction she began writing in the 1920s. Hurston came into prominence in the 1930s for both her fiction and her nonfiction. Her best-known book, *Their Eyes Were Watching God* (1937), combined her personal past, her learning, and her fiction into a powerful story of a black woman's refusal to accept the limitations and expectations of her time. Hurston, suffering from criticisms of her work and personal problems, faded into poverty and obscurity in the 1940s and 1950s and died before critics rediscovered her works in the 1970s.

Janie saw her life like a great tree in leaf with the things suffered, things enjoyed, things done and undone. Dawn and doom were in the branches.

"Ah know exactly what Ah got to tell yuh, but it's hard to know where to start at."

"Ah ain't never seen mah papa. And Ah didn't know 'im if Ah did. Mah mama neither. She was gone from round dere long before Ah wuz big enough tuh know. Mah grandma raised me. Mah grandma and de white folks she worked wid. She had a house out in de back-yard and dat's where Ah wuz born. They was quality white folks up dere in West Florida. Named Washburn. She had four gran'chillun on de place and all of us played together and dat's how come Ah never called mah Grandma nothin' but Nanny, 'cause dat's what everybody on de place called her. Nanny used to ketch us in our devilment and lick every youngun on de place and Mis' Washburn did de same. Ah reckon dey never hit us ah lick amiss 'cause dem three boys and us two girls wuz pretty aggravatin', Ah speck.

"Ah was wid dem white chillun so much till Ah didn't know Ah wuzn't white till Ah was round six years old. Wouldn't have found it out then, but a man come long takin' pictures and without askin' anybody, Shelby, dat was de oldest boy, he told him to take us. Round a week later de man brought de picture for Mis' Washburn to see and pay him which she did, then give us all a good lickin'.

"So when we looked at de picture and everybody got pointed out there wasn't nobody left except a real dark little girl with long hair standing by Eleanor. Dat's where Ah wuz s'posed to be, but Ah couldn't recognize dat dark chile as me. So Ah ast, 'where is me? Ah don't see me.'

"Everybody laughed, even Mr. Washburn. Miss Nellie, de Mama of de chillun who come back home after her husband dead, she pointed to de dark one and said, 'Dat's you, Alphabet, don't you know yo' ownself?'

"Dey all useter call me Alphabet 'cause so many people had done named me different names. Ah looked at de picture a long time and seen it was mah dress and mah hair so Ah said:

"'Aw, aw! Ah'm colored!'

"Den dey all laughed real hard. But before Ah seen de picture Ah thought Ah wuz just like de rest.

"Us lived dere havin' fun till de chillun at school got to teasin' me 'bout livin' in de white folks' backyard. Dere wuz uh knotty head gal name Mayrella dat useter git mad every time she look at me. Mis' Washburn useter dress me up in all de clothes her gran'chillun didn't need no mo' which still wuz better'n whut de rest uh de colored chillun had. And then she useter put hair ribbon on mah head fuh me tuh wear. Dat useter rile Mayrella uh lot. So she would pick at me all de time and put some others up tuh do de same. They'd push me 'way from de ring plays and make out they couldn't play wid nobody dat lived on premises. Den they'd tell me not to be takin' on over mah looks 'cause they mama told 'em 'bout de hound dawgs huntin' mah papa all night long. 'Bout Mr. Washburn and de sheriff puttin' de bloodhounds on de trail tuh ketch mah papa for whut he done tuh mah mama. Dey didn't tell about how he wuz seen tryin' tuh git in touch wid mah mama later on so he could marry her. Naw, dey didn't talk dat part of it atall. Dey made it sound real bad so as tuh crumple mah feathers. None of 'em didn't even remember whut his name wuz, but dey all knowed de bloodhound part by heart. Nanny didn't love tuh see me wid mah head hung down, so she figgered it would be mo' better fuh me if us had uh house. She got de land and everything and then Mis' Washburn helped out uh whole heap wid things."

Pheoby's hungry listening helped Janie to tell her story. So she went on thinking back to her young years and explaining them to her friend in soft, easy phrases while all around the house, the night time put on flesh and blackness.

She thought awhile and decided that her conscious life had commenced at Nanny's gate. On a late afternoon Nanny had called her to come inside the house because she had spied Janie letting Johnny Taylor kiss her over the gatepost.

It was a spring afternoon in West Florida. Janie had spent most of the day under a blossoming pear tree in the back-yard. She had been spending every minute that she could steal from her chores under that tree for the last three days. That was to say, ever since the first tiny bloom had opened. It had called her to come and gaze on a mystery. From barren brown stems to glistening leaf-buds; from the leaf-buds to snowy virginity of bloom. It stirred her tremendously. How? Why? It was like a flute song forgotten in another existence and remembered again. What? How? Why? This singing she heard that had nothing to do with her ears. The rose of the world was breathing out smell. It followed her through all her waking moments and caressed her in her sleep. It connected itself with other vaguely felt matters that had struck her outside observation and buried themselves in her flesh. Now they emerged and quested about her consciousness.

She was stretched on her back beneath the pear tree soaking in the alto chant of the visiting bees, the gold of the sun and the panting breath of the breeze when the inaudible voice of it all came to her. She saw a dust-bearing bee sink into the sanctum of a bloom; the thousand sister-calyxes arch to meet the love embrace and the ecstatic shiver of the tree from root to tiniest branch creaming in every blossom and frothing with delight. So this was a marriage! She had been summoned to behold a revelation. Then Janie felt a pain remorseless sweet that left her limp and languid.

After a while she got up from where she was and went over the little garden field entire. She was seeking confirmation of the voice and vision, and everywhere she found and acknowledged answers. A personal answer for all other creations except herself. She felt an answer seeking her, but where? When? How? She found herself at the kitchen door and stumbled inside. In the air of the room were flies tumbling and singing, marrying and giving in marriage. When she reached the narrow hallway she was reminded that her grandmother was home with a sick headache. She was lying across the bed asleep so Janie tipped on out of the front door. Oh to be a pear tree—*any* tree in bloom! With kissing bees singing of the beginning of the world! She was sixteen. She had glossy leaves and bursting buds and she wanted to struggle with life but it seemed to elude her. Where were the singing bees for her? Nothing on the place nor in her grandma's house answered her. She searched as much of the world as she could from the top of the front steps and then went on down to the front gate and leaned over to gaze up and down the road. Looking, waiting, breathing short with impatience. Waiting for the world to be made.

Through pollinated air she saw a glorious being coming up the road. In her former blindness she had known him as shiftless Johnny Taylor, tall and lean. That was before the golden dust of pollen had beglamored his rags and her eyes.

In the last stages of Nanny's sleep, she dreamed of voices. Voices far-off but persistent, and gradually coming nearer. Janie's voice. Janie talking in whispery snatches with a male voice she couldn't quite place. That brought her wide awake. She bolted upright and peered out of the window and saw Johnny Taylor lacerating her Janie with a kiss.

"Janie!"

The old woman's voice was so lacking in command and reproof, so full of crumbling dissolution, — that Janie half believed that Nanny had not seen her. So she extended herself outside of her dream and went inside of the house. That was the end of her childhood.

Nanny's head and face looked like the standing roots of some old tree that had been torn away by storm. Foundation of ancient power that no longer mattered. The cooling palma christi leaves that Janie had bound about her grandma's head with a white rag had wilted down and become part and parcel of the woman. Her eyes didn't bore and pierce. They diffused and melted Janie, the room and the world into one comprehension.

"Janie, youse uh 'oman, now, so—"

"Naw, Nanny, naw Ah ain't no real 'oman yet."

The thought was too new and heavy for Janie. She fought it away.

Nanny closed her eyes and nodded a slow, weary affirmation many times before she gave it voice.

"Yeah, Janie youse got yo' womanhood on yuh. So Ah mout ez well tell yuh whut Ah been savin' up for uh spell. Ah wants to see you married right away."

"Me married? Naw, Nanny, no ma'am! Whut Ah know 'bout uh husband?"

"Whut Ah seen just now is plenty for me, honey, Ah don't want no trashy nigger, no breath-and-britches, lak Johnny Taylor usin' yo' body to wipe his foots on."

Nanny's words made Janie's kiss across the gatepost seem like a manure pile after a rain.

"Look at me, Janie. Don't set dere wid yo' head hung down. Look at yo' ole grandma!" He voice began snagging on the prongs of her feelings. "Ah don't want to be talkin' to you lak dis. Fact is Ah done been on mah knees to mah Maker many's de time askin' *please*—for Him not to make de burden too heavy for me to bear."

"Nanny, Ah just—Ah didn't mean nothin' bad."

"Dat's what makes me skeered. You don't mean no harm. You don't even know where harm is at. Ah'm ole now. Ah can't be always guidin' yo' feet from harm and danger. Ah wants to see you married right away."

"Who Ah'm goin' tuh marry off-hand lak dat? Ah don't know nobody."

"De Lawd will provide. He know Ah done bore de burden in de heat uh de day. Somebody done spoke to me 'bout you long time ago. Ah ain't said nothin' 'cause dat wasn't de way Ah placed you. Ah wanted yuh to school out and pick from a higher bush and a sweeter berry. But dat ain't yo' idea, Ah see."

"Nanny, who—who dat been askin' you for me?"

"Brother Logan Killicks. He's a good man, too."

"Naw, Nanny, no ma'am! Is dat whut he been hangin' round here for? He look like some ole skullhead in de grave yard."

The older woman sat bolt upright and put her feet to the floor, and thrust back the leaves from her face.

"So you don't want to marry off decent like, do yuh? You just wants to hug and kiss and feel around with first one man and then another, huh? You wants to make me suck de same sorrow yo' mama did, eh? Mah ole head ain't gray enough. Mah back ain't bowed enough to suit yuh!"

The vision of Logan Killicks was desecrating the pear tree, but Janie didn't know how to tell Nanny that. She merely hunched over and pouted at the floor.

"Janie."

"Yes, ma'am."

"You answer me when Ah speak. Don't you set dere poutin' wid me after all Ah done went through for you!"

She slapped the girl's face violently, and forced her head back so that their eyes met in struggle. With her hand uplifted for the second blow she saw the huge tear that welled up from Janie's heart and stood in each eye. She saw the terrible agony and the lips tightened down to hold back the cry and desisted. Instead she brushed back the heavy hair from Janie's face and stood there suffering and loving and weeping internally for both of them.

"Come to yo' Grandma, honey. Set in her lap lak yo' use tuh. Yo' Nanny wouldn't harm a hair uh yo' head. She don't want nobody else to do it neither if she kin help it. Honey, de white man is de ruler of everything as fur as Ah been able tuh find out. Maybe it's some place way off in de ocean where de black man is in power, but we don't know nothin' but what we see. So de white man throw down de load and tell de nigger man tuh pick it up. He pick it up because he have to, but he don't tote it. He hand it to his womenfolks. De nigger woman is de mule uh de world so fur as Ah can see. Ah been prayin' fuh it tuh be different wid you. Lawd, Lawd, Lawd!"

For a long time she sat rocking with the girl held tightly to her sunken breast. Janie's long legs dangled over one arm of the chair and the long braids of her hair swung low on the other side. Nanny half sung, half sobbed a running chant-prayer over the head of the weeping girl.

"Lawd have mercy! It was a long time on de way but Ah reckon it had to come. Oh Jesus! Do, Jesus! Ah done de best Ah could."

Finally, they both grew calm.

"Janie, how long you been 'lowin' Johnny Taylor to kiss you?"

"Only dis one time, Nanny. Ah don't love him at all. Whut made me do it is—oh, Ah don't know."

"Thank yuh, Massa Jesus."

"Ah ain't gointuh do it no mo', Nanny. Please don't make me marry Mr. Killicks."

"'Tain't Logan Killicks Ah wants you to have, baby, it's protection. Ah ain't gittin' ole, honey. Ah'm *done* ole. One mornin' soon, now, de angel wid de sword is gointuh stop by here. De day and de hour is hid from me, but it won't be long. Ah ast de Lawd when you was uh infant in mah arms to let me stay here till you got grown. He done spared me to see de day. Mah daily prayer now is tuh let dese golden moments rolls on a few days longer till Ah see you safe in life."

"Lemme wait, Nanny, please, jus' a lil bit mo'."

"Don't think Ah don't feel wid you, Janie, 'cause Ah do. Ah couldn't love yuh no more if Ah had uh felt yo' birth pains mahself. Fact uh de matter, Ah loves yuh a whole heap more'n Ah do yo' mama, de one Ah did birth. But you got to take in consideration you ain't no everyday chile like most of 'em. You ain't got no papa, you might jus' as well say no mama, for de good she do yuh. You ain't got nobody but me. And mah head is ole and tilted towards de grave. Neither can you stand alone by yo'self. De thought uh you bein' kicked around from pillar tuh post is uh hurtin' thing. Every tear you drop squeezes a cup uh blood outa mah heart. Ah got tuh try and do for you befo' mah head is cold."

A sobbing sigh burst out of Janie. The old woman answered her with little soothing parts of the hand.

"You know, honey, us colored folks is branches without roots and that makes things come round in queer ways. You in particular. Ah was born back due in slavery so it wasn't for me to fulfill my dreams of whut a woman oughta be and to do. Dat's one of de hold-backs of slavery. But nothing can't stop you from wishin'. You can't beat nobody down so low till you can rob 'em of they will. Ah didn't want to be used for a work-ox and a brood-sow and Ah didn't want mah daughter used dat way neither. It sho wasn't mah will for things to happen lak they did. Ah even hated de way you was born. But, all de same Ah said thank God, Ah got another chance. Ah wanted to preach a great sermon about colored women sittin' on high, but they wasn't no pulpit for me. Freedom found me wid a baby daughter in mah arms, so Ah said Ah'd take a broom and a cook-pot and throw up a highway through de wilderness for her. She would expound what Ah felt. But somehow she got lost offa de highway and next thing Ah knowed here you was in de world. So whilst Ah was tendin' you of nights Ah said Ah'd save de text for you. Ah been waitin' a long time, Janie, but nothin' Ah been through ain't too much if you just take a stand on high ground lak Ah dreamed."

Old Nanny sat there rocking Janie like an infant and thinking back and back. Mind-pictures brought feelings, and feelings dragged out dramas from the hollows of her heart.

"Dat mornin' on de big plantation close to Savannah, a rider come in a gallop tellin' 'bout Sherman takin' Atlanta. Marse Robert's son had done been kilt at Chickamauga. So he grabbed his gun and straddled his best horse and went off wid de rest of de gray-headed men and young boys to drive de Yankees back into Tennessee.

"They was all cheerin' and cryin' and shoutin' for de men dat was ridin' off. Ah couldn't see nothin' cause yo' mama wasn't but a week old, and Ah was flat uh mah back. But pretty soon he let on he forgot somethin' and run into mah cabin and made me let down mah hair for de last time. He sorta wropped his hand in it, pulled mah big toe, lak he always done, and was gone after de rest lak lightnin'. Ah heard 'em give one last whoop for him. Then de big house and de quarters got sober and silent.

"It was de cool de evenin' when Mistis come walkin' in mah door. She throwed de door wide open and stood dere lookin' at me outa her eyes and her face. Look lak she been livin' through uh hundred years in January without one day of spring. She come stood over me in de bed.

"'Nanny, Ah come to see that baby uh yourn.'

"Ah tried not to feel de breeze off her face, but it got so cold in dere dat Ah was freezin' to death under the kivvers. So Ah couldn't move right away lak Ah aimed to. But Ah knowed Ah had to make haste and do it.

"'You better git dat kivver offa dat youngun and dat quick!' she clashed at me. 'Look lak you don't know who is Mistis on dis plantation, Madam. But Ah aims to show you.'

"By dat time I had done managed tuh unkivver mah baby enough for her to see de head and face.

"'Nigger, whut's yo' baby doin' wid gray eyes and yaller hair?' She begin tuh slap mah jaws ever which a'way. Ah never felt the fust ones 'cause Ah wuz too busy gittin' de kivver back over mah chile. But dem last lick burnt me lak fire. Ah had too many feelin's tuh tell which one tuh follow so Ah didn't cry and Ah didn't do nothin' else. But then she kept on astin me how come mah baby look white. She asted me dat maybe twenty-five or thirty times, lak she got tuh sayin' dat and couldn't help herself. So Ah told her, 'Ah don't know nothin' but what Ah'm told tuh do, 'cause Ah ain't nothin' but uh nigger and uh slave.'

"Instead of pacifyin' her lak Ah thought, look lak she got madder. But Ah reckon she was tired and wore out 'cause she didn't hit me no more. She went to de foot of de bed and wiped her hands on her handksher. 'Ah wouldn't dirty mah hands on yuh. But first thing in de mornin' de overseer will take you to de whippin' post and tie you down on yo' knees and cut de hide offa yo' yaller back. One hundred lashes wid a raw-hide on yo' bare back. Ah'll have you whipped till de blood run down to yo' heels! Ah mean to count de licks mahself. And if it kills you Ah'll stand de loss. Anyhow, as soon as dat brat is a month old Ah'm going to sell it offa dis place.'

"She flounced on off and left her wintertime wid me. Ah knowed mah body wasn't healed, but Ah couldn't consider dat. In de black dark Ah wrapped mah baby de best Ah knowed how and made it to de swamp by de river. Ah knowed de place was full uh moccasins and other bitin' snakes, but Ah was more skeered uh whut was behind me. Ah hide in dere day and night and suckled de baby every time she start to cry, for fear somebody might hear her and Ah'd git found. Ah ain't sayin' uh friend or two didn't feel mah care. And den de Good Lawd seen to it dat Ah wasn't taken. Ah don't see how come mah milk didn't kill mah chile, wid me so skeered and worried all de time. De noise uh de owls skeered me; de limbs of dem cypress trees took to crawlin' and movin' round after dark, and two three times Ah heered panthers prowlin' round. But nothin' never hurt me 'cause de Lawd knowed how it was.

"Den, one night Ah heard de big guns boomin' lak thunder. It kept up all night long. And de next mornin' Ah could see uh big ship at a distance and a great stirrin' round. So Ah wrapped Leafy up in moss and fixed her good in a tree and picked mah way on down to de landin'. The men was all in blue and Ah heard people say Sherman was comin' to meet de boats in Savannah, and all of us slaves was free. So Ah run got mah baby and got in quotation wid people and found a place Ah could stay.

"But it was a long time after dat befo' de Big Surrender at Richmond. Den de big bell ring in Atlanta and all de men in gray uniforms had to go to Moultrie, and bury their swords in de ground to show they was never to fight about slavery no mo'. So den we knowed we was free.

"Ah wouldn't marry nobody, though Ah could have uh heap uh times, 'cause Ah didn't want nobody mistreating mah baby. So Ah got with some good white people and come down here in West Florida to work and make de sun shine on both sides of de street for Leafy.

"Mah Madam help me wid her just lak she been doin' wid you. Ah put her in school when it got so it was a school to put her in. Ah was 'spectin' to make a school teacher outa her.

"But one day she didn't come home at de usual time and Ah waited and waited, but she never come all dat night. Ah took a lantern and went round askin' everybody but nobody ain't seen her. De next mornin' she come crawlin' in on her hands and knees. A sight to see. Dat school teacher had done hid her in de woods all night long, and he had done raped mah baby and run on off just before day.

"She was only seventeen, and somethin' lak dat to happen! Lawd a'mussy! Look lak Ah kin see it all over agin. It was a long time before she was well, and by dat time we knowed you was on de way. And after you was born she took to drinkin' likker and stayin' out nights. Couldn't git her to stay here and nowhere else. Lawd knows where she is right now. She ain't dead, 'cause Ah'd know it by mah feelings, but sometimes Ah wish she was at rest.

"And, Janie, maybe it wasn't much, but Ah done de best Ah kin by you. Ah raked and scraped and bought dis lil piece uh land so you wouldn't have to stay in de white folks' yard and tuck yo' head befo' other chillun at school. Dat was all right when you was little. But when you got big enough to understand things, Ah wanted you to look upon yo'self. Ah don't want yo' feathers always crumpled by folks throwin' up things in yo' face. And Ah can't die easy thinkin' maybe de menfolks white or black is makin' a spit cup outa you: Have some sympathy fuh me. Put me down easy, Janie, Ah'm a cracked plate."

"Death of a Traveling Salesman"

Eudora Welty (1909–)

The daughter of a successful insurance executive in Jackson, Mississippi, Eudora Welty witnessed the growing tension between New South boosterism and those values associated with an older society. After graduating from the University of Wisconsin and completing a three-year stint with the New Deal's Works Progress Administration in Mississippi, she began producing fiction in 1936. In stories like "Death of a Traveling Salesman" (1941), in her first collection, Welty writes of the loneliness of modern life, suggesting some of the human costs related to South-erners' growing attachment to modernity. She was awarded the 1973 Pulitzer Prize for the novel *The Optimist's Daughter.*

R. J. Bowman, who for fourteen years had traveled for a shoe company through Mississippi, drove his Ford along a rutted dirt path. It was a long day! The time did not seem to clear the noon hurdle and settle into soft afternoon. The sun, keeping its strength here even in winter, stayed at the top of the sky, and every time Bowman stuck his head out of the dusty car to stare up the road, it seemed to reach a long arm down and push against the top of his head, right through his hat—like the practical joke of an old drummer, long on the road. It made him feel all the more angry and helpless. He was feverish, and he was not quite sure of the way.

This was his first day back on the road after a long siege of influenza. He had had very high fever, and dreams, and had become weakened and pale, enough to tell the difference in the mirror, and he could not think clearly. . . . All afternoon, in the midst of his anger, and for no reason, he had thought of his dead grandmother. She had been a comfortable soul. Once more Bowman wished he could fall into the big feather bed that had been in her room. . . . Then he forgot her again.

This desolate hill country! And he seemed to be going the wrong way — it was as if he were going back, far back. There was not a house in sight. . . . There was no use wishing he were back in bed, though. By pay-ing the hotel doctor his bill he had proved his recovery. He had not even been sorry when the pretty trained nurse said good-bye. He did not like illness, he distrusted it, as he distrusted the road without sign-posts. It angered him. He had given the nurse a really expensive bracelet, just because she was packing up her bag and leaving.

But now—what if in fourteen years on the road he had never been ill before and never had an accident? His record was broken, and he had even begun almost to question it.... He had gradually put up at better hotels, in the bigger towns, but weren't they all, eternally, stuffy in summer and drafty in winter? Women? He could only remember little rooms within little rooms, like a nest of Chinese paper boxes, and if he thought of one woman he saw the worn loneliness that the furniture of that room seemed built of. And he himself—he was a man who always wore rather wide-brimmed black hats, and in the wavy hotel mirrors had looked something like a bullfighter, as he paused for that inevitable instant on the landing, walking downstairs to supper.... He leaned out of the car again, and once more the sun pushed at his head.

Bowman had wanted to reach Beulah by dark, to go to bed and sleep off his fatigue. As he remembered, Beulah was fifty miles away from the last town, on a graveled road. This was only a cow trail. How had he ever come to such a place? One hand wiped the sweat from his face, and he drove on.

He had made the Beulah trip before. But he had never seen this hill or this petering-out path before—or that cloud, he thought shyly, looking up and then down quickly—any more than he had seen this day before. Why did he not admit he was simply lost and had been for miles? ... He was not in the habit of asking the way of strangers, and these people never knew where the very roads they lived on went to; but then he had not even been close enough to anyone to call out. People standing in the fields now and then, or on top of the haystacks, had been too far away, looking like leaning sticks or weeds, turning a little at the solitary rattle of his car across their countryside, watching the pale sobered winter dust where it chunked out behind like big squashes down the road. The stares of these distant people had followed him solidly like a wall, impenetrable, behind which they turned back after he had passed.

The cloud floated there to one side like the bolster on his grandmother's bed. It went over a cabin on the edge of a hill, where two bare chinaberry trees clutched at the sky. He drove through a heap of dead oak leaves, his wheels stirring their weightless sides to make a silvery melancholy whistle as the car passed through their bed. No car had been along this way ahead of him. Then he saw that he was on the edge of a ravine that fell away, a red erosion, and that this was indeed the road's end.

He pulled the brake. But it did not hold, though he put all his strength into it. The car, tipped toward the edge, rolled a little. Without doubt, it was going over the bank.

He got out quietly, as though some mischief had been done him and he had his dignity to remember. He lifted his bag and sample case out, set them down, and stood back and watched the car roll over the edge. He heard something — not the crash he was listening for, but a slow, unuproarious crackle. Rather distastefully he went to look over, and he saw that his car had fallen into a tangle of immense grapevines as thick as his arm, which caught it and held it, rocked it like a grotesque child in a dark cradle, and then, as he watched, concerned somehow that he was not still inside it, released it gently to the ground.

He sighed.

Where am I? he wondered with a shock. Why didn't I do something? All his anger seemed to have drifted away from him. There was the house, back on the hill. He took a bag in each hand and with almost childlike willingness went toward it. But his breathing came with difficulty, and he had to stop to rest.

It was a shotgun house, two rooms and an open passage between, perched on the hill. The whole cabin slanted a little under the heavy heaped-up vine that covered the roof, light and green, as though forgotten from summer. A woman stood in the passage.

He stopped still. Then all of a sudden his heart began to behave strangely. Like a rocket set off, it began to leap and expand into uneven patterns of beats which showered into his brain, and he could not think. But in scattering and falling it made no noise. It shot up with great power, almost elation, and fell gently, like acrobats into nets. It began to pound profoundly, then waited irresponsibly, hitting in some sort of inward mockery first at his ribs, then against his eyes, then under his shoulder blades, and against the roof of his mouth when he tried to say, "Good afternoon, madam." But he could not hear his heart—it was as quiet as ashes falling. This was rather comforting; still, it was shocking to Bowman to feel his heart beating at all.

Stock-still in his confusion, he dropped his bags, which seemed to drift in slow bulks gracefully through the air and to cushion themselves on the gray prostrate grass near the doorstep.

As for the woman standing there, he saw at once that she was old. Since she could not possibly hear his heart, he ignored the pounding and now looked at her carefully, and yet in his distraction dreamily, with his mouth open.

She had been cleaning the lamp, and held it, half blackened, half clear, in front of her. He saw her with the dark passage behind her. She was a big woman with a weather-beaten but unwrinkled face; her lips were held tightly together, and her eyes looked with a curious dulled brightness into his. He looked at her shoes, which were like bundles. If it were summer she would be barefoot. . . . Bowman, who automatically judged a woman's age on sight, set her age at fifty. She wore a formless garment of some gray coarse material, rough-dried from a washing, from which her arms appeared pink and unexpectedly round. When she never said a word, and sustained her quiet pose of holding the lamp, he was convinced of the strength in her body.

"Good afternoon, madam," he said.

She stared on, whether at him or at the air around him he could not tell, but after a moment she lowered her eyes to show that she would listen to whatever he had to say.

"I wonder if you would be interested—" He tried once more. "An accident—my car . . ."

Her voice emerged low and remote, like a sound across a lake. "Sonny he ain't here."

"Sonny?"

"Sonny ain't here now."

Her son—a fellow able to bring my car up, he decided in blurred relief. He pointed down the hill. "My car's in the bottom of the ditch. I'll need help."

"Sonny ain't here, but he'll be here."

She was becoming clearer to him and her voice stronger, and Bowman saw that she was stupid.

He was hardly surprised at the deepening postponement and tedium of his journey. He took a breath, and heard his voice speaking over the silent blows of his heart. "I was sick. I am not strong yet. . . . May I come in?"

He stooped and laid his big black hat over the handle on his bag. It was a humble motion, almost a bow, that instantly struck him as absurd and betraying of all his weakness. He looked up at the woman, the wind blowing his hair. He might have continued for a long time in this unfamiliar attitude; he had never been a patient man, but when he was sick he had learned to sink submissively into the pillows, to wait for his medicine. He waited on the woman.

Then she, looking at him with blue eyes, turned and held open the door, and after a moment Bowman, as if convinced in this action, stood erect and followed her in.

Inside, the darkness of the house touched him like a professional hand, the doctor's. The woman set the half-cleaned lamp on a table in the center of the room and pointed, also like a professional person, a guide, to a chair with a yellow cowhide seat. She herself crouched on the hearth, drawing her knees up under the shapeless dress.

At first he felt hopefully secure. His heart was quieter. The room was enclosed in the gloom of yellow pine boards. He could see the other room, with the foot of an iron bed showing, across the passage. The bed had been made up with a red-and-yellow pieced quilt that looked like a map or a picture, a little like his grandmother's girlhood painting of Rome burning.

He had ached for coolness, but in this room it was cold. He stared at the hearth with dead coals lying on it and iron pots in the corners. The hearth and smoked chimney were of the stone he had seen ribbing the hills, mostly slate. Why is there no fire? he wondered.

And it was so still. The silence of the fields seemed to enter and move familiarly through the house. The wind used the open hall. He felt that he was in a mysterious, quiet, cool danger. It was necessary to do what? . . . To talk.

"I have a nice line of women's low-priced shoes . . ." he said.

But the woman answered, "Sonny 'll be here. He's strong. Sonny 'll move your car."

"Where is he now?"

"Farms for Mr. Redmond."

Mr. Redmond. Mr. Redmond. That was someone he would never have to encounter, and he was glad. Somehow the name did not appeal to him. . . . In a flare of touchiness and anxiety, Bowman wished to avoid even mention of unknown men and their unknown farms.

"Do you two live here alone?" He was surprised to hear his old voice, chatty, confidential, inflected for selling shoes, asking a question like that —a thing he did not even want to know.

"Yes. We are alone."

He was surprised at the way she answered. She had taken a long time to say that. She had nodded her head in a deep way too. Had she wished to affect him with some sort of premonition? he wondered unhappily. Or was it only that she would not help him, after all, by talking with him? For he was not strong enough to receive the impact of unfamiliar things without a little talk to break their fall. He had lived a month in which nothing had happened except in his head and his body—an almost inaudible life of heartbeats and dreams that came back, a life of fever and privacy, a delicate life which had left him weak to the point of—what? Of begging. The pulse in his palm leapt like a trout in a brook.

He wondered over and over why the woman did not go ahead with cleaning the lamp. What prompted her to stay there across the room, silently bestowing her presence upon him? He saw that with her it was not a time for doing little tasks. Her face was grave; she was feeling how right she was. Perhaps it was only politeness. In docility he held his eyes stiffly wide; they fixed themselves on the woman's clasped hands as though she held the cord they were strung on.

Then, "Sonny's coming," she said.

He himself had not heard anything, but there came a man passing the window and then plunging in at the door, with two hounds beside him. Sonny was a big enough man, with his belt slung low about his hips. He looked at least thirty. He had a hot, red face that was yet full of silence. He wore muddy blue pants and an old military coat stained and patched. World War? Bowman wondered. Great God, it was a Confederate coat. On the back of his light hair he had a wide filthy black hat which seemed to insult Bowman's own. He pushed down the dogs from his chest. He was strong, with dignity and heaviness in his way of moving. . . . There was the resemblance to his mother.

They stood side by side. . . . He must account again for his presence here.

"Sonny, this man, he had his car to run off over the prec'pice an' wants to know if you will git it out for him," the woman said after a few minutes.

Bowman could not even state his case.

Sonny's eyes lay upon him.

He knew he should offer explanations and show money — at least appear either penitent or authoritative. But all he could do was to shrug slightly.

Sonny brushed by him going to the window, followed by the eager dogs, and looked out. There was effort even in the way he was looking, as if he could throw his sight out like a rope. Without turning Bowman felt that his own eyes could have seen nothing: it was too far.

"Got me a mule out there an' got me a block an' tackle," said Sonny meaningfully. "I *could* catch me my mule an' git me my ropes, an' before long I'd git your car out the ravine."

He looked completely around the room, as if in meditation, his eyes roving in their own distance. Then he pressed his lips firmly and yet shyly together, and with the dogs ahead of him this time, he lowered his head and strode out. The hard earth sounded, cupping to his powerful way of walking—almost a stagger.

Mischievously, at the suggestion of those sounds, Bowman's heart leapt again. It seemed to walk about inside him.

"Sonny's goin' to do it," the woman said. She said it again, singing it almost, like a song. She was sitting in her place by the hearth.

Without looking out, he heard some shouts and the dogs barking and the pounding of hoofs in short runs on the hill. In a few minutes Sonny passed under the window with a rope, and there was a brown mule with quivering, shining, purple-looking ears. The mule actually looked in the window. Under its eyelashes it turned target-like eyes into his. Bowman averted his head and saw the woman looking serenely back at the mule, with only satisfaction in her face.

She sang a little more, under her breath. It occurred to him, and it seemed quite marvelous, that she was not really talking to him, but rather following the thing that came about with words that were unconscious and part of her looking.

So he said nothing, and this time when he did not reply he felt a curious and strong emotion, not fear, rise up in him.

This time, when his heart leapt, something—his soul—seemed to leap too, like a little colt invited out of a pen. He stared at the woman while the frantic nimbleness of his feeling made his head sway. He could not move; there was nothing he could do, unless perhaps he might embrace this woman who sat there growing old and shapeless before him.

But he wanted to leap up, to say to her, I have been sick and I found out then, only then, how lonely I am. Is it too late? My heart puts up a struggle inside me, and you may have heard it, protesting against emptiness. . . . It should be full, he would rush on to tell her, thinking of his heart now as a deep lake, it should be holding love like other hearts. It should be flooded with love. There would be a warm spring day. . . . Come and stand in my heart, whoever you are, and a whole river would cover your feet and rise higher and take your knees in whirlpools, and draw you down to itself, your whole body, your heart too.

But he moved a trembling hand across his eyes, and looked at the placid crouching woman across the room. She was still as a statue. He felt ashamed and exhausted by the thought that he might, in one more moment, have tried by simple words and embraces to communicate some strange thing — something which seemed always to have just escaped him. . . .

Sunlight touched the furthest pot on the hearth. It was late afternoon. This time tomorrow he would be somewhere on a good graveled road, driving his car past things that happened to people, quicker than their happening. Seeing ahead to the next day, he was glad, and knew that this was no time to embrace an old woman. He could feel in his pounding temples the readying of his blood for motion and for hurrying away.

"Sonny's hitched up your car by now," said the woman. "He'll git it out the ravine right shortly."

"Fine!" he cried with his customary enthusiasm.

Yet it seemed a long time that they waited. It began to get dark. Bowman was cramped in his chair. Any man should know enough to get up and walk around while he waited. There was something like guilt in such stillness and silence.

But instead of getting up, he listened.... His breathing restrained, his eyes powerless in the growing dark, he listened uneasily for a warning sound, forgetting in wariness what it would be. Before long he heard something—soft, continuous, insinuating.

"What's that noise?" he asked, his voice jumping into the dark. Then wildly he was afraid it would be his heart beating so plainly in the quiet room, and she would tell him so.

"You might hear the stream," she said grudgingly.

Her voice was closer. She was standing by the table. He wondered why she did not light the lamp. She stood there in the dark and did not light it.

Bowman would never speak to her now, for the time was past. I'll sleep in the dark, he thought, in his bewilderment pitying himself.

Heavily she moved on to the window. Her arm, vaguely white, rose straight from her full side and she pointed out into the darkness.

"That white speck's Sonny," she said, talking to herself.

He turned unwillingly and peered over her shoulder; he hesitated to rise and stand beside her. His eyes searched the dusky air. The white speck floated smoothly toward her finger, like a leaf on a river, growing whiter in the dark. It was as if she had shown him something secret, part of her life, but had offered no explanation. He looked away. He was moved almost to tears, feeling for no reason that she had made a silent declaration equivalent to his own. His hand waited upon his chest.

Then a step shook the house, and Sonny was in the room. Bowman felt how the woman left him there and went to the other man's side.

"I done got your car out, mister," said Sonny's voice in the dark. "She's settin' a-waitin' in the road, turned to go back where she come from."

"Fine!" said Bowman, projecting his own voice to loudness. "I'm surely much obliged—I could never have done it myself—I was sick...."

"I could do it easy," said Sonny.

Bowman could feel them both waiting in the dark, and he could hear the dogs panting out in the yard, waiting to bark when he should go. He felt strangely helpless and resentful. Now that he could go, he longed to stay. From what was he being deprived? His chest was rudely shaken by the violence of his heart. These people cherished something here that he could not see, they withheld some ancient promise of food and warmth and light. Between them they had a conspiracy. He thought of the way she had moved away from him and gone to Sonny, she had flowed toward him. He was shaking with cold, he was tired, and it was not fair. Humbly and yet angrily he stuck his hand into his pocket.

"Of course I'm going to pay you for everything—"

"We don't take money for such," said Sonny's voice belligerently.

"I want to pay. But do something more. . . . Let me stay—tonight. . . ." He took another step toward them. If only they could see him, they would know his sincerity, his real need! His voice went on, "I'm not very strong yet, I'm not able to walk far, even back to my car, maybe, I don't know— I don't know exactly where I am—"

He stopped. He felt as if he might burst into tears. What would they think of him!

Sonny came over and put his hands on him. Bowman felt them pass (they were professional too) across his chest, over his hips. He could feel Sonny's eyes upon him in the dark.

"You ain't no revenuer come sneakin' here, mister, ain't got no gun?"

To this end of nowhere! And yet *he* had come. He made a grave answer. "No."

"You can stay."

"Sonny," said the woman, "you'll have to borry some fire."

"I'll go git it from Redmond's," said Sonny.

"What?" Bowman strained to hear their words to each other.

"Our fire, it's out, and Sonny's got to borry some, because its dark an' cold," she said.

"But matches—I have matches—"

"We don't have no need for 'em," she said proudly. "Sonny's goin' after his own fire."

"I'm goin' to Redmond's," said Sonny with an air of importance, and he went out.

After they had waited a while, Bowman looked out the window and saw a light moving over the hill. It spread itself out like a little fan. It zig-zagged along the field, darting and swift, not like Sonny at all. . . . Soon enough, Sonny staggered in, holding a burning stick behind him in tongs, fire flowing in his wake, blazing light into the corners of the room.

"We'll make a fire now," the woman said, taking the brand.

When that was done she lit the lamp. It showed its dark and light. The whole room turned golden-yellow like some sort of flower, and the walls smelled of it and seemed to tremble with the quiet rushing of the fire and the waving of the burning lampwick in its funnel of light.

The woman moved among the iron pots. With the tongs she dropped hot coals on top of the iron lids. They made a set of soft vibrations, like the sound of a bell far away.

She looked up and over at Bowman, but he could not answer. He was trembling. . . .

. . .

"Have a drink, mister?" Sonny asked. He had brought in a chair from the other room and sat astride it with his folded arms across the back. Now we are all visible to one another, Bowman thought, and cried, "Yes sir, you bet, thanks!"

"Come after me and do just what I do," said Sonny.

It was another excursion into the dark. They went through the hall, out to the back of the house, past a shed and a hooded well. They came to a wilderness of thicket.

"Down on your knees," said Sonny.

"What?" Sweat broke out on his forehead.

He understood when Sonny began to crawl through a sort of tunnel that the bushes made over the ground. He followed, startled in spite of himself when a twig or a thorn touched him gently without making a sound, clinging to him and finally letting him go.

Sonny stopped crawling and, crouched on his knees, began to dig with both his hands into the dirt. Bowman shyly struck matches and made a light. In a few minutes Sonny pulled up a jug. He poured out some of the whisky into a bottle from his coat pocket, and buried the jug again. "You never know who's liable to knock at your door," he said, and laughed. "Start back," he said, almost formally. "Ain't no need for us to drink out-doors, like hogs."

At the table by the fire, sitting opposite each other in their chairs, Sonny and Bowman took drinks out of the bottle, passing it across. The dogs slept; one of them was having a dream.

"This is good," said Bowman. "This is what I needed." It was just as though he were drinking the fire off the hearth.

"He makes it," said the woman with quiet pride.

She was pushing the coals off the pots, and the smells of corn bread and coffee circled the room. She set everything on the table before the men, with a bone-handled knife stuck into one of the potatoes, splitting out its golden fiber. Then she stood for a minute looking at them, tall and full above them where they sat. She leaned a little toward them.

"You all can eat now," she said, and suddenly smiled.

Bowman had just happened to be looking at her. He set his cup back on the table in unbelieving protest. A pain pressed at his eyes. He saw that she was not an old woman. She was young, still young. He could think of no number of years for her. She was the same age as Sonny, and she belonged to him. She stood with the deep dark corner of the room behind her, the shifting yellow light scattering over her head and her gray form-less dress, trembling over her tall body when it bent over them in its sud-den communication. She was young. Her teeth were shining and her eyes glowed. She turned and walked slowly and heavily out of the room, and he heard her sit down on the cot and then lie down. The pattern on the quilt moved.

"She's goin' to have a baby," said Sonny, popping a bite into his mouth.

Bowman could not speak. He was shocked with knowing what was really in this house. A marriage, a fruitful marriage. That simple thing. Anyone could have had that.

Somehow he felt unable to be indignant or protest, although some sort of joke had certainly been played upon him. There was nothing remote or mysterious here — only something private. The only secret was the ancient communication between two people. But the memory of the woman's waiting silently by the cold hearth, of the man's stubborn journey a mile away to get fire, and how they finally brought out their food and drink and filled the room proudly with all they had to show, was suddenly too clear and too enormous within him for response. . . .

"You ain't as hungry as you look," said Sonny.

The woman came out of the bedroom as soon as the men had finished, and ate her supper while her husband stared peacefully into the fire.

Then they put the dogs out, with the food that was left.

"I think I'd better sleep here by the fire, on the floor," said Bowman.

He felt that he had been cheated, and that he could afford now to be generous. Ill though he was, he was not going to ask them for their bed. He was through with asking favors in this house, now that he understood what was there.

"Sure, mister."

But he had not known yet how slowly he understood. They had not meant to give him their bed. After a little interval they both rose and looking at him gravely went into the other room.

He lay stretched by the fire until it grew low and dying. He watched every tongue of blaze lick out and vanish. "There will be special reduced prices on all footwear during the month of January," he found himself repeating quietly, and then he lay with his lips tight shut.

How many noises the night had! He heard the stream running, the fire dying, and he was sure now that he heard his heart beating, too, the sound it made under his ribs. He heard breathing, round and deep, of the man and his wife in the room across the passage. And that was all. But emotion swelled patiently within him, and he wished that the child were his.

He must get back to where he had been before. He stood weakly before the red coals and put on his overcoat. It felt too heavy on his shoulders. As he started out he looked and saw that the woman had never got through with cleaning the lamp. On some impulse he put all the money from his billfold under its fluted glass base, almost ostentatiously.

Ashamed, shrugging a little, and then shivering, he took his bags and went out. The cold of the air seemed to lift him bodily. The moon was in the sky.

On the slope he began to run, he could not help it. Just as he reached the road, where his car seemed to sit in the moonlight like a boat, his heart began to give off tremendous explosions like a rifle, bang bang bang.

He sank in fright onto the road, his bags falling about him. He felt as if all this had happened before. He covered his heart with both hands to keep anyone from hearing the noise it made.

But nobody heard it.

from *Lanterns on the Levee*

William Alexander Percy (1885–1942)

William Alexander Percy enjoyed a youth of privilege in Greenville, Mississippi. The son of a prosperous planter-lawyer, he was educated at Sewanee College and Harvard Law School. While he enjoyed some minor success as a poet, following law school he returned to Mississippi where, in the course of his father's unsuccessful reelection campaign for U.S. Senate, he was introduced to the rough-and-tumble world of Mississippi politics. Resigned to live in a world he found increasingly chaotic, Percy dedicated himself to raising his dead cousin's three sons — one of whom was the future novelist Walker Percy. He composed *Lanterns on the Levee*, published in 1941, as an homage to his ancestors, an example to his young nephews, and an answer to critics of the South.

Gervys Lusk left home a wastrel and returned a hero; he departed with a black eye and came back with a D.S.C. During that spirtual interregnum when both of us were fumbling to become good citizens (an undertaking in which he was entirely successful) Gervys confided to me that the home town had felt distinctly let down when I returned from the wars intact. It reasoned that not having been outstandingly useful — "indispensable" would have been Major Jones's adjective — I could have afforded to be ornamental by making "the supreme sacrifice." I was cast for the role — a poet (so they had heard), young (at least youngish), slender (thin, in moments of non-exaltation). It seemed churlish of me not to have seized the opportunity. I felt rather the same way about it, now that the opportunity was safely out of hand.

My destiny apparently is to pick up the pieces and start over. A lame start it was in 1919. I spent the first few months tinkering with the manuscript of *In April Once* and almost ruined it — April was over; I made numerous speeches over the state for something like the Second Liberty Loan; for six months I again taught at Sewanee, and would probably be teaching there now had not one or two of the dignitaries questioned my papist affiliations. Briefly I did a deal of floundering before I could settle down all over again to living, mere living.

During that period I evidently did some thinking about our Southern race problem because I recently came across this letter addressed to the *New Republic* (though of course never published nor acknowledged):

Sewanee, Tennessee
September 6, 1919

The New Republic
New York City

Sirs:

Your intellectual fearlessness and sincerity prompt me to write you regarding the recent outbreak of lawlessness in Knoxville, Tennessee, which the newspapers have delighted to call a "race riot." I am an average educated Southerner and I want to give you the point of view of my class. The Northern press will doubtless see in this occurrence merely another instance of what it imagines to be the South's hostility and cruelty to the Negro, its inability to deal justly with him without Northern interference. But the moral is not so stereotyped. Viewed in its true relations, the Knoxville outrage is indicative of a situation more complex, and full of pathos, and difficult of adjustment, than any our well-meaning Northern friends conceive. This was no race riot. It was a burst of hoodlumism which protected itself under the local excitement and indignation at a ghastly and terrifying crime committed by a Negro.

It is clear from the newspaper reports that the mob at first made no attack on the Negroes, but turned against the jail from which they know the Negro they wanted had been taken. The jail was wrecked, the criminals within released, jail records and property destroyed or stolen, and finally the house of the sheriff, who at that time was on his way to Chattanooga with the prisoner, ransacked and rifled. Hardware stores were next broken into for ammunition and arms. Thereafter conflicts between these hoodlums and terrified blacks were inevitable. A good Southerner considers this incident, as does any other good American, a national disgrace.

You in the North always assume there are two attitudes toward the race question — one pre-empted by the enlightened benign citizen of Northern birth, the other peculiar to the narrow heartless citizen of Southern birth. There is no such difference. I live in the Mississippi Delta, where a full half of the white population, outnumbered ten to one by the Negro population, is Northern by birth and rearing. Yet the attitude of that one half differs in no wise from the attitude of the other half born and bred in the South. Under similar conditions, and it matters not where those conditions arise, it may be Chicago, South Africa, Washington, or Knoxville, white men of Anglo-Saxon descent, whether Northern or Southern born, act in precisely the same way toward the Negro. Inhabitants of Maine, and France and Finland, can afford to toy mentally with the race problem and the theories they arrive at may be widely divergent. But among white men for whom the problem is a bitter and pressing fact, who live with it, there is no difference of opinion as to the problem's solution, based on difference of place of birth or of education. There is only a difference on this as on all questions between those Southerners who through poverty, lack of inheritance, and ignorance misunderstand and dislike the Negro, and those who by training and opportunity feel themselves his friend and protector.

Here are the two questions, or rather the two phases of one question, with which we live: first, how best to protect and educate and deal fairly with a race which at its present stage of development is inferior in character and intellect to our own (this is the phase of the question in which the North is perennially interested); second, how best to develop so upright a character in our own people that they will resist the ever present temptation to prey and batten on this inferior race (this is the phase of the question in which the North is never interested, of which indeed it is hardly cognizant). To solve these questions in wisdom, justice, and kindness is difficult under any circumstances, but there are thousands of unadvertised leaders of thought in the South capable of working out such a solution if left to themselves — not quickly nor easily, but through the years. And they are the only people who can: it is their problem, their burden, their heavy heritage.

And the Knoxville crime illustrates the strongest force against which these leaders have to fight; to wit, the lawlessness and hoodlumism of our uneducated whites. The same force at work in politics produces vicious unworthy Southern governors and congressmen. Our fight to protect the Negro is merely part of our fight for decency in politics, for law-enforcement. The fight is often lost, but it never ceases; indeed, it gains in strength and in the end it is certain of victory.

You will wonder perhaps why I am telling you our troubles. My reason is quite simple: I want you to know why it is that we whose hearts are essentially as yours in this matter fear unjust criticism, unwise advice from the North. It makes a good Southerner's task only the harder. We could afford to be indifferent to your misunderstanding were it not that the inflammable, uneducated whites whom the best part of our lives is spent in controlling and teaching seize on the indiscreet utterances and unmerited strictures of the Northern press as excuses for their own excesses and injustices. Nor is the effect on the Negro himself less deplorable. Doing no good in themselves, these utterances and strictures greatly lessen our force for good.

To you our tragic situation, calling for courage and wisdom and unselfishness and patience, is a theory, a subject for criticism, suggested panaceas, scorn. We know the solution, the only one; for there is no short cut. It is in the first place education for the whites and in the second education, simple and practical, for the Negro. For the rest common kindness must be the guide in this as in all human affairs. My plea to you is that you trust us who are fighting the fight in the South, and that you accept my assurance we are not a corporal's guard.

Respectfully yours,
W. A. *Percy*

I drag in this communication because after twenty years it still seems to me to point out the South's two major deficiencies—character and education—which, after all, are world deficiencies, and to indicate the lines along which the "solution" of our race problem must proceed. Of course the letter expresses the Southern point of view of a so-called conservative, which is deplored to the point of tears by the so-called liberals. There's an enduring quality to truth exceedingly irritating to fidgety minds. In the South our anxiety is not to find new ideas, but to bring to realization old ones which have been tested and proved by years of anguish—a far more difficult undertaking. We Southerners aren't as bright as we are right. But when we do hit on a new idea, it's not only wrong, it's inconceivable.

The years following the war were a time of confusion not only to ex-soldiers but to all Americans. The tension of high endeavor and unselfish effort snapped, and Americans went "ornery." In the South the most vital matter became the price of cotton, in the North the price of commodities. Idealism was followed by the grossest materialism, which continues to be the order of the day.

Our town of about ten thousand population was no better or worse, I imagine, than other little Southern towns. My townsfolk had got along pretty well together—we knew each other so well and had suffered so much together. But we hadn't suffered a common disaster, one that was local and our very own, like a flood or a yellow-fever epidemic, since the flood of 1913, and that had failed as a binder because it didn't flood the town. Unbeknownst, strangers had drifted in since the war—from the hills, from the North, from all sorts of odd places where they hadn't succeeded or hadn't been wanted. We had changed our country attractively for them. Malaria had been about stamped out; electric fans and ice had lessened the terror of our intolerable summer heat; we had good roads and drainage and schools, and our lands were the most fertile in the world. We had made the Delta a good place in which to live by our determination and our ability to endure hardships, and now other folks were attracted by the result of our efforts. The town was changing, but so insidiously that the old-timers could feel but could not analyze the change. The newcomers weren't foreigners or Jews, they were an alien breed of Anglo-Saxon.

Although I was always traveling to strange places, I loved Greenville and never wanted any other place for home. Returning to it was the most exciting part of a trip. You could find friendly idlers round the post-office steps pretending they were waiting for the mail. You could take a coke any time of day with someone full of important news. There'd be amiable people running in and out of the house, without knocking, for tennis or golf or bridge or poker or to join you at a meal or just to talk. It was a lovable town.

I suppose the trait that distinguished it from neighboring towns was a certain laxity in church matters. We didn't regard drunkenness and lechery, Sabbath-breaking and gambling as more than poor judgment or poor taste. What we were slow to forgive was hardness of heart and all unkindness. Perhaps we were overstocked with sinners and pariahs and publicans, but they kept the churches in their places and preserved the tradition of sprightliness. Of course we had church folk, plenty of them — Episcopalians, not numerous but up-stage, whose forebears came from Virginia, Kentucky, or South Carolina; Catholics from Italy or Ireland or New Orleans; Methodists, indigenous and prolific; Baptists, who loved Methodists less but Catholics least, swarms of them; Presbyterians, not directly from Geneva or Edinburgh, but aged in the wood, fairly mellow considering they were predestined; and Jews too much like natives even to be overly prosperous. There were bickerings and fights during election time, but day in and day out we were pretty cozy and neighborly, and nobody cared what to hell was the other fellow's route to heaven. There was no embattled aristocracy, for the descendants of the old-timers were already a rather seedy remnant, and there was no wealth. White folks and colored folks—that's what we were—and some of us were nice and some weren't.

I never thought of Masons. Most of my friends wore aprons at funerals and fezzes (over vine leaves) at knightly convocations. Even Père had been a Mason, to the scandal of the Church and the curtailment of his last rites, but he took it easy. I thought Masonry a good thing for those who liked that sort of thing.

We had read in the newspapers that over in Atlanta some fraud was claiming to have revived the old Ku Klux Klan which during reconstruction days had played so desperate but on the whole so helpful a part in keeping the peace and preventing mob violence. This Atlanta monstrosity was not even a bastard of the old organization which General Forrest had headed and disbanded. This thing obviously was a money-making scheme without ideals or ideas. We were amused and uninterested. Even in Forrest's day the Klan had never been permitted to enter our country. It couldn't happen here. But reports of the Atlanta organization's misdeeds—masked night parades to terrorize the Negro, threatening letters, forcible closing of dance-halls and dives, whippings, kidnappings, violent brutalities — crowded the headlines. As citizens of the South we were ashamed; as citizens of Greenville we were not apprehensive.

Then in the spring of 1922 a "Colonel" Camp was advertised to speak in our courthouse for the purpose of forming a branch of the Klan in Greenville. Thoroughly aroused, we debated whether to permit the speech in the courthouse or to answer it there. We couldn't learn who had invited him to speak or who had given him permission to use the court-

house, but evidently some of our own people were already Klansmen —
fifth-column tactic before there was a Hitler. Our best citizens, those who
thought for the common good, met in Father's office and agreed almost
unanimously that the Colonel should be answered and by Father.

The Klan organizer made an artful speech to a tense crowd that packed
every cranny of the room; and every man was armed. Who killed Garfield?
A Catholic. Who assassinated President McKinley? A Catholic. Who had
recently bought a huge tract of land opposite West Point and another
overlooking Washington? The Pope. Convents were brothels, the confes-
sional a place of seduction, the basement of every Catholic church an
arsenal. The Pope was about to seize the government. To the rescue,
Klansmen! These were statements which any trained mind recognized as
lies, but which no man without weeks of ridiculous research could disprove. It was an example of Nazi propaganda before there were Nazis. The
very enormity and insolence of the lie carried conviction to the simple
and the credulous. The Colonel was listened to with courtesy.

To his surprise, Father answered him: he had never been answered
before. I have never heard a speech that was so exciting and so much fun.
The crowd rocked and cheered. Father's ridicule was amusing but bitter;
and as he continued, it became more bitter, until it wasn't funny, it was
terrifying. And the Colonel was terrified: he expected to be torn limb
from limb by the mob. I don't blame him. At the close of Father's speech
the crowd went quite mad, surging about, shouting and cheering, and
thoroughly dangerous. A resolution was passed condemning the Klan.
Colonel Camp scuttled out of a side door, appealing to a passing deputy
for protection. The deputy, an Irish Catholic and the kindliest of men (out
of *Henry IV*), escorted him ceremoniously to his hotel.

It was a triumphant meeting, but for the next two years our town was
disintegrated by a bloodless, cruel warfare, more bitter and unforgiving
than anything I encountered at the front. In the trenches soldiers felt
sorry for one another, whether friend or enemy. In Father's senatorial
fight, we were surrounded by ferocious stupidity rather than by hatred. But
in the Klan fight the very spirit of hatred materialized before our eyes. It
was the ugliest thing I have ever beheld. You didn't linger on the post-
office steps or drink cokes with random companions: too many faces were
hard and set, too many eyes were baleful and venomous. You couldn't go
a block without learning by a glance that someone hated you.

The Klan did not stand for, but against. It stood against Catholics, Jews,
Negroes, foreigners, and sin. In our town it chose Catholics as the object
of its chief persecution. Catholic employees were fired, Catholic business-
men were boycotted, Catholic office-holders opposed. At first this seemed
strange to me, because our Catholics were a small and obscure minority,

but I came to learn with astonishment that of all the things hated in the South, more hated than the Jew or the Negro or sin itself, is Rome. The evangelical sects and Rome — as different and uncomprehending of each other as youth and old age! One seems never to have glimpsed the sorrowful pageant of the race and the other, profoundly disillusioned, profoundly compassionate, sees only the pageant. One has the enthusiasm and ignorance of the pioneer, the other the despair of the sage. One's a cheer-leader, the other an old sad-eyed family doctor from Samaria. We discovered that the Klan had its genesis, as far as our community was involved, in the Masonic Temple. The state head of that fraternal organization, a well-meaning old simpleton, had been preaching anti-Catholicism for years when conferring Masonic degrees. He joined the Klan early and induced other Masonic leaders to follow his example. These composed the Klan leadership in our county, though they were aided by a few politicians who knew better but who craved the Klan vote. It was a pretty leadership — fanatics and scalawag politicians. But not all Masons or all the godly were so misguided. The opposition to the Klan at home was led by a Protestant committee (and every denomination was represented in its ranks), who fought fearlessly, intelligently, and unceasingly this evil which they considered as unchristian as it was un-American. Father was not only head of the Protestant anti-Klan committee but of the anti-Klan forces in the South. He spoke as far north as Chicago and published probably the first article on the Klan in any distinguished magazine. It was reprinted from the *Atlantic Monthly* and distributed over the whole country. He felt the Klan was the sort of public evil good citizens could not ignore. Not to fight it was ineffectual and craven.

It's hard to conceive of the mumbo-jumbo ritual of the Klan and its half-wit principles — only less absurd than the Nazi principles of Aryan superiority and lebensraum — as worthy of an adult mind's attention. But when your living, your self-respect, and your life are threatened, you don't laugh at that which threatens. If you have either sense or courage you fight it. We fought, and it was high time someone did.

The Klan's increasing atrocities culminated in the brutal murders at Mer Rouge, where Skipwith was Cyclops. Mer Rouge is across the river from us, on the Louisiana side. It is very near and the murders were very ghastly. The Klan loathed and feared Father more than any other man in the South. For months I never let him out of my sight and of course we both went armed. Never before nor since have our doors been shut and locked at night.

One Sunday night of torrential rain when Father, Aunt Lady, and I sat in the library and Mother was ill upstairs I answered a knock at the door. It was early and I opened the door without apprehension. A dark, heavy-set man with two days' growth of beard and a soft-brimmed black hat stood there, drenched to the skin. He asked for Father and I, to his obvious surprise, invited him in. He wouldn't put down his hat, but held it in front of him. I didn't like his looks, so while Father talked to him I played the piano softly in the adjoining room and listened. The man's story was that he came from near our plantation, his car had run out of gas a few miles from town, he'd left his sister in the car and walked to town, he couldn't find a service station open, and would Father help him? Father, all sympathy, started phoning. The stranger seemed neither interested nor appreciative. I watched him with mounting suspicion. Father's effort to find a service station open having failed, he said: "My car is here. We might run out and get your sister—I suppose you can drive my car?" The stranger brightened and observed he could drive any make of car. The two of them were still near the phone when Father's three bridge cronies came stamping in, laughing and shaking out the rain. As they came toward Father, the stranger brushed past them and had reached the door when I overtook him. "Say, what's the matter with you?" I asked. "Wait a minute and some of us will get you fixed up." He mumbled: "Got to take a leak," walked into the rain, and disappeared.

We waited for him, but we did not see him again for two years. Then he was in jail charged with a string of robberies. When he saw I recognized him, he grinned sourly and remarked: "Old Skip nearly put that one over." He refused to enlarge on this statement, which presumably referred to Skipwith, Cyclops of Mer Rouge. We found from the neighbors that the night of his visit to us he had arrived in a car with another man and parked across the street from our house.

It looked too much like an attempt at kidnapping and murder for me to feel easy. I went to the office of the local Cyclops. He was an inoffensive little man, a great Mason, and partial to anti-Catholic tirades. I said: "I want to let you know one thing: if anything happens to my Father or to any of our friends you will be killed. We won't hunt for the guilty party. So far as we are concerned the guilty party will be you."

There were no atrocities, no whippings, no threatening letters, no masked parades in our town. The local Klan bent all of its efforts toward electing one of its members sheriff. If they could have the law-enforcement machinery under their control, they could then flout the law and perpetrate such outrages as appealed to them. Our fight became a political fight to prevent the election of the Klan's choice for sheriff. The whole town was involved and the excitement was at fever heat. What appalled and terrified us most was the mendacity of Klan members. You never knew if the man you were talking to was a Klansman and a spy. Like German parachute jumpers, they appeared disguised as friends. For the Klan advised its members to lie about their affiliation with the order, about anything that concerned another Klansman's welfare, and about anything pertaining to the Klan—and its members took the advice. The most poisonous thing the Klan did to our town was to rob its citizens of their faith and trust in one another. Everyone was under suspicion: from Klansmen you could expect neither frankness nor truth nor honor, and you couldn't tell who was a Klansman. If they were elected judges and law-enforcement officers, we would be cornered into servility or assassination.

Our candidate for sheriff was George B. Alexander, a powerful, square-bearded, Kentucky aristocrat drawn by Holbein. He was one of those people who are always right by no discernible mental process. His fearlessness, warm-heartedness, and sheer character made him a person you liked to be with and for. He was Father's favorite hunting companion and friend.

On election night the town was beside itself with excitement. Crowds filled the streets outside the voting booths to hear the counting of the ballots as it progressed. Everyone realized the race was close and whoever won would win by the narrowest of margins. The whole population was in the street, milling, apprehensive, silent. When the count began, Father went home and started a bridge game. I waited at the polls. About nine o'clock a sweating individual with his collar unbuttoned and his wide red face smeared with tears rushed out on the steps and bellowed: "We've won, we've won! Alexander's elected! God damn the Klan!" Pandemonium broke loose. Men yelled and screamed and hugged one another. Our town was saved, we had whipped the Klan and were safe. I ran home with the news and Father's bridge game broke up in a stillness of thanksgiving that was almost religious.

Mother was away. Being a Frenchwoman, she had been neither hysterical nor sentimental during the months and months of tension and danger. But none of us knew what she went through silently and it was then that her health began to fail.

While we were talking about the victory, a tremendous uproar came to us from the street. We rushed out on the gallery. From curb to curb the street was filled with a mad marching crowd carrying torches and singing. They swarmed down the street and into our yard. It was a victory celebration. Father made a speech, everybody made a speech, nobody listened and everybody cheered. Klansmen had taken to cover, but the rest of the town was there, seething over the yard and onto the gallery. They cut Mr. Alexander's necktie to bits for souvenirs. And still they cheered and swarmed.

Father, nonplussed, turned to Adah and me and laughed: "They don't seem to have any idea of going home and I haven't a drop of whisky in the house—at least, I'm not going to waste my *good* liquor on them." Adah and Charlie dashed off in their car and returned with four kegs. Father called to the crowd: "Come on in, boys," and into the house they poured. That was a party never to be forgotten. While Adah was gone, Lucille and her band appeared, unsummoned save by instinct. Lucille, weighing twenty stone, airily pulled the grand piano into her lap, struck one tremendous chord — my Steinway's been swayback ever since — and the dancing began. Adah never touches a drop, but she mixes a mighty punch. Things got under way. There were few inhibitions and no social distinctions. Dancers bumped into knots of heroes who told one another at the same time their harrowing exploits and unforgettable adventures. A banker's wife hobnobbed with the hot-tamale man, a lawyer's careened with a bootlegger. People who hadn't spoken for years swore deathless loyalty on one another's shoulders. The little town had come through, righteousness had prevailed, we had fought the good fight and for once had won. Everybody was affectionate with everybody else, all men were equal, and all were brothers-in-arms.

Hazlewood, the gentlest and most courageous of men, kept on making speeches from the front gallery long after his audience had adjourned to the dining-room and were gyrating like flies around Adah. He was so mortified at this treatment (when it came to his attention) that he joined them and was consoled and liberally refreshed. When at a late hour he started to leave, he couldn't find his hat and became whimpery. After discovering it under the radiator, he couldn't pick it up. When he was hatted at last and started on his way, Fletcher met him on the steps, gasped: "Oh, Hazlewood!" and kissed him. Hazlewood exclaimed! "Fletch, Fletch, you shouldn't have done that," burst into tears, and walked home down the middle of the street, sobbing bitterly.

From down Lake Washington way the swarthy tribe of Steins journeyed in, all seven of them, one behind another, the old man, broad-shouldered, arrogant, and goateed, leading the advance through the side door. You felt certain they'd left a tent and a string of camels under the porte-cochere. Solemnly they shook hands with everyone down the line, curved into the dining-room around the punch bowl, shook hands again, told everyone good-night, and left through the front door. We had barely recovered from this princely visitation when they again hove into view through the side door, went through the same exchange of courtesies, pausing a bit longer at the punch bowl, and disappeared out the front door. All during the evening, just about time you were getting settled in your mind, this apparition of a Tartar tribe would materialize, unhinge you, and withdraw, always with decorum but with mounting elation. The last time I expected them to produce cymbals and go to it, but instead Mrs. Stein staged a thrilling fandango with Mr. George B.

Old man Finch, bolt upright in a throne-like chair, fell sound asleep in the very center of the revelry. Well-wishers bore him to a car, drove him home, and deposited him with the greatest tact in the swing on his own front gallery. Later he fell off and cut his forehead. Wakened by the bump, his daughters swarmed out, found him unconscious and bathed in blood, summoned half the doctors in town, and went to keening. Next morning Louise telephoned asking if I'd found Papa's teeth. I'm afraid another guest wore them off.

Long after midnight I looked into the pantry and beheld my favorite barber, a plumber acquaintance, an ex-sergeant, and the hot-tamale man seated at the pantry table eating supper. They'd raided the ice-box and found besides a bottle of liquor. They graciously invited me to join them. Instead I routed out my husky soldier friend, Howard Shields, and admonished him to get those people out of the house, one way or another. Howard bowed stiffly and answered: "Certainly, leave it to me." A bit later I again looked into the pantry; Howard was standing with a glass full of straight whisky in his hand making an undisciplined speech about the virtues of his squad. His four listeners beamed foolishly. One of them managed to observe: "Didn't know Howard waised squabs," and went off into giggles, then into hiccups, then into tears. I addressed Howard sternly: "Go to bed," and he disappeared upstairs. On the way to my room I looked in on him: he was sound asleep. Actually, he hadn't taken off a stitch, he was lying under the sheet fully clothed and anticipating my inspection. The coast being clear, he slipped out, found his buddy, George Crittenden, knocked him cold, and lit out in his car for Clarksdale.

It was a memorable evening. On the way home people fell off bicycles and into gutters, ran over street signs and up trees—and all happy (except Hazlewood). The police radiantly gathered them up and located their destinations.

We decided it was just as well, after all, that Mother had been out of town. It wasn't her sort of party. She'd have started clearing the house at the first drunk, victory or no victory.

Our Ku Klux neighbors stood on their porch watching—justified and prophesying Judgment Day.

It had been a great fight. It was also a ruthless searchlight on character, of one kind or another. My generation still remembers it, though it all happened eighteen or nineteen years ago, and that's a century of any other time. An old Klansman, one who, being educated, had no excuse for being one, asked me the other day why I'd never forgiven him. I had to answer: "Forgiveness is easy. I really like you. The trouble is I've got your number and people's numbers don't change."

from *Let Us Now Praise Famous Men*

James Agee (1909–1955)

Born and raised in east Tennessee, James Agee joined the ranks of Southern expatriates when, at the age of fifteen, he entered Phillips Exeter Academy in New Hampshire. A lackluster student, he developed a passion for writing that he nurtured through four years at Harvard. Upon graduation, Agee embarked on a writing career that would take him through the New York offices of *Fortune*, *Time*, and the *Nation*, and to the Hollywood studio of director John Huston. Despite his long absence, the South continued to stir Agee's imagination. In 1936, accompanied by photographer Walker Evans, Agee traveled to rural Alabama to prepare a story on cotton sharecroppers. What began as a *Fortune* magazine article turned into a five-year book project in which Agee examined the spiritual and material lives of three sharecropper families and his relationship to those families. Garnering little critical or popular acclaim when published in 1941, *Let Us Now Praise Famous Men* enjoyed a resurgence of popularity in the 1960s. Agee, who died of a heart attack in 1955, was awarded a Pulitzer Prize posthumously in 1957 for his novel *A Death in the Family*.

There are on this hill three such families I would tell you of: the Gudgers, who are sleeping in the next room; and the Woods, whose daughters are Emma and Annie Mae; and besides these, the Ricketts, who live on a little way beyond the Woods; and we reach them thus:

Leave this room and go very quietly down the open hall that divides the house, past the bedroom door, and the dog that sleeps outside it, and move on out into the open, the back yard, going up hill: between the tool shed and the hen house (the garden is on your left), and turn left at the long low shed that passes for a barn. Don't take the path to the left then: that only leads to the spring; but cut straight up the slope; and down the length of the cotton that is planted at the crest of it, and through a space of pine, hickory, dead logs and blackberry brambles (damp spider webs will bind on your face in the dark; but the path is easily enough followed); and out beyond this, across a great entanglement of clay ravines, which finally solidify into a cornfield. Follow this cornfield straight down a row, go through a barn, and turn left. There is a whole cluster of houses here; they are all negroes'; the shutters are drawn tight. You may or may not waken some dogs: if you do, you will hardly help but be frightened, for in a couple of minutes the whole country will be bellowing in the darkness, and it is over your movements at large at so late and still an hour of the night, and the sound, with the knowledge of wakened people, their heads lifted a little on the darkness from the crackling hard straw pillows of their iron beds, overcasts your very existence, in your own mind, with a complexion of guilt, stealth, and danger:

But they will quiet.

They will quiet, the lonely heads are relaxed into sleep; after a little the whippoorwills resume, their tireless whipping of the pastoral night, and the strong frogs; and you are on the road, and again up hill, that was met at those clustered houses; pines on your left, one wall of bristling cloud, and the lifted hill; the slow field raised, in the soft stare of the cotton, several acres, on the right; and on the left the woods yield off, a hundred yards; more cotton; and set back there, at the brim of the hill, the plain small house you see is Woods' house, that looks shrunken against its centers under the starlight, the tin roof scarcely taking sheen, the floated cotton staring:

The house a quarter-mile beyond, just on the right of the road, standing with shade trees, that is the Ricketts'. The bare dirt is more damp in the tempering shade; and damp, tender with rottenness, the ragged wood of the porch, that is so heavily littered with lard buckets, scraps of iron, bent wire, torn rope, old odors, those no longer useful things which on a farm are never thrown away. The trees: draft on their stalks their clouds of heavy season; the barn: shines on the perfect air; in the bare yard a twelve-foot flowering bush: in shroud of blown bloom slumbers, and within: naked, naked side by side those brothers and sisters, those most beautiful children; and the crazy, clownish, foxy father; and the mother; and the two old daughters; crammed on their stinking beds, are resting the night:

Fred, Sadie, Margaret, Paralee, Garvrin, Richard, Flora Merry Lee, Katy, Clair Bell; and the dogs, and the cats, and the hens, and the mules, and the hogs, and the cow, and the bull calf:

Woods, and his young wife, and her mother, and the young wife's daughter, and her son by Woods, and their baby daughter, and that heavy-browed beast which enlarges in her belly; Bud, and Ivy, and Miss-Molly, and Pearl, and Thomas, and Ellen, and the nameless plant of unknown sex; and the cat, and the dog, and the mule, and the hog, and the cow, and the hens, and the huddled chickens:

And George, and his wife, and her sister, and their children, and their animals; and the hung wasps, lancing mosquitoes, numbed flies, and browsing rats:

All, spreaded in high quietude on the hill:

. . .

Sadie the half-sister of Bud, and drowned in their remembrance: that long and spiral shaft they've climbed, from shacks on shale, rigid as corn on a cob, out of the mining country, the long wandering, her pride of beauty, his long strength in marriage, into this: this present time, and this near future:

George his lost birthright, bad land owned, and that boyhood among cedars and clean creeks where no fever laid its touch, and where in the luminous and great hollow night the limestone shone like sheep: and the strong, gay girls:

Fred, what of him: I can not guess. And Annie Mae, that hat; which still, so broken, the death odor of feathers and silk in menthol, is crumpled in a drawer; and those weeks when she was happy, and to her husband and to her heart it was pleasing to be alive:

She is dreaming now, with fear, of a shotgun: George has directed it upon her; and there is no trigger:

Ivy, and her mother: what are the dreams of dogs?

Margaret, of a husband, and strong land, and ladies nodding in the walks.

And all these children:

These children, still in the tenderness of their lives, who will draw their future remembrance, and their future sorrow, from this place: and the strangers, animals: for work, for death, for food: and the scant crops: doing their duty the best they can, like temperless and feeble-minded children: rest now, between the wrenchings of the sun:

O, we become old; it has been a long, long climb; there will not be much more of this; then we will rest: sorrow nor sweating nor aching back, sickness, nor pity, hope gone, heaven's deafness; nothing shall take or touch us more: not thunder nor the rustling worms nor scalding kettle nor weeping child shall rouse us where we rest: these things shall be the business of others: these things shall be the business of our children, and their children; we will rest:

In what way were we trapped? where, our mistake? what, where, how, when, what way, might all these things have been different, if only we had done otherwise? if only we might have known. Where lost that bright health of love that knew so surely it would stay; how, how did it sink away, beyond help, beyond hope, beyond desire, beyond remembrance; and where the weight and the wealth of that strong year when there was more to eat than we could hold, new clothes, a grafanola, and money in the bank? How, how did all this sink so swift away, like that grand august cloud who gathers — the day quiets dark and chills, and the leaves lather — and scarcely steams the land? How are these things?

In the years when we lived down by the river we had all the fish we wanted, and yellow milk, enough to sell, and we bought two mules:

When we moved in here I wanted to make the house pretty, I folded a lot of pattern-paper and cut it into a pretty lace pattern and hung it on the mantelpiece: but now I just don't care any longer, I don't care how anything looks:

My mother made me the prettiest kind of a dress, all fresh for school; I wore it the first day, and everyone laughed and poked fun at me; it wasn't like other dresses, neither the cloth, nor the way it was cut, and I never . . .

I made her such a pretty dress and she wore it once, and she never wore it away from home again:

Oh, thank God not one of you knows how everyone snickers at your father.

I reckon we're just about the *meanest* people in this whole country.

George Gudger? Where'd you dig *him* up? I haven't been back out that road in twenty-five year.

Fred Ricketts? Why, that dirty son-of-a-bitch, he *brags* that he hasn't bought his family a bar of soap in five year.

Ricketts? They're a bad lot. They've got Miller blood mixed up in them. The children are a bad problem in school.

Why, Ivy Pritchert was one of the worst whores in this whole part of the country: only one that was worse was her own mother. They're about the lowest trash you can find.

Why, she had her a man back in the woods for years before *he* married her; had two children by him.

Gudger? He's a fair farmer. Fair cotton farmer, but he hain't got a mite a sense.

None of these people has any sense, nor any initiative. If they did, they wouldn't be farming on shares.

Give them money and all they'll do with it is throw it away.

Why, times when I envy them. No risk, we take all the risk; all the clothes they need to cover them; food coming up right out of their land.

So you're staying out at Gudgers', are you? And how do you like the food they give you? Yeah, aheh-heh-heh-heh, how do you like that fine home cookin'; how do you like that good wholesome country food?

Tell you the honest truth, they owe us a big debt. Now you just tell me, if you can, what would all those folks be doing if it wasn't for us?

How did we get caught? Why is it things always seem to go against us? Why is it there can't ever be any pleasure in living? I'm so tired it don't seem like I ever could get rest enough. I'm as tired when I get up in the morning as I am when I lay down at night. Sometimes it seems like there wouldn't never be no end to it, nor even a let-up. One year it'll look like things was going to be pretty good; but you get a little bit of money saved, something always happens.

   I tell you *I* won't be sorry when I die. I wouldn't be sorry this minute if it wasn't for Louise and Squinchy-here. Rest vmd git along all right:

(But *I* am young; and I am young, and strong, and in good health; and I am young, and pretty to look at; and I am too young to worry; and so am I, for my mother is kind to me; and we run in the bright air like animals, and our bare feet like plants in the wholesome earth: the natural world is around us like a lake and a wide smile and we are growing: one by one we are becoming stronger, and one by one in the terrible emptiness and the leisure we shall burn and tremble and shake with lust, and one by one we shall loosen ourselves from this place, and shall be married, and it will be different from what we see, for we will be happy and love each other, and keep the house clean, and a good garden, and buy a cultivator, and use a high grade of fertilizer, and we will know how to do things right; it will be very different:) (? :)

((?)   )   :)

How were we caught?

What, what is it has happened? What is it has been happening that we are living the way we are?

The children are not the way it seemed they might be:

She is no longer beautiful:

He no longer cares for me, he just takes me when he wants me:

There's so much work it seems like you never see the end of it:

I'm so hot when I get through cooking a meal it's more than I can do to
sit down to it and eat it:

How was it we were caught?

> And seeing the multitudes, he went up into a mountain; and when
>   he was set, his disciples came unto him:
> And he opened his mouth and taught them, saying:
> Blessed are the poor in spirit: for theirs is the kingdom of heaven.
> Blessed are they that mourn: for they shall be comforted.
> Blessed are the meek: for they shall inherit the earth.
> Blessed are they which do hunger and thirst after righteousness: for
>   they shall be filled.
> Blessed are the merciful: for they shall obtain mercy.
> Blessed are the pure in heart: for they shall see God.
> Blessed are the peacemakers: for they shall be called the children of
>   God.
> Blessed are they which are persecuted for righteousness' sake: for
>   theirs is the kingdom of heaven.
> Blessed are ye when men shall revile you, and persecute you, and
>   shall say all manner of evil against you falsely, for my sake.
> Rejoice, and be exceeding glad: for great is your reward in heaven:
>   for so persecuted they the prophets which were before you.

from *Black Boy*

Richard Wright (1908–1960)

Richard Wright, the son of an illiterate tenant farmer and a country schoolteacher, endured a difficult early childhood as his family, in pursuit of some measure of stability and prosperity, moved across the Mississippi Delta. After being selected valedictorian of his ninth-grade class, determined both to make himself into a writer and move north, he went to Memphis where he worked at various jobs and continued to read voraciously. Arriving in Chicago in 1927, Wright began his writing career, which he mingled with political activism. In his coming-of-age autobiography *Black Boy* (1945), Wright reminds us that experience remained the cruelest teacher for many young black Southerners.

Having grown taller and older, I now associated with older boys and I had to pay for my admittance into their company by subscribing to certain racial sentiments. The touchstone of fraternity was my feeling toward white people, how much hostility I held toward them, what degrees of value and honor I assigned to race. None of this was premeditated, but sprang spontaneously out of the talk of black boys who met at the crossroads.

It was degrading to play with girls and in our talk we relegated them to a remote island of life. We had somehow caught the spirit of the role of our sex and we flocked together for common moral schooling. We spoke boastfully in bass voices; we used the word "nigger" to prove tough fiber of our feelings; we spouted excessive profanity as a sign of our coming manhood; we pretended callousness toward the injunctions of our parents; and we strove to convince one another that our decisions stemmed from ourselves and ourselves alone. Yet we frantically concealed how dependent we were upon one another.

Of an afternoon when school had let out I would saunter down the street, idly kicking an empty tin can, or knocking a stick against the palings of a wooden fence, or whistling, until I would stumble upon one or more of the gang loitering at a corner, standing in a field, or sitting upon the steps of somebody's house.

"Hey." Timidly.

"You eat yet?" Uneasily trying to make conversation.

"Yeah, man. I done really fed my face." Casually.

"I had cabbage and potatoes." Confidently.

"I had buttermilk and black-eyed peas." Meekly informational.

"Hell, I ain't gonna stand near you, nigger!" Pronouncement.

"How come?" Feigned innocence.

"'Cause you gonna smell up this air in a minute!" A shouted accusation.

Laughter runs through the crowd.

"Nigger, your mind's in a ditch." Amusingly moralistic.

"Ditch, nothing! Nigger, you going to break wind any minute now!" Triumphant pronouncement creating suspense.

"Yeah, when them black-eyed peas tell that buttermilk to move over, that buttermilk ain't gonna wanna move and there's gonna be war in your guts and your stomach's gonna swell up and bust!" Climax.

The crowd laughs loud and long.

"Man, them white folks oughta catch you and send you to the zoo and keep you for the next war!" Throwing the subject into a wider field.

"Then when that fighting starts, they oughta feed you on buttermilk and black-eyed peas and let you break wind!" The subject is accepted and extended.

"You'd win the war with a new kind of poison gas!" A shouted climax.

There is high laughter that simmers down slowly.

"Maybe poison gas is something good to have." The subject of white folks is associationally swept into the orbit of talk.

"Yeah, if they hava race riot round here, I'm gonna kill all the white folks with my poison." Bitter pride.

Gleeful laughter. Then silence, each waiting for the other to contribute something.

"Them white folks sure scared of us, though." Sober statement of an old problem.

"Yeah, they send you to war, make you lick them Germans, teach you how to fight and when you come back they scared of you, want to kill you." Half boastful and half complaining.

"My mama says that old white woman where she works talked 'bout slapping her and Ma said: 'Miz Green, if you slaps me, I'll kill you and go to hell and pay for it!'" Extension, development, sacrificial boasting.

"Hell, I woulda just killed her if she hada said that to me." An angry grunt of supreme racial assertion.

Silence.

"Man, them white folks sure is mean." Complaining.

"That's how come so many colored folks leaving the South." Informational.

"And, man, they sure hate for you to leave." Pride of personal and racial worth implied.

"Yeah. They wanna keep you here and work you to death."

"The first white sonofabitch that bothers me is gonna get a hole knocked in his head!" Naïve rebellion.

"That ain't gonna do you no good. Hell, they'll catch you." Rejection of naïve rebellion.

"Ha-ha-ha... Yeah, goddammit, they really catch you, now." Appreciation of the thoroughness of white militancy.

"Yeah, white folks set on their white asses day and night, but leta nigger do something, and they get every bloodhound that was ever born and put 'em on his trail." Bitter pride in realizing what it costs to defeat them.

"Man, you reckon these white folks is ever gonna change?" Timid, questioning hope.

"Hell, no! They just born that way." Rejecting hope for fear that it could never come true.

"Shucks, man. I'm going north when I get grown." Rebelling against futile hope and embracing flight.

"A colored man's all right up north." Justifying flight.

"They say a white man hit a colored man up north and that colored man hit that white man, knocked him cold, and nobody did a damn thing!" Urgent wish to believe in flight.

"Man for man up there." Begging to believe in justice.

Silence.

"Listen, you reckon them buildings up north is as tall as they say they is?" Leaping by association to something concrete and trying to make belief real.

"They say they gotta building in New York forty stories high!" A thing too incredible for belief.

"Man, I'd be scareda them buildings!" Ready to abandon the now suppressed idea of flight.

"You know, they say that them buildings sway and rock in the wind." Stating a miracle.

"Naw, nigger!" Utter astonishment and rejection.

"Yeah, they say they do." Insisting upon the miracle.

"You reckon that could be?" Questioning hope.

"Hell, naw! If a building swayed and rocked in the wind, hell, it'd fall! Any fool knows that! Don't let people maka fool outta you, telling you them things!" Moving body agitatedly, stomping feet impatiently, and scurrying back to safe reality.

Silence. Somebody would pick up a stone and toss it across a field.

"Man, what makes white folks so mean?" Returning to grapple with the old problem.

"Whenever I see one I spit." Emotional rejection of whites.

"Man, ain't they ugly?" Increased emotional rejection.

"Man, you ever get right close to a white man, close enough to smell 'im?" Anticipation of statement.

"They say we stink. But my ma says white folks smell like dead folks." Wishing the enemy was dead.

"Niggers smell from sweat. But white folks smell *all* the time." The enemy is an animal to be killed on sight.

And the talk would weave, roll, surge, spurt, veer, swell, having no specific aim or direction, touching vast areas of life, expressing the tentative impulses of childhood. Money, God, race, sex, color, war, planes, machines, trains, swimming, boxing, anything . . . The culture of one black household was thus transmitted to another black household, and folk tradition was handed from group to group. Our attitudes were made, defined, set, or corrected; our ideas were discovered, discarded, enlarged, torn apart, and accepted. Night would fall. Bats would zip through the air. Crickets would cry from the grass. Frogs would croak. The stars would come out. Dew would dampen the earth. Yellow squares of light would glow in the distance as kerosene lamps were lit in our homes. Finally, from across the fields or down the road a long slow yell would come:

"Youuuuuuuu, Daaaaaaaavee!"

Easy laughter among the boys, but no reply.

"Calling the hogs."

"Go home, pig."

Laughter again. A boy would slowly detach himself from the gang.

"Youuuuuuuu, Daaaaaaaavee!"

He would not answer his mother's call, for that would have been a sign of dependence.

"I'll do you-all like the farmer did the potato," the boy would say.

"How's that?"

"Plant you now and dig you later!"

The boy would trot home slowly and there would be more easy laughter. More talk. One by one we would be called home to fetch water from the hydrant in the back yard, to go to the store and buy greens and meal for tomorrow, to split wood for kindling.

On Sundays, if our clothes were presentable, my mother would take me and my brother to Sunday school. We did not object, for church was not where we learned of God or His ways, but where we met our school friends and continued our long, rambling talks. Some of the Bible stories were interesting in themselves, but we always twisted them, secularized them to the level of our street life, rejecting all meanings that did not fit into our environment. And we did the same to the beautiful hymns. When the preacher intoned:

Amazing grace, how sweet it sounds

we would wink at one another and hum under our breath:

A bulldog ran my grandma down

We were now large enough for the white boys to fear us and both of us, the white boys and the black boys, began to play out traditional racial roles as though we had been born to them, as though it was in our blood, as though we were being guided by instinct. All the frightful descriptions we had heard about each other, all the violent expressions of hate and hostility that had seeped into us from our surroundings, came now to the surface to guide our actions. The roundhouse was the racial boundary of the neighborhood, and it had been tacitly agreed between the white boys and the black boys that the whites were to keep to the far side of the roundhouse and we blacks were to keep to our side. Whenever we caught a white boy on our side we stoned him; if we strayed to their side, they stoned us.

Our battles were real and bloody; we threw rocks, cinders, coal, sticks, pieces of iron, and broken bottles, and while we threw them we longed for even deadlier weapons. If we were hurt, we took it quietly; there was no crying or whimpering. If our wounds were not truly serious, we hid them from our parents. We did not want to be beaten for fighting. Once, in a battle with a gang of white boys, I was struck behind the ear with a piece of broken bottle; the cut was deep and bled profusely. I tried to stem the flow of blood by dabbing at the cut with a rag and when my mother came from work I was forced to tell her that I was hurt, for I needed medical attention. She rushed me to a doctor who stitched my scalp; but when she took me home she beat me, telling me that I must never fight white boys again, that I might be killed by them, that she had to work and had no time to worry about my fights. Her words did not sink in, for they conflicted with the code of the streets. I promised my mother that I would not fight, but I knew that if I kept my word I would lose my standing in the gang, and the gang's life was my life.

My mother became too ill to work and I began to do chores in the neighborhood. My first job was carrying lunches to the men who worked in the roundhouse, for which I received twenty-five cents a week. When the men did not finish their lunches, I would salvage what few crumbs remained. Later I obtained a job in a small café carting wood in my arms to keep the big stove going and taking trays of food to passengers when trains stopped for a half hour or so in a near-by station. I received a dollar a week for this work, but I was too young and too small to perform the duties; one morning while trying to take a heavy loaded tray up the steps of a train, I fell and dashed the tray of food to the ground.

Inability to pay rent forced us to move into a house perched atop high logs in a section of the town where flood waters came. My brother and I had great fun running up and down the tall, shaky steps.

Again paying rent became a problem and we moved nearer the center of town, where I found a job in a pressing shop, delivering clothes to hotels, sweeping floors, and listening to Negro men boast of their sex lives.

Yet again we moved, this time to the outskirts of town, near a wide stretch of railroad tracks to which, each morning before school, I would take a sack and gather coal to heat our frame house, dodging in and out between the huge, black, puffing engines.

My mother, her health failing rapidly, spoke constantly now of Granny's home, of how ardently she wanted to see us grow up before she died. Already there had crept into her speech a halting, lisping quality that, though I did not know it, was the shadow of her future. I was more conscious of my mother now than I had ever been and I was already able to feel what being completely without her would mean. A slowly rising dread stole into me and I would look at my mother for long moments, but when she would look at me I would look away. Then real fear came as her illness recurred at shorter intervals. Time stood still. My brother and I waited, hungry and afraid.

One morning a shouting voice awakened me.

"Richard! Richard!"

I rolled out of bed. My brother came running into the room.

"Richard, you better come and see Mama. She's very sick," he said.

I ran into my mother's room and saw her lying upon her bed, dressed, her eyes open, her mouth gaped. She was very still.

"Mama!" I called.

She did not answer or turn her head. I reached forward to shake her, but drew back, afraid that she was dead.

"Mama!" I called again, my mind unable to grasp that she could not answer.

Finally I went to her and shook her. She moved slightly and groaned. My brother and I called her repeatedly, but she did not speak. Was she dying? It seemed unthinkable. My brother and I looked at each other; we did not know what to do.

"We better get somebody," I said.

I ran into the hallway and called a neighbor. A tall, black woman bustled out of a door.

"Please, won't you come and see my mama? She won't talk. We can't wake her up. She's terribly sick," I told her.

She followed me into our flat.

"Mrs. Wright!" she called to my mother.

My mother lay still, unseeing, silent. The woman felt my mother's hands.

"She ain't dead," she said. "But she's sick, all right. I better get some more of the neighbors."

Five or six of the women came and my brother and I waited in the hallway while they undressed my mother and put her to bed. When we were allowed back in the room, a woman said:

"Looks like a stroke to me."

"Just like paralysis," said another.

"And she's so young," someone else said.

My brother and I stood against a wall while the bustling women worked frantically over my mother. A stroke? Paralysis? What were those things? Would she die? One of the women asked me if there was any money in the house; I did not know. They searched through the dresser and found a dollar or two and sent for a doctor. The doctor arrived. Yes, he told us, my mother had suffered a stroke of paralysis. She was in a serious condition. She needed someone with her day and night; she needed medicine. Where was her husband? I told him the story and he shook his head.

"She'll need all the help that she can get," the doctor said. "Her entire left side is paralyzed. She cannot talk and she will have to be fed."

Later that day I rummaged through drawers and found Granny's address; I wrote to her, pleading with her to come and help us. The neighbors nursed my mother day and night, fed us and washed our clothes. I went through the days with a stunned consciousness, unable to believe what had happened. Suppose Granny did not come? I tried not to think of it. She *had* to come. The utter loneliness was now terrifying. I had been suddenly thrown emotionally upon my own. Within an hour the half-friendly world that I had known had turned cold and hostile. I was too frightened to weep. I was glad that my mother was not dead, but there was the fact that she would be sick for a long, long time, perhaps for the balance of her life. I became morose. Though I was a child, I could no longer feel as a child, could no longer react as a child. The desire for play was gone and I brooded, wondering if Granny would come and help us. I tried not to think of a tomorrow that was neither real nor wanted, for all tomorrows held questions that I could not answer.

When the neighbors offered me food, I refused, already ashamed that so often in my life I had to be fed by strangers. And after I had been prevailed upon to eat I would eat as little as possible, feeling that some of the shame of charity would be taken away. It pained me to think that other children were wondering if I were hungry, and whenever they asked me if I wanted food, I would say no, even though I was starving. I was tense during the days I waited for Granny, and when she came I gave up, letting her handle things, answering questions automatically, obeying, knowing that somehow I had to face things alone. I withdrew into myself.

I wrote letters that Granny dictated to her eight children—there were nine of them, including my mother—in all parts of the country, asking for money with which "to take Ella and her two little children to our home." Money came and again there were days of packing household effects. My mother was taken to the train in an ambulance and put on board upon a stretcher. We rode to Jackson in silence and my mother was put abed upstairs. Aunt Maggie came from Detroit to help nurse and clean. The big house was quiet. We spoke in lowered voices. We walked with soft tread. The odor of medicine hung in the air. Doctors came and went. Night and day I could hear my mother groaning. We thought that she would die at any moment.

Aunt Cleo came from Chicago. Uncle Clark came from Greenwood, Mississippi. Uncle Edward came from Carters, Mississippi. Uncle Charles from Mobile, Alabama. Aunt Addie from a religious school in Huntsville, Alabama. Uncle Thomas from Hazelhurst, Mississippi. The house had an expectant air and I caught whispered talk of "what is to become of her children?" I felt dread, knowing that others—strangers even though they were relatives—were debating my destiny. I had never seen my mother's brothers and sisters before and their presence made live again in me my old shyness. One day Uncle Edward called me to him and he felt my skinny arms and legs.

"He needs more flesh on him," he commented impersonally, addressing himself to his brothers and sisters.

I was horribly embarrassed, feeling that my life had somehow been full of nameless wrong, an unatonable guilt.

"Food will make him pick up in weight," Granny said.

Out of the family conferences it was decided that my brother and I would be separated, that it was too much of a burden for any one aunt or uncle to assume the support of both of us. Where was I to go? Who would take me? I became more anxious than ever. When an aunt or an uncle would come into my presence, I could not look at them. I was always reminding myself that I must not do anything that would make any of them feel they would not want me in their homes.

At night my sleep was filled with wild dreams. Sometimes I would wake up screaming in terror. The grownups would come running and I would stare at them, as though they were figures out of my nightmare, then go back to sleep. One night I found myself standing in the back yard. The moon was shining bright as day. Silence surrounded me. Suddenly I felt that someone was holding my hand. I looked and saw an uncle. He was speaking to me in a low, gentle voice.

"What's the matter, son?"

I stared at him, trying to understand what he was saying. I seemed to be wrapped in a kind of mist.

"Richard, what are you doing?"

I could not answer. It seemed that I could not wake up. He shook me. I came to myself and stared about at the moon-drenched yard.

"Where are we going?" I asked him.

"You were walking in your sleep," he said.

Granny gave me fuller meals and made me take naps in the afternoon and gradually my sleepwalking passed. The uneasy days and nights made me resolve to leave Granny's home as soon as I was old enough to support myself. It was not that they were unkind, but I knew that they did not have money enough to feed me and my brother. I avoided going into my mother's room now; merely to look at her was painful. She had grown very thin; she was still speechless, staring, quiet as stone.

One evening my brother and I were called into the front room where a conference of aunts and uncles was being held.

"Richard," said an uncle, "you know how sick your mother is?"

"Yes, sir."

"Well, Granny's not strong enough to take care of you two boys," he continued.

"Yes, sir," I said, waiting for his decision.

"Well, Aunt Maggie's going to take your brother to Detroit and send him to school."

I waited. Who was going to take me? I had wanted to be with Aunt Maggie, but I did not dare contest the decision.

"Now, where would you like to go?" I was asked.

The question caught me by surprise; I had been waiting for a fiat, and now a choice lay before me. But I did not have the courage to presume that anyone wanted me.

"Anywhere," I said.

"Any of us are willing to take you," he said.

Quickly I calculated which of them lived nearest to Jackson. Uncle Clark lived in Greenwood, which was but a few miles distant.

"I'd like to live with Uncle Clark, since he's close to the home here," I said.

"Is that what you really want?"

"Yes, sir."

Uncle Clark came to me and placed his hand upon my head.

"All right. I'll take you back with me and send you to school. Tomorrow we'll go and buy clothes."

My tension eased somewhat, but stayed with me. My brother was happy. He was going north. I wanted to go, but I said nothing.

A train ride and I was in yet another little southern town. Home in Greenwood was a four-room bungalow, comprising half of a double house that sat on a quiet shady road. Aunt Jody, a medium-sized, neat, silent, mulatto girl, had a hot supper waiting on the table. She baffled me with her serious, reserved manner; she seemed to be acting in conformity with a code unknown to me, and I assumed that she regarded me as a "wrong one," a boy who for some reason did not have a home; I felt that in her mind she would push me to the outskirts of life and I was awkward and self-conscious in her presence. Both Uncle Clark and Aunt Jody talked to me as though I were a grownup and I wondered if I could do what was expected of me. I had always felt a certain warmth with my mother, even when we had lived in squalor; but I felt none here. Perhaps I was too apprehensive to feel any.

During supper it was decided that I was to be placed in school the next day. Uncle Clark and Aunt Jody both had jobs and I was told that at noon I would find lunch on the stove.

"Now, Richard, this is your new home," Uncle Clark said.

"Yes, sir."

"After school, bring in wood and coal for the fireplaces."

"Yes, sir."

"Split kindling and lay a fire in the kitchen stove."

"Yes, sir."

"Bring in a bucket of water from the yard so that Jody can cook in the mornings."

"Yes, sir."

After your chores are done, you may spend the afternoon studying."

"Yes, sir."

I had never been assigned definite tasks before and I went to bed a little frightened. I lay sleepless, wondering if I should have come, feeling the dark night holding strange people, strange houses, strange streets. What would happen to me here? How would I get along? What kind of woman was Aunt Jody? How ought I act around her? Would Uncle Clark let me make friends with other boys? I awakened the next morning to see the sun shining into my room; I felt more at ease.

"Richard!" my uncle was calling me.

I washed, dressed, and went into the kitchen and sat wordlessly at the table.

"Good morning, Richard," Aunt Jody said.

"Oh, good morning," I mumbled, wishing that I had thought to say it first.

"Don't people say good morning where you come from?" she asked.

"Yes, ma'am."

"I thought they did," she said pointedly.

Aunt Jody and Uncle Clark began to question me about my life and I grew so self-conscious that my hunger left me. After breakfast, Uncle Clark took me to school, introduced me to the principal. The first half of the school day passed without incident. I sat looking at the strange reading book, following the lessons. The subjects seemed simple and I felt that I could keep up. My anxiety was still in me; I was wondering how I would get on with the boys. Each new school meant a new area of life to be conquered. Were the boys tough? How hard did they fight? I took it for granted that they fought.

At noon recess I went into the school grounds and a group of boys sauntered up to me, looked at me from my head to my feet, whispering among themselves. I leaned against a wall, trying to conceal my uneasiness.

"Where you from?" a boy asked abruptly.

"Jackson," I answered.

"How come they make you people so ugly in Jackson?" he demanded.

There was loud laughter.

"You're not any too good-looking yourself," I countered instantly.

"Oh!"

"Aw!"

"You hear what he told 'im?"

"You think you're smart, don't you?" the boy asked, sneering.

"Listen, I ain't picking a fight," I said. "But if you want to fight, I'll fight."

"Hunh, hard guy, ain't you?"

"As hard as you."

"Do you know who you can tell that to?" he asked me.

"And you know who you can tell it back to?" I asked.

"Are you talking about my mama?" he asked, edging forward.

"If you want it that way," I said.

This was my test. If I failed now, I would have failed at school, for the first trial came not in books, but in how one's fellows took one, what value they placed upon one's willingness to fight.

"Take back what you said," the boy challenged me.

"Make me," I said.

The crowd howled, sensing a fight. The boy hesitated, weighing his chances of beating me.

"You ain't gonna take what that new boy said, is you?" someone taunted the boy.

The boy came close. I stood my ground. Our faces were four inches apart.

"You think I'm scared of you, don't you?" he asked.

"I told you what I think," I said.

Somebody, eager and afraid that we would not fight, pushed the boy and he bumped into me. I shoved him away violently.

"Don't push me!" the boy said.

"Then keep off me!" I said.

He was pushed again and I struck out with my right and caught him in the mouth. The crowd yelled, milled, surging so close that I could barely lift my arm to land a blow. When either of us tried to strike the other, we would be thrown off balance by the screaming boys. Every blow landed elicited shouts of delight. Knowing that if I did not win or make a good showing I would have to fight a new boy each day, I fought tigerishly, trying to leave a scar, seeking to draw blood as proof that I was not a coward, that I could take care of myself. The bell rang and the crowd pulled us apart. The fight seemed a draw.

"I ain't through with you!" the boy shouted.

"Go to hell!" I answered.

In the classroom the boys asked me questions about myself; I was someone worth knowing. When the bell rang for school to be dismissed, I was set to fight again; but the boy was not in sight.

On my way home I found a cheap ring in the streets and at once I knew what I was going to do with it. The ring had a red stone held by tiny prongs which I loosened, took the stone out, leaving the sharp tiny prongs jutting up. I slid the ring on to my finger and shadow boxed. Now, by God, let a goddamn bully come and I would show him how to fight; I would leave a crimson streak on his face with every blow.

But I never had to use the ring. After I had exhibited my new weapon at school, a description of it spread among the boys. I challenged my enemy to another fight, but he would not respond. Fighting was not now necessary. I had been accepted.

No sooner had I won my right to the school grounds than a new dread arose. One evening, before bedtime, I was sitting in the front room, reading, studying. Uncle Clark, who was a contracting carpenter, was at his drawing table, drafting models of houses. Aunt Jody was darning. Suddenly the doorbell rang and Aunt Jody admitted the next-door neighbor, the owner of the house in which we lived and its former occupant. His name was Burden; he was a tall, brown, stooped man and when I was introduced to him I rose and shook his hand.

"Well, son," Mr. Burden told me, "it's certainly a comfort to see another boy in this house."

"Is there another boy here?" I asked eagerly.

"My son was here," Mr. Burden said, shaking his head. "But he's gone now."

"How old is he?" I asked.

"He was about your age," Mr. Burden mumbled sadly.

"Where did he go?" I asked stupidly.

"He's dead," Mr. Burden said.

"Oh," I said.

I had not understood him. There was a long silence. Mr. Burden looked at me wistfully.

"Do you sleep in there?" he asked, pointing to my room.

"Yes, sir."

"That's where my boy slept," he said.

"In *there?*" I asked, just to make sure.

"Yes, right in there."

"On *that* bed?" I asked.

"Yes, that was his bed. When I heard that you were coming, I gave your uncle that bed for you," he explained.

I saw Uncle Clark shaking his head vigorously at Mr. Burden, but he was too late. At once my imagination began to weave ghosts. I did not actually believe in ghosts, but I had been taught that there was a God and I had given a kind of uneasy assent to His existence, and if there was a God, then surely there must be ghosts. In a moment I built up an intense loathing for sleeping in the room where the boy had died. Rationally I knew that the dead boy could not bother me, but he had become alive for me in a way that I could not dismiss. After Mr. Burden had gone, I went timidly to Uncle Clark.

"I'm scared to sleep in there," I told him.

"Why? Because a boy died in there?"

"Yes, sir."

"But, son, that's nothing to be afraid of."

"I know. But I am scared."

"We all must die someday. So why be afraid?"

I had no answer for that.

"When you die, do you want people to be afraid of *you?*"

I could not answer that either.

"This is nonsense," Uncle Clark went on.

"But I'm scared," I told him.

"You'll get over it."

"Can't I sleep somewhere else?"

"There's nowhere else for you to sleep."

"Can I sleep here on the sofa?" I asked.

"*May* I sleep here on the sofa?" Aunt Jody corrected me in a mocking tone.

"May I sleep here on the sofa?" I repeated after her.

"No," Aunt Jody said.

I groped into the dark room and fumbled for the bed; I had the illusion that if I touched it I would encounter the dead boy. I trembled. Finally I jumped roughly into the bed and jerked the covers over my face. I did not sleep that night and my eyes were red and puffy the next morning.

"Didn't you sleep well?" Uncle Clark asked me.

"I can't sleep in that room," I said.

"You slept in it before you heard of that boy who died in there, didn't you?" Aunt Jody asked me.

"Yes, ma'am."

"Then why can't you sleep in it now?"

"I'm just scared."

"You stop being a baby," she told me.

The next night was the same; fear kept me from sleeping. After Uncle Clark and Aunt Jody had gone to bed, I rose and crept into the front room and slept in a tight ball on the sofa, without any cover. I awakened the next morning to find Uncle Clark shaking me.

"Why are you doing this?" he asked.

"I'm scared to sleep in there," I said.

"You go back into that room and sleep tonight," he told me. "You've got to get over this thing."

I spent another sleepless, shivering night in the dead boy's room—it was not my room any longer—and I was so frightened that I sweated. Each creak of the house made my heart stand still. In school the next day I was dull. I came home and spent another long night of wakefulness and the following day I went to sleep in the classroom. When questioned by the teacher, I could give no answer. Unable to free myself from my terror, I began to long for home. A week of sleeplessness brought me near the edge of nervous collapse.

Sunday came and I refused to go to church and Uncle Clark and Aunt Jody were astonished. They did not understand that my refusal to go to church was my way of silently begging them to let me sleep somewhere else. They left me alone in the house and I spent the entire day sitting on the front steps; I did not have enough courage to go into the kitchen to eat. When I became thirsty, I went around the house and drank water from the hydrant in the back yard rather than venture into the house. Desperation made me raise the issue of the room again at bedtime.

"Please, let me sleep on the sofa in the front room," I pleaded.

"You've got to get out of that fear," my uncle said.

I made up my mind to ask to be sent home. I went to Uncle Clark, knowing that he had incurred expense in bringing me here, that he had thought he was helping me, that he had bought my clothes and books.

"Uncle Clark, send me back to Jackson," I said.

He was bent over a little table and he straightened and stared at me.

"You're not happy here?" he asked.

"No, sir," I answered truthfully, fearing that the ceiling would crash down upon my head.

"And you really want to go back?"

"Yes, sir."

"Things will not be as easy for you at home as here," he said. "There's not much money for food and things."

"I want to be where my mother is," I said, trying to strengthen my plea.

"It's really about the room?"

"Yes, sir."

"Well, we tried to make you happy here," my uncle said, sighing. "Maybe we didn't know how. But if you want to go back, then you may go."

"When?" I asked eagerly.

"As soon as school term has ended."

"But I want to go now!" I cried.

"But you'll break up your year's schooling," he said.

"I don't mind."

"You will, in the future. You've never had a single year of steady schooling," he said.

"I want to go home," I said.

"Have you felt this way a long time?" he asked.

"Yes, sir."

"I'll write Granny tonight," he said, his eyes lit with surprise.

Daily I asked him if he had heard from Granny only to learn that there had been no word. My sleeplessness made me feel that my days were a hot, wild dream and my studies suffered at school. I had been making high marks and now I made low ones and finally began to fail altogether. I was fretful, living from moment to moment.

One evening, in doing my chores, I took the water pail to the hydrant in the back yard to fill it. I was half asleep, tired, tense, all but swaying on my feet. I balanced the handle of the pail on the jutting tip of the metal faucet and waited for it to fill; the pail slipped and water drenched my pants and shoes and stockings.

"That goddamn lousy bastard sonofabitching bucket!" I spoke in a whisper of hate and despair.

"Richard!" Aunt Jody's amazed voice sounded in the darkness behind me.

I turned. Aunt Jody was standing on the back steps. She came into the yard.

"What did you say, boy?" she asked.

"Nothing," I mumbled, looking contritely at the ground.

"Repeat what you said!" she demanded.

I did not answer. I stooped and picked up the pail. She snatched it from me.

"What did you say?" she asked again.

I still kept my head down, vaguely wondering if she were intimidating me or if she really wanted me to repeat my curses.

"I'm going to tell your uncle on you," she said at last.

I hated her then. I thought that hanging my head and looking mutely at the ground was a kind of confession and a petition for forgiveness, but she had not accepted it as such.

"I don't care," I said.

She gave me the pail, which I filled with water and carried to the house. She followed me.

"Richard, you are a very bad, bad boy," she said.

"I don't care," I repeated.

I avoided her and went to the front porch and sat. I had had no intention of letting her hear me curse, but since she had heard me and since there was no way to appease her, I decided to let things develop as they would. I would go home. But where was home? Yes, I would run away.

Uncle Clark came and called me into the front room,

"Jody says that you've been using bad language," he said.

"Yes, sir."

"You admit it?"

"Yes, sir."

"Why did you do it?"

"I don't know."

"I'm going to whip you. Pull off your shirt."

Wordlessly I bared my back and he lashed me with a strap. I gritted my teeth and did not cry.

"Are you going to use that language again?" he asked me.

"I want to go home," I said.

"Put on your shirt."

I obeyed.

"I want to go home," I said again.

"But this is your home."

"I want to go to Jackson."

"You have no home in Jackson."

"I want to go to my mother."

"All right," he relented. "I'll send you home Saturday." He looked at me with baffled eyes. "Tell me, where did you learn those words Jody heard you say?"

I looked at him and did not answer; there flashed through my mind a quick, running picture of all the squalid hovels in which I had lived and it made me feel more than ever a stranger as I stood before him. How could I have told him that I had learned to curse before I had learned to read? How could I have told him that I had been a drunkard at the age of six?

When he took me to the train that Saturday morning, I felt guilty and did not want to look at him. He gave me my ticket and I climbed hastily aboard the train. I waved a stiff good-bye to him through the window as the train pulled out. When I could see his face no longer, I wilted, relaxing. Tears blurred my vision. I leaned back and closed my eyes and slept all the way.

I was glad to see my mother. She was much better, though still abed. Another operation had been advised by the doctor and there was hope for recovery. But I was anxious. Why another operation? A victim myself of too many hopes that had never led anywhere, I was for letting my mother remain as she was. My feelings were governed by fear and I spoke to no one about them. I had already begun to sense that my feelings varied too far from those of the people around me for me to blab about what I felt.

I did not re-enter school. Instead, I played alone in the back yard, bouncing a rubber ball off the fence, drawing figures in the soft clay with an old knife, or reading what books I found about the house. I ached to be of an age to take care of myself.

Uncle Edward arrived from Carters to take my mother to Clarksdale for the operation; at the last moment I insisted upon being taken with them. I dressed hurriedly and we went to the station. Throughout the journey I sat brooding, afraid to look at my mother, wanting to return home and yet wanting to go on. We reached Clarksdale and hired a taxi to the doctor's office. My mother was jolly, brave, smiling, but I knew that she was as doubtful as I was. When we reached the doctor's waiting room the conviction settled in me that my mother would never be well again. Finally the doctor came out in his white coat and shook hands with me, then took my mother inside. Uncle Edward left to make arrangements for a room and a nurse. I felt crushed. I waited. Hours later the doctor came to the door.

"How's my mother?"

"Fine!" he said.

"Will she be all right?"

"Everything'll clear up in a few days."

"Can I see her now?"

"No, not now."

Later Uncle Edward returned with an ambulance and two men who carried a stretcher. They entered the doctor's office and brought out my mother; she lay with closed eyes, her body swathed in white. I wanted to run to the stretcher and touch her, but I could not move.

"Why are they taking mama that way?" I asked Uncle Edward.

"There are no hospital facilities for colored, and this is the way we have to do it," he said.

I watched the men take the stretcher down the steps; then I stood on the sidewalk and watched them lift my mother into the ambulance and drive away. I knew that my mother had gone out of my life; I could feel it.

Uncle Edward and I stayed at a boardinghouse; each morning he went to the rooming house to inquire about my mother and each time he returned gloomy and silent. Finally he told me that he was taking my mother back home.

"What chance has mama, really?" I asked him.

"She's very sick," he said.

We left Clarksdale; my mother rode on a stretcher in the baggage car with Uncle Edward attending her. Back home, she lay for days, groaning, her eyes vacant. Doctors visited her and left without making any comment. Granny grew frantic. Uncle Edward, who had gone home, returned and still more doctors were called in. They told us that a blood clot had formed on my mother's brain and that another paralytic stroke had set in.

Once, in the night, my mother called me to her bed and told me that she could not endure the pain, that she wanted to die. I held her hand and begged her to be quiet. That night I ceased to react to my mother; my feelings were frozen. I merely waited upon her, knowing that she was suffering. She remained abed ten years, gradually growing better, but never completely recovering, relapsing periodically into her paralytic state. The family had stripped itself of money to fight my mother's illness and there was no more forthcoming. Her illness gradually became an accepted thing in the house, something that could not be stopped or helped.

My mother's suffering grew into a symbol in my mind, gathering to itself all the poverty, the ignorance, the helplessness; the painful, baffling, hunger-ridden days and hours; the restless moving, the futile seeking, the uncertainty, the fear, the dread; the meaningless pain and the endless suffering. Her life set the emotional tone of my life, colored the men and women I was to meet in the future, conditioned my relation to events that had not yet happened, determined my attitude to situations and circumstances I had yet to face. A somberness of spirit that I was never to lose settled over me during the slow years of my mother's unrelieved suffering, a somberness that was to make me stand apart and look upon excessive joy with suspicion, that was to make me self-conscious, that was to make me keep forever on the move, as though to escape a nameless fate seeking to overtake me.

At the age of twelve, before I had had one full year of formal schooling, I had a conception of life that no experience would ever erase, a predilection for what was real that no argument could ever gainsay, a sense of the world that was mine and mine alone, a notion as to what life meant that no education could ever alter, a conviction that the meaning of living came only when one was struggling to wring a meaning out of meaningless suffering.

At the age of twelve I had an attitude toward life that was to endure, that was to make me seek those areas of living that would keep it alive, that was to make me skeptical of everything while seeking everything, tolerant of all and yet critical. The spirit I had caught gave me insight into the sufferings of others, made me gravitate toward those whose feelings were like my own, made me sit for hours while others told me of their lives, made me strangely tender and cruel, violent and peaceful.

It made me want to drive coldly to the heart of every question and lay it open to the core of suffering I knew I would find there. It made me love burrowing into psychology, into realistic and naturalistic fiction and art, into those whirlpools of politics that had the power to claim the whole of men's souls. It directed my loyalties to the side of men in rebellion; it made me love talk that sought answers to questions that could help nobody, that could only keep alive in me that enthralling sense of wonder and awe in the face of the drama of human feeling which is hidden by the external drama of life.

from *Invisible Man*

Ralph Ellison (1914–1994)

Raised in Oklahoma City in a family that encouraged his interests in music and books, Ralph Ellison received a music scholarship from Tuskegee Institute in Alabama. At Tuskegee, he befriended fellow music aficionado and future writer Albert Murray and began the serious study of literature. By 1938, Ellison was in New York studying the techniques of other novelists and working as a researcher with the New York Federal Writers' Project, a job writer Richard Wright helped him obtain. In the summer of 1945, Ellison began work on what would become the novel *Invisible Man*. Following its publication in 1952, Ellison was honored with the National Book Award. Much as the narrator of his novel, a young black Southerner, comes to reject those identities fashioned for him by others, Ellison, while a staunch supporter of civil rights, refused to support black nationalism. He argued that blacks and whites had created a culture that was unintelligible if interpreted solely in terms of color.

It goes a long way back, some twenty years. All my life I had been looking for something, and everywhere I turned someone tried to tell me what it was. I accepted their answers too, though they were often in contradiction and even self-contradictory. I was naïve. I was looking for myself and asking everyone except myself questions which I, and only I, could answer. It took me a long time and much painful boomeranging of my expectations to achieve a realization everyone else appears to have been born with: That I am nobody but myself. But first I had to discover that I am an invisible man!

And yet I am no freak of nature, nor of history. I was in the cards, other things having been equal (or unequal) eighty-five years ago. I am not ashamed of my grandparents for having been slaves. I am only ashamed of myself for having at one time been ashamed. About eighty-five years ago they were told that they were free, united with others of our country in everything pertaining to the common good, and, in everything social, separate like the fingers of the hand. And they believed it. They exulted in it. They stayed in their place, worked hard, and brought up my father to do the same. But my grandfather is the one. He was an odd old guy, my grandfather, and I am told I take after him. It was he who caused the trouble. On his death-bed he called my father to him and said, "Son, after I'm gone I want you to keep up the good fight. I never told you, but our life is a war and I have been a traitor all my born days, a spy in the enemy's country ever since I give up my gun back in the Reconstruction. Live with your head in the lion's mouth. I want you to overcome 'em with yeses, undermine 'em with grins, agree 'em to death and destruction, let 'em swoller you till they vomit or bust wide open." They thought the old man had gone out of his mind. He had been the meekest of men. The younger children were rushed from the room, the shades drawn and the flame of the lamp turned so low that it sputtered on the wick like the old man's breathing. "Learn it to the younguns," he whispered fiercely; then he died.

But my folks were more alarmed over his last words than over his dying. It was as though he had not died at all, his words caused so much anxiety. I was warned emphatically to forget what he had said and, indeed, this is the first time it has been mentioned outside the family circle. It had a tremendous effect upon me, however. I could never be sure of what he meant. Grandfather had been a quiet old man who never made any trouble, yet on his deathbed he had called himself a traitor and a spy, and he had spoken of his meekness as a dangerous activity. It became a constant puzzle which lay unanswered in the back of my mind. And whenever things went well for me I remembered my grandfather and felt guilty and uncomfortable. It was as though I was carrying out his advice in spite of myself. And to make it worse, everyone loved me for it. I was praised by the most lily-white men of the town. I was considered an example of desirable conduct—just as my grandfather had been. And what puzzled me was that the old man had defined it as *treachery*. When I was praised for my conduct I felt a guilt that in some way I was doing something that was really against the wishes of the white folks, that if they had understood they would have desired me to act just the opposite, that I should have been sulky and mean, and that that really would have been what they wanted, even though they were fooled and thought they wanted me to act as I did. It made me afraid that some day they would look upon me as a traitor and I would be lost. Still I was more afraid to act any other way because they didn't like that at all. The old man's words were like a curse. On my graduation day I delivered an oration in which I showed that humility was the secret, indeed, the very essence of progress. (Not that I believed this — how could I, remembering my grandfather? — I only believed that it worked.) It was a great success. Everyone praised me and I was invited to give the speech at a gathering of the town's leading white citizens. It was a triumph for our whole community.

It was in the main ballroom of the leading hotel. When I got there I discovered that it was on the occasion of a smoker, and I was told that since I was to be there anyway I might as well take part in the battle royal to be fought by some of my schoolmates as part of the entertainment. The battle royal came first.

All of the town's big shots were there in their tuxedoes, wolfing down the buffet foods, drinking beer and whiskey and smoking black cigars. It was a large room with a high ceiling. Chairs were arranged in neat rows around three sides of a portable boxing ring. The fourth side was clear, revealing a gleaming space of polished floor. I had some misgivings over the battle royal, by the way. Not from a distaste for fighting, but because I didn't care too much for the other fellows who were to take part. They were tough guys who seemed to have no grandfather's curse worrying their minds. No one could mistake their toughness. And besides, I suspected that fighting a battle royal might detract from the dignity of my speech. In those pre-invisible days I visualized myself as a potential Booker T. Washington. But the other fellows didn't care too much for me either, and there were nine of them. I felt superior to them in my way, and I didn't like the manner in which we were all crowded together into the servants' elevator. Nor did they like my being there. In fact, as the warmly lighted floors flashed past the elevator we had words over the fact that I, by taking part in the fight, had knocked one of their friends out of a night's work.

We were led out of the elevator through a rococo hall into an anteroom and told to get into our fighting togs. Each of us was issued a pair of boxing gloves and ushered out into the big mirrored hall, which we entered looking cautiously about us and whispering, lest we might accidentally be heard above the noise of the room. It was foggy with cigar smoke. And already the whiskey was taking effect. I was shocked to see some of the most important men of the town quite tipsy. They were all there — bankers, lawyers, judges, doctors, fire chiefs, teachers, merchants. Even one of the more fashionable pastors. Something we could not see was going on up front. A clarinet was vibrating sensuously and the men were standing up and moving eagerly forward. We were a small tight group, clustered together, our bare upper bodies touching and shining with anticipatory sweat; while up front the big shots were becoming increasingly excited over something we still could not see. Suddenly I heard the school superintendent, who had told me to come, yell, "Bring up the shines, gentlemen! Bring up the little shines!"

We were rushed up to the front of the ballroom, where it smelled even more strongly of tobacco and whiskey. Then we were pushed into place. I almost wet my pants. A sea of faces, some hostile, some amused, ringed around us, and in the center, facing us, stood a magnificent blonde—stark naked. There was dead silence. I felt a blast of cold air chill me. I tried to back away, but they were behind me and around me. Some of the boys stood with lowered heads, trembling. I felt a wave of irrational guilt and fear. My teeth chattered, my skin turned to goose flesh, my knees knocked. Yet I was strongly attracted and looked in spite of myself. Had the price of looking been blindness, I would have looked. The hair was yellow like that of a circus kewpie doll, the face heavily powdered and rouged, as though to form an abstract mask, the eyes hollow and smeared a cool blue, the color of a baboon's butt. I felt a desire to spit upon her as my eyes brushed slowly over her body. Her breasts were firm and round as the domes of East Indian temples, and I stood so close as to see the fine skin texture and beads of pearly perspiration glistening like dew around the pink and erected buds of her nipples. I wanted at one and the same time to run from the room, to sink through the floor, or go to her and cover her from my eyes and the eyes of the others with my body; to feel the soft thighs, to caress her and destroy her, to love her and murder her, to hide from her, and yet to stroke where below the small American flag tattooed upon her belly her thighs formed a capital V. I had a notion that of all in the room she saw only me with her impersonal eyes.

And then she began to dance, a slow sensuous movement; the smoke of a hundred cigars clinging to her like the thinnest of veils. She seemed like a fair bird-girl girdled in veils calling to me from the angry surface of some gray and threatening sea. I was transported. Then I became aware of the clarinet playing and the big shots yelling at us. Some threatened us if we looked and others if we did not. On my right I saw one boy faint. And now a man grabbed a silver pitcher from a table and stepped close as he dashed ice water upon him and stood him up and forced two of us to support him as his head hung and moans issued from his thick bluish lips. Another boy began to plead to go home. He was the largest of the group, wearing dark red fighting trunks much too small to conceal the erection which projected from him as though in answer to the insinuating low-registered moaning of the clarinet. He tried to hide himself with his boxing gloves.

And all the while the blonde continued dancing, smiling faintly at the big shots who watched her with fascination, and faintly smiling at our fear. I noticed a certain merchant who followed her hungrily, his lips loose and drooling. He was a large man who wore diamond studs in a shirtfront which swelled with the ample paunch underneath, and each time the blonde swayed her undulating hips he ran his hand through the thin hair of his bald head and, with his arms upheld, his posture clumsy like that of an intoxicated panda, wound his belly in a slow and obscene grind. This creature was completely hypnotized. The music had quickened. As the dancer flung herself about with a detached expression on her face, the men began reaching out to touch her. I could see their beefy fingers sink into the soft flesh. Some of the others tried to stop them and she began to move around the floor in graceful circles, as they gave chase, slipping and sliding over the polished floor. It was mad. Chairs went crashing, drinks were spilt, as they ran laughing and howling after her. They caught her just as she reached a door, raised her from the floor, and tossed her as college boys are tossed at a hazing, and above her red, fixed-smiling lips I saw the terror and disgust in her eyes, almost like my own terror and that which I saw in some of the other boys. As I watched, they tossed her twice and her soft breasts seemed to flatten against the air and her legs flung wildly as she spun. Some of the more sober ones helped her to escape. And I started off the floor, heading for the anteroom with the rest of the boys.

Some were still crying and in hysteria. But as we tried to leave we were stopped and ordered to get into the ring. There was nothing to do but what we were told. All ten of us climbed under the ropes and allowed ourselves to be blindfolded with broad bands of white cloth. One of the men seemed to feel a bit sympathetic and tried to cheer us up as we stood with our backs against the ropes. Some of us tried to grin. "See that boy over there?" one of the men said. "I want you to run across at the bell and give it to him right in the belly. If you don't get him, I'm going to get you. I don't like his looks." Each of us was told the same. The blindfolds were put on. Yet even then I had been going over my speech. In my mind each word was as bright as flame. I felt the cloth pressed into place, and frowned so that it would be loosened when I relaxed.

But now I felt a sudden fit of blind terror. I was unused to darkness. It was as though I had suddenly found myself in a dark room filled with poisonous cottonmouths. I could hear the bleary voices yelling insistently for the battle royal to begin.

"Get going in there!"

"Let me at that big nigger!"

I strained to pick up the school superintendent's voice, as though to squeeze some security out of that slightly more familiar sound.

"Let me at those black sonsabitches!" someone yelled.

"No, Jackson, no!" another voice yelled. "Here, somebody, help me hold Jack."

"I want to get at that ginger-colored nigger. Tear him limb from limb," the first voice yelled.

I stood against the ropes trembling. For in those days I was what they called ginger-colored, and he sounded as though he might crunch me between his teeth like a crisp ginger cookie.

Quite a struggle was going on. Chairs were being kicked about and I could hear voices grunting as with a terrific effort. I wanted to see, to see more desperately than ever before. But the blindfold was tight as a thick skin-puckering scab and when I raised my gloved hands to push the layers of white aside a voice yelled, "Oh, no you don't, black bastard! Leave that alone!"

"Ring the bell before Jackson kills him a coon!" someone boomed in the sudden silence. And I heard the bell clang and the sound of the feet scuffling forward.

A glove smacked against my head. I pivoted, striking out stiffly as someone went past, and felt the jar ripple along the length of my arm to my shoulder. Then it seemed as though all nine of the boys had turned upon me at once. Blows pounded me from all sides while I struck out as best I could. So many blows landed upon me that I wondered if I were not the only blindfolded fighter in the ring, or if the man called Jackson hadn't succeeded in getting me after all.

Blindfolded, I could no longer control my motions. I had no dignity. I stumbled about like a baby or a drunken man. The smoke had become thicker and with each new blow it seemed to sear and further restrict my lungs. My saliva became like hot bitter glue. A glove connected with my head, filling my mouth with warm blood. It was everywhere. I could not tell if the moisture I felt upon my body was sweat or blood. A blow landed hard against the nape of my neck. I felt myself going over, my head hitting the floor. Streaks of blue light filled the black world behind the blindfold. I lay prone, pretending that I was knocked out, but felt myself seized by hands and yanked to my feet. "Get going, black boy! Mix it up!" My arms were like lead, my head smarting from blows. I managed to feel my way to the ropes and held on, trying to catch my breath. A glove landed in my mid-section and I went over again, feeling as though the smoke had become a knife jabbed into my guts. Pushed this way and that by the legs milling around me, I finally pulled erect and discovered that I could see the black, sweat-washed forms weaving in the smoky-blue atmosphere like drunken dancers weaving to the rapid drum-like thuds of blows.

Everyone fought hysterically. It was complete anarchy. Everybody fought everybody else. No group fought together for long. Two, three, four, fought one, then turned to fight each other, were themselves attacked. Blows landed below the belt and in the kidney, with the gloves open as well as closed, and with my eye partly opened now there was not so much terror. I moved carefully, avoiding blows, although not too many to attract attention, fighting from group to group. The boys groped about like blind, cautious crabs crouching to protect their mid-sections, their heads pulled in short against their shoulders, their arms stretched nervously before them, with their fists testing the smoke-filled air like the knobbed feelers of hypersensitive snails. In one corner I glimpsed a boy violently punching the air and heard him scream in pain as he smashed his hand against a ring post. For a second I saw him bent over holding his hand, then going down as a blow caught his unprotected head. I played one group against the other, slipping in and throwing a punch then stepping out of range while pushing the others into the melee to take the blows blindly aimed at me. The smoke was agonizing and there were no rounds, no bells at three minute intervals to relieve our exhaustion. The room spun round me, a swirl of lights, smoke, sweating bodies surrounded by tense white faces. I bled from both nose and mouth, the blood spattering upon my chest.

The men kept yelling, "Slug him, black boy! Knock his guts out!"

"Uppercut him! Kill him! Kill that big boy!"

Taking a fake fall, I saw a boy going down heavily beside me as though we were felled by a single blow, saw a sneaker-clad foot shoot into his groin as the two who had knocked him down stumbled upon him. I rolled out of range, feeling a twinge of nausea.

The harder we fought the more threatening the men became. And yet, I had begun to worry about my speech again. How would it go? Would they recognize my ability? What would they give me?

I was fighting automatically when suddenly I noticed that one after another of the boys was leaving the ring. I was surprised, filled with panic, as though I had been left alone with an unknown danger. Then I understood. The boys had arranged it among themselves. It was the custom for the two men left in the ring to slug it out for the winner's prize. I discovered this too late. When the bell sounded two men in tuxedoes leaped into the ring and removed the blindfold. I found myself facing Tatlock, the biggest of the gang. I felt sick at my stomach. Hardly had the bell stopped ringing in my ears than it clanged again and I saw him moving swiftly toward me. Thinking of nothing else to do I hit him smash on the nose. He kept coming, bringing the rank sharp violence of stale sweat. His face was a black blank of a face, only his eyes alive—with hate of me and aglow with a feverish terror from what had happened to us all. I became anxious. I wanted to deliver my speech and he came at me as though he meant to beat it out of me. I smashed him again and again, taking his blows as they came. Then on a sudden impulse I struck him lightly and as we clinched, I whispered, "Fake like I knocked you out, you can have the prize."

"I'll break your behind," he whispered hoarsely.

"For *them?*"

"For *me*, sonofabitch!"

They were yelling for us to break it up and Tatlock spun me half around with a blow, and as a joggled camera sweeps in a reeling scene, I saw the howling red faces crouching tense beneath the cloud of blue-gray smoke. For a moment the world wavered, unraveled, flowed, then my head cleared and Tatlock bounced before me. That fluttering shadow before my eyes was his jabbing left hand. Then falling forward, my head against his damp shoulder, I whispered,

"I'll make it five dollars more."

"Go to hell!"

But his muscles relaxed a trifle beneath my pressure and I breathed, "Seven?"

"Give it to your ma," he said, ripping me beneath the heart.

And while I still held him I butted him and moved away. I felt myself bombarded with punches. I fought back with hopeless desperation. I wanted to deliver my speech more than anything else in the world, because I felt that only these men could judge truly my ability, and now this stupid clown was ruining my chances. I began fighting carefully now, moving in to punch him and out again with my greater speed. A lucky blow to his chin and I had him going too—until I heard a loud voice yell, "I got my money on the big boy."

Hearing this, I almost dropped my guard. I was confused: Should I try to win against the voice out there? Would not this go against my speech, and was not this a moment for humility, for nonresistance? A blow to my head as I danced about sent my right eye popping like a jack-in-the-box and settled my dilemma. The room went red as I fell. It was a dream fall, my body languid and fastidious as to where to land, until the floor became impatient and smashed up to meet me. A moment later I came to. An hypnotic voice said FIVE emphatically. And I lay there, hazily watching a dark red spot of my own blood shaping itself into a butterfly, glistening and soaking into the soiled gray world of the canvas.

When the voice drawled TEN I was lifted up and dragged to a chair. I sat dazed. My eye pained and swelled with each throb of my pounding heart and I wondered if now I would be allowed to speak. I was wringing wet, my mouth still bleeding. We were grouped along the wall now. The other boys ignored me as they congratulated Tatlock and speculated as to how much they would be paid. One boy whimpered over his smashed hand. Looking up front, I saw attendants in white jackets rolling the portable ring away and placing a small square rug in the vacant space surrounded by chairs. Perhaps, I thought, I will stand on the rug to deliver my speech.

Then the M.C. called to us, "Come on up here boys and get your money."

We ran forward to where the men laughed and talked in their chairs, waiting. Everyone seemed friendly now.

"There it is on the rug," the man said. I saw the rug covered with coins of all dimensions and a few crumpled bills. But what excited me, scattered here and there, were the gold pieces.

"Boys, it's all yours," the man said. "You get all you grab."

"That's right, Sambo," a blond man said, winking at me confidentially. I trembled with excitement, forgetting my pain. I would get the gold and the bills, I thought. I would use both hands. I would throw my body against the boys nearest me to block them from the gold.

"Get down around the rug now," the man commanded, "and don't anyone touch it until I give the signal."

"This ought to be good," I heard.

As told, we got around the square rug on our knees. Slowly the man raised his freckled hand as we followed it upward with our eyes.

I heard, "These niggers look like they're about to pray!"

Then, "Ready," the man said. "Go!"

I lunged for a yellow coin lying on the blue design of the carpet, touching it and sending a surprised shriek to join those rising around me. I tried frantically to remove my hand but could not let go. A hot, violent force tore through my body, shaking me like a wet rat. The rug was electrified. The hair bristled up on my head as I shook myself free. My muscles jumped, my nerves jangled, writhed. But I saw that this was not stopping the other boys. Laughing in fear and embarrassment, some were holding back and scooping up the coins knocked off by the painful contortions of the others. The men roared above us as we struggled.

"Pick it up, goddamnit, pick it up!" someone called like a bass-voiced parrot. "Go on, get it!"

I crawled rapidly around the floor, picking up the coins, trying to avoid the coppers and to get greenbacks and the gold. Ignoring the shock by laughing, as I brushed the coins off quickly, I discovered that I could contain the electricity—a contradiction, but it works. Then the men began to push us onto the rug. Laughing embarrassedly, we struggled out of their hands and kept after the coins. We were all wet and slippery and hard to hold. Suddenly I saw a boy lifted into the air, glistening with sweat like a circus seal, and dropped, his wet back landing flush upon the charged rug, heard him yell and saw him literally dance upon his back, his elbows beating a frenzied tattoo upon the floor, his muscles twitching like the flesh of a horse stung by many flies. When he finally rolled off, his face was gray and no one stopped him when he ran from the floor amid booming laughter.

"Get the money," the M.C. called. "That's good hard American cash!"

And we snatched and grabbed, snatched and grabbed. I was careful not to come too close to the rug now, and when I felt the hot whiskey breath descend upon me like a cloud of foul air I reached out and grabbed the leg of a chair. It was occupied and I held on desperately.

"Leggo, nigger! Leggo!"

The huge face wavered down to mine as he tried to push me free. But my body was slippery and he was too drunk. It was Mr. Colcord, who owned a chain of movie houses and "entertainment palaces." Each time he grabbed me I slipped out of his hands. It became a real struggle. I feared the rug more than I did the drunk, so I held on, surprising myself for a moment by trying to topple *him* upon the rug. It was such an enormous idea that I found myself actually carrying it out. I tried not to be obvious, yet when I grabbed his leg, trying to tumble him out of the chair, he raised up roaring with laughter, and, looking at me with soberness dead in the eye, kicked me viciously in the chest. The chair leg flew out of my hand and I felt myself going and rolled. It was as though I had rolled through a bed of hot coals. It seemed a whole century would pass before I would roll free, a century in which I was seared through the deepest levels of my body to the fearful breath within me and the breath seared and heated to the point of explosion. It'll all be over in a flash, I thought as I rolled clear. It'll all be over in a flash.

But not yet, the men on the other side were waiting, red faces swollen as though from apoplexy as they bent forward in their chairs. Seeing their fingers coming toward me I rolled away as a fumbled football rolls off the receiver's fingertips, back into the coals. That time I luckily sent the rug sliding out of place and heard the coins ringing against the floor and the boys scuffling to pick them up and the M.C. calling, "All right, boys, that's all. Go get dressed and get your money."

I was limp as a dish rag. My back felt as though it had been beaten with wires.

When we had dressed the M.C. came in and gave us each five dollars, except Tatlock, who got ten for being last in the ring. Then he told us to leave. I was not to get a chance to deliver my speech, I thought. I was going out into the dim alley in despair when I was stopped and told to go back. I returned to the ballroom, where the men were pushing back their chairs and gathering in groups to talk.

The M.C. knocked on a table for quiet. "Gentlemen," he said, "we almost forgot an important part of the program. A most serious part, gentlemen. This boy was brought here to deliver a speech which he made at his graduation yesterday . . ."

"Bravo!"

"I'm told that he is the smartest boy we've got out there in Greenwood. I'm told that he knows more big words than a pocket-sized dictionary."

Much applause and laughter.

"So now, gentlemen, I want you to give him your attention."

There was still laughter as I faced them, my mouth dry, my eye throbbing. I began slowly, but evidently my throat was tense, because they began shouting, "Louder! Louder!"

"We of the younger generation extol the wisdom of that great leader and educator," I shouted, "who first spoke these flaming words of wisdom: 'A ship lost at sea for many days suddenly sighted a friendly vessel. From the mast of the unfortunate vessel was seen a signal: "Water, water; we die of thirst!" The answer from the friendly vessel came back: "Cast down your bucket where you are." The captain of the distressed vessel, at last heeding the injunction, cast down his bucket, and it came up full of fresh sparkling water from the mouth of the Amazon River.' And like him I say, and in his words, 'To those of my race who depend upon bettering their condition in a foreign land, or who underestimate the importance of cultivating friendly relations with the Southern white man, who is his next-door neighbor, I would say: "Cast down your bucket where you are"—cast it down in making friends in every manly way of the people of all races by whom we are surrounded ...'"

I spoke automatically and with such fervor that I did not realize that the men were still talking and laughing until my dry mouth, filling up with blood from the cut, almost strangled me. I coughed, wanting to stop and go to one of the tall brass, sand-filled spittoons to relieve myself, but a few of the men, especially the superintendent, were listening and I was afraid. So I gulped it down, blood, saliva and all, and continued. (What powers of endurance I had during those days! What enthusiasm! What a belief in the rightness of things!) I spoke even louder in spite of the pain. But still they talked and still they laughed, as though deaf with cotton in dirty ears. So I spoke with greater emotional emphasis. I closed my ears and swallowed blood until I was nauseated. The speech seemed a hundred times as long as before, but I could not leave out a single word. All had to be said, each memorized nuance considered, rendered. Nor was that all. Whenever I uttered a word of three or more syllables a group of voices would yell for me to repeat it. I used the phrase "social responsibility" and they yelled:

"What's that word you say, boy?"

"Social responsibility," I said.

"What?"

"Social ..."

"Louder."

"... responsibility."

"More!"

"Respon—"

"Repeat!"

"—sibility."

The room filled with the uproar of laughter until, no doubt, distracted by having to gulp down my blood, I made a mistake and yelled a phrase I had often seen denounced in newspaper editorials, heard debated in private.

"Social . . ."

"What?" they yelled.

". . . equality—"

The laughter hung smokelike in the sudden stillness. I opened my eyes, puzzled. Sounds of displeasure filled the room. The M.C. rushed forward. They shouted hostile phrases at me. But I did not understand.

A small dry mustached man in the front row blared out, "Say that slowly, son!"

"What, sir?"

"What you just said!"

"Social responsibility, sir," I said.

"You weren't being smart, were you, boy?" he said, not unkindly.

"No, sir!"

"You sure that about 'equality' was a mistake?"

"Oh, yes, sir," I said. "I was swallowing blood."

"Well, you had better speak more slowly so we can understand. We mean to do right by you, but you've got to know your place at all times. All right, now, go on with your speech."

I was afraid. I wanted to leave but I wanted also to speak and I was afraid they'd snatch me down.

"Thank you, sir," I said, beginning where I had left off, and having them ignore me as before.

Yet when I finished there was a thunderous applause. I was surprised to see the superintendent come forth with a package wrapped in white tissue paper, and, gesturing for quiet, address the men.

"Gentlemen, you see that I did not overpraise this boy. He makes a good speech and some day he'll lead his people in the proper paths. And I don't have to tell you that that is important in these days and times. This is a good, smart boy, and so to encourage him in the right direction, in the name of the Board of Education I wish to present him a prize in the form of this . . ."

He paused, removing the tissue paper and revealing a gleaming calfskin brief case.

". . . in the form of this fist-class article from Shad Whitmore's shop."

"Boy," he said, addressing me, "take this prize and keep it well. Consider it a badge of office. Prize it. Keep developing as you are and some day it will be filled with important papers that will help shape the destiny of your people."

I was so moved that I could hardly express my thanks. A rope of bloody saliva forming a shape like an undiscovered continent drooled upon the leather and I wiped it quickly away. I felt an importance that I had never dreamed.

"Open it and see what's inside," I was told.

My fingers a-tremble, I complied, smelling the fresh leather and finding an official-looking document inside. It was a scholarship to the state college for Negroes. My eyes filled with tears and I ran awkwardly off the floor.

I was overjoyed; I did not even mind when I discovered that the gold pieces I had scrambled for were brass pocket tokens advertising a certain make of automobile.

When I reached home everyone was excited. Next day the neighbors came to congratulate me. I even felt safe from grandfather, whose deathbed curse usually spoiled my triumphs. I stood beneath his photograph with my brief case in hand and smiled triumphantly into his stolid black peasant's face. It was a face that fascinated me. The eyes seemed to follow everywhere I went.

That night I dreamed I was at a circus with him and that he refused to laugh at the clowns no matter what they did. Then later he told me to open my brief case and read what was inside and I did, finding an official envelope stamped with the state seal; and inside the envelope I found another and another, endlessly, and I thought I would fall of weariness. "Them's years," he said. "Now open that one." And I did and in it I found an engraved document containing a short message in letters of gold. "Read it," my grandfather said. "Out loud!"

"To Whom It May Concern," I intoned. "Keep This Nigger-Boy Running."

I awoke with the old man's laughter ringing in my ears.

(It was a dream I was to remember and dream again for many years after. But at that time I had no insight into its meaning. First I had to attend college.)

from *I Know Why the Caged Bird Sings*

Maya Angelou (1928–)

Maya Angelou, an accomplished poet, is best known for her autobiographical works. The first and most popular installment of the five volumes of her life story, *I Know Why the Caged Bird Sings* (1970), tells of Angelou's early childhood in Stamps, Arkansas, where she was raised by her grandmother, Annie Henderson. Because Henderson ran a general store, the young Maya enjoyed a central vantage point on life in the small Southern town. Angelou moved to California when she was eight and looked back on her Southern childhood with the distance born of learning, experience, and success.

"What you looking at me for?
I didn't come to stay . . ."

I hadn't so much forgot as I couldn't bring myself to remember. Other things were more important.

"What you looking at me for?
I didn't come to stay . . ."

Whether I could remember the rest of the poem or not was immaterial. The truth of the statement was like a wadded-up handkerchief, sopping wet in my fists, and the sooner they accepted it the quicker I could let my hands open and the air would cool my palms.

"What you looking at me for . . . ?"

The children's section of the Colored Methodist Episcopal Church was wiggling and giggling over my well-known forgetfulness.

The dress I wore was lavender taffeta, and each time I breathed it rustled, and now that I was sucking in air to breathe out shame it sounded like crepe paper on the back of hearses.

As I'd watched Momma put ruffles on the hem and cute little tucks around the waist, I knew that once I put it on I'd look like a movie star. (It was silk and that made up for the awful color.) I was going to look like one of the sweet little white girls who were everybody's dream of what was right with the world. Hanging softly over the black Singer sewing machine, it looked like magic, and when people saw me wearing it they were going to run up to me and say, "Marguerite [sometimes it was 'dear Marguerite'], forgive us, please, we didn't know who you were," and I would answer generously, "No, you couldn't have known. Of course I forgive you."

Just thinking about it made me go around with angel's dust sprinkled over my face for days. But Easter's early morning sun had shown the dress to be a plain ugly cut-down from a white woman's once-was-purple throwaway. It was old-lady-long too, but it didn't hide my skinny legs, which had been greased with Blue Seal Vaseline and powdered with the Arkansas red clay. The age-faded color made my skin look dirty like mud, and everyone in church was looking at my skinny legs.

Wouldn't they be surprised when one day I woke out of my black ugly dream, and my real hair, which was long and blond, would take the place of the kinky mass that Momma wouldn't let me straighten? My light-blue eyes were going to hypnotize them, after all the things they said about "my daddy must of been a Chinaman" (I thought they meant made out of china, like a cup) because my eyes were so small and squinty. Then they would understand why I had never picked up a Southern accent, or spoke the common slang, and why I had to be forced to eat pigs' tails and snouts. Because I was really white and because a cruel fairy stepmother, who was understandably jealous of my beauty, had turned me into a too-big Negro girl, with nappy black hair, broad feet and a space between her teeth that would hold a number-two pencil.

"What you looking . . ." The minister's wife leaned toward me, her long yellow face full of sorry. She whispered, "I just come to tell you, it's Easter Day." I repeated, jamming the words together, "Ijustcometotellyouit's Easter Day," as low as possible. The giggles hung in the air like melting clouds that were waiting to rain on me. I held up two fingers, close to my chest, which meant that I had to go to the toilet, and tiptoed toward the rear of the church. Dimly, somewhere over my head, I heard ladies saying, "Lord bless the child," and "Praise God." My head was up and my eyes were open, but I didn't see anything. Halfway down the aisle, the church exploded with "Were you there when they crucified my Lord?" and I tripped over a foot stuck out from the children's pew. I stumbled and started to say something, or maybe to scream, but a green persimmon, or it could have been a lemon, caught me between the legs and squeezed. I tasted the sour on my tongue and felt it in the back of my mouth. Then before I reached the door, the sting was burning down my legs and into my Sunday socks. I tried to hold, to squeeze it back, to keep it from speeding, but when I reached the church porch I knew I'd have to let it go, or it would probably run right back up to my head and my poor head would burst like a dropped watermelon, and all the brains and spit and tongue and eyes would roll all over the place. So I ran down into the yard and let it go. I ran, peeing and crying, not toward the toilet out back but to our house. I'd get a whipping for it, to be sure, and the nasty children would have something new to tease me about. I laughed anyway, partially for the sweet release; still, the greater joy came not only from being liberated from the silly church but from the knowledge that I wouldn't die from a busted head.

If growing up is painful for the Southern Black girl, being aware of her displacement is the rust on the razor that threatens the throat.

It is an unnecessary insult.

. . .

What sets one Southern town apart from another, or from a Northern town or hamlet, or city high-rise? The answer must be the experience shared between the unknowing majority (it) and the knowing minority (you). All of childhood's unanswered questions must finally be passed back to the town and answered there. Heroes and bogey men, values and dislikes, are first encountered and labeled in that early environment. In later years they change faces, places and maybe races, tactics, intensities and goals, but beneath those penetrable masks they wear forever the stocking-capped faces of childhood.

Mr. McElroy, who lived in the big rambling house next to the store, was very tall and broad, and although the years had eaten away the flesh from his shoulders, they had not, at the time of my knowing him, gotten to his high stomach, or his hands or feet.

He was the only Negro I knew, except for the school principal and the visiting teachers, who wore matching pants and jackets. When I learned that men's clothes were sold like that and called suits, I remember thinking that somebody had been very bright, for it made men look less manly, less threatening and a little more like women.

Mr. McElroy never laughed, and seldom smiled, and to his credit was the fact that he liked to talk to Uncle Willie. He never went to church, which Bailey and I thought also proved he was a very courageous person. How great it would be to grow up like that, to be able to stare religion down, especially living next door to a woman like Momma.

I watched him with the excitement of expecting him to do anything at any time. I never tired of this, or became disappointed or disenchanted with him, although from the perch of age, I see him now as a very simple and uninteresting man who sold patent medicine and tonics to the less sophisticated people in towns (villages) surrounding the metropolis of Stamps.

There seemed to be an understanding between Mr. McElroy and Grandmother. This was obvious to us because he never chased us off his land. In summer's late sunshine I often sat under the chinaberry tree in his yard, surrounded by the bitter aroma of its fruit and lulled by the drone of flies that fed on the berries. He sat in a slotted swing on his porch, rocking in his brown three-piece, his wide Panama nodding in time with the whir of insects.

One greeting a day was all that could be expected from Mr. McElroy. After his "Good morning, child," or "Good afternoon, child," he never said a word, even if I met him again on the road in front of his house or down by the well, or ran into him behind the house escaping in a game of hide-and-seek.

He remained a mystery in my childhood. A man who owned his land and the big many-windowed house with a porch that clung to its sides all around the house. An independent Black man. A near anachronism in Stamps.

Bailey was the greatest person in my world. And the fact that he was my brother, my only brother, and I had no sisters to share him with, was such good fortune that it made me want to live a Christian life just to show God that I was grateful. Where I was big, elbowy and grating, he was small, graceful and smooth. When I was described by our playmates as being shit color, he was lauded for his velvet-black skin. His hair fell down in black curls, and my head was covered with black steel wool. And yet he loved me.

When our elders said unkind things about my features (my family was handsome to a point of pain for me), Bailey would wink at me from across the room, and I knew that it was a matter of time before he would take revenge. He would allow the old ladies to finish wondering how on earth I came about, then he would ask, in a voice like cooling bacon grease, "Oh Mizeriz Coleman, how is your son? I saw him the other day, and he looked sick enough to die."

Aghast, the ladies would ask, "Die? From what? He ain't sick."

And in a voice oilier than the one before, he'd answer with a straight face, "From the Uglies."

I would hold my laugh, bite my tongue, grit my teeth and very seriously erase even the touch of a smile from my face. Later, behind the house by the black-walnut tree, we'd laugh and laugh and howl.

Bailey could count on very few punishments for his consistently outrageous behavior, for he was the pride of the Henderson/Johnson family.

His movements, as he was later to describe those of an acquaintance, were activated with oiled precision. He was also able to find more hours in the day than I thought existed. He finished chores, homework, read more books than I and played the group games on the side of the hill with the best of them. He could even pray out loud in church, and was apt at stealing pickles from the barrel that sat under the fruit counter and Uncle Willie's nose.

Once when the Store was full of lunchtime customers, he dipped the strainer, which we also used to sift weevils from meal and flour, into the barrel and fished for two fat pickles. He caught them and hooked the strainer onto the side of the barrel where they dripped until he was ready for them. When the last school bell rang, he picked the nearly dry pickles out of the strainer, jammed them into his pockets and threw the strainer behind the oranges. We ran out of the Store. It was summer and his pants were short, so the pickle juice made clean streams down his ashy legs, and he jumped with his pockets full of loot and his eyes laughing a "How about that?" He smelled like a vinegar barrel or a sour angel.

After our early chores were done, while Uncle Willie or Momma minded the Store, we were free to play the children's games as long as we stayed within yelling distance. Playing hide-and-seek, his voice was easily identified, singing, "Last night, night before, twenty-four robbers at my door. Who all is hid? Ask me to let them in, hit 'em in the head with a rolling pin. Who all is hid?" In follow the leader, naturally he was the one who created the most daring and interesting things to do. And when he was on the tail of the pop the whip, he would twirl off the end like a top, spinning, falling, laughing, finally stopping just before my heart beat its last, and then he was back in the game, still laughing.

Of all the needs (there are none imaginary) a lonely child has, the one that must be satisfied, if there is going to be hope and a hope of wholeness, is the unshaking need for an unshakable God. My pretty Black brother was my Kingdom Come.

In Stamps the segregation was so complete that most Black children didn't really, absolutely know what whites looked like. Other than that they were different, to be dreaded, and in that dread was included the hostility of the powerless against the powerful, the poor against the rich, the worker against the worked for and the ragged against the well dressed.

I remember never believing that whites were really real.

Many women who worked in their kitchens traded at our Store, and when they carried their finished laundry back to town they often set the big baskets down on our front porch to pull a singular piece from the starched collection and show either how graceful was their ironing hand or how rich and opulent was the property of their employers.

I looked at the items that weren't on display. I knew, for instance, that white men wore shorts, as Uncle Willie did, and that they had an opening for taking out their "things" and peeing, and that white women's breasts weren't built into their dresses, as some people said, because I saw their brassieres in the baskets. But I couldn't force myself to think of them as people. People were Mrs. LaGrone, Mrs. Hendricks, Momma, Reverend Sneed, Lillie B, and Louise and Rex. Whitefolks couldn't be people because their feet were too small, their skin too white and see-throughy, and they didn't walk on the balls of their feet the way people did—they walked on their heels like horses.

People were those who lived on my side of town. I didn't like them all, or, in fact, any of them very much, but they were people. These others, the strange pale creatures that lived in their alien unlife, weren't considered folks. They were whitefolks.

. . .

"Thou shall not be dirty" and "Thou shall not be impudent" were the two commandments of Grandmother Henderson upon which hung our total salvation.

Each night in the bitterest winter we were forced to wash faces, arms, necks, legs and feet before going to bed. She used to add, with a smirk that unprofane people can't control when venturing into profanity, "and wash as far as possible, then wash possible."

We would go to the well and wash in the ice-cold, clear water, grease our legs with the equally cold stiff Vaseline, then tiptoe into the house. We wiped the dust from our toes and settled down for schoolwork, cornbread, clabbered milk, prayers and bed, always in that order. Momma was famous for pulling the quilts off after we had fallen asleep to examine our feet. If they weren't clean enough for her, she took the switch (she kept one behind the bedroom door for emergencies) and woke up the offender with a few aptly placed burning reminders.

The area around the well at night was dark and slick, and boys told about how snakes love water, so that anyone who had to draw water at night and then stand there alone and wash knew that moccasins and rattlers, puff adders and boa constrictors were winding their way to the well and would arrive just as the person washing got soap in her eyes. But Momma convinced us that not only was cleanliness next to Godliness, dirtiness was the inventor of misery.

The impudent child was detested by God and a shame to its parents and could bring destruction to its house and line. All adults had to be addressed as Mister, Missus, Miss, Auntie, Cousin, Unk, Uncle, Buhbah, Sister, Brother and a thousand other appellations indicating familial relationship and the lowliness of the addressor.

Everyone I knew respected these customary laws, except for the powhitetrash children.

Some families of powhitetrash lived on Momma's farm land behind the school. Sometimes a gaggle of them came to the Store, filling the whole room, chasing out the air and even changing the well-known scents. The children crawled over the shelves and into the potato and onion bins, twanging all the time in their sharp voices like cigar-box guitars. They took liberties in my Store that I would never dare. Since Momma told us that the less you say to white-folks (or even powhitetrash) the better, Bailey and I would stand, solemn, quiet, in the displaced air. But if one of the playful apparitions got close to us, I pinched it. Partly out of angry frustration and partly because I didn't believe in its flesh reality.

They called my uncle by his first name and ordered him around the Store. He, to my crying shame, obeyed them in his limping dip-straight-dip fashion.

My grandmother, too, followed their orders, except that she didn't seem to be servile because she anticipated their needs.

"Here's sugar, Miz Potter, and here's baking powder. You didn't buy soda last month, you'll probably be needing some."

Momma always directed her statements to the adults, but sometimes, Oh painful sometimes, the grimy, snotty-nosed girls would answer her.

"Naw, Annie . . ." — to Momma? Who owned the land they lived on? Who forgot more than they would ever learn? If there was any justice in the world, God should strike them dumb at once! — "Just give us some extry sody crackers, and some more mackerel."

At least they never looked in her face, or I never caught them doing so. Nobody with a smidgen of training, not even the worst roustabout, would look right in a grown person's face. It meant the person was trying to take the words out before they were formed. The dirty little children didn't do that, but they threw their orders around the Store like lashes from a cat-o'-nine-tails.

When I was around ten years old, those scruffy children caused me the most painful and confusing experience I had ever had with my grandmother.

One summer morning, after I had swept the dirt yard of leaves, spearmint-gum wrappers and Vienna-sausage labels, I raked the yellow-red dirt, and made half-moons carefully, so that the design stood out clearly and mask-like. I put the rake behind the Store and came through the back of the house to find Grandmother on the front porch in her big, wide white apron. The apron was so stiff by virtue of the starch that it could have stood alone. Momma was admiring the yard, so I joined her. It truly looked like a flat redhead that had been raked with a big-toothed comb. Momma didn't say anything but I knew she liked it. She looked over toward the school principal's house and to the right at Mr. McElroy's. She was hoping one of those community pillars would see the design before the day's business wiped it out. Then she looked upward to the school. My head had swung with hers, so at just about the same time we saw a troop of the powhite-trash kids marching over the hill and down by the side of the school.

I looked to Momma for direction. She did an excellent job of sagging from her waist down, but from the waist up she seemed to be pulling for the top of the oak tree across the road. Then she began to moan a hymn. Maybe not to moan, but the tune was so slow and the meter so strange that she could have been moaning. She didn't look at me again. When the children reached halfway down the hill, halfway to the Store, she said without turning, "Sister, go on inside."

I wanted to beg her, "Momma, don't wait for them. Come on inside with me. If they come in the Store, you go to the bedroom and let me wait on them. They only frighten me if you're around. Alone I know how to handle them." But of course I couldn't say anything, so I went in and stood behind the screen door.

Before the girls got to the porch I heard their laughter crackling and popping like pine logs in a cooking stove. I suppose my lifelong paranoia was born in those cold, molasses-slow minutes. They came finally to stand on the ground in front of Momma. At first they pretended seriousness. Then one of them wrapped her right arm in the crook of her left, pushed out her mouth and started to hum. I realized that she was aping my grandmother. Another said, "Naw, Helen, you ain't standing like her. This here's it." Then she lifted her chest, folded her arms and mocked that strange carriage that was Annie Henderson. Another laughed, "Naw, you can't do it. Your mouth ain't pooched out enough. It's like this."

I thought about the rifle behind the door, but I knew I'd never be able to hold it straight, and the .410, our sawed-off shotgun, which stayed loaded and was fired every New Year's night, was locked in the trunk and Uncle Willie had the key on his chain. Through the fly-specked screen-door, I could see that the arms of Momma's apron jiggled from the vibrations of her humming. But her knees seemed to have locked as if they would never bend again.

She sang on. No louder than before, but no softer either. No slower or faster.

The dirt of the girls' cotton dresses continued on their legs, feet, arms and faces to make them all of a piece. Their greasy uncolored hair hung down, uncombed, with a grim finality. I knelt to see them better, to remember them for all time. The tears that had slipped down my dress left unsurprising dark spots, and made the front yard blurry and even more unreal. The world had taken a deep breath and was having doubts about continuing to revolve.

The girls had tired of mocking Momma and turned to other means of agitation. One crossed her eyes, stuck her thumbs in both sides of her mouth and said, "Look here, Annie." Grandmother hummed on and the apron strings trembled. I wanted to throw a handful of black pepper in their faces, to throw lye on them, to scream that they were dirty, scummy peckerwoods, but I knew I was as clearly imprisoned behind the scene as the actors outside were confined to their roles.

One of the smaller girls did a kind of puppet dance while her fellow clowns laughed at her. But the tall one, who was almost a woman, said something very quietly, which I couldn't hear. They all moved backward from the porch, still watching Momma. For an awful second I thought they were going to throw a rock at Momma, who seemed (except for the apron strings) to have turned into stone herself. But the big girl turned her back, bent down and put her hands flat on the ground—she didn't pick up anything. She simply shifted her weight and did a hand stand.

Her dirty bare feet and long legs went straight for the sky. Her dress fell down around her shoulders, and she had on no drawers. The slick pubic hair made a brown triangle where her legs came together. She hung in the vacuum of that lifeless morning for only a few seconds, then wavered and tumbled. The other girls clapped her on the back and slapped their hands.

Momma changed her song to "Bread of Heaven, bread of Heaven, feed me till I want no more."

I found that I was praying too. How long could Momma hold out? What new indignity would they think of to subject her to? Would I be able to stay out of it? What would Momma really like me to do?

Then they were moving out of the yard, on their way to town. They bobbed their heads and shook their slack behinds and turned, one at a time:

" 'Bye, Annie."

" 'Bye, Annie."

" 'Bye, Annie."

Momma never turned her head or unfolded her arms, but she stopped singing and said, " 'Bye, Miz Helen, 'bye, Miz Ruth, 'bye, Miz Eloise."

I burst. A firecracker July-the-Fourth burst. How could Momma call them Miz? The mean nasty things. Why couldn't she have come inside the sweet, cool store when we saw them breasting the hill? What did she prove? And then if they were dirty, mean and impudent, why did Momma have to call them Miz?

She stood another whole song through and then opened the screen door to look down on me crying in rage. She looked until I looked up. Her face was a brown moon that shone on me. She was beautiful. Something had happened out there, which I couldn't completely understand, but I could see that she was happy. Then she bent down and touched me as mothers of the church "lay hands on the sick and afflicted" and I quieted.

"Go wash your face, Sister." And she went behind the candy counter and hummed, "Glory, glory, hallelujah, when I lay my burden down."

I threw the well water on my face and used the weekday handkerchief to blow my nose. Whatever the contest had been out front, I knew Momma had won.

I took the rake back to the front yard. The smudged footprints were easy to erase. I worked for a long time on my new design and laid the rake behind the wash pot. When I came back in the Store, I took Momma's hand and we both walked outside to look at the pattern.

It was a large heart with lots of hearts growing smaller inside, and piercing from the outside rim to the smallest heart was an arrow. Momma said, "Sister, that's right pretty." Then she turned back to the Store and resumed, "Glory, glory, hallelujah, when I lay my burden down."

Momma intended to teach Bailey and me to use the paths of life that she and her generation and all the Negroes gone before had found, and found to be safe ones. She didn't cotton to the idea that white-folks could be talked to at all without risking one's life. And certainly they couldn't be spoken to insolently. In fact, even in their absence they could not be spoken of too harshly unless we used the sobriquet "They." If she had been asked and had chosen to answer the question of whether she was cowardly or not, she would have said that she was a realist. Didn't she stand up to "them" year after year? Wasn't she the only Negro woman in Stamps referred to once as Mrs.?

That incident became one of Stamps' little legends. Some years before Bailey and I arrived in town, a man was hunted down for assaulting white womanhood. In trying to escape he ran to the Store. Momma and Uncle Willie hid him behind the chifforobe until night, gave him supplies for an overland journey and sent him on his way. He was, however, apprehended, and in court when he was questioned as to his movements on the day of the crime, he replied that after he heard that he was being sought he took refuge in Mrs. Henderson's Store.

The judge asked that Mrs. Henderson be subpoenaed, and when Momma arrived and said she was Mrs. Henderson, the judge, the bailiff and other whites in the audience laughed. The judge had really made a gaffe calling a Negro woman Mrs., but then he was from Pine Bluff and couldn't have been expected to know that a woman who owned a store in that village would also turn out to be colored. The whites tickled their funny bones with the incident for a long time, and the Negroes thought it proved the worth and majesty of my grandmother. . . .

. . .

Stamps, Arkansas, was Chitlin' Switch, Georgia; Hang 'Em High, Alabama; Don't Let the Sun Set on You Here, Nigger, Mississippi; or any other name just as descriptive. People in Stamps used to say that the whites in our town were so prejudiced that a Negro couldn't buy vanilla ice cream. Except on July Fourth. Other days he had to be satisfied with chocolate.

A light shade had been pulled down between the Black community and all things white, but one could see through it enough to develop a fear-admiration-contempt for the white "things" — white folks' cars and white glistening houses and their children and their women. But above all, their wealth that allowed them to waste was the most enviable. They had so many clothes they were able to give perfectly good dresses, worn just under the arms, to the sewing class at our school for the larger girls to practice on.

Although there was always generosity in the Negro neighborhood, it was indulged on pain of sacrifice. Whatever was given by Black people to other Blacks was most probably needed as desperately by the donor as by the receiver. A fact which made the giving or receiving a rich exchange.

I couldn't understand whites and where they got the right to spend money so lavishly. Of course, I knew God was white too, but no one could have made me believe he was prejudiced. My grandmother had more money than all the powhitetrash. We owned land and houses, but each day Bailey and I were cautioned, "Waste not, want not."

Momma bought two bolts of cloth each year for winter and summer clothes. She made my school dresses, underslips, bloomers, handkerchiefs, Bailey's shirts, shorts, her aprons, house dresses and waists from the rolls shipped to Stamps by Sears and Roebuck. Uncle Willie was the only person in the family who wore ready-to-wear clothes all the time. Each day, he wore fresh white shirts and flowered suspenders, and his special shoes cost twenty dollars. I thought Uncle Willie sinfully vain, especially when I had to iron seven stiff starched shirts and not leave a cat's face anywhere.

During the summer we went barefoot, except on Sunday, and we learned to resole our shoes when they "gave out," as Momma used to say. The Depression must have hit the white section of Stamps with cyclonic impact, but it seeped into the Black area slowly, like a thief with misgivings. The country had been in the throes of the Depression for two years before the Negroes in Stamps knew it. I think that everyone thought that the Depression, like everything else, was for the whitefolks, so it had nothing to do with them. Our people had lived off the land and counted on cotton-picking and hoeing and chopping seasons to bring in the cash needed to buy shoes, clothes, books and light farm equipment. It was when the owners of cotton fields dropped the payment of ten cents for a pound of cotton to eight, seven and finally five that the Negro community realized that the Depression, at least, did not discriminate.

Welfare agencies gave food to the poor families, Black and white. Gallons of lard, flour, salt, powdered eggs and powdered milk. People stopped trying to raise hogs because it was too difficult to get slop rich enough to feed them, and no one had the money to buy mash or fish meal.

Momma spent many nights figuring on our tablets, slowly. She was trying to find a way to keep her business going, although her customers had no money. When she came to her conclusions, she said, "Bailey, I want you to make me a nice clear sign. Nice and neat. And Sister, you can color it with your Crayolas. I want it to say:

1 5 LB. CAN OF POWDERED MILK IS WORTH 50¢ IN TRADE
1 5 LB. CAN OF POWDERED EGGS IS WORTH $1.00 IN TRADE
10 #2 CANS OF MACKEREL IS WORTH $1.00 IN TRADE.

And so on. Momma kept her store going. Our customers didn't even have to take their slated provisions home. They'd pick them up from the welfare center downtown and drop them off at the Store. If they didn't want an exchange at the moment they'd put down in one of the big gray ledgers the amount of credit coming to them. We were among the few Negro families not on relief, but Bailey and I were the only children in the town proper that we knew who ate powdered eggs every day and drank the powdered milk.

Our playmates' families exchanged their unwanted food for sugar, coal oil, spices, potted meat, Vienna sausage, peanut butter, soda crackers, toilet soap and even laundry soap. We were always given enough to eat, but we both hated the lumpy milk and mushy eggs, and sometimes we'd stop off at the house of one of the poorer families to get some peanut butter and crackers. Stamps was as slow coming out of the Depression as it had been getting into it. World War II was well along before there was a noticeable change in the economy of that near-forgotten hamlet.

from *Train Whistle Guitar*

Albert Murray (1916–)

Noted essayist and novelist Albert Murray, born and raised in the south Alabama town of Nakomis, began what would be a lifelong friendship with future writer Ralph Ellison while attending Tuskegee Institute. After a twenty-year career in the U.S. Air Force, Murray turned to a writing career in the early 1960s. Disturbed by what he considered to be an exaggeration of "the fakelore of white supremacy and the filthlore of black pathology," Murray attempted to breathe life into the abstractions peddled by many social scientists. In his semiautobiographical novel *Train Whistle Guitar*, published in 1974, Murray reminds the reader that black life in the South cannot be understood if thought of exclusively in terms of oppression and degradation.

There was a chinaberry tree in the front yard of that house in those days, and in early spring the showers outside that window always used to become pale green again. Then before long there would be chinaberry blossoms. Then it would be maytime and then junebugtime and no more school bell mornings until next September, and when you came out onto the front porch and it was fair there were chinaberry shadows on the swing and the rocking chair, and chinaberry shade all the way from the steps to the gate.

When you climbed up to the best place in the chinaberry tree and looked out across Gins Alley during that time of the year the kite pasture, through which you took the short cut to the post office, would be a meadow of dog fennels again. So there would also be jimson weeds as well as ragworts and rabbit tobacco along the curving roadside from the sweet gum corner to the pump shed, and poke-salad from there to the AT & N.

You couldn't see the post office flag from the chinaberry tree because it was down in Buckshaw Flat at the L & N whistlestop. You couldn't see the switch sidings for the sawmills along that part of Mobile River either, because all that was on the other side of the tank yard of the Gulf Refining Company. All you could see beyond the kite pasture were the telegraph poles and the sky above the pine ridge overlooking Chickasabogue Creek and Hog Bayou.

You couldn't see the blackberry slopes near the L & N Section Gang Quarters because first there were the honeysuckle thickets and then Skin

379

Game Jungle where the best muscadine vines were and in which there were also some of the same owl tree holes you knew about from fireside ghost stories about treasures buried by the pirates and the Confederates.

Southeast of all of that was the L & N clearing, across which you could see the trains and beyond which you could also see that part of the river. Next on the horizon due south was Three Mile Crest, which blocked off Dodge Mill Bottom and that part of Three Mile Creek. So you couldn't see the waterfront either, nor any part of the downtown Mobile, Alabama skyline, not even with real binoculars.

Nor could you see One Mile Bridge beyond the treeline to the southwest. Nor the pecan orchard which you knew was due west looking out over the gate and the sunflowers and across the AT & N cut, which you couldn't see either. Nor African Baptist Hill. But between that neighborhood and the Chickasaw Highway was the Southern Railroad, whose night whistles you could sometimes hear as sometimes after midnight you could also hear the M & O, the GM & O and the GM & N en route to St. Louis, Missouri and Kansas City by way of Meridian, Mississippi.

All you could see due north up Dodge Mill Road beyond Buckshaw Corner and the crawfish pond that was once part of a Civil War artillery embankment was the sky above Bay Poplar Woods fading away into the marco polo blue horizon mist on the other side of which were such express train destinations as Birmingham, Alabama and Nashville, Tennessee, and Cincinnati, Ohio, and Detroit, Michigan, plus the snowbound Klondike of Canada plus the icebound tundras of Alaska plus the North Pole.

The Official name of that place (which is perhaps even more of a location in time than an intersection on a map) was Gasoline Point, Alabama, because that was what our post office address was, and it was also the name on the L & N timetable and the road map. But once upon a time it was also the briarpatch, which is why my nickname was then Scooter, and is also why the chinaberry tree (that was ever as tall as any fairy tale beanstalk) was, among other things, my spyglass tree.

I still cannot remember ever having heard anybody saying anything about Luzana Cholly's mother and father. Most of the time you forgot all about that part of his existence just as most people had probably long since forgotten whether they had ever heard his family name. Nobody I know ever heard him use it, and no sooner had you thought about it than you suddenly realized that he didn't seem ever to have had or to have needed any family at all. Nor did he seem to need a wife or steady woman either. But that was because he was not yet ready to quit the trail and settle down. Because he had lived with more women from time to time and place to place than the average man could or would even try to shake a stick at.

The more I think about all of that the more I realize that you never could tell which part of what you heard about something he had done had actually happened and which part somebody else had probably made up. Nor did it ever really matter which was which. Not to anybody I ever knew in Gasoline Point, Alabama, in any case, to most of whom all you had to do was mention his name and they were ready to believe any claim you made for him, the more outrageously improbable the better. All you had to do was say Luzana Cholly old Luzana Cholly old Luze. All you had to do was see that sporty limp walk. Not to mention his voice, which was as smoke-blue sounding as the Philamayork-skyline-blue mist beyond blue steel railroad bridges. Not to mention how he was forever turning guitar strings into train whistles which were not only the once-upon-a-time voices of storytellers but of all the voices saying what was being said in the stories as well.

Not that I who have always been told that I was born to be somebody did not always know on my deepest levels of comprehension that the somebody-ness of Luzana Cholly was of its very nature nothing if not legendary. Which no doubt also has something to do with why I almost always used to feel so numb and strange when somebody other than kinfolks called out the name that Mama had given me and Miss Tee had taught me how to spell and write. I always jumped, even when I didn't move. And in school I wanted to hide, but you had to answer because it was the teacher calling the roll so I said Present and it didn't sound like myself at all. It was not until Uncle Jerome nicknamed me scooter that I could say That's me, that's who I am and what I am and what I do.

Anyway, such somehow has always been the nature of legends and legendary men (which probably exist to beget other legends and would-be legendary men in the first place) that every time Little Buddy Marshall and I used to do that sporty-blue limp-walk (which told the whole world that you were ready for something because at worst you had only been ever so slightly sprained and bruised by all the terrible situations you had been through) we were also reminding ourselves of the inevitability of the day when we too would have to grab ourselves an expert armful of lightning special L & N freight train rolling north by east to the steel blue castles and patent leather avenues of Philamayork, which was the lodestone center of the universe.

That is why we had started practicing freight train hopping on the tanks and boxcars in the switchyard as soon as we had gained enough leeway to sneak that far away from the neighborhood. That was the first big step, and you were already running a double risk (of being caught and of getting maimed for life at the very least) as soon as you started playing with something as forbidden as that, which was what they told you every-thing you had ever heard about old Peg Leg Nat to keep you from doing. Old Peg Leg Nat Carver, who had a head as bald and shiny as the nick-elplated radiator of the Packard Straight Eight and who prided himself on being able to butt like a billy goat, and who now spent most of his time fishing and selling fresh fish and shrimp and crabs from the greenness of his palm frond covered wheelbarrow. Somebody was always reminding you of what had happened to him. Mama for instance, who could never pass up a chance to say Here come old Peg Leg Nat and a peg leg or some-thing worse is just exactly what messing around with freight trains will get you. And she had had me scared for a while, but not for long. Because then Little Buddy Marshall and I found out that what had happened prob-ably never would have happened if Old Nat, who was then known as old Butt Head Nat, had not been drunk and trying to show everybody how fancy he was. And anyway anybody could see that getting his leg cut off hadn't really stopped old Nat for good, since not only did he still do it again every time he got the itch to go somewhere, he also could still beat any two-legged man except Luzana Cholly himself snagging anything rolling through Gasoline Point.

. . .

Then Little Buddy found out that Luzana Cholly himself was getting ready to leave town again soon and I myself found out which way he was going to be heading (but not where) and which day, so we also knew which train; and that was when we got everything together and started waiting.

Then at long last after all the boy blue dreaming and scheming and all the spyglass scanning it was that day and we were there in that place because it was time to take the next step. I was wearing my high top bro-gan shoes and I had on my corduroy pants and a sweater under my over-alls with my jumper tucked in. I was also wearing my navy blue baseball cap and my rawhide wristband and I had my pitcher's glove folded fingers up in my left hip pocket. And Little Buddy was wearing and carrying the same amount of the very same traveling gear except for his thin first base pad instead of big thick Sears Roebuck catcher's mitt. Our other things plus something to eat were rolled up in our expertly tied blanket rolls so that we could maneuver with both arms free.

Little Buddy was also carrying Mister Big Buddy Marshall's pearl han-dled .38 Smith & Wesson. And our standard equipment for any trip out-side that neighborhood in those days always included our all-purpose jack-knives, which we had learned to snap open like a switchblade and could also flip like a Mexican dagger. Also, buckskin pioneers and wilderness scouts that we would always be, we had not forgotten hooks and twine to fish with. Nor were we ever to be caught in any root hog or die poor situation without our trusty old Y-stock (plus inner tube rubber plus shoe tongue leather) slingshots and a drawstring Bull Durham pouch of birdshot babbitt metal plus at least a handful of peewee sized gravel pebbles.

It was May but school was not out of session yet, so not only were we running away from home we were also playing hooky, for which the Truant Officer also known as the School Police could take you to Juvenile Court and have you detained and then sent to the Reformatory School. (Mt. Meigs and Wetumpka were where they used to send you in those days. No wonder I still remember them as being two of the ugliest place names in the whole state of Alabama. Not as ugly as Bay Minette, which I still remember as a prototype of all the rattlesnake nests of rawboned hawkeyed nigger-fearing lynch-happy peckerwoods I've ever seen or heard tell of. But ugly enough to offset most of the things you didn't like about grade school.)

It was hot even for that time of year, and with that many clothes on, we were already sweating. But you had to have them, and that was the best way to carry them. There was a thin breeze coming across the railroad from the river, the marsh and Polecat Bay, but the sun was so hot and bright that the rail tracks were shimmering under the wide open sky as if it were the middle of summer.

We were waiting in the thicket under the hill between where the Dodge Mill Road came down and where the oil yard switching spurs began, and from where we were you could see up and down the clearing as far as you needed to.

. . .

I have now forgotten how long we had to stay there waiting and watching the place from where we had seen Luzana Cholly come running across the right of way to the tracks so many times. But there was nothing you could do but wait then, as we knew he was doing, probably strumming his guitar and humming to himself.

Man, I wish it would hurry up and come on, Little Buddy said all of a sudden.

Man, me too, I probably said without even having to think about it.

Man, got to get to goddamn splitting, he said and I heard his fingers touching the package of cigarettes in his bib pocket.

We were sitting on the blanket rolls with our legs crossed Indian fire circle fashion. Then he was smoking another One Eleven, holding it the way we both used to do in those days, letting it dangle from the corner of your curled lips while tilting your head to one side with one eye watching and the other squinted, like a card sharper.

Boy, goddammit, you just watch me nail the sapsucker, he said.

Man, and you just watch me.

You could smell the mid-May woods up the slope behind us then, the late late dogwoods, the early honeysuckles, and the warm earth-plus-green smell of the pre-summer undergrowth. I can't remember which birds you used to hear during each season, not like I used to; but I do remember hearing a woodpecker somewhere on a dead hollow tree among all the other bird sounds that day because I also remember thinking that wood-peckers always sounded as if they were out in the open in the very bright-est part of the sunshine.

Waiting and watching, you were also aware of how damp and cool the sandy soft ground was underneath you there in the gray and green shade; and you could smell that smell too, even as the Gulf Coast states breeze blew all of the maritime odors in to you from the river and the marshlands. Little Buddy finished his cigarette and flipped the stub out into the sun-shine and then sat with his back against a sapling and sucked his teeth. I looked out across the railroad to where the gulls were circling over the reeds and the water.

You know something? Goddammit, when I come back here to this here little old granny-dodging burg, boy I'm going to be a goddamn man and a goddamn half, Little Buddy said, breaking the silence again.

As before, he was talking as much to himself as to me. But I said: And don't give a goddamn who knows it. Then he said: Boy, Chicago. And I said: Man, Detroit. And he said: Man, St. Louis. And I said: And Kansas City. Then: Hey, Los Angeles. Hey, San Francisco. Hey, Denver, Colorado. Him calling one and me adding another until we had leapfrogged all the way back down to the Florida Coast Line, with him doing that old section gang chant: Say I don't know but I think I will make my home in Jacksonville (Hey big boy cain't you line em).

Then I was the one, because that is when I said: Hey, you know who the only other somebody else in the world I kinda wish was here to be going too? And little Buddy said: Old Cateye Gander. Me too. Old Big-toed Gander. Man, shit I reckon.

Man, old Gander Gallagher can steal lightning if he have to.

Man, who you telling?

Man, how about that time? You know that time getting them wheels for that go-cart. That time from Buckshaw.

Right on out from under that nightwatchman's nose, man.

And everybody know they got some peckerwoods down there subject to spray your ass with birdshot just for walking too close to that fence after dark.

Man, shit I reckon. And tell you you lucky it wasn't that other barrel, because that's the one with triple ought buckshot.

Hey man but old Luze though.

Man, you know you talking about somebody now.

Talking about somebody taking the cake.

Goddammit man, boy, just think. We going!

Me and you and old hard cutting Luze, buddy.

Boy, and then when we get back, I said that and I could see it. Coming back on that Pan American I would be carrying two leather suitcases, and have a money belt and an underarm holster for my special-made .38 Special. And I would be dressed in tailor-made clothes and handmade shoes from London, England by way of Philamayork.

Hey Lebo, I said, thinking about all that then. How long you think it might take us to get all fixed up to come back.

Man, shoot, I don't know and don't care.

You coming back when old Luze come back?

Man, I don't know. Just so we go. Man, me I just want to go.

I didn't say anything else then. Because I was trying to think about how it was actually going to be then. Because what I had been thinking about before was how I wanted it to be. I didn't say anything else because I was thinking about myself then. And then my stomach began to feel weak and I tried to think about something else. But I couldn't. Because what I suddenly remembered as soon as I closed my eyes that time was the barbershop and them talking about baseball and boxing and women and politics with the newspapers rattling and old King Oliver's band playing "Sugarfoot Stomp" on the Victrola in Papa Gumbo's cookshop next door, and I said I want to and I don't want to but I got to, then I won't have to anymore either and if I do I will be ready.

Then I looked over at Little Buddy again, who now was lying back against the tree with his hands behind his head and his eyes closed, whose legs were crossed, and who was resting as easy as some baseball players always seem able to do before gametime even with the band hot timing the music you always keep on hearing over and over when you lose. I wondered what he was really thinking. Did he really mean it when he said he didn't know and didn't even care? You couldn't tell what he was thinking, but if you knew him as well as I did it was easy enough to see that he was not about to back out now, no matter how he was feeling about it.

So I said to myself: Goddammit if Little Buddy Marshall can go goddammit I can too because goddammit ain't nothing he can do I cain't if I want to because he might be the expert catcher but I'm the ace pitcher and he can bat on both sides but I'm the all-round infield flash and I'm the prizefighter and I'm also the swimmer.

But what I found myself thinking about again then was Mama and Papa, and that was when I suddenly realized as never before how worried and bothered and puzzled they were going to be when it was not only that many hours after school but also after dark and I still was not back home yet. So that was also when I found myself thinking about Miss Tee again. Because she was the one whose house would be the very first place I was absolutely certain Mama would go looking for me, even before asking Mister Big Buddy about Little Buddy.

Hey, Lebo.
Hey, Skebo.
Skipping city.
Man, you tell em.
Getting further.
Man, ain't no lie.
Getting long gone.
Man, ain't no dooky.

Goddammit to hell, Little Buddy said then, why don't it come on?
Son-of-a-bitch, I said.
Goddamn granny-dodging son-of-a-bitching mother-fucking mother-fucker, he said lighting another One Eleven, come on here son-of-a-bitching motherfucking son-of-a-bitch.
I didn't say anything else because I didn't want him to say anything else. Then I was leaning back against my tree looking out across the sandy clearing at the sky beyond the railroad and the marsh territory again, where there were clean white pieces of clouds that looked like balled up sheets in a wash tub, and the sky itself was blue like rinse water with bluing in it; and I was thinking about Mama and Papa and Uncle Jerome and Miss Tee again, and I couldn't keep myself from hoping that it was all a dream.

That was when I heard the whistle blowing for Three Mile Creek Bridge and opened my eyes and saw Little Buddy already up and slinging his roll over his shoulder.
Hey, here that son-of-a-bitch come. Hey, come on, man.
I'm here, son, I said snatching my roll into place, Don't be worrying about me. I been ready.
The engine went by, and the whistle blew again, this time for the Chickasabogue, and we were running across the sandy crunch-spongy clearing. My ears were ringing then, and I was sweating, and my neck was hot and sticky and my pants felt as if the seat had been ripped away. There was nothing but the noise of the chugging and steaming and the smell of coal smoke, and we were running into it, and then we were climbing up the fill and running along the high bed of crosstie slag and cinders.

We were trotting along in reach of it then, that close to the um chuckchuck um chuckchuck um chuckchuckchuck, catching our breath and remembering to make sure to let at least one empty boxcar go by. Then when the next gondola came Little Buddy took the front end, and I grabbed the back. I hit the hotbox with my right foot and stepped onto the step and pulled up. The wind was in my ears then, but I knew all about that from all the practice I had had by that time. So I climbed on up the short ladder and got down on the inside, and there was old Little Buddy coming grinning back toward me.

Man, what did I tell you!

Man, did you see me lam into that sucker?

Boy, we low more nailed it.

Hey, I bet old Luze he kicking it any minute now.

Man, I'm talking about cold hanging it, man.

Boy, you know it, man, I said. But I was thinking I hope so, I hope old Luze didn't change his mind, I hope we don't have to start out all by ourselves.

Hey going, boy, Little Buddy said.

Man, I done told you!

We crawled up into the left front corner out of the wind, and there was nothing to do but wait again then. We knew that this was the northbound freight that always had to pull into the hole for Number Four once she was twelve miles out, and that was when we were supposed to get to the open boxcar.

So we got the cigarettes out and lit up, and there was nothing but the rumbling thunder-like noise the wide open gondola made then, plus the far away sound of the engine and the low rolling pony tail of gray smoke coming back. We were just sitting there then, and after we began to get used to the vibration, nothing at all was happening except being there. You couldn't even see the scenery going by.

You were just there in the hereness and nowness of that time then, and I don't think you ever really remember very much about being in situations like that except the way you felt, and all I can remember now about that part is the nothingness of doing nothing, and the feeling not of going but of being taken, as of being borne away on a bare barge or even on the bare back of a storybeast.

All you could see after we went through the smokey gray lattice-work of Chickasabogue Bridge was the now yellow blue sky and the bare floor and the sides of the heavy rumbling gondola, and the only other thing I have ever remembered is how I wished something would happen because I definitely did not want to be going anywhere at all then, and I already felt lost even though I knew good and well that I was not yet twelve miles from home. Because although Little Buddy Marshall and I had certainly been many times farther away and stayed longer, this already seemed to be farther and longer than all the other times together!

. . .

Then finally you could tell it was beginning to slow down, and we stood up and started getting ready. Then it was stopping and we were ready and we climbed over the side and came down the ladder and struck out forward. We were still in the bayou country, and beyond the train-smell there was the sour-sweet snakey smell of the swampland. We were running on slag and cinders again then and with the train quiet and waiting for Number Four you could hear the double crunching of our brogans echoing through the waterlogged moss-draped cypresses.

Along there the L & N Causeway embankment was almost as high as the telegraph lines, and the poles were black with a fresh coat of creosote and there were water lilies floating on the slimy green ditch that separated the railroad right of way from the edge of the swamp. Hot-collared and hustling to get to where we estimated the empty boxcar to be, we came pumping on. And then at last we saw it and could slow down and catch our breath.

And that was when we also saw that old Luzana Cholly himself was already there. We had been so busy trying to get there that we had forgotten all about him for the time being. Not only that but this was also the part that both of us had completely forgotten to think about all along. So we hadn't even thought about what we were going to say, not to mention what he was going to say.

And there he was now standing looking down at us from the open door with an unlighted cigarette in his hand. We had already stopped without even realizing it, and suddenly everything was so quiet that you could hear your heart pounding inside your head. It was as if the spot where you were had been shut off from everything else in the world. I for my part knew exactly what was going to happen then, and I was so embarrassed that I could have sunk into the ground, because I also thought: Now he's going to call us a name. Now he just might never have anything to do with us anymore.

We were standing there not so much waiting as frozen then, and he just let us stay there and feel like two wet puppies shivering, their tails tucked between their legs. Then he lit his cigarette and finally said something.

Oh no you don't oh no you don't neither. Because it ain't like that ain't like that ain't never been like that and ain't never going to be not if I can help it.

He said that as much to himself as to us, but at the same time he was shaking his head not only as if we couldn't understand him but also as if we couldn't even hear him.

Y'all know it ain't like this. I know y'all know good and well it *cain't* be nothing like *this.*

Neither one of us even moved an eye. Little Buddy didn't even dig his toe into the ground.

So this what y'all up to. Don't say a word. Don't you open your mouth.

I could have crawled into a hole. I could have sunk into a pond. I could have melted leaving only a greasy spot. I could have shriveled to nothing but an ash.

Just what y'all call y'allself doing? That's what I want to know. So tell me that. Just tell me that. Don't say a word. Don't you say one word. Don't you say a goddamn mumbling word to me. Neither one of you.

We weren't even about to make a sound.

What I got a good mind to do is whale the sawdust out of both you little crustbusters. That's what I ought to be doing right now instead of talking to somebody ain't got no better sense than that.

But he didn't move. He just stood where he was looking down.

Well, I'm a son-of-a-bitch. That's what I am. I'm a son-of-a-bitch. I'm a thick-headed son-of-a-bitch. Hell, I musta been deaf dumb and blind to boot not to know this. Goddamn!

That was all he said then, and then he jumped down and walked us to where the side spur for the southbound trains began, and all we did was sit there near the signal box and feel terrible until Number Four had come whistling by and was gone and we heard the next freight coming south. Then what he did when it finally got there was worse than any name he could ever have called us. He wouldn't let us hop it even though it was only a short haul and pickup local that was not much more than a switch engine with more cars than usual. He waited for it to slow down for the siding and then he picked me up (as they pick you up to put you in the saddle of a pony because you're not yet big enough to reach the stirrups from the ground on your own) and put me on the front end of the first gondola, and did the same thing to Little Buddy; and then he caught the next car and came forward to where we were.

So we came slow-poking it right back toward the Chickasabogue and were back in Gasoline Point before the sawmill whistles even started blowing the hands back to work from noontime. I could hardly believe that so little time had passed. But then such is the difference between legendary time and actuality, which is to say, the time you remember and the time you measure.

We came on until the train all but stopped for Three Mile Creek Bridge, and then he hopped down and took Little Buddy off first and then me, and we followed him down the steep, stubble covered embankment and then to the place the hobos used under the bridge. He unslung the guitar and sat down and lit another cigarette and flipped the match stem into the water and watched it float away. Then he sat back and looked at us again, and then he motioned for us to sit down in front of him.

That was when we found out what we found out directly from Luzana Cholly himself about hitting the road, which he (like every fireside knee-pony uncle and shade tree uncle and tool shed uncle and barbershop uncle since Uncle Remus himself) said was a whole lot more than just a notion. He was talking in his regular matter-of-fact voice again then, so we knew he was not as exasperated with us as he had been. But as for myself I was still too scandalized to face him, and as for Little Buddy, he seldom if ever looked anybody straight in the eye anyway. Not that he was ever very likely to miss any move you made.

That time was also when Luzana Cholly told me and Little Buddy what he told us about the chain gang and the penitentiary: and as he talked, his voice uncle-calm and his facts first-hand and fresh from the getting-place, he kept reaching out every now and then to touch the guitar. But only as you stroke your pet or touch a charm, or as you finger a weapon or tool or your favorite piece of sports equipment. Because he did not play any tunes or even any chords, or make up any verse for us that day. But even so, to this day I remember what he said precisely as if it had actually been another song composed specifically for us.

Then, after he had asked us if it wasn't about time for two old roustabouts like us to eat something and the two of us had shared a can of sardines while he worked on a bite from his plug of Brown's Mule Chewing Tobacco, the main thing he wanted to talk about was going to school and learning to use your head like the smart, rich and powerful whitefolks, (nor did he or anybody else I can remember mean whitefolks in general. So far as I know the only white people he thought of as being smart were precisely those who were either rich and powerful or famous. The rest were peckerwoods, about whom you had to be careful not because they were smart but because so many of them were so mean and evil about not being smart and powerful and famous). He said the young generation was supposed to take what they were already born with and learn how to put it with everything the civil engineers and inventors and doctors and lawyers and bookkeepers had found out about the world and be the one to bring about the day the old folks had always been prophesying and praying for.

The three of us just sat looking across the water then. And then we heard the next northbound freight coming, and he stood up and got ready; and he said we could watch him but we better not try to follow him this time, and we promised, and we also promised to go to school the next morning.

So then we came back up the embankment, because the train was that close, and he stood looking at us, with the guitar slung across his back. Then he put his hands on our shoulders and looked straight down into our eyes, and you knew you had to look straight back into his, and we also knew that we were no longer supposed to be ashamed in front of him because of what we had done. He was not going to tell. And we were not going to let him down.

Make old Luze proud of you, he said then, and he was almost pleading. *Make old Luze glad to take his hat off to you some of these days. You going further than old Luze ever dreamed of. Old Luze ain't been nowhere. Old Luze don't know from nothing.*

And then the train was there and we watched him snag it and then he was waving goodbye.

from *A Childhood, the Biography of a Place*

Harry Crews (1935–)

Harry Crews traveled a route familiar to many poor white Southerners born in rural communities in the mid-twentieth century: he left for the city. After graduating from high school—the first in his family to do so—and serving a stint in the marines, Crews studied creative writing under Andrew Lytle, a former member of the Vanderbilt-based Agrarian literary movement, at the University of Florida. His first novel, *The Gospel Singer*, was published in 1968. Like many of his fictional characters, poor white Southerners trying to make sense out of the modern world, Crews, in his autobiography, *A Childhood, the Biography of a Place* (1978), goes back to his childhood days spent on the farm with his black friend Willalee in order to gain some perspective on the distance he has traveled.

It has always seemed to me that I was not so much born into this life as I awakened to it. I remember very distinctly the awakening and the morning it happened. It was my first glimpse of myself, and all that I know now—the stories, and everything conjured up by them, that I have been writing about thus far—I obviously knew none of them, particularly anything about my real daddy, whom I was not to hear of until I was nearly six years old, not his name, not even that he was my daddy. Or if I did hear of him, I have no memory of it.

I awoke in the middle of the morning in early summer from the place I'd been sleeping in the curving roots of a giant oak tree in front of a large white house. Off to the right, beyond the dirt road, my goats were trailing along in the ditch, grazing in the tough wire grass that grew there. Their constant bleating shook the warm summer air. I always thought of them as my goats although my brother usually took care of them. Before he went to the field that morning to work, he had let them out of the old tobacco barn where they slept at night. At my feet was a white dog whose name was Sam. I looked at the dog and at the house and at the red gown with pearl-colored buttons I was wearing, and I knew that the gown had been made for me by my Grandma Hazelton and that the dog belonged to me. He went everywhere I went, and he always took precious care of me.

Precious. That was my mama's word for how it was between Sam and me, even though Sam caused her some inconvenience from time to time. If she wanted to whip me, she had to take me in the house, where Sam was never allowed to go. She could never touch me when I was crying if Sam could help it. He would move quietly—he was a dog not given to barking very much—between the two of us and show her his teeth. Unless she took me somewhere Sam couldn't go, there'd be no punishment for me.

The house there just behind me, partially under the arching limbs of the oak tree, was called the Williams place. It was where I lived with my mama and my brother, Hoyet, and my daddy, whose name was Pascal. I knew when I opened my eyes that morning that the house was empty because everybody had gone to the field to work. I also knew, even though I couldn't remember doing it, that I had awakened sometime in mid-morning and come out onto the porch and down the steps and across the clean-swept dirt yard through the gate weighted with broken plow points so it would swing shut behind me, that I had come out under the oak tree and lain down against the curving roots with my dog, Sam, and gone to sleep. It was a thing I had done before. If I ever woke up and the house was empty and the weather was warm—which was the only time I would ever awaken to an empty house—I always went out under the oak tree to finish my nap. It wasn't fear or loneliness that drove me outside; it was just something I did for reasons I would never be able to discover.

I stood up and stretched and looked down at my bare feet at the hem of the gown and said: "I'm almost five and already a great big boy." It was my way of reassuring myself, but it was also something my daddy said about me and it made me feel good because in his mouth it seemed to mean I was almost a man.

Sam immediately stood up too, stretched, reproducing, as he always did, every move I made, watching me carefully to see which way I might go. I knew I ought not to be outside lying in the rough curve of root in my cotton gown. Mama didn't mind me being out there under the tree, but I was supposed to get dressed first. Sometimes I did; often I forgot.

So I turned and went back through the gate, Sam at my heels, and across the yard and up the steps onto the porch to the front door. When I opened the door, Sam stopped and lay down to wait. He would be there when I came out, no matter which door I used. If I went out the back door, he would somehow magically know it and he would be there. If I came out the side door by the little pantry, he would know that, too, and he would be there. Sam always knew where I was, and he made it his business to be there, waiting.

I went into the long dim, cool hallway that ran down the center of the house. Briefly I stopped at the bedroom where my parents slept and looked in at the neatly made bed and all the parts of the room, clean, with everything where it was supposed to be, just the way mama always kept it. And I thought of daddy, as I so often did because I loved him so much. If he was sitting down, I was usually in his lap. If he was standing up, I was usually holding his hand. He always said soft funny things to me and told me stories that never had an end but always continued when we met again.

He was tall and lean with flat high cheekbones and deep eyes and black thick hair which he combed straight back on his head. And under the eye on his left cheek was the scarred print of a perfect set of teeth. I knew he had taken the scar in a fight, but I never asked him about it and the teeth marks in his cheek only made him seem more powerful and stronger and special to me.

He shaved every morning at the water shelf on the back porch with a straight razor and always smelled of soap and whiskey. I knew mama did not like the whiskey, but to me it smelled sweet, better even than the soap. And I could never understand why she resisted it so, complained of it so, and kept telling him over and over again that he would kill himself and ruin everything if he continued with the whiskey. I did not understand about killing himself and I did not understand about ruining everything, but I knew the whiskey somehow caused the shouting and screaming and the ugly sound of breaking things in the night. The stronger the smell of whiskey on him, though, the kinder and gentler he was with me and my brother.

I went on down the hallway and out onto the back porch and finally into the kitchen that was built at the very rear of the house. The entire room was dominated by a huge black cast-iron stove with six eyes on its cooking surface. Directly across the room from the stove was the safe, a tall square cabinet with wide doors covered with screen wire that was used to keep biscuits and fried meat and rice or almost any other kind of food that had been recently cooked. Between the stove and the safe sat the table we ate off of, a table almost ten feet long, with benches on each side instead of chairs, so that when we put in tobacco, there would be enough room for the hired hands to eat.

I opened the safe, took a biscuit off a plate, and punched a hole in it with my finger. Then with a jar of cane syrup, I poured the hole full, waited for it to soak in good, and then poured again. When the biscuit had all the syrup it would take, I got two pieces of fried pork off another plate and went out and sat on the back steps, where Sam was already lying in the warm sun, his ears struck forward on his head. I ate the bread and pork slowly, chewing for a long time and sharing it all with Sam.

When we had finished, I went back into the house, took off my gown, and put on a cotton undershirt, my overalls with twin galluses that buckled on my chest, and my straw hat, which was rimmed on the edges with a border of green cloth and had a piece of green cellophane sewn into the brim to act as an eyeshade. I was barefoot, but I wished very much I had a pair of brogans because brogans were what men wore and I very much wanted to be a man. In fact, I was pretty sure I already was a man, but the only one who seemed to know it was my daddy. Everybody else treated me like I was still a baby.

I went out the side door, and Sam fell into step behind me as we walked out beyond the mule barn where four mules stood in the lot and on past the cotton house and then down the dim road past a little leaning shack where our tenant farmers lived, a black family in which there was a boy just a year older than I was. His name was Willalee Bookatee. I went on past their house because I knew they would be in the field, too, so there was no use to stop.

I went through a sapling thicket and over a shallow ditch and finally climbed a wire fence into the field, being very careful of my overalls on the barbed wire. I could see them all, my family and the black tenant family, far off there in the shimmering heat of the tobacco field. They were pulling cutworms off the tobacco. I wished I could have been out there with them pulling worms because when you found one, you had to break it in half, which seemed great good fun to me. But you could also carry an empty Prince Albert tobacco can in your back pocket and fill it up with worms to play with later.

Mama wouldn't let me pull worms because she said I was too little and might damage the plants. If I was alone in the field with daddy, though, he would let me hunt all the worms I wanted to. He let me do pretty much anything I wanted to, which included sitting in his lap to guide his old pickup truck down dirt roads all over the county.

I went down to the end of the row and sat under a persimmon tree in the shade with Sam and watched as daddy and mama and brother and Willalee Bookatee, who was—I could see even from this distance—putting worms in Prince Albert cans, and his mama, whose name was Katie, and his daddy, whose name was Will, I watched them all as they came toward me, turning the leaves and searching for worms as they came.

The moment I sat down in the shade, I was already wondering how long it would be before they quit to go to the house for dinner because I was already beginning to wish I'd taken two biscuits instead of one and maybe another piece of meat, or else that I hadn't shared with Sam.

Bored, I looked down at Sam and said: "Sam, if you don't quit eatin my biscuit and meat, I'm gone have to cut you like a shoat hog."

A black cloud of gnats swarmed around his heavy muzzle, but I clearly heard him say that he didn't think I was man enough to do it. Sam and I talked a lot together, had long involved conversations, mostly about which one of us had done the other wrong and, if not about that, about which one of us was the better man. It would be a good long time before

I started thinking of Sam as a dog instead of a person. But I always came out on top when we talked because Sam could only say what I said he said, think what I thought he thought.

"If you was any kind of man atall, you wouldn't snap at them gnats and eat them flies the way you do," I said.

"It ain't a thing in the world the matter with eatin gnats and flies," he said.

"It's how come people treat you like a dog," I said. "You could probably come on in the house like other folks if it weren't for eatin flies and gnats like you do."

That's the way the talk went until daddy and the rest of them finally came down to where Sam and I were sitting in the shade. They stopped beside us to wipe their faces and necks with sweat rags. Mama asked if I had got something to eat when I woke up. I told her I had.

"You all gone stop for dinner now?"

"I reckon we'll work awhile longer," daddy said.

I said: "Well then, can Willalee and me go up to his house and play till dinnertime?"

Daddy looked at the sun to see what time it was. He could come within five or ten minutes by the position of the sun. Most of the farmers I knew could.

Daddy was standing almost dead center in his own shadow. "I reckon so," he said.

Then the whole thing had to be done over again. Willalee asked his daddy the same question. Because my daddy had said it was all right didn't mean Willalee's daddy would agree. He usually did, but not always. So it was necessary to ask.

We climbed the fence and went across the ditch and back through the sapling thicket to the three-track road that led up to the shack, and while we walked, Willalee showed me the two Prince Albert tobacco cans he had in his back pockets. They were both filled with cutworms. The worms had lots of legs and two little things on their heads that looked like horns. They were about an inch long, sometimes as long as two inches, and round and fat and made wonderful things to play with. There was no fence around the yard where Willalee lived and the whole house leaned toward the north at about a ten-degree tilt. Before we even got up the steps, we could smell the food already cooking on the wood stove at the back of the house where his grandma was banging metal pots around over the cast-iron stove. Her name was Annie, but everybody called her Auntie. She was too old to work in the field anymore, but she was handy about the house with ironing and cooking and scrubbing floors and canning vegetables out of the field and berries out of the woods.

She also was full of stories, which, when she had the time—and she usually did—she told to me and Willalee and his little sister, whose name was Lottie Mae. Willalee and my brother and I called her Snottie Mae, but she didn't seem to mind. She came out of the front door when she heard us coming up on the porch and right away wanted to know if she could play in the book with us. She was the same age as I and sometimes we let her play with us, but most of the time we did not.

"Naw," Willalee said, "git on back in there and help Auntie. We ain't studying you."

"Bring us the book," I said.

"I git it for you," she said, "if you give me five of them worms."

"I ain't studying you," said Willalee.

She had already seen the two Prince Albert cans full of green worms because Willalee was sitting on the floor now, the lids of the cans open and the worms crawling out. He was lining two of them up for a race from one crack in the floor to the next crack, and he was arranging the rest of the worms in little designs of diamonds and triangles in some game he had not yet discovered the rules for.

"You bring the book," I said, "and you can have two of them worms."

Willalee almost never argued with what I decided to do, up to and including giving away the worms he had spent all morning collecting in the fierce summer heat, which is probably why I liked him so much. Lottie Mae went back into the house, and got the Sears, Roebuck catalogue and brought it out onto the porch. He handed her the two worms and told her to go back in the house, told her it weren't fitting for her to be out here playing with worms while Auntie was back in the kitchen working.

"Ain't nothing left for me to do but put them plates on the table," she said.

"See to them plates then," Willalee said. As young as she was, Lottie Mae had things to do about the place. Whatever she could manage. We all did.

Willalee and I stayed there on the floor with the Sears, Roebuck catalogue and the open Prince Albert cans, out of which deliciously fat worms crawled. Then we opened the catalogue at random as we always did, to see what magic was waiting for us there.

In the minds of most people, the Sears, Roebuck catalogue is a kind of low joke associated with outhouses. God knows the catalogue sometimes ended up in the outhouse, but more often it did not. All the farmers, black and white, kept dried corncobs beside their double-seated thrones, and the cobs served the purpose for which they were put there with all possible efficiency and comfort.

The Sears, Roebuck catalogue was much better used as a Wish Book, which it was called by the people out in the country, who would never be able to order anything out of it, but could at their leisure spend hours dreaming over.

Willalee Bookatee and I used it for another reason. We made up stories out of it, used it to spin a web of fantasy about us. Without that catalogue our childhood would have been radically different. The federal government ought to strike a medal for the Sears, Roebuck company for sending all those catalogues to farming families, for bringing all that color and all that mystery and all that beauty into the lives of country people.

I first became fascinated with the Sears catalogue because all the people in its pages were perfect. Nearly everybody I knew had something missing, a finger cut off, a toe split, an ear half-chewed away, an eye clouded with blindness from a glancing fence staple. And if they didn't have something missing, they were carrying scars from barbed wire, or knives, or fishhooks. But the people in the catalogue had no such hurts. They were not only whole, had all their arms and legs and toes and eyes on their unscarred bodies, but they were also beautiful. Their legs were straight and their heads were never bald and on their faces were looks of happiness, even joy, looks that I never saw much of in the faces of the people around me.

Young as I was, though, I had known for a long time that it was all a lie. I knew that under those fancy clothes there had to be scars, there had to be swellings and boils of one kind or another because there was no other way to live in the world. And more than that, at some previous, unremembered moment, I had decided that all the people in the catalogue were related, not necessarily blood kin, but knew one another, and because they knew one another there had to be hard feelings, trouble between them off and on, violence, and hate between them as well as love. And it was out of this knowledge that I first began to make up stories about the people I found in the book.

Once I began to make up stories about them, Willalee and Lottie Mae began to make up stories, too. The stories they made up were every bit as good as mine. Sometimes better. More than once we had spent whole rainy afternoons when it was too wet to go to the field turning the pages of the catalogue, forcing the beautiful people to give up the secrets of their lives: how they felt about one another, what kind of sicknesses they may have had, what kind of scars they carried in their flesh under all those bright and fancy clothes.

Willalee had his pocketknife out and was about to operate on one of the green cutworms because he liked to pretend he was a doctor. It was I who first put the notion in his head that he might in fact be a doctor, and since we almost never saw a doctor and because they were mysterious and always drove cars or else fine buggies behind high-stepping mares, quickly healing people with their secret medicines, the notion stuck in Willalee's head, and he became very good at taking cutworms and other things apart with his pocketknife.

The Sears catalogue that we had opened at random found a man in his middle years but still strong and healthy with a head full of hair and clear, direct eyes looking out at us, dressed in a red hunting jacket and wading boots, with a rack of shotguns behind him. We used our fingers to mark the spot and turned the Wish Book again, and this time it opened to ladies standing in their underwear, lovely as none we had ever seen, all perfect in their unstained clothes. Every last one of them had the same direct and steady eyes of the man in the red hunting jacket.

I said: "What do you think, Willalee?"

Without hesitation, Willalee said: "This lady here in her step-ins is his chile."

We kept the spot marked with the lady in the step-ins and the man in the hunting jacket and turned the book again, and there was a young man in a suit, the creases sharp enough to shave with, posed with his foot casually propped on a box, every strand of his beautiful hair in place.

"See, what it is," I said. "This boy right here is seeing that girl back there, the one in her step-ins, and she is the youngun of him back there, and them shotguns behind'm belong to him, and he ain't happy."

"Why he ain't happy?"

"Cause this feller standing here in this suit looking so nice, he ain't nice at all. He's mean, but he don't look mean. That gal is the only youngun the feller in the jacket's got, and he loves her cause she is a sweet child. He don't want her fooling with that sorry man in that suit. He's so sorry he done got hisself in trouble with the law. The high sheriff is looking for him right now. Him in the suit will fool around on you."

"How it is he fool around?"

"He'll steal anything he can put his hand to," I said. "He'll steal your hog, or he'll steal your cow out of your field. He's so sorry he'll take that cow if it's the only cow you got. It's just the kind of feller he is."

Willalee said: "Then how come it is she mess around with him?"

"That suit," I said, "done turned that young girl's head. Daddy always says if you give a man a white shirt and a tie and a suit of clothes, you can find out real quick how sorry he is. Daddy says it's the quickest way to find out."

"Do her daddy know she's messing round with him?"

"Shore he knows. A man allus knows what his youngun is doing. Special if she's a girl." I flipped back to the man in the red hunting jacket and the wading boots. "You see them shotguns behind him there on the wall? Them his guns. That second one right there, see that one, the double barrel? That gun is loaded with double-ought buckshot. You know how come it loaded?"

"He gone stop that fooling around," said Willalee.

And so we sat there on the porch with the pots and pans banging back in the house over the iron stove and Lottie Mae there in the door where she had come to stand and listen to us as we talked even though we would not let her help with the story. And before it was over, we had discovered all the connections possible between the girl in the step-ins and the young man in the knife-creased suit and the older man in the red hunting jacket with the shotguns on the wall behind him. And more than that we also discovered that the man's kin people, when they had found out about the trouble he was having with his daughter and the young man, had plans of their own to fix it so the high sheriff wouldn't even have to know about it. They were going to set up and wait on him to take a shoat hog out of another field, and when he did, they'd be waiting with their own guns and knives (which we stumbled upon in another part of the catalogue) and they was gonna throw down on him and see if they couldn't make two pieces out of him instead of one. We had in the story what they thought and what they said and what they felt and why they didn't think that the young man, as good as he looked and as well as he stood in his fancy clothes, would ever straighten out and become the man the daddy wanted for his only daughter.

Before it was over, we even had the girl in the step-ins fixing it so that the boy in the suit could be shot. And by the time my family and Willalee's family came walking down the road from the tobacco field toward the house, the entire Wish Book was filled with feuds of every kind and violence, maimings, and all the other vicious happenings of the world.

Since where we lived and how we lived was almost hermetically sealed from everything and everybody else, fabrication became a way of life. Making up stories, it seems to me now, was not only a way for us to understand the way we lived but also a defense against it. It was no doubt the first step in a life devoted primarily to men and women and children who never lived anywhere but in my imagination. I have found in them infinitely more order and beauty and satisfaction than I ever have in the people who move about me in the real world. And Willalee Bookatee and his family were always there with me in those first tentative steps. God knows what it would have been like if it had not been for Willalee and his people, with whom I spent nearly as much time as I did with my own family.

There was a part of me in which it did not matter at all that they were black, but there was another part of me in which it had to matter because it mattered to the world I lived in. It mattered to my blood. It is easy to remember the morning I found out Willalee was a nigger.

It was not very important at the time. I do not know why I have remembered it so vividly and so long. It was the tiniest of moments that slipped by without anybody marking it or thinking about it.

It was later in the same summer I awoke to a knowledge of myself in the enormous, curving oak roots. It was Sunday, bright and hot, and we were on the way to church. Everybody except daddy, who was sick from whiskey. But he would not have gone even if he were well. The few times he ever did go he could never stand more than five or ten minutes of the sermon before he quietly went out a side door to stand beside the pickup truck smoking hand-rolled Prince Albert cigarettes until it was all over.

An aunt, her husband, and their children had come by to take us to the meeting in their car. My aunt was a lovely, gentle lady whom I loved nearly as much as mama. I was out on the porch waiting for my brother to get ready. My aunt stood beside me, pulling on the thin black gloves she wore to church winter and summer. I was talking nonstop, which I did even as a child, telling her a story — largely made up — about what happened to me and my brother the last time we went to town.

Robert Jones figured in the story. Robert Jones was a black man who lived in Bacon County. Unlike any other black man I knew of, though, he owned a big farm with a great shining house on it. He had two sons who were nearly seven feet tall. They were all known as very hard workers. I had never heard anybody speak of Robert Jones and his family with anything but admiration.

"... so me and Hoyet was passing the cotton gin and Mr. Jones was standing there with his wife and ..."

My aunt leaned down and put her arm around my shoulders. Her great soft breast pressed warmly at my ear. She said: "No, son. Robert Jones is a nigger. You don't say 'mister' when you speak of a nigger. You don't say 'Mr. Jones,' you say 'nigger Jones.'"

I never missed a stroke in my story. "... so me and him was passing the cotton gin and nigger Jones was standing there with his wife ..."

We were all dutiful children in Bacon County, Georgia.

I don't know what difference it ever made that I found out Willalee Bookatee was a nigger. But no doubt it made a difference. Willalee was our friend, my brother's and mine, but we sometimes used him like a toy. He was always a surefire cure for boredom because among other things he could be counted on to be scared witless at the mention of a bull. How many afternoons would have been endless if we couldn't have said to one another: "Let's go get Willalee Bookatee and scare the shit out of him."

It didn't take much encouragement or deception to get Willalee out in the cornfield with us just after noon, when it was hot as only a day can be hot in the middle of an airless field in Georgia.

Hoyet turned to Willalee Bookatee and said: "You ever seen this here bull?"

"Which air bull?" Willalee rolled his eyes and shuffled his feet and looked off down the long heat-distorted rows of corn, the corn so green it seemed almost purple in the sun.

"The bull that stays in this field," I said.

My brother said: "To hook little boys that won't tote a citron."

Willalee was out in the middle of a twenty-acre field of corn, equidistant from all fences, brought there by design by Hoyet and me to see if we could make him carry a heavy citron to the gate. A citron is a vine that grows wild in the field, and it puts out a fruit which is also called a citron and looks in every way like a watermelon except it's slightly smaller. Its rind was sometimes pickled and used in fruitcakes, but by and large, it was a worthless plant and farmers did everything they could think of to get rid of them, but they somehow always managed to survive.

"Hook little boys," said Willalee.

It wasn't a question; it was only repeated into the quiet dust-laden air. There had been no rain in almost two weeks, and when you stepped between the corn rows, the dust rose and hung, not falling or blowing in the windless day, but simply hanging interminably between the purple shucks of corn.

"No siree, it's got to be bigger than that one," I said when Willalee rushed to snatch a grapefruit-sized citron off the ground. "That old bull wants you to tote one bigger'n that."

Willalee was scared to death of bulls. He had been trampled and caught on the horns of one when he was about three years old, and he never got over it. At the mention of a bull, Willalee would go gray and his eyes would get a little wild and sometimes he would get out of control with his fear. Willalee was struggling with an enormous citron, staggering in the soft dirt between the corn rows.

"That's better," I said. "That's a lot better. That old bull will never touch you with that in your arms."

Willalee couldn't have weighed more than about sixty-five pounds, and the citron he caught against his skinny chest must have weighed twenty pounds.

"How come it is you ain't got no citron?" said Willalee.

My brother and I walked on either side of him. He could hardly see over the citron he was carrying.

"We already carried ourn," I said. "That bull don't make you tote but one. After you tote one citron, you can take and come out here in the field anytime you want to and that bull don't pay no more mind than if you was a goat."

Willalee was a long way from the gate, and he had already started crying, soundlessly, tears tracking down through the dust on his cheeks. That citron was hurting him a lot.

"But you ain't toted your citron yet," I said, "and that big bull looking to hook into your ass if you put it down, that bull looking to hook him some ass, some good tender little-boy ass, cause that the kind he likes the best."

"I know," whispered Willalee through his tears. "I know he do."

And so Willalee made it to the fence with his citron and felt himself forever safe from the bull. He didn't hesitate at the fence but went right over it, still carrying his citron in case the bull was watching, and once over it, he didn't say anything but took off in a wild run down the road.

But Willalee was not entirely helpless, and he gave back about as good as he got. He once took a crabapple and cut the core out of it, put some cow plop down in the bottom of the hole, and then covered it over all around the top with some blackberry jam his mama had canned.

"Jam in a apple?" I said.

"Bes thing *you* ever put in your mouth," he said.

My brother, who had seen him fix the apple, stood there and watched him offer it to me, did in fact encourage me to take it.

"Had one myself," he said. "That thing is some gooooood eatin."

"I ain't had nair one with jam in it," I said.

"Take you a great big bite," said Willalee.

I not only took a great big bite, I took *two* great big bites, getting right down to the bottom. Anybody else would have known what he was eating after the first bite. It took me two. Even then, I did not so much taste it as I smelled it.

"I believe this thing is ruint," I said.

"Nawwwww," said Willalee.

"Nawwwww," said my brother.

"It smells just like . . . like . . ." And then I knew what he had fed me.

Willalee was laughing when he should have been running. I got him around the neck and we both went into the dust, where we wallowed around for a while before my brother got tired of watching it and pulled us apart. No matter what we did to one another, though, Willalee and I never stayed angry at each other for more than an hour or two, and I always felt welcome at his family's house. Whatever I am, they had a large part in making. More, I am convinced Willalee's grandma, Auntie, made the best part of me. She was thin and brittle with age, and her white hair rode her fleshless face like a cap. From daylight to dark she kept a thick cud of snuff working in her caving, toothless mouth, and she was expert at sending streams of brown spit great distances into tin cans.

The inside of their tiny house was dark on the brightest day and smelled always of ashes, even in the summer. Auntie did not like much light inside the house, so most of the time she kept the curtains drawn, curtains she had made from fertilizer sacks and decorated with bits of colored cloth. Bright light was for the outside, she said, and shade—the more the better—was for the inside.

I ate with them often, as often as mama would let me, and the best thing I ever got from their table was possum, which we *never* got at home because mama would not cook it. She said she knew it would taste like a wet dog smells. But it did not. Auntie could cook it in a way that would break your heart. Willalee and I would stand about in her dark, ash-smelling little kitchen and watch her prepare it: She would scald and scrape it just like you would scald and scrape a hog, gut it, remove the eyes, which she always carefully set aside in a shallow dish. The head, except for the eyes, would be left intact. After she parboiled it an hour and a half, she would take out the teeth, stuff the little body with sweet potatoes, and then bake the whole thing in the oven for two hours.

The reason mama would never cook a possum, of course, was because a possum is just like a buzzard. It will eat anything that is dead. The longer dead the better. It was not unusual to come across a cow that had been dead in the woods for three or four days and see a possum squeezing out of the swollen body after having eaten a bellyful of rotten flesh. But it never occurred to me to think of that when we all sat down to the table and waited for Willalee's daddy to say the only grace he ever said: "Thank the Lord for this food."

The first possum I ever shared with them was in that first summer in my memory of myself, and with the possum we had fresh sliced tomatoes and steamed okra—as well as fried okra—and corn on the cob, butter beans, fried pork, and biscuits made out of flour and water and lard.

Because I was company, Auntie gave me the best piece: the head. Which had a surprising amount of meat on it and in it. I ate around on the face for a while, gnawing it down to the cheekbones, then ate the tongue, and finally went into the skull cavity for the brains, which Auntie had gone to some pains to explain was the best part of the piece.

After we finished the possum, Willalee and Lottie Mae and I stayed at the table sopping cane syrup with biscuits. Will and Katie had gone out on the front porch to rest, and we were left alone with Auntie, who was already working over the table, taking plates to the tin tub where she would wash them, and putting whatever food had been left over into the screen-wire safe.

Finally, she came to stand beside where I sat at the table. "Come on now, boy," she said, "an ole Auntie'll show you."

"Show me what?" I said.

She was holding the little shallow saucer with the possum's eyes in it. The eyes were clouded in a pink pool of diluted blood. They rolled on the saucer as I watched.

"Nem mind," she said. "Come on."

We followed her out the back door into the yard. We didn't go but a step or two before she squatted down and dug a hole. The rear of the house was almost covered with stretched and nailed hides of squirrels and rabbits and coons and even a fox which Willalee's daddy had trapped. I would find out later that Auntie had tanned the hides by rubbing the animals' hides on the flesh side with their own brains. It caused the hair to fall out of the hide and left it soft and pliable.

"You eat a possum, you bare its eyes," she said, still squatting beside the little hole she had dug.

I motioned toward Sam where he stood at my heels. "You gone bury it," I said, "you better bury it deeper'n that. Don't he'll dig it up. You might as well go on and give it to'm now."

"Won't dig up no possum's eyes," she said. "Sam's got good sense."

Sam did not, either.

"Know how come you got to barum?" she said.

"How come?" I said.

"Possums eat whatall's dead," she said. Her old, cracked voice had gone suddenly deep and husky. "You gone die too, boy."

"Yes," I said, stunned.

"You be dead an in the ground, but you eat this possum an he gone come lookin for you. He ain't ever gone stop lookin for you."

I could not now speak. I watched as she carefully took the two little clouded eyes out of the dish and placed them in the hole, arranging them so they were looking straight up toward the cloudless summer sky. They seemed to watch me where I was.

Auntie smiled, showing her snuff-colored gums. "You ain't got to think on it, boy. See, we done put them eyes looking up. But you gone be *down*. Ain't never gone git you. Possum be looking for you up, an you gone be six big feets under the ground. You gone allus be all right, you put the eyes lookin up."

Auntie made me believe we live in a discoverable world, but that most of what we discover is an unfathomable mystery that we can name—even defend against—but never understand.

from *Oral History*

Lee Smith (1944–)

Raised in Grundy, Virginia, and educated at Hollins College, Lee Smith has attained a reputation as a fine short story writer and interpreter of Appalachia. *Oral History* (1983) turns around one of the major themes of this anthology: the difficulty of seeing Southern life without illusion. In the selection here, Smith views mountain people through the eyes of a documentary photographer ironically distanced from the lives he observes by his confidence that he sees things as they really are.

RICHARD BURLAGE DISCOURSES UPON THE CIRCUMSTANCES CONCERNING HIS COLLECTION OF APPALACHIAN PHOTOGRAPHS, C. 1934.

I parked my automobile carefully in front of the bank, wrapped my new English scarf about my neck and put on my hat, adjusting it in the mirror. The scarf and the hat were important to me, affording — or so I thought—a kind of disguise. The mustache helped, too. And the mirror pleased me because of its frame, the way it entrapped my image and framed it so nicely, reassuring me again that here was a new man, a confident man, so different from the boy who had left here ten years back. Even my eyes were different: no longer startled and wild, but melancholy and wise in the mirror's frame, betraying a knowledge beyond my years. And why not? I mused upon the singular pain to which I had been privy in these hills. Now I returned as a mature man, an artist, having in that interim deserted literature for the relatively new field of photography — this vocation, in fact, having occasioned my present visit. For I wished— foolish notion—to capture a bit of the past. I checked my film, my lenses. I stepped out into the cold clear light of early mountain spring, and turned to lock the door.

A crowd of little boys had gathered around my automobile, giggling and poking at each other, yet retaining still that judgmental solemnity I always found so unsettling among the mountain youngsters.

"Hey mister," one of them said. "Hey mister, how much you pay for that car?"

Glancing up and down the narrow, rutted street, I noted then that mine was the only new automobile among all those parked cars and battered muddy trucks which lined it. The pale sunlight glinted somehow obscenely off the outstretched wings of the silver eagle on the hood.

"Hey mister, you gotta nickel?" The boys kicked at my tires. I considered asking them not to, yet refrained from so doing when they were joined by several older friends, lean and hard-faced, who hung back against the bank's streaked marble façade and gathered beneath the green-striped flapping awning of Stinson's Pharmacy next door. The possibility of an unpleasant incident dawned on me. I smiled uncertainly, I hoped disarmingly, in the general direction of them all, checking my camera again, for these fellows were nothing if not picturesque.

"Hey mister, take my picture! Hey mister, looky here!" The little boys went into a frenzy.

"You'll have to stand very still then," I told them, focusing, relieved to have diverted their attention away from the automobile. "Stand still," I repeated.

"Like this?" one said, pushing another, so that three of them fell in a struggling heap until one sat up bawling, with a bloody nose.

I snapped the shutter.

This photograph caught the boy sitting flat in the muddy street, legs stretched out straight before him so that one can plainly see the hole in the sole of his shoe and how it has been patched with cardboard—"Hoover leather," they call it—the boy digging one fist into his face crying, his expression one of anger and loss so extreme as to be obviously inappropriate to the momentary injustice which occasioned it, blood running down from his torn nose into his mouth and dribbling back out the corner of his mouth, his other hand with its pudgy fingers splayed childishly in the dirt. I captured this boy in the foreground, sharp relief: even the patches on his overalls stand out. Behind him, blurred and grinning, stand the other boys and the shiny new automobile, an incongruous, ironic juxtaposition!

The other photographs I made that day captured beautifully, I feel, the essence of that mountain town in those depressing times, including, as they did, the following:

—The older boys, bashful and hateful, in a sullen row before the bank with its boarded-up windows and doors. A skinny rat-faced dog walks out the side of this photograph, one of the boys kicking at it but kicking with his foot only, body stiff and unmoving, no expression on his face except for that ominous squint they all have, squinting straight into the sun.

—An old man, stooped and worn, leaning on his cane in front of the new monument to the WWI dead which the V.F.W. had put up in front of the courthouse. The monument, white and shining, the old man gray, shades of gray deepening to the final dark blur of his face beneath the lowered black brim of his hat.

—A store window empty except for a glassy-eyed naked doll, rampantly blond, with one eye wildly open and one eye flatly closed with its uniform black-brush lashes lying flat against its dimpled cheek, several pieces of chipped, flowered china, a messy pile of clothes in the corner, and a sign that says "Out of Buisness" (sic!).

—A young mother sitting patiently on the curb waiting for somebody as if she has all day or perhaps all month to wait, which perhaps she has, a filthy squirming barefoot baby on her lap, her plaid dress torn at the armpit, her eyes huge and dark and tubercular and staring straight into the camera, her lips parted slightly as if to utter something she cannot articulate, something which I feel I captured, nonetheless, in this photograph.

After I had knocked for at least five minutes — the place still looked open, at any rate, if run-down — Justine Poole herself unlocked the door. Justine had grown hugely, grossly fat in these lean years, shrewd eyes nearly hidden within their bulging pouches of fat, a series of chins cascading down into some kind of billowing Chinese robe. The lobby behind her lay furred in shadow, drapery drawn, the desk empty.

I stood stunned, blinking in the light on the threshold.

"Richard," Justine said promptly. "You haven't changed a bit." I confess I was taken aback!

I professed gallantly, "Nor have you," as it seemed the thing to say, but she threw back her head at this and laughed uproariously, the old Justine, and flung open the door.

I seated myself on a maroon velvet wing chair I remembered, terrible tufted imitation velvet, and took the liquor she brought me in a glass which looked none too clean although it was difficult to tell, the lobby being so full of shadow, and the room itself seemed larger than it had been. Emptier. Yet I felt we were not alone; indistinct murmurings reached my ears from time to time, muffled footsteps above. The light was of course insufficient for me to make photographs and I felt suddenly disoriented, or perhaps it was the effect of the liquor after the long hard drive. Justine spoke at length of what had happened since I left.

"You'll hear folks say hell, it don't make hardly no difference" — she referred to the Depression which she had already characterized as "old Hoover's fault" — "and for them in the hollers it's true, I reckon, you know how things was up there all along" — I nodded in agreement — "but down here in town it's a different story. You see them banks closed? and such as that? I could tell you stories after stories, like old Ludie Davenport whose husband, God rest his soul, finally died after lingering all those years, and so she sold the farm hit'll be two year ago come April, and got a pretty penny for it, all that bottom land, and then she come into town and put every cent of that sixteen-hundred dollars into the Miners and Merchants Bank, and two days later it closed down flat, there's lots of stories I could tell you, Richard. . . ."

In the gloom, Justine's rustling form billowed and spread on the chaise longue, growing larger and larger, it seemed to me, while her voice grew more and more indistinct and seemed to be floating away. I wondered if she was drunk.

"Ah," she said finally, after telling me that the best she could do these days was to give hobos a room in exchange for chopping wood, and telling me how she had to cook rabbits and how she had to make coffee out of roasted sweet potatoes, information so first-hand as to make me—I admit it—distinctly uneasy, as, indeed, this whole conversation made me uneasy what with the occasional murmuring sounds and a girl's high sudden giggle coming from nowhere out of the stories above us and then nothing, a hush, except for Justine's whispery recital of hard times.

"Ah," she said, pouring more whiskey into my glass then leaning forward, a monstrous effort, "you want to know whatever happened to Dory Cantrell."

I felt the liquor flaming up inside me, burning out my whole stomach suddenly so that I was unable to speak. I felt again exactly as I had felt then, caught fast in the grip of something I had thought (hoped) was dead. It seemed that the years burned away to reduce me to what I was then, red-hot flame and ash, awful and elemental: I fought to maintain my carefully wrought control.

"Oh, not necessarily," I said.

Justine Poole laughed her huge and genuine laugh. *"Not necessarily!"* she mimicked me, and for an instant I hated her, and became unreasonably frightened of her, and offended. I stood to take my leave.

I had opened my mouth to say something appropriately chilling, something to the effect that I am happily married thank you to the daughter of an Episcopal bishop, a woman wise and warm and intelligent beyond my wildest dreams, that I am the father of two handsome children etc., when I heard loud deliberate steps descending and I turned, hat in hand, to see who it might be. A coarse-looking man of about fifty, wearing overalls and a thick dark suit coat, walked heavily through the dim lobby and out the front door. He did not speak or nod to Justine or myself.

Disconcerted, I sat back down abruptly.

"She married Luther Wade, Richard." Justine's voice came to me through the wake which I imagined the man had made through the lobby's still, dusty air. "She's a wife now, with a husband better than most, and children, and you are not to go up there and bother her any more. They live in the Blackey coal camp up in the holler that used to be Granny Younger's, if you want to know that. Now you can go on back to Richmond and stay there." Justine's words hung in the air like the dust. Of course she was right. Still, I had thought I might give Dory some money perhaps, and I hoped—oh God, what *had* I hoped? I felt as much of a fool as ever. I had been inspired to make this trip by a passage from *Ecclesiastes*. Oh God!

Justine struggled to heave herself up from the chaise longue. Her ankles, I saw, remained as white and tiny as ever, and I wondered how they could possibly support her.

"Take care of yourself," she enjoined, enveloping me in a hug from which I feared I might never recover. She was so huge and soft it was like embracing a cloud and sinking down and down into it; she smelt of liquor, nicotine, and cheap perfume and powder — loose powder, the kind one finds for sale in dime stores. I broke free at last and gave her soft fat hands a final squeeze, wondering, queasily, if I would bruise them. She sank back onto the chaise.

"Oh yes," I said, turning back at the door. "Aldous. Do you think I could find him at home right now?"

Justine laughed low in her throat; I fancied she had misunderstood the question.

"Aldous," I said, louder, and Justine said, "Dead."

"He's been dead for seven years now," she said in her whispery voice, "and if you go out the way he went, you'll be a lucky man, Richard — a lucky man."

Thus I departed, shaken, buoyed out the door on the wave of her ghostly laughter. *Dead!* I shook my head to clear it and gulped cold air, astounded at the brightness of the day and at the very fact that it *was* still day, still February, after all. Dead. Full of fiery unmanageable energy then, I adjusted my camera and clicked away rapidly, framing everything:

—The peeling door as Justine closed it, her puffy fingers visible around its edge, the rest of her a great unseen burgeoning presence within the dark slit which is all that is left now of the interior of the Smith Hotel, façade merely, in this photograph of the door.

— A blank bottom-story window with its shade drawn tightly down, white woodwork and white shade in the pale flat glare of the sun.

— The corner porch viewed from an odd angle so that the hanging swing appears to be in motion, although empty. An overturned flowerpot spilling earth in the foreground on the corner of the porch. And Justine's foolish forsythia, wildly ahead of its time, blooming enthusiastically in the muddy dirt by the front steps, the only intricate thing and in fact the only living thing in this photograph of flat surfaces, square angles, diminishing planes.

—And finally, the long view, which I gained from a vantage point in the middle of the busy street where I was almost (twice) run down while I made this picture: the whole of the Smith Hotel, the Gothic lettering on the small sign in its window still an anomaly, promising something quaint or charming, something clearly not present here, the whole hotel rising flat and white up from its tiny wrecked yard, porch on the side like an afterthought, a joke perpetrated by somebody who had once been somewhere else, the illogical forsythia down in the corner of the photograph, Black Rock Mountain behind, no sky—and then, on the second story, the surprise: that far left window with the shade momentarily raised and the two girls in their white slips pressed giggling against the glass, their breasts flattened against it, their bare white shoulders indistinct in the gloom behind them.

I confess I leaped for my magnifying glass when, upon development, these girls emerged! They were quite a shock to me, validating somehow my theory of photography if not life itself: the way a frame, a photograph, can illumine and enlarge one's vision rather than limit it. Frankly, I find in this theory an *apologia* for the settled life, for the lovely woman I have married who manages things so well yet understands the worth of my artistic pursuits.

This photograph, one of the best, I entitled "Whorehouse, c. Hard Times."

Although it was three o'clock already and I knew all too well how soon the sun set there, I found myself unable to leave without photographing, at least, Hoot Owl Mountain, and the schoolhouse at Tug, and the store (although I had no desire to encounter Wall!), Grassy Creek perhaps: I was obsessed by capturing these scenes. It proved slow going, however, the road treacherous, wide enough for only one vehicle at a time, but, thank God, there was truly a road, at least! Everything that had happened to me seemed to have happened a million years ago, or seemed to be, in some inexplicable way, *still* happening, over and over again as it has, I suppose, been happening on some level ever since these events took place, *as all events that ever happened always do, are never ever over*, I realized, surprised, jerking the wheel so the automobile veered suddenly off onto the shoulder of the road in the dark patch through the pines. Shuddering, I gripped the wheel again with sweaty palms and steered the car back onto the unpaved road, still ascending. I saw the sycamore tree.

—The sycamore stands hugely white and stark against the dark mountain beyond it, the lowering sky. The Cantrell homestead, nestled high among the three mountains, has a snug dreamy other-worldliness; a ribbon of mist clings to the peak of Snowman Mountain.

— The store at Tug, added onto now in several different directions, squats on its patch of litter-covered bare clay like something built by ignorant children out of whatever came to hand, the people around it stopped dead in their tracks to stare at the camera and beyond it with their habitual resigned distrust, their old wariness.

I found myself astounded by the changes along the road. Tiny ugly frame houses and makeshift shacks had mostly replaced the log cabins I remembered; or those cabins had been fronted and boarded out of all resemblance to the kind of homemade simplicity I used to love. Nothing had been done with thought or care of consequence, I noted — lumber stripped and the land left, machine parts everywhere rusting, trash and refuse out in the yards in front of the homes, if you could call them that, and children — children everywhere, ragged and dirty, in the road and in the filthy bare yards along it. Even the creek itself looked different, brown and swollen, trash along its banks where evidently it had flooded, and not so long ago. I drove slowly and deliberately up the hazardous hairpin turns of Hurricane Mountain; rounding a final curve, I found myself on a kind of overlook from which I could make wide-angle shots of the Blackey Coal Camp which occupied now the entire holler where the old woman named Granny Younger used to live.

I had never seen anything like it. The lumber companies had stripped the timber out all the way up the mountain, on both sides of the holler. They were doing it, I recalled, logging this holler, even while I was here, the logs on the narrow-gauge line going down to the Levisa River, filling it bank to bank, the loggers waiting for high water to raft them down to Catlettsburg, Ky. Somehow I had thought nothing of it at the time, which caused me to wonder what else I might have missed! what else might have made no impression. I did not enjoy the uneasiness which this idea produced, nor the way this holler made me feel, this coal camp.

One mountainside was layered with small identical company houses, rickety coal-blackened flimsy squares each with its door in the middle, its two windows giving out onto the porch, the porch itself on stilts as the houses were set back against the steep mountain. Dogs and chickens, sometimes children, could be glimpsed beneath the houses. The houses appeared to be in imminent danger of falling off the mountain. The unpaved roads leading up to them were muddy, full of potholes. Trash, rusting machine parts, and bodies of cars lay everywhere, along that road, in all the yards (where no grass grew!). At the bottom of the holler stood a structure of yellow bricks — the company store — surrounded by other cement-block and frame buildings which appeared to be offices. Behind these, the jumble of trucks and equipment, the railroad, the coal cars, and the giant black hulk of the tipple hanging over it all. The air was acrid, sulfurous. Looking up beyond the tipple to the top of the mountain, I saw the hulking slag heap, black and vast and smooth and slightly smoking, always on fire. The sulfur came from there.

My vantage point on the hairpin turn of Hurricane Mountain, facing this coal camp, made me feel omniscient: I could view it all and view it whole, the people tiny, not real people, not at all, the cars and trucks nothing but toys. I was taking wide-angle shots when the man approached me silently, the way they always come, and hunkered down to watch me for a while before he spoke.

"You got some business here, buddy?" The voice was flat and nasal, absolutely without intonation.

I whirled, almost dropping the camera.

The man hunkered silently, watching. He was so still he looked of a piece with the mountainside, rock cropped bare and left there weathering, his face seamed, the telltale black circles or coaldust ringing his pale colorless eyes so that he resembled, I thought, some giant ominous raccoon. Before I could stop myself, I was giggling wildly! Cold sweat prickled under my arms.

"What's so goddamn funny?" The man stood up slowly, then advanced.

"Nothing," I said finally. "Nothing." I stood poised by the automobile, my hand on the door.

The man looked at me. "You'll be one of them government fellers, I reckon," he said.

Christ, yes! "W.P.A. Administration." I fell into it quickly. "From Charleston."

The man came closer, squinting at me. "Then I'll tell you some things," he said. "I'll tell you some things. We been eating wild greens at my house since January this year, greens that the goddamn pigs eat. The children needs milk and we can't get none of it, you hear me mister? None of it."

"But surely," I protested, "at the company store . . . " I gestured toward Granny Younger's holler.

"Store, my ass," the man said. His voice was so flat that he might have been saying "It's going to rain": he might have been saying anything. "I owe that store so much I ain't never going to pay it, I'll die owing the company everything I got. You got to buy your powder from the store, see, you can't blast coal without no powder, and you can't get it noplace but the store, and it keeps going up on you — then they pay you by the ton, see, and then they have went and gone up on the ton too." The man fell silent, looking out at the coal camp.

"You can't win for losing," he said.

I confess I have never been able to hold my peace when I should.

"But the union," I protested. "This new man, Lewis, don't you think—"

"I don't think shit," the man said. "Ain't nobody paying me to think."

"I guess not," I stammered. "I mean, I guess so."

"Hell, they talk big," the man said, "but they ain't done nothing yet. The only thing they done so far is get Mr. Blossom all riled up so he's got him some Gatling guns and a bunch of Pinkertons up here. Hit's coming on fer a bad time," he said, almost as if to himself, then suddenly grinned a wide feral grin, exposing his yellowed broken teeth. "You heard enough?" he asked. "You want to hear some more?"

"I have to be on my way," I responded quickly. "Perhaps I could ask you, however, do you know the family of Luther Wade? I'm told they live up here someplace."

"That second row of houses over there," the man said, pointing. "The one on the end," he said. "I reckon you come up here to hear him sing. You gonna write it down or what?"

"Something like that."

"They was some other fellers up here already, doing that."

I remained silent, vastly relieved.

"Didn't none of them have a car like thisun, though."

I got into the automobile and locked the door.

"Didn't none of 'em have such a fancy car."

The man pulled a gun (!) out from somewhere — shoulder holster? — and looked at it, turning it in his hands. The gun was black and seemed to absorb the sunlight. The man looked at it carefully, blew in the barrel.

"Look, you want money?" I said — I think I said. "Is that it? Here." I struggled with my overcoat.

"I don't want nothing you've got."

Carelessly, grinning, the man lifted the gun and shot out the rearview mirror attached to the car on the driver's side. Glass splintered against the car and down onto the packed red clay.

The sound of the gun ricocheted deafeningly from the mountain wall. The man grinned.

I threw the car into gear and screeched off down the narrow road into the holler, not the way I had intended going, not at all, but the man stood behind me there in the middle of the road still grinning so I could not turn the car and I had simply no choice at all.

Children ran beside me as I drove past the company store; everybody stared. I drove on, ascending now, at last almost within shooting range of the house I knew to be hers, then braked and turned and put the automobile out of gear and leaned out for a couple of quick shots.

By this time, the light was nearly gone. This series of photographs has an indistinct, grainy surface, as if coal dust were blowing palpably through the air.

The first photograph shows the house itself with the clothes flapping on the line beside it, children out playing in the dirt of the yard, such as it is, beyond the fence, children taking a trip of their own in the rusted-out Dodge or part of a Dodge in the yard.

—Then two lovely girls, apparently twins, holding hands as they come down the steps, frail and angelic: they've got no business here in this darkening yard. The twins, their dresses, and the wringer washer on the porch all seem to glow in this photograph; the yard, the house, the other children blurry and dark.

Finally Dory herself appeared in the lighted rectangle of the door.

"You girls!" she called. "Sally! Lewis Ray! Billy! You all come on, now."

I drew my breath in sharply, clicking away.

But these pictures did not turn out because the light had gone by then! because Dory, at the door, picked just that moment to turn her head. She was reduced to an indistinct, stooped shape, the posture of an older woman—they age so fast in those mountains anyway—or perhaps it was simply the angle of her head and the way she stood at the door, her head a mere bright blur.

Even when I blew it up, there was nothing there.

I drove for most of the night, beyond Claypool Hill and Tazewell to a hotel outside Christiansburg, desperate to put as much distance as possible between myself and the mountains. When I awakened the next day, in the late morning after seven hours of deep black sleep, I felt exhausted, drugged. Driving on, I was suddenly struck by the way my splintered rearview mirror fractured the noonday sun and sent it out in a splatter of light: like a prism, in all truth. I stopped the car and stared into this phenomenon until I was nearly blinded, and when I looked back at the rolling landscape of Lynchburg around me, it appeared all different, all new, as if cleansed by a silvery wash. I felt as I had felt several years ago upon hearing the news that a ninth planet — Pluto — had been found revolving around the sun, a planet that of course *had been there* all along: oh God! I thought. Nothing is ever over, nothing is ever ended, and worlds open up within the world we know. I was anxious to rejoin my family. Yet I sat there for quite some time, just east of Lynchburg, looking out at the first faint springing green on the earth's wide rolling field.

from *I Am One of You Forever*

Fred Chappell (1936–)

Poet, short story writer, and novelist Fred Chappell uses the Appalachian region where he was born and raised as the setting for his work. Chappell's early works explored the twin themes of madness and violence. Later novels such as *I Am One of You Forever*, published in 1985, and *Brighten the Corner Where You Are*, published in 1989, follow the coming of age of young Jess Kirkman. Through Jess's story, Chappell, alternating between humor and pathos, examines the meaning of community and manhood.

The first time my father met Johnson Gibbs they fought like tomcats. My father was still feisty in 1940—he was thirty years old—and restless, maybe a little wild beneath the yoke of my mother's family. He truly had married not only my mother but my grandmother as well, and also the mule and the two elderly horses and the cows and chickens and the two perilous-looking barns and the whole rocky hundred acres of Carolina mountain farm.

The sheer amount of labor was enormous. The corn, for instance. Three huge fields stretched in the bottomland on both sides of Trivet Creek toward Ember Mountain. Even standing above in the hillside road, you couldn't see the ends of these fields.

Evidences of toil lay scattered about the barns: old hoes with handles broken off or split down the grain, with blades rounded off to cookie shapes. My father dislodged one from a corner to show me; the blade was no bigger than a jar lid. "Look at that," he said. "You don't think your grandma got her money's worth out of this hoe?" He flung it in disgust and it flew up clattering against the long tobacco tier-poles, scattering sparrows out of the barn eaves.

But the hoeing that was agonizing tedium for us seemed none so hard for her. The three of us would begin hoeing rows at the same time. I was ten years old and was soon left behind. In ten minutes my grandmother would have pulled ahead of my father; in half an hour she would have lapped him, coming back the other way on a new row, and clucking like a guinea hen. "You boys better hurry along now. Don't know but it might rain soon."

My father would give her an unbelieving stare, lean on his hoe until she passed, and then dig savagely, swinging like a lone Saracen knight fighting off Christians.

But no matter how hard the three of us labored, the farm was too much; and so we came to meet Johnson Gibbs.

I can't say how the arrangement was made. Johnson was eighteen years old and had come from an orphanage to live with us on the farm. Perhaps it wasn't entirely legal. My father put it that Johnson had been as good as sold into bondage down in Egypt land and that if he were wise he'd head back to the orphanage and lock and double-bolt his door so my grandmother couldn't get at him.

He was a big handsome red-faced man with an easy temperament. He smiled easily and blushed—which made his red face look positively fiery —and he seemed to have an endless supply of chewing gum and a talent for cracking it loudly. I knew he liked me because he tousled my hair and gave me gum. The Beechnut was his way of disarming strangers. He was a young man who had been mistreated. We found out later that his parents were drunkards, that Johnson had been taken to the orphanage for his own protection.

My mother—who was no help at the farm, since she taught school all day—took to him immediately. She loved boys—that was probably a big reason she married my father. She loved most of all boys who were quiet and cheerful and well-mannered, as Johnson was. And he was good-looking besides. When my mother was introduced to him her hands went automatically to her hips, smoothing her skirt.

Johnson's eyes were of a light blue color, and when he met my father they became lighter, almost transparently blue. His smile tightened, a quick animal reaction. There would be conflict between them—that was inevitable—but the introduction went off affably enough, and took place on a Sunday.

They didn't fight until the next day. It was a law woven into the fabric of the universe that these two young men were going to have at it; and Monday was as good a day as the Lord ever made.

They began in the road in front of the barn, continued down into the mucky cow lot, and over the fence, tumbled down the hill into the cornfield, then rampaged through the field into Trivet Creek, and it ended there in the thigh-deep water. In my school playground we would have called it a fair fight, no gouging or biting and not much kicking, but a great deal of awkward punching and grunty wrestling. My grandmother called it hog-wallering.

The predictable result was that they became inseparable friends. There they sat in the creek, torn, bleeding, smeared with mud and cow manure, laughing in companionable lunacy. They laughed and splashed one another and then began washing themselves in the muddy creek water. They floundered up the slick bank and, both on all fours, shook water from themselves like puppies. My father barked like a little squeak-dog, and Johnson began to laugh anew.

My grandmother and I were staring transfixed from the upper road. "Lord a-mercy," she said. "Just look what them crazy boys done. Your daddy's worse than that other one. Don't he understand he's a grown man with a family? And him acting like a shirttail youngun without a lick."

She described truly, then and after. My father seemed no older than Johnson, not really much older than I was. We three males might have been the same age. The women in the family represented good sense and authority and our rebellion against the situation formed us into a tight high-spirited company. The time soon came when we could hardly look at one another without grinning.

"What were they fighting about?" I asked her.

"To see which was the silliest, and it was a draw. Would you just look what they done?"

Two sections of the cow lot fence were torn away, the ragweed and jewelweed on the hillside flattened. They had trampled a shaggy roadway through the corn, the knee-high stalks lying broken and shiny where they oozed juice.

"Got brains as big as June peas," she said.

They were coming back through the field now, still laughing. Their progress faltered when they got to the bottom of the hill and looked up into the roadway where she stood. It was easy to guess what they dreaded.

"I ought to take a tobacco stick to both of them."

They arrived and stood looking down at the gravel while she scolded. "Ain't there enough work around here, you want to go and make more for us?"

My father turned and surveyed the broken fence, the trampled corn. He sighed, then brightened. "We'll get it done now we got ole Johnson here," he said.

"I pray so," she said.

Her prayer was about half answered. Johnson was a willing and cheerful laborer, and as strong as he looked. But he was easily led astray, and my father was born to lead him there. Conspiracies bloomed between them like thistles along a fencerow. It soon became clear that they would do the work, all right, but that they would streamline it, discarding all my grandmother's intricate little prescriptions. No more hilling the corn with meticulous care. And if something needed repair, they would get the tools

and repair it; no more propping gates and doors with fanciful arrangements of rocks and board ends. When milking time came they led the
cows to the stalls and milked them, forgoing the traditional protocol of
having Red and Daisy in first to milk, and then Little Jersey and Blossom.

They did the work and claimed it was done. She claimed it was only
half done; but now for the first time in her life, perhaps, she was over-
matched. And when there was nothing to do they were by God not working. It vexed my grandmother's conscience to see someone sit down and
take an easy smoke. The sight of someone not working for a moment or
two caused great catalogs of useless tasks to fret her mind, and she would
send the idler to oil doorlatches or soak milk strainers or to find a length
of twine just so long.

"While you're setting there you could at least swat some of these flies,"
she said.

My father said, "Who swats flies in a barn?"

He now produced instruments of idleness and perdition. He persuaded
my mother to produce a baseball and a couple of broken-down gloves from
her high school and he and Johnson stood in the road playing catch. They
were owlishly serious about their games of catch, zinging the ball hard and
sharp.

But the work did get done. The weeds no longer stood as tall as the
corn, the alfalfa was pitched into the barns before the summer showers
came to rot it on the ground, the milk was set out in time for the Pet Dairy
pickup, the tobacco was suckered, wormed, and topped in due season. All
this in spite of that infernal baseball and the other deviltry.

We had a dozen or so pullets in those years, and we would come across
thumb-sized eggs in the grass everywhere. My father found a use for them.
In the big brick house was a room—she called it a "sun parlor"—which
my grandmother forbade us to enter on pain of her most fearsome displeasure. Here she entertained her infrequent formal company, the
preacher, or ladies from her Bible Circle. Here she kept hidden away—
though of course my father found it early on—the huge box of deluxe
chocolates that Uncle Luden had brought to her from foreign parts, from
St. Louis or Memphis or Asheville.

My father sneaked Johnson and me into the sun parlor on tiptoe and
showed us the candy. "How's this for fancy?" he asked. Each candy lay
shining in colored foil wrappers, bright green, red, gold, purple, nested in
the velveteen-lined box. Only a few pieces were missing.

"Fancy, I reckon. Looks good enough to eat," Johnson said.

"Looks can be deceiving," my father said. "We'll be doing Grandma a
favor, I reckon, if we test this stuff." He handed each of us a piece and we

unwrapped them and ate in awed silence. Mine was a maple cream, and I've never tasted anything so good since that delicious hour.

"Now give me back those wrappers," he said, and when we did he took three fragile pullet eggs from his pockets, wrapped them in the red and green foil, and replaced them in their little nests. "Does that look okay?"

"Can't tell the difference," Johnson said. "Not by a frog hair."

He looked at me. I nodded, round-eyed. Conspiracy loomed out of the air everywhere.

We didn't stop until we'd eaten a good two-thirds of the box over the weeks, carefully substituting the disguised pullet eggs.

Then one Sunday afternoon two of my grandmother's Bible Circle friends, two chattering bespectacled ladies, came to call and she took them into the sun parlor. We knew we were caught, and the three of us met in earnest conclave behind the corncrib. Johnson counseled that we move to Australia; he'd heard that there was a lot of dairy farming in Australia.

"Hell with farming forever," my father said.

"Go to Europe, then," Johnson said. "See what them French women look like, what you hear all the talk about."

"Don't you know there's a war in Europe?"

Johnson nodded solemnly. He was eighteen years old; he knew about the war in Europe. "What're we going to do then?"

"We'll stand and face the music. You ain't afraid of an old woman, are you?"

"Yes."

My father looked up into the top of a black oak tree. "Me too," he said. Then he brightened. "But say, wouldn't you like to be in that sun parlor now to see their faces?"

Johnson grinned. "Yes."

My father instructed me to peep around the crib toward the house and tell what was coming.

"Nothing," I said.

They rolled cigarettes and smoked and looked at one another, smiling thin smiles. It seemed they wanted to laugh aloud but had better not; it would be bad luck.

"What do you think?" my father asked.

"I think we're pure fools to still be in this county," Johnson said.

"I wonder what's happening."

I peered around the crib again and reported that my grandmother was indeed coming.

"Let me have a look," Johnson said. He stuck his head out and pulled it quickly back. "She's coming, all right."

"How's she look?" my father asked. "Does she look mad? I mean, does she look real real *real* mad?"

"She looks like she's carrying a shotgun," Johnson said.

"Well then, I'm satisfied she's a little upset."

"Which way?" Johnson asked.

My father closed his eyes, deliberating like a prime minister. "Due east, I'd say."

And with that they took off running like ponies before wildfire. They leaped across the brooklet at the bottom of the slope, vaulted over the barbwire fence on the other side, and tore through the hillside of ragweed at amazing speed.

When my grandmother reached the corncrib she was calm and smiling; she was carrying not a shotgun but one of my grandfather's black-varnished walking canes. "Where's them trifling boys at?" she asked.

"They went off somewhere," I said.

"Yes, I expect they did," she said. She looked down at me fondly. "You weren't any part of these trashy doings, were you, Jess?"

In the past weeks I had learned a lot. "Part of what doings?" I asked.

"I didn't think so," she said. She patted my head. My grandmother foretold that they would return when they got good and hungry, and they did. They had to be hungry to eat the meals that came to their plates. My mother and grandmother and I ate very well indeed, never better. Fresh cornbread and tomatoes and fried okra and chicken and biscuits with sawmill gravy. But my father and Johnson ate eggs three times a day. They got fried eggs, scrambled eggs, boiled eggs, eggs any old how, for breakfast, dinner, and supper. When we worked in the back fields their paper bags held greasy egg sandwiches.

"Say, Johnson," asked my father, "do you ever have a strange craving these days to scratch dust and cluck?"

"I have stopped dreaming about the underwear girls in the Sears catalog," Johnson said. "When I lay down to sleep, it's all pork chops."

Finally one evening they did get pork chops, which was the signal my grandmother was making peace with them. Better than that, even, was that she gave us a brief account of the society news. "Ellen Louise and Mary ain't too certain about their storebought teeth," she said. "They're afraid to eat hard candy or chewy candy that will pull their plates loose. So they set there and squeezed all them pullet eggs in the candy box and they would break and smear their white gloves and the box got all runny. I saw what it was right from the first, but they just kept on. They must have busted I guess twenty of them eggs."

Johnson and my father looked hard at the tablecloth; their faces got redder and redder.

"Now I know you boys didn't eat all that candy at one go. Because some of them eggs had been there for a while. A lot of them eggs were spoiled."

"Spoiled?" My father sounded like there was a stone in his throat.

"Spoiled rotten," she said.

"Smell bad?" he asked.

"Awfullest smell there is."

At this, Johnson and my father burst from the table, overturning their chairs, and rushed outdoors. We heard them laughing out there under the walnut trees, laughter so explosive it sounded like light bulbs popping.

My grandmother sat where she was, but tears streaked down her cheeks.

My mother asked her if she was all right.

"I'm all right," she said, "but I wasn't going to laugh in front of them. If they seen me laughing, Lord only knows what they'd do next time." She reached and patted me on the head again. "Don't you never grow up to be like them two," she said.

"No ma'am," I said, promising myself that I was going to grow up to be exactly like them two.

Johnson roomed with me in the bedroom at the top of the stairs of the old brick house. It was exciting to have a roommate, someone to talk to in the dark when the wind moved the big oak branches across the windows and stars winked through the leaves one at a time. I slept in the iron bed against the south wall and he in the tall wooden bed on the other side of the dormer.

We lay staring into our separate darknesses and I asked Johnson to tell me a ghost story. What better hour for one?

"I ain't no hand at ghostally tales," he said. "Hunting, fishing, baseball: that's my line. I go for he-man stuff."

"Tell me a hunting story then. In the jungle."

And he obliged, but he wasn't much hand at jungle stories either. I was ten years old and knew for a fact that tigers didn't prey on kangaroos. He left out so many important details that I had to keep interrupting with questions.

"Wait a minute. How did the crocodile get up on the swinging bridge?"

"Why, he crawled up the bank. How else would he get up there?"

"Yes, but you had him pinned to a tree trunk with a spear through his nose. How did he get loose from that?"

"He just shook his head like a big dog till he come loose. You going to let me tell this story?"

"Sure, go on. I was just wondering."

"All right, then . . . Where was I at?"

"On the swinging footbridge with a mean gorilla at one end and the crocodile coming at you from the other. How did you get out of that?"

"I jumped in the river."

"You jumped in a river full of rocks one thousand feet straight down? You'd've been mashed like a bug."

"Well, I would've been," he said, "but there was a flood come along and filled the river up. I didn't have to jump no more than two hundred feet, I guess it was."

"It was a mighty quick flood."

"It was a great big old flash flood and a lucky thing for me. I floated along on it as easy as you please till I come to a nice big dry rock ledge and grabbed on and started climbing out. Only trouble was, there was a great big old snake sunning hisself on the rock. Big old boa constrictor snake about twenty yards long, and he struck at me like a flash of lightning . . ."

I turned on my side and fell asleep in utter disgust.

If Johnson was rather frail with jungle stories in the dark, he made up for it with his baseball stories in the daylight. He used to be star pitcher for the orphanage team, he told me, and by his own account the most stupefying phe-nom on either side of the Mason-Dixon. "They marched to the plate whistling a tune and slunk back cussing a blue streak," he said. "They never got good wood on me and only bad wood when I wanted to give my fielders something to do. I had them looking every place but where the ball was. I had them hypnotized, hornwoggled, and hooligated. They prayed rain on when I was going to pitch and I prayed it off again."

I balked at Johnson's boa constrictors but swallowed his pitching stories like they'd been soaked in hot lard. "Show me one more time how you grip that pitch," I said.

"Which one?" he asked. "I got so many I can't keep track of half." He scrunched his fingertips together on the edge of a seam and laid the ball in the heel of his palm. "This one here is what I call my Drunkard's Fancy. There ain't no way to hit this pitch because there ain't no way to expect where it'll be. Just somewhere around the plate is all you can count on. I seen many a heavy hitter jerk his backbone in a knot trying to get at it."

He had a cornucopia of pitches, all right, and enough names for them to fill a telephone book. Besides the Drunkard's Fancy, there was the Submarine Surprise, the Blue Flash, the Blitzkrieg, the Snaky Shaker, King of the Hill, Shortstop's Delight, Hole-in-the-Bucket, the Step-Away-Lively, the Chin Music Special, the Simplified Bat Dodger and the Advanced Bat Dodger, Easy Roller, Sissie's Powderpuff, Slow Boat to China, the Rare-Back-&-Letter-Rip, and of course there was always and finally, Old Reliable. There were others too, but I got lost in the thicket of them.

I tried to grip some of these pitches the way he showed me, but my hand must have been too small. It was amazing the number of awkward ways Johnson could take hold of our old tobacco-stained, chipped horsehide.

"I don't see how you can hold it like that and get anything on it," I said.

"All in the wrist," he told me. "I got a wrist snap like a bear trap. And the arm. I got an arm half steel and half rubber. It's a great blessing because I can hurl these pitches for a hundred years and never do my arm the least bit of damage."

I was highly impressed by whatever he said about pitching, partly because I'd never heard anyone use the word *hurl* before. I'd never heard *hooligate* either; and haven't since. I was so impressed, in fact, that I carried these stories to my father, who appeared to consider them thoughtfully before approaching Johnson.

"Jess tells me you're a pretty fair country pitcher," he said.

Johnson didn't back off a smidgin. "I didn't tell him the half of it," he said. "I didn't want to seem like I was bragging, but I can throw a baseball through a brick wall or around it or over it or under it."

"No, you wouldn't want to brag," my father said. "I hear bragging swells up your head and makes your eyes bug out."

"I heard that too," Johnson said. "I heard that bragging weakens a man down so much he don't even enjoy shoveling horseshit no more."

"You still look pretty stout to me," my father admitted. "And that's a good thing because I've heard of a baseball team needs a pitcher come Saturday afternoon. You know Virgil Campbell that keeps a grocery store down by the bridge? He's got together a pickup team and wants to play some Free Will Baptist team out of Caviness Cove. He thinks he's got a pretty steady team, all but a pitcher."

"I'm the man he's looking for," Johnson said. "If he looks any farther he won't find nothing but worse."

"Of course now, these are just old farm boys you might be ashamed to play against. They wouldn't be in your league, I can see that."

Johnson grinned, magnanimous as Roosevelt. "Do them good to watch me. They'll get a baseball education."

"All right then," my father said. "I'm going to tell Virgil. He's awful anxious to whip this church team. He can't abide the hardshell holy rollers of any species. It means right much to him to show them up."

"I'll be there to mow them down and rake them into windrows," Johnson said.

I was nervous as a flea from Wednesday until Saturday, wondering how Johnson would get along with the True Light Rainbow Baptist team. They had a substantial reputation in our part of the county, and I'd seen them play once, rough and tough, a fair bunch of flail-away hitters. Johnson didn't seem worried in the least; didn't mention the game or even pick up a baseball until it was time to ride out to the game. He tousled my hair. "What you fretting about, Jess?" he asked. "You're as jumpy as a frog in heat."

We drove out to Caviness Cove and stopped at a scrubby level patch of cow pasture, got through the longwinded preliminaries, and started the game.

I am not going to make an elaborate chronicle of this game, which certainly did not achieve epic stature. The Rainbows came to bat first, and we might have guessed that trouble was ours when Johnson's first pitch rolled off his fingertips and fell with a soft thud on the lip of the mound. He walked three batters before he got the ball anywhere near the plate. But it was better when it didn't get there because when it did the big raw Baptist boys whacked it to the long empty outfield. A hailstorm of baseballs out there. The Rainbows would smile and mumble in the on-deck circle as they watched Johnson wind up and *hurl*. I believe they were saying *Hallelujah Jesus how grateful we are for Thy bountiful gifts.*

Johnson's wind-up was a spectacle of some magnitude. It proceeded with grave deliberateness as he raised the baseball to eye-level, then lowered it with agonizing slowness to his belly button. Then he closed his eyes and made a frightening tortured grimace. Then he lifted his left leg shoulder high and rocked his torso back back back until the knuckles of his pitching hand nearly scraped the ground, and. Stopped. Stopped dead still with his left leg cocked like a dog aiming to pee on a cloud and with his righthand knuckles brushing the grass blades behind him: a hunk of nightmare statuary. . . . Then he came to the plate in a windmill melee. Arms, legs, head, shoulders, and torso flew apart in every direction. The body of Johnson Gibbs seemed to disintegrate like flung confetti. How would these scattered limbs ever come together again to compose a man?

This delivery flabbergasted me but confused the Rainbow batters not the slightest. They stood watching this human snow flurry with patient amusement and, when the baseball finally floated out of the uproar, swatted it into the blue reaches where the angels dwelt. *Blessed be the name of the Lord,* and so forth.

By the middle of the third inning, the score was 23–2, and not in our favor. My father conferred with Virgil Campbell, that eccentric man, and they went over to the coach of the Rainbow team and stopped the game, conceding defeat. He told me later that he would have stopped it earlier if he'd been able.

"But I couldn't," he said. "The first time I saw Johnson go into his wind-up I started giggling. By the time he delivered the ball—I mean, by the time he dropped it on his toe—I was on my knees with laughing. I laughed so hard I couldn't stand up. The more he pitched the more I laughed. I could've quit laughing maybe if I didn't look at him, but it was irresistible. Finally I was rolling on the ground like I had a green apple bellyache and laughing so hard the tears came out of my eyes like water through a sieve. If I hadn't remembered to get away from that barbwire fence I'd be all in crazy-quilt scraps."

He had a point and I had to admit it, no matter how profound my worship of Johnson. I was puzzled how to behave around Johnson during the next few days. Should I commiserate with him or avoid mentioning the game at all? I decided that Johnson would be so gloomy that I had better try to cheer him up. The man capable of pitching a game like that might be capable of any kind of self-destruction.

Johnson was as cheerful about the game as if he'd pitched a clean no-hitter. "Anybody might have a bad day," he said. "Some days the old arm just ain't there, that's all. There's days when even Lefty Grove and ole Dizzy Dean would get knocked around pretty good."

"You don't feel too bad about it then?"

"One bad day. That's the breaks."

"I guess you didn't have many days like that when you pitched for the orphanage team."

"What team? That orphanage is so broke they don't have diapers to go around for the babies. They surely ain't got no baseball team. I never saw no kind of a ball the whole time I was there."

"What about those games you pitched that built you such a big reputation?"

"Now I don't hold with lying," Johnson told me gravely. "It ruins a feller's character something awful. You tell lies and people will get to where they don't believe one word you say and then where'll you be? But—"

"What but?"

"But I was bound to pitch me a ball game. I've watched baseball and read about it till my head was full. So when I seen me a chance to pitch I jumped at it. You think they'd let me pitch if I told them I ain't never pitched a game but I sure would like to try it one time? Thing to do was let on I was the hottest thing since Walter Johnson. Then they'd pay me some mind."

"Well, now that you've pitched, what do you think about it?"

"I think I better practice some," he said. "Maybe work me up a whole new assortment of pitches. I don't let it get me down."

427

"That's nice," I said.

He rumpled my hair. "One single man can't be the best at everything. Now what I'm really good at is trout fishing. With a fly rod. I can pull trout out of the sand and the dry rocks. You never seen anything like it. Them fish come flocking to me like I was their mama."

The bright happy days darted past us like minnows. We had the farm in pretty fair running order now. The weather held good and the corn and alfalfa were tender and green. We had already reset tobacco twice. Mucked out the milking barn. Cleaned the fencerows and mended the wire. And now when I remember it, it seems we were laughing and joking from one hour to the next.

We pleased our womenfolk, and teased and exacerbated them too. "Got to keep them on their toes," my father said. "Otherwise they'll go out and rent another farm just to keep us busy."

We had running jokes, pranks, passwords, and private signals. It got to the point that my father could look at Johnson with a certain facial expression and Johnson would turn scarlet and giggle. There was a way Johnson could wiggle his shoulders that I found intolerably funny. A stranger observing us from cooler vantage would have certified us for the county asylum.

Johnson had a secret to tell me, though, which was no joke. He swore me solemnly to absolute silence. "When your folks hear about this they're going to have a tizzy fit," he said. "And that'll be soon enough. So let's don't worry them no more than we have to. But I'll bust in half, trying to keep it plumb to myself."

"What is it then?"

"I've enlisted," he said gravely. "I went down to the post office and joined up."

"Joined up what?"

"I've joined the army," he said. "Don't you tell nobody, Jess, not a soul."

"Don't worry," I said. "I won't tell, never." But I didn't understand the reason for secrecy. I knew that Johnson had joined the army so he could go to Europe and whip Hitler's sorry ass. What was wrong with that? My father was continually saying that somebody had to do it, and so Johnson, taking him at his word, had signed up for the job. It was a straightforward proposition. I only hoped Johnson wasn't thinking of taking on Hitler in a baseball game.

But then the army would train him to throw a better curve; the army was famous for training men.

"All right," Johnson said. "Now you know. Just as long as you don't tell."

"I done said I wouldn't and I won't." I kept my word.

For his birthday Johnson received a fly rod from my parents. He also got a shiny new reel and a box of dry flies. It was a first-rate rig and as soon as I laid eyes on it I was discontent with my old cane pole which had served me perfectly well for the past two years.

Johnson gazed at it with watery eyes. "It's a Shakespeare," he said in a choked voice. He laid it across a chair and walked out of the living room into the hall, going in private to wipe his tears away. He came back in and said, "I never seen one before, except the pictures in magazines. I never thought—" Then he left the room again, his face redder than I'd ever seen it before.

My father and mother stood by the wood heater, hugging one another. When Johnson returned once more, my father said, "That's all right."

Johnson said, "No it ain't either. You don't know—"

"That's all right," he said. "Nothing to say. Best thing you can do is, you boys get yourselves together and I'll drop you off up West Fork Pigeon and you bring us back a good mess of trout. That'll do it. That'll do it fine."

"I'm ready to go," I said, and Johnson said he would be ready in a minute.

The stream where he let us off wasn't much wider than a kitchen table, but it rushed by fast and we knew there'd be pools and broad quiet stretches above. We struck out upstream, dodging through laurel thickets and clambering over rock faces. We came to a pool all dark and silent except at the head, where the cold breathing water boiled beneath an eight-foot waterfall.

"This one just might do," Johnson said. "Let me try it a little bit with the fly and then you can bait fish it with the cane pole. Fly fishers have to go first, you know. All right?" He began to tie a fly to the long leader.

"What kind are you going to use?" I asked.

"Female Adams," he said. He showed me a bit of gray and brown fluff with a fuzzy gray collar which I didn't find impressive. "Sure fire," he said.

He began casting, standing ankle deep at the outlet of the pool. First he hung the fly in some low hanging sweet gum branches behind his left shoulder, then he hung it on a big lichenous rock in the middle of the stream. He grinned over his shoulder at me. "Buck fever," he said.

I settled on the bank to wait my turn.

He got the fly caught in the sleeve of his blue cotton shirt and while he was working it free the line wrapped around the rod tip. Then the fly hooked into his shirt collar. Now he couldn't see it so he took off his shirt, setting the butt of the rod on a stone. When the hook came out of the cloth the rod nearly flipped into the stream and he grabbed at it with both hands. His shirt dropped in and floated down toward me. I lifted it out dripping with my cane pole.

"Just spread it out on that bush," he said. "It'll dry in a jiffy."

"Looks like it might take you some time to get used to the new rig," I said and might have said more if I'd trusted his temper.

His expression was distant, his eyes glazed with obsession. "I don't believe this pool is just right for a fly rod."

How'd you know? You ain't got a hook in it yet. But I didn't speak aloud.

"I'll move on upstream and give this one to you. Ought to be a good baiting pool. Come on when you finish and catch up with me."

"Okay."

While he skirted a patch of sawbriar to head east, I bit a couple of lead shot onto my line and slipped a greasy white grub headfirst over the hook, careful not to squash his innards out. When I thought the pool had quieted sufficiently I tossed the hook into an oily ripple in the middle of the stream. In just a moment I got a strike as solid as a blow on the shoulder. I took my time and pulled out a black-filigreed brook trout about nine inches long. I disengaged the hook and knocked his head on a rock. I broke off a forky twig, slipped it through his mouth and gill, and stuck the twig deep into the bank so he could dangle in the water and keep fresh.

The sunlight then was edging over the treetops, and after I'd caught three more nice fish, it was level with my left shoulder, full and warm. I decided to clean what I had, and started after Johnson to borrow his pocket knife. I strung the fish on a willow withy, twisted it round my belt, and set off.

I found Johnson half a mile upstream. He was lying on a big rock in the sunlight with just his underwear drawers on. His tan cotton pants were spread out beside him; they were soaking. He was lying so still he might have been dead.

"What happened to you?"

He sat up with a jerk. "I hooked a fish!" he shouted. Then he relaxed and spoke in a quieter tone. "I swear to God, Jess, he was as big as my leg. Swear to God. But I was standing in an unsteady place and I fell off in the water."

"Did he get away?"

He nodded solemnly. "I'll get him. We'll come back again and I'll catch him next time for sure." He lay back again and closed his eyes.

"Where's your rod?"

"Right over yonder. Ain't it a dandy? Come over here and set a minute, I'll tell you something."

I went and sat. "What?" I said.

He opened his eyes and talked in confidential tones to the blue sky above. "I ain't never been fishing before. This is the first time. But I've thought a lot about it."

"You mean you ain't never been fly fishing."

"I never been fishing period. Where's a orphan boy going to go fishing?"

"I never thought."

"This is the best thing that ever happened. This is the best time I ever had."

I listened to the rush and gurgle of the stream; there were a thousand voices in it.

"There ain't nothing better than this," Johnson said. "From here on out it's all downhill." He sat up and hugged his knees. "I bet the best time is over for me after this."

We fell silent to hear the water and the woods. Downstream below us two tall poplars stood on either side. The space between their branches was like a big window and while Johnson and I watched, a bird cut straight and quick through the space, gliding from one shadow to the other. But I couldn't say what kind of bird, dark against the light.

.   .   .

It seemed that there were four of us in a hunting cabin high on a mountain near the Tennessee border, Uncle Luden, Johnson Gibbs, my father, and me. And it seemed that it began to snow the second day we were there; in the late afternoon little bitter papery flakes came down in nervous spirals. It wasn't supposed to amount to much, but when we woke early the third morning there was well over a foot of the fluffy stuff, driven in scallops by a bluff wind. We decided to wait our deer hunting until the weather improved.

But it kept on snowing.

We amused ourselves with poker and setback and eating. The others drank a little whiskey, but I was too young. We didn't worry, but by that evening had started to feel a little cabin-bound. Our manners grew gentler; four of us in close quarters might prove a tedious business.

That night we stayed awake late, swapping lies and jokes about hunting, cars, sports. The others pulled a little more steadily at the whiskey, and a cozy lassitude suffused their talk and there were long passages of silence.

I began to feel a little as a stranger among them. They knew different things than I did. It seemed that they were willing to tell me, but I didn't know what to ask. If they had talked about women I would have had some questions, but they never entered upon the subject. I thought it curious that they hadn't; maybe they were regarding my youth. No, that wouldn't be the reason.

After midnight the pauses lengthened and the comfy drowsiness deepened, the fire sinking to orange-and-red embers. They decided it was time for bed. I was still wide awake, but did not demur. I kicked off my unlaced boots and stripped off my shirt and heavy pants and climbed into a top bunk. There I lay on my back with my hands beneath my head, staring at the ceiling in which I could barely make out the board edges and pine knots. I heard the wind sifting the papery snow in the oak trees and laurels.

They fell asleep one by one, their breathing steadied and slowed and purred. Now and then one of them would shift in his bunk like a log shifting in a camp-fire. I lay thinking of many things, but nothing of winter. In my mind was the light of summer and its grass smells and sweat and dusty roads. I thought a lit-tle why we had come here, what it would be like to kill a deer.

My thoughts were interrupted when Johnson Gibbs in the lower bunk spoke in his sleep. I couldn't make out the word the first time. He spoke again, thickly but comprehensibly in the reddened dark: "Helen." Then he said nothing more, but now there was true silence in the cabin, no one turning or half-snoring, and I realized I was holding my breath. I let it out carefully. And then Uncle Luden asleep in the top bunk on my right spoke the word: "Helen."

I could tell from his voice that he was asleep, and at first I thought he was only repeating in dream the name Johnson had uttered. But wouldn't it have changed in his mind, undergone the usual alchemy? Maybe it was someone they both knew, someone they happened to be dreaming about at the same time. It was a farfetched notion, but it amused me and I elaborated upon the fancy for a while.

Then I heard my father in the other lower bunk roll over and mutter a word. I couldn't hear it distinctly, only a liquid-nasal murmur: ". . . llnn . . ." But now I took it for granted that it was a transfiguration of the familiar name Helen.

There was a woman I had never heard of before and she was powerful in their three lives. No, that was not possible. There was no secret like that for them to share. They didn't share secrets anyhow.

The room waited; I couldn't hear them breathe now. The fire had gone all down, only a pinkish gleam furred over with gray ash. Suddenly — all at the same time — each of the three stirred in his bed. I couldn't see them, but recog-nized from the sound of the movement that they now sat bolt upright in their bunks, their hands flat on the mattresses. They were still not awake, but each of them stared open-eyed and sightless into the space of the room in front of the fire-place. As one man they gasped, like divers coming out of the ocean. They remained sitting, all three, breathing hoarsely, staring and not seeing.

I couldn't see them. I couldn't see anything, but I knew what they were doing. I too stared forward into the room, straining to see . . . what? I knew I couldn't look into their dreams, I had no desire to. But the tension caught me up, and I tried to sculpt from the darkness a shape I might recognize.

Little by little—yet all in a single instant—I saw something. I thought that I saw. Framed by glossy black hair, a face appeared there, the features blurred by a veil and yet familiar to me, I fancied, if I could remember something long ago and in a distant place. Then there was no face. If something had actually appeared, it lasted no longer than an after-image upon the retina. But if I had seen something, then it was her, Helen, I had glimpsed.

Now the others lay back again. Their breathing slowed and quietened. Now they would dream no more of Helen; each would follow his own strange travels in the forests of dream; their sleepings would no longer touch.

I was disturbed most of all by the unplaceable familiarity of the vision. Who was this woman with thick black hair and those penetrating brown eyes? I thought and thought with no success and grew irritated and tired of myself. The room began to gray with predawn light reflecting from the snow and I fell asleep and dreamed of summer and a bright yellow field of oats.

I woke to the sound of sausage sizzling and water pouring. They were all up and about, and I scrambled down quickly and got dressed. In the kitchen, the only other room here, they went about their tasks, a little dull maybe from the evening whiskey. They gave me Good morning as I sat at the table and began to observe them closely.

No secret seemed to obtain among them. They were as open and careless as ever before. Even so, I felt myself at a distance from them, left out, and I felt too a small gray sense of shame, as if I'd gone through their pockets while they slept. But nothing passed among them that I could detect.

During breakfast my father informed me that we were leaving. Though the snow had stopped, they had decided the weather was no good for hunting and that we were returning home. I nodded dumbly.

They packed up and I packed hurriedly and went back to the cast-iron range to wash the tin plates and cups. They stripped the bunks and swept. When I finished washing up and had damped down the cook stove fire, I sat at the table while they loaded the gear. They waited in the car and still I sat there, gazing about the cabin.

In a few minutes I heard the sound of boots on the rough porch planking. The door opened and Johnson Gibbs stood solidly in it. His blue eyes were very bright. There was full sunlight now and it made a burning glare on the snow. Against this harsh light Johnson's figure loomed black, black as velvet, blackly burning, and his voice sounded deep and hollow:

"Well, Jess, are you one of us or not?"

The Turning

World War II changed the South more deeply than any event since the Civil War. Whether serving in the military or entering the industrial workplace for the first time, many Southerners encountered challenges to long-held assumptions concerning race, religion, work, and regional identity. An infusion of government spending and outside investment brought a prosperity to the South of the 1950s and 1960s that the region had not seen for a century. The landscape changed with remarkable speed, as interstate highways, suburbs, and fast-food franchises sprouted up in fields. Television introduced Southerners to styles of life earlier generations had only glimpsed during brief visits to the cities of the North.

Black Southerners enjoyed some of the benefits of this prosperity. Proud black neighborhoods grew in every Southern county and black people enjoyed the exciting consumer culture no less than whites. But black Southerners saw much of the region's new bounty from a distance. Kept out of high-paying industrial jobs, prevented from participating in politics, and forced to accept a separate and less-than-equal school system for their children, they organized to protest these and other injustices. They scored startling and inspiring victories in the 1954 *Brown* decision and in the Montgomery bus boycott of 1955, when the prophetic Martin Luther King, Jr., burst into national prominence.

The movement for black civil rights built slowly and in the face of bitter white opposition. The late 1950s saw few major successes, but the crusade grew from within, building on the support of African Americans in every Southern county. Some white Southerners joined in, and many others gave the movement tacit support, but the struggle was led by black people of diverse backgrounds. The early 1960s registered one stirring victory after another, from the sit-ins to voting rights. By 1965, the legal battles had been won, with, ironically, the support of a white Southerner in the White House.

Since then, change in the region has been both widespread and muted. Southern incomes have risen markedly but remain the lowest in the nation. Southern cities have grown with breathtaking speed but remain segregated in the most fundamental ways. Southern religion has become a major force for change in the nation but speaks in ways that clash with much of modern life. Southern music has been adopted by the entire country, but it is still delivered in Southern accents. Southern voters have switched their party allegiances and have elected black candidates to major offices, but politics remains deeply divided by race and charged with fear and resentment.

Though many people in the South and beyond assume that regions are fading artifacts of an older America, Southerners of both races embrace their Southernness. Black Southern exiles have begun to return to the region with a hopefulness few of their ancestors could have imagined. White Southerners, though still burdened with stereotypes of racism and backwardness, proclaim themselves proud to be both Southern and modern. Accents refuse to fade; churches remain strong; tradition receives loyalty. And Southern writing flourishes.

The selections in this final section chronicle much of the tumultuous change in the years since 1945, sometimes directly and sometimes obliquely. A number of writers, black and white, devote themselves to the struggles for social justice that stood at the center of Southern life in the twenty years following the second world war. Others talk of the costs and temptations of the new order, worrying over spiritual and moral confusion. They all describe a richly complicated and nuanced society, one that has folded into itself the experiences of the more than two hundred years chronicled in the pages of this book.

from *Killers of the Dream*

Lillian Smith (1897–1966)

To Lillian Smith, the killers of the dream, the subject and title of her 1949 book, were those Southerners who honored and passed on a flawed Southern culture. The daughter of a prominent white businessman and civic leader in Jasper, Florida, Smith abandoned a musical career in 1925 to run her parents' Laurel Falls Camp for Girls. While directing the camp, she pursued a writing career as a novelist, social critic, and magazine editor. Seemingly immune to social pressure and criticism, Smith began calling for the end of racial and sexual discrimination in the 1930s.

We cannot understand the church's role as a teacher of southern children without realizing the strength of religion in the lives of us all, rich and poor. Whether we lived in a big house on College Street, a cottage on the side street or a shanty in mill town, most of us loved church. Sunday was a fiesta, a time for our prettiest dresses, the only day of the week when we wore hats, the only time in summer when little boys slicked back their hair and put on their shoes. And the only day when the church bells rang, Baptist and Methodist, clashing their sounds together in friendly proselyting.

I do not remember that we felt a profound reverence for the Unknown when we entered our church, or that our hearts stretched to touch something bigger than the mind can find words for. I am afraid we were too busy looking at each other's clothes or watching the veins swell out on old Mr. Amster's neck as he sang the Gloria, or staring at little Mr. Pusey as he led the tenors through the vagaries of the anthem.

Church was our town—come together not to kneel in worship but to see each other. God was our Host, we were guests in His House, the altar flowers were fresh and fragrant, and if it was Communion Day the cloth was starched and white and the silver cup out of which every one drank was shining. And though we willingly listened to the sermon if it was not too long, and felt a deep flowing sense of togetherness when we sang the Doxology, we were there also to mend the little broken places in our knowledge of each other.

To children, church was more interesting than school, for the grown folks were there and one's eyes could not get enough of their movements, their quick glances, the sudden stiff droop of those who fell asleep under the minister's soothing words. We liked to be with them. But we liked best of all, classes at Sunday school where we said the golden text and emptied our mite boxes and repeated the stories of Daniel in the lion's den and David and his slingshot.

After church, there would be a good dinner at home, and always guests could be invited.

It was a day set aside, made special, with no empty moment in it. Sunday school, morning worship, junior choir practice, and a walk in the woods to pick violets.

In a few homes, like my own, it was also a time when your father heard you name the books of the Bible, or listened encouragingly as you repeated ten Psalms from memory, or asked you odd questions about the old Prophets and tripped you flat with verses whose source you must identify. But we liked the old mouth-filling names, the strange adventures which the Israelites had, and the indignant invectives so eloquently hurled by the prophets at the weak ones on that long troubled journey that seemed never to end but went on from Sunday to Sunday.

The revival meetings in August were different.

The church's emphasis on revival meetings and the revival's effect upon southern personality are difficult to understand unless we let our minds fill with echoes of distance and darkness and ignorance and violence and worn-out bodies and land. For all are tied up with each other and have much to do with the quality of the southern conscience that is stretched so tightly on its frame of sin and punishment and God's anger.

Belief in Some One's right to punish you is the fate of all children in Judaic-Christian culture. But nowhere else, perhaps, have the rich seedbeds of Western homes found such a growing climate for guilt as is produced in the South by the combination of a warm moist evangelism and racial segregation. This flowering of revivals, conversions, deathbed repentance, mourners' bench, love feasts, and fundamentalism must be credited in part also to the historical circumstance of the Brothers John and Charles Wesley's and George Whitfield's visits to Georgia. We can hardly overestimate the influence of these three preachers of God on the mind of the South, for they were men of powerful personality, burning with a powerful belief in the importance of the common man's uncommon soul, and a powerful talent for making men believe in their soul's sacredness by giving size to their sins. It was a curious inversion, this proving a man's stature by the great black shadow he cast, but it worked. Men believed in their importance by believing in the importance of their sins and grew a pride in possessing a conscience that persecuted them.

These young giants of Methodism—not long out of Oxford and full of their discovery of the poor man's soul — came to the New World with their new way of preaching that was intimate and direct and deeply sincere. They went straight to the anxiety in the minds of these tough settlers and whipped it up to a froth that obliterated rational processes, then released them from it by showing them a clear narrow road to salvation. Circuit riders who followed them for more than a century continued this emphasis on the rebirth of the soul, as they moved from settlement to settlement preaching the Gospel. They were brave, tireless, passionate men who traveled on horseback, like old Peter Cartwright, three hundred miles a week, preaching four or five times a week, sometimes two or three times a day. Devoted to God and terrified of Him, they made Him into the Despot the people had left behind them when they fled Europe; and by threats of hell, they turned the rebels once more into meek lambs. They did far more than this of course, for men *were* reborn; they did, as it were, re-enter their mother's womb, and many of them found a peace that was real and a way of life that added kindness and decency to a South that had much too little of either.

The loneliness, ignorance, and isolation of the rural South made these old preachers welcome everywhere. In spite of their lashing sermons — perhaps because of them — wherever they went, the crossroads saloonkeeper vied with pillars of the church for the privilege of putting them up for the night, for all were hungry for news of a world they were completely cut off from, and fascinated by the power of men who believed and lived their belief.

They were brave men, these circuit riders, who could kill a rattler or swamp panther or wild turkey with casual accuracy or throw a drunken bully out of their meeting with no more than a comma's pause in their sermon. They were veterans pioneering for God, taking danger and death as quietly as they took their sleep. When they spoke, men listened. They preached on the sins that tough frontiersmen committed: drinking, fighting to kill, fornication, self-abuse, gambling, and stealing. And because they made these sins of heroic size by a passionate eloquence that modern preachers cannot equal, no other sins have ever seemed real to the southern imagination but become merely vexatious problems that do not belong in church. They preached, at times, of Jesus too and his love, and turned their brush-arbor congregation into wistful blubbering children who, there in the lonely woods, wept for something lost that they knew they could never find again on this earth but hoped to find in heaven.

Such men there were in both Methodist and Baptist churches (whose combined membership is about eighty per cent of the South's churchgoing people) — eloquent, fiery, compelling — and for more than a century they shaped and gave content to the conscience of southerners, rich and poor.

Camp meetings and revivals are the South's past, and once were a heroic part of that past. Today, though often cheapened and vulgarized to the point of obscenity, they are still part of the South's present. Guilt was then and is today the biggest crop raised in Dixie, harvested each summer just before cotton is picked. No wonder that God and Negroes and Jesus and sin and salvation are baled up together in southern children's minds and in many an old textile magnate's also.

When I was a child the annual revivals were a source of enormous terror and at the same time a blessed respite from rural monotony. Nothing but a lynching or a political race-hate campaign could tear a town's composure into as many dirty little rags or give as many curious satisfactions. Like political demagogues, the evangelists enjoyed people. And, like them, they won allegiance by bruising and then healing a deep fear within men's minds. They loved God too, but they feared Him far more than they loved Him and they urgently wanted their fellowmen to be saved from His wrath. They believed their way of salvation was "right," as did the old circuit riders, and could not conceive of another way of avoiding destruction. And their faith released an enormous energy which in most of us is locked tight in a struggle between the two halves of our nature.

They preached asceticism but preached it with the libertine's words. And, as they preached, they looked as unlike an ascetic as you can imagine. These were potent men—anyone is wrong to think otherwise—who used their potency in their ardent battle for souls.

How can such men be called hypocrites, as they are grossly represented by most novels and plays written about them? They have had numerous counterfeit followers who were — mean nasty tight men who today wander up and down Tobacco Road in Dixie and Tobacco Road in Detroit spreading their gospel of fear and hate; men who preach more against the evils of communism than the evils of sex but are concerned almost wholly with these two "sins." These are the rotted culls of an evangelism that once was a respected and important part of protestant religion.

The revivalists I knew as a child lived their religion as they saw it and lived it honestly. It is true that they were ambivalent men who had healed themselves by walling off one segment of their life and who kept many doors open in their personality by keeping one door securely locked. And they were men whose powerful instincts of sex and hate were woven together into a sadism that would have devastated their lives and broken their minds had they acknowledged it for what it was. Instead, they bound it into verbal energy and with this power of the tongue they drove men in herds toward heaven, lashing out at them cruelly when they seemed to be stampeding, persuading them with laughter and tears when they moved in the right direction but too slowly. And in doing this, they felt that they were doing God's will. They were saving souls and they believed that any method was justified, if by using it, they could say, "Here, Lord, is one more for Thy Kingdom."

They were sincere if ham actors—a few of them almost touched greatness now and then—and they brought to a South bereft of entertainment and pleasure a brief surcease from the gnawing monotony that ate our small-town lives away. They often presented this entertainment with style and always with drama, for they were unafraid to explore the deep forbidden places of man's heart. There are few artists today who would dare probe so ruthlessly the raw sores of our life as did these evangelists, though they ignored the patterns of culture and the profound needs that produced the sores. They were not wise men but they were shrewd in the use of mob psychology. They were curiously indifferent to cultural patterns or else in violent loyalty defended the barbed wires crisscrossing our age on which their own lives had been wounded. And they could turn into stupid foolish men when confronted with questions that ask "Why?" Wherever their answers came from, that place did not send them answers to the problems of poverty, of race segregation, unions, wages, illness and ignorance, war, and waste of forest and soil and human relations, or answers to the old question of human freedom which Jesus turned around and around until its light blinded men with fury and drove them to build institutions to shut out its shining.

Their religion was too narcistic to be concerned with anything but a man's body and a man's soul. Like the child in love with his own image and the invalid in love with his own disease, these men of God were in love with Sin that had come from such depths within that they believed they had created it themselves. This belief in the immaculate conception of Sin they defended with a furious energy and stubbornly refused to assent to the possibility that culture had had any role in its creation.

They were twisted men, and often fanatics, but they were delightful companions. I know this is true, for many of the southern revivalists whose names all Methodists know were guests in our home for the duration of the August revival. These men were remarkable storytellers, with a warm, near-riotous sense of humor; brilliantly adept with words, soft and gentle with the children of their host, and courteous and considerate of their hostess. We liked them. My mother and father, neither of whom was easily drawn to the mediocre, respected them. We admired them and were influenced by them, for they had two of the essential qualities of leadership: They were free of personal anxiety, and they were close to their instinctual feelings. They were saved men. And they were sure of it. At the same time, what they were "saved from" was still accessible to them. The return of the repressed, which most of us puny folk fear as we fear the ghosts of our beloved, were to these powerful evangelists something they could whistle back at will, giants made impotent by the "power of God." No wonder they hypnotized us all!

They were fine looking men, strong, bold, with bodies of athletes. They had to be, for they put themselves through a killing routine: three sermons a day, with prayer circles before breakfast and midday dinners with the town's leading citizens at which every one gorged himself on fried chicken, corn and okra and butter beans, iced tea, peach ice cream, and lemon cheese cake; and after the evening sermon, an altar service which was often prolonged for hours by those under conviction of sin who agonized and prayed and yet could not secure release from their guilt. I shall never forget how I suffered with these strong men of our town — the butcher or the pitcher on the baseball team or the tenor in the choir—as they knelt there sobbing like children. Strangely enough, I cannot remember one time when the banker or millowner or principal of the school, or cotton broker or politician went to the altar. They were always among "the saved." Perhaps it is as well—for one little penitent journey might have caused a run on the bank or a cultural panic.

What an awesome gift these revivalists possessed for palpating the source of our anxiety! By means of threats, hypnotic suggestion, and a recall of the earliest fears of childhood, they plunged deep into our unconscious and brought up sins we had long ago forgotten. There were few of us whose souls did not pale out in the sulphurous glow of their sermons. Though they knew no word of psychoanalysis, they directed their attention to buried memories quite as much as the Freudians do, though the process was more like a butcher with a cleaver than a surgeon performing a skilled and delicate operation.

I have sometimes wondered why there were not suicides afterward, for surely enough terror and anxiety were released in unstable personalities to produce a collapse of the will to live. Perhaps we were saved from self-destruction simply because no matter how miserable and torn we were, life in Dixie seemed far better to the most unstable of us than any possible satisfactions that might accrue from succumbing to death wishes. For men believed in hell after death in those days and the belief restrained many a potential suicide from that infantile act of getting even with his world or himself. The revivals probably drove many more than we know into mental hospitals and into less conspicuous, because ambulatory, illnesses.

But when we were children, we did not analyze the motivations and consequences and costs of revivals, we accepted them. Hymns, sermons on hell, invitations (called "propositions") to come to the altar and be saved, the dirge-like singing that embroidered our nerves, the revivalist's soft whispers and prayers when one finally broke down and went scuttling to kneel at the altar — all of these phenomena we accepted with what seems, as I think of it now, a most extraordinary flexibility. There were such generous compensations: the sheet-lightning glimpses into the dark places of the human mind, the very real sense of being "saved," and scene after scene of drama and farce when an individual, strong in his refusal to give up his right to sin, stood night after night adamant to the preacher's pleading though sometimes his name was called aloud.

This was strong meat for children but we loved it. There was excitement too in the setting of big tent, lanterns swinging high in the shadows, fresh clean smell of sawdust that covered the ground to make a suitable place for kneeling in prayer. There were always on the platform two pianos, and two pianos to small children were of the same exciting stuff as calliopes. There was a singer too who led the congregation with fine sweeping gestures that turned old hymns into hit tunes.

For a town whose opera house rarely had the spider webs dusted out, whose citizens depended for theater on the annual play given by the high school, and for gaiety on a minstrel show and a circus each winter, the big tent was a magnet which drew not only the rural folks but the most literate and wealthy from Main Street.

Once in the tent, we were shown monstrosities that Mr. Barnum would not have dared exhibit to his gawking audiences. Queer misshapen vices, strange abnormal sins were marched out before our young eyes, amazing, titillating us as no circus could do. [We learned about the horrors of delirium tremens and the lush temptations that scarlet women dangle before men's eyes. *Whore, harlot, unnatural sins, self-abuse*—words which we had never heard in our homes and would not have dared repeat outside the church, became an August vocabulary that was pressed deep in our memory]. Adolescents, whose parents could not bring themselves to tell them where babies came from, sat on the edge of benches, wet-lipped and tense, learning rococo lessons in Sin from the revivalist who seemed magnificiently experienced in such matters. The sermon titled *For Men Only* lifted the lid from the flaming pit of things one should not know. And even little girls and their mamas safe at home watched eagerly for bits of ash that might fall from the big fire.

For the adventurous, such sins as these became irresistible. Any risk, even of hell, was worth running if one could but taste of this steamy dish which the preacher held so close, daring you, with awful threats of punishment, to touch. But for the tender-minded, the sensitive, the dish turned to vomit, and sometimes all of life seemed as nasty, as dangerous, as this portion of it with which so many sermons were concerned. Children without one protest quietly locked doors they had almost opened, forever shutting out life's natural spontaneous rhythms and curiosities.

In the sermons for children which revivalists customarily held in the afternoons, a lighter tone was sustained. The presence of little girls, sitting so stiffly in front of them with flushed-up cheeks and tight pigtails, may have made them a bit shy about pushing matters too ruthlessly. Or perhaps they needed to relax from their major efforts. Whatever their reasons, they made of the children's services rather pleasant divertisements, full of games and animal stories. We laughed on these afternoons, I remember that. Sin was shrunken to a stature that our small egos could cope with. The preacher quoted more from the New Testament than from the Old, and that was a relief. Many words about love were said, and few about vengeance. We were told that Jesus came to earth because God so loved the world that He gave His only begotten Son — which seemed to us a fine thing for God to do. We were told that Jesus loved us, that He was gentle, that soft little lambs curled up at His feet without fear, that He said, "Suffer little children to come unto Me." And for one radiant, luminous moment we knew Jesus, whatever The Rest did, would never hurt us for our mistakes. We gratefully sang, "What a Friend we have in Jesus," and cheerily piped, "Brighten the corner where you are," and gradually every one of us whose viscera had been squeezed into tight little knots by the threats of everlasting torture heard at the grown-up services, grew limp and sleepy and went home quietly and ate a good supper.

It was late at night, after the evening sermon with its persistent propositions and compulsive songs like "Almost persuaded ... almost, but lost"; it was after the preacher had sent the town home vibrating with guilt and fear, after the grown folks were asleep and so remote from us who lay terribly awake; it was then that we remembered the threats. Then, in the darkness, hell reached out bright long red fingers and seared the edge of our beds. Sometimes we would doggedly whisper to ourselves, "We are saved too," but even as we said it, we believed ourselves liars. I remember how impossible it was for me to feel "saved." Though I went up to the altar and stayed until the revivalist pried me off my knees, I was never convinced that my kneeling had effected a change in either my present or future life. But sometimes, wanting it so badly, I lied and stood up with the rest when the evangelist asked all who were sure that they would go to heaven to arise and be counted. My younger sister, more certain of her place in the family, was naturally more certain of her place in heaven, and rarely went to the altar. I remember how I admired her restraint.

But even she shivered as the Unpardonable Sin, cold, silent, implacable, slid through the room just before we fell asleep. I can feel it even now, coiling around our memories like the rattlesnakes we had seen under palmettos, daring us to believe, as we lay there listening to the rustling of our past, that we had a chance at eternal life. Whatever the theologians thought about this most cruel of human ideas, which grew through the centuries into a dragon that devoured the minds of the children of Christendom, to me as a child the Unpardonable Sin had to do with one's forbidden dreams. And I think many other children shared this feeling that somehow it was tangled up with our secret hates and loves and all the passional temptations that tear at the human heart when it is three and four years old. The poets have sometimes viewed it as man's defiance of God as he stubbornly wrests from Him His knowledge of the universe, but we children thought of it more simply, and perhaps more profoundly, in terms of our own small past, and trembled, knowing our guilt.

So our learnings on sin and sex, often taught gently at home, were welded together by the flames of hell. Always we had the feeling of punishment about to fall upon us. We too were "under arrest," we too were being tried. We never knew our crime, we never saw the Authorities face to face, but we knew we would ascend from court to court to higher court, like Kafka's Joseph K., and only death would yield up the final verdict.

No wonder we children feared Death as if he lived next door! For always he was slyly reaching out to snag our lives on his bony fingers if we once passed him carelessly. Graveyards full of baby dreams planted themselves in our past and stayed there, mouldering greenly. Tombstones stiffened in our minds, carving their inscriptions restlessly at night when we could not sleep. Born ... died ... born ... died. We sometimes did not know how we were born, but we knew how we would die. And the littlest of us knew what might happen to us after death. Thinking of death sometimes made the living of life seem vague and shadowy as if it were no more than a few dark steps through the swamp that led toward eternal————. We could never finish that sentence. It hung in our minds, curving into a big question-mark, and sometimes wrapping itself around our spirit until we could not move.

Our old nurse would say, "Law, honey, hit'll all change up deah. When us gets to heaven everything'll be right. Hit'll be right, honey," and she'd say it when she was moaning her own trouble with her husband or white folks and say it when she was picking sandspurs out of our bare feet. And sometimes we white children nestling close against the warm soft breasts of these strong old women could almost believe in the colored folks' heaven but more often with a passion for hopelessness we believed in the white folks' hell.

And everywhere there were the ghosts wandering restlessly through our everyday lives. Stories about haunted houses on the edge of town—what southerner does not remember!—merely took our minds off our own haunted lives and gave us reasons for our fears. We gratefully accepted the ghosts because they did give names to our fears and we urged the grown-ups to tell us again and again about them. And sometimes we learned to lay these ghosts by resurrecting them at will. We even grew fond of them as we walked the lonely curving paths across our trembling earth and felt them following us, like invisible pet dogs, wherever we went.

The physical setting for these tangled dreams and anxieties, the place we lived, was a backdrop to our Deep South childhood that seemed no more than a giant reflection of our own hearts. Back of our little town was the swamp, tangled green, oozing snakes and alligators and water lilies and sweet-blooming bays, weaving light and shadow into awful and tender designs, splotching our lives with brightness and terror. Green cypress blowing through the memory, held firmly to the past by its dark old knobby knees lost in brown water ... rivers that go underground and creep up miles away ... earth that shakes as you walk carefully on it, in swamp and edge of old moss-shadowed lakes.

This is the South I knew as a child. Swamp and palmetto and "sinks" and endless stretches of pines slashed and dripping their richness into little tin cups that glint like bright money. Twisting sand roads ... warm soft sand that you play in; quicksand in which you die. Fields that flatten the eye until there is no curve left in it. Rows of crazy-leaning little grey shanties pushed over by the years. Cows wandering slow through palmetto, across the roads, mute and gaunt like the acres of stumps that do not move but stare at you like the cows. The hills were there, too, but beyond us. And beyond us were bright rolling lands that hold the sun in winter and red gullied earth so beautiful in its injury. All this is the South that we remember, curving gently and more and more steeply until stopped by mountains. Beyond the mountains was the North: the Land of Damyankees, where live People Who Cause All of Our Trouble; and at the end of the North was Wall Street, that fabulous crooked canyon of evil winding endlessly through the southern mind which is, like the dark race, secretly visited by those who talk loudest against it.

Our lessons were learned against this backdrop which rubbed on the senses day in, day out, confirming all that our feelings told us was true of life.

Here also, we unlearned our lessons.

"Letter from Birmingham Jail"

Martin Luther King, Jr. (1929–1968)

The son of an influential preacher in Atlanta, Martin Luther King, Jr., grew up in a world in which the discrepancy between the promise of New Canaan and life in the South presented a challenge to people of faith. Educated at Morehouse College, Crozer Theological Seminary, and Boston University, King began what would be his lifelong struggle with that discrepancy when, in 1955, he was elected president of the Montgomery Improvement Association, the group that led the successful Montgomery bus boycott. Committed to the strategy of nonviolence and the Christian idea of universal brotherhood, King, assailed by the right wing for asking too much and the left wing for asking too little, appealed to what he referred to as the "moral law or law of God" in his 1963 "Letter from Birmingham Jail." Acknowledging man's capacity for iniquity, King nonetheless believed that New Canaan was a real possibility. King was assassinated in Memphis, Tennessee, on April 4, 1968.

April 16, 1963

My Dear Fellow Clergymen:

While confined here in the Birmingham city jail, I came across your recent statement calling my present activities "unwise and untimely." Seldom do I pause to answer criticism of my work and ideas. If I sought to answer all the criticisms that cross my desk, my secretaries would have little time for anything other than such correspondence in the course of the day, and I would have no time for constructive work. But since I feel that you are men of genuine good will and that your criticisms are sincerely set forth, I want to try to answer your statement in what I hope will be patient and reasonable terms.

I think I should indicate why I am here in Birmingham, since you have been influenced by the view which argues against "outsiders coming in." I have the honor of serving as president of the Southern Christian Leadership Conference, an organization operating in every southern state, with headquarters in Atlanta, Georgia. We have some eighty-five affiliated organizations across the South, and one of them is the Alabama Christian Movement for Human Rights. Frequently we share staff, educational and financial resources with our affiliates. Several months ago the affiliate here in Birmingham asked us to be on call to engage in a non-violent direct-action program if such were deemed necessary. We readily consented, and when the hour came we lived up to our promise. So I, along with several members of my staff, am here because I was invited here. I am here because I have organizational ties here.

But more basically, I am in Birmingham because injustice is here. Just as the prophets of the eighth century B.C. left their villages and carried their "thus saith the Lord" far beyond the boundaries of their home towns, and just as the Apostle Paul left his village of Tarsus and carried the gospel of Jesus Christ to the far corners of the Greco-Roman world, so am I compelled to carry the gospel of freedom beyond my own home town. Like Paul, I must constantly respond to the Macedonian call for aid.

Moreover, I am cognizant of the interrelatedness of all communities and states. I cannot sit idly by in Atlanta and not be concerned about what happens in Birmingham. Injustice anywhere is a threat to justice everywhere. We are caught in an inescapable network of mutuality, tied in a single garment of destiny. Whatever affects one directly, affects all indirectly. Never again can we afford to live with the narrow, provincial "outside agitator" idea. Anyone who lives inside the United States can never be considered an outsider anywhere within its bounds.

You deplore the demonstrations taking place in Birmingham. But your statement, I am sorry to say, fails to express a similar concern for the conditions that brought about the demonstrations. I am sure that none of you would want to rest content with the superficial kind of social analysis that deals merely with effects and does not grapple with underlying causes. It is unfortunate that demonstrations are taking place in Birmingham, but it is even more unfortunate that the city's white power structure left the Negro community with no alternative.

In any nonviolent campaign there are four basic steps: collection of the facts to determine whether injustices exist; negotiation; self-purification; and direct action. We have gone through all these steps in Birmingham. There can be no gainsaying the fact that racial injustice engulfs this community. Birmingham is probably the most thoroughly segregated city in the United States. Its ugly record of brutality is widely known. Negroes have experienced grossly unjust treatment in the courts. There have been more unsolved bombings of Negro homes and churches in Birmingham than in any other city in the nation. These are the hard, brutal facts of the case. On the basis of these conditions, Negro leaders sought to negotiate with the city fathers. But the latter consistently refused to engage in good-faith negotiation.

Then, last September, came the opportunity to talk with leaders of Birmingham's economic community. In the course of the negotiations, certain promises were made by the merchants — for example, to remove the stores' humiliating racial signs. On the basis of these promises, the Reverend Fred Shuttlesworth and the leaders of the Alabama Christian Movement for Human Rights agreed to a moratorium on all demonstrations. As the weeks and months went by, we realized that we were the victims of a broken promise. A few signs, briefly removed, returned; the others remained.

As in so many past experiences, our hopes had been blasted, and the shadow of deep disappointment settled upon us. We had no alternative except to prepare for direct action, whereby we would present our very bodies as a means of laying our case before the conscience of the local and the national community. Mindful of the difficulties involved, we decided to undertake a process of self-purification. We began a series of workshops on nonviolence, and we repeatedly asked ourselves: "Are you able to accept blows without retaliating?" "Are you able to endure the ordeal of jail?" We decided to schedule our direct-action program for the Easter season, realizing that except for Christmas, this is the main shopping period of the year. Knowing that a strong economic-withdrawal program would be the by-product of direct action, we felt that this would be the best time to bring pressure to bear on the merchants for the needed change.

Then it occurred to us that Birmingham's mayoral election was coming up in March, and we speedily decided to postpone action until after election day. When we discovered that the Commissioner of Public Safety, Eugene "Bull" Connor, had piled up enough votes to be in the run-off, we decided again to postpone action until the day after the run-off so that the demonstrations could not be used to cloud the issues. Like many others, we waited to see Mr. Connor defeated, and to this end we endured postponement after postponement. Having aided in this community need, we felt that our direct-action program could be delayed no longer.

You may well ask: "Why direct action? Why sit-ins, marches and so forth? Isn't negotiation a better path?" You are quite right in calling for negotiation. Indeed, this is the very purpose of direct action. Nonviolent direct action seeks to create such a crisis and foster such a tension that a community which has constantly refused to negotiate is forced to confront the issue. It seeks so to dramatize the issue that it can no longer be ignored. My citing the creation of tension as part of the work of the nonviolent-resister may sound rather shocking. But I must confess that I am not afraid of the word "tension." I have earnestly opposed violent tension, but there is a type of constructive, nonviolent tension which is necessary for growth. Just as Socrates felt that it was necessary to create a tension in the mind so that individuals could rise from the bondage of myths and half-truths to the unfettered realm of creative analysis and objective appraisal, so must we see the need for nonviolent gadflies to create the kind of tension in society that will help men rise from the dark depths of prejudice and racism to the majestic heights of understanding and brotherhood.

The purpose of our direct-action program is to create a situation so crisis-packed that it will inevitably open the door to negotiation. I therefore concur with you in your call for negotiation. Too long has our beloved Southland been bogged down in a tragic effort to live in monologue rather than dialogue.

One of the basic points in your statement is that the action that I and my associates have taken in Birmingham is untimely. Some have asked: "Why didn't you give the new city administration time to act?" The only answer that I can give to this query is that the new Birmingham administration must be prodded about as much as the outgoing one, before it will act. We are sadly mistaken if we feel that the election of Albert Boutwell as mayor will bring the millennium to Birmingham. While Mr. Boutwell is a much more gentle person than Mr. Connor, they are both segregationists, dedicated to maintenance of the status quo. I have hope that Mr. Boutwell will be reasonable enough to see the futility of massive resistance to desegregation. But he will not see this without pressure from devotees of civil rights. My friends, I must say to you that we have not made a single gain in civil rights without determined legal and nonviolent pressure. Lamentably, it is an historical fact that privileged groups seldom give up their privileges voluntarily. Individuals may see the moral light and voluntarily give up their unjust posture; but, as Reinhold Niebuhr has reminded us, groups tend to be more immoral than individuals.

We know through painful experience that freedom is never voluntarily given by the oppressor; it must be demanded by the oppressed. Frankly, I have yet to engage in a direct-action campaign that was "well timed" in the view of those who have not suffered unduly from the disease of segregation. For years now I have heard the word "Wait!" It rings in the ear of every Negro with piercing familiarity. This "Wait" has almost always meant "Never." We must come to see, with one of our distinguished jurists, that "justice too long delayed is justice denied."

We have waited for more than 340 years for our constitutional and God-given rights. The nations of Asia and Africa are moving with jetlike speed toward gaining political independence, but we still creep at horse-and-buggy pace toward gaining a cup of coffee at a lunch counter. Perhaps it is easy for those who have never felt the stinging darts of segregation to say, "Wait." But when you have seen vicious mobs lynch your mothers and fathers at will and drown your sisters and brothers at whim; when you have seen hate-filled policemen curse, kick and even kill your black brothers and sisters; when you see the vast majority of your twenty million Negro brothers smothering in an airtight cage of poverty in the midst of an affluent society; when you suddenly find your tongue twisted and your speech stammering as you seek to explain to your six-year-old daughter why she can't go to the public amusement park that has just been advertised on television, and see tears welling up in her eyes when she is told that Funtown is closed to colored children, and see ominous clouds of inferiority beginning to form in her little mental sky, and see her beginning to distort her personality by developing an unconscious bitterness toward white people; when you have to concoct an answer for a five-year-old son who is asking: "Daddy, why do white people treat colored people so mean?"; when you take a cross-country drive and find it necessary to sleep night after night in the uncomfortable corners of your automobile because no motel will accept you; when you are humiliated day in and day out by nagging signs reading "white" and "colored"; when your first name becomes "nigger," your middle name becomes "boy" (however old you are) and your last name becomes "John," and your wife and mother are never given the respected title "Mrs."; when you are harried by day and haunted by night by the fact that you are a Negro, living constantly at tiptoe stance, never quite knowing what to expect next, and are plagued with inner fears and outer resentments; when you are forever fighting a degenerating sense of "nobodiness" — then you will understand why we find it difficult to wait. There comes a time when the cup of endurance runs over, and men are no longer willing to be plunged into the abyss of despair. I hope, sirs, you can understand our legitimate and unavoidable impatience.

You express a great deal of anxiety over our willingness to break laws. This is certainly a legitimate concern. Since we so diligently urge people to obey the Supreme Court's decision of 1954 outlawing segregation in the public schools, at first glance it may seem rather paradoxical for us consciously to break laws. One may well ask: "How can you advocate breaking some laws and obeying others?" The answer lies in the fact that there are two types of laws: just and unjust. I would be the first to advocate obeying just laws. One has not only a legal but a moral responsibility to obey just laws. Conversely, one has a moral responsibility to disobey unjust laws. I would agree with St. Augustine that "an unjust law is no law at all."

Now, what is the difference between the two? How does one determine whether a law is just or unjust? A just law is a man-made code that squares with the moral law or the law of God. An unjust law is a code that is out of harmony with the moral law. To put it in the terms of St. Thomas Aquinas: An unjust law is a human law that is not rooted in eternal law and natural law. Any law that uplifts human personality is just. Any law that degrades human personality is unjust. All segregation statutes are unjust because segregation distorts the soul and damages the personality. It gives the segregator a false sense of superiority and the segregated a false sense of inferiority. Segregation, to use the terminology of the Jewish philosopher Martin Buber, substitutes an "I-it" relationship for an "I-thou" relationship and ends up relegating persons to the status of things. Hence segregation is not only politically, economically and sociologically unsound, it is morally wrong and sinful. Paul Tillich has said that sin is separation. Is not segregation an existential expression of man's tragic separation, his awful estrangement, his terrible sinfulness? Thus it is that I can urge men to obey the 1954 decision of the Supreme Court, for it is morally right; and I can urge them to disobey segregation ordinances, for they are morally wrong.

Let us consider a more concrete example of just and unjust laws. An unjust law is a code that a numerical or power majority group compels a minority group to obey but does not make binding on itself. This is *difference* made legal. By the same token, a just law is a code that a majority compels a minority to follow and that it is willing to follow itself. This is *sameness* made legal.

Let me give another explanation. A law is unjust if it is inflicted on a minority that, as a result of being denied the right to vote, had no part in enacting or devising the law. Who can say that the legislature of Alabama which set up that state's segregation laws was democratically elected? Throughout Alabama all sorts of devious methods are used to prevent Negroes from becoming registered voters, and there are some counties in which, even though Negroes constitute a majority of the population, not a single Negro is registered. Can any law enacted under such circumstances be considered democratically structured?

Sometimes a law is just on its face and unjust in its application. For instance, I have been arrested on a charge of parading without a permit. Now, there is nothing wrong in having an ordinance which requires a permit for a parade. But such an ordinance becomes unjust when it is used to maintain segregation and to deny citizens the First-Amendment privilege of peaceful assembly and protest.

I hope you are able to see the distinction I am trying to point out. In no sense do I advocate evading or defying the law, as would the rabid segregationist. That would lead to anarchy. One who breaks an unjust law must do so openly, lovingly, and with a willingness to accept the penalty. I submit that an individual who breaks a law that conscience tells him is unjust, and who willingly accepts the penalty of imprisonment in order to arouse the conscience of the community over its injustice, is in reality expressing the highest respect for law.

Of course, there is nothing new about this kind of civil disobedience. It was evidenced sublimely in the refusal of Shadrach, Meshach and Abednego to obey the laws of Nebuchadnezzar, on the ground that a higher moral law was at stake. It was practiced superbly by the early Christians, who were willing to face hungry lions and the excruciating pain of chopping blocks rather than submit to certain unjust laws of the Roman Empire. To a degree, academic freedom is a reality today because Socrates practiced civil disobedience. In our own nation, the Boston Tea Party represented a massive act of civil disobedience.

We should never forget that everything Adolf Hitler did in Germany was "legal" and everything the Hungarian freedom fighters did in Hungary was "illegal." It was "illegal" to aid and comfort a Jew in Hitler's Germany. Even so, I am sure that, had I lived in Germany at the time, I would have aided and comforted my Jewish brothers. If today I lived in a Communist country where certain principles dear to the Christian faith are suppressed, I would openly advocate disobeying that country's antireligious laws.

I must make two honest confessions to you, my Christian and Jewish brothers. First, I must confess that over the past few years I have been gravely disappointed with the white moderate. I have almost reached the regrettable conclusion that the Negro's great stumbling block in his stride toward freedom is not the White Citizen's Counciler of the Ku Klux Klanner, but the white moderate, who is more devoted to "order" than to justice; who prefers a negative peace which is the absence of tension to a positive peace which is the presence of justice; who constantly says: "I agree with you in the goal you seek, but I cannot agree with your methods of direct action"; who paternalistically believes he can set the timetable for another man's freedom; who lives by a mythical concept of time and who constantly advises the Negro to wait for a "more convenient season." Shallow understanding from people of good will is more frustrating than absolute misunderstanding from people of ill will. Lukewarm acceptance is much more bewildering than outright rejection.

I had hoped that the white moderate would understand that law and order exist for the purpose of establishing justice and that when they fail in this purpose they become the dangerously structured dams that block the flow of social progress. I had hoped that the white moderate would understand that the present tension in the South is a necessary phase of the transition from an obnoxious negative peace, in which the Negro passively accepted his unjust plight, to a substantive and positive peace, in which all men will respect the dignity and worth of human personality. Actually, we who engage in nonviolent direct action are not the creators of tension. We merely bring to the surface the hidden tension that is already alive. We bring it out in the open, where it can be seen and dealt with. Like a boil that can never be cured so long as it is covered up but must be opened with all its ugliness to the natural medicines of air and light, injustice must be exposed, with all the tension its exposure creates, to the light of human conscience and the air of national opinion before it can be cured.

In your statement you assert that our actions, even though peaceful, must be condemned because they precipitate violence. But is this a logical assertion? Isn't this like condemning a robbed man because his possession of money precipitated the evil act of robbery? Isn't this like condemning Socrates because his unswerving commitment to truth and his philosophical inquiries precipitated the act by the misguided populace in which they made him drink hemlock? Isn't this like condemning Jesus because his unique God-consciousness and never-ceasing devotion to God's will precipitated the evil act of crucifixion? We must come to see that, as the federal courts have consistently affirmed, it is wrong to urge an individual to cease his efforts to gain his basic constitutional rights because the quest may precipitate violence. Society must protect the robbed and punish the robber.

I had also hoped that the white moderate would reject the myth concerning time in relation to the struggle for freedom. I have just received a letter from a white brother in Texas. He writes: "All Christians know that the colored people will receive equal rights eventually, but it is possible that you are in too great a religious hurry. It has taken Christianity almost two thousand years to accomplish what it has. The teachings of Christ take time to come to earth." Such an attitude stems from a tragic misconception of time, from the strangely irrational notion that there is something in the very flow of time that will inevitably cure all ills. Actually, time itself is neutral; it can be used either destructively or constructively. More and more I feel that the people of ill will have used time much more effectively than have the people of good will. We will have to repent in this generation not merely for the hateful words and actions of the bad people but for the appalling silence of the good people. Human progress never rolls in on wheels of inevitability; it comes through the tireless efforts of men willing to be co-workers with God, and without this hard work, time itself becomes an ally of the forces of social stagnation. We must use time creatively, in the knowledge that the time is always ripe to do right. Now is the time to make real the promise of democracy and transform our pending national elegy into a creative psalm of brotherhood. Now is the time to lift our national policy from the quicksand of racial injustice to the solid rock of human dignity.

You speak of our activity in Birmingham as extreme. At first I was rather disappointed that fellow clergymen would see my nonviolent efforts as those of an extremist. I began thinking about the fact that I stand in the middle of two opposing forces in the Negro community. One is a force of complacency, made up in part of Negroes who, as a result of long years of oppression, are so drained of self-respect and a sense of "somebodiness" that they have adjusted to segregation; and in part of a few middle-class Negroes who, because of a degree of academic and economic security and because in some ways they profit by segregation, have become insensitive to the problems of the masses. The other force is one of bitterness and hatred, and it comes perilously close to advocating violence. It is expressed in the various black nationalist groups that are springing up across the nation, the largest and best-known being Elijah Muhammad's Muslim movement. Nourished by the Negro's frustration over the continued existence of racial discrimination, this movement is made up of people who have lost faith in America, who have absolutely repudiated Christianity, and who have concluded that the white man is an incorrigible "devil."

I have tried to stand between these two forces, saying that we need emulate neither the "do-nothingism" of the complacent nor the hatred and despair of the black nationalist. For there is the more excellent way of love and non-violent protest. I am grateful to God that, through the influence of the Negro church, the way of nonviolence became an integral part of our struggle.

If this philosophy had not emerged, by now many streets of the South would, I am convinced, be flowing with blood. And I am further convinced that if our white brothers dismiss as "rabble-rousers" and "outside agitators" those of us who employ nonviolent direct action, and if they refuse to support our nonviolent efforts, millions of Negroes will, out of frustration and despair, seek solace and security in black-nationalist ideologies—a development that would inevitably lead to a frightening racial nightmare.

Oppressed people cannot remain oppressed forever. The yearning for freedom eventually manifests itself, and that is what has happened to the American Negro. Something within has reminded him of his birthright of freedom, and something without has reminded him that it can be gained. Consciously or unconsciously, he has been caught up by the *Zeitgeist*, and with his black brothers of Africa and his brown and yellow brothers of Asia, South America and the Caribbean, the United States Negro is moving with a sense of great urgency toward the promised land of racial justice. If one recognizes this vital urge that has engulfed the Negro community, one should readily understand why public demonstrations are taking place. The Negro has many pent-up resentments and latent frustrations, and he must release them. So let him march; let him make prayer pilgrimages to the city hall; let him go on freedom rides—and try to understand why he must do so. If his repressed emotions are not released in nonviolent ways, they will seek expression through violence; this is not a threat but a fact of history. So I have not said to my people: "Get rid of your discontent." Rather, I have tried to say that this normal and healthy discontent can be channeled into the creative outlet of nonviolent direct action. And now this approach is being termed extremist.

But though I was initially disappointed at being categorized as an extremist, as I continued to think about the matter I gradually gained a measure of satisfaction from the label. Was not Jesus an extremist for love: "Love your enemies, bless them that curse you, do good to them that hate you, and pray for them which despitefully use you, and persecute you." Was not Amos an extremist for justice: "Let justice roll down like waters and righteousness like an ever-flowing stream." Was not Paul an extremist for the Christian gospel: "I bear in my body the marks of the Lord Jesus." Was not Martin Luther an extremist: "Here I stand; I cannot do otherwise, so help me God." And John Bunyan: "I will stay in jail to the end of my days before I make a butchery of my conscience." And Abraham Lincoln: "This nation cannot survive half slave and half free." And Thomas Jefferson: "We hold these truths to be self-evident, that all men are created equal . . ." So the question is not whether we will be extremists, but what kind of extremists we will be. Will we be extremists for hate or for love? Will we be extremists for the preservation of injustice or for the extension of justice? In that dramatic scene on Calvary's hill three men were crucified. We must never forget that all three men were crucified for the same crime—the crime of extremism. Two were extremists for immorality, and thus fell below their environment. The other, Jesus Christ, was an extremist for love, truth and goodness, and thereby rose above his environment. Perhaps the South, the nation and the world are in dire need of creative extremists.

I had hoped that the white moderate would see this need. Perhaps I was too optimistic; perhaps I expected too much. I suppose I should have realized that few members of the oppressor race can understand the deep groans and passionate yearnings of the oppressed race, and still fewer have the vision to see that injustice must be rooted out by strong, persistent and determined action. I am thankful, however, that some of our white brothers in the South have grasped the meaning of this social revolution and committed themselves to it. They are still all too few in quantity, but they are big in quality. Some — such as Ralph McGill, Lillian Smith, Harry Golden, James McBride Dabbs, Ann Braden and Sarah Patton Boyle — have written about our struggle in eloquent and prophetic terms. Others have marched with us down nameless streets of the South. They have languished in filthy, roach-infested jails, suffering the abuse and brutality of policemen who view them as "dirty nigger-lovers." Unlike so many of their moderate brothers and sisters, they have recognized the urgency of the moment and sensed the need for powerful "action" antidotes to combat the disease of segregation.

Let me take note of my other major disappointment. I have been so greatly disappointed with the white church and its leadership. Of course, there are some notable exceptions. I am not unmindful of the fact that each of you has taken some significant stands on this issue. I commend you, Reverend Stallings, for your Christian stand on this past Sunday, in welcoming Negroes to your worship service on a nonsegregated basis. I commend the Catholic leaders of this state for integrating Spring Hill College several years ago.

But despite these notable exceptions, I must honestly reiterate that I have been disappointed with the church. I do not say this as one of those negative critics who can always find something wrong with the church. I say this as a minister of the gospel, who loves the church; who was nurtured in its bosom; who has been sustained by its spiritual blessings and who will remain true to it as long as the cord of life shall lengthen.

When I was suddenly catapulted into the leadership of the bus protest in Montgomery, Alabama, a few years ago, I felt we would be supported by the white church. I felt that the white ministers, priests and rabbis of the South would be among our strongest allies. Instead, some have been outright opponents, refusing to understand the freedom movement and misrepresenting its leaders; all too many others have been more cautious than courageous and have remained silent behind the anesthetizing security of stained-glass windows.

In spite of my shattered dreams, I came to Birmingham with the hope that the white religious leadership of this community would see the justice of our cause and, with deep moral concern, would serve as the channel through which our just grievances could reach the power structure. I had hoped that each of you would understand. But again I have been disappointed.

I have heard numerous southern religious leaders admonish their worshipers to comply with a desegregation decision because it is the law, but I have longed to hear white ministers declare: "Follow this decree because integration is morally right and because the Negro is your brother." In the midst of blatant injustices inflicted upon the Negro, I have watched white churchmen stand on the sideline and mouth pious irrelevancies and sanctimonious trivialities. In the midst of a mighty struggle to rid our nation of racial and economic injustice, I have heard many ministers say: "Those are social issues, with which the gospel has no real concern." And I have watched many churches commit themselves to a completely otherwordly religion which makes a strange, un-Biblical distinction between body and soul, between the sacred and the secular.

I have traveled the length and breadth of Alabama, Mississippi and all the other southern states. On sweltering summer days and crisp autumn mornings I have looked at the South's beautiful churches with their lofty spires pointing heavenward. I have beheld the impressive outlines of her massive religious-education buildings. Over and over I have found myself asking: "What kind of people worship here? Who is their God? Where were their voices when the lips of Governor Barnett dripped with words of interposition and nullification? Where were they when Governor Wallace gave a clarion call for defiance and hatred? Where were their voices of support when bruised and weary Negro men and women decided to rise from the dark dungeons of complacency to the bright hills of creative protest?"

Yes, these questions are still in my mind. In deep disappointment I have wept over the laxity of the church. But be assured that my tears have been tears of love. There can be no deep disappointment where there is not deep love. Yes, I love the church. How could I do otherwise? I am in the rather unique position of being the son, the grandson and the great-grandson of preachers. Yes, I see the church as the body of Christ. But, oh! How we have blemished and scarred that body through social neglect and through fear of being nonconformists.

There was a time when the church was very powerful — in the time when the early Christians rejoiced at being deemed worthy to suffer for what they believed. In those days the church was not merely a thermometer that recorded the ideas and principles of popular opinion; it was a thermostat that transformed the mores of society. Whenever the early Christians entered a town, the people in power became disturbed and immediately sought to convict the Christians for being "disturbers of the peace" and "outside agitators." But the Christians pressed on, in the conviction that they were "a colony of heaven," called to obey God rather than man. Small in number, they were big in commitment. They were too God-intoxicated to be "astronomically intimidated." By their effort and example they brought an end to such ancient evils as infanticide and gladiatorial contests.

Things are different now. So often the contemporary church is a weak, ineffectual voice with an uncertain sound. So often it is an archdefender of the status quo. Far from being disturbed by the presence of the church, the power structure of the average community is consoled by the church's silent—and often even vocal—sanction of things as they are.

But the judgment of God is upon the church as never before. If today's church does not recapture the sacrificial spirit of the early church, it will lose its authenticity, forfeit the loyalty of millions, and be dismissed as an irrelevant social club with no meaning for the twentieth century. Every day I meet young people whose disappointment with the church has turned into outright disgust.

Perhaps I have once again been too optimistic. Is organized religion too inextricably bound to the status quo to save our nation and the world? Perhaps I must turn my faith to the inner spiritual church, the church within the church, as the true *ekklesia* and the hope of the world. But again I am thankful to God that some noble souls from the ranks of organized religion have broken loose from the paralyzing chains of conformity and joined us as active partners in the struggle for freedom. They have left their secure congregations and walked the streets of Albany, Georgia, with us. They have gone down the highways of the South on tortuous rides for freedom. Yes, they have gone to jail with us. Some have been dismissed from their churches, have lost the support of their bishops and fellow ministers. But they have acted in the faith that right defeated is stronger than evil triumphant. Their witness has been the spiritual salt that has preserved the true meaning of the gospel in these troubled times. They have carved a tunnel of hope through the dark mountain of disappointment.

I hope the church as a whole will meet the challenge of this decisive hour. But even if the church does not come to the aid of justice, I have no despair about the future. I have no fear about the outcome of our struggle in Birmingham, even if our motives are at present misunderstood. We will reach the goal of freedom in Birmingham and all over the nation, because the goal of America is freedom. Abused and scorned though we may be, our destiny is tied up with America's destiny. Before the pilgrims landed at Plymouth, we were here. Before the pen of Jefferson etched the majestic words of the Declaration of Independence across the pages of history, we were here. For more than two centuries our forebears labored in this country without wages; they made cotton king; they built the homes of their masters while suffering gross injustice and shameful humiliation — and yet out of a bottomless vitality they continued to thrive and develop. If the inexpressible cruelties of slavery could not stop us, the opposition we now face will surely fail. We will win our freedom because the sacred heritage of our nation and the eternal will of God are embodied in our echoing demands.

Before closing I feel impelled to mention one other point in your statement that has troubled me profoundly. You warmly commended the Birmingham police force for keeping "order" and "preventing violence." I doubt that you would have so warmly commended the police force if you had seen its dogs sinking their teeth into unarmed, nonviolent Negroes. I doubt that you would so quickly commend the policemen if you were to observe their ugly and inhumane treatment of Negroes here in the city jail; if you were to watch them push and curse old Negro women and young Negro girls; if you were to see them slap and kick old Negro men and young boys; if you were to observe them, as they did on two occasions, refuse to give us food because we wanted to sing our grace together. I cannot join you in your praise of the Birmingham police department.

It is true that the police have exercised a degree of discipline in handling the demonstrators. In this sense they have conducted themselves rather "nonviolently" in public. But for what purpose? To preserve the evil system of segregation. Over the past few years I have consistently preached that nonviolence demands that the means we use must be as pure as the ends we seek. I have tried to make clear that it is wrong to use immoral means to attain moral ends. But now I must affirm that it is just as wrong, or perhaps even more so, to use moral means to preserve immoral ends. Perhaps Mr. Connor and his policemen have been rather nonviolent in public, as was Chief Pritchett in Albany, Georgia, but they have used the moral means of nonviolence to maintain the immoral end of racial injustice. As T. S. Eliot has said: "The last temptation is the greatest treason: To do the right deed for the wrong reason."

I wish you had commended the Negro sit-inners and demonstrators of Birmingham for their sublime courage, their willingness to suffer and their amazing discipline in the midst of great provocation. One day the South will recognize its real heroes. They will be the James Merediths, with the noble sense of purpose that enables them to face jeering and hostile mobs, and with the agonizing loneliness that characterizes the life of the pioneer. They will be old, oppressed, battered Negro women, symbolized in a seventy-two-year-old woman in Montgomery, Alabama, who rose up with a sense of dignity and with her people decided not to ride segregated buses, and who responded with ungrammatical profundity to one who inquired about her weariness: "My feets is tired, but my soul is at rest." They will be the young high school and college students, the young ministers of the gospel and a host of their elders, courageously and nonviolently sitting in at lunch counters and willingly going to jail for conscience' sake. One day the South will know that when these disinherited children of God sat down at lunch counters, they were in reality standing up for what is best in the American dream and for the most sacred values in our Judaeo-

Christian heritage, thereby bringing our nation back to those great wells of democracy which were dug deep by the founding fathers in their formulation of the Constitution and the Declaration of Independence.

Never before have I written so long a letter. I'm afraid it is much too long to take your precious time. I can assure you that it would have been much shorter if I had been writing from a comfortable desk, but what else can one do when he is alone in a narrow jail cell, other than write long letters, think long thoughts and pray long prayers?

If I have said anything in this letter that overstates the truth and indicates an unreasonable impatience, I beg you to forgive me. If I have said anything that understates the truth and indicates my having a patience that allows me to settle for anything less than brotherhood, I beg God to forgive me.

I hope this letter finds you strong in the faith. I also hope that circumstances will soon make it possible for me to meet each of you, not as an integrationist or a civil-rights leader but as a fellow clergyman and a Christian brother. Let us all hope that the dark clouds of racial prejudice will soon pass away and the deep fog of misunderstanding will be lifted from our fear-drenched communities, and in some not too distant tomorrow the radiant stars of love and brotherhood will shine over our great nation with all their scintillating beauty.

Yours for the cause of Peace and Brotherhood,
Martin Luther King, Jr.

"Everything that Rises Must Converge"

Flannery O'Connor (1925–1964)

Flannery O'Connor's first novel, *Wise Blood*, which appeared in 1952, baffled the majority of reviewers who did not recognize her sympathy for the protagonist, religious fundamentalist Hazel Motes. A devout Catholic raised in Savannah and Milledgeville, Georgia, O'Connor's religious convictions shaped her imagination's response to the world. Dismayed at a culture that increasingly trivialized religious convictions while promoting the idea of man-made perfectibility, O'Connor highlighted the twin themes of original sin and man's capacity for self-deception. In her story "Everything that Rises Must Converge" (1965), O'Connor portrays the consequences of self-delusion in the context of the newly integrated South.

Her doctor had told Julian's mother that she must lose twenty pounds on account of her blood pressure, so on Wednesday nights Julian had to take her downtown on the bus for a reducing class at the Y. The reducing class was designed for working girls over fifty, who weighed from 165 to 200 pounds. His mother was one of the slimmer ones, but she said ladies did not tell their age or weight. She would not ride the buses by herself at night since they had been integrated, and because the reducing class was one of her few pleasures, necessary for her health, and *free*, she said Julian could at least put himself out to take her, considering all she did for him. Julian did not like to consider all she did for him, but every Wednesday night he braced himself and took her.

She was almost ready to go, standing before the hall mirror, putting on her hat, while he, his hands behind him, appeared pinned to the door frame, waiting like Saint Sebastian for the arrows to begin piercing him. The hat was new and had cost her seven dollars and a half. She kept saying, "Maybe I shouldn't have paid that for it. No, I shouldn't have. I'll take it off and return it tomorrow. I shouldn't have bought it."

Julian raised his eyes to heaven. "Yes, you should have bought it," he said. "Put it on and let's go." It was a hideous hat. A purple velvet flap came down on one side of it and stood up on the other; the rest of it was green and looked like a cushion with the stuffing out. He decided it was less comical than jaunty and pathetic. Everything that gave her pleasure was small and depressed him.

She lifted the hat one more time and set it down slowly on top of her head. Two wings of gray hair protruded on either side of her florid face, but her eyes, sky-blue, were as innocent and untouched by experience as they must have been when she was ten. Were it not that she was a widow who had struggled fiercely to feed and clothe and put him through school and who was supporting him still, "until he got on his feet," she might have been a little girl that he had to take to town.

"It's all right, it's all right," he said. "Let's go." He opened the door himself and started down the walk to get her going. The sky was dying violet and the houses stood out darkly against it, bulbous liver-colored monstrosities of a uniform ugliness though no two were alike. Since this had been a fashionable neighborhood forty years ago, his mother persisted in thinking they did well to have an apartment in it. Each house had a narrow collar of dirt around it in which sat, usually, a grubby child. Julian walked with his hands in his pockets, his head down and thrust forward and his eyes glazed with the determination to make himself completely numb during the time he would be sacrificed to her pleasure.

The door closed and he turned to find the dumpy figure, surmounted by the atrocious hat, coming toward him. "Well," she said, "you only live once and paying a little more for it, I at least won't meet myself coming and going."

"Some day I'll start making money," Julian said gloomily—he knew he never would—"and you can have one of those jokes whenever you take the fit." But first they would move. He visualized a place where the nearest neighbors would be three miles away on either side.

"I think you're doing fine," she said, drawing on her gloves. "You've only been out of school a year. Rome wasn't built in a day."

She was one of the few members of the Y reducing class who arrived in hat and gloves and who had a son who had been to college. "It takes time," she said, "and the world is in such a mess. This hat looked better on me than any of the others, though when she brought it out I said, 'Take that thing back. I wouldn't have it on my head,' and she said, 'Now wait till you see it on,' and when she put it on me, I said, 'We-ull,' and she said, 'If you ask me, that hat does something for you and you do something for the hat, and besides,' she said, 'with that hat, you won't meet yourself coming and going.'"

Julian thought he could have stood his lot better if she had been selfish, if she had been an old hag who drank and screamed at him. He walked along, saturated in depression, as if in the midst of his martyrdom he had lost his faith. Catching sight of his long, hopeless, irritated face, she stopped suddenly with a grief-stricken look, and pulled back on his arm.

"Wait on me," she said. "I'm going back to the house and take this thing off and tomorrow I'm going to return it. I was out of my head. I can pay the gas bill with that seven-fifty."

He caught her arm in a vicious grip. "You are not going to take it back," he said. "I like it."

"Well," she said, "I don't think I ought . . ."

"Shut up and enjoy it," he muttered, more depressed than ever.

"With the world in the mess it's in," she said, "it's a wonder we can enjoy anything. I tell you, the bottom rail is on the top."

Julian sighed.

"Of course," she said, "if you know who you are, you can go anywhere." She said this every time he took her to the reducing class. "Most of them in it are not our kind of people," she said, "but I can be gracious to anybody. I know who I am."

"They don't give a damn for your graciousness," Julian said savagely. "Knowing who you are is good for one generation only. You haven't the foggiest idea where you stand now or who you are."

She stopped and allowed her eyes to flash at him. "I most certainly do know who I am," she said, "and if you don't know who you are, I'm ashamed of you."

"Oh hell," Julian said.

"Your great-grandfather was a former governor of this state," she said. "Your grandfather was a prosperous landowner. Your grandmother was a Godhigh."

"Will you look around you," he said tensely, "and see where you are now?" and he swept his arm jerkily out to indicate the neighborhood, which the growing darkness at least made less dingy.

"You remain what you are," she said. "Your great-grandfather had a plantation and two hundred slaves."

"There are no more slaves," he said irritably.

"They were better off when they were," she said. He groaned to see that she was off on that topic. She rolled onto it every few days like a train on an open track. He knew every stop, every junction, every swamp along the way, and knew the exact point at which her conclusion would roll majestically into the station: "It's ridiculous. It's simply not realistic. They should rise, yes, but on their own side of the fence."

"Let's skip it," Julian said.

"The ones I feel sorry for," she said, "are the ones that are half white. They're tragic."

"Will you skip it?"

"Suppose we were half white. We would certainly have mixed feelings."

"I have mixed feelings now," he groaned.

"Well let's talk about something pleasant," she said. "I remember going to Grandpa's when I was a little girl. Then the house had double stairways that went up to what was really the second floor — all the cooking was done on the first. I used to like to stay down in the kitchen on account of the way the walls smelled. I would sit with my nose pressed against the plaster and take deep breaths. Actually the place belonged to the God-highs but your grandfather Chestny paid the mortgage and saved it for them. They were in reduced circumstances," she said, "but reduced or not, they never forgot who they were."

"Doubtless that decayed mansion reminded them," Julian muttered. He never spoke of it without contempt or thought of it without longing. He had seen it once when he was a child before it had been sold. The double stairways had rotted and been torn down. Negroes were living in it. But it remained in his mind as his mother had known it. It appeared in his dreams regularly. He would stand on the wide porch, listening to the rustle of oak leaves, then wander through the high-ceilinged hall into the parlor that opened onto it and gaze at the worn rugs and faded draperies. It occurred to him that it was he, not she, who could have appreciated it. He preferred its threadbare elegance to anything he could name and it was because of it that all the neighborhoods they had lived in had been a torment to him — whereas she had hardly known the difference. She called her insensitivity "being adjustable."

"And I remember the old darky who was my nurse, Caroline. There was no better person in the world. I've always had a great respect for my colored friends," she said. "I'd do anything in the world for them and they'd . . ."

"Will you for God's sake get off that subject?" Julian said. When he got on a bus by himself, he made it a point to sit down beside a Negro, in reparation as it were for his mother's sins.

"You're mighty touchy tonight," she said. "Do you feel all right?"

"Yes I feel all right," he said. "Now lay off."

She pursed her lips. "Well, you certainly are in a vile humor," she observed. "I just won't speak to you at all."

They had reached the bus stop. There was no bus in sight and Julian, his hands still jammed in his pockets and his head thrust forward, scowled down the empty street. The frustration of having to wait on the bus as well as ride on it began to creep up his neck like a hot hand. The presence of his mother was borne in upon him as she gave a pained sigh. He looked at her bleakly. She was holding herself very erect under the preposterous hat, wearing it like a banner of her imaginary dignity. There was in him an evil urge to break her spirit. He suddenly unloosened his tie and pulled it off and put it in his pocket.

She stiffened. "Why must you look like *that* when you take me to town?" she said. "Why must you deliberately embarrass me?"

"If you'll never learn where you are," he said, "you can at least learn where I am."

"You look like a—thug," she said.

"Then I must be one," he murmured.

"I'll just go home," she said. "I will not bother you. If you can't do a little thing like that for me . . ."

Rolling his eyes upward, he put his tie back on. "Restored to my class," he muttered. He thrust his face toward her and hissed, "True culture is in the mind, the *mind*," he said, and tapped his head, "the mind."

"It's in the heart," she said, "and in how you do things and how you do things is because of who you *are*."

"Nobody in the damn bus cares who you are."

"I care who I am," she said icily.

The lighted bus appeared on top of the next hill and as it approached, they moved out into the street to meet it. He put his hand under her elbow and hoisted her up on the creaking step. She entered with a little smile, as if she were going into a drawing room where everyone had been waiting for her. While he put in the tokens, she sat down on one of the broad front seats for three which faced the aisle. A thin woman with protruding teeth and long yellow hair was sitting on the end of it. His mother moved up beside her and left room for Julian beside herself. He sat down and looked at the floor across the aisle where a pair of thin feet in red and white canvas sandals were planted.

His mother immediately began a general conversation meant to attract anyone who felt like talking. "Can it get any hotter?" she said and removed from her purse a folding fan, black with a Japanese scene on it, which she began to flutter before her.

"I reckon it might could," the woman with the protruding teeth said, "but I know for a fact my apartment couldn't get no hotter."

"It must get the afternoon sun," his mother said. She sat forward and looked up and down the bus. It was half filled. Everybody was white. "I see we have the bus to ourselves," she said. Julian cringed.

"For a change," said the woman across the aisle, the owner of the red and white canvas sandals. "I come on one the other day and they were thick as fleas—up front and all through."

"The world is in a mess everywhere," his mother said. "I don't know how we've let it get in this fix."

"What gets my goat is all those boys from good families stealing automobile tires," the woman with the protruding teeth said. "I told my boy, I said you may not be rich but you been raised right and if I ever catch you in any such mess, they can send you on to the reformatory. Be exactly where you belong."

"Training tells," his mother said. "Is your boy in high school?"

"Ninth grade," the woman said.

"My son just finished college last year. He wants to write but he's selling typewriters until he gets started," his mother said.

The woman leaned forward and peered at Julian. He threw her such a malevolent look that she subsided against the seat. On the floor across the aisle there was an abandoned newspaper. He got up and got it and opened it out in front of him. His mother discreetly continued the conversation in a lower tone but the woman across the aisle said in a loud voice, "Well that's nice. Selling typewriters is close to writing. He can go right from one to the other."

"I tell him," his mother said, "that Rome wasn't built in a day."

Behind the newspaper Julian was withdrawing into the inner compartment of his mind where he spent most of his time. This was a kind of mental bubble in which he established himself when he could not bear to be a part of what was going on around him. From it he could see out and judge but in it he was safe from any kind of penetration from without. It was the only place where he felt free of the general idiocy of his fellows. His mother had never entered it but from it he could see her with absolute clarity.

The old lady was clever enough and he thought that if she had started from any of the right premises, more might have been expected of her. She lived according to the laws of her own fantasy world, outside of which he had never seen her set foot. The law of it was to sacrifice herself for him after she had first created the necessity to do so by making a mess of things. If he had permitted her sacrifices, it was only because her lack of foresight had made them necessary. All of her life had been a struggle to act like a Chestny without the Chestny goods, and to give him everything she thought a Chestny ought to have; but since, said she, it was fun to struggle, why complain? And when you had won, as she had won, what fun to look back on the hard times! He could not forgive her that she had enjoyed the struggle and that she thought *she* had won.

What she meant when she said she had won was that she had brought him up successfully and had sent him to college and that he had turned out so well—good looking (her teeth had gone unfilled so that his could be straightened), intelligent (he realized he was too intelligent to be a success), and with a future ahead of him (there was of course no future ahead of him). She excused his gloominess on the grounds that he was still growing up and his radical ideas on his lack of practical experience. She said he didn't yet know a thing about "life," that he hadn't even entered the real world — when already he was as disenchanted with it as a man of fifty.

The further irony of all this was that in spite of her, he had turned out so well. In spite of going to only a third-rate college, he had, on his own initiative, come out with a first-rate education; in spite of growing up dominated by a small mind, he had ended up with a large one; in spite of all her foolish views, he was free of prejudice and unafraid to face facts. Most miraculous of all, instead of being blinded by love for her as she was for him, he had cut himself emotionally free of her and could see her with complete objectivity. He was not dominated by his mother.

The bus stopped with a sudden jerk and shook him from his meditation. A woman from the back lurched forward with little steps and barely escaped falling in his newspaper as she righted herself. She got off and a large Negro got on. Julian kept his paper lowered to watch. It gave him a certain satisfaction to see injustice in daily operation. It confirmed his view that with a few exceptions there was no one worth knowing within a radius of three hundred miles. The Negro was well dressed and carried a briefcase. He looked around and then sat down on the other end of the seat where the woman with the red and white canvas sandals was sitting. He immediately unfolded a newspaper and obscured himself behind it. Julian's mother's elbow at once prodded insistently into his ribs. "Now you see why I won't ride on these buses by myself," she whispered.

The woman with the red and white canvas sandals had risen at the same time the Negro sat down and had gone further back in the bus and taken the seat of the woman who had got off. His mother leaned forward and cast her an approving look.

Julian rose, crossed the aisle, and sat down in the place of the woman with the canvas sandals. From this position, he looked serenely across at his mother. Her face had turned an angry red. He stared at her, making his eyes the eyes of a stranger. He felt his tension suddenly lift as if he had openly declared war on her.

He would have liked to get in conversation with the Negro and to talk with him about art or politics or any subject that would be above the comprehension of those around them, but the man remained entrenched behind his paper. He was either ignoring the change of seating or had never noticed it. There was no way for Julian to convey his sympathy.

His mother kept her eyes fixed reproachfully on his face. The woman with the protruding teeth was looking at him avidly as if he were a type of monster new to her.

"Do you have a light?" he asked the Negro.

Without looking away from his paper, the man reached in his pocket and handed him a packet of matches.

"Thanks," Julian said. For a moment he held the matches foolishly. A NO SMOKING sign looked down upon him from over the door. This alone would not have deterred him; he had no cigarettes. He had quit smoking some months before because he could not afford it. "Sorry," he muttered and handed back the matches. The Negro lowered the paper and gave him an annoyed look. He took the matches and raised the paper again.

His mother continued to gaze at him but she did not take advantage of his momentary discomfort. Her eyes retained their battered look. Her face seemed to be unnaturally red, as if her blood pressure had risen. Julian allowed no glimmer of sympathy to show on his face. Having got the advantage, he wanted desperately to keep it and carry it through. He would have liked to teach her a lesson that would last her a while, but there seemed no way to continue the point. The Negro refused to come out from behind his paper.

Julian folded his arms and looked stolidly before him, facing her but as if he did not see her, as if he had ceased to recognize her existence. He visualized a scene in which, the bus having reached their stop, he would remain in his seat and when she said, "Aren't you going to get off?" he would look at her as at a stranger who had rashly addressed him. The corner they got off on was usually deserted, but it was well lighted and it would not hurt her to walk by herself the four blocks to the Y. He decided to wait until the time came and then decided whether or not he would let her get off by herself. He would have to be at the Y at ten to bring her back, but he could leave her wondering if he was going to show up. There was no reason for her to think she could always depend on him.

He retired again into the high-ceilinged room sparsely settled with large pieces of antique furniture. His soul expanded momentarily but then he became aware of his mother across from him and the vision shriveled. He studied her coldly. Her feet in little pumps dangled like a child's and did not quite reach the floor. She was training on him an exaggerated look of reproach. He felt completely detached from her. At that moment he could with pleasure have slapped her as he would have slapped a particularly obnoxious child in his charge.

He began to imagine various unlikely ways by which he could teach her a lesson. He might make friends with some distinguished Negro professor or lawyer and bring him home to spend the evening. He would be entirely justified but her blood pressure would rise to 300. He could not push her to the extent of making her have a stroke, and moreover, he had never been successful at making any Negro friends. He had tried to strike up an acquaintance on the bus with some of the better types, with ones that looked like professors or ministers or lawyers. One morning he had sat down next to a distinguished-looking dark brown man who had answered his questions with a sonorous solemnity but who had turned out to be an undertaker. Another day he had sat down beside a cigar-smoking Negro with a diamond ring on his finger, but after a few stilted pleasantries, the Negro had rung the buzzer and risen, slipping two lottery tickets into Julian's hand as he climbed over him to leave.

He imagined his mother lying desperately ill and his being able to secure only a Negro doctor for her. He toyed with that idea for a few minutes and then dropped it for a momentary vision of himself participating as a sympathizer in a sit-in demonstration. This was possible but he did not linger with it. Instead, he approached the ultimate horror. He brought home a beautiful suspiciously Negroid woman. Prepare yourself, he said. There is nothing you can do about it. This is the woman I've chosen. She's intelligent, dignified, even good, and she's suffered and she hasn't thought it *fun*. Now persecute us, go ahead and persecute us. Drive her out of here, but remember, you're driving me too. His eyes were narrowed and through the indignation he had generated, he saw his mother across the aisle, purple-faced, shrunken to the dwarf-like proportions of her moral nature, sitting like a mummy beneath the ridiculous banner of her hat.

He was tilted out of his fantasy again as the bus stopped. The door opened with a sucking hiss and out of the dark a large, gaily dressed, sullen-looking colored woman got on with a little boy. The child, who might have been four, had on a short plaid suit and a Tyrolean hat with a blue feather in it. Julian hoped that he would sit down beside him and that the woman would push in beside his mother. He could think of no better arrangement.

As she waited for her tokens, the woman was surveying the seating possibilities — he hoped with the idea of sitting where she was least wanted. There was something familiar-looking about her but Julian could not place what it was. She was a giant of a woman. Her face was set not only to meet opposition but to seek it out. The downward tilt of her large lower lip was like a warning sign: DON'T TAMPER WITH ME. Her bulging figure was encased in a green crepe dress and her feet overflowed in red shoes. She had on a hideous hat. A purple velvet flap came down on one side of it and stood up on the other; the rest of it was green and looked like a cushion with the stuffing out. She carried a mammoth red pocketbook that bulged throughout as if it were stuffed with rocks.

To Julian's disappointment, the little boy climbed up on the empty seat beside his mother. His mother lumped all children, black and white, into the common category, "cute," and she thought little Negroes were on the whole cuter than little white children. She smiled at the little boy as he climbed on the seat.

Meanwhile the woman was bearing down upon the empty seat beside Julian. To his annoyance, she squeezed herself into it. He saw his mother's face change as the woman settled herself next to him and he realized with satisfaction that this was more objectionable to her than it was to him. Her face seemed almost gray and there was a look of dull recognition in her eyes, as if suddenly she had sickened at some awful confrontation. Julian saw that it was because she and the woman had, in a sense, swapped sons. Though his mother would not realize the symbolic significance of this, she would feel it. His amusement showed plainly on his face.

The woman next to him muttered something unintelligible to herself. He was conscious of a kind of bristling next to him, a muted growling like that of an angry cat. He could not see anything but the red pocketbook upright on the bulging green thighs. He visualized the woman as she had stood waiting for her tokens — the ponderous figure, rising from the red shoes upward over the solid hips, the mammoth bosom, the haughty face, to the green and purple hat.

His eyes widened.

The vision of the two hats, identical, broke upon him with the radiance of a brilliant sunrise. His face was suddenly lit with joy. He could not believe that Fate had thrust upon his mother such a lesson. He gave a loud chuckle so that she would look at him and see that he saw. She turned her eyes on him slowly. The blue in them seemed to have turned a bruised purple. For a moment he had an uncomfortable sense of her innocence, but it lasted only a second before principle rescued him. Justice entitled him to laugh. His grin hardened until it said to her as plainly as if he were saying aloud: Your punishment exactly fits your pettiness. This should teach you a permanent lesson.

Her eyes shifted to the woman. She seemed unable to bear looking at him and to find the woman preferable. He became conscious again of the bristling presence at his side. The woman was rumbling like a volcano about to become active. His mother's mouth began to twitch slightly at one corner. With a sinking heart, he saw incipient signs of recovery on her face and realized that this was going to strike her suddenly as funny and was going to be no lesson at all. She kept her eyes on the woman and an amused smile came over her face as if the woman were a monkey that had stolen her hat. The little Negro was looking up at her with large fascinated eyes. He had been trying to attract her attention for some time.

"Carver!" the woman said suddenly. "Come heah!"

When he saw that the spotlight was on him at last, Carver drew his feet up and turned himself toward Julian's mother and giggled.

"Carver!" the woman said. "You hear me? Come heah!"

471

Carver slid down from the seat but remained squatting with his back against the base of it, his head turned slyly around toward Julian's mother, who was smiling at him. The woman reached a hand across the aisle and snatched him to her. He righted himself and hung backwards on her knees, grinning at Julian's mother. "Isn't he cute?" Julian's mother said to the woman with the protruding teeth.

"I reckon he is," the woman said without conviction.

The Negress yanked him upright but he eased out of her grip and shot across the aisle and scrambled, giggling wildly, onto the seat beside his love.

"I think he likes me," Julian's mother said, and smiled at the woman. It was the smile she used when she was being particularly gracious to an inferior. Julian saw everything lost. The lesson had rolled off her like rain on a roof.

The woman stood up and yanked the little boy off the seat as if she were snatching him from contagion. Julian could feel the rage in her at having no weapon like his mother's smile. She gave the child a sharp slap across his leg. He howled once and then thrust his head into her stomach and kicked his feet against her shins. "Be-have," she said vehemently.

The bus stopped and the Negro who had been reading the newspaper got off. The woman moved over and set the little boy down with a thump between herself and Julian. She held him firmly by the knee. In a moment he put his hands in front of his face and peeped at Julian's mother through his fingers.

"I see yooooooooo!" she said and put her hand in front of her face and peeped at him.

The woman slapped his hand down. "Quit yo' foolishness," she said, "before I knock the living Jesus out of you!"

Julian was thankful that the next stop was theirs. He reached up and pulled the cord. The woman reached up and pulled it at the same time. Oh my God, he thought. He had the terrible intuition that when they got off the bus together, his mother would open her purse and give the little boy a nickel. The gesture would be as natural to her as breathing. The bus stopped and the woman got up and lunged to the front, dragging the child, who wished to stay on, after her. Julian and his mother got up and followed. As they neared the door, Julian tried to relieve her of her pocketbook.

"No," she murmured, "I want to give the little boy a nickel."

"No!" Julian hissed. "No!"

She smiled down at the child and opened her bag. The bus door opened and the woman picked him up by the arm and descended with

472

him, hanging at her hip. Once in the street she set him down and shook him.

Julian's mother had to close her purse while she got down the bus step but as soon as her feet were on the ground, she opened it again and began to rummage inside. "I can't find but a penny," she whispered, "but it looks like a new one."

"Don't do it!" Julian said fiercely between his teeth. There was a street-light on the corner and she hurried to get under it so that she could better see into her pocketbook. The woman was heading off rapidly down the street with the child still hanging backward on her hand.

"Oh little boy!" Julian's mother called and took a few quick steps and caught up with them just beyond the lamppost. "Here's a bright new penny for you," and she held out the coin, which shone bronze in the dim light.

The huge woman turned and for a moment stood, her shoulders lifted and her face frozen with frustrated rage, and stared at Julian's mother. Then all at once she seemed to explode like a piece of machinery that had been given one ounce of pressure too much. Julian saw the black fist swing out with the red pocketbook. He shut his eyes and cringed as he heard the woman shout, "He don't take nobody's pennies!" When he opened his eyes, the woman was disappearing down the street with the little boy staring wide-eyed over her shoulder. Julian's mother was sitting on the sidewalk.

"I told you not to do that," Julian said angrily. "I told you not to do that!"

He stood over her for a minute, gritting his teeth. Her legs were stretched out in front of her and her hat was on her lap. He squatted down and looked her in the face. It was totally expressionless. "You got exactly what you deserved," he said, "Now get up."

He picked up her pocketbook and put what had fallen out back in it. He picked the hat up off her lap. The penny caught his eye on the sidewalk and he picked that up and let it drop before her eyes into the purse. Then he stood up and leaned over and held his hands out to pull her up. She remained immobile. He sighed. Rising above them on either side were black apartment buildings, marked with irregular rectangles of light. At the end of the block a man came out of a door and walked off in the opposite direction. "All right," he said, "suppose somebody happens by and wants to know why you're sitting on the sidewalk?"

She took the hand and, breathing hard, pulled heavily up on it and then stood for a moment, swaying slightly as if the spots of light in the darkness were circling around her. Her eyes, shadowed and confused, finally settled on his face. He did not try to conceal his irritation. "I hope this teaches you a lesson," he said. She leaned forward and her eyes raked his face. She seemed trying to determine his identity. Then, as if she found nothing familiar about him, she started off with a headlong movement in the wrong direction.

"Aren't you going on to the Y?" he asked.

"Home," she muttered.

"Well, are we walking?"

For answer she kept going. Julian followed along, his hands behind him. He saw no reason to let the lesson she had had go without backing it up with an explanation of its meaning. She might as well be made to understand what had happened to her. "Don't think that was just an uppity Negro woman," he said. "That was the whole colored race which will no longer take your condescending pennies. That was your black double. She can wear the same hat as you, and to be sure," he added gratuitously (because he thought it was funny), "it looked better on her than it did on you. What all this means," he said, "is that the old world is gone. The old manners are obsolete and your graciousness is not worth a damn." He thought bitterly of the house that had been lost for him. "You aren't who you think you are," he said.

She continued to plow ahead, paying no attention to him. Her hair had come undone on one side. She dropped her pocketbook and took no notice. He stooped and picked it up and handed it to her but she did not take it.

"You needn't act as if the world had come to an end," he said, "because it hasn't. From now on you've got to live in a new world and face a few realities for a change. Buck up," he said, "it won't kill you."

She was breathing fast.

"Let's wait on the bus," he said.

"Home," she said thickly.

"I hate to see you behave like this," he said. "Just like a child. I should be able to expect more of you." He decided to stop where he was and make her stop and wait for a bus. "I'm not going any farther," he said, stopping. "We're going on the bus."

She continued to go on as if she had not heard him. He took a few steps and caught her arm and stopped her. He looked into her face and caught his breath. He was looking into a face he had never seen before. "Tell Grandpa to come get me," she said.

He stared, stricken.

"Tell Caroline to come get me," she said.

Stunned, he let her go and she lurched forward again, walking as if one leg were shorter than the other. A tide of darkness seemed to be sweeping her from him. "Mother!" he cried. "Darling, sweetheart, wait!"

Crumpling, she fell to the pavement. He dashed forward and fell at her side, crying, "Mamma, Mamma!" He turned her over. Her face was fiercely distorted. One eye, large and staring, moved slightly to the left as if it had become unmoored. The other remained fixed on him, raked his face again, found nothing and closed.

"Wait here, wait here!" he cried and jumped up and began to run for help toward a cluster of lights he saw in the distance ahead of him. "Help, help!" he shouted, but his voice was thin, scarcely a thread of sound. The lights drifted farther away the faster he ran and his feet moved numbly as if they carried him nowhere. The tide of darkness seemed to sweep him back to her, postponing from moment to moment his entry into the world of guilt and sorrow.

from *The Last Gentleman*
Walker Percy (1916–1991)

By the time Walker Percy reached the age of thirteen, he had lost his father to suicide and his mother to an automobile accident. He was raised, along with his two
brothers, by his father's cousin, the planter, lawyer, and writer William Alexander
Percy in Greenville, Mississippi. There, he forged what would turn out to be a lifelong friendship with future writer Shelby Foote. Trained as a physician, Percy
turned to writing after he contracted tuberculosis in 1942. His first novel, *The
Moviegoer*, appeared in 1961 and was awarded the National Book Award. No
longer comfortable with the old assumptions about the South or Southern identity, Percy's protagonists, like Will Barret in *The Last Gentleman* (1966), search out
new if not always satisfying ways to explain themselves to themselves and others.

The South he came home to was different from the South he had left.
It was happy, victorious, Christian, rich, patriotic and Republican.

The happiness and serenity of the South disconcerted him. He had felt
good in the North because everyone else felt so bad. True, there was a happiness in the North. That is to say, nearly everyone would have denied
that he was unhappy. And certainly the North was victorious. It had
never lost a war. But Northerners had turned morose in their victory.
They were solitary and shut-off to themselves and he, the engineer, had
got used to living among them. Their cities, rich and busy as they were,
nevertheless looked bombed out. And his own happiness had come from
being onto the unhappiness beneath their happiness. It was possible for
him to be at home in the North because the North was homeless. There
are many things worse than being homeless in a homeless place—in fact,
this is one condition of being at home, if you are yourself homeless. For
example, it is much worse to be homeless and then to go home where
everyone is at home and then still be homeless. The South was at home.
Therefore his homelessness was much worse in the South because he had
expected to find himself at home there.

The happiness of the South was very formidable. It was an almost
invincible happiness. It defied you to call it anything else. Everyone was
in fact happy. The women were beautiful and charming. The men were
healthy and successful and funny; they knew how to tell stories. They had
everything the North had and more. They had a history, they had a place

redolent with memories, they had good conversation, they believed in God and defended the Constitution, and they were getting rich in the bargain. They had the best of victory and defeat. Their happiness was aggressive and irresistible. He was determined to be as happy as anyone, even though his happiness before had come from Northern unhappiness. If folks down here are happy and at home, he told himself, then I shall be happy and at home too.

As he pressed ever farther south in the Trav-L-Aire, he passed more and more cars which had Confederate plates on the front bumper and plastic Christs on the dashboard. Radio programs became more patriotic and religious. More than once Dizzy Dean interrupted his sportscast to urge the listener to go to the church or synagogue of his choice. "You'll find it a rich and rewarding experience," said Diz. Several times a day he heard a patriotic program called "Lifelines" which praised God, attacked the United States government, and advertised beans and corn.

What was wrong with a Mr. and Mrs. Williston Bibb Barrett living in a brand-new house in a brand-new suburb with a proper address: 2041 Country Club Drive, Druid Hills, Atlanta, Georgia?

Nothing was wrong, but he got worse anyway. The happiness of the South drove him wild with despair.

What was wrong with marrying him a wife and living a life, holding Kitty's charms in his arms the livelong night?

Nothing, but his memory deteriorated and he was assaulted by ghostly legions of *déjà vus* and often woke not knowing where he was. His knee leapt like a fish. It became necessary to unravel the left pocket of his three pairs of pants in order to slip a hand down and keep his patella in place.

It was unsettling, too, coming among a people whose radars were as sensitive as his own. He had got used to good steady wistful post-Protestant Yankees (they were his meat, ex-Protestants, post-Protestants, para-Protestants, the wistful ones who wanted they knew not what; he was just the one to dance for them) and here all at once he found himself among as light-footed and as hawk-eyed and God-fearing a crew as one could imagine. Everyone went to church and was funny and clever and sensitive in the bargain. Oh, they were formidable, born winners (how did they lose?). Yet his radar was remarkable, even for the South. After standing around two or three days, as queer and nervous as a Hoosier, he quickly got the hang of it. Soon he was able to listen to funny stories and tell a few himself.

The Vaughts liked him fine of course and did not notice that he was worse. For he was as prudent and affable as ever and mostly silent, and that was what they expected of him. All but Sutter. He had not yet met Sutter. But one day he saw his car, as he and Jamie were sitting in the sunny quarter of the golf shelter just off number 6 fairway in front of the Vaughts' house.

Jamie was still reading *The Theory of Sets*. The engineer was pondering, as usual, the mystery of the singularity of things. This was the very golf links, he had reason to believe, where his grandfather had played an exhibition round with the great Bobby Jones in 1925 or thereabouts. It was an ancient sort of links, dating from the golden age of country clubs, with sturdy rain shelters of green-stained wood and old-fashioned ball-washers on each tee and soft rolling bunkers as peaceful as an old battlefield. Deep paths were worn through the rough where caddies cut across from green to fairway. The engineer's amnesia was now of this order: he forgot things he had seen before, but things he had heard of and not seen looked familiar. Old new things like fifty-year-old golf links where Bobby Jones played once were haunted by memory.

How bad off was he, he wondered. Which is better, to walk the streets of Memphis in one's right mind remembering everything, what one has done yesterday and must do tomorrow — or to come to oneself in Memphis, remembering nothing?

Jamie had asked him what he was thinking about. When he told him, Jamie said: "You sound like Sutter."

"Have you seen him?"

"I went to see him yesterday. Yonder he goes now."

But he saw no more than the car, a faded green Edsel which swung out of the steep driveway and disappeared down the links road. Jamie told him that Sutter drove an Edsel to remind him of the debacle of the Ford Motor Company and to commemorate the last victory of the American people over marketing research and opinion polls. The engineer wasn't sure he liked the sound of this. It had the sound of a quixotic type who admires his own gestures.

The Vaughts lived in a castle fronting on a golf links. It was an old suburb set down in a beautiful green valley across a ridge from the city. There were other ridges, the last wrinkles of the Appalachians, which formed other valleys between them, and newer suburbs and newer country clubs.

The houses of the valley were built in the 1920's, a time when rich men still sought to recall heroic ages. Directly opposite the castle, atop the next ridge to the south, there stood a round, rosy temple. It was the dwelling of a millionaire who had admired a Roman structure erected by the Emperor Vespasian in honor of Juno and so had reproduced it in good Alabama red brick and Georgia marble. At night a battery of colored floodlights made it look redder still.

The Vaught castle was made of purplish bricks which had been broken in two and the jagged side turned out. It had beam-in-plaster gables and a fat Norman tower and casement windows with panes of bottle glass. Mr. Vaught, it turned out, was richer even than the engineer had supposed. He had made his first fortune by inventing and manufacturing a new type of journal box for coal cars. After the second war he branched out into insurance companies, real estate, and auto dealerships. Now he owned and operated the second largest Chevrolet agency in the world. His talent, as the engineer divined it, was the knack of getting onto the rhythm of things, of knowing when to buy and sell. So that was the meaning of his funny way of hopping around like a jaybird with his ear cocked but not really listening to anybody! Rather was he tuned in to the music and rhythm of ventures, himself poised and nodding, like a schoolboy waiting to go into a jump rope. The engineer soon learned to pay no attention to him either: his talk was not talk at all, one discovered, that is, a form of communication to be attended to, but rather a familiar hum such as Lugurtha the cook made when she was making beaten biscuits.

There were other persons living in the castle. The "Myra" of whom Mrs. Vaught often spoke to the engineer as if he knew her, turned out to be Myra Thigpen, Mr. Vaught's stepdaughter by an earlier marriage. The Thigpens were staying in the Vaught castle while their own house was being built across the golf links. Lamar Thigpen worked for Mr. Vaught as personnel manager. Myra ran a real-estate agency. A handsome woman with strong white arms and a cloud of heavy brown hair, she reminded the engineer of the Business and Professional Women he had seen turning out for luncheons at Holiday Inns from Charleston to Chattanooga. If Mrs. Vaught had thrown him off earlier by acting as if he ought to know whom she was talking about, Myra dislocated him now by acting as if she had known him all along. Had she? "You remember that old boy Hoss Hart from Greenwood who went to Mississippi State and later moved to Ithaca?" she asked him. "You mean Mr. Horace Hart who used to sell for Checkerboard Feed?" asked the engineer, who did in fact perfectly remember such a person, having heard his name once or twice fifteen years ago. "I saw him the other day," Myra went on, "selling fruitcake for Civitan over at Boys' State. He told me about when you and he and your daddy went duck-hunting on a houseboat on the White River." "The White River?" The engineer scratched his head. Had Hoss Hart remembered something he had forgotten? "When you see Hoss," said Myra, giving him a sisterly jostle such as coeds at Mississippi State give you, "just ask him if he remembers Legs." "Yes ma'am." "Don't say Miss Homecoming of 1950, just say Legs and see what he says." "Yes ma'am, I will."

Sutter was nowhere to be seen, but the engineer made sure he would see him when he did come — as he was told Sutter occasionally did to spend the night. Sutter's old apartment was next to the quarters assigned to the two young men, on the second floor above the great four-car garage. Not two hours passed after his arrival before he explored the apartment and discovered two things. One was a bottle of three-dollar whiskey in the cupboard of the kitchenette between the two apartments. The other thing was a knot-hole in the wall of his closet which looked straight into Sutter's bedroom. He hung his Val-Pak over the hole.

I'm not well, reflected the engineer, and therefore it is fitting that I should sit still, like an Englishman in his burrow, and see what can be seen.

It was a good place to live and collect one's thoughts. In the daytime the valley echoed with the faint far-off cries of the golfers. At night a yellow harvest moon hung over the ridge and the floodlights played on the fat rosy temple of Juno. His duties were light. Indeed he had no duties. Nothing more was said after Sea Island about Jamie's plans to go live with his sister in the pine barrens or with his brother in the city. The sick youth seemed content to move into the garage apartment. Within three weeks of their arrival the two young men and Kitty had registered at the university forty miles away and two weeks later the engineer and Jamie had pledged Phi Nu and learned the grip. Kitty realized her ambition and became not a Tri Delt but a Chi Omega.

On the morning of registration they had set out for the university, the three of them, the engineer driving, Kitty in the middle, in Mrs. Vaught's Lincoln, and came home early enough to sit on the garden grass and leaf through their brand-new textbooks with the glazed glittering pages and fragrant fresh print. The engineer, who had just received his October check from Mr. Vaught, bought a $25 slide rule as thick and slick as a mahjong tile and fitted at the rear with a little window.

Later in the afternoon he played golf, borrowing Jamie's clubs and making a foursome with Mr. Vaught and two pleasant fellows, Lamar Thigpen and a man from the agency. The engineer's skill at golf stood him in good stead. (Golf he was good at, it was living that gave him trouble. He had caddied for his father and broke eighty when he was thirteen.) It was not that he was so much better than the others but rather that he was strong and had a good swing. So that when the old man, who somehow knew this, had mumbled something about "my potner" and got his bets down and waved him onto the first tee, after he and Justin and Lamar had driven, he had happened to hit a dandy. The driver sang in the air and the ball went *chack*, flattening, it seemed like, and took off low, then went high and overdrove the par four green. The two opponents exchanged great droll thunderstruck comical mid-South looks.

"Well now, what is this," said Justin, the agency man, who was a big slow easy fellow, the sort referred to in these parts as a good old boy.

"Looka here now," said Lamar.

"Sho," said Mr. Vaught, already striking out down the fairway. "Come on, potner."

He hit five more towering drives and scored a lucky-after-the-layoff 36.

"Well now goddamn," said Lamar.

They called him Bombo, the son of Tarzan, and Mr. Clean. The engineer had to laugh. They were good fellows and funny.

The sixth hole fairway of the second nine ran in front of the castle. It had got to be the custom after teeing off to mark the balls and veer over to the patio, where David, the butler, had toddies ready. Custom also required that the talk, unlike other occasions, be serious, usually about politics but sometimes even about philosophical questions. The tone of the sixth-hole break was both pessimistic and pleasurable. The world outlook was bad, yes, but not so bad that it was not a pleasant thing to say so of a gold-green afternoon, with a fair sweat up and sugared bourbon that tasted as good as it smelled. Over yonder, a respectful twenty yards away, stood the caddies, four black ragamuffins who had walked over the ridge from the city and now swung the drivers they took from the great compartmented, zippered, pocketed, studded, bonneted golf bags.

The golfers gazed philosophically into their whiskey and now and then came out with solemn *Schadenfreude* things, just like four prosperous gents might have done in old Virginny in 1774.

"The thing is, you just don't get integrity where you need it most," said Lamar Thigpen, a handsome fellow who sat slapping his bare brown arm and looking around. He was maybe forty-five and just going slack and he worried about it, pushing his sleeve up and hardening his biceps against his chest.

"I'm going to tell yall the truth," Justin might say. "If they want the country all that bad, I'm not all that much against letting them have it."

But even these dire things were not said in ill humor.

"Ain't nobody here but us niggers anyway," somebody else would say finally. "Let's play golf."

They would get up a little creakily, their sweat having cooled and muscles stiffened, and walk to their lies. Mr. Vaught always took his second shot first because he seldom drove over a hundred yards but that always straight down the middle. And now he wound up with his brassie, drawing back slowly and swaying backward too and with a ferocious deliberation; then, for all the world as if he had been overtaken by some dread mishap, went into a kind of shiver and spasm and, like a toy wound too tight and shooting its springs, came down on the ball from all directions —Poppy drives, Lamar told Justin, like a man falling out of a tree—uttering at the end of it, as he always did, a little cry both apologetic and deprecating: "Voop!", calculated to conjure away all that was untoward and out of the ordinary—and off he would march, hopping along like a jaybird.

Living as he did in the garage apartment and hanging out as he did in the pantry and not with Mrs. Vaught's coterie of patriots and anti-fluoridationists who kept to the living room, the engineer met the servants first of all. Met, not got to know. The engineer was the only white man in the entire South who did not know all there was to know about Negroes. He knew very little about them, in fact nothing. Ever since he was a child and had a nurse, he had been wary of them and they of him. Like many others, he had had a little black boy for a friend, but unlike the others, who had enjoyed perfect love and understanding with their little black friends, he had been from the beginning somewhat fuddled and uneasy. At the age of thirteen he was avoiding Negroes like a queasy middle-aged liberal.

No doubt these peculiar attitudes were a consequence of his nervous condition. Anyhow it was the oddest encounter imaginable, that between him and the Vaught servants. He baffled the Negroes and they him. The Vaught servants were buffaloed by the engineer and steered clear of him. Imagine their feeling. They of course lived by their radars too. It was their special talent and it was how they got along: tuning in on the assorted signals about them and responding with a skill two hundred years in the learning. And not merely responding. Not merely answering the signals but providing home and sustenance to the transmitter, giving him, the transmitter, to believe that he dwelled in loving and familiar territory. He must be made to make sense, must the transmitter; must be answered with sense and good easy laughter: sho now, we understand each other. But here came this strange young man who transmitted no signal at all but who rather, like them, was all ears and eyes and antennae. He actually looked at them. A Southerner looks at a Negro twice: once when he is a child and sees his nurse for the first time; second, when he is dying and there is a Negro with him to change his bedclothes. But he does not look at him during the sixty years in between. And so he knows as little about Negroes as he knows about Martians, less, because he knows that he does not know about Martians.

But here come this strange young man who act' like one of them but look at you out of the corner of his eye. What he waiting for? They became nervous and jumped out of the way. He was like a white child who does not grow up or rather who grows up in the kitchen. He liked to sit in the pantry and watch them and talk to them, but they, the Negroes, didn't know what to do with him. They called him "he," just as they used to call the madam of the house "she." "Where he is?" one might say, peeping out of the kitchen door and as often as not look straight into his eyes. "Uh-oh."

"He," the engineer, usually sat in the pantry, a large irregular room with a single bay window. It was not properly a room at all but rather the space left over in the center of the house when the necessary rooms had been built. Mr. Vaught, who also did not know what he did not know, had been his own architect. The ceiling was at different levels; many doors and vestibules opened into the room. David usually sat at one end, polishing silver in the bay. The dark end of the room let into the "bar," a dusty alcove of blue mirrors and buzzing fluorescent lights and chrome stools. It was one of the first of its kind, hailing from the 1920's and copied from the swanky bars used by Richard Barthelmess and William Powell in the movies. But it had not been used as such for years and now its mirror shelves were lined with Windex bottles, cans of O-Cedar and Bab-O and jars of silver polish stuffed with a caked rag. It fell out somehow or other that both Negro and white could sit in the pantry, perhaps because it was an intermediate room between dining room and kitchen, or perhaps because it was not, properly speaking, a room at all.

David Ross was different from the other Negroes. It was as if he had not caught onto either the Negro way or the white way. A good-humored seventeen-year-old, he had grown too fast and was as raw as any raw youth. He was as tall as a basketball player and wore summer and winter the same pair of heavy damp tweeds whose cuffs were swollen as if they had a chronic infection. He was supposed to be a butler and he wore a butler's jacket with little ivory fasten-on buttons but his arms stuck out a good foot from the sleeves. He was always polishing silver, smiling as he did so a great white smile, laughing at everything (when he did not laugh, his face looked naked and strange) a hissing laugh between his teeth, *ts-ts-ts.* Something about him irritated the engineer, though. He was not cunning enough. He, the engineer, was a thousand times more cunning and he didn't have to be. He, David, was too raw. For example, he was always answering advertisements in magazines, such as *Learn Electronics! Alert Young Men Needed! Earn Fifty Dollars a Day! Send for Selling Kit!* And the selling kit would come and David would show it to everybody, but his long black-and-pink fingers could never quite work the connections and the soldering iron. He was like a rich man's son! The engineer would never have dreamed of spending such money ($10 for a selling kit!). Hell no, David, the engineer told him, don't send off for that. Damnation, why didn't he have better sense? He should either be cunning with a white man's cunning or cunning with a black man's cunning. As it was, he had somehow managed to get the worst of each; he had both white sappiness and Negro sappiness. Why doesn't somebody tell him? One day he did tell him. "Damnation, David," said he as David showed him a selling kit for an ice-cube dispenser which was supposed to fit any kind of refrigerator. "Who do you think you're going to sell that to?"

"All the folks around here," cried David, laughing ts-ts-ts and waving a great limp hand in the direction of the golf links. "Folks out here got plenty money and ain't one in ten got a dispenser-type box" (he'd been reading the brochure). "It only come with GE and Servel!"

"Well, what in the world do they want it for," moaned the flabbergasted engineer.

"When the he'p gone in the evenings and folks want to fix they drinks! They ain't going to want to fool with no old-fashioned knuckle-bruising trays" (more from the brochure). "It's not S.E. on the other boxes."

"S.E.?" asked the engineer.

"Standard Equipment."

"Oh. Then you're just going to walk up to some lady's house at ten o'clock in the morning and ring the doorbell and when she comes to the door you're going to ask her to let you show this ice dispenser."

"Sho," said David and began laughing at the sour-looking engineer, ts-ts-ts.

"Well, you're not," the engineer would groan. Damnation, David couldn't even polish silver. There was always silver cream left in the grooves. Still, the engineer liked to watch him at work. The morning sunlight fell among the silver like fish in the shallows. The metal was creamy and satiny. The open jar of silver cream, the clotted rag, the gritty astringent smell of it, put him in mind of something but he couldn't say what.

But damn this awful vulnerability of theirs, he ranted, eyes fixed on the glittering silver. It's going to ruin us all, this helplessness. Why, David acted as if everybody was going to treat him well! If I were a Negro, I'd be tougher than that. I'd be steadfast and tough as a Jew and I'd beat them. I'd never rest until I beat them and I could. I should have been born a Negro, for then my upsidedownness would be right side up and I'd beat them and life would be simple.

But Oh Christ, David, this goddamn innocence, it's going to ruin us all. You think they're going to treat you well, you act like you're baby brother at home. Christ, they're not going to treat you well. They're going to violate you and it's going to ruin us all, you, them, us. And that's a shame because they're not that bad. They're not bad. They're better than most, in fact. But you're going to ruin us all with your vulnerability. It's God's

terrible vengeance upon us, Jamie said Val said, not to loose the seven
plagues upon us or the Assyrian or even the Yankee, but just to leave you
here among us with this fearful vulnerability to invite violation and to be
violated twenty times a day, day in and day out, our lives long, like a young
girl. Who would not? And so the best of us, Jamie said she said, is only
good the way a rapist is good later, for a rapist can be good later and even
especially good and especially happy.

But damn him, he thought, him and his crass black inept baby-brother
vulnerability. Why should I, for Christ's sake, sit here all asweat and solic-
itous of his vulnerability. Let him go sell his non-knuckle-bruising ice
trays and if he gets hurt: well, I'm not well myself.

David's mother, Lugurtha Ross, was cook. She was respectable and
black as black, with a coppery highlight, and had a straight Indian nose.
She wanted no trouble with anybody. All she wanted in the world was to
find fervent areas of agreement. She spoke to you only of such things as
juvenile delinquency. "Chirren don't have any respect for their parents
any more," she would cry. "You cain't even correck them!"—even though
David was her only living child and it was impossible to imagine him as a
delinquent. She made it sound as if everybody were in the same boat; if
only children would have more respect, our troubles would be over. She
often made beaten biscuits in the evening, and as she sifted flour on the
marble and handled the mitt of dough, she sang in a high decorous dea-
coness voice, not spirituals but songs she made up.

Up in an airplane
Smoking her sweet cigarette
She went way up in an airplane
Smoking her sweet cigarette

John Houghton, the gardener, lived in a room under the engineer's
apartment. An ancient little Negro with dim muddy eyes and a face
screwed up like a prune around a patch of bristling somewhere near the
middle of which was his mustache, he was at least sixty-five and slim and
quick as a boy. He had come from the deep country of south Georgia and
worked on the railroad and once as a hod carrier forty years ago when they
built the dam at Muscle Shoals. He had been night watchman for the construction company when Mr. Vaught built his castle. Mr. Vaught liked
him and hired him. But he was still a country Negro and had country
ways. Sometimes Jamie and David would get him in a card game just to
see him play. The only game he knew was a strange south Georgia game
called pitty-pat. You played your cards in turn and took tricks but there
was not much rhyme or reason to it. When John Houghton's turn came,

he always stood up, drew back, and slapped the card down with a tremendous *ha-a-a-a-umph!*, just as if he were swinging a sledge hammer, but pulling up at the last second and setting the card down soft as a feather. David couldn't help laughing *ts-ts-ts*. "What game we gon' play, John," he would ask the gardener to get him to say pitty-pat. "Lessus have a game of pitty-pat," John Houghton would say, standing up also to shuffle the cards, which he did by chocking them into each other, all the while making terrific feints and knee-bends like a boxer. *"Pitty-pat,"* cried David and fell out laughing. But John Houghton paid no attention and told them instead of his adventures in the city, where, if the police caught you playing cards, they would sandbag you and take you to jail.

"What do you mean, sandbag?" asked the puzzled engineer.

"That's what I mean!" cried John Houghton. "I mean they sandbag you."

Of an evening John Houghton would don his jacket, an oversize Marine drawstring jacket with deep patch pockets, turn the collar up around his ears so that just the top of his gnarled puckered head showed above it, thrust his hands deep into the patch pockets, and take a stroll down the service road which wound along the ridge behind the big houses. There he met the maids getting off work.

At night and sometimes all night long there arose from the room below the engineer's the sounds of scuffling and, it seemed to him, of flight and pursuit; of a chair scraped back, a sudden scurry of feet and screams, he could have sworn more than one voice, several in fact, screams both outraged and risible as pursuer and quarry rounded the very walls, it seemed like.

from *North Toward Home*

Willie Morris (1934–)

The title of Willie Morris's 1967 autobiography, *North Toward Home*, suggests the estrangement he felt toward his home state of Mississippi. Educated at the University of Texas and, as a Rhodes scholar, at Oxford University, he joined a growing rank of Southern expatriates when he went to work for *Harper's* magazine in 1963, later serving as editor in chief from 1967 to 1971. Morris came to recognize, if not reconcile, the existence of two independent Mississippis—one the Mississippi of his youth where he played baseball, hunted, fished, and went to parties in the Delta, the other the Mississippi of the civil rights struggle where activists feared for their lives and venomous politicians spoke of preserving "order."

In 1964, after the Mississippi "Freedom Summer," I spent an evening with a group of young people who had been there with SNCC. Several of us, after dinner in an Italian place in the Village, lingered over coffee. I had been talking with a Negro girl; she was from the Mississippi delta, and she had come to New York to make money so she could return to college in Jackson. All of a sudden, for no apparent reason, she began sobbing; a few minutes later she left to go home. One of the white girls walked her to her apartment down the street. When she returned I asked what had been wrong. The white Snick girl said, "She told me you're the first Mississippi white person she was ever with socially. You made her nervous as hell. Her emotions got the better of her."

The Mississippi these young people talked of was a different place from the one I had known, the things they said were not in context with mine; it was as if we were talking of another world—one that *looked* the same, that had the same place names, the same roads and rivers and landmarks, but beyond that the reality was awry, removed from my private reality of it. After the riots at Ole Miss, I had written a magazine article in *Dissent* about Mississippi; in it I had called the delta "beautiful," a land of great romance and sorcery to me in my childhood. One of the civil rights activists at the table, a young Mississippi Negro, had written me a letter: "Your delta," he had said, "was not mine." Now he and his friends sat talking matter-of-factly about beatings in the jailhouses of delta towns — towns whose social graces and weekend celebrations I had enjoyed as a boy. They discussed a shooting in Greenwood, where I had once played baseball and gone to "Red Top" dances as a happy, oblivious senior in high school. They described the places of my youth, the quiet hill towns I had known—one was "tough," another "damned spooky," another "getting a lot better"—as if they were objects on some sliding scale to perdition. The world of a sensitive young person growing up remains fixed in one's emotions as it was years ago, it endures in the memory dreamlike and motionless, despite even what later knowledge discloses. The words of my companions intruded on this world of my past like harsh accusations, and made it complicated and unreal to me: I had changed a great deal, and yet in other ways I had changed hardly at all; although my mind accepted what they said, my emotional recollection of these old places and things was threatened and unsure. In America, perhaps more than any other place, and in the South, perhaps more than any other region, we go back to our home in dreams and memories, hoping it remains what it was on a lazy, still summer's day twenty years ago—and yet our sense of it is forever violated by others who see it, not as home, but as the dark side of hell.

I was confronted with this feeling even more vividly when, a few days later, I met a white girl from Texas, one of the first Snick workers who had gone to Mississippi. We had mutual friends in Texas; the talk was cordial. She was leaving for Mississippi again the following week. Near the end of the evening I said, "Think of me next time you're in Yazoo." This struck a raw nerve. "Think of it yourself, you son-of-a-bitch," she said. "It's your hometown, not mine." As I sat trying to think of what to reply, she got up and walked away, and I never saw her again.

. . .

Mississippi. In the little frame house on Grand Avenue, where we were to stay one night, I showed my son the mementos from my high school: the framed scrolls and certificates and documents on the walls of my room, testifying still that I had once indulged myself in all the official trinkets and the glittering medals. Under the bed I discovered a whole shoebox full of love letters from the blond majorette from Belle Prairie Plantation; I took them into the back yard, arranged them in a neat pile near the place where my dog Skip was buried and where my father once hid from the visiting preachers, and put a match to them, gazing down at one phrase not yet burned: *"I'll meet you in front of the drugstore at 7:30 in my green sweater."* My mother and my grandmother Mamie fixed fried chicken and huge steaming casseroles, and chocolate cake and meringue pie, and while we digested this feast, spurning "Bonanza" on television, my mother played, on the grand piano, some of the old hymns: "Faith of Our Fathers," "Bringing in the Sheaves," "Living with Jesus," "Abide with Me." Outside, on the street, the teen-agers sped by, shouting and blowing the horns of their family cars, and the pecan trees in the yard rustled and moaned in the wind, stirring up too many ghosts.

Our plane for New York was to leave Jackson, forty miles away, at noon the next day, and since I had resolved not to see anyone, since old friendships suddenly brought together again . . . had always embarrassed me, we got up at dawn to drive around town. The streets of Yazoo were so settled in my consciousness after all those years that the drive was unnecessary, for I still knew where every tree was, the angles on the roofs of every house, the hidden alleys and paths and streams. Coming around some bend I would know exactly the sights that would be there — and there they were, the memory of them even more real than the blurred shapes of reality. We drove through niggertown, some of its old dirt roads now paved and with curbs and sewers, past the grocery store where the colored men had seen my dog propped against the steering wheel of my car and shouted: "Look at that ol' dog drivin' a car!" Back again in the white section, every street corner and side street had meanings for me; I had sat on the curb at Grand Avenue and Second Street, near Bubba Barrier's house, one summer afternoon in 1943, wearing a Brooklyn Dodger baseball cap, dreaming of the mythical cities of the North, and bemoaning my own helpless condition. Grand Avenue, with the same towering elms and oaks, had changed hardly at all, and only the occasional new chain store or supermarket marred my memory of it. Driving down that broad boulevard, my mother pointed out the houses in which people I had known had died, by simple attrition or by violent, tragic causes; each house represented a death or more, and the knowledge of it, after my having been away so long, gave to the whole town a vague presence of inevitable death. My old schoolhouse on Main Street, where the ineffable Miss Abbott had taught my fourth-grade class enough Bible verses to assure our salvation, had a new coat of paint; the schoolyard where I had played football against the Graball boys still had its Confederate monument; the soldier on top with the gun in one hand and the other hand extended to take the flag from the Confederate lady had not moved an inch since 1939. On Main Street the Dixie Theater had vanished from the face of the earth, as had some of the smaller stores, replaced now by the Yankee chains advertised on national television; but many of the familiar places remained: the *Yazoo Herald*, where I had turned in my first sports articles at the age of twelve, the radio station where I had played Beethoven instead of Tennessee Ernie Ford, Tommy Norman's, Henick's Store, where my taps-playing colleague Henjie now sold tires and tire accessories. But most of the young people I had known here, in the 1940s, were gone long before, living now in the prosperous 1960s in the sprawling and suburbanized cities of the New South—Atlanta, Memphis, New Orleans, Birmingham, Nashville.

Out on the edges of town, where the bootleggers had once flourished before Mississippi legalized liquor, I noticed that Yazoo had even developed its own suburbia. I was suffused with a physical feeling of lost things, with a tangible hovering presence of old dead moments; it was time to get out, and I drove as fast as I could up Broadway, that fantastic hill, for Highway 49 and Jackson.

We drove through the lush rolling hills toward Jackson. Along the highway a huge billboard had a picture of Martin Luther King, surrounded by throngs of Negroes, and the words on the sign said: "M. L. King Meets His Fellow Commies." Near Jackson I saw a more ambitious suburbia, sprung up fullborn from the pastures and cottonfields I remembered from my childhood, row after row of split-levels that seemed not much different from Pleasantville or Hawthorne on the Harlem River Line.

Mamie said, "Let's drive by the old house and see what they've done with it." We headed down Jefferson Street, and there was the brick house just as it was, the same magnolia tree, the sticker bushes where my great-aunts had gotten trapped in their endless peregrinations, the rickety garage where my grandfather Percy had built for me the miniature steamboats with names like *The Robert E. Lee* and *The Belle of Memphis*. Then down the street Percy and I had walked to the Jackson "Senator" baseball games, past the old house where the man who "stole the money from the state" had once lived, to the old capitol building at the corner of Capitol and State. Mamie turned to my son, who had been looking at many of these unfamiliar landmarks with a Yankee's skepticism. "Son," she said, "you see that building there? My father — your great-great-grandfather Harper—was in the legislature there, and one day when I was a little girl my brother Winter took me inside and told the guards, 'She's Mr. George's girl, and I want her to sit in our Papa's chair.' See that balcony yonder? That's where your uncle Henry Foote — he was Governor of Mississippi many years ago—made a speech in 18-and-60, tellin' folks not to believe a word ol' Jefferson Davis said." The boy looked out at the object of these words, the graceful building that had been restored by the State to its previous grace and eminence, and then smiled sheepishly at me, still a trifle disbelieving.

We took the road out to Raymond and drove by the Harper house, also "restored" so that its picture now appeared in the travelogues, and then on to the town cemetery; neither my mother nor my grandmother had visited here in years. The old section was overgrown with weeds and Johnson grass, the iron fences rusted and fallen, the tombstones crumbled or vanished entirely. I parked the car on a ridge and the four of us, of our four different generations, got out and walked around. It was a bright, crisp October morning, but the terrain itself was damp and gray, casting an odor heavy with decay and ruin. We looked hard enough, but we could not find the Harpers, not a single one of them — not my great-grandfather nor great-grandmother, nor my great-aunts, nor even my grandfather Percy. We searched in the weeds and stickers on the hill where Mamie thought they had been laid away. "Well, I *thought* they were around here some-where," she said. Fifty yards away was a well-kept plot of graves, soldiers who had been killed in some minor skirmish attendant to the siege of Vicksburg, watered and manicured now by the ladies of the town, and my son went over to look at these while we explored the countryside for our vanished kin. Finally we found what must have been the plot—the rem-nants of a fence, the unrecognizable stumps of gravestones, covered over now with the dank, moist weeds. "I guess they're here somewhere," Mamie said, "but you'd never know it."

I took Mamie by the arm and we wandered farther down the hill, stum-bling occasionally over a stretch of barbed wire or what remained of a tombstone. I was impressed, even as I had been as a child my son's age, by her steady good humor. One of the old broken stones marked the grave of Miss Lucy McGee, born in 1820, died in 1850. "Mamie," I said, "this is where Miss Lucy McGee is. Did you ever hear of her?" "*Lucy McGee!*" she said. "Why, of course, son. I remember Papa and Mamma talkin' about the McGees when I was a girl. I believe she died very young for her age."

The airport was a new one, bright and shining and strangely quiet on this morning. As I confirmed our tickets back to New York, my mother and grandmother spotted some TV star on "Hollywood Circus" having coffee in the restaurant, and went up near to his table to get a closer look. Then we walked down the broad corridor toward the landing field, waiting near the door in that awkward moment that always precedes some long depar-ture for me. The loudspeaker announced the flight, and we made our goodbyes. "You come back now, you *heah?*" my mother said, and my son and I walked down the ramp and got on the plane.

Why was it, in such moments just before I leave the South, did I always feel some easing of a great burden? It was as if someone had taken some terrible weight off my shoulders, or as if some old grievance had suddenly fallen away. The big plane took off, and circled in widening arcs over the city, over the landmarks of my past, and my people's. Then, slowly, with a lifting heavy as steel, it circled once more, and turned north toward home.

"The Sky Is Gray"

Ernest J. Gaines (1933–)

Ernest J. Gaines has created a fictional world out of the people and places in and around his home in New Roads, Louisiana. Raised in Louisiana until the age of fifteen, when he left for California to pursue the further education denied him at the time in his home state, Gaines published his first two short stories in 1963. While his fiction never denies the hardships faced by poor, rural blacks, Gaines is most interested in exploring the dignity and self-respect his characters wrestle from such a hard life. Widely known for his 1971 novel *The Autobiography of Miss Jane Pittman*, Gaines has also written the prizewinning *A Gathering of Old Men* (1983) and *A Lesson Before Dying* (1993). The selection here is from his 1968 collection of stories entitled *Bloodline*.

Go'n be coming in a few minutes. Coming round that bend down there full speed. And I'm go'n get out my handkerchief and wave it down, and we go'n get on it and go.

I keep on looking for it, but Mama don't look that way no more. She's looking down the road where we just come from. It's a long old road, and far 's you can see you don't see nothing but gravel. You got dry weeds on both sides, and you got trees on both sides, and fences on both sides, too. And you got cows in the pastures and they standing close together. And when we was coming out here to catch the bus I seen the smoke coming out of the cows's noses.

I look at my mama and I know what she's thinking. I been with Mama so much, just me and her, I know what she's thinking all the time. Right now it's home — Auntie and them. She's thinking if they got enough wood—if she left enough there to keep them warm till we get back. She's thinking if it go'n rain and if any of them go'n have to go out in the rain. She's thinking 'bout the hog—if he go'n get out, and if Ty and Val be able to get him back in. She always worry like that when she leaves the house. She don't worry too much if she leave me there with the smaller ones, 'cause she know I'm go'n look after them and look after Auntie and everything else. I'm the oldest and she say I'm the man.

I look at my mama and I love my mama. She's wearing that black coat and that black hat and she's looking sad. I love my mama and I want to put my arm round her and tell her. But I'm not supposed to do that. She say that's weakness and that's crybaby stuff, and she don't want no crybaby round her. She don't want you to be scared, either. 'Cause Ty's scared of ghosts and she's always whipping him. I'm scared of the dark, too, but I make 'tend I ain't. I make 'tend I ain't 'cause I'm the oldest, and I got to set a good sample for the rest. I can't ever be scared and I can't ever cry. And that's why I never said nothing 'bout my teeth. It's been hurting me and hurting me close to a month now, but I never said it. I didn't say it 'cause I didn't want to act like a crybaby, and 'cause I know we didn't have enough money to go have it pulled. But, Lord, it been hurting me. And look like it wouldn't start till at night when you was trying to get yourself little sleep. Then soon 's you shut your eyes—ummm-ummm, Lord, look like it go right down to your heartstring.

"Hurting, hanh?" Ty'd say.

I'd shake my head, but I wouldn't open my mouth for nothing. You open your mouth and let that wind in, and it almost kill you.

I'd just lay there and listen to them snore. Ty there, right 'side me, and Auntie and Val over by the fireplace. Val younger than me and Ty, and he sleeps with Auntie. Mama sleeps round the other side with Louis and Walker.

I'd just lay there and listen to them, and listen to that wind out there, and listen to that fire in the fireplace. Sometimes it'd stop long enough to let me get little rest. Sometimes it just hurt, hurt, hurt. Lord, have mercy.

Auntie knowed it was hurting me. I didn't tell nobody but Ty, 'cause we buddies and he ain't go'n tell nobody. But some kind of way Auntie found out. When she asked me, I told her no, nothing was wrong. But she knowed it all the time. She told me to mash up a piece of aspirin and wrap it in some cotton and jugg it down in that hole. I did it, but it didn't do no good. It stopped for a little while, and started right back again. Auntie wanted to tell Mama, but I told her, "Uh-uh." 'Cause I knowed we didn't have any money, and it just was go'n make her mad again. So Auntie told Monsieur Bayonne, and Monsieur Bayonne came over to the house and told me to kneel down 'side him on the fireplace. He put his finger in his mouth and made the Sign of the Cross on my jaw. The tip of Monsieur Bayonne's finger is some hard, 'cause he's always playing on that guitar. If we sit outside at night we can always hear Monsieur Bayonne playing on his guitar. Sometimes we leave him out there playing on the guitar.

Monsieur Bayonne made the Sign of the Cross over and over on my jaw, but that didn't do no good. Even when he prayed and told me to pray some, too, that tooth still hurt me.

"How you feeling?" he say.

"Same," I say.

He kept on praying and making the Sign of the Cross and I kept on praying, too.

"Still hurting?" he say.

"Yes, sir."

Monsieur Bayonne mashed harder and harder on my jaw. He mashed so hard he almost pushed me over on Ty. But then he stopped.

"What kind of prayers you praying, boy?" he say.

"Baptist," I say.

"Well, I'll be — no wonder that tooth still killing him. I'm going one way and he pulling the other. Boy, don't you know any Catholic prayers?"

"I know 'Hail Mary,'" I say.

"Then you better start saying it."

"Yes, sir."

He started mashing on my jaw again, and I could hear him praying at the same time. And, sure enough, after a while it stopped hurting me.

Me and Ty went outside where Monsieur Bayonne's two hounds was and we started playing with them. "Let's go hunting," Ty say. "All right," I say; and we went on back in the pasture. Soon the hounds got on a trail, and me and Ty followed them all 'cross the pasture and then back in the woods, too. And then they cornered this little old rabbit and killed him, and me and Ty made them get back, and we picked up the rabbit and started on back home. But my tooth had started hurting me again. It was hurting me plenty now, but I wouldn't tell Monsieur Bayonne. That night I didn't sleep a bit, and first thing in the morning Auntie told me to go back and let Monsieur Bayonne pray over me some more. Monsieur Bayonne was in his kitchen making coffee when I got there. Soon 's he seen me he knowed what was wrong.

"All right, kneel down there 'side that stove," he say. "And this time make sure you pray Catholic. I don't know nothing 'bout that Baptist, and I don't want know nothing 'bout him."

Last night Mama say, "Tomorrow we going to town."

"It ain't hurting me no more," I say. "I can eat anything on it."

"Tomorrow we going to town," she say.

And after she finished eating, she got up and went to bed. She always go to bed early now. 'Fore Daddy went in the Army, she used to stay up late. All of us sitting out on the gallery or round the fire. But now, look like soon 's she finish eating she go to bed.

This morning when I woke up, her and Auntie was standing 'fore the fireplace. She say: "Enough to get there and get back. Dollar and a half to

have it pulled. Twenty-five for me to go, twenty-five for him. Twenty-five
for me to come back, twenty-five for him. Fifty cents left. Guess I get little piece of salt meat with that."

"Sure can use it," Auntie say. "White beans and no salt meat ain't
white beans."

"I do the best I can," Mama say.

They was quiet after that, and I made 'tend I was still asleep.

"James, hit the floor," Auntie say.

I still made 'tend I was asleep. I didn't want them to know I was listening.

"All right," Auntie say, shaking me by the shoulder. "Come on. Today's
the day."

I pushed the cover down to get out, and Ty grabbed it and pulled it
back.

"You, too, Ty," Auntie say.

"I ain't getting no teef pulled," Ty say.

"Don't mean it ain't time to get up," Auntie say. "Hit it, Ty."

Ty got up grumbling.

"James, you hurry up and get in your clothes and eat your food," Auntie
say. "What time y'all coming back?" she say to Mama.

"That 'leven o'clock bus," Mama say. "Got to get back in that field this
evening."

"Get a move on you, James," Auntie say.

I went in the kitchen and washed my face, then I ate my breakfast. I
was having bread and syrup. The bread was warm and hard and tasted
good. And I tried to make it last a long time.

Ty came back there grumbling and mad at me.

"Got to get up," he say. "I ain't having no teefes pulled. What I got to
be getting up for?"

Ty poured some syrup in his pan and got a piece of bread. He didn't wash
his hands, neither his face, and I could see that white stuff in his eyes.

"You the one getting your teef pulled," he say. "What I got to get up for.
I bet if I was getting a teef pulled, you wouldn't be getting up. Shucks;
syrup again. I'm getting tired of this old syrup. Syrup, syrup, syrup. I'm go'n
take with the sugar diabetes. I want me some bacon sometime."

"Go out in the field and work and you can have your bacon," Auntie
say. She stood in the middle door looking at Ty. "You better be glad you
got syrup. Some people ain't got that—hard 's time is."

"Shucks," Ty say. "How can I be strong."

"I don't know too much 'bout your strength," Auntie say; "but I know
where you go'n be hot at, you keep that grumbling up. James, get a move
on you; your mama waiting."

I ate my last piece of bread and went in the front room. Mama was standing 'fore the fireplace warming her hands. I put on my coat and my cap, and we left the house.

I look down there again, but it still ain't coming. I almost say, "It ain't coming yet," but I keep my mouth shut. 'Cause that's something else she don't like. She don't like for you to say something just for nothing. She can see it ain't coming, I can see it ain't coming, so why say it ain't coming. I don't say it, I turn and look at the river that's back of us. It's so cold the smoke's just raising up from the water. I see a bunch of pool-doos not too far out—just on the other side the lilies. I'm wondering if you can eat pool-doos. I ain't too sure, 'cause I ain't never ate none. But I done ate owls and blackbirds, and I done ate redbirds, too. I didn't want kill the redbirds, but she made me kill them. They had two of them back there. One in my trap, one in Ty's trap. Me and Ty was go'n play with them and let them go, but she made me kill them 'cause we needed the food.

"I can't," I say. "I can't."

"Here," she say. "Take it."

"I can't," I say. "I can't. I can't kill him, Mama, please."

"Here," she say. "Take this fork, James."

"Please, Mama, I can't kill him," I say.

I could tell she was go'n hit me. I jerked back, but I didn't jerk back soon enough.

"Take it," she say.

I took it and reached in for him, but he kept on hopping to the back.

"I can't, Mama," I say. The water just kept on running down my face. "I can't," I say.

"Get him out of there," she say.

I reached in for him and he kept on hopping to the back. Then I reached in farther, and he pecked me on the hand.

"I can't, Mama," I say.

She slapped me again.

I reached in again, but he kept on hopping out my way. Then he hopped to one side and I reached there. The fork got him on the leg and I heard his leg pop. I pulled my hand out 'cause I had hurt him.

"Give it here," she say, and jerked the fork out my hand.

She reached in and got the little bird right in the neck. I heard the fork go in his neck, and I heard it go in the ground. She brought him out and helt him right in front of me.

"That's one," she say. She shook him off and gived me the fork. "Get the other one."

"I can't, Mama," I say. "I'll do anything, but don't make me do that."

She went to the corner of the fence and broke the biggest switch over there she could find. I knelt 'side the trap, crying.

"Get him out of there," she say.

"I can't, Mama."

She started hitting me 'cross the back. I went down on the ground, crying.

"Get him," she say.

"Octavia?" Auntie say.

'Cause she had come out of the house and she was standing by the tree looking at us.

"Get him out of there," Mama say.

"Octavia," Auntie say, "explain to him. Explain to him. Just don't beat him. Explain to him."

But she hit me and hit me and hit me.

I'm still young—I ain't no more than eight; but I know now; I know why I had to do it. (They was so little, though. They was so little. I 'member how I picked the feathers off them and cleaned them and helt them over the fire. Then we all ate them. Ain't had but a little bitty piece each, but we all had a little bitty piece, and everybody just looked at me 'cause they was so proud.) Suppose she had to go away? That's why I had to do it. Suppose she had to go away like Daddy went away? Then who was go'n look after us? They had to be somebody left to carry on. I didn't know it then, but I know it now. Auntie and Monsieur Bayonne talked to me and made me see.

Time I see it I get out my handkerchief and start waving. It's still 'way down there, but I keep waving anyhow. Then it come up and stop and me and Mama get on. Mama tell me go sit in the back while she pay. I do like she say, and the people look at me. When I pass the little sign that say "White" and "Colored," I start looking for a seat. I just see one of them back there, but I don't take it, 'cause I want my mama to sit down herself. She comes in the back and sit down, and I lean on the seat. They got seats in the front, but I know I can't sit there, 'cause I have to sit back of the sign. Anyhow, I don't want sit there if my mama go'n sit back here.

They got a lady sitting 'side my mama and she looks at me and smiles little bit. I smile back, but I don't open my mouth, 'cause the wind'll get in and make that tooth ache. The lady take out a pack of gum and reach me a slice, but I shake my head. The lady just can't understand why a little boy'll turn down gum, and she reach me a slice again. This time I point to my jaw. The lady understands and smiles little bit, and I smile little bit, but I don't open my mouth, though.

They got a girl sitting 'cross from me. She got on a red overcoat and her hair's plaited in one big plait. First, I make 'tend I don't see her over there, but then I start looking at her little bit. She make 'tend she don't see me, either, but I catch her looking that way. She got a cold, and every now and then she h'ist that little handkerchief to her nose. She ought to blow it, but she don't. Must think she's too much a lady or something.

Every time she h'ist that little handkerchief, the lady 'side her say something in her ear. She shakes her head and lays her hands in her lap again. Then I catch her kind of looking where I'm at. I smile at her little bit. But think she'll smile back? Uh-uh. She just turn up her little old nose and turn her head. Well, I show her both of us can turn us head. I turn mine too and look out at the river.

The river is gray. The sky is gray. They have pool-doos on the water. The water is wavy, and the pool-doos go up and down. The bus go round a turn, and you got plenty trees hiding the river. Then the bus go round another turn, and I can see the river again.

I look toward the front where all the white people sitting. Then I look at that little old gal again. I don't look right at her, 'cause I don't want all them people to know I love her. I just look at her little bit, like I'm looking out that window over there. But she knows I'm looking that way, and she kind of look at me, too. The lady sitting 'side her catch her this time, and she leans over and says something in her ear.

"I don't love him nothing," that little old gal says out loud.

Everybody back there hear her mouth, and all of them look at us and laugh.

"I don't love you, either," I say. "So you don't have to turn up your nose, Miss."

"You the one looking," she say.

"I wasn't looking at you," I say. "I was looking out that window, there."

"Out that window, my foot," she say. "I seen you. Everytime I turned round you was looking at me."

"You must of been looking yourself if you seen me all them times," I say.

"Shucks," she say, "I got me all kind of boyfriends."

"I got girlfriends, too," I say.

"Well, I just don't want you getting your hopes up," she say.

I don't say no more to that little old gal 'cause I don't want have to bust her in the mouth. I lean on the seat where Mama sitting, and I don't even look that way no more. When we get to Bayonne, she jugg her little old tongue out at me. I make 'tend I'm go'n hit her, and she duck down 'side her mama. And all the people laugh at us again.

. . .

Me and Mama get off and start walking in town. Bayonne is a little bitty town. Baton Rouge is a hundred times bigger than Bayonne. I went to Baton Rouge once — me, Ty, Mama, and Daddy. But that was 'way back yonder, 'fore Daddy went in the Army. I wonder when we go'n see him again. I wonder when. Look like he ain't ever coming back home. . . . Even the pavement all cracked in Bayonne. Got grass shooting right out the sidewalk. Got weeds in the ditch, too; just like they got at home.

It's some cold in Bayonne. Look like it's colder than it is home. The wind blows in my face, and I feel that stuff running down my nose. I sniff. Mama says use that handkerchief. I blow my nose and put it back.

We pass a school and I see them white children playing in the yard. Big old red school, and them children just running and playing. Then we pass a café, and I see a bunch of people in there eating. I wish I was in there 'cause I'm cold. Mama tells me keep my eyes in front where they belong.

We pass stores that's got dummies, and we pass another café, and then we pass a shoe shop, and that bald-head man in there fixing on a shoe. I look at him and I butt into that white lady, and Mama jerks me in front and tells me stay there.

We come up to the courthouse, and I see the flag waving there. This flag ain't like the one we got at school. This one here ain't got but a handful of stars. One at school got a big pile of stars—one for every state. We pass it and we turn and there it is—the dentist office. Me and Mama go in, and they got people sitting everywhere you look. They even got a little boy in there younger than me.

Me and Mama sit on that bench, and a white lady come in there and ask me what my name is. Mama tells her and the white lady goes on back. Then I hear somebody hollering in there. Soon 's that little boy hear him hollering, he starts hollering, too. His mama pats him and pats him, trying to make him hush up, but he ain't thinking 'bout his mama.

The man that was hollering in there comes out holding his jaw. He is a big old man and he's wearing overalls and a jumper.

"Got it, hanh?" another man asks him.

The man shakes his head—don't want open his mouth.

"Man, I thought they was killing you in there," the other man says. "Hollering like a pig under a gate."

The man don't say nothing. He just heads for the door, and the other man follows him.

"John Lee," the white lady says. "John Lee Williams."

The little boy jugs his head down in his mama's lap and holler more now. His mama tells him go with the nurse, but he ain't thinking 'bout his mama. His mama tells him again, but he don't even hear her. His mama picks him up and takes him in there, and even when the white lady shuts the door I can still hear little old John Lee.

"I often wonder why the Lord let a child like that suffer," a lady says to my mama. The lady's sitting right in front of us on another bench. She's got on a white dress and a black sweater. She must be a nurse or something herself, I reckon.

"Not us to question," a man says.

"Sometimes I don't know if we shouldn't," the lady says.

"I know definitely we shouldn't," the man says. The man looks like a preacher. He's big and fat and he's got on a black suit. He's got a gold chain, too.

"Why?" the lady says.

"Why anything?" the preacher says.

"Yes," the lady says. "Why anything?"

"Not us to question," the preacher says.

The lady looks at the preacher a little while and looks at Mama again.

"And look like it's the poor who suffers the most," she says. "I don't understand it."

"Best not to even try," the preacher says. "He works in mysterious ways —wonders to perform."

Right then little John Lee bust out hollering, and everybody turn they head to listen.

"He's not a good dentist," the lady says. "Dr. Robillard is much better. But more expensive. That's why most of the colored people come here. The white people go to Dr. Robillard. Y'all from Bayonne?"

"Down the river," my mama says. And that's all she go'n say, 'cause she don't talk much. But the lady keeps on looking at her, and so she says, "Near Morgan."

"I see," the lady says.

"That's the trouble with the black people in this country today," somebody else says. This one here's sitting on the same side me and Mama's sitting, and he is kind of sitting in front of that preacher. He looks like a teacher or somebody that goes to college. He's got on a suit, and he's got a book that he's been reading. "We don't question is exactly our problem," he says. "We should question and question and question—question everything."

The preacher just looks at him a long time. He done put a toothpick or something in his mouth, and he just keeps on turning it and turning it. You can see he don't like that boy with that book.

"Maybe you can explain what you mean," he says.

"I said what I meant," the boy says. "Question everything. Every stripe, every star, every word spoken. Everything."

"It 'pears to me that this young lady and I was talking 'bout God, young man," the preacher says.

"Question Him, too," the boy says.

"Wait," the preacher says. "Wait now."

"You heard me right," the boy says. "His existence as well as everything else. Everything."

The preacher just looks across the room at the boy. You can see he's getting madder and madder. But mad or no mad, the boy ain't thinking 'bout him. He looks at that preacher just 's hard 's the preacher looks at him.

"Is this what they coming to?" the preacher says. "Is this what we educating them for?"

"You're not educating me," the boy says. "I wash dishes at night so that I can go to school in the day. So even the words you spoke need questioning."

The preacher just looks at him and shakes his head.

"When I come in this room and seen you there with your book, I said to myself, 'There's an intelligent man.' How wrong a person can be."

"Show me one reason to believe in the existence of a God," the boys says.

"My heart tells me," the preacher says.

" 'My heart tells me,' " the boys says. " 'My heart tells me.' Sure, 'My heart tells me.' And as long as you listen to what your heart tells you, you will have only what the white man gives you and nothing more. Me, I don't listen to my heart. The purpose of the heart is to pump blood throughout the body, and nothing else."

"Who's your paw, boy?" the preacher says.

"Why?"

"Who is he?"

"He's dead."

"And your mom?"

"She's in Charity Hospital with pneumonia. Half killed herself, working for nothing."

"And 'cause he's dead and she's sick, you mad at the world?"

"I'm not mad at the world. I'm questioning the world. I'm questioning it with cold logic, sir. What do words like Freedom, Liberty, God, White, Colored mean? I want to know. That's why *you* are sending us to school, to read and to ask questions. And because we ask these questions, you call us mad. No sir, it is not us who are mad."

"You keep saying 'us'?"

"'Us.' Yes—us. I'm not alone."

The preacher just shakes his head. Then he looks at everybody in the room—everybody. Some of the people look down at the floor, keep from looking at him. I kind of look 'way myself, but soon 's I know he done turn his head, I look that way again.

"I'm sorry for you," he says to the boy.

"Why?" the boy says. "Why not be sorry for yourself? Why are you so much better off than I am? Why aren't you sorry for these other people in here? Why not be sorry for the lady who had to drag her child into the dentist office? Why not be sorry for the lady sitting on that bench over there? Be sorry for them. Not for me. Some way or the other I'm going to make it."

"No, I'm sorry for you," the preacher says.

"Of course, of course," the boy says, nodding his head. "You're sorry for me because I rock that pillar you're leaning on."

"You can't ever rock the pillar I'm leaning on, young man. It's stronger than anything man can ever do."

"You believe in God because a man told you to believe in God," the boy says. "A white man told you to believe in God. And why? To keep you ignorant so he can keep his feet on your neck."

"So now we the ignorant?" the preacher says.

"Yes," the boy says. "Yes." And he opens his book again.

The preacher just looks at him sitting there. The boy done forgot all about him. Everybody else make 'tend they done forgot the squabble, too.

Then I see that preacher getting up real slow. Preacher's a great big old man and he got to brace himself to get up. He comes over where the boy is sitting. He just stands there a little while looking down at him, but the boy don't raise his head.

"Get up, boy," preacher says.

The boy looks up at him, then he shuts his book real slow and stands up. Preacher just hauls back and hit him in the face. The boy falls back 'gainst the wall, but he straightens himself up and looks right back at that preacher.

"You forgot the other cheek," he says.

The preacher hauls back and hit him again on the other side. But this time the boy braces himself and don't fall.

"That hasn't changed a thing," he says.

The preacher just looks at the boy. The preacher's breathing real hard like he just run up a big hill. The boy sits down and opens his book again.

"I feel sorry for you," the preacher says. "I never felt so sorry for a man before."

The boy makes 'tend he don't even hear that preacher. He keeps on reading his book. The preacher goes back and gets his hat off the chair.

"Excuse me," he says to us. "I'll come back some other time. Y'all, please excuse me."

And he looks at the boy and goes out the room. The boy h'ist his hand up to his mouth one time to wipe 'way some blood. All the rest of the time he keeps on reading. And nobody else in there say a word.

Little John Lee and his mama come out the dentist office, and the nurse calls somebody else in. Then little bit later they come out, and the nurse calls another name. But fast 's she calls somebody in there, somebody else comes in the place where we sitting, and the room stays full.

The people coming in now, all of them wearing big coats. One of them says something 'bout sleeting, another one says he hope not. Another one says he think it ain't nothing but rain. 'Cause, he says, rain can get awful cold this time of year.

All round the room they talking. Some of them talking to people right by them, some of them talking to people clear 'cross the room, some of them talking to anybody'll listen. It's a little bitty room, no bigger than us kitchen, and I can see everybody in there. The little old room's full of smoke, 'cause you got two old men smoking pipes over by that side door. I think I feel my tooth thumping me some, and I hold my breath and wait. I wait and wait, but it don't thump me no more. Thank God for that.

I feel like going to sleep, and I lean back 'gainst the wall. But I'm scared to go to sleep. Scared 'cause the nurse might call my name and I won't hear her. And Mama might go to sleep, too, and she'll be mad if neither one of us heard the nurse.

I look up at Mama. I love my mama. I love my mama. And when cotton come I'm go'n get her a new coat. And I ain't go'n get a black one, either. I think I'm go'n get her a red one.

"They got some books over there," I say. "Want read one of them?"

Mama looks at the books, but she don't answer me.

"You got yourself a little man there," the lady says.

Mama don't say nothing to the lady, but she must've smiled, 'cause I seen the lady smiling back. The lady looks at me a little while, like she's feeling sorry for me.

"You sure got that preacher out here in a hurry," she says to that boy.

The boy looks up at her and looks in his book again. When I grow up I want be just like him. I want clothes like that and I want keep a book with me, too.

"You really don't believe in God?" the lady says.

"No," he says.

"But why?" the lady says.

"Because the wind is pink," he says.

"What?" the lady says.

The boy don't answer her no more. He just reads in his book.

"Talking 'bout the wind is pink," that old lady says. She's sitting on the same bench with the boy and she's trying to look in his face. The boy makes 'tend the old lady ain't even there. He just keeps on reading. "Wind is pink," she says again. "Eh, Lord, what children go'n be saying next?"

The lady 'cross from us bust out laughing.

"That's a good one," she says. "The wind is pink. Yes sir, that's a good one."

"Don't you believe the wind is pink?" the boys says. He keeps his head down in the book.

"Course I believe it, honey," the lady says. "Course I do." She looks at us and winks her eye. "And what color is grass, honey?"

"Grass? Grass is black."

She bust out laughing again. The boy looks at her.

"Don't you believe grass is black?" he says.

The lady quits her laughing and looks at him. Everybody else looking at him, too. The place quiet, quiet.

"Grass is green, honey," the lady says. "It was green yesterday, it's green today, and it's go'n be green tomorrow."

"How do you know it's green?"

"I know because I know."

"You don't know it's green," the boy says. "You believe it's green because someone told you it was green. If someone had told you it was black you'd believe it was black."

"It's green," the lady says. "I know green when I see green."

"Prove it's green," the boy says.

"Sure, now," the lady says. "Don't tell me it's coming to that."

"It's coming to just that," the boy says. "Words mean nothing. One means no more than the other."

"That's what it all coming to?" that old lady says. That old lady got on a turban and she got on two sweaters. She got a green sweater under a black sweater. I can see the green sweater 'cause some of the buttons on the other sweater's missing.

"Yes ma'am," the boy says. "Words mean nothing. Action is the only thing. Doing. That's the only thing."

"Other words, you want the Lord to come down here and show Hisself to you?" she says.

"Exactly, ma'am," he says.

504

"You don't mean that, I'm sure?" she says.

"I do, ma'am," he says.

"Done, Jesus," the old lady says, shaking her head.

"I didn't go 'long with that preacher at first," the other lady says; "but now — I don't know. When a person say the grass is black, he's either a lunatic or something's wrong."

"Prove to me that it's green," the boy says.

"It's green because the people say it's green."

"Those same people say we're citizens of these United States," the boy says.

"I think I'm a citizen," the lady says.

"Citizens have certain rights," the boy says. "Name me one right that you have. One right, granted by the Constitution, that you can exercise in Bayonne."

The lady don't answer him. She just looks at him like she don't know what he's talking 'bout. I know I don't.

"Things changing," she says.

"Things are changing because some black men have begun to think with their brains and not their hearts," the boy says.

"You trying to say these people don't believe in God?"

"I'm sure some of them do. Maybe most of them do. But they don't believe that God is going to touch these white people's hearts and change things tomorrow. Things change through action. By no other way."

Everybody sit quiet and look at the boy. Nobody says a thing. Then the lady 'cross the room from me and Mama just shakes her head.

"Let's hope that not all your generation feel the same way you do," she says.

"Think what you please, it doesn't matter," the boy says. "But it will be men who listen to their heads and not their hearts who will see that your children have a better chance than you had."

"Let's hope they ain't all like you, though," the old lady says. "Done forgot the heart absolutely."

"Yes ma'am, I hope they aren't all like me," the boy says. "Unfortunately, I was born too late to believe in your God. Let's hope that the ones who come after will have your faith — if not in your God, then in something else, something definitely that they can lean on. I haven't anything. For me, the wind is pink, the grass is black."

The nurse comes in the room where we all sitting and waiting and says the doctor won't take no more patients till one o'clock this evening. My mama jumps up off the bench and goes up to the white lady.

"Nurse, I have to go back in the field this evening," she says.

"The doctor is treating his last patient now," the nurse says. "One o'clock this evening."

"Can I at least speak to the doctor?" my mama asks.

"I'm his nurse," the lady says.

"My little boy's sick," my mama says. "Right now his tooth almost killing him."

The nurse looks at me. She's trying to make up her mind if to let me come in. I look at her real pitiful. The tooth ain't hurting me at all, but Mama say it is, so I make 'tend for her sake.

"This evening," the nurse says, and goes on back in the office.

"Don't feel 'jected, honey," the lady says to Mama. "I been round them a long time — they take you when they want to. If you was white, that's something else; but we the wrong color."

Mama don't say nothing to the lady, and me and her go outside and stand 'gainst the wall. It's cold out there. I can feel that wind going through my coat. Some of the other people come out of the room and go up the street. Me and Mama stand there a little while and we start walking. I don't know where we going. When we come to the other street we just stand there.

"You don't have to make water, do you?" Mama says.

"No, ma'am," I say.

We go on up the street. Walking real slow. I can tell Mama don't know where she's going. When we come to a store we stand there and look at the dummies. I look at a little boy wearing a brown overcoat. He's got on brown shoes, too. I look at my old shoes and look at his'n again. You wait till summer, I say.

Me and Mama walk away. We come up to another store and we stop and look at them dummies, too. Then we go on again. We pass a café where the white people in there eating. Mama tells me keep my eyes in front where they belong, but I can't help from seeing them people eat. My stomach starts to growling 'cause I'm hungry. When I see people eating, I get hungry; when I see a coat, I get cold.

A man whistles at my mama when we go by a filling station. She makes 'tend she don't even see him. I look back and I feel like hitting him in the mouth. If I was bigger, I say; if I was bigger, you'd see.

We keep on going. I'm getting colder and colder, but I don't say nothing. I feel that stuff running down my nose and I sniff.

"That rag," Mama says.

I get it out and wipe my nose. I'm getting cold all over now—my face, my hands, my feet, everything. We pass another little café, but this'n for white people, too, and we can't go in there, either. So we just walk. I'm so cold now I'm 'bout ready to say it. If I knowed where we was going I wouldn't be so cold, but I don't know where we going. We go, we go, we go. We walk clean out of Bayonne. Then we cross the street and we come back. Same thing I seen when I got off the bus this morning. Same old trees, same old walk, same old weeds, same old cracked pave—same old everything.

I sniff again.

"That rag," Mama says.

I wipe my nose real fast and jugg that handkerchief back in my pocket 'fore my hand gets too cold. I raise my head and I can see David's hardware store. When we come up to it, we go in. I don't know why, but I'm glad.

It's warm in there. It's so warm in there you don't ever want to leave. I look for the heater, and I see it over by them barrels. Three white men standing round the heater talking in Creole. One of them comes over to see what my mama want.

"Got any axe handles?" she says.

Me, Mama and the white man start to the back, but Mama stops me when we come up to the heater. She and the white man go on. I hold my hands over the heater and look at them. They go all the way to the back, and I see the white man pointing to the axe handles 'gainst the wall. Mama takes one of them and shakes it like she's trying to figure how much it weighs. Then she rubs her hand over it from one end to the other end. She turns it over and looks at the other side, then she shakes it again, and shakes her head and puts it back. She gets another one and she does it just like she did the first one, then she shakes her head. Then she gets a brown one and do it that, too. But she don't like this one, either. Then she gets another one, but 'fore she shakes it or anything, she looks at me. Look like she's trying to say something to me, but I don't know what it is. All I know is I done got warm now and I'm feeling right smart better. Mama shakes this axe handle just like she did the others, and shakes her head and says something to the white man. The white man just looks at his pile of axe handles, and when Mama pass him to come to the front, the white man just scratch his head and follows her. She tells me come on and we go on out and start walking again.

We walk and walk, and no time at all I'm cold again. Look like I'm colder now 'cause I can still remember how good it was back there. My stomach growls and I suck it in to keep Mama from hearing it. She's walking right 'side me, and it growls so loud you can hear it a mile. But Mama don't say a word.

When we come up to the courthouse, I look at the clock. It's got quarter to twelve. Mean we got another hour and a quarter to be out here in the cold. We go and stand 'side a building. Something hits my cap and I look up at the sky. Sleet's falling.

I look at Mama standing there. I want stand close 'side her, but she don't like that. She say that's crybaby stuff. She say you got to stand for yourself, by yourself.

"Let's go back to that office," she says.

We cross the street. When we get to the dentist office I try to open the door, but I can't. I twist and twist, but I can't. Mama pushes me to the side and she twist the knob, but she can't open the door, either. She turns 'way from the door. I look at her, but I don't move and I don't say nothing. I done seen her like this before and I'm scared of her.

"You hungry?" she says. She says it like she's mad at me, like I'm the cause of everything.

"No, ma'am," I say.

"You want eat and walk back, or you rather don't eat and ride?"

"I ain't hungry," I say.

I ain't just hungry, but I'm cold, too. I'm so hungry and cold I want to cry. And look like I'm getting colder and colder. My feet done got numb. I try to work my toes, but I don't even feel them. Look like I'm go'n die. Look like I'm go'n stand right here and freeze to death. I think 'bout home. I think 'bout Val and Auntie and Ty and Louis and Walker. It's 'bout twelve o'clock and I know they eating dinner now. I can hear Ty making jokes. He done forgot 'bout getting up early this morning and right now he's probably making jokes. Always trying to make somebody laugh. I wish I was right there listening to him. Give anything in the world if I was home round the fire.

"Come on," Mama says.

We start walking again. My feet so numb I can't hardly feel them. We turn the corner and go on back up the street. The clock on the courthouse starts hitting for twelve.

The sleet's coming down plenty now. They hit the pave and bounce like rice. Oh, Lord; oh, Lord, I pray. Don't let me die, don't let me die, don't let me die, Lord.

Now I know where we going. We going back of town where the colored people eat. I don't care if I don't eat. I been hungry before. I can stand it. But I can't stand the cold.

I can see we go'n have a long walk. It's 'bout a mile down there. But I don't mind. I know when I get there I'm go'n warm myself. I think I can hold out. My hands numb in my pockets and my feet numb, too, but if I keep moving I can hold out. Just don't stop no more, that's all.

The sky's gray. The sleet keeps on falling. Falling like rain now — plenty, plenty. You can hear it hitting the pave. You can see it bouncing. Sometimes it bounces two times 'fore it settles.

We keep on going. We don't say nothing. We just keep on going, keep on going.

I wonder what Mama's thinking. I hope she ain't mad at me. When summer come I'm go'n pick plenty cotton and get her a coat. I'm go'n get her a red one.

I hope they'd make it summer all the time. I'd be glad if it was summer all the time — but it ain't. We got to have winter, too. Lord, I hate the winter. I guess everybody hate the winter.

I don't sniff this time. I get out my handkerchief and wipe my nose. My hands's so cold I can hardly hold the handkerchief.

I think we getting close, but we ain't there yet. I wonder where everybody is. Can't see a soul but us. Look like we the only two people moving round today. Must be too cold for the rest of the people to move round in.

I can hear my teeth. I hope they don't knock together too hard and make that bad one hurt. Lord, that's all I need, for that bad one to start off.

I hear a church bell somewhere. But today ain't Sunday. They must be ringing for a funeral or something.

I wonder what they doing at home. They must be eating. Monsieur Bayonne might be there with his guitar. One day Ty played with Monsieur Bayonne's guitar and broke one of the strings. Monsieur Bayonne was some mad with Ty. He say Ty wasn't go'n ever 'mount to nothing. Ty can go just like Monsieur Bayonne when he ain't there. Ty can make everybody laugh when he starts to mocking Monsieur Bayonne.

I used to like to be with Mama and Daddy. We used to be happy. But they took him in the Army. Now, nobody happy no more. . . . I be glad when Daddy comes home.

Monsieur Bayonne say it wasn't fair for them to take Daddy and give Mama nothing and give us nothing. Auntie say, "Shhh, Etienne. Don't let them hear you talk like that." Monsieur Bayonne say, "It's God truth. What they giving his children? They have to walk three and a half miles to school hot or cold. That's anything to give for a paw? She's got to work in the field rain or shine just to make ends meet. That's anything to give for a husband?" Auntie say, "Shhh, Etienne, shhh." "Yes, you right," Monsieur Bayonne say, "Best don't say it in front of them now. But one day they go'n find out. One day." "Yes, I suppose so," Auntie say. "Then what, Rose Mary?" Monsieur Bayonne say. "I don't know, Etienne," Auntie say. "All we can do is us job, and leave everything else in His hand . . ."

We getting closer, now. We getting closer. I can even see the railroad tracks.

We cross the tracks, and now I see the café. Just to get in there, I say. Just to get in there. Already I'm starting to feel little better.

We go in. Ahh, it's good. I look for the heater; there 'gainst the wall. One of them little brown ones. I just stand there and hold my hands over it. I can't open my hand too wide 'cause they almost froze.

Mama's standing right 'side me. She done unbuttoned her coat. Smoke rises out of the coat, and the coat smells like a wet dog.

I move to the side so Mama can have more room. She opens out her hands and rubs them together. I rub mine together, too, 'cause this keep them from hurting. If you let them warm too fast, they hurt you sure. But if you let them warm just little bit at a time, and you keep rubbing them, they be all right every time.

They got just two more people in the café. A lady back of the counter, and a man on this side the counter. They been watching us ever since we come in.

Mama gets out the handkerchief and count up the money. Both of us know how much money she's got there. Three dollars. No, she ain't got three dollars, 'cause she had to pay us way up here. She ain't got but two dollars and a half left. Dollar and a half to get my tooth pulled, and fifty cents for us to go back on, and fifty cents worth of salt meat.

She stirs the money round with her finger. Most of the money is change 'cause I can hear it rubbing together. She stirs it and stirs it. Then she looks at the door. It's still sleeting. I can hear it hitting 'gainst the wall like rice.

"I ain't hungry, Mama," I say.

"Got to pay them something for they heat," she says.

She takes a quarter out the handkerchief and ties the handkerchief up again. She looks over her shoulder at the people, but she still don't move. I hope she don't spend the money. I don't want her spending it on me. I'm hungry, I'm almost starving I'm so hungry, but I don't want her spending the money on me.

She flips the quarter over like she's thinking. She's must be thinking 'bout us walking back home. Lord, I sure don't want walk home. If I thought it'd do any good to say something, I'd say it. But Mama makes up her own mind 'bout things.

She turns 'way from the heater right fast, like she better hurry up and spend the quarter 'fore she change her mind. I watch her go toward the counter. The man and the lady look at her, too. She tells the lady something and the lady walks away. The man keeps on looking at her.

Her back's turned to the man, and she don't even know he's standing there.

The lady puts some cakes and a glass of milk on the counter. Then she pours up a cup of coffee and sets it 'side the other stuff. Mama pays her for the things and comes on back where I'm standing. She tells me sit down at the table 'gainst the wall.

The milk and the cake's for me; the coffee's for Mama. I eat slow and I look at her. She's looking outside at the sleet. She's looking real sad. I say to myself, I'm go'n make all this up one day. You see, one day, I'm go'n make all this up. I want say it now; I want tell her how I feel right now; but Mama don't like for us to talk like that.

"I can't eat all this," I say.

They ain't got but just three little old cakes there. I'm so hungry right now, the Lord knows I can eat a hundred times three, but I want my mama to have one.

Mama don't even look my way. She knows I'm hungry, she knows I want it. I let it stay there a little while, then I get it and eat it. I eat just on my front teeth, though, 'cause if cake touch that back tooth I know what'll happen. Thank God it ain't hurt me at all today.

After I finish eating I see the man go to the juke box. He drops a nickel in it, then he just stand there a little while looking at the record. Mama tells me keep my eyes in front where they belong. I turn my head like she say, but then I hear the man coming toward us.

"Dance, pretty?" he says.

Mama gets up to dance with him. But 'fore you know it, she done grabbed the little man in the collar and done heaved him 'side the wall. He hit the wall so hard he stop the juke box from playing.

"Some pimp," the lady back of the counter says. "Some pimp."

The little man jumps up off the floor and starts toward my mama. 'Fore you know it, Mama done sprung open her knife and she's waiting for him.

"Come on," she says. "Come on. I'll gut you from your neighbo to your throat. Come on."

I go up to the little man to hit him, but Mama makes me come and stand 'side her. The little man looks at me and Mama and goes on back to the counter.

"Some pimp," the lady back of the counter says. "Some pimp." She starts laughing and pointing at the little man. "Yes sir, you a pimp, all right. Yes sir-ree."

"Fasten that coat, let's go," Mama says.

"You don't have to leave," the lady says.

Mama don't answer the lady, and we right out in the cold again. I'm warm right now—my hands, my ears, my feet—but I know this ain't go'n last too long. It done sleet so much now you got ice everywhere you look.

We cross the railroad tracks, and soon's we do, I get cold. That wind goes through this little old coat like it ain't even there. I got on a shirt and a sweater under the coat, but that wind don't pay them no mind. I look up and I can see we got a long way to go. I wonder if we go'n make it 'fore I get too cold.

We cross over to walk on the sidewalk. They got just one sidewalk back here, and it's over there.

After we go just a little piece, I smell bread cooking. I look, then I see a baker shop. When we get closer, I can smell it more better. I shut my eyes and make 'tend I'm eating. But I keep them shut too long and I butt up 'gainst a telephone post. Mama grabs me and see if I'm hurt. I ain't bleeding or nothing and she turns me loose.

I can feel I'm getting colder and colder, and I look up to see how far we still got to go. Uptown is 'way up yonder. A half mile more, I reckon. I try to think of something. They say think and you won't get cold. I think of that poem, "Annabel Lee." I ain't been to school in so long—this bad weather—I reckon they done passed "Annabel Lee" by now. But passed it or not, I'm sure Miss Walker go'n make me recite it when I get there. That woman don't never forget nothing. I ain't never seen nobody like that in my life.

I'm still getting cold. "Annabel Lee" or no "Annabel Lee," I'm still getting cold. But I can see we getting closer. We getting there gradually.

Soon 's we turn the corner, I see a little old white lady up in front of us. She's the only lady on the street. She's all in black and she's got a long black rag over her head.

"Stop," she says.

Me and Mama stop and look at her. She must be crazy to be out in all this bad weather. Ain't got but a few other people out there, and all of them's men.

"Y'all done ate?" she says.

"Just finish," Mama says.

"Y'all must be cold then?" she says.

"We headed for the dentist," Mama says. "We'll warm up when we get there."

"What dentist?" the old lady says. "Mr. Bassett?"

"Yes, ma'am," Mama says.

"Come on in," the old lady says. "I'll telephone him and tell him y'all coming."

Me and Mama follow the old lady in the store. It's a little bitty store, and it don't have much in there. The old lady takes off her head rag and folds it up.

"Helena?" somebody calls from the back.

"Yes, Alnest?" the old lady says.

"Did you see them?"

"They're here. Standing beside me."

"Good. Now you can stay inside."

The old lady looks at Mama. Mama's waiting to hear what she brought us in here for. I'm waiting for that, too.

"I saw y'all each time you went by," she says. "I came out to catch you, but you were gone."

"We went back of town," Mama says.

"Did you eat?"

"Yes, ma'am."

The old lady looks at Mama a long time, like she's thinking Mama might be just saying that. Mama looks right back at her. The old lady looks at me to see what I have to say. I don't say nothing. I sure ain't going 'gainst my mama.

"There's food in the kitchen," she says to Mama. "I've been keeping it warm."

Mama turns right around and starts for the door.

"Just a minute," the old lady says. Mama stops. "The boy'll have to work for it. It isn't free."

"We don't take no handout," Mama says.

"I'm not handing out anything," the old lady says. "I need my garbage moved to the front. Ernest has a bad cold and can't go out there."

"James'll move it for you," Mama says.

"Not unless you eat," the old lady says. "I'm old, but I have my pride, too, you know."

Mama can see she ain't go'n beat this old lady down, so she just shakes her head.

"All right," the old lady says. "Come into the kitchen."

She leads the way with that rag in her hand. The kitchen is a little bitty little old thing, too. The table and the stove just 'bout fill it up. They got a little room to the side. Somebody in there laying 'cross the bed—'cause I can see one of his feet. Must be the person she was talking to: Ernest or Alnest—something like that.

"Sit down," the old lady says to Mama. "Not you," she says to me. "You have to move the cans."

"Helena?" the man says in the other room.

"Yes, Alnest?" the old lady says.

"Are you going out there again?"

"I must show the boy where the garbage is, Alnest," the old lady says.

"Keep that shawl over your head," the old man says.

"You don't have to remind me, Alnest. Come, boy," the old lady says.

We go out in the yard. Little old back yard ain't no bigger than the store or the kitchen. But it can sleet here just like it can sleet in any big back yard. And 'fore you know it, I'm trembling.

"There," the old lady says, pointing to the cans. I pick up one of the cans and set it right back down. The can's so light, I'm go'n see what's inside of it.

"Here," the old lady says. "Leave that can alone."

I look back at her standing there in the door. She's got that black rag wrapped round her shoulders, and she's pointing one of her little old fingers at me.

"Pick it up and carry it to the front," she says. I go by her with the can, and she's looking at me all the time. I'm sure the can's empty. I'm sure she could've carried it herself—maybe both of them at the same time. "Set it on the sidewalk by the door and come back for the other one," she says.

I go and come back, and Mama looks at me when I pass her. I get the other can and take it to the front. It don't feel a bit heavier than the first one. I tell myself I ain't go'n be nobody's fool, and I'm go'n look inside this can to see just what I been hauling. First, I look up the street, then down the street. Nobody coming. Then I look over my shoulder toward the door. That little old lady done slipped up there quiet 's mouse, watching me again. Look like she knowed what I was go'n do.

"Ehh, Lord," she says. "Children, children. Come in here, boy, and go wash your hands."

I follow her in the kitchen. She points toward the bathroom, and I go in there and wash up. Little bitty old bathroom, but it's clean, clean. I don't use any of her towels; I wipe my hands on my pants legs.

When I come back in the kitchen, the old lady done dished up the food. Rice, gravy, meat—and she even got some lettuce and tomato in a saucer. She even got a glass of milk and a piece of cake there, too. It looks so good, I almost start eating 'fore I say my blessing.

"Helena?" the old man says.

"Yes, Alnest?"

"Are they eating?"

"Yes," she says.

"Good," he says. "Now you'll stay inside."

The old lady goes in there where he is and I can hear them talking. I look at Mama. She's eating slow like she's thinking. I wonder what's the matter now. I reckon she's thinking 'bout home.

The old lady comes back in the kitchen.

"I talked to Dr. Bassett's nurse," she says. "Dr. Bassett will take you as soon as you get there."

"Thank you, ma'am," Mama says.

"Perfectly all right," the old lady says. "Which one is it?"

Mama nods toward me. The old lady looks at me real sad. I look sad, too.

"You're not afraid, are you?" she says.

"No, ma'am," I say.

"That's a good boy," the old lady says. "Nothing to be afraid of. Dr. Bassett will not hurt you."

When me and Mama get through eating, we thank the old lady again.

"Helena, are they leaving?" the old man says.

"Yes, Alnest."

"Tell them I say good-bye."

"They can hear you, Alnest."

"Good-bye both mother and son," the old man says. "And may God be with you."

Me and Mama tell the old man good-bye, and we follow the old lady in the front room. Mama opens the door to go out, but she stops and comes back in the store.

"You sell salt meat?" she says.

"Yes."

"Give me two bits worth."

"That isn't very much salt meat," the old lady says.

"That's all I have," Mama says.

The old lady goes back of the counter and cuts a big piece off the chunk. Then she wraps it up and puts it in a paper bag.

"Two bits," she says.

"That looks like awful lot of meat for a quarter," Mama says.

"Two bits," the old lady says. "I've been selling salt meat behind this counter twenty-five years. I think I know what I'm doing."

"You got a scale there," Mama says.

"What?" the old lady says.

"Weigh it," Mama says.

"What?" the old lady says. "Are you telling me how to run my business?"

"Thanks very much for the food," Mama says.

"Just a minute," the old lady says.

"James," Mama says to me. I move toward the door.

"Just one minute, I said," the old lady says.

Me and Mama stop again and look at her. The old lady takes the meat out of the bag and unwraps it and cuts 'bout half of it off. Then she wraps it up again and juggs it back in the bag and gives the bag to Mama. Mama lays the quarter on the counter.

"Your kindness will never be forgotten," she says. "James," she says to me.

We go out, and the old lady comes to the door to look at us. After we go a little piece I look back, and she's still there watching us.

The sleet's coming down heavy, heavy now, and I turn up my coat collar to keep my neck warm. My mama tells me turn it right back down.

"You not a bum," she says. "You a man."

from *Meridian*

Alice Walker (1944–)

As a writer who explores the nuances of race and gender relations in her fiction, Alice Walker can write with the authority of experience. The child of share-croppers, Walker came of age in Eatonton, Georgia, graduating as valedictorian of her high school class. While working as an activist in Mississippi in the summer of 1966, she met her future husband, Melvyn Leventhal, a white civil rights attor-ney. Married in 1967, they became the first legally married biracial couple to reside in Jackson, the state capital. They divorced in 1976. In her second novel, *Meridian*, which appeared the same year, the characters confront the question of the significance of color in personal relationships. Educated at Spelman College and Sarah Lawrence College, Walker was awarded the Pulitzer Prize for her 1982 novel *The Color Purple*.

His feelings for Lynne had been undergoing subtle changes for some time. Yet it was not until the shooting of Tommy Odds in Mississippi that he noticed these changes. The shooting of Tommy Odds happened one evening just as he Truman, Tommy Odds and Trilling (a worker from Oklahoma since fled and never seen again) were coming out of the door of the Liberal Trinity Baptist Church. There had been the usual meeting with songs, prayers and strategy for the next day's picketing of downtown stores. They had assumed, also, that guards had been posted; not verifying was their mistake. As they stepped from the church and into the light from an overhanging bulb on the porch, a burst of machine-gun fire came from some bushes across the street. He and Trilling jumped off the sides of the steps. Tommy Odds, in the middle, was shot through the elbow.

When he went to visit Tommy Odds in the hospital he thought, as the elevator carried him to the fourth floor, of how funny it would be when the two of them talked about the frantic jump he and Trilling made. "You know one thing," he was going to say, laughing, to Tommy Odds, "you're just one *slow* nigger." Then they would wipe the tears of laughter from their eyes and open the bottle of Ripple he had brought. But it had not gone that way at all. First of all, Tommy Odds was not resting up after a flesh wound, as earlier reports had said; he had lost the lower half of his arm. He was propped up in bed now with a clear fluid dripping from a bot-tle into his other arm. But his horrible gray coloring, his cracked bloodless lips, his glazed eyes, were nothing compared to the utter lack of humor apparent in his face. Impossible to joke, to laugh, without tearing his insides to shreds.

Yet Truman had tried. "Hey, man!" he said, striding across the room with his bottle of Ripple under his arm. "Look what I brought you!" But Tommy Odds did not move his head or his eyes to follow him across the room. He lay looking at a spot slightly above the television, which was high in one corner of the room.

"Lynne says hurry up and get your ass out of here," he continued. "When you get out of here we gon' party for days."

"Don't mention that bitch to me, man," Tommy Odds said.

"What you say?"

"I said"—Tommy Odds turned his head and looked at him, moving his lips carefully so there would be no mistake—"don't mention that bitch to me. Don't mention that white bitch."

"Wait a minute, man," Truman stammered in surprise, "Lynne had nothing to do with this." And yet, while he was saying this, his tongue was slowed down by thoughts that began twisting like snakes through his brain. How could he say Lynne had nothing to do with the shooting of Tommy Odds, when there were so many levels at which she could be blamed?

"All white people are motherfuckers," said Tommy Odds, as listlessly but clearly as before. "I want to see them destroyed. I could watch their babies being torn limb from limb and I wouldn't lift a finger. The Bible says to dash out the brains of your enemy's children on the rocks. I understand that shit, now."

At this level, Truman thought, sinking into a chair beside his friend, is Lynne guilty? That she is white is true. That she is therefore a killer, evil, a motherfucker—how true? Not true at all! And yet—

"Man, all I do is think about what these crackers did with my motherfucking arm," said Tommy Odds.

"You want me to find out?"

"No, I guess not."

By being white Lynne was guilty of whiteness. He could not reduce the logic any further, in that direction. Then the question was, is it possible to be guilty of a color? Of course black people for years were "guilty" of being black. Slavery was punishment for their "crime." But even if he abandoned this search for Lynne's guilt, because it ended, logically enough, in racism, he was forced to search through other levels for it. For bad or worse, and regardless of what this said about himself as a person, he could not — after his friend's words — keep from thinking Lynne was, in fact, guilty. The thing was to find out how.

"I'm sorry, man," said Tommy Odds. "I shouldn't have come down on your old lady that way."

"It's okay, man, no sweat," Truman mumbled, while his thoughts continued to swirl up, hot and desperate. It was as if Tommy Odds had spoken the words that fit thoughts he had been too cowardly to entertain. On what other level might Lynne, his wife, be guilty?

"It's just that, you know, white folks are a bitch. If I didn't hate them on principle before, I hate them now for personal and concrete reasons. I've been thinking and thinking, lying here. And what I've thought is: Don't nobody offer me marching and preaching as a substitute for going after those jokers' *balls.*"

Was it because she was a white woman that Lynne was guilty? Ah, yes. That was it. Of course. And Truman remembered one night when he and Tommy Odds and Trilling and Lynne had gone to the Moonflower café for a sandwich. They shouldn't have done it, of course. They had been warned against it. They knew better. But there are times in a person's life when to risk everything is the only *affirmation* of life. That night was such a time. What had they been celebrating? Oh, yes. Tommy Odds's niggers-on-the-corner.

For months Tommy Odds had hung out every Saturday evening at the pool hall on Carver Street, talking and shooting pool. He had been playing with the niggers-on-the-corner for almost a month before he ever opened his mouth about the liberating effects of voting. At first he had been hooted down with shouts of "Man, I don't wanna hear that shit!" and "Man, let's keep this a clean game!" But the good thing about Tommy Odds was his patience. At first he just shut up and worked out with his cue. But in a few days, he'd bring it up again. By the end of the first month his niggers-on-the-corner liked him too much not to listen to him. At the end of three months they'd formed a brigade called "The Niggers-on-the-Corner-Voter-Machine." It was through them that all the derelicts, old grandmamas and grandpas and tough young hustlers and studs, the prostitutes and even the boozy old guy who ran the pool hall registered to vote in the next election. And on this particular Saturday night they decided to celebrate at the Moonflower, a greasy hole-in-the-wall that still had "Whites Only" on its door.

The food was so bad they had not been able to eat it. But they left in high spirits, Lynne giggling about the waitress's hair that was like a helmet made of blonde foil. But as they walked down the street a car slowly followed them until, turning down Carver Street, they were met by some of Tommy Odds's NOTC, who walked them to safety in front of the pool hall. After that night he and Lynne were careful not to be seen together. But since Lynne was the only white woman in town regularly seen only with black people, she was easily identified. He had not thought they would be, too.

So for that night, perhaps Lynne was guilty. But why had she been with them? Had she invited herself? No. Tommy Odds had invited them both to his little party. Even so, it was Lynne's presence that had caused the car to follow them. So she *was* guilty. Guilty of whiteness, as well as stupidity for having agreed to come.

Yet, Lynne loved Tommy Odds, she admired his NOTC. It was Lynne who designed and sewed together those silly badges that they wore, that gave them so much pride.

"What do NOTC mean?" asked the old grandmamas who were escorted like queens down the street to the courthouse.

"Oh, it mean 'Not Only True, but Colored,'" the hustlers replied smoothly. Or, "Not on Time, but Current," said the prostitutes to the old grandpas, letting the old men dig on their cleavage. Or, "Notice of Trinity, with Christ," the pool sharks said to the religious fanatics, who frowned, otherwise, on pool sharks.

So Lynne was guilty on at least two counts; of being with them, and of being, period. At least that was how Tommy Odds saw it. And who was he to argue, guilty as he was of loving the white bitch who caused his friend to lose his arm?

Thinking this, he shot up from his chair by the bed as if from an electric shock. The bottle of Ripple slipped from his fingers and crashed to the floor.

"Just don't tell me you done wasted the wine," said Tommy Odds, groaning. "I was just working myself up for a taste."

"I'll bring another bottle," Truman said, getting towels from the bathroom and mopping up. He cut his finger on a piece of glass and realized he was trembling. When he'd put the wastebasket outside the door for the janitor he looked back at Tommy Odds. Some small resemblance of his friend remained on the bed. But he could feel the distance that already separated them. When he went out that door they would both be different. He could read the message that Tommy Odds would not, as his former friend, put into words. "Get rid of your bitch, man." That was all.

Getting rid of a bitch is simple, for bitches are dispensable. But getting rid of a wife?

He had read in a magazine just the day before that Lamumba Katurim had gotten rid of his. She was his wife, true, but apparently she was even in that disguise perceived as evil, a castoff. And people admired Lamumba for his perception. It proved his love of his own people, they said. But he was not sure. Perhaps it proved only that Lamumba was fickle. That he'd married his bitch in the first place for shallow reasons. Perhaps he was considering marrying a black woman (as the article said he was) for reasons just as shallow. For how could he state so assuredly that he would marry a black woman next when he did not appear to have any *specific* black woman in mind?

If his own sister told him of her upcoming marriage to Lamumba he would have to know some answers before the nuptial celebration. Like, how many times would Lamumba require her to appear on television with him, or how many times would he parade her before his friends as proof of his blackness.

He thought of Randolph Kay, the Movie Star, who also shucked his white bitch wife, to black applause. But now Randolph Kay *and* his shiny new black wife had moved into the white world completely, to the extent of endorsing the American bombing of civilian targets in Vietnam. Randolph Kay, in fact, now sang love songs to the President! But perhaps it was perverse of him to be so suspicious. Perhaps, after all, he was just trying to cover up his own inability to act as decisively and to the public order as these men had done. No doubt these *were* great men, who perceived, as he could not, that to love the wrong person is an error. If only he could believe it *possible* to love the wrong person he would be home free. As it was, how difficult hating his wife was going to be. He would not even try.

But of course he had.

There was a man he despised, whose name was Tom Johnson. Tom had lived with a white woman for years, only most people didn't know about it. He shuttled her back and forth from his house to a friend's house down the street. Whenever he had important guests, Margaret was nowhere to be found. She was waiting at their friend's house. She was a fleshy blonde, with big tits and a hearty laugh. Once he asked Tom—who was thinking of running for political office—why he didn't marry her. Tom laughed and said, "Boy, you don't understand anything yet. Margaret is a sweet ol' thing. We been living together in harmony for five years. But she's white. Or hadn't you noticed?" Tom had reached out a chubby hand to bring Truman's head closer to his own and his small eyes danced. "It's just a matter of pussy. That's all. Just a matter of my *personal* taste in pussy." And then he had pulled Truman's head even closer and said with conspiratorial glee, "It's *good* stuff. Want some?"

"I used to believe that—" he had begun, but Tom cut him off.

"This is war, man, *war*! And all's fair that fucks with the suckers' minds!"

Then he had begun to see them together. Not in public, but with small groups of men, in the back rooms of bars. Margaret could play poker and he liked to see her when she won. She jumped up, squealing, in her small-girl voice, her big tits bouncing at the top of her low-cut blouse, and all the men looked at her tolerantly, in amusement, their curiosity about her big body already at rest. After what Tom had told him this did not surprise him: the exhibition of her delight in winning, the men's amused solidarity, their willingness to share her in this position of secrecy. And Margaret? Those squeals of delight—what did she feel? Or was it unmanly, unblack now, even to care, to ask?

When the community center was built, he began painting a mural of the struggle along one wall. The young men who would use the center for dances, Ping-Pong, card games, etc., were building tables and chairs. They were a shy, sweet bunch, country boys and naïve as possible, who were literally afraid of white women. Their first meeting with Lynne had been comic. Nobody wanted to be seen talking to her alone, and even as a group they would only talk to her from a distance. She could, just by speaking to them and walking up to them as she spoke, force them back twenty yards. This shamed him now as he thought of Tommy Odds.

Why should they be afraid of her? She was just a woman. Only they could not see her that way. To them she was a route to Death, pure and simple. They felt her power over them in their bones; their mothers had feared her even before they were born. Watching their fear of her, though, he saw a strange thing: They did not even see her as a human being, but as some kind of large, mysterious doll. A thing of movies and television, of billboards and car and soap commercials. They liked her hair, not because it was especially pretty, but because it was long. To them, *length* was beauty. They loved the tails of horses.

Against this fear, Lynne used her considerable charm. She baked cookies for them, allowed them to drink wine in her house, and played basketball with them at the center. Jumping about in her shorts, tossing her long hair, she laughed and sweated and shouted and cursed. She forced them to like her.

But while this building of trust and mutual liking was coming into being, the Movement itself was changing. Lynne was no longer welcome at any of the meetings. She was excluded from the marches. She was no longer allowed to write articles for the paper. She spent most of her time in the center or at home. The boys, unsure now what their position as young black men should be, remained inexplicably loyal. They came to visit her, bringing news she otherwise would not have heard. For Truman too was under pressure of ostracism from the group, and though he remained a member of all Movement discussions it was understood he would say nothing to his wife.

"Why I Like Country Music"

James Alan McPherson (1943–)

Following in the tradition of Ralph Ellison and Albert Murray, James Alan McPherson's fiction challenges rigid notions of black culture. Reared in the multi-cultural city of Savannah, Georgia, during the height of the civil rights movement, McPherson earned degrees from Morris Brown College, Harvard Law School, and the University of Iowa. Warned early in his writing career by Ellison never to "seg-regate himself," McPherson's work, while acknowledging the tragic element of black Southerners' lives, emphasizes his characters' emotional complexity. In "Why I Like Country Music"(1977), the narrator explains, to what he knows is a disbelieving audience, how a black Southerner could remain attached to a musi-cal genre historically detached from black culture.

No one will believe that I like country music. Even my wife scoffs when told such a possibility exists. "Go on!" Gloria tells me. "I can see blues, bebop, maybe even a little buckdancing. But not bluegrass." Gloria says, "Hillbilly stuff is not just music. It's like the New York Stock Exchange. The minute you see a sharp rise in it, you better watch out."

I tend to argue the point, but quietly, and mostly to myself. Gloria was born and raised in New York; she has come to believe in the stock exchange as the only index of economic health. My perceptions were shaped in South Carolina; and long ago I learned there, as a waiter in pri-vate clubs, to gauge economic flux by the tips people gave. We tend to dis-agree on other matters too, but the thing that gives me most frustration is trying to make her understand why I like country music. Perhaps it is because she hates the South and has capitulated emotionally to the hor-ror stories told by refugees from down home. Perhaps it is because Gloria is third generation Northern-born. I do not know. What I do know is that, while the two of us are black, the distance between us is sometimes as great as that between Ibo and Yoruba. And I do know that, despite her protestations, I like country music.

"You are crazy," Gloria tells me.

I tend to argue the point, but quietly, and mostly to myself.

Of course I do not like all country stuff; just pieces that make the right connections. I like banjo because sometimes I hear ancestors in the strum-ming. I like the fiddle-like refrain in "Dixie" for the very same reason. But most of all I like square dancing—the interplay between fiddle and caller, the stomping, the swishing of dresses, the strutting, the proud turnings, the laughter. Most of all I like the laughter. In recent months I have wondered why I like this music and this dance. I have drawn no general conclusions, but from time to time I suspect it is because the square dance is the only dance form I ever mastered.

"I wouldn't say that in public," Gloria warns me.

I agree with her, but still affirm the truth of it, although quietly, and mostly to myself.

Dear Gloria: This is the truth of how it was:

In my youth in that distant country, while others learned to strut, I grew stiff as a winter cornstalk. When my playmates harmonized their rhythms, I stood on the sidelines in atonic detachment. While they shimmied, I merely jerked in lackluster imitation. I relate these facts here, not in remorse or self-castigation, but as a true confession of my circumstances. In those days, down in our small corner of South Carolina, proficiency in dance was a form of storytelling. A boy could say, "I traveled here and there, saw this and fought that, conquered him and made love to her, lied to them, told a few others the truth, just so I could come back here and let you know what things out there are really like." He could communicate all this with smooth, graceful jiggles of his round bottom, synchronized with intricately coordinated sweeps of his arms and small, unexcited movements of his legs. Little girls could communicate much more.

But sadly, I could do none of it. Development of these skills depended on the ministrations of family and neighbors. My family did not dance; our closest neighbor was a true-believing Seventh Day Adventist. Moreover, most new dances came from up North, brought to town usually by people returning to riff on the good life said to exist in those far Northern places. They prowled our dirt streets in rented Cadillacs; paraded our brick sidewalks exhibiting styles abstracted from the fullness of life in Harlem, South Philadelphia, Roxbury, Baltimore and the South Side of Chicago. They confronted our provincial clothes merchants with the arrogant reminder, "But people ain't wearin' this in New *Yokkk!*" Each of their movements, as well as their world-weary smoothness, told us locals meaningful tales of what was missing in our lives. Unfortunately, those of us under strict parental supervision, or those of us without Northern connections, could only stand at a distance and worship these envoys of culture. We stood on the sidelines — styleless, gestureless, danceless, doing nothing more than an improvised one-butt shuffle — hoping for one of them to touch our lives. It was my good fortune, during my tenth year on the sidelines, to have one of these Northerners introduce me to the square dance. My dear, dear Gloria, her name was Gweneth Lawson:

She was a pretty, chocolate-brown little girl with dark brown eyes and two long black braids. After all these years, the image of these two braids evokes in me all there is to remember about Gweneth Lawson. They were plaited across the top of her head and hung to a point just above the back of her Peter Pan collar. Sometimes she wore two bows, one red and one blue, and these tended to sway lazily near the place on her neck where the smooth brown of her skin and the white of her collar met the ink-bottle black of her hair. Even when I cannot remember her face, I remember the rainbow of deep, rich colors in which she lived. This is so because I watched them, every weekday, from my desk directly behind hers in our fourth-grade class. And she wore the most magical perfume, or lotion, smelling just slightly of fresh-cut lemons, that wafted back to me whenever she made the slightest movement at her desk. Now I must tell you this much more, dear Gloria: whenever I smell fresh lemons, whether in the market or at home, I look around me—not for Gweneth Lawson, but for some quiet corner where I can revive in private certain memories of her. And in pursuing these memories across such lemony bridges, I rediscover that I loved her.

Gweneth was from the South Carolina section of Brooklyn. Her parents had sent her south to live with her uncle, Mr. Richard Lawson, the brick mason, for an unspecified period of time. Just why they did this I do not know, unless it was their plan to have her absorb more of South Carolina folkways than conditions in Brooklyn would allow. She was a gentle, soft-spoken girl; I recall no condescension in her manner. This was all the more admirable because our unrestrained awe of a Northern-born black person usually induced in him some grand sense of his own importance. You must know that in those days older folks would point to someone and say, "He's from the North," and the statement would be sufficient in itself. Mothers made their children behave by advising that, if they led exemplary lives and attended church regularly, when they died they would go to New York. Only someone who understands what London meant to Dick Whittington, or how California and the suburbs function in the national mind, could appreciate the mythical dimensions of this Northlore.

But Gweneth Lawson was above regional idealization. Though I might have loved her partly because she was a Northerner, I loved her more because of the world of colors that seemed to be suspended above her head. I loved her glowing forehead and I loved her bright, dark brown eyes; I loved the black braids, the red and blue and sometimes yellow and pink ribbons; I loved the way the deep, rich brown of her neck melted into the pink or white cloth of her Peter Pan collar; I loved the lemony vapor on which she floated and from which, on occasion, she seemed to be inviting me to be buoyed up, up, up into her happy world; I loved the way she caused my heart to tumble whenever, during a restless moment, she seemed about to turn her head in my direction; I loved her more, though torturously, on the many occasions when she did not turn. Because I was a shy boy, I loved the way I could love her silently, at least six hours a day, without ever having to disclose my love.

My platonic state of mind might have stretched onward into a blissful infinity had not Mrs. Esther Clay Boswell, our teacher, made it her business to pry into the affair. Although she prided herself on being a strict disciplinarian, Mrs. Boswell was not without a sense of humor. A round, full-breasted woman in her early forties, she liked to amuse herself, and sometimes the class as well, by calling the attention of all eyes to whomever of us violated the structure she imposed on classroom activities. She was particularly hard on people like me who could not contain an impulse to daydream, or those who allowed their eyes to wander too far away from lessons printed on the blackboard. A black and white sign posted under the electric clock next to the door summed up her attitude toward this kind of truancy: NOTICE TO ALL CLOCKWATCHERS, it read, TIME PASSES, WILL YOU? Nor did she abide timidity in her students. Her voice booming, "Speak up boy!" was more than enough to cause the more emotional among us, including me, to break into convenient flows of warm tears. But by doing this we violated yet another rule, one on which depended our very survival in Mrs. Esther Clay Boswell's class. She would spell out this rule for us as she paced before her desk, slapping a thick, homemade ruler against the flat of her brown palm. "There ain't no *babies* in here," she would recite. *Thaap!* "Anybody thinks he's still a *baby* ..." *Thaap!* ... "should crawl back home to his mama's *titty.*" *Thaap!* "You little bunnies shed your *last water* ..." *Thaap!* "... the minute you left home to come in here." *Thaap!* "From now on, you g'on do all your *cryin'* ..." *Thaap!* "... in *church!*" *Thaap!* Whenever one of us compelled her to make this speech it would seem to me that her eyes paused overlong on my face. She would seem to be daring me, as if suspicious that, in addition to my secret passion for Gweneth Lawson, which she might excuse, I was also in the habit of throwing fits of temper.

She had read me right. I was the product of too much attention from my father. He favored me, paraded me around on his shoulder, inflated my ego constantly with what, among us at least, was a high compliment: "You my nigger if you don't get no bigger." This statement, along with my father's generous attentions, made me selfish and used to having my own way. I *expected* to have my own way in most things, and when I could not, I tended to throw tantrums calculated to break through any barrier raised against me.

Mrs. Boswell was also perceptive in assessing the extent of my infatuation with Gweneth Lawson. Despite my stealth in telegraphing emissions of affection into the back part of Gweneth's brain, I could not help but observe, occasionally, Mrs. Boswell's cool glance pausing on the two of us. But she never said a word. Instead, she would settle her eyes momentarily on Gweneth's face and then pass quickly to mine. But in that instant she seemed to be saying, "Don't look back now, girl, but I *know* that bald-headed boy behind you has you on his mind." She seemed to watch me daily, with a combination of amusement and absolute detachment in her brown eyes. And when she stared, it was not at me but at the normal focus of my attention: the end of Gweneth Lawson's black braids. Whenever I sensed Mrs. Boswell watching I would look away quickly, either down at my brown desk top or across the room to the blackboard. But her eyes could not be eluded this easily. Without looking at anyone in particular, she could make a specific point to one person in a manner so general that only long afterward did the real object of her attention realize it had been intended for him.

"Now you little brown bunnies," she might say, "and you black buck rabbits and you few cottontails mixed in, some of you starting to smell yourselves under the arms without knowing what it's all about." And here, it sometimes seemed to me, she allowed her eyes to pause casually on me before resuming their sweep of the entire room. "Now I know your mamas already made you think life is a bed of roses, but in *my* classroom you got to know the footpaths through the *sticky* parts of the rosebed." It was her custom during this ritual to prod and goad those of us who were developing reputations for meekness and indecision; yet her method was Socratic in that she compelled us, indirectly, to supply our own answers by exploiting one person as the walking symbol of the error she intended to correct. Clarence Buford, for example, an oversized but good-natured boy from a very poor family, served often as the helpmeet in this exercise.

"Buford," she might begin, slapping the ruler against her palm, "how does a tongue-tied country boy like you expect to get a wife?"

"I don't want no wife," Buford might grumble softly.

Of course the class would laugh.

"Oh yes you do," Mrs. Boswell would respond. "All you buck rabbits want wives." *Thaap!* "So how do you let a girl know you're not just a bump on a log?"

"I know! I know!" a high voice might call from a seat across from mine. This, of course, would be Leon Pugh. A peanut-brown boy with curly hair, he seemed to know everything. Moreover, he seemed to take pride in being the only one who knew answers to life questions and would wave his arms excitedly whenever our attentions were focused on such matters.

It seemed to me his voice would be extra loud and his arms waved more strenuously whenever he was certain that Gweneth Lawson, seated across from him, was interested in an answer to Mrs. Esther Clay Boswell's question. His eager arms, it seemed to me, would be reaching out to grasp Gweneth instead of the question asked.

"Buford, you twisted-tongue, bunion-toed country boy," Mrs. Boswell might say, ignoring Leon Pugh's hysterical arm waving, "you gonna let a cottontail like Leon get a girlfriend before you?"

"I don't want no girlfriend," Clarence Buford would almost sob. "I don't like no girls."

The class would laugh again while Leon Pugh manipulated his arms like a flight navigator under battle conditions. "I know! I know! I swear to God I know!"

When at last Mrs. Boswell would turn in his direction, I might sense that she was tempted momentarily to ask me for an answer. But as in most such exercises, it was the worldly-wise Leon Pugh who supplied this. "What do *you* think, Leon?" she would ask inevitably, but with a rather lifeless slap of the ruler against her palm.

"My daddy told me ..." Leon would shout, turning slyly to beam at Gweneth, "... my daddy and my big brother from the Bronx New York told me that to git *anythin'* in this world you gotta learn how to blow your own horn."

"Why, Leon?" Mrs. Boswell might ask in a bored voice.

"Because," the little boy would recite, puffing out his chest, "because if you don't blow your own horn ain't nobody else g'on blow it for you. That's what my daddy said."

"What do you think about that, Buford?" Mrs. Boswell would ask.

"I don't want no girlfriend anyhow," the puzzled Clarence Buford might say.

And then the cryptic lesson would suddenly be dropped.

This was Mrs. Esther Clay Boswell's method of teaching. More than anything written on the blackboard, her questions were calculated to make us turn around in our chairs and inquire in guarded whispers of each other, and especially of the wise and confident Leon Pugh, "What does she mean?" But none of us, besides Pugh, seemed able to comprehend what it was we ought to know but did not know. And Mrs. Boswell, plump brown fox that she was, never volunteered any more in the way of confirmation than was necessary to keep us interested. Instead, she paraded around us, methodically slapping the homemade ruler against her palm, suggesting by her silence more depth to her question, indeed, more implications in Leon's answer, than we were then able to perceive. And during such moments, whether inspired by selfishness or by the peculiar way Mrs. Boswell looked at me, I felt that finding answers to such questions was a task she had set for me, of all the members of the class.

Of course Leon Pugh, among other lesser lights, was my chief rival for the affections of Gweneth Lawson. All during the school year, from September through the winter rains, he bested me in my attempts to look directly into her eyes and say a simple, heartfelt "hey." This was my ambition, but I never seemed able to get close enough to get her attention. At Thanksgiving I helped draw a bounteous yellow cornucopia on the blackboard, with fruits and flowers matching the colors that floated around Gweneth's head; Leon Pugh made one by himself, a masterwork of silver paper and multicolored crepe, which he hung on the door. Its silver tail curled upward to a point just below the face of Mrs. Boswell's clock. At Christmas, when we drew names out of a hat for the exchange of gifts, I drew the name of Queen Rose Phipps, a fairly unattractive squash-yellow girl of absolutely no interest to me. Pugh, whether through collusion with the boy who handled the lottery or through pure luck, pulled forth from the hat the magic name of Gweneth Lawson. He gave her a set of deep purple bows for her braids and a basket of pecans from his father's tree. Uninterested now in the spirit of the occasion, I delivered to Queen Rose Phipps a pair of white socks. Each time Gweneth wore the purple bows she would glance over at Leon and smile. Each time Queen Rose wore my white socks I would turn away in embarrassment, lest I should see them pulling down into her shoes and exposing her skinny ankles.

After class, on wet winter days, I would trail along behind Gweneth to the bus stop, pause near the steps while she entered, and follow her down the aisle until she chose a seat. Usually, however, in clear violation of the code of conduct to which all gentlemen were expected to adhere, Leon Pugh would already be on the bus and shouting to passersby, "Move off! Get away! This here seat by me is reserved for the girl from Brooklyn New York." Discouraged but not defeated, I would swing into the seat next nearest her and cast calf-eyed glances of wounded affection at the back of her head or at the brown, rainbow profile of her face. And at her stop, some eight or nine blocks from mine, I would disembark behind her along with a crowd of other love-struck boys. There would then follow a well-rehearsed scene in which all of us, save Leon Pugh, pretended to have gotten off the bus either too late or too soon to wend our proper paths homeward. And at slight cost to ourselves we enjoyed the advantage of being able to walk close by her as she glided toward her uncle's green-frame house. There, after pausing on the wooden steps and smiling radiantly around the crowd like a spring sun in that cold winter rain, she would sing, "Bye, y'all," and disappear into the structure with the mystery of a goddess. Afterward I would walk away, but slowly, much slower than the other boys, warmed by the music and light in her voice against the sharp, wet winds of the February afternoon.

I loved her, dear Gloria, and I danced with her and smelled the lemony youth of her and told her that I loved her, all this in a way you would never believe:

You would not know or remember, as I do, that in those days, in our area of the country, we enjoyed a pleasingly ironic mixture of Yankee and Confederate folkways. Our meals and manners, our speech, our attitudes toward certain ambiguous areas of history, even our acceptance of tragedy as the normal course of life—these things and more defined us as Southern. Yet the stern morality of our parents, their toughness and penny-pinching and attitudes toward work, their covert allegiance toward certain ideals, even the directions toward which they turned our faces, made us more Yankee than Cavalier. Moreover, some of our schools were named for Confederate men of distinction, but others were named for the stern-faced believers who had swept down from the North to save a people back, back long ago, in those long-forgotten days of once upon a time. Still, our schoolbooks, our required classroom songs, our flags, our very relation to the statues and monuments in public parks, negated the story that these dreamers from the North had ever come. We sang the state song, memorized the verses of homegrown poets, honored in our books the names and dates of historical events both before and after that Historical Event which, in our region, supplanted even the division of the millennia introduced by the followers of Jesus Christ. Given the silent circumstances of our cultural environment, it was ironic, and perhaps just, that we maintained a synthesis of two traditions no longer supportive of each other. Thus it became traditional at our school to celebrate the arrival of spring on May first by both the ritual plaiting of the Maypole and square dancing.

On that day, as on a few others, the Superintendent of Schools and several officials were likely to visit our schoolyard and stand next to the rusty metal swings, watching the fourth, fifth, and sixth graders bob up and down and behind and before each other, around the gaily painted Maypoles. These happy children would pull and twist long runs of billowy crepe paper into wondrous, multicolored plaits. Afterward, on the edges of thunderous applause from teachers, parents and visiting dignitaries, a wave of elaborately costumed children would rush out onto the grounds in groups of eight and proceed with the square dance. "*Doggone!*" the Superintendent of Schools was heard to exclaim on one occasion. "Y'all do it so good it just makes your *bones* set up and take notice."

Such was the schedule two weeks prior to May first, when Mrs. Boswell announced to our class that as fourth graders we were now eligible to participate in the festivities. The class was divided into two general sections of sixteen each, one group preparing to plait the pole and a second group, containing an equal number of boys and girls, practicing turns for our part in the square dance. I was chosen to square dance; so was Leon Pugh. Gweneth Lawson was placed with the pole plaiters. I was depressed until I remembered, happily, that I could not dance a lick. I reported this fact to Mrs. Boswell just after drawing, during recess, saying that my lack of skill would only result in our class making a poor showing. I asked to be reassigned to the group of Maypole plaiters. Mrs. B. looked me over with considerable amusement tugging at the corners of her mouth. "Oh, you don't have to *dance* to do the square dance," she said. "That's a dance that was made up to mock folks that couldn't dance." She paused a second before adding thoughtfully: "The worse you are at dancing, the better you can square dance. It's just about the best dance in the world for a stiff little bunny like you."

"I want to plait the Maypole," I said.

"You'll square dance or I'll grease your little butt," Mrs. Esther Clay Boswell said.

"I ain't gonna do *nothin'!*" I muttered. But I said this quietly, and mostly to myself, while walking away from her desk. For the rest of the day she watched me closely, as if she knew what I was thinking.

The next morning I brought a note from my father. "Dear Mrs. Boswell:" I had watched him write earlier that morning, "My boy does not square dance. Please excuse him as I am afraid he will break down and cry and mess up the show. Yours truly . . ."

Mrs. Boswell said nothing after she had read the note. She merely waved me to my seat. But in the early afternoon, when she read aloud the lists of those assigned to dancing and Maypole plaiting, she paused as my name rolled off her tongue. "You don't have to stay on the square dance team," she called to me. "You go on out in the yard with the Maypole team."

I was ecstatic. I hurried to my place in line some three warm bodies behind Gweneth Lawson. We prepared to march out.

"Wait a minute," Mrs. Boswell called. "Now it looks like we got seventeen bunnies on the Maypole team and fifteen on the square dance. We have to even things up." She made a thorough examination of both lists, scratching her head. Then she looked carefully up and down the line of stomping Maypoleites. "Miss Gweneth Lawson, you cute little cottontail you, it looks like you gonna have to go over to the square dance team. That'll give us eight sets of partners for the square dance . . . but now we have another problem." She made a great display of counting the members of the two squads of square dancers. "Now there's sixteen square dancers all right, but when we pair them off we got a problem of higher mathematics. With nine girls and only seven boys, looks like we gotta switch a girl from square dancing to Maypole and a boy from Maypole to square dancing."

I waited hopefully for Gweneth Lawson to volunteer. But just at that moment the clever Leon Pugh grabbed her hand and began jitterbugging as though he could hardly wait for the record player to be turned on and the dancing to begin.

"What a cute couple," Mrs. Boswell observed absently. "Now which one of you other girls wants to join up with the Maypole team?"

Following Pugh's example, the seven remaining boys grabbed the girls they wanted as partners. Only skinny Queen Rose Phipps and shy Beverly Hankins remained unclaimed. Queen Rose giggled nervously.

"Queen Rose," Mrs. B. called, "I know you don't mind plaiting the Maypole." She waved her ruler in a gesture of casual dismissal. Queen Rose raced across the room and squeezed into line.

"*Now,*" Mrs. Boswell said, "I need a boy to come across to the square dancers."

I was not unmindful of the free interchange of partners involved in square dancing, even though Leon Pugh had beat me in claiming the partner of my choice. All I really wanted was one moment swinging Gweneth Lawson in my arms. I raised my hand slowly.

"Oh, not *you*, little bunny," Mrs. Boswell said. "You and your daddy claim you don't like to square dance." She slapped her ruler against her palm. *Thaap! Thaap!* Then she said, "Clarence Buford, I *know* a big-footed country boy like you can square dance better than anybody. Come on over here and kiss cute little Miss Beverly Hankins."

"I don't like no girls *noway*," Buford mumbled. But he went over and stood next to the giggling Beverly Hankins.

"Now!" said Mrs. B. "March on out in that yard and give that pole a good plaiting!"

We started to march out. Over my shoulder, as I reached the door, I glimpsed the overjoyed Leon Pugh whirling lightly on his toes. He sang in a confident tone:

"*I saw the Lord give Moses a pocketful of roses.*
I skid Ezekiel's wheel on a ripe banana peel.
I rowed the Nile, flew over a stile,
Saw Jack Johnson pick his teeth
With toenails from Jim Jeffries' feets . . ."

"Grab your partners!" Mrs. Esther Clay Boswell was saying as the oak door slammed behind us.

I had been undone. For almost two weeks I was obliged to stand on the sidelines and watch Leon Pugh allemande left and do-si-do my beloved Gweneth. Worse, she seemed to be enjoying it. But I must give Leon proper credit: he was a dancing fool. In a matter of days he had mastered, and then improved on, the various turns and bows and gestures of the square dance. He leaped while the others plodded, whirled each girl through his arms with lightness and finesse, chattered playfully at the other boys when they tumbled over their own feet. Mrs. Boswell stood by the record player calling, "Put some *strut* in it, Buford, you big potato sack. Watch Leon and see how *he* does it." I leaned against the classroom wall and watched the dancers, my own group having already exhausted the limited variations possible in matters of Maypole plaiting.

At home each night I begged my father to send another note to Mrs. Boswell, this time stating that I had no interest in the Maypole. But he resisted my entreaties and even threatened me with a whipping if I did not participate and make him proud of me. The real cause of his irritation was the considerable investment he had already made in purchasing an outfit for me. Mrs. Boswell had required all her students, square dancers and Maypole plaiters alike, to report on May first in outfits suitable for square dancing. My father had bought a new pair of dungarees, a blue shirt, a red and white polka-dot bandanna and a cowboy hat. He was in no mood to bend under the emotional weight of my new demands. As a matter of fact, early in the morning of May first he stood beside my bed with the bandanna in his left hand and his leather belt in his right hand, just in case I developed a sudden fever.

I dragged myself heavily through the warm, blue spring morning toward school, dressed like a carnival cowboy. When I entered the classroom I sulked against the wall, being content to watch the other children. And what happy buzzings and jumping and excitement they made as they compared costumes. Clarence Buford wore a Tom Mix hat and a brown vest over a green shirt with red six-shooter patterns embossed on its collar. Another boy, Paul Carter, was dressed entirely in black, with a fluffy white handkerchief puffing from his neck. But Leon Pugh caught the attention of all our eyes. He wore a red and white checkered shirt, a loose green bandanna clasped at his throat by a shining silver buffalo head, brown chaps sewed onto his dungarees, and shiny brown cowboy boots with silver spurs that clanked each time he moved. In his hand he carried a carefully creased brown cowboy hat. He announced his fear that it would lose its shape and planned to put it on only when the dancing started. He would allow no one to touch it. Instead, he stood around clanking his feet and smoothing the crease in his fabulous hat and saying loudly, "My daddy says it pays to look good no matter what you put on."

The girls seemed prettier and much older than their ages. Even Queen Rose Phipps wore rouge on her cheeks that complemented her pale color. Shy Beverly Hankins had come dressed in a blue and white checkered bonnet and a crisp blue apron; she looked like a frontier mother. But Gweneth Lawson, my Gweneth Lawson, dominated the group of girls. She wore a long red dress with sheaves and sheaves of sparkling white crinoline belling it outward so it seemed she was floating. On her honey-brown wrists golden bracelets sparkled. A deep blue bandanna enclosed her head with the wonder of a summer sky. Black patent leather shoes glistened like half-hidden stars beneath the red and white of her hemline. She stood smiling before us and we marveled. At that moment I would have given the world to have been able to lead her about on my arm.

Mrs. Boswell watched us approvingly from behind her desk. Finally, at noon, she called, "Let's go on out!" Thirty-two living rainbows cascaded toward the door. Pole plaiters formed one line. Square dancers formed another. Mrs. Boswell strolled officiously past us in review. It seemed to me she almost paused while passing the spot where I stood on line. But she brushed past me, straightening an apron here, applying spittle and a rub to a rouged cheek there, waving a wary finger at an overanxious boy. Then she whacked her ruler against her palm and led us out into the yard. The fifth and sixth graders had already assembled. On one end of the playground were a dozen or so tall painted poles with long, thin wisps of green and blue and yellow and rust-brown crepe floating lazily on the sweet spring breezes.

"Maypole teams *up!*" called Mr. Henry Lucas, our principal, from his platform by the swings. Beside him stood the white Superintendent of Schools (who said later of the square dance, it was reported to all the classes, "Lord y'all square dance so *good* it makes me plumb *ashamed* us white folks ain't takin' better care of our art stuff"). "Maypole teams up!" Mr. Henry Lucas shouted again. Some fifty of us, screaming shrilly, rushed to grasp our favorite color crepe. Then, to the music of "Sing Praise for All the Brightness and the Joy of Spring," we pulled and plaited in teams of six or seven until every pole was twisted as tight and as colorfully as the braids on Gweneth Lawson's head. Then, to the applause of proud teachers and parents and the whistles of the Superintendent of Schools, we scattered happily back under the wings of our respective teachers. I stood next to Mrs. Boswell, winded and trembling but confident I had done my best. She glanced down at me and said in a quiet voice, "I do believe you are learning the rhythm of the thing."

I did not respond.

"Let's go!" Leon Pugh shouted to the other kids, grabbing Gweneth Lawson's arm and taking a few clanking steps forward.

"Wait a minute, Leon," Mrs. Boswell hissed. "Mr. Lucas has to change the record."

Leon sighed. "But if we don't git out there first, all them other teams will take the best spots."

"Wait!" Mrs. Boswell ordered.

Leon sulked. He inched closer to Gweneth. I watched him swing her hand impatiently. He stamped his feet and his silver spurs jangled.

Mrs. Boswell looked down at his feet. "Why, Leon," she said, "you can't go out there with razors on your shoes."

"These ain't razors," Leon muttered. "These here are spurs my brother in Bronx New York sent me just for this here dance."

"You have to take them off," Mrs. Boswell said.

Leon growled. But he reached down quickly and attempted to jerk the silver spurs from the heels of his boots. They did not come off. "No time!" he called, standing suddenly. "Mr. Lucas done put the record on."

"Leon, you might *cut* somebody with those things," Mrs. Boswell said. "Miss Gweneth Lawson's pretty red dress could get caught in those things and then she'll fall as surely as I'm standin' here."

"I'll just go out with my boots off," Leon replied.

But Mrs. Boswell shook her head firmly. "You just run on to the lunchroom and ask Cook for some butter or mayo. That'll help 'em slip off." She paused, looking out over the black dirt playground. "And if you miss the first dance, why, there'll be a second and maybe even a third. We'll get a Maypole plaiter to sub for you."

My heart leaped. Leon sensed it and stared at me. His hand tightened on Gweneth's as she stood radiant and smiling in the loving spring sunlight. Leon let her hand drop and bent quickly, pulling at the spurs with the fury of a Samson.

"Square dancers *up!*" Mr. Henry Lucas called.

"Sonofa*bitch!*" Leon grunted.

"Square dancers *up!*" called Mr. Lucas.

The fifth and sixth graders were screaming and rushing toward the center of the yard. Already the record was scratching out the high, slick voice of the caller. "*Sonofabitch!*" Leon moaned.

Mrs. Boswell looked directly at Gweneth, standing alone and abandoned next to Leon. "Miss Gweneth Lawson," Mrs. Boswell said in a cool voice, "it's a cryin' shame there ain't no prince to take you to that ball out there."

I do not remember moving, but I know I stood with Gweneth at the center of the yard. What I did there I do not know, but I remember watching the movements of others and doing what they did just after they had done it. Still, I cannot remember just when I looked into my partner's face or what I saw there. The scratchy voice of the caller bellowed directions and I obeyed:

> *"Allemande left with your left hand*
> *Right to your partner with a right and left grand . . ."*

Although I was told later that I made an allemande right instead of left, I have no memory of the mistake.

> *"When you get to your partner pass her by*
> *And pick up the next girl on the sly . . ."*

Nor can I remember picking up any other girl. I only remember that during many turns and do-si-dos I found myself looking into the warm brown eyes of Gweneth Lawson. I recall that she smiled at me. I recall that she laughed on another turn. I recall that I laughed with her an eternity later.

> *". . . promenade that dear old thing*
> *Throw your head right back and sing* be-*cause, just* be-*cause . . ."*

I do remember quite well that during the final promenade before the record ended, Gweneth stood beside me and I said to her in a voice much louder than that of the caller, "When I get up to Brooklyn I hope I see you." But I do not remember what she said in response. I want to remember that she smiled.

I know I smiled, dear Gloria. I smiled with the lemonness of her and the loving of her pressed deep into those saving places of my private self. It was my plan to savor these, and I did savor them. But when I reached New York, many years later, I did not think of Brooklyn. I followed the old, beaten, steady paths into uptown Manhattan. By then I had learned to dance to many other kinds of music. And I had forgotten the savory smell of lemon. But I think sometimes of Gweneth now when I hear country music. And although it is difficult to explain to you, I still maintain that I am no mere arithmetician in the art of the square dance. I am into the calculus of it.

"Go on!" you will tell me, backing into your Northern mythology. "I can see the hustle, the hump, maybe even the Ibo highlife. But no hillbilly."

These days I am firm about arguing the point, but, as always, quietly, and mostly to myself.

"Good-bye, Good-bye, Be Always Kind and True"

George Garrett (1929–)

Novelist, short story writer, poet, and critic, George Garrett explores, when he turns his imagination southward to his homeland, the lot of Southerners who find themselves in a somewhat disconcerting modern world. Unhappy with the new highway being built across his family's land, Peter Joshman, confined to a rocking chair on his son-in-law's porch as a result of a war injury, devises a scheme in the story "Good-bye, Good-bye, Be Always Kind and True"(1985) that purports to remind travelers hurtling down the new stretch of road that they are part of the flesh-and-blood human community. What happens to that reminder suggests the fragile state of affairs in the modern South.

At first Peter Joshman hadn't known what to make of it all, how to take it. In the beginning came the scouts, surveyors, and engineers, crisp in khaki, their white pith helmets shining, driving state-owned trucks and jeeps, and supported by little galaxies of rodmen and assistants in T-shirts. They came to look at the lay of the land, studied it, measured it, marked it, and departed. Then (and it was not long afterwards) came the axes and chain saws, the bulldozers, and the dynamite. They shook the earth and rattled the windowpanes, jarred cups and glasses on the shelves, troubled old things from their accustomed places and left behind them a clay-colored raw swathe cut through the intense monotonous green of the pinewoods and across the field from west to east, like a new scar, so close he could have thrown a stone from his chair on the porch and landed it in the center with a little puff of dust. After that big machines, the rollers and levelers and graders, hurried through the early spring, smoothing the wound that had been made in his field of vision. There were men in khaki and explorers' helmets again, overseeing, writing and writing on their clipboards, and there were the young men, all lithe arrogance and bronzed bravado as, shirtless in the Florida sun, wheeling their huge machines, laughing brilliantly and shouting profanely at each other, they created a dusty chaos.

Inevitably convicts from the State Camp followed, sweating men, black and white, in gray prison uniforms with their shovels and rakes and pick mattocks, working slowly forward day by day along the smoothed earth, spreading gravel and finally the asphalt (that smelled at first good enough to eat), all under the scrutiny of the squat, relaxed, almost motionless guards who peered squint-eyed from beneath broad-brimmed hats into the glare of light studying the work, cradling their shotguns lightly in their arms like living things. One of the convicts, a trusty probably, had come to the house for a bucket of water and Peter Joshman jabbed with his cane in the direction of the pump.

"What's a man like you doing with a walking cane?" the convict asked him. "You ain't that old, is you?"

"I'm a wounded man."

"Somebody shot you?"

"Sure they did," Peter said. "In the War. I got a wooden leg, but you wouldn't know it."

"No, you wouldn't to look at you," the convict said. "Now you got it made, though, huh? Sit on your ass and draw a government pension."

"This here's my son-in-law's house," Peter said. "This here is his farm. I can't do no heavy work. I can't do much of nothing but sit in my rocker and watch things."

"Well, you going to have something to look at from now on with this new highway."

"I don't know as I can get used to what they done."

"Hell!" the convict said, moving now toward the pump. "After a while you can get used to most anything."

"You don't have to like it though," Peter Joshman said, laughing, surprised to hear himself laughing out loud like that. "No sir, you don't have to like it a damn sight."

They poured sweet thick asphalt and they rolled it and leveled it, and soon it was really a road. Pretty soon the tourists would be coming down it, making a shortcut to the East Coast with its splendid beaches, sun and waves, and the sand as white and fine as sugar there. Peter sat in his rocker, gripping his heavy cane with knuckles whitened from impotent anger, and saw them finish up the job. Some people seemed to like it fine. The children, his grandchildren, and all the devious wolf pack of them from the other farms around, ran when they could with shrill excitement — like a flock of little birds, they were so swift and aimless — around the fringes of all the action. They would be happy to see all the cars come by. And up at Evergreen, the nearest crossroads town, the gas-station owner, the storekeeper, and even the preacher took it for a good sign that now they were going to have a real paved highway passing through. His son-in-law, S. Jay, took it badly. They had gouged out a piece of his land, split one field in two, and though it meant some cash money for him, it meant fencing, too, and crossing the highway to do his work.

"What good does it do me, anyhow?" S. Jay grumbled. "I never go to the beach anyway, except on the Fourth of July."

"Get a new car, Daddy," the children hollered and pestered. "Get us a new car."

"Sure," he replied. "And while I'm at it I might just as well buy me a patch of ground on the moon."

"We could set up a stand by the road," his wife (old Peter's daughter) said. "We could make money selling garden vegetables and fresh eggs."

"This is nothing but a long lonely stretch of straight road," S. Jay answered. "Those folks won't even slow down. They got something else in mind. Fresh vegetables! Eggs!"

"Well, it's an idea."

"Won't anything come of it. Who's going to build you a shack to sell from?"

"And maybe the children could sell ice-cold lemonade."

"Lemonade!" S. Jay snorted. "Oh my God! You don't know nothing about this world, nothing at all."

Still, Peter thought that they ought to do something. It's hard, it's wrong even, he thought, to sit still and watch a great change, something new and something that will never, in one lifetime, be the same again, and not give at least a signal or a sign of approval or discontent. When the cars at last began to come, shiny new ones, and he could see the bright relaxed people in their bright unlikely clothes heading to and from the ocean, hear radios playing, hear the rhythms of their voices and occasionally a burst of their laughter, then he suddenly felt better about the whole thing. That was entirely different, a road with people on it. Suddenly everything was happening. He'd hear them coming, and they'd flash into his view, and tires humming or purring or swishing, and the sun exploding in little balls of brightness off the gloss and chrome of auto bodies, and, for a fabulous instant, he saw them in profile, lean as arrows in flight, going or coming, framed against the green pines, the rich green fields they crossed.

It came to him that he ought to participate, share in some way in the appreciation of that hurtling unbelievable moment of gleaming speed. He wanted to offer his benediction. So, he had the boys, his grandchildren, move the rocker out into the front yard, close to the road, under the shade of a mulberry tree where he could wave at them and they, seeing him, could wave back. They smiled and laughed, shouted or waved in solemn silence, and the children, the children always seemed to catch his signal and return it.

S. Jay was a little angry, even a little ashamed.

"It must be nice," he said, "it must be mighty nice to have nothing to do with yourself but sit by the side of the road and watch cars go by."

And Peter Joshman, in spite of himself, sensitive of his position as a paying guest in the house, lonely, too, fell upon self-pity grimly:

"Lose your leg sometime and see how much you like it."

"S. Jay don't mean any harm, Daddy," his daughter said. "You know how he is."

"Never mind about that leg," S. Jay said. "I don't grudge you a thing. But it seems like you could find something besides just sitting and waving at strangers. What do those folks mean to you anyhow?"

"They cease to be strangers when I see them pass by."

"Listen," S. Jay said. "Those folks are laughing at you. You're a joke."

"It don't do nobody no harm," Peter said. "It does me a whole world of good."

"It isn't even good for you, Daddy," his daughter said, siding at last with her husband. "You ought to sit in the shade of the porch, at least."

"They won't be able to see me from the road."

"Well, why don't you hang up a sign or something?" S. Jay said. "Run up a flag."

"Don't laugh at him, Jay," his daughter said. "It's wrong to make fun of an older man like that."

"He makes fun of hisself."

Still, it was S. Jay who put the notion in his mind. Why not sit comfortable in the shade of the porch and still have a way to communicate with them, the drivers and the riders? How to do this, with wit and wisdom, was his problem. Wisdom, yet; for what stranger, moving however swiftly over whatever strange or alien landscape, where he knows no one, owns nothing, between departure and arrival, is not touched, deeply, by a salute, a sign of some kind coming from a stranger by the road saying *I acknowledge you as flesh and blood, as a creature of dust and breath like myself.* Saying to himself like the children, his grandchildren, saying to himself, to be truthful, like the song they always sing at the end of Sunday school —"Good-bye, good-bye, be always kind and true." But to say this with wit because (and Peter Joshman knew this, though often irascible, embittered too, and, like everyone, self-pitying) he knew that any shared truth needs a disguise. Laughter will do. Otherwise, like Adam and Eve without the wit of fig leaves, the naked truth would shame to the quick.

The beginning was more or less accidental. An old dressmaker's dummy was in the barn from the days when first his wife and then his daughter, now another man's wife and the mother of her own children, sewed for a living. It was an easy thing to dress the dummy in his old-fashioned Army uniform, to place it on a stump at the edge of the road, to rig the right arm something like his own artificial leg so that, sitting on his rocker on the porch, he could at just the right time jerk a cord attached to the dummy's arm. And then up went that stiff right arm to wave in clumsy benediction, bringing in reply almost invariably laughter from the passers-by. Rain or shine, night and day, the wooden soldier sat on the stump and during most of the daylight hours Peter Joshman sat in his rocking chair, alert, attentive.

S. Jay, believe it or not, was tickled.

"What the hell!" he said. "The old man always was a little crazy. At least it keeps him out of trouble."

The children, never surfeited, wanted more of the same. And that was something to do with his evenings, to fashion a whole family to go with the wooden soldier, a plump wife and a child, a Negro servant in a white coat, to seat some, stand the others. What a spectacle when they all waved to you at once as you were passing by! By the end of a year since the road had been opened, this curious gallery was something to look forward to, a landmark almost, almost a work of art.

There were three of them, machines, motorcycles, three drivers, keen- and hard- and brown-faced as hawks, cut like figures from old coins, trim in tight Levi's and glossy leather jackets that caught like sails at the breeze of their speed, and behind them the three girls, each plump-thighed, straddling the lean, agile machines, each, hair blowing like the hair of mermaids in the waves, clinging to the wide-belted waists of the drivers. The road sang beneath them. The landscape fled, glazed, past the wind-whipped corners of their eyes. The sun dazzled off the asphalt in fragments like breaking glass. And the highway was theirs; they owned it, weaving among the placid and safe cars, slashing around and about them as, say, the trout, fine as a blade, moves among the drowned shadows of swans. The road sang for them, tormented, and the conventional landscape shivered and hurtled backwards, unnoticed.

Rounding a curve, the Leader came on a long straight piece of road. It stretched toward the horizon and vanished there, empty, glistening, a holy invitation and a challenge, and, hearing his companions coming behind him, he leaned forward, crouched, and opened up with a great soaring lunge of speed. He grinned, hearing his girl squeal, hearing his friends' and rivals' engines take on the same defiant tone, accepting his dare. Nothing on either side to contend with, only the green, shocked slash pines and ahead the regular pale fields of truck farms, a few shacks, and perhaps what was a few people bunched at one place like clod-footed dummies by the roadside. Give them something to remember, something to talk about, he was thinking, edging close to that side of the road so that he'd shower them with the noise and the dust of his passage. Let them have something to dream about. The leader grinned to himself.

Peter Joshman was dozing. The road had been empty for quite a while. It was late in the day, not late enough for people to start returning from the beaches, but too late for ordinary tourists to be going there. Peter dozed and listened to the bees in the garden, heard a humming in his half-dream—louder and more profound now than the bees, and much nearer—blinked, looked slowly, and then saw the three machines in the very instant of their passing, almost too late to wave. And with a start he jerked his rigging of cords and all the wooden arms popped up at once waving wildly. Startled, the three seemed to explode, shot away from each other, skidded, reeled, whizzed, tilted on the edge of the drainage ditches on either side, amid the clear soprano of girls' screaming, somehow righted themselves unscathed, and resumed their proper course a half mile or so down the road, though he could see, laughing to himself, they were moving much slower now, abreast, in solemn formation going away.

When they reached the gas station at the crossroads called Evergreen, they stopped, pulled up under the shade of the roof, and dismounted. The three girls fled, rubber-jointed as drunks, to the door marked *Ladies*. The Leader leaned back, breathless, against a gas pump and spat into a rainbow smear of oil and grease by his feet.

"Jesus Christ! Did you see what I did?"

"A bunch of loonies!"

"What were they trying to do, kill us?"

"Christ!" the Leader again, recovered, composed. "I thought we was all gone. Liquidated, you know, dead."

They laughed together. Then they asked Smalley, who owned the station, what it was they had seen, and he told them about Peter Joshman and his wooden dummies.

"What is it with him?"

"What's he trying to prove?"

"I wouldn't know," Smalley said. "He sure gets a kick out of it."

"The son of a bitch liked to have killed all of us."

"This must be the first time you boys ever come down this road."

"Yeah, but we'll know all about it coming back."

There came at twilight a summer cloudburst. For more than an hour Peter Joshman had been watching the dark clouds massing, swelling. Just as the sun went down and the whole flat countryside seemed to glow with an inner light, the rain began to fall in rich thick drops, soon pelting the dusty yard, rattling on the roof, shining on the slick road. He watched half-sadly, his forlorn wooden figures, unable to come in out of the rain, standing, sitting, their weathered clothing steaming. Something would have to be done about them. Then he heard S. Jay come into the house by the back door, heavy-footed, stamping his feet, breathing hard from running across the field in the rain, and Peter stood up, stretched, and limped inside for his supper.

"Old-timer," S. Jay said, his wide young white-toothed mouth full of food, "how was your road today?"

"Is it Granddaddy's road?" one of the children asked.

"No, honey," his daughter answered for him. "The road belongs to the state."

"Be nice if it was your road," S. Jay said. "You could put up a tollgate out there. If you charged everybody who went by a dime, you'd be a rich man in no time. Then we could all sit on the front stoop and watch."

"Let's charge everybody ten cents, Granddaddy."

"You could at least charge them to look at your dummies," S. Jay said. "Maybe just ten cents a wave would be a good price."

"You-all hush picking on Daddy," his daughter said. "He loves those dummies."

"Well, that's something, anyway," S. Jay said. "It's nice to know he cares about something."

After the rain stopped it was cooler and Peter sat again on the porch, in the first dark, the first stars, watching the cars coming back. Sometimes if they happened to drive close to the shoulder of the road, their head-lights suddenly picked up the group of wooden figures, bathed them in expensive light, and he in reply gave his cords a pull and blessed those night riders with a lackadaisical wave.

The three, his enemies now, though he had no way to know it, were already on the road, returning. It hadn't been the day it might have been for them. Once they had arrived at the beach, they headed south, leaving the resort town with its motels and neon gardens, its drugstores and bars and camera shops behind them, the rows of cottages along the dunes, troubling the dust of a narrow road which ran along just behind the dunes, past even the forlorn and separate nigger beach and far on to a place where at last even the road ended, came to a circle centered on a huge clump of palmetto, the road ending abruptly at a clump of green growth, higher than any dune. Said to be an old Indian burial mound. They parked their motorcycles out of sight and climbed over the dunes to the beach.

"What did we come down here for?" one of the girls asked. Just like a girl.

"We're going swimming, ain't we?" the Leader said.

"I thought . . ." the girl answered. "But I didn't bring my bathing suit. I thought you said we could rent one."

"You know something," he said. "Neither did I."

The others laughed, but laughter did not work at all. With one of the girls reluctant, unpersuadable, the other two were forced by some immemorial tribal custom to side with her, to come to her defense, and in the end the three girls sat on the dunes and smoked and chatted with each other while the three young men frolicked, halfhearted, in lean tan naked exhibition amid the crisp surf. There was no hope for them and, after a while, the men, feeling foolish now, dressed and started back, grim, frustrated.

When they reached the resort town again, they met at a red light.

"That sonofabitch!" the Leader said.

"Who?"

"That bastard with the dummies by the road."

So with a mounting rage against the injustice of this afternoon, the three drivers, hating the hands now that clung to their belts, hating the rich, unseen knowledge of blown hair behind them, drove back the way they had come. It had been raining and the highway was slick and thrilling. They frightened their rivals in fat cars, forced them to clear the way.

Peter Joshman must have heard them coming. It was a solemn unison of buzzing sound that preceded the grim trinity of avengers as they came, slowing down as they passed through Evergreen, looking for their victims, three lights as bright and single as the Cyclops' furious eye, in formation as if passing in review. He must have heard them before he saw them and may have guessed then, for the first time, what was going to happen. Anyway, he didn't move. What could he do? From aimless, really impersonal malice like that of the trench mortar that shredded and took away his leg, there was no moving, only a waiting to suffer or, by sheer luck, to be saved. He may even have closed his eyes and not seen them when they stopped and fell on the foolish wooden figures in the dark. Shouting, cursing as they stripped off clothing, they broke the wooden bodies to pieces, stamped heads into the dust.

S. Jay heard them, though, and came out of his bedroom in his undershorts roaring, across the porch in one long-legged leap, his shotgun bursting forth, both barrels at once, an orange choleric mushroom against the astounded night sky, hitting nothing, or nothing important (one of the girls squealed like a frightened pig, but maybe it was nothing more than the noise and the shock of bird shot in the air). He ran toward them then, as they clambered on the motorcycles, stamped furiously on starters, cursing them as they fled down the road, knelt to reload, kneeling among the shattered corpses of the figures and the debris, the stuffing, glass eyes and torn clothing, but he was too late. Still in a rage, S. Jay fired again high and pointlessly into the trees, and the leaves sighed. He came back to the house slowly, dragging his gun butt in the dust.

"Sonofabitches!" he said. "Old-timer, they wrecked all your dummies."

"Maybe it's just as well."

"What do you mean, *just as well?*" S. Jay yelled at him. "It's my land, ain't it? I'll kill the son of a bitches if they ever come back."

"I say maybe it's just as well," Peter said. "It was a crazy idea in the first place. I let it get a hold to me and started to care too much. Nothing is worth caring that much about."

"I can't figure you out for the life of me," S. Jay said. "Ain't you going to try and fix them up again?"

"I don't know," Peter Joshman said. "I'll sleep on it."

from *Keeper of the Moon: A Southern Boyhood*
Tim McLaurin (1954–)

Raised in the midst of whites, blacks, and Indians in western North Carolina, Tim McLaurin draws his readers into a world defined by hard work, fast times, and the promise of religious redemption. Prompted by the appearance of Lawrance Williams, an old black friend of the family, at his father's funeral, McLaurin traces the trajectory of his friendship with Lawrance Junior in his autobiography *Keeper of the Moon* (1991). As we witness the slow deterioration of their relationship, we are reminded of the fragility of childhood bonds.

L awrance Williams stood to himself toward the back of the crowd, a single, lean black man, dressed in a black suit and white shirt. I had not seen him in years, but recognized him immediately. I was walking at the front corner of my father's coffin, a brother holding to each of the other corners, two uncles grasping the brass handles on each side. We were laying the old man to rest. One of his last requests had been that his sons carry him to the earth.

The grave was cut clean into the lawn: a green tarp had been fitted perfectly to cover the raw dirt. I knew we must set the coffin on top of the pulley structure, that I must not let my leg go into the hole, or trip and tip my end. I tried to ignore all the faces. Probably two hundred friends and family were gathered on that bright July day, but as I planted my feet carefully, I thought of Lawrance, remembered his son and how in my youth we had been close friends. It struck me that little had changed. We share the South now publicly, eat together, even marry, but there is still a distance, a final separation that will never end.

I called him LJ, for Lawrance Junior, a wiry black kid who lived a half mile down the road. We were of the same age and grade. The Williamses lived in a rambling, wide-porched unpainted house that sat under a huge willow and several large oaks. Their seven kids rose in age like stair steps. Our fathers were both laborers by trade who worked farming on the side, our mothers about the same age, women who could wring a chicken's neck with a baby in one arm. Socially and economically, our families could not brag above each other, except for the fact that the Williamses were black. I called LJ's father Lawrance. LJ called my father Mr. Reese.

LJ lived just off the edge of civilized, white earth. The paved road stopped just beyond our house, and with the end of the tar stopped mail delivery, the telephone line, and school-bus service. In the mornings in winter when the weather was good, we often met on the road beyond my house to wait for separate buses to the segregated schools we attended. Our ages were similar, Mabel the oldest sister, Sheryl an older brother, LJ, Kareen, Jackie, a baby or two that stayed home. We usually carried bag lunches to school, mine filled with a bologna sandwich on white bread, maybe a banana and vanilla wafers with peanut butter, a nickle buried in my pocket for milk. LJ's sack smelled of home-cooked biscuits split with salt pork. We wore clothes that looked similar, a match and mismatch of originals and hand-me-downs. Both our noses tended to run during cold weather, our lips would chap from the wind. I sometimes used a tube of Chap Stick, making ceremony as I coated extra on the corners of my mouth. I never offered him any and he never asked. We would talk, skip rocks, or hug ourselves for warmth until our separate buses came. His bus, a fixed-up hand-me-down from the white school system, usually came first, for it had a greater circuit to cover. The windows would be slam full of dark faces all pressed toward me when his bus stopped, all ages because the black school went from first to twelfth grade. He'd wave goodbye and step inside, jostle for seating along with his brothers and sisters. Winters we were only roadside acquaintances, both of us too busy staying warm to really be friends.

The coming of summer vacation brought down the barriers of clothes and color. As the sun deepened, my own skin turned darker like LJ's, both our heads were cut close of hair. The distinction of what bus we rode to school or the quality of our clothes lessened until a parity was reached where we were basically just two kids with idle time. Maybe it related to our common age and grade, maybe similar interests, but for several years, LJ and I were close friends. The other members of our families played together, but they were of mostly opposite sex, a barrier not tampered with in that era in the rural South. LJ and I roamed the woods and fields like wild creatures.

Neither of us cared to play the role of Jungle Jim when we were "natives" hunting wild game in the pine-thicket jungle that bordered my house. LJ, myself, my younger brothers, we'd strip down to only our briefs, and for hours we'd hunt the imaginary lion and rhino that inhabited those brushy twenty acres. We spoke in grunts and hand sign except for when only words would do, and were content to be equal warriors. In my mind, Jungle Jim was a sissy for wearing boots and a hat and I wanted no part of him.

Our weapon of choice was a spear cut from a reed. Sliced off at the base and trimmed of the leaves, the long, thin stems whistled a straight path through the air, and if honed with a pocketknife or piece of broken bottle, would stick end first into the ground. They were quite capable of putting out an eye.

Occasionally when game was scarce, we'd ambush the traffic that used the road through the pine thicket. In those days a car came along seldom, more likely a tractor or someone on foot. We'd follow at the woods' edge, make noise, flash our spears, and then retreat. We were being unusually bold the day we spied a pickup coming, the four of us massing at the edge of the ditch, spears raised.

We were in full war paint. I had acquired a dog-eared copy of *National Geographic*, and we had used natural resources at hand to mimic the garb of a real African tribe. Red clay mixed with water, purple poke salad berries, a tube of old lipstick I'd found lying behind our couch, fresh skullcap haircuts—we looked as if pulled from under a log in the deepest jungle of Zaire. As the truck approached, we lifted our spears and crouched, and as it was passing, slung our arms forward, pretending we had launched our spears. We grinned broadly at a white man driving the truck.

Our arms had hardly stopped moving forward when the man driving the truck locked brakes and slid sideways in his effort to stop. He opened his door and stood on the running board. I recognized him as a man who lived a few miles down on the dirt roads beyond our house, the father of several ragged children who seldom got on the school bus. He glared at us for a moment, his jaw swelled with a plug of tobacco.

"You throw at my truck again, nigger, I'll cut your goddam throat," he said.

We all stood in silence.

"You hear me, jig? I seen you sling that rock."

LJ gave me a sidelong glance. "We didn't throw nothing, mister," I answered.

"That little nigger did. Rock or something. If it had dented my truck, I'd be rolling his black ass in the dirt right now."

"He ain't no nigger," I heard my voice say.

"He's blacker than the inside of my asshole. What y'all doing playing half-naked with a nigger, anyhow?"

For the life of me, I couldn't see a hair of difference between LJ and myself. Every exposed inch of skin was covered with either mud or berry juice. The man spit once on the road.

"You boys, I know your daddy. He wouldn't like you running around trying to act like a nigger. The nigger can't help it, but y'all can."

He slid back under the steering wheel and roared off. We never ambushed cars again.

At that early point in our lives, the end of the paved road between our houses seemed to divide our lives more than color. Not only did the mail service and telephone lines stop there, but so did the amenities that a few dollars a week difference in our fathers' salaries made possible. In the early years, I don't believe LJ envied my lighter shade of skin, but it was obvious he coveted my access to a bologna sandwich on white, store-bought bread with mayonnaise.

"It got to be on light bread," LJ stated emphatically. "Not no corn bread or biscuit."

"We got three loaves of white bread," I assured him.

"Mayonnaise too," he continued. "You sure y'all got mayonnaise?"

"There's a jar full."

LJ's eyes sparkled as he reconsidered the proposal. A whole bologna sandwich made with two slices of light bread and plenty of mayonnaise, in exchange for mowing the grass in our front lawn. Deal!

In a family blessed with an abundance of stale bread, sliced bologna was a staple of life. The exchange of a second-class sandwich for two hours of LJ's labor was an easy agreement for me. I wondered at his eagerness: his own lunches of smoked pork on homemade pan bread looked especially hot and crusty and good.

"You got to cut close to the fence too," I reminded him. "So the cows won't lean over the wire."

"I'll cut it. Let's go 'fore the sun gets any higher."

I studied the sun, and considered that my father didn't really care who mowed the grass as long as it was done. He wouldn't know, anyhow.

I'd stretch out in the shade of a tree while LJ labored behind the splay-wheeled lawn mower, his dark skin running with creeks of sweat. Occasionally I'd rise and direct him to a spot he'd missed. The air would fill with the good smell of clipped clover and fescue, toads and insects would flee the path of the steel tornado. In the shortened grass, my brothers and I would rediscover baseballs, dog-chewed Frisbees, a fork or spoon or top. At last, LJ would mow over the last spot, he'd pull the lever that shut off the gas, and again we'd hear birds, the whine of the radio from where my older sister danced inside. He'd brush off the grass that had clung to his sweaty legs, the crease of a grin turning up the corners of his mouth. He wouldn't mention the sandwich, and neither would I, but we'd start for the back door.

I think he enjoyed seeing the sandwich made almost half as much as eating it. He'd follow me as I took a loaf of bread from a shelf on the cabinet and laid it on the table, then to the refrigerator where a large jar of A&P mayonnaise sat cooling, the bologna one of those large economy packages, thick-sliced. He'd prop on his elbows and watch while I unscrewed the jar lid, laid out two slices of bread—never, never an end piece—took a spoon, and began lathering the mayonnaise on.

"Add little more to dat slice," he'd usually advise me.

When the proper amount of mayonnaise gleamed on each slice, I'd lift a piece of bologna from the package and peel off the casing around the edge. LJ savored the casing, would pull it between his teeth and scrape off the skim of bologna. He would insist that I center the slice of meat between the bread, no edges hanging off, and place the top slice of bread on carefully, not mash the imprint of my hand. The result wouldn't have excited a hobo, but LJ found it exotic.

He drank his water before eating, two glassfuls straight out the cold-water faucet in the kitchen. While I was the sandwich architect, drawing the water was his privilege. He was fascinated by the frothy water that gushed from the spigot. It tasted slightly of plastic pipe and had warmed in its long travel from the ground—in my opinion, it was a poor second to the pump water that gushed cold and clear in his backyard. He'd drink down two full glasses, never pausing while his throat pulsed. Then we'd go outside and sit in the shade, and he'd eat the sandwich slowly with small bites, rolling the sticky mass over his tongue, straining it well between his teeth and gums. The sweat would have dried now on his arms and legs like gullies cut through the film of dust. He'd chew slowly, thoughtfully. I'd feel guilty knowing that in an instant I would trade him two sandwiches for one of the fat, homemade biscuits filled with salt pork that he disdained.

As the world moved into the sixties and our radio was replaced by a television, I became increasingly aware that a war was beginning between whites and blacks.

"You mark my words, somebody's gonna put a bullet through his head," my Uncle Jesse said. "People ain't gonna listen to such talk."

We were eating fried Virginia mullet, my dad and his older brother watching the television news as Martin Luther King paraded down a street backed by several hundred young blacks. The Porter Waggoner show had just ended, his twangy guitar and voice replaced by the oiled speech of a young Dan Rather. I was ten years old and stared uneasily at the television at signs and placards held aloft, demanding equal rights, blacks in clean,

pressed clothes huddled together while surrounded by groups of angry white people.

"It ain't nothing but Communists," my father said. "Trying to stir up trouble. You look at Lawrance Williams right down the road there. Now, I respect that man. He works, looks after his family. You won't see him out there acting like that."

"The nigger needs a bullet," Jesse said, his eyes narrowing as King spoke into a microphone.

"Y'all hush that kind of talk in front of the children," my mother exclaimed.

"Well, it's the truth," my uncle continued. "Somebody'll get him."

After supper my brothers and cousins and I were herded outside while the adults enjoyed a cup of coffee. Twilight was settling, doves beginning to call, a few early bats swooped for insects. One of my older cousins thought of the game, and soon we were all lined up, marched in goose step, chanting "Equal rights" over and over. The parade wound through the yard, circling trees and moving along the edge of the road. Soon we were laughing so hard we could barely walk.

I spied LJ from the corner of my eye, and my laughter caught like a burr in my throat. He stood on the far side of the road, staring straight into my face, his arms straight by his side. I stopped, and the marchers passed m by and continued on, still goose-stepping, still shouting. LJ turned at th moment and began walking toward his house, but I ran to him and caug him by the arm.

"You want to cut the grass tomorrow?" I blurted. "The grass is gett high, and you can cut it if you want. We got plenty of bologna."

"Maybe I cut it," he said, staring at the line of marchers now roun the corner of the house, their chant of "Equal rights" drowning ou animal calls of twilight.

"It needs cutting," I assured him. "My dad was complaining ab today. Mama brought home a new package of bologna just this afterr

We parted with goodbyes in the tepid air of that early evening breach of trust had been committed and was the first crack in our against time and change.

In rural North Carolina, white was king, but being pure black sidered higher than the jumble of blood and genes that consti members of the Croatan Indian tribe.

"They all mixed up, ain't black, ain't white, might be anythin me the day a beat-up panel truck showed up at our farm to drill

A rawboned brown man with matted hair, a wide nose, and pale green eyes began unloading his tools. He was helped by two boys about my and LJ's age, mongrel-looking kids, part black and part white, a little Indian thrown in, their features muddled together as if God hadn't given their mold much thought.

"What y'all be, anyway?" LJ asked one of the kids. Their father drove a pipe inch by inch into the ground.

"Indians," one said, picking at a scab at the corner of his mouth.

"Indians?" LJ said, disbelief rising in his voice. "I never knowed there was Indians around here."

"We Indians for sure."

The only Indians I was familiar with were the ones in western movies, lean, painted men with long narrow noses and shoulder-length straight black hair.

"I'm a black man," LJ said, sounding very boastful to be only ten. "There ain't no doubt I black. But I never known there to be Indians round here."

The boy picked his scab, his eyes jerky and nervous. "We Croatan Indians."

LJ stared at me, his eyes saying that maybe he and I were different, but at least we were pure in our race. But here were two lowbrows, trying to pass as something they weren't.

"Well, we Indians. You ask my dad."

LJ stared at the kid, and in his black, glistening eyes I observed deep thought. "I always thought Indians, they run real fast and jump like deers."

The Croatan pushed out his bottom lip. "Yeah, we pretty fast."

"I bet I'm faster than you," LJ answered.

"Might be," the older kid answered. "But we pretty fast. Can jump too."

"I got a quarter in my pocket says I'm faster," LJ answered.

I was surprised at his bet. LJ did have a quarter, but I knew he was saving it for going into town. He was not the kind of person to challenge others unprovoked. LJ looked to see where the kids' father was, then pushed the matter further.

"What you say, Tonto? I bet ya a quarter I can beat you from that tall pine over there to that big gum tree."

I don't know if the Croatan kid really had a quarter, but his pride made him accept the bet. His father was busy driving the pump pipe, and paid us no attention when we started for the pine thicket. Within a couple of minutes, we had shed our sneakers and were lined up at a starting gate I had scratched in the soft dirt.

"We race all the way to that tree, now, ya hear?" LJ instructed. "Don't count 'less you pass that tree."

My legs trembled from excitement. We argued for a moment over who was going to say go, then finally decided that I would toss a stick into the air. When the stick hit earth, it was every man for himself.

I slung that stick high as I could. Four sets of eyes watched it tumble end over end, four sets of legs cocked, arms ready to pump forward. The stick struck ground with a thud and we came off that line, our toes snatching the dirt and throwing it backwards in a shower. We were pretty evenly matched, and for the first fifty yards were dead even. As the finish line grew closer, LJ and I held back and let the Croatans gain on us. The older boy glanced to his side and saw we were failing, grinned, and kicked his legs and arms even harder.

Months before, we had dug a hole in the edge of the pine thicket at the base of the gum tree. The hole was head-deep and big around as a bed. Just the day before, we had carefully covered the hole with reeds, then a layer of pine straw in hopes of trapping a rabbit. The two Croatans hit the hole running wide open.

Both kids were swallowed whole by the earth. I heard the crisp snap of reeds as they fell through, then two solid thuds as their momentum slammed them against the far wall of the hole. I heard only silence for a second, then the wail of the younger kid. LJ and I peered into the trap. We laughed like hyenas. Both kids were on their knees at the bottom of the hole, pine straw clinging to their clothes. The oldest kid appeared to have had the wind knocked from his lungs, for he was moving his mouth in silence, his eyes squinted as if he too was trying to cry. His brother was wailing now, his hand held to his forehead. They looked pathetic, but we laughed and pointed. The older kid finally got his wind and began cussing a streak as talented as would a grown man. He squinted up at LJ and said, "I'll get you, you black son of a bastard."

As the two Croatans tried to climb out of the hole, LJ and I stomped at their hands and kicked dirt down in their faces. The two kids scrambled and dived at us, but the hole was deep to the crown of their heads, the sides carved straight, the dirt slick from frequent summer rain. They cussed us as we ran around the edges of the hole stomping back their attempts at escape. LJ came up with the ultimate humiliation.

At a sudden, anguished cry from one of the Croatans, I looked up to see that LJ was peeing on him. Standing slightly spread-legged, penis in hand, he directed a stream of urine on the older boy's head. In my heart, I knew it a shameful act, one that God would write down, that my mother would take up switch for. I hesitated not one second, but directed my own urine on the head of the younger kid. Broken, both of them slumped in the bottom of the hole, their curses now rent with huge sobs. The dirt we had kicked in their faces ran in dirty brown rivers. When our bladders were empty, we forced out the last drops, then sprinted for the safety of the deep pine woods where we knew even Tarzan couldn't find us. When we emerged at early evening, the Indian man had set the pump, loaded his tools and sodden boys, and gone. My mother was not waiting for me with a stick. The two boys had had either too much pride or shame to tell on us. We didn't use the fort for several days afterwards. It smelled of urine and guilt.

But in a couple of days, I had forgotten my shame. I excused our actions as necessary to defend our home turf. But later that same summer, another incident happened, something private and unknown to anyone but myself, that proved my own heart was infected with the concept that other human beings might be inferior to me for the matter of their skin colors.

My parents had driven seventy miles down to South Carolina to a quick, cheap dental clinic to get a set of false teeth made for my dad. We were left for the day in the care of LJ's older sister, Mabel. She was an olive-skinned girl in her mid-teens, quiet and studious, and was later to move north and attend college.

Lunchtime came, and she fixed us banana sandwiches as instructed by my mom. She laid on the table slices of light bread and lathered each in turn with a coating of mayonnaise. I had to tell her how to cut the bananas — not in slices like coins, for they slide out, but in lengths like planks. She complied. I doubt she had ever made a banana sandwich before, had ever wanted one. She finished each sandwich and laid it on a plate, then poured glasses full of cold, fresh cow milk. The buzz of talk and argument among us ceased as arms moved to fill our mouths.

I had lifted my sandwich and taken my first bite when I noticed the print of her fingers mashed in the soft bread. No dirt, just a ghost left where her slender fingers had closed the halves. I stared at the bread, chewed what was in my mouth, and felt it grow larger and larger.

She had touched my food. Plain and simple. I had watched her wash her hands with soap before starting to make the sandwich, a hundred times I had eaten at LJ's house — plates of collard greens, corn bread, side meat — but she had physically touched my food, the evidence staring at me in the soft belly of bread.

I could not swallow. The wad of banana and bread grew in my mouth until I thought I might gag. I bolted from the table and hurried through the back door and went around the corner of the house. I backed into the refuge of a fig bush, squatted, and spit the food from my mouth. Joe, the hound, had followed me from the porch. He sniffed the white glob, then without hesitation bolted it down. I fed him the rest of the sandwich. I heard Mabel calling me from the steps and returned.

"I had to go to the bathroom," I lied, hoping my embarrassment did not show in my face.

"Where your lunch?" she asked. "You already eat your lunch?"

"Yeah," I lied. "It was good."

She smiled, laugh lines creasing her pretty face. "You gonna get a tummyache. Bolt your food worse than a dog do. You want another sand-wich?"

I vigorously shook my head. "I'm full."

The hunger I felt that afternoon was small compensation for the shame that gnawed me.

The autumn of 1969 when the completion of a new high school ended segregation, LJ discovered Black Power. Whether powered by the hor-mones of being fourteen, by daily confrontation with a majority of hostile whites, or simply by the appeal of belonging to a movement that was pop-ular and exciting, he changed. I'd see him in the halls at school, but our hellos became increasingly brief. He wore his hair longer, Afro-style, took to dressing in red, black, and green, adopted the black soul shake. The fol-lowing summer, we saw little of each other. He spent more and more time in Fayetteville, removed from the tobacco fields and outhouses of his youth, I had discovered girls and sports. The few times we did meet on the road or visited each other's house, our conversation was measured and forced, no thought given to roaming the fields and woods again.

In my junior year in high school, we had race riots. I had become a star athlete and the pack leader of a group of guys who drank beer and made grades just minimal enough to stay in school. I considered the riots great fun—classes were disrupted, police roamed the halls. LJ was among a core group of blacks demanding certain grievances be addressed. They wanted more blacks on the Student Council and a black to run for Homecoming Queen. Between classes I saw him in the hall and proposed that he and I keep both sides of the argument stirred-up, that with a little prompting we might even get the school closed down for a few days. His bewilderment made me realize then how totally different we had become. I considered the riots a joke—to him, they were a matter of basic right and wrong.

I was graduated from high school and discharged from the Marines when I heard of LJ being accused of raping a white woman. According to the paper, he and two other black men had picked up a woman downtown and carried her to an isolated gravel pit where he and I swam as kids. In court, the woman was proved to be a prostitute, the rape a business deal that had gone sour. LJ was acquitted. He went north to live. I hope his memory has been kind and that he has been able, as I, to recall that time early in our lives when for a brief few years, we ignored racial, cultural, or social differences and accepted each other simply as friends.

I thought of LJ and of those simple early summers while the preacher spoke of my father and of the rewards of the dead. I avoided looking at the flower-draped coffin by staring at Lawrance. He shifted his weight from leg to leg, his eyes trained on a space of ground as if his thoughts too were remembering a better time. I made up my mind that I would go to him following the prayer and tell him how I appreciated him coming, inquire about LJ and the rest of his family. But when the final prayer ended, we were hustled toward the big black car. I reached out my arm and shook Lawrance's hand and said I was glad to see him. But I did not tarry, people were watching and waiting. I got in the limousine and closed the door against the world.

"The Decline and Fall of the Episcopal Church (in the Year of Our Lord 1952)"

Peter Taylor (1917–1993)

A Tennessee native, Peter Taylor enjoyed a childhood of privilege as the grandson of prominent lawyer-politicians and the son of a successful lawyer-businessman. Educated at Vanderbilt University and Kenyon College, where he studied under John Crowe Ransom, Taylor's fiction explores the upper-middle-class South he knew well. His fictional characters, like Mr. Thurston Roundtree in "The Decline and Fall of the Episcopal Church" (1993), often appear uncomfortable in a modern South where social status and order appeared tenuous at best. Employing an understated style, Taylor focused on the effects of time and changing circumstances on Southern families. He was awarded the Gold Medal for Fiction in 1979 by the National Academy of Arts and Letters.

Tom Elkins was sitting on Mr. Thurston Roundtree's front porch, uninvited. Moreover, he was about to say a kind of thing he didn't often say. He said, "Mr. Roundtree, sir, it's your decision." Such directness wasn't customary in the talk between the two men. An inevitable silence followed. During the silence old Mr. Roundtree didn't look at Tom Elkins. The old man was sitting alone at one end of the porch swing. Every now and then he would give himself a push with the toe of his soft-sole house slipper. And all the while he kept his eyes fixed on some point far down in the lawn beyond the area where the largest clump of white lilac bushes grew.

After a minute or so had passed, still not looking at Tom Elkins, the old man said, "So far as any decision from me is concerned, I made it years ago. It didn't matter, though. I didn't care, of course. But all the same the church wasn't doing any harm, Tom."

"It was a hazard, Mr. Roundtree," said Tom, returning to his usual tone of inexhaustible patience with people. He was a lawyer who was not very effective in the courtroom but who had a reputation for being very persuasive in private consultation, very effective in negotiated settlements. As a member of the town council he had, during the past two years and more, spent a good many hours on Mr. Roundtree's front porch, uninvited.

"Yes, Tom, the church was a hazard," Mr. Roundtree consented, still continuing to gaze off into the shady lawn which stretched away in grassy undulations toward the narrow macadam street. Mr. Roundtree's old house was set at least fifty yards back from the street, and besides the clumps of lilacs and yellow jasmine and Christmas honeysuckle there were a half-dozen or so old forest trees that broke the monotony of the lawn's gentle roll. "The church was a hazard, Tom," said Mr. Roundtree, "a hazard to those who went snooping around inside when they had no call to be there." Until this point the old man had continued to gaze off into the lawn. Then, seeming to realize how harsh and unfeeling he sounded in the light of the boy who had been badly hurt falling from the gallery of the abandoned church and the hobo who was found dead behind the altar rail two years before, Mr. Roundtree did look directly at Tom. But he looked with raised eyebrows that seemed to say, Now, see what an ugly thing you have driven me to saying? Now, see the position you have forced me into? The old gentleman was known for his kindliness and tolerance and for his philosophical acceptance of most of the changes he had seen in the world. He was generally regarded as being different from the rest of the old-timers in town. Yet he was a man of firm character—nobody ever doubted that —and in all matters pertaining to the old church building he had taken a firm, an almost obstinate stand. He had taken a firmly and obstinately indifferent stand, that is to say, in a case where some expression of bias might have made things a bit easier. Even Tom Elkins, the very soul of personal consideration and long-suffering patience with other men, was driven to the wall in this case. It was not often in his career that Tom had said anything so severe and so final-sounding as "Well, Mr. Roundtree, sir, it's your decision" — either to a client of his own or even to the "other party" in a case.

The church in question had been an Episcopal church — an "Episcopalian" church most people called it. Its congregation, never large out there in that little West Tennessee town, had so diminished during the first years of the present century that services were finally discontinued. At last the old building fell into such a bad state of repair that — after a number of unfortunate incidents — the town council condemned the property and had the structure torn down. This action took place more than thirty years ago — back in the middle twenties — and it was only a few weeks after the actual demolition that Tom Elkins came to sit on Mr. Roundtree's front porch, that afternoon, for their final consultation.

Mr. Thurston Roundtree was not only the sole surviving vestryman of the vanished St. John's; after the death of his spinster sister, three or four years previously, he had become the only member of the otherwise dispersed congregation still living in the town of Blackwell. In later years, other Episcopalians have moved into Blackwell, and a new, very tiny church has been built on the outskirts of town. But the new Episcopalians are different from the old sort that used to be there. One feels that they are all converts from other denominations. One feels this even about the Episcopal rector himself, nowadays. And the services in the new church are so high that they seem almost Roman. At any rate, as sole survivor of the old Episcopalians, Mr. Roundtree was the man the town council had consulted during every step of the condemnation and demolition pro-ceedings. He had not made difficulties for them in any legal way. He had not written to the diocesan headquarters in Memphis, where some claim to the property might have been made. And he had not tried to get in touch with former parishioners of the church who were scattered about the country. He had made no formal protest whatsoever. But every time Tom Elkins was sent to see him he would only say, "If I were you, Tom, I'd just let the old church stand. It doesn't matter to me, though. I don't care, of course. But it's doing no harm." If only he had said it mattered. If only he had said he cared. Then some kind of settlement might have been arranged, and everybody's conscience would have been put to rest.

Even after the town council had employed Sam Flemming and his wrecking crew, even after the work of destruction was underway, Mr. Roundtree said nothing. And yet while the building was coming down he disturbed many people by going each day to stand quietly for several hours under a rangy black walnut tree across the street from the church. Although his presence didn't seem to disturb Sam Flemming or Sam's rough crew of men, the sight of him there worried all conscientious souls like Tom Elkins when they drove past. Somehow it must have made them feel guilty. Sam Flemming, a great hulking fellow with a fine, manly stom-ach and a shock of black hair as coarse as a horse's mane, would sometimes lean against the clapboard wall of the church, eating his lunch or enjoy-ing a plug of tobacco, and frankly return old Mr. Roundtree's silent stare. They eyed each other across the asphalt street and spoke not a word. Each was as open in his staring as if he thought the other did not see him there. It seemed no embarrassment to either of them that there was no conver-sation, and it was certainly not a question of their not being acquainted. They knew each other as all men in such a little country town know each other, or as they used to know each other in those days.

Yet the way the two men looked at each other perturbed other people who passed by. And Tom Elkins bore the brunt of the general perturbation. Tom was not a married man, but for more than twenty years he had been informally engaged to a fine girl named Emma Broadhead. Literally speak-ing, Emma was no longer a girl, of course, but in a town like Blackwell a single woman will often be spoken of as a girl so long as she continues to receive attentions from any man. It was mostly through Emma that Tom was kept informed of how upset the town was by the two men's silent confrontations. Emma said that what she and others feared was that Sam Flemming and Mr. Roundtree *would* speak and that there would be an ugly incident in which Mr. Roundtree was bound to get hurt. As a responsible citizen and councilman Tom must *not* permit that to happen.

Emma had a very strong sense of social responsibility, and Tom Elkins respected her for it. She had not developed this sense until fairly recent years. It was connected, curiously, to her continuing in the single state. Perhaps it grew out of the gratitude she felt toward friends and neighbors who had cherished and comforted her when they might have ostracized her. For although she had never married Tom Elkins — it was her dying father's wish, a wish which he did not fail to mention in his will, that she remain single and at home as long as her invalid mother lived; and finally it seemed the mother would live forever — although she had never married Tom, she and he had made no secret of their true relationship. Many an early dawn saw one of them leaving the house of the other. And hardly a month passed without both of them being simultaneously out of town for a long weekend. The effect upon Emma was to inspire liberal feelings in her in nearly all matters. And since Tom was a lawyer with vague, if frustrated, political ambitions, she quite naturally came to express her sense of social responsibility in vaguely political terms. She was concerned for the common good and she did not forget the rights of the individual. (It was she, for instance, who had urged the tearing down of the church to protect hoboes and children who wandered in there.) Tom's ineffectiveness in the courtroom and in the rôle of a public speaker was, of course, what served to frustrate his political ambitions. But with Emma's encouragement he had come to see himself as the town's public peacemaker and great conciliator. Emma kept this ideal polished bright for him, and it was her scrupulosity that would not let Tom blind himself to dangers that might lie ahead in the demolition of the Episcopal church. "You must do what you know in your heart is right," Emma said to him. "And what you know in your heart is right is that such matters must not be allowed to drift."

Tom felt quite certain that there would be no real altercation between Mr. Roundtree and Mr. Flemming. The two men, being of very different sorts, were merely curious about each other. But although no altercation ever occurred, there were indeed two occasions when Tom went away as upset as if he had witnessed the ugly incident which Emma and some of her friends feared. Once he had come on the scene when stacks of rotten rafters were being carried out and thrown on a truck. Observing the rotted rafters, Tom had crossed the street to Mr. Roundtree and said cheerfully, "You can't deny that the old place was pretty dilapidated, can you, sir?" And Mr. Roundtree's reply had sent Tom away deeply concerned about the old man's state of mind and perhaps even the state of his soul.

"It wasn't dilapidated," Mr. Roundtree had said, smiling a rather puzzling smile. "It may have been a shambles, but it wasn't dilapidated. It was originally roofed with cedar shingles, its timbers were white oak and heart of pine, and the bricks in the foundation were hard bricks made on my own grandfather's farm, a mile west of town. It was a good building. But still there was no rock in it. The church wasn't built of rock, Tom, and so we couldn't properly say it was dilapidated, could we?"

The old man's smile at that moment bothered Tom more than what he had said. But when he reported the incident to Emma, she paid more attention to Mr. Roundtree's words. Was he merely being pedantic, she asked, or did that business about the rock mean that Mr. Thurston Roundtree had lost his faith? "I think it may have something to do with Miss Jenny," she said, remembering how close the old man had been to his dead sister. Perhaps he was a disillusioned man. Perhaps a secret loss of faith explained his unwillingness either to fight or to condone the condemnation of the church building.

Another time when Tom stopped to chat with Mr. Roundtree under the black walnut tree, something even more upsetting occurred. Tom and Mr. Roundtree had chatted for some five or ten minutes when Tom realized that Sam Flemming had left the work he had been doing with his crew and had come to lean against the wall of the church. The clapboard siding had been mostly stripped away by then, but the old lathing with the thick plaster bulging through in places was still there, and Sam leaned heavily against one of the uprights. Tom resented the man's common stare and he felt somehow that it would be an act of rudeness to Mr. Roundtree for him to acknowledge Sam's presence. While Tom and Mr. Roundtree continued talking, a number of cars passed along the street. Inside the cars were other good citizens of Blackwell, and Tom could see them rubbernecking as they rode by. Presently matters grew worse. Tom realized that Sam Flemming had now come forward and was standing at the curb on the opposite side of the street. At last Tom turned and gave the man what was intended as an angry look. Meanwhile, more cars were passing along the asphalt street between them. Tom felt that the whole town was participating in the moment. He even sensed that certain cars had passed more than once. Then, before he could turn his attention back to Mr. Roundtree, Tom understood that he was about to be addressed by Sam Flemming.

"Tom, tell him," Sam's voice boomed forth, as another carload of rubbernecks passed slowly between them, "tell him if there's a thing or two inside he'd like to have, he can have it—and free. The whole frame of the building will be a-coming down tomorrow or the next day; so let him speak. If there's something he craves, Tom, he can have it." Since all material coming out of the building would belong to him, Sam spoke with genuine authority. He kept his eyes on Tom as he spoke, and when Tom glanced back at Mr. Roundtree he found the old man's eyes also on him —not on Sam. Moreover, the old man pretended that he had not heard what Sam had said. His lifted eyebrows demanded that Tom repeat Sam's offer. Yet when Tom did repeat it, Mr. Roundtree only burst into laughter.

"Why, what in the world would I want with any of it?" he drawled in the most casual, good-natured tone. "What is any of it to me?" And without saying more, he lifted his hat to Tom, gave him the most genial smile, and so took his leave.

Tom Elkins gazed after the old man for a moment as he ambled away up the street. Then he turned back to Sam. Sam seemed still to be waiting for an answer from him. Tom simply shook his head. When he did so, he saw Sam Flemming's face go crimson. Then presently the man turned away and began shouting orders to his crew of workmen. Tom Elkins went and got into his car and drove off to lunch, continuing to shake his head now and again all along the way. He had lunch with Emma at the Blue Bird Tea Room on the public square, and they agreed that all Tom could do was watch and wait.

Only a few days after that, the church was leveled. Neither Tom Elkins nor anyone else observed whether it was on the very day that the demolition job was finished, or perhaps a few days later, that a marble birdbath appeared in Sam Flemming's side yard. Sam lived in an unpainted ramshackle cottage on the main street of Blackwell. Since the widening of that street, back in the twenties, the old cottage with its narrow, bannistered porch was left perched right on the sidewalk with no front yard. When the Depression had come, Sam had bought the place for a song and had moved his family over from the Mill Hill. Two of the town's finest old houses were on either side of him, and they were set back from the street in groves of maples and elms and ancient white oaks. But on Sam's place there were no trees left, and the little bit of a side yard had long since been denuded of grass by the play of Sam's half-dozen children.

Awareness of the birdbath's presence in Sam's side yard dawned slowly on everyone. (Perhaps people usually avoided looking at the run-down place.) And the realization that the new birdbath could be nothing other than the baptismal font from the erstwhile Episcopal church came more slowly still. Or perhaps realization did not come so slowly as it appeared to. At any rate, a good many days passed before anyone spoke to anyone else of what the birdbath really was. Finally Emma Broadhead said to Tom,

"There is no use in our not admitting to each other what Sam Flemming's birdbath really is." Simultaneously other honest souls seemed to have spoken their minds to those nearest them. And when at last the word *was* spoken, it seemed for a time that no one could speak any other word. Tom was made to understand that a sacrilege had been committed that must somehow be righted! The town council was blamed by everybody, and the members of the council were informed that the font must be removed from Sam's yard.

Sam Flemming, however, not resting after the completion of the church demolition, knew his rights. He had contracted to tear down the church for a very small sum and on the condition that all the building materials and all he found inside would belong to him. He had found the font locked in a closet that opened off the sacristy, where the last rector had no doubt placed it for safekeeping against vandals. Sam recognized it at once as a thing of value. His first thought had been of old Mr. Thurston Roundtree. Old Roundtree was a queer duck, and was a man who held himself too high for Sam's liking. He was one of those old-time Episcopalians. You couldn't go to him directly about something like this. But then, with the aid of Tom Elkins, Sam had got his chance to hint to the old man that there was something valuable inside. He was sure the old codger knew what he meant, and yet the man was too proud to meet him halfway. Sam was vexed. He meditated long on how he should dispose of his treasure. Then absentmindedly one night he mentioned it to his wife. It seemed an awful mistake at the time. She was down at the church next morning, calling the thing a birdbath and talking on about how she *would* have it. She wasn't a woman who complained much of her lot and of things she didn't have in life. She worked hard, spent sparingly, and nearly always let Sam have his way about things. But now and then she would forget herself — forget her children even, Sam told her, and forget *him* even — and take a fancy to some pretty piece of foolishness like bantam chickens or inside plumbing, or this birdbath! He didn't mind. He liked it in her except when she carried it too far. Besides, he knew that his work would be finished there at the church within a few days. He might not have a chance to approach old Roundtree again. What else could he do with it, for the moment, but take it home with him?

After the font had been set up in the Flemmings' side yard for only a few days, the wife and the two youngest girls had worked the earth all around it into a circular bed for flowers. How strange that the town was so slow to observe it there. It was not only the Flemmings' first birdbath; it was also the first flower bed the Flemming family had ever had.

Naturally, Tom Elkins was the person to go to Sam Flemming and suggest that the birdbath was bound to give offense to Mr. Thurston

Roundtree, the only surviving Episcopalian. Others had already appealed to Sam on the grounds that it was an offense against religion in general. But Tom knew that Sam was a godless man, and though it was in their behalf that he went to see Sam, Tom knew that the sensitive feelings of the Baptists and Presbyterians and Methodists in Blackwell would not be something to move the man. It was clear to Tom, however, that Sam had some special feeling about Mr. Roundtree and about that old church building. He went to Sam's house and stood on the sidewalk talking to Sam, who sat on the porch with his sock feet on the bannister rail. Tom talked first about how strange it was that Mr. Roundtree had come and watched the church being torn down. Then he said that when Mr. Roundtree had laughed at the idea of wishing to have anything out of the church he must have been only covering up his real feelings. Tom could see that Sam was listening carefully to all he said, but he made no direct reference to the birdbath until he was turning to leave. Even then he said only that it was "bound" to offend the old man, because he could not truthfully say that Mr. Roundtree had voiced complaint. Without taking formal leave, Tom had walked off across the street and was already behind the wheel of his car when he heard Sam call his name. "Tom!" came Sam's resonant voice across the asphalt. He was still seated on the porch and was looking out at Tom between his two black-socked feet on the bannister rail. "Tom, tell him," he called, "tell him he can still have it if he wants it. If he wants it, Tom, and if he sends me word direct, he can have it."

Tom looked back at Sam but made no reply. Behind Sam, in the shadowy doorway to the house, Tom could see Mrs. Flemming. She was a woman of slight build and with dark hair pulled tight back on her head. She stood in the doorway, clearly watching and listening, with one hand raised and resting on the doorjamb.

The result of Sam's offer was, of course, that final consultation between Tom Elkins and Mr. Thurston Roundtree. Tom went the very next afternoon to sit on the old gentleman's front porch. After a respectable preamble, in which the history of the condemnation and demolition of the church was traced once again, Tom at last got round to asking permission to say that he, Mr. Roundtree, would like to own the baptismal font. He asked it in the name of all their fellow Christians, who were greatly offended by the use being made of the font. He told Mr. Roundtree that he was there only in an effort to serve the community, that he was giving time to this business that he ought to be devoting to his own law practice.

But Mr. Roundtree declined to send the word that Sam Flemming required. He would only shrug his narrow, rather humped, old shoulders, smile to himself, and say that it simply didn't matter about the font. In the end, it was really as much the church as the font that the two men were talking about, because from the outset Mr. Roundtree was clearly determined to show the same unconcern for the one as for the other. And after their exchange over whether or not the old church had been a hazard, Tom knew that they were now exactly where they had started two years before. He was inclined now to consider the incident closed. But he wondered if Emma would consider it so.... Surely there was no more he should or could undertake.

But somehow he found himself still unwilling to stir from the big wicker chair on Mr. Roundtree's porch. He was not comfortable in the chair. Little broken sticks of wicker stuck in his back however much he shifted about. And the sight of the toe of Mr. Roundtree's house slipper pushing at the porch floor every so often was now irritating to him. He had found it painful to have to say anything as direct as, "Well, Mr. Roundtree, sir, it's your decision." One didn't say that sort of thing to an old gentleman in Blackwell, Tennessee. And yet now he *wished* to say something that would sound even more insolent. He felt a need to understand Mr. Roundtree's stubborn indifference to the whole affair. He longed to look the old man in the eye and speak the one word "Why?" Yet this was Mr. Roundtree, this was an old gentleman of one of those old-time Blackwell families—one of the old-time Episcopalians.

Tom himself was a Methodist. His mother had been a Methodist and his father a Cumberland Presbyterian. He was one of the regular, easy hybrids that the town was made up of. Emma represented a similar mélange. But the Episcopalians, the little band that once existed in Blackwell, had been different. At this time — the time of the church's demolition — Tom was a man in his early forties, and so he was able to remember back to the turn of the century when there were still enough parishioners to justify services being held at St. John's. What a different breed they had been from their Methodist and Presbyterian contemporaries. They danced and they played cards, of course, and they drank whiskey, and they did just about whatever they wanted on Sunday. They indulged in what their Baptist neighbors called "that barbarous ritual, infant baptism." They starved themselves during Lent, and they attended services on Christmas Day, even when it didn't fall on a Sunday. There were no graven images in the old church, and there was no altar stone, of course, but the Episcopalians had talked about the church as though it were the temple in Jerusalem itself. That was what their neighbors resented. Yes, they always spoke of it as "*the* Church," as though there were no other church in town. They lavished a loving care on the church building that no other church received. It was not merely that they were the richest congregation; they were, in all respects, the most attentive. Everyone else felt that there was something idolatrous in the congregation's affection for and pride in the old building. The grass on the little lot was always neatly cut. If one of the boxwoods that lined the brick walk to the entrance died, it was immediately replaced. The English ivy on the brick foundation and about the front steps was meticulously trimmed. And a great fuss was made about obtaining the right, deep shade of green paint for the window blinds. About the interior there was quite as much fuss made — by the ladies. Somebody was forever doing new needlepoint covers for the kneeling stools or sewing new velvet covers for the altar rail. And there was the somewhat mysterious and embarrassing business about the care of the altar cloths and the polishing of the silver chalice and the candelabra. The care of the church kept the whole congregation busy. And then almost overnight, it seemed—in one short decade—the Episcopalians, all but Mr. Roundtree, either died out or moved away from Blackwell.

Sitting that last afternoon on Mr. Roundtree's front porch, Tom Elkins felt, momentarily, a revival in himself of all the old resentments the town had once had against the Episcopalians — primarily, it seemed now, against their pride in their old church. It was Mr. Roundtree's obstinate indifference to its ultimate decay and destruction that stirred the old feelings. His indifference seemed but the same old pride in a different garment! Suddenly he heard Mr. Roundtree address him. "Tom," the old man began, and then paused. Tom had his eyes focused on the worn toe of the old man's house slipper. He looked up, embarrassed to be caught staring at the threadbare toe of the slipper. But he found he wasn't, after all, caught. Mr. Roundtree was once again gazing off in the general direction of that largest clump of lilac bushes. "Tom," he said, "you see that Corinthian capital on the ground down at the foot of my yard, beyond where those lilacs are? It came off the old courthouse."

Tom couldn't, from his position, actually see the capital but he knew where it was and he knew where it had come from without being told. He knew that Mr. Roundtree had had it put there when the old courthouse was replaced by a modern structure a few years earlier. Without making any effort to see it now, he replied, "Yes, sir, I do."

"I had it placed there," said Mr. Roundtree, still not looking at Tom, "because I have a romantic fondness for ruins. I don't attach any importance to this feeling of mine. But I indulge myself in it so long as it does nobody any harm. And I suppose that's how I felt about the old church, Tom. My feelings had nothing at all to do with religion, of course. Perhaps the building had, after all, become a hazard. I don't know. I simply enjoyed seeing it there. Nothing more or less."

"But, Mr. Roundtree," Tom began, hardly knowing what he was going to say, yet sitting up very straight in his chair as though he were going to make a lengthy objection to the old man's confession. It flashed through his mind that Mr. Roundtree was not telling the truth. Or perhaps the old man was merely trying to end all these months of talk on an amiable note. That was the more likely explanation. But Tom could not let it go at that. The questions in his mind were too pressing. And the opportunity presented was too good to be missed. He fairly stammered out, "But, sir, that church was your house of worship. Wasn't it a sacred place to you? Wasn't everything in it sacred? We—on the council—have been afraid that you would feel—"

But he was interrupted by the intense gaze which Mr. Roundtree settled on him. Simultaneously giving himself a little push in the swing, the old man turned his eyes from the distant Corinthian capital and the lilac bushes to Tom Elkins there on the porch. He looked at him with an amazed and amused expression. "Why, no, Tom," he said, "not at all. No, not at all." And then he actually laughed in just the ironic way he had laughed at Sam Flemming's offer that day. "I suppose it isn't generally known," he then went on, wearing a somewhat more serious expression, as if only now grasping Tom's failure to comprehend. "I suppose it isn't generally known, but at the insistence of my late sister Jenny the Bishop came out here some fifteen years ago and held a little deconsecration ceremony. One couldn't regard the old building as a sacred place after that. It would have been sacrilegious, in the most literal sense of the word. Old St. John's hasn't been a holy place for nearly fifteen years."

Tom sank into his chair, again insensible of the piercing pieces of broken wicker at his back. He could hardly believe what he had just heard. Was the old man trying to make a fool of him? Was this something he had invented to cover up the real truth of the matter? Somehow it didn't ring true. Something was still missing. And yet, after all, that was what Episcopalians *were* like! For them it was as simple as that: the holiness was removed with the wave of that bishop's hand. It was as primitive as that. It was a matter of pure magic. And why hadn't the old man mentioned it before now? Suddenly it seemed plain to Tom that Mr. Roundtree had not wanted anybody to know how little he cared about the church building. He had been laughing at Tom's efforts at conciliation all along, or simply being contrary. Tom yearned to wash his hands of the whole business. He would go to Emma and tell her finally that nothing more could be done, that his conscience as a public servant was clear.

Yet when Tom Elkins rose to leave, Mr. Thurston Roundtree seized his hand warmly and told him to come again soon. He didn't have many visitors, said Mr. Roundtree, and would always welcome a chance to chat with someone as intelligent and as generous with his time as Tom was. The old man even walked halfway down the path toward the street with his visitor. It was as though he were parting from a dear friend. Mr. Thurston Roundtree was experiencing, momentarily, that cordial feeling toward Tom that one inevitably feels toward someone to whom he has confided an old, long-locked-up secret. For, yes, Tom was the first person in Blackwell he had ever told about Jenny's deconsecration ceremony. It was something he was sure other people would not understand, might even interpret as a reflection upon the town. He had himself been strongly opposed to having the ceremony. But Jenny had insisted she was acting, as much as anything else, for *his* own good. In their long years together—an unmarried sister and brother living in the same house—they had got on famously, without any quarrels or squabbles. Yet in the very realm in which they seemed most solidly united there was the one great division between them—that is to say, in their religion. It was simply that Jenny questioned her brother's inner piety and spiritual depth. As they grew older she accused him more and more often of caring only for the ritual, the music, and the general attractiveness of the little church itself. When the church was finally no longer in use, and she and he were forced to travel twenty miles into the next county to attend services, she disapproved of his continuing to see after the upkeep of St. John's. Several times when the bishop was in the next county for confirmations, she threatened to have him over to deconsecrate the building. Each time, Mr. Roundtree would give up having the grass cut for a while and neglect to have broken windowpanes replaced. But then one year he made the mistake of having the window blinds taken down and repainted. That was when she struck the blow. The bishop came, and the building was no longer a church. His sister lived only a few years after that, but she had lived to see his idolatrous spirit broken. He had not imagined how the deconsecration would affect him. But somehow *she* must have known. For from that day forward old St. John's was to him but another of the town's outdated, picturesque buildings. When Jenny lay on her deathbed he had to confess to her that she had been right, that he had cared too much for the mere trappings of religion. He knelt beside her bed, and together they prayed God for forgiveness of His faithful but errant servant, Thurston.

Tom went directly from Mr. Roundtree's to Emma Broadhead's house. "Enough," he said to Emma, "is enough."

But Emma, whose figure was just beginning to acquire a middle-aged heaviness, settled herself in a large chintz-covered armchair, gazed up at Tom with her still girlishly soulful eyes, and said, "I know my Tom better than that."

"But there's no more to be done," Tom tried to insist. "Mr. Roundtree doesn't care a fig for that font."

"It is not Mr. Roundtree's feelings, is it," said Emma quietly, "and not yours or mine, that you are concerned about, Tom. The offense is against the good people of this town. That is what one mustn't forget if one is to serve the community."

"But what more am I to do, my dear?"

"You will have to see Sam Flemming again."

"And what can I say to him?"

"It is not for us women to tell you men what to say to each other. *That* is not our function. *That's* the other side of the coin. You will know what to say."

Tom didn't wait even till the next day to go see Sam. He went that very afternoon. And he didn't talk to Sam from the sidewalk this time. He went up to the narrow porch, without being invited to do so, and sat down beside Sam. He was ready, if necessary, to take off his shoes and put his feet on the bannister rail beside Sam's. He didn't know what the terms were going to be. It had not really occurred to him yet. But he knew he was going to meet them somehow.

Tom sat there on Sam's porch in silence for several minutes. Finally, in an offhand tone, he asked, "What church do you belong to, Sam?"

Sam looked at Tom and grinned. He ran his long, rough fingers through his black hair. Then he leaned forward a little and spat a stream of tobacco juice between his two big toes and out into the gutter beyond the sidewalk. "I call myself a lapsed Free Will Baptist," he said and laughed.

Another silence ensued. Then Tom said, "Is that so?" After a moment he said it again: "Is that so?" He was recalling that Sam and his family had once upon a time attended some church over on the Mill Hill. But they had apparently given up religion altogether since their move. People had supposed that they might begin attending one of the churches in the new neighborhood, but it was never urged on them. "What made you lapse?" Tom asked.

"It wasn't much of a church," Sam said. He spat between his toes again, hitting almost precisely the same mark in the gutter as before. "They were all so bone-ignorant, even the preachers. It was just a lot of talk and shouting and going on, nothing you could put your finger on or spit at." He grinned at Tom again and said, "It was all a lot of loose talk, and I guess I never *was* a good listener with ignorant folks."

"Didn't you ever think of trying another church?" Tom asked. Was it possible that Sam Flemming's conversion to one of the regular denominations might yet be the solution to their problem?

"Not me," said Sam. All at once he took his feet off the rail, slapping them resoundingly on the wooden floor of the porch. And he turned such a suspicious look on Tom that Tom felt sure the man had read his thoughts.

In reply—in denial—Tom Elkins merely shrugged and began examining his fingernails. When an interrogation took a wrong turn, he was the first to sense it. He knew that silence was often the best policy at such a moment. He waited now for something else to occur to him, and it wasn't long in doing so.

"I don't know how you vote, Sam," Tom began cautiously.

Sam looked at him out of the corner of his eye. "I don't vote," he said abruptly. Then after a moment he explained. "My old daddy was a Republican, like his own daddy before him. I don't know how they ever come to be so. But I know, sure God, it never done them no good hereabouts." Sam bent forward over the bannister rail and spat out his chew of tobacco. "Generally speaking, Tom," he then went on, "I don't know much. But I know enough to keep out of politics and to keep to myself what little I know about politics."

"All I was going to say," Tom said, trying to sound reassuring, "is that I guess you do believe that what the majority of people in a place want is what that place ought to have."

"In most matters, I'd say as much," said Sam with a certain caginess in his tone. Presently he touched first one and then the other of the two breast pockets on his denim shirt, feeling for his tobacco. There was none there. He slapped each of his trousers pockets and found none there, either. Since his gestures were self-explanatory, he got up and went inside the house to get a new packet of tobacco without making any explanation to Tom Elkins. In the doorway, as he was returning, he stopped to break off a plug from the new packet he had opened. Easing it into his mouth and masticating slowly and thoughtfully, he gazed out through the screen door at his visitor, who still sat by the porch bannisters, facing the street. The back of Tom Elkins's head, the hair thin on the flat plane of his double crown, struck Sam as just a little bit pathetic. He wondered if the thinning hair didn't come from wearing a hat too much; he smiled slyly at the notion. And the white shirt collar showing above Tom's suit jacket made Sam lift his own chin and twist his neck about. There the poor fellow sat, waiting to ask more questions. There was *nothing* such a fellow wouldn't ask you. Off to his left, Sam could see the marble birdbath in the side yard.

Sam knew, of course, it was the business of the birdbath Tom had come about. It was a bad business, too, and wasn't going to end well for anybody. How could it? From the moment he had got that closet door open, at the church, and had first laid eyes on it he knew it had some kind of worth— some kind he couldn't put his finger on, couldn't spit at. The wife hadn't had to tell him that. He knew *that* before the wife had ever come down to look at it and name it a birdbath. Both before and after she saw it he had tried his damnedest to get Old Roundtree to claim the thing. He hadn't for a moment kidded himself about *giving* it away. Whatever the thing was worth to Old Roundtree, Old Roundtree would have paid in full—of his own accord. That's the sort of gentleman the old man was, but somehow the old man was fouled up about whatever was connected with that church. Just how and why was beyond knowing. But it was plain now that he wasn't ever going to take the birdbath off Sam's hands. That's what made the mess. . . . And it was always bad luck to bring home something you couldn't afford to own. A birdbath with flowers all around it! In Sam Flemming's yard! He couldn't stop the wife from setting it up out there for the time being. Moreover, it was all right—for the time being. He knew the woman *had* to like it. A woman had to be the one to ask some foolishness in life. *He* liked it, too. But a man doesn't kid himself about how much foolishness he can afford. Well, she wasn't going to make it easy for him this time, he knew that. Not this time nor next, either. She didn't change. But when it was done it would be done. And she would still be his wife. He would still, also, be the man.

Presently Sam's two black sock-feet, with a perfectly round hole showing the white flesh of each heel, returned to the bannister rail. Tom watched the feet go back to their place. He said nothing. It was Sam who spoke first. "It wasn't just me," Sam said, "who thought the Free Will Baptists hadn't much of a church. My old daddy didn't think so, either. He used to be what they called the section for old St. John's. I was a little fellow then and he used to take me up there with him sometimes when he was cutting the grass or cleaning outside. He'd point out how pretty and dignified the place was and how they even had it printed in a little book what they was going to do every Sunday of the year. Daddy told me how one time he said to one of the ladies—Mr. Roundtree's sister, it was—that he thought he'd leave the Baptists and join the Episcopalians. But she said to him, 'No, Jack, you have your church and we have ours. It's better to keep it that way.'" Sam, while he spoke, had been looking directly at Tom, but when he quoted the Episcopal lady he dropped his eyes momentarily, and a smile came to his lips, a somewhat mechanical smile that parted his lips and showed a row of uneven, tobacco-stained teeth. "That's why I was kind of glad," he said presently, raising his eyes again and looking quite solemn, "to keep something out of the old church like my woman's birdbath yonder—sort of in memory of my old man. Of course, the wife and the kids set great store by it too. They would hate to part with it. I don't know what they might do. They think it's about the prettiest thing they ever saw."

Under Sam's seemingly honest gaze and listening to his expression of sentiment about his dead father and his delight in the pleasure which the font gave to his wife and children, Tom wondered now if he could ever broach the subject he had come to discuss with him. He had promised himself that he *would* come to terms with Sam that very day; yet the kind of terms that had come into his mind just now seemed suddenly so crass, and so vile even, that he felt quite ashamed of himself. All at once he felt so humble in the presence of this honest, hard-working, tenderhearted Sam Flemming that he could not resist the impulse to confess his own wicked intentions. "Sam," he said, "I have to tell you that I was just now about to offer you money for that—that birdbath out there."

He was watching Sam's face closely as he spoke the words. In the straight lines on either side of the serious mouth he read strength of character. In the wide, brown eyes he read gentleness and charity. Here was a face Tom had known most of his life, and he felt now that he had never seen it before. Wasn't the coarseness he had attributed to it really a rugged loftiness? Wasn't Sam Flemming, after all, the very salt of the earth, a man whose kind of virtue was incorruptible? Yet at the very moment when Tom was really making such acknowledgment of Sam's virtue he observed a smile beginning to form on the man's lips. Moreover, he recognized it as the same smile that had played momentarily when Sam quoted the Episcopal lady speaking to his father. There was something unreal about it. It was the smile a man smiles in his sleep. And though Sam's eyes were open, it was somehow as though the lids had closed over them again. "Well, Tom," he began, his voice growing thicker and taking on more perceptibly the accent of that particular West Tennessee county in which Blackwell is situated, "I'll tell you, Tom, money speaks louder than most anything I know of." His smile broadened until all of his tobacco-browned teeth were showing. "What kind of money was you of a mind to offer?" he asked.

Tom rose from his chair and turned his face away from the man. So it was all a lie—all that about Sam's old daddy and his wife and kiddies. Even the bits about his daddy's being the sexton and about Mr. Roundtree's sister. But why would he take the pains to make up such stuff? What went on inside such a man? He tried to look at him again but found himself looking over his head and out toward the baptismal font in the side yard. His eyes refused to be directed toward those heavy features and that sly smile. Pursing his lips, he pretended to be reckoning the value of the font. "I'll give you fifteen bucks," he said at last.

"Make it twenty," said Sam. And he spat once again between his toes and out into the gutter.

Meanwhile, Tom had drawn two ten-dollar bills from his wallet. Instead of handing them to Sam, he placed the bills neatly, one on top of the other, on the bannister rail just next to Sam's right foot.

"I'm much obliged to you," said Sam, lifting his heel and putting it down on the two bills.

"I'll send someone to fetch the font after dinner tomorrow," Tom Elkins said and went down the porch steps to the sidewalk.

. . .

The exact hour when Tom Elkins would send for the baptismal font became generally known in Blackwell by midmorning of the next day. Word had got round through some mysterious grapevine of information which neither Tom nor Sam would willingly have acknowledged feeding. Mr. Thurston Roundtree, for instance, as well as those rubbernecks who had witnessed the scenes at the church, knew that at half past one o'clock two members of Sam Flemming's own demolition crew, temporarily in the hire of Tom Elkins, would appear at Sam's place for the purpose of removing the birdbath from his yard. The general knowledge was so accurate that Tom himself, who had planned to direct the operation, was later than the spectators in arriving on the spot.

Tom, as a matter of fact, was so late in arriving that when he drew up to the curb, on the opposite side of the street, he saw his two workmen already standing in Sam's side yard. Their rusty old pickup truck was parked nearby, and it was clear that they would require hardly three minutes to do their work. It would not really be necessary, Tom reflected, to get out of his car, even. Yet when he presently observed that Sam Flemming was seated on his porch, staring out into the street between his two feet, and that just opposite Sam on the far side of the street stood Mr. Roundtree with his old eyes shaded by the broad brim of his felt hat, and that between them was moving a fairly steady stream of slow, rubbernecking traffic, Tom then feared it might seem cowardly of him to remain concealed in his car. He stepped out into the street and went and leaned against his front fender. He nodded first to Mr. Roundtree and next to Sam Flemming. Each man returned his nod and somehow did so as though the other were not present. Cars moved along the street at a snail's pace. At last, Tom gestured to his two workmen that they should proceed.

From his porch, Sam Flemming suddenly called out, "Tom, you tell him he can have it still, and I'll give you your money back."

Tom, almost despite himself, turned his eyes to Mr. Roundtree. Mr. Roundtree's eyes were not visible under the hat brim, but Tom could feel that he was waiting to have the message relayed. It was like something from a dream, or something remembered from another existence. "Sam says you can still have the font, Mr. Roundtree," Tom said without spirit, without conviction, even.

The old man threw back his head and laughed. And with his face still tilted and exposed to view he said, "Tell him I think it looks pretty up there, Tom. Why not leave it there?"

At that precise moment, a woman followed by two barefoot little girls, came running unheralded from Sam Flemming's house. They came out a side door onto a little wooden stoop there. And before the screen door had well slammed behind them, they were scurrying down the steps to the yard, and all three of them were crying out at the top of their voices. The woman's voice was more shrill even than the children's and she was shouting the sort of angry words a woman shouts when animals have got into her garden: "Shoo! No! Stoopid! Git!" She was Sam Flemming's wife, of course, and her cries along with her daughters' were directed at the workmen tampering with their birdbath. It happened also that at that moment in time two bluejays and a catbird were just swooping down to the birdbath to refresh themselves. Whether the birds' fury was directed also at the workmen or merely at each other, they gave forth fierce, almost human cries, and with a great fluttering of wings they stirred the air about the two men's bare heads.

"Don't you dare! Don't you dare!" Mrs. Flemming was shouting as she came up to the two men. Stepping into the flower bed, she threw herself forward on the rim of the font, shouting again, "Don't you dare! Don't you dare lay a hand on it!" But the men had already laid hands on the bowl of the font and were trying to lift it off the pedestal. With a quick glance over her shoulder at her husband on the porch, Mrs. Flemming called out, "Sam! Sam!" Sam didn't so much as turn his head to look at her.

One of the workmen said to her in a sympathetic voice, "He's sold it on you, Mrs. Flemming."

"No! Hit ain't for sale," Mrs. Flemming screeched. "He mought give it away, but hit ain't for sale." And with that she took her hands off the font and threw herself upon the man who had spoken to her, pulling at his fingers with one hand and at the collar of his khaki shirt with the other. Like her husband, the woman was of a sallow complexion, and her hair was perhaps thicker and blacker than his. But her face was thin and hollow-eyed, and her figure lean almost to boniness. Seeing her, ordinarily, one would not have supposed that she possessed any of her husband's vigor, nor that she was capable of the frenzy she had thrown herself into. She was shouting now at the older of her two dark-haired daughters, both of whom were moving threateningly against the other workman. "Sarah," she cried out, "grab his leg!" And then to the younger girl, who was no more than seven or eight years old, "Emmaline, sink your little teeth into his arm, honey!" Both girls obeyed her instructions with energy and with obvious relish. But the workman whom they attacked was a big man like

Sam and he shook them off like flies, hardly seeming to notice their bites and blows. And Mrs. Flemming's attack upon the other man was equally ineffective. He and his colleague were now lifting the stone basin and emptying the water on the ground.

For Tom, the spilling of the clear water onto the ground acted as a totally unexpected release. Suddenly his spirits soared. It was as if he had seen a miracle performed. And he could not understand why he felt such joy. He had failed utterly, hadn't he, to moderate among the various parties. And he still could not understand the nature of the conflict itself. Moreover, he was disenchanted with the characters of both Mr. Roundtree and Sam Flemming. He turned his eyes slowly toward Sam, who had even now not removed his two feet from the porch railing. Then he looked at Mr. Roundtree, whose face was in the shadow of his wide-brimmed hat but who obviously had his eyes fixed on the sprawling figure of Sam. Had the old man perhaps known all along what Sam was trying to offer him from the church and had he counted on finally witnessing such a scene as this one? And why? Why? And now Tom looked at Sam again. What low manner of man was this that he could not be moved by that spectacle in the yard? He cursed the man under his breath. But even so he was not able to dispel his own state of near rapture.

Despite the unremitting attacks from the woman and the two little girls, the workmen carried first the basin and then the pedestal out to the street and hoisted them into the truck bed. And meanwhile Sam Flemming continued to sit on his porch, occasionally spitting a stream of amber juice between his two feet, giving no notice to the ruckus his wife and daughters were creating. At last some of the other bystanders began to appeal at first to Tom and then to old Roundtree, imploring them to intervene. Mr. Roundtree responded only by taking off his hat to some of the ladies who were beseeching him. Tom merely shook his head sadly. Only once did the two men's eyes meet. And Mr. Roundtree's eyes said, "Take back your money, Tom." And Tom's eyes said, "Accept the Episcopal baptismal font." But each was as deaf to the other's appeal as to that of the bystanders.

Both men stood seemingly in a kind of transport until after the bird-bath, slipping and sliding about the floor of the truck and making a noise like thunder, had been hauled away down the street and out of sight. In fact, they continued to stand there just so until Mrs. Flemming and her two little daughters, straightening their dresses and pushing back their disarrayed hair, had reentered the Flemming cottage by the same side door they had emerged from. Then without any exchange with Sam Flemming or between themselves, the two men turned and went their separate ways.

The workmen had their instructions to dispose of the baptismal font however they might wish to, so long as it was never seen again in Blackwell. When, years later, the new St. John's was built, some effort was made to locate the old font for tradition's sake. But the workmen had done their work well. The font seemed to have vanished from the face of the earth, as even the two workmen themselves had. During the intervening years they had drifted away from Blackwell to some other community, and no trace of them or of the font they had carted off in their truck that day was to be found. Tom Elkins was by then married to Emma Broadhead (her mother having not, after all, lived forever) but neither he nor Emma could give any clue as to the font's whereabouts. Mr. Roundtree had by that time, of course, joined his sister Jenny in the town cemetery. Sam Flemming was not dead, but he had had a disabling stroke and in his immobile and speechless condition was being cared for by the wife and daughters whose birdbath he had sold. The fate of the font remained unknown, and the parishioners of the new St. John's have had to establish their new church without any relic from the past.

from *Salvation on Sand Mountain*

Dennis Covington (1949–)

Sent to Scottsboro, Alabama, to cover the trial of Glendel Buford Summerford, the snake-handling pastor of the Church of Jesus with Signs Following who stood accused of trying to kill his wife with poisonous snakes, Birmingham native Dennis Covington uncovered his own family connection to the evangelical sect. Raised by a generation of Southerners who directed their children's attention to the future and the idea of progress, Covington's discovery inspired him to complete a task his father tackled shortly before his death: tracing his family history back to the hills of northeast Alabama. Befriended by many members of the congregation, he revealed in *Salvation on Sand Mountain* (1995) a sympathy for the group's critique of the modern world, a critique strikingly similar to the one implicit in Flannery O'Connor's work.

An hour before sundown we reached another barren region inhabited by "poor white trash." Their houses were of the worst imaginable description, and how they managed to obtain a living upon such a soil, was a problem to us. Yet hither the pitiless monopoly of the slaveholding class had driven them, and, by some means or other, they manage to wring sufficient food to keep themselves and their children from starving, out of these inhospitable rocks.

— *dispatch from* The New York Times *dated April 14, 1862, "Advance into Alabama"*

Right before he died, my father got interested in genealogy. "As far as I know," he said, "no Covington has ever left anything to anybody, and I'm not going to be the one to break the tradition." Dad meant it as a joke. He had already given me the best gifts—unqualified love, a moral education, and a good name. But there were three tangibles that he left as well. Before his death he deeded me two and a half acres of palmetto scrubland in central Florida, fifty miles south of Orlando. It was part of a massive real estate venture that had turned belly-up, the largest bankruptcy in the history of the state. River Ranch Acres, it had been called. *Ranch*, because it wasn't on the coast. *River*, because there was supposed to be one nearby. The sales literature had been filled with drawings of horses and cattle. But the development had no roads, no power, no water. The plots hadn't even

577

been surveyed. My dad bought the two and a half acres anyway, as an investment, he said, the only investment he had ever made. But I think he really bought the land because he had always loved Westerns. His favorite movie was *Gunfight at the O.K. Corral.*

The second thing Dad left was a wooden cigar box that had belonged to my grandfather Covington. In it were a straight razor, two shaving brushes still caked with dried lather, my father's tortoiseshell pocketknife, and a few yellowing buttons.

The third thing Dad left me was a green binder containing what little family research he'd been able to do before his lungs gave out. I couldn't bear to look at it, the spidery handwriting on green ledger paper, done in pencil in case of mistakes. My father had been a supervisor in the production planning department at Tennessee Coal and Iron. His responsibilities included seeing to it that Continental Can received the exact quantity of tin they had been promised, and on time. He was, therefore, a perfectionist. Decades after his office moved to a hill overlooking the mills, he continued to get his hair cut by the same black barber downtown because the man always remembered, without having to be asked, to clip the hairs in his nose. The records Dad kept on his 1977 orange Astre station wagon included the original car dealership's ad cut neatly from the paper. He had kept that ad for nearly twelve years. At the time of his death, he had the warranties for every electrical device, including can openers and toasters, that he and my mother had ever purchased, arranged in labeled envelopes. It broke my heart to open the green binder and see him hard at work again, trying to get one last record straight.

I can tell you the exact moment I decided to take a closer look at the binder. It was New Year's Eve, 1992, at the Church of the Lord Jesus Christ in Kingston, Georgia. Brother Carl Porter's church. We were attending an all-night watch service, complete with snake handling, Holy Communion, laying on of hands, and chicken and egg salad sandwiches in the basement after we'd washed each other's feet.

We arrived in mid-service. The moment occurred when the music got cranked up, and the snakes started coming out of the boxes. Vicki had been to a snake-handling church before, but this was the first time we'd brought our daughters, Ashley, then seven, and Laura, then five. We normally took them everywhere we went, but I was a little nervous this time. Our daughters are resilient and adventuresome. I didn't want to press them too much, though.

Laura, like my mother, is an artist. She took one look at Brother Junior McCormick dancing in front of the pulpit with two rattlesnakes draped across his shoulders and decided to spend some time outside in the van, where she drew pictures of rattlesnakes and tambourines. Vicki and I took turns keeping her company. Ashley, though, was transfixed. It was a surprise to me. Physically, Ashley is a dead ringer for a Covington. She has the Covington long arms and the Covington chin. And like my father, she is a careful person—exact in her reckonings and stubborn in her defense of what she believes to be right. But she doesn't like to be startled, and she has no use for loud noises or extravagant gestures. I was afraid a serpent-handling service would be more than she could handle. But when the music started, she looked up at me wide eyed and grinning, and in no time she was clapping her hands and stomping her feet. The snakes didn't seem to faze her one bit. "Cool!" she exclaimed over the uproar. It was as though the shouting and the shrieking and the raw hillbilly music had been imprinted on her genes, like something deep within her she was remembering. I thought of this thing called cell memory. I thought of a part of her—an ancestor—resurrected, alive, caught by surprise.

The sight of my daughter, so clearly a Covington, so clearly at home in the chaos of a snake-handling service, made me quicken. *Were we actually kin to these people?* I was going to look more closely at my father's notes in the green binder. I wanted more. Who were my people? Who were my daughters kin to?

When the snakes had been put away, and the music had stopped, Vicki and Laura came back into the sanctuary. Brother Carl placed a bottle of Welch's Sparkling Concord Grape Juice on one side of the pulpit, where minutes before a rattlesnake had stretched. On the other side, he put a bottle of Manischewitz wine. Between them sat a pan of unleavened bread. And I knew we were going to have Communion.

It was the first time Carl had celebrated Communion in the new sanctuary, which was three years old. Rituals like Communion are rare events in snake-handling churches, anyway; snake handlers don't stand on ceremony or pay much attention to the traditional church calendar. I'd been in a snake-handling church on Easter morning when the word *Easter* was not even mentioned. But Carl's church seemed to be striving for a measure of respectability, and he wanted to make sure that if they did something like this, they did it right.

Carl opened his Bible to a passage in Matthew. "*And as they were eating,*" he read, "*Jesus took bread, and blessed it, and broke it, and gave it to the disciples, and said, Take, eat; this is my body.*"

Carl looked up from the book. "Now, he didn't mean it was really his body."

Amen.

"They weren't cannibals."

Thank God.

"Can you imagine me taking a big bite of Brother Junior over there, and him not even cooked? He's forty something years old. He'd be tough as foot leather!"

Bless him, sweet Jesus!

Carl looked back at the book. "*And he took the cup,*" he read, "*and gave thanks, and gave it to them, saying, Drink ye all of it; For this is my blood of the new testament, which is shed for many for the remission of sins.*"

Again, he glanced up. "I sure ain't gonna drink nobody's blood."

Amen.

"I ain't no vampire."

Praise God!

Carl solemnly closed his Bible and held it up in one hand. "This book here," he said, "will tell you everything you need to know. It'll tell you how to bake bread. It'll tell you how to raise a garden, how to treat your wife, how to wash your feet. It'll tell you how to comb your hair."

Then he blessed the grape juice, wine, and unleavened bread. A certain awkwardness descended on us all, but at Carl's encouragement everybody lined up either in front of the Welch's or in front of the Manischewitz. Vicki and the girls and I chose the grape juice. Charles and Aline McGlocklin chose the wine. Drinking unfermented grape juice, Charles confided, would be like taking up a nonpoisonous snake. Bill Pelfrey, another snake-handling preacher from Newnan, Georgia, helped Carl serve the Communion in Dixie cups. As each member of the congregation took his cup, he also reached into the pan for a piece of unleavened bread and popped it into his mouth. The women stepped off to the side to drink their grape juice or wine. The men threw theirs back right where they stood, then crumpled the cups and looked around for a trash can. Occasionally one of them would throw his arms out and praise God. Carl's cousin, Gene Sherbert, spoke rapidly in tongues.

It wasn't quite like the Communions I'd taken in my family's Methodist church in Birmingham. Back then, we went to the altar by pews and knelt. The organist played softly in the background. Brother Jack Dillard, in the black choir robe he wore only for this occasion, would serve the Welch's grape juice in tiny glasses arranged on a circular silver tray. The host, also served from a silver tray, consisted of crumbled-up Premium saltines. But except for those details, the spirit within the churches was not so different. We Methodists just didn't speak in tongues, and prior to Communion we didn't handle rattlesnakes.

After everybody in Brother Carl's church had been served, he held up his Bible and said, "It says here they ate his flesh and drunk his blood and sang a hymn and went out to the Mount of Olives."

So we sang a hymn, accompanied by guitars, drums, and Carl himself on cymbals, and then Junior McCormick and Gene Sherbert brought out pans and pitchers filled with water for the foot washing. I'd been waiting for this part. I'd heard of foot washing, but had never done it. I liked what it was supposed to represent—the idea of following Jesus by becoming a servant to others.

Carl put down his cymbals and got his Bible out again. "*If I then, your Lord and Master, have washed your feet; ye also ought to wash one another's feet.*" Then he looked up. "I want the women to go downstairs now," he said. They would wash their feet in private. I watched the women file out. Vicki had dressed the girls in Holiness fashion, in modest, long dresses. Ashley's was teal-blue, Laura's ivory. Vicki had attempted to make herself plain, too, tossing aside her dangling earrings at the last moment. Once the women disappeared down the wooden stairs, the men gathered on the deacons' bench and began taking off their shoes and socks. Brother Carl didn't say anything.

The bare feet were gray and bruised looking in the fluorescent light. Most of the feet had thick yellow nails and crooked toes, rough heels, tufts of hair. I was a little apprehensive as I took off my shoes and socks and rolled up the legs of my jeans. I didn't want to go first, and was relieved I didn't have to. Brother Carl volunteered to do that. Junior McCormick and Gene Sherbert sat on either side of him on the deacons' bench. When Carl put his feet into the pan of water, he also placed his hands on the shoulders of Junior and Gene as they leaned over to rub his feet and splash water against his legs. All the other men gathered around. It was like a rugby scrum. Everybody tried to get a hand in the water, which was slick with the olive oil Carl had poured in. Carl's head was thrown back, his eyes closed. "Lift him up, Lord," said Brother Bill Pelfrey.

I was sandwiched in between Brother Bill and Charles McGlocklin. They were jiggling against me as they stirred the water in the pan. Brother Bill stomped his foot twice. The keys he wore on a chain through his belt loop jangled. "*Ah-canna-helimos,*" he said. "*Co-taka-helican.*"

"Thank God," Carl said.

"Yes, Jesus," said Brother Charles.

I groped around in the water. I felt Carl's ankle, his stiff toes, and the hands of the other men. It was peculiar and intimate to touch other men like that.

The men began praying out loud. The voices spiraled louder and faster. "Thy will be done!" shouted Bill Pelfrey.

"We ask it in the name of Jesus!" echoed Brother Charles.

"Jesus!" shouted the other men.

"Sweet Jesus!" said a blond-haired boy with buck teeth.

Carl opened his eyes and looked at the boy with studied surprise, as though he were seeing him for the first time.

"Do you want to go next?" he asked.

The boy nodded. I don't know whose son he was, although I remembered seeing him earlier in the service with a large family Bible in his hand. Carl lifted his feet out of the water, and Gene Sherbert dried them off with a towel. Then Carl and the boy changed places.

The movement of the men changed now. They were more methodical, more delicate. During the washing, Bill Pelfrey offered up a long and intricate prayer that collapsed into tongues at intervals, like the breaking of a wave. I stepped back from the men and looked at the boy's face through their shoulders and heads. His shirt had miniature sailboats on it. His eyes were closed, his lips parted. His front teeth, one of which was chipped, glistened in the overhead light. And his body seemed to rock with the motion of the men's hands on his feet. I was moved by something I could not name. It was like desire, and not like desire, a longing for something that could not be possessed. It was what I felt sometimes when I looked in on my daughters sleeping and was suddenly aware that they were not merely bursts of restless energy and sound, but bodies, solid and temporal, that had been entrusted to me.

"You next?" Brother Charles asked me. I'd lost track of what was going on. The boy had already moved to another spot on the bench, where one of the men was drying his feet.

I nodded and sat in the boy's place on the bench. When I put my feet into the water, I immediately felt the men's hands all over them. They were praying aloud and invoking the name of Jesus. Brother Carl put his hand on my head, and I felt a vibration move along it and into my scalp. But the washing of my own feet seemed anticlimactic. The heart of the experience was watching the boy's chipped tooth glisten as his feet were washed by men.

The next morning, when we got back to Birmingham, I took out my father's green binder, which had sat since his death in a bookcase underneath a stack of magazines and unanswered correspondence. Until then, I hadn't really felt a need to know where my people had come from. But there was something about the way Ashley had responded to the snake-handling service, the sight of her clapping her hands and stomping her feet, that convinced me we were connected in some way to a distinctive mountain culture. Ashley would write in her school journal: "Mother and Daddy took me to a snake-handling church for New Year's Eve. They had copperheads, rattlesnakes, tambourines, and we got our feet washed at midnight." Her teacher would casually bring the journal out at a parent-teacher conference, and tilt her head as if to say, "And do you want to elaborate?"

I had grown up in the 1950s, with radio and television and *Reader's Digest*, and I had assumed that everyone around us was pretty much alike. The past didn't matter. The only history we knew was who we'd fought against in World War II. All we cared about was the present. And all our parents seemed to care about was the future.

East Lake was a solid neighborhood, just shy of middle class, with families trying to do things right, making sure that teeth got filled, shot records were up to date, church attendance pins got won, spelling words learned. Our parents were preparing us to do better than they had, as they had done better than their parents, but beyond that we had no idea who we were. All we knew was that wherever we came from, we didn't want to go back there.

My mother and her sister had been born in a rural crossroads town southeast of Birmingham, but their father had moved them in and out of the city numerous times, following rumors of work. They'd grown up poor in the mining camps of Jefferson County, where, for a time, my grandfather was a hired gun for the coal company. My mother remembers hiding in the cellar while striking miners broke out all their windows with bats. She and her sister found a dead man in their yard one time, no questions asked. They often went hungry. Their mother, my grandmother Nellie Russell, washed coal dust off their clothes outdoors in a number-ten tub. She had never smoked in her life, but she wound up dying of emphysema anyway. My grandfather, Charlie Russell, the strike buster and eventual railroad detective, died in the state mental hospital of the syphilis he'd contracted riding the rails. For many years my mother kept his revolver in a wooden box on the top shelf of her closet. Before he got too sick, he and my grandmother had lived in a big rock house in Pinson, Alabama. But it was the mental hospital I remember best. We'd visit him on weekends, picnic on the grounds. I used to think of the gold-domed mental hospital as our equivalent of Tara.

My father had fared better as a child. His father, though, had been born in Summit, Alabama, a ridgetop west of Sand Mountain. Only one of my grandfather Covington's four siblings survived past adolescence. Her name was Tetie. She died in 1916, at the age of forty-six. She was the first of the children to be born in Alabama, which meant that the Covington family had come to the state sometime between 1862 and 1869. But exactly where the Covingtons began their journey, where they crossed the mountains, how they lived, what they believed, who they were, nobody knew. Nobody asked. The Covingtons were a people who'd left their pasts behind. A door had been shut somewhere.

Most of what my father had written in the green binder were the names, birthdays, weddings dates, and deaths of his eleven siblings and their children, a hefty enough task. The history of the family, though, was slim. Dad's paternal grandfather, Richard Covington, had been born somewhere in North Carolina around 1826 and had married a Mary Clark from South Carolina in 1858. Their oldest child, Anna, was born in 1860 in North Carolina. The family disappeared after that and reappeared in the 1880 census in Summit, Alabama. Five more children had been born by then. Three of them had already died. The remaining two, Tetie and my grandfather, John, would be the only children of Richard and Mary Covington to live into the twentieth century.

Dad didn't know who the parents of Richard and Mary Covington were or where exactly they had lived in North Carolina or what had happened between 1860 and 1880, years during which they migrated from North Carolina to Alabama. Searching the microfilm at the Southern Collection of the Birmingham Public Library, I finally found the family at another location in Alabama in the 1870 census. Prior to the years in Summit, Richard and Mary Covington and their children had lived just south of Huntsville, at a place called Valhermosa Springs. The census taker had described both my great-grandfather and great-grandmother as illiterate. He had also checked the boxes for deaf, dumb, blind, insane, and idiotic. That was the end of what I knew about the Covingtons.

But Dad had been able to go back one generation further on his mother's side. My grandmother Covington had been a Howell. Her father had been born near Morristown, Tennessee, her mother in Nashville; at some point, they had migrated to that ridgetop called Summit, Alabama, where my grandmother, Hattie, was born. Hattie's mother's people had been Leas, and it was this line that my father had gotten the most information about. In particular, he had discovered that my great-great-grandfather, Benjamin Franklin Lea, also a Tennessean by birth, had served for three and a half years in the Confederate Army, and had been captured and held for six months in a Union prison camp. After the war, he became a Methodist circuit-riding preacher in northeastern Alabama. The center of his first circuit was Larkinsville, a town four miles west of Scottsboro.

Scottsboro. Glenn Summerford's home.

I felt as though I were closing in on the resolution of a mystery. I wondered what kind of doctrine my great-great-grandfather had been preaching in the precise area where snake handling would spring up less than a generation after his death. My reading in the history of American religion suggested an answer. John Wesley, the founder of Methodism, had challenged believers, through his doctrine of sanctification, to lead lives that were holy and set apart from sin. After the Civil War, with America's rapid urban industrialization and secularization, the calls for holiness became more strident and pervasive within American Methodism. The chief tenet of this Holiness movement was that after "salvation" or "new birth," there occurred a second act of grace, which believers called the "Baptism of the Holy Spirit." The result of this baptism, whether immediate or gradual, was moral purification. Later, the phrase also came to mean, for many believers, anyway, an imbuement of power from on high, as evidenced by spiritual gifts. Signs and wonders. Healing, prophecy, casting out devils, and ultimately speaking in tongues. My great-great-grandfather rode on horseback to preach baptism of the Holy Spirit to congregations around Scottsboro and most likely on top of Sand Mountain, where Methodist camp meetings, complete with brush arbors, drew enthusiastic crowds. *My great-great-grandfather had probably preached brush-arbor meetings on top of Sand Mountain.* I have no reason to believe he took up serpents, but I do have reason to believe he was a precursor of those who eventually did. In 1870, when he began his circuit-riding ministry in Alabama, Methodism was in the sway of the Holiness movement. It flourished for the next two decades, and broke out of Methodism only in the years immediately following his death, when the Methodist Church, its ranks swollen by middle-class urbanites, officially distanced itself from the rural and generally lower-class believers in sanctification and spiritual gifts. Out of Methodism came Holiness. Out of Holiness came Pentecostalism. Out of the Holiness-Pentecostal belief in spiritual signs and gifts came those who took up serpents.

Carl Porter's father, for instance, had gotten the Holy Ghost in a Methodist church in Alabama. Whether we were blood related or not, the handlers and the Covingtons at least shared the same spiritual ancestry. And about the time I came to this realization, a librarian in the Southern Collection of the Birmingham Public Library handed me a clip file containing, among other pieces, an Associated Press article from 1953, datelined Florence, Alabama:

SNAKE-HANDLING BROTHERS FINED $20 AND COSTS

FLORENCE, JULY 25 (AP) — Three snake handling brothers today were fined $20 and costs for disturbing religious worship by carrying a rattlesnake into a rural church.

Lauderdale County Law and Equity Court Judge Raymond Murphy imposed the fines on Allen Covington, 37, and Mansel and George Covington, 39.

The brothers had been held in the Lauderdale County Jail since July 14, after they were arrested for a disturbance at the Bumpas Creek Church.

Pat Murphy, one of the state witnesses, said that when the brothers brought the snake into the church "The people sort of scrounged back and acted like they were kind of afraid of it."

When asked by solicitor Frank Potts if the brothers broke up the service, Allen Covington replied, "The people broke it up themselves by leaving."

Mansel Covington, a big man dressed in overalls, held a Bible in his hands throughout the trial.

He said he and his brothers walked into the church and sat down in the "Amen corner." Mansel said they were praising the Lord.

George Covington testified that he had heard of an Alabama law against snake-handling and the brothers were expecting to be jailed.

"But we felt that we were obeying the spirit of the Lord," he asserted.

The brothers were tried under a disturbing the peace statute, not under Alabama's anti-snake handling law.

Snake-handling Covington brothers! But there was more. Two years later, Mansel Covington and his sister, Anna Marie Covington Yost, were bitten by rattlesnakes during a service in Savannah, Tennessee. Both were under suspended sentences for snake handling at the time. Mansel stubbornly refused treatment until the county coroner physically dragged him to a doctor for antivenin injections and then to jail. Anna Marie also refused treatment, and the next morning she died.

There were seven children in this family of Covington snake handlers, three daughters and four sons. All were born in Alabama. The sons are dead now. But Anna Marie's two sisters are still alive. Edna Covington, eighty, still lives in Savannah, Tennessee. I tracked her down and visited with her in the living room of the modest brick home to which she had retired after thirty-one years as a registered nurse, most spent at the Veterans Administration Hospital in Louisville, Kentucky.

Edna was compact and athletic looking, with short-cropped sandy hair and a clipped accent. She invited me to join her on the floor, where she had been thumbing through a genealogy book in preparation for my visit. I didn't know whether Edna and I were related, but she looked like a member of our family. She had our sharp chin and deep-set eyes. Her Covingtons, she said, had settled on the north bank of the Tennessee River, at a place called Rogersville, Alabama. My great-grandfather and his family, on the other hand, had settled on the south bank of the Tennessee River, forty miles away, at Valhermosa Springs.

In 1932 Edna's family followed the natural curve of the Tennessee River up to Savannah, Tennessee, a stone's throw from Shiloh, where the seeds of the South's defeat had been sown, and the twentieth century conceived. That's where Edna's brothers and one of her sisters took up serpents. Edna never handled any.

"My brothers got into snake handling at outdoor camp meetings," she said. "They were just fooling around. They didn't keep busy enough."

Mansel Covington was the most outspoken of the brothers, she said. He was a big man in later life, but he had been born prematurely. "He was like a little rat," she said, continuing to flip through the pages of her book. "We'd put him on pillows to handle him. He couldn't talk till he was seven or eight." She paused to scan a list of names that may or may not have been her Covingtons. "Mansel and William were both eunuchs," she said matter-of-factly.

I asked what she meant.

Edna gave me a sharp look. "They had high voices and couldn't grow beards."

I wanted to hear more about this.

"They were born without testicles," she enunciated clearly, as though I were dense, and then lay her book aside.

As a young man, she said, Mansel worked in the freezer department at the Peabody Hotel in Memphis. He took hormone shots and began to shave, but he didn't like his job in the city, so he came back to Savannah and started going to outdoor revivals, where he eventually took up serpents. Edna's sister Anna Marie married and moved to Akron, Ohio, but she came back to Savannah alone and began going to snake-handling services with her brothers.

When Anna Marie got bit and died at the end of a two-week revival in 1956, Edna was working the night shift at the VA Hospital in Louisville. She didn't see any reason to rush back to Savannah, since Anna Marie was already dead, but her brother George, the one with the harelip, insisted that she leave work right then and drive all night to get back. George said he and his brothers were going to raise Anna Marie from the dead through prayer, and since Edna was a nurse, he wanted her to be there to check her sister's vital signs.

"There was a big full moon that night," Edna said.

I left Edna's house in Savannah, Tennessee, with that image in my head, of a woman driving all night under a full moon so that she could check her dead sister's vital signs while their brothers attempted to pray her back to life. I still didn't know whether Edna's family and mine were related. All I knew was that we had settled on opposite banks of the same river. Edna's band of Covingtons went one way, toward Shiloh, and wound up handling snakes. Our band kept coming south, first to Summit, and finally, in 1907, to Birmingham, where my father would be born and

I would be born and my daughters would be born. Borderers. Hill people. New Lights.

When I told Carl Porter that I might have run across some handlers in my family tree, he seemed amused, but not surprised. "Who knows but that God sent you up here to write about Glenn's trial so you could find out that very thing?" he said.

Brother Carl had come from a family of Alabama sharecroppers. He knew even less about his ancestors than I knew about mine. Unlike me, though, Carl seemed to have an intuitive grasp of the sort of people they were, and he had accepted it as the natural order of things. I was a city boy still trying to make sense of the notes in my father's green binder. My journey with the snake handlers had become not so much a linear progression through time as a falling through levels of platitude toward some hard understanding of who I was. I did not know where or when I would arrive at my destination. All I knew for certain was that snakes would be waiting for me there.

Acknowledgments

Agee, James: From *Let Us Now Praise Famous Men* by James Agee and Walker Evans. Copyright © 1939 and 1940 by James Agee. Copyright © 1941 by James Agee and Walker Evans. Copyright © renewed 1969 by Mia Fritsch Agee and Walker Evans. Reprinted by permission of Houghton Mifflin Co. All rights reserved.

Angelou, Maya: From *I Know Why the Caged Bird Sings* by Maya Angelou. Copyright © 1969 by Maya Angelou. Reprinted by permission of Random House, Inc. and Virago Press c/o Little Brown and Company (UK).

Caldwell, Erskine: "Kneel to the Rising Sun" by Erskine Caldwell from *The Stories of Erskine Caldwell*, published by the University of Georgia Press. Copyright © 1935 by Erskine Caldwell. Reprinted by permission of McIntosh and Otis, Inc.

Cash, W. J.: From *The Mind of the South* by W. J. Cash. Copyright 1941 by Alfred A. Knopf, Inc. and renewed 1969 by Mary R. Maury. Reprinted by permission of the publishers, Alfred A. Knopf, Inc. and Thames & Hudson Ltd.

Chappell, Fred: Reprinted by permission of Louisiana State University Press from *I Am One of You Forever* by Fred Chappell. Copyright © 1985 by Fred Chappell.

Chesnutt, Charles W.: "Dave's Neckliss" by Charles W. Chesnutt first appeared in the *Atlantic Monthly* 1889. Rights in the British Commonwealth administrated by the Estate of Charles W. Chesnutt. Reprinted by permission of John C. Slade.

Covington, Dennis: From *Salvation on Sand Mountain* by Dennis Covington. Text copyright © 1995 by Dennis Covington. Reprinted by permission of Addison-Wesley Longman Inc.

Crews, Harry: From *A Childhood: The Biography of a Place* by Harry Crews. Published in 1978 by Harper & Row. Copyright © 1978 by Harry Crews. Reprinted by permission of John Hawkins & Associates, Inc.

Du Bois, W. E. B.: From *The Souls of Black Folk* by W. E. B. Du Bois. First published in 1903. Rights in the British Commonwealth administrated by the Estate of W. E. B. Du Bois. Reprinted by permission of David G. Du Bois.

Ellison, Ralph: From *Invisible Man* by Ralph Ellison. Copyright © 1948 by Ralph Ellison. Reprinted by permission of Random House, Inc.

Faulkner, William: "Wash" by William Faulkner from *The Collected Stories of William Faulkner*. Copyright © 1934 by William Faulkner and renewed 1962 by William Faulkner. Reprinted by permission of Random House, Inc. and Curtis Brown Ltd.

Gaines, Ernest J.: "The Sky Is Gray" from *Bloodline* by Ernest J. Gaines. Copyright © 1963 by Ernest J. Gaines. Used by permission of Doubleday, a division of Bantam Doubleday Dell Publishing Group, Inc. and JCA Literary Agency.

Garrett, George: "Good-bye, Good-bye, Be Always Kind and True" from *An Evening Performance* by George Garrett. Copyright © 1985 by George Garrett. Used by permission of Doubleday, a division of Bantam Doubleday Dell Publishing Group, Inc., the author, and Gelfman Schneider Literary Agents, Inc.

Percy, William Alexander: From *Lanterns on the Levee* by William Alexander Percy. Copyright 1941 by Alfred A. Knopf, Inc. and renewed 1969 by LeRoy Pratt Percy. Reprinted by permission of the publisher.

Robertson, Ben: From *Red Hills and Cotton: An Upcountry Memory* by Ben Robertson. First published in 1942. Reprinted by permission of the University of South Carolina Press.

Settle, Mary Lee: From *Know Nothing* by Mary Lee Settle. First published by The Viking Press in 1960. Reprinted by permission of the University of South Carolina Press.

Smith, Lee: "Richard Burlage" is reprinted by permission of G. P. Putnam's Sons and the Darhansoff & Verrill Agency from *Oral History* by Lee Smith. Copyright © 1983 by Lee Smith.

Smith, Lillian: "Trembling Earth" from *Killers of the Dream* by Lillian Smith. Copyright 1949, © 1961 by Lillian Smith. Reprinted by permission of W. W. Norton & Company, Inc.

Styron, William: From *The Confessions of Nat Turner* by William Styron. Copyright © 1966, 1967 by William Styron. Copyright renewed 1995 by William Styron. Reprinted by permission of Random House, Inc. and Don Congdon Associates, Inc.

Taylor, Peter: "The Decline and Fall of the Episcopal Church (in the Year of Our Lord 1952)" from *The Oracle at Stoneleigh Court* by Peter Taylor. Copyright © 1993 by Peter Taylor. Reprinted by permission of Alfred A. Knopf, Inc.

Twelve Southerners: Introduction reprinted by permission of Louisiana State University Press from *I'll Take My Stand: The South and the Agrarian Tradition* by Twelve Southerners. Copyright 1930 by Harper & Brothers. Copyright renewed 1958 by Donald Davidson.

Walker, Alice: "Of Bitches and Wives" from *Meridian* by Alice Walker. Copyright © 1976 by Alice Walker. Reprinted by permission of Harcourt Brace & Company and David Higham Associates.

Walker, Margaret: From *Jubilee* by Margaret Walker. Copyright © 1966 by Margaret Walker Alexander. Reprinted by permission of Houghton Mifflin Company. All rights reserved.

Walton, Anthony: From *Mississippi* by Anthony Walton. Copyright © 1996 by Anthony Walton. Reprinted by permission of Alfred A. Knopf, Inc.

Warren, Robert Penn: From *The Legacy of the Civil War* by Robert Penn Warren. Published in 1983 by Harvard University Press. Copyright © 1961 by Robert Penn Warren. Reprinted by permission of the William Morris Agency, Inc. for the estate of the author.

Welty, Eudora: "Death of a Traveling Salesman" from *A Curtain of Green and Other Stories* by Eudora Welty. Copyright 1941 and renewed 1969 by Eudora Welty. Reprinted by permission of Harcourt Brace & Company and Russell & Volkening, Inc.

Williams, Sherley Anne: From *Dessa Rose* by Sherley Anne Williams. Copyright © 1986 by Sherley Anne Williams. By permission of William Morrow & Company, Inc.

Author Index

Themis Bar Review
Multistate

Constitutional Law
Contracts
Criminal Law
Criminal Procedure
Evidence
Real Property
Sales
Torts

Constitutional Law

CONSTITUTIONAL LAW

Table of Contents

CONSTITUTIONAL LAW

PART ONE: POWERS OF THE FEDERAL GOVERNMENT

I. JUDICIAL POWER

A. SOURCE AND SCOPE

1. Source—Article III

Article III, Section 1 of the United States Constitution provides that "[t]he judicial power of the United States shall be vested in one Supreme Court and in such inferior courts as the Congress may from time to time ordain and establish."

Federal courts are generally created by the United States Congress under the constitutional power described in Article III. As noted above, Article III requires the establishment of a Supreme Court and permits the Congress to create other federal courts and place limitations on their jurisdiction. Although many specialized courts are created under the authority granted in Article I, greater power is vested in Article III courts because they are independent of Congress, the President, and the political process.

2. Scope

Article III, Section 2 delineates the jurisdiction of federal courts as limited to **cases or controversies**:

i) Arising under the Constitution, laws, and treaties of the United States;

ii) Affecting foreign countries' ambassadors, public ministers, and consuls;

iii) Involving admiralty and maritime jurisdiction;

iv) When the United States is a party;

v) Between two or more states, or between a state and citizens of another state;

vi) Between citizens of different states or between citizens of the same state claiming lands under grants of different states; or

vii) Between a state, or its citizens, and foreign states, citizens, or subjects.

a. Judicial review of congressional and executive actions

The judiciary has the power—although it is not enumerated in the text of the Constitution—to review an act of another branch of the federal government and to declare that act unconstitutional, *Marbury v. Madison*, 5 U.S. 137 (1803), as well as the constitutionality of a decision by a state's highest court, *Martin v. Hunter's Lessee*, 1 Wheat. 304 (1816). The central ideas of *Marbury v. Madison* are that (i) the Constitution is paramount law, and (ii) the Supreme Court has the final say in interpreting the Constitution.

b. Judicial review of state actions

The federal judiciary has the power, under the Supremacy Clause (Article VI, Section 2), to review state actions (e.g., court decisions, state statutes, executive orders) to ensure conformity with the Constitution, laws, and treaties of the United States. *Fletcher v. Peck*, 10 U.S. 87 (1810).

3.   **Limitations—Eleventh Amendment**

The Eleventh Amendment is a jurisdictional bar that prohibits the citizens of one state from suing another state in federal court. It immunizes the state from suits for money damages or equitable relief when the state is a defendant in an action brought by a citizen of another state. Although state officials may be enjoined from violating federal law, the Eleventh Amendment bars suits against state officials for violating **state** law.

The Supreme Court has expanded the amendment's reach to also preclude citizens from suing their own state in federal court.

Note that the Supreme Court has also barred federal-law actions brought against a state government without the state's consent in **state** court as a violation of **sovereign immunity**. *Alden v. Maine*, 527 U.S. 706 (1999).

a.   **Exceptions**

There are, however, a few notable exceptions to the application of the Eleventh Amendment.

1)   **Consent**

A state may consent to suit by expressly waiving its Eleventh Amendment protection (e.g., removing the case to federal court).

2)   **Injunctive relief**

The Eleventh Amendment bars only suits for damages, not those for injunctive or declaratory relief, unless the state itself is enjoined. When a state official is named as the defendant, the state official may be sued in federal court to prevent enforcement of an unconstitutional state statute. *Ex parte Young*, 209 U.S. 123 (1908). A state cannot invoke its sovereign immunity to prevent a lawsuit by a state agency seeking to enforce a federal right against a state official. *Virginia Office for Prot. & Advocacy v. Stewart*, 563 U.S. ___, 131 S. Ct. 1632 (2011).

3)   **Damages to be paid by an individual**

An action for damages against a state officer is not prohibited, as long as the officer himself (rather than the state treasury) will have to pay. Such is the case when an officer acts outside the law; the action is against the officer as an individual and not in his representative capacity.

4)   **Prospective damages**

As long as the effect of a lawsuit is not to impose retroactive damages on a state officer to be paid from the state treasury, a federal court may hear an action against a state officer, even if the action will force a state to pay money to comply with a court order.

5) Congressional authorization

Congress may abrogate state immunity from liability if it is clearly acting to enforce rights created by the Fourteenth Amendment (e.g., equal protection) and does so expressly. *Fitzpatrick v. Bitzer*, 427 U.S. 445 (1976). Congress generally may not abrogate state immunity by exercising its powers under Article I. *Seminole Tribe of Florida v. Florida*, 517 U.S. 114 (1996).

b. Not barred by the Eleventh Amendment

1) Actions against local governments

The Eleventh Amendment applies only to states and state agencies. Local governments (e.g., counties, cities) are not immune from suit.

2) Actions by the United States government or other state governments not barred

The Eleventh Amendment has no application when the plaintiff is the United States or another state.

3) Bankruptcy proceedings

The Eleventh Amendment does not bar the actions of a Bankruptcy Court that impacts state finances. *Central Cmty. Coll. v. Katz*, 546 U.S. 356 (2006).

B. JURISDICTION OF THE SUPREME COURT

1. Original

Article III, Section 2 gives the Supreme Court "original jurisdiction" (i.e., the case may be filed first in the Supreme Court) over "all cases affecting ambassadors, other public ministers and consuls and those in which a State shall be a party." Congress may not expand or limit this jurisdiction. *Marbury v. Madison*, 5 U.S. 137 (1803). It may, however, grant concurrent original jurisdiction to lower federal courts.

2. Appellate

Article III, Section 2 also provides that "in all other cases before mentioned, the Supreme Court shall have appellate jurisdiction...with such exceptions, and under such regulations as the Congress shall make."

a. Means

There are two means of establishing appellate jurisdiction in the Supreme Court: certiorari (discretionary review) and direct appeal.

1) Certiorari

Almost all cases now come to the Supreme Court by way of a petition for a writ of certiorari, i.e., discretionary review. The Court takes jurisdiction only if at least four Justices vote to accept the case (the "rule of four").

2) Direct appeal

The Supreme Court **must** hear by direct appeal only a small number of cases—those that come from a decision on injunctive relief issued by a special three-judge district court panel. 28 U.S.C. § 1253. Although these panels (and appeals) were once fairly common, they are now limited to cases brought under a few specific statutes (e.g., the Voting Rights Act).

b. Limitations

Congress has some power to limit the Supreme Court's appellate jurisdiction. *Ex parte McCardle*, 74 U.S. 506 (1868). There are constraints on this power, because to deny all Supreme Court jurisdiction over certain types of cases would undermine the constitutional system of checks and balances. *Boumediene v. Bush*, 553 U.S. 723 (2008) (Congress and President cannot remove Supreme Court's authority to say "what the law is" (quoting *Marbury v. Madison*, 5 U.S. 137 (1803))).

Note that most federal cases are filed in district court and appealed, if at all, to the courts of appeals. The jurisdiction of the federal courts is set, within the framework of Article III, by statute. For example, Congress has set the minimum amount in controversy necessary for federal jurisdiction over a case between citizens of different states at more than $75,000. 28 U.S.C. § 1332.

c. Adequate and independent state grounds

A final state-court judgment that rests on adequate and independent state grounds may not be reviewed by the U.S. Supreme Court (or it would be an advisory opinion). The state-law grounds must fully resolve the matter (i.e., be adequate) and must not incorporate a federal standard by reference (i.e., be independent). When it is not clear whether the state court's decision rests on state or federal law, the Supreme Court may hear the case, decide the federal issue, and remand to the state court for resolution of any question of state law. *Michigan v. Long*, 463 U.S. 1032 (1983).

C. JUDICIAL REVIEW IN OPERATION

Standing, timing (mootness or ripeness), and other issues of justiciability may dictate whether a case may be heard by a federal court.

1. Standing

Article III, Section 2 restricts federal judicial power to "cases" and "controversies." A federal court cannot decide a case unless the plaintiff has standing—a concrete interest in the outcome—to bring it. Congress cannot statutorily eliminate the constitutional standing requirement simply by allowing citizen suits, *Lujan v. Defenders of Wildlife*, 504 U.S. 555 (1992), but it can create new interests, the injury to which may establish standing, *Massachusetts v. EPA*, 549 U.S. 497 (2007).

a. General rule

To have standing, a plaintiff bears the burden of establishing three elements:

i) **Injury in fact**;

ii) **Causation** (the injury must be caused by the defendant's violation of a constitutional or other federal right); and

iii) **Redressability** (the relief requested must prevent or redress the injury).

See, e.g., Lujan v. Defenders of Wildlife, 504 U.S. 555 (1982); *Valley Forge Christian College v. Americans United for Separation of Church and State, Inc.*, 454 U.S. 464 (1982).

EXAM NOTE: When answering questions about standing, eliminate answer choices involving only the substance of the claim and focus on whether the plaintiff is legally qualified to press a claim, regardless of merit.

---

1) Injury in fact

The injury must be **concrete** and **particularized.**

a) Individualized injury

When a plaintiff has been directly injured "it does not matter how many people" were also injured; when "a harm is concrete, though widely shared," there is standing. *Massachusetts v. EPA*, 549 U.S. 497 (2007). However, even though an injury may satisfy the injury-in-fact standard, the court may refuse to adjudicate a claim by the application of the principles of prudence. Under this prudential-standing principle, an injury that is shared by all or a large class of citizens (i.e., a generalized grievance) is not sufficiently individualized to give the plaintiff standing. *Warth v. Seldin*, 422 U.S. 490 (1975).

b) Type of injury

The injury need not be physical or economic. *United States v. SCRAP*, 412 U.S. 669 (1973). While a generalized harm to the environment does not confer standing, if the alleged harm affects recreational "or even mere esthetic interests," that will be sufficient. *See Summers v. Earth Island Inst.*, 555 U.S. 488 (2009).

c) Future injury

While the threat of future injury can suffice, it cannot be merely hypothetical or conjectural, but must be actual and imminent. When a future injury is alleged, damages cannot be obtained, but an injunction can be sought.

2) Causation

The plaintiff must show that the injury was fairly traceable to the challenged action—that is, that the defendant's conduct caused the injury. *Warth v. Seldin*, 422 U.S. 490 (1975).

3) Redressability

It must be likely (as opposed to speculative) that a favorable court decision will redress a discrete injury suffered by the plaintiff.

b. Taxpayer status

Usually, a taxpayer does not have standing to file a federal lawsuit simply because the taxpayer believes that the government has allocated funds in an improper way. However, a taxpayer does have standing to litigate whether, or how much, she owes on her tax bill.

> **EXAM NOTE:** The standing of taxpayers is frequently tested on the MBE. A taxpayer has standing when the taxpayer challenges governmental expenditures as violating the Establishment Clause.

1) Governmental conduct

The conduct of the federal government, or of any state government, is too far removed from individual taxpayer returns for any injury to the taxpayer to be traced to the use of tax revenues. *DaimlerChrysler Corp. v. Cuno*, 547 U.S. 332 (2006). Long-standing precedent, however, suggests that a municipal taxpayer does have standing to sue a municipal government in federal court. *Crampton v. Zabriskie*, 101 U.S. 601 (1879).

2) Exception—Establishment Clause challenge

There is an exception for a taxpayer suit challenging a **specific congressional appropriation** made under the taxing and spending powers for violation of the Establishment Clause. *Flast v. Cohen*, 392 U.S. 83 (1968). This exception does not apply to the transfer of property to a religious organization by Congress under the Property Power, *Valley Forge Christian College v. Americans United for Separation of Church and State*, 454 U.S. 464 (1982), nor to expenditures made by the President to religious organizations from monies appropriated by Congress to the President's general discretionary fund, *Hein v. Freedom From Religion Foundation*, 551 U.S. 587 (2007).

c. Third-party standing

A litigant generally has no standing to bring a lawsuit based on legal claims of a third party. There are a few notable exceptions to this rule, however:

i) If the third parties would experience difficulty or are **unable to assert their own rights,** such as a Caucasian defendant raising equal protection and due process objections to discrimination against African-American people in the selection of grand juries, *Campbell v. Louisiana*, 523 U.S. 392 (1998);

ii) If there is a **special relationship between the plaintiff and the third parties,** such as an employer asserting the rights of its employees, a doctor asserting the rights of his patients in challenging an abortion ruling, *Singleton v. Wulff*, 428 U.S. 106 (1976), or a private school asserting its students' rights to attend despite a statute requiring attendance at public schools, *Pierce v. Society of Sisters*, 268 U.S. 510 (1925); and

iii) If a plaintiff suffers an injury, and **the injury adversely affects the plaintiff's relationship with a third party,** the plaintiff may assert the third-party's rights. *Craig v. Boren*, 429 U.S. 190 (1976).

The rule that a litigant has no standing to bring a lawsuit on behalf of a third party is based on prudential or discretionary considerations. The federal courts may refuse to hear any case on prudential-standing grounds. *Elk Grove Unified School Dist. v. Newdow*, 542 U.S. 1 (2004).

1) Organizational standing

An organization may bring an action when it has suffered an injury. In addition, an organization may bring an action on behalf of its members (even if the organization has not suffered an injury itself) if:

i) Its members would have standing to sue in their own right; and

ii) The interests at stake are germane to the organization's purpose.

Hunt v. Washington State Apple Adver. Comm'n., 432 U.S. 333 (1977). When damages are sought, generally neither the claim asserted nor the relief requested can require the participation of individual members in the lawsuit. But note that the damages limitation is not constitutionally mandated and can be waived by Congress. *United Food & Commer. Workers Union Local 751 v. Brown Group*, 517 U.S. 544 (1996).

2) Parental standing

Generally, a parent has standing to bring an action on behalf of the parent's minor child. However, after a divorce, the right to bring such an action may be limited to only one of the child's parents. Moreover, when the right to bring such an action is based on family-law rights that are in dispute, the federal courts should not entertain an action if prosecution of the lawsuit may have an adverse effect on the child. *Elk Grove Unified School District v. Newdow*, 542 U.S. 1 (2004) (noncustodial parent with joint legal custody could not challenge school policy on behalf of his daughter when the custodial parent opposed the action).

d. Assignee standing

An assignee of a claim has standing to enforce the rights of an assignor, even when the assignee is contractually obligated to return any litigation proceeds to the assignor (e.g., an assignee for collection), provided the assignment was made for ordinary business purposes and in good faith. *Sprint Commc'ns Co., L.P. v. APCC Servs., Inc.*, 554 U.S. 269 (2008).

e. Citizenship standing

Citizens do not have standing to assert a claim to enforce a constitutional provision merely because they are citizens, although a citizen may bring an action against the government to compel adherence to a specific federal statute. Even in such a case, the plaintiff must have directly suffered an injury in fact.

f. Standing to assert a Tenth Amendment violation

A party has standing to challenge the constitutionality of a federal statute on the grounds that it exceeds Congress's enumerated powers and intrudes upon the powers reserved to the states by the Tenth Amendment. *Bond v. United States*, 564 U.S. ___, 131 S. Ct. 2355 (2011) (defendant prosecuted for violation of federal statute).

2. Timeliness

An action that is brought too soon ("unripe") or too late ("moot") will not be heard.

a. Ripeness

"Ripeness" refers to the readiness of a case for litigation. A federal court will not consider a claim before it has fully developed; to do so would be premature, and any potential injury would be speculative.

For a case to be "ripe" for litigation, the plaintiff must have experienced a **real injury** (or imminent threat thereof). Hence, if an ambiguous law has a long history of non-enforcement, a case challenging that law may lack ripeness. *See Poe v. Ullman*, 367 U.S. 497 (1961).

b. Mootness

A case has become moot if further legal proceedings would have no effect; that is, if there is no longer a controversy. A **live controversy** must exist **at each stage of review,** not merely when the complaint is filed, in order for a case to be viable at that stage.

> **Example:** The classic example of mootness is the case of *DeFunis v. Odegaard*, 416 U.S. 312 (1974). The plaintiff was a student who had been denied admission to law school and had then been provisionally admitted while the case was pending. Because the student was scheduled to graduate within a few months at the time the decision was rendered, and there was no action that the law school could take to prevent it, the Court determined that a decision on its part would have no effect on the student's rights. Therefore, the case was dismissed as moot.

1) Exception—capable of repetition, yet evading review

A case will not be dismissed as moot if the controversy is a type that may often recur ("capable of repetition") but that will not last long enough to work its way through the judicial system ("yet evading review").

> **Example:** The most cited example of this exception is *Roe v. Wade*, 410 U.S. 113 (1973), when the state argued that the case was moot because the plaintiff, who was challenging a Texas statute forbidding abortion, was no longer pregnant by the time the case reached the Supreme Court. Because of the relatively short human gestation period (compared to a lawsuit), abortion litigation was readily capable of being repeated, but also likely to evade review, and the case was not dismissed as moot.

2) Exception—voluntary cessation

A court will not dismiss as moot a case in which the defendant voluntarily ceases its illegal or wrongful action once litigation has commenced. The court must be assured that "there is no reasonable expectation that the wrong will be repeated." *United States v. W.T. Grant Co.*, 345 U.S. 629 (1953).

3) Exception—class actions

If the named plaintiff's claim in a certified class action is resolved and becomes moot, that fact does not render the entire class action moot. *United States Parole Comm'n. v. Geraghty*, 445 U.S. 388 (1980).

3. Justiciability—Further Issues

Federal courts may invoke a variety of other reasons not to decide a case.

a. Advisory opinions

Federal courts may not render advisory opinions on the basis of an abstract or a hypothetical dispute. An actual case or controversy must exist.

> **EXAM NOTE:** Fact patterns involving a request for declaratory judgment are likely testing advisory opinion prohibition.

b. Declaratory judgments

The courts are not prohibited from issuing declaratory judgments, however, that determine the legal effect of proposed conduct without awarding damages or injunctive relief. The challenged action must pose a real and immediate danger to a party's interests for there to be an actual dispute (as opposed to a hypothetical one).

c. Political questions

A federal court will not rule on a matter in controversy if the matter is a political question to be resolved by one or both of the other two branches of government. *Baker v. Carr*, 369 U.S. 186 (1962).

A political question not subject to judicial review arises when:

  i) The Constitution has assigned decision making on this subject to a different branch of the government; or

  ii) The matter is inherently not one that the judiciary can decide.

> **Example:** Details of Congress's impeachment procedures (constitutionally assigned to a branch other than the judiciary) and the President's conduct of foreign affairs (not within judicial competence) are examples of political questions.

4. Abstention

A federal court may abstain from deciding a claim when strong state interests are at stake:

a. *Pullman* doctrine

A court may refrain from ruling on a federal constitutional claim that depends on resolving an unsettled issue of state law best left to the state courts. *Railroad Comm'n of Texas v. Pullman*, 312 U.S. 496 (1941).

b. *Younger* abstention

A court will generally not enjoin a pending state criminal case or a state enforcement proceeding in which an especially strong state interest is involved. *Younger v. Harris*, 401 U.S. 37 (1971). The exception to this abstention is seen in cases of proven harassment or prosecutions taken in bad faith.

II. THE POWERS OF CONGRESS

Just as the federal courts are courts of limited jurisdiction, the powers of Congress are not plenary or exclusive. As the Tenth Amendment makes clear, the federal government may exercise only those powers specifically enumerated by the Constitution; it is state governments and the people, not the national government, that retain any powers not mentioned in the federal charter. Any action by the federal government must be supported by a source of power originating in the Constitution. Article I, Section 1 vests all legislative powers of the federal government in Congress.

> **EXAM NOTE:** Congress has no general police power to legislate for the health, safety, welfare, or morals of citizens. The validity of a federal statute on the bar exam may not be justified based on "federal police power."

A. COMMERCE

Article I, Section 8, Clause 3 of the Constitution, known as the Commerce Clause, empowers Congress "[t]o regulate Commerce with foreign Nations, and among the several States, and with the Indian Tribes." The term "commerce" has been defined to include essentially all activity—including transportation, traffic, or transmission of gas, electricity, radio, TV, mail, and telegraph—involving or affecting two or more states.

1. Interstate Commerce

a. Power to regulate

Congress has the power to regulate (i) the **channels** (highways, waterways, airways, etc.) and (ii) the **instrumentalities** (cars, trucks, ships, airplanes, etc.) of interstate commerce, as well as (iii) any activity that **substantially affects** interstate commerce, provided that the regulation does not infringe upon any other constitutional right. *United States v. Lopez*, 514 U.S. 549 (1995).

b. Construed broadly

The Supreme Court has upheld acts of Congress seeking to prohibit or restrict the entry of persons, products, and services into the stream of interstate commerce, as well as acts regulating the interstate movement of kidnap victims, stolen vehicles, and telephone transmissions.

2. "Substantial Economic Effect"

Congress has the power to regulate any activity, intra- or interstate, that in and of itself or in combination with other activities has a "substantial economic effect upon" or "effect on movement in" interstate commerce.

a. Aggregation

With respect to an intrastate activity that does not have a direct economic impact on interstate commerce, such as growing crops for personal consumption, as long as a court can imagine a **rational basis** for concluding that the "total incidence" of the activity in the aggregate substantially affects interstate commerce, Congress may regulate even a minute amount of that total. *Gonzales v. Raich*, 545 U.S. 1 (2005) (prohibition on personal cultivation and use of medical marijuana upheld due to effect on overall interstate trade). The practical effect of this rule is that with regard to economic activity, a substantial economic effect is presumed.

> **Example:** The Supreme Court upheld congressional restriction of wheat production, even when applied to a farmer growing only 23 acres of wheat, primarily for personal use. The rationale behind the decision was that if every small farmer were allowed to grow an unrestricted amount of wheat, the combined effect could have an impact on supply and demand in the interstate market. *Wickard v. Filburn*, 317 U.S. 111 (1942).

3. Non-Economic Activity

Congress's power under the Commerce Clause to regulate **intrastate** activity that is not obviously economic (so-called "non-economic" activity) is limited to some degree by principles of federalism, at least when the regulation involves an area of traditional state concern. To prevent judicial invalidation of such a regulation, Congress must set forth facts establishing a connection between the activity and a substantial economic effect on interstate commerce. *United States v. Morrison*, 529 U.S. 598 (2000) (federal civil remedy for victims of gender-motivated violence held invalid); *United States v. Lopez*, 514 U.S. 549 (1995) (federal statute regulating possession of a firearm within 1,000 feet of a public school struck down).

B. TAXATION AND SPENDING

Article I, Section 8 provides: "Congress shall have power to lay and collect taxes, duties, imposts and excises, to pay the debts and provide for the common defense and general welfare of the United States; but all duties, imposts and excises shall be uniform throughout the United States."

> **EXAM NOTE:** If you see the word "appropriation" on the exam, the power to tax and spend is likely a consideration.

1. Taxing

A tax by Congress will generally be upheld if it has a **reasonable relationship to revenue production,** or if Congress has the **power to regulate** the activity being taxed, subject to certain limitations.

a. Power is plenary

Article I, Section 8 of the Constitution gives Congress the plenary (i.e., exclusive) power to raise revenue through the imposition of taxes. The government has no burden to prove that the tax is necessary to any compelling governmental interest. Instead, the General Welfare Clause has been interpreted as permitting Congress to exercise its power to tax for any public purpose. (Note: This clause has been interpreted as having the same effect on the spending power, as discussed at II.B.2. Spending, *infra*.)

> While the General Welfare Clause gives Congress broad power in exercising its spending and taxing powers, it does not give Congress the specific power to legislate for the public welfare in general. Such "police power" is reserved for the states.

b. Uniformity

The requirement that all federal taxes must be uniform throughout the United States has been interpreted to mean **geographical** uniformity only; the product or activity at issue must be identically taxed in every state in which it is found. Differences in state law do not destroy this uniformity. *Fernandez v. Wiener*, 326 U.S. 340 (1945) (federal estate tax on "community property" valid despite variation in state laws regarding marital property).

c. Direct tax

Article I, Section 2 provides that "[r]epresentatives and direct taxes shall be apportioned among the several states," and Article I, Section 9 provides that "no...direct tax shall be laid, unless in proportion to the Census...." A direct tax (one imposed directly on property or persons, such as an ad valorem property tax) would therefore have to be apportioned evenly among the states. The difficulty of ensuring this outcome explains Congress's reluctance to enact such taxes—or perhaps the Supreme Court's reluctance to find that federal taxes are "direct." The Sixteenth Amendment gave Congress the power to lay and collect **income tax** without apportionment among the states.

d. Export tax

Goods exported to foreign countries may not be taxed for that reason by Congress or the states. Article I, Sections 9, 10.

2. Spending

The spending power has been interpreted very broadly. Congress has the power to **spend for the "general welfare"**—i.e., any public purpose—not just to pursue its other enumerated powers. *U.S. v. Butler*, 297 U.S. 1 (1936). For example, Congress can provide for the public funding of presidential nominating conventions as well as election campaigns. *Buckley v. Valeo*, 424 U.S. 1 (1976). Although there are areas in which Congress cannot directly regulate, it can use its spending power to accomplish such regulation indirectly by conditioning federal funding. *See South Dakota v. Dole*, 483 U.S. 203 (1987) (statute upheld withholding federal highway funds from states unless they barred the sale of alcoholic beverages to individuals under the age of 21).

> Congress cannot impose unconstitutional conditions, such as requiring distribution of the Ten Commandments to patients as a condition of Medicaid funding. *Dole*, 483 U.S. 203.

C. WAR AND DEFENSE POWERS

Article I, Section 8 gives Congress the power to declare war, raise and support armies, provide and maintain a navy, make rules for governing and regulating the land and naval forces, and provide for the organizing of a militia.

1. Providing for the National Defense

The authority granted to Congress under the war power is very broad. Congress may take whatever action it deems necessary to provide for the national defense in both wartime and peacetime. The Court has upheld the military draft and selective service; wage, price, and rent control of the civilian economy during wartime (and even during the post-war period); and the exclusion of civilians from restricted areas.

2. Courts and Tribunals

Congress has the power to establish military courts and tribunals under Article I, Section 8, Clause 14 and the Necessary and Proper Clause. These courts may try enemy soldiers, enemy civilians, and current members of the U.S. armed forces, but they do not have jurisdiction over U.S. civilians. U.S. citizens captured and held as "enemy combatants" are entitled, as a matter of due process, to contest the factual basis of their detention before a neutral decision maker. *Hamdi v. Rumsfeld*, 542 U.S. 507 (2004). Under the Suspension Clause of Article I, Section 9, Clause 2, all persons held in a territory over which the United States has sovereign control are entitled to habeas corpus (or similar) review of the basis for their detention, unless the privilege of seeking habeas corpus has been suspended. *Boumediene v. Bush*, 553 U.S. 723, (2008).

Because military tribunals are not Article III courts, not all constitutional protections apply (such as the right to a jury trial or grand jury indictment).

3. National Guard

The President has the authority to order units of the National Guard into federal service without the consent of the governor of the respective state. Generally, the National Guard will be called to service to assist in times of national emergency. However, this authority extends to circumstances when no national emergency exists.

D. INVESTIGATORY POWER

Congress does not have an express power to investigate, but the Necessary and Proper Clause allows Congress broad authority to conduct investigations incident to its power to legislate. *McGrain v. Daugherty*, 273 U.S. 135 (1927).

1. Scope

The investigatory power may extend to any matter within a "legitimate legislative sphere." According to the Speech and Debate Clause of Article I, Section 6, members of Congress cannot be questioned in regard to activities such as speech or debate taking place during a session in either House of Congress in relation to the business before it. This provides an absolute immunity from judicial interference. *Eastland v. Unites States Servicemen's Fund*, 421 U.S. 491 (1975).

2. Enforcement and Witness's Rights

A subpoenaed witness who fails to appear before Congress or refuses to answer questions may be cited for contempt. The witness is entitled to certain rights, including procedural due process (e.g., presence of counsel) and the privilege against self-incrimination.

E. PROPERTY POWER

Article IV, Section 3 gives Congress the "power to dispose of and make all needful rules and regulations respecting the territory or other property belonging to the United States." There is no express limit on Congress's power to **dispose** of property owned by the United States. Under the Fifth Amendment, however, Congress may only **take** private property for public use (eminent domain) with just compensation and in order to effectuate an enumerated power.

F. POSTAL POWER

Congress has the exclusive power "to establish post offices and post roads" under Article I, Section 8, Clause 7. Congress may impose reasonable restrictions on the use of the mail (such as prohibiting obscene or fraudulent material to be mailed), but the postal power may not be used to abridge any right guaranteed by the Constitution (e.g., the First Amendment).

G. POWER OVER ALIENS AND CITIZENSHIP

1. Aliens

Congress has plenary power over aliens. *Fiallo v. Bell*, 430 U.S. 787 (1977). Aliens have no right to enter the United States and may be refused entry for reasons such as their political beliefs. *Kleindienst v. Mandel*, 408 U.S. 753 (1972). However, this power is subject to the constraints of the Fifth Amendment Due Process Clause for an alien within the United States. *Zadvydas v. Davis*, 533 U.S. 678 (2001). An alien may generally be removed from the United States, but only after notice and a removal hearing. 8 U.S.C. §§ 1229, 1229a.

2. Naturalization

Congress has exclusive authority over naturalization. Article I, Section 8, Clause 4 allows Congress to "establish a uniform rule of naturalization."

> **Example:** Children born abroad whose parents are U.S. citizens are not automatically entitled to U.S. citizenship. Congress can grant citizenship conditioned on the child's return to the U.S. within a specified timeframe or for a specified duration. *Rogers v. Bellei*, 401 U.S. 815 (1971).

However, the right of national citizenship in the Fourteenth Amendment prevents Congress from taking away the citizenship of any citizen without her consent, unless that citizenship was obtained by fraud or in bad faith. *Afroyim v. Rusk*, 387 U.S. 253 (1967) (federal statute that stripped citizenship for voting in a foreign election struck down); *Costello v. United States*, 365 U.S. 265 (1961) (citizen's willful failure to accurately state his occupation on a naturalization application resulted in loss of citizenship).

H. OTHER ARTICLE I POWERS

Congress has power over **bankruptcies, maritime matters, coining of money,** fixing of **weights and measures,** and **patents and copyrights.**

1. Power Over the District of Columbia

Article I, Section 8 provides that Congress shall have the power to: "exercise exclusive Legislation in all Cases whatsoever, over such District (not exceeding ten Miles square) as may, by Cession of particular States, and the acceptance of Congress, become the Seat of the Government of the United States." Thus, Congress has supreme authority over Washington, D.C., and may legislate freely with regard to D.C. law.

2. Elections Clause

Article I, Section 4 of the Constitution provides: "The times, places and manner of holding elections for Senators and Representatives shall be prescribed by each state legislature, but Congress may...make or alter such regulations." The Elections Clause explicitly empowers Congress to override state laws concerning federal elections.

3. Necessary and Proper Clause

Congress is given the power to enact any legislation necessary and proper to execute any authority granted to any branch of the federal government. *McCulloch v. Maryland*, 17 U.S. 316 (1819). The Necessary and Proper Clause is not an independent source of power, but it permits Congress's otherwise designated authority to be exercised fully.

> **EXAM NOTE:** Because the Necessary and Proper Clause is not an independent source of power, it is not a correct answer choice by itself unless it carries into effect other enumerated powers.

I. POWER TO ENFORCE THE THIRTEENTH, FOURTEENTH, AND FIFTEENTH AMENDMENTS

Each of the Thirteenth, Fourteenth, and Fifteenth Amendments contains a provision that authorizes Congress to pass "appropriate legislation" to enforce the civil rights guaranteed by those amendments.

1. Thirteenth Amendment—Ban on Slavery

Congress has the power to adopt legislation rationally related to eliminating racial discrimination, as it is among the "badges or incidents" of slavery. *Jones v. Alfred H. Mayer Co.*, 392 U.S. 409 (1968). This power has been broadly interpreted to allow Congress to regulate both private and government action, including racial discrimination by private housing sellers, private schools, and private employers. (This is the only amendment that authorizes Congress to regulate purely private conduct.)

2. Fourteenth Amendment—Equal Protection and Due Process

The Fourteenth Amendment, Section 5 Enabling Clause permits Congress to pass legislation to enforce the equal protection and due process rights guaranteed by the amendment, but not to expand those rights or create new ones. Under the separation of powers doctrine, the job of defining such rights falls to the Supreme Court. In enforcing such rights, there must be a **"congruence and proportionality"** between the injury to be prevented or remedied and the means adopted to achieve that end. *City of Boerne v. Flores*, 521 U.S. 507 (1997) (Religious Freedom Restoration Act held invalid for failure to show widespread religious discrimination and for disproportion to any purported remedial goal). Congress may override state government action that infringes upon Fourteenth Amendment rights, but it may not under this amendment regulate wholly private conduct. In the exercise of Fourteenth Amendment powers, Congress can override the Eleventh Amendment immunity of states.

3. Fifteenth Amendment—Voting

The Fifteenth Amendment prohibits both the state and federal governments from denying any citizen the right to vote on the basis of race, color, or previous condition of servitude. The courts have interpreted the right to vote to include the right to have that vote meaningfully counted.

J. QUALIFICATIONS OF MEMBERS

The qualifications for members of Congress are set forth in Article I and cannot be altered by Congress or the states. *United States Term Limits, Inc. v. Thornton*, 514 U.S. 779 (1995) (state-mandated term limits for federal representatives invalid); *Powell v. McCormack*, 395 U.S. 486 (1969) (House of Representatives could not refuse to seat a scandal-plagued member who satisfied constitutional criteria for service).

III. THE POWERS OF THE PRESIDENT

Article II, Section 1 grants the "executive power" to the President. The extent of this power has been interpreted broadly by the Supreme Court, which has emphasized that the President has no power to make laws but does have the power to enforce them; this enforcement power includes the exercise of prosecutorial discretion. *Davis v. U.S.*, 512 U.S. 452 (1994). Generally speaking, the President's authority is broader in the area of foreign affairs than in domestic matters.

A. DOMESTIC POWER

1. Pardon Power for Federal Offenses

Article II, Section 2 provides the President with the power to "grant reprieves and pardons for offenses against the United States, except in cases of impeachment." This power applies only to federal cases; the President may not grant pardons for state crimes.

2. Veto Power

Article I, Section 7 gives the President the power to veto any bill presented to him (i.e., passed) by Congress. Upon presentment, the President has 10 days to act on proposed legislation. If the President signs the bill, it becomes law. The President may also veto the bill by sending it back, with objections, to the house in which it originated. Congress may override the veto and enact the bill into law by a two-thirds vote in each house.

A third option is that the President does nothing at all. If Congress is still in session at the end of the 10-day period, the bill becomes law without the President's signature. If Congress has adjourned during that time, however, the bill does not become law, because the President could not have returned it to its originating house. The President's failure to act on a bill in this situation is known as the "pocket veto" and cannot be overridden.

The President may not exercise a "line item" veto, refusing part of a bill and approving the rest, because it violates the Presentment Clause. *Clinton v. City of New York*, 524 U.S. 417 (1988).

3. Appointment and Removal of Officials

a. Appointment

Article II, Section 2 authorizes the President, **with the advice and consent of the Senate,** to appoint all "officers of the United States," including ambassadors and Justices of the Supreme Court. Congress may, however, delegate the appointment of "inferior" officials to the President alone (i.e., without Senate approval), the heads of executive departments, or the courts. "Inferior" officials are those supervised by Senate-confirmed appointees. Congress may not itself appoint members of a body with administrative or enforcement powers; such persons are "officers of the United States" and must be appointed by the President. *Buckley v. Valeo*, 424 U.S. 1 (1976) (makeup of the Federal Election Commission invalidated because a majority of its members were to be appointed by the President Pro Tem of the Senate and the Speaker of the House; the FEC's tasks were executive in nature, therefore, Congress had no right to appoint such federal officers).

b. Removal

The Constitution says nothing about the President's power to remove executive officers, but it is generally accepted that the President may remove any executive appointee without cause (and without Senate approval). Congress may not shield appointees from removal by the President by imposing a multi-tiered system in which persons at each level may be removed from office only for good cause. *Free Enterprise Fund v. Public Company Accounting Oversight Bd.*, 561 U.S. ___, 130 S. Ct. 3138 (2010) (holding 15 U.S.C.S. §§ 7211(e)(6) and 7217(d)(3) unconstitutional and invalid because the multilevel protection from removal of members of the Public Company Accounting Oversight Board was contrary to Article II's vesting of the executive power in the President and contravened the Constitution's separation of powers).

Federal judges, however, are protected under Article III, Section 1, which provides that they may "hold their offices during good behavior"; they may be removed only by impeachment.

4. Authority as Chief Executive

The scope of the President's power to issue executive orders and to govern domestic affairs is extensive but not clearly delineated. The best-known exposition holds that the President's authority varies with the degree of congressional authorization of the action. Thus, when the President acts:

i)   With the express or implied authorization of Congress, presidential authority is at its highest, and the action is strongly presumed to be valid;

ii) When Congress has not spoken, presidential authority is diminished, and the action is invalid if it interferes with the operations or power of another branch of government; and

iii) When Congress has spoken to the contrary, presidential authority is "at its lowest ebb," and the action is likely invalid. *Hamdan v. Rumsfeld*, 548 U.S. 557 (2006) (military commission had no jurisdiction to proceed because the executive order authorizing the commission exceeded congressional limitations placed on the President to convene commissions).

B. FOREIGN AFFAIRS

1. Commander in Chief

Although the President is the commander in chief of the military, only Congress may formally declare war. The President may take military action without a declaration of war in the case of actual hostilities against the United States. Congress may in turn limit the President's military activities through exercise of its military appropriation (i.e., funding) power. The questions of whether and to what extent the President may deploy troops overseas without congressional approval is unsettled; presidents routinely do so, and Congress routinely asserts its authority to approve the deployment. The courts have generally left the question to the political branches.

2. Treaties

The President represents and acts for the United States in day-to-day international affairs. In addition to appointing and receiving ambassadors, the President has the exclusive power to negotiate treaties, although a treaty may only be ratified with the concurrence of two-thirds of the Senate. A ratified treaty is "the supreme law of the land," so long as it does not conflict with any provision of the Constitution, and it takes precedence over any inconsistent state law. A treaty has the same authority as an act of Congress; should the two conflict, the one most recently adopted controls. Note that a non-self-executing treaty (one that requires legislation in order to implement its provisions) does not have the same force of law as an act of Congress until legislation is passed effectuating the treaty; the treaty serves as an independent source of authority for Congress to legislate, separate from its enumerated powers. The Constitution is superior to a treaty, and any conflict is resolved in favor of the Constitution. *Medellin v. Texas*, 552 U.S. 491 (2008) (in the absence of implementing legislation by Congress, the President did not have the authority to make a non-self-executing treaty binding on the states); *Youngstown Sheet & Tube v. Sawyer*, 343 U.S. 579 (1952) (Jackson, J., conc.).

3. Executive Agreements

The President has the power to enter into executive agreements with foreign nations (e.g., reciprocal trade agreements) that do not require the approval of two-thirds of the Senate. Although not expressly provided for in the Constitution, executive agreements may be made pursuant to prior (or subsequent) congressional authorization or pursuant to the President's authority over foreign affairs.

Conflicting federal statutes and treaties take precedence over executive agreements, but executive agreements take precedence over conflicting state laws.

IV. FEDERAL INTERBRANCH RELATIONSHIPS

The separation of powers doctrine, which is inherent in the structure of the Constitution, ensures that the executive, legislative, and judicial branches of government remain separate and distinct in order to provide a system of checks and balances.

A. CONGRESSIONAL LIMITS ON THE EXECUTIVE

1. Impeachment

Article II, Section 4 states: "The President, Vice President and all civil officers of the United States shall be removed from office on impeachment for, and conviction of, treason, bribery, or other high crimes and misdemeanors." The House of Representatives determines what constitutes "high crimes and misdemeanors" and **may impeach (i.e., bring charges) by a majority vote.** The Senate tries the impeached official, and **a two-thirds vote is necessary for conviction.**

2. Appropriation

If Congress explicitly mandates an expenditure of funds, the President has no power to impound those funds (i.e., refuse to spend them or delay the spending). The President is permitted to exercise spending discretion if the authorizing legislation so provides.

> **EXAM NOTE:** Separation of powers questions often center on the President trying to impound funds appropriated by Congress. Remember that if Congress fails to mandate that the funds are to be spent, then impoundment is not a separation of powers violation.

3. Legislative Veto

It is unconstitutional for Congress to attempt a "legislative veto" of an executive action—that is, to retain direct control over the actions of an executive agency, rather than going through the proper channels of passing a bill.

> **Example:** In *INS v. Chadha*, 462 U.S. 919 (1983), a provision of law permitted either house of Congress to overturn a decision by the Attorney General granting an alien relief from deportation. The Supreme Court held such a one-house congressional "veto" of a matter delegated to the executive to be unconstitutional as violating the carefully wrought legislative procedures set forth in Article I, which require passage of legislation by both Houses of Congress (i.e., bicameralism) and sending to the President pursuant to the Presentment Clauses for his approval or return. Thus, the Court made clear that a two-house legislative veto would be equally unconstitutional.

B. DELEGATION OF LEGISLATIVE POWER

Because Congress is vested by Article I with "all legislative powers," it may not delegate that power to any other branch of government. This principle is known as the "nondelegation doctrine." However, delegation of some of Congress's authority to the executive branch has consistently been held constitutional, so long as Congress specifies an "intelligible principle" to guide the delegate. *Whitman v. Am. Trucking Ass'ns, Inc.*, 531 U.S. 457 (2001).

Example: The IRS has been given the power to collect taxes that are assessed under the Internal Revenue Code. Although Congress has determined the amount to be taxed, it has delegated to the IRS the power to determine how such taxes are to be collected.

Almost any legislative delegation passes the "intelligible standards" requirement, so even broadly phrased standards have been upheld.

Examples: A delegation of authority to an executive agency to regulate broadcast licenses to the extent that "public interest, convenience, and necessity require" has been upheld. *Nat'l Broad. Co. v. United States*, 319 U.S. 190 (1943). Similarly, an administrative agency could set "just and reasonable" rates for natural gas sold in interstate commerce. *FPC v. Hope Natural Gas Co.*, 320 U.S. 591 (1944).

Certain powers, however, are nondelegable, such as the power of impeachment and the power to declare war.

EXAM NOTE: Because there is almost no limitation on the ability of Congress to delegate to the executive and judiciary branches, an answer choice on the MBE indicating that Congress has "exceeded its power to delegate" is almost always incorrect.

C. JUDICIAL LIMITATION OF CONGRESSIONAL POWER

Under the doctrine of separation of powers, Congress may not reinstate the right to bring a legal action after the Supreme Court has definitely rejected that right.

Example: The Supreme Court opinion had the effect of making a pending action time-barred. Accordingly, the defendant was granted summary judgment. A statute that revived the plaintiff's right to bring the action was struck down as a violation of the separation of powers doctrine. *Plaut v. Spendthrift Farm, Inc.*, 514 U.S. 211 (1995).

D. IMMUNITIES AND PRIVILEGES

1. Judicial

A judge is absolutely immune from civil liability for damages resulting from her judicial acts, including grave procedural errors and acts done maliciously or in excess of authority unless there is a clear absence of all jurisdiction. *Butz v. Economou*, 438 U.S. 478 (1987); *Stump v. Sparkman*, 435 U.S. 349 (1978). The judge is not immune, however, to lawsuits regarding nonjudicial activities, such as hiring and firing court employees. *Forrester v. White*, 484 U.S. 219 (1988).

Prosecutors are subject to similar immunity rules. *Imbler v. Pachtman*, 424 U.S. 409 (1976). Court officers who perform ministerial duties, such as court reporters, are entitled only to qualified, not absolute, immunity. *Antoine v. Byers & Anderson*, 508 U.S. 429 (1993).

Under 42 U.S.C. § 1983, a damage claim can be brought against a state official personally for violation of constitutional rights. The Supreme Court has recognized that a similar claim can be brought against federal officials. *Bivens v. Six Unknown Named Agents of Fed. Bureau of Narcotics*, 403 U.S. 388 (1971).

2. Legislative

The Speech or Debate Clause of Article I, Section 6 protects members of Congress from civil and criminal liability for statements and conduct made **in the regular**

course of the legislative process, including a speech given on the floor of Congress, committee hearings, and reports. The activities of congressional aides are also protected if a legislator performing the same acts would be immune. *Gravel v. United States*, 408 U.S. 606 (1972).

> **State legislators:** The Speech or Debate Clause does not apply to state legislators, but under the principles of federalism, state legislators are immune from liability for actions within the sphere of legitimate legislative activity (*see* § VI.B.1.b.2, State legislators, *infra*).

This protection does not foreclose prosecution for a crime, including the taking of bribes, when the crime does not require proof of legislative acts or inquiring into the motive behind those acts. *United States v. Brewster*, 408 U.S. 501 (1972). This protection also does not apply to speeches made outside Congress, or the "re-publication" (i.e., repeating) of a defamatory statement originally made in Congress. *Hutchinson v. Proxmire*, 443 U.S. 111 (1979).

3. **Executive**

   a. **Executive privilege**

      Executive privilege is a privilege with respect to the disclosure of confidential information by the executive branch to the judiciary or Congress. This privilege and the more narrow presidential privilege, which applies to communications made in the performance of a president's responsibilities to shape policies and make decisions, have been recognized by the Supreme Court. The presidential privilege survives an individual president's tenure, but this privilege is not absolute. *Cheney v. United States*, 542 U.S. 367 (2004); *United States v. Nixon*, 418 U.S. 683 (1974).

      1) **Criminal trial**

         Presidential communications must be made available in a criminal case if the prosecution demonstrates a need for the information. A judge may examine the communications in camera to determine whether the communications fall within the privilege. *United States v. Nixon, supra.*

      2) **Civil proceedings**

         An executive branch decision to withhold production of information in civil proceedings will be given greater deference than in a criminal trial because the need for information is "weightier" in the latter case. In a civil case, the court may be required to consider the issue of separation of powers without first requiring the executive branch to assert executive privilege. *Cheney v. United States Dist. Court, supra.*

      3) **Historical preservation**

         Congress can require the preservation of presidential papers and tape recordings. *Nixon v. Adm'r of Gen. Servs.*, 433 U.S. 425 (1977).

      4) **State secrets**

         Claims of privilege based on national security are generally accorded enhanced deference. *United States v. Reynolds*, 345 U.S. 1 (1953) (recognizing a "state secrets" privilege). *But see In re NSA Telcoms. Records Litig.*, 564 F. Supp. 2d 1109 (2008) (the "state secrets" privilege was a common-law privilege that could be limited by congressional action).

b. Executive immunity

1) Official duties

The President may not be sued for civil damages with regard to any acts performed as part of the President's **official responsibilities.** *Nixon v. Fitzgerald*, 457 U.S. 731 (1982). The President has no immunity, however, from a civil action based on conduct alleged to have occurred **before the President took office** or completely unrelated to carrying out his job. Moreover, the President may be subject to such a suit even while in office. *Clinton v. Jones*, 520 U.S. 681 (1997).

a) Presidential advisor

A senior presidential advisor (e.g., cabinet member) is not automatically entitled to enjoy derivatively the protection of absolute executive immunity. Although the Supreme Court has stated that such an advisor may be entitled to such protection when performing special functions that are vital to national security or foreign policy, the Court has also held that an Attorney General did not qualify for absolute immunity with respect to the authorization of a warrantless wiretap for national security purposes. The burden for establishing such immunity rests with the advisor. *Harlow v. Fitzgerald*, 457 U.S. 800 (1982); *Mitchell v. Forsyth*, 472 U.S. 511 (1985).

b) Federal officials

A federal official, in performing a discretionary (as opposed to ministerial) act, is entitled to qualified immunity from liability for civil damages when the official's conduct does not violate clearly established statutory and constitutional rights of which a reasonable person would have known. This is an objective standard; a plaintiff's bare allegations of malice are insufficient to overcome this immunity. *Harlow v. Fitzgerald*, 457 U.S. 800 (1982).

Example: The Attorney General, in authorizing a warrantless wiretap for national security purposes, while not entitled to absolute immunity, was entitled to qualified immunity. The unconstitutionality of this authorization was not clearly established at the time of the authorization. *Mitchell v. Forsyth*, 472 U.S. 511 (1985).

PART TWO: THE FEDERAL SYSTEM

V.   FEDERAL AND STATE POWERS

The federal system, under which the federal and state governments each have exclusive authority over some areas, yet share authority over other areas, is one of the Constitution's basic checks on governmental power.

A.   EXCLUSIVE FEDERAL POWERS

The Constitution explicitly provides for some powers of the federal government to be exclusive, such as the powers to coin money or enter into treaties. Other powers are by their nature exclusively federal, such as the power to declare war and the power over citizenship; a state's attempt to exercise authority in these areas would essentially subvert the power of the federal government.

B.   EXCLUSIVE STATE POWERS

The Tenth Amendment provides that all powers not assigned by the Constitution to the federal government are reserved to the states, or to the people. In theory, this gives the states expansive, exclusive power. In practice, however, given the broad interpretation of the Commerce Clause and the spending power, the federal government has very broad authority, making state power rarely exclusive.

C.   CONCURRENT FEDERAL AND STATE LAWS—SUPREMACY CLAUSE

It is possible (and common) for the federal and state governments to legislate in the same area. When this happens, the Supremacy Clause (Article VI, paragraph 2) provides that federal law supersedes conflicting state law (*see* § VIII. Federal Preemption of State Law, *infra*).

VI.   INTERGOVERNMENTAL IMMUNITIES

A.   FEDERAL IMMUNITY

1.   Regulation by the States

The states have no power to regulate the federal government—for example, by imposing state wage-and-hour laws on local federal offices—unless Congress permits the state regulation or unless the state regulation is not inconsistent with existing federal policy.

2.   Taxation by the States

The federal government and its instrumentalities (such as a national bank) are immune from taxation by the states. *McCulloch v. Maryland*, 17 U.S. 316 (1819). States may, however, impose generally applicable indirect taxes so long as they do not unreasonably burden the federal government (e.g., state income taxes on federal employees).

B.   STATE IMMUNITY

1.   Federal Regulation

The federal government has virtually unlimited power to regulate the states.

a. Congressional action

As long as Congress is exercising one of its enumerated powers, Congress generally may regulate the states. For example, a federal minimum wage and overtime statute enacted under the commerce power can be applied to state employees. *Garcia v. San Antonio Metropolitan Transit Authority*, 469 U.S. 528 (1985). Similarly, Congress could prohibit the disclosure by state officials of personal information obtained from driver's license applications because such information constitutes an article of commerce that is being sold in interstate commerce. *Reno v. Condon*, 528 U.S. 141 (2000).

If Congress determines that a state is violating a person's civil liberties, it can place limits on that state's activities by using the power of the Fourteenth and Fifteenth Amendments. *See Oregon v. Mitchell*, 400 U.S. 112 (1970).

1) "Commandeering" limitation

Congress cannot "commandeer" state legislatures by commanding them to enact specific legislation or administer a federal regulatory program, and it may not circumvent that restriction by conscripting a state executive officer directly. *Printz v. United States*, 521 U.S. 898 (1997); *New York v. United States*, 505 U.S. 144 (1992). However, through the use of the taxing and spending powers, Congress may encourage state action that it cannot directly compel.

Example: In *South Dakota v. Dole*, 483 U.S. 203 (1987), the Court held that Congress could condition a provision of five percent of federal highway funds on the state's raising its drinking age to 21; the amount at issue did not exceed the point at which "pressure turns into compulsion."

b. Judicial action

1) Remedying constitutional violations

The federal judiciary has broad equitable powers in fashioning a remedy for a constitutional violation. For example, while a court may not directly impose a tax in order to fund a racial-discrimination remedy, it may order a local government with taxing authority to levy such a tax, and it may do so despite a state statutory limitation that would otherwise prevent such action. *Missouri v. Jenkins*, 495 U.S. 33 (1990).

2) State legislators

State legislators are absolutely immune from suit for damages and for declaratory and injunctive relief for actions within the sphere of legitimate legislative activity. *Supreme Court of Virginia v. Consumers Union of U.S., Inc.*, 446 U.S. 719 (1980); *Tenney v. Brandhove*, 341 U.S. 367 (1951).

2. Federal Taxation

States are not immune from federal taxation unless the tax would discourage essential governmental functions. *Helvering v. Gerhardt*, 304 U.S. 405 (1938). This is particularly true when the taxed state activity is a business similar to federally taxed businesses run by private individuals, such as railroads or liquor stores. *New York v. United States*, 326 U.S. 572 (1946).

3. **Litigation Involving the United States and Its Officers**

In suits between a state and the United States, the United States must consent before the state can file suit against it; conversely, the United States does not need to obtain consent from a state to file suit against that state. As between states, no consent is needed for one state to file suit against another state.

Suits against federal officers are limited, and generally prohibited, because such suits are considered to be brought against the United States if payment of the award will be made from the public treasury. However, if the federal officer acted outside the scope of his professional capacity, then a suit may be instituted against the officer individually.

VII. STATE REGULATION AND TAXATION OF COMMERCE

The Constitution contemplates a system of regulation of commerce and taxation that includes both the federal and state governments.

A. THE DORMANT COMMERCE CLAUSE

The Dormant Commerce Clause (sometimes referred to as the negative implication of the commerce clause) is a doctrine that limits the power of states to legislate in ways that impact interstate commerce. The Commerce Clause (Article I, Section 8, Clause 3) reserves to Congress the power "[t]o regulate commerce with foreign nations, and among the several states, and with the Indian tribes"; as a corollary, individual states are limited in their ability to legislate on such matters.

1. General Rule

If Congress has not enacted legislation in a particular area of interstate commerce, then the states are free to regulate, so long as the state or local action does not:

i) **Discriminate** against out-of-state commerce;

ii) **Unduly burden** interstate commerce; and

iii) Regulate **extraterritorial** (wholly out-of-state) activity.

2. Discrimination Against Out-of-State Commerce

A state or local regulation discriminates against out-of-state commerce if it protects local economic interests at the expense of out-of-state competitors. *See City of Philadelphia v. New Jersey*, 437 U.S. 617 (1978) (state statute prohibiting importation of out-of-state garbage discriminated in favor of local trash collectors); *Dean Milk Co. v. City of Madison*, 340 U.S. 349 (1959) (state law discriminated against out-of-state milk suppliers by requiring all milk sold in the city to be processed and bottled locally).

a. Necessary to important state interest

If a state or local regulation, on its face or in practice, is discriminatory, then the regulation may be upheld if the state or local government can establish that:

i) An important local interest is being served; and

ii) No other nondiscriminatory means are available to achieve that purpose.

Discriminatory regulation has rarely been upheld. In a few instances, a discriminatory state or local regulation that furthers an important, non-economic state interest, like health and safety, has not been struck down. *Maine v. Taylor,* 477 U.S. 131 (1986) (upheld a prohibition against importation into the state of out-of-state live baitfish that may pose contamination hazards to local waters).

b. **Market-participant exception**

A state may behave in a discriminatory fashion if it is acting as a market participant (buyer or seller), as opposed to a market regulator. If the state is a market participant, it may favor local commerce or discriminate against nonresident commerce as could any private business. *E.g., Reeves, Inc. v. Stake,* 447 U.S. 429 (1980) (state-owned cement plant may, in times of shortage, sell only to in-state buyers).

c. **Traditional government function exception**

State and local regulations may favor state and local **government** entities, though not local **private** entities, when those entities are performing a traditional governmental function, such as waste disposal. For example, an ordinance may require all trash haulers to deliver to a local **public** waste-treatment facility, but **not** to a local **private** facility. *Compare United Haulers Ass'n, Inc. v. Oneida-Herkimer Solid Waste Mgmt. Auth.,* 550 U.S. 330 (2007) (public facility), *with C & A Carbone, Inc. v. Town of Clarkstown,* 511 U.S. 383 (1994) (private facility). Similarly, a state may discriminate against out-of-state interests when raising money to fund state and local government projects. *Dep't of Revenue of Kentucky v. Davis,* 553 U.S. 328 (2008) (upholding state income tax exemption for income earned on state and local bonds, but not out-of-state bonds).

d. **Subsidy exception**

A state may favor its own citizens when providing for subsidy. For example, a state may offer in-state residents a lower tuition rate to attend a state college or university than out-of-state residents. *Vlandis v. Kline,* 412 U.S. 441 (1973).

e. **Exception—congressionally permitted discrimination**

Because Congress has exclusive authority over interstate commerce, it may explicitly permit states to act in ways that would otherwise violate the Dormant Commerce Clause. *Prudential Ins. Co. v. Benjamin,* 328 U.S. 408 (1946) (state tax only on out-of-state insurance companies upheld when Congress had enacted a law permitting states to regulate insurance in any manner consistent with federal statutes). It must be unmistakably clear that Congress intended to permit the otherwise impermissible state regulation; Congress must expressly allow or "affirmatively contemplate" such state legislation. The fact that the state policy appears to be consistent with federal policy or that the state policy furthers the goals that Congress had in mind is insufficient. *South–Central Timber Dev., Inc. v. Wunnicke,* 467 U.S. 82, 90 (1984).

3. **Undue Burden on Interstate Commerce**

a. **Balancing test**

A state regulation that is not discriminatory may still be struck down as unconstitutional if it imposes an undue burden on interstate commerce. The courts will balance, case by case, the objective and purpose of the state law against the burden on interstate commerce and evaluate whether there are less restrictive alternatives. If the benefits of the state law are grossly outweighed by the burdens on interstate commerce, then even nondiscriminatory regulation may be struck down. *Pike v. Bruce Church, Inc.*, 397 U.S. 137 (1970). This balancing test is not a cost-benefit analysis or a form of close scrutiny of state economic regulation. *United Haulers Ass'n v. Oneida-Herkimer Solid Waste Mgmt. Auth.*, 550 U.S. 330 (2007).

b. **"Extraterritoriality"**

States may not regulate conduct that occurs wholly beyond their borders. Thus, Connecticut could not require that beer sold in Connecticut not be priced higher than beer sold in any of the four neighboring states, because the Connecticut regime had the practical effect of regulating beer prices in those states. *Healy v. Beer Inst., Inc.*, 491 U.S. 324 (1989). There may be an exception for the regulation of the internal affairs of corporations. *CTS Corp. v. Dynamics Corp.*, 481 U.S. 69 (1987).

B. **STATE TAXATION OF COMMERCE**

1. **Interstate Commerce**

Much as with regulation, the states may tax interstate commerce only if Congress has not already acted in the particular area and if the tax does not discriminate against or unduly burden interstate commerce.

a. *Complete Auto* **Test**

The Supreme Court applies a four-part test to determine whether a state tax on interstate commerce comports with the Commerce Clause. *Complete Auto Transit, Inc. v. Brady*, 430 U.S. 274 (1977).

1) **Substantial nexus**

There must be a **substantial nexus** between the activity being taxed and the taxing state. A substantial nexus requires significant (i.e., more than minimum) contacts with, or substantial activity within, the taxing state. *E.g., Quill Corp. v. North Dakota*, 504 U.S. 298 (1992) (mailing of catalogs and shipment of goods to consumers in a state is not a sufficient nexus).

2) **Fair apportionment**

The tax must be fairly apportioned according to a rational formula (e.g., taxing only the state's portion of the company's business), such that interstate commerce does not pay total taxes greater than local commerce by virtue of having to pay tax in more than one state. The burden is on the taxpaying business to prove unfair apportionment.

3) Nondiscrimination

The tax may not provide a direct commercial advantage to local businesses over their interstate competitors (unless Congress specifically authorizes such a tax). A tax that is neutral on its face still may be unconstitutional if its effect is to favor local commerce. *West Lynn Creamery Inc. v. Healy*, 512 U.S. 186 (1994) (tax affecting all milk dealers, the revenue from which went to a fund used to subsidize in-state dairy farmers, violated the Commerce Clause). In addition, the denial of tax exemption to a state entity unless the entity operates primarily for the benefit of state residents may be unconstitutional. *Camps Newfound/Owatonna v. Town of Harrison*, 520 U.S. 564 (1997).

4) Fair relationship to services provided

The tax must be fairly related to the services provided by the taxing state. *Evansville-Vanderburg Airport Auth. Dist. v. Delta Airlines, Inc.*, 405 U.S. 707 (1972) (tax on airline passengers was related to benefits the passengers received from the state airport facilities).

b. Discrimination under other constitutional provisions

A discriminatory tax may violate more than just the Commerce Clause.

i) A tax that discriminates against nonresident individuals—for example, an income tax that exempts local residents—may violate the **Comity Clause** of Article IV. *Austin v. New Hampshire*, 420 U.S. 656 (1975).

ii) A discriminatory tax on out-of-state businesses, even if authorized by Congress and therefore allowed under the Commerce Clause, may still violate the **Equal Protection Clause** of the Fourteenth Amendment, if there is no rational basis to support it. *Metropolitan Life Ins. Co. v. Ward*, 470 U.S. 869 (1985).

c. Types of taxes

1) Ad valorem property tax

An ad valorem tax is based on the value of real or personal property and is often assessed at a particular time (e.g., tax day). Such taxes, which may be imposed on the full value of the property, are generally valid, but a state may **not** levy ad valorem taxes on **goods in the course of transit** (from the time the goods are delivered to an interstate carrier or begin their interstate journey until they reach their destination). *Standard Oil Co. v. Peck*, 342 U.S. 382 (1952). However, once the goods are stopped for a business purpose (i.e., obtain a "taxable situs"), they may be taxed.

A state may tax the "instrumentalities of commerce" (airplanes, railroad cars, etc.), provided that:

i) The instrumentality has a **taxable situs** within—or **sufficient contacts** with—the taxing state (i.e., it receives benefits or protection from the state); and

ii) The tax is **fairly apportioned** to the amount of time the instrumentality is in the state.

2) Sales tax

A sales tax imposed on the seller of goods is valid as long as the sale takes place within the state. Sales tax generally does not discriminate against interstate commerce as long as there is a substantial nexus between the taxpayer and the state (e.g., his business is there), and the tax is properly apportioned.

3) Use tax

A use tax on goods purchased out of state but used within the taxing state is valid so long as the use tax rate is not higher than the sales tax rate on the same item. Even though a use tax does, on its face, seem to discriminate against out-of-state purchases, the rationale for its validity is that such a tax equalizes the tax on in-state and out-of-state goods. *Henneford v. Silas Mason Co., Inc.*, 300 U.S. 577 (1937).

4) "Doing business" taxes

Taxes levied against companies for the privilege of doing business in a state (made up of privilege, license, franchise, or occupation taxes) are valid as long as they meet the basic taxation requirements:

i) The activity taxed must have a substantial nexus to the taxing state;

ii) The tax must be fairly apportioned;

iii) The tax may not discriminate against interstate commerce; and

iv) The tax must be fairly related to the services provided by the state.

Such a tax may be measured by a flat annual fee or by a graduated rate proportional to the amount of revenue derived from the taxing state. The burden of showing that a tax is unfairly apportioned is on the taxpayer.

2. Foreign Commerce

The Import-Export Clause of Article I, Section 10 prohibits the states, without the consent of Congress from imposing any tax on any imported or exported goods, or on any commercial activity connected with imported goods, except what is absolutely necessary for executing its inspection laws. *Brown v. Maryland*, 25 U.S. 419 (1827).

The Commerce Clause restricts state taxation of commerce with other countries because it vests in Congress the exclusive power to regulate foreign commerce. A state tax on foreign commerce must, in addition to meeting the same requirements as a tax on interstate commerce, not (i) create a substantial risk of *international* multiple taxation or (ii) prevent the federal government from "speaking with one voice" regarding international trade or foreign affairs issues. *Barclays Bank PLC v. Franchise Tax Board*, 512 U.S. 298 (1994).

C. ALCOHOLIC BEVERAGE REGULATION

The Twenty-First Amendment repealed prohibition and gave the authority to regulate the distribution of alcoholic beverages within each state to the states. However, regulations that economically favor local liquor businesses over out-of-state liquor businesses can violate the Commerce Clause. *Granholm v. Heald*, 544 U.S. 460 (2005). In addition,

Congress, under the spending power, can impose conditions on the grant of federal funds that affect state regulation of alcohol. *South Dakota v. Dole, supra.*

VIII. FEDERAL PREEMPTION OF STATE LAW

The Supremacy Clause of Article VI, Section 2 provides that the "Constitution, and the laws of the United States" are the "supreme law of the land." Any state law that directly or indirectly conflicts with a federal law is void under this clause. However, the Supreme Court has frequently stated that there is a presumption against preemption, especially in areas in which states have traditionally exercised police power. *Wyeth v. Levine,* 555 U.S. 555 (2009) (health and safety).

A. EXPRESS PREEMPTION

Federal law **expressly** preempts state law in cases in which the Constitution makes the federal power exclusive (such as the powers to coin money or declare war) or when Congress has enacted legislation that explicitly prohibits state regulation in the same area (e.g., the Federal Cigarette Labeling and Advertising Act forbids state laws that regulate either cigarette labels or the "advertising or promotion" of labeled cigarettes "based on smoking and health," 15 U.S.C. § 1334).

1. Narrow Construction

An express federal preemption must be narrowly construed. *Altria Group, Inc. v. Good,* 555 U.S. 70 (2008) (Federal Cigarette Labeling and Advertising Act did not preempt a suit based on a state's general deceptive-practices statute because such a statute was not based on smoking and health).

> **Example:** The National Bank Act prohibited states to "exercise visitorial powers with respect to national banks, such as conducting examinations, inspecting or requiring the production of books or records," but it was not clear from the Act's language whether it completely prohibited the state from exercising enforcement powers when state law is violated. The Court concluded that the Act's structure and purpose differentiate between the sovereign's "visitorial powers" and its power to enforce the law. While the state could not issue administrative subpoenas to banks, it could file suit to punish violations of state banking laws. *Cuomo v. Clearing House Ass'n,* 557 U.S. ___, 129 S. Ct. 2710 (2009).

2. Savings Clause

Federal law may also contain "savings clauses" that explicitly preserve or allow state laws that regulate in the same area (e.g., the Clean Water Act preserves "any right which any person (or class of persons) may have under any statute or common law," 33 U.S.C. § 1365).

B. IMPLIED PREEMPTION

Federal preemption is **implied** when any of the following circumstances exist:

i) Congress intended for federal law to **occupy the field** (*e.g., Hines v. Davidowitz,* 312 U.S. 52 (1941) (new federal law requiring registration of all aliens preempted preexisting state law requiring registration of aliens within the state);

ii) The state law **directly conflicts** with the federal law by, for example, requiring conduct that is forbidden by the federal law or making it impossible (or nearly so) to comply with both, *e.g., Rose v. Arkansas State Police,* 479 U.S. 1 (1986) (federal law providing that federal death benefits for state law-enforcement officers be in addition to other state benefits preempted contrary state law requiring that other benefits be reduced by the amount of death benefits); or

Example 1: Under 42 U.S.C. § 1983, all persons who violate federal rights while acting under color of state law may be sued for damages. A state law shielding state corrections officers from liability under § 1983 by excluding claims brought against them from being heard in state court violated the Supremacy Clause. *Haywood v. Drown*, 556 U.S. 729 (2009).

Example 2: Although a federal statute provides for preemption of state tort claims with regard to medical devices approved by the Federal Drug Administration, 21 U.S.C. § 360(k), there is no express preemption with regard to prescription drugs. However, a state-imposed duty on generic drug manufacturers to warn users of dangers through labeling was preempted by an FDA rule that required the label on generic drugs to match the label of the corresponding brand name drug. The court found that it was impossible for the generic drug manufacturers to comply with both federal regulations and state law. *PLIVA, Inc. v. Mensing*, __ U.S. __, 131 S. Ct. 2567 (2011).

Compare: The manufacturer of a brand-name drug failed to establish preemption of a state-law duty to warn when the manufacturer was permitted under FDA regulations to change the drug label and then request FDA approval for the change. *Wyeth v. Levine, supra.*

iii) The state law **indirectly conflicts** with federal law by creating an obstacle to or frustrating the accomplishment of that law's purpose (*e.g., Perez v. Campbell*, 402 U.S. 637 (1971) (state law suspending licenses of all drivers with unpaid accident judgments frustrates the purpose of federal bankruptcy laws to provide a fresh start)).

1. Absence of Preemption

If Congress does not intend to occupy the field completely, a state is free to enact similar legislation. *Colorado Anti-Discrimination Comm'n. v. Continental Air Lines, Inc.*, 372 U.S. 714 (1963) (state statute prohibiting racial discrimination valid despite the existence of identical federal law). If there has not been federal preemption in a given area, a state is free to set more stringent standards than those imposed by the federal government. In addition, a state may recognize individual rights that exceed those granted by the federal constitution or federal statutes. *Pruneyard Shopping Ctr. v. Robbins*, 447 U.S. 74 (1980) (California's constitutional grant of greater free speech rights than the federal constitution confers upheld).

EXAM NOTE: Under the Supremacy Clause, federal law sets a **floor** below which state law generally cannot go, but it does **not** set a **ceiling** beyond which state law cannot go.

IX. RELATIONS AMONG STATES

A. INTERSTATE COMPACTS

An interstate compact is an agreement, similar to a treaty or a contract, between two or more states. Article I, Section 10, Clause 3 (the "Interstate Compact Clause") allows states to enter into such agreements only with the consent of Congress. However, the only agreements that qualify as "compacts" requiring the consent of Congress are those that either affect a power delegated to the federal government or alter the political balance within the federal system.

B. FULL FAITH AND CREDIT

The Full Faith and Credit Clause of Article IV, Section 1 provides that "[f]ull faith and credit shall be given in each state to the public acts, records, and judicial proceedings of every other state."

1. Judgments

Full faith and credit requires that out-of-state **judgments** be given in-state effect. *Baker v. General Motors Corp.*, 522 U.S. 222 (1998). However, to be given full faith and credit, a decision must meet three requirements:

i) The court that rendered the judgment must have had **jurisdiction** over the parties and the subject matter;

ii) The judgment must have been **on the merits** rather than on a procedural issue; and

iii) The judgment must be **final**.

2. Laws (Public Acts)

The Full Faith and Credit Clause is "less demanding" with respect to choice of law (i.e., which state's law should apply in a situation when either might).

PART THREE: INDIVIDUAL RIGHTS

> **EXAM NOTE:** Approximately half of the Constitutional Law questions on the MBE will cover Individual Rights—that is, everything from here to the end of the outline.

X. STATE ACTION AND THE ROLE OF THE COURTS

The Constitution generally protects against wrongful conduct by the government, not private parties (with the exception of the Thirteenth Amendment's prohibition against slavery, which applies to private and government action). In other words, state action is a necessary prerequisite to triggering constitutional protections. A private person's conduct must constitute state action in order for these protections to apply. For example, state action may exist in cases of private parties carrying out traditional governmental functions or significant state involvement in the activities.

A. TRADITIONAL GOVERNMENTAL FUNCTION

State action is found when a private person carries on activities that are **traditionally performed exclusively by the state,** such as running primary elections or governing a "company town." *Terry v. Adams*, 345 U.S. 461 (1953); *Marsh v. Alabama*, 326 U.S. 501 (1946). By contrast, a shopping center that is open to the public does not thereby assume or exercise municipal functions, and therefore is not treated as a state actor. *Hudgens v. NLRB*, 424 U.S. 507 (1976) (shopping mall not required to permit picketing on its private sidewalks). Similarly, merely providing a product or service that the government **could** offer is not sufficient to make the provider a state actor. *Flagg Brothers v. Brooks*, 436 U.S. 149 (1978). However, the use of peremptory challenges, even by private litigants, constitutes state action because the selection of jurors is a traditional state function and because the judge (i.e., the government) plays a significant role in the process. *Edmonson v. Leesville Concrete*, 500 U.S. 614 (1992).

B.   SIGNIFICANT STATE INVOLVEMENT

State action may also exist if there are sufficient mutual contacts between the conduct of a private party and the government, which is a question of the degree of involvement. The Supreme Court has not laid out a test to determine what constitutes significant state involvement, but some general guidelines exist. Mere licensing or regulation of a private party does not constitute state action; the state must **act affirmatively** to facilitate, encourage, or authorize the activity. State action also exists if the actions of a private party and the government are so intertwined that a mutual benefit results, such as if the parties are involved in a joint venture. *Lugar v. Edmondson Oil Co.,* 457 U.S. 922 (1982) (state action was present when a clerk and sheriff acted together with a private citizen to obtain attachment against a property of the debtor.) Even when the state explicitly prohibits behavior that violates a person's civil rights, state action may exist if it appears the state has sanctioned the violative act.

> States are constitutionally forbidden from facilitating or authorizing discrimination, but they are not required to make discrimination illegal.

C.   INSIGNIFICANT STATE INVOLVEMENT

Businesses that the government substantially regulates or to which the government grants a monopoly, such as utility companies, do not exercise state action. Further exclusions include nursing homes that accept Medicaid, schools that receive government funds but are operated by a private corporation, and congressional grants of a corporate charter.

XI.   PROCEDURAL DUE PROCESS

The Due Process Clause of the **Fifth Amendment,** which applies against the **federal government,** provides that "[n]o person shall be...deprived of life, liberty, or property, without due process of law."

The Due Process Clause of the **Fourteenth Amendment,** which applies against the **states,** provides that "no state shall make or enforce any law which shall...deprive any person of life, liberty, or property, without due process of the law."

A.   DUE PROCESS GENERALLY

These clauses operate at a number of levels to protect the rights of individuals and other "persons"—e.g., corporations—against the government. At the most basic level, each clause ensures that the federal and state governments must follow certain procedures before depriving any person of "life, liberty, or property." These safeguards, like notice and a hearing, are the cornerstone of **procedural due process.**

At another level, the Fourteenth Amendment, through its guarantee of rights respecting life, liberty, and property, has been interpreted to make **most provisions of the Bill of Rights** (which by its terms applies to the federal government) **applicable against the states as well.** That is, the Fourteenth Amendment Due Process Clause **incorporates** the protections of the First, Second, and Fourth Amendments, as well as most of the protections of the Fifth, Sixth, and Eighth Amendments. (However, the Fifth Amendment right to grand jury indictment and the Sixth Amendment right to a unanimous jury verdict in a criminal trial are not incorporated. While the Eighth Amendment protections against cruel and unusual punishment and excessive bail are incorporated, it has not been determined whether the Eighth Amendment protection against excessive fines is incorporated.) The Seventh Amendment right to a jury in civil trials has been held not applicable to the states.

Finally, both Due Process Clauses contain a "substantive" component that guarantees certain fundamental rights to all persons. This **substantive due process** acts as something of a catchall for rights not explicitly set forth elsewhere in the Constitution.

B. PROCEDURAL DUE PROCESS APPLIED

1. General Principles

The concept of "fundamental fairness" is at the heart of the right to procedural due process. It includes an individual's right to be **notified** of charges or proceedings against him and the opportunity to be **heard** at those proceedings. When one's liberty or property interests are adversely affected by governmental action, two questions are asked:

   i)   Is the threatened interest a **protected** one?

   ii) If so, **what process** is due?

a. Neutral decision maker

Due process entitles a person to a fair decision maker. A judge must recuse herself when she has a direct, personal, substantial, pecuniary interest in a case (i.e., actual bias) or there is a serious objective risk of actual bias. In the latter instance, proof of actual bias is not required, and subjective impartiality is not sufficient to justify a refusal to recuse. *Caperton v. A. T. Massey Coal Co.*, 556 U.S. 868 (2009).

> **Example:** An attorney running for a judgeship on the state supreme court had received a $3 million contribution that had a significant and disproportionate influence on the electoral outcome. The contribution exceeded the sum total of all other contributions the attorney had received and exceeded by 50% the combined amount spent by the attorney's and his opponent's campaigns. The contribution was made by the president of a company that had received an adverse $50 million verdict in a lower court of the state prior to the election. It was foreseeable that the judgment would be appealed to the state supreme court at the time that the contribution was made. Consequently, the Due Process Clause required the judge who had received the contribution to recuse himself. *Caperton v. A. T. Massey Coal Co., supra.*

b. Intentional conduct

Due process addresses injury that results from an intentional governmental act. Mere negligent conduct by a government employee does not trigger a due process right. *Daniels v. Williams*, 474 U.S. 327 (1986) (prisoner's injury due to correction officer's negligence was not a deprivation of liberty).

2. Protected Interests

a. Liberty

An impingement on liberty is generally construed to mean **significant** governmental restraint on one's **physical freedom,** exercise of **fundamental rights** (i.e., those guaranteed by the Constitution), or **freedom of choice or action.**

Examples of loss of liberty include commitment to a mental institution, parole revocation, and loss of parental rights. Injury to reputation alone is not a deprivation of liberty, unless the injury is so great that the individual has lost **significant employment or associational rights.**

b. Property

A cognizable property interest involves more than an abstract need or desire; there must be a "legitimate claim of entitlement" by virtue of statute, employment contract, or custom. *Board of Regents v. Roth*, 408 U.S. 564, 577 (1972) (non-tenured professor with a one-year contract had no liberty or property interest in being rehired).

The rights to public education, to government-issued licenses, and to continued welfare and disability benefits are legitimate property interests. For example, although a patient may have a legitimate property interest in the continued receipt of medical benefits to pay for the patient's stay in a qualified nursing home, there is no legitimate property interest in the patient's continued residence in the nursing home of the patient's choice. As a result, a patient is not entitled to a hearing before the government disqualifies a nursing home from participating in a public benefits program. *O'Bannon v. Town Court Nursing Ctr.*, 447 U.S. 773 (1980).

There is a legitimate property interest in continued public employment only if there is an employment contract or a clear understanding that the employee may be fired only for cause. *Arnett v. Kennedy*, 416 U.S. 134 (1974). An "at will" governmental employee has no right to continued employment. *Bishop v. Wood*, 426 U.S. 341 (1976). If, however, the government gives the "at will" public employee assurances of continual employment or dismissal for only specified reasons, then there must be a fair procedure to protect the employee's interests if the government seeks to discharge the employee from his position. Such entitlement to procedural due process can also result from statutory law, formal contract terms, or the actions of a supervisory person with authority to establish terms of employment.

Note, though, that even those employees who lack any entitlement to continued employment cannot be discharged for reasons that in and of themselves violate the Constitution. Thus, an "at-will" governmental employee cannot be fired for having engaged in speech protected by the First Amendment. *Board of Regents v. Roth*, 408 U.S. 564 (1972). To be entitled to a hearing, however, the employee must make a prima facie claim that she is being discharged for reasons that violate specific constitutional guarantees. *Mt. Healthy City School Dist. Bd. of Educ. v. Doyle*, 429 U.S. 274 (1977). A dismissal will be upheld if the government can prove that the employee would have been discharged in any event for reasons unrelated to any constitutionally protected activities.

3. Notice and Hearing

If a protected interest is threatened by governmental action, the next step is to determine what type of process is due. The Court considers three factors in determining the amount of process that is due:

i) The **private interest** affected by the governmental action;

ii) The risk of erroneous deprivation of that interest using current procedures and the probable **value of additional or substitute safeguards**; and

iii) The **burden (fiscal and administrative cost)** involved in providing the additional process.

Mathews v. Eldridge, 424 U.S. 319 (1976). The greater the importance of the threatened interest, the greater the likelihood that the Court will require extensive procedural safeguards prior to the termination of the interest. Generally, the person whose interest is being deprived is entitled to **notice** of the government's action by an unbiased decision maker and an **opportunity to be heard,** although the hearing need not necessarily occur before the termination of the interest.

> **Example:** While the state must give notice and hold a hearing prior to terminating **welfare benefits,** in cases of terminating **disability benefits or public employment,** the state must give prior notice, but only a post-termination evidentiary hearing is required. *Goldberg v. Kelly*, 397 U.S. 254 (1970), *Mathews v. Eldridge, supra.*

a. Enemy combatants

United States citizens held as enemy combatants are entitled to meaningful opportunity to dispute the facts of their detention by a neutral decision maker, albeit the opportunity is adapted to reduce burdens on executive authority brought on by an ongoing military conflict. *Boumediene v. Bush*, 553 U.S. 723, (2008).

b. Parental status

Different burdens of proof are applied to termination of parental rights and paternity actions. Because termination of parental rights deprives parents of a fundamental right, the state must use clear and convincing evidence to support allegations of neglect.

When a mother or child is initiating a paternity suit, due process requires proof by only a preponderance of evidence. In a paternity action initiated by the state, the state must pay for the necessary blood work used in determining paternity.

c. Forfeitures

Forfeiture is an involuntary relinquishment of property that the government alleges is connected to criminal activity. Generally, the government is required to provide the owner with notice and a hearing prior to seizure of real property. However, the government does not need to provide notice prior to the seizure of personal property.

d. Public employees

A public employee who may be discharged only for cause has a property interest in his job and therefore is entitled to **notice** of termination and a **pre-termination opportunity to respond.** A formal hearing is not required, as long as there is pre-termination notice, an opportunity to respond to the decision maker, and a **post-termination evidentiary hearing.** *Cleveland Bd. of Educ. v. Loudermill*, 470 U.S. 532 (1985). If there is a significant reason for immediately removing a "for-cause" employee from the job, a prompt post-suspension hearing with reinstatement and back pay if the employee prevails constitutes sufficient due process. *Gilbert v. Homar*, 520 U.S. 924 (1997).

4. Court Access

The government cannot deny an indigent person access to the court system because of his inability to pay the required court fees, if such imposition of fees acts to deny a fundamental right to the indigent. Due process requires such fees to be waived. Conversely, if the matter does not involve a fundamental right, no waiver is required.

XII. SUBSTANTIVE DUE PROCESS

The guarantee of substantive due process is based upon the idea that laws should be reasonable and not arbitrary.

A. STANDARD OF REVIEW

The standard of review in substantive due process cases is generally twofold: a governmental action that infringes upon a **fundamental right** is subject to **strict scrutiny.** If the interest infringed upon is not fundamental, then there need be only a **rational basis** for the regulation.

1. Strict Scrutiny

a. Test

The law must be the **least restrictive** means to achieve a **compelling** governmental interest.

1) Least restrictive means

For the law to be the least restrictive means to achieve the government's interest, there cannot be a way to achieve the same interest that is less restrictive of the right at issue. A law will not fail simply because there are other methods of achieving the goal that are equally or more restrictive.

Under strict scrutiny, the law should be neither over-inclusive (reaching more people or conduct than is necessary) nor under-inclusive (not reaching all of the people or conduct intended).

2) Compelling interest

Although there is no precise definition of what is "compelling," it is generally understood to be something that is necessary or crucial, such as national security or preserving public health or safety.

3) Strict in theory, fatal in fact

The strict scrutiny standard is very difficult to meet. The great majority of laws reviewed under strict scrutiny are struck down.

b. Burden of proof

The burden is on the government to prove that the law is necessary to achieve a compelling governmental interest.

c. Applicability

The strict scrutiny test is applied if a **fundamental right** is involved.

2. Rational Basis

a. Test

A law meets the rational basis standard of review if it is **rationally related** to a **legitimate** state interest. This is a test of minimal scrutiny and generally results in the law being upheld.

b. Burden of proof

Laws are presumed valid under this standard, so the burden is on the challenger to overcome this presumption by establishing that the law is **arbitrary or irrational.**

In court, the government's stated interest in enacting the law need not be one that it offered when the law was passed. Any legitimate reason will suffice.

> This factor distinguishes rational basis review from strict scrutiny, when the government must defend the interest that it stated at the outset.

c. Applicability

The rational basis standard is used in all cases to which strict scrutiny or intermediate scrutiny does not apply. In practice, most legislation related to lifestyle, zoning, and punitive damages is reviewed under this standard.

Although punitive damages do not violate due process, excessive damages may. The court considers whether the defendant had fair notice of the possible magnitude before it will bar a punitive-damages award.

The government cannot presume facts about an individual that will deprive that individual of certain benefits or rights. By doing so, the government creates an arbitrary classification that may violate due process as well as equal protection.

1) Retroactive legislation

The retroactive application of a statute does not in and of itself violate substantive due process. Consequently, a law that is applied retroactively must merely meet the rational basis test. *United States v. Carlton*, 512 U.S. 26 (1994) (retroactive application of estate tax law that resulted in denial of a deduction upheld). Similar treatment applies to a statutory change that is remedial in nature (i.e., affects a remedy but does not create or abolish a right). *Chase Securities Corp. v. Donaldson*, 325 U.S. 304 (1945) (lengthening of statute of limitations that permitted an otherwise time-barred lawsuit to be maintained upheld). Note, however, that the extension of a criminal statute of limitations may violate the prohibition on an ex post facto law (*see* § XVI.B. Ex Post Facto Laws, *infra*).

B. FUNDAMENTAL RIGHT

Some rights are so deeply rooted in our nation's tradition and history that they are considered fundamental. These rights include: (i) the right to vote; (ii) the right to travel; (iii) the right to privacy (including marriage, sexual relations, abortion, child rearing, and the right of related persons to live together); and (iv) all First Amendment rights. Under **strict scrutiny,** a law interfering with a fundamental right will generally be upheld only if it is **necessary** to achieve a **compelling governmental interest.**

Government infringement upon **nonfundamental rights**—those related to social or economic interests such as business, taxation, lifestyle, or zoning—requires only a **rational relationship** between the law and a **legitimate governmental interest.**

> **EXAM NOTE:** If, on a question, a fundamental right is being infringed upon for all persons, the issue is likely one of substantive due process. If the right is being denied to only a particular class of persons, then equal protection is in play.

1. Travel

a. Interstate

There is a fundamental right to travel from state to state. *Shapiro v. Thompson*, 394 U.S. 618 (1969). This includes the right to enter one state and leave another, to be treated as a welcome visitor, and, for those who wish to become permanent residents, the right to be treated equally to native-born citizens with respect to state benefits. *Saenz v. Roe*, 526 U.S. 489 (1999) (state statute denying full welfare benefits to people who had not resided in the state for one year struck down; state's interests in discouraging fraud and establishing an objective residency test were not compelling). Reasonable residency restrictions may be imposed on the receipt of government benefits (i.e., in-state tuition); however, once a person qualifies as a resident, she must be treated equally.

b. International

Although there is a right to travel internationally, it is not a fundamental right invoking strict scrutiny. Hence, the U.S. government may limit travel to Cuba, for example, as long as it has a rational basis for doing so.

2. Voting and Ballot Access

a. Right to vote

Under the Twenty-Sixth Amendment, the right to vote is fundamental to all U.S. citizens who are 18 years of age or older. This right applies to all federal, state, and local elections, including primary elections. The level of scrutiny to which a governmental restriction of this right is subject depends on the degree to which the restriction affects the exercise of this right; the more significant the impact, the greater the degree of scrutiny.

1) Residency

A governmental unit may restrict, subject to a rational basis, the right to participate in its political process to those who reside within its borders; nonresidents generally may be prohibited from voting. *Holt Civic Club v. City of Tuscaloosa*, 439 U.S. 60 (1978) (citizens who lived outside city boundaries could be denied the right to vote in city elections, even though they were subject to business licensing fees imposed by the city).

A person must be given the opportunity to prove residency before being denied the right to vote because of lack of residency. *Carrington v. Rash*, 380 U.S. 89 (1965).

a) Length of residency

A governmental unit may require, subject to strict scrutiny, that a person be a resident for a short period prior to an election in order to vote in that election. *Marston v. Lewis*, 410 U.S. 679 (1973) (50-day period upheld); *Dunn v. Blumstein*, 405 U.S. 330 (1972) (three-month and one-year periods struck down).

b) Presidential elections

Congress can supersede state residency requirements with respect to presidential elections. *Oregon v. Mitchell*, 400 U.S. 112 (1970).

2) Property ownership

Generally, property ownership is not a valid ground upon which to restrict the right to vote. *Kramer v. Union Free School District No. 15*, 395 U.S. 621 (1969) (restriction of the right to vote on school board members to property owners or parents of school-age children struck down). A limited exception exists for elections involving special-purpose entities, such as a water-storage district. *Ball v. James*, 451 U.S. 355 (1981).

3) Poll tax

Payment of a fee in order to vote (i.e., a poll tax) in an election for federal office is prohibited by the Twenty-Fourth Amendment. More broadly, the imposition of a poll tax in order to vote in any election violates the Equal Protection Clause, as a poll tax is unrelated to voter qualifications. *Harper v. Virginia Bd. of Elections*, 383 U.S. 663 (1966).

4) Voter ID

A state may require that a citizen who votes in person present a government-issued photo ID. Applying a balancing test to a facial challenge to this neutral, nondiscriminatory requirement, the state's interests, including the prevention of voter fraud and the advancement of public confidence in the integrity of the electoral process, outweighed the limited burden on the right to vote. *Crawford v. Marion County Election Bd.*, 553 U.S. 181 (2008).

5) Felon

Pursuant to Section 2 of the Fourteenth Amendment, a state may prohibit a felon from voting, even one who has unconditionally been released from prison. *Richardson v. Ramirez*, 418 U.S. 24 (1974).

6) Write-in voting

A person's right to vote does not extend to the right to vote for any possible candidate. A state may ban all write-in candidates in both primary and general elections, at least when the state provides reasonable means by which a candidate can get on the ballot. *Burdick v. Takushi*, 504 U.S. 428 (1992).

b. Public office and ballot access

There is no fundamental right to hold office through election or appointment, but all persons do have a constitutional right to be considered for office without the burden of invidious discrimination. *Turner v. Fouche*, 396 U.S. 346 (1970).

1) Property ownership

The ownership of property cannot be made a condition of holding public office. *Turner v. Fouche, supra* (appointment to local school board).

2) Filing fee

A candidate for elected public office generally may be required to pay a reasonable filing fee, but an exorbitant filing fee, such as one that imposes the entire cost of the election on the candidates, is unconstitutional. Moreover, alternative provisions must be made for a candidate who is unable to pay the fee. *Lubin v. Parish*, 415 U.S. 709 (1974); *Bullock v. Carter*, 405 U.S. 134 (1972).

3) Public support requirements

An independent candidate for elected public office can be required to obtain the signatures of voters on a petition in order to appear on the ballot, but such a requirement cannot deny independent candidates ballot access. *Jenness v. Fortson*, 403 U.S. 431 (1971) (state requirement that an independent candidate obtain five percent of the number of registered voters at the last general election for the office in question upheld); *Williams v. Rhodes*, 393 U.S. 23 (1968) (state election scheme that prohibited independent candidacies struck down). In addition, a state can deny a candidate access to the general-election ballot if the candidate failed to receive a sufficient number of votes in the primary election. *Munro v. Socialist Workers Party*, 479 U.S. 189 (1986) (minor party senatorial candidate who failed to receive one percent of the votes cast in primary election not entitled to appear on the general ballot).

4) Write-in candidates

A state may ban all write-in candidates in both primary and general elections, at least when the state provides other reasonable means by which a candidate can get on the ballot. *Burdick v. Takushi, supra*.

5) Candidate for other office

A state may prohibit a state office holder from becoming a candidate for another state office; the office holder must resign his current office in order to run for another office. *Clements v. Fashing*, 457 U.S. 957 (1982).

6) Replacement of elected official

A state may permit a political party to name a replacement for an elected public official from that party who dies or resigns while in office. *Rodriguez v. Popular Democratic Party*, 457 U.S. 1 (1982). The governor must call an election to fill a vacant congressional seat. Article I, Section 2 (House member); Seventeenth Amendment (Senator). (Note: The Seventeenth

Amendment permits the state legislature to authorize the governor to appoint a temporary replacement senator.)

3. **Privacy**

Various privacy rights have been deemed fundamental, and any infringement upon them must be examined using strict scrutiny.

a. **Marriage**

The right of a man and a woman to enter into matrimony is fundamental, and substantial state interference with that right invokes strict scrutiny. *Loving v. Virginia*, 388 U.S. 1 (1967); *Zablocki v. Redhail*, 434 U.S. 374 (1978).

b. **Contraception**

Married persons have the right to use contraceptives, *Griswold v. Connecticut*, 381 U.S. 479 (1965), as do unmarried persons, *Eisenstadt v. Baird*, 405 U.S. 438 (1972). A state may not limit the sale of contraceptives to dispensation only by pharmacists or only to individuals older than age 16. *Carey v. Population Services International*, 431 U.S. 678 (1977).

c. **Intimate sexual behavior**

There is no legitimate state interest in making it a crime for fully consenting adults to engage in private sexual conduct—including homosexual conduct—that is not commercial in nature. *Lawrence v. Texas*, 539 U.S. 558 (2003).

d. **Abortion**

The landmark case of *Roe v. Wade*, 410 U.S. 113 (1973), established the principle that a woman has a fundamental right to an abortion. The Court acknowledged that this privacy right must be considered along with the state's compelling interests in protecting both the health of the pregnant woman and the potential life of the fetus. The resulting rule allowed for varying degrees of state restriction based on the trimester of the pregnancy. The decades since *Roe* have resulted in numerous, often conflicting, judicial opinions on the subject. The current standard is the "undue burden" test, the meaning of which depends on whether the fetus is viable (likely to survive outside the womb).

1) **Pre-viability**

An undue burden exists when the purpose or effect of a state law places **substantial obstacles** in the way of a woman's right to seek an abortion before the fetus attains viability. *Planned Parenthood of Southeastern Pennsylvania v. Casey*, 505 U.S. 833 (1992).

The following requirements have been held **not** to impose an undue burden:

i) A requirement that only a licensed physician may perform an abortion;

ii) A requirement that the physician must provide the woman with truthful information about the nature of the abortion procedure, the associated health risks, and the probable gestational age of the fetus;

iii) A requirement that a woman must wait 24 hours after giving informed consent before the abortion is performed;

iv) A requirement that a minor obtain her parents' consent, or if consent is not required, provide the parents with notice of the abortion. However, this requirement has been found to be an undue burden unless, at least for mature minors, the consent requirement can be judicially bypassed. *Planned Parenthood Association of Kansas City Missouri Inc. v. Ashcroft*, 462 U.S. 476 (1983).

v) A ban on a particular uncommon abortion technique, *Gonzales v. Carhart*, 550 U.S. 124 (2007).

An undue burden has been found when a state requires a woman to notify her husband before having an abortion.

2) Post-viability

Once the fetus reaches viability, the state may regulate, and even prohibit, abortion, as long as there is an exception to preserve the health or life of the mother. In other words, at the point of viability, the state's interest in protecting fetal life may supersede a woman's right to choose; because the state's interest in protecting fetal life cannot supersede its interest in protecting a woman's health, however, there must be an exception for the woman's health.

3) Government funding

There is no constitutional right to have the government provide indigent women with funding for an abortion or for medical care related to an abortion, even if the government does provide indigent funding for medical care at childbirth. *Maher v. Roe*, 432 U.S. 464 (1977). Furthermore, a state may prohibit all use of public facilities and public employees in performing abortions. *Webster v. Reproductive Health Services*, 492 U.S. 490 (1989).

e. Parental rights

The fundamental parental right to make decisions regarding the care, custody, and control of one's children includes the right to privately educate one's child outside the public school system, *Pierce v. Society of Sisters*, 268 U.S. 510 (1925), and to limit visitation of grandparents, *Troxel v. Granville*, 530 U.S. 57 (2000).

f. Family relations

Related persons, including extended family members, have a fundamental right to live together in a single household. *Moore v. City of East Cleveland*, 431 U.S. 494 (1977).

g. Obscene material

There is a fundamental right to possess obscene material in the privacy of one's home, *Stanley v. Georgia*, 394 U.S. 557 (1969), with the exception of child pornography, *Osborne v. Ohio*, 495 U.S. 103 (1990). The state, however, may severely restrict the sale, purchase, receipt, transport, and distribution of obscene material. *Paris Adult Theater v. Slaton*, 413 U.S. 49 (1973).

h. Right to refuse medical treatment

It is an established liberty interest that a person may not be forced to undergo unwanted medical procedures, including lifesaving measures, but the Court has not ruled on whether this right is "fundamental." *Cruzan v. Missouri Department of Health*, 497 U.S. 261 (1990).

There is no fundamental right to commit suicide; therefore, the state may ban the assistance of suicide. *Washington v. Glucksberg*, 521 U.S. 702 (1997). The Court distinguished this decision from *Cruzan* by stating that forced medication is a battery, and there is a long tradition of protecting the decision to refuse unwanted medical treatment.

4. The Second Amendment

The Second Amendment guarantees **an individual's right to possess a firearm** unconnected with service in a militia and to use that firearm for traditionally lawful purposes, such as self-defense within the home. *District of Columbia v. Heller*, 554 U.S. 570 (2008) (ban on handgun possession in the home violates Second Amendment). As mentioned previously, the Second Amendment is applicable to the states through the Fourteenth Amendment. *McDonald v. Chicago*, 561 U.S. ___, 130 S. Ct. 3020 (2010).

Like most rights, the Second Amendment right to bear arms is not unlimited. Examples of lawful regulations include imposing conditions and qualifications on the commercial sale of arms, as well as prohibitions on (i) concealed weapons, (ii) possession of firearms by felons and the mentally ill, and (iii) carrying guns in schools, government buildings, and other sensitive places are presumed to be legitimate. *District of Columbia v. Heller, supra.*

XIII. EQUAL PROTECTION

A. GENERAL CONSIDERATIONS

1. Constitutional Basis

a. State action

The Equal Protection Clause of the Fourteenth Amendment provides that "no state shall...deny to any person within its jurisdiction the equal protection of the laws." This clause applies only to states and localities.

b. Federal action

Although there is no federal equal protection clause, the Supreme Court has held that the Fifth Amendment Due Process Clause includes the rights guaranteed by the Equal Protection Clause, thereby making discrimination by the federal government subject to review under the same standards as discrimination by the states. *Bolling v. Sharpe*, 347 U.S. 497 (1954).

2. Standards of Review

When reviewing government action under equal-protection theories, the Court applies one of three levels of review, depending on the classification of persons or the type of right concerned.

a. Strict scrutiny

1) Test

The law must be the **least restrictive** means to achieve a **compelling** governmental interest.

2) Burden of proof

The burden is on the government to prove that the law is necessary. Because the strict scrutiny test is a very difficult one to pass, the government rarely meets its burden, and most laws subjected to this standard of review are struck down.

3) Applicability

The strict scrutiny test is applied if a **fundamental right** or a **suspect classification** is involved. The suspect classifications are race, ethnicity, national origin, and, if the classification is by state law, alienage. (*See* § XIII.B., *infra,* for a complete discussion of suspect classifications.)

b. Intermediate scrutiny

1) Test

To be constitutional, the law must be **substantially related** to an **important** governmental interest.

2) Burden of proof

Although the Court has not clearly stated the rule, the burden appears generally to be on the government to prove that the law in question passes intermediate scrutiny. As with strict scrutiny (and unlike rational basis review), the government must defend the interest(s) it stated when the law was enacted, not just some conceivable legitimate interest.

3) Applicability

Intermediate scrutiny is used when a classification is based on **gender** or status as a **nonmarital child** (legitimacy). Note that in gender cases there must be an "exceedingly persuasive justification" for the classification, which may bring the standard in such cases closer to strict scrutiny. *See United States v. Virginia*, 518 U.S. 515 (1996).

c. Rational basis

1) Test

A law passes the rational basis standard of review if it is **rationally related** to a **legitimate** state interest. This is a test of minimal scrutiny. It is not required that there is actually a link between the means selected and a legitimate objective. However, the legislature must *reasonably believe* there is a link.

2) Burden of proof

Laws are presumed valid under this standard, so the burden is on the challenger to overcome this presumption by establishing that the law is **arbitrary or irrational.**

3) Applicability

The rational basis standard is used in all cases in which one of the higher standards (intermediate or strict scrutiny) does not apply. Thus, rational basis review applies to laws drawing distinctions based on age, wealth, weight, or most other classifications, as well as to any distinctions drawn for business or economic reasons.

The Court generally gives extreme deference to the legislature's right to define its objectives. In order to determine the legislature's purpose, the Court will look at the statute and the preamble. If the legislative purpose is not clear from the statute, the Court may consider any conceivable purpose that may have motivated the legislature. *U.S. Railroad Retirement Bd. v. Fritz,* 449 U.S. 166 (1980).

Some classifications, although nominally subject to rational basis review, in practice receive heightened scrutiny. *See e.g., Romer v. Evans,* 517 U.S. 620 (1996) (sexual orientation); *Cleburne v. Cleburne Living Center, Inc.,* 473 U.S. 432 (1985) (developmental disability). When the government has acted out of animus toward or fear of a particular group, that action—even if not involving a suspect or a quasi-suspect classification—will be searchingly reviewed and may be struck down even under a rational basis test.

3. Proving Discrimination

To trigger strict or intermediate scrutiny, there must be **discriminatory intent** on the part of the government. The fact that legislation has a disparate effect on people of different races, genders, etc., without intent, is insufficient. Discriminatory intent can be shown facially, as applied, or when there is a discriminatory motive.

a. Facial discrimination

A law that, by its very language, creates distinctions between classes of persons is discriminatory on its face.

Example: An ordinance states that only males will be considered for a city's training academy for firefighters.

b. Discriminatory application

A law that appears neutral on its face may be applied in a discriminatory fashion. If the challenger can prove that a discriminatory purpose was used when applying the law, then the law will be invalidated.

Example: A city's ordinance concerning the police academy says nothing about gender, but in practice only men are considered for admission.

c. Discriminatory motive

A law that is neutral on its face and in its application may still result in a disparate impact. By itself, however, a disparate impact is not sufficient to trigger strict or intermediate scrutiny; proof of discriminatory motive or intent is required to show a violation of the Equal Protection Clause. *Arlington Heights v. Metropolitan Hous. Dev. Corp.*, 429 U.S. 252 (1977).

> **Example:** A city's paramedic training school is theoretically open to both men and women, but the entrance test includes a height requirement that disproportionately excludes women.

B. SUSPECT CLASSIFICATIONS

Laws that categorize based on race, ethnicity, national origin, or (in some cases) alienage are considered suspect and therefore require closer judicial examination. Such laws are subject to strict scrutiny and are invalid unless they are **necessary** to achieve a **compelling** governmental interest.

1. Race, Ethnicity, and National Origin

Laws or regulations that intentionally disadvantage on the basis of race, ethnicity, or national origin have almost always been struck down for failing to advance a compelling state interest. One exception was *Korematsu v. United States*, 323 U.S. 214 (1944), in which the internment of Japanese-Americans during World War II was upheld in the name of national security.

a. School integration

Because discrimination must be intentional in order to violate the Constitution, only intentional (de jure) segregation in schools violates the Equal Protection Clause. *Keyes v. Sch. Dist. No. 1*, 413 U.S. 189 (1973). Moreover, a court cannot impose a remedy that involves multiple school districts unless there is evidence of intentional segregation in each district. *Milliken v. Bradley*, 418 U.S. 717 (1974); *Missouri v. Jenkins*, 515 U.S. 70 (1995) (state not compelled to create magnet schools in order to attract students from outside the district).

If a school board does not take steps to eliminate intentional racial segregation of schools, a court can order the district to implement measures, such as busing, to remedy the discrimination. Court-ordered busing is temporary, however, and must be terminated once the "vestiges of past discrimination" have been eliminated. *Bd. of Educ. v. Dowell*, 498 U.S. 237 (1991).

b. Affirmative action

Programs that favor racial or ethnic minorities are also subject to strict scrutiny. *Adarand Constructors, Inc. v. Pena*, 515 U.S. 200 (1995) (overruling application of the intermediate standard to federal discrimination).

1) Past discrimination by government

For a governmental affirmative action program to survive, the relevant governmental entity must show more than a history of societal discrimination. The government—whether federal, state, or local—must itself be guilty of specific past discrimination against the group it is seeking to favor, and the remedy must be narrowly tailored to end that discrimination and eliminate its effects. In other words, the elimination of past discrimination in a particular governmental institution is a compelling state interest; attempting to remedy general societal injustice through affirmative action is not.

2) Diversity in public universities and colleges

Race may be used as a "plus factor" (i.e., one of a range of factors to consider) in determining whether a student should be admitted to a public college or university, as there is a compelling interest in obtaining the educational benefits of a diverse student body. The use of racial quotas or of race as a determinative criterion, however, violates equal protection and is unconstitutional. *Grutter v. Bollinger*, 539 U.S. 306 (2003); *Gratz v. Bollinger*, 539 U.S. 244 (2003); *Regents of University of California v. Bakke*, 438 U.S. 265 (1978).

3) Diversity in public elementary and high schools

A school district may not assign students to schools on the basis of race unless it is necessary to accomplish a compelling interest—e.g., remedy past discrimination. However, a district may use facially race-neutral criteria that may have the same effect, such as strategic site selection for new schools or the redrawing of attendance zones. *Parents Involved in Community Schools v. Seattle School Dist. No. 1*, 551 U.S. 701 (2007).

4) Private affirmative action

Recall that the Equal Protection Clause applies only to governmental action, so private employers are not restricted by it. Discrimination by private employers is nonetheless regulated by federal statute pursuant to Congress's power under the enabling clauses of the Thirteenth and Fourteenth Amendments and the Commerce Clause.

c. Racial gerrymandering

Race may not be the predominant factor in determining the boundary lines of legislative districts (*see* § XIII.E.2.a., Racial discrimination, *infra*).

2. Alienage

Classifications based on status as a lawful resident of the United States (as opposed to a citizen) are subject to a variety of different standards, depending on the level of government and the nature of the classification.

a. Federal classification

Because Congress has plenary power over aliens under Article I, a federal alienage classification is likely valid unless it is **arbitrary** and **unreasonable.**

Example: Medicare regulations may require a five-year residency period for eligibility despite thereby excluding many lawful resident aliens. *Matthews v. Diaz*, 426 U.S. 67 (1976).

b. State classifications

1) Generally struck down

The Court will generally apply the strict scrutiny test and strike down state laws that discriminate against aliens, such as laws prohibiting aliens from owning land, obtaining commercial fishing licenses, or being eligible for welfare benefits or civil service jobs.

2) Exception—participation in government functions

A growing exception exists, however, for state laws that restrict or prohibit an alien's **participation in government functions.** Such laws need only have a **rational relationship** to a legitimate state interest. Laws prohibiting aliens from voting, serving on a jury, or being hired as police officers, probation officers, or public-school teachers have been upheld as preventing aliens from having a direct effect on the functioning of the government.

> **EXAM NOTE:** When determining whether a position or license from which aliens are excluded falls under the government function or political function exception, consider whether the position or license would allow the alien to "participate directly in the formulation, execution, or review of broad public policy" or would allow the alien to exercise "broad discretion."

c. Undocumented aliens

Undocumented aliens are not a suspect class, but the states may not deny primary or secondary public education benefits to undocumented aliens. *Plyler v. Doe*, 457 U.S. 202 (1982).

C. QUASI-SUSPECT CLASSIFICATIONS

1. Gender

Discrimination based on gender is "quasi-suspect" and subject to **intermediate scrutiny,** which is less stringent than strict scrutiny but tougher than the rational basis test. Just as with suspect classifications and fundamental rights, there must be **discriminatory intent** by the government to trigger intermediate scrutiny; disparate impact is not enough. Under intermediate scrutiny, the burden is on the state to show that a statute or regulation that treats the sexes differently is **substantially related** to an **important** governmental interest. This test applies whether the classification is invidious or benign, and it is now applied rather stringently, requiring the government to show that an "exceedingly persuasive justification" exists for the distinction, and that separate facilities (such as separate sports team facilities as state universities) are "substantially equivalent." *United States v. Virginia*, 518 U.S. 515 (1996).

a. Discrimination against women

Intentional discrimination through gender classification will generally be struck down under the intermediate scrutiny standard. For example, a state law giving preference to men over women to be administrators of decedents' estates was invalid. *Reed v. Reed*, 404 U.S. 71 (1971) (ease in determining who should serve as administrator is not an important interest). *See also United States v.*

Virginia, 518 U.S. 515 (1996) (Virginia Military Institute could not exclude women from admission to public college based on overbroad generalizations about the physical capabilities and preferred educational methods of males and females).

b. Discrimination against men

Intentional discrimination against males is generally struck down for violating equal protection. However, there have been some instances of discrimination against men being upheld because of the important governmental interest:

    i)   Draft registration of males, but not females, *Rostker v. Goldberg*, 453 U.S. 57 (1981) (interest of preparing combat troops); and

    ii)   A statutory rape law that held only men criminally liable for such conduct, *Michael M. v. Sonoma County Superior Court*, 450 U.S. 464 (1981) (interest in preventing teenage pregnancy).

c. Affirmative action (benign discrimination)

The Court has upheld affirmative action regulations granting beneficial treatment to women over men (such as tax exemptions, increased social security benefits, and increased protection from mandatory armed forces discharge) because providing a remedy for past gender-based discrimination is an important governmental interest. *See Califano v. Webster*, 430 U.S. 313 (1977); *Schlesinger v. Ballard*, 419 U.S. 498 (1975).

2. Legitimacy

Classifications on the basis of status as a nonmarital child (i.e., those that distinguish between "legitimate" and "illegitimate" children) are subject to **intermediate scrutiny**—they must be **substantially related** to an **important** governmental interest. The Court will closely examine the purpose behind the distinction, and it will not uphold legislation designed to punish the offspring of a nonmarital relationship. To that end, states may not prohibit children of unmarried parents from receiving welfare benefits, *New Jersey Welfare Rights Org. v. Cahill*, 411 U.S. 619 (1973), workers' compensation benefits upon the death of a parent, *Weber v. Aetna Cas. and Sur. Co.*, 406 U.S. 164 (1972), or an inheritance from an intestate father, *Trimble v. Gordon*, 430 U.S. 762 (1977). In addition, a state cannot require a paternity action brought on behalf of an illegitimate child to be commenced within a limited time after birth in order to secure child support, while imposing a similar time limit on a legitimate child seeking child support from a parent. *Clark v. Jeter*, 486 U.S. 456 (1988).

D. NONSUSPECT CLASSIFICATIONS

1. Age

Age discrimination in violation of the Age Discrimination in Employment Act of 1967 does not provoke heightened scrutiny; laws and other governmental actions classifying on the basis of age are reviewed under the **rational basis** standard. *See, e.g., Massachusetts Bd. of Ret. v. Murgia*, 427 U.S. 307 (1976) (police officers may be forced to retire at age 50, even if they are as physically fit as younger officers).

2. Poverty

Most statutes and regulations that classify on the basis of wealth (i.e., discriminate against the poor) are subject only to **rational basis** scrutiny and will be upheld. There is an exception for cases in which governmental action prohibits the poor from exercising a fundamental right because of a government-imposed fee; strict scrutiny will usually apply in those situations. For example, the availability of appeal in a criminal case cannot hinge on ability to pay for a trial transcript. *Griffin v. Illinois*, 351 U.S. 12 (1956). Also, poll taxes are unconstitutional because wealth is unrelated to a citizen's ability to vote intelligently. *Harper v. Virginia Bd. of Elections*, 383 U.S. 663 (1966).

3. Sexual Orientation

Discrimination on the basis of sexual orientation does not provoke heightened scrutiny. The government, however, cannot impose a burden or deny a benefit on a group of persons solely based on animosity toward the class that it affects. *Romer v. Evans*, 517 U.S. 620 (1996).

E. FUNDAMENTAL RIGHTS UNIQUE TO EQUAL PROTECTION

The fundamental rights guaranteed by substantive due process are often protected by equal protection principles as well. Thus, impingement of the right to vote, to travel, or to marry may trigger an inquiry under either the Due Process Clause or the Equal Protection Clause. However, certain rights and principles are particular to equal protection.

> **EXAM NOTE:** The right to *travel* and the right to *vote* are the most frequently tested fundamental rights in the area of **equal protection.** (Often, both the Due Process Clause and the Equal Protection Clause will apply. Equal protection predominates if the question emphasizes denial of a right to a particular group, and it does not apply if the denial of the right is universal.)

1. One Person, One Vote

The principle of "one person, one vote" holds that one person's vote must be essentially equal to any other person's vote. To that end, when the government establishes voting districts for the election of representatives, the number of persons in each district must be approximately equal. *Reynolds v. Sims*, 377 U.S. 533 (1964). Voter approval of a redistricting plan will not justify a violation of the "one person, one vote" rule. *Lucas v. Colorado General Assembly*, 377 U.S. 713 (1964).

a. Congressional districts

When states establish districts for congressional elections, they must achieve nearly precise mathematical equality between the districts. This restriction is imposed on the states by Article I, Section 2, which requires members of the House to be chosen by "the People of the several States." An unexplained deviation of less than one percent may invalidate the statewide congressional district plan. Variations may be justified by the state on the basis of consistently applied, legitimate state objectives, such as respecting municipal political subdivision boundaries, creating geographic compact districts, and avoiding contests between incumbent representatives. In addition, variations based on anticipated population shifts may be acceptable when such shifts can be predicted with a high degree of accuracy, and population trends are thoroughly documented. *Kirkpatrick v. Preisler*, 394 U.S. 526 (1969) (variation in population of slightly less than six percent violated the "one person, one vote" rule); *Karcher v. Daggett*, 462 U.S. 725 (1983) (variation of slightly less than 0.7 percent violated the "one person, one vote" rule).

1) Congressional apportionment of House members

Congress, in apportioning members of the House among the states pursuant to Article I, Section 2, is not held to the "mathematical equality" standard. The method adopted by Congress is entitled to judicial deference and is assumed to be in good faith. *Dept. of Commerce v. Montana*, 503 U.S. 442 (1992) (Montana's loss of a congressional seat upheld, even though retention of the seat would have placed Montana closer to the ideal population size for a congressional district).

b. State and local districts

The size of electoral districts may vary much more in the case of state and local elections, as long as the variance is not unjustifiably large. A variation of less than 10% is rebuttably presumed to be a minor deviation that does not constitute a prima facie case for discrimination. *Cox v. Larios*, 300 F. Supp. 2d 1320 (N.D. Ga.), *aff'd*, 542 U.S. 947 (2004); *Brown v. Thompson*, 462 U.S. 835 (1983). When the maximum variation is 10% or greater, the state must show that the deviation from equality between the districts is reasonable and designed to promote a legitimate state interest. *Mahan v. Howell*, 410 U.S. 315 (1973) (maximum difference of 16% in size of population between state legislative districts permitted when the state respected the boundaries of political subdivisions).

1) Bodies performing governmental functions

The "one person, one vote" rule applies to local elections of entities that perform governmental functions, even when the functions are specialized rather than general in nature. *Hadley v. Junior College Dist.*, 397 U.S. 50 (1970) (election of trustees to junior college district). In addition to requiring relative equality with respect to the weight of a person's vote, the Equal Protection Clause subjects the restriction of voting of a particular class of persons to strict scrutiny, which generally results in the invalidation of the law. *Kramer v. Union Free School District No. 15*, 395 U.S. 621 (1969) (state law that restricted voting in school board election to property owners and parents with school-aged children struck down). The restriction of voting to a class of persons (e.g., landowners) and the allocation of voting weight on a basis other than personhood (e.g., the amount of land owned) has been upheld only with regard to water-district elections. *Ball v. James*, 451 U.S. 355 (1981).

c. At-large elections

While an election in which members of a governmental unit (e.g., county council members) are elected by all voters within that unit (i.e., an at-large election) does not violate the one-person, one-vote rule, it may conflict with another constitutional provision, such as the Equal Protection Clause. *Rogers v. Lodge*, 458 U.S. 613 (1982) (use of countywide system to elect county board unconstitutionally diluted the voting power of African-American citizens).

Note: Federal law bans at-large elections for congressional representatives in states that have more than one House member (i.e., the single-member district rule). 2 U.S.C.S. § 2c.

2. Gerrymandering

a. Racial discrimination

1) Vote dilution

When a state draws election districts for the purpose of scattering a racial or ethnic minority among several districts in order to prevent the minority from exercising its voting strength, the state's action is a violation of the Equal Protection Clause. *Gomillion v. Lightfoot*, 364 U.S. 339 (1960) (redrawing city boundaries to exclude African-American voters unconstitutional); *Rogers v. Lodge, supra*.

2) Majority-minority districts

Under the Equal Protection Clause, election districts for public office may not be drawn using race as the predominant factor in determining the boundary lines, unless the district plan can survive strict scrutiny. This restriction applies even when the district is drawn to favor historically disenfranchised groups. The state can use traditional factors—such as compactness, contiguity, or honoring political subdivisions—as the bases for the district, and it may only consider race if it does not predominate over other considerations. *Miller v. Johnson*, 515 U.S. 900 (1995).

A district's bizarre shape can be used as evidence that race was a predominating factor, but such a shape is not necessary for a finding of racial gerrymandering. *Shaw v. Reno*, 509 U.S. 630 (1993).

a) Voting Rights Act

The Voting Rights Act (42 U.S.C. § 1973 et seq.) requires racial gerrymandering to ensure minority success in elections by creating majority-minority districts (i.e., affirmative gerrymandering). The Act also requires federal pre-clearance for changes in voting rules, including redistricting, for specific southern states and a few other local governmental units. Receiving federal pre-clearance for a redistricting plan does not ensure that plan will avoid conflicting with the Equal Protection Clause. *Miller v. Johnson*, 515 U.S. 900 (1995).

b. Political discrimination

Partisan political gerrymandering may violate the Equal Protection Clause if the challenger can show "both intentional discrimination against an identifiable political group and an actual discriminatory effect on that group." *Davis v. Bandemer*, 478 U.S. 109, 127 (1986). However, lack of comprehensive and neutral principles for drawing electoral boundaries as well as the absence of rules to confine judicial intervention can prevent adjudication of political gerrymandering claims. *Vieth v. Jubelirer*, 541 U.S. 267 (2004).

XIV. PRIVILEGES AND IMMUNITIES CLAUSES

A. ARTICLE IV

Article IV, Section 2, known as the Comity Clause, provides that "the citizens of each state shall be entitled to all privileges and immunities of citizens in the several states."

1. Prohibits State Discrimination against Nonresidents

The Comity Clause, in essence, prohibits one state from discriminating against the citizens of another state. In this context, the term "citizen" does not include corporations or aliens.

2. Rights Protected

Nonresident citizens are protected against discrimination with respect to fundamental rights or essential activities. Examples include the pursuit of employment, transfer of property, and access to state courts.

> **Example:** Discrimination against out-of-state residents in setting the fee for a *commercial* activity, such as a commercial shrimping license, violates the Privileges and Immunities Clause of Article IV, but similar discrimination for a *recreational* activity, such as a recreational hunting license, does not, if there is a rational basis for the fee differential. *Compare Toomer v. Witsell*, 334 U.S. 385 (1948) (fee for out-of-state commercial shrimper that was 100 times greater than the fee for an in-state shrimper unconstitutional), *with Baldwin v. Fish & Game Comm'n*, 436 U.S. 371 (1978) (fee for out-of-state resident to hunt elk that was 25 times greater than the fee for an in-state hunter constitutional).
>
> Note that discrimination against an out-of-state resident with regard to access to a state's natural resources may violate the Dormant Commerce Clause. *New England Power Co. v. New Hampshire*, 455 U.S. 331 (1982) (prohibition on sale of hydroelectric power outside the state unconstitutional).

3. Exception—Substantial Justification

Discrimination against out-of-state citizens may be valid if the state can show a substantial reason for the difference in treatment. A substantial reason exists if:

i) The nonresidents either cause or are a part of the problem that the state is attempting to solve; and

ii) There are no less-restrictive means to solve the problem.

An example is discrimination against nonresidents with respect to the use of scarce water resources when the purpose was to preserve natural state-owned resources. *Sporhase v. Nebraska*, 458 U.S. 941 (1982).

EXAM NOTE: Although the Privileges and Immunities Clause of Article IV and the Commerce Clause are not coextensive, they tend to mutually support each other; thus, consider both when analyzing a bar exam question.

B. FOURTEENTH AMENDMENT—NATIONAL CITIZENSHIP

The Fourteenth Amendment provides that "[n]o state shall make or enforce any law which shall abridge the privileges or immunities of citizens of the United States." This clause protects citizens (not corporations or aliens) from infringement by the states upon the privileges or immunities of **national** citizenship.

The privileges or immunities of national citizenship include the right to travel interstate, to petition Congress for redress of grievances, to vote for national offices, to enter public lands, to be protected while in the custody of U.S. marshals, and to peaceably assemble. *Twining v. New Jersey*, 211 U.S. 78 (1908). The guarantees of the Bill of Rights, however, are not privileges or immunities of national citizenship within the context of the Fourteenth Amendment. *Slaughterhouse Cases*, 83 U.S. 36 (1873). Therefore, those rights are protected from state action only by the Due Process Clause and the Equal Protection Clause.

This provision is seldom successfully invoked; under the limiting interpretation of the *Slaughterhouse Cases*, the rights that the clause provides are redundant to rights provided elsewhere in the Constitution. Although the Supreme Court has since relied on the clause to underscore the right to move freely among states, *Saenz v. Roe*, 526 U.S. 489 (1999) (invalidating a duration requirement for welfare benefits), there has been no subsequent expansion of use; the Fourteenth Amendment's Privileges or Immunities Clause applies, in practice, only to the right to travel.

XV. TAKINGS CLAUSE

The power of the government to take private property for public purposes is known as **"eminent domain."** The Takings Clause of the Fifth Amendment acts as a check on this power; it provides that private property may not "be taken for public use, without just compensation." The Fourteenth Amendment Due Process Clause makes the Takings Clause applicable to the states.

A. PROPERTY INTEREST

For a person to challenge a governmental action as an unconstitutional taking, the person must have a property interest. When a person does not have an interest in the property that the government takes, the Takings Clause does not apply.

> **Example:** An organization of homeowners challenged a beach restoration project undertaken by a state agency and local governments. The homeowners objected to the creation of land beyond the mean high water line, which represented the boundary of the homeowners' property, because this infringed upon their right as owners of property along a shore to receive accretions and because they lost the right to control public access to the shoreline. However, because, under state law, the newly created land belonged to the state, and the homeowners did not enjoy property rights with respect to this land, there was no taking of their property rights. *Stop the Beach Renourishment, Inc. v. Fla. Dep't of Envtl. Prot.*, 560 U.S. ___, 130 S. Ct. 2592 (2010). (Note: A plurality of the Supreme Court justices also found that the Takings Clause applies to a judicial taking.)

1. Types of Property

Property that may be subject to the protection of the Takings Clause includes not only land and other real property, but also tangible personal property as well as intangible property, such as contract and patent rights and trade secrets. *Ruckelshaus v. Monsanto Co.*, 467 U.S. 986 (1984); *Lynch v. United States*, 292 U.S. 571 (1934); *James v. Campbell*, 104 U.S. 356 (1882).

2. Types of Interests

In addition to the transfer of a fee simple interest in property, a taking may involve an easement, leasehold interest, or a lien. *Nollan v. California Coastal Commission*, 483 U.S. 825 (1987); *Armstrong v. United States*, 364 U.S. 40 (1960); *United States v. General Motors*, 323 U.S. 373 (1945). A taking may involve the rights of a property owner, such as the right to control access to the property. *Kaiser Aetna v. United States*, 444 U.S. 164 (1980) (federal government's imposition of public-access servitude on a waterway created on private property constituted a taking).

B. TYPES OF TAKING

1. Seizure of Property

The classic application of the Takings Clause is the seizure of private property for governmental use, such as acquiring privately held land in order to construct a courthouse or other government building. In such a case, the property owner's primary challenge to the seizure is whether he has received just compensation (*see* § XV.C., Just Compensation, *infra*).

a. Public-use challenge

A government may seize private property not only for its own direct use but also to transfer the property to another private party. Although such a seizure is subject to challenge as not being made for a public use, the taking need merely be **"rationally related to a conceivable public purpose."** *Hawaii Hous. Auth. v. Midkiff*, 467 U.S. 229 (1984). This is a highly deferential standard, and the burden is on the person challenging the taking to prove a lack of legitimate interest or rational basis. In addition to traditional health, safety, and welfare justifications, economic redevelopment goals constitute a sufficient public purpose to justify the seizure. *Kelo v. City of New London*, 545 U.S. 469 (2005). Moreover, a government-mandated transfer of property from one private party directly to another (e.g., from lessor to lessee) may nevertheless be for a public use. *Hawaii Housing Authority v. Midkiff*, 467 U.S. 229 (1984).

2. Damage to or Destruction of Property

A destruction of property or property rights by the federal, state, or local government can also result in a taking. The destruction need not directly benefit the government.

> **Example:** A federal statute that prevented the transfer by devise or descent of fractional shares of an interest in tribal land upon the death of the owner and instead provided for such interest to escheat to the tribe constituted an unconstitutional taking when there was no provision for compensation of the owner. *Hodel v. Irving*, 481 U.S. 704 (1987).

Similarly, physical damage to property or interference with a property owner's rights by governmental action can result in a taking.

> **Example:** County ownership of an airport that resulted in an invasion of the airspace of nearby property owners by planes taking off and landing at the airport constituted a taking. *Griggs v. Allegheny County*, 369 U.S. 84 (1962).

Note: A statute that requires an owner of property rights to take action in order to preserve an unused right does not result in a taking if the owner fails to take such action. *Texaco, Inc. v. Short,* 454 U.S. 516 (1982).

a. Exception—public peril

The governmental destruction of private property in response to a public peril does not trigger the right to compensation.

> **Example:** The owners of infected cedar trees located near apple orchards were not entitled to compensation when the cedar trees were destroyed pursuant to a state statute in order to prevent the spread of the infection to the orchards. *Miller v. Schoene,* 276 U.S. 272 (1928).

3. Characterization of Property

The Takings Clause prevents a government from recharacterizing private property as public property.

> **Example:** Interest on the purchase price of an insolvent corporation placed by the buyer in an account with the court as part of an interpleader action involving the corporation's creditors was private property. A state court's interpretation of a statutory provision that the interest was public money constituted a taking. *Webb's Fabulous Pharmacies, Inc. v. Beckwith,* 449 U.S. 155 (1980).

4. Regulatory Taking

Generally, a governmental regulation that adversely affects a person's property interest is not a taking, but it is possible for a regulation to rise to the level of a taking. In determining whether a regulation creates a taking, the following factors are considered:

i) The economic impact of the regulation on the property owner;

ii) The extent to which the regulation interferes with the owner's reasonable, investment-backed expectations regarding use of the property; and

iii) The character of the regulation, including the degree to which it will benefit society, how the regulation distributes the burdens and benefits among property owners, and whether the regulation violates any of the owner's essential attributes of property ownership, such as the right to exclude others from the property.

Penn Central Transportation Co. v. City of New York, 438 U.S. 104 (1978).

a. Public-use challenge

In the context of a regulation, a state or local government can act under its police power for the purposes of health, safety, and welfare. In addition, a public purpose can encompass aesthetic and environmental concerns. Moreover, it is generally inappropriate for a court to examine whether a regulation substantially advances a legitimate governmental interest. (Note, however, that an arbitrary or irrational regulation may constitute a due-process violation.) *Lingle v. Chevron U.S.A. Inc.,* 544 U.S. 528 (2005).

b. Per se takings

In two instances, a regulation clearly results in a taking.

1) Physical occupation

A taking has occurred when the governmental regulation results in a **permanent physical occupation** of the property.

> **Example:** A law requiring a landlord to permit a cable company to install equipment on the landlord's property that would remain indefinitely constituted a taking, even though the installation had only a minimal economic impact on the landlord. *Loretto v. Teleprompter Manhattan CATV Corp.*, 458 U.S. 419 (1982).

2) No economically viable use

When a regulation results in a **permanent total loss of the property's economic value,** a taking has occurred. *Lucas v. South Carolina Coastal Council*, 505 U.S. 1003 (1992) (zoning ordinance precluding owner of coastal property from erecting any permanent structure on the land was a taking); *Tahoe-Sierra Preservation Council, Inc. v. Tahoe Regional Planning Agency*, 535 U.S. 302 (2002) (32-month building moratorium was not a taking).

> **Adverse economic impact:** A regulation that results in a dramatic decline in the value of the regulated property does not necessarily constitute a taking.

c. Post-adoption acquisition

A person who acquires property rights after the adoption of a regulation that affects those rights may nevertheless challenge the regulation as an unconstitutional taking. *Palazzolo v. Rhode Island.*, 533 U.S. 606 (2001).

5. Exaction as a Taking

A local government may exact promises from a developer, such as setting aside a portion of the land being developed for a park in exchange for issuing the necessary construction permits. Such exactions do not violate the Takings Clause if there is:

i) An **essential nexus** between legitimate state interests and the conditions imposed on the property owner (i.e., the conditions substantially advance legitimate state interest); and

ii) A **rough proportionality** between the burden imposed by the conditions on property owner and the impact of the proposed development.

Nollan v. California Coastal Commission, 483 U.S. 825 (1987) (state-required grant of an easement across beachfront property as a condition on the issuance of a building permit was a taking due to lack of essential nexus); *Dolan v. City of Tigard*, 512 U.S. 374 (1994) (state-required dedication of land to the city for use as a greenway and pedestrian/bicycle pathway in exchange for permit to expand a store and parking lot was a taking due to lack of rough proportionality).

In determining whether there is rough proportionality between the burden and the impact, the government must make an individualized determination that the conditions are related both in nature and extent to the impact.

These requirements are limited to exactions; they do not apply to regulatory takings. *Linge v. Chevron U.S.A. Inc., supra,* (rent cap was not an exaction taking, but instead was a valid regulation under the Takings Clause).

C. JUST COMPENSATION

The phrase "just compensation" has been interpreted to mean **fair market value,** which is the reasonable value of the property at the time of the taking. This value is measured in terms of the loss to the owner, not the benefit to the government.

1. Worthless Property

Property that is worthless to the owner but has value to the government may be taken without compensation.

> **Example:** A state law that required interest on clients' funds deposited by lawyers in a trust account to be paid to an entity in order to provide legal services for the poor constituted a taking because each client's funds would not separately have earned interest. *Brown v. Legal Foundation of Washington,* 538 U.S. 216 (2003).

2. Only Portion Taken

When only a portion of an owner's property is taken, the owner may also receive compensation for any diminution in value of the remaining portion that is attributable to the taking but must reduce any compensation by the value of any special and direct benefits (e.g., a highway access) conferred on the remaining portion.

3. Return of Property

When governmental action constitutes a taking, the government cannot escape all liability by returning the property to its owner, but instead must pay the owner compensation for the period that the government possessed the property. *First English Evangelical Church v. County of Los Angeles,* 482 U.S. 304 (1987).

D. MANNER OF TAKING

Typically, when a property owner objects to the seizure of his property by the government, the government will institute condemnation proceedings, and the property owner can raise the Takings Clause as a defense to this action. When the governmental action that allegedly constitutes a taking is a statute, regulation, or ordinance, the property owner may institute a suit seeking an injunction or a declaratory judgment; this type of legal action is sometimes referred to as an inverse condemnation.

XVI. PROHIBITED LEGISLATION

A. BILLS OF ATTAINDER

A bill of attainder is a **legislative** act that declares a person or group of persons guilty of some crime and punishes them without a trial. Article I, Sections 9 and 10 forbid the federal government and the states, respectively, from enacting such "legislative trials." It applies only to criminal or penal measures.

Barring particular individuals from government employment qualifies as punishment under the prohibition against bills of attainder. *United States v. Lovett,* 328 U.S. 303 (1946).

B.   EX POST FACTO LAWS

The constitutional prohibition on an "ex post facto" law is confined to a retroactive change to a **criminal or penal** law. A law that is civil in purpose is treated as a criminal law only if its punitive effect clearly overrides its civil purpose. *Smith v. Doe*, 538 U.S. 84 (2003).

Under Article I, Sections 9 and 10, a **federal or state** statute will be struck down as being ex post facto if it:

i) **Criminalizes** an act that was not a crime when it was originally committed;

ii) Authorizes, after an act was committed, the imposition of a **more severe penalty** on that act;

iii) **Deprives the defendant of a defense** available at the time the act was committed; or

iv) **Decreases the prosecution's burden of proof** required for a conviction to a level below that which was required when the alleged offense was committed.

Collins v. Youngblood, 497 U.S. 37 (1990).

> **Example:** A change in the relevant statute of limitations that resulted in the revival of a prosecution for an act of sexual abuse for which the statute of limitations had expired violates the prohibition on ex post facto laws; the change retroactively withdrew a complete defense to the crime after it had vested. *Stogner v. California*, 539 U.S. 607 (2003).
>
> **Compare:** The retroactive application of state law that required registration of convicted sex offenders and child kidnappers, and public notification of information about the convicts, including name, current address, and place of employment did not constitute an ex post facto law. The law was a nonpunitive regulatory scheme enacted for the protection of the public. *Smith v. Doe, supra.*

C.   OBLIGATION OF CONTRACTS

Article I, Section 10 prohibits the states from passing any law "impairing the obligation of contracts." This prohibition applies only to **state legislation**—not state-court decisions and not federal legislation—that **retroactively** impairs contractual rights. It does not apply to contracts not yet entered into.

1.   Private Contracts

State legislation that **substantially** impairs a contract between private parties is invalid, unless the government can demonstrate that the interference was **reasonable** and **necessary** to serve an **important** governmental interest. *Allied Structural Steel Co. v. Spannaus*, 438 U.S. 234 (1978); *Energy Reserves Group, Inc. v. Kansas Power and Light Co.,* 459 U.S. 400 (1983).

2.   Public Contracts

Impairment by the state of a **public contract** (one to which the state or local government is a party) is subject to essentially the same "reasonable and necessary" test as private contracts, but with a somewhat stricter application. The state must show that its important interest cannot be served by a less-restrictive alternative and that the impairment it seeks is necessary because of unforeseeable circumstances. *U.S. Trust Co. v. New Jersey*, 413 U.S. 1 (1977).

Note that there is no substantial impairment if the state reserved—by statute, law, or in the contract itself—the right to revoke, alter, or amend.

XVII. FREEDOM OF RELIGION

The First Amendment provides that "Congress shall make no law respecting an establishment of religion, or prohibiting the free exercise thereof." Both the Establishment Clause and the Free Exercise Clause have been incorporated into the Due Process Clause of the Fourteenth Amendment and are therefore applicable to the states.

A. ESTABLISHMENT

When a governmental program shows preference to one religion over another, or to religion over nonreligion, strict scrutiny applies. *Bd. of Educ. v. Grumet*, 512 U.S. 687 (1994) (creation of special school district to benefit members of one religion invalid).

1. Standard of Review

Not every governmental action that impacts religion is unconstitutional. To determine whether a particular program violates the Establishment Clause, the Court may apply the three-part test developed in *Lemon v. Kurtzman*, 403 U.S. 602 (1971).

A governmental action that benefits religion is valid if:

i) It has a **secular purpose**;

ii) Its principal or primary effect **neither advances nor inhibits** religion; and

iii) It does not result in **excessive government entanglement** with religion.

Though still applied, the *Lemon* test has often been modified or set aside in the Supreme Court's more recent Establishment Clause cases.

2. Financial Aid

Programs that provide aid to religiously affiliated institutions, such as hospitals and schools, are tested under the three-part *Lemon* test and generally fall into one of the following three categories.

a. Indirect aid to schoolchildren

Financial assistance by the government that is widely available to a class of persons (not defined by religion) is likely valid, even if the aid benefits religion in some way. For example, aid to elementary- and high-school students, including students at parochial schools, in the form of textbooks, computers, standardized tests, bus transportation, and school lunches have all been upheld. Under the *Lemon* test, these forms of financial aid all have a secular primary purpose, neither advance nor inhibit religion, and have an extremely low risk of excessive entanglement.

Giving parents tuition vouchers to assist them in paying religious-school tuition does not violate the Establishment Clause if the vouchers may also be used in non-religious private schools. *Zelman v. Simmons-Harris*, 536 U.S. 639 (2002).

b. Direct aid to colleges and hospitals

Government grants to religiously affiliated colleges and hospitals are upheld only if the government requires that the aid be **used only for nonreligious purposes.** *Tilton v. Richardson*, 403 U.S. 672 (1971).

c. Tax exemptions

Property-tax exemptions for religious institutions have been held valid as being equivalent to exemptions given to other charitable organizations and therefore neither advancing nor inhibiting religion. *Walz v. Tax Comm'n*, 397 U.S. 664 (1970). Tax exemptions that are available only for religious activities or organizations, however, violate the Establishment Clause as an endorsement of religion. *Texas Monthly v. Bullock*, 489 U.S. 1 (1989).

Similarly, tax deductions given to reimburse tuition expenses only for parents of students in religious schools are invalid. If such a deduction is available to *all* parents for actual educational expenses of attending any public or private school (including parochial schools), it is valid. *Mueller v. Allen*, 463 U.S. 388 (1983).

3. School Activities

Generally, religious activities conducted in public schools violate the Establishment Clause. The following practices have been held invalid as clearly promoting religion:

i) **Prayer** and **Bible reading,** *Engel v. Vitale*, 370 U.S. 421 (1962);

ii) A designated period of silence for **"meditation or voluntary prayer,"** *Wallace v. Jaffree*, 472 U.S. 38 (1985);

iii) **Nondenominational prayer** led by a cleric at graduation ceremonies, *Lee v. Weisman*, 505 U.S. 577 (1992);

iv) Posting the **Ten Commandments** on public-school classroom walls, *Stone v. Graham*, 449 U.S. 39 (1980); and

v) **Prohibiting the teaching of Darwinism** (i.e., human biological evolution), or mandating that such teaching be accompanied by instruction regarding "creation science," *Edward v. Aguillard*, 482 U.S. 578 (1987); *Epperson v. Arkansas*, 393 U.S. 97 (1968).

If a public school allows student groups or organizations to use its facilities when classes are not in session, allowing a religious organization to use those facilities does not violate the Establishment Clause. Furthermore, to prohibit such a group from using those facilities because religious topics would be discussed would violate the First Amendment guarantee of **free speech.** *Good News Club v. Milford Central School*, 533 U.S. 98 (2001); *Widmar v. Vincent*, 454 U.S. 263 (1981). The Court has often responded to public educational institutions' Establishment Clause concerns by focusing on the free speech rights of religious students. *E.g., Rosenberger v. Univ. of Virginia*, 515 U.S. 819 (1995) (state university could not refuse to pay for printing of religious student newspaper on Establishment Clause grounds when it funded nonreligious papers).

4. Religious Displays

a. Ten Commandments

A display of the Ten Commandments on public property is an impermissible violation of the Establishment Clause if the display has a **"predominantly religious purpose."** *McCreary County v. ACLU*, 545 U.S. 844 (2005) (Ten Commandments posted in courthouse impermissible). If the display also communicates a secular moral message, or its context conveys a historical and social meaning, it may be upheld. *Van Orden v. Perry*, 545 U.S. 677 (2005) (Ten Commandments monument on the state capitol grounds displaying 17 monuments and 21 historical markers commemorating the state's "people, ideals, and events that compose its identity" was permitted because the "Ten Commandments have an undeniable historical meaning" in addition to their "religious significance." Because of the unique historical message, which is separate from any religious message, installing the Ten Commandments in a public park did not violate the Establishment Clause). This is a highly context-dependent, case-specific inquiry.

b. Holiday displays

Government holiday displays will generally be upheld unless a reasonable observer would conclude that the display is an **endorsement** of religion. The context of the display is key—a nativity scene in a courthouse under a banner reading *"Gloria in Excelsis Deo"* was struck down as endorsing religion, but a nearby outdoor display of a Christmas tree, Chanukah menorah, and other seasonal symbols was upheld as mere recognition that Christmas and Chanukah are both parts of a highly secularized winter holiday season. *County of Allegheny v. ACLU*, 492 U.S. 573 (1989).

B. FREE EXERCISE

The Free Exercise Clause of the First Amendment has been construed to include two freedoms: the freedom to believe and the freedom to act. The degree of protection that individuals are afforded from governmental interference in religion depends on whether religious belief or conduct is involved.

1. Religious Belief

The freedom to believe in any religion or none at all is absolutely protected and cannot be restricted by law. The government may not deny benefits or impose burdens based on religious belief, *Cantwell v. Connecticut*, 310 U.S. 296 (1940); it may not require affirmation of a belief, *West Virginia State Bd. of Educ. v. Barnette*, 319 U.S. 624 (1943); and it may not determine the reasonableness of a belief, although it may determine the sincerity of the person asserting that belief, *United States v. Ballard*, 322 U.S. 78 (1944).

2. Religious Conduct

Religious conduct, on the other hand, is not absolutely protected. Generally, only laws that **intentionally target** religious conduct are subject to strict scrutiny. Neutral laws of general applicability that have an impact on religious conduct are subject only to the rational basis test.

a. Targeting religious conduct

Strict scrutiny applies when the government purposely targets conduct because it is religious or displays religious beliefs. *Church of the Lukumi Babalu Aye, Inc. v. City of Hialeah*, 508 U.S. 520 (1993) (city ordinance banning all ritual sacrifice of animals not for the purpose of food consumption struck down as targeting the Santeria religion). A law that is designed to suppress activity because it is religiously motivated is valid only if it is necessary to achieve a compelling governmental interest.

Other laws that have been struck down as violating the Free Exercise Clause include compulsory school attendance for the Amish, *Wisconsin v. Yoder*, 406 U.S. 205 (1972), and denial of unemployment benefits to one whose faith prevented her from taking a job that required her to work on the Sabbath, *Sherbert v. Verner*, 374 U.S. 398 (1963).

b. Generally applicable laws

Neutral laws of general applicability that have the incidental effect of interfering with one's ability to engage in religious practices are subject only to the rational basis test. *Employment Div. v. Smith*, 494 U.S. 872 (1990) (criminalization of peyote that did not contain an exception for use in Native American religious rituals upheld, as the ban was not motivated by any desire to burden religious conduct).

> **Example:** A parent's right to pray over a child who has contracted meningitis, rather than seeking medical assistance, may be limited by state child-neglect and manslaughter laws. Parents do not have the right to endanger the lives of their children on the grounds of freedom of religion. *See Prince v. Massachusetts*, 321 U.S. 158 (1944).

XVIII. FREEDOM OF EXPRESSION AND ASSOCIATION

In addition to its religion clauses, the First Amendment provides that "Congress shall make no laws...abridging the freedom of speech, or of the press; or the right of the people to peaceably assemble, and to petition the Government for a redress of grievances." These aspects of the First Amendment are applicable to the states via the Fourteenth Amendment.

Freedom of expression is not absolute. While governmental regulation of the content of speech is severely constrained, governmental regulation of the time, place, and manner of speech is subject to less restriction.

A. REGULATION OF SPEECH

1. Expressive Conduct

Protected speech can include not only written, oral, and visual communication, but also activities such as picketing and leafleting. Expressive conduct (or symbolic speech) may be protected as speech, but it is subject to a lesser degree of protection. Governmental regulation of expressive conduct is upheld if:

i) The regulation is **within the government's power** to enact (e.g., through a local government's police power);

ii) The regulation furthers an **important governmental interest**;

iii) The governmental interest is **unrelated to the suppression of ideas**; and

iv) The burden on speech is **no greater than necessary.**

United States v. O'Brien, 391 U.S. 367 (1968) (prohibition against burning draft cards upheld as furthering the important governmental interest in a smoothly functioning draft system).

An example of permissible regulation of expressive conduct includes upholding a ban on public nudity, such as nude dancing in adult entertainment venues, pursuant to the important governmental interest in preventing the "harmful secondary effects" of adult entertainment on neighborhoods, which is unrelated to the suppression of expression. *City of Erie v. Pap's A.M.*, 529 U.S. 277 (2000).

Examples of impermissible regulation of expressive conduct include:

i) A ban against students wearing black armbands to protest the war in Vietnam, because the government's only interest in banning the conduct was prohibiting communication, *Tinker v. Des Moines Indep. Cmty. Sch. Dist.*, 393 U.S. 503 (1969); and

ii) A federal prohibition against burning the American flag because the law was intended to suppress messages of disapproval of governmental policy, rather than any conduct-related consequences of the burning of a flag. *United States v. Eichman*, 496 U.S. 310 (1990).

The act of signing a petition constitutes expressive conduct. Public disclosure of the petition, and, thereby, the names of the individuals who signed the petition does not violate the First Amendment because such disclosure is substantially related to the important interest of preserving the integrity of the electoral process. *Doe v. Reed*, 561 U.S. ___, 130 S. Ct. 2811 (2010).

2. **Overbreadth**

A law that burdens substantially more speech than is necessary to protect a compelling governmental interest is **"overbroad"** and therefore void. A statute's overbreadth must be substantial both in an absolute sense and relative to the statute's plainly legitimate reach. The mere fact that some impermissible applications of a statute can be conceived of is not sufficient to render a statute overbroad. *United States v. Williams*, 553 U.S. 285 (2008).

In order to prevent a **"chilling effect"** on protected speech (i.e., frightening people into not speaking for fear of prosecution), overbroad statutes may be challenged as **"facially invalid"** even by those who are validly regulated on behalf of those who are not. *Watchtower Bible and Tract Soc'y of New York, Inc. v. Vill. of Stratton*, 536 U.S. 150 2080 (2002) (municipal ordinance requiring a permit in order to engage in door-to-door canvassing and solicitation violated Free Speech Clause); *Bd. of Airport Comm'rs v. Jews for Jesus*, 482 U.S. 569 (1987) (administrative rule banning "all First Amendment activities" in a large airport terminal held overbroad).

3. **Vagueness**

A statute is **"void for vagueness"** if it fails to provide a person of ordinary intelligence with fair notice of what is prohibited. *United States v. Williams, supra.*

As with overbreadth, vagueness is impermissible for fear that constitutionally protected speech will be "chilled." In addition, the "void for vagueness" doctrine is grounded in the due process requirement of notice. Statutes that tie criminal culpability to conduct that involves subjective judgments without providing statutory definitions, narrow context, or settled legal meanings have been struck down for vagueness. *Reno v. ACLU*, 521 U.S. 844 (1997) (indecent speech); *Coates v. Cincinnati*, 402 U.S. 611 (1971) (annoying conduct).

4. Prior Restraints

A prior restraint is a regulation of speech that occurs in advance of its expression (e.g., publication or utterance).   Prior restraints are generally presumed to be unconstitutional, with limited exceptions. *Bantam Books, Inc. v. Sullivan*, 372 U.S. 58 (1963). These rare exceptions require at a minimum that:

i)   There is a **particular harm** to be avoided (like publication of troop movements); and

ii)   Certain **procedural safeguards** are provided to the speaker.   Examples of such safeguards include:

a)   The standards must be narrowly drawn, reasonable, and definite, *Butterworth v. Smith*, 494 U.S. 624 (1990);

b)   The censoring body must promptly seek an injunction, *Teitel Films v. Cusack*, 390 U.S. 139 (1968); and

c)   There must be a prompt and final judicial determination of the validity of the restraint, *National Socialist Party v. Village of Skokie*, 432 U.S. 43 (1977).

The **burden is on the government** to prove that the material to be censored is not protected speech. *Freedman v. Maryland*, 380 U.S. 51 (1965).

Prior restraints have been rejected even when national security was at issue, *New York Times v. United States*, 403 U.S. 713 (1971) (Pentagon Papers), and even when press coverage threatened the fairness of a trial, *Nebraska Press Ass'n v. Stewart*, 427 U.S. 539 (1976) (prior restraint must be the only way to accomplish a goal).

5. Unfettered Discretion

A law or regulation that permits a governmental official to restrict speech (e.g., requires an official to issue a permit before a rally can be held) must provide definite standards as to how to apply the law in order to prevent governmental officials from having unfettered discretion over its application.   Such a law or regulation must be related to an important governmental interest and contain the procedural safeguards mentioned above.   A statute that gives officials unfettered discretion is void on its face; speakers need not apply for a permit and may not be punished for violating the licensing statute. *Lovell v. City of Griffin*, 303 U.S. 444 (1938).

6. Freedom Not to Speak

The First Amendment protects not only freedom of speech, but also the freedom not to speak. One such example is a child's right not to recite the Pledge of Allegiance. *West Virginia State Board of Education v. Barnette*, 319 U.S. 624 (1943). Similarly, the private organizers of a parade cannot be compelled by the government to include in the parade a group that espouses a message with which the organizers disagree. *Hurley v. Irish-American Gay, Lesbian & Bisexual Group of Boston*, 515 U.S. 557 (1995). However, a state can compel a private entity (e.g., a shopping mall) to permit individuals to exercise their own free-speech rights when the private entity is open to the public and the message is not likely to be attributable to the private entity. *Pruneyard Shopping Center v. Robins*, 447 U.S. 74 (1980).

a. Compelled financial support

Although one can be compelled to join or financially support a group with respect to one's employment, one cannot be forced to fund political speech by that group. *Abood v. Detroit Bd. of Educ.*, 431 U.S. 209 (1977) (teacher required to pay union dues); *Keller v. State Bar of California*, 496 U.S. 1 (1990) (lawyer required to join a bar association). A student, however, can be required to pay a university activity fee even though the fee may support groups that espouse messages with which the student disagrees, at least when the fee is allocated in accord with a viewpoint-neutral scheme. *Board of Regents v. Southworth*, 529 U.S. 217 (2000).

7. Government Speech

When the government itself speaks, it is not constrained by the First Amendment. Therefore, government speech (public service announcements, agricultural marketing campaigns, etc.) need not be viewpoint-neutral. *Johanns v. Livestock Mkt'ing Ass'n*, 544 U.S. 550 (2005). This Government Speech Doctrine, however, is subject to the requirements of the Establishment Clause (*See* § XVII.A., *supra*).

a. Monuments on public property

The display of a monument on public property, even if the monument has been donated by a private person, constitutes government speech. *Pleasant Grove City v. Summum*, 555 U.S. 460 (2009) (government installed a Ten Commandments monument donated by a private person in a public park; the Court held that governmental entities may exercise "selectivity" in choosing a monument being offered by a private donor).

b. Funding of private messages

The government may fund private messages. However, it must generally do so on a viewpoint-neutral basis. *Rosenberger v. Rector and Visitors of the University of Virginia*, 515 U.S. 819 (1995). The exception to this is when the government decides to fund artists; the decision of which artist to fund is necessarily based on the content of the artist's work. *National Endowment for the Arts v. Finley*, 524 U.S. 569 (1998).

c. Speech by government employees

Attempts to fire or penalize a government employee for speech on matters of "public concern" will be strictly scrutinized. *Connick v. Myers*, 461 U.S. 138 (1983). However, speech on matters of public concern made in furtherance of the public employee's job functions receives less protection under the First Amendment than speech made by a person acting outside of his job. *Garcetti v. Ceballos*, 547 U.S. 410 (2006). Courts balance the First Amendment interest of the employee against the interest of the state, as an employer, in promoting the efficiency of the public services it provides through its employees. *Pickering v. Bd. of Educ.*, 391 U.S. 563 (1968). Speech by a government employee, including a petition for redress related to the employee's job, that does not relate to a matter of public concern, is not constitutionally protected. *Borough of Duryea v. Guarnieri*, 564 U.S. ___, 131 S. Ct. 2488 (2011).

8. **Campaign Related Speech**

a. **Political campaign contributions**

Statutes limiting campaign contributions are subject to intermediate scrutiny: they must be "closely drawn" to correspond with a sufficiently important interest. *McConnell v. Federal Election Commission*, 540 U.S. 93 (2003); *Randall v. Sorrell*, 548 U.S. 230 (2006).

1) **Contributions to candidates**

The government may limit contributions to individual candidates because excessive contributions to candidates create a danger of corruption and the appearance of corruption. *Buckley v. Valeo*, 424 U.S. 1 (1976). Limits on campaign contributions to candidates for state office ranging from $275 to $1,000 have been upheld. *Nixon v. Shrink Missouri Gov't PAC*, 528 U.S. 377 (2000). However, the government cannot set differential contribution limits that penalize a candidate who finances his own campaign. *Davis v. Federal Election Commission*, 554 U.S. 724 (2008)

2) **Contributions to political parties**

The government may limit contributions to a political party that are used to expressly advocate for the election or defeat of a particular candidate (also known as "hard money") as well as contributions that are used for other purposes, such as promoting the party itself (also known as "soft money"). *McConnell v. Federal Election Commission, supra.* In addition, the government may require a political party to disclose contributors and recipients unless the party can show that such disclosure would cause harm to the party. *Brown v. Socialist Workers '74 Campaign Committee*, 454 U.S. 112 (1982).

3) **Contributions to political action committees (PACs)**

The government may limit contributions to a political action committee (PAC). *California Medical Assn. v. FEC*, 453 U.S. 182 (1981).

b. **Political campaign expenditures**

In contrast to campaign contributions, restrictions on expenditures by individuals and entities (including corporations and unions) on communications during an election campaign regarding a candidate are subject to strict scrutiny. So long as the source of the funding is disclosed, there is no legal limit to the amount that corporations and unions may spend on "electioneering communications." *Citizens United v. Federal Election Commission*, 558 U.S. ___, 130 S. Ct. 876 (2010). In addition, expenditures by a candidate on her own behalf cannot be limited. *Buckley v. Valeo, supra; Davis v. Federal Election Commission, supra.*

c. **Political speakers**

In addition to individuals, corporations enjoy First Amendment protection with regard to political speech. *Citizens United, supra.* Similarly, a candidate for a judgeship has a First Amendment right to express his views on disputed legal or political issues. *Republican Party of Minnesota v. White*, 536 U.S. 765 (2002).

B. REGULATION OF TIME, PLACE, AND MANNER OF EXPRESSION

The government's ability to regulate the time, place, and manner of speech varies with the forum in which the speech takes place.

1. Public Forum

A **"public forum"** may be **traditional** or **designated.** Traditional public forums are those that are historically associated with expression, such as sidewalks, streets, and parks. A designated (or limited) public forum is one that has not historically been used for speech-related activities, but which the government has opened for such use, such as civic auditoriums, publicly owned theaters, or school classrooms that the public is allowed to use afterhours. The practical difference between the two is that the government can change a designated forum to a nonpublic forum, but it cannot do the same with a traditional forum.

In either type of public forum, the government may impose reasonable restrictions on the time, place, or manner of protected speech, provided the restrictions:

i) Are **content-neutral** as to both subject matter and viewpoint (i.e., it is not necessary to hear what is said in order to apply the regulation);

ii) Are **narrowly tailored** to serve a **significant governmental interest**; and

iii) Leave open ample **alternative channels for communication** of the information.

Ward v. Rock Against Racism, 491 U.S. 781 (1989). Restrictions that are not content-neutral are subject to **strict scrutiny** (*see* § XVIII.C., Regulation of Content, *infra*).

a. Residential areas

There is no right to focus picketing on a particular single residence. However, a person may solicit charitable funds in a residential area. Door-to-door solicitation does not require a permit, as long as the solicitation is for noncommercial or nonfundraising purposes. *Cantwell v. Conn.*, 310 U.S. 296, 306 (1940).

b. Injunctions

The test for the constitutionality of injunctions in public forums depends on whether the injunction is content-neutral or content-based. If an injunction is **content-neutral**, then the test is whether it burdens **no more speech than is necessary** to achieve an **important** governmental interest. On the other hand, if the injunction is **content-based,** it must be **necessary** for the government to achieve a **compelling** governmental interest.

c. Public schools

When a public school, as a designated (limited) public forum, permits the public to use its facilities, it cannot discriminate against organizations based on its beliefs. *Lamb's Chapel v. Center Moriches Union Free School District,* 508 U.S. 384 (1993) (religious organizations); *Widmar v. Vincent,* 454 U.S. 263 (1981); *Healy v. James,* 408 U.S. 169 (1972) (political organization). Similarly, a public school may provide funding and other benefits (e.g., free use of facilities) to student groups, but it must do so on a viewpoint-neutral basis.

Example 1: A university that provided funds to various student publications could not withhold funds from a student religious publication on the grounds that the publication espoused religion. *Rosenberger v. Rector and Visitors of the University of Virginia*, 515 U.S. 819 (1995).

Example 2: A public university law school could adopt an "all comers policy" with which student organizations must comply in order to receive school funding and other benefits. Under the policy, a student organization had to admit any student as a member and permit any student to hold office in the organization. Because the policy was viewpoint-neutral, its application to a religious organization was constitutional. *Christian Legal Soc'y Chapter of Univ. of California, Hastings Coll. of Law v. Martinez*, 561 U.S. ___, 130 S. Ct. 2971 (2010).

2. Nonpublic Forum

A nonpublic forum is essentially all public property that is not a traditional or designated public forum. Examples include government offices, schools, jails, and military bases. Sidewalks on postal service property and airport terminals are also considered nonpublic forums. The government may regulate speech-related activities in nonpublic forums as long as the regulation is (i) **viewpoint-neutral** and (ii) **reasonably related to a legitimate governmental interest.**

Note that a governmental fundraising campaign is a nonpublic forum for the expression of speech. The decision to exclude some charities (but not others) cannot be made because the government disagrees with a particular organization's political views; such a decision must be ideologically neutral. *Cornelius v. NAACP Legal Def. and Educ. Fund, Inc.*, 473 U.S. 788 (1985).

a. Viewpoint-neutral

The regulation need not be content-neutral, but it must be viewpoint-neutral. In other words, the government may prohibit speech on certain issues altogether, but it may not allow only one side of an issue to be presented. For example, while a restriction on all public speeches related to abortion on military bases would likely be upheld, a restriction only on pro-life speeches would not.

b. Reasonable

The restriction on speech-related activities in nonpublic forums must only be rationally related to a legitimate governmental interest. For example, a city may sell commercial advertising space inside city buses but refuse to sell such space for political advertising in order to avoid the appearance of favoritism and imposition on a captive audience. *Lehman v. City of Shaker Heights*, 418 U.S. 298 (1974).

3. Personal Property

Governmental regulation of speech on a person's own private property will rarely be upheld, particularly content-based regulations. While the government has some limited powers to regulate speech on private property, outright bans on certain types of speech, such as signs in a person's yard or window, are impermissible. *City of Ladue v. Gilleo*, 512 U.S. 43 (1994) (statute banning all residential signs in order to fight "visual clutter" was found unconstitutional).

C. REGULATION OF CONTENT

In general, the government may regulate the **content** of speech only if the regulation is necessary to achieve a compelling governmental interest and is narrowly tailored to meet that interest (i.e., the **strict scrutiny** test). *Brown v. Entm't Merchs. Ass'n*, 564 U.S ___, 131 S. Ct. 2729 (2011) (state law that prohibited the sale of violent video games to minors is an unconstitutional content restriction on speech); *Simon & Schuster, Inc. v. Members of the New York State Crime Victims Board*, 502 U.S. 105 (1991). The government must identify an actual problem, and the regulation of speech must be necessary to solve that problem. This standard is incredibly stringent and is not often met. *U.S. v. Playboy Entm't Group, Inc.*, 529 U.S. 803 (2000).

However, the government may restrict speech on the basis of content if the speech falls into one of the following categories: obscenity, subversive speech, fighting words, defamation, or commercial speech. States are not free to create new categories of content-based restrictions without persuasive evidence that such restrictions have a long-standing history of proscription. *Brown v. Entm't Merchs. Ass'n, supra.*

1. Obscenity and Child Pornography

Neither obscene speech nor child pornography is protected by the First Amendment Free Speech Clause. *Roth v. United States*, 354 U.S. 476 (1957).

a. Obscenity test

To be considered obscene, speech must meet each part of a three-prong test developed in *Miller v. California*, 413 U.S. 15 (1973). Under the *Miller* test, the **average person,** applying **contemporary community standards,** must find that the material, **taken as a whole**:

  i) Appeals to the **"prurient interest"**;

  ii) Depicts sexual conduct in a **patently offensive** way; and

  iii) **Lacks serious literary, artistic, political, or scientific value.**

> **EXAM NOTE: *Standards Distinguished* –** The first two prongs of this test use a contemporary **community** standard, which may be national but is generally considered to be local or statewide. A **national** standard must be applied, however, to the third prong of the test—determining the value of the work—because the work may merit constitutional protection despite local views to the contrary. *Pope v. Illinois*, 481 U.S. 497 (1987). With regard to the third prong, the judge, not the jury, determines whether this standard has been met.

Either an appellate court or a jury can assess whether the material is obscene. Evidence of similar material on newsstands is not automatically admissible, nor is expert testimony required to make such a determination.

b. Prohibited activities

The sale, distribution, and exhibition of obscene material may be prohibited. *Stanley v. Georgia*, 394 U.S. 557 (1969). However, the right to privacy precludes criminalization of possession of obscenity in one's own home. *Stanley v. Georgia, supra.*

c. Land-use restrictions

Narrowly drawn zoning ordinances may be used to restrict the location of adult theaters if the purpose of the regulation is to reduce the impact on the neighborhood of such establishments, but they may not be used to ban such establishments entirely. It does not matter that such establishments may be found in adjoining jurisdictions. *Los Angeles v. Alameda Books*, 535 U.S. 425 (2002); *City of Renton v. Playtime Theatres, Inc.*, 475 U.S. 41 (1986).

d. Minors

Material that appeals to the prurient interests of minors may be regulated as to minors, even if it would not be considered obscene to an adult audience. *Ginsberg v. New York*, 390 U.S. 629 (1968). The government may not, however, block adults' access to indecent materials in order to prevent them from reaching children. *Reno v. ACLU*, 521 U.S. 844 (1997).

e. Child pornography

The First Amendment also does not protect child pornography, which is sexually explicit visual portrayals that feature children. Because of the state's compelling interest in protecting minor children from exploitation, the sale, distribution, and even private possession of child pornography may be prohibited, even if the material would not be obscene if it involved adults. *Osborne v. Ohio*, 495 U.S. 103 (1990); *New York v. Ferber*, 458 U.S. 747 (1982).

Simulated child pornography (i.e., pornography using young-looking adults or computer-generated images) may not be banned as child pornography. *Ashcroft v. Free Speech Coalition*, 535 U.S. 234 (2002). However, offers to sell or buy simulated child pornography that contain actual depictions of children even though the sexually explicit features are simulated may be criminalized when the material is presented as actual child pornography. *United States v. Williams*, 553 U.S. 285 (2008).

f. Violence

Violence is not included in the definition of obscenity that may be constitutionally regulated. *Brown v. Entm't Merchs. Ass'n, supra*; *Winters v. New York*, 333 U.S. 507 (1948).

2. Incitement to Violence

A state may forbid speech that advocates the use of force or unlawful action if:

i) The speech is **directed to inciting or producing imminent lawless action**; and

ii) It is **likely to incite or produce such action** (i.e., creates a clear and present danger).

Brandenburg v. Ohio, 395 U.S. 444 (1969).

Advocacy requires the use of language reasonably and ordinarily calculated to incite persons to such action. *Yates v. United States*, 354 U.S. 298 (1957). The abstract expression of ideas, including the teaching of the moral propriety or even moral necessity for a resort to force and violence, is not the same as the actual incitement of violence. There must be substantial evidence of a strong and pervasive call to violence. *Noto v. United States*, 367 U.S. 290 (1960).

3. Fighting Words

A speaker may be criminally punished for using "fighting words," which are words that **by their very nature** are likely to incite an immediate breach of the peace. *Chaplinsky v. New Hampshire*, 315 U.S. 568 (1942). Words that are simply annoying or offensive are not fighting words; there must be a genuine likelihood of imminent violence by a hostile audience. *Cohen v. California*, 403 U.S. 154 (1971).

> **EXAM NOTE:** Attempts to forbid fighting words almost always fail as vague, overbroad, or otherwise constitutionally infirm.

Statutes designed to punish only fighting words that express certain viewpoints are unconstitutional. *R.A.V. v. City of St. Paul*, 505 U.S. 377 (1992) (the Court struck down an ordinance that applied only to fighting words that insulted or provoked on the basis of race, religion, or gender).

However, actual threats of violence are outside the protection of the First Amendment, given the need to protect individuals from (i) the fear of violence, (ii) the disruption that fear engenders, and (iii) the possibility that the threatened violence will occur. *R.A.V. v. City of St. Paul*, 505 at 388.

4. Defamation

Limits on punishment for defamatory speech may apply in cases in which the plaintiff is a public official or public figure, or when a defamatory statement involves a matter of public concern. In addition to the elements of a prima facie case of defamation, the plaintiff must in these cases prove both **fault** and the **falsity** of the statement.

a. Public figure or official

A public figure is someone who is known to the general public and includes any person who has voluntarily injected herself into the public eye. The plaintiff must prove that the defendant acted with **actual malice,** i.e., knowledge of the statement's falsity or reckless disregard for whether it was true or false. *New York Times v. Sullivan*, 376 U.S. 254 (1964). Scientists who publish in scientific journals, criminals, and spouses of wealthy persons are not considered public figures.

b. Public concern

If the plaintiff is a private figure but the defamatory statement involves a matter of public concern, then the standard is lower, but the plaintiff still must establish negligence with respect to the falsity of the statement. *Gertz v. Robert Welch, Inc.*, 418 U.S. 323 (1974).

[See the Themis Torts outline for a full discussion of defamation actions.]

5. Commercial Speech

Commercial speech—advertising and similarly economically oriented expression—is entitled to an intermediate level of First Amendment protection. Restrictions on commercial speech are reviewed under a **four-part test**:

i) The commercial speech must **concern lawful activity** and be **neither false nor misleading** (fraudulent speech or speech which proposes an illegal transaction may be prohibited);

ii) The asserted governmental interest must be **substantial**;

iii) The regulation must **directly advance** the asserted interest; and

iv) The regulation must be **narrowly tailored** to serve that interest. In this context, narrowly tailored does not mean the least restrictive means available; rather, there must be a **"reasonable fit"** between the government's ends and the means chosen to accomplish those ends. *Board of Trustees of State University of New York v. Fox*, 492 U.S. 469 (1989).

Central Hudson Gas & Elec. v. Pub. Svc. Comm'n, 447 U.S. 557 (1980). Under this test, the Court has struck down laws prohibiting truthful advertising of legal abortions, contraceptives, drug prices, alcohol prices, and attorneys' fees and regulation of billboards on the basis of aesthetic value and safety.

> **Example:** A Massachusetts regulation that prohibited tobacco billboards within 1,000 feet of a school was struck down because the means—effectively barring most outdoor tobacco advertising in urban areas—were not narrowly tailored to the ends of protecting children. *Lorillard Tobacco Co. v. Reilly*, 533 U.S. 525 (2001).

Note that solicitation of funds, however, is recognized as a form of protected speech. *See Village of Schaumburg v. Citizens for a Better Env't*, 444 U.S. 620 (1980).

D. REGULATION OF THE MEDIA

Although the First Amendment specifically mentions freedom of the press, the media has no greater First Amendment rights than the general public.

1. General Considerations

The press has the right to publish information about matters of public concern, and the viewers have a right to receive it. This right may be restricted only by a regulation that is narrowly tailored to further a compelling governmental interest (i.e., strict scrutiny applies).

a. Gag orders

A gag order is a judicial order prohibiting the press from publishing information about court proceedings. Such orders are subject to prior-restraint analysis. Gag orders are almost always struck down because they are rarely the least restrictive means of protecting the defendant's right to a fair trial. The trial judge has other alternatives available, such as change of venue, postponement of the trial, careful voir dire, or restricting the statements of lawyers and witnesses. *Nebraska Press Ass'n v. Stuart*, 427 U.S. 539 (1972).

b. Attending trials

The public and the press both have the right to attend criminal trials, but this right is not absolute. It may be outweighed if the trial judge finds an **overriding** interest that cannot be accommodated by less restrictive means. The Supreme Court has not determined whether this right also applies to civil trials. However, the Supreme Court has held that the defendant's right to a public trial extended to voir dire, and the trial court must consider reasonable alternatives to closing the voir dire to the public in addressing the trial court's concerns. *Presley v. Georgia*, 558 U.S. ___, 130 S. Ct. 721 (2010).

c. No constitutional privilege to protect sources

A journalist has no First Amendment right to refuse to testify before a grand jury regarding the content and source of information relevant to the criminal inquiry. *Branzburg v. Hayes*, 408 U.S. 665 (1972).

d. Illegally obtained and private information

The First Amendment shields the media from liability for publishing information that was obtained illegally by a third party as long as the information involves a matter of public concern and the publisher neither obtained it unlawfully nor knows who did. *Bartnicki v. Vopper*, 532 U.S. 514 (2001).

Similarly, the First Amendment shields the media from liability for publication of a lawfully obtained private fact, e.g., the identity of a rape victim, so long as the news story involves a matter of public concern. *See Florida Star v. BJF*, 491 U.S. 524 (1989); *Cox Broadcasting v. Cohn*, 420 U.S. 469 (1975).

e. First Amendment conflict with state right of publicity

Some states recognize a right of publicity—the right of a person to control the commercial use of his or her identity. The right is an intellectual property right derived under state law, the infringement of which creates a cause of action for the tort of unfair competition. In *Zacchini v. Scripps-Howard Broad. Co.*, 433 U.S. 562 (1977), the Supreme Court considered a conflict between the First Amendment and a person's state-law right of publicity. A news program had televised a videotape of a daredevil's entire 15-second performance at a local fair when he was shot out of a cannon. The lower court held that the First Amendment protected the telecast from a tort suit regarding the right of publicity. The Supreme Court reversed, holding that the First and Fourteenth Amendments do not immunize the news media from civil liability when they broadcast a performer's entire act without his consent, and the Constitution does not prevent a state from requiring broadcasters to compensate performers. Note that a state government may pass a law shielding the press from liability for broadcasting performers' acts.

f. No immunity from laws of general applicability

As mentioned previously, the press has no greater First Amendment rights than does the general public, i.e., there is no special privilege allowing the press to invade the rights of others. As such, members of the press are not immune from the application of generally applicable laws, even if the application of such laws has a negative incidental effect on the ability to gather and report the news. *Cohen v. Cowles Media Co.*, 501 U.S. 663 (1991).

Example: A reporter who trespasses on another's property while investigating a story is not shielded from liability by the First Amendment.

2. Broadcast

Because the broadcast spectrum is a limited resource, radio and television broadcasters are said to have a greater responsibility to the public, and they therefore can be more closely regulated than print and other media. Broadcasters may be sanctioned, therefore, for airing "patently offensive sexual and excretory speech," even if such speech does not qualify as obscene under the *Miller* test, in the interest of protecting children likely to be listening. *FCC v. Pacifica Found.*, 438 U.S. 726 (1978).

3. Cable Television

The First Amendment protection provided to cable television falls somewhere between the extensive protection given to print media and the more limited protection for broadcasting. As such, a law requiring cable operators to carry local television stations is subject to intermediate scrutiny. *Turner Broad. Sys., Inc. v. FCC*, 512 U.S. 622 (1994).

Content-based regulations of cable broadcasts are subject to **strict scrutiny,** however. *United States v. Playboy Entm't. Group, Inc.*, 529 U.S. 803 (2000).

4. Internet

Because the Internet is not composed of scarce frequencies as are the broadcast media, and because of the reduced risk of an unexpected invasion of privacy over the Internet, any regulation of Internet content is subject to strict scrutiny. *Reno v. ACLU*, 521 U.S. 844 (1997).

E. REGULATION OF ASSOCIATION

Freedom of association protects the right to form or participate in any group, gathering, club, or organization virtually without restriction, although the right is not absolute. An infringement upon this right may be justified by a compelling state interest. *See, e.g., Board of Dirs. of Rotary Int'l v. Rotary Club of Duarte*, 481 U.S. 537 (1987) (discrimination against women was not in furtherance of or necessary for any of the expressive activity undertaken by the organization); *but see Boy Scouts of America v. Dale*, 530 U.S. 640 (2000) (requiring the Boy Scouts to accept leaders who acted in a manner contrary to Boy Scout principles would unduly intrude upon the Boy Scouts' expressive associational rights).

1. Public Employment

An individual generally cannot be denied public employment based simply upon membership in a political organization. *Keyishian v. Board of Regents*, 385 U.S. 589 (1967).

a. Test

A person may only be punished or deprived of public employment based on political association if that individual:

i) Is an active member of a **subversive organization**;

ii) Has **knowledge** of the organization's illegal activity; and

iii) Has a **specific intent** to further those illegal objectives.

Scales v. United States, 367 U.S. 203 (1961) (conviction based on membership in an organization advocating the violent overthrow of the government upheld).

b. Loyalty oaths

Public employees may be required to take loyalty oaths promising that they will support the Constitution and oppose the forceful, violent, or otherwise illegal or unconstitutional overthrow of the government. *Connell v. Higgenbotham*, 403 U.S. 207 (1971). Such oaths are often found to be vague or overbroad, however. *E.g.*, *Cramp v. Board of Public Instruction*, 368 U.S. 278 (1961) (striking down as vague a statute requiring public employees to swear that they have not and will not lend "aid, support, advice, counsel, or influence to the Communist Party"); *Shelton v. Tucker*, 364 U.S. 479 (1960) (striking down as overbroad a statute requiring teachers to file an affidavit listing every organization to which they have belonged or regularly contributed during the past five years).

2. Bar Membership

Although the state can inquire into the character of a candidate for bar admission, such admission cannot be denied on the basis of political association unless the candidate knowingly belongs to a subversive organization with specific intent to further its illegal ends. *Schware v. Board of Bar Exam'rs*, 353 U.S. 232 (1957). The state may, however, deny bar membership to a candidate who refuses to answer questions about political affiliations if that refusal obstructs the investigation of the candidate's qualifications. *Konigsberg v. State Bar of California*, 366 U.S. 36 (1961).

3. Elections and Political Parties

a. Voters in primary elections

A state cannot require a local political party to select presidential electors in an open primary (i.e., a primary in which any voter, including members of another party, may vote) when the national party prohibits nonparty members from voting. *Democratic Party v. LaFolette*, 450 U.S. 107 (1981). A state can require a semi-closed primary system, in which only registered party members and independents can vote in the party's primary, even if the party wants to permit anyone to vote. *Clingman v. Beaver*, 544 U.S. 581 (2005). On the other hand, a state may not prohibit a political party from allowing independents to vote in its primary. *Tashjian v. Republican Party of Connecticut*, 479 U.S. 208 (1986).

1) Blanket primary

A state may adopt a blanket primary system (i.e., a primary in which all voters regardless of party affiliation or lack thereof vote) that is nonpartisan. Under a nonpartisan primary system, the voters choose candidates for the general election without regard for their party affiliation. A nonpartisan blanket primary system in which a candidate identifies his own party preference or his status as an independent and that identification appears on the ballot has withstood a facial challenge, despite assertions that this self-designation violates the party's First Amendment rights as compelled speech and forced association. *Washington State Grange v. Washington State Republican Party*, 552 U.S. 442 (2008). By contrast, a partisan blanket primary system in which a party's nominees are chosen violates the party's First Amendment rights of free speech and association. *Cal. Democratic Party v. Jones*, 530 U.S. 567 (2000).

b. **Ballot access to general election**

A state may refuse to grant a political party's candidate access to the general-election ballot unless the party demonstrates public support through voter signatures on a petition, voter registrations, or previous electoral success. *Timmons v. Twin Cities Area New Party*, 520 U.S. 351 (1997); *Munro v. Socialist Workers Party*, 479 U.S. 189 (1986).

c. **Fusion candidate**

A state may prohibit a fusion candidate (i.e., a candidate who is nominated by more than one political party) from appearing on the general-election ballot as a candidate of multiple parties. This limitation on the associational rights of political parties is justified by the state's interests in ballot integrity and political stability. *Timmons v. Twin Cities Area New Party*, 520 U.S. 351 (1997).

d. **Replacement candidate**

When a state gives a political party the right to select an interim replacement for an elected state official who was a member of that party, the party may select the replacement through an election at which only party members may vote. *Rodriguez v. Popular Democratic Party*, 457 U.S. 1 (1982).

Contracts

CONTRACTS

Table of Contents

CONTRACTS

EXAM NOTE: When analyzing a contracts question on the MBE, always apply common law, unless a UCC rule that differs from common law applies. In general, Article 2 of the UCC will apply whenever the transaction at issue is a sale of goods (generally, tangible personal property). When a transaction involves both the sale of goods and the rendering of services, the "predominant purpose" test applies to determine which law applies to the entire transaction. For a more extensive discussion of UCC Article 2, see the Themis *Sales* outline.

I. FORMATION OF CONTRACTS

A binding contract is created through the process of mutual assent (i.e., offer and acceptance) and consideration, and when no valid defenses to contract exist.

A. MUTUAL ASSENT

Mutual assent occurs upon acceptance of a valid offer to contract.

1. Objective Theory of Contracts

In contract law, intent is determined by the so-called "objective theory" of contracts and not by the subjective intent or belief of a party. The objective theory is key to determining whether an offer or acceptance is valid.

Whether a party intends to enter into a contract is judged by outward objective facts, as interpreted by a reasonable person. The intent of a party is what a reasonable person in the position of the other party would believe as a result of that party's objective manifestation of intent. Thus, when the other party knew or should have known that the party lacked the intent to enter into a contract, a contract is not formed, whereas the party's mere subjective lack of intent is not sufficient to prevent the formation of a contract.

Objective facts may include things that the party said when entering into the contract, the way the party acted or appeared at such time, and the circumstances surrounding the transaction. The circumstances surrounding the statement can be critical to determining what would be reasonable to believe.

2. Offer and Acceptance

a. Offer

An offer is an objective manifestation of a willingness by the offeror to enter into an agreement that creates the power of acceptance in the offeree. In other words, it is a communication that gives power to the recipient to conclude a contract by acceptance.

1) Intent

A statement is an offer only if the person to whom it is communicated could *reasonably interpret* it as an offer. It must express the **present intent** to be legally bound to a contract. As noted above, the primary test of whether a communication is an offer is based on the objective theory of contracts; i.e., whether an individual receiving the communication would believe that he could enter into an enforceable deal by satisfying the condition.

2) Knowledge by the offeree

The offeree must have knowledge of the offer in order to have the power to accept the offer.

3) Terms

For a contract to exist, the terms of the contract must be certain and definite, or the contract fails for indefiniteness. Under common law, all essential terms (i.e., the parties, subject matter, price, and quantity) must be covered in the agreement.

The UCC allows for a more liberal contract formation. Under the UCC, a contract is formed if both parties intend to contract and there is a reasonably certain basis for giving a remedy. As long as the parties intend to create a contract, the UCC "fills the gap" when a contract is silent as to a term, such as the time or place for delivery, or even the price for the goods. In addition to identifying the parties and subject matter, an agreement to sell goods generally must specify the quantity to be sold, but requirements or output contracts satisfy UCC contract formation requirements even without naming specific quantities. (Note: The UCC also implies good faith as a contract term.)

a) Duration term

In most ongoing contracts, if a duration term is not specified in the agreement, courts will imply that the contract will last for a reasonable period of time.

i) Employment contracts

If an employment contract does not state duration, there is a rebuttable presumption that the employment is "at will." In an employment-at-will relationship, either party can terminate the relationship at any time, without the termination being considered a breach of the contract (unless the termination is against public policy, such as when the employee is discharged for filing a discrimination claim).

If an employment contract provides for "permanent employment," most courts hold that, in the absence of a proven contrary intention, the employment is "at will," because the duration term in the contract is considered too vague. If the offer promises "lifetime employment," some courts hold that the agreement is for "at will" employment, while others take the term literally.

b) Missing terms

A contract may still be formed when price and quantity are missing, if it appears that the parties intended to create a contract. The court may supply the missing terms because there is a presumption that the parties intended to include a reasonable term. However, the contract must have an objective standard for the court to reference.

c) Vague terms

When the terms of the contract are vague, the same presumption cannot be made because the parties have manifested an intent that cannot be determined due to the vagueness of the terms.

4) Language

The offer must contain words of promise, undertaking, or commitment (as distinguished from words that merely indicate intention to sell or interest in buying). The offer must also be targeted to a number of people who could actually accept.

If a return promise is requested, then the contract is a bilateral contract. If an act is requested, then the contract is a unilateral contract.

5) Invitation to deal

Offers must be distinguished from invitations to deal.

Compare, for example, the question, "what is your lowest price?" with the response to that question, "we can quote you $5 per gross for immediate acceptance." The first question is merely an inquiry, whereas the second statement is an offer. (Note that for the offeree to accept the offer, the offeree must supply the quantity term in order for the contract to meet the definiteness requirement.)

Advertisements generally are considered invitations to receive offers from the public, unless associated with a stated reward. An advertisement that is sufficiently specific and limiting as to who may accept may also qualify as an offer (e.g., "Used car for sale for $5,000. First come, first served.").

> **EXAM NOTE:** Be careful not to mistake a true offer for language that sounds like an offer but is actually just an invitation to receive offers. The more definite the statement (e.g., "I will sell you X for…"), the more likely it is to be an offer.

b. Termination of offers

An offer can be accepted only when it is still outstanding (i.e., before the offer is terminated). Offers can be terminated in the following ways.

1) Lapse of time in offer

If the offer specifies a date on which the offer terminates, the offer terminates at midnight on that date. If the offer states that it will terminate after a specified number of days, the time starts to run from the time the offer is received.

If the offer does not set a time limit for acceptance, the power of acceptance terminates at the end of a reasonable period of time.

2) Death or mental incapacity

An offer terminates upon the death or mental incapacity of the offeror. An exception exists for an offer that is an option, which does not terminate upon death or mental incapacity because consideration was paid to keep the offer open during the option period, and the offer is therefore made irrevocable during that period.

Compare accepted offer: If an offer has been accepted, death of the offeror does not automatically terminate the contract. The contract may be enforceable unless there is some reason, such as impracticability, that justifies discharge of the contractual obligation.

3) Destruction or illegality

An offer involving subject matter that is destroyed is terminated. Similarly, an offer that becomes illegal is terminated.

4) Revocation

In general, an offer can be revoked by the offeror at any time prior to acceptance, even if the offer states that it will remain open for a specific amount of time. A revocation is not effective until communicated. A revocation sent by mail is not effective until received. If the offeree acquires reliable information that the offeror has taken definite action inconsistent with the offer, the offer is automatically revoked.

Example: On day 1, A mails an offer to B. On day 2, A mails a revocation to B. If B receives the offer and accepts before receiving the revocation, a contract is formed.

An offeror's power to revoke an offer will be limited by the following.

a) Option

An option is an independent contract that limits the offeror's power to revoke an offer. The offeree must generally give consideration in order for an option to be enforceable. However, with regard to a sale of goods, a merchant's promise to keep an offer open need not be supported by consideration if it is in writing and signed.

b) Promissory estoppel

When the offeree detrimentally relies on the offeror's promise prior to acceptance, the doctrine of promissory estoppel may make the offer irrevocable. It must have been reasonably foreseeable that such detrimental reliance would occur in order to imply the existence of an option contract. The offeror is liable to the extent necessary to avoid injustice, which may result in holding the offeror to the offer, reimbursement of the costs incurred by the offeree, or restitution of the benefits conferred.

c) Partial performance

If the offer is for a unilateral contract, the offeror cannot revoke the offer once the offeree has begun performance. The same holds true for a bilateral contract. Once the offeree has begun performance, the contract is complete. Note, though, that the offeree must have had knowledge of the offer when she began performance.

Once performance has begun, the offeree will have a reasonable amount of time to complete performance but cannot be required to complete the performance.

d) UCC firm offer rule

Under the UCC, an offer to buy or sell goods is irrevocable if:

i)   The offeror is a merchant (i.e., one who deals in the type of goods involved in the transaction or holds himself out as having special knowledge in the goods);

ii)   There are assurances that the offer is to remain open; and

iii) The assurance is contained in an authenticated writing (such as a signature, initials, or other inscription) from the offeror.

If the time period during the option is to be held open is not stated, a reasonable term is implied. Whether or not a time period is stated, irrevocability cannot exceed 90 days under this rule.

No consideration by the offeree is needed to keep the offer open under the UCC firm offer rule. UCC § 2-205.

> **Example:** Merchant A sends a signed offer to B that reads, "Will sell you 100 widgets at $5 each. This offer will remain open for 15 days." Three weeks later, B faxes A a note accepting the offer. Although the offer became revocable after 15 days, B's acceptance is binding because A failed to revoke the offer.

5) Revocation of general offers

A "general offer" is an offer made to a large number of people, generally through an advertisement. A general offer can be revoked only by notice that is given at least the same level of publicity as the offer. So long as the appropriate level of publicity is met, the revocation will be effective even if a potential offeree does not learn of the revocation and acts in reliance on the offer. Restatement (Second) of Contracts § 46. Note that if a person has actual knowledge of the intent to revoke but did not see the notice, then the revocation will be effective as to such person.

6) Rejection by offeree

An offer is terminated by rejection. In other words, the offeree clearly conveys to the offeror that the offeree no longer intends to accept the offer. Under the mailbox rule, a rejection is usually **effective upon receipt.** An offeree cannot accept an offer once it has been terminated.

A counteroffer acts as a rejection of the original offer and creates a new offer. An exception exists for an option holder, who has the right to make counteroffers during the option period without terminating the original offer.

> **EXAM NOTE:** Remember that a **counteroffer** is both a **rejection and a new offer.** Examine the offeree's statement closely. It may be a rejection, but it may also be only an inquiry (e.g., "Is that a 2005 model car?") or merely indecision (e.g., "Maybe not, but I should ask my wife first."), in which case the offer remains open.

7) Revival of offer

A terminated offer may be revived by the offeror. As with any open offer, the revived offer can be accepted by the offeree. For example, if A offers to paint B's house for $500, and B rejects the offer, then A can revive the offer by stating that the offer remains open. B can change her mind and accept.

c. Acceptance

Only a party to whom an offer is extended may accept (or, if the offer is extended to a class, a party who is a member of the class may accept), and the acceptance forms a contract between the parties. An acceptance is an objective manifestation by the offeree to be bound by the terms of the offer.

An offeree must know of the offer upon acceptance for it to be valid. In addition, the offeree must communicate the acceptance to the offeror.

Commencement of performance of a bilateral contract operates as a promise to render complete performance. Restatement (Second) of Contracts § 62.

1) Method of acceptance

The offeror can detail the manner of proper acceptance.

a) Bilateral versus unilateral offer

A **bilateral contract** is one in which a promise by one party is exchanged for a promise by the other. The exchange of promises is enough to render them both enforceable. An offer requiring a promise to accept can be accepted either with a return promise or by starting performance. Commencement of performance of a bilateral contract operates as a promise to render complete performance.

A **unilateral contract** is one in which one party promises to do something in return for an act of the other party (e.g., a monetary reward for finding a lost dog). Unlike in a bilateral contract, in a unilateral contract, the offeree's promise to perform is insufficient to constitute an acceptance; the offeree must perform the act to accept the offer. Note that merely starting performance is not enough to accept a unilateral contract, which requires complete performance of the act, but it will make the offer irrevocable for a reasonable period of time to allow for complete performance. Restatement (Second) of Contracts § 62.

> **EXAM NOTE:** The offeree of a unilateral contract can accept only an offer that he is aware of. In other words, if the offeree does not become aware of the offer until after acting, then his acts do not constitute acceptance.

i) Notice of acceptance

Unless notice is requested by the offeror, an offeree of a unilateral contract who accepts by rendering the requested performance is required to give notice only if the offeree has reason to know that the offeror would not learn of the requested performance with reasonable certainty and promptness. Restatement (Second) of Contracts § 54(1).

If the offeree has reason to know that the offeror would not reasonably learn of the performance, then the offeror's duty is discharged, unless:

i) The offeree exercises reasonable diligence to notify the offeror of acceptance; or

ii) The offeror learns of the performance within a reasonable time; or

iii) The offer indicates that notification of acceptance is not required.

Restatement (Second) of Contracts § 54(2).

b) An offer to buy goods for immediate shipment

If the buyer requests that the goods be shipped, then the buyer's request will be construed as inviting acceptance by the seller either by a **promise to ship** or by **prompt shipment** of conforming or nonconforming goods.

i) Shipment of nonconforming goods

If the seller ships nonconforming goods, then the shipment is both an acceptance of the offer and a breach of the contract. The seller is then liable for any damage caused to the buyer as a result of the breach.

If, however, the seller "seasonably" notifies the buyer that the nonconforming goods are tendered as an accommodation, then no acceptance has occurred, and no contract is formed. The accommodation is deemed a counteroffer, and the buyer may then either accept (thereby forming a contract) or reject (no contract formed).

c) Mailbox rule

An acceptance sent in the mail within the allotted response time is effective **upon posting** (not upon receipt), unless the offer otherwise provides. The mailing must be properly addressed and include proper postage. E-mail, faxes, and other forms of modern communication also fall under the mailbox rule in many states.

> **EXAM NOTE:** The mailbox rule is frequently tested on the MBE. Keep in mind that the rule applies only to **acceptance,** and therefore it almost exclusively applies to bilateral contracts (when there is one promise in exchange for another promise) because unilateral contracts require action as acceptance.

i) Rejection following acceptance

If the offeree sends an acceptance and later sends a communication rejecting the offer, then the acceptance will generally control even if the offeror receives the rejection first. If, however, the offeror receives the rejection first and detrimentally relies on the rejection, then the offeree will be estopped from enforcing the contract.

ii) Acceptance following rejection

If a communication is sent rejecting the offer, and a later communication is sent accepting the contract, then the mailbox rule will **not** apply, and the first one to be received by the offeror will prevail. The offeror need not actually read the communication in order for it to prevail.

iii) Revocations effective upon receipt

Offers revoked by the offeror are effective upon receipt.

iv) Option contract

The mailbox rule does not apply in an option contract because acceptance must be received by the offeror before the option expires.

d) Means of acceptance

The offeror is master of the offer. As such, the offeror can dictate the manner and means by which an offer may be accepted. For example, the offeror can require the offeree to accept in writing or to accept by means of a phone call. However, unless the offeror specifically requires the offeree to accept in a particular manner or by using a particular means, the offeree can accept in any reasonable manner and by any reasonable means. UCC § 2-206. Even if the acceptance is by unauthorized means, it may be effective if the offeror receives the acceptance while the offer is still open.

2) Silence

Generally, silence does not operate as an acceptance of an offer, even if the offer states that silence qualifies as acceptance (or, more likely, implied acceptance), unless:

i) The offeree has reason to believe that the offer could be accepted by silence, was silent, and intended to accept the offer by silence; or

ii) Because of previous dealings or pattern of behavior, it is reasonable to believe that the offeree must notify the offeror if the offeree intends not to accept.

3) Notice

An offeree of a bilateral contract must give notice of acceptance. Because acceptance becomes valid when posted, a properly addressed letter sent by the offeree operates as an acceptance when mailed, even though the offeror has not yet received the notice.

Notice of acceptance of a unilateral contract is required only when the offeror is unlikely to become aware that the act is being performed or if the offeror requests such notice in the offer. Notice would be required under the same circumstances if a bilateral contract was being accepted by performance.

Unless notice is requested by the offeror, an offeree of a unilateral contract who accepts by rendering the requested performance is required to give notice only if the offeree has reason to know that the offeror would not learn of the requested performance with reasonable certainty and promptness. Restatement (Second) of Contracts § 54(1).

If the offeree has reason to know that the offeror would not reasonably learn of the performance, then the offeror's duty is discharged, unless:

i) The offeree exercises reasonable diligence to notify the offeror of acceptance;

ii) The offeror learns of the performance within a reasonable time; or

iii) The offer indicates that notification of acceptance is not required.

Restatement (Second) of Contracts § 54(2).

d. Counteroffers and mirror-image rule

1) Common-law mirror-image rule

Acceptance must mirror the terms of the offer. Any modification of the terms of the offer, or the addition of another term not found in the offer, acts as a rejection of the original offer and as a new counteroffer. Mere suggestions or inquiries, including requests for clarification or statements of intent, made in a response by the offeree do not constitute a counteroffer. A conditional acceptance terminates the offer and acts as a new offer from the original offeree.

2) UCC rule

The UCC does not follow the mirror-image rule. Additional terms included in an acceptance of an offer do not automatically constitute a rejection of the original offer. Generally, for a sale of goods, an acceptance that contains additional terms or modifications to the terms in the offer is nevertheless treated as an acceptance rather than a rejection and a counteroffer. An exception exists when the acceptance is expressly conditioned on assent to the additional or different terms, in which case the acceptance is a counteroffer. Whether the additional or different terms are treated as part of the contract depends on whether one of the parties is a merchant. UCC § 2-207. A merchant is a person who regularly deals in the kind of goods sold or who holds himself out as having special knowledge or skills as to those goods. UCC § 2-104(1).

a) Both parties are not merchants

When the contract is for the sale of goods between nonmerchants or between a merchant and a nonmerchant, a definite and seasonable expression of acceptance or written confirmation that is sent within a reasonable time operates as an acceptance of the original offer. This is true even if it states terms that are additional to or different from the offer, unless the acceptance is made expressly conditional on the offeror's consent to the additional or different terms. The additional or different terms are treated as a proposal for addition to the contract that must be separately accepted by the offeror in order to become a part of the contract.

b) Both parties are merchants—battle of the forms

> **EXAM NOTE:** The MBE has consistently tested the situation in which both parties to the contract are merchants. In this situation, remember that a contract exists *under the terms of the acceptance,* unless (i) the terms materially alter the agreement, (ii) the offer expressly limits the terms, or (iii) the offeror objects to the new terms within a reasonable time after notice of the new terms is received. UCC § 2-207.

When both parties to the sale of goods are merchants, often both the offer and the acceptance are made by means of forms designed for use in the typical transactions in which the merchants engage rather than for the particular sale in question. As a consequence, the acceptance often contains different and additional terms. In this "battle of the forms" over whose terms will form the basis of the contract between the merchants, the rules may vary depending on whether the terms are additional terms or different terms.

i) Acceptance includes additional terms

Under the "last shot" rule, an additional term in the acceptance is **automatically included** in the contract when both parties are merchants, unless:

i) The term materially alters the original contract;

ii) The offer expressly limits acceptance to the terms of the offer; or

iii) The offeror has already objected to the additional terms, or objects within a reasonable time after notice of them was received.

If any one of these three exceptions is met, a contract is formed, but the offeror's original terms are controlling.

Examples of terms that typically are found to have materially altered the original contract include a warranty disclaimer, a clause that flies in the face of trade usage with regard to quality, a requirement that complaints be made in an unreasonably short time period, and terms that surprise or create hardship without express awareness by the other party. Terms that usually **do not** materially alter the contract include fixing reasonable times for bringing a complaint, setting reasonable interest for overdue invoices, and reasonably limiting remedies.

ii) Acceptance includes different terms

The courts in different jurisdictions disagree as to the result when different terms are included in the merchant offeree's acceptance. A few jurisdictions treat different terms the same as additional terms and apply the "last shot" rule, as described above. Most, however, apply the so-called **"knock-out" rule,** under which different terms in the offer and acceptance nullify each other and are "knocked out" of the contract. When there are gaps in the contract, the court uses Article 2's gap-filling provisions to patch the holes.

e. Auction contracts

The UCC has special rules for auction sales.

1) Goods auctioned in lots

If goods in an auction sale are offered in lots, each lot represents a separate sale.

2) Completion of sale

An auction sale is complete when the auctioneer announces its end by the fall of the hammer or in any other customary way. When a bid is made contemporaneously with the falling of the hammer, the auctioneer may, at her discretion, reopen the bidding or declare the sale completed at the fall of the hammer.

3) Reserve and no-reserve auctions

In a reserve auction, the auctioneer may withdraw the goods any time before she announces completion of the sale. An auction is with reserve unless specifically announced as a no-reserve auction.

In a no-reserve auction, the goods cannot be withdrawn by the auctioneer unless no bid is received on the item or lot.

In either type of auction, a bidder may retract her bid until the auctioneer announces the end of the bidding. A retraction, however, does not revive earlier bids.

4) When the seller bids

When an auctioneer knowingly accepts a bid by the seller or on her behalf, or procures such a bid to drive up the price of the goods, the winning bidder may avoid the sale or, at her option, take the goods at the price of the last good-faith bid prior to the end of the auction. There are two exceptions to this rule, which are that (i) a seller may bid at a forced sale and (ii) a seller may bid if she specifically gives notice that she reserves the right to bid.

B. CONSIDERATION

1. Bargain and Exchange

In addition to an offer and acceptance, some legal detriment must be bargained for in order for a contract to exist. The exchange must be a bargained-for change in the legal position between the parties. Valuable consideration must exist on both sides of the bargain to make it fully enforceable.

a. Legal detriment and bargained-for exchange

For the legal detriment to constitute sufficient consideration, it must be bargained for in exchange for the promise. The promise must induce the detriment, and the detriment must induce the promise.

Consideration can take the form of:

i) A return promise to do something;

ii) A return promise to refrain from doing something legally permitted;

iii) The actual performance of some act; or

iv) Refraining from doing some act.

b. Gift distinguished

A promise to make a gift does not involve bargained-for consideration and is therefore unenforceable.

A promise by A to give B $1,000 when B turns 21 is not enforceable because the act of attaining the age of 21 is not bargained for and is thus not sufficient consideration. There also can be no reliance on the promise (B will turn 21 regardless of A's promise), so promissory estoppel does not apply.

Alternatively, if A offers B $1,000 to quit smoking, it is assumed that A is bargaining for B's act and that B would rely on the promise of the payment when he quit smoking.

> **EXAM NOTE:** The test to distinguish a gift from valid consideration is whether the offeree could have **reasonably believed that the intent of the offeror was to induce the action.** If yes, there is consideration, and the promise is enforceable.

A party's promise to make a gift is enforceable under the doctrine of promissory estoppel if the promisor/donor knows that the promise will induce substantial reliance by the promisee, and the failure to enforce the promise will cause substantial injustice.

2. Adequacy of Consideration

The basic concept of legal detriment is that there must be something of **substance,** either an act or a promise, that is given in exchange for the promise that is to be enforced. In general, a party cannot challenge a contract on the grounds that the consideration is inadequate. A difference in economic value between the items exchanged is not grounds for finding that a contract did not exist due to inadequate consideration.

a. Subjective value

The benefit to the promisor does not need to have an economic value. Regardless of the objective value of an item, as long as the promisor wants it, the giving of it will constitute adequate consideration.

b. Preexisting duty rule

1) Common law

At common law, a promise to perform a preexisting legal duty does not qualify as consideration because the promisee is already bound to perform (i.e., there is no legal detriment). Note that if the promisee gives something in addition to what is already owed (however small) or varies the preexisting duty in some detrimental way (however slight), there will be consideration.

Partial payment of a liquidated debt is invalid for a lack of consideration, unless there is a compromise of a claim disputed in good faith. This exception applies even if it later becomes apparent that the reason for disputing the claim was invalid. Restatement (Second) of Contracts § 74.

2) Exception for a third party

There is an exception to the pre-existing legal duty rule when a third party offers a promise contingent upon performance of a contractual obligation by a party. Under the exception, the third party's promise is sufficient consideration. Restatement (Second) of Contracts § 73.

> **Example:** C contracts with P for P to install plumbing in a house being built by C for H. C subsequently becomes insolvent and walks away from the project. H contracts with P and promises to pay P the same amount P would have received from C if P installs the plumbing. P's completion of the job constitutes consideration for the promise by H, even though P was already contractually obligated to C to do the work.

c. Past consideration

Under the common law, something given in the past is typically not adequate consideration because it could not have been bargained for, nor could it have been done in reliance upon a promise.

> **Example:** A is drowning, and B dives in and saves A. Grateful to have been saved, A promises B $500. Under the common-law approach, there is no consideration, and the promise is therefore unenforceable. It is based on a mere moral obligation arising out of past conduct.

There is a modern trend, adopted by the Second Restatement, however, toward enforcing such promises when necessary to prevent injustice, unless the promisee intended his act to be a gift, or otherwise did not expect compensation. Furthermore, courts will enforce a promise only to the extent that the value of the promise is proportional to the previous benefit conferred by the promisee.

See, e.g., First National Bankshares of Beloit, Inc. v. Geisel, 853 F.Supp. 1344 (D.Kan. 1994), Restatement (Second) of Contracts § 86.

d. Modification

1) Common law

At common law, modification of an existing contract must be supported by consideration. Agreements to modify a contract may still be enforced if:

i) There is a rescission of the existing contract by tearing it up or by some other outward sign, and then the entering into of a new contract, whereby one of the parties must perform more than she was to perform under the original contract;

ii) There are unforeseen difficulties, and one of the parties agrees to compensate the other when the difficulties are discovered if those difficulties would make performance impracticable (*see* § II.A. Impracticability, *infra*); or

iii) There are new obligations on both sides.

2) UCC and consideration

Unlike under the common law, under Article 2, no consideration is necessary to modify a contract for the sale of goods, although there is a requirement of good faith by both parties. Thus, if one party is attempting to extort a modification, it will be ineffective under the UCC. Good faith requires honesty in fact and, in the case of a merchant, fair dealing in accordance with reasonable commercial standards.

> **EXAM NOTE:** The MBE frequently tests the different common-law and UCC rules regarding contract modification. At common law, modifications require consideration; under the UCC, they require only good faith.

> **Example:** If a party demands an increase in price because the other party has no choice but to agree, the courts will invalidate such a bad-faith modification.

a) Statute of Frauds

A contract **as modified** that falls within the Statute of Frauds must generally be in writing. However, any of the Statute of Frauds exceptions apply to take a modification out of the Statute of Frauds.

b) Parties may prohibit oral modification

A provision that modifications to a written sales contract may occur only in writing is valid and binding under the UCC. If such a provision is on a form supplied by a merchant, it must be separately signed by the other party, unless that other party is also a merchant.

i) Waiver

When an oral modification violates the Statute of Frauds or is contrary to a provision against oral modification, it may be withdrawn or retracted so long as no party has relied upon it. When one party relies on an improper modification, the other party may not avoid it by reliance on the Statute of Frauds or a no-oral-modification provision. The benefitting party is deemed to waive any challenge to the modification.

ii) **Installment contracts**

Generally, a party benefited by a condition under a contract may orally waive that condition without new consideration. However, in installment contracts, the beneficiary of a waiver that is not supported by consideration may retract that waiver by reasonable notification, received by the other party, that strict performance will be required, so long as the retraction would not be unjust because of a material change of position by the other party in reliance on the waiver.

e. **Accord and satisfaction**

Under an accord agreement, one party to a contract agrees to accept different performance from the other party than what was promised in the existing contract. Generally, consideration is required for an accord to be valid. By compromising, each party surrenders its respective claim as to how much is owed. Restatement (Second) of Contracts § 74.

When a creditor agrees to accept a lesser amount in full satisfaction of the debt, the original debt is discharged **only when there is some dispute** either as to the validity of the debt or the amount of the debt, **or when the payment is of a different type than called for under the original contract.**

A "satisfaction" is the performance of the accord agreement; it will discharge both the original contract and the accord contract. However, there is no satisfaction until performance, and the original contract is not discharged until satisfaction is complete. Therefore, if an accord is breached by the debtor, the creditor can sue either on the original contract **or** under the accord agreement.

Compare accord with a substituted contract, which is a second agreement that immediately discharges the original contract, such that the remedy for breach is limited to the terms of the second contract. Whether an agreement is an accord or a substitute contract turns on how formal the agreement is; the less formal, the more likely it is an accord.

Example 1: A contracts with B to build a barn out of cherry wood for $10,000. B instead builds the barn out of particle board. A refuses to pay, and after many discussions, finally says, "Fine. I will pay you $7,500 next week." B accepts, but when A goes to pay B the following week, B says, "I changed my mind and want the original $10,000." What is the result? The $7,500 deal was an accord, which means B can recover it or the original contract price. Once A pays the $7,500, however, the accord is satisfied and B can no longer recover under the original contract.

f. **Illusory promises**

An illusory promise is one that essentially pledges nothing because it is vague or because the promisor can choose whether or not to honor it. Note that a good faith requirement is implied into contracts; otherwise, the contract would be illusory. In order to meet this good-faith requirement, parties must take reasonable steps to fulfill their obligations.

> **Example:** B promises "I will give C $100, at my option." Such promises are not legally binding.

g. Voidable and unenforceable promises

A promise that is voidable or unenforceable by a rule of law (e.g., infancy) can nevertheless constitute consideration. Restatement (Second) of Contracts § 78.

> **Example:** A car dealer promises to sell a used car to a minor for $5,000. The car dealer may not escape selling the car to the minor for $5,000 on the grounds that, since the minor's promise is voidable, the car dealer did not receive consideration for its promise.

h. Requirements and output contracts

A requirements contract is a contract under which a buyer agrees to buy all that he will require of a product from the other party. An output contract is a contract under which a seller agrees to sell all that she manufactures of a product to the buyer. There is consideration in these agreements because the promisor suffers a legal detriment. The fact that the party may go out of business does not render the promise illusory.

Under the UCC, any quantities under such a contract may not be unreasonably disproportionate to any stated estimates, or if no estimate is stated, to any normal or otherwise comparable prior requirements or output.

Good faith is required under the UCC with regard to requirements and output contracts. Thus, for example, if a buyer in good faith no longer needs the goods, he may cancel the contract.

i. Settlement of a legal claim

The promise not to bring a legal action or to assert a particular claim or defense in such an action generally can serve as consideration for a settlement agreement because the party making the promise is foregoing a legal right. The legal action need not be one that is certain of success. Instead, the party agreeing to forebear bringing the action must have only an honest belief as to the validity of the claim, and there must be a reasonable basis for that belief. Restatement (Second) of Contracts § 74.

C. PROMISES BINDING WITHOUT CONSIDERATION

There are a number of circumstances in which a promise will be enforceable despite the fact that it is not supported by consideration.

1. Promise to Pay a Debt Barred by the Statute of Limitations

A new promise to pay a debt after the statute of limitations has run is enforceable without any new consideration.

2. Promise to Perform a Voidable Duty

A new promise to perform a duty that is voidable will be enforceable despite the absence of consideration, provided that the new promise does not suffer from an infirmity that would make it, in turn, voidable.

Example: X, who is 15, enters into a contract with Y that is voidable because of X's infancy. Upon reaching the age of majority, X promises to perform the contract. Such promise will be enforceable without any new consideration. Note that if X reaffirmed the promise before reaching the age of majority, such promise would be voidable (because of X's continued infancy).

3. Promise to Pay Benefits Received—Material Benefit Rule

Under the material benefit rule, when a party performs an unrequested service for another party that constitutes a material benefit, the modern trend permits the performing party to enforce a promise of payment made by the other party after the service is rendered, even though, at common law, such a promise would be unenforceable due to lack of consideration.

This rule is not enforced when the performing party rendered the services without the expectation of compensation (e.g., as a gift). In addition, the promise is enforced only to the extent necessary to prevent injustice, and it is not enforceable to the extent that the value of the promise is disproportionate to the benefit received, or the promisor has not been unjustly enriched.

Example: P sees D's horse running free and knows that D is out of town. P feeds and houses the horse for two weeks at a cost of $30 while awaiting D's return. When D returns, D thanks P and promises to pay P $50 at the end of the month. At common law, this promise is unenforceable due to lack of consideration. Under the material benefit rule, the promise is not enforceable to the extent that it is disproportionate to the benefit received. Thus, P's promise can be enforced to the extent of $30.

Note: Apart from a contract remedy, the provider of services may also be able to recover under a quasi-contract theory (*see* § I.G.2., *infra*).

Requested services distinguished: If one party requests another party to perform a service but does not indicate a price, and the service is performed, this generally creates an "implied-in-fact" contract. The party who performed the requested service is generally entitled to recover the reasonable value of her services in a breach-of-contract action in which the party who enjoyed the benefit of the services refused to pay. An exception applies, however, when the services were rendered without the expectation of payment.

4. Promissory Estoppel

The doctrine of promissory estoppel (detrimental reliance) can be used under certain circumstances to enforce a promise that is not supported by consideration.

a. Requirements

A promise is binding if:

   i)   The promisor should reasonably expect it to induce action or forbearance on the part of the promisee or a third person;

ii) The promise does induce such action or forbearance; and

iii) Injustice can be avoided only by enforcement of the promise.

> Note that, in general, the promisee must actually rely on the promise, and such reliance must have been reasonably foreseeable to the promisor. See below, however, for an exception regarding charitable subscriptions.

The remedy may be limited or adjusted as justice requires. Generally, this results in the award of reliance damages rather than expectation damages.

> **Example:** X, who is very wealthy, knows that her nephew Y is poor but wants to go to college. X promises to pay Y $100,000 when Y gets his diploma. Y then chooses to go to a state college and takes out $50,000 in loans to cover all tuition and expenses. In April of his senior year, Y is told by X that she won't pay anything. Y gets his degree in May and sues X. While there is no consideration for X's promise, the promise is still enforceable under the doctrine of promissory estoppel. X reasonably should have expected that Y would rely on her promise. Y did in fact rely by going to college, and it would seem unjust not to enforce the promise. Note, though, that Y's remedy can be limited "as justice requires." The proper amount would likely be $50,000 (the amount of Y's out-of-pocket expenses in reliance), not the $100,000 that X originally promised.

> **EXAM NOTE:** Always consider whether there is a valid contract before considering promissory estoppel as the correct answer choice.

b. Exception to the reliance requirement for charitable subscriptions

Courts often apply the doctrine of promissory estoppel to enforce promises to charitable institutions. In some cases, they presume that the charity detrimentally relied on the promised contribution. A charitable subscription (i.e., a written promise) is enforceable under the doctrine of promissory estoppel without proof that the charity relied on the promise. Restatement (Second) of Contracts § 90(2).

> **Example:** A promises in writing to give a university a $10,000 donation. Under the Second Restatement, the university may enforce the promise under the doctrine of promissory estoppel, even though the university does not establish that it relied to its detriment on A's promise.

c. Construction contracts and promissory estoppel

In the construction industry, it would be unjust to permit a subcontractor to revoke a bid after inducing justifiable and detrimental reliance in the general contractor. Thus, an agreement not to revoke a sub-bid offer is enforceable under the theory of promissory estoppel.

Because the sub-bid is only an outstanding offer, the **general contractor is not bound** to accept it upon becoming the successful bidder for the general contract. A general contractor can enter into a subcontract with another subcontractor for a lower price.

D. ENFORCEABILITY

The absence of an essential element (capacity, consent, legality, form, etc.) may render the contract void, voidable, or unenforceable.

1. **Void Contracts**

   A void contract results in the entire transaction being regarded as a nullity, as if no contract existed between the parties.

2. **Voidable Contracts**

   A voidable contract operates as a valid contract, unless and until one of the parties takes steps to avoid it.

3. **Unenforceable Contracts**

   An unenforceable contract is a valid contract that cannot be enforced if one of the parties refuses to carry out its terms.

   > **EXAM NOTE:** Remember that a void contract cannot be enforced, but a party may opt to avoid a voidable contract.

E. DEFENSES TO FORMATION

A person who is asserted to be in breach of a contract can defend the action by showing that there has not been a valid offer and acceptance or that valid consideration was not exchanged (and no consideration substitute exists). The agreement will also not be enforced if a party can show that there was no "meeting of the minds" due to a mistake or misunderstanding, misrepresentation or fraud, undue influence or duress, or the party's own lack of capacity.

1. **Mistake**

   A mistake is a belief that is not in accord with the facts as to a basic assumption on which the contract was made that materially affects performance. Note that the mistake must be with regard to a belief about an existing fact and not with regard to something that will happen in the future. Risks with regard to changing facts are governed by the doctrines of impracticability and frustration of purpose.

   a. **Unilateral mistake**

      When only one of the parties is mistaken as to an essential element of the contract, either party can generally enforce the contract on its terms. However, the mistaken party can void the contract if the mistaken party did not bear the risk of the mistake and either:

      i)   The mistake would make enforcement of the contract unconscionable; or

      ii) The non-mistaken party:

           a) Failed to disclose the mistake despite knowing or having a reason to know that the other party was mistaken or having a duty to disclose the fact about which the other party was mistaken; or

           b) Caused the mistake.

      Finally, for a unilateral mistake to form the basis for rescission, there must be an **absence of serious prejudice to the other party.** Evidence of these conditions must be clear and positive.

b. Mutual mistake

Mutual mistake occurs when both parties are mistaken as to an essential element of the contract. In such a situation, there must be a substantial difference between the deal as it was contemplated and the actual deal, with *no intent by the parties to take a risk on that element* of the transaction.

The contract will generally be **voidable** by the party that was adversely affected by the mistake if the mistake materially affects the bargain between the parties.

> **Example:** Rescission of a contract to sell a cow was granted on grounds of mutual mistake when both parties completed the exchange of the cow on the mistaken understanding that the cow was barren. *Sherwood v. Walker*, 33 N.W. 919 (Mich. 1887).

When reformation of the contract is available to cure a mistake, neither party can avoid the contract.

1) Conscious ignorance

A party may bear the risk of a mistake, however, when she is aware, at the time of the contract, that she has only limited knowledge of the facts to which the mistake relates, and she accepts her limited knowledge as sufficient. Note that the risk created by conscious ignorance rests on the party being aware of her limited knowledge. Restatement (Second) of Contracts § 154.

2) Mistaken party's ability to void the contract

When the mistake is attributable to a party's failure to know or discover facts before entering into the contract, such failure does not bar the mistaken party from asserting the defense of mistake, unless the failure constitutes a failure to act in good faith and in accordance with the reasonable standards of fair dealing. The mistaken party's negligence with regard to the mistake is not sufficient to prevent the mistaken party from avoiding the contract. Restatement (Second) of Contracts § 157.

c. Reformation for mistake

When a writing that evidences or embodies an agreement in whole or in part fails to express the agreement because of a mistake of both parties as to the contents or effect of the writing, the court may, at the request of a party, reform the writing to express the agreement, except to the extent that rights of third parties who have relied on the document, such as good-faith purchasers for value, will be unfairly affected. Restatement (Second) of Contracts § 155.

Reformation of a writing for mistake is available if:

i)   There was a prior agreement (either oral or written) between the parties;

ii) There was an agreement by the parties to put that prior agreement into writing; and

iii) As a result of a mistake, there is a difference between the prior agreement and the writing.

Note that if one party, without the consent of the other party, intentionally omits a term from the writing that had been agreed upon by the parties, reformation would be available on the grounds of misrepresentation. (*See* § I.E.3.f. Avoidance or reformation for misrepresentation, *infra*.)

2. Misunderstanding

A misunderstanding occurs when both parties believe that they are agreeing to the same material terms, but in fact they agree to different terms.

a. Neither party knows or should know of the misunderstanding

If the misunderstanding involves a material term, and neither party knows or should know that there is a misunderstanding, then there is no contract. Restatement (Second) of Contracts § 20(1).

b. One party knows or should know of the misunderstanding

If a material term in the offer and acceptance is ambiguous, and one party knows or should know that the other party has a different understanding of the meaning of the ambiguous term, then there will be a contract formed based on the meaning of the term as understood by the unknowing party.

c. Both parties know of the misunderstanding

There is no contract if both parties at the time of contract knew that the terms were ambiguous, unless both parties intended the same meaning.

d. Waiver of the misunderstanding

Even if there is a misunderstanding, one party may waive the misunderstanding and choose to enforce the contract according to the other party's understanding.

3. Misrepresentation, Nondisclosure, and Fraud

A misrepresentation is an assertion that is contrary to the existing facts. Affirmative conduct to conceal a fact from another is equivalent to a statement that the fact does not exist. A misrepresentation may prevent the formation of the contract or make the contract voidable by the adversely affected party. The misrepresentation must be of fact and not of law or of opinion. Note that the use of an "as is" provision in a contract can shift the risk to a buyer in the absence of unconscionability.

Misrepresentation can be innocent, negligent, or fraudulent. Avoidance of a contract can be based on any of these standards, but different rules will apply. Thus, a fraudulent misrepresentation need not be material, but an unintentional misrepresentation is required to be material.

EXAM NOTE: The rules regarding misrepresentation and nondisclosure are frequently tested on the MBE.

a. Fraudulent misrepresentation

Fraud exists if the misrepresentation is made:

i)   Knowingly;

ii) Without confidence in the assertion; and

iii) When the person making the assertion knows that no basis exists for the assertion.

b. Nondisclosure

Nondisclosure of a known fact is tantamount to an assertion that the fact does not exist, if the party not disclosing the fact knows that:

i) Disclosure is necessary to prevent a previous assertion from being a misrepresentation or fraudulent;

ii) Disclosure would correct a mistake of the other party as to a basic assumption, and the failure to disclose would constitute lack of good faith and fair dealing;

iii) Disclosure would correct a mistake of the other party as to the contents or effect of a writing evidencing their agreement; or

iv) The other party is entitled to know the fact because of a confidential or fiduciary relationship.

c. Effect

1) Fraud in the factum

Fraud in the factum (or fraud in the execution) occurs when the fraudulent misrepresentation prevents a party from knowing the character or essential terms of the transaction. In such a case, no contract is formed, and the apparent contract is **void** (i.e., not enforceable against either party), unless reasonable diligence would have revealed the true terms of the contract.

2) Fraud in the inducement

Fraud in the inducement occurs when a fraudulent misrepresentation is used to induce another to enter into a contract. Such a contract is **voidable** by the adversely affected party if she justifiably relied on the misrepresentation in entering into the agreement.

d. Non-fraudulent misrepresentation

Even if non-fraudulent, a misrepresentation (innocent or negligent) can still render a contract **voidable** by the adversely affected party. The misrepresentation must be *material* (i.e., information that would cause a reasonable person to agree, or that the person making the misrepresentation knows would cause this particular person to agree), the adversely affected party's assent to the contract has been induced by the misrepresentation, and the adversely affected party must have justifiably relied on the misrepresentation.

e. Cure of a misrepresentation

If, following a misrepresentation but before the deceived party has avoided the contract, the facts are cured so as to be in accord with the facts that were previously misrepresented, then the contract will no longer be voidable by the deceived party.

f. Avoidance or reformation for misrepresentation

When one party misrepresents the content or legal effect of a writing to another party, the other party may elect to avoid the contract or to reform it to express what had been represented.

4. Undue Influence

A party to a contract who is a victim of undue influence can void the contract. Restatement (Second) of Contracts § 177.

a. Unfair persuasion

Undue influence is the unfair persuasion of a party to assent to a contract. It can occur by virtue of a relationship between the parties in which one party justifiably assumes that the other party will not act in a manner that is inconsistent with his welfare. It can also occur in a relationship in which one party is dominant and the other dependent, either due to lack of expertise or experience, or because the dependent person has diminished mental capacity. Such relationships include trustee-beneficiary, lawyer-client, doctor-patient, financial advisor–client, and, in some cases, parent-child.

Compare duress and misrepresentation: Undue influence can provide a party with relief in circumstances in which the behavior of the other party to the contract does not rise to the level of duress or misrepresentation.

The key is whether a party has been able to exercise free and competent judgment or whether the persuasion of the other party has seriously impaired that judgment. Relevant factors can include the fairness of the bargain, the availability of independent advice, and the susceptibility of a party to being persuaded.

Caution: While a person who is mentally or physically infirm may be more susceptible to persuasion, the mere existence of an infirmity is not grounds for avoiding a contract. Similarly, the existence of a confidential relationship, by itself, is not grounds for avoiding a contract.

b. Confidential relationship—fairness and disclosure

When a confidential relationship between contracting parties is established, the burden of proving that the contract is fair may be placed upon the dominant party. The dominant party to the contract may also be held to a higher standard of disclosure than she would be in a contract between arms-length parties. Restatement (Second) of Contracts § 173.

c. Third-party undue influence

When the undue influence is caused by the person who is not a party to the contract, the victim may void the contract, unless the non-victim party to the contract gave value or materially relied on the contract while acting in good faith and without reason to know of the undue influence. Restatement (Second) of Contracts § 177(3).

d. Damages

Restitution damages may be available to the party induced to enter a contract because of undue influence.

5. Duress

Duress is an **improper threat** that deprives a party of meaningful choice.

a. Improper threat

Examples of improper threats include threats of a crime, a tort, or criminal prosecution, or the threat of pursuing a civil action (when made in bad faith). In addition, it is improper to threaten to breach a contract if doing so would violate the duty of good faith and fair dealing. Restatement (Second) of Contracts § 176.

1) Threat of criminal prosecution

The threat of criminal prosecution is an improper means by which to induce a person to enter into a contract. It does not matter that the person making the threat honestly believes that the person who would be subject to criminal prosecution is guilty. Nor does it matter that the person threatened with prosecution is in fact guilty of the crime.

2) Threat of civil action

Unlike the threat of criminal prosecution, the threat of a civil action is generally not improper. The lack of success in pursuing a civil action does not make the threat improper unless the civil action is pursued in bad faith.

b. Deprivation of meaningful choice

A person is deprived of meaningful choice only when he does not have a reasonable alternative to succumbing to the threat. Thus, with regard to the threat of a civil action, a person generally has the reasonable alternative of defending against the action. However, if the threat also involves the seizure of property in conjunction with the civil action, or causes the person to be unable to fulfill other contractual obligations, then the person may be deprived of a meaningful choice. Restatement (Second) of Contracts § 175.

> **EXAM NOTE:** In assessing the effect of the threat, the test is a subjective one: Did the threat induce the person's assent?

c. Effect on the contract

When a party's agreement to enter into a contract is physically compelled by duress, such as the threat to inflict physical violence, the contract is **void.** In other instances when a party is induced to enter into a contract by duress, such as when the threat is a breach of the duty of good faith and fair dealing, the contract is **voidable.**

When the duress is caused by the person who is not a party to the contract, the victim may void the contract, unless the non-victim party to the contract gave value or materially relied on the contract while acting in good faith and without reason to know of the undue influence. Restatement (Second) of Contracts § 177(3).

Generally, restitution damages are available to the party induced to enter a contract under duress. Restatement (Second) of Contracts §§ 174, 175.

6. Capacity to Contract

Parties to a contract must be competent (i.e., have the legal capacity to be held to contractual duties). Incompetency arises because of infancy, mental illness or defect, guardianship, intoxication, and corporate incapacity.

a. Infancy

Infants (in most states, individuals who are under the age of 18) do not have the capacity to contract. When a contract is made by an infant, it is **voidable** by the infant but not by the other party. This means that the infant may either disaffirm (void) the contract and avoid any liability under it or choose to hold the adult party to the contract. The disaffirmance must be effectuated either before the infant reaches majority (or within a reasonable time thereafter). If the contract is not disaffirmed within a reasonable time after the infant reaches majority, then the infant will be held to have ratified the contract as an adult. The infant must restore any benefits received under the contract, if possible. Restatement (Second) of Contracts § 14.

1) Liability for necessities

The purpose behind the infancy doctrine is to protect minors, a class of people who are generally immature and require protection from poor judgment and advantageous adults. An exception to the infancy rule exists when the contract is based on necessities. When necessities are furnished to the infant, the infant must pay for them, but the recovery by the person furnishing the necessities is limited to the **reasonable value** of the services or goods (not the agreed upon price). Recovery is under a theory of quasi-contract.

2) Statutory exceptions

By statute, an education loan made to a minor student may not be voidable by the student but instead may be fully enforceable by the lender. Similar treatment may also be accorded an insurance contract entered into by a minor.

b. Mental illness

If an individual is adjudicated mentally incompetent, a purported contract made by the individual is **void**. On the other hand, if there has been no adjudication, a contract is **voidable** and may be disaffirmed if the individual is unable to

i)   Understand the nature and consequences of the transaction; or

ii) Act in a reasonable manner with regard to the transaction, **and** the other party has reason to know of this fact.

If a contract is made during a lucid period, the contract is fully enforceable, unless the person has been adjudicated incompetent. A mentally incompetent person may be liable for the reasonable value of necessities furnished by another party. Restatement (Second) of Contracts § 15.

c. Guardianship

If an individual's property is under guardianship by reason of an adjudication (such as for mental illness or defect, habitual intoxication, narcotics addiction), that individual has no capacity to contract, and a purported contract made by the individual is void. A person under guardianship may be liable for the reasonable value of necessities furnished by another party. Restatement (Second) of Contracts § 13.

d. Intoxication

A contract entered into while intoxicated due to alcohol or drugs is **voidable** by the intoxicated party if that person was unable to understand the nature and consequences of the transaction, and the other party had reason to know of the intoxication. The intoxicated party must act promptly to disaffirm the contract and is required to return any value received, if possible. Generally, the intoxicated party may be liable in quasi-contract for the fair value of the goods or services furnished. Restatement (Second) of Contracts § 16.

e. Corporate incapacity

When a corporation acts ultra vires (outside its powers), the contract is voidable. Most states allow recovery in quantum meruit if one party performs on the contract.

F. DEFENSES TO ENFORCEMENT

A party to a contract can assert that the nature of the agreement or the manner in which it was arrived at should prevent its enforcement.

1. Illegality

If the consideration or performance that is to occur under a contract is illegal, then the contract itself is illegal and is unenforceable. If a contract contemplates illegal conduct, it is void. If a contract becomes illegal after it is formed, the duty to perform under the contract is discharged.

Examples of illegal contracts include contracts that are usurious, contracts for the commission of a tort or crime, or contracts in restraint of trade.

a. Effect of illegality

Illegal transactions are not recognized or enforceable, restitution is not awarded for consideration, and no remedy is available for partial performance.

b. Exceptions

1) Ignorance

When one party is justifiably ignorant of the facts that make the contract illegal, that party may recover if the other party to the contract acted with knowledge of the illegality.

2) Party lacks illegal purpose

If only one party has an illegal purpose, then the other party can recover if he did not know of the illegal purpose, or if he knew of the illegal purpose but did not facilitate that purpose, and the purpose does not involve serious moral turpitude.

Example: A seller of gambling equipment can recover the price, as long as he did not become involved in illegal gambling using the equipment. *This is true even if the seller knows of the illegal purpose.*

3) Divisible contracts

Some contracts can be easily separated into legal and illegal parts so that recovery is available on the legal part(s) only.

4) Licensing violation

When a party fails to comply with a licensing, registration, or similar requirement and, as a consequence, is prohibited from performing an act, the other party's promise made in consideration for the performance of the prohibited act or a promise to perform that act is unenforceable under public-policy grounds if the requirement has a regulatory (e.g., health, safety), rather than economic (e.g., revenue-raising) purpose, **and** public policy for the requirement clearly outweighs the interest in enforcing the promise. Restatement (Second) of Contracts § 181.

5) Restitution

Generally, a party to an illegal contract not only cannot enforce the contract, but also is not entitled to restitution with respect to a performance rendered. Restatement (Second) of Contracts § 197.

a) Not *in pari delicto*

When the parties are equally at fault (*in pari delicto*), neither party is entitled to restitution for a performance rendered. But, if the parties are not *in pari delicto,* the less guilty party may be able to recover restitutionary damages. Restatement (Second) of Contracts § 198.

b) Withdrawal

A party to an illegal contract who withdraws from the transaction before the improper purpose has been achieved may be entitled to restitution for a performance that the party has rendered when the party has not engaged in serious misconduct. Restatement (Second) of Contracts § 199.

2. Unconscionability

The UCC provides that a court may modify or refuse to enforce a contract or part of a contract on the grounds that it is unconscionable. UCC § 2-302.

A contract (or part of a contract) is unconscionable when it is so unfair to one party that no reasonable person in the position of the parties would have agreed to it. The contract or part of the contract at issue must have been offensive at the time it was made. Unconscionability may also be applied to prevent unfair surprise. Boilerplate contract provisions that are inconspicuous, hidden, or difficult for a party to understand have been held unconscionable. Courts have also applied the doctrine of unconscionability when the contract is a contract of adhesion (a take-it-or-leave-it contract) and there is greatly unequal bargaining power between the parties.

The question of whether a contract is unconscionable is a question of law for the court to decide; the issue does not go to the jury.

3. Public Policy

Even if a contract is neither illegal nor unconscionable, it may be unenforceable if it violates a significant public policy (e.g., contracts in restraint of marriage).

G. IMPLIED-IN-FACT CONTRACTS AND QUASI-CONTRACTS

1. Implied-in-Fact Contracts

When words express the intent of the parties, the contract is an express contract. When conduct indicates assent or agreement, the agreement is considered implied in fact.

Example: Without paying, B joins a tour group that is walking through a downtown area learning about landmark buildings. The tour guide can charge B the fee for the tour because B's conduct of joining the group implied agreement with the contract.

2. Implied-in-Law ("Quasi") Contracts

a. In general

When one party confers a benefit on another and has a reasonable expectation of compensation, allowing the benefited party to receive the benefit without any cost would be unjust. In this case, the court can imply a contract (quasi-contract) as a method of recovery that **prevents unjust enrichment.**

b. Requirements

A court will imply a contract to prevent unjust enrichment when:

i) The plaintiff has conferred a "measurable benefit" on the defendant;

ii) The plaintiff acted without gratuitous intent; and

iii) It would be unfair to let the defendant retain the benefit because either the defendant had an opportunity to decline the benefit but knowingly accepted it, or the plaintiff had a reasonable excuse for not giving the defendant such opportunity, usually because of an emergency.

In such a case, a promise is implied that requires the defendant to make restitution to the plaintiff (such as money damages equal to the fair value of the benefit).

Implied-in-law contracts can be found in cases in which there is (i) a failed contract, (ii) no contract, or (iii) a divisible contract.

> **EXAM NOTE:** Always keep in mind the possibility of quasi-contractual relief. Even when a party is not entitled to contractual relief, if she has provided services or suffered a loss, she may be entitled to quasi-contractual relief.

c. Remedies

Generally, a successful quasi-contract action results in the award of restitution damages, although reliance damages may occasionally be awarded. Expectation damages are almost never awarded.

d. Quasi-contractual recovery by a plaintiff in breach

If a plaintiff has not substantially performed, but the defendant has still benefited from the plaintiff's performance, the plaintiff can generally recover her restitution interest less the defendant's damages for the breach. Such recovery is often referred to as "quantum meruit" ("as much as he has deserved").

To recover under quantum meruit, one must show that the recipient:

    i)   Acquiesced in the provision of services;

    ii)   Knew that the provider expected to be compensated; and

    iii)   Was unjustly enriched.

1) Willful breach

Most courts hold that a plaintiff in breach is permitted to recover in quasi-contract only if her breach is not willful. If the breach is willful, then she cannot recover anything in quasi-contract.

2) UCC allows for partial restitution to the breaching buyer

For contracts for the sale of goods, a defaulting buyer's right to restitution is governed by UCC § 2-718. The buyer is entitled to a refund of any payments made on the contract less damages provable by the seller and either the amount to which the seller is entitled by virtue of an enforceable liquidated damages provision or a penalty of "twenty percent of the value of the total performance for which the buyer is obligated under the contract or $500, whichever is smaller."

H. WARRANTIES IN SALE-OF-GOODS CONTRACTS

UCC Article 2 allows not only for express warranties, but also for the implied warranties of merchantability and fitness for a particular purpose.

1. Express Warranty

Any promise, affirmation, description, or sample that is part of the basis of the bargain is an express warranty, **unless it is merely the seller's opinion** or commendation of the value of the goods. The use of a sample or model will create a warranty that the goods the buyer is to receive will be like the proffered sample or model. UCC § 2-313.

An express warranty can be made subsequent to the contract for sale. Although this would modify the original agreement, under the UCC, no consideration is needed to make a modification enforceable.

Disclaimer clauses that conflict with the express warranties, such as "all warranties, express or implied, are disclaimed," are ignored. UCC § 2-316.

2. Implied Warranty of Merchantability

A warranty of merchantability is implied whenever the seller is a **merchant.** To be merchantable, goods must be **fit for their ordinary purpose** and pass without objection in the trade under the contract description. A breach of this warranty must have been present at the time of the sale. UCC § 2-314.

Unless the circumstances indicate otherwise, the warranty can be disclaimed by use of "as is," "with all faults," or similar language that makes plain that there is no implied warranty. The disclaimer may be oral, but it must use the term "merchantability" and must be conspicuous if in writing. UCC § 2-316.

If the buyer, before entering into the contract, has examined the goods or a sample or model as fully as the buyer desires, or has refused to examine the goods, then there is no implied warranty with respect to defects that an examination ought to have revealed to the buyer. UCC § 2-316(3).

3. Implied Warranty of Fitness for a Particular Purpose

A warranty that the goods are fit for a particular purpose is implied whenever the seller has reason to know (from any source, not just from the buyer) that the buyer has a particular use for the goods, and the buyer is relying upon the seller's skill to select the goods. UCC § 2-315.

Note that the seller need not be a merchant for this implied warranty to apply.

An implied warranty of fitness for a particular purpose can be disclaimed by general language (including by the use of "as is"), but the **disclaimer must be in writing and be conspicuous.** UCC § 2-316(2).

II. DISCHARGE

The promisor may not be liable for nonperformance if some supervening event or change in circumstances arises after the formation of the contract that discharges the promisor's duty to perform.

A. IMPRACTICABILITY

A party's duty to perform can be dismissed by impracticability. The defense of impracticability is available if:

i) Performance becomes **illegal** after the contract is made;

ii) The specific subject matter of the contract (e.g., the goods) is **destroyed**;

iii) In a personal services contract, the performing party to the contract **dies or becomes incapacitated**; or

iv) Performance becomes **impracticable.**

UCC § 2-615; Restatement (Second) of Contracts § 265.

If the contract is to perform services that can be delegated, it is not discharged by the death or incapacity of the party who was to perform the services.

Impossibility: Traditionally, courts referred to this defense as "impossibility." Under the modern view, adopted by the Restatement, "impracticability" better expresses the extent of the increased burden that is required.

1. **Elements of Impracticability**

    For the defense of impracticability to be available, the following conditions must also be met:

    i)   An **unforeseeable event** has occurred;

    ii) **Non-occurrence** of the event was a basic assumption on which the contract was made; and

    iii) The **party seeking discharge is not at fault.**

    When performance becomes impracticable for a seller of goods, the seller must notify the buyer. Restatement (Second) of Contracts § 265.

2. **Other "Events Sufficient for Discharge" of a Contract**

    Unforeseen natural disasters, wars, trade and military embargoes, strikes, and local crop failures have all been found sufficient to excuse performance. However, non-extraordinary increases in the cost of performance are not.

3. **Assumption of the Risk**

    If a party assumes the risk of an event happening that makes performance impracticable, then the defense of impracticability will not apply.

    Note that impracticability is not available merely when a party has made a bad deal and will have to pay more, even a lot more, than originally contemplated. It requires some totally unexpected occurrence that completely upsets the parties' expectations. Generally, the cost increase must be extreme.

4. **Partial Impracticability**

    When impracticability does not prevent a seller from delivering some of the goods, the goods actually produced must be apportioned among all of the buyers with whom the seller has contracted. The buyer, however, may refuse to accept and may cancel the contract. UCC §§ 2-615(b), 2-616.

5. **Failure of a Particular Source of Supply**

    If the contract provided that a specific source of supply be used, and that source of supply fails, performance is discharged. This is so even when other sources are readily available. Courts will excuse performance when the parties have specifically identified the source in the contract.

6. **Failure of Agreed-Upon Method of Transportation**

    If, without the fault of either party, the agreed-upon delivery facilities or method of transportation or payment become unavailable or commercially impracticable, any commercially reasonable delivery method may be tendered and must be accepted.

B. FRUSTRATION OF PURPOSE

The doctrine of frustration of purpose applies when unexpected events arise that destroy one party's purpose in entering into the contract, even if performance of the contract is not rendered impossible. The frustrated party is entitled to rescind the contract without paying damages. The event that arises must not be the fault of the frustrated party, and its nonoccurrence must have been a basic assumption of the contract. If this is the case, the party's duty to render performance is discharged, unless the language of the agreement or the circumstances otherwise indicate. Restatement (Second) of Contracts § 265.

The occurrence need not be completely unforeseeable to the parties. It must, however, be unexpected and not a realistic prospect. For the doctrine of frustration of purpose to be applicable, the frustration must be so severe that it is not within the assumed risks inherent under the contract. Restatement (Second) of Contracts §§ 261, comments b and c, 265, comment a.

Example: A contracts with B to rent B's apartment for one day in order to get a prime view of a marathon run that will occur on that day. A agrees to pay a price that is far more than the typical rental value of the apartment. The marathon run is cancelled because of a terrorist threat. A may be excused from performance under the doctrine of frustration of purpose because her essential purpose in renting the apartment has been frustrated, and the event that arose was not her fault and was completely unexpected.

C. RESCISSION

Rescission is the cancelling of a contract so as to restore the parties to their positions before the contract was made. Parties may seek to rescind a contract for a variety of reasons, including mutual mistake, fraud, misrepresentation, or even unilateral mistake, if the other party knew or should have known of the mistake. The grounds for rescission must have existed at the time the contract was made.

The non-defaulting party to a contract can cancel or rescind the contract, which requires a return of any deposits or other benefit conferred on the other party.

Rescission can also occur by the mutual agreement of the parties. The surrender of rights under the original contract by each party is consideration for the rescission by mutual agreement.

In cases of third-party beneficiaries, a contract is **not** discharged by mutual rescission if the rights of the third-party beneficiary have already vested.

D. RELEASE

A release is a writing that manifests intent to discharge another party from an existing duty. For common-law contracts, the release must generally be supported by consideration to discharge the duty.

Under the UCC, however, a claim or right can be discharged in whole or in part without consideration by a written waiver or renunciation signed and delivered by the aggrieved party. No consideration is needed to support the release.

E. DESTRUCTION OR INJURY TO IDENTIFIED GOODS

If a contract calls for the delivery of goods identified at the time the contract is made, and the goods are destroyed without the fault of either party before the risk of loss passes to the buyer, then the contract is avoided. Both parties are discharged; neither party must perform, and neither party has breached. If the goods are damaged, but not destroyed, then the contract is avoided, unless the buyer chooses to take the goods at a reduced price without any other claim against the seller. (Note: If the risk of loss has passed to the buyer, then the contract is not avoided, and the seller may demand performance by the buyer (*see* § VIII.F.3. Risk of Loss, *infra*).)

III. THIRD-PARTY BENEFICIARY CONTRACTS

A third-party beneficiary contract results when two parties enter into a contract with the understanding and intent that the performance by one of the parties is to be rendered to a third person. Jurisdictions are split as to whether the First or Second Restatement of Contracts applies.

> **EXAM NOTE:** On the MBE, if the question is silent as to the applicable law, assume that the jurisdiction follows the Second Restatement of Contracts.

A. CREDITOR AND DONEE BENEFICIARIES

The First Restatement classifies third-party beneficiaries as creditor or donee beneficiaries. If performance of a promise would satisfy an actual, supposed, or asserted duty of the promisee to a third party, and the promisee did not intend to make a gift to the third party, then the third party is called a **creditor beneficiary.** A creditor beneficiary has the right to sue either the promisor or the promisee to enforce the contract.

> **Example:** A agrees to paint B's house in return for B's promise to pay $500 to C because A owes C $500. C is an intended beneficiary and can recover the $500 from B.

If the promisee entered the contract for the purpose of conferring a gift on a third party, then the third-party **donee beneficiary** is given the right to sue the promisor.

> **Example:** A pays B to build a house for C. C is a donee beneficiary of the contract between A and B.

B. INTENDED AND INCIDENTAL BENEFICIARIES

The Second Restatement abandons the donee beneficiary and creditor beneficiary categories. Instead, a third party can recover if she is an intended beneficiary. Otherwise, she is said to be an incidental beneficiary with no rights to enforce the contract.

An intended beneficiary is one to whom the promisee wishes to make a gift of the promised performance or to satisfy an obligation to pay money owed by the promisee to the beneficiary. The promisee must have an intention (explicit or implicit) to benefit the third party, or the beneficiary is incidental.

> **Example:** If A agrees to paint B's house in return for B's promise to pay $500 to C, then C is an intended beneficiary and can recover the $500 from B.

An incidental beneficiary is one who benefits from a contract even though there is no contractual intent to benefit that person. An incidental beneficiary has no rights to enforce the contract.

> **Example:** A promises to buy B a car manufactured by C. Here, C is an incidental beneficiary with no grounds upon which to recover if A reneged on the promise.

To bring an action for breach of a third-party beneficiary contract, the third party must establish:

i) A contract between A and B;

ii) The "clear" or "manifest" intent of A and B that the contract primarily and directly benefit the third party (or class of persons to which that party belongs);

iii) A breach of the contract by either A or B; and

iv) Damages to the third party resulting from the breach. An incidental beneficiary has no enforceable rights under a contract.

Restatement (Second) of Contracts § 302.

> **EXAM NOTE:** On the exam, if the promise indicates that the promisor will pay the third party directly to relieve the promisee from a debt, then the third party is likely an intended beneficiary. In contrast, if the promisor is to pay the promisee in order that she may pay the third party, then the third party is most likely an incidental beneficiary.

C.   VESTING OF BENEFICIARY'S RIGHTS

Only an intended beneficiary has a right to bring an action on the contract. An intended beneficiary of a "gift promise" (a donee beneficiary) may sue only the promisor. If the promisee tells the donee beneficiary about the contract and should reasonably foresee reliance, and the beneficiary does so rely to his detriment, then promissory estoppel would apply. An intended beneficiary to whom the promisee owed money (a creditor beneficiary) may sue either the promisor or the promisee, or both, on the underlying obligation, but only one recovery is allowed.

1.   When Rights Vest

The rights of an intended beneficiary vest when the beneficiary:

i) **Detrimentally relies** on the rights created;

ii) **Manifests assent** to the contract at one of the parties' request; or

iii) **Files a lawsuit** to enforce the contract.

2.   Effect of Vesting on Original Parties

Once the beneficiary's rights have vested, the original parties to the contract are both bound to perform the contract. Any efforts by the promisor or the promisee to rescind or modify the contract after vesting are void, **unless the third party agrees** to the rescission or modification.

D.   DEFENSES

The promisor can raise any defense against the third-party beneficiary that the promisor had against the original promisee. Therefore, the beneficiary also becomes liable for counterclaims on the contract that the promisor could establish against the promisee. This liability can never exceed the amount that the promisor owes under the contract.

> **Example:** A agrees to paint B's house in return for B's promise to pay $500 to C, to whom A owes $500. If the statute of limitations (or any other contractual defense) precludes A (the promisee) from recovering against B (the promisor), then it will also preclude C (the intended creditor beneficiary) from recovering against B on the contract.

The promisor may not assert any defenses that the promisee would have had against the intended beneficiary.

> **Example:** In the example above, if the statute of limitations precluded C from recovering against A on the debt that A owed to C, then B's obligation to C would not be affected.

IV. ASSIGNMENT OF RIGHTS AND DELEGATION OF DUTIES

A. ASSIGNMENT OF RIGHTS

"Assignment" is the **transfer of rights** under a contract, and **"delegation"** is the **transfer of duties** and obligations under a contract.

> **EXAM NOTE:** Although the two terms are clearly distinct in concept, the term "assignment" is often used to refer to either assignment or delegation on the MBE.

Almost all contract rights can be assigned. Partial assignments are permissible, as is the assignment of future or unearned rights.

1. When Disallowed

Assignments are not allowed when they materially increase the duty or risk of the obligor or materially reduce the obligor's chance of obtaining performance. Generally, prohibitions against assignment in the contract are strictly construed, and the assignment is permissible. Even if validly prohibited by the contract, the power to assign is retained by the parties, and the only consequence is that an assignment operates as a breach of the contract.

2. Requirements

No formalities are needed for an assignment, but there must be a present intent to transfer the right immediately. No consideration is needed, but the lack of consideration would affect revocability of the assignment. If an assignment is for consideration, it is irrevocable. If no consideration supports the assignment (a gratuitous assignment), then it will generally be revocable, unless the obligor has already performed or promissory estoppel applies. If the contract right that is being assigned is evidenced by a document that symbolizes the right (e.g., a bank book, insurance policy, or stock certificates), then delivery of the document makes the assignment irrevocable. A gratuitous assignment will be automatically revoked upon the death, incapacity, or bankruptcy of the assignor. Restatement (Second) of Contracts § 332.

3. Rights of the Assignee

An assignee **takes all of the rights of the assignor as the contract stands at the time of the assignment,** but she takes **subject to any defenses that could be raised against the assignor.** The rights of the assignee are subject to set-off if the transaction giving rise to the set-off occurred prior to the time the obligor was given notice of the assignment. In addition, the rights of the assignee are subject to a set-off that arises out of the same transaction. The assignee is also subject to any modification of the contract made prior to the time the obligor obtained notice of the assignment. Thus, payment by the obligor to the assignor can be raised as a defense, provided the payment was made before the obligor had notice of the assignment.

A subsequent assignment of the same right(s) revokes any prior *revocable* assignment. If the first assignment was an *irrevocable* assignment, then the first assignee will have priority over the second assignee, unless the second assignee is a bona fide purchaser for value without notice of the first assignment, in which case the assignee who obtains payment from the obligor or judgment first will have priority. If the second assignee knows about a prior assignment, then he is estopped from asserting a claim over the first assignee even if he would have otherwise prevailed.

B. DELEGATION OF DUTIES

1. In General

Generally, obligations under a contract can be delegated. Delegation is not permitted when the other party to the contract has a substantial interest in having the delegating individual perform (for example, in a personal services contract involving taste or a special skill), or the delegation is prohibited by the contract.

When obligations are delegated, the **delegator is not released from liability,** and recovery can be had against the delegator if the delegatee does not perform.

2. Novation

A novation is the substitution of a new contract for an old one when the original obligor is released from his promises under the original agreement. A novation may be express or implied after delegation if (i) the original obligor repudiates liability to the original promisee and (ii) the obligee subsequently accepts performance of the original agreement from the delagatee without reserving rights against the obligor.

3. Effect of Delegation of Performance

Any delegation of performance under a contract for the sale of goods may be treated by the other party as creating reasonable grounds for insecurity. UCC § 2-210(5). The other party may, without prejudice to his rights against the delegator, demand assurances from the delegatee (UCC § 2-609, *see* §§ VIII.B.2–3., *infra*).

A delegation does not relieve the delegating party of her obligations under the contract unless the other party to the contract agrees to release that party and substitute a new one (a novation). Merely consenting to a delegation does not create a novation. UCC § 2-210.

A contractual assignment is typically treated as both an assignment of rights and a delegation of duties, the acceptance of which constitutes a promise to perform. Further, the promise is enforceable by either the assignor or the other party to the contract. Therefore, the UCC treats the other party as a third-party beneficiary of the assignment and delegation.

V. STATUTE OF FRAUDS

A. WRITING REQUIRED

Contracts that fall within the Statute of Frauds are **unenforceable** unless they are **in writing.** The memorandum must:

i) Be in writing;

ii) Be signed by the party to be charged (i.e., the person against whom enforcement is sought); and

iii) Contain the essential elements of the deal.

The memorandum need not be formal (i.e., receipts or correspondence can serve as memoranda). The essential elements may be in more than one writing only if one of the writings references the other(s). The memorandum need not be delivered. Even if it is lost or destroyed, it still operates to satisfy the Statute of Frauds, and its prior existence can be proved by oral evidence.

> **EXAM NOTE:** Note that a memorandum sufficient to satisfy the Statute of Frauds does not need to be written at the time a promise is made and can be subsequently reduced to writing. The memorandum also does not have to be addressed to the promisee to be enforceable by the promisee.

B. TYPES OF CONTRACTS WITHIN THE STATUTE OF FRAUDS

Most states require that these five categories of contracts be in writing:

Marriage - A contract made upon consideration of marriage;

Suretyship - A contract to answer for the debt or duty of another;

One year - A contract that cannot be performed within one year from its making;

UCC - Under the UCC, a contract for the sale of goods for a price of $500 or more; and

Real property contract - A contract for the sale of an interest in real property.

> **EXAM NOTE:** Statute of Frauds issues are often tested on the MBE. You can remember which types of contracts are governed by the Statute by using the mnemonic **Mr. SOUR** (Marriage, Suretyship, One year, UCC, Real property).

1. Marriage Provision

Any agreement in consideration of marriage is within the Statute of Frauds, except the promises by each to marry the other (i.e., the marriage contract itself). A prenuptial agreement is the paradigm of an agreement made in consideration of marriage that is subject to the Statute of Frauds. A promise made in consideration of marriage does not become enforceable merely because the marriage has taken place in reliance on it. However, additional part performance or action in reliance may make such a promise enforceable. Restatement (Second) of Contracts § 124.

2. Suretyship Provision

a. Rule

Suretyship is a three-party contract, wherein one party (the surety) promises a second party (the obligee) that the surety will be responsible for any debt of a third party (the principal) resulting from the principal's failure to pay as agreed. A suretyship induces the second party to extend credit to the third party. A promise to answer for the debt of another must generally be in writing to be enforceable.

b. Exceptions

1) Indemnity contracts

An indemnity contract (i.e., a promise to reimburse for monetary loss) does not fall within the Statute of Frauds as a suretyship provision.

2) Main purpose exception

If the main purpose of the surety in agreeing to pay the debt of the principal is for the surety's own economic advantage, rather than for the principal's benefit, then the contract does not fall within the Statute of Frauds, and an oral promise by the surety is enforceable.

3. Real Property Contracts

a. Types

A promise to transfer or receive **any interest in real property** is within the Statute of Frauds. The Statute does not apply to the conveyance itself (which is governed by a separate statute), but it does apply to a **contract providing for** the subsequent conveyance of an interest in real property. The Statute of Frauds also applies to a promise to create an interest in real property, the assignment of a right to purchase real property, an option contract for the sale of an interest in real property, and a promise to give a mortgage or other lien as security. While leases and easements, as property interests, are generally subject to the Statute of Frauds, a lease or easement for one year or less is usually not covered by the Statute. In addition, licenses and assignments of mortgages are typically not within the Statute.

b. Part performance

Even if an oral contract for the transfer of an interest in real property is not enforceable at the time it is made, **subsequent acts** by either party that show the existence of the contract may make it enforceable, even without a memorandum. Thus, if the seller of an interest in real property conveys it to the purchaser, then the seller will be able to enforce the purchaser's oral promise to pay. Full or partial payment alone, however, would not be sufficient to take the transaction out of the Statute of Frauds. Payment must be accompanied by something more, such as possession of the property or valuable improvements, in order for the part performance doctrine to apply.

4. One-Year Provision

Contracts that **cannot** be performed within one year due to the constraints of the terms of the agreement must be in writing. The year starts **the day after** the contract is made. It is the time that the contract is made that is important, not the length of performance.

> The fact that a contract is not completed within one year does not mean that it is voidable under the Statute of Frauds. For the Statute to apply, the *actual terms* of the contract must make it impossible for performance to be completed within one year.

Full performance will generally take the contract out of the Statute of Frauds. While part performance would not take the contract out of the Statute of Frauds, restitution would be available to the party who performed.

5. Sale of Goods for $500 or More

> **EXAM NOTE:** The UCC Statute of Frauds requirements and exceptions for goods when the price is at least $500 are frequently tested on the MBE.

a. Sufficiency of the writing

When the price of goods is at least $500, the UCC requires a memorandum of the sale that must:

i) Indicate that a contract has been made;

ii) Identify the parties;

iii) Contain a quantity term; and

iv) Be signed by the party to be charged.

The memorandum needs to be signed only by the party being sued; it does not need to be signed by both parties.

1) Type of writing required

To satisfy the Statute of Frauds, the above terms must be in writing, but that writing need not be an actual contract. It doesn't even need to be contained on one piece of paper—a series of correspondence between the parties may suffice.

2) Mistake in writing

A mistake in the memorandum or the omission of other terms does not destroy the memorandum's validity. An omitted term can be proved by parol evidence. However, enforcement is limited to the quantity term actually stated in the memorandum.

> **EXAM NOTE:** Some states have raised the threshold amount from $500 to $5,000. On the exam, assume that the amount is $500, unless stated otherwise.

b. Exceptions—writing not required

1) Specially manufactured goods

No writing is required if (i) the goods are to be specially manufactured for the buyer, (ii) the goods are not suitable for sale to others, and (iii) the seller has made "either a substantial beginning of their manufacture or commitments for their procurement." UCC § 2-201.

2) Part payment

When part of the purchase price for a single item has been paid, the contract is enforced and the partial payment falls outside the UCC Statute of Frauds only to the extent of the purchase.

3) Receipt and acceptance

The contract is outside the UCC Statute of Frauds to the extent that goods are received and accepted.

4) Judicial admission

If the party to be charged admits in pleadings, testimony, or otherwise in court that a contract was made, then the contract is enforceable only to the extent of the quantity admitted.

5) Failure to respond to a memorandum (when both parties are merchants)

If both parties are merchants and a memorandum sufficient against one party is sent to the other party who has reason to know its contents, and the receiving party does not object in writing **within 10 days,** then the contract is enforceable against the receiving party even though he has not signed it.

c. Modifications

Under UCC § 2-209(3), the requirements of the Statute of Frauds must be satisfied if the contract as modified is within its provisions. Any of the above exceptions would apply, though, to take a modification out of the Statute of Frauds.

The UCC would also enforce a provision in a contract for the sale of goods that required a modification to be in writing. Thus, even if the contract was for a sale of goods valued at less than $500 or involved one of the exceptions discussed above, if the contract specifically provided that any modification be in writing, then the UCC would enforce that requirement. *See* UCC § 2-209(2). Note that under a common-law contract, a provision requiring a modification to be in writing even though the modification would not otherwise fall within the Statute of Frauds would not be enforceable.

VI. PAROL EVIDENCE RULE

Before signing a written agreement, parties typically negotiate their contract through a series of conversations, phone calls, letters, faxes, e-mails, etc. When the written contract is finally signed, it may include all of the terms of these negotiations, or it may fail to include some of the terms, or it may change the terms in some way. The parol evidence rule generally prevents a party to a written contract from presenting prior extrinsic evidence that contradicts the terms of the contract as written. The rule is concerned with the issue of whether any of the earlier oral or written terms are part of the parties' contract, even though they are absent from the parties' written agreement.

A. INTEGRATION

The first step is to determine whether the parties' writing is "integrated," meaning that the parties intended it to be their final agreement. The parol evidence rule applies only to a document that is an integration.

If the document is determined not to be an integration (i.e., not to be the final expression of the parties' agreement), such as a preliminary negotiation document or tentative draft agreement, then the parol evidence rule will not apply.

1. **Total versus Partial Integration**

   If the writing is determined to be an integration, then the second step is to decide whether it completely expresses all of the terms of the parties' agreement.

   a. **Total integration**

      If the writing completely expresses all of the terms of the parties' agreement, then it is a **total integration,** and the parties cannot introduce any extrinsic evidence (oral or written) of prior or contemporaneous understandings or negotiations.

   b. **Partial integration**

      If, on the other hand, the writing sets forth the parties' agreement about some terms, but not all terms, then it is a **partial integration.** The parties are then permitted to introduce supplementary extrinsic evidence (oral or written) of other terms as long as the evidence is **consistent** with the writing, but not if the evidence contradicts the terms of the writing.

2. **Intent of the Parties**

   The intent of the parties determines whether there is total, partial, or no integration.

   a. **Common-law "four corners" rule**

      Under the common law, in determining whether the parties intended the written contract to be the final and complete expression of their agreement, a court was only permitted to look to the writing itself for evidence of intent. This is called the "four corners" rule because the court could not look outside the four corners of the parties' document. If the written contract appeared to be detailed, then a court would likely conclude that it was final and totally integrated. Such a conclusion was especially true if the contract had an explicit integration or "merger" clause, which usually said something like: "This contract is the final and complete expression of the parties' agreement and supersedes all prior contracts, agreements, understandings, negotiations, assurances, guarantees, or statements."

   b. **Second Restatement rule**

      The Second Restatement adopts a different approach to the parol evidence rule. If, under the circumstances, an extrinsic term of an agreement would "naturally be omitted" from a writing, then that term can be introduced, so long as it does not contradict the writing. Restatement (Second) of Contracts § 213.

   c. **UCC rule**

      In contrast to the common law and Second Restatement parol evidence rules, the UCC rule is much more lenient. The UCC essentially presumes that a written contract is only a "partial integration" of the parties' agreement, and therefore it lets in any outside terms unless a court concludes that they "certainly" would have been included in the written contract. UCC § 2-202. It is typically very difficult for courts to conclude that parties "certainly" would have included any particular term in their written contract. Thus, under the UCC, parties usually can bring in outside evidence.

B. WHEN THE PAROL EVIDENCE RULE IS INAPPLICABLE

The parol evidence rule does not apply to communications that occur after the execution of the written contract; it applies only to agreements reached before or contemporaneously with the execution of the written contract.

1. Raising an Excuse

The parol evidence rule does not apply when a party is raising an excuse, such as mistake, misunderstanding, or misrepresentation. Parties may always introduce evidence that would show that no valid contract exists or that the contract is voidable.

2. Establishing a Defense

Similarly, the parol evidence rule does not apply to evidence offered to establish a defense such as incompetence, illegality, duress, or lack of consideration. Again, if the evidence would make the contract void or voidable, then the parol evidence rule will not apply.

3. Separate Deal

Even when there is full integration, evidence may be offered if it represents a distinct and separate contract.

4. Condition Precedent

Parol evidence may also be admitted to prove a condition precedent to the existence of the contract.

5. Ambiguity and Interpretation

Evidence may be admitted for the purpose of interpreting or clarifying an ambiguity in the agreement. This can include evidence of trade usage or even local custom to show that a particular word or phrase had a particular meaning. Courts approach interpretation in two ways:

a. Plain meaning rule

This rule provides that the objective definitions of contract terms control the meaning of the contract, regardless of whether this meaning corresponds with the actual intent of the parties. Sometimes courts will go outside the document to clarify the ordinary meaning of terms that are ambiguous or overly vague.

b. Context rule

Some states permit courts to use a contextual approach to contract interpretation. Under the context rule, judges determine the contract's meaning by considering all evidence of the facts and circumstances related to the transaction. The goal is to effectuate the parties' actual contract objectives and purposes.

6. Subsequent Agreements

The parol evidence rule does not apply to evidence of agreements between the parties subsequent to execution of the writing.

7. UCC Rule—Trade Usage and Course of Dealings or Performance

Even if the terms of a written contract for the sale of goods appear to be unambiguous, a party may explain or supplement the terms by evidence of trade usage or course of dealings or performance. UCC § 2-202.

VII. CONDITIONS AND PERFORMANCE

A condition is a future and uncertain event that must take place before a party's contractual rights or obligations are created, destroyed, or enlarged. By contrast, a promise constitutes a party's obligation to act or refrain from acting.

Example: A buyer and seller enter into a contract for the sale of a house if the buyer can obtain a loan. Under the contract, the seller has promised to sell the house to the buyer, and the buyer has correspondingly promised to buy the house. However, both promises are conditioned on the buyer obtaining a loan.

Ambiguity as to whether a statement creates a promise or a condition is usually resolved in favor of a promise over a condition. Restatement (Second) of Contracts § 227.

EXAM NOTE: Remember, the failure of a **condition** relieves a party of the **obligation** to perform; the failure of a party to perform a **promise** constitutes **breach**.

A. TYPES OF CONDITIONS

A condition may be express (clearly stated in the agreement) or implied (presumed based on the nature of a transaction).

1. Express

Express conditions are expressed in the contract. Words in the contract such as "on condition that" or "provided that" are typical examples of express conditions. Express conditions must be complied with fully; substantial performance will not suffice. Arbitration clauses are enforceable, except when a consumer might be waiving an important substantive right.

2. Implied Conditions

Implied conditions are those that are deemed to be part of the contract because the nature of the agreement suggests that the parties truly intended the condition but failed to expressly include it, or because fairness requires including the condition to prevent an unjust result (also called "constructive condition"). The most common types of implied conditions are called "constructive conditions of exchange" and arise most frequently in construction and employment contracts. A court will imply that the builder or employee must perform first (at least "substantially") before the other side's performance (the payment of money) becomes due.

Substantial performance is all that is required to satisfy an implied condition.

B. TIMING OF CONDITIONS

Performance by one or both of the parties may be made expressly conditional in the contract, and the conditions may precede the obligation to perform (**condition precedent**) or may excuse the duty to perform after a particular event occurs (**condition subsequent**). A condition subsequent exists only with respect to duty that is absolute. (Note: Under the Restatement (Second) of Contracts, a condition subsequent is treated as a discharging event rather than as a condition. Restatement (Second) of Contracts §§ 224, 230.)

> **Example:** A agrees to hire B if B passes the bar exam. B agrees to work as a clerk for C until B passes the bar exam. B's passing of the bar exam is a condition precedent to being hired by A, and a condition subsequent to B's employment with C.

If a defendant's duty is subject to a condition precedent, the plaintiff has the burden of proving that the condition occurred in order to recover. If the defendant's duty is subject to a condition subsequent, then the defendant must prove the happening of the condition to avoid liability.

C. SATISFACTION OF CONDITIONS

In most contracts, a party's duty to perform is absolute because it is easy to conclude that all conditions have been satisfied. In unusual cases, the occurrence of the condition may be more difficult to determine.

1. Satisfaction Clause

When the aesthetic taste of an individual is a condition of satisfactory performance, and that individual in good faith determines that the work is not satisfactory, then that person is not liable on the contract. Conditions requiring satisfaction of performance not involving aesthetics are examined against a reasonable person standard.

2. Time of Payment Clause

A clause in a contract making payment conditioned on the occurrence of an event is usually construed as a mere guide as to time for payment rather than as an absolute condition that must occur before payment is due.

D. DISPUTES ABOUT PERFORMANCE

A party to a contract cannot recover until performance is tendered to the other party. When parties expressly agree to a condition, they are generally held strictly to that condition, meaning that there must be full compliance. With implied conditions or constructive conditions of exchange, courts permit less than full compliance with the constructive conditions. This doctrine is known as "substantial performance."

> The doctrine of substantial performance does not apply either to express conditions or to contracts for the sale of goods under the UCC.

1. Substantial Performance

a. Meaning

The doctrine of substantial performance provides that a party who substantially performs can recover on the contract even though full performance has not been tendered. If the failure of a constructive condition of exchange is minor, then it will not negate substantial performance. If the failure of a constructive condition of exchange is material, however, it will negate substantial performance.

b. Willful failure

No recovery is allowed for a willful failure, which implies some attempt to cheat the other party or to provide less than was called for by the contract.

Under the doctrine of prevention, a party must refrain from conduct that prevents or hinders the occurrence of a condition. Restatement (Second) of Contracts §§ 225, 245 cmt. a.

c. Damages

In general, the party who substantially performed the contract can recover the contract price minus any amount that it will cost the other party to obtain complete performance as had been promised. Note that even if there is no substantial performance, a party who performed to some degree and cannot recover in contract can still potentially recover through restitution.

2. Strict Performance under the UCC

Under the UCC, the basic obligations of a seller are to **transfer ownership** of the goods to the buyer and to **tender goods** conforming to the warranty obligations. In general, the UCC requires "perfect tender," and substantial performance will not suffice. Substantial performance applies to installment contracts under the UCC and when the parties agree that it applies. In addition, the UCC provides that if a buyer rejects goods as nonconforming and time still remains to perform under a contract, the seller has a right to cure and tender conforming goods.

a. Transferring ownership

The UCC implies a warranty of title in all sales contracts, providing that the seller automatically warrants that (i) it is conveying good title, (ii) the transfer is rightful, and (iii) the goods are delivered free from any security interest of which the buyer has no knowledge at the time of the contract. Actual knowledge by the buyer of a security interest on the goods nullifies the warranty of title. UCC § 2-312(1).

The UCC permits disclaimer of the warranty of title, but such disclaimer must be by specific language or circumstances that give the buyer reason to know that the seller does not claim rightful title, or that the seller is only purporting to sell such rights as the seller or a third person possesses. UCC § 2-312(2).

b. Tendering goods

The seller must tender the goods in accordance with the contract provisions or in accordance with the UCC if the contract is silent on tender. UCC § 2-503.

1) Time of tender

In the absence of a specific contract provision, the goods must be tendered within a reasonable time after the contract is made. UCC § 2-309.

2) Manner of tender

The goods are to be delivered in one delivery, unless otherwise provided in the contract, or the circumstances give either party a right to make or demand delivery in lots (as when a party would clearly have no room to store the goods if delivered all at once). UCC § 2-307.

3) Place of tender

Unless otherwise provided in the contract, the place of tender will be the seller's place of business (or residence, if the seller has no place of business), unless the goods are identified and the parties know that they are at some other location, in which case that location will be the place of tender. UCC § 2-308.

4) Method of tender

The four methods of tender are as follows.

a) Seller's place of business

If the goods are tendered at the seller's place of business, then the seller must place the goods at the disposition of the buyer and give the buyer notice, if notice is necessary to enable the seller to take delivery. UCC § 2-504.

b) Shipment contract

If the contract is a shipment contract (often identified by the words "F.O.B. (free on board) seller's place of business"), then the seller must deliver the goods to the carrier, make a proper contract for their shipment, obtain and deliver any document necessary for the buyer to obtain possession of the goods, and give the buyer notice that the goods have been shipped. UCC § 2-319(1)(a).

c) Destination contract

If the contract is a destination contract (often identified by the words "F.O.B. (free on board) buyer's place of business"), then the seller must deliver the goods to a particular place (specified in the contract) and tender them there by holding the goods at the buyer's disposition and giving the buyer notice. UCC § 2-319(1)(b).

d) Goods in the hands of a bailee

The seller must bargain for a negotiable document of title or obtain acknowledgment from the bailee of the buyer's rights in the goods. UCC § 2-509(2).

A contract that requires the seller to ship goods to the buyer by a third-party carrier is either a shipment contract or a destination contract. When the contract is otherwise silent, a shipment contract is presumed when the contract requires shipment by a third-party carrier. UCC § 2-503 cmt. 5.

5) C.I.F. (cost, insurance, and freight) and C & F (cost and freight)

In a C.I.F. contract, the price includes the cost of the goods, the cost of transporting the goods, and the cost of insuring the goods during shipment.

In a C & F contract, the price includes the cost of the goods plus the cost of shipment.

6) F.A.S. contracts

When a contract specifies F.A.S. (free alongside ship), the seller is obligated to deliver the goods **alongside** a designated vessel in a manner that comports with the ordinary course of business of the port of delivery, or at a specified dock.

c. Buyer's obligations

When a conforming tender is made, the buyer is obligated to accept and pay the price under the contract. UCC § 2-507. Rejection amounts to breach of contract.

An agreement that is otherwise sufficiently definite will not be made invalid merely because it omits details regarding the performance to be specified by one of the parties. The UCC implies an obligation of good faith within the parameter of "commercial reasonableness." UCC § 2-311(1).

When a contract fails to specify the assortment of goods, the UCC imposes a duty on the buyer to specify, whereas arrangements relating to shipment are the seller's duty to specify. UCC § 2-311(2).

If the buyer fails to specify the assortment of goods, then the seller can treat the failure as a breach by failure to accept the contracted-for goods only if the buyer's failure materially impacts the seller's performance. UCC § 2-311(3).

1) Non-carrier cases versus carrier cases

Unless otherwise specified in the contract, when goods are shipped by carrier, payment is due from the buyer at the moment the buyer receives the goods. In non-carrier cases, payment is due upon tender of delivery by the seller.

2) Shipment under reservation

A seller who ships by carrier under a contract that does not specify the method or form of payment may send the goods **under reservation,** meaning that the carrier will hold the goods until the buyer pays. This is accomplished by the seller's obtaining a negotiable or nonnegotiable bill of lading.

3) Tender of payment

a) Generally required to trigger delivery obligation

Unless otherwise agreed, tender of payment is a condition to the seller's duty to tender and complete any delivery.

b) Sufficiency of tender of payment

Tender of payment is sufficient when made by any means or in any manner consistent with the ordinary course of business, unless the seller

(i) demands payment in legal tender (i.e., cash) and (ii) gives any extension of time reasonably necessary to procure such legal tender.

c) Payment by check

If payment is made by check, payment is conditional until the check is paid or dishonored.

d. Buyer's right to inspect

A buyer has a right to inspect goods that are tendered, delivered, or identified to the contract for sale, unless the contract provides otherwise.

1) Prior to payment

A buyer's right to inspect is a condition to payment. An inspection may occur at any reasonable time and place and in any reasonable manner, even when the goods are held under reservation. However, the parties can agree that inspection can occur in a particular form, time, or place. If the seller is required or authorized to send the goods to the buyer, then the inspection may be after their arrival.

2) When not entitled to inspect

Unless otherwise agreed, the buyer is **not** entitled to inspect the goods before payment of the price if the contract (i) provides for delivery "C.O.D." or (ii) is on other terms that, under the applicable course of performance, course of dealing, or usage of trade are interpreted to preclude inspection before payment. Similarly, the buyer is not entitled to inspect the goods before payment, unless otherwise agreed, if the contract provides for payment against documents of title, except when such payment is due only after the goods are to become available for inspection.

3) Expenses of inspection

Expenses of inspection must be paid by the buyer, but they may be recovered from the seller if the goods do not conform and are rejected.

3. Divisible or Installment Contracts

a. Common law

A divisible or installment contract is one in which the various units of performance are divisible into distinct parts. Recovery is limited to the amount promised for the segment of the contract performed. Damages are recoverable for breach of the other segments.

b. UCC

1) Multiple shipments

Under the UCC, an installment contract is defined as one in which the goods are to be delivered in multiple shipments, and each shipment is to be separately accepted by the buyer. Payment by the buyer is due upon each delivery, unless the price cannot be apportioned. UCC § 2-612.

2) Nonconforming segment

If the seller makes a nonconforming tender or tenders nonconforming goods under one segment of an installment contract, then the buyer can reject only if the nonconformity:

i) Substantially impairs the value of that shipment to the buyer; and

ii) Cannot be cured.

If the seller makes adequate assurances that he can cure the nonconformity, then the buyer must accept the shipment. UCC § 2-612(2).

3) Remaining segments

When there is a nonconforming tender or a tender of nonconforming goods under one segment of an installment contract, the buyer may cancel the contract only if the nonconformity substantially impairs the value of the entire contract to the buyer.

E. SUSPENSION OR EXCUSE OF CONDITIONS

If a condition is suspended, then the condition is restored upon expiration of the suspension, whereas if the condition is excused, then the party having the benefit of the condition can never raise it as a defense.

1. Waiver

A party whose duty is subject to the condition can waive the condition, either by words or by conduct. Courts will find waiver of a condition only if the condition is not a material part of the agreement.

The condition may be reinstated if:

i) The waiving party communicates a retraction of the waiver before the condition is due to occur; and

ii) The other party has not already suffered detrimental reliance.

2. Wrongful Interference

A duty of good faith and fair dealing is implied into **all** (both common law and UCC) contracts. Included in this duty is a duty not to hinder the other party's performance and a duty to cooperate, when necessary. Accordingly, if the party whose duty is subject to the condition wrongfully interferes with the occurrence of that condition, then the condition is excused and the party wrongfully interfering has an absolute duty to perform.

3. Election

A party who chooses to continue with a contract after a condition is broken effectively elects to waive that condition.

4. Estoppel

A party who indicates that a condition will not be enforced may be estopped from using that condition as a defense if the other party reasonably relied on the impression that the condition had been waived.

VIII. BREACH OF CONTRACT AND REMEDIES

A. BREACH OF CONTRACT

Once a duty to perform exists, nonperformance is a breach of contract unless the duty is discharged (by agreement, statute, inability to perform, waiver, etc.).

1. Common Law

Under common law, a material breach of contract (i.e., when the non-breaching party does not receive the substantial benefit of its bargain) allows the non-breaching party to withhold any promised performance and to pursue remedies for the breach, including damages. If the breach is minor (i.e., the breaching party has substantially performed), then the non-breaching party is entitled to any remedies that would apply to the nonmaterial breach. If a minor breach is accompanied by an anticipatory repudiation, then the non-breaching party may treat the breach as a material breach.

The party who commits a material breach of his contract obligations cannot sue for contract damages but would ordinarily be entitled to the fair value of any benefit conferred on the non-breaching party.

> **EXAM NOTE:** Keep in mind that under a minor breach, the non-breaching party may be able to recover damages, but also still must perform under the contract. If the breach is material, the non-breaching party does not need to perform.

2. UCC

Under the UCC, the seller generally must strictly perform all obligations under the contract or be in breach. The doctrine of material breach applies only in the context of installment contracts or when the parties so provide in their contract.

B. ANTICIPATORY REPUDIATION

1. Anticipatory Repudiation Under the Common Law

a. Repudiation of promise

The doctrine of anticipatory repudiation is applicable when a promisor repudiates a promise before the time for performance arises or elapses. The repudiation must be **clear and unequivocal** (as opposed to mere insecurity) and may be by acts or words.

b. Nonbreaching party's options

Repudiation excuses the occurrence of any condition that would otherwise prevent the repudiating party's duty from being absolute. Upon repudiation, the promisee can treat the repudiation as a breach or ignore it and demand performance. If the repudiation is ignored, then continued performance by the promisee must be suspended if the performance would increase the damages of the promisor.

In a situation in which the date of performance has not passed and the only performance left is payment, the aggrieved party must wait until performance is due before filing suit (to allow the potentially breaching party to change his mind and perform). In other words, in this limited situation, anticipatory breach is inapplicable; the aggrieved party must wait for actual breach before filing suit.

c. Retraction of repudiation

Repudiation may be retracted until such time as the promisee (i) acts in reliance on the repudiation, (ii) signifies acceptance of the repudiation, or (iii) commences an action for breach of contract. Notice of the retraction must be sufficient enough to allow for the performance of the promisee's obligations.

d. Unilateral contracts

The doctrine of anticipatory repudiation *does **not** apply to unilateral contracts* and may not be used if the promisee has completed performance prior to the repudiation.

2. Anticipatory Repudiation under the UCC

According to the UCC, anticipatory repudiation occurs when there has been an **unequivocal refusal** of the buyer or seller to perform, or when a party creating reasonable grounds for insecurity fails to provide adequate assurances within 30 days of demand for assurances. UCC § 2-609. The repudiation can be retracted if the other party has not canceled the contract or materially changed position. Repudiation allows the nonrepudiating party to resort to any remedy given by the contract or code.

3. Prospective Inability to Perform

A party's expectations of performance may be diminished by an event that occurs after the contract was made.

> **EXAM NOTE:** On the exam, be reluctant to excuse a party from performing solely on the ground that he or she does not expect counter-performance to be given.

Under the UCC, either party can demand assurance of performance if there are reasonable grounds for insecurity about the other party's ability or willingness to perform. Once such assurances are requested, performance may be suspended until they are provided. Failure to give adequate assurances within a reasonable time, not exceeding 30 days, can be treated as repudiation. UCC § 2-609.

a. Commercial standards for merchants

Between merchants, the reasonableness of grounds for insecurity and the adequacy of any assurance offered are determined according to commercial standards. Thus, for example, if a supplier writes to a manufacturer demanding assurances of financial solvency, and the manufacturer provides its latest audited financial statements as well as a satisfactory credit report from its banker, then that would likely constitute adequate assurances of its financial status.

b. Effect of acceptance

The acceptance of any improper delivery or payment does not preclude an aggrieved party from demanding adequate assurance of future performance.

C. REMEDIES: DAMAGES FOR BREACH OF CONTRACT

Remedies are meant to compensate the nonbreaching party for actual economic losses. Actual economic losses are calculated depending on how the contract was formed (e.g., through consideration or through promissory estoppel) and what type of contract it was (e.g., sale of goods versus services).

1. Expectation Damages

a. In general

Expectation damages are intended to put the injured party in the same position as if the contract had been performed. They are those damages that arise naturally and obviously from the breach and are normally measured by the market value of the promised performance less the consideration promised by the non-breaching party. Thus, to calculate expectation damages, subtract from the contract price from the market value of performance. The market value of performance is whatever it reasonably costs to get the performance that was promised in the contract. Expectation damages must be foreseeable and the non-breaching party must be able to prove them with reasonable certainty.

> **Example:** B breaches a contract with A to fix A's car for $500. A finds another mechanic, C, to fix A's car for $700, which is the market value of performance. A can recover $200 from B.

1) Construction contracts

In construction contracts, the general measure of damages for a contractor's failure to begin or to complete the building or other structure is the difference between the contract price and the cost of construction by another builder, plus compensation for delay in completion of the construction. The general measure of damages for the owner's failure to pay the contract price, in whole or in part, is the profits that the builder would have earned, plus any costs incurred by the builder, less the amount of any payments made by the owner to the contractor and any materials purchased by the contractor that are used by the contractor on another job.

2) Sale of goods contracts

Damages for failing to deliver goods are measured by the difference between the contract price and the market value of the goods (or the cost of cover).

3) Real estate contracts

Damages for failing to perform a real estate sales contract also are measured by the difference between the contract price and the market value.

4) Formula

The general expectation formula can be computed as follows:

> Expectation Damages = loss in value + other loss − cost avoided − loss avoided

Loss in value is the difference between the performance that the non-breaching party should have received under the contract and what was actually received, if anything.

Other loss includes consequential and incidental damages, if any.

The cost avoided is the additional costs that the non-breaching party can avoid by rightfully discontinuing performance under the contract as a result of the other party's breach.

Loss avoided is the beneficial effect of the breach due to the non-breaching party's ability to salvage or reallocate resources that otherwise would have been devoted to performing under the contract. Loss avoided is subtracted only if the savings results from the injured party not having to perform rather than from some unrelated event. Restatement (Second) of Contracts § 347.

b. Partial performance

A partially performing party can generally recover for work performed, plus expectation damages for the work not yet performed.

> **Example:** B agrees to paint A's house for $500, which covers $400 in supplies and labor and $100 in profit. After B paints half of the house and incurs $200 in costs, A breaches. B can recover the $200 for costs already incurred and the $100 of profit, but not the remaining $200 for costs not yet incurred.

If at the time of a breach the only remaining duties of performance are (i) those of the party in breach and (ii) for the payment of money in installments not related to one another, then breach by nonperformance as to less than the whole, whether or not accompanied or followed by a repudiation, does not give rise to a claim for damages for total breach and is a partial breach of contract only. Restatement (Second) of Contracts § 243(3).

> **Example:** A borrows $10,000 from B. The loan is to be paid back in monthly installments with interest over a one-year period of time. A fails to make the first installment payment and tells B that he will be unable to make the other payments as well. B has a claim for partial breach of the contract but cannot sue for a total breach of the contract. (Note: Lenders circumvent this rule by including in the loan agreement an acceleration clause that causes the entire loan to become due upon the failure by the borrower to timely make an installment payment.)

c. Defective performance

1) Construction contracts

In construction contracts, damages for defective or incomplete construction are measured by the cost of repair or completion. The general measure of damages for failing to perform a construction contract is the difference between the contract price and the cost of construction by another builder.

2) Sale of goods contracts

By contrast, in contracts for the sale of goods, damages for nonconformity with the contract generally are measured by the difference between the value of the goods as warranted and the actual value of the tendered nonconforming goods.

The purpose of both measures is to place the plaintiff in as good a position as if the defendant had performed the contract according to its specifications.

d. Waste

Economic waste occurs when the amount of damages awarded is disproportional to any economic benefit or utility gained as a result of the award. If the award of expectation damages would result in economic waste, then courts may instead, at their discretion, award damages equal to diminution in value. *See Jacob & Youngs v. Kent,* 129 N.E. 889 (N.Y. 1921).

> **Example:** Landowner grants Mining Company a five-year license to remove coal from his property. In return for the license, Mining Company agreed to restore the property to its original state at the end of the five-year period. After five years, Mining Company refused to restore the land. The restoration work would cost $29,000, but, if completed, would result in only a $300 increase in the property's value. The court may elect to award only $300 in damages, instead of the usual $29,000 expectation award. *Peevyhouse v. Garland Coal and Mining Co.,* 382 P.2d 109 (Okla. 1962).

However, if the breach is willful, and only completion of the contract will give the nonbreaching party the benefit of its bargain, then a court may award expectation damages even if that award would result in economic waste. *See Rock Island Improvement Co. v. Helmerich & Payne, Inc.,* 698 F.2d 175 (10th Cir. 1983).

2. Consequential Damages and Foreseeability

a. Consequential damages

Consequential damages are **reasonably foreseeable losses** to a nonbreaching party that go beyond expectation damages, such as loss of profits.

b. Foreseeability

Damages are recoverable if they were the natural and probable consequences of breach, or if they were "in the contemplation of the parties at the time the contract was made," or were otherwise foreseeable. *Hadley v. Baxendale,* 156 Eng. Rep. 145 (Ex. Ch. 1854).

Because it is assumed that a borrower will be able to obtain a substitute bank loan, the borrower's lost profit is considered unforeseeable at the time of contract formation.

c. Causation

A defendant can defend on the ground that the losses that the plaintiff seeks to recover would have occurred even if the defendant had not breached the contract.

d. Reasonable certainty

To recover damages, a plaintiff must prove the dollar amount of the damages with reasonable certainty. Courts are hesitant to award damages for lost profits, as they are difficult to prove. When lost profits are considered too speculative, such as with a new venture, courts often limit a party's recovery to reliance damages (i.e., reasonable expenditures made in connection with the contract).

e. UCC—Breach of warranty

While generally consequential damages for breach of warranty may be limited or excluded unless the limitation or exclusion is unconscionable, limitation of consequential damages for injury to the person in the case of consumer goods is prima facie unconscionable. Limitation of damages when the loss is commercial is not. UCC § 2-719(3).

> **EXAM NOTE:** Although courts are hesitant to award damages for lost profits and lost opportunities, such damages are still recoverable for breach of contract claims. Beware of questions on the exam that conclude in absolute terms that such damages are not recoverable. They are not likely, but they are still possible.

3. Liquidated Damages and Penalties

Liquidated damages are an amount contractually stipulated as a reasonable estimation of actual damages to be recovered by one party if the other party breaches. A term fixing unreasonably large liquidated damages is unenforceable on grounds of public policy as a penalty. A provision for liquidated damages is enforceable and not construed as a penalty if the amount of damages stipulated in the contract is reasonable in relation to either the actual damages suffered or the damages that might be anticipated at the time the contract was made. However, if the provision is construed as a penalty, then it is unenforceable.

When the contract contains a liquidated damages clause, the party seeking to repudiate that clause must show that the agreed-to damage is so exorbitant as to be in the nature of a penalty.

a. Enforceability

There is no fixed rule applicable to all liquidated damages provisions, and each is evaluated on its own facts and circumstances. To validate a liquidated damages clause, the following three-prong test must be met:

i) The **parties intended to agree** in advance to the settlement of damages that might arise from the breach;

ii) The **amount of liquidated damages was reasonable** at the time of contracting, bearing some relation to the damages that might be sustained; and

iii) **Actual damages would be uncertain** in amount and difficult to prove.

Bear Stearns Gov't Sec., Inc. v. Dow Corning Corp., 419 F.3d 543 (6th Cir. 2005).

Thus, if the liquidated damages are disproportionate to the actual damages, then the clause will not be enforced, and recovery will be limited to the actual damages proven.

b. Uncertainty of actual damages

When determining whether actual damages would be uncertain in amount and difficult to prove, courts look to the time of contracting, not to the time of breach. Additionally, the damages contained in a liquidated damages clause must be for a **specific amount for a specific breach**; the provision may not merely serve as a threat to secure performance or as a means to punish nonperformance. Although exculpatory language in the contract stating that the liquidated damages provision is not a penalty does not control, it should be given some weight.

4. Incidental Damages

Incidental damages may be awarded to the non-breaching party. In the sale of goods, such damages may include the cost of inspecting, transporting, caring for, or maintaining custody over goods.

5. Punitive Damages

Punitive damages are very rarely available in contract actions. Some statutes apply them for the purpose of punishing fraud, violation of fiduciary duty, and acts of bad faith, and for deterrence. Under the Restatement (Second) of Contracts § 355, punitive damages are not recoverable "unless the conduct constituting the breach is also a tort for which punitive damages [can be recovered]."

6. Nominal Damages

Damages do not need to be alleged in a cause of action for breach. If no damages are alleged or none are proved, the plaintiff is still entitled to a judgment for "nominal" damages (e.g., one dollar).

7. Mitigating Damages

A party to a contract must avoid or mitigate damages to the extent possible by taking such steps as do not involve undue risk, expense, or inconvenience. The non-breaching party is held to a standard of reasonable conduct in preventing loss.

Although often phrased as a "duty to mitigate damages," a non-breaching party's failure to mitigate does not give the breaching party a right to sue the non-breaching party for such failure; it only reduces the damages that may be recovered by the non-breaching party. For example, with regard to a sale of goods, a non-breaching buyer's failure to take reasonable steps to mitigate damages by buying substitute goods (i.e., cover) will prevent a claim for consequential damages but will not deprive the buyer of damages measured by the difference between the contract and market prices. In addition, the measure of damages for breach of a contract to lend money is the additional cost of obtaining a loan from another lender (e.g., the difference in cost over time between the interest rates of the original loan and the subsequent loan).

Note that reasonable expenses incurred as a result of efforts to mitigate damages can be recovered, even if the mitigation attempt was unsuccessful.

D. RESTITUTION AND RELIANCE RECOVERIES

Restitution awards the fair market value of the benefit conferred, while reliance damages are reasonable out-of-pocket losses by the non-breaching party.

1. Restitutionary Damages

Restitutionary damages restore to the plaintiff whatever benefit was conferred upon the defendant prior to the breach. Generally, the benefit may be measured by either the reasonable value of the defendant obtaining that benefit from another source or the increase in the defendant's wealth (e.g., the increase in value of property owned by the defendant) from having received that benefit. However, when justice requires, recovery may be limited to one of the two measurements. For example, if the plaintiff has breached a contract, recovery is generally limited to the increase in the defendant's wealth.

Under some circumstances, restitutionary damages may be recovered even though the plaintiff would have suffered a loss had the defendant not breached.

Thus, if A contracts with B to paint B's house for $500, and B repudiates the contract after A has done some, but not all, of the painting, and A shows that the fair value of the work that has been done is actually $1,000, most courts allow recovery of restitutionary damages ($1,000) on the theory that otherwise the defendant would be profiting from the breach.

If, however, at the time of the defendant's breach, the plaintiff has **fully performed the contract,** and the defendant owes only money and not some other kind of performance, then the plaintiff is not permitted to recover restitutionary damages and is limited to expectation damages (generally the contract price minus the cost of completion).

Restitutionary damages are also available in quasi-contract when there is no contract between the parties or when a contract is unenforceable, and a lack of any recovery would be unjust given that a benefit was conferred on the other party. Recovery is limited to the fair value of the benefit conferred.

2. Reliance Damages

Reliance damages may be recovered if a non-breaching party incurs expenses in reasonable reliance upon the promise that the other party would perform. Unlike with restitutionary damages, with reliance damages, there is no requirement that the defendant benefit from the plaintiff's expenditures. **A party cannot recover both reliance and expectation damages.**

The injured party can choose to pursue reliance damages instead of expectation damages, but those damages are then mitigated by any losses that the plaintiff would have sustained if the contract had been performed. Restatement (Second) of Contracts § 349.

E. SPECIFIC PERFORMANCE AND DECLARATORY JUDGMENT

1. Specific Performance

When damages are an inadequate remedy, the non-breaching party may pursue the equitable remedy of specific performance.

a. Factors considered

In determining whether damages are adequate, consider the:

i) Difficulty of proving damages with reasonable certainty;

ii) Difficulty of procuring a suitable substitute performance by means of money awarded as damages; and

iii) Likelihood that an award of damages will be collected.

b. Real property

Contracts involving the transfer of an interest in real property may be enforced by an order of specific performance because every parcel of **real property is considered unique.**

c. UCC

Specific performance may be granted when the goods are rare or unique, or in other circumstances—such as for breach of a requirements contract when there is not another convenient supplier. UCC § 2-716.

d. Limitations

Even if the remedy of damages is inadequate, specific performance will not be granted when the court cannot supervise enforcement. Thus, courts rarely grant specific enforcement of contracts for personal services, although they may restrain the breaching party from working for another when the contract contains a noncompete clause.

e. Defenses

Equitable defenses, such as laches (prejudicial delay in bringing the action) or unclean hands (when the non-breaching party is guilty of some wrongdoing in the transaction at issue) may be raised by the breaching party. A party may also wish to enter an injunction against the breaching party to enforce the contract.

2. Declaratory Judgment

If the rights and obligations of the parties under a contract are unclear, and an actual dispute exists between the parties concerning those rights and obligations, then either party may bring a declaratory judgment action to obtain an adjudication of those rights and duties. Declaratory judgment is not available, however, to resolve moot issues or theoretical problems that have not risen to an actual dispute.

F. REMEDIES UNDER THE UCC

The following sections more specifically address the remedies that are available to buyers and sellers under the UCC. These rules are frequently tested on the MBE.

1. Buyer's Remedies

When the seller's time for performance arises, the seller may:

i) Do **nothing** (breach by the seller);

ii) Make a **nonconforming tender** (breach by the seller); or

iii) Make a **conforming tender** (performance by the seller).

a. Failure to tender

Under the UCC, the buyer has several alternative remedies if the seller fails to tender the goods.

1) Damages

The buyer may recover the market price minus the contract price. The market price is the price that existed at the time of the breach at the place where tender was to occur under the contract. UCC § 2-713.

The UCC also permits recovery for incidental and consequential damages resulting from the seller's breach. Incidental damages are damages that are incidental to the seller's failure to perform, such as the costs of warehousing, transportation, inspection, etc. Consequential damages are any losses resulting from general or particular requirements and needs of which the seller, at the time of contracting, had reason to know and which could not be reasonably prevented by purchasing substitute goods or otherwise. Consequential damages may be limited or excluded under the UCC unless such limitation or exclusion would be unconscionable. UCC § 2-719(3).

2) Cover

Alternatively, the buyer may purchase similar goods elsewhere and recover the replacement price minus the contract price. UCC § 2-712.

3) Specific performance

The buyer may demand specific performance for **unique** goods. In addition, specific performance may be had in other proper circumstances. An inability to cover is strong evidence of such circumstances. The court may grant specific performance on terms and conditions that the court deems just. UCC § 2-716(1).

4) Replevin

a) Payment by the buyer

When the buyer has made at least partial payment for identified goods, the buyer can obtain the undelivered goods from the seller if:

i) The seller becomes insolvent within 10 days of receiving the first payment from the buyer; or

ii) The goods were for family, personal, or household purposes, and the seller has repudiated or failed to deliver the goods as required by contract.

To obtain the goods, the buyer must tender any unpaid portion of the price to the seller. UCC § 2-502.

b) Buyer's inability to cover

The buyer can also obtain identified, undelivered goods from the seller if:

i) The buyer is unable to affect cover;

ii) The circumstances reasonably indicate that such effect will be unavailing; or

iii) The goods have been shipped under reservation, and satisfaction of the security interest in the goods has been made or tendered.

UCC § 2-716(3).

b. Nonconforming tender

Under the UCC, if either the tender or the goods are nonconforming, then the buyer has the **right to accept or reject** all or part of the goods. UCC § 2-601.

The buyer has the **right to inspect** the goods before deciding whether to accept or reject. Payment does not constitute "acceptance" if there is no right of inspection before payment (e.g., C.O.D., C.I.F., or C & F contracts). UCC § 2-513.

1) Rejection

a) Valid rejection

A valid rejection requires that the buyer:

i) Give notice to the seller;

ii) Within a reasonable time; and

iii) Before acceptance.

UCC § 2-602. Upon a rightful rejection, the buyer is entitled to a return of any payments made on the goods. UCC § 2-711(3).

b) Retain possession

The buyer must retain possession of rejected goods for a reasonable time to allow for the seller to reclaim them. UCC § 2-602(2).

c) Perishable and non-perishable goods

In the absence of other instructions from the seller, the buyer may store non-perishable goods at the seller's expense, reship them to the seller, or sell them for the seller's account. If the goods are perishable and the seller has no local agent to whom they can be returned, in the absence of other instructions from the seller, the buyer is required to sell the goods on the seller's behalf. UCC § 2-603.

d) Remedies

The same remedies are available to the buyer after rejection as if no tender was made by the seller, i.e., damages (including incidental and consequential damages, unless properly limited or excluded), cover, specific performance, or replevin.

Need for notice: A failure to give notice of the breach to the seller within a reasonable time after the buyer discovers or should have discovered the breach will preclude the buyer from any remedies.

i) Conversion

The remedy for conversion is the fair market value of the goods at the time of the conversion.

2) Acceptance

Under the UCC, the buyer accepts goods by:

i) **Expressly stating** acceptance;

ii) **Using** the goods; or

iii) **Failing to reject** the goods.

UCC § 2-606.

The buyer can revoke acceptance (which amounts to rejection) if acceptance was with a reasonable expectation that the seller would cure and the seller did not cure or if the defect was hidden. The revocation must occur within a reasonable time after the nonconformity or defect was or should have been discovered, and notice must be given to the seller. UCC § 2-608.

A buyer's original refusal to accept may be withdrawn by a later acceptance if the seller indicates that he is holding the tender open. UCC § 2-601. However, if the buyer attempts to accept after his original rejection caused the seller to arrange for other disposition of the goods, then the buyer is liable for any ensuing damage. The buyer is liable even if the seller chooses to treat his action as acceptance rather than conversion. UCC § 2-601 cmt. 2.

Note that a buyer's attempts in good faith to dispose of defective goods when the seller fails to give instructions within a reasonable time are not to be regarded as an acceptance.

3) Right to cure

The seller has a right to cure a defective tender if:

i) The **time for performance** under the contract has not yet elapsed; or

ii) The seller had **reasonable grounds** to believe that the buyer would accept despite the nonconformity.

The seller must give notice of the intent to cure and make a new tender of conforming goods, which must be accepted by the buyer. Once cured, the tender is considered proper and valid. UCC § 2-508.

2. Seller's Remedies

a. Right to price upon acceptance

Under the UCC, the price is due after the goods are physically delivered to the buyer and the buyer has an opportunity to inspect, unless the contract provides otherwise. If the buyer refuses to pay the price, the seller may sue for the price set forth in the contract. If the contract omits a price term, then the UCC supplies a reasonable price at the time for delivery. If the contract provides that the parties will agree to a price in the future and they do not so agree, then the UCC would impose a reasonable price. UCC § 2-305.

b. Right to reclaim goods

1) Insolvent buyer

When an insolvent buyer receives goods on credit, and the seller learns that the buyer is insolvent, the seller may reclaim the goods, provided a demand is made **within 10 days** after the buyer's receipt of the goods. This 10-day limitation does not apply if the buyer has misrepresented solvency to the seller in writing within three months before delivery. Otherwise, the seller cannot base a right to reclaim goods on the buyer's fraudulent or innocent misrepresentation of solvency or of intent to pay. In addition, this right is subordinate to the rights of a buyer in the ordinary course or other good-faith purchaser, and, if exercised, precludes all other remedies with respect to the reclaimed goods. UCC § 2-702.

Pre-delivery insolvency: As a condition for the seller to reclaim goods from a buyer, the buyer must have received the goods on credit while insolvent. If the buyer becomes insolvent **after** delivery, then the seller may not reclaim the goods.

2) C.O.D. sale

In a C.O.D. (cash on delivery) sale, the seller can reclaim the goods if the buyer's check bounces. UCC §§ 2-511, 512.

c. Stoppage of goods in transit

1) Buyer's breach

A seller can stop the goods in transit because of the buyer's breach; goods can be stopped in transit only if shipped in large-sized (e.g., carload, truckload) lots. The seller cannot stop goods in transit once the:

    i)   Buyer has received the goods;

    ii) Carrier or warehouseman has acknowledged the buyer's rights;

    iii) Goods have been reshipped by the carrier; or

    iv) Title has been given or negotiated to the buyer.

UCC § 2-705(1),(2).

2) Buyer's insolvency

If the buyer becomes insolvent before the delivery of the goods, then the seller can stop goods in transit and refuse delivery except for cash. UCC § 2-705(1).

Compare buyer's breach: When a buyer is insolvent, the seller can stop goods in transit, regardless of the size of the shipment.

d. Wrongful rejection

If the buyer wrongfully rejects, then the seller has three alternative remedies and would also be entitled to incidental damages and lost profits. UCC § 2-703.

1) Collect damages

The seller would ordinarily be entitled to the contract price minus the market price at the time and place for tender, together with any incidental damages, less any expenses saved as a result of the buyer's breach. UCC § 2-708(1).

If that measure does not put the seller in as good a position as performance would have done, then the measure of damages will be the profit (including reasonable overhead) that the seller would have made from full performance by the buyer, together with any incidental damages, less any payments received or the proceeds of a resale of the goods. UCC § 2-708(2).

2) Resell the goods

If the seller elects to resell and sue for the contract price minus the resale price, then the resale must be (i) only of goods identified to the contract and (ii) commercially reasonable. UCC § 2-706.

3) Recover the price

The seller can recover the price after rejection only if the goods are not sellable in the seller's ordinary course of business. UCC § 2-709.

The price is the price as defined in the contract or, if no price is defined in the contract, a reasonable price. The seller can retain deposits paid by the buyer up to the amount stated in a liquidated-damages clause, or, in the absence of such a provision, 20% of the value of performance, or $500, whichever is less.

4) Incidental damages

Note that in **addition to** any of the remedies listed above, the seller is entitled to recover incidental damages (including storage and shipping costs). UCC § 2-710.

5) Lost profits

In some circumstances, a seller cannot be made whole through resale at the contract price. This is true for volume sellers (those sellers who have an unlimited supply of the goods and who make a profit per item). Although they can resell the goods at the same price as the contract price, they have lost the opportunity to sell them in the first instance when the seller breached or repudiated. They are, therefore, entitled to those lost profits. To qualify as a "lost volume" seller, the seller needs to show only that it could have supplied both the breaching purchaser and the resale purchaser with the goods. In general, the measure of lost profit would be the list price minus the cost to the dealer or manufacturer. UCC § 2-708(2).

Example: S, a high-volume maker of personal computers, contracts to sell 100 computers to B for $100,000 (their list price). B subsequently repudiates the contract, and S resells the computers to another customer. S can recover its lost profit (i.e., the list price of $100,000 minus its manufacturing cost), as well as any incidental damages from B.

3. Risk of Loss

a. General rules—non-identified goods, no breach

If goods that have not been identified are damaged or destroyed without the fault of either party to the contract, then the risk of loss is generally on the seller until the seller satisfies the contractual delivery obligations. Upon the happening of that event, the risk of loss shifts to the buyer. UCC § 2-509.

1) Goods to be shipped by a third-party carrier

If the contract requires or authorizes the seller to ship the goods by carrier, the event necessary to shift the risk of loss is dependent upon whether the contract is a "shipment" or "destination" contract.

a) Shipment contract

If the contract is a shipment contract, then risk of loss passes to the buyer when the seller gives possession of the goods to the carrier and makes a proper contract for their shipment.

b) Destination contract

If the contract is a destination contract, then risk of loss passes to the buyer when the seller tenders at the place specified in the contract.

Example: B orders a computer from S that is identical to a display model shown on the floor of S's store. The contract specifies that the computer is to be tendered by S at B's place of residence. In transit, the computer is destroyed by the shipping company through no fault of S. S is still required to perform the contract.

2) Goods held by a bailee

When goods that are held by a bailee are to be transferred without being moved, the risk of loss generally passes to the buyer on the buyer's receipt of a negotiable document of title covering the goods or on acknowledgment by the bailee of the buyer's right to possession of the goods.

3) All other cases

Unless the parties agree otherwise, in other cases (e.g., the buyer picks up the goods from the seller or the seller delivers the goods to the buyer), risk of loss passes to the buyer upon the taking of physical possession if the seller is a merchant; otherwise, risk passes on tender of delivery.

b. Identified goods, no breach

If the **contract deals with identified goods** (e.g., a specific painting or specifically identified items of inventory), then the seller is excused if the goods are totally destroyed without the seller's fault prior to the risk of loss being shifted to the buyer. Neither party is required to perform; neither party has breached. If the specifically identified goods are damaged, but not totally destroyed, then the contract is avoided unless the buyer chooses to take the goods at a reduced price without any other claim against the seller. UCC § 2-613.

c. Effect of breach of contract

1) Seller's Breach

If the seller delivers nonconforming goods, the risk of loss remains on the seller until the buyer accepts or there is a cure. If the buyer rightfully revokes acceptance, the risk of loss shifts back to the seller to the extent of any lack of insurance coverage by the buyer.

2) Buyer's Breach

If the **buyer repudiates or breaches** after the goods have been identified but before the risk of loss shifts, then the risk of loss is immediately shifted to the buyer to the extent of any lack of insurance coverage by the seller.

4. Insurable Interest in Goods

a. Seller's insurable interest

The seller of goods retains an insurable interest in the goods as long as the seller retains title to the goods or has a security interest in them. Unless the contract specifies otherwise, the title passes from the seller to the buyer when the seller completes his delivery obligations. At that point, the seller's insurable interest ceases unless the seller retains a security interest in the goods. When the seller alone identifies the goods, the seller may substitute other goods for those identified until default, insolvency, or notification to the buyer that the identification is final. UCC §§ 2-401; 2-501(2).

b. Buyer's insurable interest

The buyer of goods obtains an insurable interest in the goods as soon as the goods are identified to the contract. Identification can be made at any time by the parties' explicit agreement. In the absence of such an agreement, identification occurs when the contract is made if it is for the sale of goods already existing and identified; for future goods, identification occurs when the goods are shipped, marked, or otherwise designated by the seller as the goods to which the contract refers. UCC § 2-501(1).

5. Title and Good-Faith Purchasers

a. Entrusting provisions

The UCC provides that entrustment of goods by the owner to one who sells goods of that kind gives the transferee the power to convey good title to a buyer in the ordinary course. A "buyer in the ordinary course" is one who in good faith and without knowledge of a third party's ownership rights or security interest buys goods from someone selling goods of that kind. UCC § 2-403.

"Entrusting" includes any delivery and acquiescence in possession regardless of any condition expressed between the parties and regardless of whether the procurement of the entrusting or the possessor's disposition of the goods have been larcenous. UCC § 2-403(3).

b. Voidable title

When the true owner of goods sells them to another, but the sale is voidable because of fraud, because of lack of capacity, or because it was a cash sale and the buyer failed to pay or paid with a dishonored check, the buyer may transfer good title to a good-faith purchaser. UCC § 2-403.

6. Statute of Limitations on Breach of Sales Contract

a. Period of limitations

Under Article 2, an action for breach of any sales contract must be commenced within **four years** after the cause of action accrues.

b. When a cause of action accrues

In general, a cause of action accrues when the breach occurs, regardless of whether the aggrieved party knows of the breach. A breach of warranty accrues when delivery is made. If a warranty expressly extends to the future performance of the goods, the cause of action will accrue when the breach is or should have been discovered by the aggrieved party.

c. Modification of limitations period

By their original agreement, the parties may reduce the four-year limitations period of Article 2 to not less than one year, but they may not extend it.

Criminal Law

CRIMINAL LAW

Table of Contents

CRIMINAL LAW

I.   GENERAL PRINCIPLES

The elements of a criminal offense include the *mens rea*, or guilty mind; the *actus reus*, the bad or unlawful act; and causation. With the exception of strict liability crimes, which have no *mens rea*, every statute defining a substantive criminal offense proscribes a particular *mens rea* and *actus reus* that must be proved by the prosecution beyond a reasonable doubt in order for criminal liability to result.

A.   *ACTUS REUS*—ACTS AND OMISSIONS

Before there can be a crime, there must be a criminal act (*actus reus*). The criminal act must be a voluntary, affirmative act causing a criminally proscribed result. The act requirement may also be satisfied by an "omission" or failure to act under circumstances imposing a legal duty to act. A bad thought standing alone cannot result in criminal liability.

1.   Voluntary Act

The criminal act must be physical and voluntary. Actions during unconsciousness, sleep, or hypnosis are not voluntary. Other acts that are not considered voluntary are reflexive or convulsive acts, and conduct that is not the product of the actor's determination.

Example: Person A pushes Person B into a bystander, injuring the bystander. Person B cannot be held criminally liable.

If an epileptic knows of the possibility of a seizure and engages in the voluntary act of driving a car, has a seizure while driving, and causes a fatal accident, the epileptic is criminally responsible.

Example: An epileptic may still be criminally responsible if (i) he knows of the possibility of seizure; and (ii) the last act was voluntary.

The best example of when liability is not generally imposed is for acts committed while sleepwalking.

2.   Failure to Act When Duty Exists

A legal duty to act and the failure to do so results in criminal liability in these five instances:

i)   Imposed by statute (e.g., obligation to file tax return);

ii)   Contract (e.g., lifeguard saving drowning person);

iii)   Special relationship (e.g., parent's duty to her child, or duty to one's spouse);

iv)   Detrimental undertaking (e.g., leaving victim in worse condition after treatment); and

v)   Causation (e.g., failing to aid after causing victim's peril).

The defendant must have knowledge of the facts giving rise to the duty to act and fail to act. Additionally, it must be reasonably possible for the defendant to perform the duty.

Contrast absence of a duty: When there is not a duty to act, a defendant is not criminally liable by failing to help others in trouble. A mere bystander has no duty to act.

B. *MENS REA*—STATE OF MIND

Mens rea is the requirement of a guilty mind or legally proscribed mental state a defendant must possess in order to commit a crime. Except for strict liability crimes, a crime is committed when a criminal act (*actus reus*) is coupled with a guilty mind—both the mental and physical elements exist at the same time. Strict liability crimes have no *mens rea* requirement and only require an *actus reus*.

1. Specific Intent Crimes

Specific intent crimes require that the defendant possess **a subjective desire, specific objective, or knowledge to accomplish a prohibited result**. When dealing with specific intent crimes, it is necessary to identify specific intent for two reasons. First, the prosecution must prove the specific intent in order to prosecute the defendant; and second, certain defenses (e.g., voluntary intoxication and unreasonable mistake of fact) are applicable only to specific intent crimes.

The specific intent crimes include:

i) **F**irst-degree murder;

ii) **I**nchoate offenses (attempt, solicitation, conspiracy);

iii) **A**ssault with intent to commit a battery; and

iv) **T**heft offenses (larceny, larceny by trick, false pretenses, embezzlement, forgery, burglary, robbery).

EXAM NOTE: A simple way to remember the specific intent crimes is by using the mnemonic "FIAT." Whenever a fact pattern defines the crime as requiring "the intent to…," the crime is a specific intent crime.

2. Malice Crimes

The crimes of common law murder and arson require malice, **a reckless disregard of a high risk of harm**. Although these two crimes appear to have an "intent" requirement (e.g., intent to kill), malice only requires a criminal act without excuse, justification, or mitigation. Intent can be inferred from the accomplishment of the act.

3. General Intent Crimes

General intent crimes require only the **intent to perform an act** that is unlawful. Generally, acts done knowingly, recklessly, or negligently under the Model Penal Code are general intent crimes. Examples include battery, rape, kidnapping, and false imprisonment.

Motive is not the same as intent. The motive is the reason or explanation for the crime and is immaterial to the substantive criminal offense.

a. Transferred intent

When a defendant acts with an intent to cause harm to one person or object and that act directly results in harm to another person or object, the defendant can be liable for the harm caused under the doctrine of transferred intent.

> **Example:** D points a gun at A, intending to shoot and kill A, but accidentally shoots and kills B instead. D is guilty of two crimes: the murder of B under the doctrine of transferred intent, and the attempted murder of A.

Transferred intent, also known as the unintended victim rule, is usually confined to homicide, battery, and arson. Any defenses that the defendant could assert against the intended victim (e.g., self-defense) may also transfer to the unintended victim.

> The Model Penal Code, while not specifically recognizing the doctrine of transferred intent, does recognize liability when purposely or knowingly causing a particular result is an element of an offense. This element can be established even if the actual result is not within the purpose or contemplation of the defendant, so long as the result differs from the intended or contemplated result only insofar as (i) a different person or different property is harmed or (ii) the contemplated injury or harm would have been more serious or more extensive than the harm actually caused. MPC 203.2(2).

4. Minority View: Model Penal Code

A crime defined by statute generally states the requisite *mens rea*. The following levels of culpability are based on the Model Penal Code ("MPC"). The MPC is the minority view. The MBE tests the common law majority position unless otherwise expressly stated in the question. The MPC has no application to federal law. The following mental states are defined by the MPC:

a. Purposely

When a defendant acts "purposely," his conscious objective is to engage in the conduct or to cause a certain result. MPC 2.02(2)(a).

b. Knowingly or willfully

"Knowingly" or "willfully" requires that the defendant be **aware that his conduct is of the nature required by the crime** or that circumstances required by the crime exist. In other words, the defendant must be aware or know that **the result is practically certain to occur** based on his conduct. MPC 2.02(2)(b).

c. Recklessly

"Recklessly" requires the defendant **to act with a conscious disregard of a substantial and unjustifiable risk** that a material element of a crime exists or will result from his conduct. The risk must constitute a gross deviation from the standard of conduct of a law-abiding person. MPC 2.02(2)(c). Mere realization of the risk is not enough.

d. Negligently

A defendant acts "negligently" when that defendant **should be aware of a substantial and unjustifiable risk** that a material element of a crime exists or will result from his conduct. The risk must constitute a gross deviation from the standard of care of a reasonable person in the same situation. MPC 2.02(2)(d). Furthermore, similarly to tort law, violation of a statute or ordinance may be evidence of liability.

e. *Mens rea* not stated

If the requisite *mens rea* is not stated in a criminal statute, it is established if the defendant acted purposely, knowingly, or recklessly. MPC 2.02(3). If the *mens rea* does not state the culpable mind applicable to all material elements of the crime, then the *mens rea* applicable to one material element is applicable to all material elements, unless noted to the contrary in the statute.

5. Strict Liability Crimes

A strict liability crime does not require a *mens rea*. Examples of strict liability crimes include statutory rape, bigamy, regulatory offenses for public welfare, regulation of food, drugs, and firearms, and selling liquor to minors.

a. Public welfare offense

A public welfare offense is a strict liability crime for which no *mens rea* is required. Conduct that is subject to stringent public regulation includes that which could seriously threaten the public's health or safety or is inherently dangerous.

Examples: Typical examples include adulteration of food or drugs, regulation of waste disposal, and selling liquor to minors.

b. Degree of penalty

In general, when courts look to determine whether a crime is a public welfare offense, the degree of the penalty imposed by the statute can often be determinative if the statute is unclear. Thus, if the penalty imposed is severe (e.g., the crime is classified as a felony), a court looking at the issue may find an intent requirement in the statute and treat the offense as not a strict liability crime.

6. Vicarious Liability

Vicarious liability differs from strict liability in that strict liability crimes require a personal act on the part of the defendant (*actus reus*), but not mental fault (*mens rea*). Conversely, vicarious liability crimes do not require an *actus reus*, but they do retain a *mens rea* requirement. Many times, courts impose vicarious liability for strict liability crimes. However, there generally is no indication that the legislature intended for vicarious liability to apply in strict liability offenses. Further, imprisonment for a faultless crime may have constitutional due process implications. Thus, generally, vicarious liability crimes are limited to regulatory crimes and punishment is limited to fines.

When dealing with corporations, common law held that corporations had no criminal liability because a corporation could not form the necessary *mens rea*. Modern statutes, on the other hand, impose vicarious liability on corporations when the offensive act is performed by an agent of the corporation acting within the scope of his employment or when the act is performed by a high-ranking corporate agent who likely represents corporate policy. Under the MPC, a corporation may be held criminally liable if (i) the corporation fails to discharge a specific duty imposed by law, (ii) the board of directors or a high ranking agent of the corporation acting within the scope of his employment authorizes or recklessly tolerates the offensive act, or (iii) the legislative purpose statutorily imposes liability on a corporation for a specific act. The individual agent of the corporation who violated the statute may also be held criminally liable, and the corporation's conviction does not preclude conviction of the individual.

7. Causation

When intent is required, the criminal act must occur as a result of the intent. In other words, the defendant's act must cause the particular result made unlawful by statute.

8. Mistake as a Defense

a. Mistake of fact

1) Negation of intent

Mistake of fact may negate criminal intent but it must be an "honest mistake." The defense applies differently between specific and general intent crimes. Mistake of fact is never a defense to a strict liability crime because strict liability offenses do not have a *mens rea.*

2) Reasonableness of mistake

a) Specific intent crimes

A mistake of fact is a defense to a specific intent crime, even if the mistake is unreasonable.

> **Example:** An athlete takes an expensive gold watch from a table mistakenly thinking that it was her inexpensive black plastic sports watch. Even though the athlete's mistake of fact is unreasonable, the athlete lacks the intent to steal necessary to commit larceny, a specific intent crime.

b) General intent and malice crimes

A mistake of fact must be reasonable in order to be a defense to a general intent or malice crime.

3) MPC approach

Under the MPC, a mistake of fact that negates the required state of mind for a material element of a crime is a defense.

b. Mistake of law

Mistake or ignorance of the law generally is not a valid defense, except when:

i) There is reliance on the decision of a court, administrative order, or official interpretation of the law determined to be erroneous after the conduct;

ii) A statute defining a *malum prohibitum* crime (i.e., a crime for engaging in conduct not obviously wrong, such as a failure to obtain a license) was not reasonably made available prior to the conduct; or

iii) An honestly held mistake of law negates the required intent.

> **Example:** A forcibly takes money from B to settle a debt that B owed to A. A has the mistaken belief that the law allows for self-help in such situations. A's belief negates the specific intent required for the crime of robbery (i.e., the specific intent to gain control over the property of another person).

Incorrect or bad legal advice from an attorney is not a valid mistake-of-law defense.

C. JURISDICTION

Criminal jurisdiction addresses the authority of the federal and state governments to create criminal laws and the courts to enforce those laws. (Procedural rules that affect the conduct of a trial, such as the admissibility of a defendant's confession, are discussed in the Themis Criminal Procedure outline.)

1. Constitutional Limits on Authority

a. State authority

State authority to create crimes is based on the states' broad, inherent police power that is implicitly recognized by the Tenth Amendment.

b. Federal authority

Federal authority to create crimes is limited. There is no federal common law of crimes; all are statutory. Under the U.S. Constitution, Congress is granted power over only a handful of crimes, including treason and currency counterfeiting.

c. State and federal authority

Under the Constitution, neither federal nor state governments may criminalize conduct that has already occurred (i.e., an ex post facto law) or impose punishment without a trial (i.e., a bill of attainder). The Due Process Clauses of the Fifth and Fourteenth Amendments prevent both federal and state governments from imposing criminal liability without giving clear warnings as to the conduct prohibited. *Papachristou v. City of Jacksonville*, 405 U.S. 156, 162-63 (1972) (vagrancy ordinance struck down as "void for vagueness").

Additionally, many jurisdictions are in the process of eliminating multiple convictions against a defendant with more than one offense if those multiple offenses were all part of the same criminal transaction. Some states have statutorily prohibited such convictions, while other states apply the doctrine of merger or double jeopardy to eliminate the multiple convictions.

2. Territorial Considerations

a. Federal

Congress has the power to criminalize conduct occurring over federally owned or controlled territory (national parks or the District of Columbia), United States nationals abroad, and conduct on ships or airplanes.

b. State authority

A state has the authority to prosecute a person for a crime committed within the state and for a crime that is only partly committed within the state if an element of the crime is committed within the state. In addition, the following actions may also be prosecuted by the state:

i) Conduct outside the state that constitutes an attempt to commit a crime within the state;

ii) Conduct outside the state that constitutes a conspiracy to commit an offense within the state when an overt act in furtherance of the conspiracy occurs within the state;

iii) Conduct within the state to commit attempt, solicitation, or conspiracy of a crime in another jurisdiction when the state and the other jurisdiction recognize the crime; and

iv) The failure to perform outside the state a duty imposed by the state.

D. PARTIES TO A CRIME

Under the modern rule, in most jurisdictions the parties to a crime can be a principal, an accessory before the fact, and an accessory after the fact.

At common law, the principal was called the principal in the first degree and the accessory before the fact was called the principal in the second degree, if the accessory was actually or constructively present at the scene of the crime. An accomplice was simply called an accessory before the fact if he was not present at the crime scene.

1. Principal

A principal is the person whose **acts or omissions are the *actus reus*** of the crime, or, in other words, the perpetrator of the crime. The principal must be actually or constructively present at the scene of the crime. A principal is constructively present when some instrumentality he left or controlled resulted in the commission of the crime.

If two or more people are directly responsible for the *actus reus*, they are joint principals (i.e., co-principals).

2. Accomplice Liability

An accessory before the fact, principal in the second degree, or an accomplice is a person who, with intent that the crime be committed, aids or abets a principal prior to or during the commission of the crime and is present at the commission of the offense. Presence may be actual or constructive. For example, a getaway driver some distance from the scene is deemed constructively present.

a. Accessory before the fact

The difference between an accessory before the fact and a principal in the second degree is presence. The accomplice's assistance to the principal may be verbal encouragement, financial assistance, or physical assistance, provided that the accomplice has the requisite intent to encourage or assist in the commission of the crime. Mere knowledge that a crime will result is not enough.

b. Accomplice's criminal liability

An accomplice is responsible for the crime to the same extent as the principal. If the principal commits crimes other than the crimes for which the accomplice has provided encouragement or assistance, an accomplice is liable for the other crimes if the crimes are the natural and probable consequences of the accomplice's conduct.

Example: D encourages E to burn V's house and E does so. The fire spreads to W's house and it was foreseeable that it would do so. D is an accomplice to the burning of W's house.

An accomplice may be criminally liable even though the accomplice cannot be a principal.

Example: A woman who cannot commit rape as a principal can be liable for rape if she aids the male principal (e.g., restraining the victim) in his rape of the victim.

c. Withdrawal

To legally withdraw (and therefore avoid liability for the substantive crime), the accomplice must (i) repudiate prior aid, (ii) do all that is possible to countermand prior assistance, and (iii) do so before the chain of events is in motion and unstoppable.

A mere change of heart, flight from the crime scene, arrest by law enforcement, or an uncommunicated decision to withdraw is ineffective. Notification to the legal authorities must be timely and directed toward preventing others from committing the crime.

> **EXAM NOTE:** Be careful not to confuse these rules with the rules regarding withdrawal for inchoate offenses such as solicitation, attempt, and conspiracy. The rules are different.

d. Persons not accomplices

A person who is a member of the class protected by a statute cannot be an accomplice. Similarly, when the crime requires another party, the other party is not, simply by engaging in the criminal act, guilty of the crime as an accomplice. For example, the buyer of drugs is not guilty of the crime of distributing drugs simply by purchasing the drugs.

e. Effect of principal's status

At common law, the accomplice could only be convicted of a crime if the principal was also previously convicted of the crime. A small minority of jurisdictions still subscribes to this approach. By modern statute, however, in most jurisdictions, an accomplice may be convicted of a crime even if the principal is not tried, is not convicted, has been given immunity from prosecution, or is acquitted.

3. Accessory After the Fact

An accessory after the fact is a person who aids or assists a felon in avoiding apprehension or conviction after commission of the felony. An accessory after the fact must know that a felony was committed, act specifically to aid or assist the felon, and give the aid or assistance for the purpose of helping the felon avoid apprehension or conviction. An accessory after the fact is not subject to punishment for the crime committed by the felon, but instead has committed a *separate crime*, frequently labeled "obstruction of justice" or "harboring a fugitive."

a. Failure to report a crime

The mere failure to report a crime is not generally itself a crime. However, a person who gives false information to the police in order to prevent the apprehension of a felon can be an accessory after the fact.

b. Misprision

Misprision is a common law misdemeanor that amounts to a failure to report or prosecute a known felon.

The defendant must have (i) had full knowledge that the principal committed and completed the felony alleged, (ii) failed to notify the authorities, and (iii) taken an affirmative step to conceal the crime. *U.S. v. Ciambrone*, 750 F.2d 1416, 1417 (1986).

c. Compounding a crime

A person who receives valuable consideration for agreeing not to prosecute a crime may be guilty of compounding a crime.

E. RESPONSIBILITY

1. Insanity

Insanity encompasses mental abnormalities that may affect legal responsibility. It is a legal term rather than a psychiatric term. The four tests for insanity are the M'Naghten test, the Irresistible Impulse test, the Durham rule, and the Model Penal Code test. These expressly exclude the "sociopathic" or "psychopathic" criminals who have a tendency to commit antisocial and sometimes violent acts and are incapable of experiencing guilt. A defendant who puts his sanity in issue can be compelled to submit to psychiatric testing after being informed of his Fifth Amendment rights.

a. M'Naghten test

Under the M'Naghten test, the defendant is not guilty if, because of a defect of reason due to a mental disease, the defendant did not know either (i) the nature and quality of the act or (ii) the wrongfulness of the act.

Without knowing the act is wrong, a defendant could not have formed the requisite criminal intent. Therefore, it is important to assess whether the defendant's actions would have been criminal if the facts, as he believed them to be, supported his delusions. However, a defendant is not exculpated simply because he believes his acts to be morally right. Loss of control because of mental illness is not a defense under this test. This is the "right from wrong" test.

b. Irresistible impulse test

Under the "irresistible impulse" test, the defendant is not guilty if he lacked the capacity for self-control and free choice because mental disease or defect prevented him from being able to conform his conduct to the law. The loss of control need not be sudden. This is an impulse the defendant cannot resist.

c. Durham rule

Under the Durham rule, a defendant is not guilty if the unlawful act was the product of the defendant's mental disease or defect, and would not have been committed but for the disease or defect. This is the "but for" test.

d. Model Penal Code test

The Model Penal Code combines the M'Naghten and irresistible impulse tests. The defendant is not guilty if, at the time of the conduct, he, as a result of a mental disease or defect, did not have substantial capacity to appreciate the wrongfulness of the act, or to conform the conduct to the law.

e. Burden of proof

The defendant is presumed sane and has the initial burden of raising the issue of mental capacity and responsibility. The burden of production then shifts to the prosecution, which also has the burden of persuasion on the issue. Depending on the jurisdiction, the level of proof required of the prosecution on the issue can be by a preponderance of the evidence, clear and convincing evidence, or beyond a reasonable doubt.

2. Intoxication

Intoxication can be caused by any substance (e.g., alcohol, drugs, or prescription medicine). There are two types of intoxication defenses, voluntary and involuntary.

a. Voluntary intoxication

Voluntary intoxication is the intentional taking of a substance known to be intoxicating; actual intoxication need not be intended.

1) Specific intent crimes

Voluntary intoxication is a defense to specific intent crimes if it prevents the formation of the required intent. For example, intoxication may prevent the formation of the premeditation required for first-degree murder, but not second-degree murder.

2) When inapplicable

Voluntary intoxication is not a defense when the intent was formed before intoxication, or the defendant becomes intoxicated for the purpose of establishing the defense of voluntary intoxication. Voluntary intoxication is not a defense to crimes involving malice, recklessness, or negligence, or for strict liability crimes.

> **Note:** Although common law murder and arson sound like specific intent crimes as they require the "intent to kill" or the "intent to burn," they are malice crimes and the specific intent defenses (e.g., voluntary intoxication) do not apply.

b. Involuntary

Involuntary intoxication is a defense when the intoxication serves to negate an element of the crime, including general as well as specific intent and malice crimes. To be considered involuntary, the intoxicating substance must have been taken:

i) Without knowledge of the intoxicating nature of the substance, including substances taken pursuant to medical advice; or

ii) Under duress.

In addition, although intoxication and insanity are two separate defenses, excessive drinking and drug use may bring on actual insanity. Thus, involuntary intoxication can give rise to an insanity defense if the requirements for that defense are met.

3. Immaturity/Infancy

At common law, a child under the age of seven could not be convicted of a crime. A child at least seven years old but less than 14 years old was rebuttably presumed to be incapable of committing a crime. A child at least 14 years old could be charged with a crime as an adult.

Modern statutes have modified this and provide that no child can be convicted of a crime until a certain age is reached, usually between the ages of 11 and 14.

F. TYPES OF CRIMES

There are two basic types of crimes—felonies and misdemeanors. A felony is a crime that is punishable by death or imprisonment for more than one year; a misdemeanor is a crime punishable by imprisonment for one year or less or by a fine or by both.

II. HOMICIDE

A. DEFINITION

Homicide includes the offenses of murder and manslaughter. At common law, homicide was divided into three categories: (i) homicide justified by law, (ii) criminal homicide, and (iii) excusable homicide. Criminal homicides were divided into three offenses: murder, voluntary manslaughter, and involuntary manslaughter.

Murder was defined as the unlawful killing of another living human being with malice aforethought. In most modern statutory jurisdictions "malice aforethought," which is difficult to define or approximate, has been replaced by four main categories of murder: (i) intent to kill, (ii) intent to do serious bodily injury, (iii) depraved heart murder, and (iv) felony murder. Only the first category is an intentional killing. The remaining categories involve conduct that results in the death of another not accompanied by the intent to kill. Manslaughter includes two types: voluntary and involuntary. Voluntary manslaughter involves an intentional killing and involuntary manslaughter is an unintentional killing.

1. Killing a Person

In order for a homicide to occur, a living person must die. A body need not be found; death can be established by circumstantial evidence.

A person cannot be killed twice. Shooting a corpse is not homicide, but can be a crime (e.g., abuse of a corpse).

At common law, a fetus is not a living person.

2. Causation

To prove a homicide, the prosecution must show that the defendant caused the victim's death. The prosecution must prove both actual and proximate causation.

a. Actual cause

If the victim would not have died **but for** the defendant's act, then the defendant's act is the actual cause (i.e., cause-in-fact) of the killing. When the defendant sets in motion forces that led to the death of the victim, the defendant is the actual cause of the victim's death.

> **Example:** A mechanical device set up by the defendant kills an individual. The defendant is considered to have caused that individual's death.

1) Substantial factor

Actual causation can be found when there are multiple causes, (i.e., other persons are also responsible for the victim's death) and the defendant's act was a substantial factor in causing the death.

2) Independent cause

A defendant's act will not be deemed to be the cause when a victim is killed by an independent cause before the defendant's act can kill the victim. Simultaneous acts may be considered adequate causes of a single result. Additionally, a victim's pre-existing condition that predisposes him to death does not break the chain of causation.

> **Example:** A plans to kill B by stabbing him. A approaches B, finding him lying on the bed in a nonresponsive state. A assumes that B is asleep, and stabs him multiple times. However, in reality, B had died an hour ago due to a massive heart attack. A's actions did not cause B's death, therefore there is no homicide (but there may be attempted murder).

3) Mercy killing

Providing a person with the **means** by which that person can commit suicide generally does not make the provider guilty of murder as an accomplice, but instead guilty of a lesser crime, such as assisting a suicide. Note, however, that consent is not a defense to homicide, so a "mercy killing" (i.e., euthanasia) can be a criminal homicide, even if the person was willing to die due to a painful, terminal illness.

b. Proximate cause

Proximate cause (i.e., legal cause) exists only when the defendant is deemed to be legally responsible for a homicide. To be legally responsible for a homicide, the death must be foreseeable. A defendant's conduct is deemed to be foreseeable if death is the natural and probable result of the conduct. Actions by a third party (e.g., medical malpractice by the doctor treating the victim) as well as actions by the victim (e.g., suicide to escape the pain that resulted from the injuries inflicted by the defendant) are generally foreseeable. Actions by a force of nature that are not within the defendant's control (e.g., a victim who is tied to a tree by a defendant who is later killed by lightning striking the tree) are generally not foreseeable. An act that accelerates the death is a legal cause of that death.

> **EXAM NOTE:** Proximate cause is commonly tested in the context of the felony murder rule. A frequently applied standard is that the homicide must be a natural and probable consequence of the defendant's actions.

c. Year and one day rule

At common law, the defendant's act was conclusively presumed not to be the proximate cause of the killing if the victim died more than one year and one day after the act was performed. Most states have either abolished this rule or have extended the time period of responsibility.

B. TYPES OF HOMICIDE

1. Murder

Murder is the:

i)   Unlawful (i.e., without a legal excuse);

ii) Killing;

iii) Of a human being;

iv) Committed with **malice aforethought**.

"Malice aforethought" includes the following mental states: intent to kill, intent to inflict serious bodily injury, reckless indifference to an unjustifiably high risk to human life (depraved heart), or the intent to commit certain felonies (felony murder).

a. Intent to kill

Conduct, accompanied by the intent to kill, which is the legal cause of the death of a living person, constitutes intent-to-kill murder unless the legal circumstances surrounding the homicide are such that the crime is reduced to voluntary manslaughter. An inference of intent to kill may be made if an intentional use of a deadly weapon was used in the commission of the crime.

> **Example:** A intends to kill B, and by his conduct of shooting B, kills him.

b. Intent to inflict serious bodily harm

A person who intends to do serious bodily injury or "grievous bodily harm," but actually succeeds in killing, is guilty of murder despite the lack of intention to kill.

> **Example:** A intentionally hits B over the head with a baseball bat, intending to hurt B but not kill him, and B later dies from a skull fracture.

Intent to inflict serious bodily harm is an unintentional killing that results in death.

Intent to inflict serious bodily harm can be inferred from the use of a deadly weapon to inflict the bodily injury.

c. Depraved heart

A killing that results from reckless action by a defendant that manifests an extreme indifference to human life is a depraved heart murder.

> **Example:** A stands on top of a highway overpass and for a joke drops a bowling ball into on-coming traffic, resulting in the death of B, a passing motorist.

Depraved heart murder is an unintentional killing that results in death. There is a split among jurisdictions as to whether the requisite depravity exists when a defendant is unaware of the risk involved in the conduct, but even states that ordinarily follow a subjective standard allow a conviction if the reason the defendant failed to appreciate the risk was due to voluntary intoxication.

d. Felony murder

Felony murder is an unintended killing proximately caused by and during the commission or attempted commission of an inherently dangerous felony. The felonies traditionally considered inherently dangerous are: **B**urglary, **A**rson, **R**ape, **R**obbery, and **K**idnapping. [Mnemonic: **BARRK**]. (Common-law felonies also include murder, manslaughter, mayhem, and sodomy, but the BARRK crimes are most commonly tested in the context of felony murder.) To convict a defendant of felony murder, the prosecution must establish the underlying felony and that the defendant committed that felony. In addition, in most states, any aggravated felony committed with the use of a dangerous weapon is subject to the felony murder rule.

> **Examples:** X accidentally shoots the owner of a home while committing a burglary. X could be charged with felony murder.

There is no charge of attempted felony murder if the unintended victim does not die. Generally, co-felons (including accessories) are vicariously liable for the death if the death is a foreseeable consequence of the underlying inherently dangerous felony.

If one of two co-felons kills the other during the commission or attempted commission of a dangerous felony, this will also constitute felony murder. If the co-felon is killed by a victim or a police officer, though, the defendant is generally not guilty of felony murder.

> **Note:** The underlying felony will generally merge into the crime of felony murder. For example, a defendant who kills the proprietor of a store while committing a robbery can only be convicted of felony murder; the robbery conviction would merge into the felony murder conviction.

1) Defenses to felony murder

To successfully defend against a felony murder charge, the defendant must establish one of the following circumstances:

i) A valid defense to the underlying felony;

ii) The felony was not distinct from or independent of killing itself (e.g., aggravated battery);

iii) Death was not a foreseeable result or a natural and probable consequence of the felony (i.e., there was no proximate causation); or

iv) Death occurred after the commission of the felony and the ensuing flight from the scene of the crime.

2) Killing of felony victim or police

a) Death of bystander

When **a third party (e.g., a bystander)** is killed by a police officer or due to resistance by the victim of the felony, liability will depend on whether an agency theory or proximate cause theory is applied. Under an agency theory, the death of a bystander caused by a felony victim or police officer does not fall within the rule because neither is an agent of the perpetrator of the felony. Under the proximate cause theory, the bystander's death may fall within the rule because the death is a direct consequence of the felony.

> **EXAM NOTE:** Proximate cause theory is the majority position and should be applied on the MBE unless the question specifically indicates that the jurisdiction is an agency theory jurisdiction.

b) Death of co-felon

When a co-felon is killed by a victim or a police officer either in self-defense or to prevent escape, under the *Redline* doctrine (*Commonwealth v. Redline*, 391 Pa. 486 (1958)), the defendant is generally not guilty of felony murder. The killing by the victim or the police officer is considered justifiable homicide.

2. Statutory Crimes of Murder

At common law, there were no degrees of murder. Under modern statutory rules, murder is generally divided into two degrees: first-degree and second-degree murder.

> **EXAM NOTE:** Because degrees of murder do not exist at common law, the fact pattern on the MBE must supply a statute if you are to consider degrees of murder.

a. First-degree murder

First-degree murder is generally defined as a deliberate and premeditated murder. In addition, felony murder is frequently classified as first-degree murder.

1) Created by statute

Because the specific criteria for first-degree murder are established only by statute, a homicide cannot be first-degree murder without a corresponding statute.

2) Premeditation

The distinguishing element of first-degree murder is premeditation, meaning the defendant reflected on the idea of killing or planned the killing. The amount of time needed for premeditation may be brief. It must be long enough after forming the intent to kill for the defendant to have been fully conscious of the intent and to have considered the killing (i.e., a time for reflection). This requirement does not apply to felony murder.

3) During the commission of an inherently dangerous felony

If a murder is committed during the perpetration of an enumerated felony, it may be first-degree murder. The most commonly enumerated felonies are **B**urglary, **A**rson, **R**ape, **R**obbery, and **K**idnapping. [Mnemonic: **BARRK**].

NOTE: A homicide committed during the commission of an inherently dangerous felony may be treated as first or second-degree murder depending upon the jurisdiction.

4) Heinous murder

A murder resulting from an egregious act, such as ambush (i.e., lying in wait), torture, bombing, terrorism, or poisoning, may be classified as first-degree murder.

b. Second-degree murder

Second-degree murder is a homicide committed with the necessary malicious intent: the intent to kill, the intent to do great bodily injury, or a depraved-heart murder. In addition, a murder that occurs during the commission of a felony other than the felonies that trigger first-degree murder may statutorily be treated as second-degree murder.

EXAM NOTE: Be sure to differentiate between second-degree murder and first-degree murder when answering exam questions. First-degree murder is a specific intent crime, whereas second-degree murder, like common law murder, is a malice crime.

3. Voluntary Manslaughter

Voluntary manslaughter is murder committed in response to adequate provocation (i.e., in the "heat of passion").

a. "Heat of passion"

The defendant acts in the heat of passion if she was provoked by a situation that would inflame the passion of a reasonable person to the extent that it would cause that person to momentarily act out of passion rather than reason. The defendant cannot have been set off by something that would not bother most people.

> **EXAM NOTE:** Remember that "heat of passion" is NOT a defense; it merely reduces murder to voluntary manslaughter.

1) Sufficient provocation

A serious battery, a threat of deadly force, or discovery of adultery by a spouse constitutes sufficient provocation. Usually words, such as taunts, do not.

2) "Cooling off"

If there was sufficient time between the provocation and the killing for a reasonable person to cool off, murder is not mitigated to manslaughter. If there was sufficient time to cool off for a reasonable person but the defendant himself did not regain self-control, the murder is not mitigated to manslaughter.

Second provocation: Even when the defendant has "cooled off," a second encounter with the victim may give rise to another situation in which the defendant acts in the "heat of passion."

b. Causation

There must be a causal connection between provocation, passion, and the fatal act. There will be no mitigation if the intent to kill was formed prior to the provocation.

c. Imperfect defense

Murder may be reduced to voluntary manslaughter even if the defendant started the altercation or the defendant unreasonably but truly believed in the necessity of using deadly force.

While an intentional killing committed when resisting arrest is generally murder, an intentional killing can be manslaughter if the arrest is unlawful and the defendant acts in the "heat of passion."

d. Transferred provocation

When, due to a reasonable mistake of fact, the defendant is in error in identifying her provoker or accidentally kills the wrong person, she will be guilty of voluntary manslaughter if that would have been her crime if she had killed the provoker. If, however, the defendant, in her passion, intentionally kills another person known to her to be an innocent bystander, there will be no mitigation and murder, rather than voluntary manslaughter, will apply.

4. **Involuntary Manslaughter**

Involuntary manslaughter is an unintentional homicide committed with criminal negligence or during an unlawful act.

a. **Criminal negligence**

Criminal negligence is reckless action (or inaction when there is a duty to act) that puts another person at a significant risk of injury or death. It requires more than ordinary negligence for tort liability and something less than extremely negligent conduct required for depraved heart murder. For example, the failure of a parent, under a duty of care, to provide medical care to a sick minor child constitutes criminal negligence.

b. **Unlawful act**

The unlawful act may occur in one of two ways:

i) Under the misdemeanor-manslaughter rule, which is a killing committed in the commission of a *malum in se* (wrong in itself) misdemeanor; or

ii) A killing committed in the commission of a felony that is not statutorily treated as first-degree felony murder or second-degree murder.

The term "*malum in se*" means "wrong in itself," or "inherently evil," and includes crimes such as assault and battery. "*Malum prohibitum*" refers to wrongs that are merely prohibited, (i.e., not inherently immoral or hurtful, but wrong due to a statute), such as a parking violation, smuggling, or failure to obtain a license. A homicide resulting from a wrong that is *malum prohibitum* will constitute involuntary manslaughter only if the unlawful act was willful or constituted criminal negligence.

c. **Causation**

There must be a causal connection between the unlawful act and the death for involuntary manslaughter to apply.

III. OTHER CRIMES

A. CRIMES AGAINST PROPERTY

1. **Larceny**

Larceny is the:

i) Trespassory;

ii) Taking and;

iii) Carrying away;

iv) Of the personal property;

v) Of another;

vi) With the intent to permanently deprive that person of the property (i.e., intent to steal).

a. Trespass

The property must be taken without the owner's consent. If the original taking was without consent, yet was not unlawful because there was no intent to steal at the time of the taking, larceny may be committed at a later time if the intent to steal is later formed. Under the "continuing trespass" rule, the original trespass is deemed to be "continuing" in order for the criminal act to coincide with the criminal intent. The defendant's original taking must have been wrongful (e.g., a taking based on knowledge that the property belonged to another, such as a taking with the intent to borrow and return the property).

b. Taking

The taking (also known as caption) requirement is satisfied by any trespassory removal of the property from the owner's possession into another's control.

1) Destruction of property in owner's possession

The destruction of property while it is in the owner's possession (e.g., breaking an object held by the owner) is not a taking.

2) Use of agent

If the defendant uses an agent, even one unaware of the defendant's criminal intent, a taking occurs.

c. Carrying away (asportation)

The carrying away requirement (also known as asportation) is satisfied by even a slight movement of the property (e.g., inches).

d. Personal property

The property taken must be personal, not real property. Electricity or gas supplied by a utility constitutes personal property.

1) Intangibles

Documents that represent the rights to property (e.g., stocks, bonds) are treated as personal property.

2) Services

Modern theft statutes usually criminalize obtaining services without paying for them (i.e., the theft of services).

> **EXAM NOTE:** Services taken without paying for the services (e.g., a massage) do not constitute personal property for purposes of the MBE.

3) Real property items

The taking of fixtures (i.e., items affixed to real property) or real property items (e.g., trees, unharvested crops) is not larceny when the defendant's act of severance occurs immediately before the carrying away of the fixture or other real property items. However, when the real property items have previously been severed from the land by the owner, they become personal property (e.g., picked apples), and the carrying away of such items can be larceny.

e. Another's property

The property must be in the possession of someone other than the defendant.

> **Contrast with embezzlement:** For embezzlement, the defendant is legally entrusted with the property by the owner and then the defendant later fraudulently converts the property to his own use. With larceny, the initial taking must be trespassory; there cannot be lawful entrustment by the owner. This is the main difference between the two crimes.

1) Owner of property

The owner of property (i.e., a person who has title to it) can commit larceny when someone other than the owner (e.g., lessee) is entitled to current possession of the property.

2) Thief

Larceny may even be committed against a thief. Stolen property taken from a thief can constitute larceny unless the taker has a superior possessory interest in the property (e.g., an owner or a lessee of the property).

3) Joint owners

A joint owner of property who takes possession of the property from a co-owner is not guilty of larceny because the taker has an equal right to possess the property.

4) Constructive possession

"Constructive possession" means legal possession when factual possession does not exist.

> An owner has constructive possession of property when actual possession, but not title, is taken from her by fraud. The crime is called "larceny by trick." *See* § III.A.2, *infra*.

a) Employee's control over employer's property

Low-level employees can only be guilty of larceny whereas high-level employees are typically guilty of embezzlement. An employer generally has constructive possession of property in the hands of a lower-level employee. Such an employee has custody, not possession, of the employer's property. A higher-level employee (e.g., company president) who has greater authority with respect to the employer's property may have possession of, rather than custody of, such property and may be guilty of embezzlement, rather than larceny, for taking the property.

b) Bailee possession

A bailee is guilty of larceny if, with intent to steal, the bailee opens and takes property from closed containers belonging to the bailor. Otherwise, the bailee simply has possession.

5) Abandoned vs. lost property

Property that has been abandoned by its owner (i.e., the owner has surrendered all rights to the property) is not subject to larceny. Property that has been lost by its owner can be the subject of larceny if, at the time of the finding, the finder knows the owner or believes that he can locate the owner and the finder possesses the necessary intent to permanently deprive the owner of the property.

6) Mistakenly delivered property

Property that has been mistakenly delivered may be the subject of larceny if the recipient of the property realizes that a mistake has been made at the time of the receipt of the property and the recipient possesses the necessary intent to permanently deprive.

a) Special problems

When a defendant takes legitimate possession of an item, but he discovers another item enclosed in the larger item (the container), the issue arises as to whether the defendant had possession of the enclosed item at the time the defendant legitimately possessed the larger item. If so, there is no larceny because the defendant has not taken the property from another's possession. However, determining whether or not there is possession is a difficult task. Larceny may depend on whether or not the parties intended to transfer the container. If the intent is to transfer, then no larceny is committed because the defendant effectively takes immediate possession of both items. A few states hold that the defendant does not take possession of the enclosed property until he discovers it. At which point, if he forms the intent to keep the property, then he is guilty of larceny.

f. Intent to permanently deprive

Larceny is a **specific intent** crime. At the time of the taking, the intent to permanently deprive the owner of the property must be present. There is no defense of restoration if the defendant later has a change of heart and restores the property to the rightful owner. The crime is complete at the time of the taking.

Examples: The intent to permanently deprive the owner of the property can occur when the defendant takes property with the intent to claim a reward, the defendant intends to throw away or abandon the property, the defendant intends to sell the property back to the owner, or the defendant intends to pledge or pawn the property without being able to redeem it.

1) Insufficient intent

The necessary specific intent does not exist when the defendant's intent is to:

i) Borrow property with the ability to return it;

ii) Pay for merchandise that she has the means to buy; or

iii) Take money as repayment of a debt.

a) Intent to borrow

If the defendant intends only to borrow the property with the ability to do so, then larceny does not occur because there is no intent to permanently deprive the owner of the property, (e.g., borrowing a car to run an errand).

If property is taken with the intent to return the property and is accidently damaged or destroyed, larceny has not occurred.

> **Example:** D takes A's car to run an errand. On the way back to A's house, D is in a car accident and A's car is totaled. D will be found not guilty of larceny.

b) Intent to pay

A defendant's intent to pay for property is not sufficient to prevent larceny when the property is not offered for sale.

c) Repayment of debt

If a defendant takes property with the honest belief that she is entitled to the property as repayment of a debt then larceny does not occur.

d) Rewards

A defendant intending to return property in expectation of claiming a reward has not committed larceny, unless his intent is to return the property only upon receiving the reward.

2) Sufficient intent

There is sufficient intent if the defendant intends to create a substantial risk of loss or if the defendant intends to sell the goods back to the owner.

3) Time for measuring intent

The intent to permanently deprive is generally measured at the time of the taking. The continuing trespass rule may apply to stretch the time at which intent is measured. *See* § III.A.1.a, *supra*.

2. Larceny by Trick

One who obtains possession of but not title to property owned by another through fraud or deceit, with the intent to unlawfully convert and later does so, is guilty of larceny by trick. Larceny by trick occurs when the defendant fraudulently induces the victim to deliver possession of the property to the defendant.

a. False representation of material present or past fact

The representation (whether oral, written, or by actions) must be false in fact and be of a material past or present fact. A prediction about a future event, a false promise, or an opinion such as sales talk or puffing is not sufficient.

b. Reliance by the victim

The victim must rely upon the false representation, and that reliance must cause the victim to give possession to the defendant. This standard is subjective, not objective.

Contrast with false pretenses: Under larceny by trick, the defendant obtains possession. Under larceny by false pretenses, the defendant obtains title. *See* § III.A.5, *infra.*

3. Forgery

Forgery is the:

i) Fraudulent;

ii) Making;

iii) Of a false writing;

iv) With apparent legal significance; and

v) With the intent to defraud (i.e. make wrongful use of the forged document).

a. Fraudulent

The defendant must intend to make a wrongful use of the writing, (e.g., cashing a check with a forged drawer's signature). There must be intent to defraud, even if no one actually is defrauded.

b. Making

Making includes creating, altering, or fraudulently inducing another to sign a document when that person is unaware of the significance of the document. The defendant need not use the document; the crime is complete upon the "making" of the document. When property is acquired by use of the forged document, the defendant may also be guilty of another crime, such as false pretenses (*see* § III.A.5, *infra*).

c. False writing

The writing itself must be false, instead of merely including false information in an otherwise genuine document. (Note: Signing another person's name on a check or other commercial paper makes the check itself false.) When there is an alteration, the alteration must be material.

d. Apparent legal significance

A document has legal significance if it has value beyond its own existence. A contract, deed, will, or check has value beyond the document itself; a painting does not.

4. Embezzlement

Embezzlement is the:

i) Fraudulent;

ii) Conversion;

iii) Of the property;

iv) Of another;

v) By a person who is in lawful possession of the property.

a. Conversion

Conversion is a serious interference with the owner's rights to the property by inappropriately using property held pursuant to a trust agreement either by selling it, damaging it, or unreasonably withholding possession. The defendant need not personally benefit from the conversion. No movement or carrying away of the property is required. If it is unclear whether there was a conversion of the property, the victim must demand a return of the property and the embezzler must refuse to return the property before a claim for embezzlement can be made.

b. Intent to defraud

The defendant must intend to defraud the owner of the property. If the defendant intends to return the exact property that is converted and has the ability to do so at the time that the intent is formed, the defendant lacks the intent to defraud the property owner. If the defendant intends to return similar property or the cash equivalent of the value of the property, the defendant has the intent necessary to commit embezzlement. A conversion pursuant to a claim of right also is not embezzlement.

c. Type of property

Property that is subject to larceny is also subject to embezzlement. In some states, real property, as well as personal property, may be embezzled.

d. Another's property

The property embezzled must belong to another. The inability to fulfill a contractual obligation (e.g., pay back a loan) is not embezzlement.

e. Lawful possession

The embezzler must be in lawful possession of the property at the time that the intent to defraud occurs, although some states limit embezzlement to property entrusted to the embezzler.

5. False Pretenses

The crime of false pretenses is a false representation of a past or present material fact made by the defendant with the intent to cause the victim to pass title to the defendant and title is passed. False pretenses requires:

i) Obtaining title to the property;

ii) Of another person;

iii) Through the reliance of that person;

iv) On a known false representation of a material past or present fact; and

v) The representation is made with the intent to defraud.

a. Title must pass

Title to the property must pass from the victim to the defendant. Title can be obtained without possession of the property, but mere possession does not constitute false pretenses.

Contrast larceny by trick: Mere possession of the property without legal title by a defendant can be sufficient for larceny by trick.

b. Type of property

Generally, property that may be subject to larceny is also subject to false pretenses.

c. False factual representation

The representation must be false and must be of a material past or present fact. A prediction about a future event, a false promise, or an opinion, such as sales talk or puffing, is not sufficient. The representation may be made orally, in writing, or by actions (e.g., resetting a car's odometer). Silence does not constitute a representation, even when the defendant is aware of the owner's misunderstanding, unless the defendant caused the misunderstanding.

d. Reliance by the victim

The victim must rely upon the false representation, and that reliance must cause the victim to pass title to the defendant. This standard is subjective, not objective.

e. Intent to defraud

The defendant must know that the representation is false and specifically intend to defraud. Most courts find that a defendant acts knowingly and has knowledge of a particular fact when he is aware of a high probability of the fact's existence and deliberately avoids learning the truth. A few states require actual knowledge of a particular fact.

A defendant has the intent to defraud required to establish false pretenses when she intends that the person to whom the false representation is made will rely upon it.

6. Robbery

Robbery is:

i) Larceny;

ii) By force or intimidation;

iii) Where the taking of the property is from the person or presence of the victim.

a. Elements of larceny

All of the elements of larceny are necessary for robbery. Larceny is the (i) trespassory, (ii) taking and carrying away, (iii) of the personal property of another, (iv) with the intent to steal.

b. From the person or presence

The property taken must be on the victim's person or within the victim's reach or control (from the presence of the victim). For example, if a victim is restrained by the defendant within the victim's home prior to the seizure of the property, items taken from the entire house can be treated as "from the victim's presence."

c. By force or intimidation

The taking of the property must be accomplished by force or intimidation.

1) Force

The force used by the defendant must be more than the amount necessary to effectuate taking and carrying away the property. When a pickpocket takes the victim's property without the victim's knowledge, the taking does not constitute robbery unless the victim notices the taking and resists.

> **EXAM NOTE:** The MBE often tests the degree of force necessary for robbery. Remember that slight force is sufficient, but the force must be manifested immediately before or at the same time as the taking.

2) Intimidation

The threat must be of immediate serious physical injury to the victim, a close family member, or other person present. A threat to damage or destroy property, other than the victim's home, is not sufficient.

d. Merger

Larceny, assault, and battery all merge into robbery.

> **EXAM NOTE:** Merger of these crimes is often tested on the MBE by asking, "which is the highest crime D can be convicted of?"

7. Extortion

a. Common law

At common law, extortion was the unlawful taking of money by a government officer.

b. Modern approach

Most jurisdictions have enacted statutes that more broadly define extortion as the taking of money or property from another by threat. In most jurisdictions, it is the making of threats (rather than obtaining the property) that is the essence of the crime. In a minority of jurisdictions, however, the accused must actually obtain the property to be guilty.

Extortion differs from robbery in two respects:

i) The threats need not be of immediate harm, nor need they be of a physical nature (e.g., threatening to expose the victim's marital infidelity in the future is sufficient); and

ii) The property intended to be taken need not be on the victim or in his presence.

8. Burglary

Common law burglary is the:

i) Breaking and;

ii) Entering;

iii) Of the dwelling;

iv) Of another;

v) At nighttime;

vi) With the specific intent to commit a felony therein.

a. Breaking

Breaking is accomplished by using force to create an opening into a dwelling, such as by shattering a window or kicking in a door. The force used may be slight, such as opening an unlocked door or window.

Note: It is not a breaking to enter a dwelling through an open door or window, unless the opening must be enlarged in order to allow the entry.

1) Breaking without use of force

If entry is obtained by fraud or threat, there is a breaking. If the defendant had consent by the owner to enter, no breaking occurs unless the consent was obtained by fraud or the defendant exceeded the scope of such consent.

2) Breaking within dwelling

If entry is gained with consent, a breaking can still occur if the defendant breaks into a part of the dwelling structure, such as by opening a closet door or wall safe. The mere opening of an object within the dwelling, such as a desk drawer, trunk, or box, does not constitute a breaking.

3) Use of force to exit—No breaking

The use of force to exit a dwelling does not constitute a breaking.

Most states now require only that the defendant enter the premises; a breaking is not required. The common law requires a breaking.

b. Entering

Entering occurs when any portion of the defendant's body (e.g., a hand through a broken windowpane) or an instrument used by the defendant to gain entry (e.g., rock thrown through a window), crosses into the dwelling without permission through the opening created by the breaking.

Breaking and entering need not happen at the same time.

c. Dwelling of another

A dwelling is a structure regularly occupied for habitation. It need not be occupied at the time of the breaking, but must not be abandoned.

> All states have statutes that expand the type of structure to include non-dwellings, such as businesses, buildings, or cars, and surrounding areas, such as the yard.

The dwelling must be that of another person. A person cannot burglarize his own dwelling, unless a possessory interest has been transferred to another (e.g., a tenant).

d. Nighttime

Nighttime occurs during the period of darkness between sunset and sunrise. It is not considered nighttime if there is sufficient natural daylight to see the burglar's face.

> The common law required that the breaking and entering had to occur during nighttime. No states require that all forms of burglary be committed at night, although more severe penalties may be imposed on nighttime burglaries.

e. Specific intent to commit a felony

At the time of the breaking and entering, the defendant must have the intent to commit a felony (e.g., larceny, robbery, rape, murder) inside the dwelling.

A defendant who fails to commit the underlying felony may nevertheless be guilty of burglary as well as attempt to commit the underlying felony. If the underlying felony is completed, it does **not** merge with the burglary.

Many states have broadened the scope of the crimes intended to be committed to include misdemeanor thefts.

9. Arson

Arson is the:

i) Malicious;

ii) Burning;

iii) Of the dwelling;

iv) Of another.

a. Malice

Malice does not require ill will. The defendant is not required to intend to burn the dwelling of another; it is sufficient that the defendant performs an act with reckless disregard that creates a substantial risk of such burning.

b. Burning

The damage to the dwelling must be caused by fire. Smoke damage alone is insufficient. In addition, the damage must affect the structure of the building; mere scorching (i.e., discoloration due to heat) of the walls and burning of the contents of the dwelling are insufficient. When the dwelling is constructed of wood, there must be at least a charring of the wood (i.e., damage to the wood itself).

c. Another's dwelling

Ownership is not required. The test is whether a person has the right to possession or occupancy of the dwelling. Many states have expanded arson to include the burning of one's own dwelling. At common law, however, the burning of one's dwelling (house burning) that was located near other houses or in a city was only a misdemeanor, and burning one's own building for insurance fraud was not considered arson.

> Most states have expanded arson to include the burning of buildings other than dwellings, but burning the contents of a building alone does not constitute arson.

> **EXAM NOTE:** The MBE has not always been consistent with regard to the definition of arson in its questions. Some questions in the past have included the burning of non-dwellings or of the defendant's own dwelling as arson, without indicating a statutory definition. If a situation looks like "arson" from a common-sense point of view, it generally will be considered arson on the MBE.

10. Possession Offenses

Possession of a prohibited object (e.g., drug paraphernalia, burglar's tools) or a substance (e.g., illegal narcotics) is unlawful if the defendant exercises control over such object or substance. The defendant is not required to be aware that possession of the object is illegal. Dominion and control must exist for a period long enough to have provided the defendant with an opportunity to cease such dominion and control.

11. Receiving Stolen Goods

Receiving stolen property is a statutory crime that requires:

i)   Receiving control of stolen property;

ii) Knowledge that the property is stolen; and

iii) Intent to permanently deprive the owner.

Knowledge that the property is stolen must coincide with the act of receiving the property. Only control, not possession, is necessary. The goods must have actually been stolen at the time they are received and the defendant must believe that they have been stolen.

> **Example:** If police recover stolen property from a thief and use the property with the owner's permission, it is not considered stolen; the defendant can only be convicted of attempt, not of receipt of stolen property.

12. Legislative Changes to Theft Crimes

There are several changes made to the common law property offenses under the MPC and through states' criminal codes. Larceny, false pretenses, embezzlement, and receipt of stolen goods are treated as a single statutory crime of theft. The definition of property has been expanded to cover intangibles, services, and documents. In addition, the defendant need only have unauthorized control over the property.

B. CRIMES AGAINST THE PERSON

1. Battery

Battery is the:

    i) Unlawful;

    ii) Application of force;

    iii) To another person;

    iv) That causes bodily harm to that person; or

    v) Constitutes an offensive touching.

a. Unlawful

"Unlawful" means that the force is applied without legal excuse. Excessive use of force by a police officer during an arrest is unlawful.

b. Application of force

The touching, however slight, must result in bodily harm (e.g., a bruise) or an offensive touching (e.g., an unwanted kiss). The force can be applied by a third party acting under the defendant's direction or by an object controlled by the defendant (e.g., a brick thrown by the defendant).

c. To the person of another

The application of force to an object near, carried by, or attached to the victim constitutes a battery if the victim suffers bodily harm or an offensive touching.

Example: A battery occurs if a defendant kicks a cane used by a victim for support causing the victim to fall and injure herself.

d. Requisite intent

Battery is a general intent crime that includes not only intentional conduct but also criminal negligence (i.e., conduct that carries a high degree of risk to others).

e. Consent defense

Although consent is generally not a defense to a crime, consent may be a defense to a battery. Consent may be explicit (e.g., a signed authorization for surgery) or implicit (e.g., participation in an athletic event).

f. Aggravated battery

Battery may carry a greater penalty, by statute, when serious bodily injury is inflicted or bodily injury is caused by the use of a deadly weapon.

2. Assault

Assault is:

i)   An attempt to commit a battery; or

ii) Intentionally placing another in apprehension of imminent bodily harm.

Assault requires an absence of contact with the victim. The attempted-battery assault is a specific intent crime. The fear-of-harm assault is a general intent crime.

> ***Battery Distinguished:*** The defendant **must** actually touch the victim or something attached to his person in order for a battery to occur. An assault can occur even if the defendant does not touch the victim.

a. Attempted battery

The defendant must take a substantial step toward the commission of a battery. Like all attempt crimes, the defendant must have the specific intent to commit a battery.

b. Fear of harm

The "fear of harm" type of assault (also called "apprehension assault") is a general intent crime—the defendant must intend to cause bodily harm or apprehension of such harm. The victim's apprehension must be reasonable. Unlike attempted battery, because actual apprehension is necessary, the victim's lack of awareness of the threat of harm is a defense to this type of assault.

c. Consent defense

As is the case with battery, consent may be a defense to assault.

d. Aggravated assault

Assault may carry a greater penalty, by statute, when a deadly weapon is used.

3. Mayhem

Mayhem is a common-law battery that causes the dismemberment or permanent disfigurement of a person. It is the equivalent of modern statutory aggravated battery.

4. Kidnapping

Kidnapping is the:

i)   Unlawful;

ii)   Confinement of a person;

iii) Against that person's will;

iv)   Coupled with either:

    a) The movement; or

    b) Hiding of that person.

Note: There is no requirement for a ransom demand in order to establish kidnapping.

a. Unlawful

The unlawful requirement excludes legally sanctioned actions, such as the imprisonment of a felon by the state after his conviction.

b. Confinement

The victim's freedom of movement must be significantly restricted. It is not enough that the victim is prevented from taking a path or entering an area; the victim must be prevented from leaving an area or compelled to go to a place the victim does not want to go.

c. Against the victim's will

The confinement must be accomplished by force, threats, or fraud.

Consent of the victim to the confinement is a defense if given by a person with the capacity to consent. A child cannot consent to be taken out of the control of a parent or guardian.

d. Movement

The victim need only be moved a short distance (e.g., forced from driver's seat into the trunk of car). If the kidnapping occurs incident to another crime (e.g., robbery), the movement must be more than is necessary for the commission of that crime in order for a defendant to be liable for both kidnapping and the separate offense.

e. Hidden location

Instead of movement, the victim may be concealed for a substantial period of time at a hidden location.

f. Enhanced punishment

A kidnapping that results in bodily injury, interferes with a governmental function, or is done for the purpose of collecting a ransom may be subject to enhanced punishment, by statute.

5. False Imprisonment

False imprisonment is the:

i) Unlawful;

ii) Confinement of a person;

iii) Without consent.

a. Unlawful

The confinement is unlawful unless is it consented to or specifically authorized by law.

b. Confinement

Confinement may be effected by forcing a person to go where he does not want to, or preventing him from going where he does want so long as no alternative routes are available to him. This may be done by actual force, threat of force, or a show of force.

c. Consent

To be effective, consent must be given freely, and the one consenting must have the capacity to do so.

C. RAPE AND OTHER SEX CRIMES

1. Rape

Rape is:

i)   Unlawful;

ii) Sexual intercourse;

iii) With a female;

iv) Against her will by force or threat of immediate force.

Most modern statutes have removed the force requirement.

a. Unlawful—exclusion of husband

At common law, a husband could not rape his wife. Most states have either abolished this restriction or removed the immunity if the husband and wife have separated or filed for divorce.

b. Sexual intercourse

Actual penetration, however slight, is required; emission is not.

c. With a female

Traditionally, the victim of rape could only be a woman. Most states recognize homosexual rape as a crime labeled "sexual assault" rather than rape. Some states have defined rape in a gender-neutral manner; under such statutes, a woman could be the perpetrator of a rape.

d. Without consent

When a woman consents to sexual intercourse, rape has not occurred. Consent does not exist if intercourse is procured by force or threat of harm, or when the female is unable to consent due to a drug-induced stupor or unconsciousness.

1) Threat of harm

Consent is ineffective if a woman consents to sexual intercourse due to threat of harm, although the harm threatened must be imminent and must involve bodily harm. Economic duress is not sufficient.

2) Fraud

Fraud rarely negates consent. Consent obtained by fraud regarding the nature of the act itself—fraud in factum (e.g., the defendant convinces victim the act is not intercourse but part of a medical exam)—is not a valid defense. Consent obtained by fraud in inducement (e.g., a promise of marriage in exchange for sex) is a valid defense.

3) Resistance of victim

Resistance of the victim is not required, but can be evidence of the victim's lack of consent.

e. Intent

Rape is a general intent crime requiring only the intent to commit intercourse without consent of the female. Intent is negated if a defendant reasonably believes the victim's lack of resistance indicates consent.

2. Statutory Rape

Statutory rape is sexual intercourse with a female under the age of consent. It is a strict liability crime. Consent by the underage female is not a defense. A defendant's reasonable mistake of fact concerning the victim's age is not a defense.

3. Adultery and Fornication

Adultery and fornication are considered misdemeanor offenses in some states. Adultery involves sexual intercourse or cohabitation with a person who is not a spouse. Fornication is open and notorious cohabitation or sexual intercourse between unmarried persons.

4. Crimes Against Nature

There are two crimes under this category, sodomy and bestiality, both considered common law felonies. However, in light of *Lawrence v. Texas*, 539 U.S. 558 (2003), it is most improbable that a defendant could be successfully prosecuted for the crime of sodomy. Because the majority in *Lawrence* held that intimate consensual sexual conduct was part of the liberty protected by the Fourteenth Amendment, *Lawrence* effactually invalidated similar laws that purport to criminalize sodomy. Bestiality, sexual intercourse with an animal by a human, continues to survive.

5. Incest

In most jurisdictions, incest is marriage or sexual acts between persons that are too closely related. However, there is no uniformity in classifying the degree of relationship. While some states restrict incest to blood relatives, many other states extend the felony to non-blood relatives as well.

6. Bigamy

A strict liability offense, bigamy is the act of marrying someone while still legally married to someone else. Common law considered a defendant guilty even when the defendant incorrectly believed that an alleged divorce was valid or that his spouse was dead.

7. Seduction

Seduction occurs when a man induces a woman to have sexual intercourse with him on the false promise of marriage. Subsequent marriage may be a defense in some jurisdictions.

D. PERJURY AND BRIBERY

1. Perjury

Perjury involves the willful act of falsely promising to tell the truth, either verbally or in writing, about material matters that affect the outcome of the case. A witness cannot be prosecuted for making two contradictory statements if they are made during the same proceeding and the witness admits, prior to the end of the proceeding, that one of the statements is false. All witnesses are absolutely immune from civil liability based on their alleged perjured testimony in litigation brought under the Civil Rights Act, 42 U.S.C. § 1983.

2. Subornation of Perjury

At common law, subornation of perjury was a separate offense committed when one persuaded or induced another to commit perjury. Some states have eliminated subornation of perjury from the perjury statute.

3. Bribery

Under common law, bribery was a misdemeanor involving the corrupt payment of something of value for the purpose of influencing the action of an official in the discharge of his public or legal duties. Under modern law, bribery can be a felony and may extend to persons who are not public officials. Mutuality is not required. Further, the offering or taking of a bribe may constitute a felony as well. In some jurisdictions, failure to report a bribe constitutes a misdemeanor.

IV. INCHOATE CRIMES

The term "inchoate" literally means "unripened." With an inchoate offense, the intended crime need not be committed to be guilty. The inchoate offenses are solicitation, conspiracy, and attempt. Inchoate offenses are specific intent crimes.

A. MERGER

Traditionally, under the doctrine of merger, if a person's conduct constitutes both a felony and a misdemeanor, the misdemeanor merges into the felony, and the person can be convicted of the felony, but not the misdemeanor. However, if the crimes are of the same degree, i.e., all felonies or all misdemeanors, there is no merger of the crimes.

Modern law does not subscribe to the doctrine of merger except in cases of solicitation and attempt. A defendant may be tried, but not punished, for solicitation and the completed crime or for attempt and the completed crime. Solicitation and attempt are said to "merge" into the completed crime.

Contrast conspiracy: Unlike a solicitation and attempt conviction, a conviction for conspiracy does *not* merge into a conviction for the completed crime.

Note: The Double Jeopardy Clause prohibits a defendant from being convicted of both a crime and a lesser-included offense (i.e., an offense all the elements of which are also elements of the more significant crime), such as robbery and larceny. Many jurisdictions characterize this prohibition as a "merger" of the lesser-included offense into the greater. For further discussion of Double Jeopardy, please refer to the Themis Criminal Procedure outline.

B. SOLICITATION

Solicitation is the:

i) Enticing, encouraging, or advising of another person;

ii) To commit a crime;

iii) With the intent that the other person commits the crime.

1. Encouragement

The encouragement may take the form of enticement, incitement, request, or command. The crime is completed upon the encouragement. The other person need not agree to commit the crime.

2. Relationship to Other Crimes

If the other person does agree, the solicitor and the person being solicited may also become co-conspirators unless the person being solicited is merely feigning agreement.

3. Defenses to Solicitation

a. Renunciation

At common law, renunciation was no defense to solicitation. Under the Model Penal Code, voluntary renunciation may be a defense, provided the defendant thwarts the commission of the solicited crime.

b. Factual impossibility

Factual impossibility is not a defense to solicitation. If a solicitor is part of group that was meant to be exempted by the statute, the solicitor cannot be guilty of solicitation (e.g., minor female soliciting sex cannot be guilty of statutory rape).

C. CONSPIRACY

Conspiracy is:

i) An agreement;

ii) Between two or more persons;

iii) To accomplish an unlawful purpose; and

iv) With the intent to accomplish that purpose.

The majority rule and federal law, as well as the MPC, now require the commission of an overt act, which can be legal or illegal, in furtherance of the conspiracy to complete the formation of the conspiracy. At common law, no overt act was required for the conspiracy to be complete.

1. Agreement

The agreement need not be a formal document, or even in writing; an oral agreement is sufficient. An agreement need not be specifically articulated, but can be inferred from a concerted action by the defendants.

2. Number of Conspirators

At common law and under the majority rule, there is no such thing as a unilateral conspiracy. Two or more persons are required to form a conspiracy. The Model Penal Code, however, does permit unilateral conspiracies, but that is the minority rule. A unilateral conspiracy may be formed when only one party *actually agrees*, such as when another party merely feigns agreement, or if the alleged co-conspirators are ultimately acquitted.

a. Feigned agreement

When only one conspirator has the intent to agree, such as when the other conspirator is a governmental agent or pretends to go along with the crime to warn police, there is no conspiracy, unless another participant is involved.

b. Protected by statute

When the purpose of a criminal statute is to protect a type of person (e.g., a statutory rape statute protects underage females), there is no conspiracy between the protected party and the targeted defendant.

c. Wharton Rule

Under the Wharton Rule, if a crime requires two or more participants (e.g., adultery) there is no conspiracy unless more parties than are necessary to complete the crime agree to commit the crime. Although there is no conspiracy, they may be found guilty of the underlying crime itself.

d. Corporation and its agents

A corporation can conspire with its own agents with some limitations. In some jurisdictions, there can be no conspiracy between a corporation and a single agent of that corporation. A conspiracy between the corporation and multiple agents of the same corporation may in most jurisdictions satisfy the plurality requirement. A corporation or its agents can enter into a conspiracy with another corporation or agents of that corporation. In the federal system, there are no such limitations on a conspiracy between the corporation and its own agents.

e. Prosecution of other conspirators

A conspirator cannot be convicted of conspiracy if all other conspirators are acquitted at the same trial. In other circumstances, such as when co-

conspirators are never tried or apprehended, a conspirator may be convicted of conspiracy if the prosecution proves the existence of a conspiracy.

f. Spouses as co-conspirators

Common law did not consider husband and wife as co-conspirators because the law viewed them as a single entity. However, they could, as an entity, conspire with a third person. Nearly every jurisdiction has abolished this common law concept.

3. Unlawful Purpose

Under federal law and the modern trend, "unlawful purpose" is limited to criminal conduct. In some states, even the achievement of a lawful purpose through illegal means can be the subject of a conspiracy.

4. Specific Intent

Conspiracy is a specific intent crime. A conspirator must have the intent to agree, and the intent to commit the criminal objective. The intent to agree may be inferred from conduct of the parties.

> **Example:** Conspiracy to commit arson requires specific intent; the substantive offense of arson, however, is a general intent crime. Similarly, a conspiracy to commit a strict liability crime requires intent.

Because intent to agree and to commit the crime are elements of conspiracy, criminal liability for a conspiracy cannot be based solely on knowledge of the existence of the conspiracy. For example, a merchant who supplies goods to a conspirator knowing that the conspirator intends to use the goods in furtherance of the objective of the conspiracy is not a member of the conspiracy simply because the merchant possessed such knowledge. Instead, the merchant must take an additional step to show such intent, such as selling the goods at an exorbitant price, basing the price of the goods on a percentage of the conspiracy's "take," or ordering specially manufactured goods that the merchant does not normally sell.

5. Overt Act Requirement

An overt act was not required at common law, but is now a required element of a conspiracy under federal law, the Model Penal Code, and in a majority of the states. When an overt act is required, the conspiracy crime is not complete until the overt act is performed in furtherance of the conspiracy. The overt act can be performed by any co-conspirator, with or without the knowledge of all co-conspirators. The overt act can be lawful or unlawful.

> **Contrast attempt:** To constitute attempt, the defendant must have taken a substantial step towards commission of the crime. A mere preparatory act is insufficient for attempt.

6. Scope of Conspiracy

a. Crimes committed by co-conspirators

Under the Pinkerton Rule, a conspirator can be convicted of both the offense of conspiracy and all substantive crimes committed by any other co-conspirators acting in furtherance of the conspiracy. Under the Model Penal Code, the minority view, a member of the conspiracy is not criminally liable for such crimes unless that member aids and abets in commission of the crimes.

b. Multiple crimes, single conspiracy

A single conspiracy may have numerous criminal objectives. Not all of the co-conspirators even need to know the identities of all of the other co-conspirators or all of the details of the criminal organization. It is only necessary that all co-conspirators agree to further the common scheme or plan. Multiple conspiracies arise when the objectives and/or crimes are not committed in furtherance of the same agreement, common scheme, and plan.

c. Unknown conspirators, single conspiracy

1) Chain relationship

Persons who do not know each other can be members of the same conspiracy if there is a **community of interest** in the achievement of the object of the conspiracy. A community of interest is usually found when the activities of each person resemble links of a chain, such as a scheme to acquire and distribute drugs. In such a conspiracy, all of the members of the community of interest are liable for the acts of the others in furtherance of the conspiracy.

2) Hub-spoke relationship

A scheme that resembles a hub with spokes, such as the processing of fraudulent loans by one person that were submitted by numerous other individuals, is less likely to have a community of interest. In such case, the "hub" and each "spoke" is usually treated as having formed a separate conspiracy with the other hubs. Thus, the common hubs will be liable for all of the other conspiracies, but the spoke members are not liable for the acts of the other conspirators.

7. Impossibility

Factual impossibility (that it was factually impossible to complete the intended crime) is not a defense to conspiracy. Legal impossibility (that the intended act is not criminal in nature) may be a defense if the object of the agreement is not a crime.

8. Withdrawal

a. Effect on liability for conspiracy

At common law, withdrawal was not a defense to conspiracy because the conspiracy is complete as soon as the parties enter into the agreement. Under the federal rule, which is also the majority rule, withdrawal is possible between the date of the agreement and the commission of the overt act. In order to withdraw, notice must be communicated to the other co-conspirators, or the police must be advised of the existence of a conspiracy in a timely manner. Upon completion of the overt act, the conspiracy is formed and withdrawal is no longer possible. Under the MPC and the minority view, subsequent withdrawal or renunciation is possible only if there is timely notification that is sufficient to "thwart the success" of the conspiracy.

b. Effect on liability for substantive crimes

A co-conspirator may limit his liability for the substantive crimes that are the subject of the conspiracy by withdrawing from the conspiracy at any time after it is formed. For this purpose, he may withdraw by giving notice to his co-conspirators or timely advising legal authorities of the existence of the conspiracy even though such an action does not thwart the conspiracy.

9. Termination

It is important to determine when a conspiracy ends for purposes of determining the statute of limitations and the admissibility of acts or declarations made by the conspirators in furtherance of the crime. Generally, the act of concealing the conspiracy is not treated as a part of the conspiracy.

10. Punishment

Jurisdictions vary widely with respect to penalty provisions for conspiracies. Some jurisdictions make conspiracy a misdemeanor regardless of the objective, while other jurisdictions provide maximum sentencing depending on the objective. Still others allow for a permissible maximum, regardless of the objective. Nevertheless, sometimes the sentencing for conspiracy is more severe than the punishment for the crime itself.

D. ATTEMPT

An attempt requires a specific intent to commit a criminal act coupled with a substantial step taken toward the commission of the intended crime, which fails to be completed. An attempt is:

i) A **substantial step** towards the commission of a crime; coupled with

ii) Intent to commit the crime.

If the crime is successfully completed, the attempt is merged into the completed crime.

1. Substantial Step Test

A subjective test, called the "substantial step" test, is applied to determine whether an attempt has occurred. Under this test, conduct does not constitute a substantial step if it is in mere preparation; the act must be conduct that tends to effect the commission of a crime.

a. Preparatory acts

Any of the following preparatory acts may constitute a substantial step if they corroborate the defendant's criminal purpose:

i) Lying in wait, searching for, or following the intended victim;

ii) Unlawful entry into the place contemplated for the commission of the crime;

iii) Enticing the intended victim to go to such place;

iv) Possession of materials specially designed for committing the crime;

v) Possession of materials to be used in the commission of the crime at or near the place of commission; and

vi) Soliciting an innocent agent to engage in criminal conduct.

b. "Dangerous proximity" test

Some states continue to apply the traditional "dangerous proximity" test. Under this test, an attempt does not occur until the defendant's acts result in a dangerous proximity to completion of the crime.

2. Specific Intent

The defendant must possess the specific intent to perform an act or attain a result, which, if completed, would constitute the target crime, even if the target crime is not a specific intent crime.

Example: Arson is not a specific intent crime, but attempted arson is. An attempt to commit a strict liability crime is also a specific intent crime.

There is no attempt to commit negligent crimes like involuntary manslaughter because a defendant's act cannot be both intentional and negligent.

3. Impossibility

Impossibility is not a defense to attempt if the crime attempted is factually impossible to commit due to circumstances unknown to the defendant. If, however, the act intended is not a crime (i.e., a legal impossibility), the defendant is not guilty of attempt. In such a case, even when statutes purport to have done away with the impossibility defense, there is always a provision that allows for legal impossibility.

Example: D shoots V, believing that V is sleeping. V actually was already dead. D is guilty of attempted murder, but not murder.

4. Abandonment

At common law, once the defendant has taken a substantial step toward the commission of the offense, the defendant may not legally abandon the attempt to commit the crime because of a change of heart. Upon the completion of a substantial step, the crime of attempt is completed; there can be no abandonment or withdrawal.

Some states do recognize voluntary abandonment as a defense to attempt. Even then, abandonment is not voluntary if it is motivated by a desire to avoid detection, a decision to delay commission of the crime until a more favorable time, or the selection of another similar objective or victim. Abandonment by the defendant does not constitute a defense for an accomplice who did not join in the abandonment or withdrawal.

5. Prosecution and Punishment

A defendant who does not complete a crime may only be charged with attempt of the completed crime. However, if a defendant completes a crime, he may be charged with either attempt of the completed crime or with the completed crime itself. Punishment for attempt is usually less severe than the sentence for the completed offense.

V. DEFENSES

A. GENERALLY

1. Justification and Excuse

Defenses may be divided into the categories of justification and excuse. When the defendant's actions, despite being criminal, are socially acceptable, the defendant has acted justifiably. Self-defense and defense of others are examples of justification defenses. When the defendant has a disability that makes the defendant not responsible for her actions, the defendant's criminal behavior is excused. Insanity, intoxication, and duress are examples of excuse defenses. This distinction does not affect the applicability or operation of these defenses.

2. Mistake of Fact

When a defendant is factually mistaken (e.g., the defendant thinks that the victim is holding a pistol that instead is a toy gun), the defendant may generally rely on a defense if the mistake is a reasonable one. In determining the reasonableness of the mistake, the defendant's physical characteristics, experiences, and knowledge are taken into account. An unreasonable factual mistake is a defense only to a specific intent crime.

B. SPECIFIC DEFENSES

1. Self-Defense

One who is not the aggressor is justified in using reasonable force against another person to prevent immediate unlawful harm to himself. The harm to the defendant must be imminent, not a threat of future harm. The defendant can use only as much force as is required to repel the attack.

a. Deadly force

Deadly force is force that is intended or likely to cause death or serious bodily injury. Deadly force may be justified in self-defense only when it is reasonably necessary to prevent death or serious injury; to prevent the commission of a serious felony; or in some cases, to apprehend a fleeing felon who may endanger the safety of the community.

b. Nondeadly force

Nondeadly force is force that is not intended or likely to cause death or serious bodily injury and may be used to repel nondeadly force.

c. Retreat

There is never an obligation to retreat before employing nondeadly force. Under the majority view, retreat is not required even when deadly force is used in self-defense. Under the minority view (states that follow the so-called "retreat doctrine"), retreat is required if it can be safely accomplished. Even under the minority view, however, retreat is never required when the person employing deadly force is in his own home.

d. Imperfect right of self-defense

Imperfect self-defense occurs when the person claiming self-defense unjustifiably kills the attacker. The purpose of the rule is to reduce the charge from murder to voluntary manslaughter. The rule is applied when for some reason the defendant cannot claim perfect self-defense. For example, a defendant honestly, but unreasonably believes that deadly force is required to prevent death or serious bodily injury.

e. Aggressor's right to use self-defense

It is possible for an initial aggressor to gain the right to act in self-defense in two circumstances: (i) an aggressor using nondeadly force is met with deadly force, or (ii) the aggressor must, in good faith, completely withdraw from the altercation, and must have communicated that fact to the victim.

2. Defense of Others

A person has the right to defend others under the same circumstances that self-defense would be acceptable. Defense of others is not limited to defending family members, but extends to anyone the defendant reasonably believes has the right of self-defense.

3. Defense of Property

A person in lawful possession of property that is threatened by the conduct of another, and who has no time to seek assistance from law enforcement, may take reasonable steps, including the use of nondeadly force to protect the property. To use force, the defender must reasonably believe that the real property is in immediate danger of unlawful trespass or that personal property is in immediate danger of being carried away and that the use of force is necessary to prevent either. The force cannot be unreasonably disproportionate to the perceived harm.

There is no right to use deadly force in defending property, with one exception. Generally, a person may use deadly force to prevent or terminate a forcible felony in the dwelling, arson, burglary, or robbery. The use of deadly force against an intruder exiting the dwelling is generally not permitted. Mechanical devices cannot be used to protect property.

4. Arrest

A police officer or a person acting under police direction is justified in using reasonable force to make a lawful arrest or to prevent the escape from one already in lawful custody.

a. Right to arrest

The right of a police officer to arrest a suspect is often specified by statute. A police officer can lawfully arrest a suspect, with or without a warrant, if the suspect has committed a crime in the officer's presence or the officer has probable cause to believe the defendant committed a felony offense outside of his presence. A civilian acting without police direction in making an arrest (e.g., a "citizen's arrest") who makes a mistake, even a reasonable mistake, as to the commission of the crime is not entitled to rely on this defense.

b. Use of force to arrest

A police officer can use nondeadly force to arrest a suspect. A police officer can use deadly force to arrest a suspect if the suspect represents a threat to either the officer or third parties.

c. Resisting unlawful arrest

A defendant may use nondeadly force to resist an unlawful arrest, but never deadly force. Some jurisdictions do not permit the use of force at all and require defendants to seek legal redress for an unlawful arrest.

5. Prevention of Crimes

Anyone can use deadly force to prevent the commission of a serious felony involving a risk to human life, and may use nondeadly force to prevent the commission of a felony or a breach-of-the-peace misdemeanor. A private citizen who makes a mistake, even a reasonable mistake, as to the commission of a serious felony by the victim is not entitled to rely on this defense.

6. Public Authority

Actions taken by public officials pursuant to legal authority (e.g., court ordered seizure of property, state-sanctioned executions) are justified.

7. Parental Authority

The use of reasonable force in the exercise of parental authority (i.e., discipline) by a parent or by a person in charge of a child (e.g., a teacher), is justified if exercised for the benefit of the minor child.

8. Duress

A third party's unlawful threat that causes a defendant to reasonably believe that the only way to avoid death or serious bodily injury to himself or another is to violate the law and causes the defendant to do so, allows the defendant to claim the duress defense.

Duress is not a defense to intentional murder. A defendant charged with felony murder may claim duress as a defense to the underlying felony and avoid conviction for felony murder.

9. Necessity

If natural forces of nature (e.g., storm, fire) cause the defendant to commit what would otherwise be a crime, the defendant may be justified in doing so based upon necessity. The law prefers that the defendant, when faced with two evils, avoids the greater evil by choosing the lesser evil, e.g., the destruction of property to prevent the spread of a fire.

The defendant is not entitled to assert necessity if he set the natural forces in motion (e.g., set the fire), or if there is a noncriminal alternative. In addition, economic necessity does not justify theft. For example, an unemployed worker may not steal food from the grocery store.

Necessity is a result of natural forces; duress results from human actions.

10. Consent

Consent of the victim is not a defense to a crime unless the consent negates a required element of the crime or precludes the harm sought to be avoided by the crime. Such consent must be voluntarily and freely given, involve no fraud, and given by one competent to consent.

Consent is a defense to rape (unless the woman is a minor), since rape is defined as sexual intercourse without consent. Consent is also a defense to kidnapping if an adult (but not a minor) consents to traveling with the defendant.

a. Bodily injury

Consent to bodily injury or to conduct that may cause bodily injury may constitute a defense when the injury is not serious or, with regard to a sporting event or similar activity, the conduct and injury are reasonably foreseeable (i.e., boxing).

b. Ineffective consent

Consent may be ineffective when given by a legally incompetent person; by a victim who is unable to make a reasonable judgment due to age, mental disease or defect, or intoxication; or by a victim whom the law seeks to protect. Consent obtained by fraud, duress, or deception may also be ineffective.

11. Entrapment

Entrapment is the conception and planning of an offense by a law enforcement officer, and his procurement of its commission by a defendant who would not have committed that offense except for the trickery, persuasion, or fraud of the officer. If an officer merely offers an already-predisposed person the opportunity to commit a crime, it is not entrapment. In other words, the defendant must lack any predisposition to commit the crime. Entrapment can occur through the use of an undercover agent, but not by a private citizen. The modern trend allows a defendant to deny participation in an event, yet still raise the defense of entrapment. Traditionally, the defendant was precluded from using the entrapment defense if he denied his participation in the event.

a. Subjective approach

The subjective approach to defining entrapment is the majority position among the states and has also been adopted by the U.S. Supreme Court. Under this approach, the focus is on the defendant. Entrapment occurs when (i) the crime is induced by a government official or agent, and (ii) the **defendant was not predisposed** (i.e., ready and willing) to commit the crime.

b. Objective approach

Under the objective approach, which has been advanced by the MPC and adopted by a few states, the focus is on the government's action. This approach requires the **government official or agent** to have induced or encouraged the defendant to commit a crime by employing methods of persuasion or inducement that **create a substantial risk** the crime will be committed by persons other than those who are ready to commit it. Further, the Supreme Court has ruled that the government is allowed to provide the defendant with the material needed to commit the crime, even if the material was contraband. *Hampton v. United States*, 425 U.S. 484 (1976).

12. **Alibi**

An alibi is a defense whereby a defendant denies his participation in a crime because he asserts that he was somewhere else at the time of the commission of the alleged crime.

Criminal Procedure

CRIMINAL PROCEDURE

Table of Contents

CRIMINAL PROCEDURE

I. FOURTH AMENDMENT: APPLICATION TO ARREST, SEARCH AND SEIZURE

The Fourth Amendment reads: "The right of the people to be secure in their persons, houses, papers, and effects against unreasonable searches and seizures shall not be violated, and no Warrants shall issue, but on probable cause, supported by Oath or affirmation, and particularly describing the place to be searched, and the persons or things to be seized." This amendment protects persons against unreasonable arrests or other seizures as well as unreasonable searches. In addition, when a warrant is required, it must comply with these constitutional requirements.

A. GENERAL FOURTH AMENDMENT PRINCIPLES

1. Standing

Fourth Amendment rights are personal and may not be asserted vicariously. A defendant cannot successfully challenge governmental conduct as a violation of the Fourth Amendment protection against unreasonable searches and seizures unless the defendant himself has been seized or he has a reasonable expectation of privacy with regard to the place searched or the item seized. It is not enough that the introduction as evidence of an item seized may incriminate the defendant.

> **Example:** Defendants Al and Bob are accused of burglarizing an electronics store. Police found stolen DVD players in Al's apartment after an illegal warrantless search. Only Al has standing to raise the issue of a Fourth Amendment violation; Bob may not raise it in his own defense, as his rights were not violated.

2. The Exclusionary Rule

The right to be free from unreasonable searches and seizures must be distinguished from the remedy. The primary remedy is the "exclusionary rule," which prevents the introduction at a subsequent criminal trial of evidence unlawfully seized. This remedy is judicially created, not constitutionally mandated. The remedy provided by the exclusionary rule generally applies to criminal trials; it **does not apply** in other court proceedings, including federal habeas corpus review of state convictions, grand jury proceedings, preliminary hearings, bail hearings, sentencing hearings, and proceedings to revoke parole. Evidence will also not be excluded at trial when introduced as impeachment evidence against the defendant. Finally, the exclusionary rule is not applicable to civil proceedings. *See* § I.C.6., Exclusionary Rule, *infra,* for an expanded discussion.

3. Abuse of Discretion Standard

The judge, not the jury, resolves suppression issues raised by a pretrial motion to suppress. These issues are reviewed on appeal under the "abuse of discretion" standard.

4. Threshold of Governmental Action

The Fourth Amendment limits governmental action; it does not restrict the acts of private parties unless the private person is acting as an "instrument or agent of the government." Even if governmental action exists, there still is no constitutional violation unless the individual had a reasonable expectation of privacy and either the police did not have a valid warrant or they executed an invalid warrantless search.

> **EXAM NOTE:** Remember, the Fourth Amendment applies only to searches and seizures conducted by police or someone acting under police direction.

5. Grand Jury Subpoena

Unless a grand jury subpoena is being used for harassment or is extremely broad, requiring a person to appear before the grand jury under such subpoena does not fall under the protection of the Fourth Amendment.

6. Broader Rights Possible Under State Constitution

A state may grant broader rights under its own constitution than are granted by the federal Constitution. *See Michigan v. Long*, 463 U.S. 1032 (1983). Thus, even though the Fourth (or Fifth or Sixth) Amendment may not restrict the state government, state constitutional law may.

B. ARREST: UNREASONABLE SEIZURE OF PERSONS

1. Seizure: Objective Test—Not Free to Leave

A person is seized by the police when the officer, by means of physical force or show of authority, terminates or restrains freedom of movement; there is no seizure without actual submission. *Terry v. Ohio*, 392 U.S. 1 (1968). When the actions of the police do not show an unambiguous intent to restrain or when the individual's submission to a show of governmental authority takes the form of passive acquiescence, a seizure occurs only if, in view of the totality of the circumstances, a **reasonable person would believe he was not free to leave.** The test is whether a reasonable person would feel free to decline the officers' requests or otherwise terminate the encounter.

a. Intentional detention

The police officer must intentionally employ physical force or a show of authority in order for the officer's actions to result in a seizure.

> **Example:** During a high-speed chase, an officer forced the driver of the pursued automobile off the road. The officer's intentional use of deadly force against the driver constituted a seizure. *Scott v. Harris*, 550 U.S. 372 (2007).
>
> **Compare:** During a high-speed chase, an officer accidentally struck and killed the passenger of the pursued motorcycle when the motorcycle tipped over. The officer's accidental use of deadly force against the passenger did not constitute a seizure. *County of Sacramento v. Lewis*, 523 U.S. 833 (1998).

However, as long as the officer intentionally employs force or makes a show of authority, the officer's purpose need not be to detain the defendant in order for the defendant to be seized. Consequently, when a police officer makes a traffic stop, not only the driver but also any passengers are deemed to be seized. Therefore, the passenger as well as the driver may challenge the constitutionality of the stop. *Brendlin v. California*, 551 U.S. 249, 251 (2007).

2. **Contrast Stop and Frisk**

A temporary detention for the purpose of a stop-and-frisk search is not an arrest, but it may still constitute a seizure for Fourth Amendment purposes. The test is whether the officer, by means of physical force or show of authority, has in some way restrained the liberty of the citizen. Seizure includes physical restraint or an order to stop so that the officer can frisk and ask questions on the street.

3. **Arrest Warrants**

An arrest warrant is issued by a detached and neutral magistrate upon a finding of probable cause that a crime has been committed and that it was the particular defendant who committed the particular crime. However, an arrest made pursuant to a warrant that failed to satisfy the probable cause requirement is not illegal when the officer making the arrest independently had probable cause for making the arrest.

a. **Entry into home**

A warrant to arrest an individual implicitly authorizes entry into the arrestee's home to serve the warrant if the police have probable cause to believe that the arrestee is present. A police officer may not arrest a person in another person's home without a search warrant, absent exigent circumstances or valid consent. *Steagald v. United States*, 451 U.S. 204 (1981).

4. **Warrantless Arrests**

Unlike searches, police generally do not need a warrant to make a valid arrest **in a public place,** even if they have time to get one. The police, however, must have a warrant to arrest an individual in his own home, absent exigent circumstances or valid consent. *Payton v. New York*, 445 U.S. 573 (1980).

a. **Crime committed in the presence of the arresting party**

Either a police officer or a private individual has a right to arrest without an arrest warrant if either a felony or a misdemeanor amounting to a breach of the peace is committed in the arresting party's presence.

b. **Crime committed outside the presence of the arresting party**

In situations in which a **felony** has been committed outside the presence of the one making the arrest, a police officer may arrest anyone whom he reasonably believes has committed a felony, but a private individual may make an arrest only if (i) a felony has actually been committed and (ii) the private individual reasonably believes that the person being arrested is guilty.

c. **Misdemeanor arrest**

A warrantless arrest of a person for a misdemeanor punishable only by a fine is not an unreasonable seizure under the Fourth Amendment. *Atwater v. Lago Vista*, 532 U.S. 318 (2001). Note that the misdemeanor must have been committed in the presence of the arresting party; probable cause to believe that a misdemeanor was committed, without actually witnessing the crime, is not sufficient for a valid warrantless arrest.

d. Effect of invalid arrest

An unlawful arrest alone has **no bearing** on a subsequent criminal prosecution, and it is not a defense to the crime charged. If the police have probable cause to detain a suspect, they may do so even if they illegally arrested him (e.g., in his home without a warrant).

An unlawful arrest has legal significance, however, when there is a seizure of evidence. Evidence seized pursuant to an unlawful arrest may be suppressed at trial.

C.   SEARCH AND SEIZURE

1.   Governmental Action

Searches conducted by private citizens are not protected by the Fourth Amendment—there must be governmental action. However, the police may not circumvent the Fourth Amendment by intentionally enlisting private individuals to conduct a search of a suspect or areas in which the suspect has a reasonable expectation of privacy.

2.   Defining "Search": The Violation of a Reasonable Expectation of Privacy

Only **unreasonable** searches and seizures are subject to the Fourth Amendment. A **search** occurs when governmental conduct violates a **reasonable expectation of privacy.** *Katz v. United States*, 389 U.S. 347 (1967). A search also may occur when the government physically intrudes upon private property for the purpose of obtaining information. *United States v. Jones*, 565 U.S. ___, 132 S. Ct. 945 (2012) (placement of GPS device on defendant's vehicle for the purpose of monitoring the vehicle's movements constituted a search).

> **EXAM NOTE:** Be aware of fact patterns that involve an individual with no expectation of privacy, such as when incriminating evidence is seized at another individual's home. Remember that the search is valid unless there is a legitimate expectation of privacy or the government trespassed upon the defendant's private property.

a.   Locations searched

1)   Home

Although the Supreme Court has stated that "the Fourth Amendment protects people, not places," (see *id.* at 351), the Fourth Amendment, by its terms, protects against an unreasonable governmental search of a "house." This protection extends to persons who have the right to immediate possession of a dwelling, such the renter of an apartment. *Chapman v. United States*, 365 U.S. 610 (1961).

a)   Curtilage

In addition to the home itself, an area immediately surrounding the home known as the "curtilage" may be covered by the "umbrella" of the home's Fourth Amendment protection. In determining whether the area is protected, the following four-factor test applies:

i)   The proximity of the area to the home;

ii) Whether the area is included within an enclosure surrounding the home;

iii) The nature of the uses to which the area is put; and

iv) The steps taken by the resident to protect the area from observation by passersby.

United States v. Dunn, 480 U.S. 294 (1987).

> **Example:** A barn was 60 yards away from the main house and 50 yards away from the innermost fence surrounding the house. The barn was not being used for domestic purposes and, despite being surrounded by a fence, was fenced in a manner that did not prevent persons from observing what lay inside the fence. Consequently, the barn and the area immediately surrounding it lay outside the curtilage. Information of illegal drug activity being conducted within the barn gained by drug enforcement agents while within that area did not constitute an unreasonable search. *Id.*

b) Open fields

Private property that lies outside the curtilage of a home, such as a farmer's field, is not protected by the home's umbrella of Fourth Amendment protection. Under the "open fields" doctrine, governmental intrusion on such property is not a search. The owner does **not** have a reasonable (i.e., objective) expectation of privacy, even though the owner may have a subjective expectation of privacy based on the fact that the land is fenced, protected from public view, and "no trespassing" signs are posted. *United States v. Oliver*, 466 U.S. 170 (1984).

c) Overnight guest in a home

While an overnight guest in a home does not have an ownership interest in the home, such a guest does have a reasonable expectation of privacy, at least as to the areas of the home to which the guest has permission to enter. *Minnesota v. Olson*, 495 U.S. 91 (1990). (As to the ability of the owner or guest to consent to a search of the home, *see* § I.C.4.f, Consent searches, *infra*.)

> **Contrast short-term use of home for illegal business purpose:** Short-term use of a home (e.g., several hours) with the permission of the owner does not give rise to a reasonable expectation of privacy, at least when the home is being used for an illegal business purpose (e.g., bagging cocaine for sale on the streets). *Minnesota v. Carter*, 525 U.S. 83 (1998).

2) Motel room

As with the search of a home, the search of a motel room by a government agent may be an unreasonable search. A motel clerk's consent to a governmental search of a room during the time it is rented is insufficient to justify the search. *Stoner v. California*, 376 U.S. 483 (1964).

3) Business premises

In general, business premises are protected by the Fourth Amendment. *G.M. Leasing Corp. v. United States*, 429 U.S. 338 (1977). However, such premises may be subjected to administrative searches, *see* § I.C.4.g., Administrative searches, *infra.*

4) Prison

A prison inmate has no reasonable expectation of privacy in his cell. The limitations on Fourth Amendment rights are justified by the need to maintain institutional security and preserve internal order and discipline. *Hudson v. Palmer*, 468 U.S. 517 (1984). Unlike a convict, a pretrial detainee may have a limited expectation of privacy in his cell. However, a detainee's cell may be subject to a routine search, and the detainee's person may be subject to a strip search or a full-body search after a contact visit with someone from the outside. *Bell v. Wolfish*, 441 U.S. 520 (1979).

Trespass. While the fact that a governmental agent is on property without permission may make a warrantless search unreasonable (e.g., a search of a home), the fact that a governmental agent is illegally on property does not automatically make the search illegal (*United States v. Oliver, supra*), nor does the fact that a governmental agent is legally in a public place make the search legal (*Katz v. United States, supra*).

b. Objects sought

1) Papers and effects

The Fourth Amendment, by its terms, protects "papers and effects." For example, a person retains a reasonable expectation that items placed within his luggage will be free from a purposeful, exploratory physical manipulation of the luggage. *Bond v. United States*, 529 U.S. 334 (2000).

Compare smell emanating from object. A person does *not* have a reasonable expectation of privacy with regard to a smell emanating from his luggage, at least when the smell arises from an illegal substance. *United States v. Place*, 462 U.S. 696 (1983).

When papers and effects, such as checks, deposit slips, and financial statements given to a bank, are transferred to a third party, a person no longer has a reasonable expectation of privacy in these items. *United States v. Miller*, 425 U.S. 435 (1976).

Example: A defendant who hides drugs in a friend's purse in order to avoid their detection by police has no legitimate expectation of privacy in the purse. *Rawlings v. Kentucky*, 448 U.S. 98 (1980).

2) Automobiles

Although, under the Fourth Amendment, stopping a car constitutes a seizure of the driver and any passengers, *Brendlin v. California*, 551 U.S. 249 (2007) (passenger), *Delaware v. Prouse*, 440 U.S. 648 (1979) (driver), there is a lesser expectation of privacy with regard to the automobile and its contents than with a home. *Wyoming v. Houghton*, 526 U.S. 295 (1999). Even so, officers must have an articulable, reasonable suspicion of a violation of the law in order to stop an automobile.

a) Checkpoints

Police may stop an automobile at a checkpoint without reasonable, individualized suspicion of a violation of the law if the stop is based on neutral, articulable standards and its purpose is closely related to an issue affecting automobiles. A roadblock to perform sobriety checks has been upheld, while a similar roadblock to perform drug checks has not. *Compare Michigan Dept. of State Police v. Sitz*, 496 U.S. 444 (1990) (sobriety check) *with Indianapolis v. Edmond*, 531 U.S. 32 (2000) (check for illegal drugs).

> **Compare random stops:** Police may generally *not* stop an automobile, even for a driving-related matter, without a reasonable, individualized suspicion of a violation of the law, unless the stop is effected on the basis of neutral, articulable standards. *Delaware v. Prouse*, 440 U.S. 648 (1979) (no random stop of a driver to verify driver's license and car registration).

i) Immigration law enforcement

When the purpose of the stop relates to the enforcement of immigration laws, any car may be stopped on a random basis at the border of the United States without a reasonable suspicion of wrongdoing. *Almeida-Sanchez v. United States*, 413 U.S. 266 (1973). When a search does not occur at the border or its functional equivalent, all cars may be stopped at a fixed checkpoint without a reasonable suspicion of violation of an immigration law, but a car may not be singled out and randomly stopped without a particularized and objective basis. *United States v. Cortez*, 449 U.S. 411 (1981) (holding the stop of one car proper when officers could reasonably surmise that the car was involved in criminal immigration activity); *United States v. Martinez-Fuerte*, 428 U.S. 543 (1976) (affirming convictions based on stops at checkpoints at which all cars were stopped).

ii) Search for witnesses

A checkpoint maintained by police for the purpose of finding witnesses, rather than suspects, to a hit-and-run accident is not per se unreasonable. *Illinois v. Lidster*, 540 U.S. 419 (2004).

b) Car's VIN

The driver of a car does not have a reasonable expectation of privacy in the vehicle identification number (VIN) affixed to an automobile. *New York v. Class*, 475 U.S. 106 (1986). Consequently, a police officer's moving of papers that obstructed his view of this number did not constitute a search under the Fourth Amendment, and a gun found while doing so was admissible into evidence.

3) Abandoned property

Abandoned property is not protected by the Fourth Amendment.

> **Example:** There is no reasonable expectation of privacy in garbage set curbside for pickup. *California v. Greenwood,* 486 U.S. 35 (1988).

c. Persons and their attributes

1) Physical characteristics

There is no expectation of privacy in one's physical characteristics; therefore, a demand for a handwriting or voice sample is not a search. *United States v. Mara,* 410 U.S. 19 (1973) (handwriting exemplar); *United States v. Dionisio,* 410 U.S. 1 (1973) (voice exemplar).

2) Government informants

Some surveillance and investigation techniques have been held not to implicate any reasonable expectation of privacy because the targets of the surveillance were regarded as having assumed the risk that the people with whom they were interacting would be government agents. There is no reasonable expectation of privacy in conversations carried on with government informants or undercover officers. Similarly, if one party to a telephone call consents to wiretapping or agrees to record the call at the government's request, such monitoring will not trigger the Fourth Amendment rights of any other party to the call. *United States v. White,* 401 U.S. 745 (1971). A person also runs the risk that a third party to whom she turns over information may disclose such information to the government. *United States v. Miller,* 425 U.S. 435 (1976).

d. Methods used to search

1) Fly-over

An inspection conducted from the air, whether by an airplane or a helicopter, does not violate a reasonable expectation of privacy and therefore is not a search for the purposes of the Fourth Amendment. *Florida v. Riley,* 488 U.S. 445 (1989) (helicopter); *California v. Ciraolo,* 476 U.S. 207 (1986) (airplane).

2) Technological device

With regard to automobiles, the Fourth Amendment does not prohibit the police from using technological devices to enhance their ability to search (e.g., radar detectors, computers to search license plates, surveillance equipment). *United States v. Knotts,* 460 U.S. 276 (1983) (placement of a tracking device on a car). However, physically intruding upon a suspect's property to install a technological device (e.g., a GPS tracker on a car) may constitute a search. *United States v. Jones, supra.*

> It is important to note the distinction between *Knotts* and *Jones*—in *Knotts,* the device was installed with the permission of the former owner (a person other than the suspect) before the car came into the defendant's possession; defendant Jones, on the other hand, owned the vehicle in question at the time the government installed the GPS device.

The use of a device or sense-enhancing technology (e.g., a thermal sensing device) that is not in use by the general public to explore the details of a dwelling that would previously have been unknowable without physical intrusion constitutes a search. *Kyllo v. United States*, 533 U.S. 27 (2001). Moreover, use of an electronic listening device to eavesdrop on a conversation made from a public phone booth can violate the speaker's reasonable expectation of privacy. *Katz v. United States, supra.*

Flashlight. Because flashlights are ubiquitous, the use of a flashlight at night to illuminate the inside of a car does not constitute a search for Fourth Amendment purposes. *Texas v. Brown*, 460 U.S. 730 (1983).

3) Canine sniff

Use of a trained dog to sniff for the presence of drugs does not violate a reasonable expectation of privacy. *Illinois v. Caballes*, 543 U.S. 405 (2005) (car); *United States v. Place*, 462 U.S. 696 (1983) (luggage).

Officer's sense of smell: A police officer may also rely on his own sense of smell in ascertaining the presence of illegal drugs or alcohol. *United States v. Sharpe*, 470 U.S. 675 (1985) (marijuana); *United States v. Ventresca*, 380 U.S. 102, 104, 111 (1965) (alcohol).

4) Field test of substance

A field test performed on a substance to determine if the substance is contraband is not a search for Fourth Amendment purposes. *United States v. Jacobsen*, 466 U.S. 109 (1984).

3. Search Warrant Requirements

When a search occurs, a warrant serves to protect a person's privacy interests against unreasonable governmental intrusion. A valid search warrant must be issued by a neutral and detached magistrate based on probable cause, must be supported by oath or affidavit, and must describe the places to be searched and the items to be seized.

Warrantless searches are per se unreasonable unless the search satisfies one of seven exceptions to the warrant requirement.

a. Probable cause

Facts supporting probable cause may come from any of the following sources:

i) A police officer's personal observations;

ii) Information from a reliable, known informant or from an unknown informant that can be independently verified; or

iii) Evidence seized during stops based on reasonable suspicion, evidence discovered in plain view, or evidence obtained during consensual searches.

1) Right to attack truthfulness of affidavit

Generally, a search warrant that is valid on its face may not be attacked by a defendant as lacking in probable cause. A defendant can challenge a facially valid warrant only when the defendant can establish, by a preponderance of the evidence, that:

i) The affidavit contained **false statements** that were **made** by the affiant **knowingly, intentionally, or with a reckless disregard** for their truth; and

ii) The false statements were **necessary to** the finding of **probable cause.**

Franks v. Delaware, 438 U.S. 154 (1978).

b. Particularity

A search warrant must describe with particularity the place to be searched and the objects to be seized. *United States v. Grubbs*, 547 U.S. 90 (2006). Warrants that, in addition to describing specific documents to be seized, also refer to "other fruits, instrumentalities and evidence of the crime at this [time] unknown" are not converted into illegal general warrants by the inclusion of such language. The reference to a "crime" has been interpreted as being limited to a particular crime (e.g., false pretenses), rather than any crime. *Andresen v. Maryland*, 427 U.S. 463 (1976). A warrant need not specify the manner of its execution.

c. Anticipatory warrant

Police do not have to believe that contraband is on the premises to be searched at the time the warrant is issued. The probable cause requirement is satisfied when, at the time that the warrant is issued, there is probable cause to believe that the triggering condition will occur and, if that condition does occur, there is a fair probability that contraband or evidence of a crime will be found in a particular place. *United States v. Grubbs, supra.*

d. Third-party premises

A search warrant may be issued to search the premises of a person who is not suspected of a crime. *Zurcher v. Stanford Daily*, 436 U.S. 547 (1978).

e. Execution of warrant

1) By whom

A warrant cannot be executed by a private citizen. Generally, only a police officer may execute a warrant, but administrative warrants may be executed by the appropriate governmental official (e.g., fire inspector).

2) Timing

A warrant that is not timely executed (i.e., an unreasonable delay occurs) may be subject to challenge on the grounds that probable cause ceased to exist.

3) Manner of execution

a) Knock and announce

Most states and the federal government mandate that a police officer, when executing a warrant, must generally announce his purpose before entering. The failure to "knock and announce" will invalidate the arrest. A state may permit an exception to the rule if the entry is made under exigent circumstances, such as when there is a reasonable belief of danger to the officer or destruction of evidence. *Ker v. California*, 374 U.S. 23, 34 (1963).

Note, though, that violation of the "knock and announce" rule does not trigger the exclusionary rule (*see* § I.C.6., *infra*) with respect to evidence discovered as a result of a search conducted in violation of the "knock and announce" rule. *Hudson v. Michigan*, 547 U.S. 586 (2006).

4) Seizure of evidence not specified

A search warrant confers authority to search only the places and persons named in it. Regardless, any evidence of a crime, instrumentalities or fruits of a crime, or contraband found in plain view while properly executing the warrant, whether or not specified in the warrant, may be seized (*see* § I.C.4.e., "Plain view" doctrine, *infra*).

5) Treatment of persons not specified in the warrant

Independent justification is needed to search persons not named in a search warrant; mere proximity to a named person does not supply such justification. However, in conducting a search for contraband pursuant to a warrant, any occupant of the premises to be searched may be detained in a reasonable manner, which may include the use of handcuffs, for a reasonable time while the search is conducted. *Muehler v. Mena*, 544 U.S. 93 (2005); *Michigan v. Summers*, 452 U.S. 692 (1981).

4. Exceptions to the Warrant Requirement

> **EXAM NOTE:** Warrantless searches are frequently tested on the MBE. Be aware of answer choices that include concepts that apply to one type of warrantless search when another is being tested.

a. Search incident to a lawful arrest

A warrantless search is valid if it is reasonable in scope and if it is made incident to a lawful arrest. If the arrest is invalid, any search made incident to it is likewise invalid. Therefore, if a suspect is stopped for a traffic offense and given a citation but not arrested, then there can be no search incident to lawful arrest. *Knowles v. Iowa*, 525 U.S. 113 (1999).

1) The *Chimel* standard

A lawful arrest creates a situation that justifies a warrantless contemporaneous search of the person arrested and the immediate surrounding area (his "wingspan") from which a weapon may be concealed or evidence destroyed. *Chimel v. California*, 395 U.S. 752 (1969). If the arrest occurs in a home, it is permissible to search "closets and other spaces immediately adjoining the place of arrest from which an attack could be launched." *Maryland v. Buie*, 494 U.S. 325, 334 (1990).

2) Time limitations (temporal unity)

A search incident to a valid arrest must take place promptly after the arrest in order to be valid.

3) Scope of search

The right to search incident to a lawful arrest includes the right to search pockets of clothing and to open containers found inside the pockets. The right also extends to containers "immediately associated" with the person (such as a shoulder bag or purse), **so long as the containers are large enough to conceal a weapon or evidence of a crime.**

4) Vehicle search incident to arrest

For many years, if the police had probable cause to arrest the driver or passenger of a vehicle, an officer could conduct a full search, incident to that arrest, of the passenger compartment and all containers therein, whether open or closed. This was known as the *Belton* rule. *New York v. Belton*, 453 U.S. 454, 460 (1981).

In 2009, the Supreme Court restricted the parameters for a warrantless vehicle search incident to arrest. *Arizona v. Gant*, 556 U.S. 332 (2009). The *Gant* Court held that, in order to justify a warrantless search of an automobile incident to arrest, the Fourth Amendment requires that law enforcement demonstrate either (i) that the arrestee is within reaching distance of the passenger compartment at the time of the search and, as a result, may pose an actual and continuing threat to the officer's safety or a need to preserve evidence from being tampered with by the arrestee or (ii) that it is reasonable that evidence of the offense of arrest might be found in the vehicle.

5) Impounded vehicle

A legally impounded vehicle may be searched, including closed containers, such as glove box or a backpack, as part of a routine inventory search. *South Dakota v. Opperman*, 428 U.S. 364, 369–71 (1976). The warrantless search need not take place at the time that the vehicle is seized.

b. Exigent circumstances

Warrantless entry into a home or business is presumed unlawful unless the government demonstrates both probable cause and exigent circumstances. In determining the existence of exigent circumstances, courts use the "totality of circumstances" test. As a corollary to this doctrine, police may also secure the premises for a reasonable time to enable officers to obtain a warrant when the police have reason to believe that the failure to do so could result in the destruction of evidence. *Illinois v. McArthur*, 531 U.S. 326 (2001).

The exigent-circumstances rule does not apply when the police create the exigency by engaging or threatening to engage in conduct that violates the Fourth Amendment. *Kentucky v. King*, 563 U.S. ___, 131 S. Ct. 1849 (2011).

1) Hot pursuit

If the police have probable cause to believe that an individual has committed a *felony* and they are pursuing him to arrest him, then they have the right to enter a private building during the pursuit, to search that building while they are present on the premises, and to seize evidence found there, even though the material found is "mere" evidence and neither fruits nor instrumentalities of a crime.

> No such exigency exists in pursuing someone suspected of a nonjailable traffic offense; the hot-pursuit exception is inapplicable in that instance. *Welsh v. Wisconsin*, 466 U.S. 740 (1984).

2) Emergency situations

A search without a warrant is authorized whenever there is a reasonable apprehension that the delay required in obtaining the warrant would result in the immediate danger of evidence destruction or the threatened safety of the officer or the public, or when a suspect is likely to flee before a warrant can be obtained.

> The Supreme Court has ruled that the involuntary, warrantless blood test of a drunken-driving suspect was appropriate when police could reasonably have believed that the delay necessary to obtain a search warrant would likely result in disappearance of the blood-alcohol content evidence, and the test was administered according to accepted medical practices. *Schmerber v. California*, 384 U.S. 757 (1966).

c. Stop and frisk

1) Stop—limited seizure/detention

A "stop" (also known as a "*Terry* stop") is a limited and temporary intrusion on an individual's freedom of movement short of a full custodial arrest. Merely approaching a person, but not restricting the person's movement in any way, does not constitute a detention. A stop is justified on the **reasonable suspicion,** based upon **articulable facts,** that the detainees are or were involved in criminal activity. *Terry v. Ohio*, 392 U.S. 1 (1968). Whether reasonable suspicion exists is based on the **totality of the circumstances.** It requires more than a vague suspicion, but less than probable cause, and it need not be based on a police officer's personal knowledge.

> **Example:** Police were justified in stopping a suspect who (i) was standing on a street corner in a high-crime area and (ii) fled upon noticing the police, even though neither factor alone would constitute reasonable suspicion to justify a stop. *Illinois v. Wardlow*, 528 U.S. 119 (2000).

Reasonable suspicion can be based on a flyer, a police bulletin, or an informant's tip, but only if the tip is accompanied by sufficient indicia of reliability. *United States v. Hensley*, 469 U.S. 221, 233–34 (1985).

2) Frisk—limited search

An officer who does not have probable cause to arrest may make a limited search of the person, such as a pat-down of the outer clothing, if he has **reasonable suspicion** that the suspect was or is involved in criminal activity and that the frisk is necessary for the preservation of his safety or the safety of others.

Under the **"plain feel"** exception, if an officer conducting a valid frisk feels an object that has physical characteristics that make its identity immediately obvious (i.e., he has probable cause to believe that the item is contraband), then the officer may seize the evidence. Police may also *briefly* seize items if the officers have a reasonable suspicion that the item is or contains contraband.

3) *Terry* stop of a car

Pursuant to a lawful stop of a vehicle, police may conduct a search of the passenger compartment for weapons, if:

i) The police possess a reasonable belief that the suspect is dangerous and may gain immediate control of weapons; and

ii) The search of the passenger compartment is "limited to those areas in which a weapon may be placed or hidden."

Maryland v. Buie, 494 U.S. 325, 332 (1990); *Michigan v. Long*, 463 U.S. 1032, 1048–50 (1983).

Police may order occupants out of a vehicle that they have lawfully stopped. *Maryland v. Wilson*, 519 U.S. 408 (1997).

When police lawfully detain a driver or a passenger after a traffic stop, they may frisk the person if there is reasonable suspicion that the individual has a weapon. *Arizona v. Johnson*, 555 U.S. 323 (2009).

4) Limits on time, place, and investigative method

A *Terry* stop must be temporary and last no longer than is necessary to effectuate the purpose of the stop. The investigative methods employed should be the least intrusive means reasonably available to verify or dispel the officer's suspicion in a short time.

Police may stop the person, question him for a limited period of time, and frisk him for weapons only, not evidence. Police also can require that the detained person identify himself. Failure to comply with this request can result in the arrest of the detained person.

When police hold a suspect beyond the amount of time necessary to effectuate the purpose of the stop, the seizure becomes an arrest and must be supported by probable cause.

5) Development of probable cause

If the officer conducting the stop develops probable cause, the officer may then make an arrest and conduct a full search incident to that arrest. If the stop involves a vehicle, the officer may search the passenger compartment and all containers therein, whether open or closed, if the arrestee is within reaching distance of the passenger compartment of the vehicle or if it is reasonable to believe that the vehicle contains evidence of the offense of arrest. *See* § I.C.4.a.4), Vehicle search incident to arrest, *supra,* discussing the *Gant* rule.

d. Automobile exception

The Fourth Amendment does not require police to obtain a warrant to search a vehicle if they have probable cause to believe that it contains contraband or evidence of a criminal activity. The police may search anywhere in a car that they believe there to be contraband, including the trunk and locked containers, so long as they have **probable cause** to do so. *United States v. Ross*, 456 U.S. 798, 825 (1982). The search may also extend to passengers' belongings, *Wyoming v. Houghten*, 526 U.S. 295, 302 (1999), as well as to mobile homes, *California v. Carney*, 471 U.S. 386, 393–394 (1985). Any other evidence observed in plain view may also be seized.

1) Pretextual stop

Police may use a pretextual stop to investigate whether a law has been violated, even if they have no reasonable suspicion, provided that they have probable cause to believe that the law for which the vehicle was stopped has been violated. *Whren v. United States*, 517 U.S. 806 (1996) (seizure of illegal drugs constitutional even though police stopped a car for a traffic violation as a pretext to investigate a hunch that the occupants possessed drugs).

2) Containers within a car

Probable cause to search a vehicle extends only to containers and compartments that reasonably could hold the evidence. However, if the police have probable cause to search only containers, they may search only that container, but not the entire car. *California v. Acevedo*, 500 U.S. 565, 570 (1991).

Example: A driver left a residence holding a closed paper bag, which officers had probable cause to believe contained narcotics, based on an informant's tip. The bag was placed in the trunk, and the driver drove away. Police were authorized to stop the vehicle, open the trunk, and inspect the bag. However, the search was limited to the bag only. If they did not find the bag, they could only open and search containers big enough to store the bag. *Id.* at 579–80.

3) Trunk

If police have probable cause to search the trunk, not just a container placed in the trunk, then they can search the entire trunk and every container in the trunk, even if locked.

e. "Plain-view" doctrine

1) In public view

Items in public view may be seized without a warrant because one cannot have a reasonable expectation of privacy in things that are exposed to the public (e.g., physical characteristics, vehicle identification numbers, or items in open fields).

2) In private view

In situations in which there is a reasonable expectation of privacy (e.g., in a suspect's house), a police officer may seize an item in plain view of the officer, even if it was not named in the search warrant or the discovery was not inadvertent, as long as (i) the officer is on the premises for a **lawful purpose,** and (ii) the incriminating character of the item is **immediately apparent.** If the officer is not legitimately on the premises, the plain view doctrine does not apply.

> **Example:** Officer Olivia was executing a valid warrant to search Defendant Doug's home for a gun suspected to have been used in a murder. On entering the premises, Olivia saw what appeared to be bags of cocaine piled on Doug's coffee table. Under the "plain view" doctrine, Olivia could properly seize the bags, even though the warrant applied only to a gun.

f. Consent searches

Consent can serve to eliminate the need for police to have probable cause as well as to first obtain a warrant in order to conduct a search.

1) Voluntary

For permission to constitute consent, the permission must be given voluntarily. Permission given under threats of harm or compulsion does not constitute consent. In determining whether a person's response constitutes consent, courts evaluate the **totality of the circumstances** in which the response is made.

a) False assertion of authority

Permission given in acquiescence to lawful authority (e.g., a warrant) is not voluntary. Consequently, if the officer conducting the search erroneously states that he has a warrant, then permission given in reliance on that statement does not constitute consent. *Bumper v. North Carolina,* 391 U.S. 543, 549 (1968).

b) Knowledge of the right to withhold consent

The failure by police to inform the person from whom consent is sought that she has the right to withhold consent does not invalidate the consent. *Schneckloth v. Bustamonte,* 412 U.S. 218, 233 (1973).

2) Third-party consent

When the person from whom consent is sought is not the defendant, in addition to the voluntariness of the permission, the authority of that person to consent can be an issue.

a) Property of a third party

Generally, a third party has the authority to consent to a search of property that she owns or occupies. As such, the defendant cannot suppress evidence seized during such a search on the grounds that he (the defendant) did not consent to the search.

b) Property of the defendant

Generally, a third party does not have the authority to consent to a search of property owned or occupied by the defendant. The defendant can suppress evidence seized during such a search unless (i) an agency relationship exists between the third party and the defendant that gives to the third party the right to consent on behalf of the defendant, or (ii) the defendant otherwise gives the third party such rights with respect to the property that the defendant assumes the risk that the third party would allow the property to be searched (e.g., a shared duffle bag). *Frazier v. Cupp*, 394 U.S. 731, 740 (1969).

c) Jointly controlled property

When the property to be searched is under the joint control of the defendant and a third party (e.g., co-tenants of an apartment, a house jointly owned by a husband and wife), the authority of the third party to consent turns on whether the defendant is present at the time of the search.

i) Defendant not present

If the property to be searched is under the joint control of the defendant and a third party, and the defendant is not present at the time of the search, then the third party has authority to consent. The third party has actual authority when she has joint access or control for most purposes. *U.S. v. Matlock*, 415 U.S. 164, 170–171 (1974). In addition, the third party's consent may be valid even though she lacks actual authority if the police reasonably believe that she has such authority. *Illinois v. Rodriguez*, 497 U.S. 177, 184 (1990).

ii) Defendant present

When the property to be searched is under the joint control of the defendant and a third party, and the defendant is present at the time of the search, then the police may not rely on third-party consent if the defendant objects to the search. *Georgia v. Randolph*, 547 U.S. 103, 114–116 (2006).

iii) Ownership versus current control

In some instances, ownership of the premises is not sufficient to confer authority to consent to a search. For example, a landlord may not consent to a search of the tenant's premises. *Chapman v. United States*, 365 U.S. 610, 617 (1961). Similarly, a hotel clerk cannot consent to the search of a guest's room. *Stoner v. California*, 376 U.S. 483, 489 (1964).

iv) Parental consent

When a child lives with a parent, the parent has the authority to consent to a search of a child's room even if the child is an adult. However, a parent may lack authority to consent to the search of a locked container inside the child's room, depending on the age of the child. *U.S. v. Block*, 590 F.2d 535, 540 (4th Cir. 1979).

3) Scope of consent

Although a search is limited to the area to which the consent applies, the search may extend to areas that a reasonable person would believe it extends. For example, consent by a driver to search his car for drugs extends to a closed container within the car that could contain drugs. *Florida v. Jimeno*, 500 U.S. 248, 252 (1991).

4) Burden of proof

The prosecution must prove that the permission was freely given; the defendant is not required to show that the permission was coerced.

g. Administrative searches

Administrative search warrants are generally required for nonconsensual fire, health, or safety inspections of residential or private commercial property.

1) Probable cause

The probable cause requirement for administrative searches is less stringent than that for a criminal investigation. Evidence of an existing statutory or regulatory violation or a reasonable plan supported by a valid public interest will justify the issuance of a warrant. *Camara v. Mun. Court of San Francisco*, 387 U.S. 523, 533 (1967).

2) Use of administrative searches

The government may not use administrative searches to investigate criminal activity. However, discovery of evidence during the search does not invalidate the search.

The following administrative-type searches may be validly made without a warrant:

i) Searches of people entering an **airplane boarding area,** as long as the passenger can prevent the search by not boarding the plane;

ii) Searches of businesses in **highly regulated industries** such as liquor stores, gun shops, strip-mining operations, and automobile junkyards, because of urgent public interest and under the theory that the business impliedly consented to warrantless searches by entering into a highly regulated industry;

iii) Oral statements seized by **wiretaps,** when matters of national security are at issue;

iv) Searches of students by **public school officials,** so long as they are based on reasonable grounds (this standard is lower than probable cause and calls for only a "moderate chance" of finding the expected evidence, rather than a "fair probability" or "substantial chance"), and the measures adopted for the search are reasonably related to the objectives of the search and not excessively intrusive in light of the age and sex of the student and the nature of the infraction. *New Jersey v. T.L.O.*, 469 U.S. 325, 340–341 (1985);

> Note that searches of students by public school officials must have been initiated by the school officials and not at the request of the police in order to be valid.

v) **Special needs searches,** such as drug testing for railroad employees involved in an accident or student athletes during the athletic season. To be a special need, the state interest must be a real, current, and vital problem that can be effectively addressed through the proposed search. Even if the need exists, it must be balanced against the privacy interest at stake and the character of the intrusion. *Bd. of Educ. v. Earls*, 536 U.S. 822, 829 (2002);

vi) **Inventory searches** of items in official custody, such as impounded vehicles. After lawfully taking custody of property, police may conduct a warrantless search of other property to protect the owner's property while in custody, to protect police from claims of theft, and to protect officers from danger. Inventory searches must be performed according to standardized criteria and procedures. Subjective intent of the officer is irrelevant;

vii) **Routine international border** searches of border crossers and their belongings within the United States, including (i) stops, but not searches, by roving patrols who reasonably suspect that undocumented immigrants may be in an automobile, (ii) opening of international mail if authorities have reasonable cause to suspect contraband in the mail, and (iii) subsequent reopening of mail after the item had been resealed and delivered to the recipient;

viii) **Vehicle checkpoints and roadblocks** set up to stop cars on the basis of a neutral articulable standard and designed to serve a limited purpose closely related to the problem of an automobile's inherent mobility (e.g., to get drunk drivers off the road);

ix) **Factory searches** of the entire work force to determine citizenship of workers;

x) Searches of **government employees' file cabinets and desks** if they are justified by a reasonable suspicion of work-related misconduct or a noninvestigatory, work-related need;

xi) **Detention of a traveler** whom authorities have reasonable suspicion is smuggling contraband in his stomach;

xii) Searches of **parolees and their homes,** even with no reasonable suspicion, when a parolee agrees to submit to searches by a parole officer or police officer at any time as a condition of his parole. The rationale being that because there is a greater need to search parolees since they are less likely to be law-abiding citizens, a parolee has a lower expectation of privacy;

xiii) Seizure of **contaminated or spoiled food**; and

xiv) Searches for the **cause of a fire** that occurs within a reasonable time after the fire is extinguished, but excluding searches for other evidence unrelated to the cause that would establish that the fire was attributable to arson. *Michigan v. Clifford*, 464 U.S. 287 (1984) (search of home); *Michigan v. Tyler*, 436 U.S. 499 (1978) (search of business (furniture store)).

h. Wiretapping

To obtain a warrant authorizing a wiretap, officers must satisfy the below requirements. The warrant must:

i) Be limited to a short period of time;

ii) Demonstrate probable cause that a specific crime has been or is about to be committed;

iii) Name the person or persons to be wiretapped;

iv) Describe with particularity the conversations that can be overheard; and

v) Include provisions for the termination of the wiretap.

Upon termination of the wiretap, the conversations that have been intercepted must be shown to the court. Note that a person assumes the unreliability of those to whom she speaks and has no Fourth Amendment claim if she finds out later that the listener was wired or recording the conversation. *United States v. White*, 401 U.S. 745 (1971). Furthermore, a speaker who makes no attempt to keep his conversation private has no Fourth Amendment claim. *Katz v. United States*, 389 U.S. 347 (1967).

In addition, a wiretap related to domestic security surveillance requires that a neutral and detached magistrate—not the president—make the determination that a wiretapping warrant should issue, and the wiretap must comply with the Omnibus Crime Control and Safe Streets Act. However, there is no requirement for prior authorization when a covert entry is planned to install the electronic equipment, or when a pen register is used.

5. Raising the Issue of Standing

To establish that a search violated his Fourth Amendment rights, a defendant must show a legitimate expectation of privacy with regard to the search (*see* § I.C.2., *supra*). To make such a showing, which is sometimes referred to as "standing," the defendant may have to admit facts that would incriminate him. Consequently, testimony given by the defendant to establish standing cannot be admitted as evidence against the defendant at trial.

6. Exclusionary Rule

Under the exclusionary rule, evidence obtained in violation of the Fourth, Fifth, or Sixth Amendments may not be introduced at trial to prove guilt. Under the Fourth Amendment, evidence seized during an unlawful search cannot constitute proof against the victim of the search. *Weeks v. United States*, 232 U.S. 383 (1914).

a. Fruit of the poisonous tree

Subject to some exceptions, the exclusionary rule applies not only to evidence initially seized as a result of the primary government illegality, but also to secondary "derivative evidence" discovered as a result of the primary taint, also known as the "fruit of the poisonous tree."

> **Example:** A police officer conducts an unconstitutional search of a home, finds an address book, and uses that address book to locate a witness. The witness will not be allowed to testify, because her testimony would be a "fruit" of the unconstitutional search.

b. Exceptions

Assuming the exclusionary rule is otherwise applicable to exclude the primary evidence, derivative evidence may still be admissible if one of the following exceptions to the fruit of the poisonous tree doctrine applies.

1) Inevitable discovery rule

The evidence would have been inevitably discovered through lawful means.

2) Independent source doctrine

The evidence was discovered in part by an independent source unrelated to the tainted evidence.

3) Attenuation principle

The chain of causation between the primary taint and the derivative evidence has been so attenuated as to "purge" the taint. Both the passage of time and/or intervening events may attenuate the taint.

4) Good-faith exception

The good-faith exception applies to police officers who act in good faith on either a facially valid warrant later determined to be invalid or an existing law later declared unconstitutional. Good faith is limited to the objective good faith of a reasonable police officer.

This exception does **not** apply if:

i) No reasonable officer would rely on the affidavit underlying the warrant;

ii) The warrant is defective on its face;

iii) The warrant was obtained by fraud;

iv) The magistrate has "wholly abandoned his judicial role"; or v)　The warrant was improperly executed.

5) Isolated police negligence

Isolated negligence by law-enforcement personnel will not trigger the exclusionary rule. To trigger the rule, police conduct must be sufficiently deliberate such that exclusion can meaningfully deter it. The exclusionary rule serves to deter deliberate, reckless, or grossly negligent conduct or, in some circumstances, recurring or systemic negligence. *Herring v. United States*, 555 U.S. 135, 144 (2009).

Example: Defendant Don goes to the police station to pick up an impounded vehicle. Policeman Paul believes that there might be a warrant out from another county for Don's arrest and calls the other county's sheriff to check. The sheriff tells Paul that there is a warrant out for Don's arrest. Paul immediately arrests Don and in a search incident to the arrest finds illegal drugs and an illegal weapon on Don. Minutes later, the sheriff calls back to say that the warrant had actually been recalled and she had made a mistake. The exclusionary rule will not apply to the drugs and the weapon because Paul was relying in good faith on the erroneous information from the sheriff in conducting the arrest. The exclusionary rule should be applied only if there is substantial additional deterrence of police misconduct to be gained. *Herring v. United States*, 555 U.S. 135 (2009).

6) Knock and announce

The exclusionary rule does not apply to evidence discovered as a result of a search conducted in violation of the "knock and announce" rule, if the search was otherwise authorized by a valid warrant. *Hudson v. Michigan*, 547 U.S. 586 (2006).

7) In-court identification

A witness's in-court identification of the defendant is not fruit of an unlawful detention. Thus, the identification cannot be excluded. On the other hand, live testimony may be excluded as fruit of illegal police conduct if there is a sufficient link between the illegal police conduct and the testimony.

c. Harmless error

Even if the trial court wrongfully admitted illegally seized evidence, the appellate court can refuse to order a new trial if it finds that the error was harmless beyond a reasonable doubt, meaning that the erroneously admitted evidence did not contribute to the result.

Note: The denial of the right to counsel is never a harmless error.

d. Enforcement

When the defendant challenges a confession or the admissibility of evidence, by right, a hearing is held to determine whether the confession or evidence is fruit of the poisonous tree. This hearing is held outside the presence of the jury. The defendant has a right to testify at this hearing, and the state bears the burden of establishing admissibility by a preponderance of the evidence.

e. Obtaining evidence by questionable methods

Evidence obtained in a manner that shocks the conscience is inadmissible. Examples of such methods of gathering evidence include inducements by official actions that offend the sense of justice and serious intrusions into the body, such as with surgery to remove a bullet. Contrast that, however, with drawing blood, which is a reasonable intrusion because it does not generally involve trauma or pain and is a common medical procedure.

II. FIFTH AMENDMENT RIGHTS AND PRIVILEGES

A. THE PRIVILEGE AGAINST COMPULSORY SELF-INCRIMINATION

The Fifth Amendment provides that no person shall be compelled in any criminal case to be a witness against himself. It is applicable to the states through the Fourteenth Amendment.

1. Persons

A person means an individual. Artificial entities such as corporations, partnerships, and labor unions may not assert the privilege, but a sole proprietorship may. The privilege does not extend to the custodian of corporate records, even if production would incriminate the custodian individually.

2. Testimonial Evidence

The privilege protects only testimonial evidence. Nontestimonial physical evidence (such as blood or urine samples, Breathalyzer test results, handwriting exemplars, or other evidence of physical characteristics) is not protected.

a. Business papers

The privilege does not apply to an individual's voluntarily prepared business papers, obligatory reports, or tax returns. However, a personal diary may be protected. Moreover, a person who is served with a subpoena requiring the production of possibly incriminating documents cannot invoke the privilege because the act of turning over the documents is not self-incriminating testimony.

b. Evidence must be incriminating

The testimonial evidence must also be incriminating, meaning not only those answers to questions that would support a conviction, but also those answers that would furnish a link in the chain of evidence needed to prosecute.

c. Document seizure

Law-enforcement officials may search for and seize documents that would incriminate a person.

1) Diaries

Generally, the government may not compel **production** of a diary. The contents of a diary are similar to oral testimony, and as such are considered testimonial in nature. Because one cannot be compelled to testify against himself, the government may not compel production of documents that are similarly testimonial in nature.

Note, however, that if the diary's production is not compelled, e.g., it is found incident to a lawful arrest, its contents are admissible (assuming the entries were made voluntarily).

3. Nature of Proceedings

The privilege extends to a defendant in any proceeding, whether civil or criminal, formal or informal, if the answers provide some reasonable possibility of incriminating the defendant in future criminal proceedings. However, the privilege cannot be invoked when the government requires civil records to be maintained and reported on for administrative purposes, because they are public records, unless those records fulfill a registration requirement of a select group of inherently suspect criminal activities and compliance would require self-incrimination. The privilege does not extend to identification requests at *Terry* stops. A violation occurs the moment the compelled statements are used against a person.

4. Invoking the Privilege

a. Defendant's privilege

A defendant who wishes to invoke the privilege simply invokes it by not taking the stand. Included in this right is the state's inability to ask the defendant to testify. The prosecution cannot bring the defendant's failure to take the stand to the jury's attention.

b. Witness's privilege

A witness, on the other hand, may be compelled to testify and would invoke the privilege only after listening to the question and specifically invoking the privilege rather than responding to the question.

5. Counseling Clients to Invoke the Privilege

Attorneys may counsel their clients to invoke the privilege and will not be held in contempt of court. Otherwise, the person invoking the privilege would be denied his Fifth Amendment protection.

6. Invocation of Privilege Should Not Impose a Burden

The state cannot penalize a defendant for invoking his right against self-incrimination by not testifying or cooperating with authorities. The prosecution cannot comment to the jury on the defendant's refusal to speak in accordance with his *Miranda* rights. A violation in this regard by the state triggers the harmless-error test. However, if during trial the defendant claims that he was not allowed to explain his story, then the prosecution may comment on the defendant's failure to take the stand.

7. Waiving the Privilege

A **defendant** waives the privilege by taking the witness stand and succumbing to the prosecution's questions, whereas a **witness** waives the privilege by disclosing self-incriminating information.

B. THE FIFTH AMENDMENT IN A POLICE INTERROGATION CONTEXT

In the seminal case of *Miranda v. Arizona,* the U.S. Supreme Court held that a suspect has a constitutional right not to be compelled to make incriminating statements in the police interrogation process. *Miranda v. Arizona,* 384 U.S. 436 (1966). *Miranda* once was considered to be necessary in nearly every encounter with police. However, the Supreme Court has been gradually narrowing the scope and limiting the use of *Miranda.*

Any statement, whether inculpatory or exculpatory, obtained as the result of **custodial interrogation** may not be used against the suspect at a subsequent trial **unless** the police provided procedural safeguards effective to secure the privilege against self-incrimination (i.e., informed the suspect of his *Miranda* rights).

1. Custodial Interrogation

Custodial interrogation is questioning initiated by law-enforcement officers after a person has been taken into custody.

a. "Custodial"

Custody is a substantial seizure and is defined as either a formal arrest or a restraint on freedom of movement to the degree associated with a formal arrest. *New York v. Quarles,* 467 U.S. 649, 655 (1984). A person is in custody when he is not free to leave or is otherwise deprived of his freedom in any significant way. The test is whether a **reasonable person** would **believe** that he is not free to leave. *Yarborough v. Alvarado,* 541 U.S. 652, 662 (2004). A child's age is a relevant factor to consider when determining whether the child is in custody for the purposes of *Miranda. J.D.B. v. North Carolina,* 564 U.S. ___, 131 S. Ct. 502 (2011).

> **Example:** Sarah voluntarily goes to the police station to talk about a crime. As soon as she arrives, she is informed by the officer on the case that she is free to leave at any time and is not under arrest. Even though she is speaking with the police at the police station, the totality of the circumstances establishes that she is not in "custody," and therefore *Miranda* will not apply. *See California v. Beheler,* 463 U.S. 1121 (1983); *Oregon v. Mathiason,* 429 U.S. 492 (1977).

Traffic stops generally are not considered custodial because they generally are brief and temporary.

1) Location irrelevant

There is no requirement that the interrogation take place in a police station to be deemed custodial, only that a governmental agent (e.g., police officer), not a civilian, does the interrogating.

2) Crime scene

The questioning of persons at the scene of a crime or pursuant to field investigation does not constitute "custody" for purposes of *Miranda* as long as the person questioned has the **right to leave** the presence of the questioning officer.

b. "Interrogation"

Interrogation refers not only to express questioning, but also to any words or actions that the police know or should know are **likely to elicit an incriminating response.**

1) Voluntariness of statement

Volunteered statements are not protected by *Miranda.* A confession is involuntary only if the police coerced the defendant into making the confession. Whether a statement is voluntary or coerced is determined based on the totality of the circumstances (including facts such as the conduct of the police, the characteristics of the defendant, and the time of the statement). A claim that a confession should be excluded because it is involuntary must be decided by the trial judge as a preliminary question of fact, and not by the jury.

a) Trickery

Trickery by the police or false promises made to the accused by the police may render a confession involuntary. However, deceit or fraud by the interrogators (i.e., lying about a co-conspirator's confession) does not itself make the confession involuntary.

b) Character of the defendant

The defendant's age, state of health, education, or intoxication are all factors in determining the coercive nature of the confession. Although a potentially significant factor, the defendant's mental condition alone cannot violate the voluntariness standard. There must be coercive police activity for the confession to be found involuntary. *Colorado v. Connelly,* 479 U.S. 157 (1986).

2) Break in questioning

Miranda protections carry over when there is a break in the interrogation process attributed to a second police agency continuing an interrogation after the first police agency has stopped questioning the suspect.

> **EXAM NOTE:** Remember to apply the *Miranda* warnings only when an individual is subject to a custodial interrogation. If the police have no intention of questioning the individual, or if the individual is not in police custody, then the *Miranda* warnings are not applicable.

2. Compliance

Once a custodial interrogation begins, anything the defendant says is inadmissible until the defendant is informed of the *Miranda* rights **and** the defendant intelligently waives those rights.

The failure to give a suspect the *Miranda* warnings does not require suppression of physical fruits of the suspect's "unwarned but voluntary statements." *United States v. Patane,* 542 U.S. 630, 640 (2004).

a. Content

The warnings, which must be given before interrogation begins, need not be a verbatim repetition of the language used in the *Miranda* decision. Law-enforcement officials must inform defendants:

i)   Of their right to remain **silent**;

ii) That any statement uttered may be **used in court**;

iii) Of their right to **consult an attorney** and to have the attorney present during an interrogation; and

iv) That an **attorney will be appointed** to represent indigent defendants.

b. Timing

The *Miranda* warning must be given before interrogation begins. If interrogation is stopped for a long duration, the warning must be given again.

c. Right to counsel invoked

The right to counsel under the Fifth Amendment is not the same as the constitutional requirement of the right to counsel under the Sixth Amendment. The right to counsel under the Fifth Amendment is not automatic. To invoke the right to counsel under the Fifth Amendment, the defendant must make a specific, unambiguous statement asserting his desire to have counsel present. If a suspect makes an ambiguous statement regarding the right to counsel, the police are not required to end the interrogation or to ask questions or clarify whether the suspect wants to invoke the right. *Davis v. United States*, 512 U.S. 452 (1994). However, once that right to counsel is invoked, **all** interrogation must stop until counsel is present, **unless** the defendant voluntarily initiates communication with the police, which includes statements that the defendant spontaneously blurts out.

d. Right to silence invoked

If a defendant invokes his *Miranda* right to remain silent, the interrogator(s) must "scrupulously honor" that request. However, if later (such as after a substantial development in the case) the defendant indicates a desire to speak, then a subsequent interrogation would be lawful, as long as the defendant was not coerced. The defendant must again receive fresh *Miranda* warnings.

e. Grand jury

There is no requirement to give *Miranda* warnings to a witness testifying for the grand jury. The witness may, however, consult with an attorney outside the grand jury room.

3. Exceptions to the *Miranda* requirement

a. Public safety

When the public's safety is at risk, the police are not required to give *Miranda* warnings before questioning a suspect.

b. Routine booking

The "routine booking question" exception allows police to ask a suspected drunken driver routine biographical questions and to videotape the driver's responses without first giving the driver *Miranda* warnings.

c. Undercover police

Miranda warnings are not required if the suspect being questioned is not aware that the interrogator is a police officer. *Illinois v. Perkins*, 496 U.S. 292, 294 (1990).

> **Example:** The police placed an undercover officer, posing as a criminal, in the defendant's jail cell, and the undercover officer engaged the defendant in a conversation designed to elicit details of the crime for which the defendant was suspected. Such statements were admissible in the absence of *Miranda* warnings. *Illinois v. Perkins, supra.*

4. Waiver

A defendant may knowingly, voluntarily, and intelligently waive his *Miranda* rights. The burden is on the government to demonstrate by a preponderance of the evidence that the waiver was made knowingly, voluntarily, and intelligently. (Keep in mind that a defendant's mental illness does not necessarily negate the voluntariness requirement; there must be coercive police activity for a confession to be involuntary. *Colorado v. Connelly, supra.*)

There can be no effective waiver, however, until the *Miranda* warnings are properly given. Silence on the part of the suspect is not sufficient to waive his *Miranda* rights. However, a suspect who has received and understood the *Miranda* warnings, and has not invoked his *Miranda* rights, waives the right to remain silent by making an uncoerced statement to the police. *Berghuis v. Thompkins*, 560 U.S. ___, 130 S. Ct. 2250 (2010). Once effectively waived, the police are not required to inform the suspect of the defense counsel's efforts to reach the defendant by telephone and need not inform counsel that the defendant is being questioned.

5. Use of Statements Taken in Violation of *Miranda*

The failure to give *Miranda* warnings is not a violation until a statement obtained without the use of warnings is used at trial. *Chavez v. Martinez*, 538 U.S. 760, 770–771 (2003).

a. Confessions

Involuntary confessions cannot be used either substantively or for impeachment purposes. If a coerced confession is admitted into evidence, however, reversal is not automatic; the harmless-error test is applied, and the conviction will stand if the prosecution can show other overwhelming evidence of guilt.

b. Statements other than confessions

Statements taken in violation of *Miranda* may be used to impeach the credibility of the criminal defendant if he takes the witness stand and gives testimony at variance with his previous admissions. *Harris v. New York*, 401 U.S. 222, 224 (1971). To be admissible for impeachment, the statement must be voluntary and trustworthy. The impeaching admissions may not be used directly in deciding ultimate issues of guilt or innocence; they may only be used in determining the defendant's veracity. The defendant's silence after being given his *Miranda* warnings cannot be used by the prosecution to oppose an insanity defense.

C. FRUITS OF A TAINTED CONFESSION

1. Physical Evidence

Derivative **physical evidence** (e.g., a gun) that has been obtained as a result of a confession that itself is inadmissible due to the failure by police to give *Miranda* warnings is admissible. *United States v. Patane*, 542 U.S. 630 (2004).

2. Second Confession

A *Miranda* violation does not automatically require the suppression of incriminating statements made by the defendant after receiving *Miranda* warnings. The giving of *Miranda* warnings generally removes the "taint" of the prior *Miranda* violation. *Oregon v. Elstad*, 470 U.S. 298, 305–306 (1985). However, a second confession may be suppressed when the circumstances indicate that the substance of *Miranda* has been drained away. For a plurality of the court, the test is an objective one—a reasonable person in the suspect's position would not have understood the *Miranda* warnings to convey a message that the suspect retained a choice about whether to remain silent. For the justice who cast the deciding vote (Justice Kennedy), the test is a subjective one—did the police act with an intent to circumvent the purpose of the *Miranda* warnings. *Miranda*; *Missouri v. Siebert*, 542 U.S. 600, 611 (2004).

D. FIFTH AMENDMENT IN THE TRIAL CONTEXT

1. Scope of Privilege

A defendant may refuse to testify at a criminal trial. He may also refuse to answer questions in other proceedings (i.e., civil depositions) when the answers might incriminate him in future criminal proceedings.

The privilege does not prevent the prosecutor from using prior conflicting statements to impeach the defendant once the defendant takes the stand. This is called "opening the door" by the defendant.

2. Voluntariness

Admissions of incriminating statements made during a court-ordered psychiatric examination are generally deemed involuntary and not admissible at trial unless the defendant is given *Miranda* warnings before the interview and waives his rights.

Business papers voluntarily prepared by an individual, or required records, such as tax returns, are not protected.

3. Immunity

The prosecution may compel incriminating testimony if it grants immunity to the individual and the individual must testify. The testimony cannot be used against the individual, directly or indirectly, in a subsequent prosecution.

a. Transactional immunity

Often called "blanket" or "total" immunity, "transactional immunity" fully protects a witness from future prosecution for crimes related to her testimony.

b. Use and derivative-use immunity

"Use and derivative-use" immunity only precludes the prosecution from using the witness's own testimony, or any evidence derived from the testimony, against the witness. The Supreme Court has held that the grant of "use and derivative-use" immunity is all that is constitutionally required to compel the testimony of a witness. *Kastigar v. United States*, 406 U.S. 441, 452–453 (1972). Testimony encouraged by a promise of immunity, however, is considered coerced and involuntary.

c. Federal and state immunity

Testimony under a grant of immunity may not be used by another U.S. jurisdiction to prosecute the defendant. *See United States v. Balsys*, 524 U.S. 666 (U.S. 1998); *Murphy v. Waterfront Comm'n*, 378 U.S. 52 (1964). Thus, a state grant of immunity will preclude admission of the testimony in a federal proceeding.

4. Prosecutorial Comment

The prosecutor may not comment on the defendant's exercise of the privilege against self-incrimination at trial. It is per se reversible error.

III. SIXTH AMENDMENT

The Sixth Amendment provides that the accused shall have the right to a public trial, the right to confront witnesses against him, the right to cross-examine witnesses, the right to be present at his own trial, and the right to "the assistance of counsel for his defense." The right to assistance of counsel encompasses not only the right to hire private counsel, but also the right to be provided with counsel without charge if the accused is unable to afford counsel.

A. APPLICABILITY: RIGHT TO COUNSEL

1. Types of Proceedings

The Sixth Amendment provides a constitutional right to counsel:

i) In all felony cases; and

ii) In any misdemeanor case in which actual (or suspended) incarceration is imposed.

2. When Applicable

The Sixth Amendment right to counsel applies at all **critical stages** of a prosecution, after formal proceedings have begun. The right automatically **attaches** when the State initiates prosecution with an **indictment or formal charge** and **ends at the sentencing stage** of the trial.

> **EXAM NOTE:** Unlike the Fifth Amendment right to counsel, the defendant does not need to invoke the Sixth Amendment right to counsel. The failure to provide counsel results in automatic reversal of a conviction.

a. Critical stages

The Supreme Court recently summarized its definition of "critical stage" as those proceedings between an individual and an agent of the state that amount to trial-like confrontations, at which counsel would help the accused in coping with legal problems or meeting his adversary. *Rothgery v. Gillespie County*, 554 U.S. 191, 212 (2008).

Generally, the right to counsel attaches at the following critical stages:

  i) Post-indictment lineups and identifications;

  ii) Custodial police interrogations;

  iii) Post-indictment interrogations, whether custodial or otherwise;

  iv) Arraignment and preliminary hearing to determine probable cause to prosecute;

  v) Guilty pleas and sentencing; and

  vi) Appeals as a matter of right.

b. Noncritical stages

The right to counsel generally does not apply to the following events:

  i) A witness viewing photos of the alleged defendant;

  ii) Precharge (investigative) lineups;

  iii) Taking of fingerprints, handwriting exemplars, voice exemplars, or blood samples;

  iv) Hearings to determine probable cause to detain the defendant (*Gerstein* hearing);

  v) Discretionary appeals; and

  vi) Post-conviction proceedings, such as parole or probation hearings (except habeas corpus).

3. Indigence

When the right to counsel exists, an indigent defendant has the right to the appointment of counsel. However, this right does not entitle an indigent defendant to the appointment of counsel of his own choosing. *See United States v. Gonzalez-Lopez*, 548 U.S. 140, 147–148 (2006) (defendant who retains his own counsel has the right to be represented by that attorney); *Wheat v. United States*, 486 U.S. 153 (1988).

4. Waiver

A defendant has the constitutional right to refuse counsel and proceed pro se at trial unless the request is untimely or the defendant is unable or unwilling to abide by the rules of procedure or protocol. *Faretta v. California*, 422 U.S. 806 (1975). A defendant who is competent to stand trial may nevertheless be found incompetent to represent himself. *Indiana v. Edwards*, 554 U.S. 164 (2009). In addition, a defendant does not have a right to proceed without an attorney on an appeal. *Martinez v. Court of Appeal*, 528 U.S. 152 (2000).

In the Fifth Amendment context, once an individual in custody asserts the Fifth Amendment right to counsel, no subsequent waiver of that right is valid in a police-initiated interrogation. *Edwards v. Arizona*, 451 U.S. 477, 484 (1981). However, police may re-open interrogation of a suspect who has asserted his Fifth Amendment right to counsel if there has been a 14-day or more break in custody (such as a the suspect's release back into the general prison population). *Maryland v. Shatzer*, 559 U.S. ___, 130 S. Ct. 22 (2010). The Sixth Amendment right to counsel can be waived "so long as relinquishment of the right is voluntary, knowing and intelligent." *Montejo v. Louisiana*, 556 U.S. 778 (2009). Thus, as long as the defendant is given *Miranda* warnings and a valid waiver occurs, evidence obtained voluntarily from the interrogation without the presence of counsel is admissible.

> **EXAM NOTE:** Remember, even if the defendant has made a valid waiver of his right to counsel, statements made during interrogation must be **voluntary** to be admissible at trial, i.e., the police still cannot use compelled statements.

B. OFFENSE-SPECIFIC

Once the Sixth Amendment right to counsel is properly invoked, it applies **only** to the specific offense at issue in those proceedings. *McNeil v. Wisconsin*, 501 U.S. 171, 175–176 (1991).

1. *Blockburger* Test

Two crimes committed in one criminal transaction are deemed to be the same offense for Sixth Amendment purposes unless each offense requires proof of an element that the other does not. *Texas v. Cobb*, 532 U.S. 162 (2001); *Blockburger v. United States*, 284 U.S. 299, 304 (1932).

2. Compare to *Miranda*

Unlike under the *Miranda* standard, under the Sixth Amendment standard, the requirement for counsel to be present applies only to interrogations about the offense charged. However, like with *Miranda,* the defendant may make a knowing and voluntary waiver of the right to counsel being present.

> **Example:** Defendant Dave has been charged with burglary and is out on bail awaiting trial. The police also suspect Dave in an unrelated arson case, and they bring him to the police station to question him about the arson. Dave is given the *Miranda* warnings and waives his right to remain silent, but he asks to see his attorney. The police do not call Dave's attorney but continue to interrogate Dave until he confesses to the arson. While the police did violate Dave's Fifth Amendment right to have an attorney present during questioning, they did not violate his Sixth Amendment right to counsel, as the arson was unrelated to the burglary.

C. REMEDIES FOR DENIAL OF COUNSEL

1. Effect on Conviction

If a right to counsel at a trial proceeding under the Sixth Amendment is denied, the defendant's conviction should be automatically reversed, even without a specific showing of unfairness. *Gideon v. Wainwright*, 372 U.S. 335, 339 (1963). Automatic reversal also applies to a conviction obtained after a court has erroneously refused to permit an attorney chosen by the defendant to represent him, when that attorney is not supplied by the state. *United States v. Gonzalez-Lopez*, 548 U.S. 140 (2006).

2. Effect on Guilty Plea

If the defendant has pleaded guilty at a preliminary hearing, without being given the opportunity to have counsel, then the defendant has the right to withdraw the plea, and it may not be used against the defendant as an evidentiary admission. *White v. Maryland*, 373 U.S. 59, 60 (1963).

3. Effect on Denial of Counsel at Nontrial Proceedings

A denial of counsel at a nontrial proceeding, such as a lineup, is subject to harmless-error analysis. *United States v. Wade*, 388 U.S. 218, 223 (1967).

4. Admissibility of a Defendant's Statements to Informants

Post-indictment statements that a defendant makes to a police informant are inadmissible when the police intentionally create a situation likely to induce the defendant into making incriminating statements without the assistance of counsel. *United States v. Henry*, 447 U.S. 264, 274–275 (1980). There is no Sixth Amendment violation, however, if the police place an informant in the defendant's cell simply to listen and report the defendant's statements, without questioning the defendant. *Kuhlmann v. Wilson*, 477 U.S. 436, 456 (1986).

5. Exclusionary Rule Under the Sixth Amendment

a. Fruits doctrine

The fruit of the poisonous tree doctrine is applicable to violations of the Sixth Amendment right to counsel. *Nix v. Williams*, 467 U.S. 431 (1984). Both statements and physical evidence obtained as a result of a Sixth Amendment violation are inadmissible.

b. Impeachment

If the police initiate a conversation with an accused individual who has requested counsel, any incriminating statements made by the defendant may still be used for impeachment purposes, despite the fact that the improper police conduct precludes admission of the statements as part of the prosecution's case in chief. *Michigan v. Harvey*, 494 U.S. 344, 350–351 (1990).

D. INEFFECTIVE ASSISTANCE OF COUNSEL

1. Standard of Competence

The right to counsel encompasses the right to be assisted by a reasonably competent attorney and is presumed. The right to effective counsel extends to the defendant's first appeal. To reverse a conviction on the ground of ineffective counsel, the claimant has the burden to show that:

i) Counsel's representation fell below an objective standard of reasonableness; and

ii) Counsel's deficient performance prejudiced the defendant, resulting in an unreliable or fundamentally unfair outcome in the proceeding.

Strickland v. Washington, 466 U.S. 668, 687 (1984). Counsel's mere inexperience, strategy, choice of appellate issues, or even failure to produce mitigating evidence have all been found insufficient to rise to the level of ineffective counsel. *Bell v. Cone*, 535 U.S. 685 (2002); *Jones v. Barnes*, 463 U.S. 745 (1988); *United States v. Cronic*, 466 U.S. 648 (1984). The failure of defense counsel to raise a federal constitutional issue that was law at the time of the trial, but was later overruled, does not constitute ineffective assistance of counsel. *Lockhart v. Fretwell*, 506 U.S. 364 (1993).

2. **Conflict of Interest**

The representation of defendants with conflicting interests may amount to ineffective assistance of counsel. In general, to overturn a conviction on the basis of a conflict of interest, a defendant must show that there was an actual conflict of interest and that such conflict adversely affected the attorney's performance.

a. **Actual conflict**

To find an actual conflict, a court must determine that the defense attorney is subject to an obligation or unique personal interest that, if followed, would lead her to adopt a strategy other than that most favorable to the defendant.

b. **Adverse impact**

Adverse impact can be established by demonstrating that some plausible alternative defense strategy or tactic might have been pursued and such strategy or tactic was inherently in conflict with, or not undertaken, due to the attorney's other loyalties or interests. The conflicting character of the strategy is not sufficient if the strategy actually was rejected because another strategy was viewed as even more favorable to the accused.

c. **Knowledge of the court**

If an attorney representing codefendants makes a timely motion for appointment of separate counsel based on a potential conflict of interest, then the trial judge must either grant the motion or at least conduct a hearing to determine whether appointment of separate counsel is warranted under the circumstances. Failure of the judge to do so requires automatic reversal of a subsequent conviction. *Holloway v. Arkansas*, 435 U.S. 475, 484 (1978). Actual conflict and prejudice are presumed under such circumstances.

Unless the trial court knows or reasonably should know that a conflict exists, however, the court is not required to inquire about multiple representations. *Cuyler v. Sullivan*, 446 U.S. 335, 347–348 (1980). Actual conflict (rather than potential conflict) is required to be shown on appeal if the issue of separate trials was not brought up during the trial, and the defendant must show that the conflict adversely affected counsel's performance. *Mickens v. Taylor*, 535 U.S. 162, 173 (2002).

d. Rule 44(c)

When co-defendants are represented by the same attorney, Rule 44(c) of the Federal Rules of Criminal Procedure requires the court to conduct a prompt inquiry into potential conflicts of interest and advise the defendants of the right to separate representation. Failure to comply with the Rule, though, will not constitute a per se reversible error, and an appellate court will likely ask whether the end result was representation by counsel under an actual conflict.

e. Disqualification despite waiver

A trial court has the authority to disqualify a defense attorney, even over the objection of the defendant, if the court concludes that there is serious potential of a conflict of interest. *Wheat v. United States*, 486 U.S. 153, 158–159 (1988).

3. Right to Confidential Communications

No type of discovery device may be used by the prosecution to obtain information about the defense of the case.

IV. PRETRIAL PROCEDURES

A. EYEWITNESS IDENTIFICATION PROCEDURES

1. Types

There are two types of identification procedures: corporeal and noncorporeal. Corporeal identifications are "in-person," as in lineups. Noncorporeal identifications are not in-person and involve police officers using photo arrays for a witness to identify the suspect.

2. Sixth Amendment Right to Counsel at Lineups

A defendant is entitled to have counsel present at any post-indictment lineup in which the defendant is required to participate. Testimony about a post-indictment, pre-trial identification in the absence of counsel is inadmissible at trial, but the witness may still identify the defendant at trial if the prosecution can show that the identification has independent reliability. *Kirby v. Illinois*, 406 U.S. 682, 690–691 (1972). The right to counsel does not apply to any pre-indictment eyewitness identification. *Id.*

a. Waiver

The defendant can waive the right to have counsel present, provided that waiver is made knowingly and intelligently.

b. Remedy

A violation of the defendant's right to have counsel present at a lineup results in the exclusion of the identification.

3. Admissibility of Pre- and Post-Indictment Identification

a. Two-prong test

Courts use a two-prong test to determine the admissibility of a pre- or post-indictment lineup identification: (i) the defendant must prove that the identification procedure was **impermissibly suggestive**, and (ii) the court must determine whether the testimony was **nonetheless reliable**, using five factors:

i) The witness's **opportunity to view** the defendant at the time of the crime;

ii) The witness's **degree of attention** at the time of the crime;

iii) The **accuracy of the witness's description** of the defendant prior to the identification;

iv) The **level of certainty** at the time of the identification; and

v) The **length of time** between the crime and the identification.

Neil v. Biggers, 409 U.S. 188, 199–200 (1972).

b. Remedy

1) Hearing

A suppression hearing will be held to determine the admissibility of the evidence. It usually is held outside the presence of the jury, although exclusion of the jury is not constitutionally required. The government has the burden of proving that the defendant waived counsel or that counsel was present, and the defendant has the burden of demonstrating a violation of due process.

2) Suggestiveness finding

A finding of "impermissibly suggestive procedures" will result in suppression of the out-of-court identification. However, an in-court identification of the defendant by the witness is admissible if the prosecution can establish by clear and convincing evidence that the identification at trial was reliable.

3) Standard of review

A conviction as the result of a trial in which an illegal identification was admitted will be overturned **unless,** under the doctrine of harmless error, the appellate court is convinced beyond a reasonable doubt that the improperly admitted identification did not contribute to the verdict.

4. Non-Corporeal Identifications

There is no right to counsel during a pre- or post-indictment photo spread.

A photo spread is not a critical stage of the prosecution, but the prosecution is required to turn over the photographic display in discovery, and the defendant may file a motion to suppress based upon suggestiveness of the photo array. The two-prong test for determining the validity of an in-court identification in which the witness has previously identified the defendant at a lineup (*see* § 3.a., *supra*) also applies when the witness has previously identified the defendant through a photo array.

B. PRELIMINARY PROCEEDINGS

Subsequent to the defendant's arrest, various court proceedings may be held. These pretrial proceedings, which take various forms depending on the jurisdiction, can include a hearing to determine probable cause to detain (a *Gerstein* hearing), an initial appearance, an arraignment, a detention or bail hearing, and a preliminary hearing to determine probable cause to prosecute the defendant. Some of these proceedings may be combined, and some may not be required. In addition, the defendant may make various motions, including motions to suppress evidence obtained in violation of the defendant's constitutional rights.

1. Probable Cause to Detain (*Gerstein* Hearing)

Under the Fourth Amendment, a preliminary hearing must be held after the defendant's arrest to determine whether probable cause exists to hold the defendant, unless such determination has already been made before the defendant's arrest through a grand jury indictment or the judicial issuance of an arrest warrant. *Gerstein v. Pugh*, 420 U.S. 103 (1975). This hearing, known as a *Gerstein* hearing, need not be adversarial. There is no right to counsel at this hearing, and hearsay evidence may be introduced, but a hearing not held within 48 hours after arrest is presumptively unreasonable. *County of Riverside v. McLaughlin*, 500 U.S. 44 (1991). However, the failure to hold this hearing does not affect the prosecution of the defendant for the charged offense, other than the exclusion of any evidence discovered as a consequence of the unlawful detainment. Under the Fifth Amendment, all felony charges must be by indictment of a federal grand jury, unless waived by the defendant.

2. Initial Appearance

Soon after the defendant is arrested, the defendant must be brought before a judge who advises the defendant of the charges against him and of his rights and who appoints counsel if the defendant is indigent. During this initial appearance, which may be held in conjunction with a *Gerstein* hearing, the judge may also determine whether the defendant should be released prior to trial and the conditions of the release (e.g., bail), accept a plea from the defendant, and set a date for a preliminary hearing.

3. Arraignment

At an arraignment, the court informs the defendant of the crime with which the defendant has been charged and elicits the defendant's response (i.e., plea) to those charges. At this time, the court may appoint counsel for an indigent defendant. These events may also take place at the initial appearance.

4. Detention Hearing

In conjunction with the defendant's initial appearance or at a separate hearing, the court may determine whether to release the defendant and any conditions upon such release. At such time, the court may set bail (*see* § C. Right to Bail, *infra*).

5. Preliminary Hearing to Determine Probable Cause to Prosecute

Subsequent to the defendant's initial appearance, a preliminary hearing may be held to determine whether there is probable cause to believe that the defendant has committed a specific crime. At this hearing, which is an adversarial proceeding, the defendant has the right to counsel. *Coleman v. Alabama*, 399 U.S. 1 (1970). A defendant who has been indicted by a grand jury is not entitled to this hearing.

C. RIGHT TO BAIL

There is no explicit constitutional right to bail. However, any denial of bail must comply with the Due Process Clause. Therefore, the setting of excessive bail or the refusal to set bail is immediately appealable. Furthermore, bail set higher than an amount reasonably calculated to ensure the defendant's presence at trial is "excessive" under the Eighth Amendment.

1. Statutory Bail Provisions

The Bail Reform Act of 1984 governs release or detention determinations in federal courts in criminal proceedings. Many states have modeled similar statutory bail provisions on the Act.

2. Presumptions Pre- and Post-Conviction

There is a presumption in favor of pre-trial release. A detention hearing must be held at the initial appearance for there to be a release. However, there is a presumption against bail post-conviction, pending appeal. The Federal Rules of Evidence do not apply at detention hearings.

3. Pre-Trial Detention

Certain pretrial detention practices that are reasonably related to maintaining jail security are permissible and do not violate due process or the Fourth Amendment. These include routine inspections of inmates' cells, prohibiting receipt of outside food or personal belongings, body-cavity searches, and double bunking.

D. COMPETENCY

Incompetency is a bar to trial. The judge has a constitutional duty to investigate and determine the competence of the defendant to stand trial if such evidence is apparent to the judge. A separate hearing is held to assess the defendant's competency. The test for whether a defendant is competent to stand trial is the same test for determining whether the defendant is competent to plead guilty: whether the defendant comprehends the nature of the proceedings against him and has the ability to consult with a lawyer with a reasonable degree of rational understanding.

If the defendant is declared mentally incompetent to stand trial, and the charge is a serious criminal offense, then the government may administer antipsychotic drugs. Three conditions must be met before the defendant can receive these drugs:

i) The treatment should not cause serious side effects that would affect the fairness of the trial;

ii) The treatment is necessary and there is no less intrusive method to further the government's important interest; and

iii) The treatment is medically appropriate.

Insanity Defense Distinguished: The insanity defense considers the defendant's mental condition at the time of the crime, whereas incompetence concerns the defendant's mental condition at the time of the trial. Detention also varies depending on whether it is based on incompetency or insanity. In a successful insanity defense, the defendant may be detained in a mental hospital for a longer term than incarceration requires. If a defendant is found to be incompetent, confinement in a mental hospital must be limited to a brief period of time for evaluation.

The conviction of a legally incompetent defendant or the failure of the trial court to provide an adequate competency determination violates due-process principles by depriving the defendant of the constitutional right to a fair trial. State courts may place the burden of proving incompetence on the defendant, but they may not require the defendant to prove it by clear and convincing evidence.

E. GRAND JURIES

1. Indictment

After hearing the prosecution's evidence, the grand jury decides whether there is probable cause to charge a particular defendant with a particular crime and, if so, returns a "true bill" of indictment. (This formal charging process is mandated by the Fifth Amendment under the federal system for felonies and is used in most eastern states, but a state is not constitutionally required to use this process, as the Fifth Amendment Grand Jury Clause has not been incorporated by the Fourteenth Amendment. In most western states, the charging process is initiated by filing an information by a prosecutor.)

2. Grand Jury Proceedings

a. Defendant's rights

The grand jury is a non-adversarial proceeding. The proceedings are conducted in secret, and the defendant has no right to present or confront witnesses or to introduce evidence. The defendant is not entitled to a dismissal due to a procedural defect in grand jury proceedings, unless the defect substantially impacted the grand jury's decision to indict. However, the defendant (or any other witness) may make a motion to seal the grand jury report if he believes that he has been defamed.

1) Double jeopardy

Because jeopardy does not attach until a trial begins, the Double Jeopardy Clause does not apply to grand jury proceedings. The refusal of a grand jury to indict a defendant with respect to a specific crime does not prevent the indictment of the defendant for the same crime by another grand jury. *United States v. Williams*, 504 U.S. 36, 49 (1992). (*See* § VI.A., Double Jeopardy, *infra*.)

b. Role of the prosecutor

The prosecutor is the advisor to the grand jury. As such, the prosecutor's role is to advise the grand jury with respect to the law and assist the grand jury in its job of issuing subpoenas for witnesses and evidence. The prosecutor has no legal obligation to present evidence exculpating the defendant to the grand jury. Thus, a grand jury indictment cannot be dismissed for the prosecutor's failure to present exculpatory evidence, unless the prosecutor violated a preexisting constitutional or legislative rule. The prosecutor is subject to the grand jury secrecy rules.

c. Witness's rights

A grand jury witness has no right to counsel in the grand jury room. The witness may request permission to consult with counsel outside of the jury room before answering a grand jury question. A prosecutor's failure to give a *Miranda* warning to a witness who then lies to a grand jury does not prevent the prosecution of the witness for perjury. *United States v. Wong*, 431 U.S. 174 (1977). Further, a witness who is a target of an investigation and may become a defendant is not entitled to a warning of his putative defendant status; the failure to receive such a warning does not protect a lying witness from a perjury conviction. *United States v. Washington*, 431 U.S. 181 (1977).

d. Grand jury's role

The grand jury has subpoena power to investigate matters before it or to initiate criminal proceedings. The subpoena can be quashed by the opposing party if he can demonstrate that the evidence sought is not relevant to the investigation. However, the witness or defendant cannot attack the subpoena based on the grand jury's lack of probable cause. The grand jury is not restricted to hearing evidence that would be admissible at trial; an indictment may generally be based on hearsay or illegally obtained evidence. *United States v. Calandra*, 414 U.S. 338, 348 (1974) (illegally seized evidence admissible in grand jury proceeding); *Costello v. United States*, 350 U.S. 359 (1956) (hearsay evidence admissible in grand jury proceeding). (Note: By federal statute, information obtained from an illegal wiretap cannot be presented to a grand jury. 18 U.S.C. 2515.) The grand jury may not exclude members of minority races, regardless of whether they are the same race as the defendant. Such exclusion will lead to a reversal of the indictment without regard to the harmlessness of the error. *Campbell v. Louisiana*, 523 U.S. 392 (1998); *Vasquez v. Hillery*, 474 U.S. 254 (1986).

F.   STATE'S DUTY TO DISCLOSE

The prosecution has an affirmative duty to disclose any material evidence favorable to the defendant and relevant to the prosecution's case in chief that would negate guilt or diminish culpability or punishment. *Brady v. Maryland*, 373 U.S. 83 (1963). Failure to make such a disclosure violates the Due Process Clause and is grounds for reversal, regardless of whether the failure to disclose was intentional, if the defendant can show that (i) the evidence is favorable to the defendant (i.e., is exculpatory or impeaches) and (ii) the failure to disclose caused prejudice against the defendant. *Strickler v. Green*, 527 U.S. 263, 281-282 (1999); *United States v. Bagley*, 473 U.S. 667, 675 (1985). This duty does not extend to disclosure of impeachment evidence prior to a plea bargain agreement, *United States v. Ruiz*, 536 U.S. 622 (2002), or to post-conviction proceedings.

V.   TRIAL

A.   JURY TRIAL

In the federal system, the Sixth Amendment provides the right to jury trials. States are obligated under the Fourteenth Amendment to provide jury trials in criminal cases involving only serious offenses. *Duncan v. Louisiana*, 391 U.S. 145 (1968). States have wide latitude, though, to determine the conduct and details of jury use.

1. **Maximum Sentence to Exceed Six Months**

There is a constitutional right to a jury trial for **serious offenses**—those that carry an authorized sentence of **more than six months of imprisonment,** regardless of the actual penalty imposed. *Baldwin v. New York*, 399 U.S. 66 (1970). The right to a jury trial attaches for crimes punishable by six months of imprisonment or less only if additional statutory or regulatory penalties make the offense a "serious offense." *United States v. Nachtigal*, 507 U.S. 1 (1993) (a misdemeanor for which the maximum punishment was six months in prison and a $5,000 fine or probation not to exceed five years was not a serious offense). There is no right to trial by jury for multiple petty offenses (those that carry a combined total maximum term exceeding six months); the prison terms imposed for such convictions are not aggregated.

   a. **Contempt**

   In a civil contempt case, there is no jury trial requirement if the witness can avoid the punishment by complying with the court order. In a criminal contempt case that has no statutorily authorized punishment, the right to a jury trial is determined by the actual penalty imposed. Thus, a sentence of over six months would trigger the right to a jury trial. However, an alleged contemnor is not entitled to a jury trial simply because a strong possibility exists that upon conviction he will face a substantial term of imprisonment regardless of the punishment actually imposed. Moreover, if a sentence is imposed for contempt and it is more than six months, an appellate court may reduce the sentence to six months or less to protect the conviction against constitutional attack for lack of a jury. There is no right to a jury trial when the sentence imposed is probation, regardless of the length of the probation, at least when imprisonment following revocation of probation does not exceed six months.

2. **Waiver**

A defendant may waive the right to a jury trial and opt for a trial by judge, known as a "bench trial," by (i) obtaining the court's approval and, in some jurisdictions, the consent of the prosecutor, (ii) entering a voluntary waiver, (iii) expressing the waiver in open court knowingly and intelligently, and (iv) recording the waiver in writing.

3. **Compliance**

   a. **Jury size and unanimity**

   A jury of less than six members is a denial of due process, and a unanimous verdict is constitutionally required if a jury is made up of only six members. For juries of seven or more, the vote need not be unanimous, but there is no strict rule as to how many votes are required for conviction.

   Federal Rule of Criminal Procedure 23(b) requires a 12-member jury unless waived in writing and approved by the court. A verdict by 11 jurors is permitted if the 12th juror is excused for good cause after deliberations begin.

   b. **Composition of the jury**

      1) **Representative cross-section of the community**

      The Equal Protection Clause bars racial discrimination in the selection of juries, including grand juries. The requirement that a jury be selected from a representative cross-section of the community also extends to sexual discrimination. However, the actual jury selected need not represent a fair cross-section of the community. *Holland v. Illinois*, 493 U.S. 474, 480 (1990).

2) All defendants may challenge jury selection discrimination

The defendant has standing to challenge the jury-selection process, regardless of any showing of actual bias. *Powers v. Ohio*, 499 U.S. 400, 410–411 (1991).

3) Prima facie case

The prima facie case for absence of a representative cross-section can be established by showing that:

i) The group allegedly excluded is a **"distinctive" group** in the community;

ii) The group was not **fairly represented** in the venire from which the jury was chosen; and

iii) The underrepresentation resulted from a **systematic exclusion** of the group in the jury-selection process.

To rebut, the prosecution must show that the disproportionate exclusion manifestly and primarily advances a significant governmental interest.

4) State's right to use neutral principles

In response to a claim of intentional racial discrimination in jury selection, the state has the right to apply neutral, nonracial principles to jury selection, even though it results in a smaller percentage of minorities on juries. The state must prove "absence of discriminatory intent."

5) Peremptory challenges

Peremptory challenges are requests by both parties during the voir dire jury-selection process to disqualify potential jurors without the need to show cause.

a) Discriminatory use

The Fourteenth Amendment Equal Protection Clause prohibits both the criminal defendant and the prosecutor from exercising peremptory challenges solely based on race or gender. *J.E.B. v. Alabama*, 511 U.S. 127 (1994); *Batson v. Kentucky*, 476 U.S. 79, 84 (1986). The defendant need not be a member of the excluded group in order to have standing to contest the prosecution's use of its peremptory challenges.

If the explanation for striking a juror is deemed pretextual, then it gives rise to an inference of discriminatory intent that makes it difficult for the challenge to survive. *Snyder v. Louisiana*, 552 U.S. 472, 485 (2008).

The United States Supreme Court has set forth a three-prong test (the "*Batson*" test) to determine whether a **peremptory challenge** has been exercised on the basis of race, in violation of the Equal Protection Clause of the Fourteenth Amendment. The test requires that:

i) The moving party establishes a **prima facie case of discrimination**;

ii) The party who exercised the challenge provides a **race-neutral explanation** for the strike;

iii) The moving party carries her burden of **proving that the other party's proffered reason was pretextual** and that the strike was indeed motivated by purposeful discrimination.

Once the party who exercised the challenge offers a race-neutral explanation and the trial court has ruled on the ultimate question of intentional discrimination, the preliminary issue becomes moot. **The ultimate burden of persuasion regarding racial motivation rests with the opponent of the strike.**

b) Not constitutionally required

The loss of a peremptory challenge does not violate the right to an impartial jury. *Ross v. Oklahoma*, 487 U.S. 81, 88 (1988). A defendant's exercise of peremptory challenges is not denied or impaired when the defendant chooses to use such a challenge to remove a juror who should have been excused for cause. *United States v. Martinez-Salazar*, 528 U.S. 304, 307 (2000).

c) Harmless-error doctrine

The Constitution allows states to choose between harmless-error review and automatic reversal when a judge, acting in good faith, erroneously denies a defendant's peremptory challenge. *Rivera v. Illinois*, 556 U.S. 148 (2009). Thus, if state law permits harmless-error review of the erroneous seating of the juror, there is no constitutional requirement for automatic reversal of the defendant's conviction.

c. Impartial jury

The Sixth Amendment provides that an accused person is entitled to a trial by an impartial jury. Claims of juror bias and misconduct are subject to the harmless-error rule.

1) Views on race

A defendant is entitled to inquire on voir dire into ethnic or racial prejudice of possible jury members only when the issues to be tried involve allegations of racial or ethnic prejudice, or whenever race is "inextricably bound up in the case." *Ristiano v. Ross*, 424 U.S. 589, 597 (1976).

2) Views on capital punishment

Prospective jurors who are opposed to the death penalty may be removed for cause if their opposition to the death penalty is so strong as to prevent or substantially impair the performance of their duties at the sentencing phase of the trial. *Wainwright v. Wirr*, 469 U.S. 412, 424–425 (1985); *Adams v. Texas*, 448 U.S. 38, 44 (1980).

An improper exclusion of a juror from a jury that imposed a death sentence is subject to automatic reversal. *Gray v. Mississippi*, 481 U.S. 648, 668 (1987).

d. Sentencing

1) Enhancements

When a sentence may be increased if additional facts are established, a jury must determine the existence of such facts. Enhancement of a defendant's sentence by a judge without such a determination violates the defendant's right to a jury trial. *Apprendi v. New Jersey*, 530 U.S. 466, 476 (2000). This limitation on a judge's ability to impose an enhanced sentence also applies when the defendant has entered a guilty plea. *Blakely v. Washington*, 542 U.S. 296 (2004). However, the harmless-error test applies to determine whether a sentence enhanced in violation of a defendant's right to a jury trial must be reversed. *Washington v. Recuenco*, 548 U.S. 212 (2006).

2) Concurrent versus consecutive sentences

Judges can decide whether sentences for multiple crimes run concurrently or consecutively without violating this right. *Oregon v. Ice*, 555 U.S. 160 (2009).

e. Inconsistent verdicts

If a jury renders a verdict that a defendant is guilty of certain offenses but not guilty of other related offenses, then the verdict is not reviewable on the grounds of inconsistency, even when the jury acquits the defendant of an offense that is a predicate offense to an offense for which the same jury finds the defendant guilty. *United States v. Powell*, 469 U.S. 57 (1984). This rule, which permits inconsistent verdicts, is also applicable when a defendant is convicted of an offense for which a co-defendant, who is tried at the same time, is acquitted, even though the facts would logically dictate the same verdict for each defendant. *United States v. Dotterweich*, 320 U.S. 277 (1943). This rule extends to bench as well as jury trials. *Harris v. Rivera*, 454 U.S. 339 (1981). (Note: The defendant may challenge a jury verdict on the grounds that there was insufficient evidence to establish the defendant's commission of a crime.)

B. GUILTY PLEAS

A guilty plea is an admission of facts contained in the charging document (e.g., indictment, information).

1. Knowing and Voluntary

Because a guilty plea constitutes both a confession and a waiver of various constitutional rights, the plea must be both intelligent and voluntary. *Boykin v. Alabama*, 395 U.S. 238 (1969); *McCarthy v. United States*, 394 U.S. 459 (1969). The record must reflect that the judge has determined that the defendant knows and understands the following:

i) The nature of the charges and their essential elements;

ii) The consequences of the plea (i.e., the maximum and minimum possible sentences); and

iii) The rights that the defendant is waiving (e.g., right to a trial).

(Note: The judge does not personally need to explain each element of the crime. It is sufficient for the defendant's counsel to explain the nature and elements of the crime to him. *Bradshaw v. Stumpf*, 545 U.S. 175 (2005).) The judge must also determine that the plea did not result from force or improper threats or from promises other than those contained in the plea agreement.

a. Factual basis for plea

Although the federal rules of criminal procedure require a judge to ascertain that there is factual basis for the defendant's plea, a judge is generally not constitutionally required to ascertain that there is a factual basis for the plea, nor does the defendant need to admit guilt. However, when the defendant, despite entering a plea, also asserts his innocence, the judge must determine that there is a factual basis for the plea. *North Carolina v. Alford*, 400 U.S. 25, 37 (1970).

b. Effect of violation

When the court fails to ensure that the plea was knowing and voluntary, the defendant is entitled to withdraw his plea.

2. Right to Counsel

In entering a plea, a defendant has the right to counsel. *White v. Maryland*, 373 U.S. 59 (1963).

3. Plea Bargain

A plea bargain between the prosecutor and the defendant is treated as a contract. The bargain may involve the crimes with which the defendant has been charged, such as a promise by the prosecutor to drop specific charges in exchange for the defendant's promise to plead guilty to other charges, or the defendant's sentence, such as a promise by the prosecutor to recommend a particular sentence in exchange for the defendant's guilty plea.

a. No right to bargain

A defendant cannot compel the prosecutor to bargain; the defendant does not have a constitutional right to plea bargain. *Weatherford v. Bursey*, 429 U.S. 545 (1977).

b. Pressure to bargain

A defendant's plea made in response to the prosecution's threat to bring more serious charges does not violate the protection of the Due Process Clause against prosecutorial vindictiveness, at least when the prosecution has probable cause to believe that the defendant has committed the crimes. *Bordenkircher v. Hayes*, 434 U.S. 357 (1978). Similarly, the bringing of felony charges against a defendant after the defendant asserted his right to a jury trial for misdemeanor offenses related to the same incident does not in itself constitute prosecutorial vindictiveness. *United States v. Goodwin*, 457 U.S. 368 (1982).

c. No duty to disclose impeachment information

The prosecution is not required to disclose impeachment information or information related to an affirmative defense to a defendant when the defendant enters into a plea bargain agreement prior to trial. The failure to disclose such information does not render the defendant's plea bargain involuntary. *United States v. Ruiz*, 536 U.S. 622 (2002).

d. Enforcement of the bargain

1) Court

When entering into a plea bargain, the agreement is enforceable against the defendant and the prosecutor, but not against the judge. If the judge is not satisfied with the bargain, he can reject the plea. A defendant does not have a constitutional right to have his plea accepted by the court.

2) Prosecution

Should the prosecution violate the provisions of the plea bargain, the judge decides whether specific performance of the plea is required or whether the defendant can withdraw his plea. *Santobello v. New York*, 404 U.S. 257 (1971).

3) Defense

If a defendant fails to abide by the plea agreement (e.g., fails to testify in another trial), then the prosecution can have the sentence vacated and reinstate the original charge. *Ricketts v. Adamson*, 483 U.S. 1 (1987).

4. Effect of the Plea on the Defendant's Rights

Generally, a defendant, by entering a guilty plea, waives his constitutional rights, such as the right to a trial, the privilege against self-incrimination, and the right to confront his accusers. However, a defendant may challenge a guilty plea on the due-process grounds that it was not a knowing and voluntary waiver of such rights. *Boykin v. Alabama*, 395 U.S. 238 (1969). In addition, a guilty plea does not constitute a waiver of a double jeopardy challenge unless the waiver is agreed to in the plea agreement. *Menna v. New York*, 423 U.S. 61 (1975). A defendant may also attack a guilty plea that is due to ineffective assistance of counsel. *Hill v. Lockhart*, 474 U.S. 52 (1985). (Note: A defendant may also challenge a guilty plea on the grounds that the court lacked jurisdiction. *Menna v. New York, supra*.)

C. SPEEDY TRIAL

The Due Process Clause and federal statutes protect defendants from intentional and prejudicial **pre-accusation** delay. The Sixth Amendment speedy trial guarantee, the Fourteenth Amendment, the Speedy Trial Act of 1974, and other federal and state statutes protect defendants from undue **post-accusation** delay.

1. Commencement of the Right

Statutes of limitations are the primary safeguards against pre-accusation delay. However, the Due Process Clause may be violated if the delay was used to obtain a tactical advantage for the prosecution or to harass the defendant. *United States v. Marion*, 404 U.S. 307 (1971). Delay resulting from an investigation conducted in good faith does not violate the Due Process Clause. *United States v. Lovasco*, 431 U.S. 783 (1977).

Under the Sixth and Fourteenth Amendments, the time period commences at the time of arrest or formal charge, whichever comes first. The defendant need not know about the charges against him for the right to attach.

2. Balancing Test

The factors to be considered in determining whether the defendant has been deprived of a speedy trial post-accusation are the:

i) Length of the delay;

ii) Reason for the delay;

iii) Defendant's assertion of a right to a speedy trial; and

iv) Prejudice to the defendant.

Courts weigh these factors and determine whether the state made a "diligent, good-faith effort" to bring the defendant to trial. *Barker v. Wingo*, 407 U.S. 514, 530 (1972). A delay caused by the inaction of an attorney assigned by the state to represent the defendant may be attributable to the defendant, but a delay caused by the court's failure to promptly appoint replacement counsel when an assigned attorney withdraws or by a breakdown in the public-defender system is attributable to the state. *Vermont v. Brillon*, 556 U.S. 81 (2009).

3. Remedy

If the defendant's right to a speedy trial is violated, the charges are dismissed with prejudice.

D. PUBLIC TRIAL

1. Defendant's Right

The Sixth Amendment guarantees a criminal defendant the right to a public trial. The defendant may waive the right and request a closed proceeding. However, because the request also implicates the First Amendment right of access of the press and the public, the court must consider several factors, and the likelihood of a closed proceeding is slight. The court may even allow the proceedings to be televised over the defendant's objection.

The right to a public trial extends to preliminary hearings and suppression hearings. A suppression hearing may be closed if (i) there is an overriding interest likely to be prejudiced by an open trial, (ii) the closure is not in excess of the interest, (iii) other alternatives have been considered, and (iv) the court enters adequate findings to support closure.

2. Public's Right

Regardless of the wishes of the defendant or prosecutor, a trial must be public unless there is either a *substantial likelihood* of prejudice to the defendant or a need to limit access to ensure an orderly proceeding. *Press-Enterprise Co. v. Superior Court of CA (Press-Enterprise I)*, 464 U.S. 501, 509–10 (1984).

E. FAIR TRIAL

1. Impartial Judge

Due process requires that a judge possess neither actual nor apparent bias. If actual or apparent bias exists, the judge must follow a recusal process in the federal or state jurisdiction. The impermissible bias or prejudice usually must stem from an extrajudicial source.

2. Fair Conduct by the Prosecutor

a. Examples of misconduct

A prosecutor may not:

i) Make material misstatements of law or fact;

ii) Elicit information from the defendant outside the presence of his counsel;

iii) Express opinions about the defendant's guilt or innocence;

iv) Make unfair or improper remarks about the defendant, his counsel, or witnesses;

v) Comment on the defendant's failure to testify at trial; or

vi) Make improper remarks to the jury to inflame their passions to convict for an improper reason.

b. No use of false testimony

A prosecutor may not knowingly use perjured or false testimony for the case in chief, for sentencing, or to impeach the credibility of a witness.

c. No suppression of favorable evidence

As discussed in IV.F., *supra,* due process requires the prosecution to disclose evidence favorable to the accused when such evidence is material to guilt or punishment. Evidence is material if there is a "reasonable probability" that disclosure would have changed the outcome of the proceeding; a reasonable probability is "a probability sufficient to undermine confidence in the outcome." *United States v. Bagley,* 473 U.S. 667, 682 (1985). The prosecution's failure to disclose evidence in its possession both favorable and material to the defense entitles the defendant to a new trial. *Brady v. Maryland,* 373 U.S. 83 (1963). Under *Bagley,* the prosecution's failure to turn over specifically requested evidence will seldom, if ever, be excused.

Similarly, police violate due process when, in bad faith, they destroy evidence that would have been useful to the defendant at trial. The defendant does not, however, have the right to require police to preserve all evidence if it is not certain that the evidence would have been exculpatory.

F. RIGHT TO CONFRONTATION

1. Trial

The accused has the right to directly encounter adverse witnesses, to cross-examine adverse witnesses, and to be present at any stage of the trial that would enable the defendant to effectively cross-examine adverse witnesses as guaranteed by the Sixth and Fourteenth Amendments. Not only does this right allow the defendant to cross-examine the adverse witness, but it also allows the defendant to observe the demeanor of the adverse witness. A witness may invoke the right against self-incrimination; however, such an invocation after testimony has already been made may violate the defendant's right to confrontation, guaranteed by the Sixth and Fourteenth Amendments, because the witness's invocation will prevent adequate cross-examination by the defendant. If the defendant was instrumental in preventing a witness from testifying, then he forfeits his right to confrontation.

2. Compliance

a. Face-to-face confrontation

Face-to-face confrontation is not an absolute right. A criminal defendant has the right to confront witnesses against him under the Sixth Amendment, unless preventing such confrontation is necessary to further an important public policy and the reliability of the testimony is otherwise assured. A defendant who voluntarily leaves the courtroom or a disruptive defendant whom the judge removes from the courtroom has not had his right to confrontation violated. This is to be determined on a case-by-case basis.

The state's interest in protecting child witnesses from more than *de minimis* trauma as a result of testifying in the defendant's presence is considered an important public purpose under this rule. *Maryland v. Craig*, 497 U.S. 836, 855–856 (1990).

b. Cross-examination of witnesses

The right to confrontation means more than being allowed to confront the witness physically. The principal purpose of confrontation is to secure for the defendant the opportunity of cross-examination of the prosecution's witnesses.

1) Impeachment for bias

A denial of the opportunity to cross-examine a prosecution witness with regard to bias violates the Confrontation Clause. *Delaware v. Van Arsdall*, 475 U.S. 673, 679 (1986). However, such denial is subject to harmless-error analysis. Moreover, trial judges retain wide latitude to impose reasonable limits on such cross-examination based on concerns about, among other things, harassment, prejudice, confusion of the issues, the safety of the witness, or interrogation that is repetitive or only marginally relevant. *Id.*

2) Memory loss by the witness

The fact that a witness has a memory loss does not by itself violate the Confrontation Clause. *Delaware v. Fensterer*, 474 U.S. 15, 19–20 (1985). The Supreme Court has held that the Confrontation Clause does not bar testimony concerning a prior out-of-court identification when the identifying witness is unable, because of memory loss, to explain the basis for the identification. A defendant may conduct an effective cross-examination if given the opportunity to address the very fact of the poor memory of the witness. *United States v. Owens*, 484 U.S. 554, 564 (1988).

3) Confrontation Clause and the hearsay rule

The Confrontation Clause limits the use of hearsay evidence in a criminal trial. Out-of-court statements by witnesses that are "testimonial" are barred under the Confrontation Clause, unless the witnesses are unavailable and the defendant had a prior opportunity to cross-examine those witnesses, regardless of whether such statements are deemed reliable by the court. If, however, the declarant appears for cross-examination at trial, then the Confrontation Clause places no constraints at all on the use of the declarant's prior out-of-court testimonial statements. *Crawford v. Washington*, 541 U.S. 36, 59 (2004).

Out-of-court testimonial statements are not barred by the Confrontation Clause when they are used for a purpose other than establishing the truth of the matter asserted (i.e., when they are not used for a hearsay purpose). *Id. See also Tennessee v. Street*, 471 U.S. 409, 417 (1985).

The Confrontation Clause has no application to "non-testimonial" out-of-court statements. *Whorton v. Bockting*, 549 U.S. 406, 420 (2007).

a) Testimonial statements

A statement is considered "testimonial" if the declarant would reasonably expect it to be used in a prosecution. Such statements include affidavits, custodial examinations, prior testimony, and statements given in response to police interrogation. *Crawford v. Washington*, 541 U.S. 36, 40 (2004). The Supreme Court has also held that certificates of analysis, which state the results of state laboratory tests, are testimonial evidence that may not be admitted without accompanying live testimony by the analyst who conducted the tests. *Melendez-Diaz v. Massachusetts*, 129 S. Ct. 2527, 2549 (2009). It is not sufficient to substitute the testimony of another analyst who is familiar with the testing protocol but did not perform or observe the tests or sign the report. *Bullcoming v. New Mexico*, 564 U.S. ___, 131 S. Ct. 2705 (2011).

b) Non-testimonial statements

The Confrontation Clause permits the admission of non-testimonial statements, even if they lack indicia of reliability. *Whorton v. Bockting*, 549 U.S. 406, 411 (2007). Statements made for the primary purpose of assisting the police in the investigation of an ongoing emergency are not testimonial. Examples of non-testimonial statements include statements made to a 911 operator during a domestic dispute, *Davis v. Washington*, 547 U.S. 813, 822 (2006), and statements made to police officers by the victim of a mortal gunshot wound as he lay in a gas-station parking lot. *Michigan v. Bryant*, 562 U.S. ___, 131 S. Ct. 1143 (2011).

4) Witness unavailable

The right of confrontation is satisfied if the defense counsel had a right to cross-examine the witness at an earlier hearing, provided that the prosecution failed in a good-faith effort to produce the witness at the trial and the declarant is now unavailable. However, if the witness is unavailable because of the defendant's conduct, then testimonial hearsay is admissible. *Giles v. California*, 554 U.S. 353, 373 (2008).

5) Confession of a non-testifying co-defendant at a joint trial

a) *Bruton* rule

The admission of a confession by a non-testifying co-defendant at a joint trial against the defendant violates the Sixth Amendment, even when it merely corroborates the defendant's own confession. *Bruton v. United States*, 391 U.S. 123, 132 (1968). A limiting instruction will not cure the defect. If the co-defendant testifies, then the rule does not apply. The rule does not apply at a bench trial. *Lee v. Illinois*, 476 U.S. 530, 539 (1986). It also does not apply to the statements of an accomplice who is not tried as a co-defendant or to a co-defendant who takes the stand and denies making such a statement. *Nelson v. O'Neil*, 402 U.S. 622, 629–630 (1971); *Dutton v. Evans*, 400 U.S. 74, 88–89 (1970).

b) Harmless error

Admission of a co-defendant's statement in violation of *Bruton*, however, is subject to harmless-error analysis. *Schneble v. Florida*, 405 U.S. 427, 430 (1972).

c) Severance

The accused may assert a demand for a severance of the trial of his case from a co-defendant's case whenever the prosecution intends to introduce a confession that is hostile to one co-defendant, and the confession:

i) Implicates the confessing defendant but is not admissible against the non-confessing defendant; and

ii) Cannot be edited to exclude inculpation of the non-confessing defendant.

Bruton v. United States, 391 U.S. 123, 132 (1968). The prosecutor may avoid severance if the court denies the use of the statement or the prosecutor chooses not to use it at trial.

G.   DUE PROCESS

1.   Right to Testify

A defendant has a right to testify and to present evidence on his own behalf.

2.   Burden of Proof

a. Presumptions

1) Presumption of innocence

While a defendant is not automatically entitled to a jury instruction apprising the jury of the presumption of innocence doctrine, the presumption is a basic tenet of a fair trial, and it may be required when necessary for a fair trial. *Kentucky v. Whorton*, 441 U.S. 786, 789 (1979).

2) Presumptions of facts

a) Permissive presumption

A permissive presumption (i.e., a presumption that the trier of fact is not compelled to accept and that does not shift the burden of proof) regarding an element of an offense does not violate the due-process requirement that the prosecution must prove each element of an offense unless the presumption is irrational. A presumption is not irrational if it is more likely than not to flow from the proven fact on which it depends. *County Court v. Allen*, 442 U.S. 140, 163–164 (1979) (upholding the statutory presumption that the occupants of a car in which firearms are found are in possession of the firearms).

b) Mandatory presumption

A mandatory presumption (i.e., a presumption that the trier of fact is compelled to accept or that shifts the burden of proof) regarding an element of an offense violates the due-process requirement. *Sandstrom v. Montana,* 442 U.S. 510, 522 (1979) (jury instruction that a person intends the ordinary consequences of his voluntary acts constituted a mandatory presumption when the crime—deliberate homicide—required proof of intent).

b. Elements of the prosecution's case

The Due Process Clause requires that the prosecution prove all of the elements of the case beyond a reasonable doubt. Due process does not require the court to use any particular words to advise the jury of the government's burden of proof. In some jurisdictions, the failure to instruct on reasonable doubt may result in reversible error, whereas in other jurisdictions, the lack of such an instruction is per se reversible error.

Sentencing factors need not be proved beyond a reasonable doubt unless the fact is being used to increase the penalty beyond the proscribed statutory maximum, in which case proof beyond a reasonable doubt is required. *Apprendi v. New Jersey*, 530 U.S. 466, 492 (2000).

c. Affirmative defenses

The state is not forbidden by the Due Process Clause from placing the burden of proving an affirmative defense—such as insanity, self-defense, entrapment, or duress—on the defendant. *Dixon v. United States*, 548 U.S. 1, 13 (2006).

d. Directed verdict

In a criminal case, a judge may order a directed verdict only for acquittal; the power to convict is reserved to the jury.

H. CRUEL AND UNUSUAL PUNISHMENT

1. Applicability

The Eighth Amendment to the U.S. Constitution prohibits the federal government from imposing cruel and unusual punishment for federal crimes, or "such punishment as would amount to torture or barbarity, any cruel and degrading punishment not known to the common law, or any fine, penalty, confinement, or treatment so disproportionate to the offense as to shock the moral sense of the community." U.S. Const. amend. VIII.

2. Compliance

a. Non-death penalty

1) Physical conditions of incarceration

The physical conditions of incarceration amount to cruel and unusual punishment only if the prisoner can show that prison officials had actual knowledge of a substantial risk to the prisoners.

2) Physical force

A prisoner need not show serious injury to recover for a violation of the Eighth Amendment prohibition against cruel and unusual punishment. The inquiry is whether the physical force was applied in a good-faith effort to maintain or restore discipline, rather than applied maliciously and sadistically to cause harm.

3) Sentence proportionality

A sentence that is grossly disproportionate to the crime constitutes cruel and unusual punishment. *Compare Weems v. United States*, 217 U.S. 349 (1910) (reversing punishment of 20 years' imprisonment for falsifying a public record) *with Harmelin v. Michigan*, 501 U.S. 957 (1991) (upholding punishment of life imprisonment without the possibility of parole for drug dealing based on possession of more than 650 grams of cocaine) *and Ewing v. California*, 538 U.S. 11 (2003) (upholding punishment of an indeterminate sentence of 25 years to life for theft of merchandise valued at about $1,200 after conviction of at least two other felonies, at least one of which was serious or violent).

4) Equal protection limitations on punishment

A jail sentence is impermissible if it is imposed only because the defendant was unable to pay a fine. If a defendant has made reasonable bona fide efforts to pay the fine, then revocation of probation without consideration of alternative punishments is fundamentally unfair under the Fourteenth Amendment.

5) Repeat offenders

Some jurisdictions have statutes imposing mandatory indeterminate life sentences (e.g., 25 years to life) on defendants who commit three felonies, even if the felonies are non-violent property-related offenses. These recidivist statutes are not unconstitutional under either the Double Jeopardy Clause of the Fifth Amendment or the Cruel and Unusual Punishment Clause of the Eighth Amendment. *Ewing v. California*, 538 U.S. 11 (2003).

6) Defendant's perjured testimony

If a trial judge believes that the defendant perjured himself during the trial, then the judge may take this belief into consideration when determining the sentence.

b. Capital punishment

The death penalty may be imposed only under a statutory scheme that provides:

i) Clear and objective standards;

ii) Specific and detailed guidance; and

iii) An opportunity for rational review of the process.

1) Homicide crimes

a) Aggravating circumstances

A defendant in a homicide case cannot be sentenced to death unless the trier of fact convicts the defendant of murder and finds at least one "aggravating circumstance" at either the guilt phase or penalty phase. *Brown v. Sanders*, 546 U.S. 212, 218–19 (2006). The aggravating circumstance must meet two requirements:

i) It must not apply to every defendant convicted of murder; and

ii) It must not be unconstitutionally vague. (For example, "especially heinous, atrocious, or cruel" conduct definition is unconstitutionally vague.)

The trier of fact can consider both statutory and non-statutory aggravating circumstances, but the death penalty cannot be imposed without one statutorily defined aggravating factor being found.

b) Mitigating circumstances

A death sentence violates the Eighth and Fourteenth Amendments if the sentencing judge refuses to review or admit mitigating evidence. Mitigating evidence must be presented if it meets a low threshold test for relevance. *Woodson v. North Carolina*, 428 U.S. 280, 316 (1976).

Note: When the death penalty is not imposed (e.g., when the defendant receives a sentence of life in prison without parole), a mandatory sentence may be imposed without the presentation of mitigating evidence. *Harmelin v. Michigan*, 501 U.S. 957, 965 (1991).

2) Non-homicide crimes

Punishment that is disproportionately excessive in relation to the crime committed is prohibited by the Eighth Amendment. The death penalty is considered excessive in a rape case when the victim was an adult woman or a child, *Coker v. Georgia*, 433 U.S. 584 (1977); *Kennedy v. Louisiana*, 554 U.S. 407 (2008), and in felony-murder cases when the defendant did not intend to kill or intend that lethal force be used.

3) Defendant insane

The Eighth Amendment prohibits states from inflicting the death penalty on a prisoner who is insane or can "demonstrate a severe mental disorder." *Panetti v. Quarterman*, 551 U.S. 930, 960 (2007).

4) Mental retardation of the defendant

The Eighth Amendment prohibits execution of mentally retarded persons. *Atkins v. Virginia*, 526 U.S. 504 (2002).

5) Age of the defendant

The Eighth Amendment prohibition against "cruel and unusual punishment" prohibits the execution of a defendant who was younger than 18 years of age at the time of the commission of a crime. *Roper v. Simmons*, 543 U.S. 551, 569 (2005). In addition, the Eighth Amendment prohibits the imposition of a sentence of life without the possibility of parole on a defendant who was younger than 18 years of age at the time of the commission of the crime if the crime was not a homicide. *Graham v. Florida*, 560 U.S. ___, 130 S. Ct. 2011 (2010).

6) Fairness of sentencing proceedings

To minimize the risk of arbitrary action, a capital sentencing process must satisfy, at a minimum, two general requirements:

i) The process must channel or limit the sentencer's discretion in order to genuinely narrow the class of persons eligible for the death penalty and reasonably justify the imposition of a more severe sentence on the defendant compared to others found guilty of murder; and

ii) The court must allow the jury to consider any relevant mitigating evidence that might lead the sentencer to decline to impose the death penalty. The sentencer is also allowed to take into consideration victim impact statements.

7) Racial discrimination claims

Under *McCleskey v. Kemp*, 481 U.S. 279 (1987), the Supreme Court held that despite serious statistical evidence of racial disparity in the imposition of the death penalty (e.g., African-American defendants who kill white victims are more likely to receive the death penalty), it was not imposed as a result of unconstitutional discrimination.

8) Lethal injection

Lethal injection is not considered cruel and unusual punishment because there is only a mere possibility that the condemned may receive an improperly administered shot that would cause him unnecessary pain.

c. Adequate medical care

Although prison inmates have a right to adequate medical care, such care constitutes "cruel and unusual punishment" under the Eighth Amendment only when there is a deliberate indifference to the serious medical needs of an inmate. Mere negligence in assessing an inmate's medical condition or in providing treatment is not sufficient to trigger a constitutional violation. *Estelle v. Gamble*, 429 U.S. 97, 104–105 (1976).

VI. POST-TRIAL CONSIDERATIONS

A. DOUBLE JEOPARDY

The Fifth Amendment protection against double jeopardy applies to the federal government. It has been incorporated by the Due Process Clause of the Fourteenth Amendment, and consequently it also applies to the states. *Benton v. Maryland*, 395 U.S. 784 (1969).

1. Protection Against Prosecution and Punishment

The Fifth Amendment Double Jeopardy Clause provides three protections:

i) Protection against a second prosecution for the same offense after acquittal;

ii) Protection against a second prosecution for the same offense after conviction; and

iii) Protection against multiple punishments for the same offense.

a. Definition of "same offense"

1) Shared elements

If a defendant's conduct may be prosecuted as two or more crimes, then the *Blockburger* test is applied to determine whether the crimes constitute the same offense for double jeopardy purposes. Under this test, each crime must require the proof of an element that the other does not in order for each to be considered as a separate offense. *Blockburger v. United States*, 284 U.S. 299, 304 (1932).

> **Example 1—No Jeopardy:** A defendant robs a store and shoots and kills the store clerk. The state prosecutes the defendant for premeditated murder. The defendant is acquitted. The state then brings charges against the defendant for robbery. The protection against double jeopardy does not apply because robbery and murder each require the proof of an element that the other does not. Robbery requires, among other elements, the proof that the defendant took the victim's personal property; murder requires, among other elements, the death of the victim.
>
> **Example 2—Jeopardy:** A defendant robs a store and shoots and kills the store clerk. The state prosecutes the defendant for felony murder based on the robbery. The defendant is acquitted. The state then brings charges against the defendant for robbery. The protection against double jeopardy applies because the state, in order to prove felony murder in the first trial, had to prove that the defendant committed a robbery. *Harris v. Oklahoma*, 433 U.S. 682, 683 (1977).

As a consequence of *Blockburger,* the Double Jeopardy Clause generally bars successive prosecutions for greater and lesser included offenses. A lesser included offense is one that does not require proof of an element beyond those required by the greater offense.

2) Occurrence of a necessary subsequent event

When jeopardy has attached with respect to a lesser included offense prior to the occurrence of an event necessary to establish the greater offense, the defendant may be subsequently tried for the greater offense.

> **Example:** If a defendant who physically harms a victim is tried for a crime such as battery, and the victim subsequently dies as a consequence of the defendant's conduct, then the defendant may be tried for murder without running afoul of the Double Jeopardy Clause. *Diaz v. United States*, 223 U.S. 442, 449 (1912).

3) Statutory offenses

At a single trial, a defendant may be convicted of two offenses, one of which is a lesser included offense of the other, if both offenses are statutory and the legislature has specifically authorized cumulative punishment. *Missouri v. Hunter*, 459 U.S. 359, 368–369 (1983) (first-degree robbery and armed criminal action).

4) Conspiracy

An offense and the conspiracy to commit that offense are not the same offense for double-jeopardy purposes because each requires proof of different elements. *United States v. Felix*, 503 U.S. 378, 389 (1992).

5) Sentence enhancement use

The use of a defendant's prior conviction to enhance the sentence imposed on a defendant for a current conviction does not violate the Double Jeopardy Clause. *Witte v. United States*, 515 U.S. 389, 400 (1995).

b. Acquittal

A defendant who has been acquitted of a crime generally may not be retried for the same crime. A grant of a demurrer or motion to dismiss in favor of the accused at the close of the state's case is the equivalent of an acquittal.

2. Attachment of Jeopardy

The protection against double jeopardy is not triggered until jeopardy attaches. In a jury trial, jeopardy attaches when the jury is empaneled and sworn in. In a bench trial, jeopardy attaches when the first witness is sworn in.

3. Different Jurisdictions

Under the dual-sovereignty doctrine, the protection against double jeopardy does not preclude prosecution of a crime by both federal and state governments. Consequently, a defendant may be charged and convicted for the same type of crime in a federal court and a state court. Similarly, a defendant may be prosecuted by two different states for the same conduct. However, a state and state-created entity, such as a municipality, cannot both prosecute a defendant for the same conduct. *Waller v. Florida*, 397 U.S. 387, 394 (1970) (municipality's conviction of defendant for violation of city ordinance for destruction of city property precluded state prosecution for grand larceny).

4. Civil Actions

The Double Jeopardy Clause does not preclude a criminal punishment and civil penalty for the same conduct. Therefore, even if a defendant has been found guilty in a criminal action, the state may still bring a civil action against the defendant that arises out of the same conduct. The protection does not apply to administrative proceedings such as a disciplinary hearing stemming from criminal conduct, nor does it apply to a parole, probation, or bond-revocation hearing related to a criminal charge or punishment.

A civil penalty may be treated as a criminal punishment when the penalty amount is grossly disproportionate to governmental loss and it serves only a deterrent or retributive purpose. *Dep't of Revenue of Montana v. Kurth Ranch*, 511 U.S. 767, 783 (1994) (tax imposed on possession of illegal drugs after satisfaction of state and federal fines and forfeitures). However, a civil forfeiture proceeding is typically not punitive in nature. *United States v. Ursery*, 518 U.S. 267, 275 (1996) (forfeiture of property used in the commission of drug crimes).

Note: Juvenile adjudicatory proceedings are criminal, not civil, actions for purposes of the Double Jeopardy Clause. A minor who is subject to an adjudicatory hearing regarding conduct that would constitute a crime if committed by an adult cannot subsequently be tried as an adult for a crime based on such conduct. *Breed v. Jones*, 421 U.S. 519, 541 (1975).

5. Guilty Plea

A defendant does not automatically waive her double-jeopardy rights by entering a guilty plea, but the plea agreement may include a provision that the charges against the defendant may be reinstated if the defendant breaches the agreement. *Ricketts v. Adamson*, 483 U.S. 1, 11 (1987). A guilty plea to a lesser included offense does not preclude prosecution for a greater offense if the greater offense has been charged before the plea is entered. *Ohio v. Johnson*, 467 U.S. 493, 501 (1984).

6. Mistrial

The Double Jeopardy Clause does not prohibit a retrial following a mistrial if "taking all the circumstances into consideration, there is a manifest necessity for [declaring a mistrial]." *United States v. Perez*, 22 U.S. 579, 580 (1824). For example, if a mistrial is declared because the judge or a juror is ill or dies, or because of a hung jury, then the defendant generally may be retried. On the other hand, if the judge grants an acquittal instead of declaring a mistrial after there has been a hung jury, then a retrial is not permitted. Moreover, if the prosecution asks for a mistrial because of its inability to locate a witness, then double jeopardy prevents a retrial.

If the defendant asks for or consents to a mistrial, then she generally can be retried, unless the request is based on bad-faith conduct by the prosecutor or judge directed toward goading the defendant into seeking a mistrial. The manifest necessity standard does not apply when the defendant requests a mistrial. *United States v. Dinitz*, 424 U.S. 600, 606–607 (1976).

7. Appeal

a. By the prosecution

The government may appeal an adverse ruling in a criminal case only when authorized by statute. If the trial judge grants an acquittal on an issue that does not relate to the defendant's guilt or innocence, such as the failure to give the defendant a speedy trial, then the prosecution may appeal and, if the appeal is successful, the defendant may be retried. In addition, a prosecutor may appeal an order dismissing an indictment or suppressing evidence, a bail determination, the sentence imposed on a defendant, and a post-verdict new-trial order.

b. By the defendant

The Double Jeopardy Clause generally does not prevent the retrial of a defendant after an appeal on the basis of an error made at trial, such as the admission of improper hearsay evidence or improper jury instructions. *Lockhart v. Nelson*, 488 U.S. 33, 38 (1988). This is true even when a conviction is overturned due to the weight of the evidence. *Tibbs v. Florida*, 457 U.S. 31, 42 (1982). However, a retrial after reversal of a conviction due to **insufficiency** of the evidence is barred by the Double Jeopardy Clause. A conviction is based upon insufficient evidence if the evidence presented, when viewed in the light most favorable to the prosecution, is such that **no rational fact-finder** could have found the defendant guilty beyond a reasonable doubt. *Burks v. United States*, 437 U.S. 1, 18 (1978).

8. Retrial Offenses

A defendant who was tried for a crime but convicted only of a lesser included offense may not be retried on the originally charged crime even if the conviction is reversed. *Price v. Georgia*, 398 U.S. 323, 329 (1970).

> **Example:** A defendant on trial for murder is found guilty of voluntary manslaughter. The conviction is overturned on appeal due to trial error. The defendant's retrial for murder violates the Double Jeopardy Clause, even if on retrial the defendant again is convicted only of voluntary manslaughter.

9. Retrial Punishment

The Double Jeopardy Clause generally does not preclude a greater sentence from being imposed on a defendant upon reconviction after a successful appeal. However, the Due Process Clause does prevent the imposition of a greater sentence upon reconviction if the greater sentence is imposed as a penalty for the exercise of a statutory right to appeal or to seek a collateral remedy. Consequently, when imposing a greater sentence upon reconviction, the judge must articulate reasons for the greater sentence that are based on objective information concerning identifiable conduct by the defendant that occurred after the original sentencing proceeding. *Alabama v. Smith*, 490 U.S. 794 (1989). In a jurisdiction where a jury rather than the judge determines the sentence, the jury in the retrial may impose a greater sentence unless it has been told of the defendant's original sentence. *Chaffin v. Stynchcombe*, 412 U.S. 17, 24 (1973).

a. Capital sentencing procedures

The Double Jeopardy Clause is applicable to capital sentencing proceedings when there is a determination that the government failed to establish an aggravating factor that would justify the death penalty. Consequently, if a jury imposes a life sentence rather than the death penalty, then the defendant, upon retrial, may not be sentenced to death. *Bullington v. Missouri*, 451 U.S. 430, 445 (1981).

> A capital-sentencing procedure under which the sentencing judge may override the jury's recommendation and impose the death penalty does not violate the Double Jeopardy Clause.

10. Collateral Estoppel

The Double Jeopardy Clause recognizes the doctrine of collateral estoppel. For collateral estoppel to apply, the earlier decision must have necessarily determined the issue on which collateral estoppel is sought by the defendant.

> **Example 1:** Several victims were robbed at the same time. The defendant is initially tried for the crime with respect to only one of the victims. The sole contested issue at the trial is whether the defendant was a perpetrator of the crime. The defendant is acquitted of the crime. The acquittal prevents the defendant's prosecution for the robbery with respect to any other victim. The fact that the jury determined that the defendant was not a perpetrator of a robbery estops the government from trying the defendant for robbery of any of the other victims. *Ashe v. Swenson*, 397 U.S. 436 (1970).

If a jury renders a verdict against a defendant on one crime but deadlocks on another crime that contains the same element, then the jury's verdict may serve to prevent retrial on the crime over which the jury was deadlocked. In such a case, issue preclusion applies to the issue(s) that the jury did determine.

> **Example 2:** A defendant was charged with both insider trading and fraud. An element of both crimes is the possession of insider information. The jury acquitted the defendant of fraud but deadlocked over insider trading. By acquitting the defendant, the jury determined that the defendant did not possess insider information. Consequently, under the doctrine of collateral estoppel, the government could not retry the defendant for fraud. *Yeager v. United States*, 557 U.S. 110, (2009).

The burden is on the defendant to prove that the jury's verdict **necessarily** determined the issue that the defendant seeks to foreclose. Because a jury usually renders a general verdict in a criminal trial, it is rare that a defendant will be able to meet this burden.

B. APPEAL

The Constitution neither provides for nor guarantees an individual the right to appeal. Nevertheless, appeals are commonplace in the U.S. justice system. Individuals are guaranteed certain rights during their appeal, among them equal protection and the right to counsel. However, despite this latter right, if an attorney believes that the appeal is frivolous, she may withdraw so long as the appellant's right to counsel continues to be protected. There is also no right of self-representation during an appeal.

C. CONVICTIONS

1. Writ of Habeas Corpus

Defendants may attack their convictions, even if their appeal was unsuccessful or not available, by challenging the lawfulness of the detention under a writ of habeas corpus. The defendant does not have to be in custody; she may be out on bail, probation, or parole. However, if the defendant's sentence has expired and her prior conviction is being used to enhance a later one, then the defendant does not satisfy the in-custody requirement to petition for the habeas writ.

A writ of habeas corpus proceeding is civil in nature. Therefore, the "beyond a reasonable doubt" standard is not applicable. The petitioner must demonstrate only the unlawfulness of the detention by a preponderance of the evidence. If the petitioner is granted the writ, then the state may appeal, and double jeopardy does not apply to either the appeal or the retrial after the granting of the writ. An indigent person does not have a right to have counsel appointed to assist in perfecting her habeas petition.

2. Parole and Probation

If a new sentence will be imposed upon the revocation of parole, then the right to counsel is activated, and the parolee is entitled to representation to the same extent as a trial. On the other hand, if an already-imposed sentence is triggered by parole revocation, then the right to counsel is limited. The right to counsel applies only if it is necessary for a fair hearing.

3. Access to Courts

Reasonable access to courts, with no unreasonable limitations on presenting arguments, is a right of prison inmates. In addition, inmates cannot be prohibited from consulting with other inmates if there is no reasonable alternative in the prison, such as a law library.

4. Disenfranchisement

Some states disenfranchise a convicted felon. This prohibition on voting does not violate the Fourteenth Amendment, even when it applies to felons who have been released from incarceration. *Richardson v. Ramirez*, 418 U.S. 24, 54 (1974).

D. SENTENCING

1. Applicable Rights

Sentencing is considered a critical stage triggering the Sixth Amendment right to counsel. A defendant may have the right to confrontation and cross-examination at sentencing, particularly in death-penalty cases, or when a sentence is based upon a finding of new facts beyond those necessary to prove the offense charged. *Gardner v. Florida*, 430 U.S. 349, 358 (1977); *Specht v. Patterson*, 386 U.S. 605, 610 (1967).

2. Enhancement Over the Statutory Maximum

Any fact, other than a prior conviction, that can be used to increase a sentence beyond the statutorily prescribed maximum must be charged in an indictment, submitted to a jury, and established beyond a reasonable doubt. A fact is considered an element of a crime, as opposed to a sentencing enhancement, when it can increase the maximum sentence imposed. The failure to abide by the above procedure is a violation of the defendant's due-process rights under the Fifth Amendment and Sixth Amendment rights to notice and a jury trial, both of which are incorporated against the states through the Fourteenth Amendment. *Apprendi v. New Jersey*, 530 U.S. 466, 476 (2000).

It is not a Sixth Amendment violation for a judge to impose consecutive sentences based on facts that were not found by the jury, but rather by the judge. *Oregon v. Ice*, 555 U.S. 160 (2009). The rule of *Apprendi v. New Jersey, supra,* is thus limited to sentencing for single crimes, not to the arrangement for punishing multiple offenses.

Harmless-error analysis applies in deciding whether or not to overturn a sentence for a judge's failure to submit a sentencing factor to the jury. *Washington v. Recuenco*, 548 U.S. 212, 222 (2006).

Evidence

EVIDENCE

Table of Contents

EVIDENCE

I.   PRESENTATION OF EVIDENCE

With some exceptions, the Federal Rules apply to all civil and criminal proceedings before United States district courts, courts of appeal, Bankruptcy Court, and Claims Court, and in proceedings before United States magistrates. Fed. R. Evid. 1101(a).

The Federal Rules do not apply to:

  i)   The court's determination of a preliminary question of fact governing admissibility (*see* § I.B.1.a. Judicial control of process, *infra*);

  ii) Grand jury proceedings; and

  ii) Criminal proceedings for the following purposes:

       a) The issuance of a search or arrest warrant or a criminal summons;

       b) A preliminary examination in a criminal case;

       c) Extradition or rendition;

       e) Consideration of bail or other release;

       f) Sentencing; and

       g) Granting or revoking probation or supervised release.

Fed. R. Evid. 1101(c), (d).

A.   INTRODUCTION OF EVIDENCE

1.   Role of Judge and Jury

In a jury trial, the jury is traditionally the trier of fact and the judge the trier of law.

a.   Judge

The trial judge generally decides **preliminary questions** regarding the competency of evidence, including the admissibility of evidence, whether privilege exists, and whether a person is qualified to be a witness. The court is not bound by the Federal Rules in deciding these questions, except with respect to privileges, and it may consider otherwise inadmissible evidence. Fed. R. Evid. 104(a). With respect to preliminary questions, the party offering the evidence ordinarily bears the burden to persuade the trial judge by a preponderance of the evidence. *Bourjaily v. United States*, 483 U.S. 171 (1987) (confession of co-conspirator as admission of party opponent); *Daubert v. Merrell Dow Pharm.*,

509 U.S. 579 (1993) (expert opinion); Rule 702, Notes of Advisory Committee (2000).

Hearings on preliminary matters must be conducted outside the presence of the jury when the hearing involves the admissibility of confessions, when a defendant in a criminal case is a witness and so requests, or when justice requires it. Fed. R. Evid. 104(c).

b. Jury

A party has the right to present evidence (e.g., bias) that is relevant to the weight and credibility of other evidence (e.g., the testimony of a witness). Once evidence has been admitted, it is the role of the jury to determine the **weight and credibility** of the evidence. Fed. R. Evid. 104(e).

2. Challenge to Evidence Ruling

A party may challenge an evidentiary ruling as erroneous only if the ruling affects a substantial right of a party, and the party notifies the judge of the error. There are two ways to call the court's attention to the error—objection and offer of proof. Fed. R. Evid. 103(a). (Note: While the judge in a jury trial must permit a party to challenge the court's ruling, the judge must also conduct the trial to the extent practicable so that inadmissible evidence is not suggested to the jury. Fed. R. Evid. 103(d).)

a. Objection to admission of evidence

If the ruling **admits** evidence, a party must make a timely **objection** or motion to strike and must usually state the specific ground for the objection or motion in order to preserve the admissibility issue for appeal. A party is not required to state the ground if it is apparent from the context. Fed. R. Evid. 103(a)(1).

b. Offer of proof for exclusion of evidence

If the ruling **excludes** evidence, a party must make an **offer of proof** in order to preserve the evidence for appellate review of the ruling. An offer of proof is an oral or written explanation of the relevance and admissibility of the evidence made on the record. The court may direct that an offer of proof be made in question-and-answer form. An offer of proof is not necessary if the substance of the evidence is apparent from the context. Fed. R. Evid. 103(a)(2),(c).

c. Consequence of a definitive ruling

Once a judge has made a definitive ruling on the admissibility of evidence, a party need not renew an objection or offer of proof, even if the ruling was made before the trial began. Fed. R. Evid. 103(b).

d. Plain error rule

A plain error—an error that affects a substantial right—is grounds for reversal, even if no objection or offer of proof was made. Fed. R. Evid. 103(e). A court may take notice of a plain error to prevent a miscarriage of justice or to preserve the integrity and the reputation of the judicial process.

3. Limited Admissibility

Evidence may be admissible for one purpose but not for another (e.g., for impeachment but not substantive purposes), or against one party but not against another. In these cases, if a party makes a timely request, the court must restrict the evidence to its proper scope and instruct the jury accordingly. Fed. R. Evid. 105.

4. Completeness Rule

Under the rule of completeness, when a party introduces part of a writing or recorded statement, an adverse party may compel the introduction of an omitted portion of the writing or statement if, in fairness, it should be considered at the same time, such as when the omitted portion explains or clarifies the admitted portion. This rule also applies to a separate writing or recorded statement that relates to the introduced writing or recorded statement, such as the original letter when the reply letter has been introduced. Fed. R. Evid. 106. The rule of completeness does not require the admission of irrelevant portions of a statement. *United States v. Kopp*, 562 F.3d 141 (2d Cir. 2009).

> **Timing of introduction of omitted evidence:** While the rule of completeness permits an adverse party to compel the immediate introduction of evidence during the presentation of related evidence, the rule does not *require* the adverse party to do so. The adverse party may instead choose to present the omitted evidence subsequently, such as during cross-examination.

5. Judicial Notice

Judicial notice is the court's acceptance of a fact as true without requiring formal proof. The Federal Rules only address judicial notice of adjudicative facts, which are the facts of the case at hand—those that relate to the parties and their activities, and that typically are decided by the jury. The Federal Rules do not apply to judicial notice of legislative facts, which are policy facts related to legal reasoning and the lawmaking process. Fed. R. Evid. 201.

> **Example (adjudicative fact):** A witness testifies that an accident happened on a Saturday. The accident report indicates that the accident happened on July 21, 2007. Whether July 21, 2007, was indeed a Saturday is an adjudicative fact.
>
> **Example (legislative fact):** A judge must decide whether to recognize an exception to the common-law marital privilege. The fact that allowing the exception would undermine the sanctity of marriage is a legislative fact.

a. Facts subject to judicial notice

Not all adjudicative facts are subject to judicial notice. Judicial notice may be taken of an adjudicative fact only if it is **not subject to reasonable dispute** because (i) it is **generally known** within the territorial jurisdiction of the trial court, or (ii) it can be **accurately and readily determined** from sources whose accuracy cannot reasonably be questioned. Fed. R. Evid. 201(b).

1) Generally known facts within jurisdiction

A fact does not need to be known by everyone to be "generally known"; it must only be well known within the community. Fed. R. Evid. 201(b).

> **Example:** A judge could take judicial notice that a bank provides a checking account customer with a monthly account statement. *Kaggen v. IRS*, 71 F.3d 1018 (2d Cir. 1995).

Despite being termed "judicial notice," a judge may not take notice of a fact based solely on his own personal knowledge.

> **Example:** A judge could not take judicial notice of informal judicial procedures for the issuance of court orders within a jurisdiction. *Switzer v. Coan*, 261 F.3d 985 (10th Cir. 2001).

2) Accurately and readily determined facts

A fact that can be accurately and readily determined need not be generally known as long as it can be determined from a source whose accuracy cannot be reasonably questioned, such as a geographic and historical fact obtained from a respected reference source.

> **Example:** A judge could take judicial notice of the state's statutory rate for post-judgment interest in determining the appropriate interest rate for pre-judgment interest. *Fox v. Kane-Miller Corp.*, 398 F. Supp. 609 (D. Md. 1975).

> **Contrast:** A judge could not take judicial notice of information about a company found on the company's website, because such information is often self-serving and subject to puffery. *Victaulic Co. v. Tieman*, 499 F.3d 227 (3d Cir. 2007).

b. Procedure

A court may take judicial notice at any time during a proceeding, including on appeal, whether upon request of a party or by the court's own initiative. Note, however, that a court may not take judicial notice against a criminal defendant for the first time on appeal. *U.S. v. Jones*, 580 F.2d 219 (6th Cir. 1978). If a party makes a request and the court is supplied with the necessary information, then the court must take notice of the fact. Fed. R. Evid. 201(c), (d).

1) Party's opportunity to be heard

When a party makes a timely request, the judge must give the party an opportunity to be heard on the propriety of taking judicial notice and the nature of the fact to be noticed. This right to be heard exists even if the court has taken judicial notice of a fact before notifying the party. Fed. R. Evid. 201(e).

2) Instructing the jury

a) Civil case

In a civil case, the jury must be instructed to accept the noticed fact as **conclusive**. Fed. R. Evid. 201(f).

b) Criminal case

In a criminal case, the jury must be instructed that it **may or may not accept** any judicially noticed fact as conclusive. Fed. R. Evid. 201(f).

B. MODE AND ORDER OF PRESENTATION OF EVIDENCE

1. Trial Process

A trial traditionally begins with the plaintiff's case-in-chief, followed by the defendant's case, followed by the plaintiff's rebuttal.

a. Judicial control of process

Subject to the evidentiary rules, a party is generally free to present evidence in the manner and order that the party feels is most effective. The order of the witnesses and presentation of the case, however, are within the discretion of the court, in order to effectively determine the truth, avoid wasting time, and protect witnesses from harassment. Fed. R. Evid. 611(a).

b. Judicial presentation of evidence

A judge may question, or even call, a witness. If the judge calls a witness, all parties may cross-examine that witness. A party objecting to the judge's calling or interrogation of a witness may wait to object until the next opportunity when the jury is not present. Fed. R. Evid. 614.

2. Examination of Witness

A party who calls a witness may examine the witness subject to the evidentiary rules. Another party may then cross-examine that witness.

a. Scope of cross-examination

The scope of cross-examination generally is limited to the subject matter of the direct examination and the credibility of the witness; however, the court may allow inquiry into additional matters. Fed. R. Evid. 611(b).

b. Additional examination

After cross-examination, the party who called the witness may engage in redirect examination, ordinarily to reply to any significant new matter raised on cross-examination. Recross-examination is also generally permissible with respect to significant new matters brought up during redirect examination. For both redirect and recross, the court has discretion to permit inquiry into other matters.

c. Examination of a defendant

The Fifth Amendment privilege against self-incrimination protects a defendant in a criminal case from being compelled to testify. A defendant in a criminal case who testifies as to a preliminary question, such as the voluntariness of the defendant's confession, has not opened himself up to cross-examination on other issues in the case. Fed. R. Evid. 104(d).

3. Form of Questions

a. Leading questions

1) Direct examination

On direct examination of a witness, a leading question—that is, a question that suggests the answer within the question—generally is not permitted. Fed. R. Evid. 611(c).

> **Example:** The question "Didn't you start the fire at 10:00?" suggests when the person being questioned started the fire. In contrast, the question "When did you start the fire?" does not suggest the answer.

a) Exceptions

A leading question is permitted on direct examination when it is necessary to develop the witness's testimony. For example, a leading question is usually permitted to elicit preliminary background information that is not in dispute. In addition, a leading question is typically permitted on direct examination of a witness who has difficulty communicating due to age or a physical or mental condition. Finally, when a party calls a witness who is likely to be antagonistic, such as an adverse party or a person associated with an adverse party, or a witness who presents adverse testimony (i.e., a hostile witness), even if such testimony is unanticipated, then the party ordinarily is permitted to use leading questions.

2) Cross-examination

There is no restriction on the use of leading questions during cross-examination. Fed. R. Evid. 611(c).

b. Improper questions

1) Compound question

A question that requires answers to multiple questions is compound and is not permitted.

> **Example:** "Didn't you leave the house at 7:00, lock the door behind you, get in your car, and drive away?" (A "no" answer could mean that the witness did not leave at all, left at a time other than 7:00, did not lock the door, etc.)

2) Assumes facts not in evidence

A question that assumes as true facts that have not been established is not permitted.

> **Example:** "When did you stop beating your wife?" (The question assumes that the witness is married and used to beat his wife. If neither fact has been established, this question is objectionable.)

3) Argumentative

A question that is intended to provoke an argument, rather than elicit a factual response, is not permitted.

Example: "You don't really expect the jury to believe you, do you?"

4) Calls for a conclusion or opinion

A question that requires the witness to draw a conclusion or state an opinion that he is not qualified to make is not permitted.

Example: "How did your mother feel after you told her the news?" (The witness cannot know how her mother felt and would have to give an opinion to answer the question.)

5) Repetitive

A question that has been asked and answered is not permitted, although judges may allow some repetition, particularly on cross-examination.

4. Exclusion of Witnesses

At a party's request or upon the court's own initiative, the court must exclude witnesses from the courtroom so that they do not hear the testimony of other witnesses. Some witnesses, however, may not be excluded under this rule, including:

i) A party who is a natural person;

ii) An officer or employee of a party that is not a natural person, after the individual has been designated as the party's representative by its attorney;

iii) A person whose presence is essential to a party's presentation of its case, such as a police officer in charge of the investigation in a criminal case; or

iv) A person, such as a victim, whose presence is permitted by statute.

Fed. R. Evid. 615. Note that a victim may be excluded if the court determines, by clear and convincing evidence, that the victim's testimony would be materially altered by the victim hearing other testimony. 18 U.S.C. § 3771.

C. BURDENS AND PRESUMPTIONS

1. Burden of Proof

The burden of proof comprises two distinct burdens: the burden of production and the burden of persuasion.

a. Burden of production

The party with the burden of production (or burden of going forward) must produce legally sufficient evidence as to each element of a claim or defense, so that a reasonable trier of fact could infer that the alleged fact has been proved. In meeting this burden, a plaintiff or prosecutor has made a **prima facie** case. Failure to meet this burden can result in a directed verdict against the party bearing the burden. The determination of whether it has been met rests with the court. The burden of production may shift during trial.

> **Example:** In a negligence action in which the plaintiff produces uncontroverted evidence of the defendant's negligence, the defendant who does not have an affirmative defense bears the burden of producing evidence that challenges the case made by the plaintiff.

b. Burden of persuasion

The burden of persuasion (or standard of proof) is the degree to which legally sufficient evidence must be presented to the trier of fact. For example, in a civil case, this burden usually lies with the plaintiff to prove the allegations in the complaint and with the defendant to prove any affirmative defenses. This burden does not shift. Typically, determination of whether it has been met rests with the trier of fact.

1) Civil standards

The standard in most civil cases is a **preponderance of the evidence.** A fact is proven by a preponderance of the evidence if it is more likely to exist than not.

A higher standard used in some civil cases (such as fraud) is **clear and convincing evidence.** Under this standard, the existence of a fact must be highly probable or reasonably certain.

2) Criminal standard

In criminal cases, the prosecution must prove each element of a crime **beyond a reasonable doubt** to overcome the defendant's presumption of innocence. *In re Winship*, 397 U.S. 358 (1970).

2. Presumptions

A presumption is a conclusion that the trier of fact is required to draw upon a party's proof of an underlying fact or set of facts (i.e., basic facts). For example, a presumption arises that a person is dead when a party establishes that the person has been missing and not heard from for more than seven years. A rebuttable presumption may be overcome by evidence to the contrary; a conclusive presumption may not.

a. Rebuttable

A rebuttable presumption shifts the burden of production, but not the burden of persuasion, to the opposing party. Under the "bursting bubble" approach followed by the Federal Rules in a civil case, a presumption "bursts" (i.e., no longer has a preclusive effect) after the introduction of sufficient evidence by the opposing party to sustain a contrary finding. If no contrary evidence is introduced, the judge must instruct the jury to accept the presumption. If contrary evidence is introduced, the burden of persuasion remains on the party who had it originally. While the presumption no longer has preclusive effect after the introduction of contrary evidence, a judge may instruct the jury that it may, but is not required to, draw the conclusion (e.g., a person is dead) from the basic facts (e.g., the person has been missing for seven years). Fed. R. Evid. 301.

> **Limitation:** The "bursting bubble" approach does not apply when a federal statute or another Federal Rule of Evidence, such as Federal Rule 302 (*see* § c. Diversity cases, *below*), provides otherwise.

b. Conclusive

Conclusive (or irrebuttable) presumptions are treated as rules of substantive law and may not be challenged by contrary evidence, no matter how strong the proof. One example is the presumption in some states that a child under the age of four lacks the ability to form the intent necessary to commit an intentional tort; no evidence to the contrary is permitted to disprove this assumption.

c. Diversity cases

In a federal diversity action, the federal court generally applies the Federal Rules to determine the resolution of evidentiary issues. However, when state substantive law is determinative of the existence of claim or defense under the *Erie* doctrine, then state law, rather than the Federal Rules, also governs the effect of a presumption related to the claim or defense. Fed. R. Evid. 302.

3. Destruction of Evidence

In general, the intentional destruction of evidence relevant to a case raises a presumption or inference that such evidence would have been unfavorable to the party that destroyed the evidence. To be entitled to such an inference, the alleged victim of the destruction of the evidence must establish that (i) the destruction was intentional, (ii) the destroyed evidence was relevant to the issue about which the party seeks such inference, and (iii) the alleged victim acted with due diligence as to the destroyed evidence. The presumption that arises from the destruction of evidence is rebuttable.

II. RELEVANCE

A. GENERAL CONSIDERATIONS

As a rule, evidence must be relevant to be admissible, and all relevant evidence is admissible unless excluded by a specific rule, law, or constitutional provision. Fed. R. Evid. 402. Evidence is relevant if:

i) It has any tendency to make a fact more or less probable than it would be without the evidence (i.e., **probative**); and

ii) The fact is of consequence in determining the action (i.e., **material**).

Fed. R. Evid. 401.

> **Sufficiency Distinguished:** To be relevant, evidence need not, by itself, establish an element that a party must prove (e.g., the death of an individual in a homicide prosecution) or serve to refute such an element (e.g., a defendant's lack of a duty in a negligence action). The test of sufficiency of a party's evidence focuses on all evidence submitted by a party and admitted by the court. By contrast, under the test of relevancy, evidence is admissible even if it is only a single brick that is part of a wall of evidence establishing a party's position. Fed. R. Evid. 401, Notes of Advisory Committee, referring to Professor McCormick's famous statement, "A brick is not a wall."

1. **Direct and Circumstantial Evidence**

   a. **Direct evidence**

   Direct evidence is identical to the factual proposition that it is offered to prove. An eyewitness who testifies that she saw the defendant shoot the victim dead is an example of direct evidence that the defendant committed a homicide.

   > **Conviction without direct evidence:** There is no rule that requires the presentation of direct evidence in order to convict a defendant. In other words, a defendant can be convicted solely upon circumstantial evidence.

   b. **Circumstantial evidence**

   Evidence that tends to indirectly prove a factual proposition through inference from collateral facts is circumstantial. An eyewitness who testifies that, moments before entering a room, she heard a shot, and upon entering the room saw the defendant standing over the body of the victim holding a smoking gun is circumstantial evidence that the defendant committed a homicide.

   > **Compare direct evidence:** While it is sometimes said that direct evidence is better than circumstantial evidence, circumstantial evidence may have greater probative value. For example, testimony as to the identity of a thief based on a fleeting glimpse by an eyewitness with poor vision may not be as persuasive as testimony that the stolen item was found in the defendant's home.

2. **Exclusion of Relevant Evidence**

   Relevant evidence may be excluded if its probative value is **substantially outweighed** by the danger of unfair prejudice, confusing the issues, misleading the jury, undue delay, wasting time, or needlessly presenting cumulative evidence. This exclusion is often denominated by the applicable rule; that is, it is referred to as a "Rule 403" exclusion. Fed. R. Evid. 403.

   > **Matter of degree:** Evidence may be admissible even if the danger of prejudice or other factors outweigh the probative value, so long as the danger does not do so **substantially.**

3. **Relevance Dependent on Existence of Fact**

   When the relevance of evidence depends upon whether a fact exists, proof must be introduced sufficient to support a finding that the fact does exist. The court may admit the proposed evidence on the condition that the proof is introduced later. Fed. R. Evid. 104(b). In making its determination that sufficient evidence has been introduced, the court must examine all of the evidence and decide whether the jury could reasonably find the conditional fact by a preponderance of the evidence; the court itself is not required to find that the conditional fact exists by a preponderance of the evidence. *Huddleston v. United States*, 485 U.S. 681 (1988).

4. **Admission of Irrelevant Evidence—Curative Admission**

   Generally, irrelevant evidence is inadmissible. However, when a court admits evidence that is not relevant, the court may permit the introduction of additional irrelevant evidence to rebut the previously admitted evidence. Known as a curative admission, such evidence is admitted when necessary to remove unfair prejudice.

The failure of a party to object to the admission of the initial irrelevant evidence is a factor to be considered in determining whether the party was unfairly prejudiced by it. *United States v. Hall*, 653 F.2d 1002 (5th Cir. 1981); *Crawford v. United States*, 198 F.2d 976 (D.C. Cir. 1952).

B. CHARACTER EVIDENCE

Character evidence, which is generalized information about a person's behavior—such as information that the defendant is a criminal, a bad parent, or an inattentive driver—is generally inadmissible.

1. Civil Cases

a. Inadmissible to prove conforming conduct

Evidence of a person's character (or character trait) generally is inadmissible to prove that the person acted in accordance with that character (or character trait) on a particular occasion. Fed. R. Evid. 404(a)(1).

Example: A plaintiff cannot introduce evidence that the defendant is a reckless driver to prove that the defendant drove recklessly on the day in question.

Evidence concerning the past sexual behavior of a victim of sexual misconduct (e.g., rape) is admissible in limited circumstances (*see* § V.B.6. Sexual Conduct, *infra*).

b. Character at issue

Character evidence is admissible, however, when character is an **essential element** of a claim or defense, rather than a means of proving a person's conduct. Character is most commonly an essential element in defamation (character of the plaintiff), negligent hiring or negligent entrustment (character of the person entrusted), and child-custody cases (character of the parent or guardian). Fed. R. Evid. 404, Notes of Advisory Committee.

2. Criminal Cases

a. Defendant's character

1) By prosecution—defendant's bad character

In general, the same rule that applies in a civil action applies to the prosecution in a criminal case. The prosecution is not permitted to introduce evidence of a defendant's **bad character** to prove that the defendant has a **propensity** to commit crimes and therefore is likely to have committed the crime in question. Fed. R. Evid. 404(a)(1).

Example: A defendant is charged with brutally murdering his wife. The prosecution may not present evidence of the defendant's violent nature.

2) By defendant—defendant's good character

A defendant is **permitted** to introduce evidence of his **good character** as being inconsistent with the type of crime charged.

> **Example 1:** A defendant is charged with brutally murdering his wife. The defendant may present evidence of his peaceable nature.

The defendant's character evidence must be pertinent to the crime charged.

> **Example 2:** A defendant is charged with embezzling money from her employer. The defendant may not present evidence of her peaceable nature.

Proof of good character offered by the defendant must be in the form of **reputation** testimony or **opinion** testimony. Reputation evidence is defined as a defendant's reputation in the community. "Community" includes people with whom the defendant engages on a regular basis.

3) Defendant "opens the door"

Although the prosecution cannot introduce evidence of the defendant's bad character, the defendant makes his character an issue in the case if he offers evidence of his good character. When the defendant **"opens the door,"** the prosecution is free to rebut the defendant's claims by attacking the defendant's character. Fed. R. Evid. 404(a)(2)(A).

> **Defendant as witness:** The defendant does not "open the door" to character evidence merely by taking the stand, but as a witness, the defendant is subject to impeachment.

In addition, the defendant "opens the door" for the prosecution to introduce evidence of his bad character by introducing evidence of the victim's bad character. The prosecution's evidence regarding the defendant must relate to the same character trait (e.g., violence) that the defendant's evidence about the victim did. Fed. R. Evid. 404(a)(2)(A).

b. Victim's character

1) By defendant—victim's bad character

A criminal defendant may introduce reputation or opinion evidence of the victim's character when it is relevant to the defense asserted. Fed. R. Evid. 404(a)(2)(B). (Note: The introduction of evidence of the character of a victim of sexual misconduct in a criminal case, however, is subject to significant limitations (*see* § V.B.6. Sexual Conduct, *infra*).)

> **Example:** A defendant is charged with assault. The defendant may offer evidence of the victim's character trait of violence to support a claim of self-defense by showing that the victim was the aggressor. The prosecution may then rebut with evidence of the victim's character trait of peacefulness or the defendant's character trait of violence.

2) By prosecution—victim's good character

The prosecution may offer rebuttal evidence of the victim's good character only when the defendant has introduced evidence of the victim's bad character. In a homicide case, the prosecution may offer evidence of the victim's trait for peacefulness to rebut evidence that the victim was the first aggressor. Fed. R. Evid. 404(a)(2)(B), (C).

> **Example:** A defendant is charged with assault. The defendant presents evidence of the victim's character trait of violence to support a claim of self-defense. The prosecution may then rebut the defendant's evidence with evidence of the victim's character trait of peacefulness. The prosecution may also offer evidence of the defendant's character trait of violence.

3. Methods of Proving Character

When character evidence is admissible, it may always be proved by testimony about the person's reputation or in the form of the witness's opinion. Fed. R. Evid. 405(a). For use of specific instances of conduct, *see* § II.C.2. Introduction of Specific Acts as Character Evidence, *infra*.

4. Impeachment

Character evidence is admissible for impeachment purposes. Character evidence about the witness may be introduced to show that the witness is not a person whose testimony should be believed. In such instances, the witness's character for untruthfulness is relevant. When permitted, the witness's testimony may be supported by testimony as to the witness's character for truthfulness. Fed. R. Evid. 404(a)(3). *See* § III.B. Impeachment, *infra*.

C. BAD ACTS

In addition to general evidence of a person's character (or character trait), evidence of a prior bad act is not admissible to prove a person's character in order to show that the person acted in accordance with that character on a particular occasion. Fed. R. Evid. 404(b)(1).

> **Example 1:** A driver is sued to recover for injuries inflicted on the plaintiff allegedly due to the driver's negligent failure to stop at a stop sign. The plaintiff cannot introduce testimony by a witness that the driver failed to stop at the same stop sign the day before the accident in question for the purpose of proving that the plaintiff failed to stop at the stop sign on the day of the accident.

Although a defendant's crimes or other wrongful acts are not admissible to show his criminal propensity in order to prove that he committed the crime for which he is charged, such bad acts are admissible for another purpose, such as proving motive, opportunity, intent, preparation, plan, knowledge, identity, absence of mistake, or lack of accident. Fed. R. Evid. 404(b)(2).

> **Example 2:** A defendant is charged with murder. Evidence that the defendant was previously convicted of robbery is likely admissible when the murder victim was the person who prosecuted the robbery. Such evidence establishes the defendant's motive for killing the victim.

MIMIC evidence: This type of evidence is sometimes referred to as "MIMIC" evidence (**M**otive, **I**ntent, absence of **M**istake, **I**dentity, or **C**ommon plan), but it is important not to treat this list as all-inclusive. Subject to the other restrictions on the admissibility of evidence (e.g., relevancy, Rule 403 exclusion), a defendant's bad act may be introduced for any purpose so long as that purpose is not to prove that, because the defendant had a propensity to commit crimes, the defendant committed the charged crime.

1. Advance Notice

When a criminal defendant requests, the prosecution must provide reasonable notice of the general nature of such evidence that the prosecution intends to offer at trial. Such notice must generally be given before trial, but it can be given during trial when the court, for good cause, excuses the lack of pretrial notice. Fed. R. Evid. 404(b)(2).

2. Introduction of Specific Acts as Character Evidence

a. Civil cases

When character evidence is admissible as evidence in a civil case (i.e., evidence that is an essential element of a claim or defense), it may be proved by specific instances of a person's conduct as well as either by testimony about the person's reputation or by testimony in the form of an opinion. Fed. R. Evid. 405(b).

b. Criminal cases

Generally, when character evidence is admissible as evidence in a criminal case (e.g., evidence of good character introduced by the defendant), specific instances of a person's conduct are not admissible. Character must be proved by either reputation or opinion testimony. Fed. R. Evid. 405(a).

Non-propensity use: When a defendant's bad act is not used to show the defendant's criminal propensity but for another purpose (e.g., motive, identity), such instance of conduct may be admissible for that purpose.

c. Cross-examination of character witness

When a character witness is cross-examined, the court may allow a party to inquire into specific acts committed by the person about whom the witness is testifying. Fed. R. Evid. 405(a).

Rule 403: Keep in mind that evidence of a prior bad act that is otherwise admissible is especially subject to challenge under Federal Rule 403, which permits the court to exclude evidence when its probative value is substantially outweighed by the danger of unfair prejudice (*see* § II.A.2. Exclusion of Relevant Evidence, *supra*).

D. HABIT EVIDENCE

Evidence of a **person's habit** or an **organization's routine** is admissible to prove that the person or organization acted in accordance with the habit or routine on a particular occasion. A habit is a person's particular routine reaction to a specific set of circumstances.

Example: A person drives the same route to work and parks in the same spot every day.

Habit evidence may be admitted without corroboration and without an eyewitness. Fed. R. Evid. 406.

EXAM NOTE: Habit is more specific than character evidence. On the MBE, words like "always" or "every time" generally refer to habit, whereas "often" or "frequently" are more likely to imply character evidence.

III. WITNESSES

A. COMPETENCE

Generally, every person is presumed to be competent to be a witness. Common-law prohibitions on a witness's ability to testify because of a lack of religious belief or conviction of a crime are inapplicable in proceedings governed by the Federal Rules. Questions of mental competence go to the weight rather than the admissibility of the testimony. However, in cases that turn on state law, such as diversity cases, a witness's competency is determined by state law. Fed. R. Evid. 601.

1. Personal Knowledge

A non-expert witness must have personal knowledge of a matter in order to testify about that matter. Personal knowledge may be established by the witness's own testimony as well as through other means. Fed. R. Evid. 602.

2. Oath or Affirmation

A witness must give an oath or affirmation to testify truthfully. The oath or affirmation must be in a form designed to impress that duty on the witness's conscience. Fed. R. Evid. 603. An interpreter must give an oath or affirmation to make a true translation. Fed. R. Evid. 604.

3. Judge as Witness

The presiding judge is absolutely barred from testifying as a witness in the trial. A party is not required to object in order to preserve the issue. Fed. R. Evid. 605.

4. Juror as Witness

a. At trial

A juror may not testify as a witness at trial in front of the members of the jury. If a juror is called to testify, the opposing party must be given the opportunity to object outside the presence of the jury. A juror may be called to testify outside the presence of the other jurors as to matters that occur during the trial, such as the bribery of a juror or a juror's failure to follow the court's instruction (e.g., discussing the case with family members). Fed. R. Evid. 606(a).

b. After trial

During an inquiry into the validity of a verdict, a juror generally may not testify about:

i) Any statement made or incident that occurred during the course of the jury's deliberations (e.g., refusal to apply the court's instructions);

ii) The effect of anything upon that juror's, or any other juror's, vote; or

iii) Any juror's mental processes concerning the verdict.

Fed. R. Evid. 606(b).

1) Exceptions

A juror may testify about whether:

i) Extraneous prejudicial information was brought to the jury's attention (e.g., the circulation of a newspaper article not introduced into evidence about the trial and the defendant's guilt);

ii) An outside influence was improperly brought to bear on a juror (e.g., a threat on the life of a juror's spouse); or

iii) A mistake was made in entering the verdict onto the verdict form.

The mistake exception, item iii above, does not extend to mistakes about the consequences of the agreed-upon verdict. Fed. R. Evid. 606(b).

Grand jury: The same rule applies with regard to a challenge to the validity of an indictment by a grand jury.

5. Child as Witness

The competence of a child depends on his intelligence, his ability to differentiate between truth and falsehood, and his understanding of the importance of telling the truth. *Wheeler v. United States*, 159 U.S. 523, 524, 526 (1895) (finding a five-year-old child competent to testify at a capital murder trial). A witness who is so young that he is unable to understand the requirement to tell the truth would be disqualified. There is, however, no specific age at which a person becomes competent. The decision with regard to competency is one for the court.

6. Dead Man's Statutes

At common law, a party with a financial interest in the outcome could not testify in a civil case about a communication or transaction with a deceased person whose estate was party to the suit and the testimony was adverse to the decedent's estate, unless there was a waiver. Dead Man's Statutes do not apply in criminal cases.

The Federal Rules do not include such a restriction, but most jurisdictions have adopted such "Dead Man's Statutes," which may be applicable in federal cases when state law applies (i.e., diversity cases).

a. Protected parties

The rationale of a Dead Man's Statute is to protect a decedent's estate from parties with a financial interest in the estate. Therefore, protected parties generally include an heir, a legatee, a devisee, an executor, or an administrator of an estate.

b. Disqualified witnesses

Any person directly affected financially by the outcome of the case may be disqualified as a witness under a Dead Man's Statute. A predecessor in interest to the party may be disqualified in order to prevent circumvention of the statute by transference of property to a relative or friend.

c. Interested person

A personal representative of the decedent or a successor in interest may also be protected under a Dead Man's Statute as an interested person.

d. Waiver

An interested person or protected party may waive the protection afforded by a Dead Man's Statute in several ways, including (i) failing to object to the introduction of testimony by a disqualified witness or (ii) introducing evidence of a conversation or transaction to which the statute applies.

B. IMPEACHMENT

A witness may be impeached by calling into question her credibility. Typically, a witness's testimony is challenged based on her character for truthfulness, bias, ability to perceive or testify accurately, or prior statement that contradicts the witness's testimony at trial. In addition, a witness may be impeached by another witness or by evidence that contradicts the witness's testimony.

1. Who May Impeach a Witness

Any party, including the party that called the witness to testify, may attack the credibility of a witness. Fed. R. Evid. 607.

2. Witness's Character for Truthfulness

a. Reputation and opinion testimony

A witness's credibility may be attacked by testimony regarding the witness's character for untruthfulness. Generally, this testimony must be about the witness's **reputation** for having a character for untruthfulness or in the form of an **opinion** of the witness's character for untruthfulness. Fed. R. Evid. 608(a).

b. Truthful character evidence

The credibility of a witness may not be bolstered. Evidence of the truthful character of the witness is admissible only after the witness's character for truthfulness has been attacked. Evidence that impeaches the witness but does not specifically attack the witness's character for truthfulness, such as testimony that the witness is biased, does not constitute an attack. As with evidence regarding a witness's character for untruthfulness, evidence as to a witness's character for truthfulness is generally admissible only in the form of reputation or opinion testimony. Fed. R. Evid. 608(a).

c. Specific instances of conduct

Generally, a specific instance of conduct (e.g., lying on a job application) is not admissible to attack or support the witness's character for truthfulness. However, on cross-examination, a witness may be asked about specific instances of conduct if it is probative of the truthfulness of (i) the witness or (ii) another witness about whose character the witness being cross-examined has testified. Fed. R. Evid. 608(b).

a) Limitations

The judge may refuse to allow such questioning of a witness under either Federal Rule 403 (the probative value is substantially outweighed by the danger of unfair prejudice) or Federal Rule 611 (protection of the witness from harassment or undue embarrassment). In addition, the lawyer who examines the witness must have a good-faith basis for believing that the misconduct occurred before asking the witness about it. *United States v. Davenport*, 753 F.2d 1460 (9th Cir. 1985).

b) Arrest

Because an arrest for misconduct is not itself misconduct, a witness may not be cross-examined about having been arrested solely for the purpose of impeaching the witness's character for truthfulness; however, the witness may be cross-examined about the underlying conduct that lead to the arrest. *See Michelson v. United States*, 335 U.S. 469 (1948).

c) Use of extrinsic evidence

When, on cross-examination, the witness denies a specific instance of conduct, extrinsic evidence is not admissible to prove that instance in order to attack or support the witness's character for truthfulness. This prohibition also bars references to any consequences that a witness may have suffered because of the conduct (e.g., suspension from a governmental job for improper personal use of governmental property). (An exception exists for criminal convictions, *see* § 3. Criminal Conviction, *below.*)

Note, however, that extrinsic evidence of specific conduct can be admissible to impeach the witness on other grounds, such as bias. Fed. R. Evid. 608(b), Notes of Advisory Committee (2003).

While a document is generally considered to be extrinsic evidence, *United States v. Elliott*, 89 F.3d 1360, 1368 (8th Cir. 1996), when the foundation for the document is established through the witness being impeached, it is possible that the document might be admissible to impeach the witness's character for truthfulness. Kevin C. McMunigal & Calvin W. Sharpe, *Reforming Extrinsic Impeachment*, 33 Conn. L. Rev. 363, 372–73 (2001).

d) Privilege against self-incrimination

By testifying on another matter, a witness does not waive the privilege against self-incrimination for testimony that relates only to the witness's character for truthfulness. Fed. R. Evid. 608(b).

3. Criminal Conviction

A witness's character for truthfulness may be impeached with evidence that the witness has been convicted of a crime, subject to the limitations discussed below. It does not matter whether the conviction is for a state or federal crime. Fed. R. Evid. 609.

a. Crimes involving dishonesty or false statement

Subject to the 10-year restriction (*see below*), **any witness** may be impeached with evidence that he has been convicted of **any crime**—felony or misdemeanor—**involving dishonesty or false statement,** regardless of the punishment imposed or the prejudicial effect of the evidence. A crime involves dishonesty or false statement if establishing the elements of the crime requires proof (or admission) of an act of dishonesty or false statement, such as perjury, fraud, embezzlement, or false pretense. Crimes of violence, such as murder, assault, and rape, are not crimes involving dishonesty or false statement, even though the perpetrator acted deceitfully in committing the crime of violence. Fed. R . Evid. 609(a)(2).

b. **Crimes not involving dishonesty or false statement**

Subject to the 10-year restriction (*see below*), a conviction for a crime not involving fraud or dishonesty is admissible to impeach a witness only if the crime is **punishable by death or imprisonment for more than one year** (typically, a felony). Fed. R. Evid. 609(a)(1).

1) **Criminal defendant**

When the witness is a criminal defendant, evidence of a felony conviction for a crime not involving dishonesty or false statement is admissible **only if** its probative value outweighs the prejudicial effect to that defendant. This stricter-than-usual balancing test gives extra protection to a criminal defendant who takes the stand in his own defense.

2) **Other witnesses**

For witnesses other than a criminal defendant, such evidence generally must be admitted. The court does have the discretion, however, to exclude the evidence when the party objecting to the impeachment shows that its probative value is **substantially outweighed** by its prejudicial effect (i.e., the Rule 403 standard).

c. **Convictions more than 10 years old**

If more than 10 years have elapsed since the conviction (or release from confinement, whichever is later), then evidence of the conviction is admissible only if:

i) The probative value of the conviction, supported by specific facts and circumstances, **substantially outweighs** its prejudicial effect; and

ii) The proponent gives an adverse party reasonable written notice of the intent to use such evidence so that the adverse party has a fair opportunity to contest the use of such evidence.

Fed. R. Evid. 609(b).

d. **Effect of pardon**

Evidence of a witness's conviction is not admissible if the conviction has been the subject of a pardon, annulment, or other action based on a finding of innocence. This rule also applies to an action based on a finding that the witness has been rehabilitated, provided that the witness has not been convicted of a later crime punishable by death or imprisonment in excess of one year (typically, a felony). Fed. R. Evid. 609(c).

e. Juvenile adjudications

Evidence of a juvenile adjudication is not admissible to impeach a defendant. When the witness is not the defendant, evidence of a juvenile adjudication can be used to impeach the witness's character for truthfulness only if:

i)   It is offered in a criminal case;

ii) An adult's conviction for that offense would be admissible to attack the adult's credibility; and

iii) Admitting the evidence is necessary to fairly determine guilt or innocence.

Fed. R. Evid. 609(d).

> **Used to show bias:** Under the Sixth Amendment Confrontation Clause, evidence of a witness's juvenile adjudication can also be used by a criminal defendant to impeach a witness's credibility by showing bias, such as when the witness's juvenile adjudication could provide a motive for the witness to lie. *Davis v. Alaska*, 415 U.S. 308 (1974).

f. Manner of proof

Evidence of a prior conviction may be produced by way of an admission by the witness, whether during direct testimony or on cross-examination, as well as by extrinsic evidence (e.g., a record of the conviction). Fed. R. Evid. 609, Notes of Advisory Committee (1990).

g. Pendency of appeal

A witness's conviction may be used for impeachment purposes even if an appeal is pending. Evidence of the pendency is also admissible. Fed. R. Evid. 609(e).

4.   Prior Inconsistent Statements

A witness's prior statement that is inconsistent with a material part of the witness's testimony may be used to impeach the witness.

a.   Disclosing the statement to the witness

A party who is examining a witness about the witness's prior statement is not required to show it or disclose its contents to the witness, but the statement must be shown, or its contents disclosed, to an adverse party's attorney upon request. Fed. R. Evid. 613(a).

b.   Extrinsic evidence

Extrinsic evidence of a witness's prior inconsistent statement may be introduced only if the witness is given the opportunity to **explain or deny** the statement, and the opposing party is given the opportunity to **examine the witness** about it. The witness's opportunity to explain or deny the statement need not take place before the statement is admitted into evidence.

1)   Exceptions to the opportunity to explain

The opportunity to explain or deny a prior inconsistent statement does not apply when the statement (i) impeaches a hearsay declarant (*see* § 7. Impeachment of a Hearsay Declarant, *below*) or (ii) qualifies as an opposing party's statement under Rule 801(d)(2) (*see* § VI.B.2., "Opposing Party's Statement," *infra*). Fed. R. Evid. 806, 613(b).

2) Collateral matter

Extrinsic evidence of a prior inconsistent statement cannot be used to impeach a witness regarding a collateral (i.e., irrelevant) matter; the questioning party is bound by the witness's answer.

5. Bias or Interest

Because a witness may be influenced by his relationship to a party (e.g., employment), his interest in testifying (e.g., avoidance of prosecution), or his interest in the outcome of the case (e.g., receipt of an inheritance), a witness's bias or interest is always relevant to the credibility of his testimony, and consequently, a witness may be impeached on that ground.

Although the Federal Rules do not expressly require that a party ask the witness about an alleged bias before introducing extrinsic evidence of that bias, many courts require that such a foundation be laid before extrinsic evidence of bias can be introduced.

> **EXAM NOTE:** MBE questions typically test bias in the form of witnesses who are employed by one of the parties, or witnesses for the prosecution who testify in exchange for reduced or dropped charges.

6. Sensory Competence

A witness may be impeached by showing a deficiency in her testimonial capacities to perceive, recall, or relate information. This can be achieved by demonstrating that the witness is physically or mentally impaired, or through evidence of outside interference with the witness's abilities, such as thunder impeding the ability to hear or darkness impeding the ability to see.

7. Impeachment of a Hearsay Declarant

When a hearsay statement is admitted into evidence, the credibility of the declarant may be attacked (and, if attacked, supported) by any evidence that would be admissible if the declarant had testified as a witness. The declarant need not be given the opportunity to explain or deny any inconsistent statement or conduct, whether such statement or conduct occurred before or after the hearsay statement. If the party against whom a hearsay statement has been admitted calls the declarant as a witness, then the party is entitled to examine the declarant on the statement as if under cross-examination. Fed. R. Evid. 806.

Similar impeachment treatment is accorded a nonhearsay statement made by a co-conspirator, agent, or authorized spokesperson for an opposing party that has been admitted into evidence.

8. Rehabilitation of a Witness

A witness who has been impeached may be "rehabilitated" by the introduction of rebuttal evidence by either party to support the witness's credibility. Rehabilitation may be accomplished by:

i) **Explanation** or clarification on redirect examination;

ii) Reputation or opinion evidence of his **character for truthfulness,** if the witness's character was attacked on that ground under Fed. R. Evid. 608(a); or

iii) A **prior consistent statement** offered to rebut an express or implied charge that the witness lied due to improper motive or influence.

Fed. R. Evid. 801(d)(1)(B).

9. Religious Opinions and Beliefs

Evidence of a witness's religious opinions or beliefs is not admissible to attack or support a witness's credibility. Fed. R. Evid. 610. However, such evidence may be admissible to show bias or interest, such as when the witness is affiliated with a church that is a party to a lawsuit.

10. Impeachment by Contradictory Evidence

A witness may be impeached by evidence that contradicts the witness's testimony. Impeachment may be by extrinsic evidence as well as by cross-examination.

> **Example:** The plaintiff in a negligence action based on a car accident testifies that, due to the defendant's reckless driving, the plaintiff's car was damaged. The defense may introduce a record of an insurance claim filed by the plaintiff prior to the accident for such damage due to another incident. Alternatively, the defense attorney may cross-examine the plaintiff about that claim.

11. Collateral Issues

While the Federal Rules do not explicitly prohibit impeachment on collateral issues, a court may refuse to admit evidence related to a collateral issue under the Rule 403 balancing test. Generally, a party may not impeach the credibility of a witness by introducing extrinsic evidence of a collateral matter. Instead, the party must accept the witness's testimony.

> **Example:** A defendant is charged with assault. A prosecution witness testifies that the defendant assaulted the victim, who was wearing a plaid shirt. The defense may not call another witness to testify that the victim was wearing a striped shirt in order to establish the type of shirt that the victim was wearing.

C. RECOLLECTION REFRESHED

1. Present Recollection Refreshed

A witness may examine any item (e.g., writing, photograph) to "refresh" the witness's present recollection. The witness's testimony must be based on the witness's refreshed recollection, not on the item itself (e.g., the witness cannot read from the refreshing document).

a. Adverse party's options

When the item used to refresh a witness's recollection is a writing, the adverse party is entitled to have the document produced, to inspect the document, to cross-examine the witness about it, and to introduce any relevant portion into evidence. If the producing party claims that the document contains unrelated matter, the court may examine the document in camera and delete any unrelated portion before ordering that the rest be delivered to the adverse party.

The adverse party may object to the deletion, in which case the deleted portion must be preserved in the record. Fed. R. Evid. 612(b).

> **Evidentiary purpose:** When an adverse party seeks to introduce a writing used to refresh a witness's memory, the writing typically will be admissible for only the purpose of impeaching the witness's credibility. It will be admissible for substantive purposes only if it satisfies the other restrictions on admissibility, such as the hearsay rule.

When the refreshing of a witness's memory with a writing takes place before the witness testifies, the court may permit an adverse party to utilize these options, if justice so requires. Fed. R. Evid. 612(a).

b. Failure to produce or deliver the writing

In a criminal case, if the prosecution refuses to comply with a court order to produce or deliver a writing, the court must strike the witness's testimony, or may, when justice requires, declare a mistrial. In other circumstances, the court is free to issue any appropriate order. Fed. R. Evid. 612(c).

2. Past Recollection Recorded

A memorandum or record about a matter that a witness once had knowledge of but now has insufficient recollection of to testify to it may be admissible under a hearsay exception (*see* § VII.B.5. Recorded Recollection, *infra*). Although the record may be read into evidence, it is received as an exhibit only if offered by an adverse party.

> **Refreshed and recorded recollections distinguished:** The item used to refresh a witness's present recollection is generally not admitted into evidence, but a document introduced under the recorded recollection hearsay exception may be.

D. OPINION TESTIMONY

1. Lay Witness

A lay (non-expert) witness is generally not permitted to testify as to his opinion. However, lay opinions are admissible with respect to common-sense impressions such as appearance, intoxication, speed of a vehicle, or another's emotions. To be admissible, the opinion must be:

i) Rationally **based on the perception** of the witness; and

ii) Helpful to a **clear understanding** of the witness's testimony or the determination of a fact in issue.

Additionally, the opinion must **not** be based on scientific, technical, or specialized knowledge. Fed. R. Evid. 701.

2. Expert Witness

a. Subject matter of testimony

Before an expert witness may testify, the court must first determine that the subject matter of the witness's testimony:

i) **Is scientific, technical, or other specialized knowledge,** which focuses on the *reliability* of the testimony; and

ii) Will **help the trier of fact** understand the evidence or determine a fact in issue, which focuses on the *relevance* of the testimony.

b. Qualified expert

Once the testimony is determined to be reliable and relevant, an expert witness may testify as to her opinion, provided:

i) The witness is **qualified as an expert** by knowledge, skill, experience, training, or education;

ii) The testimony is based on **sufficient facts or data**;

iii) The testimony is the product of **reliable principles and methods** (i.e., the factual data, principles, and methods used as a basis for the testimony are of the type reasonably relied on by experts in the field, although the data need not be admissible itself); and

iv) The witness **applied the principles and methods reliably to the facts** of the case.

Fed. R. Evid. 702. The expert must also possess a reasonable degree of certainty in her opinion, which may be expressed using language such as "probably." *United States v. Mornan*, 413 F.3d 372 (3d Cir. 2005); *see also, Kumho Tire Co. v. Carmichael*, 526 U.S. 137 (1999); *Daubert v. Merrell Dow Pharm.*, 509 U.S. 579 (1993).

c. Ultimate issue

Generally, an expert's opinion may be admissible even though the opinion embraces an ultimate issue in the case (including the defendant's state of mind). However, an expert **may not** state an opinion about whether a criminal defendant had the **requisite mental state** of any element of the crime charged or of a defense. That determination lies in the province of the trier of fact. Fed. R. Evid. 704.

d. Basis of opinion

The expert's opinion may be based on facts and data that the expert has personally observed or about which the expert has been made aware. When such facts and data are not admissible, the opinion itself may nevertheless be admissible if experts in the particular field would reasonably rely on those kinds of facts and data in forming an opinion on the subject. If such facts are inadmissible, the proponent nevertheless may disclose them to the jury if their probative value in helping the jury evaluate the opinion substantially outweighs their prejudicial effect. Fed. R. Evid. 703.

1) Disclosure of underlying facts and data

An expert may state an opinion and give the reasons for it without first testifying as to the underlying facts or data, unless the court orders otherwise. Another party, when cross-examining the expert, may, of course, require the expert to disclose those facts or data. Fed. R. Evid. 705.

2) Use of hypothetical

In making facts known to the expert at trial, use of a hypothetical question is not required.

e. Court-appointed expert

The court may appoint an expert witness and must inform the expert, either orally or in writing, of the expert's duties. Such a witness must advise each party of any findings. Each party may depose the witness, call the witness to testify, and cross-examine the witness. The court may authorize disclosure to the jury that the court appointed the expert. In a criminal case, the expert is paid by funds provided by law; in most civil cases, the expert's compensation is paid by the parties. Fed. R. Evid. 706.

f. Interpreter

An interpreter is subject to the rules for expert witnesses. Fed. R. Evid. 604.

IV. TANGIBLE EVIDENCE

Tangible evidence is evidence that is not presented in the form of testimony by a witness; it includes both documentary evidence (e.g., a written contract, a letter) and physical objects (e.g., a gun, torn clothing, an injured foot, a sound recording).

A. AUTHENTICATION

All tangible evidence must be authenticated. To authenticate an item, the proponent must produce sufficient evidence to support a finding that the thing is what its proponent claims it is. This is a lesser standard than a preponderance of the evidence. Fed. R. Evid. 901(a).

1. Physical Objects

a. Personal knowledge

A physical object may be authenticated by testimony of **personal knowledge** of the object. Fed. R. Evid. 901(b)(1).

Example: The owner of a stolen pocket watch may authenticate the watch by simply identifying it, "Yes, that is my pocket watch that was stolen."

b. Distinctive characteristics

A physical object may be authenticated by testimony of its **distinctive** characteristics. Fed. R. Evid. 901(b)(4).

Example: An electronically stored document may be authenticated by its metadata (e.g., filename, file type, creation date, permissions).

c. Chain of custody

Authentication by chain of custody must be used with respect to a physical object that could easily be tampered with or confused with a similar item, such as a blood sample. The witness testifying must account for the whereabouts of the item from the time it was obtained up until its introduction at the trial.

d. Reproductions and explanatory evidence

When reproductions (e.g., photographs, diagrams, maps, movies) are introduced into evidence, they may be authenticated by the testimony of a witness with personal knowledge that the object accurately depicts what its proponent claims it does. It is generally not necessary to call the person who created the reproduction to authenticate it. However, the creator may be called to authenticate the reproduction and may do so by testifying that the reproduction method produces an accurate result. Fed. R. Evid. 901(b)(9).

e. X-ray images and electrocardiograms

X-ray images, electrocardiograms, and similar items are physical representations of things that cannot otherwise be seen (i.e., the inner workings and functionality of a human body), and, as such, unlike other reproductions, they cannot be authenticated merely by the testimony of a witness that they are accurate reproductions of the facts. To authenticate such an item, it must be shown that an accurate process was used, that the machine used was working properly, and that the operator of the machine was qualified to operate it. The chain of custody must also be established.

2. Documentary Evidence

Documentary evidence is commonly authenticated by stipulation, testimony of an eyewitness, or handwriting verification.

a. Ancient documents and data compilations

A document or data compilation, including data stored electronically, is considered authentic if it is (i) at least **20 years old,** (ii) in a **condition unlikely to create suspicion** as to its authenticity, and (iii) **found in a place where it would likely be** if it were authentic. Fed. R. Evid. 901(b)(8).

b. Public records

A public record may be authenticated by evidence that the document was recorded or filed in a public office as authorized by law or that the document is from the office where items of that kind are kept. Fed. R. Evid. 901(b)(7).

c. Reply letter doctrine

A document may be authenticated by evidence that it was written in response to a communication, so long as it is unlikely, based on the contents, that it was written by someone other than the recipient of the first communication.

d. Handwriting verification

There are two methods by which handwriting verification may be used to authenticate a writing.

1) Comparison

An expert witness or the trier of fact may compare the writing in question with another writing that has been proven to be genuine in order to determine the authenticity of the writing in question. Fed. R. Evid.

901(b)(3). This method may also be used for authenticating other items, such as fingerprints, cloth fibers, and hair.

2) Non-expert opinion

A lay witness with personal knowledge of the claimed author's handwriting may testify as to whether the document is in that person's handwriting. The lay witness must not have become familiar with the handwriting for the purposes of litigation. Fed. R. Evid. 901(b)(2).

e. Self-authenticating documents

The following items of evidence are self-authenticating—they do not require extrinsic evidence of authenticity in order to be admitted:

i) Public documents bearing a governmental seal and a signature of an authorized governmental official or that are not sealed but are signed by an authorized governmental official and certified by another authorized governmental official;

ii) Certified copies of public records;

iii) Official publications issued by a public authority;

iv) Newspapers and periodicals;

v) Trade inscriptions (e.g., labels affixed in the course of business that indicate ownership);

vi) Notarized (acknowledged) documents;

vii) Commercial paper (including the signature thereon, and related documents);

viii) Any document, signature, or other item declared by federal statute to be authentic; and

ix) Records of a regularly conducted activity (e.g., a business) certified by a custodian of the records.

Although a proponent of a self-authenticating document generally is not required to give an adverse party advance notice of the intent to introduce the document, the proponent of business records (item ix, *above*) must give an adverse party reasonable written notice prior to the trial or hearing of the intent to offer the record and must make the record available for inspection so that the party has a fair opportunity to challenge them. Fed. R. Evid. 902.

f. Attesting witness

The testimony of a witness who attests or subscribes to a document generally is not required to authenticate a document. However, such testimony may be required by state law, such as to authenticate a will. Fed. R. Evid. 903.

3. Oral Statements

Oral statements may need to be authenticated as to the identity of the speaker in cases in which that identity is important (e.g., an opposing party's statement).

a. Voice identification

A voice can be identified by **any person** who has heard the voice **at any time** (including one made familiar solely for the purposes of litigation, in contrast to the rule for handwriting verification). It makes no difference whether the voice was heard firsthand or through mechanical or electronic transmission or recording. Fed. R. Evid. 901(b)(5).

b. Telephone conversations

A party to a telephone conversation may authenticate statements made during that conversation by testifying that:

    i) The caller recognized the speaker's voice;

    ii) The speaker knew facts that only a particular person would know;

    iii) The caller dialed a number believed to be the speaker's, and the speaker identified himself upon answering; or

    iv) The caller dialed a business and spoke to the person who answered about business regularly conducted over the phone.

Fed. R. Evid. 901(b)(4)–(6).

B. BEST EVIDENCE RULE

The best evidence rule (also known as the original document rule) requires that the original document (or a reliable duplicate) be produced in order to prove the contents of a writing, recording, or photograph, including electronic documents, x-rays, and videos. A "writing" is defined as "letters, words, numbers or their equivalent set down in any form." A "recording" and "photograph" are similarly broadly defined. Fed. R. Evid. 1001(a)–(c).

This rule applies only when the **contents of the document are at issue** or a witness is **relying on the contents of the document** when testifying. Fed. R. Evid. 1001–08.

Caution: Despite its name, the best evidence rule does not require a party to present the most persuasive evidence, nor does it require the presentation of documentary evidence instead of a witness's testimony simply because a document is available.

Example: A witness writes down her observations of an accident immediately after it happens. The best evidence rule does not prevent the witness from testifying about the event simply because a writing of her observations exists.

EXAM NOTE: The best evidence rule is frequently an incorrect answer choice on the MBE.

1. Contents at Issue

The contents of a document are at issue when:

    i) The document is used as proof of the happening of an event, such as with a photograph of a bank robbery;

    ii) The document has a legal effect, such as with a contract or a will; or

    iii) The witness is testifying based on facts learned from the writing (as opposed to personal knowledge), such as with an x-ray image.

Fed. R. Evid. 1002, Notes of Advisory Committee.

2. **"Original"**

An original of a writing or recording includes any counterpart intended to have the same effect as the original by the person who executed or issued it. If the information is stored electronically, any legible printout (or other output readable by sight) that reflects the information accurately is an original. An original of a photograph includes the negative and any print made from it. Fed. R. Evid. 1001(d).

3. **Exceptions**

a. **Duplicates**

A duplicate is a counterpart produced by any process or technique that accurately produces the original. Fed. R. Evid. 1001(e). A duplicate is admissible to the same extent as an original unless:

i)   There is a genuine question as to the authenticity of the original; or

ii) The circumstances make it unfair to admit the duplicate, such as may be the case when only part of the original is duplicated.

Fed. R. Evid. 1003.

Handwritten copies: Handwritten copies of an original are not duplicates and are admissible only when the original or duplicate is lost, destroyed, or in the possession of an adversary who fails to produce it.

b. **Original unavailable**

The original is not required, and other evidence of its contents is admissible if:

i)   All of the originals are lost or destroyed, and not by the proponent acting in bad faith;

ii) The original cannot be obtained by any available judicial process;

iii) The party against whom the original would be offered (a) had control of the original, (b) was at that time put on notice that the original would be the subject of proof at the trial or hearing, and (c) failed to produce it at the trial or hearing; or

iv) The writing, recording, or photograph is not closely related to a controlling issue (i.e., it is a collateral matter).

In such cases, once the party has accounted for the absence of an original, the party may prove the contents of the writing, recording, or photograph by other means. Fed. R. Evid. 1004.

c. **Public records**

The contents of a public record (i.e., an official record or a document recorded or filed in a public office as authorized by law) may be, and generally are, proved by a certified copy rather than by the original record. Alternatively, a public record may be proved by a copy of the record plus the testimony of a person who has compared the copy with the original. If a certified or compared copy cannot be obtained by reasonable diligence, the contents may be proved by other evidence. Fed. R. Evid. 1005.

d. Summaries

The contents of voluminous writings, recordings, or photographs may be presented in the form of a chart, summary, or calculation, if such contents cannot be conveniently examined in court. The proponent must make the originals or duplicates available for examination and copying by other parties at a reasonable time and place. The court may order the proponent to produce the originals or duplicates in court. Fed. R. Evid. 1006.

e. Admission by party

The proponent may prove the contents of a writing, recording, or photograph by the testimony, deposition, or written statement of the party against whom the evidence is offered. In such a case, the proponent does not need to account for the original. Fed. R. Evid. 1007.

> **Oral out-of-court statement:** If a party against whom a document is offered admits to the contents of the document in an oral statement made out of court (other than during a deposition), the best evidence rule applies. The proponent must account for the original before using the adverse party's oral statement to prove the contents of the document.

4. Role of Court and Jury

Ordinarily, the court determines whether the proponent has fulfilled the conditions for admitting other evidence of the content of a document. In a jury trial, however, the jury determines any issue as to whether:

i) An asserted writing, recording, or photograph ever existed;

ii) Another writing, recording, or photograph produced at trial is the original; or

iii) Other evidence of content correctly reflects the content.

Fed. R. Evid. 1008.

C. PAROL EVIDENCE RULE

1. General Rule

The parol evidence rule operates to exclude evidence that, if introduced, would change the terms of a written agreement. The rule is based on the assumption that a written contract represents the complete agreement between the parties.

a. Complete integration

If a written agreement is a complete integration (i.e., contains all of the terms to which the parties agreed), then the parol evidence rule is in effect, and no extrinsic evidence may be introduced.

b. Partial integration

A contract that contains some, but not all, of the terms to which the parties agreed is a partial integration. In this case, extrinsic evidence that **adds to** the writing may be admitted. Evidence that **contradicts** the writing may not be admitted.

2. Exceptions

Extrinsic evidence can always be admitted for the following purposes:

i) To clarify an ambiguity in the terms of the writing;

ii) To prove trade custom or course of dealings;

iii) To show fraud, duress, mistake, or illegal purpose on the part of one or both parties; or

iv) To show that consideration has (or has not) been paid.

3. Applicable Evidence

Only evidence of **prior or contemporaneous negotiations** is subject to the parol evidence rule. In other words, evidence of negotiations conducted **after** the execution of the written contract is not prohibited by the parol evidence rule and may be offered to prove subsequent modifications of the agreement.

D. DEMONSTRATIVE AND EXPERIMENTAL EVIDENCE

A court may allow demonstrations and experiments to be performed in the courtroom. This may include exhibition of injuries in a personal injury or criminal case. A court has discretion to exclude evidence of personal injuries if the demonstration of such severe injuries would result in unfair prejudice. A court may also exclude a demonstration that cannot be effectively cross-examined. Science experiments are permitted but may be excluded if they will result in undue waste of time or confusion of the issues.

V. PRIVILEGES AND OTHER POLICY EXCLUSIONS

A. PRIVILEGES

The Federal Rules have no specific privilege provisions but instead defer to common-law privileges, except in diversity cases, when state rules generally apply. Fed. R. Evid. 501. A claim of privilege applies at all stages of a case or proceedings. Fed. R. Evid. 1101(c).

1. Confidential Communication

For a privilege to apply, there must be a confidential communication.

a. Presence of third party

Generally, if the communication is overheard by a third party, the privilege is destroyed. However, the presence of the third party does not destroy the privilege if:

i) The first two parties do not know that the third party is present (e.g., an unknown eavesdropper); or

ii) The third party is necessary to assist in the communication (e.g., a translator).

b. Waiver

A privilege may be waived if the person who holds the privilege:

i) Fails to assert the privilege in a timely manner (i.e., when the testimony is offered);

ii) Voluntarily discloses, or allows another to disclose, a substantial portion of the communication to a third party, unless the disclosure is privileged; or

iii) Contractually waives the privilege in advance.

A wrongful disclosure without the privilege holder's consent does not constitute a waiver. For limitations on waiver of the attorney-client privilege due to inadvertent disclosure, *see* § 3.c. Effect of disclosure on waiver, *below*.

2. Spousal Privilege

"Spousal privilege" comprises two distinct privileges: spousal immunity and confidential marital communications.

a. Spousal immunity

The general rule is that the spouse of a **criminal defendant** may not be called as a witness by the prosecution. Nor may a married person be **compelled** to testify against his spouse in any criminal proceeding, including a grand jury proceeding, regardless of who is the defendant.

1) Holder of the privilege

a) Federal courts

In federal courts (and a minority of states), the **witness spouse** holds the privilege and may choose to testify but cannot be compelled to do so.

b) State courts

In many jurisdictions, the **party spouse** (as opposed to the witness spouse) holds the privilege and may prevent the witness spouse from testifying, even if the witness spouse wants to testify.

2) Period to which the privilege applies

The spousal immunity privilege applies to testimony about events that occurred **before and during the marriage.**

3) Time limit on assertion of the privilege

The spousal immunity privilege can be asserted **only during a valid marriage.** The right to assert the privilege expires upon divorce or annulment.

b. Confidential marital communications

Communication made between spouses **while they were married** is privileged if the communication was made **in reliance on the sanctity of marriage.**

1) Holder of the privilege

The majority view is that the privilege is held by **both spouses.** Some courts, however, have taken the position that only the communicating spouse can assert the privilege. *See* 1 Kenneth S. Broun et al., McCormick on Evidence § 83 (6th ed. 2006).

2) Scope of the privilege

This privilege applies only to communications made **during marriage.** This privilege applies to both **civil and criminal cases.**

3) Lack of time limit on assertion of the privilege

The time for asserting this privilege extends **beyond the termination of the marriage.** Thus, either party may assert the privilege—by refusing to testify or by preventing the other party from doing so—at any time, even after divorce or the death of one spouse.

> **Comparison of timing:** Spousal immunity applies to events occurring before marriage but ends when the marriage does, whereas the confidential communication privilege begins with marriage but continues beyond the length of the marriage.

c. Exceptions

Neither of the spousal privileges applies in cases in which one spouse is suing the other, or when one spouse is charged with a crime against the other spouse or the children of either.

3. Attorney-Client Privilege

A confidential communication between a client and an attorney for the purpose of seeking legal advice or representation is privileged.

a. Elements

1) Confidential

The communication must be intended to be confidential in order to be privileged. A communication made in the presence of a third party generally is not privileged, but the presence of, or communication by or through, a representative of the client or the attorney does not destroy the attorney-client privilege.

2) Communication

The communication must be **for the purpose of seeking legal advice or representation,** but the attorney does not need to give advice or agree to the representation for the privilege to exist.

a) Non-privileged statements

A statement made to an attorney that is not about legal advice or services sought by the client is not privileged. This includes statements regarding the fact of employment, the identity of the client, and the fee arrangements for the representation. If providing such information would divulge a confidential communication or incriminate the client, then it may be protected.

Furthermore, the attorney-client privilege does not protect disclosure of the underlying facts. A client cannot be compelled to answer the question "What did you say to your attorney?" but cannot refuse to reveal a fact within her knowledge merely because she told that fact to her attorney. *Upjohn Co. v. United States*, 449 U.S. 383 (1981) (quoting *Philadelphia v. Westinghouse Electric Corp.*, 205 F.Supp. 830, 831 (E.D. Pa. 1962)).

Finally, communications are not privileged when they are made to an attorney who is acting in a capacity other than as an attorney, such as a tax preparer, business partner, or witness to a will.

b) Corporate client

When an attorney represents a corporation, some states limit the privilege to communications received by the attorney from a member of the "control group" of the corporation (employees in a position to control or take a substantial part in a decision). *See, e.g., Consolidation Coal Co. v. Bucyrus-Erie Co.*, 432 N.E.2d 250 (Ill. 1982). However, in cases in which federal law controls, the privilege extends to communications by a non-control-group employee about matters within the employee's corporate duties made for the purpose of securing legal advice for the corporation. *Upjohn Co. v. United States*, 449 U.S. 383 (1981) (protecting communications by lower-level employees who were directed by their superiors to communicate with the corporation's attorney).

3) Client holds the privilege

The client holds the privilege and is the only one who may waive it. The attorney, however, must assert the privilege on the client's behalf to protect the client's interests. The privilege exists until it is waived, and it can survive the client's death.

b. Exceptions

The attorney-client privilege does not protect these confidential communications:

i) Communications made to enable or aid the commission of what the client **knew or should have known** was a crime or fraud;

ii) Communications relevant to a dispute between attorney and client (e.g., a malpractice allegation);

iii) Communications relevant to a dispute between parties who claim through the same deceased client; and

iv) Communications between former co-clients who are now adverse to each other.

Work product documents: Documents prepared by an attorney for his own use in connection with the client's case are not covered by the attorney-client privilege because **they are not communications.** However, such documents are protected under the "work product" doctrine and are not subject to discovery unless the party seeking disclosure (i) demonstrates a substantial need for the information, and (ii) cannot obtain the information by any other means without undue hardship. The mental impressions, conclusions, and trial tactics of an attorney are always protected from discovery. Fed. R. Civ. P. 26(b)(3).

c. **Effect of disclosure on waiver**

Although the Federal Rules generally do not address the existence or scope of common-law privileges, there is one exception. Federal Rule 502 addresses the effect that a litigation-related disclosure of protected information has on the waiver of the attorney-client privilege, drawing a distinction between an intentional disclosure and an unintentional disclosure. The rule applies to confidential communications as well as material protected by the work-product doctrine. Fed. R. Evid. 502.

1) **Inadvertent disclosure—no waiver**

When made during a federal proceeding, the inadvertent disclosure of privileged communication or information does not waive the privilege if the holder of the privilege:

i) Took reasonable steps to prevent disclosure; and

ii) Promptly took reasonable steps to rectify the error.

Fed. R. Evid. 502(b). In determining whether the holder took reasonable steps to prevent disclosure, factors such as the number of documents to be reviewed, the time constraints for production, or the existence of an efficient records-management system may be relevant.

2) **Intentional disclosure—limitation on the scope of waiver**

When made during a federal proceeding, the intentional disclosure of privileged material operates as a waiver of the attorney-client privilege. The waiver extends to undisclosed information only in those unusual situations in which (i) the disclosed and undisclosed material concern the same subject matter and (ii) fairness requires the disclosure of related information because a party has disclosed information in a selective, misleading, and unfair manner. Fed. R. Evid. 502(a).

3) **Effect of disclosure made in a state proceeding**

When privileged material is disclosed in a state proceeding and the state and federal laws are in conflict as to the effect of the disclosure, the disclosure does not operate as a waiver in a subsequent federal proceeding if the disclosure (i) would not be a waiver had it been made in a federal proceeding or (ii) is not a disclosure under the law of the state where it was made. In other words, the federal court must apply the law that is most protective of the privilege. This rule does not apply if the state court has issued an order concerning the effect of the disclosure; in such a case, the state-court order would be controlling. Fed. R. Evid. 502(c).

4) **Controlling effect of a federal confidentiality order**

A federal court may order that the privilege or protection is not waived by disclosure connected with the pending litigation (i.e., a confidentiality order). In such a case, the disclosure does not constitute a waiver in any other federal or state proceeding. Fed. R. Evid. 502(d).

5) Parties' agreement

An agreement between the parties regarding the effect of a disclosure binds only the parties unless the agreement is incorporated into a court order. Fed. R. Evid. 502(e).

4. Physician-Patient Privilege

Although there is no common-law privilege covering statements made by a patient to a doctor, many states protect such communications by statute, so long as the communications were made for the purpose of obtaining medical treatment. The patient holds the privilege; thus, only the patient may decide whether to waive it.

The privilege does not exist if:

i) The information was acquired for **reasons other than treatment**;

ii) The patient's **physical condition is at issue**;

iii) The communication was made as part of the **commission of a crime or tort**;

iv) A **dispute exists** between the physician and the patient;

v) The patient contractually **agreed to waive** the privilege; or

vi) A **case is brought in federal court** and state law does not apply (e.g., most cases that involve a federal question).

> If an attorney requests that a physician consult with his client, then the physician-patient privilege applies only if treatment is contemplated during the consult.

5. Psychotherapist-Patient Privilege

The federal courts and most states recognize a privilege for confidential communications made between a psychiatrist, psychologist, or licensed social worker and a patient. The patient holds the privilege, but the psychotherapist must assert the privilege in the patient's absence.

The privilege does not exist if (i) the patient's mental condition is at issue, (ii) the communication was a result of a court-ordered exam, or (iii) the case is a commitment proceeding against the patient.

> The psychotherapist-patient privilege is more widely recognized than the traditional physician-patient privilege.

6. Self-Incrimination

a. In general

The Fifth Amendment protection against self-incrimination allows a witness in any proceeding to refuse to give testimony that may tend to incriminate the witness. The protection covers only current (not prior) statements, and it does not apply to physical characteristics or mannerisms. The privilege belongs only to human beings. A corporation or other organization is not able to assert the privilege. *Bellis v. United States*, 417 U.S. 85 (1974).

b. Comment and inference

In a criminal case, a prosecutor may not comment on the defendant's failure to take the stand and may not argue that the jury should draw a negative inference from the assertion of the privilege. *Griffin v. California*, 380 U.S. 609 (1965).

In a civil case, however, it is proper for the opposing party to ask the jury to draw an adverse inference from a witness's claim of privilege.

c. Immunity

A witness may be compelled to provide incriminating testimony if the government grants him immunity from prosecution. The witness is not entitled to "transactional" immunity, i.e., protection against prosecution for the entire transaction about which he was testifying; instead, the government is constitutionally required to offer mere "use" immunity, which prohibits only the use of the compelled testimony against the witness. *Kastigar v. United States*, 406 U.S. 441 (1972). If the government does prosecute the witness in such a case, the government has the burden to show that the compelled testimony did not provide an investigatory lead that was helpful to the prosecution.

A witness may lose the right to invoke the privilege if the danger of incrimination has been removed through acquittal or conviction of the underlying charge. If the questioning about the adjudicated crime can lead to prosecution for other crimes, however, the privilege can be invoked.

7. Other Privileges

a. Clergy-penitent

In some jurisdictions, a confidential communication made by a penitent to a member of the clergy is privileged. The penitent holds the privilege, but the clergy member must assert the privilege on the penitent's behalf.

b. Accountant-client

Although not available at common law, many jurisdictions recognize a privilege for confidential communications made by a client to his accountant. The privilege operates similarly to the attorney-client privilege.

c. Professional journalist

There is no federal privilege protecting a journalist's source of information, but some states have enacted statutes extending some protection to journalists.

d. Governmental privileges

The government, at all levels, is privileged against disclosing:

i)   The identity of an informant in a criminal case; and

ii) The communication of **official information** (i.e., information that relates to the internal affairs of the government and is not open to the public) by or to public officials.

B.   PUBLIC POLICY EXCLUSIONS

1.   Subsequent Remedial Measures

When measures are taken that would have made an earlier injury or harm less likely to occur (e.g., repairing an area where a customer slipped), evidence of the subsequent measures is **not admissible to prove negligence, culpable conduct, a defective product or design, or the need for a warning or instruction.**   However, evidence of subsequent remedial measures may be admissible for other purposes, such as impeachment or—if disputed—ownership or control of the cause of the harm (e.g., a car) or the feasibility of precautionary measures. Fed. R. Evid. 407.

> **Product liability:** The exclusion of evidence of a subsequent remedial measure applies to product liability actions based on negligence and those based on strict liability. To be excluded, the remedial measure must be undertaken **after** the plaintiff is injured; a remedial measure made after a product was manufactured but **before** the plaintiff was injured is not subject to exclusion under this rule. Fed. R. Evid. 407, Notes of Advisory Committee (1997).

2.   Compromise Offers and Negotiations

Compromise offers made by any party, as well as any conduct or statements made during compromise negotiations, are not admissible to prove or disprove the **validity or amount of a disputed claim,** nor may they be admitted for impeachment by prior inconsistent statement or contradiction. Fed. R. Evid. 408.

> **Lack of dispute:** If the claim is not disputed as to its validity or amount (e.g., a party admits to both), then a statement made in connection with an offer to settle for a lesser amount is admissible. Fed. R. Evid. 408, Notes of Advisory Committee.

a.   Exceptions

1)   Negotiation with a governmental agency

A person's conduct or statements made during compromise negotiations with a governmental agency (e.g., the IRS) during the exercise of its regulatory, investigative, or enforcement authority may be introduced in a subsequent criminal case against the person.

2)   Admissibility for other reasons

Evidence of settlement offers and negotiations is admissible to prove bias or prejudice of a witness, to negate a claim of undue delay, or to prove obstruction of a criminal investigation or prosecution.

b.   No immunization of evidence

Evidence may be admissible through means other than as an admission made during compromise negotiations. A party does not immunize (i.e., protect from admission) evidence simply by discussing it during compromise negotiations. Fed. R. Evid. 408, Notes of Advisory Committee (2006).

c. Prohibition on all parties

Compromise evidence is not admissible on behalf of **any party** who participated in the compromise negotiations, even the party who made the settlement offer or statement. The protection of this rule cannot be waived unilaterally. Moreover, when there are more than two parties, a settlement agreement entered into by a party with an adverse party cannot be used by a remaining adverse party to prove or disprove the validity or amount of an unsettled claim. Fed. R. Evid. 408, Notes of Advisory Committee (2006); *Branch v. Fid. & Cas. Co.*, 783 F.2d 1289 (5th Cir. 1986).

3. Offers to Pay Medical Expenses

Evidence of the payment, offer to pay, or promise to pay medical or similar expenses resulting from an injury is **not admissible to prove liability for the injury.** Fed. R. Evid. 409.

> **Compare compromise:** Unlike a compromise negotiation, any conduct or statement that accompanies the payment, offer to pay, or promise to pay medical expenses is admissible.

4. Plea Negotiation

In a civil or criminal case, evidence of the following is generally not admissible against the defendant who made the plea or participated in the plea discussions:

i) Withdrawn guilty pleas;

ii) Pleas of no contest (i.e., a *nolo contendere* plea);

iii) Statements made while negotiating a plea with a prosecutor (e.g., an offer to plead guilty); and

iv) Statements made during a plea proceeding (e.g., a Rule 11 proceeding under the Federal Rules of Criminal Procedure).

Fed. R. Evid. 410(a).

a. Exceptions

Statements made during pleas or negotiations are admissible, however, if another statement made during the same plea or negotiation has already been admitted, and fairness requires that the statement in question also be admitted. Such statements also are admissible in a subsequent perjury prosecution if they were false statements made under oath, on the record, and with counsel present. Fed. R. Evid. 410(b).

b. Waiver

A defendant may waive the protection of Rule 410 if the waiver is knowing and voluntary. *United States v. Mezzanatto*, 513 U.S. 196 (1995).

5. Liability Insurance

Evidence that a person was or was not insured against liability is not admissible to prove whether the person acted negligently or otherwise wrongfully. However, such evidence may be admissible for another purpose, such as to prove agency, ownership, or control, or to prove a witness's bias or prejudice. Fed. R. Evid. 411.

6. Sexual Conduct

a. Victim's conduct

Under the "rape shield" rule, evidence offered to prove the sexual behavior or sexual predisposition of a victim (or alleged victim) generally is not admissible in any civil or criminal proceeding involving sexual misconduct. The exclusion applies to the use of such evidence for impeachment as well as substantive purposes.

Sexual behavior includes not only sexual intercourse or contact but also activities that imply such sexual intercourse or contact, such as the use of contraceptives or the existence of a sexually transmitted disease. Sexual predisposition can include the victim's mode of dress, speech, or lifestyle. Fed. R. Evid. 412(a), Notes of Advisory Committee (1994).

1) Exceptions

a) Criminal cases

In a criminal case involving sexual misconduct, evidence of specific instances of a victim's sexual behavior is admissible to prove that someone other than the defendant was the source of semen, injury, or other physical evidence. In addition, evidence of sexual behavior with the person accused of sexual misconduct is admissible if offered by the defendant to prove consent or if offered by the prosecution. Fed. R. Evid. 412(b)(1).

> Note that, in contrast with the general preference under the Federal Rules for reputation or opinion testimony over evidence of specific acts, in criminal cases involving sexual misconduct, reputation or opinion evidence of a victim's sexual behavior or predisposition is not admissible.

Finally, any evidence whose exclusion would violate the defendant's constitutional rights is admissible under Rule 412. For example, under the Sixth Amendment Confrontation Clause, a defendant in a rape case may be able to cross-examine an alleged victim who testified that she lived with her mother about her cohabitation with another man in order to show that the alleged victim denied having consensual sex with the defendant in order to protect her relationship with the other man. *Olden v. Kentucky*, 488 U.S. 227 (1988).

b) Civil cases

In a civil case, evidence offered to prove a victim's sexual behavior or predisposition is admissible if its probative value **substantially outweighs** the danger of harm to any victim and of unfair prejudice to any party. Evidence of a victim's reputation is admissible only when it has been placed in controversy by the victim. Fed. R. Evid. 412(b)(2).

> The restriction on evidence of a victim's sexual behavior or predisposition applies only when the party against whom the evidence is offered can be characterized as a victim of sexual misconduct. For example, a plaintiff in a defamation action based on a statement about the plaintiff's sexual behavior is not a victim of sexual misconduct. By contrast, a plaintiff

c) Procedure for admission

In a criminal or civil case, the party intending to offer evidence of the victim's sexual behavior or predisposition must file a motion describing the evidence and stating the purpose for its introduction. The motion must be filed at least 14 days before trial unless the court sets a different time. The motion must be served on all parties, and the victim (or the victim's guardian or representative) must be notified. The court must conduct an *in camera* hearing and give the victim and the parties the right to attend and to be heard. Unless the court orders otherwise, the record of the hearing is sealed. Fed. R. Evid. 412(c).

b. Defendant's conduct

In a criminal case in which a defendant is accused of sexual assault, attempted sexual assault, or conspiracy to commit sexual assault, evidence that the defendant committed any other sexual assault is admissible to prove any relevant matter. Similarly, in a criminal case in which a defendant is accused of child molestation, evidence that the defendant committed any other child molestation is admissible to prove any relevant matter. A similar rule applies in civil cases alleging sexual assault or child molestation. Fed. R. Evid. 413–15.

Propensity evidence: Unlike Federal Rule 404(b), which applies to other crimes or bad acts committed by a defendant, these rules permit the use of a defendant's previous commission of a sexual assault or child molestation as evidence of the defendant's propensity to commit the charged sexual assault or child molestation. Consequently, for example, a defendant's prior conviction for rape can be used as evidence of the defendant's propensity to commit the charged rape, but a defendant's prior conviction for robbery cannot be used as evidence of the defendant's propensity to commit the charged robbery.

The court does have discretion to exclude such evidence under Rule 403 when the probative value is substantially outweighed by the danger of unfair prejudice. *United States v. Kelly*, 510 F.3d 433 (4th Cir. 2007); *Johnson v. Elk Lake Sch. Dist.*, 283 F.3d 138 (3d Cir. 2002).

1) Not limited to convictions

An arrest or even testimony of an incident that was unreported to the authorities may be admitted as evidence that a defendant has committed sexual assault or child molestation. Moreover, unlike Rule 609 regarding the use of a conviction to impeach a witness, there is no specific time restriction on the use of such evidence. *See, e.g., United States v. Horn*, 523 F.3d 882 (2008).

2) Pretrial disclosure

The prosecutor or plaintiff who intends to introduce such evidence must disclose it to the defendant at least 15 days before trial unless the court, for good cause, allows a later disclosure. Fed. R. Evid. 413(b), 414(b), 415(b).

VI. HEARSAY

A. WHAT IS HEARSAY

Hearsay is a statement that the declarant makes at a time other than while testifying at the current trial or hearing (i.e., an out-of-court statement) that is offered to prove the truth of the matter asserted. Fed. R. Evid. 801(c). Hearsay evidence generally is inadmissible unless it falls within an exception set out in the Federal Rules, a federal statute, or a Supreme Court rule. Fed. R. Evid. 802.

1. Declarant—Person

The declarant (i.e., the maker of the statement) must be a person. Evidence generated by a machine or an animal is not hearsay. Fed. R. Evid. 801(b). Examples of such nonhearsay evidence include:

i) A dog's bark;

ii) An automatically generated time stamp on a fax;

iii) A printout of results of computerized telephone tracing equipment; and

iv) Raw data (such as blood-alcohol level) generated by a forensic lab's diagnostic machine.

2. Statement—Assertion

A statement is a person's oral or written assertion, or it may be nonverbal conduct intended as an assertion. Fed. R. Evid. 801(a). An example of assertive conduct is a defendant nodding his head up and down to indicate a "yes" answer to a question.

Contrast nonassertive conduct: Nonassertive conduct is not hearsay. An example of nonassertive conduct is a pilot's act of flying an airplane, when such evidence is offered as evidence of the plane's safety.

3. Offered to Prove the Truth of the Matter Asserted

Statements offered to prove something other than the truth of the matter asserted are not hearsay.

> **EXAM NOTE:** A statement that is not hearsay is not automatically admissible. For exam purposes, it is important to keep in mind that the statement must be admissible under the other rules restricting admission, such as the rules on privileges.

a. Legally operative facts

A statement offered to prove that the statement was made, regardless of its truth, is not hearsay.

Example: In a slander action, the defendant's statement that the plaintiff is a murderer may be admissible to prove that the defendant made the statement but not to prove that the plaintiff is a murderer.

b. Effect on recipient

A statement offered to show the effect on the person who heard it is not hearsay.

> **Example:** In a negligence action, the defendant's statement to the plaintiff that the sidewalk in front of the defendant's house was icy may be admissible to show that the plaintiff had notice of the danger but not to show that the sidewalk was actually icy.

c. State of mind

A statement offered as circumstantial evidence of the declarant's mental state is not hearsay.

> **Example:** A testator's statement, "I am the queen of England," is not admissible to show its truth, but it is admissible to prove that the testator is not of sound mind.

d. Impeachment

A statement offered solely to impeach a witness is not being introduced for its truth and therefore is not hearsay.

4. Multiple Hearsay

A statement that contains hearsay within hearsay may be admissible as long as each part of the combined statement conforms to a hearsay exception. Fed. R. Evid. 805.

> **Example:** A plaintiff sues a defendant for battery, claiming that the defendant struck the plaintiff's kneecaps with a baseball bat. At trial, the plaintiff seeks to introduce as evidence a hospital record, which consists of a note from a physician that the plaintiff told the physician that the plaintiff's injury was caused by being struck with a baseball bat. Both the plaintiff's statement to the physician and the note are hearsay; they are out-of-court statements being offered to prove the truth of the matter asserted—the cause of the plaintiff's injury. However, because each part of the statement falls within a hearsay exception (the plaintiff's statement is a statement made for the purpose of obtaining medical treatment, and the doctor's note is a business record), the hospital record may be admissible.

B. WHAT IS NOT HEARSAY

The following types of statements, which otherwise would qualify as hearsay, are expressly defined as nonhearsay. Fed. R. Evid. 801(d).

1. Prior Statements

The Federal Rules identify three types of prior statements that are not hearsay. In all three cases, the witness who made the statement must testify at the present trial or hearing and be subject to cross-examination concerning the statement in order for it to be admissible. Fed. R. Evid. 801(d)(1).

a. Prior inconsistent statements

A prior inconsistent statement **made under penalty of perjury** at a trial, hearing, or other proceeding, or in a deposition may be admissible to **impeach** the declarant's credibility and as **substantive evidence.** Statements made in a prior legal action that is unrelated to the current action may be admitted under this rule. Fed. R. Evid. 801(d)(1)(A).

b. Prior consistent statements

A prior consistent statement, whether made under oath or not, may be admissible to rebut an express or implied charge that the declarant recently fabricated it or acted from a recent improper influence or motive in testifying. Such a statement is admissible only if it was made **before the declarant had reason to fabricate.** Fed. R. Evid. 801(d)(1)(B).

c. Prior statement of identification

A previous out-of-court identification of a person after perceiving that person (e.g., lineup or photo array) is not hearsay and may be admissible as substantive evidence. Fed. R. Evid. 801(d)(1)(C).

> **EXAM NOTE:** Beware of fact patterns involving prior out-of-court identifications by a witness who is not testifying at the current trial and therefore is not subject to cross-examination. This rule cannot apply, for instance, if the witness is dead or otherwise unavailable to testify.

2. Opposing Party's Statement

A statement made by a **party to the current litigation** is not hearsay if it is offered by an opposing party. The statement may have been made by the party in his individual or representative capacity (e.g., trustee). Fed. R. Evid. 801(d)(2)(A). This type of statement traditionally was known as an admission of a party-opponent.

Contrast statement against interest exception: Unlike with the statement against interest hearsay exception (*see* § VII.A.4. Statement Against Interest, *infra*), an opposing party's statement need not have been against the party's interest at the time that it was made.

Unlike most testimony by a lay witness, an opposing party's statement may be admitted even if it is not based on personal knowledge. In addition, an opposing party's statement in the form of an opinion may be admitted, even if the statement is about a matter that normally would be beyond the scope of lay witness opinion testimony. Fed. R. Evid. 801(d)(2), Notes of Advisory Committee.

a. Judicial admission

An admission made during the discovery process or a stipulation otherwise made during a proceeding is conclusive evidence, as is a statement made in a pleading, unless amended. Otherwise, although a statement in a pleading or an admission or stipulation made in another proceeding is usually admissible, it may generally be rebutted.

Note: A *withdrawn* guilty plea is generally not admissible in a subsequent civil or criminal proceeding (*see* § V.B.4. Plea Negotiation, *supra*.)

b. Adoptive admission

An adoptive admission is a statement of another person that a party expressly or impliedly adopts as his own. Fed. R. Evid. 801(d)(2)(B). Silence in response to a statement is considered an adoptive admission if:

i) The person was present and heard and understood the statement;

ii) The person had the ability and opportunity to deny the statement; and

iii) A reasonable person similarly situated would have denied the statement.

Post-arrest silence by a defendant who has received *Miranda* warnings may not be used as an adoptive admission of a statement made by another person (e.g., a police officer). *Doyle v. Ohio*, 426 U.S. 610 (1976).

c. Vicarious statements

A statement made by one person may be imputed to another based on the relationship between them. In determining whether a statement constitutes an opposing party's statement, the statement is considered, but the statement itself cannot establish the necessary relationship between the parties.

1) Employee or agent

A statement made by a party's agent or employee constitutes an opposing party's statement if it was made concerning a matter **within the scope of and during the course of the relationship.** Fed. R. Evid. 801(d)(2)(D).

2) Authorized speaker

A statement about a subject that is made by a person who is **authorized** by a party to make a statement on the subject constitutes an opposing party's statement. Fed. R. Evid. 801(d)(2)(C).

3) Co-conspirators

Although a statement made by one co-party is not admissible against another co-party based solely on their status as co-parties, a statement made by a co-conspirator **during and in furtherance of** the conspiracy is admissible as an opposing party's statement against other co-conspirators. Fed. R. Evid. 801(d)(2)(E). A statement made by a co-conspirator after being arrested is not admissible, since it was not made during the conspiracy.

VII. HEARSAY EXCEPTIONS

Although hearsay generally is inadmissible, the Federal Rules identify some situations in which hearsay is allowed, either because of necessity (i.e., the declarant is unavailable) or because the statements are inherently trustworthy, in which case the declarant's availability is immaterial.

A. DECLARANT UNAVAILABLE AS A WITNESS

There are five exceptions to the hearsay rule that apply only if the declarant is unavailable as a witness: former testimony, dying declaration, statement against interest, statement of personal or family history, and statement offered against a party that wrongfully caused the declarant's unavailability.

1. **Unavailable Declarant**

    An unavailable declarant is a person who:

    i)   Is exempt on the grounds of privilege;

    ii) Refuses to testify despite a court order to do so;

    iii) Lacks memory of the subject matter of the statement;

    iv) Is unable to testify due to death, infirmity, or physical or mental disability; or

    v)   Is absent and cannot be subpoenaed or otherwise made to be present.

    A declarant is not deemed unavailable if the unavailability is due to the procurement or wrongdoing of the proponent of the statement in order to prevent the declarant from testifying at or attending the trial. Fed. R. Evid. 804(a).

2. **Former Testimony**

    Testimony that was given **as a witness** at a trial, hearing, or lawful deposition is not excluded as hearsay if the party against whom the testimony is being offered (or, in a civil case, a party's predecessor-in-interest) had an **opportunity and similar motive** to develop the testimony by direct examination, redirect examination, or cross-examination. This exception applies whether the testimony was given during the current proceeding or during a different one, but the witness who gave the testimony must now be unavailable. Fed. R. Evid. 804(b)(1).

    Grand jury testimony does not fall within the former testimony exception, but it may be admissible nonhearsay evidence as a prior inconsistent statement.

3. **Dying Declaration**

    A statement qualifies as a "dying declaration" if:

    i)   The declarant **believes that her death is imminent**; and

    ii) The statement pertains to the **cause or circumstances** of her death.

    Under this exception to the hearsay rule, although the declarant must be unavailable, the declarant need not have actually died in order for the statement to avoid exclusion as hearsay. The dying-declaration exception applies only in homicide prosecutions and civil cases. Fed. R. Evid. 804(b)(2).

4. **Statement Against Interest**

    A statement made by a declarant who is unavailable to testify is not excluded as hearsay if the statement:

    i)   Was against the declarant's interest at the time it was made; and

    ii) Would not have been made by a reasonable person unless he believed it to be true.

    Under this exception to the hearsay rule, the statement must have been against the declarant's proprietary or pecuniary interest, have invalidated the declarant's claim against someone, or have exposed the declarant to civil or criminal liability. A statement that would subject the declarant to criminal liability is not admissible unless corroborating circumstances clearly indicate the trustworthiness of the statement. Fed. R. Evid. 804(b)(3).

> **Opposing party's statement distinguished:** A **statement against interest** may be made by a non-party, the declarant must be unavailable, and the statement must have been against the declarant's interest at the time it was made. An **opposing party's statement,** on the other hand, must have been made by a party, and the statement need not have been against the party's interest when it was made (*see* § VI.B.2. Opposing Party's Statement, *supra*).

5. Statement of Personal or Family History

A statement concerning the unavailable declarant's own birth, adoption, marriage, divorce, legitimacy, familial relationship, or other similar fact of personal or family history is not excluded as hearsay. Fed. R. Evid. 804(b)(4).

6. Statement Against Party That Caused Declarant's Unavailability

Formerly known as the "forfeiture against wrongdoing" exception, a statement offered against a party that wrongfully caused the declarant's unavailability is not excluded as hearsay. Under this exception, the wrongful party forfeits the right to object to the admission of the declarant's statement as hearsay. The wrongdoing, which need not be criminal, may be accomplished by a deliberate act or by acquiescing to another's act. This exception applies to all parties, including the government. Fed. R. Evid. 804(b)(6).

Note: For the effect of the Confrontation Clause on this exception, *see* § VIII.A.1.b. Unavailability of the declarant, *infra*.

B. DECLARANT'S AVAILABILITY AS A WITNESS IMMATERIAL

The following hearsay exceptions do not require that the declarant be unavailable because the circumstances under which the statements were made suggest that the statements are inherently trustworthy. Fed. R. Evid. 803.

1. Present Sense Impression

A statement describing or explaining an event or condition that is made **while or immediately after the declarant perceived it** is not excluded as hearsay. Fed. R. Evid. 803(1).

a. Res gestae

A common-law hearsay exception labeled "res gestae" (meaning "things done") existed for a statement that was precipitated by an event or was about a contemporaneous condition. The Federal Rules do not contain a general res gestae exception but instead recognize several distinct, related exceptions, including exceptions for a present sense impression; an excited utterance; a dying declaration; a statement of mental, emotional, and physical condition; and a statement made for purposes of medical treatment or diagnosis.

2. Excited Utterance

A statement made about a startling event or condition **while the declarant is under the stress of excitement that it caused** is not excluded as hearsay. Under this exception to the hearsay rule, the event must shock or excite the declarant, and the statement must relate to the event, but the declarant need not be a participant in the event (i.e., the declarant can be a bystander). Fed. R. Evid. 803(2).

Present sense impression distinguished: A present sense impression must be a **description** of the event, whereas an **excited utterance** need only **relate to** the exciting event.

Example 1: Adele looks out the window and states, "It sure is raining hard tonight." She has made a statement of present sense impression, which is admissible to prove that it rained on the night in question.

Example 2: Bob discovers that he has a winning lottery ticket and shouts, "I just won a million dollars!" He has made an excited utterance, which is admissible to prove that he won the money.

Note: There is some overlap between these exceptions, and a statement, such as one describing a murder made immediately after the murder took place, could fall into both categories.

3.   **Statement of Mental, Emotional, or Physical Condition**

A statement of the declarant's **then-existing** state of mind or emotional, sensory, or physical condition is not excluded as hearsay. Fed. R. Evid. 803(3).

a. **State of mind**

A statement of **present intent, motive, or plan** can be used to prove **conduct in conformity** with that state of mind. A statement of a **past** memory or belief is inadmissible hearsay when used to prove the fact remembered or believed, unless the statement relates to the validity or terms of the declarant's will.

EXAM NOTE: Do not confuse this "state of mind" hearsay exception with circumstantial evidence of the declarant's state of mind, which is not hearsay. (*See* § VI.A.3.c. State of mind, *supra*.) To fall under the hearsay exception, the statement must be offered to prove that the declarant acted in accordance with his stated intent.

b. **Physical condition**

When a declarant's physical condition at a particular time is in question, a statement of the declarant's mental feeling, pain, or bodily health made **at that time** can be used to prove the **existence** of that condition but not its cause.

In most states, a statement made by a patient to a doctor relating to a **past** condition is not admissible under this exception. Under the Federal Rules, such a statement is admissible under the hearsay exception for statements for purposes of medical diagnosis or treatment (*see below*).

4.   **Statement Made for Medical Diagnosis or Treatment**

A statement describing medical history or past or present symptoms is not hearsay if it is made for medical **diagnosis or treatment.** A statement of the cause or source of the condition is admissible as an exception to the rule against hearsay if it is reasonably pertinent to diagnosis or treatment. Fed. R. Evid. 803(4).

a. Statement made to a person other than a physician

The statement need not be made to a physician to fall under this exception. Statements to other medical personnel, including hospital attendants and ambulance drivers, or even to family members, may be included. Fed. R. Evid. 803(4), Notes of Advisory Committee.

b. Statement made by a person other than the patient

Under this hearsay exception, the statement need not necessarily be made by the patient, so long as it is made for the purpose of medical diagnosis or treatment. The relationship between the declarant and the patient usually determines admissibility—the closer the relationship, the stronger the motive to tell the truth, and, as such, the more presumably reliable the statement. The court must assess the probative value of the statement pursuant to Rule 403, weighing that value against the risk of prejudice, confusion, or waste of time. *See Weinstein's Evidence*, Vol. 4 (1993), p. 803-145.

5. Recorded Recollection

If a witness is unable to testify about a matter for which a record exists, that record is not excluded as hearsay if the following foundation is established:

i) The record is on a matter that the witness once knew about but now cannot recall well enough to testify fully and accurately;

ii) The record was made or adopted by the witness when the matter was fresh in the witness's memory; and

iii) The record accurately reflects the witness's knowledge.

Under this exception, the record, if admitted, may be read into evidence, but it may be received as an exhibit only if offered by an adverse party. Fed. R. Evid. 803(5).

Present recollection refreshed distinguished: An item—which need not be a writing—used to refresh a witness's recollection is not admitted into evidence (*see* § III.C.1. Present Recollection Refreshed, *supra*), so there is no hearsay problem.

6. Records of Regularly Conducted Activity (Business Records)

A record (e.g., memorandum, report, data compilation) of an act, event, condition, opinion, or diagnosis is not excluded as hearsay if:

i) The record was kept in the course of a regularly conducted activity of a business, organization, occupation, or calling;

ii) The making of the record was a regular practice of that activity; and

iii) The record was made at or near the time by (or from information transmitted by) someone with knowledge.

Although this exception is commonly referred to as the "business records" exception, it extends to any regularly conducted activity of an organization, including a nonprofit organization. Fed. R. Evid. 101(b)(4); 803(6)(A)–(C).

Recorded recollection exception distinguished: Unlike the recorded recollection exception, the business records exception does not require the inability to remember, but it does require that the record be kept in the course of a regularly conducted business activity.

a. Authentication

For the record to be admissible under the business records hearsay exception, the custodian of the record or other qualified witness may testify that the above requirements have been met. Alternatively, a record may be self-authenticated if properly certified (*see* § IV.A.2.f. Self-authenticating documents, *supra*). Fed. R. Evid. 803(6)(D).

b. Lack of trustworthiness

A business record that otherwise qualifies under this hearsay exception is nevertheless inadmissible if the source of information for the record or the method or circumstances of its preparation indicate a lack of trustworthiness. Fed. R. Evid. 803(6)(E).

Anticipation of litigation: Records prepared in anticipation of litigation, such as an employee's accident report, may not qualify under this exception due to a lack of trustworthiness. *Palmer v. Hoffman*, 318 U.S. 109 (1943).

c. Medical records

Medical records are considered business records to the extent that the entries relate to diagnosis or treatment. Statements related to fault associated with the cause of injury generally do not qualify under the business records exception.

d. Police reports

A police report can qualify under the business records exception, but a statement made by a witness that is contained in the report does not generally qualify because the witness is not acting on behalf of the police in making the statement. The statement may, however, qualify under another hearsay exception, such as an opposing party's statement.

e. Absence of a record

Evidence that a **matter is not included in a record** of a regularly conducted activity may be admissible to prove that the matter did not occur or exist, provided that a record was regularly kept for a matter of that kind. The circumstances, including the possible source of the information, must not indicate a lack of trustworthiness. Fed. R. Evid. 803(7).

7. Public Records

A hearsay exception applies to a record or statement of a public office or agency that sets out:

i) The **activities** of the office or agency;

ii) An **observation** of a person under a duty to report the observation (except for an observation of a law enforcement officer offered in a criminal case); or

iii) **Factual findings of a legal investigation,** when offered in a civil case or against the government in a criminal case.

Fed. R. Evid. 803(8).

> **Investigative reports:** In addition to factual findings, opinions, evaluations, and conclusions contained in an investigative report that are based on factual findings are included in the public records exception. *Beech Craft Corp. v. Rainey,* 488 U.S. 153 (1988).

a. Lack of trustworthiness

As with the business records exception, the court may exclude any evidence offered under this exception if the source of the information or other circumstances indicate a lack of trustworthiness. Fed. R. Evid. 803(8)(B).

b. Absence of a record

Similarly, testimony that a diligent search failed to disclose a public record or statement may be admitted to prove that the record or statement does not exist, or that a matter did not occur or exist, if a public office regularly kept a record of statements for a matter of that kind. Fed. R. Evid. 803(10).

c. Public record or vital statistics

A record of a birth, death, or marriage is not excluded as hearsay if the event is reported to a public office in accordance with a legal duty. Fed. R. Evid. 803(9).

8. Learned Treatises

A statement contained in a treatise, periodical, or pamphlet is not excluded as hearsay if:

i) An expert witness **relied on the statement during direct examination** or it was **called to the expert's attention on cross-examination**; and

ii) The publication is established as a **reliable authority** by admission or testimony of the expert witness, by another expert's testimony, or by judicial notice.

If admitted, the statement is read into evidence, but the publication itself may not be received as an exhibit. Fed. R. Evid. 803(18).

9. Judgment of Previous Conviction

Evidence of a final judgment of conviction is not excluded as hearsay if:

i) The judgment was entered after a trial or guilty plea, but not a plea of no contest (i.e., *nolo contendere*);

ii) The conviction was for a crime punishable by death or imprisonment for more than one year; and

iii) The evidence is offered to prove any fact essential to sustain the judgment.

If the prosecutor in a criminal case offers evidence of a final judgment of conviction for a purpose other than impeachment, the judgment must have been against the defendant. Fed. R. Evid. 803(22).

Traffic offense: A driver's guilty plea to a traffic offense that is punishable by a fine or imprisonment for one year or less cannot be used as evidence of the driver's negligence under this hearsay exception.

10. Other Exceptions

Other hearsay exceptions for which the declarant's availability is immaterial include:

i) A statement concerning personal or family history, such as a birth, death, marriage, or divorce contained in a regularly kept record of a religious organization (Fed. R. Evid. 803(11));

ii) A statement of fact in a marriage or baptismal certificate (Fed. R. Evid. 803(12));

iii) A statement of fact about personal or family history contained in a family record, such as a Bible or an engraving on a ring (Fed. R. Evid. 803(13));

iv) Records of, and statements in, documents affecting an interest in property (Fed. R. Evid. 803(14), (15));

v) Statements in ancient documents (i.e., authenticated documents in existence at least 20 years) (Fed. R. Evid. 803(16));

vi) Market reports and similar commercial publications generally relied upon by the public (Fed. R. Evid. 803(17));

vii) Reputation concerning personal or family history, boundaries or general history, or character (Fed. R. Evid. 803(19)–(21)); and

viii) A judgment admitted to prove a matter of personal, family, or general history or a boundary, if the matter was essential to the judgment and could be proved by evidence of reputation. Fed. R. Evid. 803(23).

C. RESIDUAL EXCEPTION

There is a "catch-all" exception for a statement that is not otherwise covered by the Federal Rules. A hearsay statement may be admissible under this exception if:

i) The statement has equivalent circumstantial guarantees of trustworthiness;

ii) It is offered as evidence of a material fact;

iii) It is more probative on the point for which it is offered than any other evidence that the proponent can reasonably obtain; and

iv) Admission will best serve the purposes of the Federal Rules and the interests of justice.

The proponent must give an adverse party reasonable notice before the trial or hearing of the intent to offer the statement as well as its particulars, including the declarant's name and address. Fed. R. Evid. 807.

VIII. CONSTITUTIONAL LIMITATIONS

A. HEARSAY EVIDENCE RESTRICTIONS

Hearsay evidence has successfully been challenged on two constitutional grounds.

1. Sixth Amendment—Confrontation Clause and Hearsay Evidence

In a criminal trial, the Confrontation Clause of the Sixth Amendment requires that, in order to admit an out-of-court testimonial statement of a declarant (i.e., hearsay) against a defendant:

i) The declarant must be unavailable; and

ii) The defendant must have had a prior opportunity to cross-examine the declarant.

Crawford v. Washington, 541 U.S. 36 (2004).

Note: The Supreme Court suggested in dicta in *Crawford* that the Confrontation Clause does not preclude the admission of a dying declaration as hearsay, even if the statement is testimonial, since this common-law exception predates the Confrontation Clause. *Crawford v. Washington*, 541 U.S. 36, 56, n.6 (2004).

a. Testimonial statements

In determining whether a statement is testimonial, an objective analysis of the circumstances, rather than the subjective purpose of the participants, is key. A statement made during a police interrogation that had the primary purpose of ascertaining past criminal conduct is testimonial, as is a certificate of a governmental laboratory analyst that a substance was an illegal drug. *Melendez-Diaz v. Massachusetts*, 557 U.S. ___, 129 S. Ct. 2527 (2009).

By contrast, a statement made to police during the course of questioning with the primary purpose of enabling police to provide assistance to meet an ongoing emergency (e.g., a 911 call) is not testimonial, *Davis v. Washington*, 547 U.S. 813 (2006), nor is a statement made by a fatally wounded victim as to the identity of his assailant in response to police questioning, because the statement was made to assist the police in addressing an on-going emergency, *Michigan v. Bryant*, ___ U.S. ___, 131 S. Ct. 1143 (2011).

b. Unavailability of the declarant

The Confrontation Clause mandates that the use of hearsay evidence based on the forfeiture-by-wrongdoing exception requires the defendant to have acted with the particular purpose of making the witness unavailable. The mere fact that the declarant is unavailable due to the defendant's act (e.g., murder of the witness) is not sufficient to establish such a purpose when the defendant is on trial for the act that made the witness unavailable. *Giles v. California*, 554 U.S. 353 (2008).

2. Fourteenth Amendment—Due Process Clause

The Due Process Clause of the Fourteenth Amendment may deny application of a hearsay rule when such rule denies the defendant the ability to present witnesses in the defendant's own defense. *Chamber v. Mississippi*, 410 U.S. 284 (1973).

B.   FACE-TO-FACE CONFRONTATION

The Confrontation Clause reflects a preference for face-to-face confrontation of a defendant and a witness in court.

Example: A defendant who is charged with committing a sex crime against a child can force the child victim to testify in open court rather than from behind a screen that blocks the witness's view of the defendant. *Coy v. Iowa*, 487 U.S. 1012 (1988).

This type of confrontation may be denied, however, if there is an important public interest at stake, such as protecting a child.

Example: A child victim of a sex crime could testify via a one-way closed circuit television when there was a specific finding that the child witness would suffer serious emotional distress if the witness was required to testify in open court. *Maryland v. Craig*, 497 U.S. 836 (1990). The Court in *Coy*, above, refused to recognize a *presumption* of trauma to witnesses who were victims of sexual abuse.

Real Property

REAL PROPERTY

Table of Contents

[x]

REAL PROPERTY

I. OWNERSHIP

Ownership of real property may be transferred from one to another by sale, gift, or devise. The seller or donor is called the grantor, and the buyer or recipient is called the grantee. This section will discuss both present and future possessory interests in land (which are subject only to the rights of others), and other sections will discuss non-possessory interests in land (which are subject to specific restrictions as to the use of the land).

A. PRESENT ESTATES

In order to be categorized as a freehold, an estate must be (i) immobile (either land or some interest derived from or affixed to land), and (ii) for an indeterminate duration (as opposed to leasehold, which is for a limited duration). The owner of a present estate has the right to currently possess the property.

1. Fee Simple Absolute

Fee simple absolute is the most common form of property ownership and the broadest ownership interest recognized by law. It is absolute ownership of potentially infinite duration, is freely alienable (i.e., easily bought or sold), and has no accompanying future interest. Although common law required words of limitation (e.g., "and heirs"), conveyances that are ambiguous are now considered fee simple by default (e.g., "to B").

Example: A conveys Blackacre "to B and his heirs." C conveys Whiteacre to "B." Both conveyances give B a fee simple absolute estate in the property.

The fee simple absolute is a present estate that does not terminate unless the owner dies intestate without heirs, in which case the property escheats to the state.

2. Defeasible Fees

As with a fee simple absolute estate, a defeasible fee is ownership of potentially infinite duration. But, unlike a fee simple absolute estate, a defeasible fee **may be terminated by the occurrence of an event**.

a. Fee simple determinable

A fee simple determinable is a present fee simple estate that is **limited by specific durational language** (e.g., "so long as," "while," "during," "until"), such that it terminates automatically upon the happening of a stated condition and full ownership of the property is returned to the grantor. The fee simple determinable is freely alienable, devisable, and descendible, but always subject to the stated condition.

> **EXAM NOTE**: Be certain the language limits the duration, not merely the purpose of the transfer before concluding a fee simple determinable was created. If the language limits only the purpose, it is treated as creating a fee simple absolute.

1) Possibility of reverter

Upon the occurrence of the stated condition, the estate automatically reverts back to the grantor. The grantor's retained future interest is called a **"possibility of reverter."**

> **Example:** A conveys Blackacre "to B and his heirs, until B gets married." The estate reverts back to A if B gets married. Therefore, B has a fee simple determinable in Blackacre, with a possibility of reverter in A.

b. Fee simple subject to condition subsequent

A fee simple subject to a condition subsequent is a present fee simple that is **limited in duration by specific conditional language.**

> **EXAM NOTE:** Typical language that indicates a fee simple subject to a condition subsequent: "provided that," "on condition that," "but if."

1) Compare to fee simple determinable

As with a fee simple determinable, the fee simple subject to a condition subsequent is freely alienable by the owner during his life, and upon his death devisable and descendible.

Unlike a fee simple determinable, termination of a fee simple subject to a condition subsequent is not automatic. Upon occurrence of the stated condition, the present fee simple **will only terminate if the grantor affirmatively demonstrates intent to terminate** (e.g., by bringing an action to recover possession).

If the language in the conveyance is ambiguous, courts typically adopt a preference for the fee simple on condition subsequent.

2) Right to terminate

In the conveyance, the grantor must explicitly retain the right to terminate the fee simple subject to a condition subsequent (known as the **"right of entry," "right of re-entry,"** or the **"power of termination"**). This right is devisable and descendible, but cannot be transferred during the owner's lifetime. The owner may waive this right, but the mere failure to assert it does not constitute a waiver.

> **Example:** A conveys Blackacre "to B and his heirs, but if B gets married, then A can reenter Blackacre." B will retain ownership until A exercises his right to reenter. B has a fee simple subject to a condition subsequent in Blackacre, and A has a right of re-entry. (Even if B gets married, B will retain his current possessory estate in Blackacre until A exercises his right to terminate B's estate.)

c. Fee simple subject to executory interest

A fee simple subject to an executory interest is a present fee simple estate that is limited in duration by either conditional language or durational language, such that it will terminate upon the occurrence of the specified condition and **title will pass to a third party** (i.e., someone other than the grantor).

Upon occurrence of the stated condition, the present fee simple terminates automatically. The future interest held by the third party is an **executory interest**.

> **Example:** A conveys Blackacre "to B for as long as the property is used as a hospital, then to C." In Blackacre, B has a fee simple subject to an executory interest, C has an executory interest, and A does not have an interest. (Note: C's interest is subject to the Rule Against Perpetuities.)

For a more detailed discussion, *see* § I.C.5., Future Interests, *infra*.

3. Fee Tail

A fee tail is a freehold estate that limits the estate to the grantee's lineal blood descendants by specific words of limitation (e.g., "heirs of the body"). The fee tail estate has been eliminated in most states because it is treated as a fee simple absolute.

4. Life Estate

A life estate is a present possessory estate that is limited in duration by a life. The language must be clear, and must be measured in terms of a life, not a number of years (e.g., "to A for life"). Upon the end of the measuring life, title reverts to the grantor or specified remainderman. This future interest is known as a reversion.

> **Example 1:** A conveys Blackacre "to B for the life of B." B has a life estate in Blackacre, which terminates upon B's death. A has a reversion; upon B's death, ownership of Blackacre reverts to A.
>
> **Example 2:** A conveys Blackacre "to B for B's life, and then to C." B has a life estate in Blackacre, which terminates upon B's death. C has a remainder; upon B's death, ownership of Blackacre vests in C.

The life estate is not subject to the Rule Against Perpetuities.

a. Measuring life is grantee

To be a life estate, the interest granted must be measured by the life of a human being, and be qualified only by non-time limitations. Unless otherwise specified, the measuring life is the grantee.

> **Example:** A conveys Blackacre to "B for life." B has a life estate that is measured by his own life.

A life estate is fully transferable during the life of the person by whom the life estate is measured. Because the interest terminates at the death of the person by whom the life estate is measured, a life estate measured by the grantee's life is generally neither devisable nor descendible. If the life estate is received by will or intestacy, the life tenant may renounce the estate if he so chooses. In the states that have done away with the common law curtesy and dower custom, a surviving spouse has a statutory right to take a portion of the estate.

In states that continue dower and curtesy, a conveyance from the husband to a bona fide purchaser without the wife's joining in the conveyance does not defeat dower. Similarly, a wife's dower rights are not defeated by the husband's creditors.

b. Measuring life is third party

A life estate measured by the life of a third party is also called a life estate *pur autre vie*.

> **Example:** A conveys Blackacre to "B for the life of C." A granted a life estate to B for the life of C.

c. Rights and obligations

A life tenant has the right of possession, the right to all rents and profits during possession, and the right to lease, sell, or mortgage the property (right of alienation). To the extent the property can produce income, life tenants have the obligation to pay all ordinary taxes on the land and interest on the mortgage. If the property is not producing an income, the life tenant is responsible for taxes and mortgage interest to the extent of the reasonable rental value of the land. The life tenant also has the duty not to commit waste.

The life tenant is under no obligation to insure the land for the benefit of the remainderman and is not responsible for damage caused by third-party tortfeasors.

> **EXAM NOTE:** Remember that the life tenant is responsible only for the interest of a mortgage on the life estate, whereas the remainderman is responsible for the mortgage itself.

d. Waste

The rights of a holder of any estate but a fee simple may be limited by the doctrine of waste. The particular rules of waste depend on the type of estate held by the present tenant and the type of waste created.

Any remainderman or grantor with a reversionary interest may enter upon the land to inspect for waste and seek an injunction to prevent waste.

1) Affirmative waste

Affirmative (or voluntary) waste is the result of overt conduct that causes a decrease in the value of the property. The holder of the vested remainder interest may bring suit for damages, and either a vested or contingent remainder holder may bring suit for an injunction. Limited exceptions exist for the exploitation of minerals and timber if such use was authorized by the grantor, in effect at the time the tenancy began, or is necessary to maintain the property.

2) Permissive waste

Permissive waste is the result of neglect, a failure to keep up the property, or a failure to reasonably protect the property. To maintain the property and avoid permissive waste, the tenant is only required to spend the amount of income generated by the property. The tenant's responsibilities include paying any property taxes and mortgage interest associated with the property.

3) Ameliorative waste

At common law, a life tenant was prohibited from engaging in acts that changed the property's value (even those that enhanced the value), unless all future interest holders were known and consented. The current majority rule allows life tenants to physically alter structures on the property when necessary to make reasonable use of the property.

B. CONCURRENT ESTATES

A concurrent estate (or co-tenancy) is ownership or possession of real property by two or more persons simultaneously. The most common concurrent estates are tenancy in common, joint tenancy, and tenancy by the entirety.

1. Tenancy in Common

Any tenancy with two or more grantees creates a tenancy in common (and is thus considered the "default" or "catch-all" co-tenancy when neither joint tenancy nor tenancy in the entirety exists). Equal right to possess or use the property (unity of possession) is required, and **no right of survivorship** exists. Each co-tenant holds an undivided interest with unrestricted rights to possess the whole property, regardless of the size of the interest. Without the right of survivorship, each tenant can devise or freely transfer his interest to anyone. A tenant in common may also transfer his interest to another by a lease. The other tenants in common are entitled to share possession with the lessee and to a share of the rental profits from the lessor-tenant in common. In most states, there is a presumption that a conveyance to two or more persons creates a tenancy in common rather than a joint tenancy.

2. Joint Tenancy

A joint tenancy exists when two or more individuals own property **with the right of survivorship** (i.e., upon the death of a joint tenant, the interest terminates and automatically goes to the surviving joint tenants). Modern law calls for a clear expression of intent along with survivorship language.

> **EXAM NOTE**: To determine if a joint tenancy was created, look for survivorship language.

a. Four unities

The joint tenancy must be created with each joint tenant having the equal right to possess or use the property (unity of **p**ossession), with each interest equal to the others (unity of **i**nterest), at the same time (unity of **t**ime), and in the same instrument (unity of **t**itle). [*Mnemonic—"**PITT**"*]

Unlike a joint tenancy, a tenancy in common only requires the unity of possession.

b. Severance

Although an interest in a joint tenancy cannot be devised, joint tenants can convey all or part of their individual interests during their lifetimes (inter vivos) to a third party, thereby severing the joint tenancy.

1) Effect of severance on remaining joint tenants

Once the joint tenancy interest is transferred inter vivos, the right of survivorship to that interest is destroyed and converted to a tenancy in common. A conveyance by only one of more than two joint tenants does not destroy the joint tenancy of the remaining joint tenants.

> Note that any lien against one joint tenant's interest also terminates upon that tenant's death, such that the lien does not encumber the surviving tenants' interest.

2) Mortgages

A joint tenant may grant a mortgage interest in the joint tenancy property to a creditor. In **lien theory** states (the majority), the mortgage is only a lien on the property and does not sever the joint tenancy absent a default and foreclosure sale. In **title theory** states (the minority), the mortgage severs title and the tenancy between the joint tenants and creditor is converted into a tenancy in common.

3) Leases

There is a split among jurisdictions with respect to how to handle joint tenancies when one joint tenant leases his interest. Some jurisdictions hold that the lease destroys the unity of interest and thus severs the joint tenancy, while other jurisdictions believe that the lease merely temporarily suspends the joint tenancy, which would resume upon expiration of the lease.

4) Intentional killings

When one co-tenant intentionally kills the other co-tenant, some states allow the felonious joint tenant to hold the property in constructive trust for the deceased joint tenant's estate. This means the surviving joint tenant does not profit from the felony, but is able to keep his interest in the property. Other jurisdictions have statutes that sever the joint tenancy upon a felonious killing of one joint tenant by another joint tenant.

3. Tenancy by the Entirety

Tenancy by the entirety is a joint tenancy between married persons with a right of survivorship. The same rules for joint tenancy apply to tenancy by the entirety, plus the joint tenants must be married when a deed is executed or the conveyance occurs (the fifth **unity of person**). Neither party can alienate or encumber the property without the consent of the other. Tenancy by the entirety is used in many states and is analogous to community property in the states that recognize that type of property ownership.

4. Rights and Obligations

a. Possession

Unless there is an agreement to the contrary, each co-tenant has the right to possess all of the property. A co-tenant is generally not required to pay rent to the other co-tenants for the value of her own use of the property, even when the other co-tenants do not make use of the property. Similarly, a co-tenant is generally not required to share profits earned from the use of the property, such as from a business conducted on the property.

As a consequence of each tenant's right to possess the entire property, a co-tenant's exclusive use of the property does not, by itself, give rise to adverse possession of the interest of another cotenant.

1) Ouster

When a co-tenant refuses to allow another co-tenant access to the property, the ousted co-tenant may bring a court action for ouster to gain access to the property and to recover the value of the use of the property for the time during which the co-tenant was denied access to the property.

2) Natural resources

A co-tenant is entitled to the land's natural resources (e.g., timber, minerals, oil, gas) in portion to their share.

b. Third party rents

A co-tenant must account to other co-tenants for rent received from third parties, but can deduct operating expenses when calculating net proceeds. Third party rents are divided based on the ownership interest of each tenant.

c. Operating expenses

A co-tenant can collect contribution from the other co-tenants for paying more than his portion of necessary or beneficially spent operating expenses (e.g., taxes or mortgage interest), unless he is the only one in physical possession of the property and the value of his use of it is equal to or outweighs the overpayment. Note that a co-tenant in sole possession can collect only for the amount that exceeds the rental value of the property.

d. Repairs and improvements

A co-tenant does not have a right to be reimbursed by other co-tenants for repairs made to the property, even when those repairs are necessary. However, the majority view is that contribution for necessary repairs can be compelled in actions for accounting or partition. A co-tenant may, in some jurisdictions, maintain a separate action for contribution, as long as the other co-tenants have been notified of the need for the repair.

Similarly, except in actions for accounting or partition, a co-tenant does not have right to reimbursement for improvements made to the property. As noted, when a third party is occupying the property, the co-tenant who collects rent from the third party can subtract expenses for necessary repairs from the rent received before sharing the rent with the other co-tenants.

e. Fiduciary obligation

In general, co-tenants do not owe fiduciary duties to each other. However, co-tenants who became co-tenants at the same time (e.g., by the same deed or will) can have a fiduciary obligation to each other, such that if one co-tenant buys back his property at a tax or mortgage foreclosure sale, the other co-tenants can reacquire their original interests by paying their due contributions.

Co-tenants share a duty of fair dealing, such that an acquisition by one co-tenant that impacts the estate owned by all co-tenants is considered an acquisition by all co-tenants.

f. Partition

1) Who may partition

A tenant in common or a joint tenant generally has the right to unilaterally partition the property, but a tenant by the entirety *does not* have this right. Property can be partitioned either voluntarily (if the co-tenants agree in writing on the division of land), or involuntarily (by court action).

The holder of a future interest who shares that interest with another (e.g., jointly held remainder interest) does not have the right to immediate possession and therefore cannot maintain an action for involuntary partition.

2) Effect of partition

In a partition action, the court divides the jointly owned property into distinct portions, or, if division of the property is not practicable or fair, the court may sell the property at a public auction and distribute the proceeds among the co-tenants.

3) Restriction on partition

An agreement by co-tenants not to seek partition is enforceable. However, the agreement must be clear and the time limitation must be reasonable.

C. FUTURE INTERESTS

A future interest is an interest in presently existing property, or in a gift or trust, which may commence in use, possession, or enjoyment sometime in the future.

1. Reversion

A reversion (or "reverter") is the future interest held by the grantor who grants a life estate or estate for years but does not convey the remaining future interest to a third party. Reversions are not subject to the Rule Against Perpetuities.

2. Possibility of Reverter

A possibility of reverter is automatically retained by a grantor when a fee simple determinable is conveyed.

3. Right of Reentry

A right of reentry (also called "right of entry" or "power of termination") is a future interest held by the grantor after a fee simple on condition subsequent is granted.

4. Remainder

A remainder is a future interest created in a grantee that is capable of becoming possessory upon the expiration of a prior possessory estate of known fixed duration that is created in the same conveyance in which the remainder is created. A remainder can either be vested or contingent. If a survivorship contingency is stated in a conveyance, the majority view is that the contingency applies at the termination of the interest that precedes distribution of the remainder. A minority approach interprets a survivorship contingency to require surviving only the testator and not the life tenant.

a. Class interests

A class interest consists of a group of unspecified persons whose number and identity and share of the interest is determined in the future (e.g., at the death of the donor). Usually, the group is of children.

Example: A conveys a gift "to my children." Here, A conveys a class gift to an unspecified group because the recipients (i.e., those who will qualify as A's children upon A's death) are not known until A dies.

1) Vested remainder

A vested remainder is an interest that is not subject to any conditions precedent, and is created in an ascertainable grantee.

Example: A conveys Blackacre "to B for life, and then to C and his heirs." Here, the grantee, C, is ascertainable.

a) Vested subject to open

If a conveyance grants a remainder to a class of grantees and at least one of the grantees receives a vested remainder at the time of the conveyance, that vested remainder is subject to open, (i.e., the property interest is uncertain because other grantees may become vested, and able to share in the grant).

Example: A conveys "to B for life, and then to B's children as they turn 18." B has three children upon death, X (10 years old), Y (15 years old), and Z (20 years old). Z has a vested remainder subject to open, because the property interest will be shared when Y and then X become vested (i.e., on their 18th birthdays).

Once a class closes, any person who might otherwise have become a class member (e.g., later born siblings) cannot claim an interest in the property as a class member.

Although those born after the class closes are generally not part of the class, *those already in gestation upon closing are* included in the class.

Absent a closing date, the rule of convenience closes the class when any member of the class becomes entitled to immediate possession of the property.

> **Example:** A conveys "to B for life, and then to C's children." If the conveyance does not specify when the class closes, the class closes when B dies, regardless of any of C's children born after B's death.

b) Vested subject to complete

A vested remainder subject to complete indicates that the occurrence of a condition subsequent will completely divest the remainder interest.

> **Example:** A conveys "to B for life, and then to C; but if C has no children, then to D's children." C has a vested remainder interest, but if he is not survived by his children at the time of B's death, then C's interest will be divested.

b. Contingent remainder

A remainder is contingent if it is created in a grantee that is unascertainable, or if it is subject to an express condition precedent to a grantee's taking. This normally occurs in one of two circumstances: (i) when the property cannot vest because the beneficiary is unknown, or (ii) when the property cannot vest because the known beneficiary is subject to a condition precedent that has not yet occurred.

> **Example:** A conveys "to B for life, remainder to C's heirs." If C is alive at the conveyance, C's heirs are not yet ascertainable, and the remainder is contingent.

Contingent remainders were destroyed at common law if they had not vested by the time the preceding estate terminated. In such a situation in most states today, the grantor's reversion becomes possessory, and the person holding the contingent remainder takes a springing executory interest (see *infra*), which becomes possessory if and when the condition precedent is met.

c. Rule in *Shelley's Case*

At common law, the rule in *Shelley's Case* prevented contingent remainders in grantee's heirs by defeating the grantor's intent and changing the interest that the grantor purported to give to the grantee and his heirs to a vested remainder in the grantee. The rule in *Shelley's Case* changes the state of the title to two successive freehold estates in the grantee. Under the doctrine of merger, both the present and future interests are merged so that the grantee takes in fee simple absolute. Most jurisdictions have abolished the rule in *Shelley's Case*, and the parties now take the present and future interests according to the language in the deed.

> **Example:** A conveys "to B for life, remainder to B's heirs." If the rule in *Shelley's Case* applies, after the merger, B will receive the property in fee simple absolute. If the rule in *Shelley's Case* has been abolished, B has a life estate and B's heirs have a contingent remainder in the subject property.

d. Doctrine of Worthier Title

The Doctrine of Worthier Title is a rule of construction similar to the rule in *Shelley's Case*, except that it prevents against remainders in the grantor's heirs, and still applies in some states. The presumption is in a reversion to grantor.

5. Executory Interests

An executory interest is a future interest in a third party that is not a remainder and that cuts the prior estate short upon the occurrence of a specified condition. **Executory interests are transferable** and are subject to the Rule Against Perpetuities.

Most courts hold that executory interests are freely transferable, although they were not transferable inter vivos at common law.

The two types of executory interests are shifting executory interest and springing executory interest.

a. Shifting executory interest

A shifting executory interest divests the interest of the grantee by cutting short a prior estate created in the same conveyance. The estate "shifts" from one grantee to another on the happening of the condition.

Example: A conveys "to B and his heirs, but if C returns from Paris, then to C." This conveyance creates a fee simple subject to an executory limitation in B, and a shifting executory interest in C.

b. Springing executory interest

A springing executory interest divests the interest of the grantor or fills a gap in possession in which the estate reverts to grantor.

Example: A conveys "to B for life, and one year after B's death to C and his heirs." This conveyance creates a life estate in B, a one-year reversion in A (in fee simple subject to an executory limitation), and a springing executory interest in C.

EXAM NOTE: Any interest held by a third party that follows a fee is always an executory interest because a remainder *never* follows a fee.

6. Transferability of Remainders and Executory Interests

Vested remainders are fully transferable inter vivos, devisable by will, and descendible by inheritance. Today, executory interests and contingent remainders are transferable inter vivos in most jurisdictions, although under common law they were not transferable; and both are devisable and descendible. It is important to note that most states permit any transferable future interest to be reached by creditors, except for those interests held by unascertainable or unborn persons.

7. Classification of Interests

It is important to classify the various interests in a disposition clause because the label given to the first interest will usually determine the labels given to the following interests. For example, a contingent remainder will follow a contingent remainder, but will not follow a fee simple; while executory interests follow vested remainders subject to complete.

Example 1: A conveys Blackacre "to B for life, then to C if C survives B; but if C does not survive B, on B's death to D."

Example 2: A conveys Blackacre "to B for life, and on B's death to C. But if C predeceases B, on B's death to D."

In example 1, B has a life estate and C has a contingent remainder because C's taking is conditioned on C surviving B. Therefore, since C's interest is a contingent remainder, D's interest must also be a contingent remainder.

In example 2, B has a life estate and C has remainder. However, in this example C's remainder is vested in fee simple because C is ascertainable **and** there is no condition precedent that C must satisfy in order to take. The next clause defeats C's interest if he predeceases B. Thus, C's vested remainder is subject to complete once the condition subsequent (C predeceasing B) is satisfied. To determine D's interest, we first consider C's interest, which is vested in fee simple, and thus D's interest cannot be a remainder because a remainder does not follow a fee simple. Since D's taking will potentially cut short C's interest, D's interest is an executory interest.

The above two examples demonstrate the importance of examining each clause independently and classifying each interest in proper order. Although they both basically reach the same conclusion (i.e., D ends up with the estate if C predeceases B), the interests in example 1 are labeled very differently than the interests in example 2.

8. Rule Against Perpetuities

Under the Rule Against Perpetuities ("Rule"), specific future interests are valid only if they must vest or fail by the end of a life in being, plus 21 years.

Example 1: A conveys Blackacre "to B for life, and then to the first male descendant of B, then to C." This provision violates the Rule because it may be many generations before there is a male descendant of B, if at all.

Example 2: A conveys Blackacre "to B for life, and then to B's first son who reaches the age of 18, then to C." This provision is valid because any son of B will attain age 18 within twenty-one years after B's death.

Note the difference in the examples above. In example 1, the opportunity for B to have a male descendant does not end after he dies. Because there is a possibility that the devise will neither vest nor fail within a life in being plus 21 years, the Rule is violated.

On the other hand, in example 2, once B dies, his opportunity to have children ends, and so the clock starts. If when he dies, B has at least one son under the age of 18, then it is certain to be less than a life in being plus 21 years before the condition either vests (son reaches 18), or fails (son dies).

a. Affected future interests

The Rule applies only to the following interests: contingent remainders, vested remainders subject to open, executory interests, powers of appointment, rights of first refusal, and options. It does *not* apply to future interests that revert to the grantor (i.e., reversion, possibility of reverter, right of reentry).

1) Trust interests

Even though a beneficiary of a trust holds only an equitable interest in the trust property, such an interest may be subject to the Rule.

b. Measuring lives

The application of the Rule is determined by one or more measuring lives. A measuring life must be human, but there can be more than one measuring life, provided the number of such lives is reasonable. If a measuring life is not specified, the measuring life is the life directly related to the future interest that is subject to the rule.

> **Example 1:** A devises Blackacre "to B for life, and then to B's children who reach the age of 25." B's life is the measuring life.

If there is not a measuring life, the applicable testing period is 21 years from the time that the future interest is created.

> **Example 2:** A devises Blackacre "to a charity for so long as the property is used as an animal shelter, and then to C." Since there is not a measuring life, C's interest must vest or fail within 21 years of the creation of C's interest in order to satisfy the Rule. Since there is not a guarantee regarding the future use to which Blackacre is put, C's interest violates the Rule.

c. Creation events

The Rule tests the future interest as of the time that it is created. For example, a future interest created by a will is tested as of the testator's death.

d. "Vest or fail" requirement

The Rule requires that the future interest either vest or fail to vest within the applicable time period. If there is *any possibility* that it will not be known whether the interest will vest or fail within that period, the Rule has not been satisfied.

e. Effect of violation of Rule

If a future interest fails to satisfy the Rule, **only the offending interest fails**. In the rare case when the voiding of the future interest undermines the grantor's intent, the entire transfer is voided.

> **EXAM NOTE:** The MBE often tests the Rule by presenting answer choices relating to the result of a failed interest. Be sure to analyze the estate without the offending interest and to consider the grantor's intent.

f. Special rule for transfer to a class

If the transfer of a future interest is made to a class and the Rule voids a transfer to any member of a class, the transfer is void as to all class members, even those whose interests are already vested (i.e., "bad as to one, bad as to all").

> **Example:** A devises Blackacre "to B for life, and then to B's children who have graduated from college." At the time of A's death, B had two children, X, who graduated from college, and Y, who had not. X has a vested remainder subject to open; Y, as well as any after-born children of B, has a contingent remainder. At the time of B's death, Y has also graduated from college and B has had a third child, Z, who is in elementary school. Because it may take Z more than 21 years

to graduate college and thereby vest his interest, not only is Z's interest void under the Rule but X and Y's interests are void as well.

1) Rule of convenience as a savior

The rule of convenience can operate to prevent the application of the Rule to a class transfer.

Example 1: A conveys Blackacre "to B for life, and then to C's children." At the time of the conveyance, C has one child, X. X has a vested remainder subject to open. Although C may have children more than 21 years after B's death, the class will close upon B's death since C has a child, X. Consequently, X and any other children born to C prior to B's death will take Blackacre. The Rule will not apply to void their interests in Blackacre.

The application of the rule of convenience to a class transfer does not automatically forestall the application of the Rule.

Example 2: In the example at f, *supra*, (A devises Blackacre "to B for life, and then to B's children who have graduated from college"), although the class closes upon B's death because both X and Y have vested remainder interests, Z, as child of B, is also a member of the class. Since Z's interest may not vest within 21 years of B's death, the remainder interests of all B's children are void due to the Rule.

EXAM NOTE: Beware of fact patterns with class gifts to grandchildren of an inter vivos grantor instead of a testator. An inter vivos transfer is more likely to violate the Rule because there is a greater chance that a donor will have later-born children than a testator.

2) Exceptions

There are two main exceptions to the "bad as to one, bad as to all" rule for class transfers. Both transfers of a specific dollar amount to each class member (e.g., "$50,000 to each grandchild who survives his parent") and transfers to a subclass that vests at a specific time (e.g., "to the children of B, and upon the death of each, to that child's issue") are tested separately. Any person who is entitled to the transferred interest is not prohibited from taking that interest simply because there are other members of the class who are prohibited from taking the interest.

g. Exceptions to rule

1) Charity-to-charity exception

If property passes from one charity to another charity, the interest of receiving charity is not subject to the Rule.

Example: Blackacre is conveyed "to charity B, as long as the premises are used for a school, and then to charity C." The executory interest of charity C may not vest within the time allotted by the Rule, but, because the Rule does not apply to charity-to-charity transfers, C's executory interest is valid.

EXAM NOTE: The Rule applies to property that passes between a charity and a non-charity.

2) Current tenant's option exception

The Rule does not apply to an option to purchase the property that is held by a current leasehold tenant. If the current tenant can transfer such an option, this exception does not apply to a subsequent holder of the purchase option.

h. Common rule violations

1) Class transfers—"survival beyond age 21" condition

If a transfer to a class is conditioned on the class members surviving to an age beyond 21 and the class is open, the transfer to the class violates the Rule.

> **Example:** A conveys Blackacre "to B for life, and then to B's children who reach the age of 30." B is alive at the time of A's death, and has one child, X, who is 35 years old. X has a vested remainder subject to open; B's potential children have a contingent remainder. The contingent remainder violates the Rule because it is possible that B could have another child who would not attain the age 30 until more than 21 years after B's death. Since the contingent remainder is invalid, X's vested remainder subject to open is also invalid as a consequence of the "bad as to one, bad as to all" rule for class transfers.

2) Fertile octogenarian

Anyone, regardless of age or physical condition, including an 80-year-old woman (i.e., the fertile octogenarian) is deemed capable of having children for the purposes of the Rule. Some states have set an age limit (e.g., 55 years old) beyond which it is rebuttably presumed that a woman cannot have a child.

> **Example:** A conveys Blackacre "to B for life, then to B's children who reach the age of 30 years old." At the time of the conveyance, B is 90 years old, with one child, X, who is 35 years old. X has a vested remainder subject to open, since B, despite her age, is assumed to be capable of having another child. Since the contingent remainder in that child would violate the Rule, X's interest is also void under the "bad as to one, bad as to all" rule.

3) Unborn spouse

If an interest following a widow's life estate cannot vest until the widow dies, it violates the Rule.

> **Example:** A conveys Blackacre "to B for life, then to B's widow for life, then to B's children who are then living." The contingent remainder in B's children violates the Rule because B's widow may be someone who is not yet alive at the time of the conveyance. The contingent remainder would not violate the rule if the life estate was conveyed to a particular person (e.g., B's current spouse) instead of "B's widow."

4) Defeasible fee followed by an executory interest

An executory interest that follows a defeasible fee violates the Rule, unless there is a time limit on the vesting of the executory interest that satisfies the Rule.

If the limit on the defeasible fee is durational (e.g., "so long as," "while"), the striking of the executory interest leaves the grantor with the possibility of reverter. If the limit on the defeasible fee is a condition subsequent (e.g., "but if," "upon the condition that"), the striking of the executory interest leaves the holder of the defeasible fee with a fee simple absolute interest in the property.

> **Example 1:** A conveys Blackacre "to B for so long as the property is used for residential purposes; if it is not, then to C." B has a fee simple subject to an executory interest; C has an executory interest. Since C's executory interest could become possessory after the expiration of the testing period for the Rule, C's interest is stricken and A has a possibility of reverter in Blackacre.
>
> **Example 2:** A conveys Blackacre "to B; but if the property is used for residential purposes, then to C." B has a fee simple subject to an executory interest; C has an executory interest. Since C's executory interest could become possessory after the expiration of the testing period for the Rule, C's interest is stricken and B owns Blackacre in fee simple absolute.

5) Conditional passage of interest

If there is a condition imposed on the passing of a future interest subject to the Rule that is not confined to a specified time limit that meets the Rule's testing period, such as probating the will, or termination of a current military conflict, the future interest runs afoul of the Rule.

i. Statutory changes

A majority of the states have adopted the Uniform Statutory Rule Against Perpetuities, which adopts a "wait and see" stance with respect to the applicability of the Rule. Under this stance, an otherwise invalid interest is valid if it does in fact vest within 90 years of its creation. A few states have simply repealed the Rule altogether.

II. LANDLORD AND TENANT

The relationship between a landlord and a tenant can create four different estates. This relationship is generally governed by a contract, called the lease, and contains the covenants of the parties. The promises are generally independent of each other. In other words, each party must perform his promises regardless of whether or not the other party performs his promise.

A. TYPES OF TENANCIES

There are four types of landlord-tenant estates:

i) Tenancy for years;

ii) Periodic tenancy;

iii) Tenancy at will; and

iv) Tenancy at sufferance.

1. Tenancy for Years

A tenancy for years is an estate measured by a fixed and ascertainable amount of time.

a. Term

A tenancy for years may be any length of time (e.g., one week, six months, five years).

b. Creation

A tenancy for years is created by an agreement between the landlord and the tenant. The Statute of Frauds applies to a tenancy for years that is longer than one year; such agreements must be in writing. A lease subject to the Statute of Frauds is voidable until the tenant takes possession and the landlord accepts rent from the tenant.

c. Termination

1) At end of term

Termination occurs automatically upon the expiration of the term; no notice is required. Any right to renew the agreement must be explicitly set out in the lease.

2) Prior to end of term

Termination may also occur before the expiration of the term, such as when the tenant surrenders the leasehold (i.e., the tenant offers and the landlord accepts return of the leasehold). In addition, although, at common law, the doctrine of independent covenants usually prevented the breach of a covenant in the lease by a tenant or landlord from giving the other party the right to terminate the lease, most states recognize that the breach of certain specific leasehold covenants (i.e., the tenant's payment of the rent, and the landlord's covenants of quiet enjoyment and implied warranty of habitability) can give rise to a right to terminate the lease.

2. Periodic Tenancy

A periodic tenancy is a repetitive, ongoing estate measured by a set period of time (e.g., a month-to-month lease), but with no predetermined termination date.

a. Term

A periodic tenancy automatically renews at the end of each period until one party gives a valid termination notice. The Statute of Frauds does not apply to a periodic tenancy because its nature is that it is for a non-fixed term.

b. Creation

A periodic tenancy can be created by express agreement, implication (e.g., the failure of an express agreement to mention a termination date), or operation of law (e.g., a hold-over tenant, *see* § II.B.5.c., *infra*).

c. Termination

Because a periodic tenancy automatically renews, notice is required to terminate.

1) At end of term

Notice of termination must be given before the beginning of the intended last period of the periodic tenancy.

> **Example 1:** A landlord who wants to terminate a month-to-month tenancy as of March 31st must give notice of the termination to the tenant before the first day of March.

Notice that is given late is generally treated as effective for the subsequent period.

> **Example 2:** A landlord who wanted to terminate a month-to-month tenancy that began on January 1st as of March 31st gave notice of the termination to the tenant on March 5th. The notice is effect to terminate the month-to-month tenancy as of the end of April.

A notice of termination is generally effective only as of the last day of the period (e.g., the end of the month for a month-to-month tenancy that began on the first day of the month).

> **Example 3:** A landlord wanted to terminate a month-to-month tenancy that began on January 1st as of March 15th. The landlord gave notice of the termination to the tenant on February 14th. The notice is effective to terminate the month-to-month tenancy as of the end of March.

> **EXAM NOTE:** The termination of year-to-year tenancy requires notice only six months rather than a year in advance.

In addition, many states have reduced the advance notice period for all periodic tenancies even further (e.g., one month).

2) Prior to end of term

The same circumstances discussed with regard to a tenancy for years may also give rise to the termination of a periodic tenancy prior to the end of a term.

3. Tenancy at Will

A tenancy at will is a leasehold estate that may be terminated by either the landlord or the tenant. If only the landlord is expressly given the right to terminate the leasehold, the tenant is given such right by implication. By contrast, if only the tenant is expressly given the right to terminate the leasehold, the landlord is *not* given a similar termination right.

a. Term

A tenancy at will is an estate that does not have a specific term, but continues until terminated by the landlord or tenant.

b. Creation

A tenancy at will can be created by the express agreement of the parties (or by implication if a person is allowed to occupy the premises), such as when the parties are negotiating a lease. Note that payment of rent by the tenant can convert a tenancy at will into a periodic tenancy.

c. Termination

A tenancy at will can be terminated by either party without notice, but a tenant must be given a reasonable time in which to vacate the premises. A tenancy at will can also be terminated by death of either party, waste or assignment by the tenant, and transfer or lease to a third party by the landlord.

4. Tenancy at Sufferance

A tenancy at sufferance is the period of time after the expiration of a lease during which the tenant remains on the premises. During a tenancy at sufferance, the tenant is bound by the terms of the lease that existed before expiration, including payment of rent.

> **EXAM NOTE:** Know the difference between a tenancy at will, which is created by the agreement of the landlord and the tenant, and a tenancy at sufferance, which is created by the actions of the tenant alone.

A tenancy at sufferance can be terminated by the departure of the tenant from the premises, the eviction of the tenant from the premises by the landlord, or by the landlord's decision to lease the premises to the tenant for another term. Thus, the landlord's remedies may include eviction, creation of a periodic tenancy, or forcible entry in some states.

B. DUTIES OF TENANT

The tenant has two basic duties: to pay rent and avoid waste. The duty to pay rent arises as a consequence of the agreement between the tenant and the landlord (i.e., a lease), which usually takes the form of a written contract. The duty to avoid waste is the same duty imposed on any holder of a current possessory property interest with respect to the holders of other interests in the same property. The duty to avoid waste may be modified by contractual or other legal obligations regarding repair of the premises.

1. Duty to Pay Rent

Although a tenant may enjoy a leasehold estate without having to pay rent (e.g., if the tenant is a relative of the landlord), most tenants are required to pay rent. Although rent was not apportionable under common law, most states today allow the tenant to pay a proportionate amount of the rent if the leasehold terminates prematurely. In addition, the landlord may require a deposit (either as security or a future rent payment) prior to commencing the leasehold.

This duty to pay rent is subject to two major exceptions: destruction of the premises and a material breach by the landlord.

a. Destruction of premises

The lease is terminated and the tenant is excused from paying rent if the premises are destroyed, such as by flood, as long as the tenant is not at fault for the destruction. At common law, the tenant's duty to pay rent was not excused simply because the leasehold premises were destroyed.

b. Material breach of lease by landlord

At common law, the doctrine of independent covenants usually prevented the tenant from avoiding the obligation to pay rent despite the landlord's material breach of the lease. However, even at common law, a landlord who breached the covenant of quiet enjoyment could give the tenant the right to terminate the lease and cease paying rent.

Most states give tenants various options with regard to the payment of rent if a landlord violates the implied warranty of habitability **in a residential lease** (e.g., establishment of an escrow account into which the rent is paid, deducting the cost of repairs incurred by the tenant from the rent paid).

2. Duty to Avoid Waste

At common law, a tenant was held to the same standards of waste imposed on a life tenant, including the duty not to commit affirmative waste (i.e., damage to property), ameliorative waste (i.e., alterations to property, even if value of property increases), or permissive waste (i.e., failure to prevent or repair damage).

a. Ameliorative waste

A tenant is entitled make changes to the physical condition of the leased property that are reasonably necessary in order for the tenant to use the property in a reasonable manner, unless the landlord and tenant agree otherwise. Restatement (Second) of Property (Landlord and Tenant) § 12.2(a).

b. Permissive waste

A tenant has a duty, unless relieved by the terms of the lease, state statute, or local ordinance, to repair the premises to the extent necessary to maintain the premises in their pre-rental condition. An exception exists for **normal wear and tear**, unless the tenant contracts otherwise.

3. Contractual Duty to Repair

If a **non-residential lease** specifies that the tenant must "repair and maintain" the property, the tenant is generally liable for all damage to the property, unless the landlord caused the damage. If the damage is significant (e.g., structural damage due to a fire) and such damage was not caused by the tenant, the modern trend is to narrowly read the tenant's duty to repair and to find that it does not cover such damage.

A **residential lease** provision that places the burden of repair on the tenant is generally void, but the tenant may be required to notify the landlord of the need for such repairs.

4. Other Duties

A tenant may have other contractual duties, such as a duty to avoid excessive noise or to use the premises only for a specified type of business. In addition, a tenant who uses the premises for illegal purposes on a regular basis (e.g., drug distribution) may violate an implied duty. Violation of such duties can give the landlord the right to terminate the lease.

5. **Landlord's Remedies for Tenant's Breach**

   a. **Failure to pay rent**

   If the tenant fails to pay rent, the landlord can sue both for damages and to remove the tenant from the property. An agreement to pay rent on or by a certain date is a material term of a lease and thus, late payment of rent is considered a material breach of the lease. Thus a landlord may bring an action for damages.

   b. **Abandonment**

   At common law, if the tenant unjustifiably abandoned the leasehold, the landlord could treat the abandonment as an offer of surrender, and accept by **retaking the premises**.

   1) **Duty to mitigate**

   Alternatively, the landlord may re-rent the premises on the tenant's behalf and hold the tenant liable for any deficiency. The majority rule today requires a landlord to mitigate damages by making an effort to re-rent the premises.

   2) **Anticipatory breach**

   Although the landlord can sue a tenant for rent as it becomes due, a landlord cannot sue for future rent due under the lease because the doctrine of anticipatory breach does not apply to leases.

   c. **Holdover tenant**

   When a tenant continues to occupy the premises without the landlord's agreement after the original lease expires, the tenant is considered to be a "holdover tenant." The landlord can continue the relationship by treating the holdover tenant as a periodic tenant or a tenant at sufferance. Alternatively, the landlord may file a lawsuit for unlawful detainer if the holdover tenant remains after serving a written notice to vacate (or, "quit").

   The tenant is not considered to be a holdover tenant if the tenant leaves a few articles of personal property behind or the tenant's occupation is only for a few hours. Circumstances out of the tenant's control (e.g., severe illness) and seasonal leases are also exempt from the holdover doctrine.

   1) **Periodic tenant**

   By accepting rent after the termination of a lease, the landlord creates a periodic tenancy, the terms of which mirror the previous terminated lease. Notwithstanding the foregoing, no periodic lease of a residence can be implied for greater than one month, and of a commercial structure no longer than one year, due to Statute of Frauds requirements.

2) Tenant at sufferance

If the landlord refuses to accept rent from a holdover tenant, the tenant is considered wrongfully in possession and the landlord may evict the tenant without notice. *See* § II.A.4, *supra*.

3) Self-help

Most states no longer allow the landlord to use self-help, but must instead (i) properly serve the tenant with notice of a lawsuit, and (ii) obtain a court judgment of possession.

4) Rent

A landlord can impose a higher rent on a holdover tenant if the landlord informed the tenant of the new rent prior to the expiration of the old lease. Otherwise, the rent of the old lease applies.

C.   DUTIES OF LANDLORD

1.   Give Possession

In most states, a tenant is relieved of the obligation to pay rent if the landlord fails to deliver actual possession of the leasehold premises. The minority rule requires only that the landlord deliver legal possession.

2.   Duty to Repair

The contract can place the duty to repair on the tenant of a commercial lease. The landlord has the duty to repair under a residential lease, even when the lease attempts to place the burden on the tenant, except for damages caused by the tenant.

3.   Warranty of Habitability

There is an implied warranty of habitability to most **residential** leases, particular when the dwelling is multi-family. The landlord must maintain the property such that it is reasonably suited for residential use. The landlord's failure to comply with applicable housing code requirements constitutes a breach of this warranty, particularly with regard to violations that substantially threaten the tenant's health and safety. This warranty generally cannot be waived by the tenant, either by express language in the lease or by taking possession of the property with knowledge of the conditions.

If the premises are not habitable, the tenant may choose to (i) refuse to pay rent, (ii) remedy the defect and offset the cost against the rent, or (iii) defend against eviction. Generally, before the tenant can withhold the rent or remedy the defect, the tenant usually must first notify the landlord of the problem and give the landlord a reasonable opportunity to correct the problem.

4.   Covenant of Quiet Enjoyment

Every lease (both commercial and residential) contains an implied covenant of quiet enjoyment, which is breached only when the landlord, someone claiming through the landlord, or someone with superior title disrupts the possession of the tenant. Off-premises actions of third parties will not suffice.

The landlord is not liable for acts of other tenants, but has a duty to take action against a tenant's nuisance-like behavior and to control the common areas. Any actions by the landlord that breach this covenant amount to an **actual or constructive eviction** of the tenant.

Not every interference with the use and enjoyment of the premises amounts to a constructive eviction. Temporary or *de minimis* acts not intended to amount to a permanent expulsion do not amount to constructive eviction.

a. Actual eviction

If the landlord removes the tenant from the premises, the total eviction terminates the lease and ends the tenant's obligation to pay rent.

b. Partial eviction

If the tenant is prevented from possessing or using a portion of the leased premises, the tenant may seek relief for a partial actual eviction. The type of relief granted depends on who prevented the possession.

1) Landlord

The tenant is completely excused from paying rent for the entire premises if the landlord is responsible for partial eviction.

2) Third parties

The tenant must pay reasonable rental value of the premises occupied if the partial eviction is by a third party with a superior claim to the property.

The tenant is not excused from paying rent if a third-party adverse possessor/trespasser partially evicts tenant.

c. Constructive eviction

If the landlord substantially interferes with the tenant's use and enjoyment of the leasehold (e.g., fails to provide heat or water), the tenant's obligation to pay rent is excused due to constructive eviction **only if the tenant gives notice and vacates** the property within a reasonable amount of time.

d. Retaliatory eviction

A landlord may not evict a residential tenant for failure to pay rent as retaliation for the tenant's reporting a housing code violation to the appropriate authorities.

D. TORT LIABILITIES

1. Tenant

The tenant is the possessor of the leasehold who owes a duty of care to invitees, licensees, and foreseeable trespassers and may be liable for dangerous conditions or activities on the leased property. However, this duty is not violated by a failure to remove a natural accumulation of snow or ice, unless an act or failure to act caused the condition to worsen.

2.   Landlord

Under common law, the landlord is only responsible for injuries occurring in **common and public areas**, or those occurring as a result of a **hidden defect** or **faulty repair** completed by the landlord. In addition, some jurisdictions extend the landlord's responsibility to furnished short-term leases.

The modern trend is to hold landlords to a general duty of reasonable care. This means that a landlord may be liable for (i) existing defects prior to tenant's occupation of premises, (ii) failure to make repairs required by a housing code, and (iii) at times, criminal activity of third persons which injure tenants.

See the Themis Torts outline for a further discussion of the liability of owners and possessors of land.

E.   ASSIGNMENT AND SUBLETTING

Absent any language to the contrary, a lease can be freely assigned or sublet. Because a lease is both a contract and a conveyance, these can be independent grounds for liability.

1.   Assignment v. Sublease

An assignment is a complete transfer of the tenant's remaining lease term. Any transfer for less than the entire duration of the lease is a sublease.

2.   Assignee's Rights and Liabilities

Assignee tenants are in privity of estate with the landlord, and are thus liable to the landlord for the rent and any other covenants in the lease that run with the lease. However, if the assignee tenant reassigns the leasehold to a subsequent tenant, the assignee tenant's privity with the landlord ends. Thus, he is no longer liable because the subsequent tenant is now in privity with the landlord.

3.   Sublessee's Rights and Liabilities

Because the sublessee is not in privity of estate or contract with the landlord, the sublessee is not liable to the landlord for the rent or any other covenants in the lease, but is liable to the lessee. However, if the sublessee expressly assumes the rent covenant (or any other covenants), he becomes personally liable to the landlord. While the sublessee can enforce all covenants made by the original lessee in the sublease, the sublessee cannot enforce any covenants made by the landlord.

4.   Original Tenant's Rights and Liabilities

The privity of estate held by the original tenant terminates upon a successful assignment by the tenant to the assignee. But, because the original tenant remains in privity of contract with the landlord (both are parties to the lease agreement), the original tenant remains liable for all the covenants in the lease—even after a successful assignment. Absent an agreement by the landlord to release the original tenant from liability (i.e., a **novation**), the original tenant remains liable to the landlord for the entire duration of the lease.

5.   Landlord Assignments

A landlord may assign his ownership interest, usually through a deed, to a third party without the tenant's consent. The tenant is required to continue his rent obligation and any other covenant under his lease to the new landlord, provided that the covenants touch and concern the land. Likewise, the assignee landlord, as well as the original landlord, is bound to the tenant by the covenants of the lease.

6. Limitations on Assignment and Subletting

a. Prohibition

When a lease prohibits the tenant from assignment or subletting the leasehold, the tenant may nevertheless assign or sublet the premises. However, the landlord generally can then terminate the lease for breach of one of its covenants and recover any damages.

b. Landlord's permission

When a lease prevents assignment or subletting of the leasehold without the permission of the landlord and the lease is silent as to a standard for exercising that permission, the majority rule is that the landlord may withhold permission only on a *commercially reasonable ground*. The minority position is that the landlord may withhold permission at his discretion. Non-assignment and non-sublease clauses are valid, but narrowly construed.

> A clause that prohibits assignment does not automatically also prohibit subleasing.

c. Waiver by landlord

An assignment or sublease may be waived if the landlord knows of either the assignment or sublease and does not object. When a landlord consents to an assignment or waives her right to object, she cannot then object to a subsequent assignment. This prohibition on an objection to a subsequent assignment does not apply to subsequent subleases, and a minority of jurisdictions does not impose such a prohibition even on a subsequent assignment.

F. CONDEMNATION

Condemnation is the taking of land either for public use or because it is unfit for use, and can be a partial taking or a complete forfeiture. If the condemnation is partial, meaning that only a portion of the leased property is condemned or the property is temporarily condemned, the tenant must continue to make his rent payments. However, he is entitled to compensation for the portion of the property that was condemned or the time he was dispossessed from the leased property.

If the condemnation is complete, meaning that the entire leased property is taken for the balance of the lease term, the tenant is discharged from his rent obligation and is entitled to compensation.

G. FAIR HOUSING AND DISCRIMINATION

The Fair Housing Act ("FHA") (Title VIII of the Civil Rights Act of 1968), 42 U.S.C.S. § 3601 *et seq.*, prohibits discrimination in the sale, rental, and financing of homes and in other housing-related transactions (such as advertising, homeowner's insurance, and zoning). Owner-occupied buildings with no more than four units and single-family housing sold or rented without the use of a broker may be exempted from the FHA in certain circumstances.

1. Protected Classes

The FHA prohibits discrimination on the basis of race, color, religion, national origin, sex, disability, and familial status. Protected familial status includes having or securing custody of children under the age of 18 and being pregnant. Exemption from familial status protection exists for certain housing for older persons.

2. Prohibited Practices

The Act prohibits taking any of the following actions on the basis of a protected characteristic:

i)   Refusing to rent or sell housing;

ii) Making housing unavailable;

iii) Providing different housing services or facilities;

iv) Setting different terms for sale or rental of a dwelling;

v)   Falsely denying that housing is available;

vi) Refusing to make a mortgage loan or imposing different terms or conditions on a loan;

vii) Refusing to allow a disabled tenant to make reasonable modifications to the dwelling or common use areas at his own expense;

viii) Refusing to make reasonable accommodations in rules, policies, practices, or services if necessary for the disabled person to use the housing (e.g., refusing to allow a visually impaired tenant to keep a guide dog in an apartment with a 'no pets' policy);

ix) Threatening, coercing, or intimidating or interfering with anyone exercising a fair housing right; and

x)   Advertising or making any statement that indicates a limitation or preference based on protected characteristics.

3. Enforcement and Compliance

The U.S. Department of Housing and Urban Development ("HUD") plays the lead role in administering the FHA. A person who believes that a violation of the FHA has occurred may file a complaint with HUD and/or file suit in federal court (a court-appointed attorney may be available). Available relief includes actual damages (including humiliation, and pain and suffering), injunctive or other equitable relief (such as making the housing available), and reasonable attorney's fees and costs. If the case is resolved by an administrative hearing, a civil penalty to vindicate the public interest may be assessed. A federal court may award punitive damages.

4. Complaint Process

Complaints filed with HUD are first investigated by the Office of Fair Housing and Equal Opportunity ("FHEO"). If it finds reasonable cause to believe that discrimination occurred, the case is heard in an administrative hearing within 120 days, unless either party elects for the case to be heard in federal court.

Before an administrative hearing is ordered, HUD attempts to reach an agreement among the parties, and any conciliation agreement will cease action on the complaint. However, in order for a conciliation agreement to cease action on the complaint, it must protect both the complainant and the public interest. The breach of a conciliation agreement may result in suit by the Attorney General.

III. DISPUTES ABOUT OWNERSHIP IN LAND

A. ADVERSE POSSESSION

The doctrine of adverse possession allows ownership to be granted to a person who exercises exclusive physical possession of a piece of property for a certain amount of time. Title acquired by adverse possession is as good as title traceable to a prior record owner. For possession to ripen into title, possession must be continuous, open and notorious, actual, exclusive, and hostile. Government-owned land cannot be adversely possessed.

1. Continuous

Possession must be continuous and uninterrupted for a period of time as defined by statute (or, 20 years at common law). Seasonal or infrequent use may be sufficiently continuous if it is consistent with the type of property that is being possessed (e.g., land at a summer camp).

a. Tacking

An adverse possessor may tack on his predecessor's time in order to satisfy the statutory period, as long as there is privity satisfied by any non-hostile nexus (such as blood, contract, deed, or will). The periods of possession must pass directly from one possessor to the next, without any gaps.

Tacking is not allowed when there is an actual, wrongful exclusion of a party entitled to possession from the property (ouster).

b. Disability of owner

The statute of limitations will not run against a true owner who is afflicted with a disability (e.g., insanity, infancy, imprisonment) at the inception of the adverse possession.

2. Actual, Open, and Notorious

Possession must be open and notorious, such that a reasonable true owner would become aware of the claim. Uses that are hidden (such as underground wiring or piping) are insufficient to satisfy this requirement.

3. Hostile

The adverse possessor must possess the land without the owner's permission and with the intent to claim the land as his own against the claims of others for it to be considered "hostile." The majority of jurisdictions do not require that the possession be hostile in the sense that the possessor purposefully seeks to defeat the owner's title. The intent of the possessor is irrelevant in many jurisdictions. Most jurisdictions that consider intent will grant title to a possessor who, in good faith, thought he had the legal right to possess (i.e., believed the property was unowned or thought he owned the property).

4. Exclusive

Possession cannot be shared with the true owner, although two or more people can join together to create a tenancy in common by adverse possession.

5. Scope of Possession

a. Constructive adverse possession

If a person enters property under color of title (a facially valid will or deed) and only actually possesses a portion of the property, constructive adverse possession can give title to the whole. The amount possessed must be a reasonable portion of the whole.

b. Below surface area

The adverse possessor acquires the rights to the subsurface (e.g., mineral rights), unless those rights belong to a third party.

c. Future interests

The adverse possessor acquires the estate held by the person who has legal possession at the time that the adverse possession began. In other words, the adverse possession period does not run against future interests that exist at the time that the adverse possession begins, but does apply to future interests created from a fee simple absolute estate after the adverse possession has begun.

B. THE LAND SALE CONTRACT

1. Formation

A contract for the sale of real property is generally negotiated by a real estate broker who acts as an intermediary between sellers and buyers of real estate. Generally, the broker has a duty of a fiduciary and must follow the same requirements as for the formation of any contract (i.e., offer, acceptance, and consideration), and is also subject to the Statute of Frauds.

> **EXAM NOTE:** The Statute of Frauds has been tested on nearly every MBE.

a. Statute of Frauds

The land sale contract must:

i)   Be in writing;

ii) Be signed by the party to be charged; and

iii) Contain all of the essential terms (i.e., parties, property description, terms of price and payment).

b. Exceptions to Statute of Frauds

1) Part performance

Under the doctrine of part performance, either party may seek specific performance where the acts of performance constitute persuasive evidence of the existence of a contract. Among the acts that may constitute such evidence are:

i) Payment of all or part of the purchase price;

ii) Possession by the purchaser; or

iii) Substantial improvement of the property by the purchaser.

2) Detrimental reliance

Specific performance may also be permitted where the party seeking enforcement has reasonably relied on the contact and would suffer such hardship that the other party will be estopped from asserting the statute of frauds as a defense to the contract.

3) Admission

A party may be able to enforce an oral land sale contract where the other party admits the existence of the contract.

c. Rescission of contract

While a writing is generally required to create an enforceable land sale contract, a majority of states permit the oral rescission of a land sale contract.

2. Performance

a. Marketable title

Absent contrary language, an implied covenant of marketable title (i.e., a title free from defects) is part of a land sale contract, regardless of the type of deed created. Marketable title is a title that is free from an unreasonable risk of litigation. Unless otherwise agreed, the seller is not required to deliver marketable title until the closing. In the case of an installment land contract, marketable title is not required to be given until delivery occurs.

Once the deed is delivered, the terms of the contract merge with the deed and the deed controls. This is known as "merger." After merger takes place, the purchaser is not able to enforce provisions of the purchase contract.

1) Defects

Defects in title rendering title unmarketable include:

i) Title acquired by adverse possession that has not yet been quieted (i.e., supported by a judicial decree);

ii) Future interests wherein the holders of such interests have not agreed to the transfer;

iii) Private encumbrance (e.g., mortgage, covenant, option, or easement);

iv) Violation of a zoning ordinance; or

v) Significant physical defect (an encroachment on the land that is incurable).

The above defects may be waived in the contract of sale.

2) Remedies for unmarketable title

A buyer may rescind and recover payments, sue for breach, or bring an action for specific performance with an abatement of the purchase price (e.g., price adjustment to compensate buyer for defect), but usually cannot do so until the date of closing.

b. Time of the essence

Generally, a court will assume that time is not of the essence in a real estate contract, unless the contract specifically states that time is of the essence, circumstances indicate that this was the intention of the parties, or one party gives the other party notice that time is of the essence. Such notice must be given at a reasonable time before the date designated for closing.

If time is not of the essence, strict adherence to the closing date set in the contract will not be required in equity. Thus, a failure to perform will generally not be grounds for rescission of the contract. A party can sue for specific performance, though, as long as the party was ready to perform within a reasonable time from the date set for performance.

Regardless of whether time is of the essence in a real estate contract, though, the party that fails to render performance on the date set for closing in the contract will be in breach and liable for damages in an action at law.

c. Implied warranty of fitness or suitability (new homes)

Replacing the doctrine of caveat emptor ("let the buyer beware"), a warranty of fitness or suitability (or implied warranty of quality, workmanlike construction, performance, habitability) is implied in a land sale contract for the purchase of a newly constructed residence. In some jurisdictions the warranty extends to repair and remodeling of an existing residence, and even to related structures (such as a detached garage or a retaining wall).

1) Construction defects

Under this warranty, the seller asserts that he used adequate materials and good workmanship in working on the residence. The implied warranty generally covers latent construction defects (i.e., defects that cannot be discovered from reasonable observation or inspection), such as a defective electrical, plumbing, or mechanical system, or a leaky roof or drainage problem that does not manifest itself until after the sale. While the buyer has a duty to conduct a reasonable inspection of the residence for patent defects, the buyer is not required to employ an expert home inspector.

2) Parties

a) Defendants

Generally, the warranties are implied against commercial builders, developers, and contractors of residences.

b) Plaintiffs

A majority of jurisdiction permit not only the initial homeowner-purchaser but also subsequent purchasers who do not contract directly with the commercial developer or builder to recover damages.

3) Timing

Generally, a suit for breach of this warranty must be brought within a reasonable time after discovery of the defect. Where the warranty is statutory, a fixed time is generally specified (generally from one to ten years), may vary with the type of defect (e.g., structural defects, foundation problems), and may begin to run with the completion of the residence or the initial buyer's possession of it, rather than discovery of the defect.

4) Damages

Damages are generally based on the cost of repairs to bring the residence into compliance with the warranty. However, where the defects cannot be corrected without substantial destruction of the residence, damages may be based on the difference between the value of the residence with the warranty and the value of the residence as built.

5) Disclaimer and waiver

This implied warranty may be disclaimed by the builder or waived by the homeowner if done so with language that is clear and unambiguous, but a general disclaimer (e.g., "property is sold as is") is generally not sufficient.

d. Disclosure duty (all homes)

In a majority of jurisdictions, a seller of a residence has a duty to disclose all known material physical defects to the buyer. The defect must not be readily observable or known to the buyer. In order to be material, the defect must substantially affect the value of the residence, impact the health or safety of a resident, or the desirability of the residence to the buyer. When a seller fails to make such disclosures, the buyer may rescind the sale or seek damages. Some states limit this duty to commercial sellers (e.g., builders); other states impose this duty on all sellers.

Even in a jurisdiction that does not require an affirmative disclosure by the seller, a buyer can sue the seller for misrepresentation or fraudulent concealment. General disclaimers (e.g., property sold as is) are not sufficient to preclude the seller's liability.)

e. Tender of performance

The seller's and the buyer's performance are concurrent conditions. Therefore, one is not obligated to perform without the other's performance. When one party, either buyer or seller, repudiates the contract, the non-repudiating party is excused from performing. However, if both parties fail to perform, the closing date is simply extended until one of the parties performs. On the other hand, the inability of the seller to produce a marketable title does not automatically create a breach; rather, the buyer must give the seller sufficient time to cure the title defect.

f. Merger

Under the doctrine of merger, obligations contained in the contract of sale, such as the seller's duty to deliver marketable title, are merged into the deed and cannot thereafter be enforced unless the deed contains the obligation. However, this doctrine generally is not applicable to obligations that are collateral to and independent of the conveyance itself, such as the obligation of the buyer to perform some act on the property after acquisition.

(Note: The term "merger" is used in other real property contexts, such as the merger of property interests (e.g., acquisition of both the land that is subject to and the land that is benefited by a restrictive covenant). Such a merger results in the extinguishment of the property right (e.g., the restrictive covenant).)

3. Remedies for Breach

a. Damages

Both the buyer and seller can recover damages based on the difference between the contract price and the market value on the date of performance. If the seller breached but acted in good faith, damages are limited to the buyer's out-of-pocket expenses.

A non-breaching seller may also collect liquidated money damages for costs relating to reselling the property, but courts likely will not enforce liquidated damage clauses if the seller suffered no loss (such as if the value of the property actually increased).

b. Specific performance

The buyer is entitled to specific performance for a seller's breach of a contract to sell land since the buyer's remedy at law is considered inadequate due to the unique nature of land. Under the theory of mutualities of remedies, the seller is also permitted to seek specific performance and force the buyer to purchase the land, even though the seller typically receives money rather than land. When the buyer seeks specific performance with respect to property for which there is a title defect (e.g., an encumbrance), the buyer may also obtain an abatement in purchase price to compensate the buyer for the defect.

4. Equitable Conversion

Under the doctrine of equitable conversion, although the seller retains legal title to real property during the pendency of the land sale contract, equitable title passes to the buyer upon entering the contract. The seller effectively holds the property in trust for the buyer, and has a duty to keep up the property. However, as the holder of legal title, the seller has the right to possess the property.

a. Action against seller

When an action is maintained against the seller for a claim that arose prior to the execution of the contract, a judgment obtained against the seller after the execution of the contract is not enforceable against the real property. Under the doctrine of equitable conversion, the seller's interest is converted by the contract into an interest in the proceeds from the sale; it is no longer an interest in the real property itself.

b. Risk of loss

Most states, following the logic of the doctrine of equitable conversion, place the risk of loss during the time between the execution of the contract and the closing **on the buyer**, regardless of whether the buyer takes possession of the property. An exception is recognized when the loss is attributable to the seller's intentional or negligent actions. The Uniform Vendor and Purchaser Risk Act (adopted by a minority of jurisdictions) keeps the risk of loss with the seller, unless and until the buyer takes possession or title is transferred. In order for the Act to apply, a material part of the property must be destroyed.

c. Insurance

Unless the contract requires otherwise, the seller does not have a duty to carry casualty insurance. Because the buyer has an equitable interest in the property, the buyer may obtain such insurance. When the risk of loss is on the buyer and the seller has casualty insurance, the seller is generally required to give the buyer credit against the purchase price in the amount of the insurance proceeds when a casualty occurs.

d. Effect of buyer's or seller's death

When one of the contracting parties dies prior to the performance date of the contract, the seller's interest may be treated as personal property and the buyer's interest may be treated as a real property interest for purposes of distributing in the property pursuant to either's will.

1) Seller's death

When the seller-decedent has devised his real property interests, the proceeds from the sale of the property under contract are treated as personal property that pass to the devisee of the seller-decedent's personal property. The devise of the real property itself is treated as having been adeemed. In jurisdictions that have adopted an anti-ademption statute, the devisee of the seller-decedent's real property is entitled to the sale proceeds.

2) Buyer's death

The devisee of the buyer-decedent's real property interest is entitled to the property under contract and can compel its transfer to her. In addition, when the property is not fully paid for, payment is made from the buyer's personal property.

5. Security Interest

a. Mortgage

Lenders and buyers use mortgages as security devices to secure repayment of a debt. Two such devices are purchase money and future advance mortgages. A **purchase money mortgage** is used when a person takes out a loan for the purpose of purchasing property. A **future advance mortgage** (sometimes considered a second mortgage on property used to secure the loan) is a line of credit often used for home equity, construction, business, and commercial loans.

The promise to repay the debt is usually contained in the mortgage note, which sets out the terms of the transaction. An agreement without a writing that encumbers property as security for a debt is an equitable mortgage that may be proven by parol evidence.

If the debtor fails to repay the debt, the lender has the power to force a judicial foreclosure sale to satisfy the debt.

1) Severance

The **majority rule** (the lien theory) treats the mortgage interest as a lien that does not affect a joint tenancy.

The **minority rule** (the title theory) severs joint tenancy upon the granting of a mortgage and converts it to a tenancy in common.

2) Equity of redemption

After default but **prior to foreclosure**, the debtor/mortgagor retains the right to reclaim clear title to the property and prevent foreclosure upon full repayment of the debt. Courts routinely reject attempts by the mortgagee to deny the mortgagor this right (i.e., to "clog" the equity of redemption) prior to default, such as by the inclusion of a waiver clause in the mortgage.

3) Statutory redemption

After the foreclosure sale is complete, some states still allow the debtor/mortgagor to redeem the property for a limited time. A statutory redemption by the mortgagor essentially nullifies the foreclosure sale because it ends the purchaser's title and restores title to the debtor/mortgagor.

Statutory redemption by the mortgagor is final.

> **Example:** A sold Blackacre to B for $300,000. B made a down payment of $100,000 and A carried a mortgage for the remaining balance. A mortgage was executed as security for a $200,000 promissory note due in 2015 with 7% interest per year. B stopped making payments on the mortgage in 2007, and A forced a foreclosure sale to settle the debt. Before the foreclosure sale, B would be able to pay off the debt and reclaim Blackacre. But, after the foreclosure sale, B can reclaim only by statutory redemption.

4) Clogging

Mortgage clauses that contain a provision that the mortgager waives the right to redeem are not valid. However, a mortgagor may waive his right to redeem after the mortgage has been executed in exchange for good and valuable consideration.

b. Mortgage alternatives

1) Deed of trust

In some states, a deed of trust (or trust deed) is used in place of a mortgage. The debtor (landowner) makes a note to a third party trustee as collateral security for the payment of the note to the beneficiary (lender), with the condition that the trustee re-convey the title to the debtor upon payment of the note. Upon default, the beneficiary instructs the trustee to sell the land to repay the note. In a defective transfer of a deed of trust transaction, an equitable lien can be argued when a property is transferred without proper payment of the mortgage.

2) Installment land contract

An installment land contract is a contract for deed. The seller retains title until the buyer makes the final payment under an installment payment plan. Usually, installment land contracts allow the seller to keep all installment payments and retake possession if the buyer fails to make a payment.

States vary in their methods to assist purchasers in default. Some jurisdictions treat an installment land contract as a mortgage, requiring the seller to foreclose on the property rather than have the purchaser forfeit payments. Other jurisdictions offer equity of redemption, similar to mortgage law; while others provide for a combination of forfeiture and restitution of payments.

3) Sale-leaseback

In a sale-leaseback, the property is simultaneously sold and leased back to the seller, usually for long term continued use.

4) Absolute deed

An absolute deed (also known as a "Deed of Absolute Sale") is free of all liens and encumbrances and is used to transfer unrestricted title to property. Unlike a mortgage deed, an absolute deed does not transfer title back to the mortgagee when the terms of the mortgage have been fulfilled.

c. Effect of transfer by mortgagor

1) Assuming mortgage—personal liability attaches

If the buyer assumes the mortgage, upon default, the lender may seek payment from both the original debtor and the buyer for payment of the debt. But, the original debtor is relieved of all liability if there is any modification of the obligation after the mortgage is assumed. (Note: Most jurisdictions do not require that an assumption agreement be in writing; if proven, an oral agreement is enforceable.)

2) "Subject to" mortgage

If the buyer takes title "subject to" an existing mortgage, the buyer is not personally liable upon default, although absent a novation, the original debtor is personally liable. The property remains subject to the security interest held by the lender. If a deed is silent, the grantee is considered to have taken subject to the mortgage.

3) Due-on-sale clauses

Mortgages employ due-on-sale and due-on-encumbrance clauses to prevent the transfer of mortgages. These clauses are enforceable and allow acceleration of the mortgage (i.e., when the principal and interest become due immediately).

4) Subrogation and Suretyship

A surety, also known as a guarantee, is a promise by a borrower's guarantor to assume the obligation to pay the debt upon default by the borrower. Subrogation provides for the substitution of a surety in the place of a creditor so that the surety succeeds to the rights, claims, and remedies of the creditor in relation to the debt to recover the cost of making payment or performing on the borrower's behalf.

d. Effect of transfer by mortgagee

1) Transfer mortgage without note

Jurisdictions are split when it comes to transferring mortgages without the note. Because the note is the principal evidence of the debt, many states hold that a transfer of the mortgage alone has no legal validity and is void. Other jurisdictions, however, consider the note and the mortgage somewhat of a single entity. Thus, they hold that the note is automatically transferred along with the mortgage, unless expressly stated to the contrary.

2) Transfer note without mortgage

Conversely, transferring the note without the mortgage is possible because the mortgage follows the note. Although it is customary for the transferee to obtain and record a mortgage assignment, no separate written assignment is necessary.

If the promissory note given by the mortgagor is a negotiable instrument, the mortgagor is generally obligated to pay the holder of the note. This is true even when the mortgagor does not have notice that the original mortgagee has transferred to the note to a third party. However, most promissory notes given in connection with a mortgage are not negotiable instruments. In such cases, the traditional view follows the rule for a promissory note that it is a negotiable instrument, but the modern trend is that the mortgagor may pay the original mortgagee until the mortgagor receives notice of the transfer. Restatement (Third) of Property-Mortgages 5.5.

e. Pre-foreclosure

1) Possession

Whether the mortgagee may take possession depends on the theory of title the jurisdiction follows.

In a **lien theory state**, the mortgagee cannot take possession prior to foreclosure because the mortgagor is considered to be the owner of the land until foreclosure.

In a **title theory state**, legal title is in the mortgagee until the mortgage has been fully satisfied. Thus, the mortgagee is entitled to take possession at any time and can certainly take possession as soon as default occurs. As such, the mortgagee can make repairs, take rent, prevent waste, and lease out vacant space. While in practice this may seem advantageous, few mortgagees take advantage of this right because of the liability risks involved. A mortgagee in possession assumes a duty to take reasonable care of the property, and incurs liability as if she were the owner. Instead, some mortgagees opt to have the court appoint a receiver to manage the property and intercept the rents prior to foreclosure.

A minority of jurisdictions follow the **intermediate theory**, which in practice is similar to the title theory. In actuality, the intermediate theory combines both lien and title theories. It allows the mortgagor to retain legal title (lien theory) until default, and on mortgagor's default, vests legal title in the mortgagee (title theory).

2) Waste

The mortgagor has a duty not to commit waste at least to the extent that the waste impairs the mortgagee's security. This duty exists even if the mortgagor is not otherwise in default.

3) Equity of redemption

After the default, but prior to a foreclosure sale, the mortgagor may regain clear title to the property under the doctrine of equity of redemption. Redemption occurs upon full repayment of the debt and any accrued interest by the mortgagor.

Some states also permit the debtor to reclaim the property after a foreclosure sale for a fixed period of time (e.g., six months).

Also, in lieu of foreclosure, a mortgagor may convey all interest in the property to the mortgagee. This is known as "deed in lieu of foreclosure." This permits the mortgagee to take immediate possession of the property without any further legal formalities, but requires the consent of both the mortgagor and mortgagee.

f. Foreclosure and its effect on interests

The two most common types of foreclosure are by judicial sale and power of sale. Judicial sale provides for the sale of mortgaged property under the supervision of a court in which all proper parties are notified. Foreclosure by power of sale is held by the mortgage holder. A few jurisdictions adhere to the strict foreclosure method in which a court orders the mortgagor to pay the mortgage within a certain time period. If the mortgagor does not pay within the time period, the mortgagor takes title free and clear.

Purchasers at a foreclosure sale take the property free and clear of any interests created after the creation of the interest being foreclosed, and take subject to any mortgages or liens that are senior to the lien of the foreclosing party. If the bid at the sale is less than the debt, even if it is for fair market value, the lender may be granted a deficiency judgment for the balance of the debt against the debtor.

1) Junior interests

All interests that are junior to the mortgage that is being foreclosed are destroyed. Thus, all junior interests must be given notice of the foreclosure and made necessary parties to the foreclosure action. This provides the junior interest with an opportunity to redeem the property by paying off a senior interest. If a subordinate interest is not made party to the action, her interests will be safeguarded, regardless of the foreclosure action.

2) Senior interests

A purchaser at a foreclosure sale takes subject to any mortgages or liens that are senior to the lien of the foreclosing party. A senior interest is generally any interest created before the interest being foreclosed, but classification of interests is subject to the applicable recording act and any subordination agreements between the mortgagees.

3) Omitted party

If a subordinate interest is not made party to the action, his interests will be safeguarded, regardless of the foreclosure action. As a result, the purchaser does not acquire an interest in the property free of the subordinate's rights.

4) Subrogation

A person who pays off another person's mortgage obligation may become the owner of the obligation and the mortgage to the extent necessary to prevent unjust enrichment. Subrogation is appropriate when the payor is under a legal duty to do so, or does so in order to protect an interest in the property subject to the mortgage or on account of misrepresentation, mistake, duress, fraud or undue influence.

5) Deficiency and surplus

Once a foreclosure sale takes place and the proceeds are not enough to pay the outstanding mortgage balance, costs, and liens on the property, there is a deficiency. The homeowner is then responsible for paying the deficiency even though she no longer owns the property. Even if the bid is for fair market value, the lender may still be granted a deficiency judgment for the balance of the debt against the debtor.

If the proceeds from the sale exceed the mortgage balance, outstanding liens, and foreclosure costs, there is a surplus of proceeds from the sale against which the homeowner may make a claim.

g. Non-judicial foreclosure

If a mortgage contains a "power of sale" clause which calls for the sale of property to pay off the balance on a loan in the event of default, a non-judicial (private) foreclosure is authorized.

h. Priority in foreclosure actions

The money from a foreclosure sale is applied first to the costs associated with the sale, second to the balance and interest of the mortgage obligation being foreclosed, and finally to the mortgage obligations owed to all junior interest holders. Any residue is paid to the debtor. If the successful bid at the sale is less than the debt, the lender may be granted a deficiency judgment.

When multiple interests must be paid out of the proceeds, generally, the earliest mortgage placed on the property has priority over the other interests. There are, however, some exceptions as noted below.

1) Exceptions

a) Purchase money mortgage exception

A purchase money mortgage (i.e., a mortgage used to finance the purchase of the property) has **priority over all other** non-purchase money mortgages, even those recorded earlier. Seller's purchase money mortgages have priority over those of third-parties (and the priority of third party purchase money mortgages is determined chronologically).

b) Unrecorded senior mortgage exception

A senior mortgage (i.e., one that is first in time), is not given priority over junior mortgagees who paid value for the mortgage without actual inquiry or constructive notice of the senior mortgage.

c) Subordination agreement between mortgagees

When a senior mortgagee agrees to subordinate his interest to a junior mortgagee, such agreement will be enforced unless the mortgage is not sufficiently described or specified.

d) Mortgage modifications

A senior mortgagee who enters into an agreement with the landowner to modify the mortgage by making it more burdensome subordinates his interest only as to the modification. The senior mortgagee's original mortgage will otherwise remain superior.

Similarly, when a senior mortgagee makes an optional advance of funds after the mortgage is executed and a junior mortgage is placed on the property with the senior mortgagee's knowledge, the advance will be subordinate to the junior interest. Otherwise, if the junior interest is placed on the property without the senior mortgagee's knowledge, the optional advance will have the same priority as the original mortgage.

i. Personal liability of mortgagor

When the mortgagor signs a note and gives a mortgage, in most states, the mortgagee is permitted to bring an action based on the note itself before bringing an action to foreclose on the mortgage. In addition, after bringing a foreclosure action, many states permit the mortgagee to bring a deficiency action against the mortgagor. Some states disallow this action when the mortgagee forecloses via a private foreclosure sale or when the mortgage is a purchase money mortgage. In addition, some states limit the amount that may be recovered in a deficiency action to the fair market value of the property when the value of the property falls below the amount of the deficiency.

j. Defenses

Mortgages are subject to the same defenses as the underlying obligation secured by the mortgage (e.g., mistake, duress, failure of consideration, or fraud). In addition, the following valid defenses can affect the application of all or part of a mortgage.

1. Usury

Usury is the act of lending money at an interest rate in excess of the legal limit. If a bank or association is a usurious lender, only the interest, not the principal, is forfeited.

2. Competency

If the parties lack the legal capacity to contract, because of minority or mental incapacity, a mortgage may be invalidated.

k. Discharge

A mortgage may be discharged by payment of the debt secured by the mortgage, acceptance by the mortgagee of a deed in lieu of foreclosure, or by the merger of the equitable and legal interests.

6. Options and Rights of First Refusal

An option to purchase real property (or a right of first refusal with respect to the transfer of property) involves special considerations. As an interest in property, each is subject to the Statute of Frauds and the applicable recording act.

a. Option contract

In an option contract, one party acquires the right to purchase property, typically during a specific time period, in exchange for consideration.

1) Protection against revocation and termination

An option contract removes the ability of a grantor to revoke the option. Otherwise, an offeror is free to withdraw the offer, even despite a promise to the contrary, unless the offeree has detrimentally relied on the offer. In addition, as a contract, the option does not terminate upon the death or incapacity of the grantor of the option, unlike the termination of an offer upon the death of the offeror.

2) Counter-offer without rejection

The holder of an option can make an offer to the grantor of the option that otherwise would constitute a counteroffer (and thereby a rejection of the original offer) without losing the right to exercise the option.

3) Acceptance

The holder of an option must exercise the option pursuant to the terms of the contract. The mailbox rule, which treats an acceptance as valid when mailed, does not apply. The holder's decision to exercise the option must be received by the grantor of the option within any time period specified in the contract.

b. Right of first refusal

A right of first refusal is a preemptive right that gives its holder the opportunity to acquire property prior to its transfer to another. The right may be limited in various ways, such as the time period during which right exists, the transactions to which it applies, and its transferability to another person.

c. Rule Against Perpetuities

The Rule Against Perpetuities does not apply to an option or right of first refusal granted to a current leasehold tenant. In addition, a significant minority of jurisdictions, following the modern trend, do not apply the rule to an option contract or a right of first refusal, particularly when the property right is created in a commercial transaction. Restatement (Third) of Property: Servitudes 3.3, cmt. a.

d. Restraints against alienability

As partial restraints on the alienability of property, both an option contract and a right of first refusal are subject to the rule of a reasonableness. Under this rule, the utility of the purpose served by the restraint is balanced against the likely harm that would result from its enforcement. Restatement (Third) of Property: Servitudes 3.4, cmt. c.

e. Marketable title

A right of first refusal as well as an option contract can constitute an encumbrance that prevents the seller of property from providing marketable title.

7. Real Estate Broker

In many instances, the sale of real property involves a real estate broker or agent. The rights and duties of the broker are generally governed by contract.

a. Seller's agent

Typically, a real estate broker serves as the seller's agent. There is usually a listing agent, who deals directly with seller, and who may help to set the selling price and assume primary responsibilities for advertising the property for sale. There is also a selling agent, who serves as a sub-agent of the listing agent and finds a buyer for the property. Generally, the listing agent and the selling agent share in the commission paid by the seller.

1) Entitlement to commission

a) Procurement of buyer

In general, to be entitled to a commission, the selling agent's efforts must be the procuring cause for the buyer's purchase of the property. In other words, the resulting sale must be induced primarily by those efforts.

b) "Ready, willing, and able" buyer

Most contracts provide for payment of a commission to the real estate broker upon the procurement of a buyer who is ready, willing, and able to purchase the property on terms that are agreeable to the seller. Consequently, a broker generally has a right to a commission when the contract of sale is executed or, if the contract is subject to conditions, when the conditions are satisfied, despite the fact that the sale does not take place. Traditionally, it made no difference whether the nonoccurrence of the sale was due to the seller or the buyer. However, in a minority of states, the broker is not entitled to a commission when the buyer, after entering into a contract, defaults ("no sale, no commission" rule), but may be entitled to a share of any recovery gained by the seller from the defaulting buyer (e.g., retention of a deposit).

While entering into a contract usually establishes that the buyer is both ready and willing, when the buyer's contractual duty to pay is subject to a condition precedent, the failure of that condition to be met will prevent the broker from being entitled to the commission.

b. Buyer's agent

More recently, a real estate broker may serve as the buyer's agent. Typically, such agent also receives a commission-based fee in an amount similar to the selling agent.

c. Dual agent

A dual agent serves as agent for both the buyer and seller of real property. Many states prohibit a person from serving as a dual agent, due to the likelihood of a conflict of interest.

d. Transaction brokers

In a few states, unless the parties to a real estate transaction specify otherwise in a written contract, the broker serves as a facilitator of the transaction but does act as an agent for either the seller or the buyer. As a transaction broker, the broker may subject to statutory rules as well as some ethical duties, such as fair dealing, honesty, care and competence, in assisting the parties with the transaction (e.g., securing a title search).

C. DELIVERY AND RECORDING OF DEED

In order to transfer a real property interest, the grantor must demonstrate the intent to make a present transfer of the interest (e.g., delivery of the deed) and the grantee must accept the interest. In addition, pursuant to the Statute of Frauds, the transfer of a real property interest must be evidenced by a writing (e.g., a valid deed). Finally, the grantee may be able to protect his property interest against others' claims by recording the deed.

1. Intent to Transfer (Delivery)

The grantor must, at the time of transfer, intend to make a present transfer of a property interest to the grantee. Note that the interest itself may be a future interest, such as when a parent retains a life estate in a residence and transfers a remainder interest to an adult child.

Typically, this intent is manifested by delivery of the deed. Delivery may be completed by physically handing or mailing the deed to the grantee or the grantee's agent. However, intent can be implied from the words and conduct of the grantor, such as when the grantor drafts and records a deed.

Although it is often stated that a deed must be delivered in order for a real property interest to pass (i.e., a delivery requirement), the term "delivery" is used as shorthand for the existence of the necessary grantor intent. Physical transfer of a deed is not required and is not conclusive evidence of the grantor's intent.

a. Retention of deed by grantor

When the grantor keeps the deed, intent to transfer is not presumed. Instead, parol evidence is admissible to establish whether the grantor had the intent to make a present transfer of the property interest.

b. Transfer of deed to grantee

Transfer of a deed to the grantee creates a presumption that the grantor intended to make a present transfer of the property interest. Parol evidence is admissible to show that the grantor lacks such intent (e.g., the grantor only intended to create a mortgage not to effect an outright transfer). However, when the grantor transferred the deed to the grantee subject to an oral condition (i.e., a condition that does not appear in the deed), parol evidence is not admissible and the condition is not enforceable.

c. Transfer of deed to third party

1) Grantor's agent

When the grantor transfers the deed to her own agent (e.g., an attorney), the transfer is treated as if the grantor had retained the deed, even where the grantor has instructed the agent to deliver the deed to the grantee at some future time or upon the happening of an event. Until the grantor's agent does deliver the deed to the grantee, the grantor can demand that the agent ignore the prior instruction and return the deed to the grantor.

2) Grantee's agent

Where the grantor transfers the deed to the grantee's agent, the transfer is treated as if it had been made to the grantee herself.

3) Independent agent-gift

If the grantor purportedly gives property to a grantee through a third party and places a condition on the transfer of the deed by the third party to the grantee, whether delivery has taken place depends on the grantor's language. If the grantor retains an absolute right to recover the deed, no valid delivery exists because transfer of title was not clearly intended.

> **Example 1:** A executes a deed that transfers real property to B. The deed itself contains no conditions. A gives the deed to C to hold and says, "Give this deed to B on his 21st birthday, unless I ask for the deed back before then." Because A retained an absolute right to recover the deed, A did not have the intent to make a present transfer.

If the grantor does not retain a right to retrieve the deed, the key is whether the grantor intends to make a present gift of a property interest. If so, the grantor cannot later void the gift. Instead, the conditional transfer is treated as creating a future property interest in the grantee.

Example 2: A executes a deed that transfers real property to B. The deed itself contains no conditions. A gives the deed to an independent third party, C, and says, "I want B to have this property when she has her first child. Please give the deed to her then." Since A gave C the deed with the intent of presently creating an executory interest in B, B currently has an executory interest in the real property.

When the third party's transfer of the deed to the grantee is conditioned on the death of the grantor, the grantor's transfer of the deed to the third party must evidence the intent to make a present gift. When the grantor's intent is that the gift itself be effective only upon the grantor's death, the transfer can be ineffective due to a failure to comply with the requirements for a testamentary transfer (i.e., the Statute of Wills).

Example 3: A executes a deed that transfers real property to B. The deed itself contains no conditions. A gives the deed to an independent third party, C, saying, "I want B to have this property upon my death. Please give the deed to her then." Because A gave C the deed with the intent of presently creating a remainder interest in B, the transfer is effective.

Example 4: A executes a deed that transfers real property to B. The deed itself contains no conditions. A gives the deed to an independent third party, C, saying, "I want B to have this property if she outlives me. Please give the deed to her then." Because A gave C the deed with the intent of making a testamentary transfer (i.e., requiring that B survive A in order to take the property), the transfer is ineffective unless the requirements for a testamentary transfer were satisfied.

4) Independent agent-contract

When a contract for the sale of real property calls for the seller to give the deed to an independent third party (i.e., an escrow agent) and conditions the release of the deed to the buyer on the happening of an event, typically payment of the purchase price, the escrow agent is obligated to transfer the deed to the buyer if and when the condition occurs.

a) Retrieval by grantor

When there is a written contract, the grantor cannot require the escrow agent to return the deed prior to the failure of the condition to occur. When the contract is oral, the grantor can reclaim the deed from the escrow agent because the Statute of Frauds requires a writing for a land sale contract to be enforceable.

b) Escrow agent

When the escrow agent delivers the deed to the buyer prior to the performance of the condition, title to the property remains with the seller. This is true even when the buyer then transfers the property to a third party, even a person who purchases the property in good faith (i.e., a bona fide purchaser). An exception exists when the seller permits the buyer to possess the property.

c) Time of transfer

In general, title to the property remains in the seller until the condition is satisfied. Once the condition is satisfied, title automatically vests in the buyer. The date of transfer can relate back to the date that the grantor deposited the deed in escrow when, before the condition is satisfied, the grantor dies, becomes incapacitated or marries, or the grantee dies.

d. Acceptance

Acceptance is required for a transfer to be complete, and the grantee is generally presumed to have accepted any beneficial conveyance. Acceptance relates back to the time the deed was transferred, unless a bona fide purchaser or creditor of the grantor would be negatively affected by doing so.

If the grantee rejects the deed, no title passes and the grantor holds the title. But, if the grantee accepts the deed and then changes his mind even a moment later, an entirely new deed must be created in order for the grantee to convey the title back to the original grantor.

2. Valid Deed

Valid deeds abide by the Statute of Frauds and include all necessary terms, such as the grantor's signature, named grantee, words of transfer, and a description of the property. Unlike a contract, **consideration is not required**. Fraudulent documents are ineffective to convey title, even if they are relied upon by bona fide purchasers. Deeds executed through duress, mistake, undue influence, or by persons younger than the age of majority or otherwise incapacitated are deemed voidable.

a. Parties

The **grantor** and **grantee** must be identified. In addition, the grantor's signature is required, but in most states it need not be witnessed nor acknowledged (notarized). The grantee need not sign the deed.

A deed that does not identify the grantee is ineffective until the grantee's name is added or determined.

Example: A executed a deed conveying Blackacre "to my neighbors." Until the intended neighbors are determined by extrinsic evidence, the deed has no effect.

b. Words of transfer

The portion of a deed that contains the words that transfer an interest from the grantor to the grantee is called a granting clause ("do grant and convey"). Any language evidencing a present intent to transfer will suffice.

c. Description of property

The description of the property must be reasonably definite, but extrinsic evidence is admissible to clarify. A habendum clause (e.g., "to have and to hold") in a deed defines the interest conveyed. When there is an irreconcilable difference between the granting clause and the habendum clause, the granting clause prevails.

Descriptions by metes and bounds or by street address are acceptable but not required to sufficiently describe the property. When there is a conflict between descriptions of the property in the deed, descriptions based on monuments (e.g., from oak tree east to tool shed) are given priority over area descriptions (e.g., "100 acres").

3. Recording Act

A deed need not be recorded to be valid and convey good title. The common law rule was "first in time, first in right," meaning that a grantee could not lose title to a subsequent grantee.

All states have enacted recording acts, which establish priorities among conflicting claims to land and promote certainty of title. Nearly all types of property interests may be recorded, including easements, covenants, leases, and mortgages. Some state statutes also require that the grantor acknowledge the deed before a notary public, in an attempt to prevent fraudulent transfers.

a. Types of statutes

The three types of recording statutes are notice, race, and race-notice.

> **EXAM NOTE:** Notice and race-notice statutes are the most frequently tested types of recording statutes on the MBE.

1) Notice statute

A purchaser need only purchase without notice of the prior interest to prevail under a notice statute. (See *infra* for a discussion of what constitutes notice.) Notice statutes tend to protect subsequent purchasers against interest holders who could have, but failed to record documents describing their interests.

> **EXAM NOTE:** Notice statutes are commonly tested on the MBE, and usually contain words like "in good faith" or "without notice."

> **Example of notice statute:** "No conveyance or mortgage of real property shall be good against subsequent purchasers for value and *without notice* unless the same be recorded according to law."

> **EXAM NOTE:** Remember that a bona fide purchaser need not record in order to prevail over a prior interest in a notice jurisdiction, but must record to prevail against a subsequent purchaser.

2) Race statute

A minority of states have race statutes, when the purchaser who records first prevails, regardless of his knowledge of any prior conflicting interests.

> **Example of race statute:** "No conveyance or mortgage of real property shall be good against subsequent purchasers for value unless the same be *first recorded* according to law."

3) Race-notice statute

A race-notice statute requires a subsequent purchaser to take the interest without notice of a prior conflicting interest, **and** be the first to record.

> **EXAM NOTE:** Look for words in the statute like "in good faith" in conjunction with phrases like "first duly recorded," which are present in a race-notice statute.

> **Example of race-notice statute:** "No conveyance or mortgage of real property shall be good against subsequent purchasers for value and *without notice* who shall *first record.*"

b. Paid value

Only a grantee who pays value for an interest in real property is entitled to protection under the recording statutes.

> **EXAM NOTE:** Most questions have the grantee clearly paying value for the property, but the more likely to be tested situations are mortgages, judgment liens, and donees.

1) Mortgages

Mortgagees are considered to have "paid value" and are protected by the recording acts, unless the mortgage is not given simultaneously with a loan (such as when the mortgage is given after the loan is created).

2) Judgment liens

Creditors are protected only against claims that arise after a judgment lien against the debtor is recorded, unless otherwise indicated by statute. But, the majority of jurisdictions protect purchasers of property at a judicial sale against all unrecorded interests subject to the recording act.

> **EXAM NOTE:** As this topic is almost always tested on the MBE, review the following example thoroughly.

> **Example:** B purchases Blackacre from A (the record owner), but B does not record the deed. C, a creditor of A, not knowing of the deed to B, then records a judgment lien against Blackacre. A judicial sale of Blackacre is scheduled. A sells Blackacre to D, who promptly records the deed.
>
> In this example, C is protected against D's claim because D purchased after C recorded the judgment lien. In the majority of jurisdictions, C is not protected against B's unrecorded interest (which preceded the recording of C's lien), unless C purchases Blackacre at the judicial sale (in which case C takes A's original title).

3) Donees, heirs, and devisees

Grantees who acquire title of property by gift, intestacy, or devise are not protected by the recording act against prior claims, even those who fail to record their claims to the same property.

Example: A sells Blackacre to B, who forgets to record the deed. In the interim, A gives a deed to his daughter, C, who promptly records her deed. C will not defeat B's ownership because C did not pay value for the property.

4) Shelter rule

Grantors who are protected by the recording act protect (or, "shelter") their grantees who would otherwise be unprotected. The **exception** to the shelter rule is that a purchaser who is not a bona fide purchaser cannot convey to a bona fide purchaser and then buy the property back to obtain the status of a bona fide purchaser.

c. Notice

As discussed *supra*, only purchasers who give value in good faith and without notice of a prior claim will prevail in notice or race-notice jurisdictions. "Notice" can be actual, by inquiry, or constructive.

1) Actual notice

A grantee possessing actual, personal knowledge of a prior interest cannot prevail under a notice or race-notice recording statute.

2) Inquiry notice

If a reasonable investigation would have disclosed the existence of prior claims, the grantee is considered to possess inquiry notice, and cannot prevail against those prior claims. The purchaser is charged with whatever knowledge a reasonable inspection of the property would have disclosed. In most states, taking a quitclaim deed does not in itself create inquiry notice of prior claims.

> **EXAM NOTE:** Examples of situations that typically give rise to inquiry notice on the MBE are (i) when someone other than the grantor has possession of the property (e.g., a tenant), or (ii) when documents are referenced in the chain of title.

Example: A's deed to B references a restrictive covenant entered into by A and B at the time of the deed. The deed is recorded, but the covenant is not contained in the deed. Any purchaser in A's chain of title will be charged with knowledge of the covenant and its contents.

3) Constructive notice

Grantees are held to have constructive notice of all prior conveyances that were properly recorded.

a) Tract index

All properties in a tract index system are listed by location on a separate page that includes all conveyances and encumbrances.

b) Grantor-grantee indexes

Each yearly index is usually alphabetized by the last names of grantors and grantees.

When searching the chain of title, the potential purchaser must first search for the grantor's name as a grantee (to ensure good title) in the grantee index, then the name of the grantor's grantor must be searched as a grantee, and so on, until the title has been searched back to its inception (common law rule) or as far back as the recording statute provides. Some states have search cut-off dates. Then, the grantors are searched as grantors to verify the chain of title.

c) Related searches

Title searches also should include a search of tax assessment and judgment lien records, as well as the marriage, divorce, and probate records for every named grantor and grantee.

d. Priorities

Interests are placed in order of priority based on the relevant statute (notice, race, and race-notice). The protected interest that is first in time is satisfied first, followed by the junior interests in order of time.

e. Rule application

Example 1: First, O conveys Blackacre to A, but A does not record. Second, O then conveys Blackacre to B, who has no notice of the earlier conveyance to A. Next, A records. Then, B records. B sues A to quiet title in Blackacre. What is the result?

i) Under a race statute, the first in time to record prevails. In the situation above, A wins because A was the first to record.

ii) Under a notice statute, regardless of who records first, those who in good faith purchase without notice prevail. So, in the above scenario, B wins because B took without notice.

iii) In a race-notice jurisdiction, B is unable to prove that he had both no notice **and** recorded first. Because A recorded first, A wins.

Example 2: First, O conveys an easement in Blackacre to A, but A does not record. Second, O then conveys Blackacre in fee simple absolute to B, who knows of the earlier conveyance to A. Next, B records. Then, A records. B sues A for title to Blackacre. What is the result?

i) Under a race statute, B wins and the easement is extinguished because B recorded first.

ii) Under a notice statute, A wins because B had notice of A's rights at the time of purchase.

iii) In a race-notice jurisdiction, A prevails and can enforce the easement against B because B is unable to show that he both recorded first **and** purchased without notice of A's prior claim.

Example 3: First, O promises A in writing that O will use Blackacre only for residential purposes, and the parties intend that this burden will run with the land. A does not record the promise. O then conveys Blackacre in fee simple absolute to B, who has no notice of O's earlier promise to A. Next, B records. Then, A records the promise. B then conveys a fee simple absolute estate in Blackacre to C, who has actual knowledge of O's promise to A. C uses Blackacre for non-residential purposes. A sues C to enforce O's promise to A, seeking damages and an injunction. What is the result?

    i) Under a race statute, C wins, even though C records after A. In this situations, A's recording is outside C's chain of title, so does not constitute "winning the race" for the purposes of a race statute. Also, because B's interest in Blackacre "wins" over A's, and C relies on B's title, C wins.

    ii) Under a notice statute, C wins even though C had notice. The shelter doctrine shelters C by making B's title marketable, because B was a good faith purchaser. Therefore, B passes his title to C, and C takes B's status as a good faith purchaser.

    iii) In a race-notice jurisdiction, C wins because the shelter doctrine applies.

f. Chain of title problems

1) Wild deed

Although an instrument is recorded and indexed in the recording office, it may not be recorded in such a way as to give notice to subsequent purchasers (i.e., the deed may not be in the "chain of title"). A deed not within the chain of title is a "wild deed."

Example 1: First, O conveys Blackacre to A, but A does not record. Second, A conveys Blackacre to B, and B records. O then conveys Blackacre to C, who has no notice of the earlier conveyances to A or B. Next, C records. Then, A records deed from O to A. B sues A for title to Blackacre. What is the result?

    i) Under a race statute, C prevails even though B recorded the deed from A to B before C recorded the deed from O to C, because the deed from A to B was a "wild deed," outside C's chain of title. In performing a standard title search, C would have searched in the grantor index for deeds listing O as grantor from the date the deed granting Blackacre to O was executed to the date C recorded the deed from O to C. No deed from O to A would have been discovered in such a search, and without finding a deed from O to A, B would not be expected to look for a deed from A to B.

    ii) Under a notice statute, C prevails because he had no actual notice of the conveyances from O to A and from A to B, and the deed from A to B did not give him constructive notice because it was a wild deed.

    iii) In a race-notice jurisdiction, C prevails for a combination of the two reasons above: C had no actual or constructive notice of O's deed to A, and B's prior recording of the deed from A to B does not count because it is a wild deed.

2) Deed recorded late

> **Example 2:** O conveys Blackacre to A, but A does not record. Next, O conveys Blackacre to B, who has actual notice of the conveyance from O to A, and B records. Then, A records. Next, B conveys to C, who has no actual notice of the O-to-A conveyance. C sues A for title to Blackacre. What is the result?

i) Under a race statute, C prevails even though A recorded the deed, because A's deed was recorded outside C's chain of title. Remember that under the standard title search, C would only research the grantor index under O's name until the date that B recorded the deed from O to B. Because O's deed to A was filed after that date, it is not considered "duly recorded" for the purposes of a race statute.

ii) Under a notice statute, C wins because C had no notice and because A's deed was recorded outside C's chain of title.

iii) In a race-notice jurisdiction, C wins because both race and notice requirements are met.

3) Deed recorded early (estoppel by deed)

Under the "estoppel by deed" doctrine, a grantor who conveys an interest to land by warranty deed before actually owning it is estopped from later denying the effectiveness of her deed. Consequently, when the grantor does acquire ownership of the land, the after-acquired title is transferred automatically to the prior grantee.

However, under the majority rule, a subsequent purchaser from the same grantor who takes without notice can obtain good title, despite the doctrine of estoppel by deed, in a notice or race-notice jurisdiction. The purchaser is generally required to search the grantee index for a grantor's name only as far back as the date on which the grantor's name appears as a grantee (i.e., the date on which the grantor acquired the property). That date is the earliest date that a grantor's name must be searched on the grantor index for a conveyance by the grantor. The recording of a transfer made by the grantor before that date is not treated as giving the purchaser constructive notice of the transfer.

4) Title insurance

Title insurance protects owners or lenders against the actual monetary loss due to such matters as title defects and lien problems. Title defects are most often created as the result of errors in the title examining process, as well as title recording errors. Forged instruments and undelivered deeds also create title defects because they do not transfer title and are void.

Lien problems result from the invalidity or unenforceability of mortgage liens. Additionally, tax liens and judgments create defects that do not allow for the proper transference of title.

4. Types of Deeds

a. General warranty deed

The grantor of a general warranty deed guarantees that he holds six covenants of title, which are discussed below.

1) Present covenants

Present covenants embodied in the general warranty deed are the covenant of seisin, right to convey, and the covenant against encumbrances.

The covenant of seisin warrants that the grantor owns the land as it is described in the deed. The covenant of the right to convey guarantees that grantor has the right to transfer title. The covenant against encumbrances guarantees that the deed contains no undisclosed encumbrances.

2) Future covenants

Future covenants run with the land, and the statute of limitations does not begin to run until the grantee's rights are encroached. The grantor of a general warranty deed promises to protect the grantee against subsequent lawful claims of title or encroachment (covenant of quiet enjoyment and covenant of warranty).

In some jurisdictions, the grantor also promises to do whatever is necessary to pass title to the grantee if it is later determined that the grantor omitted something required to pass valid title (future covenant of further assurances).

3) Breach of covenant

a) Time of breach

Breach of the present covenants occurs at the time of conveyance. A breach of the covenant of seisin and right to convey arises when the grantor is not the owner. A property that is encumbered at the time of conveyance creates a breach of the covenant against encumbrances. In most states, these present covenants do not run with the land. Consequently, a subsequent grantee cannot sue to enforce them against the original grantor. However, some states allow a remote grantee to sue the original grantor for breach of the covenant against encumbrances. *See* Uniform Land Transactions § 2-312.

Conversely, a breach of future covenants occurs only upon interference with possession and runs to successive grantees. The party seeking liability must provide the covenantor with notice of the claim.

b) Recovery

A buyer can recover for breach of the covenant against encumbrances the lesser of the difference in value between title with and without the defect, or the cost of removing the encumbrance.

Recovery for the covenants of enjoyment or warranty is the lesser of the purchase price or the cost of defending title.

Recovery for the covenants of seisin, right to convey, or further assurances is the lesser of the purchase price or the cost of perfecting title.

c) After-acquired title

When a person who purports to transfer real property that he does not own subsequently becomes owner of that property, the after-acquired title doctrine provides that title to the property automatically vests in the transferee. Most often this doctrine is applied to the grantor of a warranty deed. A related doctrine, estoppel by deed, prevents the grantor from asserting ownership of the after-acquired property. For the interplay of estoppel by deed and the recording acts, *see* § III.C.3.e.3) Deed recorded early (estoppel by deed), *supra*.

b. Special warranty deed

A special warranty deed contains the same covenants of title, but only warrants against defects arising during the time the grantor has title.

c. Quitclaim deed

Unlike a warranty deed, a quitclaim deed promises **no covenants of title.**

A common form of quitclaim deed is the tax deed, which is used by government authorities when selling properties seized for nonpayment of taxes.

The grantee in a quitclaim deed (or a grant deed or warranty deed) receives no better title than what the grantor possessed.

D. FIXTURES

A fixture is tangible personal property (i.e., chattel) that is attached to real property in a manner that it is treated as part of the real property when determining its ownership.

1. Structures and Items Incorporated into Structures

Structures built on real property (e.g., wall, dam) and materials incorporated into a structure (e.g., bricks used in making a wall) become part of the realty. The owner of the real property is generally also the owner of the structure on the real property (e.g., an improvement), including any materials used in the constructing the structure. Once incorporated into the structure, such materials become an integral part of the real property and are not subject to a separate security interest. UCC § 9-334(a).

2. Attachment of Chattel

The fee simple owner of real property is free, subject to governmental land use restrictions, to make improvements to the real property, including fixtures. For the holder of a life estate or a tenant, the right to make improvements to real property (ameliorative waste) is somewhat circumscribed. *See* § I.A.4.d.3 Ameliorative waste, *supra*, regarding life estate holders, and § II.B.2. Waste, *supra*, regarding tenants.

3. Removal of Chattel

a. Fee simple owner of real property

A fee simple owner of real property typically intends for the chattel become a fixture by attaching chattel to real property. Such intent is judged by applying an objective, reasonable person standard that examines such factors as the importance of the chattel to the real property, whether the chattel was specially designed for use on the real property, and the amount of damage to the real property that removal of the chattel would cause.

When the chattel is a fixture, the buyer of the real property is generally entitled to the chattel unless the seller reserves the right to remove the fixture in the contract of sale. Similarly, the mortgagee is entitled to the chattel upon foreclosure of the mortgage unless mortgage provides otherwise.

b. Other possessors of real property

Absent an agreement to the contrary, a non-freehold tenant, such as a tenant under a tenancy for years or a periodic tenancy, can remove a fixture that the tenant has attached to the leased property if (i) the leased property can be and is restored to its former condition after the removal, and (ii) the removal and restoration is made within a reasonable time. If the leased premises cannot be restored to its former condition, the tenant can remove the fixture only with the consent of the landlord. This rule applies to commercial tenants and the removal of trade fixtures, as well as to residential tenants and the removal of personal items, such as bookshelves attached to the wall. Restatement (Second) of Property (Landlord and Tenant) § 12.2(4), (5).

A licensee and life tenant are generally also subject to this rule.

A reasonable time for removal generally does not extend beyond the termination of the lease, but may do so when (i) the termination is not due to a breach by the tenant, and (ii) the date of termination is not foreseeable by the tenant sufficiently far enough in advance to permit removal before the termination of the lease or unless equitable factors (such as illness of the tenant) justify an extension. Restatement (Second) of Property (Landlord and Tenant) § 12.3.

c. Trespassers

Under common law, a trespasser (such as a holder tenant) is prohibited from removing a fixture attached to the land. Many jurisdictions now allow a trespasser to remove a fixture that was attached in good faith or at least to recover the value added to the property by the improvement.

d. Mortgagee v. secured party

When there is a conflict between the mortgagee of real property and the holder of a security interest in a fixture attached to the real property, the general rule is that the first to record has priority. An exception exists when the security interest is a purchase money security interest (i.e., a security interest given in connection with the acquisition of the goods). In such cases, the secured party who records her security interest before or **within 20 days** after the goods become a fixture has priority over a prior recorded mortgage. UCC § 9-334.

e. Sale of fixtures by property owner

A contract for the sale of a structure or its materials is a contract for the sale of goods governed by the U.C.C. when the structure or material is to be severed by the seller. A contract for the sale of other things that are attached to real property and are capable of severance without material harm to the real property is a contract for the sale of goods regardless of whether the seller or buyer effects the severance. UCC § 2-107(1),(2).

E. CONVEYANCE BY WILL AND BY OPERATION OF LAW

Real property can be conveyed by will and by statutes that govern intestate succession for property that does not pass by will.

1. In General

A transfer ownership of real property at death through a will can take effect through a specific devise (e.g., "I leave my residence to my son") or residuary clause (e.g., "I leave all other property to my daughter") when the property is not specifically mentioned in the will. When a decedent does not leave a valid will or the will does not specify a taker of the real property, the property is transferred pursuant to the applicable state law of intestate succession. While the intestacy rules vary by state, preference is typically given to the decedent's immediate family (e.g., spouse, children). When a decedent has no heir, as determined under state law, the property typically escheats to the state.

2. Ademption

A devise of real property may fail (or be "adeemed") because the testator no longer owns the property upon death (i.e., because the property was sold, destroyed or given away before death). If the testator gives the property to the intended beneficiary while the testator is still alive, the devise is adeemed by satisfaction. Once a devise is adeemed, the beneficiary named in the will takes nothing.

> **EXAM NOTE:** Remember that ademption can occur only with a specific devise, such as real property, and not a general devise, such as money.

> **Example:** A executes a will under which Blackacre is devised to B, but then sells Blackacre to C. When A dies, the gift is adeemed and B takes nothing.

3. Lapse

Under common law, a devise of real property can also fail (lapse) if the beneficiary under a will dies before the testator and no alternate beneficiary is named. When the testator indicates a clear intent that the devise survive the death of the beneficiary, the devise will not fail. In addition, all jurisdictions have anti-lapse statutes, which prevent gifts from lapsing if the gift is made to the parties specified by the statute (usually immediate relatives of the testator). A lapsed gift becomes part of the residuary estate.

> **Example:** By will, A devises her car to B, Blackacre to C, and the remainder of her property (the residuary estate) to D. A does not name any alternate beneficiaries. If C dies before A and the devise does not qualify for protection under the anti-lapse statute, Blackacre becomes part of the residuary estate and passes to D, along with

When a devise is made to a class (e.g., "my children") and one member of the class dies before the testator, only the surviving class members take the property. However, if an anti-lapse statute applies because the class members were related to the testator, the descendants of the predeceased class member also share in the devise. Most states apply the anti-lapse rule first before applying the class gift rule.

4. Exoneration of Liens

Under the exoneration of liens doctrine, if a testator makes a specific devise of real property that is subject to an encumbrance, such as a mortgage or a lien, the devisee is entitled to have the land "exonerated" by payment of the encumbrance from the remaining assets in the testator's estate. Although this is the majority view, many states have abolished this doctrine. In such states, the property passes subject to the encumbrance unless the will specifically requires payment of the encumbrance.

5. Abatement

A devise is reduced or abated when the assets of the estate are insufficient to pay all debts and satisfy all devises. If the testator does not choose to indicate her intended order of abatement, gifts are sacrificed to satisfy funeral expenses, expenses of administration, and creditor's claims in the following order:

i) Property not disposed of by will,

ii) Residuary devises,

iii) General devises,

iv) Specific devises.

Some states further breakdown abatement to favor various devisees, such as the testator's relatives or surviving spouse, or a type of property (e.g., real property, cash), within a particular class (e.g., specific devises).

a. Specific

A specific devise is a devise of property that can be distinguished with reasonable accuracy from other property that is part of the testator's estate (e.g., a car, a house).

Example: "I give my diamond wedding ring to A"

b. General

A general devise is a devise of personal property that the testator intends to be satisfied from the general assets of his estate.

Example: "I give $100,000 to A"

c. Demonstrative

A demonstrative devise is a general devise that is to be paid from a particular source.

A demonstrative devise is treated as a specific devise for abatement purposes to the extent that it can be satisfied from the specified source, and otherwise as a general devise.

d. Residuary

A residual devise is a devise of the estate remaining after all claims against the estate and all specific, general, and demonstrative devises have been satisfied.

e. Pro rata abatement

Within each class, the amount abated is allocated in a pro rata basis among the devisees in proportion to the amount of property each would have received if a full distribution had been made.

F. CONVEYANCE BY TRUST

A trust is essentially a situation in which property is managed by one person or entity for the benefit of another.

1. Private Trusts

The trust must have:

i) A **settlor**, the person who creates the trust;

ii) A **trustee**, the person or entity who holds legal title to the property;

iii) **Res**, the property that is subject to the trust; and

iv) **Beneficiaries**, those *identifiable* persons for whose benefit the trust is created and who hold equitable title to the property.

An inter vivos trust is created when the settlor conveys his property (res) to the trustee while the settlor is alive. Alternatively, the settlor may simply declare that he is holding certain property in trust for certain beneficiaries, without there being an actual conveyance of the property. Remember that any conveyance of real property must satisfy the Statute of Frauds.

Another form of conveyance occurs when the settlor creates a trust by language in his will and transfers the property by devise in his will. This type of trust is called a testamentary trust and comes into being only on the death of the settlor. Finally, the settlor may choose to create an inter vivos trust, but not fund the trust until his death by devise in his will. In this case, property "pours over" into the trust.

2. Charitable Trusts

A differentiating factor between a private trust and charitable trust is the beneficiaries. As noted above, a private trust must have identifiable beneficiaries; whereas in a charitable trust, the beneficiaries must be reasonably numerous and unidentifiable. Another important distinction is that the Rule Against Perpetuities does not apply to trusts that are entirely charitable. Moreover, if a charitable trust no longer serves the purpose for which it was created, the court may redirect the trust to a different purpose. This is called the doctrine of cy pres. The attorney general of the state also has the power to enforce a charitable trust, but not a private trust.

G. RESTRAINTS ON ALIENATION

1. Restraints on Legal Interests

Generally, a restraint on the right of alienation is void when it purports to prohibit alienation of the estate and render any conveyance by the grantee void. If the restraint is valid, any attempt to alienate the property in violation of the restraint is null and void. If void, the restraint is rejected and the property could be alienated in violation of the void restraint. Restatement (Second) of Property § 4.1.

Sometimes restraints only restrict the power to transfer the interest under certain specific circumstances. In such cases, the restraint may be valid if it is for a limited time and for a reasonable purpose. However, any restraint based on a person's race, ethnicity, or religion is not enforceable. Further, such discriminatory restraints are considered state action and forbidden by the Fourteenth Amendment. In addition, the federal Fair Housing Act prohibits housing discrimination on the basis of race, color, religion, gender, disability, familial status, and national origin. Among the prohibited activities are refusing to rent or sell housing or setting different terms or conditions for the sale or rental of a dwelling on a prohibited basis. There are various exceptions, including an exemption for a residential sale by an owner and a lease of an owner occupied dwelling with four or fewer units.

a. Forms of restraint

1) Disabling restraint

A disabling restraint is a prohibition on the transfer of the property interest by its owner. Such a restraint is always void.

2) Forfeiture restraint

A forfeiture restraint effects the loss of property (i.e., the property is forfeited) if the interest owner attempts to transfer his interest. Such a restraint on a future interest or a life estate can be valid.

3) Promissory restraint

A promissory restraint is a promise by the property interest holder not to transfer the property interest. Such a restraint is enforceable by an injunction against the transferor/promisor to prevent the transfer or by a suit seeking damages from the transferor/promisor for having violated the promise. Such a restraint on a life estate can be valid.

b. Permissible restraints

A restraint that is limited in time and purpose may be valid. In addition, a right of first refusal, which gives the holder of the right the opportunity to purchase the property interest if sold, is usually upheld, as are restrictions on the transfer of a lease (e.g., a prohibition on assignment). Other permissible restraints are those found in commercial transactions when the basis for the restraint is found in the parties' contractual obligations.

Compare restraints on use: Unlike restraints on the transfer of legal property interests, restraints on the *use* of property (e.g., covenants) are generally permissible.

2. Restraints on Equitable Interests

A restriction on the transferability of an equitable property interest (e.g., a beneficial property interest held in trust), such as a spendthrift clause, is valid.

IV. DISPUTES ABOUT THE USE OF LAND

The most commonly tested disputes about the use of land revolve around use of another's land (by easement, profit, or license) or restriction of use of one's own land (by covenants running with the land or equitable servitude). Other disputes concern who has the right to own or possess land; ownership is decided by a quiet-title action, while possession (often between a landlord and tenant) is decided by an action for ejectment.

A. EASEMENTS

An easement is the right held by one person to make specific, limited use of land owned by another. The land that is subject to the easement is the servient estate, whereas the land that benefits from an easement on a servient estate is the dominant estate.

> **EXAM NOTE:** When a fact pattern involves the use of another's land, consider three questions:
>
> 1. Was an easement created?
>
> 2. If so, was the easement terminated?
>
> 3. What is the scope of the easement?

1. Classification of Easements

a. Easements by grant and reservation

An affirmative easement gives another the right to use the land for a specific purpose.

An easement by reservation is created when a grantor conveys land but reserves an easement right in that land for his own use and benefit (and not for a third party).

b. Easements appurtenant and profit in gross

Easements are presumed to be appurtenant (i.e., tied to the land) unless there are clear facts to the contrary. The benefits of an easement must correspond directly to the use and enjoyment of the possessor of the dominant estate.

An easement is in gross if it was granted to benefit a particular person (as opposed to the land).

> **Example:** A owns lakefront property and grants B, who lives in a town across the lake, an easement to gain access to the lake at a certain point on A's property. A created an easement in gross because it benefits B, not any land owned by B.

2. Types of Easements

a. Express easements

An express easement arises when it is affirmatively created by the parties in a writing that is in compliance with the Statute of Frauds.

b. Easements by necessity and implication

1) Easement by necessity

An easement by necessity is generally created only when property is virtually useless (e.g., landlocked) without the benefit of an easement across neighboring property. In addition, in order for an easement for necessity to be created, both the dominant and servient estates must have been under common ownership in the past. Also, the necessity must have arisen at the time that the property was severed and the two estates were created. However, unlike an easement by implication, a quasi-easement need not have existed that the time that both estates were under common ownership (i.e., there need not be a showing of prior use). Restatement Third of Property: Servitudes 2.15.

> **Example:** B owns an undeveloped parcel of land, which B subdivides into two lots. B sells one of the lots to A and retains the other lot for himself. The only access to a public road from the lot purchased by A is through the lot retained by B. Even though the deed makes no mention of an easement across B's lot and there has not been a prior path from A's lot across B's lot to the public road, A has an easement by necessity across B's lot to the road.

> **EXAM NOTE:** On the exam, if it is not absolutely clear that an easement is required for use, it is not an easement by necessity.

2) Easement by implication

If an easement was previously used on the servient estate by an earlier owner, the court may find the parties intended the easement to continue if the prior use was continuous, apparent (open and obvious), and reasonably necessary to the dominant land's use and enjoyment (distinguish from easement by necessity, which requires strict necessity).

Because an owner cannot have an easement on his own land, this is considered a "quasi" easement. The scope of a quasi easement is determined by the prior use that gave rise to the easement, but can change over time if the changes are reasonably foreseeable at the time of conveyance.

Easements may also be implied without an existing use in a conveyance of lots sold in a subdivision with reference to a recorded plat or map that details streets leading to lots. An easement may be implied from a subdivision map or plat, may be created through eminent domain, and may arise by actual or implied dedication. Individuals who buy lots have an implied easement to be able to get to their lots that does not expire even if a public easement held by the city or county is vacated in the future.

c. Easements by prescription

Easements can be obtained by prescription similarly to the way land can be acquired by adverse possession. There must be continuous, actual, open, and hostile use for the statutory period (or 20 years). Unlike adverse possession, the use need not be exclusive (such as a public easement to access a beach).

The scope of an easement by prescription is limited to the nature and extent of the adverse use.

d. Easements by estoppel

Good faith, reasonable, detrimental reliance on permission by a servient estate holder, may create an easement by estoppel to prevent unjust enrichment.

Example: A allows B to use a road on A's land to gain access to B's land, and B builds his house with the road being its main access point, improving the road with pavement and foliage. Thereafter, A tells B he can only use the road if B pays $500; A closes off the road when B refuses. B likely has an easement by estoppel, because he relied on the ability to use the road when he built his house, and unjust enrichment may otherwise result.

Distinguish this example from easement by prescription, which requires that the use be hostile (i.e., no permission was given). To prove an easement by estoppel, there must be permission to use the property, plus detrimental reliance on that permission (as in the example above).

e. Negative easements

A negative easement prevents the owner from using land in particular ways. To be valid, a negative easement must be expressly created by a writing signed by the grantor, and is typically only recognized in relation to restricting use of light, air, support, or stream water from an artificial flow.

Example: A conveys a lot adjacent to his own to B, with an agreement that no structure will be built that would obstruct the light and air of A's land. This is a negative easement of light and air, because it deprives B from enjoying the property to the fullest extent. Negative easements are really restrictive covenants (see full discussion, *infra*).

3. Transfer

a. Easement appurtenant

An easement appurtenant is transferred with the land to which it relates. Consequently, the benefit is transferred automatically with the transfer of the dominant estate, and the burden likewise is transferred automatically with the transfer of the servient estate.

b. Easement in gross

Traditionally, an easement in gross could not be transferred, but most courts now look to the intent of the parties to determine whether the parties intended only the holder of the easement in gross to enjoy the right, in which case it is not transferable, or whether the parties intended the holder to be able to transfer it.

Whether a transferable easement in gross can be apportioned turns on whether the easement in gross is exclusive or non-exclusive. A non-exclusive easement cannot be divided up, but an exclusive easement may be. However, the division of an exclusive easement in gross is subject to the one stock rule. Under this rule, the use that the transferees make of the easement collectively is limited by the use that the transferor made of the easement (i.e., his "stock").

4. Termination

a. Release

An easement can terminate by a writing that expressly releases the easement right and complies with the Statute of Frauds.

b. Merger

An easement is terminated if the owner of the easement acquires fee title to the underlying estate (and the easement is said to "merge" into the title). Under such circumstances, the easement will not be automatically revived unless a new grant is made.

Note that the easement does not merge if the owner acquires less than fee title, and is applicable only to easements appurtenant.

c. Severance

Any attempt to convey an appurtenant easement separate from the land it benefits terminates (or "severs") the easement.

d. Abandonment

An easement can be terminated if the owner of the easement acts in an affirmative way that shows a clear intent to relinquish the easement right.

Mere statements of intent without affirmative conduct are insufficient to constitute abandonment, but may constitute estoppel (*infra*). Mere non-use of the easement is also not sufficient to extinguish the easement right.

Example: B is the owner of an easement across A's land for access to a beach. B does not like the beach, and builds a brick wall across his land, blocking the entranceway to the easement. B's easement is terminated by abandonment.

e. Destruction and condemnation

Destruction of a structure on the servient estate by natural forces can terminate an easement if the easement is related to the structure (e.g., access to a lighthouse). Condemnation of the servient estate also terminates an easement. Note that some courts permit the holder of the easement to receive compensation due to the condemnation.

f. Prescription

If an easement holder fails to protect his easement against a trespasser for the statutory period, his easement right may be terminated by prescription.

g. Estoppel

If the servient estate owner changes position to his detriment in reliance on statements or conduct of the easement holder that the easement is abandoned, the easement holder may be estopped from asserting the easement.

h. Sale to bona fide purchaser

If a **written easement** is granted but not recorded against the servient estate, the easement is not enforceable against a bona fide purchaser (i.e., a purchase with no notice of the easement). The easement is not actually terminated, but rather becomes unenforceable.

5. Scope of Easement

a. Express easements

The scope of an express easement is defined in the first instance by its terms. If the terms are ambiguous, courts look to the intent of the original parties, which may be indicated by the easement's original purpose.

When the language of an express easement is ambiguous, changes in the use of an easement are tested under a reasonableness standard, with the understanding that the original parties most likely contemplated not only its present use but its future use as well.

b. Implied easements

The scope of an easement by necessity or implication is determined by the extent of the necessity. In other words, courts examine the circumstances surrounding the easement and will consider the easement's future foreseeable use, so long as any changes in use are reasonable. The scope of an easement by prescription is limited to the nature and extent of the adverse use.

6. Profits

A profit is an easement that confers the right to enter another's land and remove specific natural resources (such as oil, gas, minerals, timber, or game).

Although a profit can be either exclusive or non-exclusive, most are construed as non-exclusive. If it is exclusive, the holder of the profit has an unlimited and exclusive right to take the subject matter of the profit from the land. If it is non-exclusive, the right to take the profit is either limited by quantity, time, or use or shared with another. Exclusive rights may be assigned and apportioned, as long as the apportionment is not wholly inconsistent with the original agreement.

Non-exclusive rights are assignable, but apportionment is not permitted when the burden on the servient estate is increased. Under the "one stock" rule, the transferees are limited to the amount of material taken by the transferor (i.e., his "stock") and this quantity is divided up by transferees taking the profit.

Profits are created and analyzed similarly to easements, except that profits cannot be created by necessity.

7. Licenses

As with an easement, a license is a non-possessory right to enter another's land for some delineated purpose. Unlike an easement, a license is freely revocable unless coupled with an interest or detrimentally relied on (e.g., if money is spent in furtherance of the license). Examples of licenses are tickets to amusement parks, theaters, or other public venues. A license coupled with an interest occurs when, for example, a grantor creates a life estate for A with the remainder to B. During A's life tenancy, B has an irrevocable license to enter the land and inspect for waste, due to his future interest in the land.

A license may be created without consideration or a writing. Because no writing is required, a license is created where there is an oral attempt to create an easement or written attempt otherwise fails due to Statute of Frauds.

In addition to a specific revocation by the licensor, a license is revoked when the licensor dies or the servient estate is transferred. Traditionally, a license could not be transferred by the licensee and the attempt to do so resulted in the loss of the license.

8. Duty to Maintain

The owner of the easement has the right and the duty to maintain the easement for its purpose unless otherwise agreed between the owner of the easement and the owner of the servient land. The duty to contribute, however, is dependent upon the reasonableness of the repair. Specifically, the repairing party must give the contributing parties adequate notification and a reasonable opportunity to participate in decisions regarding the repairs. Moreover, the repairs must be performed adequately, properly, and at a reasonable price. *See* Restatement (Third) of Property § 4.13 (2000).

B. COVENANTS RUNNING WITH THE LAND

Unlike easements, profits, and licenses, which grant affirmative rights to use land, covenants and equitable servitudes restrict the right to use land. The requirements discussed below are necessary for both the benefit and the burden to run with the land, unless otherwise indicated.

1. Requirements to Run

Covenants run with the land (subsequent owners may enforce or be burdened by the covenant).

> **EXAM NOTE:** The requirements for a covenant to run with the land have been tested on nearly every MBE.

a. Writing

In order for a covenant to be enforceable it must first comply with the Statute of Frauds. The only exception is an implied reciprocal servitude, which does not require a writing.

b. Intent

The parties must intend for the rights and duties to run with the land. Look for either explicit language like "and his heirs and assigns," or implication from the totality of the document and circumstances.

c. Touch and concern

The covenant must touch and concern the land, which means that the benefit or burden must affect both the promisee and the promissor as owners of land, and not merely as individuals.

An affirmative covenant touches and concerns the servient estate. The servient estate holder makes a promise that reduces her use and enjoyment of the property (such as a promise to pay for improvements or to pay the real estate taxed assessed against the servient estate).

d. Notice—burden only

Under the recording acts, a subsequent purchaser without notice of a burdening covenant is not bound by it in equity. In other words, notice must be constructive (recorded in the chain of title) or actual (told that the covenant exists).

e. Privity

1) Horizontal privity – burden only

The parties must have privity of estate at the time the covenant is imposed (i.e., the estate and covenant are contained in the same instrument, such as in a deed or a lease) for the burden to run. But, horizontal privity is not required for the benefit to run.

2) Vertical privity

The successor to property can be held to the covenant (i.e., the burden runs) only if title to the entire servient estate can be traced back to the promisor. The successor to the property can enforce the covenant (i.e., the benefit runs) as long as the property interest possessed by the successor is at least some portion of the property interest held by the promissee. Consequently, the holder of a life estate cannot enforce a covenant granted to the holder of a fee simple interest in the same property.

3) No privity required

The Restatement of Property relies less on privity to determine running of the benefit and the burden than on a distinction between affirmative and negative covenants. The benefits and burdens of an affirmative covenant run to the successor of an estate of the same duration as the estate of the original party. Negative covenants, on the other hand, are analyzed similarly to easements.

f. Specific examples

There are certain burdens that come with their own specific problems. First, **money** that is used in connection with the land, such as association fees, as a general rule will run with the land. With **covenants not to compete**, although the burden of restricting land use touches and concerns the land, some courts have refused to permit the benefit to run with the land because the covenant does not affect the land's physical use. Finally, a **racially-based covenant** that disallows an owner from transferring his property to another because of the person's race is never enforceable because to do so would violate the Fourteenth Amendment.

2. Equitable Servitudes

a. Requirements

For a servitude to be enforced at equity, there are the following requirements:

i) There must be an **intent** for the restriction to be enforceable by successors-in-interest for the benefit to run and enforceable against successors-in-interest for the burden to run;

ii) The person against whom the servitude is to be enforced must have notice (whether **actual, record, or inquiry notice**) of the servitude; and

iii) The servitude must **touch and concern** the land.

There is no privity requirement.

> **EXAM NOTE:** Some aspect of equitable servitudes is almost always tested on the MBE.

b. Implied reciprocal servitudes

Most jurisdictions impose the following requirements to enforce an implied reciprocal servitude: (i) an intent to create a servitude on all plots (i.e., the promise must be reciprocal), (ii) the servitude must be negative (i.e., a promise to refrain from doing something), and (iii) actual, record, or inquiry notice by the party against whom enforcement of the servitude is sought. In order to establish intent, a common scheme must be established.

> **EXAM NOTE:** Equitable servitudes in subdivisions (also called "mutual rights of enforcement" and "reciprocal negative servitudes"), are typically tested in a situation involving an owner subdividing a large tract of land into smaller lots to create a common scheme of development by:
>
> i) **Recording a map** showing the scheme;
>
> ii) **Telling purchasers** of the lots about the plan; or
>
> iii) Including a **common building restriction** in most of the lot deeds.

Note that when an equitable remedy, such as an injunction, is sought, the promise enforced need only constitute an equitable servitude; where money damages are sought, the promise enforced must meet the requirements of a real covenant.

3. Termination of Covenants

Like easements, covenants, equitable servitudes, and implied reciprocal servitudes terminate upon written release, merger of title, abandonment, estoppel, condemnation, or sale to a bona fide purchaser.

4. Changed Circumstances

EXAM NOTE: Typical equitable defenses are applicable to actions for equitable servitudes or implied reciprocal servitudes (such as laches or unclean hands), but **"changed circumstances"** is the most commonly tested.

If a restriction on a property no longer makes sense to enforce due to drastic changes in the surrounding area since the restriction was first contemplated, the restriction will not be enforced. A good indication that the neighborhood has changed is a variance in zoning ordinances.

Example: A small subdivision restricts lots to residential use. Forty years later, the subdivision is next to a major thoroughfare and the land in the surrounding area is largely commercial and industrial. The restriction for residential use will likely be unenforceable on the theory that its value was lost with the drastic change of the neighborhood.

C. WATER RIGHTS

1. Theories

a. Riparian rights

The riparian doctrine states that water belongs to those who own the land bordering the water course (known as riparians). Riparians share the right of reasonable use of the water. One riparian is liable to another for unreasonable interference with the other's use. Domestic use trumps commercial use and can be unlimited.

b. Prior appropriation

Most western states have adopted the doctrine of prior appropriation, which states that the water belongs initially to the state, but the right to divert and use it can be acquired by an individual, regardless of location. Rights are determined by priority of beneficial use. The norm for allocation is first in time, first in right. Any productive or beneficial use of the water, including use for agriculture, is sufficient to create appropriation rights.

2. Waterways

Rights in navigable waters are limited by the government's right to protect the use of the waterway for transportation. Rights to non-navigable waters vary in their treatment depending on the theory in which the jurisdiction subscribes. Most jurisdictions, including those that have adopted the doctrine of reasonable use, treat non-navigable water (including all underground water) in the same manner as surface water rights. Some jurisdictions that have adopted an appropriation system have also applied it to non-navigable waters, including underground ponds and lakes. At least one jurisdiction has adopted a correlative rights standard, which gives a landowner a proprietary right to the portion of water which correlates to his proportion of land over the underground waterway.

3. Groundwater

The majority view allows the surface owner to make "reasonable use" of the groundwater. Contrast this with the doctrine of absolute ownership followed by some eastern states, which allows the surface owner total and complete discretion over water extraction and use. The western states, on the other hand, tend to follow the prior appropriation doctrine.

4. Surface Water

Surface water (traditionally called "diffused surface water") is, as the name implies, water that lies on the surface of the land, but that is not part of a lake or waterway. Usually, the water derives from rain or melted snow. In about half of the states, the landowner may make changes or improvements to his land to combat the flow of surface water ("common enemy doctrine"). Some jurisdictions limit this right to prohibit unnecessary harm to another's land. On the other hand, about half of the states prevent the landowner from altering the rate or natural flow of water ("natural flow theory"). However, most of those states have mitigated the rule to permit **reasonable** changes in water flow. This is a growing trend and requires balancing the harm against the utility.

5. Support Rights

A landowner has the right to have the land supported in its natural state.

a. Lateral support

A landowner is strictly liable for damages to adjoining land caused by the landowner's excavation of his land, unless the adjoining land was improved in a way that contributed to the damage.

In other words, when adjoining land is in its natural state (i.e., undeveloped), a landowner who excavates on his own land is strictly liable for any damage to the adjoining land caused by the excavation. If the adjoining land has been improved (i.e., is not in its natural state), the excavating landowner is strictly liable for any damage caused by the excavation only if the land **would have collapsed in its natural state** (regardless of the improvement). However, if the weight of an improvement on adjoining land contributes to the land's collapse, the excavating landowner is not strictly liable. Instead, the adjoining landowner may recover only if the excavating landowner was negligent.

Example 1: Owner and Neighbor have adjoining parcels of land. Owner excavates on his land, causing Neighbor's undeveloped land to collapse. Owner is strictly liable.

Example 2: Owner and Neighbor have adjoining parcels of land. Owner's excavation of his land causes Neighbor's barn and the land under it to collapse. Owner is strictly liable unless the weight of Neighbor's barn contributed to the collapse. In that case, Neighbor may recover only if Owner was negligent in his excavation.

b. Subjacent support

The right to subjacent support (i.e., support from beneath the surface of the land) arises when the owner of land grants the right to mine on his land to a third party. The owner of the mineral rights is strictly liable for any failure to support the land and any buildings on the land at the time the rights were conveyed. The owner is liable only for negligence for damage to any improvements built after the conveyance of the rights.

6. Air Rights

A landowner has the right to have the air above his land be free from excessive noise and aircraft transit. This is not an exclusive right, but such intrusions may constitute a trespass.

7. Remedies for Intrusion onto Land

The possessor of land has a right to exclude trespassers and to be free from noise and odors that substantially limit his right to use and enjoyment of the land. He may seek an injunction in equity or damages at law as compensation for the intrusion.

D. GOVERNMENT REGULATION OF LAND

The following testable concepts should be read in conjunction with the detailed discussion of the Fourteenth and Fifth Amendments in the Constitutional Law outline.

1. Zoning

State and local governments may regulate the use of land through zoning laws, subject to limitations of the Fourteenth and Fifth Amendments of the Constitution.

Zoning laws may be used to segregate incompatible uses from developing in the same area. They are enacted for the protection and safety of the communities' citizens. Single family residences are normally considered the highest and best use in zoning ordinances. Commercial and industrial uses are lower uses and generally incompatible with residential neighborhoods. Unusual uses, like funeral homes, require special use permits, even if the district authorizes that type of use.

a. Exemptions and variances

In certain situations an owner may be exempt from the zoning ordinance. If an owner can demonstrate that a particular zoning ordinance exacts a unique hardship on him, he may request a variance as long as the variance is not contrary to the public welfare.

b. Relationship to covenants

A zoning restriction establishes a "ceiling" beyond which a private covenant cannot go, but does not set a "floor" below which a private covenant cannot go.

> **Example**: A zoning ordinance requires that a residence be set back at least 50 feet from the edge of the property. A covenant that requires a setback of 100 feet is enforceable. A covenant that requires a setback of 25 feet does not override the zoning restriction and cannot justify the location of a residence that is setback only 35 feet.

EXAM NOTE: Fact patterns about zoning ordinances that contain standard restrictions are typically not far enough outside the norm to be constitutional violations.

2. Eminent Domain

A taking occurs when the government takes title to land, physically invades the land, or severely restricts the use of land. Courts look to whether an essential nexus exists between the legitimate state interest stated as the justification for the taking/restriction and any conditions imposed on the property owner.

Valid exercises of police power include regulations that have the purpose of protecting the public from harm, or ensuring a public benefit.

A landowner can recover damages equal to the reduction in value for the harm to his property resulting from a partial taking.

E. NUISANCE

See a more detailed discussion of Nuisance in the Themis Torts outline.

1. Private Nuisance

A private nuisance is a **substantial unreasonable** interference with another individual's use or enjoyment of his property. The interference need not be intentional or even negligent to constitute nuisance. Anyone with possessory rights in the property may bring a nuisance claim.

a. Substantial

A substantial interference is one that would be offensive, inconvenient, or annoying to an average person in the community.

b. Unreasonable

The interference is unreasonable if the injury caused outweighs the usefulness of the defendant's actions.

2. Public Nuisance

A public nuisance is an unreasonable interference with the health, safety, or property rights of the community. In order to recover for a public nuisance, a plaintiff must show that he suffered a different kind of harm than that suffered by the rest of the community.

3. Remedies

a. Damages

The usual remedy for nuisance is damages. Damages include any depreciation in value of the property, and may be apportioned among multiple defendants.

All resulting harm is recoverable, including personal (e.g., diseases acquired from inhaling fumes), and harm to property.

b. Injunctive relief

If money damages are inadequate or unavailable, courts may impose injunctive relief. In determining whether an injunction is appropriate, the courts will balance the potential hardships to the two parties. However, the court need not consider the relative hardships if the defendant's conduct was unreasonable.

F. DEDICATION

Dedication is the giving of land by the lawful owner to the government for use by the public. The owner still retains the fee, but the public essentially holds an easement in trust such that the owner does not retain any rights that are inconsistent with the complete exercise and enjoyment of the public uses to which the property has been committed. The dedication may be express (through a deed), implied, or by adverse use by the public, but must be accepted by the public entity (which can be implied by use).

V. OTHER TYPES OF OWNERSHIP

A. CONDOMINIUMS

Condominium unit ownership is fee ownership. However, it differs from most other types of property ownership in that in a condominium, the owner owns the interior of his unit and an undivided interest in the common elements and exterior of the building. Each unit owner carries his own mortgage and is responsible for taxes, insurance, and expenses related to the upkeep of the unit and the building.

B. COOPERATIVES

Cooperatives are a type of housing in which the land and buildings are owned by corporations that lease the individual apartments to its shareholders. Residents who live in cooperatives are not fee owners of the units they live in; rather, they are tenants who own shares of the stock in the building. As a result, the residents are restricted from transferring their interest in the building. Tenants also have a legitimate concern about the other tenants' ability to pay their mortgage. Unlike condominiums, where each owner is responsible for his own mortgage, a cooperative has a blanket mortgage. This mortgage takes priority over occupancy leases, and each tenant pays a share of the mortgage. Although a tenant is not personally liable on the mortgage, a default by any tenant could initiate foreclosure proceedings on the property, which could in turn terminate all leases. Maintenance expenses in a cooperative are treated the same as in a condominium.

C. EMBLEMENTS (CROPS)

Fructus industriales and *fructus naturales* are two types of crops that, with some exceptions, are conveyed along with the land conveyance. *Fructus industriales* are produced through cultivation and are considered personalty. *Fructus naturales* are perennial; they do not require planting because they are produced by nature alone. Title to *fructus naturales* passes automatically with the land because this crop is considered real property.

1. Conveyance of Crops

Generally, both *fructus naturales* and *industriales* are conveyed along with the land conveyance because the owner of the land is presumed to be the owner of both types of crops. Since this presumption is based on the intent of the parties, a contrary intent may be shown to rebut the presumption.

2. Exceptions

Harvested crops, or crops that have been severed from the land, are not conveyed with the land. Thus, the prior owner can remove the crops and has the right to reenter the land.

Some courts also treat ripened *fructus industriales* as being constructively severed from the land because they no longer draw sustenance from the soil. Thus, in some jurisdictions, these crops are not conveyed with the land.

When crops are planted by a tenant, if the tenant's lease is for an uncertain duration and the lease is terminated through no fault of the tenant, the tenant has a right to reenter the land and remove, harvest, and cultivate crops planted prior to the termination of his tenancy. This "doctrine of emblements" applies unless there is a provision to the contrary in the lease, or the one who planted the crops is a trespasser. However, adverse possessors who plant under a claim of right are entitled to the same rights as tenants.

Sales

SALES

Table of Contents

SALES

I. INTRODUCTION

A. SCOPE OF ARTICLE 2

The Uniform Commercial Code ("UCC") Article 2 governs transactions in goods. Although UCC Article 2 adopts much of the common law of contracts, it codifies a number of modifications relating to transactions in goods. Where the common law of contracts and UCC Article 2 differ, Article 2 prevails.

B. DEFINITIONS

1. "Sale"

A sale is a contract under which title to goods passes from the seller to the buyer for a price.

2. "Goods"

The term "goods" is defined under Article 2 as all things movable at the time they are identified as the goods to be sold under the contract between the buyer and the seller. Article 2 applies to the sale of tangible things such as auto parts, toys, gasoline, etc., but it does not apply to the sale of real property, services (e.g., window cleaning, country club membership), or intangibles (e.g., intellectual property, goodwill). Where a sale involves both tangible property and services (e.g., a beauty parlor uses lotion when giving a permanent wave), a court will apply the "predominate purpose" to determine which aspect of the contract predominates (common law or Article 2) governing the predominate aspect to the entire contract. Article 2 expressly states that "goods" include "specially manufactured goods." A contract to build a car would, therefore, be covered by Article 2. The sale of investment securities is governed by UCC Article 8, not Article 2.

3. Goods Associated with Real Property

"Goods associated with real estate" are sometimes governed by Article 2 as follows:

a. Structures to be removed from land

Sales of "structures to be removed from the land," "minerals," "or the like" are governed by Article 2 when severance is to be made **by the seller**.

b. Growing crops and uncut timber

Sales of growing crops or timber to be cut, separate from a sale of the land on which the crops or timber grows, are governed by Article 2 **regardless** of whether severance is made by the buyer or the seller.

c. "Other things"

Aside from those things described above, the sale of other things that can be removed from the land without material harm to the land (such as fixtures) fall under Article 2 regardless of who severs.

4. Merchants

Article 2 applies to all sellers and buyers of goods, whether or not they are involved in the business of buying or selling. When a customer buys a hamburger at a fast-food restaurant, the transaction is governed by Article 2. However, Article 2 has some special rules for a subset of players known as **merchants.** "Merchant" is defined as a person who deals in the kind of goods involved in the transaction or holds himself out (or works for someone who holds himself out) as one with special knowledge or skill concerning the practices or goods involved in the transaction.

The UCC's special provisions as to merchants appear only in Article 2. Sections dealing with the Statute of Frauds, firm offers, confirmatory memoranda and modification (see below) rest on normal business practices, which are or ought to be typical of and familiar to any person in business. For purposes of these sections, almost every person in business would therefore be deemed a "merchant." On the other hand, as to the warranty of merchantability, such warranty is implied only "if the seller is a merchant with respect to goods of that kind."

5. Good Faith

Under Article 2, the rule for all buyers and sellers is that they act "in good faith," meaning that they behave in a way that they believe to be honest. This is a subjective standard. In the case of a merchant, "good faith" also includes observance of reasonable commercial standards of fair dealing in the trade. This is an objective standard.

6. Insolvency

Under the UCC, insolvency occurs when a party (i) cannot pay its debts when due, (ii) has ceased to pay its debts, or (iii) has liabilities that exceed its assets. Certain rules and remedies apply under Article 2 when a buyer or seller is insolvent.

C. CHOICE OF LAW AND CHOICE OF FORUM

The law of the forum state is applied to a transaction involving more than one jurisdiction so long as the transaction bears an appropriate relationship to the law of the forum. This is true even when there is also an appropriate relationship to another jurisdiction. The parties are free to agree to the appropriate law to be applied in any dispute, as long as that choice of law bears an appropriate relationship to the transaction.

II. CONTRACT FORMATION UNDER ARTICLE 2

Under Article 2, a contract for the sale of goods can be made in any manner that is sufficient to show agreement between the parties. Accordingly, a valid contract may be oral, written, or established through conduct of the parties that evidences the intent to form a contract.

A. OFFER

1. Merchant's Firm Offer

At common law, an offeror may revoke her offer at any time prior to acceptance **unless** she has received consideration to keep her offer open. Article 2 modifies that rule for certain offers by **merchants.** When a merchant signs a written offer giving assurances that the offer will be held open for an agreed period, the offer is *irrevocable* for the stated time or for a reasonable period if no period is specified. No consideration by the offeree is needed to keep the offer open under the UCC firm-offer rule.

a. Three-month limit

The period of irrevocability may not exceed three months. If the parties erroneously agree in the original writing that the period of irrevocability extends beyond three months, then the statute supersedes the contract provision and the offer becomes revocable after three months.

b. Required elements

Although no consideration is required to make a merchant's offer irrevocable, it must give words of **firmness,** be in **writing,** and be **signed by the merchant** (see below regarding signature).

Authentication, rather than a "signature," is technically what matters. The assurance must be contained in an authenticated writing. Thus, a signature, initials, or other authenticated inscription by the merchant would be binding. For example, a handwritten memo on the writer's letterhead purporting to "confirm" a firm offer already made would be enough to satisfy the rule, even though it is not "signed," because, under the circumstances, it could not be considered a memorandum of mere negotiation and it would adequately show its own authenticity. Similarly, an authorized telegram would be sufficient, even if the original draft contained only a typewritten signature.

2. Omitted Terms—"Gap-Filler" Provisions

A contract may be formed despite the absence of one or more terms, including price. Under Article 2, a court may supply **reasonable** terms for those not included by the parties. However, the parties must intend a contract. The more terms they leave open, the less likely it is that they intended to conclude a binding agreement.

a. Price

1) Absence of price term

If the parties intend to enter into a contract but (i) say nothing as to the price, (ii) leave the price to be agreed and fail to come to an agreement, or (iii) agree that the price will be fixed by a market or by another standard set by a third party and the price is not then set by that third party, the UCC will make the price under the contract a **reasonable price at the time for delivery.**

2) Fault of one party

If a price that was left to be fixed otherwise than by agreement of the parties fails to be fixed through the fault of one party, then the other party may treat the contract as canceled or fix a reasonable price. A price that is to be fixed by the seller or by the buyer means a price fixed in good faith.

3) No intent to be bound without price

If the parties intend not to be bound unless the price is fixed or agreed and it is not fixed or agreed, then there is no contract. The buyer must then return any goods already received or, if unable to do so, must pay their reasonable value at the time of delivery and the seller must return any portion of the price paid on account.

b. Quantity term required

The only term that **cannot** be supplied by a court is **quantity,** which must be certain or capable of being made certain. The failure to specify a quantity term is fatal to the contract. However, contracts for the seller's **output** or the buyer's **requirements** do not fail for lack of a quantity term because quantity in such contracts is objectively determinable.

B. ACCEPTANCE

1. Forms/Methods of Acceptance

Unless otherwise unambiguously indicated by the language or circumstances, an offer invites acceptance in the following ways:

a. In any reasonable manner or medium

An offer to make a contract is construed as inviting acceptance in any manner and by any medium reasonable in the circumstances (unless a specific medium is unambiguously required by the offer).

b. An offer to buy goods for immediate shipment

If the buyer requests that the goods be shipped, the buyer's request will be construed as inviting acceptance by the seller either by a **promise to ship** or by **prompt shipment** of conforming or nonconforming goods.

1) Shipment of nonconforming goods

If the seller ships nonconforming goods, the shipment will be both an acceptance of the offer and a breach of the contract. The seller is then liable for any damage caused to the buyer as a result of the breach.

If, however, the seller "seasonably" notifies the buyer that the nonconforming goods are tendered as an accommodation, then no acceptance has occurred, and no contract is formed. The accommodation is deemed a counteroffer. The buyer may then either accept (thereby forming a contract) or reject (no contract formed).

2) Acceptance by performance

When an offeror invites performance by the offeree as a means of acceptance, the beginning of that performance is a reasonable mode of acceptance so long as the offeror is notified of that performance within a reasonable time.

> **EXAM NOTE:** Acceptance in the context of *contract formation* is different from the concept of *acceptance of goods,* which is discussed below (*see* § VIII.C., Acceptance of Goods, *infra*).

2. Counteroffers: "Battle of the Forms" Replaces "Mirror-Image Rule"

At common law, no contract is formed unless the acceptance "mirrors" the offer. This is the so-called "mirror-image rule." Any deviation by the offeree, either with additional or different terms, is a counteroffer, not an acceptance. The rule for acceptance in Article 2 is different and is commonly applied in a context known as the "battle of the forms."

a. Between nonmerchants

If both parties are nonmerchants or if only one party is a merchant, then when the additional or different terms are included as part of a definite and seasonable expression of acceptance or a written confirmation of an existing contract, the additional or different terms do not become part of the contract **unless** the original offeror expressly assents to the terms. If the original offeree conditions acceptance on the offeror's acceptance of the additional or different terms there would be no contract unless the original offeror expressly assents. In the latter instance, the offeree's expression is a counteroffer (no contract is yet formed).

Example: Cary, a nonmerchant, makes an offer to purchase goods from Morton, a merchant. Morton accepts the offer but includes an additional term—an arbitration clause in the acceptance. Under Article 2, the contract is formed without the additional term.

b. Both parties are merchants

When both parties are merchants, the rules change.

1) Acceptance includes additional terms

When both parties are merchants, the additional terms in the acceptance will be **automatically included** in the contract unless:

   i) They materially alter the original contract;

   ii) The offer expressly limits acceptance to the terms of the offer; or

   iii) The offeror has already objected to the additional terms or objects within a reasonable time after notice of them was received.

If any one of these three conditions is met, a contract is formed, but the offeror's original terms are controlling.

Example: Mark, a merchant, makes an offer to purchase goods from Melanie, another merchant. The offer does not expressly limit acceptance to its terms. Melanie accepts the offer but includes a new term in the acceptance—that payment must be by cash or certified check. Because both parties are merchants, the additional term will be automatically included in the contract because it does not materially alter the original contract. If Mark had previously objected to the additional term, or if he objects within a reasonable time after notice of the term is received, then Mark's original terms will control.

2) Acceptance includes different terms

The courts in different jurisdictions disagree as to the result when **different** terms are included in the merchant offeree's acceptance. A few jurisdictions treat different terms the same as additional terms and apply the additional-terms test, above. Most, however, apply the so-called **"knock-out" rule,** under which different terms in the offer and acceptance between merchants nullify each other and are "knocked out" of the contract. If by knocking out these terms there are gaps in the contract, the court will use Article 2's gap-filling provisions to patch the holes.

c. Where performance occurs

If the offer and purported acceptance differ to such a degree that there is no contract, but the parties have begun to perform anyway (i.e., demonstrated conduct that recognizes the existence of a contract), then Article 2 provides that there will be a contract, and its terms will consist of those terms on which the writings of the parties agree , together with any supplementary terms filled in by the provisions of the UCC.

3. Auction Contracts

The UCC has special rules for auction sales.

a. Goods auctioned in lots

If goods in an auction sale are offered in lots, each lot represents a separate sale.

b. Completion of sale

An auction sale is complete when the auctioneer announces its end by the fall of the hammer or in any other customary way. When a bid is made contemporaneously with the falling of the hammer, the auctioneer may, at her discretion, reopen the bidding or declare the sale completed at the fall of the hammer.

c. Reserve and no-reserve auctions

In a reserve auction, the auctioneer may withdraw the goods any time before she announces completion of the sale. An auction is with reserve unless specifically announced as a no-reserve auction.

In a no-reserve auction, the goods cannot be withdrawn by the auctioneer unless no bid is received on the item or lot.

In either type of auction, a bidder may retract her bid until the auctioneer announces the end of the bidding. A retraction, however, does not revive earlier bids.

d. When the seller bids

When an auctioneer knowingly accepts a bid by the seller or on her behalf, or procures such a bid to drive up the price of the goods, the winning bidder may avoid the sale or, at her option, take the goods at the price of the last good-faith bid prior to the end of the auction. There are two exceptions to this rule: (i) a seller may bid at a forced sale; and (ii) a seller may bid if she specifically gives notice that she reserves the right to bid.

III. DEFENSES TO CONTRACT ENFORCEMENT

A. STATUTE OF FRAUDS

Under Article 2, except as provided below, contracts for the sale of goods with a price of $500 or more must satisfy the Statute of Frauds. That is, they must be in writing and signed by the party to be charged or her agent; otherwise, the contracts are not enforceable against the party that did not sign.

> **EXAM NOTE:** Under Article 2, the Statute of Frauds applies to both a present sale of goods of $500 or more and a contract to sell such goods in the future.

1. Writing Requirement

The writing need not contain formalistic words or be on a specific form. The writing need not be in a single document, and it is probably sufficient, for example, even if scribbled on a matchbook cover. The writing need only be sufficient to indicate that the parties entered into a contract.

Moreover, even if the writing omits or incorrectly states a term, it is still sufficient to satisfy the statute. The only exception is where the contract fails to state a quantity term—there is no Article 2 gap-filler for quantity.

2. Signature of the "Party to Be Charged"

The signature must be by the party against whom enforcement of the contract is sought or her agent. Under Article 2, a "signature" is more than a person's written signature; it includes any symbol adopted with the intention to accept a writing. It may be contained on any part of a writing, and it may even include, under proper circumstances, a billhead or letterhead when the writing was intended as a memorandum of an agreement.

3. "$500 or More"

Article 2 provides that the $500 threshold is measured by including any subsequent modification (discussed below) of the contract. This works in both directions. That is, a subsequent modification that brings the contract price below $500 will take the contract out of the Statute of Frauds, just as a modification that brings the price above $500 will bring it under the Statute of Frauds.

4. Quantity Term Issues

The quantity term is a required ingredient for an enforceable contract under the UCC. The rule in Article 2 is that the contract is not enforceable beyond the quantity term contained in the writing. While all other terms of the contract (e.g., price) may be proven by parol evidence, the quantity term cannot.

> **EXAM NOTE:** Remember that a quantity term is required for a contract to be enforceable. Price, on the other hand, is not a required term and can be supplied under the UCC gap-filler provisions.

5. Merchant's Confirmatory Memo

In contracts of $500 or more between merchants, if one party—within a reasonable time after an **oral** agreement has been made—sends to the other party a written confirmation of the agreement that is sufficient under the Statute of Frauds to bind the sender, then the recipient is also bound if she had **reason to know** of the confirmation's contents and **does not object** within 10 days of receipt. Thus, the merchant who receives the signed confirmation from the other merchant will be bound by that confirmation just as if she had signed it.

> **Example:** Betsy Buyer and Sharon Seller are both merchants. Betsy telephones Sharon and orders 10,000 pens at $1.00 each. Sharon then sends a signed, written confirmation of the contract, listing the price and quantity agreed to by the parties. Sharon will be bound immediately under the Article 2 Statute of Frauds. If Betsy does not object within 10 days of receiving the written confirmation from Sharon, Betsy will also be bound by the confirmation, even though she did not personally sign anything. Note that Betsy may still argue that there was no contract. By not objecting to the confirmation she merely loses her Statute of Frauds defense.

6. **Writing Not Required**

In three instances under Article 2, a contract is enforceable without a writing.

a. **Specially manufactured goods**

No writing is required if:

i)   The seller made or obtained the goods **specifically** for the buyer;

ii) The goods are **unsuitable** to any other buyer in the ordinary course of the seller's business; and

iii) The seller, in circumstances reasonably indicating that the goods are intended for the buyer, has made either:

a) **Substantial beginnings** in its manufacture; or

b) **Commitments for its purchase** before notice of repudiation is received.

The rationale for this exception is that a seller is unlikely to start producing specially manufactured items unless there really was an oral agreement to buy them.

b. **Court admission**

When a party makes a judicial admission in pleadings, in testimony, or in any other fashion that a contract was made, the contract is enforceable without a writing, up to the quantity of goods admitted.

c. **By performance**

If the goods are (i) received and accepted or (ii) paid for, the contract is enforceable up to the quantity accepted or paid for, even in the absence of a writing.

If, however, the oral agreement contemplates one indivisible item (e.g., a car), and the buyer pays a portion of the purchase price as a down payment, then courts will generally permit evidence of the contract, despite the partial payment.

B. UNCONSCIONABILITY

Article 2 of the UCC provides that a court may modify or refuse to enforce a contract or part of a contract on the grounds that it is "unconscionable." A contract or term is unconscionable when it is so unfair to one party that **no reasonable person in the position of that party would have agreed to it.** Unconscionability may also be applied to prevent unfair surprise. The contract or term at issue must have been offensive at the time it was made.

The question of whether a contract or term is unconscionable is a question of law for the court to decide; the issue does not go to the jury. Upon a finding of unconscionability, the court may invalidate the entire contract, strike only the offending provision(s), or limit the applicability of the offending provision(s) in order to avoid the unconscionable result.

Unfair boilerplate contract provisions that are inconspicuous, hidden, or difficult for a party to understand have been held unconscionable. Courts have also applied the doctrine of unconscionability when the contract is a contract of adhesion (a take-it-or-leave-it contract) and there is greatly unequal bargaining power between the parties. Still, there must be a finding of gross unfairness before the court will conclude that the contract or term is unconscionable.

IV. CONTRACT MODIFICATION AND EXCUSE OF PERFORMANCE

A. BY AGREEMENT BETWEEN THE PARTIES

Under traditional common-law principles, a contract modification must generally be supported by new consideration. In the absence of that new consideration, the modification is unenforceable. Article 2 abandons this rule.

1. Consideration Not Required

Under Article 2, a contract modification made in good faith is enforceable without new consideration.

2. Good Faith

Article 2 makes clear, in its official commentary, that modifications obtained in bad faith (for example, by extortion) are unenforceable. If a party demands an increase in price because the other party has no choice but to agree, the courts will invalidate such a bad-faith modification.

3. Statute of Frauds

A contract **as modified** that falls within the Statute of Frauds must generally be in writing. Any of the general Statute of Frauds exceptions apply, however, to take a modification out of the Statute of Frauds.

4. Parties May Prohibit Oral Modification

A provision that modifications to a written sales contract may occur only in writing is valid and binding under the UCC. Except as between merchants, such a requirement on a form supplied by the merchant must be separately signed by the other party.

a. Waiver

When an oral modification fails to satisfy the Statute of Frauds or is contrary to a provision against oral modification, it can operate as a waiver. A waiver affecting a part of the contract that has not yet been performed may be withdrawn or retracted so long as the other party has not materially relied upon it so that it would be unjust to permit retraction. If there has been no reliance, the waiver may be withdrawn by reasonable notification, received by the other party, that strict performance will be required.

B. BY OPERATION OF LAW

1. Destruction or Injury to Identified Goods

a. Before risk of loss passes to the buyer

If a contract requires the delivery of goods identified at the time the contract was made, and the goods are damaged or destroyed without the fault of either party **before the risk of loss passes to the buyer,** the following rules apply.

1) Total destruction

If the goods are destroyed, the contract is avoided—neither party must perform, and neither party has breached.

2) Partial destruction

Where the goods are damaged but not destroyed, the contract is avoided **unless** the buyer chooses to take the goods at a reduced price **without** any other claim against the seller.

b. After risk of loss passes to the buyer

If the risk of loss has passed to the buyer, then the contract is not avoided, and the seller may demand performance by the buyer.

2. Failure of Agreed-Upon Method of Transportation

If, without the fault of either party, the agreed-upon delivery facilities or method become unavailable or commercially impracticable, then any commercially reasonable delivery method must be tendered **and must be accepted.**

3. Impracticability

Article 2 contains several provisions to be applied when the seller's performance of a contract for the sale of goods becomes impossible or more difficult—often meaning more expensive—than anticipated. In some circumstances, the seller's obligations under the contract may be discharged.

a. Commercially impracticable

Article 2, by design, speaks of "impracticability" rather than the common-law concept of "impossibility." It does so to excuse the seller's performance in some situations where performance may still be objectively possible. The excuse of impracticability is usually not available, however, if the seller's performance has been rendered more expensive. In such cases, performance typically is deemed not to be commercially impracticable. A court might reach a different result if the added expense would cause a loss that is sufficiently ruinous.

b. Non-occurrence of event presumed

Impracticability is established when a circumstance arises that both parties impliedly assumed would not occur, and that circumstance has a material effect on the seller's ability to perform. This does not mean that all risk to the seller is removed. The commentary to Article 2 makes clear that only circumstances that are essentially unforeseeable will excuse performance. Bad weather, for example, is not sufficient, although an extraordinary weather condition like a tornado may be. A winter snowstorm is not sufficient, but an avalanche may be.

c. Other "events sufficient for discharge" of a contract

Unforeseen natural disasters, wars, trade and military embargoes, strikes, and local crop failures have all been found sufficient to excuse performance. However, non-extraordinary increases in the cost of performance have not.

d. Failure of a particular source of supply

If the contract provided that a specific source of supply be used, and that source of supply fails, then performance is discharged. This is so even when other sources are readily available. Courts will excuse performance when the parties have specifically identified the source in the contract.

4. The Seller's Partial Inability to Perform

When a seller is only **partially** unable to perform due to a deficiency in supply, the seller is not excused fully from the contract. The seller must allocate the available supply among its customers in any manner that is fair and reasonable, but may include regular customers not then under contract as well as the seller's own requirements for further manufacture. The seller must seasonably notify a buyer that there will be delay or nondelivery and, if allocation is required, of the estimated amount that will be made available for the buyer. If the prospective deficiency substantially impairs the value of the whole contract for the buyer, then the buyer may end the contract.

C. PROSPECTIVE INABILITY TO PERFORM

Situations may arise between the making of a contract and its performance such that one party appears to be unwilling or incapable of performing. A common example is the insolvency of one of the parties.

1. Demand of Assurance

Under Article 2, when any reasonable grounds for insecurity arise with respect to the performance of the other party, the party who fears that the other party will not perform may demand, in writing, **adequate assurance** from the other party. While waiting for adequate assurance, the party may suspend performance if it is commercially reasonable.

2. What Constitutes Adequate Assurance

The form of the assurance depends on the facts of the individual case. Between merchants, the adequacy of any assurance offered is to be determined according to commercial standards.

3. Performance Begun

The acceptance of any improper delivery or payment does not prejudice the aggrieved party's right to demand adequate assurance of future performance.

4. Adequate Assurance Not Provided

After receipt of a justified demand, the failure to provide adequate assurance within a reasonable time not to exceed 30 days will constitute a repudiation of the contract.

D. ANTICIPATORY REPUDIATION

Anticipatory repudiation occurs when a party unequivocally states her unwillingness to perform under the contract or fails to provide, upon proper demand, adequate assurances of performance.

1. Effect of Repudiation

If the repudiation "substantially impairs the value of the contract," the aggrieved party may await performance for a commercially reasonable time or may immediately seek available remedies under Article 2 for breach of contract. The aggrieved party's performance is excused.

2. Substantially Impairs the Value of the Contract

The value of a contract will be substantially impaired if material inconvenience or injustice will result if the aggrieved party is forced to wait and ultimately receives tender minus the part or aspect of the contract that was repudiated.

3. Retraction

Until the repudiating party's next performance is due, he may retract the repudiation unless the aggrieved party has since canceled the contract, changed her position, or otherwise indicated a belief that the repudiation is final. Retraction may be by any method that clearly indicates to the aggrieved party that the repudiating party intends to perform. It must include any assurances of performance that the other party has justifiably demanded about whether the retracting party will perform.

V. PAROL-EVIDENCE RULE

A. FINAL EXPRESSION OF AGREEMENT

When the terms of the contract are set forth in a writing intended by the parties to be a final expression of their agreement with regard to some of the terms (a partial integration) or all of the terms (a complete integration), the terms in the writing cannot be contradicted by extrinsic evidence of a **prior** agreement or **contemporaneous oral** agreement. The goal of this rule is to prevent uncertainty in the enforcement of contracts that may occur if evidence is allowed that contradicts the parties' final writing. If the writing is not intended as a complete and exclusive statement of the terms of the parties' agreement, then evidence of consistent additional terms may be admitted.

B. INTEGRATIONS

Writings that qualify as integrations are those that are accepted by both parties as setting forth some or all of the terms finally agreed upon at the time the writing is created. If the writing is a completely integrated, the parol evidence rule bars admission of any prior conversations or writings, such as tentative early drafts of the contract created during negotiations or internal memoranda retained by one party and not adopted by the other. Contemporaneous oral agreements are also inadmissible. If the writing is partially integrated, then it may be possible to admit evidence of prior and contemporaneous agreements regarding consistent additional terms.

C. EXPLANATION OR SUPPLEMENTATION

Terms can be **explained or supplemented** (but not contradicted) by:

i) Consistent additional terms, only if the writing is not completely integrated;

ii) Course of dealing between the parties on earlier occasions;

iii) Use of the trade or business; or

iv) Course of performance (when the contract involves repeated earlier occasions of performance that were accepted by or acquiesced to by the parties).

D. SUBSEQUENT MODIFICATIONS

Parol evidence may be offered to show subsequent modifications of a written contract.

Example: Sarah Seller and Betty Buyer enter into a written contract for the sale of a car on March 1 for $5,000. On March 2, Sarah and Betty orally agree that Betty can test drive the car for one week, and if it does not work properly during that time, she can return it to Sarah for a full refund. Because the oral agreement occurred **subsequent** to the written contract, there is no parol-evidence issue.

VI. PERFORMANCE

A. THE SELLER'S OBLIGATION OF TENDER AND DELIVERY

1. Non-Carrier Cases

These are cases in which the parties did not intend that the goods be delivered by common carrier.

a. Tender of delivery

The seller must put and hold conforming goods at the buyer's disposition for a sufficient time for the buyer to take delivery.

1) Reasonable notice and opportunity to take delivery

The seller must give the buyer reasonably sufficient notice to enable her to take possession of the goods. Tender must be at a reasonable hour.

2) Place of delivery—the seller's place of business

If there is no provision otherwise, the seller's place of business (or, if she has none, her residence) is the place of delivery. However, if at the time of the contract both parties know that the goods are elsewhere, then that place is the place of delivery.

2. **Carrier Cases**

If the agreement specifies that the goods will move by carrier, then the seller may be obligated to deliver them for shipment or to deliver them to an agreed-upon destination.

a. **Shipment contracts**

Under Article 2, the presumption is that the contract is a shipment contract. In a shipment contract, the seller is obligated to put the goods into the hands of a carrier, make a reasonable contract for shipment, promptly tender the shipping documents to the buyer, and promptly notify the buyer of the shipment.

If the seller fails to enter into a reasonable contact with the carrier or promptly notify the buyer of the shipment, then the buyer may reject the goods if a material loss or delay occurs as a result.

b. **Destination contracts**

Some contracts require that the seller tender delivery of the goods at a specified destination. Once there, the seller must hold conforming goods at the buyer's disposition. The seller must also reasonably notify the buyer of delivery and provide the necessary documents for the buyer to obtain possession.

c. **FOB contracts**

Some contracts require the seller to tender delivery of the goods FOB (free on board) at a particular point. That point becomes the delivery point. In some instances, the contract may specify FOB the seller's location, meaning that the seller must tender delivery of the goods, as in a shipment contract. If the contract specifies FOB destination, then the seller must tender delivery, as in a destination contract.

d. **FAS contracts**

When a contract specifies FAS (free alongside ship), the seller is obligated to deliver the goods **alongside** a designated vessel in a manner that comports with the ordinary course of business of the port of delivery, or at a specified dock.

e. **CIF and C&F contracts**

In a CIF (cost, insurance, and freight) contract, the price includes the cost of the goods, the cost of insuring the goods during shipment, and the cost of transporting the goods. In a C&F (cost and freight) contract, the price includes the cost of the goods plus the cost of shipment. Both types of contracts are shipment contracts.

B. THE BUYER'S OBLIGATION TO PAY

1. Carrier Cases

Unless otherwise specified in the contract, payment is due at the time and place at which the buyer is to receive the goods even though the place of shipment may, if the contract is a shipment contract, be the place where tender of delivery occurs.

2. Shipment under Reservation

A seller who ships by carrier under a contract that does not specify the method or form of payment may send the goods **under reservation,** meaning that the carrier will hold the goods until the buyer pays. This is accomplished by the seller's obtaining a negotiable bill of lading or a nonnegotiable bill of lading taken to a party other than the buyer.

3. Tender of Payment

a. Generally required to trigger delivery obligation

Unless otherwise agreed, tender of payment is a condition to the seller's duty to tender and complete any delivery.

b. Sufficiency of tender of payment

Tender of payment is sufficient when made by any means or in any manner consistent with the ordinary course of business, unless the seller (i) demands payment in legal tender (i.e., cash) **and** (ii) gives any extension of time reasonably necessary to procure such legal tender.

> **Example:** Susan Seller contracts with Barry Buyer for the sale of a used car for $10,000. Under the contract, Susan is to deliver the car to Barry on July 1. After the contract is signed, Susan learns that she could sell the car to another person for $12,000 and seeks to avoid the contract with Barry. When Susan delivers the car to Barry at 6:00 p.m. on July 1 and Barry tenders a check for $10,000, Susan refuses the check and demands payment in legal tender. Barry cannot obtain the cash because the banks have closed for the day. The next day, after the banks have opened and Barry obtains the cash, Susan claims that Barry has breached the contract by tendering payment after the July 1 due date. Under the UCC, Barry would have a reasonable extension of time to obtain the cash demanded by Susan and would be found not to have breached the contract.

c. Payment by check

If payment is made by check, payment is conditional until the check is paid or dishonored.

4. Installment Contracts

Unless otherwise agreed, all goods called for by a contract for sale must be tendered in a single delivery, and payment is due only on such tender. If goods are to be delivered in installments, however, payment may also be made or demanded for each installment, if the price can be apportioned, unless the contract specifies otherwise.

5. The Buyer's Right to Inspect

A buyer has a right to inspect goods that are tendered, delivered, or identified to the contract for sale, unless the contract provides otherwise.

a. Prior to payment

A buyer's right to inspect is a condition to payment. An inspection may occur at any reasonable time and place and in any reasonable manner, even when the goods are held under reservation. However, the parties can agree that inspection occur in a particular form, at a particular time, or at a particular place. If the seller is required or authorized to send the goods to the buyer, then the inspection may be after the arrival of the goods.

b. When not entitled to inspect

Unless otherwise agreed, the buyer is **not** entitled to inspect the goods before payment of the price if the contract provides for delivery "C.O.D." or on other terms that under the applicable course of performance, course of dealing, or usage of trade are interpreted to preclude inspection before payment. Similarly, the buyer is not entitled to inspect the goods before payment, unless otherwise agreed, if the contract provides for payment against documents of title, except when such payment is due only after the goods are to become available for inspection.

c. Expenses of inspection

Expenses of inspection must be paid by the buyer, but they may be recovered from the seller if the goods do not conform and are rejected.

VII. INSURABLE INTEREST AND RISK OF LOSS

A. UCC REPLACED CONCEPT OF TITLE

The comments to Article 2 explain that traditional property and contract law principles of "property" and "title" are arbitrary and unsatisfactory methods of allocating the risk of loss in goods. Accordingly, Article 2 contains several provisions dealing with risk of loss and related provisions for determining insurable interests. In effect, Article 2's way of allocating risk of loss is based on an assessment about which party to a sales transaction is most likely to have insurance. Once it is acknowledged that this is the essential basis for ascribing risk, it makes sense that Article 2 gives clear guidance about what interests are insurable. The message is clear—if the parties themselves do not agree as to who carries the risk of loss (which they are free to do), then Article 2 will do it for them according to which party is most likely (and should be) insured.

1. Insurable Interest

To insure the goods that are the subject matter of a sales transaction, a person must have an insurable interest in them.

a. The seller's insurable interest

A seller has an insurable interest in goods so long as she has title to them or a security interest in them.

b. The buyer's insurable interest

The buyer has an insurable interest in the goods as of the moment they are identified as the goods under the contract. The parties can agree about when identification takes place, and those agreements are generally valid. If they do not agree, Article 2 does it for them as follows:

1) Specified, ascertained, and existing goods

Identification is deemed to occur when, at the time the contract is formed, the agreement calls for the sale of specific goods already in existence.

2) Unborn animals and crops

If the contract is for the sale of unborn animals to be born within one year after the contract is made or crops to be harvested within one year after the contract is made, then identification occurs upon conception and planting, respectively.

3) Goods generally

As to goods in general, identification occurs when the goods are designated by the seller as those to be delivered under the contract. Note that a seller may delegate the right to a buyer to identify the goods.

2. Risk of Loss

Before a contract for the sale is made, the owner (prospective seller) is responsible for any loss or damage to her property. This **risk of loss,** however, will at some point shift to the buyer after a contract for the sale of those goods is executed. Article 2 leaves to the parties the freedom to determine when that risk of loss will pass. If the parties cannot or do not agree, then Article 2 provides the rules.

a. Non-carrier contracts

When the goods are not shipped by carrier or are in the possession of a bailee, if the seller is **not a merchant,** the risk of loss passes to the buyer after the seller has tendered the goods to the buyer. If the seller **is a merchant,** the risk of loss passes at the time the buyer takes physical possession of the goods.

b. Carrier contracts (Shipment)

In a shipment contract, the risk of loss shifts to the buyer when the seller gives possession of the goods to the carrier, makes an appropriate contract for shipment, and notifies the buyer that the goods have been shipped.

c. Carrier contracts (Destination)

In a destination contract, the risk of loss passes to the buyer when the seller tenders the goods to the buyer at the destination point.

d. Goods held by bailee to be delivered without being moved

If the goods are held by a bailee to be delivered without being moved, then the risk of loss passes to the buyer:

i) On the buyer's receipt of a negotiable document of title covering the goods;

ii) On acknowledgment by the bailee of the buyer's right to possession of the goods; or

iii) After the buyer's receipt of a nonnegotiable document of title or other written direction to the bailee to deliver.

3. Exceptions

When there is a breach of the contract, the rules change.

a. Nonconforming goods

When a seller tenders goods that are nonconforming so as to give the buyer a right of rejection, the risk of loss does not pass to the buyer unless and until any defect is cured or the buyer accepts the goods despite the nonconformity. Thus, for example, in a shipment contract in which nonconforming goods are destroyed in transit, the risk of loss remains with the seller.

b. Acceptance revoked

When a buyer justifiably revokes acceptance, the risk of loss remains with the seller, but only to the extent that the buyer's insurance does not cover the loss.

c. Breach or repudiation by the buyer

When conforming goods are identified to the contract and the buyer repudiates or breaches before the risk of loss has passed to him, the seller may treat the risk of loss as being on the buyer for a commercially reasonable time to the extent that the seller's insurance does not cover a loss of the goods.

B. PROVISIONS REGARDING PASSAGE OF TITLE

Despite Article 2's rejection of "title" as a primary factor in sales transactions, including risk of loss, the drafters recognized that some transactions in goods, especially documentary transactions, require reliance on the concept of "title." Accordingly, Article 2 has provisions regarding the passage of title that apply only when no other of Article 2's provisions can resolve the issue. Also worthy of note is Article 2's clear invitation for the parties to agree about when title passes from one to the other. Of course, the parties cannot agree that title pass before the goods are identified—this is logically impossible. If they do not agree, then title passes when the seller completes her performance with respect to the physical delivery of the goods.

1. Carrier Cases

In a destination contract, title passes when the goods are tendered at the destination. In all other cases, title passes to the buyer at the place and time of shipment. These rules mirror the risk-of-loss rules.

2. Non-Carrier Cases

There are two instances when delivery is made without moving the goods. When the seller must deliver a document of title to complete the sale, the delivery of that document passes title to the buyer. When the goods have been identified at the time of contracting and no document of title need be delivered, passage of title occurs at the time and place of contracting.

VIII. REMEDIES

A. THE BUYER'S REJECTION OF GOODS

After the seller has tendered delivery of the goods, responsibility shifts to the buyer to either accept them or reject them. The buyer must choose, and choose quickly. If the buyer fails to respond in a timely manner, then Article 2 will deem his silence an acceptance. Importantly, the buyer is obligated to respond **regardless of whether the tender is conforming or not.** Article 2 does not assume that the buyer will reject nonconforming goods.

> **EXAM NOTE:** For purposes of the exam, be sure you understand the difference between the process of rejection and revocation of acceptance (i.e., that rejection is based on the perfect tender rule, revocation is based on substantial impairment, and the distinction turns on whether acceptance has occurred).

1. In General

If the goods or tender of delivery fail in any respect to conform to the contract, then the buyer may reject the goods or choose to accept the goods despite the nonconformity. The buyer may also choose to accept some of the goods while rejecting the rest. A buyer who accepts a nonconforming tender does not lose any remedy otherwise available (e.g., damages for breach of contract).

2. Exceptions

The following are exceptions to the rule requiring perfect tender:

a. Shipment contract—failure to contract with carrier or notify the buyer

In a shipment contract, a seller's failure to make proper arrangements with a carrier for transportation or to notify the buyer that the goods have been shipped will be grounds for rejection by the buyer only if material loss or delay ensues.

b. Form of delivery becomes commercially impracticable

If an agreed-upon form of delivery becomes commercially impracticable, then a commercially reasonable substitute must be tendered by the seller and accepted by the buyer.

c. Installment contracts

In an installment contract, a buyer may not reject any nonconforming installment unless the nonconformity **substantially impairs** the value of that installment and cannot be cured. The entire contract may be breached if the nonconformity substantially impairs its value.

d. Course of dealing or performance and trade usage

Course of dealing, course of performance, or usage of the trade may require acceptance of goods that the buyer would otherwise have the right to reject.

e. Agreement of the parties

Acceptance is required if the parties have agreed that the buyer will accept nonconforming goods.

3. Rules for Proper Rejection

The buyer must:

a. Notify the seller of the rejection within a reasonable time

What is "reasonable" will depend on the particular facts and can depend on such factors as the difficulty of discovering the defect, the specific terms agreed to in the contract, and whether or not the goods are perishable. Remember that the buyer has a reasonable time within which to inspect the goods.

b. Notify the seller of the particular defect

To rely on a particular defect to justify a rejection or establish a breach, the buyer is required to identify the reason for rejection if the defect is ascertainable by a reasonable inspection, and the seller could have cured it if it was seasonally identified. Obviously, a seller cannot cure a defect of which she is unaware.

1) Between merchants

In a sale between merchants, after a merchant buyer has rejected goods and the time for cure has passed, a merchant seller is entitled to a final statement of the buyer's objections. If the merchant seller makes a request in writing for a full and final written statement of all defects on which the merchant buyer proposes to rely, then the failure of the merchant buyer to identify a particular defect that is ascertainable by reasonable inspection precludes the buyer from relying on the defect to justify rejection or to establish breach.

c. Hold the goods for a reasonable time

This allows the seller time to recover the goods or make other arrangements for their disposition.

4. The Buyer's Responsibility after Rejection

a. If the buyer has security interest in the goods

If the goods are rightfully rejected, the buyer will have a security interest in goods that it possesses or controls for any payments made, as well as for expenses reasonably incurred in handling the goods after rejection. The buyer may hold the goods and resell them in good faith in a commercially reasonable manner, but he must account to the seller for any excess over the amount of the buyer's security interest.

b. If the buyer has no security interest in the goods

1) In general

If, before rejection, the buyer has taken physical possession of goods in which he does not have a security interest (i.e., the buyer has not paid any part of the price of the goods and has no claim for expenses incurred in inspecting or caring for the goods), then the buyer is obligated to hold the rejected goods with **reasonable care** at the seller's disposition for a time sufficient to permit the seller to remove them.

2) When the seller fails to give instructions within a reasonable time

If the seller fails to give instructions to the buyer within a reasonable time after notification of the rejection, then the buyer has the options to (i) store the goods for the seller's account, (ii) reship them to the seller, or (iii) resell them for the seller's account. Any expenses incurred by the buyer must be reimbursed by the seller. A buyer's good-faith compliance with these rules immunizes him from any claim that he accepted the goods or that he wrongfully converted them.

3) Merchant buyer

If the seller has no agent or place of business within the market area of the place of rejection, then a merchant buyer must, after rejecting goods in its possession or control:

i) Follow any reasonable instructions the seller gives with respect to the goods; and

ii) In the absence of any instructions, make reasonable efforts to sell the goods for the seller's account if they are perishable or threaten to decline in value speedily.

Instructions are not reasonable if, on demand by the buyer, indemnity for expenses is not forthcoming.

c. When the buyer resells rejected goods

If the buyer resells goods following a rightful rejection, then the buyer is entitled to reimbursement from the seller or out of the proceeds of the resale for the reasonable expenses of caring for and selling the goods, as well as any sales commission as is usual in the trade, or, if there is no usual commission, a reasonable sum not to exceed 10 percent of the gross proceeds.

B. THE SELLER'S RIGHT TO CURE

1. In General

When any tender or delivery by the seller is rejected because it is nonconforming, and the time for performance has not yet expired, the seller may seasonably notify the buyer of his intention to cure and may then, within the contract time, make a conforming delivery.

> **Example:** Stanley Seller contracts with Brenda Buyer to deliver a blue truck on or before December 1. On November 15, Stanley delivers a silver truck and Brenda rejects it. Stanley may cure by notifying Brenda of his intention to cure and delivering a conforming blue truck by December 1.

2. The Seller Has Reasonable Grounds to Believe that Nonconforming Tender Would Be Acceptable

If a buyer rejects a nonconforming tender that the seller had **reasonable grounds** to believe would be acceptable, with or without money allowance, then the seller may, after seasonably notifying the buyer, have a further reasonable time beyond the contract time in which to substitute a conforming tender. Reasonable grounds can include prior course of dealing between the parties or trade usage that in fact reasonably led the seller to believe that the nonconforming goods would be acceptable.

> **Example:** In the above example, before signing the contract, Brenda told Stanley that the color of the truck did not matter to her and she would accept any color truck. If Brenda then rejects the silver truck, Stanley would have a reasonable time after the contract date of December 1 to cure the defect by substituting a conforming blue truck.

3. Installment Contracts

A nonconforming tender in an installment contract may not be rejected when it can be cured within the installment period.

C. ACCEPTANCE OF GOODS

To this point, the buyer has not yet accepted the goods. Once the buyer does so, the rules change for both the buyer and the seller. Acceptance occurs when the buyer:

i) After a reasonable opportunity to inspect the goods signifies to the seller that the goods are conforming or that he will take or retain them in spite of their nonconformity;

ii) Fails to make an effective rejection, but such acceptance does not occur until the buyer has had a reasonable opportunity to inspect the goods; or

iii) Engages in conduct inconsistent with the seller's ownership of the goods.

D. CONSEQUENCES OF ACCEPTANCE

The consequences of acceptance described below follow with respect to **any** goods accepted, whether conforming or nonconforming and whether or not the buyer could have rejected them. Although the buyer may have suffered damages in accepting nonconforming goods (this will be considered later), he is still bound by the following rules.

1. The Buyer Must Pay the Contract Price

The buyer must pay the full price for accepted goods, though the buyer would have remedies for any nonconformity, including seeking damages and deducting such damages from the price.

2. Right to Reject Is Extinguished

Except as described below (*see* § VIII.E. regarding revocation of acceptance), the buyer has lost the opportunity to reject.

3. Notification of Breach

The buyer must, within a reasonable time after he discovers or should have discovered any breach, notify the seller of the breach or be barred from any remedy. This provision means what it says: failure to notify the seller of a breach is a complete bar to recovery of damages.

4. Burden of Proof

The burden of proof is on the buyer to establish any breach with respect to the goods accepted.

E. REVOCATION OF ACCEPTANCE

1. In General

Issues sometimes arise when a buyer accepts goods only to discover later that they are nonconforming. Although the buyer may recover damages on a breach of warranty theory, the buyer may wish instead to revoke the original acceptance when he has no use or desire for some or all of the goods. Article 2 provides for the revocation of acceptance. A buyer who revokes his acceptance has the same rights and duties with regard to the goods as if he had rejected them.

2. When Acceptance May Be Revoked

A buyer may revoke an acceptance of the goods if the defect **substantially impairs** their value to the buyer and:

i)   The buyer accepted the goods on the reasonable belief that the seller would cure the defect, but the seller has failed to do so; or

ii) The buyer accepted the goods without discovery of the nonconformity, and such acceptance was reasonably induced either by the difficulty of discovering the nonconformity before acceptance or because the seller gave assurances that the goods were conforming.

3. Timely Revocation

The buyer must inform the seller of its decision to revoke within a reasonable time after the nonconformity was discovered or should have been discovered by the buyer. Notably, if the buyer fails to exercise due diligence in discovering a defect, then his notice to the seller may be untimely, and revocation will be barred.

4. Goods Unchanged

Revocation of acceptance must occur before any substantial change in the condition of the goods not caused by the defect. Thus, when a buyer receives nonconforming goods and later causes or allows a substantial change in the goods, the buyer may be prevented from revoking his acceptance **despite** the original nonconformity.

F. THE BUYER'S REMEDIES FOR NONDELIVERY, AFTER REJECTION, AND UPON PROPER REVOCATION OF ACCEPTANCE

When there has been nondelivery, proper rejection, or proper revocation of acceptance, the buyer's remedies are the same:

1. Damages

The buyer is entitled to benefit-of-the-bargain damages, as well as any incidental and consequential damages that may be applicable.

a. Contract price versus market price

This is the classic "benefit of the bargain" remedy. Market price is determined at the place of tender and at the time the buyer learns of the seller's failure of performance. When the buyer rejects or revokes after delivery, market price is determined at the place of delivery.

> **Example:** Bernie Buyer enters into a contract with Shelley Seller to purchase 100 barrels of oil at $50 per barrel, delivery to take place at Bernie's Texas refinery on July 1. Shelley fails to deliver the oil. On July 1, the price of oil near Bernie's Texas refinery was $75 per barrel. Under the benefit-of-the-bargain damages formula, Bernie's measure of damages will be $25 per barrel, and he is entitled to $2,500.

b. Contract price versus cost of replacement

In Article 2 parlance, this is known as **cover**. In this situation, the buyer's damages are measured by the difference between the contract price and the cost of actually replacing the goods. The buyer's cover must be reasonable, in good faith, and made without unreasonable delay.

> **Example:** Assume the same facts as the example above. When Shelley fails to deliver on July 1, Bernie, in good faith, calls a reputable local oil dealer who immediately supplies the oil to Bernie at $80 per barrel. Under the cover formula for damages, Bernie's measure of damages will be $30 per barrel, and Bernie would be entitled to $3,000.

c. Incidental and consequential damages

In addition to either of the above damage remedies, the buyer may be entitled to incidental and consequential damages. Incidental damages are damages that are incidental to the seller's failure to perform, such as the costs of warehousing, transportation, inspection, etc. Consequential damages are any loss resulting from general or particular requirements and needs of which the seller, at the time of contracting, had reason to know and which could not be reasonably prevented by purchasing substitute goods or otherwise. Consequential damages must have been foreseeable to the seller at the time of contracting.

2. The Buyer's Right to Replevin

a. When the buyer is unable to effect cover

The buyer has a right of replevin for any goods identified to the contract if, after reasonable effort, the buyer is unable to effect cover (i.e., obtain an adequate substitute) for such goods, or the circumstances reasonably indicate that such an effort would be unavailing.

> **Example:** Seller and Buyer enter into a contract for the sale of 1,000 mufflers for $100,000 by January 1. Seller identifies the mufflers from its inventory, sets them aside, and marks them for delivery to Buyer. Seller subsequently fails to deliver the mufflers by the contract date. Buyer attempts to purchase similar mufflers in the market but is unable to do so. Buyer is entitled to replevy the mufflers from Seller.

b. Partial-payment situations

The buyer may also replevy undelivered goods that have been identified under the contract when:

i) The buyer has made partial payment, and the seller becomes insolvent within 10 days of the buyer's first payment (the buyer must tender full payment at the time of replevin); or

ii) The buyer has made partial payment, and the goods are for personal, family, or household use (the buyer must tender full payment at the time of replevin).

3. Specific Performance

When the undelivered goods are unique "or in other proper circumstances," a court may order specific performance even if the goods have not yet been identified to the contract by the seller.

> Note that under the remedy of replevin, the goods must have been identified to the contract, but under the remedy of specific performance, the goods need not have been identified to the contract.

G. THE BUYER'S DAMAGES AS TO ACCEPTED GOODS

1. Measure

When the buyer accepts goods that are nonconforming, the buyer may recover damages for the resulting loss. When the buyer accepts goods that violate one of the seller's warranties (see § X., Warranties, *infra*), the buyer may recover damages measured as the difference (at the time and place of acceptance) between the value of the goods as accepted and the value they would have had if they had been as warranted, plus any appropriate consequential and incidental damages. Typically, the amount of such damages is the cost to repair or replace the goods.

2. Notice

To recover damages, the buyer must give notice to the seller of the breach within a reasonable time after the buyer discovers or should have discovered the breach. If such notice is not given, the buyer will be barred from any remedy.

3. Where the Buyer Resells Goods and is Sued by a Subsequent Buyer

If the buyer resells the goods and is sued for breach of a warranty or other obligation for which the seller would be answerable over the buyer, then the buyer may give the seller written notice of the litigation and that the seller may come in and defend, and that if the seller does not do so, the seller will be bound in any action against him by the buyer with regard to any determination of fact common to the two litigations. If the seller, after seasonable receipt of the notice, does not come in and defend, then the seller will be bound by the litigation. This is referred to as "vouching in." As a practical matter, this procedure would only be used if the buyer is unable to implead the seller because the seller has insufficient contacts with the forum jurisdiction.

IX. REMEDIES FOR SELLERS

A. THE SELLER'S RIGHT TO WITHHOLD DELIVERY

1. The Buyer's Failure to Pay

When the contract calls for payment in advance and payment is not forthcoming from the buyer, the most straightforward remedy for a seller is to refuse delivery of the goods.

2. Discovery that the Buyer on Credit Is Insolvent

If the seller discovers that a buyer on credit is insolvent, then the seller may withhold delivery unless the buyer pays the seller in cash.

B. THE SELLER'S RIGHT TO RECAPTURE GOODS

1. Delivered Goods to an Insolvent Buyer on Credit

If the seller discovers that the buyer has received goods on credit while insolvent, then the seller may reclaim/recapture the goods following a demand made within 10 days after the buyer's receipt of the goods. (Note that if a buyer tenders cash, despite his insolvency, the seller may not reclaim the goods.) If a written misrepresentation of solvency was made to the seller within three months prior to the delivery of the goods, then the 10-day limitation will not apply. The seller's right to reclaim the goods is subject to the right of a buyer in the ordinary course of business or any other good faith purchaser.

Note that as a precondition to recapture, Article 2 requires that the buyer have received the goods on credit while insolvent. If the buyer becomes insolvent **after** delivery, the seller may not reclaim.

2. Delivered Goods to a Buyer Who Pays With a Check

If the buyer pays with a check that is subsequently dishonored, then the seller may reclaim the goods following a demand made within a reasonable time. The seller's right to reclaim is subject to the right a good faith purchaser.

3. Stoppage in Transit

a. Goods in transit or stored with a bailee

If the goods are in transit in the possession of a carrier or stored with a bailee, then the seller may stop their delivery if the seller learns that the buyer is insolvent. The seller's notification must be received by the carrier/bailee in reasonable time to stop delivery. If the buyer tenders cash for the goods, then the seller is obligated to deliver them.

b. Breach by the buyer

A seller may stop delivery of carload, truckload, planeload, or larger shipments of express or freight if the buyer repudiates or fails to make a payment due before delivery or if for any other reason the seller has a right to withhold or reclaim the goods. The seller's notification must be received by the carrier/bailee in reasonable time to stop delivery.

4. When Goods May Not Be Stopped

Delivery cannot be stopped after:

i)   Receipt of the goods by the buyer;

ii) Acknowledgment to the buyer by any bailee of the goods (except a carrier) that the bailee holds the goods for the buyer;

iii) Such acknowledgment to the buyer by a carrier by reshipment or as warehouseman; or

iv) Negotiation to the buyer of any negotiable document of title covering the goods.

5. Obligations of a Carrier or Bailee

To stop delivery, the seller must notify the carrier or bailee in enough time to prevent delivery of the goods. After such notification, the carrier/bailee must hold and deliver the goods according to the directions of the seller, but the seller is liable for any charges or damages to the carrier/bailee. If a negotiable document of title has been issued for the goods, then the bailee is not obliged to obey a notification to stop delivery until surrender of the document. A carrier that has issued a nonnegotiable bill of lading is not obligated to obey a notification to stop delivery received from a person other than the consignor.

C. THE SELLER'S MONETARY DAMAGES

Regardless of a seller's success in withholding delivery or reclaiming the goods, she may still have suffered money damages and may seek to be made whole by the buyer. This is, of course, more true when efforts in withholding delivery and reclaiming the goods have failed. One important exception is when a credit seller reclaims from an insolvent buyer. In that case, the seller has no further claim against the buyer.

1. Full Contract Price

Recovery of the full contract price is an extraordinary remedy under Article 2. It is available in three circumstances:

i)   The buyer has accepted the goods;

ii) Conforming goods have been lost or damaged within a reasonable time **after** risk of loss has passed to the buyer; and

iii) Goods identified to the contract are unable to be sold by the seller after reasonable effort to resell them at a reasonable price, or the circumstances reasonably indicate that such effort will be unavailing.

2. Contract Price versus Market Price

When the buyer breaches or repudiates, the seller may choose this measure of damages, with the market price measured at the time and place for delivery.

> **Example:** Sally Seller and Billy Buyer enter into a contract for the sale of a camera for $500. Billy subsequently repudiates the contract. If the market price for the camera at the time and place of delivery is $400, then Sally may recover $100, as well as any incidental damages she suffered, minus any expenses she saved as a result of Billy's repudiation of the contract.

3. Contract Price versus Resale Price

A seller who chooses this route must exercise good faith and must conduct a commercially reasonable private sale or public auction. The buyer must be given reasonable notice of a private sale. A public auction must be held at a usual market for such goods, if reasonably available, and the seller must give the buyer reasonable notice of the time and place of the resale, except if the goods are perishable or threaten to decline in value quickly. The buyer may purchase the goods at an auction sale. A purchaser that buys in good faith at a resale takes the goods free of any rights of the original buyer.

4. Lost Profits

In some circumstances, a seller cannot be made whole through resale at the contract price. This is true for "lost volume" sellers; that is, those sellers who have an unlimited supply of the goods and who make a profit per item. Although they can resell the goods at the same price as the contract price, they have lost the opportunity to sell them in the first instance when the buyer breached or repudiated. They are, therefore, entitled to those lost profits. To qualify as a lost volume seller, the seller needs to show only that it could have supplied both the breaching purchaser and the resale purchaser with the goods. In general, the measure of lost profit would be the contract price minus the cost to the dealer or manufacturer.

> **Example:** Acme Computers, a high-volume maker of personal computers, contracts with Beverly Buyer to sell 100 computers for $100,000, their list price. Beverly subsequently repudiates the contract, and Acme resells the computers to another customer. Acme can recover from Beverly its lost profit, i.e., the contract price of $100,000 minus its manufacturing cost, as well as any incidental damages.

There are two other situations in which the lost profits formula might be used. One involves a seller who acts as a middleman and, before the seller acquires the goods, the buyer repudiates. The other type of seller is a manufacturer who chooses not to complete the goods following the buyer's repudiation. In both cases the resale formula makes no sense (the seller has nothing to resell) and the contract/market formula will undercompensate the seller.

5. Incidental Damages

Under any theory for measuring damages, the seller is entitled to incidental damages. Incidental damages to an aggrieved seller would include any commercially reasonable charges, expenses, or commissions incurred (i) in stopping delivery; (ii) in the transportation, care, and custody of goods after the buyer's breach or repudiation; or (iii) in connection with return or resale of the goods resulting from the breach or repudiation by the buyer.

X. WARRANTIES

A. WARRANTY OF TITLE

All sellers of goods warrant that the title conveyed is good and its transfer rightful. In addition, all sellers warrant that the goods will be delivered free from any security interest or other lien or encumbrance of which the buyer at the time of contracting has no knowledge. Article 2 allows disclaimer of the Title Warranty by specific language or by circumstances that give the buyer notice that the seller does not claim title or is selling only the rights that he actually has.

B. WARRANTY AGAINST INFRINGEMENT

Merchant sellers regularly dealing in goods of the kind warrant that the goods will be delivered free of the rightful claim of any third person by way of infringement (intellectual property protections) or the like. However, when a buyer furnishes specifications for the goods, the seller is held harmless against any such claims.

C. EXPRESS WARRANTIES

Any affirmation of fact or promise made by the seller to the buyer that relates to the goods and becomes part of the basis of the bargain creates an express warranty that the goods conform to that affirmation or promise. Any sample or model that is made part of the basis of the bargain creates an express warranty that the goods will conform to the sample or model. There are no "magic words" that need to be used—such as "guarantee" or "warranty"—before an express warranty is binding. Statements of opinion, affirmations of the value of the goods, or statements of commendation do not establish an express warranty.

Note that an express warranty can be made **subsequent** to the contract for sale. Technically, this would modify the original agreement, and under the UCC, no consideration is needed to make a modification enforceable.

D. IMPLIED WARRANTY OF MERCHANTABILITY

A warranty that the goods are merchantable is implied in a contract for their sale whenever the seller is a merchant with respect to goods of that kind. Under Article 2, serving food or drink for value, to be consumed either on the premises or elsewhere, is a sale subject to the implied warranty of merchantability.

To be merchantable, goods must at least:

i) Pass without objection in the trade under the contract description;

ii) In the case of fungible goods, be of fair average quality within the description;

iii) Be fit for the ordinary purposes for which such goods are used;

iv) Run, within the variations permitted by the agreement, of even kind, quality, and quantity within each unit and among all units involved;

v) Be adequately contained, packaged, and labeled as the agreement may require; and

vi) Conform to the promises or affirmations of fact made on the container or label, if any.

A breach of this warranty must have been present **at the time of the sale.**

The implied warranty of merchantability will be enforced regardless of whether the seller was aware of any breach of the warranty. The seller is strictly liable. However, if the buyer, before entering into the contract, has examined the goods or a sample or model as fully as the buyer desired, or has refused to examine the goods, then there is no implied warranty with respect to defects that an examination ought to have revealed to the buyer.

E. IMPLIED WARRANTY OF FITNESS FOR A PARTICULAR PURPOSE

When the seller at the time of contracting has reason to know (from any source, not just the buyer) of any particular purpose for which the goods are required, and that the buyer is relying on the seller's skill or judgment to select or furnish suitable goods, there is (unless excluded or modified), an implied warranty that the goods shall be fit for such purpose.

Note that the implied warranty of fitness for a particular purpose will apply to any seller (i.e., the seller need not be a merchant for it to apply).

F. EXCLUSION OR MODIFICATION OF WARRANTIES

1. Express Warranties

Under Article 2, words or conduct relevant to the creation of an express warranty and words or conduct tending to negate or limit warranty shall be construed as consistent with each other, but negation or limitation is inoperative to the extent such construction is unreasonable. Take note, however, that the parol-evidence rule may bar evidence of oral express warranties or disclaimers of such warranties.

2. Implied Warranties

a. Implied warranty of merchantability

One way for the seller to disclaim the implied warranty is to use the term "merchantability." This may be done orally. If it is in writing, the disclaimer language must be conspicuous. Unless the circumstances indicate otherwise, the implied warranty of merchantability can also be disclaimed by stating that the goods are sold "as is," "with all faults," or by using similar language that makes plain that there is no implied warranty.

b. Implied warranty of fitness for a particular purpose

An implied warranty of fitness for a particular purpose can be disclaimed **in writing** and by **conspicuous language.** Language to exclude all implied warranties of fitness is sufficient if it states, for example, that "There are no warranties that extend beyond the description on the face hereof." Unless the circumstances indicate otherwise, the fitness warranty can also be disclaimed by stating that the goods are sold "as is," "with all faults," or by using similar language that makes plain that there is no implied warranty.

c. Course of dealing or performance or trade usage

An implied warranty can also be excluded or modified by course of dealing or course of performance or usage of trade.

3. Unconscionability

Although Article 2 does not specifically provide that exclusion or modification of warranties may not be unconscionable, some courts have so held. *See* § III.B., Unconscionability, *supra*, regarding how to determine unconscionability.

4. Limitations under Federal Law

Federal consumer-protection law supersedes Article 2 to the extent that certain warranties cannot be disclaimed. Under the Magnuson-Moss Act, 15 U.S.C. §§ 2301 et seq., certain written consumer-product warranties must fully and conspicuously disclose terms and conditions of the warranty, including whether the warranty is "full" or "limited." If the warranty is described as a **full** warranty under the Act, then the warrantor must remedy a defect in the product within a reasonable time and without charge to the consumer. Under a full written warranty, implied warranties cannot be disclaimed. When a written warranty is described as a **limited warranty,** implied warranties may not be disclaimed during the warranty period.

G. LIMITATION OF DAMAGES

1. Consequential Damages

Consequential damages for breach, including a breach of warranty, may be limited or excluded unless the limitation or exclusion is unconscionable. Limitation of consequential damages for injury to the person in the case of consumer goods is prima facie unconscionable, but limitation of damages when the loss is commercial is not.

2. Liquidated Damages

Damages for breach by either party may be liquidated in the agreement, but only at an amount that is reasonable in light of the anticipated or actual harm caused by the breach, the difficulties of proof of loss, and the inconvenience or non-feasibility of otherwise obtaining an adequate remedy. A contractual term fixing unreasonably large liquidated damages is void as a penalty.

H. THIRD-PARTY RIGHTS

States are free to adopt alternative Article 2 provisions dealing with who may sue for a breach of warranty. Most states limit such causes of action to a claim against the buyer's immediate seller by the buyer and the buyer's immediate family and household guests, if it is reasonable to expect that such persons may use, consume, or be affected by the goods being warranted, and the person is personally injured as a result of the breach of warranty. A seller may not exclude or limit the operation of this provision.

Other states extend recovery against any seller in the chain of distribution byany natural person who may reasonably be expected to use, consume, or be affected by the goods being warranted and is injured in person by the breach of warranty. A seller may not exclude or limit the operation of this provision.

Still other states extend the right to sue any seller in the chain of distribution to anyone who is a foreseeable user or bystander regardless of thetype of injury involved. A seller may not exclude or limit the operation of this provision with respect to personal injury to a person to whom the provision applies but could exclude or limit the operation of the provision with respect to liability for damages other than personal injury.

I.   STRICT LIABILITY

Most states have adopted provisions making manufacturers, distributors, and retail sellers strictly liable for personal injuries or property damage caused by defective products. Lack of privity between the plaintiff and the defendant is no defense in any such action. Assumption of the risk would be a defense to such actions.

XI.   MISCELLANEOUS

A.   REMEDIES AVAILABLE TO BOTH THE BUYER AND THE SELLER

1.   Right to Proceed Against Third Parties

Article 2 has expansive rules about who may sue a third party when goods are damaged or destroyed. The seller may sue if she has either a security interest in the goods or title. The buyer may sue if the goods have been identified to the contract. Under circumstances in which a plaintiff party does not bear the risk of loss at the time of the damage, she sues as a fiduciary for the non-litigant party.

2.   Other Remedies and Limitations on Remedies

Article 2 allows the parties to agree in the contract to any remedy or limitation on a remedy that is not unconscionable. A typical provision will limit the buyer's remedy to repair or replacement of nonconforming goods or parts. If the seller refuses or is unable to provide the buyer with conforming goods, then the remedy will have "failed of its essential purpose." Where a remedy fails of its essential purpose, the buyer may resort to any appropriate remedy under Article 2.

3.   Statute of Limitations on Breach of a Sales Contract

a.   Period of limitations

Under Article 2, an action for breach of any sales contract must be commenced within **four years** after the cause of action accrues.

b.   When a cause of action accrues

In general, a cause of action accrues when the breach occurs, regardless of whether the aggrieved party knows of the breach. A breach of warranty accrues when delivery is made. If a warranty expressly extends to the future performance of the goods, then the cause of action will accrue when the breach is or should have been discovered by the aggrieved party.

c.   Modification of limitations period

By their original agreement, the parties may reduce the four-year limitations period of Article 2 to not less than one year, but they may not extend it.

B.   RIGHTS OF THIRD PARTIES

1.   Voidable Title

A buyer who obtains title unlawfully possesses a **voidable** title.

Nevertheless, Article 2 provides that a person with voidable title has power to transfer a good title to a **good-faith purchaser** for value (purchaser includes a person who, in good faith, takes a security interest in the goods) even though:

i) The seller was deceived as to the identity of the buyer;

ii) The delivery was in exchange for a check that is later dishonored;

iii) It was agreed that the transaction was to be a "cash sale"; or

iv) The delivery was procured through fraud punishable as larcenous under the criminal law.

2. Entrustment

Any entrusting of possession of goods to a merchant who deals in goods of that kind gives that merchant the power to transfer all rights of the entruster to a buyer in the ordinary course of business. "Entrusting" includes any delivery and any acquiescence in retention of possession regardless of any condition expressed between the parties to the delivery or acquiescence, and regardless of whether the procurement of the entrusting or the possessor's disposition of the goods is larcenous under the criminal law. A "buyer in the ordinary course of business" is one who in good faith and without knowledge of a third party's ownership rights or security interest buys from someone selling goods of that kind. UCC § 2-403.

3. Theft

Title cannot be obtained by theft. A thief acquires no title and, therefore, can pass no title. A good-faith purchaser from a thief does not cut off the rights of the true owner **except** when:

i) The buyer has made improvements (accessions) to the goods; or

ii) The true owner, by words or conduct, has indicated that the thief had good title to the goods.

Torts

TORTS

Table of Contents

TORTS

I. INTENTIONAL TORTS

A. GENERALLY

A prima facie case for an intentional tort must include proof of an **act**, **intent**, and **causation**.

1. Act

The act must be voluntary, meaning the defendant must have the state of mind that directed the physical muscular movement. Failure to act when there is a duty to do so also fulfills this element.

2. Intent

An act is performed intentionally if it is done deliberately and purposefully; that is, the actor desires to cause the consequences of his act, or the actor knows with **substantial certainty** that the conduct will result in the ensuing consequences. Intent is satisfied even if the actor does not intend to cause an injury.

The majority view states that minors and incompetents are also capable of having the requisite intent and can be held liable for their intentional torts.

Transferred intent exists when a person intends to commit an intentional tort against one person, but instead commits either:

i) A **different intentional tort** against that person;

ii) The intended tort **against a different person**; or

iii) A different intentional tort against a different person.

> **Example 1:** A intends to frighten B by shaking his fist at her (assault) but accidentally strikes B instead (battery). A's intent to commit assault is transferred to the ensuing battery.
>
> **Example 2:** A intends to harm B by shooting him with a gun, but A's aim is poor and he shoots C, who is standing nearby. A's intent to commit battery is transferred from the intended party (B) to the injured party (C), even though A had no intent to harm C.
>
> **Example 3:** A intends to frighten B by throwing a book at her but does not intend to hit B with the book (assault). A's aim is quite poor and he instead hits C with the book (battery). A's intent to assault B is transferred to the subsequent battery upon C.

Note that transferred intent applies only when the intended tort and the resulting tort are among the following: assault, battery, false imprisonment, trespass to land, or trespass to chattels.

3. Causation

Causation exists when the resulting harm was legally caused by the defendant's act. Causation is also established when the defendant's conduct is a substantial factor in creating the harm.

B. HARMS TO THE PERSON

1. Battery

A battery is a **harmful or offensive contact** with the **plaintiff's person** caused by the defendant's **intentional** act. The act must be volitional and must be intended to cause a harmful or offensive contact with someone. The plaintiff need not be aware of the contact when it occurs in order to recover.

a. Harmful or offensive contact

A contact is "harmful or offensive" when a reasonable person would find the contact harmful or offensive (objective test). An act is not harmful or offensive if the plaintiff consented to the act, either expressly or by virtue of participating in a particular event or situation (such as being bumped on a crowded subway or playing in a football game).

Note that a defendant may be liable if he is aware that the victim is hypersensitive but proceeds to act nonetheless. In such a case, the fact that a reasonable person would not object to the contact is not a defense.

b. Plaintiff's person

Contact with anything **connected to** the plaintiff's person qualifies as contact with the plaintiff's person for the purposes of battery (e.g., a person's clothing, a pet held on a leash, a bicycle ridden by the plaintiff).

c. Causation

The act must in fact result in contact of a harmful or offensive nature. A defendant who sets in motion a chain of events that causes contact with the plaintiff, whether the contact is direct or indirect, is liable (e.g., a trip wire set by the defendant that causes the plaintiff to fall).

d. Intent

A defendant intentionally causes contact if she acts with the desire to bring about the harm or engages in action knowing that the harm is substantially certain to occur. The doctrine of transferred intent applies to battery.

e. Damages

No proof of harm is required; the plaintiff may recover nominal damages even though no actual damage occurred (to vindicate a plaintiff's right to physical autonomy). Many states allow recovery of punitive damages if the defendant acted with malice (i.e., a wrongful motive, or a conscious or deliberate disregard of a high probability of harm).

2. Assault

An assault occurs when the defendant's **intentional overt act** causes the plaintiff to experience **reasonable apprehension** of an **imminent** battery.

a. Intent

The act must be volitional and performed with intent to place someone in apprehension of imminent harm or offensive contact. The doctrine of transferred intent applies to assault.

b. Overt act

Words alone are not enough to constitute an overt act, but words coupled with conduct or other circumstances may be sufficient.

c. Reasonable apprehension

A plaintiff's apprehension must be reasonable, and unlike a battery, he must be aware or have knowledge of the defendant's act. The defendant's apparent ability to cause harm (e.g., a toy gun) can be sufficient to place the plaintiff in apprehension of harm.

d. Immediacy

The threat of harm must be imminent—without significant delay. Threats of future harm are insufficient, as are threats made by a defendant too far away to inflict any harm.

e. Damages

No proof of harm is required. As with battery, nominal damages are available, and in many states, punitive damages may be imposed if the defendant acted with malice.

3. False Imprisonment

False imprisonment results when a person acts:

i)   Intending to **confine or restrain**;

ii) Another person;

iii) To a **bounded area**; and

iv) Those actions directly or indirectly **result in such confinement.**

a. Intent

The doctrine of transferred intent applies to false imprisonment.

b. Confine or restrain

1) Methods

a) Sufficient

The defendant may confine or restrain the plaintiff by the use of physical barriers, physical force, direct or indirect threats (to the plaintiff, a third party, or plaintiff's property), failure to provide a means of escape, or invalid use of legal authority.

> **Shopkeeper's Privilege:** A shopkeeper's reasonable (in both duration and manner) detention of a suspected shoplifter is **not** an invalid use of authority, and hence is not a false imprisonment.

b) Insufficient

The defendant's use of moral pressure or future threats does not constitute confinement or restraint. The plaintiff is not imprisoned if she submitted willingly to confinement.

2) Time

The length of time of the confinement or restraint is immaterial (except so as to determine the extent of damages).

3) Awareness

The plaintiff must be conscious of the confinement. Alternatively, under the Restatement approach, a plaintiff who is unaware of the confinement must suffer actual harm.

c. Bounded area

A bounded area is one within which the plaintiff's freedom of movement in all directions is limited. An area is not bounded if there is a **reasonable** means of safe escape.

d. Damages

It is not necessary to prove actual damages (except when the plaintiff is unaware of the confinement). Punitive damages may be imposed if the defendant acted with malice.

4. Intentional Infliction of Emotional Distress

A defendant is liable for **intentionally or recklessly** acting with **extreme or outrageous conduct**, which conduct causes the plaintiff **severe emotional distress**.

a. Intent

The defendant must intend to cause severe emotional distress or must act with recklessness as to the risk of causing such distress. Transferred intent does *not* apply.

b. Extreme or outrageous conduct

Conduct is extreme or outrageous if it exceeds the possible limits of human decency, so as to be entirely intolerable in a civilized society. Conduct that is not necessarily outrageous may become so if it is **continuous**, directed at a member of a group with a known **heightened sensitivity** (e.g., children, pregnant women, or elderly persons); or committed by a **common carrier or innkeeper** (who are held to a higher standard and may be liable for insulting remarks or indecent language) and the victim is a customer.

c. Liability for acts directed at third parties

When the defendant's conduct is directed at a third-party victim, that defendant is liable if he intentionally or recklessly causes severe emotional distress to:

i) A **member of the victim's immediate family** who is present at the time of the defendant's conduct (and the defendant is aware of such presence), whether or not such distress results in bodily injury; or

ii) Any other bystander who is present at the time of the conduct (and the defendant is aware of such presence) when the **distress results in bodily injury**.

Restatement (Second) of Torts § 46.

d. Causation

The plaintiff may establish causation by a showing that the defendant's actions were a **substantial factor** in creating the plaintiff's distress.

Special rules of causation apply in cases in which a bystander makes a claim of severe emotional distress. When the defendant has caused severe **physical** harm to a third party and the plaintiff suffers severe emotional distress as a result, the plaintiff can recover if the:

i) Plaintiff was **present** when the defendant inflicted the harm;

ii) Plaintiff was a **close relative** to the injured person; and

iii) Defendant **had knowledge** of both of the above facts.

Note that the plaintiff does not need to prove the above if the defendant's **design or purpose** was to cause severe distress to the plaintiff.

e. Damages

The plaintiff must prove actual damages, i.e., severe emotional distress beyond what a reasonable person could endure, but she does not need to prove physical injury (except in § I.B.4.c.ii, Liability for Acts Directed at Third Parties, *supra*).

> **EXAM NOTE:** The distinction between intentional infliction and negligent infliction of emotional distress (§ II.F.1., Negligent Infliction of Emotional Distress, *infra*) is often tested on the bar exam.

C. HARMS TO PROPERTY INTERESTS

1. Trespass to Land

Trespass to land occurs when the defendant's **intentional** act causes a **physical invasion** of the land of another.

a. Intent

The defendant need only have the intent to enter the land (or to cause a physical invasion), not the intent to trespass. The defendant need not know that the land belongs to another. Mistake of fact is not a defense.

> The doctrine of transferred intent applies to trespass to land.

b. Physical invasion

1) Need not enter land

The defendant need not personally enter onto the plaintiff's land; flooding the plaintiff's land, throwing rocks onto it, or chasing a third party onto it all will suffice. Additionally, the defendant's failure to leave the plaintiff's property after his lawful right of entry has expired constitutes a physical invasion.

2) What is land?

A trespass may be committed on, above, or below the surface of the plaintiff's land.

3) Distinguish from nuisance

If no physical object enters onto the plaintiff's land (e.g., the defendant's floodlights project onto plaintiff's land, or damage results from the defendant's blasting), the case is generally treated as a nuisance or strict liability action (*discussed infra*).

c. Standing

Because the right to possession is being protected, anyone in actual or constructive possession of land may bring an action for trespass (e.g., lessee, adverse possessor).

d. Damages

No proof of actual damages is required.

2. Trespass to Chattels

A defendant is liable for trespass to chattels if he **intentionally** commits an act that **interferes with a plaintiff's right of possession** of the chattel (i.e., tangible personal property) and causes **damage.**

a. Intent

Only the intent to do the interfering act is necessary; the defendant need not have intended to interfere with another's possession of tangible property. Further, mistake as to the lawfulness of the defendant's activities is no defense.

The doctrine of transferred intent applies to trespass to chattels.

b. Interference

The defendant interferes with the plaintiff's right of possession (plaintiff need not be the owner—merely one entitled to immediate possession of the property, e.g., lessee, bailee) by either:

    i) **Dispossessing** the plaintiff of her chattels; or

    ii) **Using or intermeddling** with the plaintiff's chattels.

c. Standing

An action for trespass to chattels may be brought by anyone with possession or the immediate right to possession of the chattel.

d. Damages

In a case of dispossession, a plaintiff must prove damages by either:

    i) The **actual amount caused** by the interference; or

    ii) The loss of use.

In circumstances of intermeddling, the plaintiff must show actual damages.

e. Mistake

Mistake by the defendant about the legality of his actions is no defense.

f. Remedy

The plaintiff may be entitled to compensation for the diminution in value, the cost of repair, and/or reasonable rental value.

3. Conversion

A defendant is liable for conversion if he **intentionally** commits an act of **possession or interference** with the plaintiff's chattel so **serious** that he deprives the plaintiff of the chattel and must pay its full value as of the time of the conversion.

Only personal property and intangibles that have been reduced to physical form (e.g., a promissory note) can be converted.

a. Intent

The defendant must only intend to commit the act that interferes; intent to cause damage is not necessary. Mistake of law or fact is no defense (e.g., a purchaser of stolen goods is liable to the rightful owner).

Accidentally damaging the plaintiff's chattel is **not** conversion **if** the defendant had permission to be using the property.

b. Interference

The defendant interferes with the plaintiff's chattel by exercising **dominion or control** over it. Examples of acts of conversion include wrongful acquisition, transfer, or detention; substantially changing; severely damaging or destroying; or misusing the chattel.

Note that if the acquisition was not wrongful, there must be a demand for the return of the chattel before the plaintiff may sue for conversion.

c. Seriousness

There is no specific rule as to what behavior constitutes conversion, as opposed to trespass to chattels; it is a matter of degree of seriousness. The following factors are considered:

i) **Duration and extent** of interference;

ii) The defendant's **intent to assert a right inconsistent** with the rightful possessor;

iii) The defendant's **good faith**;

iv) Expense or inconvenience to the plaintiff; and

v) **Extent of the harm** to the chattel.

Generally, the greater the degree of these factors, the greater the likelihood that a conversion has occurred.

d. Damages

The plaintiff may receive damages in the amount of the full value of the converted property at the time of the conversion. Alternatively, the plaintiff may bring an action for replevin to recover the chattel.

D. DEFENSES TO INTENTIONAL TORTS TO PERSONS AND PROPERTY

1. Consent

The majority view is that a person cannot consent to a criminal act.

a. Express

The plaintiff expressly consents if she, by words or actions, manifests the willingness to submit to the defendant's conduct. The defendant's conduct may not exceed the scope of the consent.

1) Mistake

Consent by mistake is still valid consent unless the defendant caused the mistake or knew of it and took advantage of it.

2) Fraud

Consent induced by fraud is invalid if it goes to an essential matter. If the fraud that induced the consent goes only to a collateral matter, the consent is still valid.

3) Duress

Consent given while under duress (physical force or threats) is not valid. However, the threat must be present, not a threat of future action.

b. Implied

The plaintiff's consent is implied when the plaintiff is silent (or otherwise nonresponsive) in a situation when a reasonable person would object to the defendant's actions.

1) Implied by law

Consent may be implied by law in situations when action is necessary to save a person's life or some other important interest, e.g., emergency surgery after a car accident that leaves the plaintiff unconscious.

2) Implied by custom

Consent may also be implied by custom or usage (e.g., participation in a contact sport).

c. Capacity

Youth, intoxication, and incompetence each prevent a person from being able to give valid consent.

2. Self-Defense

A person may use non-deadly force to defend against an offensive contact or bodily harm that he reasonably believes is about to be intentionally inflicted upon him. A mistaken belief that he is in danger does not invalidate the defense. He may use deadly force only if he has a reasonable belief that force sufficient to cause serious bodily injury or death is about to be intentionally inflicted upon him. The force used in self-defense must be reasonably proportionate to the anticipated harm.

a. Retreat

A person is not required to retreat under the majority rule, but there is a growing trend toward requiring retreat before using deadly force **unless** the defendant is in (or within the curtilage of) her own home. Under the Restatement (Second), a person has a duty to retreat before he may use defensive deadly force if he can do so safely.

b. Initial aggressor

The initial aggressor is not entitled to claim self-defense unless the other party has responded to non-deadly force with deadly force.

c. Third-party injuries

The actor is not liable for injuries to bystanders that occurred while exercising self-defense, so long as those injuries were accidental, rather than deliberate, and the actor was not negligent with respect to the bystander.

3. Defense of Others

Defense of another is permitted upon reasonable belief that the defended party would be entitled to use self-defense. The defender may use force that is proportionate to the anticipated harm to the other party. He is not liable for acting on a mistaken belief that another was in danger as long as his belief is *reasonable*.

4. Defense of Property

A person may use force to defend his property from the commission of a tort if he reasonably believes in the apparent necessity of that use of force and he uses only a reasonable and proportionate degree of force. He may not, however, use force to defend his property against another when the other person has a privilege to enter the land. Deadly force may not be used to defend property unless the defender reasonably believes he will personally suffer serious bodily injury or death. A person may never use a deadly mechanical device (e.g., a spring-loaded gun) to defend his property. Finally, a person is not liable for using force if he makes a reasonable mistake with respect to an intrusion occurring on his land.

5. Recapture of Chattels

a. Reasonable force

A person may use reasonable force to reclaim his personal property that has been wrongfully taken by another. If the original taking was lawful (e.g., bailment), only peaceful means may be used to reclaim the chattel.

b. Forcible entry onto land

At common law, an owner or possessor of land was permitted to use reasonable force to regain possession of that land from one who had wrongfully taken possession of it. However, modern statutes provide procedures for recovery of realty; therefore, use of force is no longer allowed.

6. Parental Discipline

A parent may use reasonable force or impose reasonable confinement as is necessary to discipline a child, taking into consideration the age of the child and the gravity of the behavior. An educator has the same privilege unless the parent places restrictions on that privilege.

7. Necessity

The privilege of necessity is available to a person who enters onto the land of another or interferes with another's personal property in order to prevent injury that is substantially more serious than the invasion or interference itself. Note that the privilege of necessity applies only to intentional torts to property.

a. Private necessity

Private necessity is a qualified privilege to protect a limited number of people. For example, entering another's land to protect one's own person or property from harm is justified by private necessity. The actor is not liable for trespass; if there are no actual damages, the landowner cannot recover nominal damages. However, the actor is responsible for any actual damages that result from his actions.

b. Public necessity

Public necessity is an unqualified privilege to protect a large number of people. Entering another's land in order to avert an imminent public disaster is a matter of public necessity. **It is an absolute privilege.** As long as the defendant acts reasonably, he is not liable for any damage to the property. He is not liable even if the original entry was not necessary, as long as he reasonably believed the necessity existed. The privilege lasts only as long as the emergency continues.

8. Privilege of Arrest

a. Felony

1) Private citizen

A private citizen is privileged to make an arrest in the case of a felony if a felony has in fact been committed and the arresting party has reasonable grounds to suspect that the person being arrested committed it.

It is a defense to make a reasonable mistake as to the identity of the felon but not as to the commission of the felony.

2) Police officer

A police officer must reasonably believe that a felony has been committed and that the person he arrests committed it. Unlike a private citizen, a police officer who makes a mistake as to the commission of a felony is not subject to tort liability.

b. Misdemeanor

In the case of a misdemeanor, an arrest may be made only if the misdemeanor is a breach of the peace that is being committed or reasonably appears about to be committed **in the presence** of the arresting party (regardless of whether an officer or private citizen).

II. NEGLIGENCE

> **EXAM NOTE:** Half of the torts questions on the MBE test the topic of negligence. In addition to memorizing the elements, be sure to know that the defendant must:
>
> i)   Fail to exercise the care that a reasonable person in his position would exercise; and
>
> ii) Act in a way that breaches the duty to prevent the foreseeable risk of harm to anyone in the plaintiff's position, and the breach must be the cause of the plaintiff's injuries.

Negligence is the commission of an act (or the failure to act), without wrongful intent, that falls below the minimum degree of ordinary care imposed by law to protect others against unreasonable risk of harm.

A prima facie case for negligence consists of four elements:

i) **Duty**, the obligation to protect another against unreasonable risk of injury;

ii) **Breach**, the failure to meet that obligation;

iii) **Causation**, a close causal connection between the action and the injury; and

iv) **Damages**, the loss suffered.

> **EXAM NOTE:** When analyzing answer choices to negligence questions, look for the threshold elements. For instance, if there is no duty, then you can dismiss answer choices involving damages, breach, or causation.

A. DUTY

Generally, a duty of care is owed to all foreseeable persons who may be injured by another's failure to follow a reasonable standard of care.

1. Failure to Act

In general, there is no affirmative duty to act; moral obligation does not create a legal obligation to render aid to or protect another from harm. However, the failure to perform an act that is **necessary** to protect or assist another person, and which the actor is **under a duty** to perform, does constitute negligent conduct.

2. Unforeseeable Plaintiffs

A duty of care is generally owed only to all foreseeable plaintiffs. (However, a defendant may also be liable to an "unforeseen" plaintiff if a breach of a duty to one plaintiff results in injury to a second plaintiff.)

The **majority rule** for determining whether a plaintiff is a "foreseeable plaintiff" was that established in *Palsgraf v. Long Island Railroad*, 162 N.E. 99 (NY 1928)—the defendant is liable only to plaintiffs who are within the **zone of foreseeable harm**. This rule is referred to as the "Cardozo view."

The Andrews (minority) view states that if the defendant has breached a duty to anyone, the same duty is owed to everyone (foreseeable or not) harmed as a result of his breach.

3. Obligations to Control the Conduct of Third Parties

There is generally no duty to control the conduct of a third party, except in cases when the defendant has a special relationship with either the actor or the foreseeable victim of the actor's conduct (*see* § II.B.6. Affirmative Duty to Act, *infra*).

> **Example:** A parent may be liable for failing to control the conduct of a child who uses a dangerous instrumentality to injure a plaintiff.

4. **Special Foreseeable Plaintiffs**

   a. **Rescuers**

   A person who comes to the aid of another is a foreseeable plaintiff. If the defendant negligently put the rescuer or himself in any danger, he is liable for the rescuer's injuries. The defendant is not liable if the rescuer is haphazard or wanton while attempting the rescue. An emergency professional, such as a police officer or firefighter, is barred from recovering damages from the party whose negligence cause the professional's injury ("firefighter's rule").

   b. **Intended beneficiaries**

   A defendant is liable to a third-party beneficiary if the legal or business transaction the beneficiary is a part of is prepared negligently and the defendant could foresee the harm of completing the transaction.

   c. **Fetuses**

   Fetuses are owed a duty of care if they are viable at the time the injury occurred. However, most states do not permit actions by a child for "wrongful life" based on the failure to properly perform a contraceptive procedure or failure to diagnose a congenital defect, even if the child is born with a disability. Conversely, many states do permit parents to recover for "wrongful birth" (failure to diagnose a defect) or "wrongful pregnancy" (failure to perform a contraceptive procedure). Generally, the mother can recover damages for the medical expenses of labor, as well as for pain and suffering. In the case of a disabled child, the parents may be able to recover damages for the additional medical expenses of caring for that child, and, in some states, may recover for emotional distress as well.

B. **THE STANDARD OF CARE**

1. **Reasonably Prudent Standard**

   In most cases, the standard of care imposed is that of a **reasonably prudent person under the circumstances**, as measured by an **objective** standard. Under this standard, the defendant is presumed to have average mental abilities and the same knowledge as an average member of the community. An actor is required to exercise the care that a reasonable person under the same circumstances (i.e., in his position, with his information and competence) would recognize as necessary to avoid or prevent an unreasonable risk of harm to another person. In determining whether particular precautions were warranted, a jury should weigh the probability and gravity of the injury against the burden of taking such precautions.

   a. **Characteristics considered**

   The defendant's own mental handicaps are not considered, but the defendant's particular **physical characteristics** (e.g., blindness) are taken into account in determining the reasonableness of the defendant's behavior. Intoxicated individuals are held to the same standards as sober individuals unless their intoxication was involuntary.

b. Customs considered

Evidence of custom in a community or industry may be offered to establish the proper standard of care, **but such evidence is not conclusive**. The entire community or industry may be negligent.

2. Other Standards

a. Children

The standard of care imposed upon a child is that of a reasonable child of similar age, intelligence, education, and experience. Restatement (Second) of Torts § 283A. Unlike the objective standard applied to adult negligent defendants, the standard applicable to minors is more subjective in nature as children are unable to appreciate the same risks as an adult. However, children engaged in adult behavior, such as driving a car, are held to the same standard as an adult. Children under the age of four are generally incapable of negligent conduct.

b. Professionals

A professional person (e.g., doctor, lawyer, or electrician) is expected to exhibit the same skill, knowledge, and care as another practitioner in the same community. A specialist may be held to a higher standard than a general practitioner if he has superior knowledge.

c. Special rule for physicians—informed consent

Physicians are under a special obligation to explain all material risks of a medical procedure to a patient in advance of a patient's decision to consent to treatment. Failure to comply with this **"informed consent"** doctrine constitutes a breach of the physician's duty toward the patient and is actionable as medical malpractice.

Doctors are not under an obligation to disclose when the:

   i) Risk is a **commonly known** risk;

   ii) **Patient waives** or refuses the information;

   iii) **Patient is incompetent** (although the physician must make a reasonable attempt to secure informed consent from a guardian); or

   iv) **Disclosure would be too harmful** to the patient (e.g., would upset the patient enough to cause extreme illness, such as a heart attack).

d. Common carriers and innkeepers

Common carriers and innkeepers are held to the highest duty of care consistent with the practical operation of the business. Accordingly, they have a broader duty to prevent unreasonable risk of injury to their customers.

> **EXAM NOTE:** Be certain to apply the carriers and innkeepers standards only to customers or guests.

e. Automobile drivers

In most jurisdictions, automobile drivers owe ordinary care to their guests as well as their passengers (those who confer an economic benefit for the ride).

However, a minority of states distinguish between the two with "guest statutes," which impose only a duty to refrain from gross or wanton and willful misconduct with a guest in the car. Proof of simple negligence by the driver will not result in recovery by the plaintiff guest.

f. Bailors-bailees

The duty of care that must be exercised by a bailor or bailee varies, depending on the type of bailment.

   i) Bailor—The bailor has a duty to inform the gratuitous bailee only of **known** dangerous defects in personal property, but must inform a bailee for hire of defects which are known or **should have been known** by the bailor had he used reasonable diligence.

   ii) Bailee—When a bailor receives the sole benefit from the bailment, the bailee has a lesser duty to care for the property and is liable only if he has been grossly negligent. In contrast, when a bailee receives the sole benefit from the bailment, he must exercise extraordinary care for the bailor's property. Slight negligence on the bailee's part will result in liability for any injuries to the property from failure to properly care for or use it. In a bailment for mutual benefit, the bailee must take reasonable care of the bailed property.

Note that the trend is toward a directive that imposes the use of ordinary care under all circumstances on the bailee.

3. Standards Applicable to Owners and Occupiers of Land

In general, possessors of land owe a duty only to those within the boundaries of their land. The term "landowner" as used here includes owners, occupiers, and possessors of land, unless indicated otherwise.

a. Trespassers

A trespasser is one who enters or remains upon the land of another without privilege or consent to do so. A landowner is obligated to refrain from willful, wanton, or intentional misconduct toward trespassers.

1) Discovered trespassers

Landowners owe a duty toward **discovered** or **anticipated** trespassers to warn or protect them from **concealed dangerous artificial conditions**. There is no duty to warn of natural conditions or artificial conditions that do not involve risk of death or serious bodily harm. Landowners also have a duty to use reasonable care while conducting activities on their land as well as to control the activities of third parties on their property.

2) Undiscovered trespassers

Landowners owe no duty to undiscovered trespassers, nor do they have a duty to inspect their property for evidence of trespassers.

Note that a majority of jurisdictions state that when a landowner should reasonably know that trespassers are consistently entering his land, the landowner owes a duty to the trespasser, regardless of the landowner's actual knowledge.

3) Attractive nuisance

Under the "attractive nuisance" doctrine, a landowner may be liable for **injuries to children** trespassing on the land if:

i) An artificial condition exists in a place the owner knows or has reason to know **children are likely to trespass**;

ii) The owner knows or has reason to know that the condition poses an **unreasonable risk** of death or serious bodily injury to children;

iii) The **children**, because of their youth, do not discover or **cannot appreciate the danger** presented by the condition;

iv) The utility to the landowner of maintaining the condition and the burden of eliminating the danger are **slight compared to the risk** of harm presented to children; and

v) The landowner fails to exercise **reasonable care** to protect children from the harm.

b. Licensees

A licensee is one privileged by virtue of the landowner's consent to enter or remain upon another's land for his own benefit. Social guests are considered licensees.

A landowner has a duty to warn a licensee of **known** dangerous conditions and must exercise **reasonable care** in conducting activities on the land.

c. Invitees

An invitee is one who enters the land of another by invitation, often, but not necessarily, for the business purposes of the landowner. Those who enter upon land held open to the public are invitees.

A landowner owes the greatest duty of care to invitees: he is under the same obligations owed to licensees (duty to **warn** and to **use reasonable care**), but he also must **conduct reasonable inspections** of his property and make the property safe for the protection of invitees. Such a landowner is liable for **any** negligence that causes an invitee to be injured due to unsafe conditions, even if the negligent party was an independent contractor (*see* § II.G.1.b., Independent contractors, *infra*).

However, the duty of care owed to an invitee does not extend beyond the scope of the invitation, and the invitee is treated as a trespasser in areas beyond that scope.

Note that a strong minority of states no longer distinguishes between invitee and licensee, and some have eliminated trespasser status as well. In these cases, a reasonable person standard is applied to dangerous conditions on land.

d. Easement and license holders

Easement holders and those licensed to use land must exercise reasonable care to protect the trespasser.

Example: Gas Company acquires an easement from Landowner to run gas lines, but negligently fails to maintain the lines. A gas line leaks causing an explosion and injuring a trespasser on landowner's property. Gas Company is liable to trespasser.

e. Lessors of land

Because the obligations associated with property are owed by the possessor of the land, a lessee assumes any duty owed by the lessor once the lessee takes possession. If only a portion of the land is leased, the lessor is still responsible for ensuring the safety of the common areas. The lessor has a duty to warn the lessee of existing defects on the premises of which the lessor knows the lessee is not likely to discover on his own reasonable inspection.

1) Exceptions

When the lessor promises to make repairs of reasonably dangerous defects, the lessor remains responsible for injuries arising from those defects. However, if the lessor voluntarily and without commitment makes those repairs, he is not liable unless he does so negligently.

A warning is insufficient when the lessor transfers property to the lessee with existing unreasonably dangerous conditions knowing that the lessee intends to admit the public and will not repair the defects. In this case, the lessor remains liable until the defect is repaired.

2) Tenant's liability

As an occupier of land, the tenant continues to be liable for injuries to third parties arising from dangerous conditions within the tenant's control, regardless of whether the landowner has liability.

f. Recreational land users

A landowner who opens his land to the public for recreational purposes is not liable for injuries sustained by recreational land users so long as he does not charge a fee for the use of his land, unless the landowner willfully and maliciously failed to warn users of a dangerous condition.

g. Off-premises persons

A landowner generally does not owe a duty to a person not on the premises (e.g., passerby, owner of adjacent land) who is harmed by a natural condition on the landowner's premises. An exception exists, however, with respect to trees in urban areas.

With respect to an artificial condition, the landowner generally owes a duty to prevent an unreasonable risk of harm to persons who are not on the premises. Similarly, with respect to an activity conducted on the premises by the owner or by someone subject to the owner's control, the landowner generally owes a duty of reasonable care to persons who are not on the premises.

h. Sellers of real property

Sellers of real property owe a duty to disclose to buyers those concealed and unreasonably dangerous conditions known to the seller. These are conditions that the buyer is unlikely to discover upon reasonable inspection. Seller's liability continues until the buyer has a reasonable opportunity, through maintenance and inspection, to discover and remedy the defect.

4. Emergencies

The applicable standard of care in an emergency is that of a reasonable person in the same situation, but only if the defendant's conduct did not cause the emergency.

5. Statutory Standards of Care

When a criminal statute or administrative regulation defines the standard of reasonable conduct, that standard supersedes common-law standards. Violation of such a statute is negligence *per se*. The plaintiff may establish a duty and breach of that duty by proving that:

i) He was **in the class** of people intended to be protected by the statute;

ii) The **interest** was of the type intended to be protected;

iii) The **harm** was of the type intended to be protected; and

iv) The harm materialized in the **manner** that was of legislative concern.

The defendant can avoid liability by proving that compliance was either impossible under the circumstances or that compliance would have been more dangerous than noncompliance. Sometimes even compliance with a statute does not necessarily prevent the defendant's liability if it is shown that compliance did not establish due care and the action required more than what the statute was designed to meet.

6. Affirmative Duty to Act

Although there is generally no affirmative duty to act, there are some notable exceptions to that rule.

i) Assumption of duty—A person who voluntarily aids or rescues another is liable for injury caused by a failure to act with reasonable ordinary care in the performance of that aid or rescue.

Note that some states have enacted "Good Samaritan" statutes to protect doctors and other medical personnel when they voluntarily render emergency care. These statutes exempt medical professionals from liability for ordinary negligence. However, they do not exempt them from gross negligence.

ii) Placing another in peril—A person who places another in peril is under a duty to exercise reasonable care to prevent further harm by rendering care or aid.

iii) By contract—There is a duty to perform contractual obligations with due care.

iv) By authority—One with actual ability and authority to control another, such as parents over children and employers over employees, has an affirmative duty to exercise reasonable control. Generally, this duty is imposed upon the defendant when the defendant knows or should know that the third person is apt to commit the injuring act.

v) By relationship—Defendants with a unique relationship to plaintiffs, such as business proprietor-patron, common carrier-passenger, employer-employee, and parent-child may have a duty to aid or assist the plaintiffs and to prevent reasonably foreseeable injury to them from third parties.

C.   PROOF OF FAULT

1.   Burden of Proof

The plaintiff must establish all four elements of negligence (duty, breach, causation, damage) by a **preponderance of the evidence**. A breach of duty occurs when the defendant departs from the conduct expected of a reasonably prudent person acting under similar circumstances. The evidence must show a greater probability than not that (i) the defendant failed to meet the required standard of care, (ii) that failure was the proximate cause of the injury, and (iii) the plaintiff suffered damages. The plaintiff can demonstrate such failure by introducing evidence of the required standard of care through custom and usage, violation of a statute, or *res ipsa loquitur*.

2.   Res Ipsa Loquitur

Under the doctrine of *res ipsa loquitur*, the trier of fact may infer the existence of negligence in the absence of direct evidence of such negligence. *Res ipsa* is circumstantial evidence of negligence that **does not** change the standard of care. For this doctrine to apply, the plaintiff must prove that:

i) The plaintiff's injury or damage was caused by an instrumentality or condition that was under the **defendant's exclusive control** or the defendant was responsible for all others in control at the relevant times;

ii) The plaintiff's harm **would not have occurred if the defendant had used ordinary care** while the instrumentality was under his control; and

iii) The plaintiff was not responsible for his injury.

With respect to the second element, the focus is on the fact that the plaintiff's injury would not have occurred in the absence of negligence. Because there is no direct evidence, the court relies on a statistical guess based on other accidents of this type, and whether they ordinarily result from negligence. However, there is not a complete guarantee that this particular plaintiff's injury resulted from negligence.

If there are multiple defendants (i.e., more than one person may have had control of the instrumentality), *res ipsa loquitur* generally does not apply. However, in medical malpractice cases, a significant minority of jurisdictions has required each defendant to exonerate himself. *See, e.g., Ybarra v. Spangard*, 25 Cal. 2d 486 (1944).

If the plaintiff establishes the above three elements (that is, a prima facie case of *res ipsa*) the trial court must deny the defendant's motion for a directed verdict, and the issue of negligence must be decided by the trier of fact. *Res ipsa* does not require that the trier of fact find negligence on the defendant's part. It simply establishes an inference of negligence sufficient to avoid dismissal of the plaintiff's action.

EXAM NOTE: *Res ipsa loquitur* does not apply if there is direct evidence of the cause of the injury.

D. CAUSATION

The plaintiff must prove that the defendant's actions were both the actual (cause-in-fact) cause and proximate (legal) cause of the plaintiff's injury.

1. Actual Cause

a. "But for" test

If the plaintiff's injury would not have occurred but for the defendant's act or omission, then the defendant's conduct is the cause-in-fact of the harm. If the injury would have occurred despite the defendant's conduct, there is no cause-in-fact.

b. Substantial factor test

In cases in which several causes/defendants may have contributed to the plaintiff's injury, the "but for" test may not be determinative. In such cases, causation can be established by proving that the defendant's conduct was a substantial factor in causing the plaintiff's injury.

c. Multiple causes

If there are multiple defendants and it is unclear which defendant caused the harm, the burden of proof shifts to each defendant to prove that he did not in fact cause the harm to the plaintiff. This burden shifting generally occurs only if there are relatively few defendants.

> **EXAM NOTE:** Beware of fact patterns involving more than one cause-in-fact. If the defendant's conduct was a **substantial factor in causing the damages**, the defendant does not escape liability solely because another person might have contributed to the plaintiff's damages.

2. Proximate Cause

In addition to actual causation, the plaintiff must also prove proximate causation, or legal responsibility. Generally, injuries suffered by individuals within the **"zone of danger"** created by the defendant's unreasonable conduct are proximately caused by the defendant. The doctrine of proximate cause is a limitation on liability; that is, even when a defendant's act is the "but for" cause of the plaintiff's injury, if that plaintiff was outside the zone of danger and was not foreseeable, the defendant is not liable (*See* § II.A.2. Unforeseeable Plaintiffs, *supra*).

> **EXAM NOTE:** Remember that there must be cause-in-fact for proximate cause to exist, and if cause-in-fact exists, then proximate cause exists unless there are intervening acts.

a. Direct cause

Proximate cause exists when the defendant's actions are the **direct** cause of the plaintiff's injuries, i.e., when the defendant starts a natural and continuous sequence of events without which the plaintiff's injury would not have occurred. In other words, the defendant is liable for all harm to the plaintiff that is a foreseeable consequence of the defendant's actions. If the type of injury suffered by the plaintiff is entirely unforeseeable as a result of the defendant's conduct, there is no proximate cause.

b. Indirect cause

When an intervening force occurs between the defendant's act and the plaintiff's injury, the question arises as to whether it was the defendant's act or the intervening force that caused the plaintiff's injury. Foreseeability is the key factor in establishing proximate cause.

1) Foreseeable intervening forces

Generally, the defendant is liable for harm caused by foreseeable intervening forces that occur between the time of the defendant's act and the plaintiff's injury. Examples of foreseeable intervening forces include subsequent medical malpractice, disease, or accident; negligence of rescuers; normal forces of nature; or efforts to protect a person or property.

2) Unforeseeable intervening forces

When an intervening force is unforeseeable, a defendant will still be liable for his acts (or omissions) if the *result* was nevertheless foreseeable.

Example: An owner is aware of a rotten tree limb overhanging a sidewalk and negligently fails to remove it. It is struck by lightning and injures a passing pedestrian. The intervening force (the lightning) was unforeseeable, but the injury was not. The unforeseeable intervening cause does not absolve the defendant of liability.

However, when both the intervening cause and the harm are unforeseeable, the intervening cause becomes a **superseding cause**, and the defendant's liability is cut off by that superseding cause. Examples of superseding causes may include acts of God and criminal acts and/or intentional torts of third parties.

EXAM NOTE: Remember that the original tortfeasors remain liable unless the results of an intervening negligent act are **unforeseeable**. In particular, keep in mind that medical malpractice is foreseeable, and therefore it is not a superseding cause that breaks the chain of causation and insulates the defendant from liability.

E. DAMAGES

1. Actual Damages

The plaintiff must prove actual injury; nominal damages are not available in negligence actions, nor are damages for the threat of future harm. In addition, a plaintiff who suffers only economic loss without any related personal injury or property damage cannot recover such loss through a negligence action.

2. Duty to Mitigate

The plaintiff has a duty to take reasonable steps to mitigate damages. Traditionally, the failure to do so precluded the plaintiff from recovering for any additional harm caused by aggravation of the injury. In comparative negligence jurisdictions, the failure to mitigate is taken into account, but does not categorically prevent recovery for such harm.

3. Personal Injury

The measure of damages in a personal injury action includes:

i) All actual damages incurred;

ii) Past and future pain and suffering (e.g., emotional distress);

iii) Medical expenses;

iv) Lost wages and any reduction in future earnings capacity; and

v) Loss of consortium.

The plaintiff's duty to mitigate requires that he seek appropriate treatment for any injuries caused by the defendant.

Under the "eggshell skull" rule, the defendant is liable for the full extent of the plaintiff's injuries due to the plaintiff's pre-existing medical condition or vulnerability, even if the extent is unusual or unforeseeable.

Attorneys' fees and interest from the date of damage in a personal injury suit are not recoverable as damages in negligence actions.

4. Property Damage

The measure of damages in property damage actions is loss of use, the reasonable cost of repair, or the fair market value at the time of the accident if the property was destroyed.

5. Collateral Source Rule

Benefits or payments provided to the plaintiff from outside sources (such as medical insurance) are not credited against the liability of any tortfeasor, nor is evidence of such payments admissible at trial.

Exception: Payments made by a tortfeasor or by a person acting for him or on his behalf (an insurance company) are credited against that tortfeasor's liability.

6. Punitive Damages

The plaintiff may be entitled to punitive damages if it can be established by clear and convincing evidence that the defendant acted willfully and wantonly, recklessly, or with malice. Punitive damages are available for inherently malicious torts (such as intentional infliction of emotional distress, which requires outrageous conduct).

F. SPECIAL RULES OF LIABILITY

1. Negligent Infliction of Emotional Distress

A plaintiff can recover for negligent infliction of emotional distress from a defendant whose negligence creates a foreseeable risk of physical injury to the plaintiff that causes a **threat of physical impact** resulting in emotional distress, which generally must manifest as some form of bodily harm (e.g., a heart attack).

Note that it is possible for a defendant to inflict severe emotional distress that results in physical symptoms without the threat of physical impact, such as when a physician negligently misdiagnoses a patient with a terminal illness that the patient does not have, and the patient goes into shock as a result.

a. Threat of impact

The threat of physical impact that causes distress must be directed at the plaintiff or someone in his immediate presence.

b. Zone of danger

Generally, a plaintiff must show that he was within the "zone of danger" of the threatened physical impact—that he feared for his own safety because of the defendant's negligence.

A plaintiff who was a bystander also generally cannot recover for emotional distress caused by witnessing the serious injury to (or death of) another person, unless the bystander is within the zone of danger.

Note, however, that there is a trend toward allowing recovery for a bystander plaintiff outside the zone of danger if the plaintiff:

i)   Is closely related to the person injured by the defendant;

ii) Was present at the scene of the injury; and

iii) Personally observed (or otherwise perceived) the injury.

A majority of jurisdictions would be unlikely to expand liability to a cohabitating fiancée. However, some jurisdictions do allow engaged cohabitants to recover.

c. Physical symptoms required

The majority rule is that damages for negligent infliction of emotional distress without accompanying **physical symptoms** (e.g., nightmares, shock, ulcers, etc.) are not recoverable.

d. Exceptions to physical injury requirement

There are exceptions to the physical injury requirement in cases of misinforming someone that a family member has died and the negligent mishandling of a corpse.

e. Tacking on emotional distress to another tort

A plaintiff who is the victim of a tort that causes physical injury may also add emotional distress as an element of damages.

Compare to intentional infliction of emotional distress, when the plaintiff must prove more than negligence (intentional or reckless extreme or outrageous conduct), but need not prove any physical injury.

2.   Wrongful Death

A decedent's spouse, next of kin, or personal representative may bring suit to recover pecuniary damages for losses suffered as a result of decedent's death. Damages include loss of support and loss of companionship, society, and affection, but not pain and suffering. Recovery, however, is limited to what the deceased would have recovered had he lived. Additionally, the decedents' creditors have no right to institute a claim against the amount awarded.

a. Survival actions

Survival actions are those brought by a decedent's estate (as if the decedent had lived), and are based on claims involving torts to property or torts resulting in personal injury. The estate may recover lost earnings, medical expenses, and pain and suffering before death.

b. Intangible personal interests

Most states do not allow survival of tort actions involving intangible personal interests (such as defamation, malicious prosecution, or invasion of privacy), as they are considered too personal to survive.

> If a jurisdiction recognizes both wrongful death and survival actions, there is no double recovery.

3. Interference with Family Relationships

a. Spouses

One spouse may recover for loss of consortium or services as a result of injuries to the other spouse resulting from the defendant's negligent, intentional, or other tortious behavior.

b. Parent-child

A parent may recover damages for loss of services if a child is injured due to the defendant's tortious conduct. A child has no such recourse for injuries to a parent.

c. Limitations

Recovery in a derivative action for interference with family relationships is limited by the injured family member's contributory actions. Thus, if the injured family member is precluded from recovering damages in his own suit, he will also be precluded from recovery in the derivative action.

G. OTHER LIABILITY ISSUES AND IMMUNITIES

1. Vicarious Liability

Vicarious liability is a form of strict liability in which one person is liable for the negligent actions of another. It arises when one person has the right, ability, or duty to control the activities of another, even though the first person was not directly responsible for the injury.

a. Respondeat superior

1) Scope of employment

An employer is liable for the tortious conduct of an employee that is within the **scope of employment**. Conduct within the scope of employment includes that which the employee is employed to perform, is within the authorized limits of time and space, and is performed for the purpose of serving the employer.

Careful instructions directed to the employee do not insulate the employer from liability.

a) Force inherent in the work

The general rule is that employers are not liable for the intentional torts of employees. However, when force is inherent in the employee's work (e.g., a bouncer at a bar), the employer may be responsible for the employee's intentional torts.

b) Opportunity to commit a tort

In addition, when the employer authorizes the employee to act on his behalf, and the employee's position provides the opportunity to commit a tort, the employer may be liable (e.g., employee with the power to sign contracts enters into a fraudulent contract with a third party—employer may be liable).

2) Detour and frolic

An employer may be liable for an employee's **detour** (a minor and permissible deviation from the scope of employment), but not for an employee's **frolic** (an unauthorized and substantial deviation).

3) Negligent hiring

An employer may be liable for the negligent hiring, supervision, entrustment, or retention of an employee. This is primary negligence; it is **not** vicarious liability.

> **EXAM NOTE:** After concluding that a defendant is not liable under a vicarious liability theory, be certain to consider whether personal negligence applies.

b. Independent contractors

Employers are generally not vicariously liable for the torts of independent contractors. However, an employer may be liable for:

i)   Negligence in selecting or instructing the independent contractor;

ii) **Non-delegable duties** arising out of a relationship with a specific plaintiff or the public (i.e., activities that are inherently risky or that affect the public at large, such as construction work adjacent to a public highway); or

iii) **Inherently dangerous activities**, even though performed by an independent contractor.

c. Business partners

Partners in a joint enterprise, when two or more parties have a common purpose and mutual right of control, may be liable for the tortious acts of each other that are committed within the scope of the business purposes.

d. Automobile owners

1) Negligent entrustment

The owner of a vehicle may be liable for the negligent acts of a driver to whom the car was entrusted if the owner knew or should have known of the driver's negligent propensies.

2) Family use

In jurisdictions with "family use" statutes, the owner of an automobile may be liable for the tortious acts of any **family member** driving the car with permission.

3) Permissive use

In jurisdictions with "permissive use" statutes, the owner of an automobile may be liable for the tortious acts of **anyone** driving the car with permission.

e. Parents and their children

Parents are not vicariously liable for their minor child's torts unless the child commits a tort while acting as the parent's agent.

Parents, however, are liable for their own negligence with respect their minor child's conduct. A parent is under a duty to exercise reasonable care to prevent a minor child from intentionally or negligently harming a third party, provided the parent:

i) Has the ability to control the child ; and

ii) Knows or should know of the necessity and opportunity for exercising such control.

In such circumstances, a parent who fails to exercise control may be liable for harm caused by her child, even though the child, because of his age, is not liable. Restatement (Second) of Torts § 316.

> **Example:** A father gives to a gun to his six-year old son. Although the son lacks the necessary maturity and judgment to operate the gun independently in a safe manner, the father allows the son to use the gun when the father is not present. The son, while aiming the gun at a toy in his yard, misses and accidentally shoots a neighbor. The father, because of his failure to properly supervise his son, can be liable for the injury suffered by the neighbor that is directly attributable to the son's conduct, even though the son himself will not be liable, because he exercised the care of a reasonable six-year old.

f. "Dram Shop" Acts

At common law, there was no remedy against the seller of intoxicating beverages if that sale resulted in harm to a third party. In order to provide such a remedy, many states have enacted "Dram Shop" laws. These laws impose strict liability against the seller of intoxicating beverages if a third party, by reason of intoxication of another, sustains personal injury, property damage, or loss of support. Because these laws impose strict liability, the plaintiff need not demonstrate negligence on the part of the seller.

g. Bailment liability

A bailor may be liable for his own negligent actions, but is not vicariously liable for the tortious acts of his bailee.

2. Immunities

a. Government immunity

Governmental entities were traditionally immune from tort actions unless they consented to be sued, but that immunity is now quite limited.

1) Federal and state governments

Under the Federal Tort Claims Act, Title 28 U.S.C., the U.S. government waives immunity in tort actions, with the following exceptions:

i) Certain enumerated torts (assault, battery, false imprisonment, false arrest, malicious prosecution, abuse of process, libel and slander, misrepresentation and deceit, and interference with contract rights);

ii) Discretionary activity (i.e., planning or decision-making, as opposed to operational acts); and

iii) Assertion of the government's immunity by a government contractor in a products liability case if the contractor conformed to government specifications and warned the government of any known dangers in the product.

Most state governments have waived tort immunity to the same extent as the federal government. However, when immunity still attaches, it covers several state and federal agencies as well.

2) Municipalities

a) Public duty

A municipality's liability may be limited by the public duty rule. That is, there is no liability to any one citizen for the failure to fulfill a duty that is owed to the public at large, unless that citizen has a special relationship with the municipality that creates a special duty. A special relationship can be shown by:

i) Promises or actions on the part of the municipality demonstrating an affirmative duty to act on behalf of the injured party;

ii) Knowledge by the municipality's agents that failure to act could lead to harm;

iii) Direct contact between the municipality's agents and the injured party; and

iv) The injured party's justifiable reliance on the municipality's affirmative duty.

b) Government versus proprietary function

Tort immunity attaches to the performance of traditional government functions (such as police and court systems), but it does not attach when a municipality is performing a "proprietary" function that traditionally is performed by a private company (such as utilities and parking lots).

3) Government officials

Tort immunity applies to government officials performing discretionary functions entrusted to them by law so long as the acts are done without malice or improper purpose. There is no tort immunity for carrying out ministerial acts.

b. Intra-family immunity

1) Inter-spousal immunity

Intra-family immunity applies only to personal injuries, not to property injuries. Traditionally, inter-spousal immunity prevented one spouse from suing another spouse in a personal injury action. In most jurisdictions today, inter-spousal immunity has been extinguished, and either spouse can now institute a cause of action for personal injury against the other spouse.

2) Parent-child immunity

In states where parent-child immunity has been abolished, parents are still given broad discretion in their exercise of authority and supervision over a child. Jurisdictions that continue to adhere to parent-child immunity do not apply immunity to car accidents and intentional tortious conduct by the parent.

c. Charitable immunity

Most states have eliminated the common-law rule of charitable immunity.

3. Multiple Defendants

a. Joint and several liability

When the acts of two or more persons combine to produce a single indivisible harm, each person is liable for the entire amount of damages. Accordingly, the plaintiff may sue any one of them, or some or all, jointly or separately, obtain judgments for the full amount of her damages against as many as she can, and then collect her judgment from a single one, or any combination of them at the discretion of the plaintiff.

Joint and several liability applies both when the defendants act in concert with one another and when they act concurrently and independently of each other (without a common design). In the case of concurrent, independent tortfeasors, the doctrine applies when the plaintiff suffers an indivisible injury.

A significant number of states now recognize pure several liability, under which a tortfeasor generally is liable only for his comparative share of the plaintiff's damages.

b. Satisfaction and release

Once a plaintiff has recovered fully from one or a combination of defendants, she is barred from pursuing further action against other tortfeasors. The plaintiff generally may not receive double recovery.

The plaintiff's release of claims against one tortfeasor does not apply to other tortfeasors unless expressly stated in the release agreement **or** the release was given because the plaintiff was paid the full amount of her damages. A plaintiff made whole may not seek a double recovery. However, the paying tortfeasor may seek contribution from other non-paying joint tortfeasors for the reimbursement of the share of damages paid by the tortfeasor on behalf of the joint tortfeasors.

c. Contribution

There is a right of contribution among joint tortfeasors, even if judgment has not been recovered against all or any of them, so long as the tortfeasor from whom contribution is sought is originally liable to the plaintiff. The traditional rule allowed the paying defendant to recover a proportional share of the damages from each tortfeasor; the modern trend is to apportion cost among the tortfeasors in proportion to the relative fault of each. It is also generally true that tortfeasors who committed an intentional tort may not seek contribution from another tortfeasor.

d. Indemnity

Indemnification is the shifting of the entire loss from one joint tortfeasor to another.

1) Scope

Indemnification generally applies when one tortfeasor is vicariously liable for the other's wrongdoing. The tortfeasor who has discharged the liability is entitled to indemnity from the actual wrongdoer who was primarily responsible for the harm (e.g., an employer (secondary tortfeasor) pays a judgment for the tort of an employee (primary tortfeasor) due to the employer's vicarious liability).

2) Complete reimbursement

The employer can then seek complete reimbursement (indemnity) from the employee) when:

i) There is a **prior indemnification agreement** between the parties (e.g., in the construction industry, a contractor may agree to indemnify a subcontractor for the latter's negligence that may occur in the future);

ii) There is a significant difference between the blameworthiness of two defendants such that **equity requires a shifting of the loss** to the more blameworthy defendant;

iii) Significant **additional harm is subsequently caused by another tortfeasor** (i.e., one defendant pays the full judgment, including for additional harm caused by the malpractice of the treating physician); and

iv) Under **strict products liability**, each supplier has a right of indemnification against all previous suppliers in a distribution chain.

3) Exceptions

Indemnity in degree of blameworthiness is rejected in jurisdictions with comparative negligence systems. These states apportion damages based on relative fault, although indemnification is allowed in other instances when it is not based on degree of fault.

H. DEFENSES

1. Contributory Fault

Contributory fault occurs when a plaintiff fails to exercise reasonable care for her own safety and thereby contributes to the legal cause of her own injury. Note that when a plaintiff is suing a defendant for the negligent rendering of services, such as medical services, the plaintiff's negligent conduct in creating the condition that defendant has been employed to remedy is not taken into account.

a. Contributory negligence

At common law, and in states that still recognize the doctrine, the plaintiff's contributory negligence (i.e., failure to exercise reasonable care for her own safety), regardless of the percentage that the plaintiff's own negligence contributed to the harm, is a complete bar to recovery.

Examples of contributory negligence include the failure to remove oneself from danger or the plaintiff's violation of a statute, except that the plaintiff's violation of a statute cannot be used as a defense when the statute places the entire responsibility for the harm suffered by the plaintiff on the defendant. In addition, a rescuer who takes extraordinary risks when attempting a rescue may also be permitted to recover despite the rescuer's negligence.

Contributory negligence is not a defense to an intentional tort, gross negligence, or recklessness.

b. Last clear chance

In contributory negligence jurisdictions, the plaintiff may mitigate the effects of her own contributory negligence by proving that the defendant had the last clear chance to avoid injuring the plaintiff but failed to do so. This doctrine has been abolished in most comparative negligence jurisdictions.

1) Helpless peril

A plaintiff who, due to his contributory negligence, is in peril from which he cannot escape is in helpless peril. In such cases, the defendant is liable in most states if she knew or should have known of the plaintiff's perilous situation and could have avoided harming the plaintiff but for her (the defendant's) own negligence.

2) Oblivious peril

A plaintiff who, due to his contributory negligence, is in peril from which he could escape if he were paying attention is in oblivious peril. The defendant is liable only if she has actual knowledge of the plaintiff's situation.

c. Comparative negligence

1) Pure comparative negligence

In jurisdictions that have adopted the doctrine of pure comparative negligence, a plaintiff's contributory negligence is **not** a complete bar to recovery. Instead, the plaintiff's full damages are calculated by the trier of fact and then reduced by the proportion that her fault bears to the total harm (e.g., if the plaintiff's full damages are $100,000, and the plaintiff is 80% at fault and the defendant is 20% at fault, the plaintiff will recover $20,000).

> **EXAM NOTE**: Always apply pure comparative negligence on the MBE unless the facts instruct you to apply a different test.

2) Modified comparative negligence

There are two types of modified or "partial" comparative negligence jurisdictions. One bars recovery when the plaintiff is equally as negligent as the defendant is. In such jurisdictions, a plaintiff who is 50% at fault recovers nothing.

In the second type of jurisdiction that has adopted a modified or "partial" comparative negligence doctrine, the plaintiff's recovery is barred if she was more negligent than the defendant was.

3) Multiple defendants

With respect to multiple defendants, a different approach is used. The plaintiff's negligence is compared to the total negligence of all defendants combined.

4) Illustrations

i) Single defendant, pure comparative—Defendant is 55% negligent and Plaintiff is 45% negligent in causing the accident. They each have $100,000 is damages. Plaintiff will recover $55,000 from Defendant ($100,000 minus $45,000, which represents Plaintiff's proportionate fault of 45%), and Defendant will recover $45,000 from Plaintiff. Plaintiff will have a net recovery of $10,000 because Defendant's damages will be offset against Plaintiff's damages.

ii) Single defendant, partial comparative—Same facts as above, except that Defendant will not recover anything because he was more than 50% at fault.

iii) Multiple defendants, partial comparative—Two defendants are negligent: Defendant 1 is 20% negligent, while Defendant 2 is 45% negligent. Combined their negligence is 65%. Plaintiff is 35% negligent. Plaintiff can recover $65,000 from either Defendant 1 or 2 under the theory of joint and several liability. The paying defendant can then seek contribution from the nonpaying defendant. If either defendant suffered damages, he also has a right of recovery against either of the other two negligent parties because each one's negligence is less than the total negligence of the other two.

When comparative negligence exists (either pure or modified), it supersedes all other affirmative defenses except assumption of the risk.

EXAM NOTE: Consider comparative negligence whenever two negligent parties are suing one another. Assume that the jurisdiction adopts pure comparative negligence unless the facts state otherwise.

d. Imputed fault

Similar to vicarious liability, imputed fault prevents or limits a plaintiff's recovery due to the contributory fault of another. For example, an employee's negligent driving may prevent or reduce an employer's recovery from a third party if the employer's car is damaged by the third party's negligence. Generally, fault is not imputed between family members.

EXAM NOTE: Common fact patterns of imputed fault to note on the bar are ones involving employer-employee and business partners. Note that imputed fault does not apply to spouses when one spouse is suing a third person; to children for a parent's contributory negligence; to parents in a child's action against a third party; nor to automobile owners against their drivers unless the owner is vicariously liable for the driver's negligence.

2. Assumption of the Risk

a. Express

Generally, a plaintiff who **voluntarily** and **knowingly** (subjective standard—what the plaintiff knew/believed) assumed the risk of harm arising from the defendant's negligent conduct is barred from recovery if that assumption of the risk was express, such as through a contractual limitation of liability.

b. Implied

In a **contributory negligence** jurisdiction, the plaintiff may be barred from recovery if the assumption of the risk was implied from his actions.

In a **comparative negligence** jurisdiction, the plaintiff's implied assumption of the risk is not treated as a separate defense. Instead, the plaintiff's awareness of the risk is taken into account in determining the degree to which the plaintiff is at fault, but it also can be considered in determining the reasonableness of the plaintiff's or the defendant's actions.

c. Exclusions

Certain situations warrant exclusion of the defense of assumption of the risk as against public policy. For example, common carriers cannot disclaim their liability for personal injury, and members of a protected class have not assumed the risk when a statute designed to protect that class is violated. Situations involving fraud, force, or emergency are also excluded from the application of assumption of the risk as a defense, as one's actions in such situations are not considered voluntary.

> ***Consent distinguished:*** Consent is a defense to intentional torts, whereas assumption of the risk applies only to negligence actions.

III. STRICT LIABILITY

A prima facie case for strict liability requires (i) an absolute duty to make the plaintiff's person or property safe, (ii) breach, (iii) actual and proximate causation, and (iv) damages.

The three general situations in which strict liability is imposed are:

i) **D**angerous activities;

ii) **A**nimals; and

iii) **D**efective or dangerous products.

MNEMONIC: **DAD**

> **EXAM NOTE:** The "DAD" situations are the only situations in which a defendant can be liable without fault. Otherwise, strict liability is generally the wrong answer choice.

A. ABNORMALLY DANGEROUS ACTIVITIES

An activity is characterized as abnormally dangerous if it is not commonly engaged in, inherently involves risk of serious harm, and cannot be performed with complete safety. One who engages in an abnormally dangerous activity is strictly liable for harm caused to the person, land, or chattels of another resulting from that activity, regardless of precautions taken to prevent the harm. Restatement (Second) of Torts § 519(1).

> Common abnormally dangerous activities include mining, blasting, using explosives, fumigation, and excavating (i.e., activities that cannot be performed with complete safety no matter how much care is taken).

1. Limitations

The strict liability is limited to the kind of harm **expected to be caused** by the activity and to **foreseeable** plaintiffs. The defendant's liability can be cut off by unforeseeable intervening forces. Furthermore, strict liability does not apply to harm that would not have resulted but for the abnormally sensitive character of the activity or when the activity is conducted pursuant to a public duty.

2. Airplanes

The owner or operator of an aircraft is strictly liable to persons and objects on the ground that have been injured by objects that fell or were dropped from the aircraft, or from the aircraft itself falling and crashing. Strict liability also applies to any physical damage to the land under such circumstances. (Note: Strict liability does not apply to harm suffered by passengers or chattel within an aircraft due to a crash.)

Crop dusting is also subject to strict liability.

B. THE RULE OF RYLANDS V. FLETCHER

An individual is strictly liable when "... for his own purposes brings on his lands and collects and keeps there anything likely to do mischief if it escapes, must keep it at his peril, and, if he does not do so, is prima facie answerable for all the damage which is the natural consequence of its escape." *Rylands v. Fletcher*, LR 3 HL 330 (1868) (involving the release of water from defendant's reservoir onto plaintiff's property). The narrow holding of *Rylands*, that an owner of property with a dam on it is strictly liable for the harm caused by the release of water due to the bursting of the dam, is still followed. However, the broader principle of strict liability for harm caused by any dangerous object brought onto property by the landowner is no longer completely followed. Instead, only abnormally dangerous activities are subject to strict liability.

C. ANIMALS

1. Trespassers

a. Humans

A landowner is **not** strictly liable for injuries inflicted by his animals against a trespasser, except for injuries inflicted by a vicious watchdog. Remember, however, that a landowner may be liable on a negligence theory.

Licensees or invitees injured by a wild or abnormally dangerous animal may recover in strict liability.

b. Animals

An animal owner is strictly liable for any reasonably foreseeable damage caused by his trespassing animal, other than household pets.

2. Wild Animals

A wild animal is an animal that, as a class, is not by custom devoted to the service of humankind in the place where it is being kept. The possessor of a wild animal is strictly liable for harm done by that animal, in spite of any precautions the possessor has taken to confine the animal or prevent the harm, as long as the plaintiff did not knowingly do anything to bring about the injury and the harm arises from a **dangerous propensity** that is **characteristic** of such wild animals or of which the owner **has reason to know**. Note that strict liability applies to an injury caused by a plaintiff's fearful reaction to the sight of an unrestrained wild animal in addition to injuries caused directly by the wild animal.

3. Domestic Animals

An animal's owner is strictly liable for injuries caused by a domestic animal if he **knows** or has reason to know of the animal's **dangerous propensities**.

D. DEFENSES TO STRICT LIABILITY

1. Contributory Negligence

The plaintiff's contributory negligence is **not** a defense to strict liability.

2.   Comparative Fault

In comparative negligence jurisdictions, comparative fault principles apply as they do in negligence actions.

3.   Assumption of the Risk

The plaintiff's assumption of the risk bars his recovery in a strict liability action. This defense is also referred to as "knowing contributory negligence."

4.   Statutory Privilege

Performance of an essential public service (e.g., construction of utility or sewer lines) exempts one from strict liability; however, liability may still exist under a negligence theory.

IV.   PRODUCTS LIABILITY

A product may be defective because of a defect in the design or manufacture of the product, or because of a failure to adequately warn the consumer of a hazard related to the foreseeable use of the product. When a plaintiff files a products liability case, he generally has three possible claims on which to base an action: negligence, strict products liability, and breach of warranty. Each type of claim requires different elements. In addition, if the defendant intended or knew with substantial certainty the consequences of the defect, the cause of action could be based on an intentional tort. As with any intentional tort claim, punitive as well as compensatory damages are recoverable. The same defenses germane to each type of tort are applicable.

A.   NEGLIGENCE

As with any negligence action, the plaintiff must prove duty, breach, causation, and damages to prevail.

1.   Duty

The commercial manufacturer, distributor, retailer, and seller of a product owe a duty of reasonable care to **any foreseeable plaintiff** (i.e., a purchaser, user, or bystander).

2.   Breach

Failure to exercise **reasonable care** in the inspection or sale of a product constitutes breach of that duty. The plaintiff must establish not only that the defect exists, but that the defendant's negligent conduct (lack of reasonable care) led to the plaintiff's harm. In other words, had the defendant exercised reasonable care in the inspection or sale of the product, the defect **would have been discovered,** and the plaintiff would not have been harmed. The plaintiff also has the option of invoking *res ipsa loquitur* if the defect could not have occurred without the manufacturer's negligence.

The individual defendant must have breached his duty to reasonably inspect or sell. Unlike in strict products liability, the negligence of others in the supply chain cannot be imputed. Rather, the plaintiff has the burden of proving the individual fault of the defendant.

3. Causation

The plaintiff must prove actual and proximate causation.

> When a seller sells a product with a known defect and without giving adequate warnings about the defect, the failure to warn may be a superseding cause, breaking the chain of causation between the manufacturer and the injury.

4. Damages

The plaintiff is entitled to recover damages for any personal injury or property damage. Claims for purely economic loss are generally not allowed under a negligence theory but must be brought as a breach of warranty action.

5. Defenses

The standard negligence defenses of contributory/comparative negligence and assumption of the risk apply.

B. STRICT PRODUCTS LIABILITY

Under strict liability, the seller or other distributor of a defective product may be liable for any harm to persons or property caused by such product.

> **EXAM NOTE:** Strict products liability is only one way a manufacturer or supplier of a product can be held liable for a plaintiff's injuries. Remember to also consider breach of warranty and negligence on the exam.

1. Defective Product

A product is defective when, at the time of the sale or distribution, it contains a manufacturing defect, contains a design defect, or contains inadequate instructions or warnings (i.e., failure to warn).

a. Manufacturing defect

To prevail on a claim of manufacturing defect, the plaintiff must prove:

i)   The product was defectively manufactured;

ii) The **defect existed** when the product left the defendant's control;

iii) The defect caused the plaintiff's injury; and

iv) The plaintiff used the product in a reasonably foreseeable way.

A manufacturing defect is a physical deviation from what the **manufacturer intended the product to be** that causes harm to the plaintiff. The test for the existence of such a defect is whether the product conforms to the defendant's own specifications.

b. Design defect

To prevail on a claim of design defect, the plaintiff must prove:

i)   The product was **defectively designed**;

ii) The **defect existed** when the product left the defendant's control;

iii) The defect caused the plaintiff's injury; and

iv) The plaintiff used the product in a reasonably foreseeable way.

Design defects are judged under two standards. The first is whether the product was dangerous **beyond the expectation of the ordinary consumer** (i.e., the "consumer expectation test").

Under the second standard (i.e., the risk-utility test), a design defect exists if there was a **reasonable alternative design** available to the defendant and the failure to use that design has rendered the product not reasonably safe. To establish the existence of the design defect, the plaintiff must show that a less-dangerous modification or alternative was economically feasible.

Merely providing a warning does not necessarily prevent a product from being unreasonably dangerous.

c. Failure to warn

An action brought under a failure to warn theory is essentially the same as a design defect claim, but the defect in question is the manufacturer's failure to provide an adequate warning related to the risks of using the product. A defect is deemed to exist if there were **foreseeable risks of harm, not readily recognized by an ordinary user of the product, which risks could have been reduced or avoided by providing reasonable instructions or warnings**.

1) Prescription drugs

Under the "learned intermediary" rule, the manufacturer of a prescription drug typically satisfies its duty to warn by informing the prescribing physician of problems with the drug rather than the patient taking the drug. An exception exists if the manufacturer is aware that the drug will be dispensed or administered without the personal intervention or evaluation of a health-care provider, such as when a vaccine is administered through a mass inoculation.

d. Inference of defect

A plaintiff is entitled to a *res ipsa loquitor*-like inference that a product defect existed if the harm suffered by the plaintiff:

i) Was of a kind that ordinarily occurs as a result of a product defect; and

ii) Was not solely the result of causes other than a product defect existing at the time of sale or distribution.

This inference is mainly applied in cases involving a manufacturing defect when the product is lost or destroyed as a consequence of the incident that causes the plaintiff's harm.

2. Plaintiffs

To bring a strict liability action, a plaintiff is not required to be in privity of contract with the defendant. Consequently, **any foreseeable user** of a defective product who is personally injured or whose property is harmed by the product may maintain a strict liability action. The user of the product need not have purchased it from a seller but can be a family member of the purchaser or even a bystander whose person or property is injured by the product.

3. Defendants

In order to be subject to strict liability for a defective product, the defendant must be in the **business of selling** or otherwise distributing products of the type that harmed the plaintiff. Included as a seller are the manufacturer of the product, its distributor, and its retail seller. As long as the seller is a commercial supplier of the product, the seller is subject to strict liability for a defective product, even if the revenue from sales of the product is not a significant portion of the seller's business. The seller is strictly liable even if the seller was not negligent in any way, and even when the product is not purchased directly from the seller.

a. Lessor

Generally, a lessor of commercial product (e.g., car, boat, tools) is subject to strict liability for a defective product.

b. Products and services

A seller that provides both products and services generally is liable if the defective product is consumed, such as food at a restaurant, but not if the product is not used, such as the vendor of a balloon ride when the balloon itself is defective. Hospitals and doctors generally are treated as providing a service, rather than a product, in cases when the defective product is used as a tool, loaned to the patient, or even implanted in the patient.

c. Seller of product component

The commercial supplier of a component, such as sand used in manufacturing cement or a switch used in an electrical device, is subject to liability if the component itself is defective, but not when the component is incorporated into a product that is defective for another reason. However, the commercial supplier of a component may be liable if that supplier substantially participates in the process of integrating the component into the design of another product and that product is defective due to the integration.

d. Exclusion—casual seller

Because the seller must be in the business of selling similar products, a casual seller, such as an individual car owner who sells the car to his neighbor or an accountant who sells her office furniture to another businessperson, is not subject to strict liability.

e. Exclusion—auctioneer

Similarly, an auctioneer of a product generally is not subject to strict liability with respect to the products auctioned.

4. Damages

As with negligence claims, the plaintiff is entitled to recover damages for any personal injury or property damage. A claim for purely economic loss generally is not allowed under a strict liability theory but must be brought as a breach of warranty action, as must a claim for harm to the product itself and consequential damages arising therefrom.

5. Defenses

a. Comparative negligence

In a comparative negligence jurisdiction, the plaintiff's negligence is a defense to a strict product liability action in the same manner as it is in a negligence action. For example, in a pure comparative negligence jurisdiction, the plaintiff's recovery is reduced by the percentage that the plaintiff's fault contributed to causing her injury.

b. Contributory negligence

In a contributory negligence jurisdiction, the plaintiff's negligence generally is not a defense to a strict product liability action when the plaintiff **misused** the product in a reasonably foreseeable way or **negligently failed to discover** the defect.

Suppliers are required to anticipate reasonably foreseeable misuses of their products.

c. Assumption of risk

Voluntary and knowing assumption of the risk is a complete bar to recovery in either type of jurisdiction. Assumption of the risk is a subjective standard. The plaintiff must be aware of the danger and knowingly expose himself to it.

d. Misuse, modification, or alteration of product by user

Misuse, modification, or alteration of a product by its user may serve as a defense to a products liability claim that is based on strict liability. However, when such actions are foreseeable, the failure to take them into account in designing the product or providing warnings may constitute a design defect or a failure to warn.

e. Substantial change in product

If the product substantially changes before it reaches the consumer (e.g., a part is reconditioned), this change may constitute a superseding cause that cuts off the liability of the original manufacturer.

f. Compliance with government standards

Compliance with government safety standards is not conclusive evidence that the product is not defective. On the other hand, failure to comply with these standards substantiates the product's defective nature.

g. Contract disclaimers, limitations, and waivers

A disclaimer or limitation of remedies or other contractual exculpation (i.e., waiver) by a product seller or other distributor does not generally bar or reduce an otherwise valid products liability claim for personal injury.

C. WARRANTIES

Product liability actions brought under the following theories generally may be brought not only against a retailer of a product, but also against a manufacturer or distributor of goods, at least when damages are sought for personal injury or property damage.

1. Implied Warranties

a. Types

The implied warranty of **merchantability** warrants that the product being sold is generally acceptable and is reasonably fit for the ordinary purposes for which it is being sold. The seller must be a merchant with respect to the kind of goods at issue.

The implied warranty of **fitness** warrants that a product is fit for a particular purpose, but only if the seller knows the particular purpose for which the product is being purchased and the buyer relies on the seller's skill or judgment in supplying the product.

b. Claims

Any product that fails to live up to either of the above warranties constitutes a breach of the defendant's warranty; the plaintiff need not prove any fault on the defendant's part.

The plaintiff may recover damages for personal injury and property damage, as well as for purely economic loss. Anyone foreseeably endangered by the product has standing to sue for bodily harm.

Assumption of the risk, comparative negligence, and contributory negligence are valid to the same extent as they are in strict liability actions. Additional defenses include the use of disclaimers and the plaintiff's failure to provide notice of the breach. However, in the case of consumer goods, the limitation of consequential damages for personal injury is prima facie unconscionable.

2. Express Warranties

A representation of fact that is part of the basis of a bargain is an express warranty, and a seller is liable for any breach of that warranty, regardless of fault. A disclaimer is potentially a defense, but only if the disclaimer is consistent with the warranty. (In practice, this is virtually impossible, since the warranty being disclaimed was expressly made.) Assumption of the risk, comparative negligence, failure to give prompt notice of breach to the defendant, and product misuse are also defenses. Generally, contributory negligence is no defense to an express warranty action.

V. OTHER TORTS

A. NUISANCE

1. Private

A private nuisance is a thing or activity that **substantially and unreasonably** interferes with another individual's use or enjoyment of his property.

The interference must be intentional, negligent, reckless, or the result of abnormally dangerous conduct to constitute nuisance.

Anyone with possessory rights in the property may bring a nuisance claim.

a. Substantial

A substantial interference is one that would be offensive, inconvenient, or annoying to a normal, reasonable person in the community. A person with special sensitivities cannot recover when the average person would not be offended, inconvenienced, or annoyed. Conversely, a person who is not offended, inconvenienced or annoyed (e.g., the "thick-skinned" plaintiff) is nevertheless entitled to recover if a normal reasonable person would be, although the amount of damages may be affected.

b. Unreasonable

The interference is unreasonable if the injury caused outweighs the usefulness of the defendant's actions.

The difference between private nuisance and trespass is physical invasion. The same thing or conduct may constitute both (e.g., a defendant's construction site sending massive amounts of dust onto a plaintiff's property).

2. Public

A public nuisance is an **unreasonable interference with a right common** to all members of the community.

Generally, a criminal prosecution or civil suit **by the government** is the exclusive remedy for a public nuisance. A private citizen has no civil cause of action for a harm that results from a public nuisance if his harm is of the same kind as that suffered by the general public. Only when an individual suffers harm that is peculiar to him and different in kind from the general public may he bring an action for public nuisance.

Example 1: A dynamiting operation causes rocks to block a public highway. All members of the community are harmed by the nuisance. Consequently, a driver who suffers economic harm, such as a loss of business, due to the blockage cannot recover.

Example 2: Same facts as in Example 1, but in this case a rock strikes the driver's car, cracking the windshield. The driver has suffered harm different from the general community and may bring an action in public nuisance.

3. Remedies

a. Damages

The usual remedy for nuisance is damages. Damages include any depreciation in value of the property, and they may be apportioned among multiple defendants. All resulting harm is recoverable, including personal injury and harm to property.

1) Utility greater than harm

Even if the utility of the conduct outweighs the gravity of the harm, damages, but not an injunction, may be available if the harm is serious and the financial burden of compensating for the harm would not make conduct unfeasible. In other words, while it may be reasonable for the defendant to engage in the conduct, it is unreasonable for the defendant to do so without paying for the harm done.

b. Injunctive relief

If money damages are inadequate or unavailable, courts may grant injunctive relief. In determining whether an injunction is appropriate, the courts will balance the potential hardships to the parties. However, the court need not consider the relative hardships if the defendant's sole purpose was to cause harm to the plaintiff or to violate the common standards of decency.

c. Abatement

1) Private nuisance

A person may enter another's land in order to abate a private nuisance after giving the defendant notice of the nuisance and the defendant's refusal to act. The amount of force used may be only that which is reasonable to abate the nuisance; the plaintiff is liable for any additional damage.

2) Public nuisance

One who is entitled to recover for a public nuisance has the right to abate that nuisance by self-help, as one would with a private nuisance. However, in the absence of unique injury, a public nuisance may be abated only by public authority.

4. Defenses

Apart from challenging the elements of nuisance, the defenses available to a defendant turn on whether the defendant's conduct is intentional, negligent, or otherwise subject to recovery. For example, the plaintiff's negligence or assumption of the risk may be a defense to a nuisance resulting from the defendant's negligence.

a. Regulatory compliance

The fact that a defendant's behavior is in compliance with a statute or administrative regulation is not a complete defense but may be evidence as to whether the behavior is unreasonable.

b. Coming to the nuisance

As long as the plaintiff purchased his land in good faith (i.e., not to initiate a harassing lawsuit), it is no defense that he "came to the nuisance" after it already existed, because a purchaser is entitled to reasonable use and enjoyment of his land.

Conversely, ownership of land prior to the defendant's entry into the neighborhood will not, by itself, make the defendant's action a nuisance. The test is whether the defendant's action is unreasonable.

c. Access to light

Courts, historically, have refused to find the obstruction of sunlight as creating a private nuisance.

B. DEFAMATION

A plaintiff may bring an action for defamation:

i) If the defendant's **defamatory language;**

ii) Is of or concerning the plaintiff;

iii) Is **published** to a third party who understands its defamatory nature; and

iv) **Damages** the plaintiff's reputation.

For matters of public concern, the plaintiff must also prove fault on the part of the defendant.

Libel and slander distinguished: Defamation by words written, printed, or otherwise recorded in permanent form is **libel**. Defamation by spoken word, gesture, or any form other than libel is **slander**.

1. Defamatory Language

Language that diminishes respect, esteem, or goodwill toward the plaintiff, or that deters others from associating with the plaintiff, is defamatory. The plaintiff may introduce extrinsic facts to establish defamation by innuendo.

An opinion is actionable if the defendant implies that there is a factual basis for that opinion. *See Gertz v. Welch, Inc.*, 418 U.S. 323 (1974); *Milkovich v. Lorian Journal Co.*, 497 U.S. 1 (1990).

A deceased individual may not be defamed. A corporation, partnership, or unincorporated association may be defamed if the language prejudices it in conducting its activities or deters others from dealing with it.

2. "Of or Concerning" the Plaintiff

A reasonable person must believe that the defamatory communication refers to this particular plaintiff and holds him up to scorn or ridicule in the eyes of a substantial number of respectable members of the community. If the defamatory language applies to a group, a member of the group can maintain a defamation action only if the group is so small that the matter can reasonably be understood to refer to that member, unless there is other evidence that the language refers to that particular member.

3. Publication

Publication of defamatory matter is its **intentional or negligent communication** to a third party, i.e., to someone other than the person being defamed.

> **EXAM NOTE:** MBE questions on defamation often center on the publication requirement. Remember that the statement must be **intentionally or negligently** made **to a third party**. Beware of fact patterns in which the publication requirement is not met, such as those involving a third party learning about the statement through no fault of the defendant's, or when no third party hears the statement at all.

A person who repeats a defamatory statement may be liable for defamation even though that person identifies the originator of the statement and expresses a lack of knowledge as to the truthfulness of the statement.

4. Fault

For matters of public concern, the plaintiff must prove fault on the part of the defendant. The standard for establishing the defendant's fault depends on the plaintiff's status as a public or private figure.

Common law distinction: The plaintiff need not prove fault or falsity for common-law defamation. Defamatory statements are presumed to be false, and the defendant must assert truth as a defense.

a. Public figure or official

A public figure is someone who is known to the general public and includes any person who has voluntarily injected himself into the public eye.

The plaintiff must prove **actual malice** on the part of the defendant, as well as the **falsity** of the language.

Malice means that the **defendant knew the statement or language was false**, or he recklessly disregarded its truthfulness. In order to establish a reckless disregard for the truthfulness of a statement, the defendant must have entertained serious doubts about its truthfulness; mere failure to check facts is not sufficient. *New York Times Co. v. Sullivan*, 376 U.S. 254 (1964); *St. Amant v. Thompson*, 390 U.S. 727 (1968).

b. Limited public figure

Private figures who voluntarily inject themselves into a public controversy are treated as public figures if the defamatory statement relates to their position in the controversy, but they are treated as private figures if the defamation relates to any other matter.

c. Private figure

If the plaintiff is a private figure and the defamatory statement involves a matter of **public concern**, the plaintiff must prove the defendant's fault regarding the falsity of the statement. Fault may be established by either negligence or actual malice. *Gertz v. Robert Welch, Inc.*, 418 U.S. 323 (1974).

In a defamation action by a private figure that does not involve a matter of public concern, the plaintiff must prove only that the defendant was at least negligent in ascertaining the truth or falsity of the statement. Restatement (Second) of Torts § 580B.

5. Damages

Depending on the type of defamation, the plaintiff may be entitled to either **general** or **special** damages. **General damages** (also called presumed damages) are compensatory for the damage to the plaintiff's reputation. **Special damages** are awarded if the plaintiff can prove that she suffered **economic** loss due to the defamation, such as loss of a job. A plaintiff may also be able recover for personal injuries, such as emotional distress, even though such harm does not qualify as special damages.

a. Libel

The general rule is that special damages need not be established in libel cases. The statement is deemed libelous "on its face" and is called libel *per se*.

This rule does not apply, however, when a plaintiff must prove extrinsic circumstances to show why a statement that otherwise appears innocent is libelous. In this case, the libel is *per quod*.

Note that even when extrinsic circumstances must be shown, there is no need to prove special damages if the words, had they been spoken, would have amounted to slander *per se*.

b. Slander

Unlike in an action for libel, in an action for slander, **special damages** must be proven **unless** the defamatory statement is slander *per se*.

Under **slander *per se***, damage to reputation is presumed by any statement:

i) **Directly relating to the plaintiff's abilities** in her profession, business, or trade;

ii) Asserting that the plaintiff suffers from a loathsome disease;

iii) Imputing unchaste behavior to a woman; or

iv) Charging that the plaintiff is guilty of a crime.

c. Constitutional limitation on presumed damages

If the plaintiff is a private figure and the matter is one of public concern, general damages may not be awarded if the plaintiff establishes the defendant's fault without proving actual malice. *Gertz v. Robert Welch Inc., supra.* However, if the plaintiff is a private figure and the matter is not one of public concern, general damages may be awarded even if the plaintiff establishes the defendant's fault without proving actual malice. *Dun & Bradstreet, Inc. v. Greenmoss Builders,* Inc., 472 U.S. 749 (1985).

6. Defenses

a. Truth

Truth is an absolute defense to a claim of defamation. A truthful statement is not defamatory. A statement that contains slight inaccuracies may nevertheless be considered to be true and therefore not defamatory. A statement that a person has engaged in conduct that is substantially different from the conduct in which the person did in fact engage is not considered to be true, even if the person's actual conduct was equally or more morally reprehensible.

> If a statement is true but seems like defamation, consider whether it constitutes intentional infliction of emotional distress or invasion of privacy.

b. Consent

Consent by the plaintiff is a defense, but as with other torts, a defendant cannot exceed the scope of the plaintiff's consent.

c. Privilege

1) Absolute privilege

Statements made under the following circumstances are shielded by absolute privilege:

i) In the course of **judicial proceedings**;

ii) In the course of **legislative proceedings**;

iii) Between **husband and wife**; and

iv) **Required publications** by radio, television, or newspaper (e.g., statements by a political candidate that a station must carry and may not censor).

> Note that statements made in the course of judicial proceedings must be related to the proceeding in order to be privileged; no such requirement exists for legislative proceedings.

2) Qualified privilege

Statements made under the following circumstances are subject to conditional privilege:

i) Affecting an important **public interest**;

ii) In the **interest of the publisher** (defendant), such as defending his reputation; or

iii) In the **interest of a third party** or the recipient.

A qualified privilege may be lost if it is abused. Generally, a privilege is abused by making statements outside the scope of the privilege or by acting **with malice**. The burden is on the defendant to prove that the privilege exists. It is, therefore, an **affirmative defense**.

C.   INVASION OF PRIVACY

The right of privacy does not extend to corporations, only to individuals. Additionally, because the right of privacy is a personal right, this right terminates upon the death of the plaintiff and does not extend to family members.

Invasion of privacy is not a single tort but includes four separate causes of action.

1. **Misappropriation of the Right to Publicity**

   A majority of states recognize an action for the misappropriation of the right to publicity, which is based on the right of an individual to control the commercial use of his identity. The plaintiff must prove the defendant's **unauthorized** use of the plaintiff's picture or name for the defendant's **commercial** advantage. Use of one's picture or name for personal benefit may not be sufficient. An action also may be maintained when the defendant uses other items closely associated with the plaintiff, such as a specially designed car with unique markings associated with a racecar driver. The states are split as to whether this right survives the death of the individual, with some states treating it as a property right that can be devised and inherited.

2. **Unreasonable Intrusion upon Plaintiff's Affairs or Seclusion**

   The defendant's act of **intruding,** physically or otherwise, into the plaintiff's **private** affairs, solitude, or seclusion must be **objectionable to a reasonable person**. Eavesdropping on private conversations by electronic devices is considered an unreasonable intrusion; photographing a person in a public place generally is not, unless the photograph is taken in manner that reveals information about the person that, even in a public place, the person expects to keep private.

   Unlike the other forms of invasion of privacy, no publication is required to establish liability, but the amount of damages usually turns on nature of publication.

3. **Placing the Plaintiff in a False Light**

   The plaintiff must prove that the defendant made public facts about that plaintiff that placed the plaintiff in a **false light**, which false light would be **objectionable to a reasonable person**. Attributing to the plaintiff **views** that he does not hold or **actions** that he did not take may constitute placing him in false light.

   If the published matter was in the public interest, the plaintiff must show **malice** on the defendant's part.

4. **Public Disclosure of Private Facts about a Plaintiff**

   The defendant's **public disclosure** of **private facts** about the plaintiff is actionable if the matter publicized is something to which a **reasonable person of ordinary sensibilities would object**. Because this action is based on the disclosure of truthful information about the plaintiff, truth is not a defense. Such disclosure is not actionable if the publication is **newsworthy** or is of legitimate interest to the public.

   MNEMONIC: **I FLAP (I**ntrusion, **F**alse **L**ight, **A**ppropriation, **P**rivate facts)

5. **Damages**

   The plaintiff need not prove special damages; emotional and mental distress are sufficient.

6. Defenses

a. Defamation defenses

The defenses of absolute and qualified privileges applicable in defamation actions also apply to privacy actions brought on "false light" or "public disclosure of private facts" grounds.

b. Consent

Consent is a defense to invasion of privacy actions. Mistake as to consent is **not** a valid defense, no matter how reasonable the mistake.

> **EXAM NOTE:** Remember that truth is not a defense to invasion of privacy, whereas it is a complete defense to defamation.

D. MISREPRESENTATION

1. Intentional Misrepresentation

A prima facie case of intentional misrepresentation is established by proof of the following six elements.

a. Defendant's false representation

The misrepresentation must be of a material fact. There generally is no duty to disclose a material fact or opinion; thus, omission of a material fact does not fulfill this element except under the following special circumstances:

i)   Existence of a **duty to disclose**;

ii)   Existence of a **fiduciary relationship**;

iii)   **Deceptive** or misleading statement;

iv)   **Active concealment** of a material fact;

v)   Concealment of a material fact about which the defendant knows the plaintiff is mistaken and the plaintiff lacks the ability to reasonably discover; or

vi)   **Failure to disclose** new information that makes a previous statement false.

b. Scienter

The defendant must have known the representation to be false or must have acted with reckless disregard as to its truthfulness.

c. Intent

The defendant must have intended to induce the plaintiff to act (or refrain from acting) in reliance on the misrepresentation.

d. Causation

The misrepresentation must have caused the plaintiff to act or to refrain from acting. That is, the plaintiff must have actually relied on the misrepresentation.

e. Justifiable reliance

The plaintiff's reliance must have been justifiable. Reliance is not justifiable if the facts are obviously false or if the defendant is stating a lay opinion. However, the plaintiff is under no duty to investigate the truth or falsity of the statement.

f. Damages

The plaintiff must prove actual economic (i.e., pecuniary) loss in order to recover; nominal damages are not awarded. Consequential damages, if proven with sufficient certainty, can be recovered.

2. Negligent Misrepresentation

The elements of negligent misrepresentation are:

i) Misrepresentation;

ii) Breach of duty toward the plaintiff;

iii) Causation;

iv) Justifiable reliance; and

v) Damages.

a. Scope

This tort generally is confined to commercial transactions; the defendant is not liable to the public in general, but only to the particular plaintiffs to whom the representation was made or to those the defendant knew would rely on it. In addition, the defendant is liable only if the plaintiff uses the information for its intended purpose or a substantially similar one.

b. Defenses

Unlike in intentional misrepresentation, in negligent misrepresentation, negligence defenses can be raised.

c. Damages

The plaintiff can recover reliance (out-of-pocket) damages, as well as consequential damages, if proven with sufficient certainty.

E. INTENTIONAL INTERFERENCE WITH BUSINESS RELATIONS

To establish a prima facie case for intentional interference with business relations, the plaintiff must prove that the defendant **knew** of a **contractual relationship** between the plaintiff and a third party (or a valid business **expectancy** of the plaintiff) and that the defendant's **intentional** interference resulted in a breach of contract (or termination of expectancy) that caused the plaintiff **damages**.

1. Interference

The defendant's actions must be shown to have **caused** the interference; it is not enough that the defendant merely took advantage of the broken contract after the fact.

a. Inducing breach of contract

A defendant may be liable for an intentional act that causes a third party to breach an existing contract with the plaintiff. The contract in question must be valid and not terminable at will. A contract that is voidable by one of the parties to the contract, such as due to a violation of the Statute of Frauds, may be the subject of tortious interference unless the party elects to void the contract.

b. Interference with contractual relations

Even if the interference does not cause a breach, the defendant may be liable if the interference makes performance under the contract unreasonably difficult.

To be considered tortious, a defendant's actions must substantially exceed fair competition and free expression, such as persuading a bank not to lend money to a competitor.

c. Interference with prospective economic advantage

The defendant may be liable for interfering with a plaintiff's expectation of economic benefit from third parties even in the absence of an existing contract.

d. Theft of trade secrets

The plaintiff must own a valid trade secret (i.e., information that provides a business advantage) that is not generally known. The owner of the secret must take reasonable precautions to protect the secret, and the defendant must have taken the secret by improper means.

2. Intent

The defendant's interference must have been intentional; negligence is insufficient.

3. Damages

The plaintiff is entitled to actual damages, but, in appropriate cases, may be awarded punitive damages or damages for emotional distress.

4. Defenses

The defendant's interference may be privileged if it was a proper attempt to obtain business or was intended to protect the defendant's interests, particularly if the interference is with a prospective economic advantage rather than an existing contract. This privilege is not absolute.

F. TRADE LIBEL

Trade libel applies to statements injurious to a plaintiff's business or products. Unlike defamation, it is not intended to remedy damage to the personal reputation of the owner/manager of the business. Proof of special damages is required. Damages for mental suffering are not available. The plaintiff must prove:

i) Publication;

ii) Derogatory statement;

iii) **Relating to the plaintiff's title to his business** property, the quality of his business, or to the quality of its products; and

iv) Interference or damage to business relationships.

G. WRONGFUL INSTITUTION OF LEGAL PROCEEDINGS

1. Malicious Prosecution

A person is liable for malicious prosecution when:

i) He **intentionally (and maliciously) institutes** or pursues, or causes to be instituted or pursued;

ii) For an improper purpose;

iii) A legal action that is brought **without probable cause**; and

iv) That **action is dismissed** in favor of the person against whom it was brought.

Most jurisdictions have extended malicious prosecution to include civil cases, as well as criminal actions. The plaintiff may recover for any damage proximately caused by the malicious prosecution, including legal expenses, lost work time, loss of reputation, and emotional distress.

Note that judges and prosecutors enjoy absolute immunity from liability for malicious prosecution.

2. Abuse of Process

Abuse of process is the misuse of the power of the court. The defendant is liable for any harm caused by his use of a legal process (criminal or civil) against the plaintiff in a wrongful manner to accomplish a purpose for which that process was not intended.

Note that abuse of process, like malicious prosecution, does not require ill will or spite, but does require proof of damages.